Missiology for the 21st Century
South Asian Perspectives

Missiology for the 21st Century
South Asian Perspectives

Edited by
Roger E. Hedlund
and
Paul Joshua Bhakiaraj

ISPCK/MIIS
2004

Missiology for the 21st Century: South Asian Perspectives—
Jointly published by The Rev. Ashish Amos of **Indian Society for Promoting Christian Knowledge (ISPCK)**, Post Box 1585, Kashmere Gate, Delhi-110006 for **Mylapore Institute for Indigenous Studies (MIIS)**, Chennai.

ISBN: 81-7214-834-8

Cover design by PAUL JOSHUA BHAKIARAJ

Laser typeset ISPCK, Post Box 1585, 1654 Madarsa Road, Kashmere Gate, Delhi-110006,
Tel: 23866323, Fax: 011-23865490
• E-Mail-ispck@ispck.org.in • publishing@ispck.org.in
Internet-www.ispck.org.in

TABLE OF CONTENTS

ACKNOWLEDGEMENTS

Many persons have contributed to the production of MISSIOLOGY FOR THE 21st CENTURY. We wish to acknowledge first of all the inspiration of Rev. Dr. James C. Gamaliel who first proposed the idea and gave the keynote address at the 'Missiology for the 21st Century' Mylapore Colloquium held during 2-4 December 1999. The substance of that address is found in the introductory chapter of this volume.

A number of topics had been suggested by Dr. Gamaliel which were then circulated to a number of potential writers with the request that they prepare a publishable paper to be presented at a symposium called for the purpose of producing a post-graduate missiology textbook for the South Asian context. Participants included Rev. Dr. James C. Gamaliel (Kerala), Rev. Dr. Martin Alphonse (Chennai), Bishop Dr. Nirmal Minz (Ranchi), Dr. O.L. Snaitang (Shillong), Mr. M.S. Vasanthakumar (Sri Lanka), Rev. Fr. Dr. Augustine Kanjamala, SVD (Mumbai), Dr. K. Rajendran (India Missions Association), Mr. Paul E. Joshua (Bangalore), Ms. Beulah Herbert (Chennai), Mr. Abey George (Bangalore), Rev. Dr. Eliya Mohol (Pune), Mr. David Emmanuel Singh (Delhi), Dr. C.V. Mathew (Chennai), Dr. Siga Arles (Serampore), and Dr. Roger E. Hedlund (Chennai). Some were unable to attend but sent their papers which were distributed, read and discussed: Dr. Jeanette Pinto (Mumbai), Rev. Dr. Ivan Satyavrata (Bangalore), Dr. John Thannickal (Bangalore), Fr.Dr. S.M. Michael, SVD (Mumbai), Fr.Dr. J. Parappalli (Pune), and Dr. Ramesh Khatry (Nepal).

The symposium was made possible by a grant from the Maclellan Foundation which has supported the publication of this volume. We express our thanks to Mr. Thomas H. McCallie, III, for his interest and encouragement as well as to Mr. Hugh O. Maclellan, Jr., and other staff of the Maclellan Foundation for their kindness.

We thank Dr. M. J. John and the staff of Farms India for hosting the colloquium. We are grateful for the writers who presented their papers at that time, but also for the many others who later contributed papers for this compendium. Their names are found in the list of contributors.

A few of the chapters were published previously and are used by permission of the publishers as well as the authors. Chapter four, Jubilee and Mission by J. B. Jeyaraj, was published earlier in the *Evangelical Review of Theology* as "Jubilee and Society: Reflections" (ERT 25,4, October 2001:337-349) and is used by permission. Chapter six, "The Place of Mission in New Testament Theology" by Andreas Köstenberger, originally was published in *Missiology: An International Review* (XXVII,3, July 1999:347-362) and is used with permission. Chapter 16, "Mission, Inter-Cultural Encounter and Change in Western India" by Mohan D. David, was published previously in *Mission Studies* (XVI-1,31, 1999:10-25) and is used by permission. Chapter 23, "The Christian Response to Hinduism," and chapter 32, "Spiritual Warfare and Worldview," both by Paul G. Hiebert, were originally presented as seminar papers in Brazil. Chapter 39, "Let There Be Light: Theological Foundations for the Care and Keeping of Creation" by Praveen (Sunil) Kapur, was first published in the *Evangelical Review of Theology* (ERT 17,2, April 1993:168-175) and is used by permission. Chapter 41,"An Alternate Reading of Poverty" by Jayakumar Christian, appeared previously as a chapter in the book *Working with the Poor* edited by Bryant L. Myers and published by World Vision International (1999), and is used by permission. We acknowledge and thank each one.

Staff of the Mylapore Institute for Indigenous Studies provided indispensable clerical, secretarial and accounting services to this project. These at various stages included Mr. Carlton Benny, Mr. M. Jayachandran, Mr. Johnson Srigiri, Ms. Thea June Hedlund, Mr.Ebenezer Immanuel, Vijaya Joshua and Ms. Jessica Richard. We thank each one and particularly acknowledge the contribution of Ms. Thea June Hedlund in editing and re-writing some of the material. This is a better book as a result. Ms. Elizabeth Alexander, Tambaram, provided excellent service as copy editor.

To everyone who contributed in many ways to the production of this work, our appreciation and thanks. All this is to the glory of God and for the extension of the Kingdom of His Son.

CONTRIBUTORS

ATUL AGHAMKAR heads the Department of Missiology at South Asia Institute of Advanced Christian Studies (SAIACS), Bangalore, where he also teaches Urban Studies. He has authored *Insights into Openness: Encouraging Urban Mission* and co-authored *Ecology and Christian Mission*.

ELIZABETH SUSAN ALEXANDER is a researcher in the area of the History of Christianity in Modern S. *India with Special Reference to Madras Presidency, 1919-1927.*

CHRISTEENA ALAICHAMY is the Head of the Missiology Department, Union Biblical Seminary, Pune. She and her husband served as missionaries among the Kukna tribe of South Gujarat and translated the New Testament into the Kukna language.

SIGA ARLES currently serves as Dean of the Consortium for Indian Missiological Education (CIME) based at Bangalore to train teachers for missiology at the doctoral level. He is author of *Theological Education for the Mission of the Church in India: 1947-1987.*

M. MANI CHACKO is Principal and Head of the Department of Old Testament Studies at Gurukul Lutheran Theological College, Chennai.

JAYAKUMAR CHRISTIAN is the Director of World Vision India. He previously served as the Director for Transformational Development for World Vision International providing leadership globally on strategic issues relating to development programmes of the organization.

MOHAN D. DAVID, Emeritus Fellow of the University Grants Commission, New Delhi, is former Professor and Head of the Department of History at the University of Mumbai. He has published a large number of books and research articles.

R. GEORGE EDWARD is a Bible Translator in the Malto language of Jharkhand. He works with the Friends Missionary Prayer Band (FMPB) and teaches regularly at Missionary Training Centers at Jhansi and Varnasi.

JAMES C. GAMALIEL directs Bethel Theological Institute near Thiruvananthapuram, Kerala. He is the author of *The Gospel of God to the Sikh* and *The Gospel of God to the Hindu* as well as other studies.

ABEY GEORGE teaches theology at Southern Asia Bible College, Bangalore. He is an ordained minister of the Assemblies of God.

ROGER E. HEDLUND is director of the Dictionary of South Asian Christianity project and managing editor of *Dharma Deepika: A South Asian Journal of Missiological Research.* He is author of *Quest for Identity: India's Churches of Indigenous Origin* and other publications.

BEULAH HERBERT is Visiting Lecturer at the Asian Institute of Theology, Bangalore, and part-time lecturer at the Indian Theological Seminary, Avadi, while continuing research on gender practice of Indian Christian women.

PAUL G. HIEBERT is the Distinguished Professor of Mission, Anthropology and South Asian Studies, Trinity Evangelical Divinity School, Deerfield, USA. He is the author of *Anthropological Reflections on Missiological Issues* and numerous other studies.

SAMUEL JAYAKUMAR is Principal, Madras Theological Seminary and College. He is the author of *Dalit Consciousness and Christian Conversion* and *Mission Reader: Historical Models for Wholistic Mission in the Indian Context*.

DANIEL JEYARAJ is currently Judson-DeFrietas Associate professor of World Christianity at Andover Newton Theological Seminary, USA, and editor of *Dharma Deepika: A South Asian Journal of Missiological Research*. He previously was the John A. Mackay Professor of World Christianity at Princeton Theological Seminary.

JESUDASON B. JEYARAJ is Director of Research at ACTS .Academy of Higher Education, Bangalore. A former Professor of Old Testament at Tamilnadu Theological Seminary and a clergy of CSI Madurai-Ramnad Diocese, he has published a number of books and articles in Tamil and English.

PAUL JOSHUA BHAKIARAJ is a commended worker from the Brethren Assemblies and the Director Designate of the Mylapore Institute for Indigenous Studies. He is presently pursuing doctoral research in the UK.

AUGUSTINE KANJAMALA, Provincial Superior of the Bombay Province of the Society of the Divine Word, previously served as Director of Ishvani Kendra in Pune. He is the author of *Religion and Modernization of India: A Case Study of Northern Orissa* and other studies.

PRAVEEN SUNIL KAPUR, Nairobi, Kenya, is the Executive Director for African Asian Concern Kenya (ASCKEN) which challenges the African Churches to reach out to the South Asian diaspora in Africa and to send missionaries into India and Pakistan. He also teaches at the Haggai Institute.

SEBASTIAN KAROTEMPREL, Professor of Missiology at Sacred Heart Theological College, Shillong, Founder-Editor of *Indian Missiological Review* (now called *Mission Today*), also served as Professor of Missiology at the Pontifical Urban University, Rome. He has published many books including *Following Christ Today*.

RAMESH KHATRY is the Executive Secretary of the Association for Theological Education in Nepal (ATEN). He teaches Bible Interpretation and Expository Preaching at Nepal Bible Ashram. He has written a number of books in Nepali and English.

SEBASTIAN C.H. KIM is Director of Christianity in Asia at the Faculty of Divinity, University of Cambridge, UK. He has recently published *In Search of Identity: Debates on Religious Conversion in India*.

ANDREAS J. KÖSTENBERGER is Professor of New Testament and Director of Ph.D./ Th.M. Studies at Southeastern Baptist Theological Seminary, Wake Forest, USA. He is co-author with P. T. O'Brien of *Salvation to the Ends of the Earth: A Biblical Theology of Mission*.

Y. VINCENT KUMARADOSS teaches Medieval and Modern Indian History at Madras Christian College, Chennai. He has published extensively on the History of Christianity in South India.

JAMES MASSEY, New Delhi, India, serves as General Secretary/Director of the all India Dalit Solidarity Peoples and is Honorary Director of the Centre for Dalit Studies. His major publications include *The Doctrine of the Ultimate Reality in Sikh Religion, Dalits in India*, and *Minorities in a Democracy: The Indian Experience*.

C.V. MATHEW is Principal of Jubilee Memorial Bible College, Chennai. He is an ordained minister of the St. Thomas Evangelical Church of India and the Chairman of the Evangelical Fellowship of India.

S.M. MICHAEL is Director of the Institute of Indian Culture, Mumbai, and Professor in the Department of Sociology, University of Mumbai. He serves as Chairman of Interreligious Dialogue, Archdiocese of Bombay, and is one of the Asian Consultors for the Pontifical Council for Interreligious Dialogue.

NIRMAL MINZ, now retired, has served as a Bishop in the Lutheran Church and as Principal of a degree college. His publications include *Mahatma Gandhi and Hindu Christian Dialogue, Rise Up My People and Claim the Promises* as well as other books and numerous articles.

SUDHAKAR MONDITHOKA is Executive Director of RZIM (Ravi Zacharias International Ministries) Life Focus Society at Chennai. He is a member of the Evangelical Philosophical Society and the Evangelical Theological Society, USA.

ELIYA MOHOL teaches Old Testament at Union Biblical Seminary, Pune, and and has served as Associate Dean for Academic Affairs and Academic Dean for Extension Studies.

T.K. OOMMEN, recently retired from the Department of Sociology at Jawarhal Nehru University, New Delhi, was President of the International Sociological Association (1990-1994) as well as President of the Indian Sociological Society (1998-1999). He has authored more than a dozen books.

LALSANGKIMA PACHUAU teaches in the Department of Mission and Ecumenics at the United Theological College, Bangalore. He is the author *Ethnic Identity and Christianity* and editor of *Ecumenical Missiology.*

AUGUSTINE PAGOLU is Academic Dean of the South Asia Institute of Advanced Christian Studies (SAIACS) at Bangalore, India. He is the author of *The Religion of the Patriarchs.*

JACOB PARAPALLY is Professor of Systematic Theology and Dean of the Faculty of Theology at Jnana-Deepa Vidyapeeth (Pontifical Institute of Philosophy and Religions), Pune, India. *Emerging Trends in Indian Christology* is one of his several publications.

JEANETTE PINTO serves as Director, Diocesan Human Life Committee for the Archdiocese of Bombay. She is the author of *Slavery in Portuguese India 1510 –1842*, and *The Indian Widow– from Victim to Victor.*

VINOTH RAMACHANDRA is Secretary for Dialogue & Social Engagement (Asia) for the International Fellowship of Evangelical Students, Colombo, Sri Lanka. He is author of *The Recovery of Mission, Gods That Fail, Faiths in Conflict?* He is co-author with Howard Peskett of *The Message of Mission.*

IVAN SATYAVRATA is the President and Professor of Theology at Southern Asia Bible College, Bangalore. He is an ordained minister of the Assemblies of God.

DAVID EMMANUEL SINGH is Lecturer in South Asian and Islamic Studies at the Oxford Centre for Mission Studies in UK. He previously served as Auxiliary Secretary of the Bible Society in North West India and as Associate Director of the Henry Martyn Institute of Islamic Studies in Hyderabad, India.

O.L. SNAITANG is currently Professor of History of Christianity at GFA Bible College, Tiruvella, Kerala. He is an ordained minister of the Church of God in Northeast India.

G.P.V. SOMARATNA is Director of Research, Colombo Theological Seminary, Sri Lanka. He is author of the six volume *Sinhala Bible Encyclopedia.*

TIMOTHY C. TENNENT is Associate Professor of World Missions and Director of Missions Programs at Gordon-Conwell Theological Seminary in South Hamilton, Massachusetts, USA. He is author of *Christianity at the Religious Roundtable: Evangelicalism in Conversation with Hinduism, Buddhism and Islam* and other books.

SAMUEL THAMBUSAMY is a research scholar currently doing the M.Th. in Theology course at Gurukul Lutheran Theological College and Research Institute in Chennai, India.

M.S. VASANTHAKUMAR is a Senior Lecturer at Lanka Bible College, Peradeniya, Sri Lanka, and Editor of a national Tamil magazine. He has authored numerous books, articles and research papers.

BRIAN WINTLE presently serves as the Regional Secretary for India of the Asia Theological Association, a regional accrediting agency of the International Council for Evangelical Theological Education. Dr. Wintle taught New Testament in the Union Biblical Seminary, Pune, 1978-1995.

ABBREVIATIONS

AB	Anchor Bible	CSI	Church of South India
ABCFM	American Board of Commissioners for Foreign Missions	CWME	Commission on World Mission and Evangelism
ABD	*Anchor Bible Dictionary*	DDM	Dornakal Diocesan Magazine
AD	*Anno Domine:* The Year of our Lord	DP	Dialogue and Proclamation
AG	*Ad gentes:* Decree on the Church's Missionary Activity	EA	Ecclesia in Asia
AIC	African Instituted Churches	EFI	Evangelical Fellowship of India
AICC	All India Christian Council	EFICOR	Evangelical Fellowship of India Commission on Relief
AUS	American University Studies	EIC	East India Company
BA	*Biblical Archaeologist*	EN	*Evangelii Nuntiandi:* Apostolic Exhortation on Evangelization
BARev	*Biblical Archaeology Review*	ERT	Evangelical Review of Theology
BC	Before Christ	ETSM	Evangelical Theological Society Monograph Series
BD	Bajrang Dal	FABC	Federation of Asian Bishops' Conferences
BCE	Before the Common Era		
BJP	Bhartiya Janata Party	GS	*Gaudium et spes:* The Pastoral Constitution on the Church in the Modern World
BKAT	*Biblischer Kommentar Altes Testament*		
CBCI	Catholic Bishops Conference of India	HAR	*Hebrew Annual Review*
		HJM	Hindu Jagran Manch
CBCNEI	Council of Baptist Church in North East India	HSM	Harvard Semitic Monographs
		HTR	*Harvard Theological Review*
CBQ	*Catholic Biblical Quarterly*	HZAT	*Handkommentar zum Alten Testament*
CE	The Common Era		
CIO	Churches of Indigenous Origins	IAMS	International Association for Mission Studies
CISRS	Christian Institute for the Study of Religion and Society		
		IB	*Interpreter's Bible*
CFTLN	Clark's Foreign Theological Library New Series	IBMR	*International Bulletin of Missionary Research*
CMS	Church Missionary Society	IDB	*Interpreter's Dictionary of the Bible*
CNI	Church of North India		
CPM	Ceylon Pentecostal Movement	ICHR	*Indian Church History Review*

IIC	Indian Instituted Churches
IMC	International Missionary Council
IMS	Indian Missionary Society
Int	*Interpretation*
IPC	Indian Pentecostal Church of God
JBL	*Journal of Biblical Literature*
JCS	*Journal of Cuneiform Studies*
JHS	*Journal of Hellenistic Studies*
JPOS	*Journal of the Palestine Oriental Society*
JSOT	*Journal for the Study of the Old Testament*
JSS	*Journal of Semitic Studies*
LCWE	Lausanne Committee for World Evangelisation
LG	*Lumen gentium:* The Dogmatic Constitution on the Church
LMS	London Missionary Society
LWCOT	Living Word Commentary on the Old Testament
NA	*Nostra aetate:* The Declaration on the Church's Relations with non-Christian Religions
NBCLC	National Biblical Catechetical and Liturgical Centre
NCC	National Christian Council National Council of Churches
NEB	New English Bible
NEFA	North East Frontier Agency
NEI	North East India
NICOT	New International Commentary on the Old Testament
NMS	National Missionary Society
OBT	Overtures to Biblical Theology
OCIC	International Catholic Association for Cinema and Audiovisual
OT	*Optatam totius:* The Decree on the Training of Priests
OUP	Oxford University Press
PEQ	*Palestine Exploration quarterly*
RM	*Redemptoris Missio*
RQ	*Revue de Qumran*
RSS	Rashtriya Swayam Sevak Sangh
RZIM	Ravi Zacharias International Ministries
SPCK	Society for the Promotion of Christian Knowledge
SPG	Society for the Propagation of the Gospel
SSA	Semantic Structure Analysis
SWFA	South West Frontier Agency
TDOT	*Theological Dictionary of the Old Testament*
TEF	Theological Education Fund
TSPM	Three Self Patriotic Movement: registered churches of China
TVG	*Die Theologische Verlagsgemeinschaft*
UCFHR	United Christian Forum for Human Rights
UNDA	(Itatian acronym) for International Catholic Association for Radio and Television
UNDP	United Nations Development Programme
VHP	Vishwa Hindu Parishad
VT	*Vetus Testamentum*
VTS	*Vetus Testamentum Supplements*
WBC	Word Biblical Commentary
WEA/WEF	World Evangelical Alliance / World Evangelical Fellowship
ZB	Zurcher Bibelkommentare

CHAPTER 1

Introduction: Evangelisation, Contextual Apologetics and Research

J.C. GAMALIEL

The foundation of missiology is in theology. Missiology must be squarely based on systematic, exegetical and historical theology but is informed by the social sciences and the study of religions leading ultimately to an integrated inter-disciplinary approach. Evangelisation, research and apologetics are brought together in the discipline of missiology, and therein lies the worthwhileness of this project—now the textbook in your hands! *Missiology for the 21st Century: South Asian Perspectives* is an effort to bring together some of the fruits of academic research which may be helpful for equipping the People of God for the mission of the Church in the world today.

Much controversy has arisen around the term 'evangelisation'. The last visit of Pope John II aggravated the situation. Some of his statements about the Church's responsibility to "evangelise India" infuriated Hindu fundamentalists who argue that evangelisation is tantamount to conversion, and conversion means that Hinduism loses an adherent. Meanwhile some church leaders also seem to shun the term 'evangelisation' and seek to deflect criticism by claiming to do mere social service among the scheduled castes and tribes. In this context, it seems appropriate to consider more closely the meaning and significance of evangelisation, contextual apologetics and research for the Church's task in South Asia today.

Evangelisation

The root word for evangelisation, *evangelizo,* means to declare, proclaim, preach. The New Testament is replete with illustrious examples of the apostles who were at it day in and day out.[1] The Lord Jesus Christ at the beginning of his own ministry refers to the prophecy concerning himself (Isaiah 61:1-4) and makes clear the grand missional vision it conceals.[2] Mark, the evangelist, puts it in terse form when he says, "Jesus came to Galilee proclaiming the good news of God, and saying, "The time is fulfilled, and the kingdom of God has come near; repent and believe in the gospel"(Mk 1:15). After the events of Christ's death and resurrection, the call to repentance continued to be proclaimed by the Apostles.

Basic to Christian ministry, distinguishing it from all other services rendered, is the gospel of Jesus Christ.[3] The whole world, the universe, all things visible and invisible, are within the kingdom of power. God is sovereign, He rules and over-rules everything. The controls are in his hands. But he has given free will to humans and

---

[1] See Rev.10:7; 14:6; Acts 16:17; Isaiah 60:6; Acts 13:32; Gal.1:16; Luke 9:6; 20:1; Acts 14:7; Rom.15:20; 1 Cor.1:17; 9:16,18.

[2] Luke 4:16-21.

[3] Mark 1:1; Acts 20:24; Rom.15:16; 2 Cor.4:9; 1 Tim.1:11; Eph.6:15.

limited freedom. But nothing goes out of God's ultimate control. Evangelisation is calling people from the kingdom of power to the kingdom of grace. God rules the kingdom of power by His love and holy laws.[4] In the kingdom of grace, the fellowship of believers, God works through His love, law and the gospel.

The people of the kingdom of power are called by the Law and the gospel of God to the conviction of sin, to repentance and faith to receive forgiveness of sin and reconciliation with God through grace alone. In Romans Paul describes how a repentant and believing person is transferred from darkness to light, from death to life, from the power of Satan to the abundant grace of God. The Holy Spirit calls people from the kingdom of power to the kingdom of grace through the gospel. Living faith produces good works which are pleasing to God and brings glory to God, edification to the Church and good to humankind. The end of the life of sanctification is the kingdom of glory, heaven.

Christian ministry is calling people from the kingdom of power and darkness, of bondage and hopelessness to the kingdom of grace and a life of fellowship with God and with fellow believers.

To have the right perspective on evangelisation, the nature of the kingdom of Satan also has to be understood. God's commission to Paul was "… to open their eyes so that they may turn from darkness to light and from the power of Satan to God, so that they may receive forgiveness of sins and a place among those who are sanctified by faith in me" (Acts 26:17-18). 'Principalities and powers' refer to Satan and the demonic powers who are with him. "Having disarmed principalities and powers, Christ made a public spectacle of them, triumphing over them on the cross" (Col.2:15). Satan has been disarmed, defeated. Still Satan has limited power, and through cunning wiles and falsehoods lures people away from God and keeps them in bondage and darkness. "Professing to be wise, they became fools, and exchanged the glory of the incorruptible God for images resembling corruptible humans and birds and animals and reptiles" (Rom.1:23). While these are facets of popular religion, subtle philosophies based on human reason also can keep people in slavery. "Though they knew God, they did not honour him as God or give thanks to him, but they became futile in their thinking, and their senseless minds were darkened" (Rom.1:21). Making reason their God, they became lost in the intricacies of their confused thinking.

The only redeeming feature in this abysmal world of contradicitions is the law of God written in the human heart at creation and still operative in every human conscience. "When Gentiles who have not the law do by nature what the law requires, they are a law to themselves, even though they do not have the law. They show that what the law requires is written on their hearts, to which their own conscience also bears witness; and their conflicting thoughts will accuse or perhaps excuse them" (Rom.2:14-15). So the law written in people's hearts and conscience become stepping stones for the proclamation of the gospel of God.

State or national government is a further dimension of the kingdom. The authorities and ordinances of the State are called God's ministers or servants (Rom.13:4,6). They are not ministers of the gospel, but ministers of the law to maintain order in the world. The police, laws and law courts exist to restrain the evil passions, greed and avarice of humans which, if unbridled, result in mutual annihilation and destruction. The role of the Church, the kingdom of grace, has to be distinguished from that of the State, God's minister with the law and the sword (Rom.13:4). A Christian has a dual citizenship. He is a citizen

---

[4] Mt.5:45; 6:25-35.

of the Church, the kingdom of grace, and also a citizen of a State. The Church has the law and the gospel. The State has only the law. The Christian's role and responsibilities differ in the Church and in the State. While the State functions at a national level, culture and various social institutions function to control life at the local level. In evangelisation it is important to discern the restraining forces of the law at work in every society.

When a person has become a believer and a forgiven sinner, the Law of God which was once an accuser becomes a guide to God's will. Motivated by the gospel and guided by the Holy Spirit operating through God's Word and the sacraments, the believer glorifies God's name by a life of obedience to the will of God. Both the Law and the gospel are holy. They come from God, and God through the Law and the Gospel works for the salvation of humankind.[5]

Evangelisation is a call to enter into the Kingdom of God in order to experience deliverance and salvation in every dimension of life. The essential tenets of the Kingdom of God, namely power, grace and the glory of God contending against the kingdom of the world and of Satan, are the core content of evangelisation. Evangelisation works to strengthen the legitimate functioning of the State for restraining evil forces and maintaining law and order in the world.

Thus evangelisation is an invitation for every person to turn away from rebellion against God's will, clearly depicted in the law, and return to the loving God perfectly revealed in Christ. Only then could anyone begin to appreciate both the law and the gospel as holy, both pointing to a righteous and loving God. The richness of the gospel and the veracity of evangelisation are such that missiology must squarely be based on systematic, exegetical and historic theology informed by the relevant disciplines of science.

This is what makes missiology an integrated, interdisciplinary field of study. Since evangelisation involves the proclamation of the gospel, the pertinent questions will concern the modes of communication. The content of the gospel, its power and wisdom, most effectively meet the deepest quests of the human heart. There is no excuse for lassitude; both with faith and gratitude the gospel is to be presented in the best possible way.

Contextual Apologetics

Missionaries from early times found a need for research and apologetics in evangelisation. In the incessant search for effective means of communicating the gospel, we can find models worth emulating even now. Robert de Nobili (1577-1656) was a great 'orientalist' and missionary apologist who came to Madurai in 1606. After a year he changed his residence, lifestyle and dress to that of an Indian sanyasi. Nobili was a scholar who wrote in Tamil, Telugu, Sanskrit, Latin, Italian and Portuguese. His apologetic works included: Refutation of Transmigration, Dialogue on Eternal Life, A Treatise on the Soul, Theodicy, Spiritual Torch. He delineated culture from religion and cultural traits from religious elements. At a time when Western culture, dress and names were imposed on converts, Nobili advocated retention of local cultural forms. That was a revolutionary idea at that time which provoked much controversy.

Similar pursuits are found in the first Protestant missionaries, Bartholomew Ziegenbalg and Henry Plütschau, who arrived in Tranquebar in 1706 where they established a church and schools, studied Tamil and completed the translation of the New Testament. Ziegenbalg's two books, *The Geneology of the Malabar Gods* and *Malabarischen Heidentum* reveal in-depth research and cultural insights. Ziegenbalg acknowledged the realities of two worlds, the

---

[5] See Ephesians 2:4-6 and Romans 10:1-5.

kingdom of Satan and the kingdom of God. The task of the missionary was to call people from darkness to light and from the power of Satan to the power of God.

After the decline of the Tranquebar Mission, the Evangelical Revival opened the age of modern missions which brought William Carey (1761-1834) to Bengal in 1793. Carey and his associates believed that a profound study of the background and thought of the non-Christian peoples was essential for the effective communication of the gospel. Carey's Sanskrit Grammar, a beautifully printed work of 1,000 pages, was a remarkable contribution. He translated the Ramayana into English and into Bengali. William Ward's *History, Literature and Mythology of the Hindus* in four volumes was a remarkable contribution.

In addition to the efforts of the missionaries enumerated above, the contributions of the orientalists Charles Wilkins, Alexander Duff, William Jones, and Max Mueller opened the vistas of the Hindu world to the Western world for understanding, appreciating and opening the possibility of dialogue.

John Nicol Farquhar (1861-1929) was an outstanding missionary scholar who recruited a group of scholars like Griswold and McNicol to launch a new era of Christian apologetics in the early decades of the twentieth century which would pave the way for deeper dialogue between Hinduism and Christianity. Farquhar wrote *Gita and Gospel* (1903), *Permanent Lessons of the Gita* (1903), *The Age and Origin of the Gita* (1904), *The Crown of Hinduism* (1913), *Modern Religious Movements in India* (1915), and *An Outline of the Religious Literature of India* (1920).

Some of the other publications in the Religious Quest of India series edited by Farquhar and Griswold were: Sinclair Stevenson, *The Heart of Jainism*; J.H. Moulten, *The Treasure of the Magi*; A.G. Hogg, *The Vedanta*; John Mackenzie, *Hindu Ethics*; K.J. Saunders, *Buddhism*; Sinclair Stevenson, *The Rites of the Twice Born*; Sydney Cave, *Redemption, Hindu and Christian*; and others.

Alfred George Hogg (1875-1954), who served in India for thirty years, wrote *Karma and Redemption* (1909), *Christ's Message of the Kingdom* (1911), *Redemption from this World* (1922) and *Christian Message to the Hindu* (1947).

Along with these developments in India, a series of ecumenical missionary conferences at Edinburgh (1910), Jerusalem (1928) and Tambaram (1938) also contributed to thinking about mission. Professor William Hocking's publication of the Laymen's Foreign Missions Inquiry report (1932) seemed to cut at the very root of the missionary movement.[6] In response, and at the request of the International Missionary Council, Hendrik Kraemer wrote his famous *The Christian Message in a Non-Christian World* which was published as study material for the IMC Tambaram conference (1938). Later Kraemer also wrote *Why Christianity of All Religions* (1962).

The scope of Christian apologetics is not restricted to the mere defence of the gospel, but can serve to invigorate Christian witness and participation in dialogue. P.D.Devanandan's efforts at urging Indian national Christians to meet the challenges of resurgent Hinduism and his tireless campaign to engage in nation building are the best examples of this way of doing Christian apologetics. Most of Devanandan's apologetic writings were brought together and published in *Preparation for Dialogue* (1964). Devanandan died in 1962, and M.M. Thomas became his successor at the Christian Institute

---

[6] William Ernest Hocking, *Re-Thinking Missions: A Laymen's Inquiry after One Hundred Years*, New York and London: Harper & Brothers, 1932.

for the Study of Religion and Society (CISRS). Thomas' *Salvation and Humanisation* (1971) gives the framework and theological assumptions of Thomas' political philosophy. He wrote as a social and political philosopher. From this time onward the primary concern of CISRS has been for liberation of the socially and politically oppressed and for the liberation of women.

This, in brief, is a survey of evangelisation and apologetics in India from the time of the early missionaries to the present.

Missiological Research

In addition to what has been written so far, something needs to be added about missiological research. I speak out of personal experience and involvement! I had the privilege of being trained under Henry Presler of the School of Research, Leonard Theological College, Jabalpur, Madhya Pradesh. He oriented his students with much enthusiasm, not only in theology, but also in sociology, anthropology and research methods. I am convinced that his massive and monumental research material, if published, would be a great contribution to the church in South Asia. Presler's work points to the need to move to new frontiers and new horizons.

My training under Presler in the pursuit of evangelisation was of immense help in my study of the religious phenomena, patterns, processes and trends of Malad near Bombay (now Mumbai). Later when I moved to Concordia Theological Seminary, Nagercoil, Tamil Nadu, I was invited to be in-charge of its Institute of Evangelism and Research out of which Bethel Theological Institute (Kerala) has emerged. Bethel exists to motivate and to equip the laity to witness through seminars, research and publications in cooperation with other like minded people and institutions. From 1974 to 1990 at Concordia Seminary some 323 study papers had been submitted by the students, as follows:

Methodology	10
Devi Temples	76
Saiva Temples	55
Vishnu Temples	14
Ashrams, Gurus	59
Tribes, Castes, Communities	31
Villages, Panchayats, Wards	19
Various Case Studies	36
Studies of Islam	7
Urban Studies	1
Church Related Studies	25

In addition there were other study papers, all an indication of what can be done. The value of such research is, in the light, it can throw on contemporary religious and social phenomena and on the practice of mission.

Evangelisation is our God-given task. Conversion is God's work. Conversion is a change of heart and mind, a spiritual transformation. McGavran's 'people movement' concept has great relevance in India. The task of the Church is not to wrench individuals out of their culture, social structure or kinship web. People should be encouraged to remain in their family structure, to receive the treasure of the gospel of God, the message of forgiveness and peace with God, and then to share this new-found joy with their fellows. In matters of faith, prayer and worship, they may differ from their kin, but in all matters social, economic and political they remain as one. Religion and culture have a close link but are not identical and have to be differentiated. Religion is one of the components of culture. When the gospel of God, the message of the Cross, becomes the center of a culture, it ultimately transforms that culture.

Philosophy, sociology, anthropology, psychology and all other intellectual disciplines have to be seen in a proper perspective to develop an integrated and inter-disciplinary missiology and harnessed for the all-important task.

The insights of McGavran combined with Presler's empirical research methodology would facilitate the production of relevant apologetic literature to meet the deepest of spiritual and ethical needs.

Evangelisation, apologetics and research ought to be at the core of missiological studies. *Missiology for the 21ˢᵗ Century: South Asian Perspectives* is an endorsement of such a conviction! It is grounded in the conviction that these three activities are necessary and urgent in this new day and era. When much controversy has arisen within and without the Church on its rationale and methodology, this is a timely and valuable resource for the Church in the region.

PART I

Biblical Studies

CHAPTER 2

Incomparability of Yahweh in the Hebrew Bible

MANI CHACKO

Introduction

The notion that Yahweh is the Incomparable One: "that you may know that there is no one like me" (Ex 8:6, 9:14); "that you may know that I, Yahweh, am in the midst of the earth" (8:18); "that you may know that the earth is Yahweh's" (9:29); "and the Egyptians shall know that I am Yahweh" (7:5, 14:4,18); "...on all the gods of Egypt, I will execute judgements: I am Yahweh" (12:12b), is a key motif in the Hebrew Bible. An examination of this religious polemic motif gives rise to several key issues. Do the expressions of Yahweh's incomparability contain any notion of definite comparison? Or has this notion of comparison fallen into the background?[1] Are these expressions merely, and nothing more than, "honorific ascriptions to God" or "exclamations of praise", borrowed from pagan context and used with reference to Yahweh? [2] Are there similar expressions found in the wider Old Testament context? If so, what is their content? What are the implications of these confessions to Israel? Does this motif particularly in the exodus tradition, project any clue to the origin of monotheism in Israel? Does this motif have any relevance in a multi religious context like South Asia? Before we deal with these issues, the exodus text itself has to be probed in order to trace the emergence of the religious polemic motif. A consideration of the key formula "I am Yahweh", a reflection on the motif of "hardening of heart" and an analysis of the plague stories are in order for a proper understanding of the motif of Yahweh's incomparability in the exodus tradition.

I am Yahweh

The frequent occurrence of this *Selbstvorstellungsformel* [3] (self-introduction formula) in Ex. 1:1-15:21 is of decisive significance, for it describes Yahweh as unique and incomparable. The opening words of the Decalogue portray this point with great precision: 'I am Yahweh your God, who brought you out of the land of Egypt, out of the house of slavery' (Ex 20:2). It is in this act of redemption that Israel saw the particular characteristic that distinguishes Yahweh from other gods: "Yahweh did something that no other god ever did - the liberation of a nation for Himself from the clutches of slavery".[4] Zimmerli's observations regarding the *Selbstvorstellungsformel* are worthy of note. Based on the Holiness code, he observes that this formula appears in two forms: the statement "I am Yahweh" and the fuller formulation, "I am Yahweh, your God". The former contains the element of self-introduction by means of the personal name in its pure form and the latter is an appropriate development of the first, which means the one introducing himself under the

---

[1] G.E. Wright, The Old Testament against its Environment, London, 1950 p. 34.

[2] *Ibid.*

[3] W. Zimmerli, 'Ich bin Yahweh' Geschichte und Altes Testament. Beiträge zur historischen Theologie, Atlanta, p.16. (1953) pp. 179-209; trs by Douglas W. Stott, I am Yahweh, pp. 1-28.

[4] C.J. Labuschagne, *The Incomparability of Yahweh in the Old Testament*, Leiden,1966, p.136.

name Yahweh also stands in a divine and lordly relationship to Israel.[5] It is his view that the *Sitz im Leben* of the formula of self-introduction lays within the priestly literature and that the formula functions within the framework of legal discussion.[6] He arrives at this conclusion by a comparative study of Ex.6 and Ezekiel 20. In Ex.6:2-3, it is perfectly clear that the use of the formula is not merely incidental but on the contrary, he argues, is a sign of fully conscious theological reflection. The self-introductory formula in Ex. 6 is integrated into the framework of a larger historico-theological vision (6:2-3). This is followed by a reference to the covenant with the Patriarchs and to the content of the promise that is to be fulfilled in response to the agonising cry of the enslaved Israelites in Egypt. Then follows the announcement of the particular task given to Moses, framed both at the beginning and at the end by the formula of self-introduction, with *hwhy yna* again appearing in the midst of the announcement: "Therefore, say to the Israelites, 'I am Yahweh, and I will bring you out from under the burdens of the Egyptians, and I will deliver you from their bondage, and I will redeem you with an outstretched arm and by great acts of judgement. And I will take you for my people and I will be your God. Then you will know that I, Yahweh, am your God, who has brought you out from under the burdens of the Egyptians. I will bring you into the land which I vowed with uplifted hand to give to Abraham, to Isaac and to Jacob, and I will give it to you as a possession. I am Yahweh'" (6:6-8).

Zimmerli compares this passage with Ezekiel 20:5-7, where the content of the above passage is recapitulated: "On the day when I chose Israel, I vowed with uplifted hand to the seed of the house of Jacob, making myself known to them in the land of Egypt. I swore to them, saying, I, Yahweh, am your God. On that day I vowed with uplifted hand to them that I would bring them out of the land of Egypt into a land that I had searched out for them, a land flowing with milk and honey, the most glorious of all lands. And I said to them, cast away the detestable things your eyes feast on, every one of you, and do not defile yourselves with the idols of Egypt; I am Yahweh your God." He observes that in the Ezekiel passage, although there is no reference to the patriarchal tradition, the giving of the law is woven totally into the departure period of the Exodus story. The first and second commandments, he argues, are clearly echoed in the command to cast away "the detestable things your eyes feast on" and the "idols of Egypt" (20:7) and that the formula "I am Yahweh," as in the Exodus passage, here also carries all the weight and becomes the denominator upon which all else rests. Zimmerli, in fact, affirms, "everything Yahweh has to announce to his people appears as an amplification of the fundamental statement, 'I am Yahweh.'"[7]

It is also his observation that this pattern of the repetition of *hwhy yna* is repeated appears in the context of the legal formulations of the Holiness code (Lev. 18:2-5). He finds definite significance in the occurrence of this pattern and remarks "this indefatigable repetition of '*nyyh wh*" at the end of individual statements or smaller groups of statements in the legal offerings is not to be understood as thoughtlessly strewn decoration; rather, this repetition pushes these legal statements into the most central position from which the Old Testament can make any statement. Each of these small groups of legal maxims thereby becomes a legal communication out of the heart of the Old Testament revelation of Yahweh."[8]

---

[5] W. Zimmerli, I am Yahweh, p.4.

[6] *Ibid.* p. 7

[7] *Ibid.* p. 9.

[8] *Ibid.* p. 12.

His scrutiny of the formula in the Old Testament also points towards its polemical dimension, which is especially evident in Deutero-Isaiah. He notes that in all the passages where the formula appears in Deutero-Isaiah Yahweh is presented as highly exalted against potential rival gods: "I am Yahweh, that is my name; my glory I give to no other, nor my praise to graven images" (42:8); "I am Yahweh, and there is no other besides me, there is no God" (45:5); "I, I am Yahweh, and besides me there is no saviour" (43:11); "Am I not Yahweh, and there is no other god besides me, a righteous god, and a saviour, there is none besides me" (45:21). He also draws attention to Hosea 13:4, "I am Yahweh, your God, from the land of Egypt; you know no God but me, and besides me there is no saviour," where Yahweh's singularity is greatly stressed and projected.[9] This polemic note is also reflected in Judges 6:10; Psalm 50:7 ff., and in Psalm 81:9 ff, but what is also notable in these verses, he argues, is that there is a juxtaposition of the formula of self-introduction and the Decalogue. Hence Zimmerli re-emphasises his view that the formula of self-introduction does indeed belong in the context of the mediation of legal maxims, and not in prophetic speech, despite its frequent appearances in Ezekiel, Deutero-Isaiah and Hosea. It is his observation that the prophets, in their encounter with God, do not experience the encounter in the kind of theophany with an "I AM" introduction, as in the context of the proclamation of the Law.[10]

W.H. Schmidt's remarks are also of due significance. To begin with, he asserts, "the self-revelation of God in his word is a basic characteristic of the Old Testament understanding of God."[11] In other religions, he argues, God appears not so much in the word which people hear, as in the image which they see and in the cultic rites which they perform. In short, he contends that the word of revelation was not a constitutive element of such religions. Secondly, it is his conjecture — the form of speech as such that emerges from polytheism. In the ancient Near East, he points out, the deity generally bears a name that characterises him or her and distinguishes from others. The most frequently quoted example from Israel's neighbours is the oracle the Assyrian king, Esarhaddon, received from the goddess Ishtar: "I am Ishtar of Arbela, O Esarhaddon, king of Assyria!.... 'Fear not, O king', I said to you."[12] He also makes reference to what the goddess Inanna says of herself in a Sumerian song:

> My father has given me the sky,
> has given me the earth;
> I am the mistress of heaven,
> Is any, a god, a match for me?[13]

Here, the formula of self-introduction is expanded with aspects of "boastful self-glorification,"[14] as also used by Deutero-Isaiah: "I am Yahweh, who made all things, who stretched out the heavens alone, who spread out the earth – who was with Me?" Thus, Schmidt observes that "the formula....changes its sense by such expansions"[15] and that "....it is found in different forms and with changing meaning throughout antiquity."[16]

Thirdly, he argues that the formula in the Old Testament is not intended to introduce someone completely unknown. Rather, it refers explicitly

---

[9] *Ibid.* pp. 17-20.

[10] *Ibid.* p. 22.

[11] W.H. Schmidt, *The Faith of the Old Testament*, Oxford, 1953) p. 53.

[12] J.B. Pritchard *Ancient Near Eastern Texts*, Princeton, 1955, p. 450.

[13] W.H. Schmidt, *op.cit.*, p.54.

[14] *Ibid.*

[15] *Ibid.* p. 55.

[16] *Ibid.*

to the history which God has experienced together with Israel, as is evident in the prologue of the Decalogue, "I am Yahweh, your God, who brought you out of Egypt, out of the house of slavery." He further contends that this prologue "is like a 'basic law' from which the individual commandments follow"[17] and that "this association of divine self-introduction and giving of commandments appears to be unknown to Israel's neighbours"[18] where "only the king can prefix his 'I' to the proclamation of the law...."[19] Fourthly, Schmidt maintains that the collections of laws such as the Decalogue and the Book of the Covenant presuppose Israel's settlement and closer contact with the Canaanite environment, and hence the Decalogue will have only gradually in the course of time obtained the dominant position which it now has in the Pentateuch. Therefore, the address of God in the theophany "I am Yahweh," he argues, was not from the beginning connected with the proclamation of the law. He thinks it is probable on the basis of many parallels of the address "I am" from the surrounding world the formula may have developed first in Canaan under foreign influence. This being the case, "....Israel took over a formula from other religions, in order....to distinguish its God from the gods of other nations and so to express the distinctive character of its faith."[20]

The polemic aspect in this formula has been also asserted by J.P. Hyatt: "For P, it is an assertion not only that this is the name of God, but that Yahweh is the only God who exists and exerts His sovereign power in the affairs of men".[21] Thus it is clear from the above examination that the sole intention of the Hebrew writer in the frequent use of the *Selbstvorstellungsformel* is to project Yahweh as the one and the only incomparable God.

The Hardening of Pharaoh's Heart

This issue has long disturbed theologians and biblical scholars. Some of the passages in Exodus 4-14 seem to say that God himself hardens the heart of Pharaoh (Ex, 4:21; 7:3; 9:12; 10:1, 20, 27; 11:10; 14:4, 8, 17) and, because of this hardening, Pharaoh continues to resist the will of Yahweh until he is destroyed. It is this deterministic view of the relationship between God and human that has puzzled most theologians, and, because of this, considerable attempts have been made to interpret the motif of "hardening" in such a way as to soften the harsh view they seem to project.[22] The motif also assumes a religious polemic intention, especially when it is noted that the Egyptian king was himself regarded as a god with a claim to incomparability because of his relation with the sun god.[23] Thus the contest in the liberation of

---

[17] *Ibid.*

[18] *Ibid.*

[19] Hammurabi introduces his collection of laws (the code of Hammurabi) by "Hammurabi the Shepherd, called by Enlil, am I", *Ancient Near Eastern Texts*, p.164.

[20] *Ibid.* p. 56

[21] J.P. Hyatt, *Exodus*, London, 1971, p. 93.

[22] For a general discussion of the motif of hardening of Pharaoh's heart See F. Hesse, *Das Verstockungsproblem im Alten Testament*, Berlin, 1955, pgs. 31-98; G von Rad, *Old Testament Theology* Vol. 2, pp. 151-55; W. Eichrodt, *Theology of the Old Testament*, Vol. 2,London, 1985, pp. 177-81; B.S. Childs, *Exodus*, London, 1974, pp. 170-171; U. Cassuto, *A Commentary on the Book of Exodus*, London, 1954, pp. 55-57; J. Plastaras, *The God of Exodus*, Milwaukee, 1955, pp. 133-37; I.L. Seeligmann, "Menschliches Heldentum und göttliche Hilfe," *TZ* 19, Gottingen, 1963, pp. 385-411; K.L. Schmidt, "Die Verstockung des Menschen durch Gott," *TZ* 1,1945, pp. 1-17; J.Gnilka, *Die Verstockung Israels, Munich, 1961*; H. Räisänen, *The Idea of Divine Hardening*, Helsinki, 1972; B. Jacob, "Gott und Pharao," *MGWJ* 68, Jerusalem, 1924, pp. 118-26.

[23] C.J. Labuschagne, *The Incomparability of Yahweh in the Old Testament*, p.60; cf. also H. Frankfort, *Kingship and the Gods*, n.d., p.42 ff.

Israel is between Yahweh and the god-king of Egypt. Labuschagne's remarks are notable here: "It was not only because he was the ruler of Egypt that he is represented as Yahweh's adversary in the dramatic contest to free Israel, but also because he was known as a god, having control not only over the Egyptians, but also over Yahweh's people whom he oppressed and enslaved. Because of this and because of the fact that he showed contempt for Yahweh (5:2), it was felt that the Pharaoh in particular had to acknowledge that 'there is no one like Yahweh' (8:6; 9:14)."[24] The position and attitude of the Pharaoh is presented as a challenge to Yahweh which offends His position and defies His rights concerning Israel. The motif, therefore, intends to vindicate Yahweh's unique and incomparable position, as God.

The way in which the motif of the "Hardening of Pharaoh's heart" serves to establish the incomparability of Yahweh needs examination. A.U. Cassuto has argued that the motif does not deal with the philosophical issues such as "the relationship between the free will of man and God's presence, or the justification of reward and punishment for human deeds that God himself brought about."[25] Rather it is an example, he asserts, of "the way in which the ancient Hebrew expresses itself," as it was customary to attribute every phenomenon to the direct action of God (I Sam.1:5; Ex. 2:13).[26] He further insists that the passages where the motif occurs should be considered according to their simple meaning and as per the reasoning of their period and not in the light of concepts that came into existence at a later period.[27]

S.R. Driver shares the same line of thought as Cassuto, when he remarks that "the Hebrews, with their vivid sense of the sovereignty of God, were in the habit of referring things done by man to the direct operation of God; and it is possible that these are merely examples of the same custom."[28] However, he cogently expresses his belief that God, especially in His dealings with His agents, does not act arbitrarily. He only hardens those who begin by hardening themselves. It would be inconsistent with the character of a righteous God, if He were to harden those whose hearts were turned towards Him. Pharaoh, he argues, from the very outset in the Exodus story, appears as a self-willed, obstinate man, who persistently hardens himself against God. God thus hardens him only because he has first hardened himself. It is also his remark that the means by which God hardens a man need not be by any extraordinary intervention on his part, but could be by the ordinary experiences of life, which are appointed by him.[29] J.P. Hyatt tends to think that the belief that it was Yahweh who hardened the heart of the Pharaoh arose as a result of the re-telling of the Exodus story and reflecting upon it, by Israel, in this process, ".....they came to believe that the will of Yahweh could not in any sense be thwarted by the will of the pagan ruler. As the story of the exodus was told and re-told, the Israelites came to increasingly believe in the complete sovereignty of their God."[30] Though Hyatt perceives a tension between divine determinism and human freedom because of J's assertions that the Egyptian king hardened his own heart, it is his belief that the weighting is in favour of the former. Thus, he argues, there is no

---

[24] *Ibid.* p. 75.
[25] U. Cassuto. *A Commentary on the Book of Exodus*, p. 55.
[26] *Ibid.* p. 56.
[27] *Ibid.*
[28] S.R. Driver, *Exodus*, Cambridge, 1911, p. 53.
[29] *Ibid.* p. 54
[30] J.P. Hyatt, *Exodus*, p.102.

contest of wills between Yahweh and Pharaoh is not really free to oppose the will of Yahweh.[31]

This notion of the absolute sovereignty of God has been also echoed by D.M. Beegle: "In trying to understand such Old Testament interpretations of events, it must be remembered that the people of the ancient biblical world did not make a distinction between primary and secondary causes. In the broader context of the ancient world, God created Pharaoh with a strong ego, determined to defend itself. While Pharaoh's part was not ignored, God himself was considered responsible for Pharaoh's actions."[32]

A similar view is seen reflected in the *Methodical and Systematic Analysis of the Categories of Obduracy in the Old Testament* by F. Hesse, where he identifies the almighty power of Yahweh and the sinful action of human in an unbelievable tension. The last section of his work *Verstockungsaussagen und Gottesverständnis* is particularly noteworthy, where he categorically affirms that God acts with absolute freedom and before Him, people must bow with humility and awe. His purpose to make for Himself a people cannot be thwarted. Only as saving history reaches its goal will all obduracy cease. But in the meantime, he insists that Israel must know that the ways of God cannot be fitted into human's narrow categories. There remains always a mystery, he remarks, of which the act of God in hardening the heart is an aspect.[33]

David Gunn has recently argued along the same lines that the element of divine causality is important to understand the significance of the motif. He summarises his observations, which he arrived at, from his study of the motif in Ex. 4-14, as follows: -

> .... while in the early stages of the story we are invited to see Pharaoh as his own master, hardening his own heart (perhaps the legacy of the J story), as the narrative develops, it becomes crystal clear that God is ultimately the only agent of heart-hardening who matters (the P legacy). 'Pharaoh's heart was hardened' thus becomes a kind of shorthand for 'Yahweh caused Pharaoh's heart to harden'. If Pharaoh may have been directly responsible for his attitude at the commencement, by the end of the story he is depicted as acting against his own better judgement, a mere puppet of Yahweh. [34]

John Rogerson also draws attention to the element of divine causality because through it is expressed the power of God, a theme which he and others see at the centre of the whole exodus story.[35] However, he also considers the J legacy in the story-Pharaoh hardens his own heart — as significant: "In the case of the hardening of Pharaoh's heart, the narrative displays some subtlety, and in its final form there is an apparent contradiction between Pharaoh hardening his own heart (8:32) (Heb. 8:28) and God hardening Pharaoh's heart (9:12)....The final narrative....seeks to express both God's complete control over the destinies of men (that is, God hardened Pharaoh's heart), and the part that can be played by a man in shaping his own destiny and those of others (that is, Pharaoh hardened his own heart)."[36]

While granting due importance to such views as listed above, it is also important to realise that

---

[31] *Ibid.* p. 54.

[32] D.M. Beegle, *Moses, The Servant of Yahweh*, Grand Rapids, 1972, p.105.

[33] F. Hesse, *op.cit.*, pgs. 31-98.

[34] D.M. Gunn, 'The "Hardening of Pharaoh's Heart": Plot, Character and Theology in Ex.1-14' in '*Art and Meaning: Rhetoric in Biblical Literature*', ed. D.J.A. Clines, D.M. Gunn and A.J. Hauser, Sheffield, 1982, pp.79-80.

[35] J. Rogerson, *The Supernatural in the Old Testament*, Guidford, 1976, p.41; *cf.* R.E. Clements, *Exodus*, Cambridge, 1972, pp. 30, 34, 38, 43; B.S. Childs *Exodus*, pp. 24-25; 118, 155.

[36] *Ibid.*

there have been other interpretations of the motif as well. Because this motif appears only in Ex. 4-14 and does not appear in later reflections of the exodus event[37] many scholars have argued that the motif was simply the creation of the authors or editors of these narratives. It is their view that the motif was not originally a part of the plague or exodus traditions and hence it was not preserved in later accounts of those traditions. A few of them have suggested that the hardening motif is simply a literary device used by the author to give the plague and crossing narratives a coherent structure.[38] Scholars using form-critical and traditio-historical approaches to the problem have suggested that the authors or editors of Ex. 4-11 created the "hardening motif" in order to link previously existing narratives of individual plagues or a sequence of plagues. G. Fohrer has been one of the recent exponents of such a view that the hardening motif is simply a technique for connecting individual plague stories.[39] Although only a few scholars state this position as sharply as Fohrer does, a number of them seem to pre-suppose views similar to his in their discussions of the plague narratives.[40] Thus there is a growing tendency among scholars to see the hardening motif as a literary device and therefore as a secondary addition to the plague traditions. B.S. Childs, however, has taken a different stand from the views above. He denies that the "hardening motif" functioned primarily as an editorial tool linking independent plague narratives. According to him, in both J and P, the motif is closely linked to divine signs; "In J hardness prevents the signs from revealing the knowledge of God; in P the hardness results in the multiplication of signs as judgement."[41] Therefore, he contends that "....all attempts to relate hardness to a psychological state or derive it from a theology of divine causality miss the mark"[42] and suggests an explanation for the frequent appearance of the motif: ".... Hardening was the vocabulary used by the biblical writers to describe the resistance which prevented the signs from achieving their assigned task."[43]

These varied interpretations of the motif, particularly Childs' position, have led Robert R. Wilson to undertake a re-examination of the use of the motif.[44] It is his view that Childs does not deal with all of the dimensions of the problem of the hardening and that it is not possible to generalise about its use in Ex. 4-14. He argues that the motif has slightly different functions in each literary source. In J the hardening motif does not exist to link previously independent plague narratives, but it is used to give literary structure to the overall narrative. In E, the hardening is seen as directly responsible for the plague and Yahweh is regarded as the agent of the hardening, thus giving a reason for the previously inexplicable repetition of Pharaoh's refusal to let the people go. Wilson also observes that E links

---

[37] Apart from Ex. 4-14, the only explicit reference to the hardening of Pharaoh's heart occurs in one of the ark narratives, 1 Sam. 6:6.

[38] B. Jacob, 'Gott und Pharao' *MGWJ* 68, 1924, pp. 202-11 cf. also U. Cassuto, *A Commentary on the Book of Exodus,* pp. 92-135; Heinisch, *Das Buch Exodus,* pp. 78-80; F.V. Winnett, *The Mosaic Tradition,* n.d., pp. 6-9.

[39] G. Fohrer, *Überlieferung und Geschichte des Exodus,* Berlin, 1964, p. 62.

[40] See for a similar view to Fohrer, W. Fuss, Die *deuteronomistische Pentateuchredaktion in Exodus 3-17,* n.d.,pp. 266-67; H. Eising, 'Die ägyptischen Plagen', *Lex tua Veritas : Festschrift für Hubert Junker,* edited by H. Gross and F. Mussner, Trier : Paulinus Verlage, 1961, pp. 85-86; M. Noth, *Exodus: A Commentary,* n.d., pp. 68-71; D.J. McCarthy, 'Moses' Dealings with Pharaoh: Ex.7, 8-10, 27, *CBQ* 27, 1965, pgs. 342-47; P. Weimar, *Untersuchungen zur priesterschriftlichen Exodusgeschichte,* n.d. pp. 195-245; H. Gressmann, Mose und seine zeit, n.d., pp.66-97.

[41] B.S Childs, *Exodus,* p.174.

[42] *Ibid.*

[43] *Ibid.*

[44] R.R. Wilson,'The Hardening of Pharaoh's Heart', *CBQ* 41,1979, pp. 18-36.

the hardening directly with the death of the first-born, thus helping to unify the whole plague cycle. For P as well, the plagues are caused by the hardening which is the work of Yahweh. P further links the motif with' the crossing narrative and uses it to portray the plagues and the crossing as part of Yahweh's holy war to bring about his divine plan for Israel and the narrative also serves as an admonition to Israel to obey Yahweh. Thus Wilson insists "...We must conclude that the hardening motif does indeed have editorial functions within Exodus 4-14..." although he is also of the opinion that this editorial function should not blind scholars to the literary and theological functions of the motif.[45] Thus it may be right to conclude that there is support in the text both for the traditional form-critical view that has redactional functions and for Childs' view that has literary and theological functions.

Among these interpretations, the view that the motif is a literary device used by the author seems to be more convincing. It is perfectly clear from the initial encounter of Moses with Pharaoh that the Pharaoh will not let the Israelites leave. Yahweh himself had made this clear to Moses, in the context of his commission: "I surely know that the king of Egypt will not permit you to go, except by a strong hand" (3:19). Besides, Yahweh had also informed Moses, prior to his encounter with Pharaoh, of his plan to harden the heart of Pharaoh: ".... But I will indeed harden his heart, and he will not let the people go" (4:21). Here of course, the view of divine causality looms large, but the question still emerges as to why the motif is repeated frequently throughout the plagues story, especially when the obdurate nature of Pharaoh and the plan of Yahweh are already clear? It is for this reason that the suggestion was made that the interpretation of the motif as a literary or narrative device is more probable.

However, it needs to be emphasised that this narrative device used by the writer functions not just as a technique to give a coherent structure to the plague narratives or just as a technique connecting individual plagues, as argued by scholars, but also as a device used by the writer in order to establish the sovereignty and incomparability of Yahweh before the Egyptians and Israel. Had Pharaoh been allowed immediately to grant the request of Moses and Aaron and let the Israelites free, there would not have been any need for the plagues. But due to his resistance a series of plagues was necessary to convince Pharaoh of his limitations and of Yahweh's sovereignty and incomparability. Had it not been for the frequent stubbornness of Pharoah all the plagues would not have occurred. The repetitive usage of this motif makes the story more picturesque and progressive. Therefore it may be a possibility to conclude that the motif is a stylistic device used by the writer for effective storytelling.

The Plagues

The motif of religious polemic has its strongest evidence in the event of the plagues. There is an element of mockery of Egyptian gods reflected in the plague episode. As noted above, the Pharaoh himself was regarded as a god and the main thrust of the plague stories is to be found in proving to Pharaoh that "there is no one like Yahweh" (8:6; 9:14). The element of mockery or polemic is seen from the very outset of the plague episode. The Egyptians had personified and deified the river and regarded the river as god with the name *Hapi*, which means "to flow, to run". As a river god, *Hapi* was pictured as a bearded man with female breasts and a hanging stomach to signify fertility. He was crowned with aquatic plants, and he held a tray of food or poured water from vases.[46] There are also hymns

---

[45] *Ibid.* p. 36.
[46] J. Finegan, *Let My People Go*, New York, 1963, p. 49

praising the river god as issuing from the earth and coming to keep Egypt alive.[47] Yet in the biblical narrative, there is a tone of mockery of this belief of the Egyptians when "...all the water in the Nile became blood. The fish that were in the Nile died and the river stank and the Egyptians were not able to drink water from the Nile...." (7:20-21), all by mere striking the water with a rod at God's command (7:20b). The nature of the 'divine' creature had degenerated and its waters ceased to be a source of blessing to Egypt. The transformation of the water by a rod removed all doubt as to where the real power lay. [48] The sole purpose of this event is clearly stated: Pharaoh is to know "that I am Yahweh" (7:17).

The episode of the frogs (7:26 - 8:11) continues to project the motif of mockery or polemic. The Egyptians attributed to the frogs a divine power, and regarded them as a symbol of fertility. The frog was associated with the goddess *Heket*, who is depicted in the form of a woman with a frog's head. *Heket* is the spouse of the god *Khnum*, to whom the Egyptians attribute the creation of human beings. *Heket* was held to blow the breath of life into the nostrils of the bodies that her husband fashioned on the potter's wheel from the dust of the earth.[49] The plague of frogs was regarded as a dreadful nuisance and annoyance. Childs' description of the plague brings the element of mockery into sharp focus: "The frogs entered the houses, climbed on the beds, into the kitchen and eating utensils. Even the most unlikely place to attract a frog, namely the dry oven, was not immune."[50] The narrative intends to convey the idea that Yahweh alone is the sovereign God and that He only bestows on his creatures, according to His will, the power of fertility and that these frogs, a symbol of fecundity

for the Egyptians, can be transformed if He so desires, from a token of blessing to one of blight.[51] The mockery element or the motif of religious polemic is seen again in the concession the obdurate Pharaoh was forced to make: "Pray to Yahweh to remove the frogs from me, and from my people; and I will let the people go to sacrifice to Yahweh" (8:4) and in the prompt removal of the plague, exactly as the Pharaoh wanted (8:9). A final note of mockery is seen in the comment that, even though the frogs were removed, "....the land stank" (8:10).

The third plague of gnats (8:12-15) expresses the religious polemic motif in the confession of the magicians. The magicians had been able to change water into blood and even to produce frogs, but they are unable to bring forth gnats. Instead they confess, "It is the finger of 'God'" (8:15). Cassuto remarks that, by saying the finger of 'God' and not Yahweh, they do not yet concede the Divinity of Yahweh, but merely acknowledge that there is some divine power at work. However the confession is interpreted, what is significant here is that the magicians made partial admission of their limitations. "This is the first explicit indication of how the author settles the question of the true and false miracle."[52]

There are two motifs inherent in the fourth plague of flies (8:16-28) that portray a religious polemic motif. First is the setting of a distinction between the Israelites and the Egyptians, through which Yahweh's sovereignty is defended; "But on that day I will make the land of Goshen, where my people dwell, separate so that no swarms of stinging flies shall be there; that you may know that I am Yahweh in the midst of the land" (8:18). Secondly, there is further concession from Pharaoh. Pharaoh picks up his earlier concession,

---

[47] J.P. Pritchard, *Ancient Near Eastern Texts*, p. 372.

[48] B.S. Childs, *Exodus*, p. 154

[49] U. Cassuto, *A Commentary on the Book of Exodus*, p.14 & 101

[50] B.S. Childs, *Exodus*, p.155

[51] U. Cassuto, *A Commentary on the Book of Exodus*, p. 101

[52] B.S.Childs, *Exodus.*, p.156

i.e., the Israelites will be allowed to sacrifice to their God, but he restricts it with the decisive stipulation "within the land" (8:21). Moses argues that their method of sacrifice would be offensive to the Egyptians and would call forth reprisals against his people. He stands firm on his demand, for a three days journey into the wilderness, which he had voiced from the very beginning (8:23). Pharaoh is compelled to broaden the terms of his assent, to allow them to go to the wilderness to sacrifice to Yahweh, but adds a restriction "only you must not go very far away" (8:24). Moses suspects Pharaoh's motives and he is shrewd enough not to trust him (8:25). Still, as Pharaoh desired, Yahweh removed all the flies, without even one remaining in the land (8:27); but Pharaoh remains stubborn and did not let the people go, exactly in accordance with Yahweh's predictions.

Though the fifth plague of animal pestilence (9:1-7) is considerably shorter and no new themes are introduced, the motif of distinction is developed. Pharaoh's fear and anxiety is evident in him sending messengers to confirm whether in fact Israel's cattle have been spared (9:7). The polemic is strong in the fact that "all the cattle of the Egyptians died, but of the cattle of the Israelites, not one died" (9:6). The sixth plague of boils (9:8-12) serves as another instance, displaying a religious polemic motif, for it brings to a conclusion the theme of the conflict between Moses and the Egyptian magicians. A clear progression is noticeable in the narrative with regard to the magicians. When the first plagues were brought upon Egypt, the magicians managed to perform the same kind of signs. When the third plague, the plague of gnats, occurred, they realised that all their efforts were in vain and they were forced to acknowledge the finger of God. Subsequently, when new plagues were inflicted on Egypt, they maintained silence and now they could not even stand silently "because the boils were on the magicians and on all the Egyptians" (9:11).

The seventh plague, of the hail (9:13-35), displays an element of intensity of the purpose of Yahweh and a growing readiness for serious negotiation on the part of Pharaoh. The intensity of Yahweh's purpose is reflected in vs. 15 and 16: "For by now I could have stretched out my hand and struck you and your people with a plague, and you would have been destroyed from the earth. But for the sake of this have I maintained you, in order to show you my power to the intent that my name may be declared in all the earth."

In vs. 14, a new series of plagues is announced where the purpose of Yahweh is still clear: "that you may know there is no-one like me in all the earth". "The announcement concerning the sending of all plagues (vs. 14), not only serves to heighten the tension in the dramatic narrative but also shows that the acknowledgement of Yahweh's incomparability did not depend on the·effect of one or a few plagues, but of all the plagues".[53] There is a new level of concession on the part of Pharaoh. He said: "Now at length I have sinned. Yahweh is in the right, and I and my people are in the wrong" (vs. 27). Pharaoh then pleads for the stoppage of thunder and hail and suggests a concession: "I will let you go and you shall stay no longer" (vs.28b). Moses, dispelling any hope that a real change has occurred with Pharaoh, is willing to intercede to demonstrate Yahweh's control over the world: "that you may know that the earth is Yahweh's" (vs. 29).

The motif of mockery or polemic becomes more explicit in the eighth plague (10:1-20), for here, for the first time, the purpose of the plagues is described explicitly as "making sport" of Pharaoh, which was to be recounted in the ears

---

[53] C.J. Labuschagne, *The Incomparability of Yahweh in the Old Testament*, p. 94.

of the children (vs. 2). Even Pharaoh's own servants, instead of being supportive, strongly react to Pharaoh's silence to the request of Moses: "Until when will this man be a snare to us? Let the people go and serve Yahweh their God. Do you not yet know that Egypt is ruined?" (vs. 7). Pharaoh does not oppose the advice of his servants and makes a concession but again with a restriction: "Go, serve Yahweh your God; but who are to go?" (vs. 8). Moses is portrayed as growing in intransigence and rejects any condition or restriction (vs. 9). Though Pharaoh again withdrew his word, he is forced by the plague of the locusts to confess, in accordance with the customary formula, declaring, "I have sinned" (vs. 16). This time, his confession becomes more comprehensive that he acknowledges his sins against Yahweh, and also against Moses and Aaron. Here a strong climax of the religious polemic motif is approaching in the phrase "....forgive my sin, I pray, only this once...." (vs.17a). Moses again intercedes and the power of Yahweh was shown once more, by the removal of the locusts (vs.19).

In the ninth plague, of darkness (10:21-29) there is a further demonstration of the greatness of Yahweh's power against the gods of Egypt. When Yahweh wills, the Sun, which is held by the Egyptians as the chief deity, will be hidden and unable to shine upon its worshippers. Pharaoh makes a concession, but again with a restriction (vs. 24). Now Moses refuses to soften his demand. The motif of distinction is explicit: "....but all the Israelites had light in their dwelling places" (vs. 23), which itself is a continuous sign of Yahweh's power. The fact that the Pharaoh finally is forced to let Israel go, exactly in accordance with Moses' demand, further displays an element of mocker□y on Pharaoh, as evident in the context of the tenth plague (11:1-11; 12:29-32) of the killing of the first born, when Pharaoh

is forced to let Israel go in haste, without any restrictions: "Rise up, go forth from among my people both you and the people of Israel; and go, serve Yahweh, as you have said" (12:31). The motif of mockery reaches its zenith in the fruitless attempt of Pharaoh and his soldiers in pursuing the Israelites, which in turn led to their own disappearance from history in the sea (14:28).

The contrast between the true God and other gods becomes apparent not only to Pharaoh and the Egyptians, but also to Israel as well: "And Israel saw the great work which Yahweh did against the Egyptians, and the people feared and believed in Yahweh and in his servant Moses" (14:31). Israel expresses this newly born conviction in the *Song of the Sea* : "Who is like You, among the gods, O Yahweh? Who is like You, majestic in holiness, worthy of awe and praise, doing wonders?" (15:11) It is highly significant to note that the Egyptian gods, with the exception of the god Pharaoh and the reference to the gods in Exod 12:12, were totally ignored in the exodus account, and, as Labuschagne remarks, it was not their existence but their significance, which was denied through the exodus story.[54]

To round of this section of our discussion we agree with the idea that 'Yahweh as the incomparable One' is the central motif of the Exodus Tradition. The *Selbstvorstel-lungsformel* "I am Yahweh," the motif of the "Hardening of Pharaoh's heart" and the story of the plagues portray this fact with great force and lucidity. Rowley has rightly remarked: "It is perfectly true there have been many cases of the adoption of a foreign religion. Sometimes it has been imposed upon a subject people or even readily adopted because of the prestige of a powerful people; sometimes, as in the case of Kenite religion among the southern tribes, it has spread by gradual penetration among the peoples closely

---

[54] *Ibid.* p 48

associated with one another and intermarrying with one another; sometimes by infiltration from a neighbouring people, as frequently in the story of Israel. But here there is nothing of such a character. Here Israel's adoption of Yahweh was the response to His adoption of Israel, and the sequel to His achieved deliverance of her."[55] What is equally noteworthy is the fact that Pharaoh who reacts with arrogance, "Who is Yahweh that I should heed his voice and let Israel go?", is forced to acknowledge who Yahweh is, that He is the incomparable One.

Some Significant Questions & Issues

Having discussed some aspects of the Exodus text let us now go on to discuss important issues, the notion of the "incomparability of Yahweh" raises.

(a) Do the expressions of Yahweh's incomparability contain any notion of definite comparison? Are these expressions really nothing more than "honorific ascriptions to God," or "exclamations of praise," borrowed from a pagan context and used of Yahweh?

The view of G.E. Wright brings the issue into focus: "In most cases...it is doubtful whether this frequent type of comparative expression involves anything more than an honorific ascription to God (e.g.:2 Sam.7:22; I Kings 8:23; Ps.35:10; 71:19; 77:13 etc). The ascription is simply borrowed from a pagan context and used of Yahweh, any definite comparative notion having fallen into the background".[56] C.J. Labuschagne has, however, challenged this view of Wright and has remarked; "...the expressions of Yahweh's incomparability cannot be detached from their context, for they are more than mere epithets of praise parenthetically strung together with other appellations, like beads in a necklace. It is therefore, wrong to characterise them as "exclamations of praise," for one can lift an exclamation of praise out of its context without disturbing the context itself. This, however, is unthinkable as far as the expressions of Yahweh's Incomparability are concerned, because they constitute the main idea, the substance of the passage, to which epithets of praise are complementary."[57] Labuschagne, citing examples from the Old Testament, further states that there can be no doubt at all that a definite comparison was made between Yahweh and the gods of the nations.[58] He also argues that this comparative notion was kept alive right through Israel's history not only by prophetic voices but also in her hymns and Psalms.[59] He thus rightly concludes that it would be wrong to think that the idea of a definite comparison has fallen into the background.[60] With regard to the question of whether the concept of the deity's incomparability was borrowed by Israel from pagan context, Labuschagne has observed: ".... in view of the sources available to us, it has not and cannot be proved on sufficient grounds that Israel borrowed the concept from its neighbours...". [61] He further remarked one might presume that Israel borrowed the concept from its neighbours because the deity was described as incomparable, not only in Israel, but also in Mesopotamia and in Egypt and because Israel had closer contact between these areas, but the phenomenon as such is not convincing proof of dependence and borrowing unless stronger arguments are brought forth.[62] He

---

[55] H.H. Rowley, "Moses and Monotheism" in *From Moses to Qumran*, London, 1963, p.58.

[56] G.E. Wright, *The Old Testament against its Environment*, p.34

[57] C.J. Labuschagne, *The Incomparability of Yahweh in the Old Testament*, p. 65

[58] *Ibid.* pp. 64-89

[59] *Ibid.*

[60] *Ibid.*

[61] *Ibid.* p.131.

[62] *Ibid.* p.130.

also draws attention to the fact that in the Assyro-Babylonian and Egyptian religions, the concept of incomparability was closely connected with the Sun cult and they came to use the attributes of incomparability independently of each other. Therefore, Labuschagne contends the possibility of considering a god incomparable is present in all religions and therefore the possibility that Israel came to call its God incomparable, independently of its neighbours, has to be reckoned with. He does not deny the possibility that Israel was acquainted with its neighbours' use of the attribute of incomparability but he categorically affirms that there are not sufficient grounds to believe that this concept was simply borrowed and applied by Israel to Yahweh. He rightly averts that "the origin of the concept should rather be sought in Hebrew idiom and in Israel's experience in history that Yahweh is a distinctive unique God, quite different from other deities, the truly Incomparable One."[63]

(b) Are there expressions that echo a religious polemic motif in the wider Old Testament context? If so, what is the content of such expressions?

A cursory glance through the biblical texts would reveal the notion is inherent in biblical passages. In Jer.10:2-16, there is a comparison of the idols with Yahweh, in order to prove that they are nothing compared to Yahweh; "Not like these is He who is the portion of Jacob" (vs. 16). The passage maintains that the idols cannot be compared with Yahweh. Faith in him is unlike heathen convictions and the way of the people of Yahweh is not like the way of the nations. The idols are the work of human hands and therefore are not to be feared. But Yahweh is great and who would not fear Yahweh? (vs. 5, 6, 7). Deut. 3:24, 4:34 reveal one of the strongest aspects of Yahweh's incomparability – His acts in history: "Yahweh, God, you have begun to show to your

servant your greatness and your might; for what god is there in heaven or on earth who can do such works and mighty acts as you do?" (Deut. 3:24); "Or has any god ever attempted to go and take a nation for himself ...as Yahweh your God did for you in Egypt before your eyes?" (4:34). Reflecting on the past, the author compares Yahweh with other gods and concludes that, since no other god has ever attempted what Yahweh did, He is incomparable, proving that "Yahweh is God; there is no other besides Him" (4:35) and that "Yahweh is God in heaven above and on earth beneath; there is no other" (4:39).

In Deutero-Isaiah, Yahweh's incomparability is expressed in the form of rhetorical questions:

> To whom then will you liken God or what likeness compare with him? (40:18);
>
> To whom will you compare me that I should be like him? says the Holy One (40:25);
>
> Who is like me? Let him proclaim it, let him declare and set it forth before me (44:7);
>
> To whom will you liken me and make me equal, and compare me, that we may be like? (46:5)

These passages occur in 'lawsuits' dealing with Yahweh's position against the idols, His uniqueness and His claim to be the only God. The people in the pagan environment were inclined to regard Yahweh as one of the many gods, on a level with the idols. Deutero-Isaiah, realising this situation emphatically stresses the uniqueness and incomparability of Yahweh. The idea of the elimination of rival gods is another aspect which is implicit in the concept of incomparability. Deut.32:1-43 clearly projects this idea. The insignificance and impotence of other gods will be proved when Yahweh judges the followers of these gods and they will realise that there is no other god but Yahweh: "See now that I, even I, am He, and there is no god beside

---

[63] *Ibid.* p.132.

me" (vs. 39). The enemies themselves will judge and come to the conclusion that their 'rock' is not as Israel's Rock (vs.31). The Psalmist (Ps.18:32) conveys the same conviction: "For who is God, but Yahweh? And who is a rock, except our God?" The Psalmist learnt from his experience that Yahweh alone as the Rock of refuge could deliver, of which the other gods are impotent, without power, and unable to save, for "they cried for help but there was none to save" (vs.42a). The Psalmist, being convinced that it was only Yahweh, in contrast to the gods of the enemy, who proved Himself to be a living God, affirms his belief: "Yahweh lives; and blessed be my rock, and exalted be the god of my salvation" (vs. 47). More references could be cited but these would suffice to show that the religious polemic motif is widespread throughout the Old Testament.

(c) What are the implications of these expressions to Israel?

The text asserts that the primary and predominant characteristic of Yahweh, as experienced by Israel, was His miraculous intervention in history as the redeeming God. It was this characteristic quality of Yahweh that distinguishes Him from other gods. This unique feature of Yahweh also enables them to proclaim Him as the only One. Israel's basic confession of faith is reflected in the *shema* (Deut.6:4): "Hear O Israel, Yahweh, our God, Yahweh is One." Thus for Israel, Yahweh was not merely a God among the host of other gods; rather Yahweh was the only God. Labuschagne observes that "...the exclusiveness of the confession is not the result of monotheistic thought, but the result of Moses' work, as well as Israel's experience in history that Yahweh is incomparable."[64] In the first commandment, after introducing himself as the God who brought Israel out of Egypt, Yahweh

forbids Israel to have other gods because through the Exodus His incomparability has been proved. Thus Israel is expected to pay undeviating allegiance and loyalty to Yahweh alone, the One incomparable God.

It also needs to be noted, at this juncture, that Israel herself is called 'incomparable' (Deut 33:29; II Sam 7:23; Deut 4:7). There seems to be a close connection between Yahweh's incomparability and that of his people. As Yahweh was incomparable among the gods, Israel was incomparable among the nations. It is note worthy that Israel, apart from being known as 'incomparable', is also known as 'alone' (Num. 23:9; Deut. 33:28; Micah 7:14); 'distinct' (Ex. 33:16); 'separated' (Esth. 3:8); 'the first of the nations' (Amos 6:1). These descriptions reiterate her place among the nations and her responsibility to manifest to the world her loyalty to the One God, Yahweh.

(d) Does the motif of incomparability of Yahweh, particularly in the exodus tradition, project any clue to the origin of monotheism in Israel?

Labuschagne remarks: "Only in the Mosaic period do we find all the conditions required by true monotheism: the appearance of a revolutionary reformer, recognition of one single God, rejection of polytheism, intolerance of the significance of other gods and a tendency toward universalism."[65] Rowley however suggests that the idea of God developed during the time of Moses "is not monotheism and it is unwise to exaggerate it. Nevertheless, it was incipient monotheism and universalism, when fully achieved in Israel, emerged not by natural evolution out of something fundamentally different, but by development of its own particular character."[66]

---

[64] *Ibid.* p.138.
[65] *Ibid.* pp. 148-9
[66] *Ibid.* p 63

This view "the antiquity of monotheism in Israel may....be dated from the time of Moses...." [67] is widely debated. What the text does assert is, through their deliverance from slavery in Egypt, the Israelites have realised that Yahweh is God and that He is incomparable.

Missiological Implications

(e) Does the motif of the Incomparability of Yahweh have any relevance to a multi religious context like South Asia?

The notion of the Incomparability of God is not a phenomenon exclusively unique to Israel alone. As it has been already noted, this phenomenon was common in other religious traditions. If this is so, the confession that Yahweh is Incomparable is to be seen as Israelite confession based on their experience of Yahweh in their history. For the Israelites history plays a significant role in their faith. Their relationship to Yahweh was established on the basis of their redemption from slavery in Egypt. To them Yahweh was a redeeming God and this affirmation was a declaration of their own history and identity.

One of the greatest temptations for the church today is to play down its own history and testimony so that society can achieve a harmonious pluralism. Some scholars suggest that we should alter our theology and mission according to this ideology. The affirmation of our experience of God in Christ they say can be altered to fit that system. We must understand however, that diluting our own faith does not help the cause of a plural society nor the Christian faith. What use is a watered down belief in Christ for society? Such ideas will be neither Christian nor a useful resource for pluralism. Just as we need to respect others who hold differing beliefs, our own identity has to be respected and its integrity valued. Whilst we should be careful how we communicate our experience of God in Jesus Christ, seeing that we do not adopt arrogant and questionable methods, at the same time we should not withdraw from expressing our own faith and experience of God in Christ humbly and in the spirit of selfless service. Yahweh formed Israel as a community after He liberated them from bondage in Egypt. They clearly expressed their faith in the "incomparability of Yahweh" in a religiously plural world. Many people and communities in our nations have likewise been liberated by the gospel of Christ and we are called to be witnesses to that liberation. For us today it is possible to see the value and relevance of the notion of Incomparability of Yahweh in South Asia. One of the most significant challenges we face is to hold on to our understanding of God and experience in Christ and seek to live by that history and identity.

---

[67] H.H. Rowley, "Moses and Monotheism," in *From Moses to Qumran*, p. 58

CHAPTER 3

The Confessional Community Of Isaiah 56-66:
A New Paradigm for Mission

ELIYA MOHOL

Introduction

In the twentieth century, mission was understood, among other things, as originating from God, mediating salvation, a quest for justice, evangelism, liberation, ministry by the whole people of God, witness to people of other faiths, theology, and action in hope.[1] Bosch suggests that all these paradigms are valid and need to be incorporated in an understanding of mission, "which transforms reality" and which, in itself, is in need of constant transforming.[2] While he has delineated the important aspects of missions, Bosch has failed to suggest any criterion to prioritize and categorize these. By failing to identify the focus of missions, Bosch has become the target of Neill's criticism: "If everything is mission, nothing is mission."[3] Understanding mission as confessing of a faith by the Faith, *i.e.*, Confessional Community, I propose, would help us not only to hold different aspects of missions together, but also to prioritize them and find the focus of mission. In this chapter, I will first look at the establishment of Zion in Isaiah 60-62 as a covenantal act, with special reference to her relationship with Yahweh and his solidarity promise. Secondly, I will reflect on the implications of solidarity for inclusions and exclusions. Thirdly, I will present examples of inclusion and exclusion as evidence of Zion Community becoming Confessional in character and open in principle to all irrespective of caste, class and gender. Fourthly, I will conclude by arguing how this model of Zion Community can be a model of the Confessional Community paradigm. Before I begin that however some basic questions need to be answered.

What Is The Confessional Community Paradigm?

The Confessional Community in Isaiah 56-66 is the Zion community, Yahweh's royal household.[4] Yahweh establishes the Confessional Community by an everlasting covenant and wants her to live out His covenantal expectations. The everlasting covenant is continuous with His previous Abrahamic, Sinaitic and Davidic covenants (59:21; 61:8; cf. 54:17-55:5). Yahweh makes "those who confess faith in Him in word and deed" members of this community, irrespective of their colour, class or caste. Into this community of faith, He then incorporates the others (56:8; 66:18-23). He excludes, however, those who cease to confess faith in Him in "word and deed" (57:6; 66:24).

---

[1] D. J. Bosch, *Transforming Mission: Paradigm shifts in Theology of Mission,* New York, 1991, pp.368-510.

[2] *Ibid.*, p.511.

[3] S. Neill, *Creative Tension: The Duff Lectures 1958,* London, 1959, p. 81.

[4] E.V. Mohol, "The Covenantal Rationale for Membership in the Zion Community Envisaged in Isaiah 56-66," an unpublished Ph.D. dissertation, University of Coventry, Coventry, 1998.

What is the Zion Community?

The Zion community is centered on Mount Zion, the temple mount at Jerusalem, with which her identity is closely bound. In the Hebrew Bible, the mount Zion is called "Zion" and the "holy mountain." By extension these designations refer to the city of Jerusalem, the land of Israel and the whole earth.[5] They also point to the two-fold role of the Zion Community:

a) Zion is called "inheritance of Yahweh" (Ex. 15:17; Clements: 1965, 52-53).[6] The title may have been borrowed from the Ras Shamra texts, which similarly describes Zaphon, Baal's dwelling place in the northern skies, as "the mountain of my heritage."[7] The title clarifies that the mountain is Yahweh's patrimony, i.e., the special property that could only be inherited by the son.[8] As Yahweh's special possession, Zion is also Yahweh's dwelling place. Yahweh is called "Yahweh Sabaoth [the Lord of hosts] who dwells [Hashaken] on Mount Zion" (Is. 8:18; Ps. 135:21). In the ANE the gods seem to have a primary association with land, but in the Hebrew Bible Yahweh is primarily associated with His people.[9] This association between Yahweh and people is particularly evident in the Core of Trito-Isaiah (60-62), and is defined in terms of kinship. The title "Yahweh of hosts," besides indicating Yahweh's kingship on Zion, also shows His kinship with Zion. He comes to her as a kinsman to redeem her (Is. 59:21). Unlike Marduk or Baal, Yahweh's royal house Zion includes within its membership also the people of Zion.[10]

b) Yahweh Sabaoth indicates Yahweh's kingship on Zion,[11] the place from which he rules (Is. 24:23). The oracles in which "My holy mountain" occurs as direct speech by Yahweh also point to His kingship. These oracles begin with "thus says Yahweh" or end with "declares Yahweh" or "Yahweh says."[12] Each of these, therefore, represents the decree of a king, Yahweh Sabaoth, who demands exclusive loyalty. Mount Zion, therefore, is the place where people come to seek instruction and pray to and worship Yahweh.[13]

Thus we can define the Zion community as Yahweh's household. Since Yahweh, the father, is also the king over the household, the Zion community is His royal household over which He has exclusive prerogative. Thus Yahweh's kingship and kinship give Him the exclusive rights of redemption and of dominion over Zion. She must look to Him alone for redemption and protection.[14]

What is the Covenantal Rationale For Membership?

The membership rationale has to do with the covenant relationship with Yahweh. This relationship is confessional in character. It has

---

[5] *cf.* R. E. Clements, *God and Temple*, Oxford, 1965; D. E. Holwerda, *Jesus & Israel: One Covenant or Two?* Grand Rapids, 1994, pp. 96-99.

[6] Ex.15:17; Ps. 48:1; Is. 10:12, 32; 11:9; 16:1; 24:23; 25:6-7; 52:1; 56:7; 64:9; 65:25b; R.E. Clements, *God and Temple, pp. 52-53; cf.* U. Cassuto, *Exodus*, Jerusalem,1967, p. 177; J. Durham, *Exodus*, Dallas Texas, WBC 3, 1987, p. 209.

[7] Ras Shamra Mythological texts 3.3.26-28, quoted by R.J. Clifford, *The Cosmic Mountain in Canaan and the Old Testament*, Cambridge, Massachusetts, 1972, p.138.

[8] R.J. Clifford, *The Cosmic Mountain in Canaan and the Old Testament*, Cambridge, Massachusetts, 1972, p.71.

[9] D.I. Block, *The Gods of the Nations: Studies in Ancient Near Eastern National Theology*, ETSM, Jackson, Mississippi , 1988, p. 23; R.E. Clements, *God and Temple*, p. 16.

[10] Ex. 15:16-18; Ps.48:2.

[11] R.J. Clifford, *The Cosmic Mountain in Canaan and the Old Testament*, p. 71.

[12] Is. 56:8; 57:19; 65: 25; 66:20

[13] Is. 2:3-4; 27:13b; 66:20; Mic. 4:2.

[14] B.C. Ollenburger, "Zion, the City of the Great King: A Theological Symbol of the Jerusalem Cult," *JSOTS* 41, Sheffield, 1987, pp. 18-19; Block, The Gods of the Nations...1988, p. 127.

dual aspects of *allegiance, i.e.* confession by word, to Yahweh and *holiness, i.e.,* confession by deed. On the basis of one's allegiance to Yahweh (or His representative) and on the basis of devotional–ethical holiness, one is included in or excluded from the Zion community of Yahweh.

Confession by Word: The rationale of faith, by which the members are established in the community, is drawn from the Abrahamic Covenant "Abraham believed God, and it was credited to him as righteousness" (Gen.15:6). It is the same faith that Yahweh puts forth, through Isaiah, before the Ahazinic community, by which to seek refuge in Him to be saved (Is. 28:16). Habakkuk, later in the aftermath of the devastation of the exile, reiterates the same faith as the key to salvation -"Righteous shall live by faith" (Hab. 2:4). It is on the models of Abraham, Isaiah and Habakkuk, that the New Testament writers develop the doctrine of justification by faith (Rom. 3:21 – 5:22,Gal. 2:15 – 4:7, I Pet. 2:1-11).

Confession By Deed: Although implicit in the Abrahamic covenant, this rationale of holiness is drawn from the Sinaitic covenant. God asks Abraham to "walk before me and be blameless" (Gen.17:1). This was a call for moral perfection (cf. 12:1-4a 15:22). "Be ye holy as I the Lord your God am holy" is a mandate, which God gives to Israel in the Sinaitic covenant (Lev.11; 19) and which finds its echo in the admonition extended to the Confessional Community, "Do justice and righteousness"(Is.56:1). The rationale for establishment or entry into the Zion Community is clearly presented in Is.52:1 as holiness. It is

addressed to Zion herself: "no longer shall enter again into you an uncircumcised and an unclean person." This refers primarily to cultic and ethical uncleanness of heart.[15]

Zion's Establishment In Isaiah 60-62: A Covenantal Act

Inclusion refers to a process by which foreigners are given membership in the Zion community of Isaiah 56-66. It involves *legitimation* of the adherents, *i.e.,* declaration that they are the rightful heirs, and their *enfranchisement, i.e.,* the giving of inheritance rights. Exclusion refers to a process by which insiders are delegitimated, their membership in the Zion community is terminated, and they are dis-enfranchised, *i.e.,* their rights to Yahweh's heritage are withdrawn.

Isaiah 60:1–62:12 is generally accepted as a literary and thematic unity. This unity is observed in the usage of the verbs denoting light or brightness corresponding with those denoting growth, so that one can see a dual "glow and grow" motif in the Core.[16] Also the verbs denoting the movement of light from Yahweh to Zion (*Bo', Zarakh*) correspond with those denoting the movement of the nations to Zion (*Bo', Halakh*).[17] This correspondence shows that the nations come to Zion to participate in the salvation, which Yahweh has wrought for her. It is the theme of the establishment of Zion, which includes her salvation that provides the whole Core with its thematic unity.

Yahweh's act of establishing Zion and its recognition by the nations is represented by two strings, each consisting of seven verbs: i) those

---

[15]A. Piepe, *Isaiah II An Exposition of Isaiah 40-66,* (German: 1919) Milwaukee, Wisconsin, 1979, p.420; J. A. Motyer, *The Prophecy of Isaiah,* Leicester, 1993, p. 416; But cf. R. N. Whybray, *Isaiah 40-66,* NCB, London, 1975 , p. 164; and J. D. W. Watts. *Isaiah 34-66,* WBC 25, Waco, Texas, 1987, p.213.

[16]D. Grossberg, "The Dual Glow/Grow Motif," *Biblica* 67, 1986, p.547.

[17] E. Achtemeier, *The Community and Message of Isaiah 56-66* Minneapolis, 1982, p.83; *cf.* C. Westermann, *Isaiah 40-66: A Commentary,* London, *1969,* p. 356; J. Muilenburg, "The Book of Isaiah: Chapters 40-66: Introduction and Exegesis," in G Buttrick, ed., *The Interpreter's Bible,* Vol. 4, New York, 1956, p.697.

denoting 'establishing': *Sim, Kun* and *Nathan*[18] and ii) those denoting 'recognition' of Zion's new identity: *Qara* and *Nakhar*.[19] The link between Yahweh's action and Zion's recognition is clear in many instances. Yahweh appoints righteous leaders over her (60:17b), and Zion recognizes that she has secure walls (60:18b). Yahweh establishes those who mourn in Zion (61:3a), and the nations recognize them as 'oaks of righteousness' (61:3b). Yahweh makes an everlasting covenant with the people (61:8b), and the nations recognize their blessed status (61:9b). This everlasting covenant is Yahweh's gracious act that establishes Zion in the majestic and exalted position of the city of Yahweh.

With Whom?

That the covenant is made with the people of Zion is clear from 59:21, which reads "And as for me this is my covenant with them." Here 'them' refers to the people of Zion, i.e., those who repent (59:20).[20] These are "everyone who thirsts" (55:1), who seek Yahweh (6-7), and include the Israelites and foreigners who are admonished to seek justice and righteousness as in 56:1-5. In 54:10, Yahweh promises to the new Zion "my mercies" and "covenant of peace," indicating that this covenant is a covenant of mercy and is the same covenant that is described in 55:3 as "sure mercies of David" and "everlasting."[21]

What Is The Content?

The term 'everlasting' is used of the Noahic (Gen. 9:16), Abrahamic (Gen.17:7,13), Sinaitic (Ex. 31:16) and Davidic (2 Sam.23:5) covenants and the new covenant in Jeremiah (32:40) and Ezekiel (16:20). Since the term is used in connection with all the covenants, it refers not to Israel's violated covenant obligations, but rather to God's covenant faithfulness in keeping his promises. The basis of the covenant in 54:10 and 55:3 is Yahweh's steadfast love or faithfulness to his promises. The permanence of the covenant made with the people of Zion in 55:3 is dependent upon the 'sure mercies of David' (Hasede David).H.G.M.Williamson has demonstrated that the term "sure mercies of David" is an objective genitive, which denotes the deeds of steadfast love that Yahweh performed for David.[22] More specifically, Motyer argues that the term refers to "world dominion" and "enduring throne," items, which are each described with the singular "mercy" in Psalm 89.[23] Though this is possible, more secure background for "sure mercies of David".lies in God's promise to David through Nathan in 2 Samuel 7 where the emphasis seems to be not so much on the enduring throne but on Yahweh's continued gracious covenantal dealings with David's sons.

The promise of the dynasty and world rule is reminiscent of Yahweh's covenant-promise to Abraham "I will establish you as a father of multitude of nations" (Gen. 17:5b). The promise also recalls the covenant of Genesis 17:7 which understands the eternal covenant as the covenant that will be renewed (continued, *Kum*) with Abraham's offspring (*Zera*) from generation to generation. At the heart of the covenant lies the relationship. The enduring throne is dependent upon and indicative of this relationship.

---

[18] *Sim* (Is. 59:21; 60:15b; 60:17b; 61:3; 62:7a); *Kun* (62:7a) and *Nathan* (61:8b).

[19] *Qara* (Is. 60:14; 60:18; 61:3; 61:4; 61:6); *Nakar* (61:9b and 62:12).

[20] T. Cheyne, *The Prophecies of Isaiah: A New Translation with Commentary and* Appendices, Vol. 2, London, 1889, p.87; E.J.Young, *The Book of Isaiah...* p. 441; J. T. Willis, *Isaiah*, LWCOT 12, Austin, Texas, 1980, p.451; J. A. Motyer, *The Prophecy of Isaiah*, 1993, p.492.

[21] *Cf.* J. Muilenburg, "The Book of Isaiah" p.646; A. Schoors, *I Am God Your Saviour: A Form-critical Study of the Main Genres in Is. XL-LV,* VTS 24, Leiden,1973, p.148.

[22] H.G.M.Williamson, "Sure Mercies of David: subjective or objective genitive [Is.55:3]," *JSS* 23,1978, pp.31-49.

[23] J.A. Motyer, *The Prophecy Of Isaiah*, p.454.

How?

How is the covenant going to last? It will last through Yahweh's gracious treatment of David's heir. This can be explained by a reference to 2 Samuel 7 where Yahweh promises David that his son Solomon's throne will endure forever. Yahweh will not break the promise. If He has to punish David's son, He would do it "with the rod of men, with flogging inflicted by men," as a father disciplines his son (14). This promise is concerned with the father-son relationship (Ps.2:7). The purpose of the promise is found in David's prayer in verse 26: 'so that your name will be great forever, your name Yahweh Sabaoth, God of Israel.'[24] Divine initiative of grace, which is explicit in "sure mercies of David," implies that it requires a response of faith from David's son. This can be inferred from the term "faithful" (Neamanim) that qualifies "sure mercies of David." In order to experience God's faithful acts

of mercy, the texts invite the people with whom the Davidic covenant is being renewed to put faith in God.

Solidarity Promise (60:12)

The solidarity promise is essentially a promise of protection given by the sovereign to his ally. By it, the sovereign validates the allegiance, which the ally gives to him. The solidarity promise given to Zion in the Core is in 60:12: '*For the nation and the kingdom that will not serve you will perish, and the nations shall be utterly destroyed*'. It only depicts what will happen when the nations do not come to serve Zion willingly. Hence, it continues the thought of the nations' submission to Zion and is in harmony with the context.[25] Isaiah 60:12 is in harmony also with the structure of Isaiah 60 as it functions as the chapter's pivot:

A1 The Lord, the Light of Zion (1-5)

B1   New status of the nations: materially and spiritually accepted by the Lord (6-7)

C1   World expectations met in the Lord (8-9)

D1   The serving nations: the Lord's compassion to Zion (10-11)

E   Zion, the Key to world destiny (12)

D2   The submissive nations: their recognition of Zion (13-14)

C2   Zion's needs met by the Lord (15-16)

B2   The transformation of Zion, materially and spiritually (17-18b)

A2 The Lord, the light of Zion (18c-22)

Finally, 60:12 is in harmony with the overall theme of Zion's establishment. In 54:11-17, in the context of the establishing of Zion, the promise of solidarity is given immediately after the declaration "I will establish [*Khun*] you in righteousness." It is promised that fear and terror will be distant from her (14b), and that any nation, weapon or tongue that rises against Zion will be defeated and any plan against her will fail (15,

17ab). Thus she is promised protection from attacks, wars and legal arguments.

After urging those who remember Yahweh, "Do not give Yahweh rest until he establishes and makes [*Sim*] Jerusalem a praise in the earth," the prophet announces Yahweh's resolve (62:8): 'Never again will I give your grain as food to your enemy. Never again will the sons of foreigners drink your wine for which you have

---

[24] H. Gese, *Vom Sinai zum Zion*, BZT 64, München.1974, p.127.

[25] R. N. Whybray, *Isaiah 40-66*, p. 235.

toiled.' This negatively stated promise of solidarity leads to a positive description of Zion's people who celebrate Yahweh's presence in their midst by offering the first-fruits and by eating and drinking in the sanctuary (62:9). In Deuteronomy, it is laid down that Israel's covenant violation will incur a curse on the fruits of the ground (28:18), of the vineyard (28:30) and of "all your labour" (28:33), specifying that unknown people will eat the fruits (33). This was to be an inevitable outcome in which Yahweh would withdraw his solidarity promise. Therefore, a resolve on Yahweh's part, in Isaiah 62:8, not to allow enemies to eat the fruit of Zion's labour, signifies a restoration of the Sinaitic solidarity promise, and, therefore of Yahweh's covenantal presence. Hence the reference to the celebration of Yahweh's presence: the "eating" and "drinking" in "my holy courts" (Is. 62:9). As in Isaiah 54:11-17, so in the Core, the context in which the promise of solidarity is given to Zion is the same: *her establishment*, as Yahweh's city, in righteousness and for glory. A threat of complete destruction is given against any nation or kingdom that assumes a confrontational stance and refuses to serve Zion or acknowledge her sovereignty (Is. 60:12).

The subject of the nations' entry into Zion, stated positively in 60:9-11 and 13-15 where the nations come to Zion along with their wealth, is stated negatively in verse 12. The nations come to Zion because Yahweh has glorified her, established the covenant relationship with her and given her the solidarity promise in verse 12, which necessarily involves a threat to the enemy of Zion. Thus, verse 12 viewed as the solidarity promise, fits within the overall context of the establishment of Zion as Yahweh's city, which is the main theme of the Core.

Therefore, 60:12 is neither odd nor nationalistic, but serves a vital function in the chapter by bestowing upon Zion the "Abrahamic" position of the blessed figure. 60:12 is in harmony with the structure and theme of 60:1-22 where it is, most likely, used by the author in order to create a parallel with Abraham.

Plan And Purpose Of Establishment of the Covenantal Community

Yahweh establishes Zion on the foundation of an everlasting covenant: on peace and righteousness and for majesty and praise in all the earth. The everlasting covenant, which Yahweh makes with the people of Zion as "their reward in truth," is the central act in the Core (61:8b),[26] whilst "majesty" and "praise," which parallel the concept of exaltation, frame the Core (60:15; 62:7). Zion is exalted to a high position as Yahweh's holy people, priests and ministers. As a result, the nations are attracted to her. Their attraction seems to be the very purpose of Zion's exaltation. The nations' response to Zion's new blessed position determines their destiny: they are either blessed or cursed. Those who enter Zion's gates in order to serve her are blessed but those who do not are cursed and destroyed (60:12). Only as she becomes the Lord's city can she function as the universal city.[27] Only as she is blessed above all can she administer blessings to all.

The purpose of Zion's establishment is to bring the Gentile nations into the plan of Yahweh's universal blessings promised to Abraham (Gen.12:3). It might seem that in the Core the Gentiles are portrayed as subordinate to the Israelites. They perform menial jobs and even pay homage to Israel (60:14; 61:5). They are not, however, inferior in status to Israel. First, the language of service is metaphorical.[28] The

---

[26] Here 60:8b, Zion receives the reward on the basis of faith by the act of God just as Abraham received the promise of reward by faith; Gen. 15:1; *cf.*40:10b; 49:4b.

[27] J.A. Motyer, *The Prophecy of Isaiah*, p.493.

[28] R.N. Whybray, *Isaiah 40-66*, p.243.

phrases "build your walls," and "bow low to you" (Is. 60:10a, 14b), which are often taken to argue for the subordination of the Gentiles to Israel,[29] however, indicate that now the Gentiles recognize the blessed status of Zion, acknowledging Yahweh's presence in her.

Secondly, even if we take the language of service literally, the list of services performed by the nations suggests that they are involved in all aspects of the city's life. The verbs that describe what the nations or their kings do or what is done to them or their wealth are: go (60:3), bring (5b), proclaim (6b), build (10), serve (10), lead forth (11), bow down (14a), worship (14b), stand (61:5a), feed the flock (5a), plough the land (5b), dress the vines (5b), know, acknowledge (9), and observe (62:2). These describe their pilgrimage to Zion, worship at the sanctuary and both menial and cultic service to Zion. This shows that the nations are not only assigned menial tasks, but partake in all aspects of the city's life. They have received full membership in the Zion community. Thirdly, Zion here does not represent the old political or ethnic Israel; it is international in its membership because some of the foreigners have become fully-fledged members (cf. 56:57; 66:21a). Therefore, if the language does indicate subordination, it is not of Gentiles as foreign races to Israel's Abrahamic race, but of the nations to Zion as a symbol of Yahweh's sovereignty.

Section Summary

In the Core, the exaltation language is used in the context of the "founding of Zion" as Yahweh's city. She is founded as Yahweh's community on the basis of the everlasting covenant. Her membership is extended to the obedient and the penitent. The nations are admitted into Zion on the basis of their allegiance to Yahweh, her King who has prerogative and exclusive right to rule over her and provide her with salvation and sustenance. Since Zion is holy and nothing unclean can enter her, holiness is the basis by which they have been accepted as members. Zion and her people are established in righteousness. The purpose of exaltation or establishment of Zion is to bring the nations into God's Zion community so that the blessings promised to Abraham for all humankind might come to fulfillment.

Inclusion of Foreigners And Eunuchs: 56:1-8

The implication of Yahweh's exclusive rule over Zion is that those in Zion who look to Him are sure to receive protection and blessing, but those who look elsewhere will be frustrated. *Those insiders who by going after other gods cease to confess allegiance to Yahweh receive the threat of exclusion, whilst those outsiders who confess allegiance in faith and holiness to Yahweh receive the promise of inclusion.* This allegiance-holiness rationale is applied, in the Framework as in the Core, in the instances of both inclusions and exclusions. The study of these inclusions and exclusions reveals a contrast of character and destiny between Yahweh-adherents, to whom the promise of inclusion is given, and Yahweh-apostates, to whom the threat of exclusion is issued.

Isaiah 56:1-8 makes the imminent salvation and righteousness of Yahweh (1b) the basis for exhorting Yahweh's community to do justice and righteousness (1a). It directs the exhortation universally in verse 2 and specifically to the Eunuchs and Foreigners in verses 3-7, prompting them to righteous action. It assures them that they will be included in Yahweh's community, the Zion Community (3-7). It then ends with the announcement of further inclusion/gathering of "yet others" (8).

---

[29] *Cf.* Is. 49:23b; see Van Winkle, 1982, p193, 243; P.A. Smith, *Rhetoric and Redaction in Trito-Isaiah: The Structure, Growth and Authorship of Isaiah 56-66*, VTS-62, Leiden, New York, Koln,1995, p.59.

Promises Of Membership

The rationale of membership is applied universally to the Israelites and the foreigners alike. Irrespective of one's descent or nationality, the Eunuchs and Foreigners in Isaiah 56:1-8 are given the right to membership in Yahweh's community on the basis of allegiance and holiness. Since in the text the qualification "who has joined himself to Yahweh" (3), applied to "foreigners," is not applied to the eunuchs, it is likely that the eunuchs were Israelites. Similarly, the foreigners of 56:1-8 were proselytes.[30] This is apparent from the two qualifying appositions 'joiner(s)' or 'adherent(s).' Since the cultic term *Sarath* is used of them, they may have been involved in some kind of temple service.[31] We will henceforth call them "Yahweh-adhering foreigners."

Legitimation

Their portrayal as the true seed of Abraham indicates that Yahweh-adhering foreigners are not, as H. M. Orlinsky would have us believe, simply servants to Israel, but legitimate heirs of Yahweh's heritage.[32] The whole section 54:17b–56:8 has to do with the issue pertaining to the rights of the true heirs.[33] This is reinforced by the occurrence in close proximity of two phrases in 54:17b: i) Nahalah and ii) Avadim.

Nahalah is inalienable heritage that cannot be parted with. It is often used in connection with the land that was allotted to the Israelites by Yahweh. There were provisions within the law that this heritage might not be permanently snatched away from individual households (1 Ki.

22) But the exile had separated the Israelites from this inheritance. Meanwhile, as they were in Babylon, other peoples, now called "the people of the land," had occupied it. At the commencement of the return from exile, these "people of the land" also claimed rights to the land. The landlessness of the returnees could have triggered the reflection on the issue of "reactivating of the rights."[34] One should not overlook, however, that in Isaiah 56–66, the reactivating of rights is linked also to the deactivating of land rights, which results fundamentally from the context of apostasy. Hence the nature of the problem is not so much sociological as it is theological. The threats contained in the covenant documents (Dt. 28:15-68) indicate that the issue of inheritance would arise whenever the relationship between Yahweh and Israel is threatened by the apostasy of Israelites. This situation is characteristic of Isaiah 56-66.

Enfranchisement

The blessed position of Yahweh-adherents, the Eunuchs and Foreigners, is described in terms of their enfranchisement, by means of the destiny-promises of the divine oracle (56:5, 7). The eunuchs complain that they have no children, implying that they will have neither inheritance nor continuation of their memory among Yahweh's people. So, the prophet assures them that their memory will be preserved by means of *Yad Washem.*

The Promise of Yad Washem: Many ancient versions, modern commentaries and translations

---

[30] R. N. Whybray, *Isaiah 40-66*, p. 199; J. T. Willis, *Isaiah*, p. 436; C.P. Stuhlmueller, "Deutero-Isaiah and Trito-Isaiah," in *The New Jerome Biblical Commentary*, 329-48, London, 1990, p. 344.

[31] J. L. McKenzie, *Second Isaiah: Introduction, Translation, and Notes*, Anchor Bible, New York, 1968, pp.150-51; J. M. Baumgarten, "Netinim and Proselytes in 4Q Flor," *Revue de Qumranm*, 87-96, 1972, p. 91.

[32] H.M. Orlinsky, " Nationalism-Universalism and Internationalism in Ancient Israel," in H.T. Frank, W. L. Reed, ed., *Translating and Understanding the Old Testament: Essays in Honour of Herbert Gordon May*, New York, 1970, pp. 206-236.

[33] J.D.W. Watts, *Isaiah 34-66*, pp. 26-28.

[34]*Ibid.*

render the phrase *Yad Washem* as two nouns joined by a conjunction.[35] *Yad Washem*, however, is a hendiadys, a two-word phrase expressing one unified concept.[36] Therefore it is rightly translated by LXX (*Septuagint*) as *topon onomaston* and by some commentators as "a memorial stele or plaque,"[37] This memorial is similar to the one mentioned in 2 Samuel 18:18, where, *Yad* and *Shem*, occur in a break-up pattern, *i.e.*, separately, but in close proximity,[38] and mean a memorial as a substitute for children (2 Sa. 14:27). The meaning of the phrase in 56:5, however, goes beyond the idea of "memorial" in the literal sense. *Yad,* in the derivative sense, can sometimes mean a portion or a piece of pastureland.[39] Therefore, Robinson takes *Yad* to mean "possession" and the phrase *Yad Washem* to mean "inheritance" *Nahalah*.[40] But what good is the inheritance if there are no children to inherit it? In 44:5 *Yad* and *Shem* refer to the future offspring of Zion, converts or reconverts. Some commentators insist that the offspring refers to the Israelites who are reaffirming their faith in Yahweh, or who, after having forsaken Yahweh whilst in exile in pagan lands, are now returning to him.[41] Others argue that it refers to the Gentiles, the spiritual offspring, who became Israelites through faith.[42] Both the groups of commentators agree, however, that the offspring here are converts. On this basis, it is better to refer to *Yad Washem* as "spiritual offspring" drawn from both Israel and the Gentile nations. The spiritual offspring can preserve memory and also hold inheritance among Yahweh's people.

The Promise Of 'Bringing Them Into His Holy Mountain' (v.7). Yahweh's promise that he will bring them into his holy mountain, according to most commentators, signifies the Yahweh-adhering foreigners' full membership in the confessional community.[43] The promise of verse 7 consists of three clauses: "And I will *bring them* to my holy mountain," "And I will *make them rejoice* in my prayer house" and "Their offerings and sacrifices will be *acceptable* upon my altar." The first of these relates primarily to Yahweh's historical guidance of Yahweh-adhering foreigners into "His holy mountain,"[44] and the last two point primarily to their cultic experience of worship and acceptance in the Zion community.

---

[35] Aq, Sym, V, Tg; ASV, NEB, NIV, RSV and HB; K.E. Kissane, *The Book of Isaiah*, p.204; E. Achtemeier, *The Community and Message of Isaiah 56-66*, p. 32; G. Fohrer, *Jesaja 40-66*, p.184 and J. A. Motyer, *The Prophecy of Isaiah*, p. 466.

[36] R. N. Whybray, *Isaiah 40-66*, p.198; C. Westermann, *Isaiah 40-66*, pp.314-15; S. Talmon, "Yad Washem: An Idiomatic Phrases In Biblical Literature And Its Variations," *HS* 25, 8-17,1984, p. 12 and G. Robinson, *The Origin and Development of the Old Testament Sabbath: A Comprehensive Exegetical Approach*, Bangalore, 1976, pp.282-284.

[37] Whybray, 1975, p.198.

[38] S. Talmon, "Yad Washem", p.10.

[39] P. R. Ackroyd, "Yad," in G. H. Botterweck, *Theological Dictionary of the Old Testament, Michigan*, 1974, p. 401; Jer. 6:3.

[40] G. Robinson, "The Meaning of éÅä in Isaiah 56:5", *ZAW* 88, pp.282-284.

[41] C. C. Torrey, *The Second Isaiah: A New Interpretation*, Edinburg, 1928, p.344; J.D.W. Watts, *Isaiah 34-66*, pp.144-45; and J. A. Motyer, *The Prophecy of Isaiah*, p.343.

[42] F. J. Delitzsch, *Jesaja*, *Die Theologische Verlagsgemeinschaft*, 1887, Vol.2 p.204;K. Elliger, *Deuterojesaja 1 Teiband Jesaja 40,1–45,7*, BKAT 2, Neue Krchen-Vluyn, 1978, p.393; Muilenburg, p.504; J.Skinner, *The Book of Prophet Isaiah chapters XL-LXVI*, Revised ed., Cmbridge,1917,p.52; C.P. Stuhlmueller, "Deutero-Isaiah and Trito-Isaiah." In *The New Jerome Biblical Commentary*, 1990, pp.130-31 and C Westermann, *Isaiah*, p.111.

[43] C. Westermann, *Isaiah 40-66*, p.315; Whybray, p. 199; Watts, p. 250; J. Blenkinsopp, "Yahweh and other Deities: Conflict and Accommodation in the Religion of Israel," Int 40, 1986, pp.362-66; van Houten, *The Alien in Israelite Law*, JSOT Shefield,1991, p. 164 and Motyer, p. 467.

[44] The phrase 'historical guidance' is used with reference to Yahweh's guidance of Israel out of Egypt to the promised land in H. D. Preuss, 19xx *Bo*, pp.20-49.

According to Westermann, the metaphor behind '*I will bring them*' means that the foreigners will participate in Yahweh's worship. This participation in worship is "completely divorced from the realm of history."[45] Against Westermann, Pauritsch proposes that the promise relates to a concrete situation of "Yahweh-adhering foreigners." It suggests a change of place, *i.e.*, the foreigners have been brought from distant lands into the temple.[46] (1971:37). The historical experience of Yahweh-adhering foreigners is both patterned after Israel's entry into the land and is considered as part of "the return of the scattered ones" (*cf.* Is. 11:16). The promise of restoration was essentially a promise of bringing people to Yahweh's own abode, since the land is viewed as the place where Yahweh's name dwells (Is. 18:7).

The expression "I will make them rejoice in my prayer house" (7b), stands for complete satisfaction and acceptance in Yahweh's house. To "rejoice before Yahweh" is a characteristic term for the celebration of public worship in Deuteronomy. The context of this rejoicing is the celebration of the harvest Festivals of Weeks and booths (16:1-15). The important feature of the Festival of the Weeks, which later came to be known as the Pentecost, was the command given by Yahweh to Israel that they should share the joy of the feast with slaves, strangers and Levites, the groups that did not have an inheritance of their own.[47] Rejoicing is linked with the blessing of Yahweh.[48] Mourners in Zion possess eternal joy and a double portion in the land (Is. 61:7). The relation between the eternal joy and the mourners' perpetual dwelling in the land is reinforced by the use of the banquet metaphor in 65:13-15. In 65:21-23, the blessings of Yahweh-adherents are described in terms of enjoying the fruits of settling and long life in the land. The rejoicing takes place in the land to which *Yahweh brings* them.[49]

'Acceptable' (Leratson), in 'their Offerings And Sacrifices Will Be Acceptable,' conveys total acceptance of the foreigners. Israelites offered to Yahweh only a blameless, domestic male animal 'so that Yahweh may accept him' (Lev. 1:3b). The general aim of the sacrifice was that ' ... the offerer may be *accepted* ... by God.' With the assurance *that their sacrifices will be accepted*, the Yahweh-adhering foreigners in 56:1-8, have, properly speaking, ceased to be foreigners and have become members of the community in full standing.[50]

Gathering Of 'Yet Others' of verse 8, functions both as the summary of the preceding oracle (56:1-7), and as the spin off for the forthcoming oracles (9-57; 66:18-23). Here Yahweh is called 'One who gathers the dispersed ones of Israel'. The 'dispersed ones' refer to those who are estranged from Yahweh, and the 'others' refer to the eunuchs, Yahweh-adhering foreigners and 'whosoever does right' of verse 2. All these are brought by Yahweh to be one people, his 'holy people.'[51]

---

[45] C. Westermann, *Isaiah 40-66*, 1969, p.314.

[46] K. Pauritsch, Die neue Gemeinde: Gott sammelt Ausgestossene und Arme (Jesaia 56 – 66): Die Botschaft des Tritojesaiah-Buches literar-,form-, gattungskritisch und redaktionsgeschichtlich untersucht, Analecta Biblica 47, Rome, 1971, p.37.

[47] R. E. Brown and J.A. Fitzmyer, eds, *The New Jerome Biblical Commentary*, London, 1990 , p172.

[48] Dt.12:12; 14:26; 16:10,15; 27:7; *cf.* Lev. 23:40 and Ps. 33:1-3; 47:2-8; 95:1-2; 96:1-4; 98:1-6; 100:2-3; 105:1-3; 149:1-5 and 150:1-6.

[49] Note the emphasis on Yahweh's initiative in making them happy, which may have a polemical significance; see Harvey, 1962,pp. 116-127.

[50] C. Westermann, 1969, p.315; cf. J. A. Motyer, *The Prophecy of Isaiah*, p.467.

[51] H.D.Preuss, 'Bo', p.25; J. Blenkinsopp, "Yahweh and other Deities," 1986, pp.362-66; van Houten, *The Alien in Israelite Law*, p.164.

Rationale For Inclusion

Allegiance: The allegiance of Yahweh-adhering foreigners to Yahweh and their membership in Yahweh's community are inseparably linked. The description of Yahweh-adhering foreigners as 'the ones who have joined Yahweh' is contrasted with the threat to their identity that 'Yahweh would certainly separate me from his people.' The implication is that those who have joined Yahweh cannot be separated from his people (3b). The concern of Yahweh-adhering foreigners that they might face separation from Yahweh's people is here alleviated first by issuing an injunction to the community to do justice and righteousness. This means that the community should relate to the marginalized people like Yahweh-adhering foreigners in such a way that they no longer fear exclusion from her (3a).[52] Secondly, Yahweh assures them that they would be accepted into his community as full members.[53]

The Designations: "Yahweh-adherents," "Covenant-keepers," and "Sabbath-keepers" are three character-designations applied to "Yahweh-adhering foreigners" who have joined Yahweh through a covenant. First, Isaiah 56:1-8 applies to Yahweh-adhering foreigners the main designation, 'adherer/s' (3, 6). It reveals a basic attitude of allegiance towards Yahweh, indicating that Yahweh-adhering foreigners have, of their own volition become Yahweh-adherents. Jeremiah 50:5b and Zechariah 2:11, by using the phrase "the everlasting covenant" and the covenantal term "my people" respectively, explain the nation's adherence to Yahweh in terms of covenant.[54] Similarly both these texts use *lawah* to indicate covenantal sense of peoples' adherence. Therefore, since 56:1-8 also employs *lawah* to express the allegiance of Yahweh-adhering foreigners to Yahweh, it does so to express their covenantal allegiance. Secondly, the designation "covenant keepers" is used for Yahweh-adhering foreigners (56:6c) as well as for the eunuchs (56:4c). Being derived from the verb *hazak*, it shows the perseverance of Yahweh-adhering foreigners, explaining the meaning of the previous designation "Yahweh-adherents" as "those who hold fast to the covenant." Thirdly, the related designation "Sabbath–keepers" extends the meaning of "covenant-keepers." It is applied universally to "everyone" (6b) and particularly to the eunuchs (4a). It further explains the practical and ethical implications of membership in Yahweh's community. Here, Sabbath-keeping represents the Ten Commandments, and obedience to his entire law. One kept Sabbath as a member of the community.

Motive clauses: In 56:6, there are three infinitival phrases used in tripartite structure. The first, "to serve [*Sarath*] him," and the third, "to be his servants," express the same objective of service, while the second, "to love the name of Yahweh," explains how this objective will be achieved. In view of the parallel in Isaiah 66:21 where *Sarath* undoubtedly refers to "a priestly service," it should here mean the same.[55] It conveys an attitude of loving devotion and faithfulness to Yahweh just as '*awad*' conveys an attitude of allegiance and obedience to Yahweh. The expression 'to love the name of Yahweh' means to love Yahweh, and to keep his commandments (Ps. 5:11; 69:36; 119:132; Ex. 20:6). Love towards Zion also implies love towards '*Amo*,' his people, both of which stand in the servant position (60:12). The love of the name of Yahweh leads one to become his

---

[52] G. Fohrer, *Jesaja 40-66,* p.187.

[53] Isaiah56:5, 7; Blenkinsopp, "Second Isaiah—Prophet of Universalism" *JSOT* 41, pp. 83-103; *cf.* 1986, pp. 362-66; van Houten, *The Alien in Israelite Law,* pp.162-65.

[54] The participle of *lawah* is also used of the *ger* joining Israel in Is. 14:1.

[55] J. Skinner, *The Book of Prophet Isaiah chapters XL-LCVI,* p. 166; Motyer: 1993,p.210.

servants, the rightful heirs to Yahweh's heritage (Ps. 69:70). Thus the designations and motive clauses indicate the covenantal nature of Yahweh-adhering foreigners' membership in the Zion community.

Entry And Holiness: The Hebrews perceived the world as consisting of things that were holy and things that were common, or, clean and unclean. Holy things could become unclean and unclean things could become holy if they passed through an intermediate state of cleanness. The holy and unclean or unholy, however, could never come in contact. They represented two opposing poles of the holiness spectrum. On the one end stood God and on the other stood humankind. It was their divine election and elaborate sacrificial atoning system that brought Israel closer to God.[56] The disenfranchised members of the Israelite community such as eunuchs and Yahweh-adhering foreigners and the Gentile world, however, remained in the realm of the unclean. How then has it become possible for the eunuchs and Yahweh-adhering foreigners to receive the promise of full membership in the *holy* Zion community?

Righteousness: The instruction in 56:1 'Keep justice and do righteousness' implies conduct of ethical holiness. The Yahweh adhering foreigners did the right, and were therefore holy and righteous before God. But it was Yahweh's righteousness that saved them and the Zion community as the parallelism between 5:16 and 1:27 reveals:

Yahweh of hosts is exalted by justice, and the holy God shows himself holy in righteousness, 5:16; Zion shall be redeemed by justice and her repentant ones in righteousness, 1:27.

Yahweh redeems his people by his righteousness but expects them, as those who have joined him through the covenant, to show themselves to be holy through righteousness.[57]

Sabbath And Holiness: In 56:1-8, in return for "Sabbath-keeping," the promise of acceptance into Yahweh's holy temple/community is given to the eunuchs and the foreigners (56:5,7). Sabbath-keeping here is radically exalted to be "the primary criterion by which one becomes and remains a member of the community."[58] It is applied in verse 2, generally, to any 'pursuer of justice and righteousness' and in verses 4 and 6, specifically, to the eunuchs and foreigners. Since the Zion Community is Yahweh's and is holy, no one can become her member without holiness (3; 52:1). If so, then the Sabbath may have something to do with imparting holiness to people so as to qualify them for the membership. Sabbath is a sign that it is Yahweh who imparts holiness to people: 'You shall keep my Sabbath, for it is a sign between me and you, throughout your generations, that you may know that I, Yahweh, sanctify you.' (Ex. 31:13). Thus Sabbath provides access to the sanctuary[59] and blessings in the land. Yahweh will feed those who keep his Sabbaths with the 'heritage of Jacob' (Is. 58:14).

---

[56] G.J. Wenham, *The Book of Leviticus,* NICOT, Grand Rapids, 1979, p.19.

[57] '*Righteousness* is holiness expressed in moral principles; *justice* is the application of the principles of righteousness'. Accordingly, Yahweh's acts of judgement and salvation are visible expressions of his holiness; Motyer, 1993, 72; H. C. Leupold, *Exposition of Isaiah: Volume I Chapters 1-39; Volume II Chapters 40-66,* Herts, England, c, 1968, 1977, Vol.1. p.117.

[58] Lev. 26:4-13; B.Schramm, *The Opponents of Third Isaiah: Reconstructing the Cultic History of the Restoration,* p. 119.

[59] Lev. 19:30; 26:2; Ez. 22:8, 26; G.Robinson, *TheOrigin and Development of the Old Testament Sabbath: A Comprehensive Exegetical Approach,*p. 266.

Proximity Of The Divine And Human: The proximity or presence of God represents the key notion of the idea of holiness in Deuteronomy.[60] In Isaiah 56:1-8 the idea of holiness is conveyed through the notion of the presence of Yahweh. The presence of Yahweh is realised in the adherents' movement to Yahweh to serve (*sharath*) him. *Sharath* particularly expresses an idea of serving Yahweh by being near him. It is therefore related to holiness. In Numbers 16, only he who is chosen by Yahweh is holy, and only he can come near to serve. Coming near requires prior election and reception of holy status. Apart from the reference in the Framework (56:6), *Sharath* is used again in the Core of Trito-Isaiah (Is. 60:7,10; 61:6). Using metaphorical language, the references in the Core depict the similar phenomenon of the foreigners' coming to do the priestly ministry for Yahweh. In 61:6a, *Sharath* is used of Zion as a substantive, 'ministers', in parallel with 'priests': 'but you shall be called priests of Yahweh, you shall be named ministers of our God'. Their initiation into the ministry of *Sharath* implied that a certain kind of holiness was *granted* to Yahweh-adhering foreigners. The rationale of holiness does not refer exclusively to what people have to do in order to enter the holy assembly of Yahweh; rather it has to do with Yahweh's election and bestowal of priestly status upon the adherents and with the human response of faithful allegiance.

Section Summary

In Isaiah 56:1-8, Yahweh promises Yahweh-adhering foreigners equal rights to membership in his assembly on the basis of allegiance and holiness. Isaiah 56:1-8 promises, through the divine oracle, to the 'sons of the foreigners' access to Yahweh's assembly. It seems, therefore, that the ban placed upon the foreigners in Deuteronomy 23:2-9 is repealed by Isaiah 56:1-8.[61] The foreigners and eunuchs are permitted into the Lord's assembly in Isaiah 56:1-8 because they observe his Sabbath and hold fast to his covenant, *i.e.*, they seek justice and righteousness enshrined in Yahweh's Law. Yahweh announces that he will also bring "to those who are already gathered," "others" who are yet to be gathered (56:8). The object of this gathering is to incorporate them into this assembly as *equal* members. This is borne out by several factors. First, the acceptance (*lerason*) of offerings and sacrifices suggests their total acceptance into the worshipping assembly. Secondly, the promise of everlasting *Yadwashem* (Inheritance) better than "sons and daughters" suggests they have been given full rights of membership. Thirdly, like the insiders, some of the foreigners, who have become members, will be given rights to priesthood (66:18-23). Confessional character means principally and logically that those who cease to confess faith in Yahweh must face exclusion from the community.

Exclusion of Insiders: Apostate Leaders And Peoples: 56:9-57:21

The section 56:9–57:21 belongs to the broader section 54:17–66:24 of which 54:17c 'this is the inheritance of the servants of Yahweh', can be considered the title.[62] The issue of who will inherit the mountain of Yahweh recurs in 56:9–57:21, in 57:6 and 13b. The key word of the section 56:9–57:21 is *Derekh*, which provides the fundamental contrast between the apostates and adherents. It describes the sinful way of the apostates in 56:11, 57:10 and 57:17-18; but in 57:14 refers to the way to peace and inheritance. Thus, a dual theme of the entire section 56:9–57:21, is the pronouncement of judgement upon

---

[60] J. G.Gammie, *Holiness in* Israel, OBT, Minneapolis,1989, pp. 106-7.

[61] E. V. Mohol, *The Covenantal Rationale for Membership in the Zion Community Envisaged in Isaiah 56-66*, p.133. After Donner, Mohol regards abrogation of Dt. 23:1-9 in Is. 56:1-8 as 'exegetical'.

[62] J. D. W.Watts, *Isaiah 40-66*, p. 244.

the wicked, and God's gracious forgiveness to the penitent (57:15-19). This section thus exhibits a thematic unity.

Threat Of Exclusion

Delegitimation: This is a process by which the apostates are shown to have ceased from being the legitimate heirs to Yahweh's heritage. There are two ways in which this process can be seen. First, it is logically derived from the unholiness which the apostates have contracted, by association with the pagan cults. Secondly, the character designations metaphorically applied to the apostates point to their illegitimacy. Illegitimacy is strongly put forth through a dominant metaphor of mother sorceress [63] and supporting metaphors of mother-adulterer, harlot and offspring of sorcery. The designations show that it is the character that gives legitimacy to one's descent and determines one's destiny. That these designations are mutually explanatory becomes clear from the way they are arranged in parallel below (57:3-4):

Sons of sorceress	3ab	a
Seed of adulterer	3ba	b
Children of rebellion	4ba	a
Seed of lie	4bb	b

The first two designations point to acts of deviation whereas the latter two indicate the attitude and character that informs these acts. The first one reveals the apostates' strong addiction to sorcery, magic and all forms of witchcraft.[64] The reference to "a mother sorceress," "an adulterer" and "a whore" points to the illegitimacy of the children they have borne. By implication, these indicate that the apostates are not the true obedient children. By designating them as such the prophet is denying the apostates their share of the inheritance.

Sorcery is used at both the metaphorical and cultic levels. This is evident in the designation "sons of sorcery." Sorcery points to the whole idolatrous system that is the very antithesis of "Yahweh's way." "Sons of sorcery" therefore provides a rationale for the pronouncement of delegitimacy on the apostates, followed by their disenfranchisement, destining them to the fate of the idols they worshipped.

Disenfranchisement: Forming an inclusion to this section on apostatising conduct (57:6b-13a) are two pronouncements assigning destinies to the people (6a, 13b). The first of these 'among the stones of the valley is your portion' ties their destiny to the pebble stones used to cast lots or to the dead whom they worshipped.[65] The ferocity of these words becomes stronger if we recall the use of the *wadi* in the reforms of Asa, Hezekiah and Josiah who used it as a place to dump all the idolatrous cult objects and the burnt Asherahs.[66] The threat of expulsion becomes obvious and final in verse 20. The stark contrast is made clear by the use of Nigerash, which in Ugaritic has to do with the sense of "expelling" since it refers to the two weapons of Baal with which he expelled Yam from his throne. In light of this meaning, the following reading is suggested by Irwin: 'But the wicked shall be like Yam, cast out because he could not keep silent, and his waters cast up mire and dirt'.[67] The second pronouncement (13a) also ties their destiny to idols and suggests what will happen to them by specifying what will happen to the idols: 'but the wind shall bear away all of them; vanity takes them'.

Rationale For Exclusion

It has been argued above that there is an addition of 'an invitation to repentance' to the judgement oracle of 57:3-13. Despite this, the

---

[63] T. J.Lewis, "Death Cult Imagery in Isaiah 57," HAR 11,1987, p.282.

[64] Leupold: 1977, 2.274.

[65] J. A. Motyer, *The Prophecy of Isaiah*, p.472; *cf* Is. 17:14.

[66] W. Irwin, "The Smooth Stones of the Wadi"?, p.38.

[67] *Ibid.* p. 279.

basic division between the apostates and adherents remains. According to this text, in the ultimate sense of the term, the apostates are those who do not repent. It is the attitude of willful deviation from Yahweh's covenant that becomes the cause of their exclusion from His community. This attitude is illustrated in the description of their disavowal and unholiness.

Disavowal: The focus of 57:3-4, a unit within the judgement oracle (57:3-13a), is to expose the apostates' disdain towards Yahweh and His servants. This disdain is not just a passive attitude of complacency seen in the sins of omission, namely not giving Yahweh priority (11), but an arrogance manifested in the sins of commission, namely their unholy involvement in the cults of the dead, child sacrifice and fertility (3-10). The disdain is manifested in the rhetorical questions and designations of 57:3-4, 11.

The Rhetorical Questions: The rhetorical questions i) 'Against whom do you rejoice?' ii) 'Against whom have you opened your mouth wide?' and iii) 'Against whom do you make wide your tongue?' are reminiscent of those in Isaiah 36–37 and 28:14-22. Sennacherib's attitude of disdain towards Yahweh, seen in his mocking and abusing of Zion, led him to his death, while Hezekiah's attitude of humility before Yahweh led him to his vindication and life.[68]

The rhetorical question 'whom did you dread and fear' (Is. 57:11) refers to the apostates being trapped in the dread and fear of the cults of the dead, thus discreetly evoking the memories of their covenantal obligation to fear Yahweh (Dt. 6:12-13; 13:5). The apostates' failure to show reverence and devotion to Yahweh is made more explicit in the rhetorical rejoinders framed almost in the form of answers: 'And me you did not remember or place upon your heart!' and 'And me you did not fear' (57:11b), 'upon your heart' reminded them of the exhortation in the *Shema*

to remember and to 'place upon your heart' the words of the commandments (Dt. 6:4-10).

Thus, the rhetorical questions accuse the apostates of the dual sin of complacency in what they were supposed to do (fear and remember Yahweh) and of apostasy (fear of other gods). The disdain of apostates implicit in the rhetorical questions becomes crystallized in the designations used for the apostates.

Designations

Children Of Rebellion; 57:4b: At the very outset of the book of Isaiah, the entire nation of Israel is designated as "rebellious sons" (1:2). This designation is then explained in 1:3-4 by means of many synonyms. We will consider two. The *first*, "Seed of Evildoers," describes activity that is contrary to Yahweh's will. The participial noun "evildoers" comes from the root, which connotes a raging and hurtful disposition (Is. 11:9; Nu. 11:10). It points to Israel's willful acts that hurt and provoke Yahweh to anger. Isaiah attributes these acts of rebellion to their lack of understanding (1:2-3; cf. Je. 4:22). So does Jeremiah to his people (4:22). Unless the people change their ways, Yahweh will inflict pain upon them (1:16, 20; cf. Je. 25:29). Later, Jeremiah noticed that people had become addicted to doing evil (13:23). This was not to be the disposition of Yahweh's people in the new Zion (Is. 11:9; 65:25b).

The *second*, 'They Have Rejected' describes an attitude of disdain. Their worship of other gods and complacency and forgetfulness towards Yahweh provoke a response of disdain within him (cf. Dt. 32:19). In his fury meted out to Israel (by exiling them) Yahweh is seen as despising his people for their act of apostasy and rebellion (Lam. 2:6). Rebellion provokes Yahweh to respond with retribution in anger and vengeance. Although the entire nation is called, "rebellious

---

[68] T.R. Hobbs, *2 Kings*, WBC 13, Waco, Texas, 1985, p.279.

sons" (Is. 1:2), in the real sense, the term refers only to those who will reject the offer of salvation extended to everyone on the condition of repentance (Is. 1:27; 59:20). In Trito-Isaiah the rebellious people are the Israelites who provoke Yahweh to anger, greatly upsetting him through their idolatry (57:3-13a), as opposed to the Gentiles who seek him (65:1, 10).

Seed Of Deception; 57:4b: The designation, "offspring of deceit" in 57:4b is to be understood in the same sense as the seed of transgression or rebellion. Israelites were commanded not to give false testimony in the court or to deal falsely (Ex. 20:16; Lev.19:11). In Leviticus 19:11 this admonition forms a part of the overall exhortation to be holy (Lev.19:2). Isaiah 57:4b uses the designation with reference to a perversion of justice in the courts and to the oppression of the innocents by the rich landlords. It could, more likely, indicate the cultic misuse of Yahweh's sanctuary and of the privileges endowed to priestly Israelite groups.

Jeremiah uses "deceit" in connection with the idol that deceives and puts to shame those who worship it (Jer.10:16a). Here, Jeremiah's purpose in depicting the deceptive nature of the idolatrous religion is to contrast it with the truthfulness of Yahweh. He also emphasizes the uniqueness of Israel that is designated as 'the tribe of his inheritance' (16). The use of the designation 'seed of deception' in Isaiah 57:4b is intended to bring out the contrast between the deceptive, illegitimate offspring, and the true and legitimate offspring of Yahweh.

Unholiness: There are only indirect references to the unholiness of the apostates in Isaiah 57:3-11. The apostates' unholiness is that which comes to them by virtue of their involvement in unholy pagan cults. Isaiah 57:3-11, together with 65:1–66:24, shares the view that the pagan cults and their adherents are

both unholy and incompatible with Yahweh's religion.

Unholiness Of Israel's Cultic Involvement : This section's closing verse, 57:11, containing the rhetorical questions, attributes Israel's apostasy, by twice repeating the word "fear"— to their lack of fear of Yahweh and to their fear of something other than Yahweh. "Fearing Yahweh" is elsewhere used to mean regarding Yahweh as holy (Dt. 8:12, 13). The rhetorical questions in verse 11 echo the similar rhetorical questions of verse 4, thus connecting their lack of reverential fear to their disdain of Yahweh. Sandwiched between the rhetorical questions are character-designations and activity-designations, which point to their involvement in the pagan cults. Thus, both in attitude and conduct, they exhibit unholiness.

In this passage there is explicit reference to the cults of fertility and child sacrifice. In addition, there are allusions to the cult of the dead, including necromancy.[69] These cults are mentioned together in an unbroken sequence: fertility cult – child slaughter – cult of the dead (57:5-6). This sequence is further repeated to form an *abc* pattern in 57:7-9. This shows that Trito-Isaiah perceives a unity between the cults of fertility, child sacrifice and the dead. He describes the whole idolatrous system before the apostate Israelites as unholy and unacceptable with a view to challenging them to abandon it and accept Yahweh's alternative option of perpetual life in the land (57:13).

Invitation To Repentance 57:13b–21

57:1-21 seems to be an intermediate judgement-salvation oracle since the oracle is turned into 'invitation to repent' by addition to 1-13, of 13b-19, which is addressed to the whole nation. The message of salvation seems to be based, like Deutero-Isaiah, on the forgiveness by

---

[69] .T. J. Lewis, *Death Cult Imagery in Isaiah 57*, pp.270-71.

Yahweh of Israel's past sins (18). The difference is, however, that those who persist in wickedness and continue to be an obstruction in the way of those who repent (14), are isolated to be picked up and destroyed (20-21). According to Whybray, "the stumbling block" of verse 14 refers to the "wicked" of verses 20-21.[70]

57:13b is of particular relevance to us: 'but, he who takes refuge in me, he will inherit the earth, and will possess my holy mountain'. In meaning, "taking refuge" corresponds to "believing" of Isaiah 28:17, which, in the context of judgment, means to find security in Yahweh, the founder and king of Zion. We have also indicated a possibility that the background to this usage of "believing" is Genesis 15:6, which presents Abraham as one who was reckoned righteous by faith.

Section Summary

In the Confessional Community Of Isaiah 56-66, faith or allegiance is the key for membership. The foreigners and eunuchs who have been promised full or equal membership by the Lord in his assembly, are those who have 'joined to the Lord' to serve him with covenant steadfastness. They are those who observe his Sabbaths and do justice and righteousness (56:1-5). On the other hand in 56:9–57:21, Yahweh-apostates are threatened with exclusion from Yahweh's community. These are those who provoke Yahweh to anger by their apostasy and idolatry. Thus they follow the way that is an abomination, illegitimate and antithetical to the way of Yahweh (Lev. 18:21; 19:29-32; 20:1-27 and Dt. 18:9-14). They also show an attitude of disdain towards Yahweh–adherents and Yahweh. Their exclusion proves that the genealogical dimension of holiness is set aside as a rationale of membership of Yahweh's community.

Hence, the qualifying titles and appended designations portray those of foreign descent as true sons having holiness of character, but those of Israel as rebellious and false. One is portrayed as Yahweh-adherents, while the other as Yahweh-apostates. One is involved in right and acceptable worship of Yahweh, but the other in syncretistic worship of other deities alongside Yahweh. In accordance with their acts and attitudes, they meet their respective destinies. One is brought into the holy mountain (56:7-8); the other is destined to the graveyard (See Is. 57:6, 13a). Thus, a complete reversal has taken place in the status of the apostate Israelites and Zion's faithful Gentiles. Faithfulness has elevated the Yahweh adhering foreigners to the status of Israel, the true sons and priests of Yahweh, while apostasy has now demoted the native apostate Israelites to the status of Gentiles.

Implications for Contemporary Mission
Gathering (Bringing/Sending)

We can see that Missio-Dei is i). establishing the Community by everlasting covenant mediated through the "sent one," the Redeemer (59:21); and ii). opening it up on confessional grounds to "everyone" irrespective of race, class and gender. Yahweh does not just leave it to people to respond and come to him on their own; but takes initiative through His community in bringing/gathering the peoples into his household, the Zion. He gives them equal rights of membership. Incorporation, therefore, of the nations as equal members is the modus operandi and goal of mission in this paradigm of the Confessional Zion community.

The role of His community, the church, in this gathering has to do with "light-giving" through their holiness and service. This includes "doing justice and righteousness" primarily (56:1). Holiness here is both given and cultivated. It is not the ritualistic but moral and devotional holiness of the Sinaitic covenant that is emphasized in Isaiah 56-66:58-59. In fact the ritualistic holiness is downplayed and devotional

---

[70] R. N. Whybray, *Isaiah*, p.211.

and moral highlighted (57:15; 66:1-2). Thus holiness in Isaiah 56-66 refers primarily to ethical and moral holiness.

Traditionally, mission was understood as 'sending', a little emphasis was given on bringing and incorporation. The Edinburgh itself highlighted that evangelism should result in "conversion to Christ and His Church."[71] The ensuing conference also stressed the vital link that exists between the church and mission; this way the mission is viewed as "the church-with-others."[72] Mission was thought to be an integral part of the Church and the Church as the singular goal of mission. How far this development in the thought world corresponded with the reality on the ground is something, which needs to be explored. The problem is not with accepting the goal of mission as 'church' but with the kind of the church we need to be and to plant. Missions have resulted in churches, but what sort of churches? Are these churches truly confessional, biblically based and mission-minded?

Interreligious Dialogue and Religious Pluralism

According to the Confessional Community Paradigm, which I have proposed, interreligious dialogue is welcome. The plurality of religions and cultures is accepted as a given factor and can be cherished.[73] In Yahweh's eschatological Zion, nations as ethnic and linguistic entities are welcomed (66:18-19). The problem, however, is with the ideological religious pluralism, which relativizes the revealed Biblical truth, that stands in opposition to this paradigm. Isaiah, like Jeremiah and Ezekiel, engages in religious dialogue with Israel at the intellectual level in order to bring out the universal validity of the Monotheistic Yahwism. He wants on the one hand, peoples belonging to all cultures and tongues to be part of the community of Yahweh and his kingdom, but on the other, quite logically, he can tolerate no ideology or philosophy that denies Yahweh his sovereignity and singularity. Isaiah envisages that peoples of all nations and tongues will come and will be brought (60; 66), but they will do so leaving behind their father's household idols and gods. Yahweh will be all in all (65:15-16; 66:23-24).

Why Is This Paradigm Viable For The Twenty First Century?

It is Biblically Based: In the ferment of conflicting ideologies, compelling Christians to swirl hither and thither, a Biblically rooted paradigm is what is needed. This will help us to face both the ideological onslaught and persecutions, having known that the cause we are fighting for is also worth dying for. In two areas is this paradigm rooted biblically. First, the very constituting of the confessional community is biblical (Gen. 15:6; Dt. 26:19; Is. 28:6; Hab. 2:4; Jn. 1:2; 1 Pet.2). Secondly, its missiological orientation is biblically rooted (Is. 56:6-7), thus conforming to the whole counsel of God.

It is Universally Relevant: Narrowly exclusive approaches to missions will not cater to the missiological goal, which is universal in scope 'through you all the families of the nations will be blessed' (Gen. 12:3). Confessional community of Isaiah fulfils the Abrahamic blessing and mandate. First, there is a reaching out from Zion to the nations. This reaching out is seen in the centrifugal outward movement of Zion's light (60:10). Zion as Israel is called to 'be the light to the nations' (42:6). Traditionally, 'being a light' is understood in passive sense of modeling an exemplary role. Given the strong

---

[71] R.E. Hedlund, *Roots of the Great Debate in Mission: Mission in Historical and Theological Perspective*, Bangalore, 1997, p30.

[72] D. J. Bosch, *Transforming Mission: Paradigm Shifts in Theology of Mission*, pp.69, 467.

[73] D.A.Carson, *The Gagging of God: Christianity Confronts Pluralism*, Leicester,1996,.

connection between 60:1 and 56:1 ('Do Justice and righteousness'), which in the context explicitly implies reaching out to the marginalized and the outsiders, the above passive interpretation of light cannot be sustained. Understood as doing justice and righteousness, the light cannot be taken as passive. The light always shines outward centrifugally. Secondly, there is a gathering in of the nations, seen in its centripetal movement of streaming of the nations towards Zion.

It is Theologically Oriented/Controlled: One of the issues in interpreting the Abrahamic blessing 'through you all families will be blessed (*Nibereku*)' is, whether to translate the Hebrew verb *niberaku* as passive 'be blessed' (NIV) or as reflexive 'bless themselves' (RSV). 'Be blessed' would put an emphasis on Abraham, the agent of blessing, but 'bless themselves' would shift the emphasis from Abraham to nations. Too much emphasis on Abraham might lead to a narrowly church-centered interpretation of missions. Similarly, heavy emphasis on 'nations' can lead to "universalism," denying any worthwhile role to Abraham.

Applying this to Zion, especially in Isaiah 60, it does seem, and many have taken it so, that exclusively Zion-centered salvation is planned for the nations 'any nation or kingdom that will not come to serve you will utterly perish' (60:12). Those who want to avoid this interpretation suggests, and majority of commentators do this, that 60:12 is a gloss. Some of these universalist commentators translate *niberaku* as 'bless themselves', in support of their universalism.[74]

To avoid falling into either of these two extremes of church-centrism or radical universalism, certain controls are necessary. These are provided by our approach by its theological orientation. The emphasis in this approach is neither on "you" nor on "they" but on the divine "I", which is implicit in Gen. 12:3c. Similarly Yahweh is the indisputable author of Zion's glory and nations' gathering to that glory in Isaiah 60-62. The emphasis on the divine sovereignity and singularity is conspicuously present in Isaiah: 'I am God, there is no other'. 'I the Lord do all these things' (45:6-7). This same Lord, the faithful one, will be 'all in all' (65:16).

It is Integrative: How does confessional community paradigm help integrate different paradigms of the missions as delineated in the introduction? First, it recognizes that mission is of God. He is the Creator, sustainer, protector and blesser of the confessional community. Mission, under this paradigm, is theocentric. Secondly, it accepts mediatory role given to the confessional community. It acts as an instrument of blessing and salvation to the nations. Thirdly, it understands mission in terms of doing justice and righteousness. Righteousness is 'doing right,' *i.e.*, believing in Yahweh as Saviour. Doing justice is obeying his commands, practicing his laws and observing his Sabbath. Fourthly, proclaiming the Gospel, Witnessing, Formulating Theology and Eschatology can be viewed as genuine or definitive tasks (confessions) of the confessional community.

The way the confessional community integrates these varied paradigm of mission is by considering them as modes of confessing her faith in Yahweh "He is the Lord, and there is no other." The intent and purpose of confession is to bring others under his lordship by bringing them into the confessional community, the family of Yahweh. This confession provided the focus and affects the synergy (effective situation) for missions.

---

[74] V. Premasagar, "God's Words to Our Father: Towards an Inclusive Missiology," *IRM* 75, July 1986, pp.282-84.

CHAPTER 4

Jubilee and Mission[1]

JESUDASON BASKAR JEYARAJ

The world has seen the dawn of the 3rd millennium. Churches and leaders in different countries have called for the redistribution of land and cancellation of the debts of Third world countries. Poor peasants in India and in the subcontinent are involved in the struggle for justice. In this paper, I will reflect on the release of the land and labourers and the cancellation of the debts as well as highlighting some of the salient features of the Jubilee institution. This study is not a thorough study of the Jubilee tradition in ancient Israel, but it is more of a reflection. Some scholars have already written on the topic of biblical Jubilee.[2]

The salient features of the biblical Jubilee tradition are more relevant to the Indian context at present than ever before. First, 60 percent of the population still lives in villages and our society is predominantly agrarian. Second, land alienation is taking place rapidly along with modernization. There is construction of industries, highways, extension of airports, leasing of water reservoirs to multinational companies, construction of new dams, shopping complexes, etc. Third, moneylenders have multiplied at every level. Policemen lend money on interest to poor rickshaw workers, auto drivers and vegetable vendors on the street. Even

Christian teachers and office assistants in mission schools operate money-lending business on a small scale among fellow teachers and neighbours. I was told that a treasurer of a local church lends the Sunday offering to local people at a high interest rate and multiplied the income for the sake of his church. Many moneylenders in India use local and state-level political forces to protect their authorised and unauthorized money-lending businesses.

This paper focuses attention on the theme "jubilee" in Leviticus 25. The word "Jubilee" is derived from the Hebrew word *Yobal* that literally means "ram's horn." The priests of ancient Israel were asked to blow the ram's horn on the completion of the forty-ninth year in order to inaugurate the fiftieth year:

> You shall count off seven weeks of years, seven times seven years, so that the period of seven weeks of years gives forty-nine years. Then you shall have the trumpet sounded loud; on the tenth day of the seventh month — on the Day of Atonement — you shall have the trumpet sounded throughout all your land. And you shall hallow the fiftieth year and you shall proclaim liberty throughout the land to all its inhabitants. It shall be a Jubilee for you; you shall return, every one of you, to your property and every one of you, to your family (Lev. 25:8-10).

---

[1] "Jubilee and Society: Reflections" was published originally in *ERT* (2001) 25:4, 337-349, and is used with permission.

[2] For example, R. North, *Sociology of the Biblical Jubilee*; Jeffrey Fager, *Land Tenure and the Biblical Jubilee*; Chris J.H. Wright, *God's People in God's Land: Family, Land and Property in the Old Testament*; Walter Brueggemann, *The Land*; and others.

Restoration

Ancient Israelite society was an agrarian society. When the people settled down in Canaan, the land was distributed, according to the size of the family, to cultivate and produce food for their families (Num.26). The land cultivated by the family was regarded as *nahala* "inheritance". The families were prohibited from selling this inheritance to anyone and becoming land less is evident from the case of Naboth's vineyard (1 Kgs.21:3 "The Lord forbid that I should give you my ancestral inheritance.") Such an inheritance gave each family employment, food and the right to be members of the village. Questions have been raised on the nature of he ownership of the land: whether the tribe or the clan, or by families, such as Naboth's vineyard, the tradition of passing on the land of the deceased person without male child to his brother, the claim of the five daughters of Zelophehad for their father's land (Num.27:1-11), Boaz redeeming the land of Naomi (Ruth 4:1-7), and the purchase of the land in Anathoth by Jeremiah (Jer.32:6-15).

Socio-economic Dimension
Land

Families as we know, cannot survive without land. Alienation from the land means poverty and bonded slavery. Poor families in ancient Israel were allowed to mortgage part of their land to their relations or neighbours, cultivate the rest and redeem the mortgaged land when they could find the money. But debt is a vicious trap. Due to an increasing burden of debt, such families had no other option except to mortgage the rest of the property and become servants to the mortgagee. People who could lend money started accumulating the land of the poor and became wealthy. Moneylenders exploited poor peasants and oppressed them so that the poor would work for them continuously.

The rich in their society added land to land, house to house and remained as the ruling class, the kings, officials at the royal court, landlords and business families never wanted to change the policies and laws or implement them to bring economic and social justice in their society. Prophets raised their voices against such injustice and inequality and demanded the ruling class to repent and render justice to the poor and marginalized (Amos 2:6-8; 5:24; 6:4-7; Micah 2:1-2; Isaiah 5:8-10). The sociological justification for the redemption of the land and labourers comes from the historical situation that developed during the monarchy.

To encounter the alienation of the land from the poor and the accumulation of wealth in the hands of a few rich, God insisted on the liberation of land from the rich and its restoration to the original families. The need to empower the poor with land, the right to cultivate it and enjoy the fruits of their labour was met by the introduction of the Jubilee Law. Since it is set in the context of Sinai, it became a legal code for them to practise.

The institution of Jubilee limited the mortgage to a maximum period of 49 years. The rich were then asked to return the land without demanding repayment of the loan or interest. Thus the Jubilee year institution put an end to the perpetual alienation of land from poor families and the accumulation of properties by the rich. It became an instrument in restoring the land and resetting the economy, if not to perfect egalitarianism, at least to reducing the widening gap between the rich and poor. It also challenged upper people at least once every 50 years. Socio-economic evils that began in one era in ancient Israel could be rectified at the end of the era and the new era could begin with justice and welfare.

Labour

When families lose their right to cultivate the land that is mortgaged to another person, the mortgagee can employ the mortgager to cultivate it for wages. This happened in ancient Israel and is still happening in India today. In such a situation, the family are labourers for their new master. The mortgagee, however, can choose to appoint another family as his labourers. The family that lost the land then has to leave and go to another landlord for work and be his servants. In both situations, the family is alienated from their land, become servants and eventually end up in bonded slavery. Restoring the land alone to the family in the 50th year is not enough. The family must also be set free from servitude so they can go back to their land and exercise the right to cultivate it. Cancelling the mortgage and restoring the land demands also the liberation of labourers.

The rich, who enjoy the servitude of the poor, do not allow them to escape their clutches and go free. If the families are not set free and enabled to reclaim their right to return to their land, cultivate it once again and enjoy the produce, then releasing the land is meaningless. The Jubilee institution, therefore, linked the liberation of the land with the liberation of labour. Families and land must be reunited to overcome alienation.

Capital

The Jubilee institution provides relief from repayment of the loan. The mortgagee cannot charge any interest on the loan or even demand that the capital be returned to him in the 50th year. Since the mortgagee uses the land, the produce from the land is valued as equal to the capital and interest. Of course, it depends upon the amount borrowed, the number of years of the mortgage and the yielding capacity of the land. When the mortgager wants to redeem the land, he needs to pay only the balance for the number of years the mortgagee cannot use the land.

If the family cannot redeem it due to their poverty, then in the 50th year the land should be restored to the family without demanding the return of the borrowed capital. Families are relieved of their debts since the money-lender has used the land till the Jubilee year and enjoyed the fruits of the land. In spite of the writing off of their debts and restoration of their land, the families also need money to start cultivating the land once again and to maintain their family until the next harvest. Mere liberation of land and labours is not enough. If financial aid is not extended, the poor family will once again need to borrow money by mortgaging their land and so become slaves again.

So another law took care of this problem (Deut. 15:12-15). This law insisted that rich landlords should provide enough food, grain, cattle, wine, oil, and money to the poor family to start their new life. Such a sharing of resources with the poor sustains them until they reap the harvest of their land. Not only the remission of debts, restoration of land and liberation of labour are important but also the sharing of resources to establish their new life.

Theological Dimension

The theological justification for providing the redemption of land and labourer is stated in Lev. 25:23-24:

> The land shall not be sold in perpetuity, for the land is mine; with me you are aliens and tenants. And in all the country you possess, you shall provide for the redemption of the land.

While Ex.19:5-6; Deut.10:14 and Ps. 24:1 speak of Yahweh's ownership of the whole earth in general, Lev. 25:23-24 speaks of the ownership of the agricultural land. That the Israelites are the tenets of the land is worth noting. First, Yahweh's explicit claim to the agricultural land is seen in the reason for prohibiting the sale of the land in Lev.25:23. Concerning the meaning of the phrase 'for the land is mine' in v.23b, two views have been expressed. One is that the word "land" (*erets*) refers in general to the ground or territory that the people of Israel will possess and dwell in. Here it signifies Yahweh's ownership of the promised territory.[3]

Another view is that it refers to the farmland or agricultural fields of the families.[4] According to this view, V.23b signifies Yahweh's ownership of the agricultural land within the promised territory. Since scholarly opinions differ regarding the meaning of the word *erets* in V.23b, and the same word appears four times in vv.23-24, it is necessary to make clear how this word is used in the text.

The word *erets* that appears in v.24a "and in all the country you possess" refers to the territory, which they are going to possess and settle down in, and live as Yahweh's sojourners and strangers. The use of the preposition "in" (*ba*), which usually refers to a location, and the instruction to grant redemption for the agricultural land in the territory which has been possessed by them, indicate that the word *erets* in v.24a means the territory of the promised land.

Erets inv.23b, however, 'for the land is mine', refers to the agricultural land and not the promised territory. For the phrase 'for the land is mine' (v.23b) is closely linked to v.23a by the casual particle (ki) and stands as the direct reason for the prohibition of permanent sale of agricultural land. This logical connection leads us to regard erets in v.23b as agricultural land rather than the promised territory. Furthermore, we know this from the main thrust of Lev. 25:1-24. Details such as giving rest to the fields in the seventh year (vv.1-7, 20-22), selling and buying fields according to the number of years for crops (vv.13-16), abundant yields of the land by the kin and returning the fields in the jubilee year (vv.10, 24, 28) are all concerned with agriculture. So, the word erets which is used in connection with selling, buying, redeeming and returning the land in v.23a and v.24b, must refer to the fields of the family.

Second, an implicit claim of Yahweh to the agricultural land is expressed through the law of rest to the land in the seventh year (Lev.25:1-7, 20-22). Although expressions such as 'your fields' and ' your vineyards' (vv.1-7,20-22) and 'each of you shall return to his property' (vv.10, 13) seem to indicate that the land ,fields and vineyards belong to the Israelites they do not. They should instead be understood in relation to the main thrust of Lev.25:1-24: these agricultural lands belong to Yahweh and they are left in the Israelite's possession like land left in the custody of tenants. The condition that the Israelites should give rest to the agricultural land in the seventh year laid down by Yahweh is to remind and make them realize that Yahweh is the owner and they cannot use the land according to their own will as they are the owners.

Such "a resting period" (*sabbat*) or "a year of solemn rest" (*sabat sabaton*) for the land is described as "sabbatical period for Yahweh" (*sabat layahweh*) in vv.2 and 4. The purpose of leaving the land fallow in the seventh year is neither for the use of the poor nor for the use of the people of Israel in general. No one is allowed to sow, plough, harvest or use that land in any way in the seventh year (vv.2-5). The land must be left completely to its rest during that period. The humanitarian dimension expressed in Ex.23:10-11 is mostly interpreted in the sense of allowing the poor to go and collect the food

---

[3] A. R. S. Kennedy, *Leviticus and Numbers: Introduction*. Rev. ed., CB: Edinburgh, T.C & E.C.Jack, n.d., p.166; J .R. Porter, *Leviticus*, CBC: Cambridge UP, 1976, p.201; M.Ottosson, "erets," *TDOT*:1, 1974, p.401; N. Micklem, *The Book of Leviticus*. Vol.2. Ed. G.A. Buttrick, IB; Nashville: Abingdon, 1953, p.123; G.J. Wenham, *The Book of Leviticus*, NICOT; London: Hodder and Stoughton, 1979, p.320.

[4] R. North, *Sociology of the Biblical Jubilee*, Anal. Bibl. 4; Roam: Pontifical Biblical Institute, 1954, p.158; N. H. Snaith, *Leviticus and Numbers*, CB; London: Nelson, 1967, p.164; R. K. Harrison, *Leviticus: An Introduction and Commentary*, TOTC, Leicester: IVP, 1980, p.226.

available in the fallow land in the seventh year. The poor always found some fallow land in their region, or nearby, year after year and so survived. Here the emphasis is on the charitable aspect of the sabbatical year.

There is some truth in this interpretation if we understand that the land left as fallow in the Sabbath year is not the same land as mortgage from another family. If the land left as fallow is the land of another family, then we can also interpret it as allowing the family that lost it to return to their land in the sabbatical year, not just to collect food, but to claim it again and keep it in their possession. The land returns to the original owner in the sabbatical year. This does not conflict with the idea of the sabbatical year of rest for the land and so he cannot cultivate that piece of land. From the perspective of the mortgager who has lost it for six years, it is a year to enter into the land collect food and thus reverse the ownership. This right is provided by the divine rule of the sabbatical year.

This aspect is further emphasised by the theological dimension of Lev.25:1-7 where the resting period of the land is called a resting year for the sake of Yahweh. To observe the rest for the land in the seventh year throughout the promised territory is to acknowledge that Yahweh has given it as his gift for their use. I also think the implication of expressions such as "a resting period for Yahweh," "sabbatical year of solemn rest" to the land in Lev.25, is that the land is redistributed in the sabbatical year and the redistribution of land.

The two conditions Yahweh placed on the Israelites, namely, not to sell the land because it belongs to him, and to give rest to the land in the seventh year, indicate that the Israelites are only tenant-workers. The idea that the Israelites are not the owners of the land is further made clear by describing their landless status as that of sojourners dwell in somebody's land with the permission of the landlord or the community to cultivate the land.[5] However, Israelites as tenants were allowed to sell the "right of use" to another family only in times of poverty (v.25) and they were not allowed to sell the "ownership" of land.

This is made clear to us, first, from the expressions "according to the number of crops after the Jubilee you shall buy," "according to the number of years for crops he shall sell" (v.15) and "the number of crops that he is selling"(v.16). The word "crops" (*tebuah*) here means a series of cultivation on the land and indicates that only the use of the land and is sold and not the ownership of the land. The families can only mortgage the land is expressed, secondly, by a prohibition, "do not sell the land for annihilation" (*lismitut,* v.23) which means the sale of land must not cancel the right of recovering the land.[6] No one in Israel has the right to sell the land to another person as if that land is in his ownership. They can only mortgage it for a period with the view to redeeming it.

Two kinds of redemption of the land are outlined in Lev. 25:25-28, namely redemption by the nearest kin of the family that mortgaged the land (v.25), and, redemption by the seller himself (vv.25-28). The theology of Yahweh's ownership of land does not deny the responsibility of the tenant or kinsman. The person who sold the land to another party is expected to redeem that part of the land on mortgage, improving his financial situation either by cultivating the rest of the land

---

[5] For details on "sojourners" and "strangers"; R de Vaux, *Ancient Israel*, pp.74-76; D. Kellermann, "*gur; ger; geruth; meghurim,*" *TDOT.* 2, 1977, pp.439-449; C. J. H. Wright, "Family, Land and property in Ancient Israel. Some Aspects of Old Testament Ethics," Ph.D. Thesis, University of Cambridge, 1976, pp.61f.

[6] Rui de Menzes. "The Pentateuchal Theology of Land" *Bible Bhashyam* 12, 1986, p.23; Wright, "Family, Land and Property," p.56.

or by some other means. If he is unable to improve his financial situation, the nearest kinsman can pay the money to the one who bought the land, presumably at some time in the middle of the sale period, reclaim the right of use and restore the land to the seller.[7]

The tenancy system demands family solidarity. If these possibilities fail, then the land should be returned in the Jubilee year to the family that mortgaged it. No payment is necessary at the time of returning the land in the Jubilee year because the price is worked out according to the number of years of cultivation, taking into consideration the marginal gain of buyer and the money received by the seller for the number of years he could not cultivate his land. If the whole capital, or part of it, has to be returned after the completion of the sale period, then the buyer gets a great bargain. He enjoys the produce for the full period of mortgage as well as getting back some money. That is why Lev.25:13-28 does not say that the capital should be returned after the completion of the sale period in order to get back the right of use, only the 'balance of payment' when the land is redeemed by the seller in the middle of the sale period.

Historical Dimension

Historical criticism raises questions regarding the origin of the idea of the Jubilee year and the actual practice of it in ancient Israel. Since this text is from the Priestly writer, it could be said that the Priestly group invented the idea of Jubilee during their exilic experience in Babylon and introduced it through their Holiness Code. As such, it is an exilic law. Jeffery Fager points out that J.R. Porter and Anton Jirku believe that the ancient Israelites and the idea of land

redemption in the Jubilee year because their patriarchs practiced tribal ethics, which insisted on the redemption of land.[8] He also quotes the view of S, Bess, who suggests that the combination of poverty and accumulation of land in the monarchical period could have created the Jubilee law.[9] Finally, the idea of land belonging to God in the Ancient Near East is another reason for a very early date for the Jubilee tradition.

These three reasons (tribal ethics, economic situation and theological ideas from the Ancient Near East) suggest the existence of a tradition of periodic redistribution of land in the pre-exilic period. Apart from these, we cannot ignore the possibility of a move to counter the Canaanite tradition of permanent ownership of land by the rulers and landlords. For example, Moses' tradition of distributing the land equally to families, insisting on the idea of *nahala*, and the tradition of redistribution of land in the pre-exilic period could counter the Canaanite system which was influencing them during the period of settlement and of the monarchy.

However, Fager believes that there could have been some sort of tradition of periodic redistribution of land in the pre-exilic period but that such a tradition could have become the law of the Jubilee under the influence of the Priestly group in the exilic period for two main reasons. First, their intention was to help the returning exiles to obtain their land. Those who left the land and went into exile needed their land in e\which to live and produce food when they returned. These exiles who underwent difficulties should not feel doubly punished-alienated from the land in exile, and landless after returning. The concern of the priests was to give economic

---

[7] M. Noth, *Levitiucs: a Commentary* , OTL; Trans. J. E. Anderson , London: SCM, 1981, p.189;North, Sociology, pp.165f.

[8] Jeffery A. Fager, "Land Tenure and the Biblical Jubilee: Uncovering Hebrew Ethics through the Sociology of Knowledge," *JSOT Supplement* 155, Sheffield: SAP, 1993, pp.27-29.

[9] Fager, "Land Tenure," pp.29-32.

power to the returning exiles by introducing the law of the returning Israelites and those already living in the land and help to create one single, united community of Yahweh.[10]

The second intention of the priestly group was to assert their authority on the community by modifying the old Mosaic tradition of distribution of land so that each family has the right to their share of land through the Jubilee law, and placing this law in the context of the legal code of Sinai. This results in the redistribution of land and overcoming of the economic disorder caused over the years by the accumulation land by purchase and money loans or the departure of families either to survive the famine or into exile.[11]

Fager is of the opinion that redistribution in every Jubilee could have been disastrous to the economy. He thinks that the Priestly group intended some sort of distribution of land to those families who lost land, not a thorough redistribution throughout the land in the Jubilee year.[12] The Priestly group made a compromise between the ideal of total redistribution and failure to redistribute the land by introducing the idea of land redistribution through the law of the Jubilee year. But how can the Priestly group speak of one thing and mean another? In my opinion, practical difficulties in the redistribution of the land in the Jubilee year and some economic problems could not be avoided. Oppressive forces would have definitely tried to hinder the implementation of the Jubilee law. Denial of redistribution is more disastrous to the community life. The gap widens between the rich and poor, and this could lead to class struggle.

The linking of the Sabbath to the land in the text of Jubilee (Lev.25) and suggestion of the calculation of the Jubilee year by multiplying Sabbaths, leads me to think that there was a periodic redistribution of land once in seven years as Yahweh cancels the tenancy right on the sabbatical year and renews it again. It seems the observance of the sabbatical year of release of land and forgiveness of debts in the earlier period by families according to their own sabbatical calendar could have failed by the 8th century. The Priestly group, who knew of this failure and the message of the 8th century prophets, modified the idea of a sabbatical year periodic redistribution to once in 50 years as a compromise for the sake of returning exiles. However, their remarkable achievement was to enable the release of land and labourer in the Jubilee year without the repayment of the capital and interest. We can notice that the Jubilee law of the Priestly code is a combination and modification of the earlier three important laws of the sabbatical year; rest to the land, release of slaves and servants and lending financial help without interest as stated in the Covenant code.

In my opinion, redistribution of land in the sabbatical year could have been revived as a practical possibility because:

- It gives a short period of six years for possessing the mortgaged land.

- The Sabbath tradition is deeply rooted in Israel both in terms of rest and releasing the slaves.

- The mortgager would also like to see the release of the land without any payment on the seventh year and reassert his economic position.

- Because of its flexibility the Sabbath year release could be worked out locally with the help of the two parties and the elders or priests in the village more easily than adhering to a uniform, national Jubilee year for the country.

---

[10] Fager, "Land Tenure," pp.60-63.
[11] Fager, "Land Tenure," pp.54-56.
[12] Fager, "Land Tenure," pp.110-111.

So it seems to me that the preferable option is to have the tradition of a local release of land and labourers once in seven years. But a national law is also needed to force the defaulters to give the land to the original owner, release the bonded labourers and forgive the debts at least once in 50years.

Having examined the situation, we can see that there are several salient features of the Jubilee institution that challenges us, whether we are involved in agriculture or in some other profession.

i) By declaring that the land belongs to God, the Jubilee institution makes the agricultural land sacred. It does not mean that people cannot enter or use it, but they cannot own it as their permanent property. Converting agricultural land, which produces food for people, into industrial or amusement parks or highways and airports in a country like India needs to be rethought.

ii) The Jubilee institution that insists on the redistribution of land to the landless stops the growth of large estates (latifundism) by a few rich people, thus giving more political and economic power to the poor.

iii) Jubilee attaches people to the land and underlines the close relationship between the two. People need the land and the land needs the people to live, produce food and take care of it.

iv) Jubilee emphasizes the economic viability of families to live, cultivate and grow food. Each family can stand on its own feet without depending on others for food. This sustainability is brought out in the Jubilee law.

v) Since redemption of land by kith and kin- the 'goel' concept –is emphasized in the jubilee regulation, family solidarity is demanded.

vi) Jubilee envisages the possibility of a new egalitarian society here and now. It is not a utopia, but rather a realistic goal that can be achieved if the community co-operates.

vii) Jubilee also implies that in any period of 50 years, the socio-economic system can go wrong and disparities can arise but Jubilee provides an on-going mechanism for periodic redistribution and the recycling of the social order.

Revitalization

By introducing the Jubilee institution, the Priestly group revitalized the tradition of the release of land, labourer and forgiveness of debts in Israel. As the 'intelligentsia' of the Israelite community, with cultic authority and in the absence of the monarchy in the post-exilic period, the priestly group could have made the effort to implement it and reorder the new community in the post-exilic period. Jubilee could have been made a meaningful celebration to the communities. Jubilee brings reconciliation and rejoicing. The poor who lost the land and went into servitude for a number of years should rejoice at receiving their land once again. The 50th year wipes away their tears after a long period of poverty and suffering. They are set free to exercise their right to enjoy their land in freedom and dignity.

Rejoicing is not just for emotional satisfaction. It has a spiritual effect. It contributes to the healing of the estranged relationships between the rich and the poor. By rejoicing in what God has initiated to set things right, the poor in society can get rid of their bitter feelings towards those who oppress them. Real joy in society is possible only when the poor forgive their oppressors. The rich need the forgiveness of the poor and powerless. The wealthy need to repent, rectify their losses to their victims. Jubilee year is a special year for repentance and forgiveness and reconciling the broken relationships in society.

The rich people also can rejoice because they are repenting and restoring the land to the families who lost it, setting them free to cultivate the land and helping them with various resources to restart their life in the new era. Real joy is not in the accumulation of wealth and enjoying the labour of others, but in sharing and enabling the poor to regain power and dignity and seeing them rejoicing. The rich should be thankful to God for the Jubilee law that counters their selfish nature and compels them, to contribute to the process of achieving equality and welfare for all. Like the Priestly group in Israel, churches today are expected to revitalize the meaningful Jubilee tradition to redeem land and the labourer and provide forgiveness of debts.

India experienced a similar distribution of land by the rich to the landless through an institution called "Boodan Movement" ("boomi" means the land; "dan" means gift) initiated in April 1951 by Acharya Vinoba Bhave, an ardent follower of Mahatma Gandhi and his ideals.[13] Soon after independence, the process of consolidation of the states into formation of union of India continued. During this period (1947-1951), peasants in different states were involved in the struggles, claiming their rights to own the land. Some of these peasant movements in West Bengal (Naxalite) and Andhra Pradesh (Telungana) were violent and many landlords were killed. Vinoba went to these riot-stricken areas and pleaded with the landlords to distribute land to landless farmers. Voluntarily giving land as a gift went on from 1951to 1961 in many parts of India.

The Gandhian School, led by Vinobha, introduced another institution called "Gramdan" ("Gram" means "Villages;" "dan" means "gift") in January 1957 after seeing the success of

Boodan Movement. It provided the opportunity for the rich to donate lands to the villages to hold them as a common property. Families in villages can only make use of these lands donated to their village to produce food and cannot claim ownership. This paved the way for cooperative farming in many villages. Even though the Boodan Movement and Gramdan Movement did not achieve a thorough redistribution of land and recycling of the economy, they proved that land distribution is possible without violence. They were timely actions to help the landless soon after our liberation from the British, who could have done a major land reform in our country during their 150 years of rule. I am not equating the Gandhian movements of Boodan and Gramdan to the biblical Jubilee institution of the Priestly group. But there is a similarity: whenever a nation is liberated from bondage (Egyptian) or exile (Babylon), or colonial rule (British), land is the foremost issue to be dealt with.

Contemporary Challenges

Biblical messages remind us of the need to make our lives more meaningful to our society. Land alienation happens quickly, and many people in India are becoming poor, leaving their villages in search of jobs in towns and cities. One of the main reasons for leaving the land and becoming bonded labourers is the problem of debt. In times of monsoon failure, extra medical or education expenses, or marriages of children, house repairs, purchase of seed and fertilizers, farmers borrow money from money-lenders by mortgaging their land. Unable to pay the capital and interest, they transfer the ownership of their land forever to the moneylenders and surrender themselves as their servants. Now they plough their land for the sake of their new master.

The reviving of the biblical idea of Jubilee in the last decade has challenged many of our

---

[13] C. B. Mamoria and B. B. Tripathi, *Agricultural Problem of India*, New Delhi: Kitab Mahal, 1989, pp.713-719.

churches and missionary organisations. The theology of land is becoming prominent in India. Three national missionaries belonging to the national missionary organisations in India have initiated a scheme to help the tribals in their area. Farmers bring the best of their wheat harvest to be stored in the church as seed to be used in the next cultivation, rather than selling all their harvest at a low price and then later borrowing money from the money- lenders to buy the seed for sowing. They use the church as the seed-bank and later as a marketing place to sell their harvest at a good price. Some of the tribals who co-operated with this scheme were able to redeem their land. The moneylenders did not like the mediating role of the church in storing the seed, promoting the sale, and clearing their debts. They accused the missionaries of converting the tribals to Christianity and finally set fire to the church. This kind of micro-level social action in redeeming the land and labourers is repeated in different parts of India.

However, loans and debts are problems not only for the farmers but also for the people who are working in organised and unorganised sectors in the cities and towns. They borrow money from the illegal moneylenders and also fall into the debt trap. Many Christians think that the Jubilee challenges are not relevant to the people living in towns and cities, since most of them do not own land or are not involved in agriculture. But some industrial workers go home without their salary and borrow again to sustain their family. Some of them hesitate to go out of the company confines, and stay inside the campus until late at night to avoid the money- lenders waiting at the gate. Some of them take leave on payday to avoid the money- lenders. If they regularly avoid the money- lenders and fail to pay them interest on their loans, they are beaten and their wives and children are ill-treated by the moneylenders.

A survey was made by our students to find out the seriousness of loans and debts of the poor living in a particular area near our seminary and the problems faced by them from the money-lenders. These moneylenders collect Rupee 1 per day as interest for a loan of Rs.100. It looks as if it is a very low interest rate, but it is calculated per day. A poor labourer who borrowed Rs.500 pays Rs.5 as daily interest that makes Rs.1825 in interest by the end of the year. The loan of Rs.500 still remains an unsettled burden. Moneylenders encourage their borrowers not to worry about the capital now but to continue to pay the interest regularly. The small capital lent is used as a hook to fetch a big income through interest. If the person is unable to return the capital borrowed, they will remain on the hook, paying the interest continuously for years. These people who are hooked to the vicious cycle of debts undergo mental agony, become sick, and resort to alcohol and drugs and even commit suicide.

Churches and missions are fighting not only against these principalities and powers but also against our government. The ruling BJP government in New Delhi (religious fundamentalist party of Hinduism) and their militant out fits like RSS and Bajrang Dal (suspected of killing the Australian missionary, Graham Staines, and his two sons in Orissa) see the Christian mission activities of evangelism and liberation as a threat to their status quo and their policy of keeping the poor as poor and rich as rich, low caste as low and the high caste as high. So, the liberative actions are accused of being conversions. This government celebrated the 50th year of Independence as a mere political function, ignoring economic and social reform. There is a great need for solidarity and co-operation of leaders in politics, religion and economics to make the ideals of Jubilee more meaningful to the people in a local area or at the national level. This is urgently needed in the light of the mounting debts of the Third World Countries.

CHAPTER 5

The Patriarchs and Religious Pluralism: An Old Testament Perspective

P. AUGUSTINE

Introduction

The subject, "religious pluralism and the Old Testament" has attracted little interest compared to "religion of the Old Testament." Two recent articles have begun to reverse that trend. They suggest that the idea of "pluralism" within ancient texts is relatively new, probably because of the general Christian consensus that the Old Testament faith is exclusivist and not open to the modern idea of "religious pluralism," which believes that the various religions are equally valid approaches to the one "Ultimate Reality." In the first Richard Hess[1] is very specific, focusing on the religious beliefs of the people of Israel during the monarchy, that is from the time of David to the fall of Jerusalem in 586 BCE and dealing with only the four "most important" inscriptions, which have been discovered. In the second John E. Goldingay and Christopher J.H. Wright deal with the whole of the Old Testament literature in six headings, each focusing on the material dealing with different periods of the Old Testament times.[2]

Hess argues that the inscriptions illustrate three different religious attitudes prevalent during the monarchy. They are: 1) Yahwistic exclusivism seen in the prophets and others writers of scripture; represented by the *Ketef Hinnom* amulets probably worn by priests, leaders and other individuals. 2) Yahwism as state religion affirmed and promoted in general by the rulers and the cult in Jerusalem, but many kings and queens displaying tolerance to other deities and even participating in those cults through political and marital alliances; represented by the inscription on the ivory pomegranate found in Jerusalem, although no mention of tolerance of other deities is made. 3) Open tolerance of a variety of deities, even participation in the fertility cult of Baal and Asherah at the popular level both in Israel and Judah, but simultaneously accepting Yahweh as the supreme God at the national level; represented by two inscriptions, namely the *Kuntillet Ajrud* and the *Khirbet el-Qom*. Both associate Asherata (identified with biblical Asherah) with Yahweh, who is mentioned first, suggesting that Yahweh was believed to be the main deity while recognizing the existence of other gods. 4) State support of a foreign god as supreme in Israel, as seen in Baal worship introduced in the northern kingdom by Ahab and Jezebel and later Athaliah, her daughter, who made similar attempts in the south. Prophets in the north and priests in the south opposed this attitude. The second essay opens with the question, "Is the Old Testament exclusivist and

---

[1]Richard S. Hess, *Yahweh and His Asherah? Epigraphic Evidence for Religious Pluralism in Old Testament Times*, ed. by Andrew D. Clarke and Bruce W. Winter, *One God One Lord in a World of Religious Pluralism*, Tyndale House: Cambridge, 1991, pp. 5-33.

[2]John E. Goldingay and Christopher J.H. Wright, *Yahweh our God Yahweh One: The Old Testament and Religious Pluralism*, ed. by Andrew D. Clarke and Bruce W. Winter, *One God One Lord in a World of Religious Pluralism*, pp. 34-52.

nationalist or open and universalist?" The authors suggest that the Old Testament recognizes other religions "as reflecting truth about God from which Israel itself may even be able to learn. But they are always in need of the illumination which can only come from knowing what Yahweh has done with Israel." The authors go on to state further:

> The biblical view is that the living God, later disclosed as Yahweh, accommodated his dealings with the ancestors of Israel to the names and forms of deity then known in their cultural setting. It does not thereby endorse every aspect of Canaanite El worship. The purpose of God's particular action in the history of Israel is ultimately that God, as the saving and covenant God Yahweh, should be known fully and worshipped exclusively by those who as yet imperfectly know him as El. The end result of what God began to do through Abram was of significance for the Canaanites precisely because it critiqued and rejected Canaanite religion.[3]

This "accommodation" idea is probably influenced by 'God of the Fathers' debate,[4] which began first with Albrecht Alt and reached its climax with F.M. Cross. It assumes that the names used for God in Genesis— the relational titles, such as *El Elohe Israel* and *El Elohe Abika* as well as the titles describing his attributes, such as *El Olam, El Elyon* and *El Shaddai*— can fit well with the known characteristics of Canaanite *El* because of their meaning and the context in which they occur in Genesis. Alt concluded that they were different clan gods before they were merged into Yahwism, while Cross argued that patriarchs worshipped *El* cult or they used the

epithets of *El* to give a wider meaning to their own God.[5] Several questions may be raised here. First, regarding interpretation: Can it be sustained that the 'living God' accommodated himself to the 'names and forms' of the deity known to the ancestors of Israel? Secondly, a theological question: Would it justify the views of present day pluralists who find the connections between the religions of other faiths and Christianity to show the need for such a view? Goldingay and Wright's attempt to cover the religious environment of the entire Old Testament period is to be commended for its broad sweep and insightful argument, but it lacks the in-depth focus on a particular period with which we are dealing here.

The present essay will be an elaboration on 'Israel's Ancestors' (sub-heading in Goldingay and Wright) and a study of patriarchal attitudes to their neighbours' religions as portrayed in Genesis 12-50. In what follows, we will explore only a small portion of the Old Testament as a test case, namely the patriarchal narratives. The reasons for this are two-fold: First, because a large number of scholars regard patriarchal religion as primitive and even animistic compared to the more developed monotheistic religion of the later Israel, it would seem to be easier to find ideas closer to religious pluralism in the patriarchal narratives than elsewhere in the Old Testament. Secondly, and more importantly, the patriarchal narratives form the foundational traditions of faith and practice for Israel. Walter Moberly argued convincingly, that God's dealings with the patriarchs are distinctly different from the way he dealt with the later Israel and so he calls the patriarchal narratives *The Old Testament of the Old Testament*.[6] If this is so, their religion, as have

---

[3]*Ibid.* p. 39.

[4]This issue will be discussed in detail below.

[5]A. Alt, "The God of the Fathers," in A. Alt, *Essays on Old Testament History and Religion*, Sheffield: Sheffield Academic Press, 1989; [German, 'Der Gott Der Vater', 1929]; F.M. Cross, *Cannanite Myth and Hebrew Epic*, Cambridge, Massachusetts: Harvard University Press, 1973, pp.55-58.

[6] Walter Moberly, *The Old Testament of the Old Testament, Patriarchal Narratives and Mosaic Yahwism* Minneapolis: Fortress, 1992.

I argued elsewhere, must be distinct from that of the later Israel.[7] But does this mean that the patriarchs were monotheists, or was their religion, as some biblical texts suggest and many scholars argue, primitive, animistic and even more pluralistic than the Yahwistic religion of the later Israel? This will be our concern in the rest of this essay.

Religious Pluralism and the Patriarchal Narratives

Method: Since the idea of religious pluralism is a modern concept and the sources we deal with are the ancient texts written from a faith point of view to a community of faith, we must take caution to avoid at least two possible mistakes. We are to resist, on the one hand, reading late Jewish and Christian ideas into them, and on the other hand, to restrain from reading into them twentieth century religious pluralism. The issues involved are – who was the God (or gods) of the Patriarchs? What is his (or their) relationship with Yahweh of Israel? Did patriarchs worship Yahweh or, as Albrecht Alt had argued, some local numina who were later amalgamated into the official Yahwism? What if the patriarchs'

religious history, as some have vigorously argued, testifies to a religious pluralism?[8] To do that there are problems in our way; first, the material available is inadequate to reconstruct a history of the religion of the Patriarchs. Secondly, the sources in their present form are centuries removed from the events they describe. Thirdly, the materials at hand are religious in nature and at times even anachronistic and yield little factual content. However, recent archaeological discoveries in Palestine, Egypt and Mesopotamia have opened up new possibilities and our sources themselves are said to preserve "an appreciable amount of ancient and trustworthy traditions."[9]

Sources: Our sources are the two great epics, J and E, coming in their present form from 10th and 8th century BCE respectively. Though this is a generally agreed scholarly opinion, J. Van Seters has lately argued that the whole of the Old Testament literature comes from the exilic and post-exilic times.[10] A methodological issue is involved here. What are the criteria that decide the antiquity or lateness of a text? And a theological issue beneath it is: how does an appeal

---

[7] Augustine Pagolu, *The Religion of the Patriarchs,* JSOT 277, Sheffield: Sheffield Academic Press, 1998, pp. 243-47. I have argued here that patriarchal religion was distinct both from the ancient Near Eastern and later Israelite religions. There is no "apologetic agenda" here, as alleged by a recent reviewer (*CBQ* 63 [2001], pp. 325-26), to search for what is unique in their religion in order to prove that theirs was the "true religion." My focus was to unravel the way authors of Genesis portrayed patriarchal religion, which most modern approaches, such as source, form and traditio-historical methods (the reviewer wrongly alleges that I have not considered them), to patriarchal stories have failed to do justice. While there are no unbiased readers, the value of any reading is to be assessed against its proposed method and not from a presupposition that the traditional source critical methods have the answer. In fact since James Muilenburg's seminal essay, "Form Criticism and Beyond" in 1969, many presuppositions of these traditional methods have been either seriously questioned or totally rejected. See R. Rendtorff, *The Problem of the Process of Transmission in the Pentateuch,* Sheffield: JSOT 1990; German 1977; R.N. Whybray, *The Making of the Pentateuch: A Methodological Study,* Sheffield: JSOT, 1987. It may be noted here that most of the material in this essay has been adapted from this book.

[8] J. A. Loader, "Theologia Religionum: From the Perspective of Israelite Religion – An Argument," *Missionalia* 13/2, 1985, pp.14-32.

[9] James Muilenberg, "History of the Religion of Israel," ed. by G. A. Buttrick et. al., *IB* Vol.1, New York, Nashville, Abingdon Press, 1952, p. 295; Martyn J. Selman, "Comparative Customs and the Patriarchal Age," ed. by A.R. Millard and D.J. Wiseman, *Essays on the Patriarchal Narratives,* Leicester: Inter Varsity Press, 1980, pp. 93-138; Claus Westermann, *Genesis 12-36,* London: SPCK, 1985; Minniapolis: Augsburg 1981, pp. 34, 40, 75, 85-86; Moberly, *The Old Testament of the Old Testament,* pp. 195-98; Augustine Pagolu, *The Religion of the Patriarchs,* pp. 22-23.

[10] John Van Seters, "The Religion of the Patriarchs in Genesis," *Biblica* 61, 1980, p. 232.

to antiquity increase the truth-claims of that text?[11] Some scholars have produced criteria to determine the antiquity of the sources, at least of the poetic texts. Van Seters and F. M. Cross are at opposite poles. For the former, a text basically illumines its own age. For the latter, our sources do contain, and reveal information relevant to the subject in question, "when they are analyzed in relation to comparative data and when typologies are developed carefully."[12] If we follow Van Seters we are forced to conclude that the patriarchal stories are nothing but a projection of exilic and post-exilic Jewish ideas of their own times. But the enormous epigraphic material and artifacts demand that we turn our attention and follow Cross's line. We shall not, however, ignore insights gained from the traditional diachronic methods of source-, form- and traditio-historical tools although they assume the composite nature of the texts and attempt to recover the original text behind the present one,[13] nor shall we set aside the fruits of the new literary criticism which gives little or no attention to the history or theology of the narratives.[14] However, since the Genesis authors/redactors seem to be concerned more with content and purpose than with the form of their materials, we shall follow a synchronic approach and focus on the 'final form' of the text as it stands before us rather than relying entirely on an often hypothetically reconstructed one.[15]

Patriarchal Religion in Scholarly Debate

There are at least two lines of thought: One argues that the patriarchal stories are a fabrication of the exilic and post-exilic community which tried to establish its identity by creating the stories in which their ancestors were promised land and numerous descendants in order that their claims to the land may be warranted in the stories themselves. Further, on the basis of elements such as calling upon the name of Yahweh through building altars, raising pillars and planting trees which were condemned in strongest terms in later Israel, they argue that if the patriarchs ever existed, their religion must be primitive and animistic and incompatible with the religion of Moses and later Israel.[16] The other line of thought stresses the historicity of the patriarchs and sees their period as pre-exodus and pre-settlement of Israel as portrayed in the pentateuchal narratives, but it largely follows the first group of scholars as far as their religion is concerned, that it was primitive and animistic and incompatible with the Mosaic religion. These scholars support their arguments by epigraphic and archaeological evidence.[17] However, recently a third option has opened up which sees the patriarchs narratives in Genesis as plausible on epigraphic and

---

[11] P. D. Miller, "Israelite Religion," eds. D. A. Knight and G. M. Tucker, *Hebrew Bible and Its Modern Interpreters*, California: Scholars Press, 1985, p. 213.

[12] *Ibid.*; F. M. Cross, *Canaanite Myth and Hebrew Epic*, Cambridge, Massachusetts: Harvard University Press, 1973.

[13] J. Wellhausen, *Prolegomena to the History of Israel*, Edinburgh: A. & C. Black, 1885, p. 9, believes that the texts have no historical value. Cf. Whybray, *The Making of the Pentateuc*, pp. 22-28. However, form- and traditio-historical methods assume that the narratives have an historical kernel and that many texts and ideas go back to the patriarchal period. Cf. *Commentaries on Genesis* by Gunkel 1902, von Rad (1965) and Claus Westermann , 1985, and Alt's article, "The God of the Fathers" in his *Essays on Old Testament History and Religion*, pp. 1-77.

[14] For a representative sample, see Paul R. House, ed., *Beyond Form Criticism: Essays in Old Testament Literary Criticism*, Winona Lake, IN: Eisenbrauns, 1992.

[15] For an exposition and justification, see B.S. Childs's many writings, especially his *Introduction to Old Testament as Scripture*, Philadelphia: Fortress, 1979.

[16] J. Wellhausen, *Prolegomena to the History of Israel*, also see the so-called Wellhausen school.

[17] W. F. Albright, *The Archaeology of Palestine and the Bible*, New York: Revell, 1932; *idem. From Stone Age to Christianity: Monotheism and the Historical Process*, New York: Doubleday, 1957; *idem. Yahweh and the Gods of Canaan: A Historical Analysis of Two Contrasting Faiths*, London: Athlone Press, 1968; also see the so-called Albright school.

archaeological grounds and also on a comparative study of customs and practices from the so called patriarchal period, the early second millennium BCE.[18] The present essay follows this line and explores the possibility of patriarchal religion being in some way continuous with the religion of Israel and compatible only with the lifestyle of the patriarchs presented in the patriarchal stories in Genesis. On the other hand, if the religion of the patriarchs is in some way discontinuous with the Mosaic religion, it would have far reaching implications for religious pluralism. We shall not explore the validity of the first option, which discredits the historicity of the patriarchs even as most of the critical commentaries during the early part of the 20th century take this view for granted. Nevertheless, we shall interact with this view as we explore the second and the third options. One of the most contentious issues in the religion of the patriarchs has been the idea of the 'God of the Fathers' to which we shall now turn.

God of the Fathers: Within the framework of those who allow historicity to the patriarchs, the discussion on the religion of the patriarchs for the most part of the 20th century, has been centred around the idea, "God of the Fathers," assuming that this would be the key to understanding the religion of the patriarchs. In this regard, no study of patriarchal religion can bypass the work of Albrecht Alt. He found two forms of worship in the Patriarchal stories. One is characterized by the element *"El"*

that is attached as a substantive or an adjective to the God worshipped by the patriarchs.[19] They are *"El Olam"* (Gen. 21:33), *"El Elyon"* (Gen. 14:18ff), *"El Elohe Israel"* (Gen. 33:20), *"El Roi"* (Gen. 16:13), *"El Bethel"* (Gen. 35:7) and *"El Shadday"* mostly in Priestly source, P. All these epithets were attached to individual patriarchal sanctuaries. Alt thought that this is a local numina worshipped by common people all over the land with its sanctuaries, sacred pillars, altars and sacred trees.[20] The other form was a group of epithets in which the god was identified by the name of a patriarch, like "the Benefactor of Abraham" (Gen. 15:1), "the Fear of Isaac." (Gen. 31:42, 53), and "the Bull of Jacob" (Gen. 49:24). Alt thought that these were originally independent gods worshipped by the individual patriarchs which in course of time combined into a single family God, (the 'God of the fathers') by fictional genealogies.[21]

Alt's suspicions, apparently, proved to be correct when he examined a passage from the so-called Elohistic source, E:

> Then Moses said to God, If I come to the people of Israel and say to them, The God of your fathers has sent me to you, and they ask me, 'What is his name?', what shall I say to them? ... God said to Moses, 'I am who I am'... and he said, 'Thus you shall say to the people of Israel, Yahweh the God of your fathers, the God of Abraham, the God of Isaac and the God of Jacob has sent me to you' (Ex. 3:13-15).

---

[18]M.J. Selman, "The Social Environment of the Patriarchs," *Tyndale Bulletin* 27 (1976): 114-36; *idem.* "Comparative Customs and the Patriarchal Age," in A.R. Millard and D.J. Wiseman , eds, *Essays on the Patriarchal Narratives,* Leicester: Inter Varsity Press, 1980, pp. 93-138, and the various articles in this volume; Claus Westermann, *Genesis 12-36,* London: SPCK, 1985; N. M. Sarna, *Genesis, Bereshith,* JPS Torah Commentary; Philadelphia: Jewish Publication Society of America, 1989; Moberly, *The Old Testament of the Old Testament;* Augustine Pagolu, *The Religion of the Patriarchs.*

[19] A. Alt, "The God of the Fathers," in A. Alt, *Essays on Old Testament History and* Religion, Sheffield: Sheffield Academic Press, 1989; cf. Cross, *Canaanite Myth and Hebrew Epic,* p. 46.

[20] Alt, "The God of the Fathers," pp. 25-30, J. Van Seters, "Patriarchs" in K. Crim et al., eds, *IDB* Sup., Nashville: Abingdon Press, 1976, p. 647. For a detailed analysis of the patriarchal religious practices see Augustine Pagolu, *The Religion of the Patriarchs,* pp. 33-85, 135-213.

[21] Alt, "The God of the Fathers," p. 32-44; Cf. Cross, *Canaanite Myth and Hebrew Epic,* p. 4.

This is crucial to Alt's analysis since the text seems "to insist that Yahweh is to be identified with the 'God of the fathers'."[22] Alt thought that these were two different religions. The so-called Priestly source, P, also pointed toward similar direction: "I am Yahweh, I revealed myself to Abraham, to Isaac, and to Jacob as *El Shadday* but was not known to them by my name Yahweh" (Ex. 6:2-3).[23] This seemed to insist of an identification and continuity of Yahwism with the "God of the fathers." With this Alt thought that the nature of the religion of the patriarchs could be discovered if we could unravel the nature of the 'God of the Fathers'. Subsequently, a number of scholars focused their attention on the 'God of the Fathers.' Alt himself tried to substantiate his theory by taking an example from the Greek and Aramaic inscriptions of Nabateans and Palmyreans (nomadic tribes, like the patriarchs, who worshipped the gods of the heads of their clans) dating between the first century BCE and fourth century CE, assuming that this would reflect the original cult of the patriarchs. Many scholars have admitted that an inquiry into patriarchal religion before Exodus would be possible but they were not convinced about his conclusions.

There are several questions raised in Alt's reconstruction of patriarchal religion. Alt's idea that the patriarchal gods were anonymous and were identified only by their worshippers, as "the God of Abraham," "the Fear of Isaac," and "the Bull of Jacob," was also found to be baseless since a high god is found to be described in similar terms in nineteenth-century Cappadocia and the real name of the God of the patriarchs was *El Shadday*. Furthermore, it is pointed out that Alt's analogy of Nabateans and Palmyreans was based on fragmentary inscriptions coming between the first century BCE and fourth century CE, which is too remote to be compared with the religion of the patriarchs.[24] Another criticism is that Alt identified '*elim*' in Genesis with local numina because his theory was advanced before the discovery of Ugaritic texts where 'El' is widely attested as the head of the Canaanite pantheon. 'El' is the primordial father of the gods. He is described as the divine father, divine warrior, king and creator, being stern sometimes and compassionate at other times, but always wise in his judgements.[25] Subsequent scholarship, Cross for example, tried to see a connection between the *El* in the Ugaritic texts and the different designations used for God in Genesis.[26]

After a thorough inquiry into the characteristics of *El* from Ugarit and elsewhere in the ancient Near East on the one hand, and the divine epithets found in Genesis on the other, Cross tried to describe the patriarchal religion as a form of *El* religion. He thought that most of the titles used for the patriarchal God in Genesis- the relational titles, such as *El Elohe* Israel and *El Elohe Abika* as well as the titles describing his attributes, such as *El Olam, El Elyon* and *El Shaddai*- can fit well with the known characteristics of Canaanite *El* because of their meaning and the context in which they occur in Genesis. *El Shaddai* proved difficult since it seemed to have no obvious parallel in the Canaanite pantheon. He attributes it to an Amorite origin and suggests that the patriarchs brought it from Mesopotamia.[27] Thus different divine

---

[22] Cross, *Canaanite Myth and Hebrew Epic*, p. 5.

[23] *Ibid.*

[24] W. S. Prinsloo, response to J. A. Loaders "Theologia Religionum," in *Missionalia* 13 No.1, 1985, pp. 33-34.

[25] Cross, *Canaanite Myth and Hebrew Epic*, pp. 40-43.

[26] M.H. Pope, *El in the Ugaritic Texts* VTSup 2; Leiden: Brill, 1955, pp. 82-89.

[27] F.M. Cross, "Yahweh and the God of the Patriarchs," *HTR* 55 (1962), pp 255-59, *idem. Canaanite Myth and Hebrew Epic*, pp. 3-75.

names of Genesis were not the different clan gods before they were merged into Yahwism as Alt thought, but were originally epithets of *El* that survived in patriarchal traditions.[28] This meant that the patriarchs worshipped *El* or they used epithets of *El* to give a wider meaning to their own God. Further, Cross suggests that this is probably the reason why *El* epithets were more readily acceptable in later Yahwism than those of Baal and this also shows basic continuity between the patriarchal religion, a form of *El* religion, and the Yahwism of the later Israel. Cross's theory was attractive to many scholars since he handled his comparative materials more carefully and since they come closer in time and place to the patriarchal times.[29] But several scholars challenge this.[30] Despite the enormous efforts of Alt and Cross the discussion on the religion of the patriarchs was confined to the "God of the patriarchs" and even here there is no consensus. Thus it has become increasingly clear that the answer to the nature of the religion of the patriarchs is to be sought elsewhere and not in the "God of the Fathers."

Historicity of the Patriarchal Stories: The third option explored the issue focusing chiefly on the social, religious and legal customs, and personal names and people movements reflected in the patriarchal narratives. The main conclusion was that the customs and practices reflected in the patriarchal narratives are surprisingly similar to the social practices known from Nuzi, Mari and Alalakh and hence patriarchal stories are to be placed in the wider context of the second millennium BCE ancient Near Eastern society, unless the biblical testimony is to be proved as entirely unhistorical.[31] We still cannot date the patriarchal period precisely, nor are we trying to prove the historicity of the patriarchs. However, on the basis of the enormous data available on the ancient Near Eastern customs and practices it is plausible to suggest that the patriarchs could have existed, although a number of scholars still remain skeptical.[32]

Nevertheless, the discussion on the religion of the patriarchs has not moved beyond the designations or names of God used in Genesis. For this we need to go back to the patriarchal stories themselves and ask a different set of questions that hitherto have not been asked. Among the few scholars who have led the discussion in this direction are Westermann and Moberly. Some of the characteristics, distinct and unique to the patriarchal religion in Genesis, recognized by these scholars are the personal relationship between the patriarchs and their God, the unconditional promises relating to the patriarchal situation, the lack of priesthood and

---

[28] Cross, *Canaanite Myth and Hebrew Epic*, pp. 60.

[29] It appears that Goldingay and Wright, p. 39, also tow Cross' line here.

[30] M.H. Pope, *El in the Ugaritic Texts*, pp. 55-58; E.L. Abel, "The Nature of the Patriarchal God 'El Shadday,'" *Numen* 20, 1973, pp 48-59; G.J. Wenham, "The Religion of the Patriarchs," ed. by A.R. Millard and D.J. Wiseman, *Essays on the Patriarchal Narratives*, Leicester: Inter-Varsity Press, 1980, p. 171. For further literature on the subject, see Augustine Pagolu, *The Religion of the Patriarchs*, pp. 18-19.

[31] S.M. Warner, "The Patriarchs and Extra-Biblical Sources," *JSOT* 2, 1977, pp 50-61; J.J. Bimson, "Archaeological Data and the Dating of the Patriarchs," in A.R. Millard and D.J. Wiseman; *Essays in the Patriarchal Narratives*, pp. 59-92; Selman, "The Social Environment of the Patriarchs," pp. 114-36; *idem.* "Comparative Customs and the Patriarchal Age," pp. 93-138; For a discussion on different views see Augustine Pagolu, *The Religion of the Patriarchs*, pp. 19-24.

[32] T.L. Thompson, *The Historicity of the Patriarchal Narratives*; *idem. Early History of the Israelite People*; Van Seters, *Abraham in History and Tradition*; *idem. Prologue to History*; P.R. Davies, *In Search of Ancient Israel*, JSOT 148, Sheffield: Sheffield Academic Press, 1992; 2nd edn. 1995. For a rebuttal of Davies's position, see Ed Noort, *History and Recent Trends in Old Testament Studies*, ed. by D.J. Muthunayagom, *Bible Speaks Today: Essays in Honour of Gnana Robinson*, Bangalore: UTC; Delhi: ISPCK, 2000, pp. 7-12.

temple, the lack of the concept of sin and judgment and the family centred patriarchal society.[33] To these, I have added my own list of features especially in regard to the patriarchal acts of piety, such as building altars, raising pillars, planting trees, offering prayers and tithes, making vows and being involved in purification rites.[34] A study on these themes led me to conclude that the religion of the patriarchs was distinct both from the ancient Near Eastern and the later Israelite religions. The present essay will take this argument further to show that the patriarchs had consciously kept themselves aloof (exclusivistic?) or even rejected the cultic practices and the gods of their neighbours and thus had little concern with the idea of "religious pluralism."

Patriarchal Religion as Unique among their Neighbours

In what follows, we shall deal briefly with the religious acts of the patriarchs as portrayed in their stories in Genesis, in order to see whether there is any hint of religious pluralism. Some of the main questions we shall keep asking would be: Why did the patriarchs involve themselves in building altars, planting trees or raising pillars, practices that were strongly condemned in later Israel? If their worship was similar to the Canaanite religious practices why did they not join in the local cult of which there was no lack in the land in which they sojourned? Were the places where they offered sacrifices or experienced theophany already holy sites as some scholars wish to argue, or were they considered holy subsequently as others suggest? We shall seek answers to these questions in the light of the ancient Near Eastern and later Israelite religious practices in order to see whether the religion of the patriarchs was closer to the former or the latter and whether it reflects the idea of a religious pluralism or religious particularism (exclusivism).

Abraham Narratives (Gen. 11:27-25:11): Abraham, for instance, offered worship on two types of occasion: Firstly, during regular worship when he built altars at different places where he chanced to pitch his tent or camp. Secondly, on special occasions, when God directed him to do so. We shall deal with each of these in turn.

Regular Worship: There are three different occasions when Abraham built altars and on another occasion he reused an altar that he had previously built (Gen. 12:7 at a place near Shechem; 12:8 between Bethel and Ai; 13:4 refers to the altar mentioned in 12:8; and 13:18 at Hebron). One may ask with regard to Abraham's altars, "why did Abraham build his altars and what did he do with them?" Three possible answers can be given for this question. First, that Abraham built altars as can be gathered from the texts, in response to a theophany (Gen. 12:7) or when he moved his tent to a new place, especially with a view to live there for a period of time (Gen. 12:8—13:18). Thus it is said that in patriarchal stories their altars usually followed their tents.[35] Secondly, Abraham built altars in order to offer sacrifices. There is no mention of sacrifices in the texts, but there is no reason to doubt that sacrifices were involved because the very word for "altar," *mizbeach,* in Hebrew, means "a place

---

[33]Claus Westermann, *Genesis 12-36*, pp. 108-13; *idem. The Promises to the Fathers,* Philadelphia: Fortress, 1976; Moberly, *The Old Testament of the Old Testament,* pp. 84-87.

[34]Augustine Pagolu, *The Religion of the Patriarchs.*

[35]Claus Westermann, *Genesis 12-36*, pp. 156-57. For a discussion on exceptions to this rule see Augustine Pagolu, *The Religion of the Patriarchs,* pp. 54-55.

[36]Archaeological evidence from Chalcolithic period at En-Gedi and from Bronze Age Megiddo, Ai, Shechem, Hazor and Gezer show the remains of ashes and animal bones at all places where different kinds of altars were identified. For relevant literature, see Augustine Pagolu, *The Religion of the Patriarchs,* p. 62.

of slaughter," suggesting that sacrifices were part and parcel of the activity of altar building.[36] Thirdly, on two occasions the texts explicitly state (Gen. 12:8; 13:4) that the purpose for which Abraham built altars was to "worship God" for which the technical phrase used is "called upon the name of Yahweh" *qara beshem Yahweh,* as in Gen. 4:26. However, an unusual phenomenon occurs in the stories of Abraham in Gen. 21:33 where two new elements, namely the planting of a tamarisk tree and *'El Olam'* are added to the expression, "called upon the name of Yahweh." While this phrase suggests that Abraham was involved in a formal worship, it is not clear what the relation of his action was with "called upon the name of Yahweh." Abraham's camping was associated with oak-like trees but this is the first time he planted a tree in relation to his worship. There are no exact parallels of this in the ancient Near East, although we find the practice of planting a fir tree on either side of the temple gate in the Hittite healing rituals.[37] The tamarisk plant in which a tree spirit was believed to live is frequently used in Babylonian healing rituals, but it is not planted or associated with worship.[38] It is uncertain if Abraham implied sanctity of the tamarisk here. Westermann suggests that worship in patriarchal narratives is described as a "two-part event." The phrase "called upon the name of Yahweh" stands for the "word" in worship and the altar building "or some other action, like the planting of a tamarisk" for the "action" in worship. ... the two basic elements of word and

action are already part of worship in its simplest form.[39] Further, *El Olam* need not refer to the local deity of Beer-sheba. The Hebrew, as Sarna argues, "does not allow the use of a proper name in the construct state joined to a noun. Hence, "El" in the phrase *El Olam* can no longer be the proper name of a god but means simply "God". Therefore, it appears from Abraham's actions of both building altars and planting of a tree that the patriarch was involved in a formal worship in an informal family setting. There are no special places, prescribed sacrifices or priests involved here, although some of the places (or nearby) where he worshipped, like Shechem and Bethel, seemed to have become important cult centres in later Israel. But Gen 12:8 clearly denies that Abraham built his altar at Bethel. In other words, Abraham neither conformed with nor participated in the local Canaanite cult.

Special Occasions: Abraham built altars twice[40] (Gen. 15 and 22) and offered sacrifices similar to those in the ancient Near East and Israel even as the occasion, the types of sacrifice and the manner of offerings were all described by God himself. The sacrifice offered in Gen. 15 by Abraham has no complete parallel in any known ancient Near Eastern text, although different aspects of the sacrifice are found in various texts from first and second millennium BCE.[41] But in Gen. 15 there is no idea of substitution or the idea of self-imprecatory oath on the part of Yahweh. Closer parallels, however, are found in Alalakh Tablets (early 2nd millennium BCE)

---

[37]J.B. Pritchard ed., *Ancient Near Eastern Texts Relating to the Old Testament* [hereafter *ANET*], Princeton, NJ: Princeton University Press, 1969, pp. 148-49.

[38]The tamarisk tree appears again and again in the process of cleansing from the evil spirits and was also used in magic by certain gods like Ea, R.C. Thompson, *The Devils and Evil Spirits of Babylonia,* I, London: Luzac, 1903, pp. xlviii, xlix, 19-23, 103, 119, 173, 197; idem. *The Devils and Evil Spirits of Babylonia,* II, London: Luzac, 1904, pp. 21, 107-111.

[39]Claus Westermann, *Genesis 12-36,* p. 156.

[40]It may be noted here that altar building is not explicitly mentioned in Gen. 15, but it could be assumed from the context of the prescription of animals, their cutting into pieces and the fire and smoke.

[41]For parallels from Neo-Assyrian and Sefire texts, see R.S. Hess, "The Slaughter of the Animals in Genesis 15," ed. by R.S. Hess, P.E. Satterthwaite and G.J. Wenham, *He Swore an Oath: Biblical Themes from Genesis 12-50,* Cambridge: Tyndale House, 1993, pp. 61-62.

where the texts are concerned with land grants that are involved in an obligation of a servant to his master and the granter taking oath, and the dismemberment of the animals.[42] Yet many aspects of the ritual, such as the number of animals, Abraham's driving away of the birds of prey hovering over the carcasses, his sleep during the ritual, and the smoke of the fire that passed between the divided parts of the victims are still unique to the ritual in Gen. 15. It can be reasonably suggested that this unusual ritual was not part of a formal or regular worship but meant to ratify once for all a treaty, as in Alalakh tablets, in which the promises God made to Abraham, such as land, descendants and a relationship, are assured.[43]

As for the sacrifice asked in Gen. 22, there are many historical, theological and ethical problems raised by interpreters down the ages, and to deal with them here will be beyond the scope of this essay.[44] However, certain features of this sacrifice may be highlighted in order to show its uniqueness to the religion of the patriarchs. Once again there are no real parallels to Abraham's attempted human sacrifice in Gen. 22. First, the occasion, a form of testing, secondly, the type, human victim, and thirdly, the procedure, a burnt offering, all decided by God himself. This is very different from the cultic practices of both the ancient Near East and Israel where sacrifices were highly organized and usually conducted by a priest. Thus the sacrifices offered in Genesis 15 and 22 are special occasions in Abraham's life although they appear to be similar to those offered in the ancient Near East and Israel. On both these occasions neither a priest nor an established cult place was involved. The transaction, being between God and the patriarch only, represents a special relationship of the patriarch with his God and does not reflect the patriarch's regular form of worship. Nevertheless, all these aspects point to a pattern of religion peculiar to patriarchal lifestyle and there is no hint of the patriarch being involved with the cult places or practices of his neighbours though, several scholars have pointed out that the places where the patriarch chanced to camp or build altars were already sacred places.

Patriarchs Worshipped at Canaanite Cult Places? : The chief evidence adduced for this view is from the use of the words such as "the place" *maqom,* "the oak of Moreh" *elon Moreh,* "the oaks of Mamre" *elone mamre,* where Abraham camped or built altars (Gen. 12:6-7; 13:4, 18; 22:3-4 etc.). From Gunkel onward scholars followed this argument[45] probably for two reasons. First, these scholars were working within the framework of the "history of religions" school, which assumes that Mosaic religion evolved from an inferior, if not animistic, religion that preceded it. The second reason is suggested by the biblical texts themselves, which say that Yahweh was not known by the patriarchs (Exod. 6:3).[46] Thus it appeared legitimate to scholars to seek a type of primitive religion behind patriarchal practices, and *maqom* and *elon* provided possible hints to confirm their

---

[42]*Ibid.* pp. 57-58.

[43]For a plausible interpretation of this ritual, see G.J. Wenham, "The Symbolism of the Animal Rite in Genesis 15: A Response to G. F. Hasel, *JSOT* 19 (1981): 61-78, *JSOT* 22, 1982, pp. 134-37. Cf. Paul R. Williamson, *Abraham, Israel and the Nations: The Patriarchal Promise and its Covenantal Development in Genesis,* Sheffield: Sheffield Academic Press, 2000, pp. 121-144.

[44]For a survey of research, see Claus Westermann, *Genesis 12-36,* pp. 351-54.

[45]H. Gunkel, *Genesis,* p. 147; O. Prockcsh, *Die Genesis,* Leipzig: Deichert, 1924, p. 98; Skinner, *Genesis,* p. 246; D. Kidner, *Genesis,* TOTC; London: Tyndale Press, 1967, p. 115; Claus Westermann, *Genesis 12-36,* pp. 153-54.

[46]Interestingly, Exod. 6:3 is assigned to P, the latest source, who seemed to have known that Yahweh was not known by the patriarchs while the earlier sources, J and E, assume that they did.

assumptions. It is not certain, however, if the author used the word, *maqom,* in a technical sense though it is possible that the word suggests a holy place. If the author had meant a sacred place, it would have been sufficient to say "to the *maqom* between Bethel and Ai," since the altar, which was as good as a sanctuary, was already there.[47] Further, the fact that Abraham builds an altar suggests at least that there was no existing or functioning altar. While the situation of cult in early second-millennium Canaan is unclear, the later Ugaritic texts indicate a highly organized cult, with the king or royal family firmly in control and it is possible that this may have been the case during Abraham's time, if the story of Melchizedek has any historical value. It thus seems unlikely that the author used *maqom* as a technical word for a sacred place.[48] If the places where Abraham built altars lay outside the settled townships, for instance the altar between Bethel and Ai, the other details of patriarchs pitching their tents where they intended to settle for a while fits well with the whole story, suggesting that these were family altars compatible with their wandering lifestyle.

The presence of oak-like trees at the places where the patriarchs often camped is claimed as further evidence to indicate the prior sanctity of the places. This probably has more claims to religious connections than the word *maqom.* In six references to oak-like trees in Genesis, three different Hebrew forms, *elon, elah* and *allon* are used,[49] but only in two instances were altars associated with these trees, while twice burials

occurred under them (35:4, 8). Nevertheless, the form, *elon,* seems to have had religious associations in all its occurrences in Genesis and Judges.[50] Aramaic commentary on Genesis, *Targum Onkelos,* renders this word as "plain," "valley," in all of its occurrences in Genesis,[51] probably to suppress the idea that the patriarchs engaged in what was later associated with pagan cults. *Elon* is coupled with *Moreh* in Gen. 12:6. *Moreh* literally means "teacher," and the phrase, *elon Moreh,* "oak of the teacher" or "the oak where oracles may be obtained" (cf. "the palm of Deborah," Judg. 4:5). Judges 9:6 describes that Abimelech was made king by the "oak of pillar," *elon mutsav* at Shechem. The association of the "pillar" with the oak and the crowning ceremony suggests the existence of a tree-shrine, probably with the practice of receiving oracles, outside the city. While opinion is divided concerning whether it is the same tree that is mentioned in Gen. 12:6, there is no archaeological evidence of an open-air shrine here during this period. If Abraham is to be dated during this period he could not have used an already existing open-air shrine which may be taken to indicate that he built his own altar here.

Of the three places where Abraham built altars, only Bethel shows clear evidence of a shrine existing before and during the time of the patriarchs, but Gen. 12:8 clearly denies that Abraham built his altar at Bethel. Therefore, there is insufficient evidence to assert that the places where Abraham built altars were already sacred places. Alternatively, some scholars have argued that the places where the patriarchs built altars

---

[47]U. Cassuto, *A Commentary on the Book of Genesis,* I, Jerusalem: Hebrew University, 1964, pp. 323-24; Gordon J. Wenham, *Genesis 1-15,* p. 279.

[48]F. Delitzsch, *A New Commentary on Genesis,* I, Edinburgh: T. & T. Clark, 1888, p. 381; Cassuto, *A Commentary on the Book of Genesis,* p. 323-24; G.C. Aalders, *Genesis,* Grand Rapids: Zondervan, 1981, pp. 271-72.

[49]*Elon:* 12:6; 13:18; 14:13; 18:1; *elah:* 35:4; *allon:* 35:8; there is only one other form, *allah* which occurs only in Joshua 24:26. RSV renders all these forms as "oak(s)."

[50]This form occurs ten times in all, four times in Genesis as shown above and twice in Judges. In the other four occurrences it refers to a landmark or boundary marker, Deut. 11:30; Josh. 19:33; Judg. 4:11; 9:37.

[51]*The Vulgate* follows this rendering in 12:6 only.

later became sanctuaries, so that the patriarchs may be viewed as founders of ancient cult centres.[52] While those who follow this view obviously affirm, directly or indirectly, that the places were not already sacred, the patriarchal stories themselves provide witness to the fact that the patriarchs themselves considered the places special or awesome in some sense. This is implied in Abraham's return to the place where he had previously built an altar. In Jacob's case, he first recognized the 'awesomeness' of the place, then promised to build a temple there, and finally was directed by God to return to Bethel where God had first appeared to him (Gen. 28:16, 17, 22; 31:13). Thus the patriarchs built altars following a theophany or at places to which they had newly moved. From the authors' point of view, Israel regarded these places as sacred because their fathers had received revelations there. It is quite possible that some of these places were Canaanite cult centres when Israel took them over, but the sanctity attached to them was not seen, at least by the authors of Genesis, as having derived from their having been Canaanite cult centres but from the fact that their patriarchs had already worshipped in those places. Once again there is no suggestion in the stories of Abraham of religious pluralism. Abraham's religious activities were informal, family centred and involved no established cult or priest even on special occasions when God directed him to offer a sacrifice.

Isaac Narratives: The Isaac narratives have only one reference to building of an altar (Gen. 26:25), but the occasion for it is similar to that of Abraham. Like Abraham, Isaac built an altar and "called on the name of Yahweh" after a theophany and a move to a new place, from Gerar to Beer-Sheba. The fact that Isaac built an altar

clearly suggests that there was no altar existing and the formulaic phrase "called upon the name of Yahweh" indicates that Isaac was involved in a formal worship of Yahweh with sacrifices and prayers. Further, it is possible to suggest that Beer-sheba had a tradition of being a patriarchal sanctuary in view of Abraham's earlier associations with it (Gen. 21:33; 22:19) and of Jacob's receiving a theophany later at this place and responding with sacrifices (Gen. 46:1-4). The same questions we asked in relation to Abraham's altars, such as "why did Abraham build altars?" and "what did he do with them?" will be relevant here also. Besides a formal act of worship compatible with the patriarchal lifestyle, it is possible that building an altar at Beer-sheba, the southern-most border of the promised land,[53] may have represented not only a claim to the land but also a legitimating of the sanctuary for later Israel.[54] Thus like Abraham, Isaac's building of an altar and being himself the officiate in a formal act of worship suggests that his religion is compatible with his own wandering lifestyle and distinct from the religions of the ancient Near East and Israel where temples, priests and cultic calendars played an important role. Although Isaac's stories are overshadowed by Abraham's stories on the one hand and Jacob's on the other, his general religious activities fit well with the overall picture of the religion of the patriarchs as distinct, if not exclusive, from the ancient Near Eastern religions.

Jacob Narratives: Jacob is said to have built altars on two occasions and on two other occasions to offer sacrifices. We shall take the former cases as regular worship and the latter as special occasions similar to those of Abraham's religious activities. There is no mention of sacrifices in the former and there is no mention

---

[52]C.F. Keil, *Genesis und Exodus,* Giessen/Basel: Brunnen Verlag, 1878, p. 167; A. Dillmann, *Genesis,* p. 15; U. Cassuto, *A Commentary on the Book of Genesis,* pp. 325-26.

[53]*Cf.* the phrase "from Dan to Beer-Sheba," Judg. 20:1; 1 Sam. 3:20; 2 Sam. 3:10; 17:11; 24:2, 15; 1 Kgs 5:5.

[54]In eighth -century Israel, pilgrims resorted to oracles from Beer-Sheba (Amos 5:5; 8:14); Skinner, *Genesis* p. 327.

of altars in the latter. It could be argued that building altars would involve sacrifices as much as offering sacrifices would involve building altars. Besides, Jacob also is said to have been involved in raising pillars, making vows and performing purification rituals. We shall discuss each of these in turn.

Regular Worship: First, we shall deal with the two occasions of altar building by Jacob, once at Shechem (Gen. 33:20) and once at Bethel (Gen. 35:7). Both these occasions appear to be like the formal worship of the other patriarchs, involving sacrifices as well. Jacob's altars, like Abraham's and Isaac's, also followed a theophany and a movement to a new place, despite the temporary stop at Succoth. A close reading of the texts themselves can see that Jacob's actions did not involve a belief in "religious pluralism". In the first case, the text clearly states that Jacob camped "before the city," (*phane hayir*) (Gen. 33:18), probably meaning outside the settled community, as was the usual practice with other patriarchs, and that Jacob built his altar in the place he had bought from the natives to erect his tent. And an extra element is added here that Jacob names the altar *El Elohe Israel* (v. 20). For the author this is none other than Jacob's own, just as were Abraham's and Isaac's. However, there is no archaeological evidence of a shrine outside the city during the patriarchal period,[55] and it is difficult to prove that Jacob worshipped at an existing shrine. Further, Jacob's naming of the altar[56] suggests that Jacob had a special reason for building this altar besides using it for formal worship. The immediate context suggests that the name of the altar was to reflect Jacob's own experience with the God who met him in his crisis and even changed his name (Gen. 32:29). In this sense, this altar may also have represented a 'memorial' of Jacob's experience. Once again, our earlier observation that patriarchal worship was distinct from the ancient Near Eastern and Israelite worship and compatible only with their lifestyle is confirmed.

The other occasion when Jacob built an altar (Gen. 35:6-7) was when he was reminded by God of the vow Jacob had made earlier at Bethel (Gen. 31:13), that was not yet fulfilled. The place to build the altar and the occasion were directed by God himself, but there were some features common to the previous occasions, in that there were no altars already existing and the patriarch was the sole officiant of the cult. However, two new elements are added to this occasion, namely the ritual preparation of purification and throwing away of foreign gods (35:2, 4), both of which are unique to this occasion, although such preparation before presenting oneself at a sanctuary was by no means uncommon in the ancient Near East.[57] While the place of Bethel had an unbroken tradition of having a shrine from the third millennium BCE, the place of Jacob's altar should be distinguished from the site of the traditional shrine, which had previously been called Luz.[58]

From these two occasions, it becomes clear once again that Jacob was following his family tradition of worshipping his own God, or the God of his fathers. There is no hint of his association with or participation in the local cult. In fact the reverse may be true at Bethel since Jacob demands that his family members part with their

---

[55]G.R.H. Wright, "Temples at Shechem," *ZAW* 80 (1968), pp 1-35; *ABD*, vol. V, pp. 1179-81.

[56]Naming of altars was not unusual in Israel, Gen. 35:7; Exod. 17:15; Judg. 6:24; Ezek. 48:35; Sarna, *Genesis*, p. 232 n.15

[57]*Ancient Near Easterm Texts*, p. 144. For a detailed discussion on the possible background for Jacob's actions for a ritual purification, see Augustine Pagolu, *The Religion of the Patriarchs*, pp. 229-41

[58]The new name given by Jacob to the place of his altar was probably extended to the traditional site so that the name Bethel then applied to the whole place. Cf. *New Bible Dictionary*, p. 133; D.L. Newlands, "Sacrificial Blood at Bethel?" *PEQ* 104, 1972, p.155.

former household gods and even their representation in their ornaments, namely earrings, before they approached Bethel. The reasons for Jacob's sudden call to his family members to part with the foreign gods is not far to seek. Jacob was probably aware of his long association with Laban and Rachel's household gods, his long stay and Dina's rape at Shechem which came very close to his integration with the Shechemites, and his sons' massacre of the Shechemites and their subsequent looting which could have included the foreign gods, as many scholars observe. Further, Jacob was shocked at the violence of his sons and feared the imminent retaliation of the natives. He was desperate for help, and wanted to ensure by every possible means that this God was favourable to him once more, as he had been in the encounter with Esau. His actions probably were meant to rally his family's allegiance to the God of Bethel who had directed him in the first place to go back and build an altar at Bethel, which he failed to do by settling down at Shechem. Thus the call for purification and the rejection of the foreign gods was Jacob's voluntary action that indicates, at the least, that Jacob wanted to find favour with the God of Bethel, although we are not certain from the texts themselves that this God demanded exclusive allegiance. Nevertheless, we can see a pattern in the religious practices of the patriarchs here. There is no hint of Mosaic monotheism here, nor is there a suggestion of polytheism either, in spite of their polytheistic forefathers and idolatrous relatives like Laban which we shall see below.

Special Occasions: Secondly, we shall deal with the two other occasions when Jacob is explicitly said to have offered sacrifices, one following a covenant between him and Laban (Gen. 31:54), and the other when he heard that Joseph, whom he thought was dead, was still living (Gen. 46:1). Once again our focus shall remain on Jacob's actions and to see whether they involve in a belief of religious pluralism.

The covenant between Jacob and Laban, like most covenants in the ancient Near East, is of a religious nature, in which each swears by his own deity, who is called to act as judge if either of them should violate the treaty, and the covenant is concluded by a common meal that followed a sacrifice. Both in their swearing and the sacrifice that followed, there are certain differences between Jacob and Laban that throw light on their religious associations and beliefs. Although Jacob married into Laban's family and worked for him over twenty years, their allegiance to their own gods seemed to have remained intact. The distinction between the gods of Laban and Jacob is nowhere clearer than here. In the episode of Jacob's flight from Laban, just before they reached an agreement, Laban charged Jacob directly with stealing *his* gods: "why did you steal *my* gods?" (Gen. 31:30) Jacob's reply makes this distinction equally clear: "Anyone with whom you find *your* gods shall not live" (Gen.31:32); "If the God of *my* father, the god of Abraham and the Fear of Isaac, had not been on my side, surely now you would have sent me away empty-handed" (Gen. 31:42, italics added; cf. vv. 29, 30, 32). Then in the covenant between them each swears by his own god: Laban says, "The God of Abraham and the God of Nahor, the God of their father (*Elohe abihem*) judge (plural verb used: *ishphatu*) between us" (Gen. 31:53). If this treaty is similar to the boundary treaties of the ancient Near East where different deities are invoked to indicate the ethnic diversity of the parties involved,[59] it is not difficult to see that Laban invoked two (or more?) different deities, the God of Abraham and the God of Nahor, (the ancestor of the Aramaeans, Gen. 22:20-23) and possibly also the god of their father. The plural verb, "judge" *(ishphatu),*

---

[59] J.C.L. Gibson, *The Text Book of Syrian Semitic Inscriptions*, Oxford: Clarendon Press, 1971-82, pp. IA, 8-12; N. M. Sarna, *Genesis*, p. 222.

indicates that Laban saw the distinction between the god of Nahor and the God of Abraham.[60] We may note a similar distinction being made by Laban in his earlier talk with Jacob (31:29, 30). The term "their father," *(abihem),* probably refers to Terah, the father of Abraham and Nahor. Elsewhere he is described as a polytheist (Josh. 24:2). So Laban probably invoked the god of their common ancestor. In response, however, Jacob ignores Laban's formula and invokes only the "Fear of Isaac" his father.[61] Thus it is reasonable to think that Jacob also knew the distinction between them. This makes sense in the light of his call to his family members to renounce "foreign gods"as observed above.

Interestingly, only Jacob is said to have offered sacrifices here, probably because Laban at that time would not have had the wherewithal to do so. Or, he was not used to informal cultic acts like the patriarchs did, with no cult place or cultic personnel involved. The word used for sacrifice here, and in 46:1, is *zebach,* which is a general term for sacrifice. Priestly regulations apply this term, combined with *shalomim,* to the particular sacrifice of "well-being offerings" (Lev. 3; 7:11-21, 34, 35), which are made as thanksgiving, votive and free-will offerings. At Ugarit and in Israel, *zebach shalomim* are meant to achieve peace between the deity and the worshipper. The context of the Jacob-Laban treaty certainly fits such a meaning.[62]

The second time that Jacob is said to have offered sacrifices was when he was about to go down to Egypt after hearing that his beloved son Joseph was still living (Gen. 46:1). The text clearly states that at Beer-sheba Jacob "offered sacrifices to the God of his father Isaac." The place, Beer-sheba, seems to have had no Canaanite settlement prior to the arrival of the patriarchs.[63] The term for sacrifice, *zebach,* is used here as in Genesis 31:54. If the priestly *zebach shalomim* is any guide here, it is quite likely that Jacob's sacrifice was a thank-offering for sparing Joseph's life. Interestingly, theophany followed the altars, contrary to the usual order of altars following the theophany in the narratives. It is possible that Jacob also sought guidance through the sacrifices before leaving for Egypt. "Such a move as Jacob is undertaking requires divine sanction, the more so in that to leave Canaan is to retreat from the Promised land."[64]

Thus Jacob's offering of sacrifices on both these occasions — once to seal the covenant between Laban and him, and once to thank God for Joseph's life and to seek guidance for his move to Egypt, while having certain parallels in the ancient Near East and Israel, are unique and compatible only with his wandering lifestyle and with the religion of the other patriarchs. His beliefs and actions show no hint of participation with the local cult. On the other hand, he insisted his family members part with their household gods and followed a pattern that was familiar with the practices of his fathers Isaac and Abraham.

Raising Pillars and Making Vows: We have seen Jacob building altars in response to theophanies, but raising pillars appears to be his

---

[60]Septuagint and Samaritan Pentateuch have a singular verb. But several commentators, like Skinner and Driver see the treaty as being made between the clans of Nahor and the clans of Abraham.

[61]"Fear of Isaac," *phachad itsachaq,* is found only here. Its exact meaning is uncertain, although the context suggests that this is another name or expression for the 'God of the father'. For various suggestions, see D.R. Hillers, "Pahad Yishaq," *JBL* 91, 1972, pp. 90-92.

[62]D.M.L. Urie, "Sacrifice among the West Semites," *PEQ* 26, 1949, pp. 67-82.

[63]The deepest stratum represents an un-walled settlement during the time of the judges and a fortified city appears only during the monarchy, so that the "city of Beer-Sheba" in Genesis 26:33 must be regarded as an editorial note.

[64]Gordon J. Wenham, *Genesis 16-50,* WBC 2; Dallas: Word Books, 1994, p. 440; cf. Balaam's (Num. 23) and Babylonian sacrifices as a means for guidance.

special response to theophanies. As has been discussed above in the context of Abraham's planting a tree, raising pillars forms part of the patriarchal pattern of worship, although it is attested to only in Jacob stories. Jacob seemed to have erected pillars on four different occasions in Genesis: i) when God appeared to him for the first time at Bethel (Gen. 28:18, 22); ii) when he made a treaty with Laban in the hill country of Gilead (31:45, 51, 52); iii) when Jacob returned from Paddan-aram (Gen. 35:14, 15), and iv) upon Rachel's grave (35:20).[65] The pillar described in the treaty of Jacob and Laban appears to be a witness to the agreement and as such may be described as a "legal" or "memorial stone."[66] These were erected to remind individuals or groups of treaties or boundaries between them. Sometimes these stones served as witnesses to a covenant treaty and as documents on which the terms of the covenant were written.[67] The pillar on Rachel's grave was probably erected as a "memorial stone" (cf. 2 Sam. 18:18), although several scholars, on the basis of the significance attached to the grave in biblical traditions, argue that the site later became a place for death cult activities in Israel (Gen. 48:7; 1 Sam. 10:2; Jer. 31:15-17; Mt. 2:17-18).[68] However, none of the texts or their context suggests cultic activity at Rachel's tomb.[69] Therefore we may not attach any deep religious significance to them. On the other two occasions, however, Jacob's pillars (items [i and iii] above) seem to have religious significance marking the sacred area where God appeared. This is clear from Jacob's words in 28:17, 22, calling the place, 'this is none other than the house of God' and the pillar "house of God," *beth elohim,* and his actions, in 28:18 and 35:14, directed to the pillars, which included anointing them with oil and pouring a drink offering over one, actions not attested elsewhere in the Hebrew Bible. While Jacob's actions were not condemned, the context in both instances suggests that they were part of his response to the theophanies that preceded them. Since both these instances are similar, I believe that the conclusions reached for the one would be applicable to the other as well, although certain important differences will be explained. i) When God appeared to Jacob for the first time at Bethel (Gen. 28:18, 22): Jacob's controversial raising of a pillar at Bethel occurs in the context of a theophany in Gen. 28:10-22. Several scholars, however, see a connection between stone and god, and suggest that Jacob worshipped the god/numen who dwelt in the stone. If this could be proved, it would have serious implications for religious pluralism in patriarchal stories. It was S. Bochart who first identified Jacob's pillar with the so called *baetylia,* "anointed stones," in the early 18ᵗʰ century: "In their attempt to imitate

---

[65]The Hebrew word for "pillar" is *matsebah,* (plural, *matseboth).* Pillars occur 11 times in Genesis alone, all in Jacob stories, Gen. 28:18, 22; 31:13, 45, 51, 52(x2); 35:14(x2); 20(x2). Elsewhere they occur 36 times in the Hebrew Bible.

[66]Archaeologists divide pillars, matseboth, into four categories, namely legal, memorial, commemorative and cultic. C.F. Graesser, "Standing Stones in Ancient Palestine," *BA* 35, 1972, pp.34-63; U. Avner, "Mazzebot Sites in the Negev and Sinai and their Significance," ed.by A. Biran and J. Aviram, *Biblical Archaeology Today, 1990: Proceedings of the Second International Congress on Biblical Archaeology,* Jerusalem: Israel Exploration Society, 1993, pp. 166-181.

[67]Examples exist already in the 3ʳᵈ millennium Sumerian city states, the famous Hammurabi code, the 8ᵗʰ century Sefire inscriptions, J.B. Pritchard, ed., *Ancient Near East in Pictures Relating to the Old Testament,* Princeton, NJ: Princeton University Press, 1954, pp. 298-3-2; J.C.L. Gibson, *Text Book of Syrian Semitic Inscriptions, II,* Oxford: Clarendon Press, 1971-82, pp. 30, 44; C.F.Graesser, "Standing Stones in Ancient Palestine," pp. 37-39; for biblical examples, see Exod. 24:4; Deut. 27:1-8; Josh. 8:30-35; 24:26-27.

[68]T.J. Lewis, *Cult of the Dead in Ancient Israel and Ugarit,* Atlanta: Scholars Press, 1989, p. 119; E. Block-Smith, *Judahite Burial Practices and Beliefs about the Dead,* Sheffield: JSOT Press, 1992, pp. 113-14.

[69]On the basis of a dubious interpretation of the word in 1 Sam. 10:2 as "in the shade of a shiny rock," L.M. Luker, "Rachel's Tomb," in *ABD,* p. 609, argues that the tombstone became smooth and shiny because of the continual anointing of it by pilgrims.

Jacob, the Phoenicians first worshipped the stone which the patriarch had set up; then they anointed and consecrated other stones, and called them *baetylia, baetyli,* in memory of the stone at Bethel."[70] Bochart's equation was subsequently repeated indiscriminately by lexicons, encyclopaedias, commentaries and archaeologists,[71] despite the objections raised by some.[72] Firm evidence is lacking to assert that stone worship lay behind Jacob's pillar at Bethel. The parallels adduced from Greek and Semitic sources are too remote and the religious views attached to them are too different to be compatible.[73] Therefore our reliable guide shall remain a plain reading of the texts themselves, to which we shall now turn.

There is no consensus among the scholars about assigning different parts of the story of Gen. 28:10-22 to different literary sources. Some attribute the dream, *matsebah* and vow to the same source, E, while others reduce the original story to the dream alone, but many assume the story of Jacob's dream is much older than J or E. It is also not certain whether this story had any antecedent in Canaanite traditions prior to its incorporation into its present context.[74] What is certain, however, is that the story in its present form reflects the perspective of the Yahwist, or of the redactor with a conscious dissociation of the previous Canaanite background of the place. Therefore it is safer to read the story from the final author's perspective than to read it from a hypothetical reconstruction of it. From this viewpoint, certain features of the story stand out in the text, such as the place as obscure, Jacob's stopover as unplanned due to the impossibility of travel after sunset, the stone as ordinary[75] and Jacob's surprise at the theophany. With these in the background, we need to look more closely at Jacob's reactions to the dream in order to see whether Jacob's actions involved worshipping the numen residing in the stone, a practice common to many primitive cultures all over the world.

First, Jacob expressed surprise at the theophany. In the ancient world devotees normally planned a "sleepover" in the sacred precincts of a shrine in order to "induce the deity to reveal its will."[76] Given the facts that Jacob's stop was unplanned, the place unnamed and the theophany unexpected, it suggests that the author is implicitly denying any sacredness to the place. Verse 19 implies that the place of Jacob's

---

[70]S. Bochart, *Geographia sacra,* Holland: Cornelium Bontesteyn & Jordanum Luchtmans, 1707, 784-85 cited in Augustine Pagolu, *The Religion of the Patriarchs,* pp. 136-37.

[71]J. Hastings, ed., *Dictionary of the Bible* I, Edinburgh: T. & T. Clark, 1900-1904, p. 27; E. Ebeling and B. Meissner, eds, *Reallexikon der Assyriologie* I, Berlin, Leipzig: W. de Gruyter, 1928-, p. 392; H. Gunkel, *Genesis,* p. 282; J. Skinner, *Genesis,* p. 38; M. Eliade, *Patterns of Comparative Religion,* pp. 228-30; A.J. Evans, "Mycenaean Tree and Pillar Cult and its Mediterranean Relations," *JHS* 21, 1901, pp.99-204; J. Teixidor, *The Pagan God: Popular Religion in the Greco-Roman Near East,* Princeton, NJ: Princeton University Press, 1977, pp.38-39; T.N.D.Mettinger, *No Graven Image?,* pp. 35, 96.

[72]A .J. A. Dillmann, *Genesis,* p. 337; W.R. Smith, *The Religion of the Semites,* London: A. & C. Black, 1927, p. 210; G.F. Moore, "Baetylia," *AJA ,*1903, pp. 203, 205, 208; S.R. Driver, *The Book of Genesis,* London: Methuen, 1948, p. 268.

[73]For a detailed analysis of the relevant sources and their interpretation, see Augustine Pagolu, *The Religion of the Patriarchs,* pp. 136-47.

[74]For different views on source- tradition- and literary analyses of the passage, see Augustine Pagolu, *The Religion of the Patriarchs,* pp. 158-161.

[75]H. Gunkel, *Genesis,* p. 280 and M. Burrows, "From Pillar to Post," *JPOS* 14, 1934, p. 45, consider the stone as so unusually large that only Jacob, being giant-like, could erect it, while H. Donner, "Zu Genesis 28,22," *ZAW* 74, 1962, pp. 68-70, J.G. Frazer, "Jacob at Bethel," in T.H. Gaster, ed., *Myth,Legend and Custom in the Old Testament,* London: Gerald Duckworth, 1969, pp.191 and C. Houtman, "What did Jacob See in his Dream at Bethel,"*VT* 27, 1977, p. 345 consider it a *baetyl* or holy stone.

[76]N. M. Sarna, *Genesis,* p. 197-98.

theophany lay near Luz and the name Bethel that Jacob gave to the place probably extended later to the settlement Luz.[77] Excavations at the traditional site of Bethel reveal the existence of an open-air shrine there from 3500 BCE, a temple from the 19th century BCE and a stone *in situ* from Middle Bronze I and II.[78] It is probable that the settlement of Luz and the shrine of Bethel occupied the same site,[79] and the Israelites took over the pagan shrine during the time of Joshua (18:21) or the Judges (1:22, 26) since Bethel became an important cult centre from then on, especially in the 8th century. Thus it is unlikely that the place of Jacob's theophany had a Canaanite shrine. Secondly, Jacob's response to the theophany was erecting a pillar, not building an altar as his fathers did. A number of scholars argue that the story in its original form was about the worship of a numen resident in the stone.[80] But one may ask, why would the author leave any traces of a belief that could be misunderstood later by his readers, if he consciously denied any Canaanite associations of the place? The author obviously stood in the tradition that viewed pillars positively, as we noted above, and not as abodes of a *numen*. We have no way of knowing exactly what the stone would have meant to Jacob, but what the author thought it meant is reasonably clear. It was a "sign" of Jacob's dream and a "witness" to his vow,[81] and probably also a marker of a sacred place. Such a meaning is quite fitting given Jacob's awe and surprise following his dream. Thirdly, Jacob anointed the pillar. While pillars were unique to Jacob stories in the patriarchal narratives, anointing of them is unique to the whole Old Testament. Altars and various cultic objects were anointed in the Old Testament and many view this as a "consecration" for cultic use.[82] On the other hand, various types of people, like leaders, kings and priests were also anointed with oil, especially when taking office. On the basis of widespread evidence among the Semites of the use of oil as a symbol of peace, friendship and fellowship, and anointing being practised effecting relationships, transacting business, buying land, contracting marriage and international treaties and liberating slaves, T.N.D. Mettinger proposes: "...the efficacy of the anointing performed by Jacob was not primarily a sanctification or a consecration of the stone, but was to establish a contractual relation between Jacob and God."[83] Therefore, we may conclude that Jacob's anointing was probably a symbolic act of establishing a contractual bond with God. Fourthly, Jacob makes a vow at Bethel as part of his reaction to the theophany (vv. 20-22). Several scholars, however, consider these verses as later expansions of the main story since they have no syntactical link with the main narrative, the oath appears to be a literary construction than a verbal

---

[77]A. Dillmann, *Genesis*, p. 229; M. Haran, *Temple and Temple-Service in Ancient Israel*, Oxford: Clarendon, 1978, p. 52.

[78]J.L. Kelso, *Excavations at Bethel 1934-60*, Cambridge, MA: American Schools of Oriental Research, 1968, pp. 20, 21, 45, 46, cf. pp. 1-3.

[79]Z. Kallai, *Historical Geography of the Bible*, Jerusalem/Leiden: Magnes/Brill, 1986, p. 130-31; *contra* Claus Westermann, *Genesis12-36*, 458. V. 19 implies that the place of Jacob's dream lay near Luz.

[80]H. Holzinger, *Genesis*, Leipzig, Tubingen: J.C.B. Mohr, 1898, p.193; H. Gunkel, *Genesis*, pp. 281-82; Prochsch, *Die Genesis*, p. 340-42; W. R. Smith, *The Religion of the Semites*, pp. 204-205; Claus Westermann, *Genesis12-36*, p. 454.

[81]N. M. Sarna, *Genesis*, p. 199.

[82]Exod. 30:22-29; 40:9-11; Lev. 8:10-11; Num. 7:1; Hos. 12:2. For an interpretation, see Driver, *The Book of Genesis*, p. 266; J. Pedersen, *Israel: Its Life and Culture*, III, IV, London: Oxford University Press, 1940, p. 209; Von Rad, *Genesis*, p. 280-81.

[83]Mettinger, *King and Messiah*, pp. 224-25; for various texts of the ancient Near East relating to the use of oil to effectuate a relationship, see pp. 211-24. Cf. N. M. Sarna, *Genesis*, p. 200.

reproduction of Jacob's words, and the words in v. 17, "it is none other than the house of God!" and v. 22, "this stone shall be a house of God" seem to contradict each other.[84] Once again it is beyond the scope of this essay to deal with the literary, form and syntactical questions of the passage here.[85] Although a certain amount of standardization in form and structure may be admitted, this does not prove that a vow like Jacob's could not have been made. T.W. Cartledge, rather humorously, points out that "any one who knew how to make a bargain could also make a vow" without consulting fixed forms available at certain cult places.[86] Thus the vow made in v. 22 as a pronouncement of the obligation implied in the anointing fits well in the context, and Jacob's modest requests and his situation described between his flight and return also fit well with the total story of Jacob. Further, it may be pointed out that there is no contradiction between the phrases in verses 17 and 22. The former should refer to the place in relation to Jacob's experience of the dream, as also the two other phrases, "Surely Yahweh is in this place" and "How awesome is this place!" while the latter must mean, as Westermann observes, "that a sanctuary is to arise from this stone" and it cannot mean that the *matsebah* would become an abode of God.[87]

However, in the other incident, iii) when Jacob raised a pillar after his return from Paddan-aram (Gen. 35:14), there is an addition of "drink offering" to the pillar compared to the mere anointing in the earlier case.[88] Would this suggest a Canaanite practice of the cult of the dead, or worship of the stone god who helped Jacob return to his country safely? It is impossible for an author, who was consciously emptying any sanctity of the place or the stone previously, to add a tradition with an extra ritual of drink offering which would give an impression of a Canaanite practice of his own time. Therefore the meaning of Jacob's actions ought to be different from the traditional view of patriarchal religion being primitive and animistic. The drink offering was possibly intended to commemorate God's appearance to Jacob, or more probably offered to God himself, while the pouring of the oil on the pillar most probably reflects the same rite as in 28:18 and has the same significance, that is to establish once again a contractual bond between God and Jacob.

Therefore, Jacob's actions in response to the theophany, together with his vow, can reasonably be explained both from the Near Eastern parallels and Jacob's own situation and lifestyle and there is no reason to suggest that the patriarch was involved in Canaanite cultic practices. In the second instance, Jacob's actions aside, the separation of God, stone and the place are more tellingly described than anywhere in the patriarchal stories. God is said to have "gone up" from the place where he was speaking with him, after which Jacob erected a pillar and called the place Bethel. For the author God, the pillar and the place are all distinct from each other in the story.

Summary and Conclusions

It is clear from our study of the patriarchal stories in Genesis, that altars and sacrifices occur in all their stories and appear to form the core of

---

[84]W. Richter, "Das Gelubde als theologische Rahmung der Jakobsuberlieferungen," *BZ* 11, 1967, pp. 44, 45, 50; Claus Westermann, *Genesis*, p. 458.

[85] See Augustine Pagolu, *The Religion of the Patriarchs*, pp. 204-206.

[86]T.W. Cartledge, *Vows in the Hebrew Bible and the Ancient Near East*, JSOTSup. 147; Sheffield: JSOT Press, 1992, p. 150.

[87]Claus Westermann, *Genesis12-36*, p. 459; Driver, *The Book of Genesis*, p. 267.

[88] For a discussion on (Gen 35:9-15), see Augustine Pagolu, *The Religion of the Patriarchs*, pp.166-68.

their worship. However, there seem to be some significant differences between their form of worship and the normal Canaanite and Israelite worship where the rituals were highly organized with established cult and cultic personnel, the type of sacrifice for each occasion was minutely prescribed and procedures and purpose of sacrifices, elaborately described. The occasions for sacrifices in all the near Eastern cultures, including Israel, are similar. There were daily sacrifices and those that were offered on special occasions, such as festivals, dedication of temples, laying palace foundations, before and after battles, averting pestilence and healing the sick. Besides, there were sacrifices offered by the individuals for thanksgiving and votive purposes and "sacrifices for the dead" at regular intervals and on special occasions, although sacrifices for the dead in Israel were seen largely as lapses on a popular level and therefore were condemned.

Regarding the patriarchal worship, however, a distinct pattern emerges. Unlike in the ancient Near East and Israel, their cultic practices were informal with no fixed cult place or cultic personnel and with no prescription of the types of sacrifice or description as to the manner of offering. In all their worship officiates were the patriarchs themselves and the places where they built altars were usually on the fringes of the settled communities probably distinct from their shrines. It is also clear from the texts that the patriarchs neither joined worship in the local shrines nor did they invoke local gods on their own. They seemed to have consciously dissociated themselves from the local cult. On the other hand, they followed a pattern of worship that is compatible only with their wandering lifestyle. The fact that the elements of pagan worship, such as trees and pillars, while condemned in later Israel, are not expunged from the stories of Israel's beginnings, suggests that their portrayal is authentic, as the authors did not see objectionable elements in them. Therefore, we may conclude that the patriarchs were "exclusivists," believed and worshipped the God who followed their tents, protected their interests and promised a future, which was believed to have unfolded in the lives of the authors who wrote their stories. We may further conclude that patriarchal religion was less syncretistic than the religion of later Israel in any period of its history.

For those whose idea of religious pluralism is based partly on the patriarchal narratives and their supposed attitude to religions of their day, we have demonstrated how for the patriarchs devotion to their own God, who was Yahweh for the authors, was to be exclusive, and polytheism, which was essentially the prevailing culture of both their forefathers and compatriots, was summarily rejected. If this is so, patriarchal religion is continuous with Mosaic Yahwism and the idolatry and polytheistic tendencies reflected in later Israel are rightly condemned as lapses by the prophets. From these early days Yahweh was seen as supreme, sovereign and the only one worthy of all their worship. As children of Abraham by faith we also are called to follow his God and worship Him, the sovereign and supreme one alone.

CHAPTER 6

The Place of Mission in New Testament Theology[1]

ANDREAS J. KÖSTENBERGER

What is the place of mission in the theology of the New Testament? After clarifying the nature of mission, New Testament theology, and Scripture, the present essay assesses the significance of mission within the scope of the New Testament's message as a whole. The author first surveys the New Testament theologies by Rudolf Bultmann, George Ladd, and N.T Wright, then the theologies of mission by Donald Senior and Carroll Stuhlmueller, and David Bosch. This is followed by a discussion of the biblical material focusing on John's Gospel. The article concludes with three important principles in determining the place of mission in New Testament theology.

****

What is the place of mission in the theology of the New Testament? Is mission at the center of the New Testament's, indeed the entire Bible's, message, as many missiologists claim? Is mission merely a marginal component of the New Testament theologies written in this century? In what follows, we will seek to locate the place of mission within the larger framework of New Testament theology. This will be done on the basis of surveys of both New Testament. But first a few preliminary remarks are in order.

Prolegomena

The task at hand makes it necessary for us to reflect on the nature of mission, New Testament theology, and Scripture.

First, determining the place of mission within the scope of New Testament requires at least a preliminary understanding of what constitutes mission according to the writings of the New Testament. In contemporary usage, *missions* generally refer to cross-cultural ministry. In biblical terminology, however, it appears that the cross-cultural aspect of Christian ministry is not a necessary part of mission. To be sure, mission may, and frequently will, involve the crossing of ethnic, cultural, or other boundaries (cf., e.g., Acts 1:8), but this is not an integral part of the New Testament concept of mission itself. Rather, mission in the New Testament usually centers around a person's (or group's) commissioning (e.g., Matthew 28:18-20; Luke 24:46-48; John 20:21-23) to a particular task, in the present case focusing on the salvation and forgiveness of sins in Christ Jesus which is to be appropriated by faith. This soteriological focus rules out an understanding of mission that is conceived so broadly that the message of salvation in Christ is submerged under more general notions of "Christian service" or even lost altogether.

At the same time, the question arises whether it is unduly narrow to limit mission, in its New Testament usage, exclusively to direct verbal gospel proclamation. For there is some indication in certain books of the New Testament that other forms of Christian activity were considered to

---

[1] "The Place of Mission in New Testament Theology" was published in *Missiology: An International Review*, Vol. XXVII, No.3, July 1999 and is used with permission.

be part of the church's overall mission. In Peter's first epistle, for example, believers are frequently exhorted to respond to suffering in a godly, -glorifying manner. To be sure, they are told always to be prepared to make a defense to everyone who asks them to give an account for the hope that is in them (1 Peter 3:15). But even where this is not possible, the Christian's godly response to suffering, whether accompanied by verbal gospel proclamation or not, to give but one example, may properly be considered to constitute *mission*, albeit more broadly conceived. Thus it appears inappropriate to dichotomize between verbal, intentional, purposeful proclamation of the gospel message. But this should not be pressed to the extent that other legitimate aspects of mission are excluded, especially if it can be shown that the New Testament itself includes these within the scope of its presentation of Christian outreach.

Second, determining the place of mission within the scope of New Testament theology also requires an understanding of the nature of New Testament theology. In the words of the eminent conservative German theologian Adolf Schlatter, it is "not the interpreter's own theology or that of his church and times that is examined but rather the theology expressed by the New Testament itself" (1997:18). Thus New Testament theology, as a subset of biblical theology, is a task that is both historical and primarily descriptive. The *historical* dimension of New Testament theology brings into play our own presuppositions, convictions, and vested interests. As those engaged in mission or biblical studies, we inevitably approach the New Testament documents with our own understanding of the nature of mission and its place within the scope of the New Testament's theology as a whole. But as Schlatter (1997:18) reminds us,

It is the historical objective that should govern our conceptual work exclusively and completely.... We turn away decisively from ourselves and our time to what was found in the men through whom the church came into being. Our main interest should be the thought as it was conceived *by them* and the truth that was valid *for them*.... This is the internal disposition upon which the success of the work depends, the commitment which must consistently be renewed as the work proceeds.

The *descriptive* nature of New Testament theology entails that we set aside for the time being our concern for the contemporary application of the biblical message. At the proper time, this will, of course, be very important, and, truth told, this is also what fuels our interest in the present subject in the first place. But unless we are willing to let the New Testament speak to us on its own terms, we only deceive ourselves. We will merely find in the pages of the Bible what we have already determined to find there on other grounds. If we thus domesticate Scripture, we deprive ourselves of an opportunity to be instructed by, and even transformed by, Scripture, and we rob Scripture of its authority and preeminence. Although no one can claim to be able to escape completely his or her own preconceived notions of a given subject (our "pre-understanding"), this must not keep us from trying, and as we make this, effort, we can do so with the expectation that our own views (and subsequent practice) will be increasingly, albeit not perfectly, conformed to the counsel of Scripture itself. This is what has in recent hermeneutical debate been called the "hermeneutical circle" or "spiral," a dialectical process between the self and the text by which the interpreter, through repeated study of the biblical message, approaches ever more closely an accurate understanding of the text on its own terms. Without this confidence in our Spirit-aided ability to apprehend the teaching of Scripture, we would sink into utter despair, into a relativism where any knowledge of absolute truth is excluded, and into a kind of epistemological solipsism (the autonomy of self in the process of arriving at knowledge) where human existence is ultimately absurd.

Third, it should be recognized at the outset that one's very conception of mission in the New Testament is closely tied to one's view of the nature of Scripture. Two primary approaches can be identified, a religion-historical one and a salvation-historical one. In its purest form, a history-of-religions model utilizes a comparative religions approach that views Scripture from an essentially evolutionary vantage point.[2] The history of Israel, the life of Jesus, and the development of the early church are viewed in terms of the evolution of human religious consciousness. This approach is anthropocentric; it focuses on the development of *humankind's* understanding of, leading to participate concepts of, forms of worship, and moral codes. Mission, likewise is understood within this framework: it is part of humanity's emerging beliefs concerning, including the understanding that these convictions ought to be persuasively shared with others. Such a religion-historical approach finds in Scripture a progression, a dynamic, but one that is entirely as a human consciousness rather than in divine revelation. This history-of-religions model has devastating effects on one's view of Scripture (it is conceived entirely as a human witness to the emergence of religious consciousness in history); on the objective nature of divine redemptive acts, ultimately centering in Christ's substitutionary cross-death and resurrection (which are, in customary liberal fashion, viewed in merely mythological or existential terms); and on the deity of Christ's (which is denied, with Jesus being viewed as merely a "Galilean peasant" or "Cynic sage" or the like), to name but a few of the most important implications. And where there

is diversity in Scripture, no underlying unity may be found or should even be sought. For where there is no inspiring, revealing, redeeming God who intervenes in human history, there is no unity of purpose, but only diversity of human religious views.

For this reason the second approach, the salvation-historical one, is to be preferred. The term "salvation history" (German: *heilsgeschichte*) of course, has been used in many different ways, not all of which are compatible with the view proposed in the present essay. A full-fledged critique far exceeds the scope of this presentation; we can only provide a brief description of a basic salvation-historical conception of Scripture as the notion of divine revelation. Salvation history is more than merely the evolution of human religious consciousness. It is rather the history of God's self-revelation in the form of both prepositional self-disclosure (e.g., the Law) and redemptive acts (e.g., the Exodus). Scripture, according to this view, is not merely a human witness to the emergence of human religious consciousness, but rather the inspired record of God's revelation and redemptive acts in human history. This, too, involves progression and dynamism, but these are at the heart rooted in the sovereign plan rather than merely in human consciousness. There may still be diversity, as well as development, along salvation-historical lines and among different biblical writers, but there will also be an underlying unity and coherence to the counsel of Scripture, derived not from any human source but from the God who revealed himself, redeemed humanity and inspired Scripture. This God is also the God of mission, the Lord of the harvest, the one who is carrying out his sovereign plan of redemption and mission in history to which the Scriptures testify.

---

[2] In the following discussion, we do not suggest that it is unhelpful to locate Judaism or Christianity within the larger religious landscape of their day. Our critique rather refers to a history-of-religions approach denying the revelatory nature of scripture with the salvation-historical dimension that entails.

We turn now to our discussion of the place of mission in the New Testament theology. We shall first survey a selected portion of the relevant literature. In view of limitations of space, interaction will be focused on three significant contributions to New Testament theology: the New Testament theologies of Rudolf Bultmann, George Ladd, and N.T. Wright, and on two major works in the biblical theology of mission, written by Donald Senior and Carroll Stuhlmueller and David Bosch.

The Place of Mission in New Testament Theology

In this section I will interact with the New Testament theologies of several major theologians, followed by a discussion of theologies of mission found in the work of several major authors.

New Testament Theology of Rudolf Bultmann

In his famous opening statement to his *New Testament Theology*, Bultmann contends that the message of Jesus is a presupposition for the theology of the New Testament rather than a part of that theology itself (1951:30). For Bultmann, the theology of the New Testament begins with the *kerygma* (preaching) of the early church and not before. Bultmann claims that the dominant concept of Jesus' message, in keeping with Jewish apocalyptic expectations, is the reign of God. This message concerning the kingdom of God, according to Bultmann, is central to Jesus' call to decision. Following Wrede, however, Bultmann adamantly denies that Jesus considered Himself to be the Messiah. Jesus, he argues, was declared such only by the early church. This church, so Bultmann claims, presented itself as an eschatological sect within Judaism, distinguished from other sects by its belief in

Jesus as Messiah and its conviction that the followers of Jesus constituted the eschatological messianic community.

Bultmann devotes an extended section of the first volume of his *New Testament Theology* to a discussion of the Gentile mission of the church (1951:65-92). Among the topics he surveys are monotheism, God as Creator and Judge of the world, repentance, the Day of the Lord, Jesus' role as the eschatological judge, the resurrection from the dead and the resurrection of Jesus, the sacrificial death of Jesus, the formation of the gospels, the proclamation of the gospel (*euangelion, kerygma*), and the requirement of faith. Bultmann's casting of the Christian message against the backdrop of the contemporary religious environment is one of the strongest sections of this work.

Overall, Bultmann's treatment is very incisive, but his failure to root the mission of the early church in Jesus' messianic consciousness[3] renders his evaluation of the Christian mission rootless if not arbitrary. Also it is unclear how Bultmann can ignore the salvation-historical unfolding of 's plan that pervades the entire Old Testament and is picked up repeatedly in the New Testament as well (viz., Luke-Acts, Galatians). The call and blessing of Abraham in Genesis 12:1-3 in particular deserves much greater attention in light of further Old and New Testament references. Thus Bultmann's discussion of the early Christian mission becomes a mere exercise in the history of religions without rooting this mission in the history of Israel culminating in Jesus. A case in point is Bultmann's discussion of the Gospel of John, which is entirely dominated by alleged parallels to Gnosticism while claiming that a salvation-historical perspective is lacking in

---

[3] See also Bultmann's interaction with the work of Adolf Schlatter (1955:II: 248-251) in which Bultmann faults Schlatter for failing to distinguish between the historical Jesus and the Christ of faith and for interpreting Jesus against the backdrop of Old Testament Jewish tradition rather than Hellenistic syncretism.

John (1955:8-9).[4] In the end, Bultmann's radical dichotomy between the Jesus' message and the missionary preaching of the early church that alone the rapid growth of Christianity in the decades subsequent to Jesus' ministry.

New Testament Theology of George Eldon Ladd

In his chapter on "The Messianic Mission," George Ladd describes Jesus' mission as the preparation of men and women for the future kingdom of (Ladd 1993:181-192), those who in the present decide for Jesus may partake of the future life of the kingdom already in the present. As the Son of , Jesus brings the Kingdom to humanity; as the servant of the Lord, Jesus is called to suffer vicariously for humankind (Mark 10:45; 14:24). Jesus' mission as the suffering servant of the lord is already given expression by the voice from heaven at Jesus' baptism where Jesus, in allusion to Psalm 2:7 and Isaiah 42:1, is called to the mission of God's servant. To quote Ladd, "This allusion to the servant passage in Isaiah indicates that Jesus realized from the very beginning that his messianic mission was to be carried out in terms of the Suffering Servant of the Lord rather than in terms of the ruling Davidic king"(1993:184). Passages such as Mark 2:20 ("the days will come when the bridegroom is taken away from them, and then they will fast on that day") indicate that Jesus expected to die from the earliest stages of his ministry. The Gospels also make clear that Jesus understood his own death in terms of ransom (Mark 10:45) and the shepherd's substitutionary sacrifice for his sheep (Mark 14:27, citing Zechariah 13:7; John 10:11,15,17).

However, while Ladd gives adequate attention to the mission of Jesus and its centrality in God's plan, he does virtually nothing to relate Jesus' mission to the mission of the early church. The reason for this may be Ladd's commitment

to biblical theology foremost as the study of individual biblical books in their own contexts. But biblical theology also entails the investigation of larger themes of Scripture (Carson 1995:24-25). In fact, if the study of the Bible stops short of this larger thematic level, it cannot be called "biblical theology" at all (Carson 1995:30-31; Gibson 1997). This major weakness in Ladd's treatment is to small extent remedied by the appendix on unity and diversity in the New Testament added in the second edition by David Wenham (1993:684-719). Taking his starting point with James Dunn, who contends that Jesus Christ as the fulfillment of Scripture and the giver of the Spirit, is the center of the new testament, Wenham argues for a broader center of new testament theology, also taking into account God's plan of salvation and reconciliation for his people and the world (1993:712). According to Wenham, New Testament theology is about "the divine mission [of restoration] to the world," which he describes as follows:

1. The one creator God, the God of Israel, in His love and in fulfillment of the scriptures, intervened through Jesus to complete His saving purposes through His people Israel and thus to bring a broken and hostile world back under His rule and to restore it to the love and perfection that God intended.

2. Jesus was the Spirit-filled Messiah of Israel and the Son of God. Through His life, teaching and supremely through His death and resurrection, He announced and inaugurated the saving rule of God, inviting others to receive the divine gift.

3. Those who receive Jesus and His salvation by faith are thorough and with Him the true Israel, children of God,

---

[4] This contention has been decisively countered in recent years by Pryor (1992).

having the Holy Spirit of sonship. They are called to live as a restored community in loving fellowship with God and with each other and to proclaim and live the good news of restoration in the world.

4. The emission of restoration will be complete at the Lord's return to judge the world, when evil will finally be overcome, God's people will be raised and perfected, and the whole of creation will be restored to its intended glory. (Wenham 1993; 712-713).

In light of our present concern the question arises whether even Wenham gives mission its due within the context of New Testament theology as a whole. Does God conceive of salvation history in its entirety as a history of mission? Did He call Israel to participate in that mission, and if so, how? What is Jesus' role in the divine mission, both in relation to Israel and to the Gentiles? And how central ought mission to be in the life of the church in the interim between the exalted Christ's sending of His Spirit at Pentecost and Christ's return? These are the questions that merit much more detailed exploration than is devoted to them by Ladd and Wenham.

New Testament Theology of N.T. Wright

In the inaugural volume of his yet to be completed five-volume theology of the New testament, N.T. Wright sketches out the contours of what remains to be developed more fully in volumes two through five (Wright 1992). Wright contends that any work on New Testament theology must do justice to the historical, theological, and literary dimensions of the biblical text. Consequently, with regard to history,

Wright's first volume focused on setting Jesus' ministry in the context of second-temple Judaism and early Christianity. With regard to theology, Wright discusses the salvation-historical interconnection between Israel, Jesus and the church. With regard to literature he notes how later versions of the biblical story line, such as the gospel accounts of Jesus' earthly ministry, pick up and further develop earlier aspects of Scripture.

In his critique of Bultmann, Wright points out that Bultmann sought to arrive at timeless theological truths by way of historical criticism and history of religions. Indeed, such a "timeless theology" is the real object of the historical quest. "Theology" thus becomes the real thing in terms of some aspects being "timelessly true" and others being "culturally conditioned." But as Wright puts it, the problem is that "the skin doesn't peel away so clearly," so that "quite a lot of fruit has been thrown away, still sticking to the discarded skin" (1992:20). As Wright contends, "All of the new testament is culturally conditioned: if that were to disqualify an idea or a theme from attaining 'relevance' to other periods or cultures, the New Testament as a whole is disqualified" (1992:20).[5] Wright's assessment of the new literary criticism is equally devastating. According to Wright, it is nothing but "an attempt to accomplish, within post modernity, what Bultmann's package failed to accomplish within modernity" (1992:25).

Wright's own alternative is a "creative synthesis" combining "the pre-modern emphasis on the test as in some sense authoritative, the modern emphasis on the text (and Christianity itself) as irreducibly integrated into history, and irreducibly involved with theology, and the post modern emphasis on the reading of the text" (1992:26-27). The solution is not found by

---

[5] Wright also has serious problems with the biblical theology school of the 1950s and 1960s (cf., esp. GE. Wright [1962]). In this model, the New Testament is given authority not because it witnesses to timeless truth, but because it testifies to the mighty acts of God in history, especially in the life of Jesus. The text is revelatory, and thus authoritative to the extent that it bears witness to the "real thing", that is, particular salvation-historical events.

absolutizing any one of the elements of history, theology, and literature, but in a balanced approach in which each one of these aspects is given its proper due.

The most important section in Wright's work for the present study is found in his survey of what he terms "the first Christian century."[6] Wright starts his discussion with the following observation: "The single most striking thing about early Christianity is its speed of growth" (1992: 359). He quotes a statement by Martin Hengel who comments that "the irresistible expansion of Christian faith in the Mediterranean world during the first 150 years is the scarlet thread running through any history of primitive Christianity (1992:360, citing Hengel 1983:48). Wright continues, "This missionary activity was not an addendum to a faith that was basically 'about' something else (e.g., a new existential self awareness). 'Christianity was never more *itself* than in the launching of the world mission' (Meyer 1986:18)" (1992:360). Wright concludes with this remarkable assertion: "World mission is thus the first and most obvious feature of early Christian praxis" (1992:361).[7]

In his survey of early literature, Wright notes that the synoptic gospels tell the story of Jesus as part of a much larger story, that is the story of Israel, a story that is to function as a foundational story for the early Christian communities (1992:369). This requires that the evangelists intended to write history, the history of Jesus for the Jewish people expected fulfillment of God's promises to the nation *in history* rather that in some symbolic or mythical sense (1992:402). What is more, the Gospels are the story of Jesus told as the history of Israel in miniature. Thus, Matthew, for example, "gives us, in his first five chapters, a Genesis (1.1), an Exodus (2.15), and

a Deuteronomy (5-7); he then gives us a royal and prophetic ministry, and finally an exile (the cross) and restoration (the resurrection)" (1992:402). The same phenomenon is also at work in John's Prologue, which includes references to creation, the giving of the Law through Moses, the Exodus, and the tabernacle (1:1-5, 14, 17-18) (1992:411-413).[8] The early Christians, according to Wright, on other part "told, and lived, a form of Israel's story which reached its climax in Jesus and which then issued in their Spirit-given new life and task," including mission (1992:456).

Wright makes no attempt in his first volume to locate mission within New Testament theology as a whole. His focus is primarily historical. What he seeks to show is how Jesus' history is rooted in that of Israel and how the early church's history in turn, is rooted in the history of Jesus. It may be fair to say, however, that of the three attempts surveyed here, Wright's treatment is the most satisfying. Where Ladd fails to integrate the various strands of theology provided by the various biblical writers, Wright provides a grand synthesis: the conviction on the part of the early Christians that the history/story of Israel culminated in the history/story of Jesus. This conviction alone, together with the early church's missionary activity, accounts adequately for the historical phenomenon of the explosive growth of Christianity in the remaining decades of the first century A.D.

Bultmann's history-or-religions treatment, on the other hand, in its isolation salvation history, fails to supply a credible rationale for the early Christian mission. If Jesus' first followers, all Jews, recognized in Jesus Israel's Messiah, a Messiah the Jews expected to come in history, and if this is the Messiah they in fact proclaimed

---

[6] See especially "2. Praxis" in N.T. Wright (1992:359-365).

[7] Besides mission, Wright also names sacrament and worship (1992:362).

[8] Whether John's prologue was indeed written with conscious reference to a passage in the Jewish intertestamental work of Sirach 24:1-28, as Wright contends, is another question.

subsequent to Jesus' crucifixion, a mythological explanation is historically implausible.

Theology of Mission of Donald Senior and Carroll Stuhlmueller

As is hinted at in the title of Senior and Stuhlmueller's work, the *Biblical Foundations for Mission* (1983), the writers are convinced that "the entire Bible...lays the foundations for mission" (1983:315). Already the Old Testament "reveals a dialectic between centripetal and centrifugal forces" (1983:316). Indeed, Old Testament theology, particularly Isaiah, has room for Israel as God's chosen people and outreach to the nations (1983:317-318). Thus, Senior and Stuhlmueller find in the Old Testament an evolving dialectic between identity and outreach (1983:318). Nevertheless, they conclude, "these elements did not coalesce into an active missionary stance" (1983:318). They elaborate, "Institutions of a collegial role for the nations remained on the periphery, especially in the postexilic period. Although some proselytizing activity took place during the intertestamental period, this was always in an ethnocentric perspective: Gentiles could become Jews and thus share in Israel's privileged status. Israel was not called to go the nations; the nations were permitted to come to Israel" (1983:318).

It was Jesus who showed compassion to those outside of Israel, challenging the narrow particularism of his contemporaries (1983:319). The Gospels use the "pattern of Jesus' ministry – a ministry that flowed from his concept of – as the norm for the universal mission of the church" (1983:331). The authors find mission prominent especially in Paul's writings (such as in Colossians and Ephesians), the Gospel of Matthew, Luke-Acts, and even the Gospel of John, concerning which they comment, "the mission question remains central" (1983:320). Senior and Stuhlmueller conclude their survey of the Bible with the following statement:

Thus throughout the Old and New Testament the question of mission is far from peripheral. In the Old Testament this motif must be sought in the complex and evolving dialectic between Israel and its sovereign God and between Israel and secular environment. With the figure of Jesus the centrifugal forces surging within the scriptures break out into the non-Jewish world. The New Testament writings represent the multiple ways in which the members of the Christian community reflected on their mission experience and its relationship to the person of Jesus and the history of Israel. (1983:320-321)

According to Senior and Stuhlmueller, four key themes provided the impetus for mission: (1) a theology of God's sovereignty, (2) a theology of history, and (3) a theology of creation, all of which were (4) formed in the crucible of religious experience of God's people. First, "the conviction that the God of Israel was sovereign over all peoples and that he was a saving God is absolutely fundamental to the Scripture" (1983:320). Second, the writers of scripture detect God's hand even in what might be considered "secular" events of world history. Third, all of creation was considered to be the arena in which God's redemptive purposes are played out. And fourth, encounters with God, such as Paul's conversion on the road to Damascus, led to an expanded vision of humanity and of history. Senior and Stuhlmueller's model might be represented as follows.

Religious Experience of God's People

Figure 1. Senior and Stuhlmueller's Model on the Missionary Impulse

For my taste, however, this model is entirely too anthropocentric. Arguing for religious experience as the key to mission, the authors refer to Peter's words quoted in Acts 11:17, "If then gave the same gift to them as he gave to us when we believed in the Lord Jesus Christ, who was I that I could withstand ?" and conclude, "This seems to imply that religious experience is an equalizer" (1983:332). This is a puzzling statement indeed. It rather seems that the key impetus for mission came from God through divine revelation, with human beings frequently being extremely reluctant to respond, as is clear in the case of both Peter and Paul in the Book of Acts. A theocentric model of mission is therefore to be preferred.

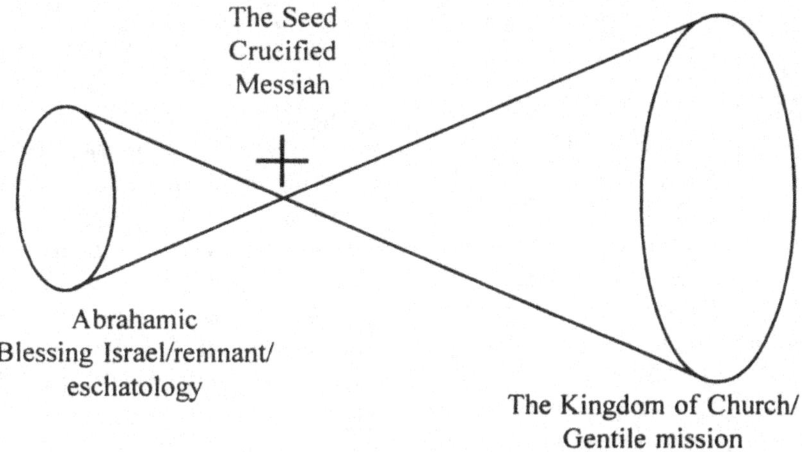

Figure 2. Israel, Jesus and the Church: The Work of God along Salvation-historical Lines

Contrary to Senior and Stuhlmueller, the centrifugal forces in Old Testament theology are primarily confined to the faithful remnant and are generally set in the framework of eschatology. Even Jesus operated within the parameters of Israel, ministering to gentiles only when the initiative came from them. As the representative Israelite, Jesus took upon himself the curses pronounced for disobedience to the Deutronomic covenant and suffered an exile of his own at the cross. As the true vine, he attracted new branches, the new messianic community replacing the old, with faith in Jesus as Messiah serving as its constitutive principle. The Gentile mission, in turn, belongs of the post-pentecost age of the church, when believers, in fulfillment of the Great Commission, go and disciple the nations in a way neither Israel nor Jesus had done.

This entails an element of mystery, an unexpected turn of events: while the nations in Old Testament expectation were to be drawn to Israel and join Israel in its worship of God, the New Testament church actively goes and seeks out converts to the Christian faith (Beale 1997). In my view, it is therefore mistaken to level, in the interest of continuity between the testaments, the missionary modalities in the Old and New Testaments by accentuating alleged centrifugal forces in the mission of Israel and by having Jesus embark already on a Gentile mission of his own. The discontinuity must rather be allowed to stand, giving, as it were, a striking testimony to the way in which the sovereign God consistently confounds human expectations and accomplishes God's plan of salvation in ways controlled by and known only to Him until the time comes.

Still, I concur with Senior and Sthulmueller that mission is a central motif in both Old and New Testament theology. Also laudable is their attention to different emphasis in the various writings of the New Testament. As they correctly point out, direct proclamation is but one, albeit the most significant, means of evangelization in the early church (1983:333). Other, complementary modes of mission include exemplary suffering or "good citizenship" (1983:336-337).

Theology of Mission of David J. Bosch

"Christianity is missionary by its own nature, or it denies its *raison d'etre,*" David Bosch states at the very outset of his magisterial volume *Transforming Mission* (Bosch 1991:9). In his first chapter, entitled "Reflections on the New Testament as a Missionary Document," he maintains, alluding to the title of Senior and Sthulmueller's work, that he is not interested in investigating the "Biblical Foundations for Mission" (1991:15). Rather, he contents that the "New Testament witnesses to a fundamental shift when compared with the Old Testament" (1991:15). According to Bosch, the advent of Jesus led to the first and cardinal paradigm shift in the history of missions. Consequently, the writer views the New Testament as a "missionary document" (1991:15, reiterated 54), contenting that mission was at the heart of the early church's theologizing. First-century theologians, such as the apostle Paul, were no ivory-tower theologians. Rather, Paul was compelled to theologize in the context of his missionary encounter with the world. As Martin Kähler remarks, mission is "the mother of theology" (Kähler 1971: 190, cited in Bosch 1991:16).

Thus Bosch devotes only five pages of his almost six-hundred-page work to the Old Testament. For "there is, in the old testament, no indication of the believers of the old covenant being sent by God to cross geographical, religious, and social frontiers in order to win others to faith in Yahweh" (1991:17). Even Jonah he denies the status of foreign missionary, and the second part of Isaiah is not considered to be a book about mission (1991:17; contra Hahn 1965:19). Still, Bosch acknowledges that the Old Testament is fundamental to the understanding of mission in the New. Bosch devotes considerably more space to Jesus, whose conduct he considers to be "the real starting point of the primitive Christian mission" (1991:31). Similar to Ladd, he focuses on Jesus' teaching on the reign of God (1991:31-35). In his discussion of the mission of the early church, Bosch stresses that mission did not gradually replace the *Natherwartung* (expectation of the imminent end of the world) of Christ's return. "Rather, mission was, in itself, an eschatological event" (1991:41). Bosch's in-depth discussion of individual New Testament writings focuses on Matthew, Luke-Acts, and Paul. It should be noted that only 180 pages, or roughly one-third of the book, are devoted to biblical material (Part 1). The remainder of Bosch's work traces historical paradigms of mission (Part 2) and seeks to advance "toward a relevant missiology" (Part 3).

By way of evaluation, we find it problematic that Bosch uses a modern-day definition, that of the sending out of *missionaries*, in his evaluation of the biblical material. This leads him to exclude the Old Testament while embracing the New Testament alone as a missionary document. But arguably Bosch's methodology is seriously flawed. Any understanding of a biblical theology of mission must derive its contours from the biblical material itself rather than being submerged by extra biblical definitions. As it is, Bosch vastly exaggerates the discontinuity between the testaments. While I believe he is right in maintaining that Israel was not called to go and evangelize the nations in Old Testament, as a document, provides in the Abrahamic blessing the foundational paradigm of mission that is realized in the history of salvation through Abraham's "seed," Jesus Christ, and the mission of the church, with the result that all nations of the earth are blessed. Bosch's radical disjunction between the Testaments obscures the underlying theological unity provided by this foundational statement.

Also, Bosch's – in part merely pragmatic – decision to focus his discussion exclusively on the Matthean-Lucan-Pauline axis of mission drowns out significant voices such as John's Gospel or Peter's First Epistle, not to mention the Book of Revelation. Bosch's claims that the writings chosen by him are "representative" sounds like special pleading and fails to convince (1991:54-55). His selective use of material leaves Bosch ill-equipped to assess the respective place of mission in the various writings of the New Testament, so that his claim that the New Testament is a missionary document ends up being, at least in part, asserted rather than actually demonstrated.

Survey of Biblical Material

In evaluating the works surveyed above, and seeking to determine the place of mission within the scope of the New Testament message as a whole, it is neither possible nor necessary to survey the New Testament writings themselves. Two volumes to which I have contributed have endeavored to do this already: the just-released *Mission in the New Testament: An Evangelical Approach* (1998), edited by William Larkin and Joel Williams, and the forthcoming *Salvation unto the Ends of the Earth: A Biblical Theology of Mission,* which I co-authored with Peter O' Brien in the new studies in Biblical Theology Series.[9] In the place of a summary of mission in the entire New testament, I will limit myself to a brief discussion of the place of mission in Johannine theology, in further development of my recently published *The Missions of Jesus and the Disciples according to the Fourth Gospel* (Köstenberger 1998).

Mission in John's Gospel

Currently, few books on Johannine theology include mission among the important themes in John's Gospel, even though an excellent case can be made for mission being one of the most important motifs in the entire book. The most natural reading on John's purpose statement already suggests that you may have life in His name" (20:31, NIV). To interpret "believing" here as first time faith in Christ is supported by the fact that this purpose statement follows shortly after the Johannine commissioning passage in 20:21, where the disciples are enjoined to forgive others their sins, again most likely referring to the pronouncement of forgiveness upon first-time faith in Jesus as Christ.

If one word is able to describe the nature of John's Gospel, it arguably is the word *universal.* No verse bears this out more clearly than the famous statement in John 3:16, "For God so loved the world that He gave His one and only Son, that *whoever* believes in Him shall not perish but have eternal life." The term "believe" occurs almost a hundred times in this gospel, and John states emphatically that faith in Jesus as Christ has become the sole criterion for membership among God's people. Also, John substitutes the universal phrase "eternal life" for the synoptic concept of "the Kingdom of God", which still conjures up particularistic Jewish expectations in fulfillment of God's promises to David. And many other Johannine terms are as universal as can be imagined: the word, the truth, or light.

This however, does not mean that John loses sight of the Jews, the old covenant community. To the contrary, the entire first half of his Gospel is devoted to Jesus' ministry to the Jews. But in his Gospel, the Jews have become part of the world (cf. 1:11) and must exercise faith in Jesus as Messiah to join His new covenant community, on equal terms with Gentiles. Is it historically

---

[9] See also my forthcoming entry on "Mission" in the *New Dictionary of Biblical Theology*.

implausible for John to try to convert Jews toward the end of the first century? Many interpreters today argue that the alleged addition of curses on Christians to the Jewish synagogue service in around A.D. 70, the so-called *Birkath-ha-minim,* precludes such an attempt. But it is doubtful whether the break was as radical as these scholars claim (Alexander 1992:6-11; Bauckham 1997:23, n.26). Moreover, how could John, himself a Jew, and convinced that Jesus was the Messiah, give up trying to convince his countrymen of this vital, all-important truth?

I submit that, rather than the curses on the Christians, another event taking place in A.D. 70 provided the occasion for John's evangelistic effort: the destruction of his Jewish temple and the city of Jerusalem (Balfour 1995). In the aftermath of this – for Jews – shocking development, John detected a window of unprecedented opportunity for the proclamation of the Christian gospel to his fellow Jews, many of whom doubtless had fled to the Diaspora where John raised and wrote (Goodman 1992:27-38). For with the destruction of the temple, Jews had lost the center of their national and religious identity, and the question arose what would take its place. Of course, it was a rabbinic form of Judaism centered on pharisaic scholasticism that emerged as the eventual substitute (Alexander 1992:1-25). But as John is trying to argue, it is Jesus, not a renewed devotion to the Hebrew scriptures or to oral traditions surrounding them, who alone is able to fill the theological and existential vacuum brought about by the destruction of the temple: hence the Johannine "replacement theme," which shows systematically how Jesus fulfilled the symbolism inherent in the most significant institutions of Jewish life, such as the temple as well as in the major Jewish feasts, such as the Passover or the Feast of Tabernacles (Carson 1988:253-256).

John thus proves to be a theologian who is also an apologete, an evangelist, and an expert in contextualizing the Christian message in the world of his day. And if the above reconstruction is correct, mission is not merely at the fringes of John's gospel but rather the impetus for John's writing of his Gospel, providing the organizing principle for his presentation of Jesus' person and work. This is but one example of the crucial significance of the theme of mission in the writings of the new testament, a fact that has yet to impact New Testament scholarship in a way that new testament theologies and works on the theology of individual new testament books reflect this reality.

Conclusion

As we determine the place of mission in New Testament theology, the following observations should be kept in mind.

1.*A tracing of mission in the entire Bible requires flexibility concerning the definition of mission.* We must allow the scriptural record itself to spell out dynamics and developments pertaining to mission over the course of salvation history rather than impose a particular abstract or modern definition of mission on the Bible. Otherwise, legitimate aspects of Scripture will inevitably be excluded and the remaining material streamlined according to the interpreter's respective definition of mission. What makes things even more difficult is that mission is an abstract term that as such is not even found in scripture itself. This has led many to advocate a semantic field approach to the study of mission in the Bible, but even there limitations remain. On the other hand, while caution in one's understanding of mission is crucial, care must be taken not to define mission so broadly as to include everything under the heading "mission"; this would render any further investigation meaningless.

2. *A salvation-historical approach to Scripture is imperative for an accurate understanding of the Bible's own teaching on mission.* The writers of the Old Testament looked forward to 's future acts on behalf of His people,

including the sending of a Messiah and the eschatological kingdom. The writers of the New Testament interpreted 's recent or present intervention in terms of Old Testament paradigms, such as the Abrahamic blessing, the Exodus, the giving of the law, the exile, or the restoration of a faithful remnant. A history-of-religions approach or an approach that focuses merely on the various theologies of mission contributed by individual biblical writers without understanding the underlying thematic unity along salvation-historical lines is therefore inadequate.

3. *Care must be taken not to compromise the Bible's own story line by imposing on Scripture an artificial uniformity concerning mission.*[10] Those who believe that mission is the central motif of Scripture could easily tend to find mission even where it is not. Moreover, they may represent Scripture's teaching on mission in a way that stresses a certain kind of uniformity in which the continuity of mission over salvation history is stressed, even where this may not be borne out by the biblical record. Two examples may be given: first, the question of whether Israel was called to an active outreach among the surrounding nations in the same way the disciples were enjoined in the great commission; and second, the issue of whether Jesus limited His earthly ministry to Israel or whether He embarked on a Gentile mission as well. This is not the place to answer either question. We may simply warn against a misguided zeal that, in an effort to demonstrate the crucial importance of mission in the entire Bible, reads one's presuppositions regarding continuity into the text even where discontinuity may be found.

This fear is, I submit, in any case unwarranted. In other words, even if Israel was not called to go and reach out to its neighbors [but rather was to showcase by godly living what life under God is like], and even if Jesus did *not*

embark on a Gentile mission [but left this to the post-Pentecost church], mission would be still a major scriptural motif. For what would have changed in that case would not be God's heart for the world, but merely God's progressive mode of operation, His way of realizing His plan of salvation in successive stages. This, of course, relates to the question of theological systems. Dispensationalists may feel more comfortable with the possible system I have just outlined; covenant theologians may tend to see a greater degree of continuity between Israel and the church, and between the missions of Jesus and His disciples.

Thus we have come full circle: as I urged in my opening comments, if we don't want our exegesis merely to become a validation of our already predetermined views, we must be open for our larger theological system to be challenged by our study of a biblical theme such as mission. This is easier said than done, but I believe it is possible. May God give us the grace to apprehend ever more closely 's plan of the ages, for us personally, and for those who still need us to tell them that Jesus Christ is Lord, to the glory of God the Father.

References Cited

Alexander, Philip S. 1992 "'The Parting of the Ways' from the Perspective of Rabbinic Judaism" in *Jews and Christians: The Parting of the Ways. A.D. 70 to 135.* James D.G. Dunn, ed. Pp. 1-25. Tubingen, Germany: J. C. B. Mohr (Paul Siebeck).

Balfour, G.M. 1995 " Is John's Gospel Anti-Semitic? With Special Reference to its Use of the Old Testament", Ph.D. dissertation, University of Nottingham, England.

Bauckham, Richard, ed. *The Gospels for All Christians: Rethinking the Gospel Audiences.* Grand Rapids, MI: Eerdmans.

---

[10] On the importance of the Bible's own story line in the current post-modern climate, see especially Carson ,1996.

Beale, Gregory "Mystery". Presentation at the annual Meeting of the Society of Biblical Literature, San Francisco, CA, 25 November.

Bosch,David J. *Transforming Mission : Paradigm Shifts in Theology of Mission.* Maryknoll, NY: Orbis Books.

Bultmann, Rudolf 1951,1955, *Theology of the New Testament.* 2 Vols. Kendrick Grobel, trans. New York: Charles Scribner's Sons.

Carson, D. A. 1988 "John and the Johannine Epistles" in *It Is Written: Scripture Citing Scripture: Essays in Honour of Barnabas Lindars.* D.A. Carson and H.G.M. Williamson, eds., Cambridge University Press, pp.245-264.

1995 "Current Issues in Biblical Theology: A New Testament Persspective" in *Bulletin of Biblical Research* 5:17-41.

1996 The Gagging of God: Christianity Confronts Pluralism. Grand Rapids, MI: Eerdmans.

Gibson, R.J., ed. *Interpretin's Plan: Biblical Theology and the Pastor.* Carlisle, UK: Paternoster. Goodman, Martin

Goodman, Martin "Diaspora Reactions to the destruction of the Temple" in *Jews and Christians: The Parting of the Ways, A.D. 70 to 135.* James D.G. Dunn, ed., Tubingen, Germany: J.C.B. Mohr (Paul Siebeck), pp 27-38.

Hahn, Ferdinand *Mission in the New Testament. Studies in Biblical Theology 47,* Frank Clarke, trans. London, UK: SCM.

Hengel, Martin *Between Jesus and Paul: Studies in the Earliest History of Christianity,* John Bowden, trans. London, UK: SCM.

Kähler, Martin 1971 [1908] Schriften zur christologie and Mission. Munich, Germany:Chr. Kaiser.

Kösttenberger, Andreas J. *The Missions of Jesus and the Disciples according to the Fourth Gospel: with implication for the Fourth Gospel's and the Mission of the Contemporary Church.* Grand Rapids, MI: Eerdmans.

Forthcoming "Mission" in *New Dictionary of Biblical Theology,* eds. Desmand Alexander and Brian Rosner, Leicester, UK: Inter-Varsity Press.

Kösttenberger, Andreas J., and Peter T. O'Brien, Forthcoming Salvation unto the Ends of the earth: A Biblical Theology of Mission . New Studies in Biblical Theology. Leicester, UK: Inter-Varsity Press; Grand Rapids, MI: Eerdmans.

Ladd, George Eldon .*A Theology of the New Testament,* Rev. ed., Grand Rapids, MI: Eerdmans.

Larkin, William J., Jr., and Joel F. Williams, eds. *Mission in the New Testament: An Evangelical Approach. American Soceity of Missiology Series No.27.* Maryknoll, NY: Orbis Books.

Meyer, Ben F. *The Early Christians: Their World Mission and Self-Discovery.* Good News Studies 16. Wilmington, DE: Michael Glazier.

Pryor, John W. *John: Evangelist of the Covenant people: The Narrative and the themes of the Fourth Gospel.* Downers Grove, IL: Inter Varsity Press.

Schlatter, Adolf. *The History of the Christ: The Foundation of the New Testament Theology.* Andreas J. Kostenberger, trans. Grand Rapids, MI: Baker.

Senior, Donald, and Carroll Stuhlmueller. *The Biblical Foundations for Mission.* Maryknoll, NY: Orbis Books.

Wenham, David. "Unity and Diverstiy in the New Testament" in *A Theology of the New Testament by George Eldonn Ladd,* Rev. ed. Grand Rapids, MI: Eerdmans, Pp. 684-719.

Wright, G. Ernest. *Who Acts: Biblical Theology as Recital.* London, UK: SCM.

Wright, N. T. 1992, *The New Testament and the People of God : Christian Origins and the Question of ...,* Volume One. Minneapolis, MN: Fortress.

CHAPTER 7

The Early Church in Mission

BRIAN WINTLE

The story of the Early Church in mission is the fascinating and multi-faceted account of how the movement, which began with a small group of Jews who believed that Jesus of Nazareth was the Messiah, gathered sufficient momentum within a few decades to spread to Rome, the imperial capital of the Roman Empire and beyond. The story can be recounted in different ways; but for the purposes of this essay, the story is divided up into two parts: In the first part, we trace the spread of the new faith from being a sect within Judaism, to becoming a faith that embraced, first of all, Samaritans, then god-fearers, and eventually Gentiles. The outline of this first section of the essay is based on the schema set out in Acts 1:8 – Jerusalem, then Judea and Samaria, and then the ends of the earth. In the second part, we will focus chiefly on Paul of Tarsus, the Apostle to the Gentiles. In conclusion, we will make a brief assessment of the strengths and weaknesses of the early church in the area of mission.

The Beginning: In Jerusalem

The story of the mission of the New Testament Church begins with the coming of the Spirit at Pentecost (Acts 2). One of the concerns that the risen Jesus apparently had was to reassure his disciples that his death as Messiah was indeed a fulfilment of the Old Testament Scriptures, just as he had already told them.[1] Since they were witnesses to his life, death, and resurrection, they were to wait in Jerusalem until they were endowed with power from on High in the person of the Holy Spirit, and then were to proclaim forgiveness of sins to the penitent in His Name (Lk.24:47-49).

Pentecost is therefore the starting point of the mission of the New Testament church. With the coming of the Holy Spirit, the community of Jewish disciples of Jesus of Nazareth was not only initiated into mission, but also guided as to its where and how. On the one hand, Pentecost marked the giving of the promised Spirit to individuals - the end-time renewal of the people of God (Acts 2:36,39), with the Twelve as the central core group; on the other, Pentecost foreshadowed the mission of this renewed people of God to the "ends of the earth."[2]

In Acts 2:5 we read that on the day of Pentecost there were *devout Jews from every nation under heaven living in Jerusalem* – and it may be presumed that when those who became believers in Jesus of Nazareth as Messiah returned to their various cities in the Diaspora, they proclaimed their new-found faith in Jesus, and started churches. This may explain the beginnings of Christian communities in such places as Damascus, Rome and Alexandria.[3]

To begin with, the disciples of Jesus had no difficulty in remaining within Judaism. We read

---

[1] Luke 24:25-27, 44-46.

[2] Acts 1:8; see Lincoln 1997:906.

[3] C.E. Arnold, "Centres of Christianity" in *Dictionary of the Later New Testament and Its Developments*, ed.by R.P. Martin & Peter H. Davids, Leicester, IVP, 1997, p.144.

that they were frequently in the Temple (Acts 2:46; 5:21,25,42), observed the regular hours of prayer (3:1,3), and, generally speaking, enjoyed the goodwill of the people (Acts 2:47; 5:13). This suggests that, from the perspective of outward observances, they continued as practising Jews. "In so far as the Gentiles entered into their thinking it would probably be in terms of the long cherished hope that in the new age the Gentiles would flock to Mount Zion (with the diaspora Jews) to worship God there as eschatological proselytes."[4] James Dunn is undoubtedly correct in his conclusion.

> The earliest community in no sense felt themselves to be a new religion, distinct from Judaism. They saw themselves simply as a fulfilled Judaism, the beginning of eschatological Israel. Only their belief in Jesus as Messiah and risen, and their belief that the last days were upon them mark them out as different from the majority of their fellow Jews. And the Jewish authorities evidently did not see them as anything very different from themselves: they held one or two eccentric beliefs, but otherwise they were wholly Jewish.[5]

On the other hand, there were distinctive features. First, there was the religious element - the apostles' teaching, the fellowship of "common religious experience",[6] the common meals at which the Lord's Supper was celebrated, and the prayers (Acts 2:42-47). Second, there was the proclamation of the good news of Jesus and his resurrection that was attested with clear evidence of supernatural power in the community – wonders and signs, healing of the sick, and deliverance from evil spirits (Acts 2:43; 5:12-16). And third, there were changed attitudes and concerns – there was a unity of mind and purpose,

"each person held his goods at the disposal of the others whenever the need arose",[7] there was a new boldness in their proclamation of the good news of Jesus, and there was a heightened sense of the seriousness of sin (as the narrative of Ananias and Sapphira makes clear) (Acts 5:1-11).

The overall impact of their witness on the population of Jerusalem was twofold: on the one hand, *everyone was filled with awe* (Acts 2:43), and *with wonder and amazement* (3:10), *all the people were praising God for what happened* (4:21), and *none of the rest dared to join them* (5:13); on the other, the Christians *enjoyed the favour of all the people* (2:47), and *the people held them in high esteem* (5:13), and *more than ever believers were added to the Lord, great numbers of both men and women* (5:14).

In Acts 3-5, Luke narrates how the witness of the early disciples brought them into conflict with the Jewish leaders, who tried unsuccessfully to prevent them from preaching. Two incidents are recorded.[8] In the first one, Peter and John healed a cripple at the gate of the temple in the name of Jesus (Acts 3:6). The significance of this is "the continuing power of the name of Jesus to perform the same gracious and healing acts that were signs in the Gospels of the coming of the kingdom or rule of God."[9] As in the case of Jesus' own miracles, the people are filled with wonder and amazement, and Peter uses the opportunity to explain what has just happened. The particular interest of what he says lies in the way in which he gives further teaching about the person of Jesus, describing him as God's servant, the Holy and Righteous One, the Author of life and the prophet like Moses. "This indicates that a

---

[4] E.g. Isa.2:2f; 56:6-8; Zeph. 3:9f; Zech.14:16.

[5] James D.G. Dunn, *Unity and Diversity in the New Testament*, London: SCM, 1997, p.238f.

[6] I. Howard Marshall, *Acts*, Leicester: IVP, 1980, p.83.

[7] *Ibid., p. 84.*

[8] Acts 3:1-4:31; 5:12-42.

[9] Marshall, *Acts*, p.86.

considerable amount of thinking about Jesus, based on study of the Jewish Scriptures, was taking place.[10] The healing and Peter's preaching aroused the opposition of the Jewish leaders who arrested both Peter and John. In their defence before the Sanhedrin, Peter repeated the essential facts concerning the resurrection of Jesus, and added that He alone could save. The Jewish leadership recognised that they were acting in the same way as Jesus had done, but contented themselves with merely threatening them if they continued to speak about Jesus in the way they were speaking.

Luke's summary in Acts 5:12-16 helps set the scene for his narrative of a further confrontation with the Jewish authorities. The emphasis is on a powerful healing ministry, on signs and wonders, and on deliverance from evil spirits. In this case, it was not just Peter and John, but "all the apostles", and the impact was such that the authorities felt that they ought to take action against them. So they arrested them, but the apostles were delivered miraculously, and returned to their preaching in the temple (Acts 5:21). When they were threatened again, the apostles refused to obey the authorities. This enraged them so much, that they would have killed the apostles had they not been stopped by the respected Rabban Gamaliel (Acts 5:33f). In the event, they flogged them and let them go. But the apostles *rejoiced that they were considered worthy to suffer dishonour for the sake of the name (of Jesus)* and continued to teach and proclaim Jesus as the Messiah.

So in these early stages, the chief concern of the disciples was to argue the case that the mission, death and resurrection of Jesus of Nazareth threw light on how the Jewish Scriptures ought to be understood. In other words, the debate with the Jewish authorities and people was essentially a hermeneutical one. The position of the disciples was that God had accredited Jesus during his lifetime by *deeds of power, wonders and signs,* which he did through him. Further, God had vindicated Jesus by raising him from the dead and exalting him to his right hand (Acts 2:23-26; 3:13-26). Therefore, scripture had to be understood in the light of these momentous events.[11] Dunn observes:

> The Jewish Scriptures remained authoritative only to the extent that they could be adequately re-interpreted by and in relation to the new revelation of Jesus. The event of Jesus, the Jesus-tradition, the belief in Jesus exalted, the new experience of the Spirit – these were the determinative elements in the process of interpretation.[12]

It is significant that mission was undertaken not out of a sense of obligation to follow a given command, but under the inspiration of the Spirit. "We cannot help speaking about what we have seen and heard," reflected the characteristic inner dynamic of the early Christian witnesses. Further, the Spirit-inspired way of life, especially the concern for the needy among them and the willingness to take the necessary steps to meet that need, was also part of the witness (Acts 2:45; 4:32-35). Multitudes were added as a result, to the number of disciples (Acts 2:47b). So though there was official opposition, by and large, the disciples continued to enjoy general acceptance among the people.

The Gospel spreads beyond Jerusalem

However, this soon changed. According to Luke's narrative in Acts, it was a Hellenistic Jewish Christian, Stephen, who first attempted to work out the implications of the coming of Messiah in the person of Jesus of Nazareth for

---

[10] *Ibid., p.90.*

[11] J. B. Green, *The Gospel of Luke,* Cambridge: CUP, 1997, p.18.

[12] James D. G. Dunn, *Unity and Diversity,* p. 101.

the Jewish temple and the Law of Moses. Stephen was promptly accused by the Jewish authorities of saying that Jesus would destroy the Temple and change the traditions of the fathers that were regarded as having come down from the time of Moses (Acts 6:13-14).

The precise nature of the charges against Stephen is unclear. Luke describes the witnesses against him as "false" (Acts 6:13). In his defence speech, Stephen himself refers to the Law as *living oracles* (Acts 7:38); and he accuses his hearers of refusing to obey the Law (Acts 7:53). In fact, the main point in the defence is that the Jews are guilty of disobedience by which they themselves have brought about the destruction of the temple. Stephen's innocence is assumed.

On the other hand, a careful reading of the speech reveals "it is a subtly slanted presentation which climaxes in an outspoken attack on the temple."[13] Perhaps the most significant clue here is that Stephen refers to the temple as *made with human hands* (7:48, NRSV). This is a description that is found elsewhere in the New Testament to contrast the work of humans with that of God,[14] and it is clear that the reference here is intended to be a critical one. So while the evidence regarding Stephen's views on the Jewish law might be somewhat unclear, there is little doubt that he was critical of the narrow cultic nationalism based on the Temple and its worship.

Now it is likely that the more conservative Aramaic-speaking Jewish Christians, including the apostles, did not agree with that analysis. In fact, it is probably correct to conclude that Stephen and his fellow-Hellenists were critical not just of orthodox Jewry, but of the Aramaic-speaking Christians as well for their parochial

conservatism, focused on Jerusalem and the temple. In the event, Stephen was executed by the enraged mob, and this marked the beginning of a period of severe persecution of the disciples, who were forced to flee the city. Although Luke tells us that the persecution was against *the church in Jerusalem* (Acts 8:1), he also informs us that the twelve apostles remained in Jerusalem. There are many who assume that Luke is exaggerating, and that it was just the Hellenistic Christians who were targeted - the local Aramaic-speaking Christians and their leaders (the Apostles) were relatively secure.[15] But this has been dubbed "an unwarranted simplification of early church history."[16] The apostles may have continued to use Jerusalem as headquarters, but the assumption that the Aramaic-speaking Christians remained in Jerusalem, strengthened their ties with Judaism, and eventually became the Judaistic church under James, goes beyond the evidence. Rather, both Aramaic-speaking and Greek-speaking Christians were scattered – the former into the regions of Judea, Samaria and Galilee, and the latter, further afield.[17]

When under persecution, the disciples were empowered by the Spirit to press forward in spite of the opposition and suffering. While still in Jerusalem, the disciples were empowered to speak boldly in the face of organised and systemic opposition (Acts 4:31). And now, when open persecution broke out and the disciples were scattered, they continued to witness to what they had seen, heard and experienced for themselves (Acts 8:4; 11:19-21). Mission was spontaneous.

Michael Green has identified three main missionary motives operative in the early church: first, a sense of gratitude; two, a sense of

---

[13] *Ibid., p. 271.*
[14] E.g. Eph.2:11; Col.2:11.
[15] See e.g. James D.G. Dunn, *Unity and Diversity, p.274.*
[16] G.B. Caird, *The Apostolic Age,* London: Duckworth, 1975, p.86.
[17] F.F. Bruce, *New Testament History,* London: Anchor Books, 1972, p.226.

responsibility; and three, a sense of concern.[18] And to this must be added the conviction that the eschatological age had arrived with the ministry of Jesus Christ and that its consummation might arrive sooner rather than later.

Their methods placed much emphasis on verbal proclamation. There was spontaneous sharing of the good news by all believers. Besides, every opportunity to preach in synagogues or in the open air was seized, and when people responded, they were then taught and nurtured as young believers. And the testimony of their changed lives made a forceful impact.[19]

To The Ends of the Earth

As a result of the persecution, and the resulting scattering of the Jewish followers of Jesus, the good news was proclaimed first to the Samaritans (Acts 8:1b-25), then to the god-fearers and Gentile proselytes (Acts 10), and eventually to people who had had nothing to do with the Jewish faith or with Jesus (Acts 13:6ff.). Each step, every fresh breakthrough, was taken under the guidance and empowering of the Holy Spirit. This comes through the narrative in the Book of Acts in a variety of ways: a) there is a strong emphasis on the purpose of God being fulfilled in the developments that took place;[20] and b) there is a persistent sense that certain things ought to take place because they are according to God's will.[21] And a sort of climax was reached with the conversion of the god-fearer Cornelius and his household. As Peter preached in this home, the Holy Spirit was given to this group of god-fearers just as He had been given to the Jewish Christians at Pentecost. Peter and his band were amazed

for they recognised the parallels immediately. With awe they drew the appropriate conclusion: God does not show favouritism (Acts 10:34). Even as by coming to faith in Jesus the Jewish Christians had become the renewed Israel, the people of God, they were now witnessing on the basis of that same faith, Gentile believers being incorporated into the one people of God.

This incorporation of Gentiles into the renewed people of God had far-reaching ramifications that had to be debated, and clarified over the period of many years and at various times and places. Traditionally, the Jewish vision of the last times had been that of the nations coming to Jerusalem.[22] However, this was to be preceded by instruction going forth out of Zion, *and the word of the Lord from Jerusalem* (Isa.2:3). It has been conjectured, and rightly so, that when Luke describes Peter's preaching on the Day of Pentecost to *Jews from every nation under heaven* (Acts 2:5), he provides us "with a programmatic account of the earliest mission strategy of the Jerusalem church."[23] But in the event, the Christian apostles and other evangelists going to the Gentiles replaced the anticipated pilgrimage of the nations to Jerusalem. So in the Book of Acts, the gospel of Jesus the Messiah is taken from Jerusalem to Samaria, Damascus and Syria, to Asia Minor, to Macedonia and Greece and on to Rome.

There are good grounds to hold that the roots of the Gentile mission can be traced back to Jesus' own teaching and practice. Although Jesus himself made His own people, the nation of Israel, His priority, there is evidence in the Gospel

---

[18] Michael Green, *Evangelism in the Early Church,* Grand Rapids, Eerdmans, 1970, *p. 236-255;* so also D. S. Lim 1997, p.354.

[19] Acts 2:40, 8:25, 18:5, 23:11, 28:23.

[20] Acts 2:23; 4:28; 13:36; 20:27.

[21] Acts 1:16,21; 3:21; 4:12; 5:29; 9:16; 14:22; 16:30; 17:3; 19:21; 20:35; 23:11; 27:24,26.

[22] Isa.2:2-5; Micah 4:1-5; Zech.8:20-23.

[23] R.J. Bauckham, "James and the Jerusalem Church" in *The Book of Acts in its Palestinian Setting,* ed. by R.J. Bauckham, Grand Rapids: Eerdmans, 1995, p. 426.

tradition that He was not totally uninterested in the Gentiles. In the first place, there were occasions when Jesus responded to individuals who sought him out.[24] But this interest was reinforced in his teaching. He clearly indicated that the Jewish assumption that it was one's Jewish ancestry that entitled one to participate in eschatological bliss was wrong and that faith was an all-important criterion. On another occasion, He announced that the consummation would not occur until the good news of the kingdom had been preached to all nations (Mt.24:14), thus implying that a mission to the ends of the earth was a necessity (Mk.13:10). And, after His death and resurrection, He commissioned His disciples to go and make disciples of all nations (Mt.28:19-20).

Schnabel lists four points that he believes confirm that the roots of the Gentile mission go back to Jesus: a) If Jesus foresaw his rejection by the Jewish authorities, it is quite probable that He replaced the Old Testament expectation of the nations streaming to the temple with a mission that would actively take the messianic salvation to the nations; b) If Jesus expected to die and then be raised, it would be quite natural for Him to leave His messianic mission to His disciples; c) Jesus' teaching implies that the kingdom has taken effect among His disciples but not as yet taken full effect in the world at large; this implies a period of worldwide evangelism; and d) It is significant that there was no debate in the early church over the Gentile mission as such, but only about the conditions for entry of Gentile believers into the church.[25]

The lead in this entire process was, to begin with, taken by the apostles (the Twelve),[26] but in due course switched to an erstwhile Jewish leader,

Saul of Tarsus. Saul was party to the execution of Stephen by stoning (Acts 8:1a) and had been, for a time, in the vanguard of the Jewish opposition to the Church; but, in a very dramatic way, he had been confronted by the risen Jesus and had become a disciple himself. Having been touched by the grace of God and commissioned as His apostle to the Gentiles (Acts 9:1-22), he soon became the spearhead of the Gentile mission.

However, before we turn to consider Paul and his mission, we must note that there were other aspects to the expanding mission of the church. To begin with, there continued to be acts of healing and deliverance from evil (Samaria, Acts 8:4-8, Lydia, Acts 9:32f., Joppa, Acts 9:36f). Further there was the impact of changed lives and high ethical and moral standards. So, for example, we have references to the disciples throughout Judea, Galilee and Samaria *living in the fear of the Lord and in the comfort of the Holy Spirit* (Acts 9:31), to *evidence of the grace of God* in Antioch (Acts 11:22), and to concern on the part of the disciples for the brothers living in Judea, when famine struck the area (Acts 11:27-30). We also have corresponding references to the church growing as a result.[27] Finally, as in the early chapters of Acts, we have repeated references here to evidence of supernatural power in the Christian community – the striking of the mercenary Simon the sorcerer (Acts 8:20ff.), the raising and restoring of Tabitha (Acts 9:36-43), and the dramatic conversion of Cornelius and his household (Acts 10:44ff.).

Paul's Missionary Practice

Through debate and controversy, it was gradually clarified that the Gentile mission had

---

[24] Cf. Mk. 5:1-20; 7:24-30; Lk.7:1-10 etc.

[25] E. J. Schnabel, "Jesus and the Beginnings of the Mission to the Gentiles," in J.B. Green & M. Turner, eds. *Jesus of Nazareth: Lord and Christ,* Grand Rapids: Eerdmans, 1997, p.753.

[26] Acts 1:13,25-26; 11:1.

[27] Acts 8:12, 9:31, 11:21, 24.

as much validity as the Jewish mission. In recognition of the legitimacy of the latter, Paul set up his base in Syrian Antioch, a city about 300 miles to the north of Jerusalem. From this base, Paul and various selected colleagues made three missionary journeys, visiting the great metropolitan centres of the first-century Roman empire, and establishing in them viable, self-supporting and self-sustaining communities of disciples of Jesus.

Paul the missionary-pastor

In Rom.15:15-21, Paul gives some important insights into his understanding of his own mission as the Apostle to the Gentiles. It is quite clear that he did not understand his task as merely that of an itinerant evangelist. He was indeed an evangelist, and through his ministry congregations of new believers sprung up in the metropolitan centres that he visited. But he remained with those who responded to his evangelistic preaching until he had grounded them in the 'faith'. His task, therefore, was not only to found but also to nurture new congregations until they were strong enough to stand and grow on their own. Of course, on occasions there were times when he was hounded out of certain cities or townships, by those who opposed his ministry for differing reasons (e.g. from Thessalonica, Acts 17:1-9). But these were the exceptions that prove the rule, and the agony and concern that are reflected in, for example, his correspondence to the Thessalonian church confirm that he was distressed because he had not had the satisfaction of seeing them established before he left them (1 Thess.2:17-3:5). Further, his practice of writing pastoral letters to the churches he founded and others that had come under his pastoral oversight, of visiting them as

and when possible or necessary, and sending his fellow-workers to visit them on certain occasions, confirms that he understood his task to be one of nurture toward spiritual maturity.

From the passage in Romans 15, we learn that at the time of writing, Paul felt that he had completed what he had set out to do in the north-eastern quadrant of the first-century Mediterranean world, and that he was now planning to move westwards to begin work in the north-western quadrant (Italy and Spain). It is quite unlikely, when Paul said, *I have fully proclaimed the good news of Christ* (vs. 19) and (*Now there is*) *no further place for me to work in these regions* (vs.23), that he meant that the regions where he had been working had become wholly Christian. What he probably meant was that there were now self-sustaining congregations that could take responsibility for evangelising the surrounding areas.[28] Besides, he expressly states that his policy was not to build on another's foundation, but rather to work in pioneer contexts. Bosch suggests that the primary reason for this was the sense of urgency and shortness of time – under the circumstances going to places that had already been evangelised by someone else would amount to bad stewardship.[29]

It is important, too, to note that Paul's strategy was to go first to his own people, the Jews. This is seen repeatedly in the Book of Acts: in Pisidian Antioch (13:46), Corinth (18:6) and Ephesus (19:8-10), and it is only when the Jews refused the gospel that the Apostle and his colleagues turned to the Gentiles (13:46-48). There is no reason to be sceptical about the historical accuracy of Luke's narrative on this point,[30] Paul confirmed this in his letters. Paul affirms the Jewish privilege, as in Rom.1:16; 2:10 et al; but

---

[28] So e.g. Marshall 2000, p.104. We know of at least one example of this – the church in Colossae was founded by one of the Christians from Ephesus.

[29] David J. Bosch, *Transforming Mission*, Mary Knoll, NY: Orbis, 1991, p.131. See also C.K. Barrett, *The Epistle to the Romans*, London: A. & C. Black, 1971, p.277.

[30] Wayne A. Meeks, *The First Urban Christians*, New Haven/London: A. & C. Black, 1971, p.277.

he also holds that their rejection of the gospel has rightly opened up the way for it to be offered to the Gentiles (Rom.10:16-21). There is good reason to hold that this aspect of Paul's missionary practice reflects Paul's conviction that the mission to the Gentiles and the mission to the Jews went hand in hand. "The shape of his mission is that he perceives himself to be driven by the conviction that his ministry is in direct continuity with the ministry given to Israel to be a light to lighten the Gentiles."[31]

Paul the Team-leader

Another noteworthy feature of Paul's strategy was that his was a team-effort. Three categories of co-workers have been identified in the Pauline circle: first, the most intimate circle, comprising Barnabas, Silas and Timothy; second, independent co-workers like Priscilla and Acquilla, and Titus; and third, representatives from the local churches such as Epaphroditus, Epaphras, Gaius and so on. And it has been suggested that these colleagues were, in some sense, representatives of their respective churches, and were commissioned to participate in Paul's mission. In this way, the different churches themselves became partners with Paul in the gospel.[32]

According to Luke's account in the Book of Acts, on all three of his missionary journeys, select colleagues accompanied Paul. The word 'select' is important, for at the beginning of the second journey, Paul and Barnabas differed strongly over whether John Mark ought to join them or not (Acts 15:37-40). John Mark had started out with them on the first journey, but for reasons that are not stated in the narrative, left his colleagues mid-way, and returned to Jerusalem. It is clear from the fact that Paul was

even prepared to forfeit the partnership of Barnabas on the second journey, that he felt very strongly that John Mark was not a suitable partner.

Now John Mark left soon after the ministry to and conversion of the Roman official, Sergius Paulus, in Cyprus (Acts 13:13). Since John Mark's home in Jerusalem was apparently one of the house-churches (see Acts 12:12), it may be assumed that he was fully aware of the debate over the Gentile mission in the Jerusalem church. If evangelising god-fearers was controversial, it could be safely conjectured that the evangelisation of a pagan like Sergius Paulus would cause even more of a furor. Under the circumstances, it appears that John Mark decided that it would be wiser to withdraw from Paul's missionary endeavours until the matter was sorted out. This would be all the more true if John Mark were in some sense, a representative of the church in Jerusalem, on the evangelistic team.

But Paul realised that behind this timidity was a lack of commitment to the cause of the Gentile mission or, at least, that John Mark was unsure of himself regarding the matter. And if there was one thing that Paul found hard to take, it was a lack of commitment or conviction. Barnabas, on the other hand, acted true to form, for it was he who had trusted Paul as a new convert and encouraged the other disciples to accept him as such (Acts 9:27-28). So, in this situation, Barnabas felt that John Mark ought to be given another chance, rather than rejected altogether. And he was prepared to pay the price of being rejected himself in his endeavour to encourage and build up people.

In the place of Barnabas and John Mark, Paul invited a young man named Timothy to join his team of missioners on the second missionary

---

[31]G. Goldsworthy, "Biblical Theology and the Shape of Paul's Mission" in *The Gospel to the Nations: Perspectives on Paul's Mission,* ed.by Peter Bolt and Mark Thompson, IVP / Apollos, 2000, p. 16.

[32] So also W. H. Ollrog, *Paulus and Seine Mitarbeiter,* Neukirchen-Vluyn: Neukirchener Verlag, 1979, pp. 119-125, cited in David J. Bosch, *Transforming Mission,* p. 132.

journey (Acts 16:1ff). Timothy was from Lystra, and probably came to faith in Christ when Paul made his first visit to Lystra (Acts 14:8ff). Paul's sensitive and meticulous mentoring of Timothy is an interesting example of his nurturing of younger leaders. Besides inviting Timothy to join him on the second missionary journey, Paul entrusted Timothy with some very sensitive and delicate missions. For example, from the Thessalonian correspondence we learn that when Paul was concerned for the new Christians in Thessalonica, he sent Timothy to Thessalonica to determine how they were doing and to strengthen and encourage them even as they faced persecution that was a carry over from the persecution that Paul had suffered at the hands of the unbelieving Jews in that city. According to 1 Thess.3:6ff. we gather that Timothy completed this task very satisfactorily and brought back encouraging news of the Thessalonians to Paul.

Some time later, Paul entrusted to Timothy another sensitive and delicate task. Although Paul had founded the Church in Corinth, his relationship with the Church had deteriorated over time, partly as a result of various persons who claimed to be apostles, but whose claim Paul regarded as false. The exact details relating to the case are unclear, but what is clear is that these "apostles" had indulged in a lot of mudslinging and undermining of Paul's authority as an apostle, in their bid to turn the church against Paul. When the relationship with the church appeared to be approaching breaking point, Paul turned to Timothy to pay a visit to Corinth on his behalf, and to explain his position to the church. But it would appear that the church did not treat Timothy very kindly, and the situation deteriorated further. Eventually, Paul had to turn to another of his colleagues, Titus, to visit Corinth bearing a "stern" or "painful" letter, and this expedient led eventually to a resolution of the problem.

The above examples give us interesting and important insights into the methods the Apostle used to initiate chosen colleagues to share his mission and eventually to take up independent charge of various mission fields. If developing a second and third line of leadership is a characteristic of a good leader, Paul was certainly a good leader.

Paul and the Church in Jerusalem

In the context of Paul's working with others, his relationship to the church in Jerusalem is important. In Galatians 1 Paul states that the gospel that he preached was not something that man made up and that he had not received it from man, nor was he taught it; rather he had received it by revelation from Jesus Christ (vs.11-12). Nevertheless, as he proceeds to narrate the events relating to his conversion and apostolic commissioning, he relates how he went up to Jerusalem and met Peter and James (vs.18-19). Besides, his narrative in Gal.2 clearly shows that Paul valued very highly the recognition on the part of the leadership of the church – "the pillars" - in Jerusalem that he had been *entrusted with the gospel for the uncircumcised, just as Peter had been entrusted with the gospel for the circumcised* (vs.7) and on that basis gave him and Barnabas the right hand of fellowship. As Dunn points out:

> The action indicates a formal agreement, clearly set out, and not simply a private arrangement or vague expression of good will. The thought here is of the hand-shake as an expression of what the pillars and Paul and Barnabas already shared in common, which here must include their common faith in Messiah Jesus and their agreement regarding the gospel, as the basis of the specific agreement on the division of responsibility.[33]

Paul himself indicates that he recognised that this relationship could have ramifications for his

---

[33]James D.G. Dunn, *The Epistle to the Galatians*, Peabody, Massachusetts Hendrickson Publishers, 1995, p.110.

mission to the Gentiles. He knew that, if there was opposition from the church in Jerusalem, his mission could be unnecessarily hindered, and he wanted to do whatever was necessary to ensure that this did not happen (Gal.2:2). "Paul's ministry thus unfolds in a creative tension between loyalty to the first apostles and their message on the one hand and an overpowering awareness of the uniqueness of his own calling and commission on the other."[34]

So there were pragmatic reasons for Paul being desirous for a good working relationship with the church in Jerusalem. However, there were theological reasons as well. On the one hand, Paul's going up to Jerusalem to *lay before (the acknowledged leaders) the gospel that (he) proclaimed among the Gentiles* was an acknowledgement – at least implicitly – of the primacy of the church in Jerusalem in salvation history; on the other hand, it was also a reflection of the importance Paul placed on the unity of Jews and Gentiles in Christ.[35]

The Man and his Message

Bernard Smyth observes:

> Preaching is truth mediated through personality. Our preaching ...(ought to) increasingly take its life from our personal immersion in life and become a reflection of our own Christian experience and enthusiasm. In a sense it becomes personal testimony to the presence and power of the Lord Jesus working in our lives. If it does not grow into something like that, it can hardly be called Christian preaching at all.[36]

The correctness of this observation can be illustrated from the life and ministry of Paul. A noteworthy aspect of Paul's missionary-leadership is his repeated exhortation to his readers to follow his example even as he followed

Christ. One of the earliest of these references is in 1 Thess.1 where Paul is reminding the Thessalonian church of his initial evangelising visit to the city when he had founded the church. In vs.6 he refers to their having become imitators "of us and of the Lord" in receiving the word in much affliction. In 2:14-16 there is a further reference to their suffering for the sake of the gospel and it becomes apparent a) that Paul saw an intrinsic connection between Christ's suffering and death, his own suffering and that of his fellow-missionaries, and the suffering of the church in Judea and Thessalonica for the sake of the gospel; and b) that God's power in the lives of his people is manifest most clearly in the context of suffering.

In 2 Thess.3:3-9 Paul refers twice to his policy of voluntary renunciation of his apostolic rights in the interest of the Gospel. Here too he speaks of himself as an example for his readers to follow, but emphasises another aspect – that of self-sacrificing industry.

The Apostle uses the same language of "imitation" of his example in two contexts in the first letter to the Corinthian church. In 3:3-4:21, he is dealing with the problem of cliques in the church, and the consequent threat of disunity. While he seeks to set right their relationship to the various Christian leaders and teachers who had come to Corinth, he holds that his relationship to them is uniquely that of a spiritual father. Therefore, he says, *be imitators of me* (1 Cor.4:16). In this context, Paul means that they ought to follow his *ways in Christ Jesus* that are based on basic principles that formed part of his teaching, and that Timothy was being sent to reiterate this.

In 10:33, Paul concludes his discussion in chapters 8-10 on *idol-meal* with an explicit

---

[34] David J. Bosch, *Transforming Mission*, p. 129.

[35] See James D. C. Dunn, *The Epistle*, p. 94.

[36] Bernard T. Smyth, *Paul: Mystic and Missionary*, Maryknoll; NY: Orbis, 1980, p. 119.

challenge to his readers to follow his example. Paul tells them that he is governed in everything he does by his concern for others and their spiritual well-being. This allusion to his own conduct is paralleled in 8:13 where he concludes the preceding argument with an emphatic assertion of his willingness to curtail his liberty in the interests of his fellow-believers.

However, 8:13 also introduces a longer section, 9:1-27, in which the Apostle states and illustrates a basic ethical principle that underlies his conduct – namely, that he has become all things to all people, that he might by all means save some (9:22). In verses 24-27 Paul reaches the crowning point of what he has to say as he develops further the theme of self-control and the voluntary restriction of one's rights and liberty in the interests of the Gospel. "The Apostle's body and everything included in physical life, his hopes, plans, ambitions, desires, comforts and pleasures – all these subjected to the one goal, the effectiveness of the gospel that he preached."[37] In other words, when the Apostle holds himself up as an example, he is referring to his self-control and the voluntary restriction of his rights and liberty in the cause of the Gospel, which he understands as his being conformed to the cross of Christian discipleship.

This is confirmed further in his letter to the Philippians, where, once again, he exhorts his readers to *join in imitating* him (3:17). In this section of the letter, Paul has been describing the change that had come about in his value-system when confronted by the risen Christ on the road to Damascus. He refers particularly to the fact that in contrast to his past confidence in his Jewish birth and upbringing, his primary concern now was to know Christ and to be conformed to him in his death and resurrection (3:10-11). He had once striven for legal righteousness, but now he strains forward to the eschatological righteousness that believers are called to in Christ. And it is this perspective that he would like his readers to have as well.

In other words, Paul was a living illustration of his message that believers are called to Christ likeness. It was clear to all who knew him that he was very serious about being conformed to the likeness of Christ, and that he would not allow anything to come between him and that goal. And that goes a long way towards explaining his extraordinary effectiveness as an evangelist.

The social impact of Paul's mission and message

First century society had its share of social evils and Paul's mission and message impacted it for good in several areas.

In Gal.3:28, Paul says, *There is no longer Jew or Greek, there is no longer slave or free, there is no longer male and female; for all of you are one in Christ Jesus.* Paul's consistent emphasis on the equality of believers helped to bring down major barriers in contemporary society. The major one was that between Jews and Gentiles. But by emphasising that God has in Christ created a new humanity, and adamantly resisting all efforts on the part of some to impose Jewish customs and legal obligations on the Gentiles, the Apostle helped establish the primacy of the unity of Christians over racial and cultural barriers.

There is little doubt that there would have been many households in the Pauline churches that had both masters and slaves.[38] The Apostle has been criticised for not attacking the institution of slavery as such. But Paul's teaching and personal contacts with masters and slaves must have had an impact. On the one hand, Paul used the metaphor of slavery to elucidate his teaching

---

[37] V.C. Pfitzner, *Paul and the Agon Motif,* Leiden, Novt Suppl. 16, p. 93.

[38] Cf. Philem; 1 Cor.7:21; Eph.6:5-9; Col.3:22-4:1; 1 Tim.6:1-2.

on salvation: like those who were once slaves, believers in Christ have been set free from sin. Further, no matter whether freedman or slave, believers are brothers and sisters in Christ and that relationship must be given priority. A good example is found in the so-called household codes in Colossians and Ephesians.[39] Paul addresses both masters and slaves, and the overall thrust is that both are accountable for their behaviour and attitudes to their common Lord, Jesus. A further example is Paul's letter to Philemon, in which he deals with the very delicate matter of the runaway slave, Onesimus, who had since become a Christian. While fulfilling his obligation to send him back to his master, he nevertheless appeals to Philemon to receive him back as a brother in the Lord. O'Brien's comments help to clarify the matter:

> The issue was not that of an acceptance of an institution sanctioned by law and part of the fabric of Graeco-Roman society; nor was it a question of how to react to a demand for its abolition. Rather, it concerned the tension between the freedom given in Christ and the "slavery" in which Christian slaves are to continue to serve their earthly masters.[40]

The impact of Paul's teaching and practice on the status of women in society must be assessed in the light of three lines of evidence: a) his teaching on marriage and on the relationship of husbands and wives; b) his teaching on women in Christian ministry; and c) the references to women among his own colleagues, co-workers and acquaintances.

While a detailed consideration of Paul's teaching on marriage or on women in ministry is out of the scope of this essay, suffice it to say that the contention of some that Paul was a misogynist goes far beyond the evidence. Paul's basic assumption is that women and men are intended to be complementary rather than wholly equal. This assumption is the basis of much of his teaching in both these areas.

However, it is worth noting that a remarkable number of women are mentioned as Paul's associates both in Acts and in his letters. Several of them were engaged in ministries of teaching and preaching.[41] Others who are described as *working hard* in Rom.16:6,12, were involved in unspecified church work, and others were members of wealthy families who supported Paul as benefactors and who dedicated their homes for use as house churches.[42] This would suggest that Paul was more progressive than chauvinistic in his attitude to women.

The Religious Context of the Pauline Mission

Religious challenges for the early Christian mission: Schnabel[43] lists various religious challenges that the early missionaries faced: a) The lack of relevant models. The task that the early missionaries set themselves – namely, to convince people to change their religious convictions, to alter patterns of behaviour in everyday life and to switch loyalty from family, city or country to a new community – was a totally unfamiliar one to both the missionaries and their audiences. b) The dissimilarity of basic beliefs and values. The good news that spoke about a Jewish Messiah who died on the cross and was raised from the dead was deeply incompatible with traditional Jewish and pagan conceptions of God and of salvation. c) The likelihood of misunderstanding. For a pagan to switch allegiance to the worship of one God while denying the existence of all the other gods would

---

[39] Col.3:22-4:1; Eph.6:5-9.
[40] P.T. O'Brien, *The Letter to the Ephesians,* Grand Rapids: Eerdmans/ Leicester: Apollos, 1999, p.448.
[41] Rom.16:1,3,7; Phil.4:2-3; Acts 18:26.
[42] Rom.16:15; Col.4:15; Philem 1-2; cf. Rom.16:13,15-16; Acts 16:4-15,40. See Ellis 1993:187.
[43] E.J. Schnabel, "Jesus and the Beginnings", 1997, p.760f.

incur the charge of atheism, which might lead to vilification and slander or to outright persecution. The success of the Christian mission in the face of such challenges is credited by Luke to the power of the Holy Spirit.[44]

Contexualisation of the good news: The Graeco-Roman world in the first century C.E. was one of religious plurality, and the Christians found it necessary to contextualise the good news of Jesus as they addressed different audiences. The setting of the narrative in the early chapters of the Book of Acts is Jerusalem and its surroundings, and the *kerygma* is appropriate to Jewish audiences: there is repeated reference to the Jewish scriptures and to the Jewish messianic hope, the terminology is Jewish, and the theme of fulfilment appears over and over again. But once the setting changes to that of the Gentile mission, the kerygma changes as well. The strong Jewish elements are now absent, and instead, we have references to God's self-revelation in creation and in human history.

Luke gives us a sample in Acts 13:13-52 of the preaching to an audience consisting of Jews and *god-fearers* in Pisidian Antioch. The first part of the sermon surveys salvation history from Abraham to David. But in verse 23, Paul suddenly moves from David to Jesus as his descendant who is the promised Saviour. He then elaborates on the prophetic message, that should have been recognised as pointing to Jesus, but has been unintentionally fulfilled in the execution of Jesus (vs.26-29). But this was followed by a spectacular climax to salvation history – the resurrection from the dead of the Lord Jesus (vs.30-41). So the theme is that of fulfilment, and the thrust is solidly Christological.

We have also two samples of the preaching to Gentile audiences. In Lystra, Paul and Barnabas heal a cripple, and the local populace try to honour them (Acts 14:1ff). But the apostles realise from their actions that the people think that they are followers of local Greek deities, and seize the opportunity to proclaim the true and living God to them. They draw attention to the fact that He is the Creator God, and that the regularity of the seasons testifies to His goodness towards His creation. On the other hand, it is also true that "He allowed all the nations to follow their own ways"(Acts 14:16). But the apostle proceeds to issue a call to repentance, and to turn from the worthless things that idols are, to the living God.

There are at least three points to note in their preaching: One, creation bears witness to God's nature as wholly Other - as the Creator God he is distinct from creation - and to His goodness to His creation. Two, God does not force himself upon His creatures, but leaves them to the consequences of their own choices. And three, by preaching Jesus as Lord, they proclaim Him as being the manifestation of the one true God and not merely as an addition to an already overcrowded pantheon.[45]

The second sample that Luke gives us is in Acts 17: 24-30. Paul is in Athens, and is deeply distressed by the idolatry all around him. He is given an opportunity to speak at the Areopagus, and uses it to the full. He begins, as he had done at Lystra, with the Creator God, who is the source and sustainer of life (17:24-25). He dismisses idolatry as wrongful thinking (17: 29), and issues a call to repentance in the light of a coming day of judgment.

There are several points of interest in this passage. To begin with, it is important to note that Paul was deeply distressed by the idolatry of the Athenians. While he was prepared to recognize that they might worship many gods and many lords, he knew, as a Christian believer, that

---

[44] Acts 8:29, 39; 10:10-20, 47; 13:4,9; 1 Thess. 1:4-6; 1 Cor.2:5.

[45] J.B. Green, *The Theology of the Gospel of Luke,* Cambridge: CUP, 1995, p. 152.

there was but one God, the Father, and but one Lord, Jesus Christ (1 Cor.8: 6). "The phrase 'but for us' (in 1 Cor.8: 6) indicates that there was a clear dividing line for the Christian community on the issue of religious pluralism."[46] With reference to this, Carson makes a significant comment, "The New Testament writers did not distinguish the pluralism of the day from the idolatry of the day."[47]

In the course of what he has to say, the Apostle says that God has created the nations from a common ancestor, and has providentially ordered their affairs so that "they would search for God and perhaps grope for him and find him" (17: 27). On the face of it, this could be taken to imply that it is possible that some that have never heard the gospel of Jesus Christ might nonetheless grope after and find God. Indeed, Paul's appeals to the Greek poets Epimenides and Aratus at this point appear to imply that this is not a hopeless quest.[48] But the reference immediately after this to the futility of idolatry (17: 29) suggests that Paul intends to say that they had been groping after idols and other gods of their own making instead of the true and living God. Consequently, they had remained ignorant of the true God. So the Apostle now issues a call to repentance, for although God was willing to overlook past ignorance, he had now appointed one who would be humankind's future Judge. Escape from this judgment "involved repentance including the repudiation of the worship of idols and the pluralism which that implied."[49]

Several scholars have drawn attention to the similarity of the line of argument in this passage and that in Rom.1: 18-32. Michael Green, for example, draws out the points of comparison: "The unity of God, the inanity of idols, and the ethical implications of idolatrous living in wilful estrangement from the true God, are made abundantly plain."[50]

It is important to note that in both these samples of Paul's preaching to Gentile audiences, the Apostle made direct comments on religious pluralism. Winter underlines the point:

> The reason that the matter of religious pluralism was discussed in public preaching was simply that it was an essential component of the gospel presentation. Conversion involved a rejection of the pluralistic perception of divinity present in an epiphany or in any idol.[51]

There is a further point that must be noted. In Acts 17:30 (cf. Acts 14:16), there is a clear implication that the "natural revelation" of God belongs to the past, for it has been superseded by his self-revelation in Christ. In this connection, Klaas Runia says, "With a few exceptions Christian theology has always recognized a general self-revelation of God in nature and in man's morality and conscience, but it also recognized that this revelation is always suppressed by man's wickedness (Rom.1:18), the result being that all religions are a mixture of truth and error, of true and false trails. For this reason a new revelation was necessary, a revelation that started immediately after the fall and had its culmination in the appearance of Jesus Christ."[52]

---

[46] Bruce W. Winter, "In Public and in Private: Early Christians and Religious Pluralism," in *One God, One Lord in a World of Religious Pluralism*, ed.by A.D. Clarke and B. Winter, Cambridge: Tyndale House, p. 145.

[47] D. A. Carson, *The Gagging of God: Christianity Confronts Pluralism*, Grand Rapids: Zondervan, 1996, p.497.

[48] So. E.g. Jacques Dupuis, *Toward a Christian Theology of Religious Pluralism*, Anand, Gujarat: Gujarat Sahitya Prakash, 2001, p. 49.

[49] Bruce W. Winter, "In Public and in Private," p. 142.

[50] Michael Green, *Evangelism in the Early Church*, 1984, pp.154-155.

[51] Bruce W. Winter, "In Public and in Private," p. 142.

[52] Klaas Runia, "Why Christianity of all Religions?", *Evangelical Review of Theology*, 22:3, 1998, p.254.

The Social Context of the Pauline Mission

Paul came from Tarsus and had apparently received a good education in Jerusalem, in the school of Gamaliel. As a Roman citizen, he was entitled to many privileges and made use of them occasionally.[53] Roman citizenship generally implied an affluent background and Paul appears to have had access to high authorities in Jerusalem.

We have already noted that whenever Paul visited a city for the first time, he usually made his way to the synagogue.[54] This appears to have been a strategy to use the existing social networks to which he related in order to make contact with people. Another aspect of his strategy was to seek out a household that would allow him to use their home as a sort of base for his missionary work.[55] In some cases, the house was identified as the place in which believers met for worship.[56]

Similarly, being a tentmaker by profession, he sought out others in the same trade, including Priscilla and Acquila.[57] On the basis of references in his letters to his "labour" and "toil"[58] it has been conjectured that tent-making was central to Paul's life. It is significant, for example, that Paul connects his work with his ministry (1 Thess.2:9). This probably means that Paul carried on his evangelistic ministry while he worked on his tents, that is, he talked about his faith in Christ to his customers.

From his letters, we gather that some of his churches resented the fact that Paul did not accept support from them, but preferred to earn his living through tent-making. In a society where it was conventional for wealthy patrons to provide for visiting preachers and teachers, his refusal of support was considered particularly offensive. If so, Paul must have had strong reasons for his insistence on supporting himself and he gives us at least two of these reasons in his letters.

First, Paul wanted to distance himself from others whom he describes as *peddlers of God's word* (2 Cor.2:17a), who *practise cunning and falsify God's word* (2 Cor.4:2) and who *prey upon* others (2 Cor.11:20). "This vocabulary implies the receipt of improper payment, the watering down of the message and the exploitation of the hearers." In contrast to all such, Paul saw himself and his colleagues in Christ as *persons of sincerity, sent from God and standing in his presence* (2 Cor.2:17b). As such, he was concerned that there was no reason at all for anyone to question his motives.

Second, Paul tells the Corinthians that he felt a sense of obligation to preach the gospel because he had been called to be an apostle. Further, although he was aware of his right to support from those to whom he ministered, he chose to forfeit that right and to proclaim the gospel free of cost (1 Cor.9:15-18). By so doing, he exemplified the message he preached – that God's grace is freely offered to all in Christ.

Although Paul refused support from the church in Corinth and Thessalonica (1 Thess.2:9), he tells the Corinthians in 2 Cor.11:9 that he accepted support from the Macedonian Christians while he was in Corinth. Further, in Phil.4:10-20, he thanks the church in Philippi for its support

---

[53] Acts 16:37; 22:22-29.

[54] Acts 13:5,14; 14:1; 17:2; 18:4; 19:8.

[55] Acts 16:15; 17:7; 18:1-3, 7-8; 1 Cor.16:15.

[56] Rom.16:5; 1 Cor.6:19; Col.4:15; Philem 2.

[57] Meeks, who rejects Luke's picture of Paul beginning in the synagogues and Jewish places of worship or prayer, holds that his fellow artisans were probably his first contacts when he visited a city for the first time. Wayne A. Meeks, *The First Urban Christians*, p. 29. Since there are references to Ananias and Sapphira being in various cities, it is likely that they were manufacturers and traders in tents and related goods, who travelled from city to city. (Acts 18:1-3, 26; Rom.16:3-4). Wayne A. Meeks, *op. cit.*, p. 29.

[58] 1 Cor.4:10-12; 2 Cor.11:27.

while he was in Thessalonica. From this it appears "that Paul did not accept support from any church when he was actively working in that church. But after he had established a church, he expected them to contribute to the cause of the gospel. This is (an) example of Paul putting the gospel first and using money in ways that furthered the preaching of the gospel rather than hindering it."[59]

Paul's Missionary Thinking

The Damascus Road Experience: There has been much scholarly debate regarding the theological underpinning of Paul's missionary vocation, which has, quite justifiably, focussed on his encounter with the risen Jesus on the road to Damascus. This momentous event is described three times in Luke's narrative in the Book of Acts[60] and Paul himself makes reference to it in several of his letters. In one of his earliest letters, the Apostle describes the encounter in terms that unmistakably echo the prophetical books. In Isa.49:1-6, the Servant says that he was called from the womb, before being sent as a light to the Gentiles. Here Paul says, *God called me through his grace,* he says, *and was pleased to reveal his Son to me* (Gal.1:15-16). This has been understood to mean that as a result of this encounter, Paul came to understand the true identity of Jesus Christ, and this is undoubtedly correct. In 2 Cor.4:4-6, Paul refers to God *who has shone in our hearts to give the light of the knowledge of the glory of God in the face of Christ,* and this confirms that the Damascus Road experience, was, in the first instance, Christological in its significance.

However, in Gal.1:16, there follows a purpose clause: *so that I might proclaim him among the Gentiles.* This suggests that the Damascus Road experience did not merely constitute his call to Christian discipleship, but was also his commissioning as missioner to the Gentiles. In Luke's narrative in Acts 9:1-22, this commissioning takes place separately through the ministry of a disciple named Ananias. But it is very much part and parcel of the one event, and the overall effect of separating it in this way is to bring out its particular significance. "His concept of apostleship is characterised by the fact of his being simultaneously converted, entrusted with the gospel, and sent to the Gentiles."[61]

If so, the question arises, what was the relationship, if any, between Paul's call and his commission to mission to the Gentiles? One suggestion is that the realisation of the true identity of Jesus necessarily led Paul to a revision of his understanding of the role of the Law in salvation history. This in turn led to the conclusion that if salvation was not related to obedience of the Jewish Law, it was not restricted to the Jews alone. In other words, salvation was universal, and this was the basis of his commission to the Gentile mission.

But this has been challenged on the grounds that universalism does not necessarily imply mission. The conviction that anyone may be admitted is not at all the same as the conviction that everyone must be actively invited. Further, Paul understands his call to Gentile mission as a specific individual assignment, which he grounds not in a common experience in Christ but in a unique personal experience that set him apart.[62] Bowers agrees with the dual understanding of Paul's Damascus road experience – both encounter and call. His encounter with Jesus as once-dead-but-now-risen called forth certain theological adjustments, and these adjustments were then worked out within the framework of

---

[59] J.M. Everts, "Financial Support," in *Dictionary of Paul and His Letters* [DPL], ed. by Gerald F. Hawthorne, Ralph P. Martin and Daniel G. Reid, Leicester: IVP, 1993, p. 300.

[60] 9:1-19; 22:4-16; and 26:9-19.

[61] Ferdinard Hahn, *Mission in the New Testament*, ed. by Frank Clarke, London: SCM, 1965, p. 98.

[62] W. P. Bowers, "Mission" in Gerald F. Hawthorne et.al., *Dictionary of Paul and His Letters*, p. 615.

a special commission to Gentile mission. "It was the christological encounter that provided the creative force in Paul's theological renovation, and the commission that determined its direction of development. Either without the other cannot adequately account for all the historical and theological data involved."[63]

Pauline Eschatology: Another aspect of Paul's theology of mission is its eschatological framework. In an important book published in 1954, Johannes Munck proposed that Paul's sense of mission vocation must be sorted out and clarified within a framework of eschatological beliefs. Paul took his Gentile mission vocation to be decisively connected with the events of the consummation. His call was to fulfil the Old Testament eschatological expectation of the ingathering of the nations, and to this end he undertook to proclaim the good news to the ends of the earth before the final day. Paul regarded himself as the one on whom the arrival of the Messianic age depends. The completion of his own Gentile mission assignment would thus precipitate the final events leading to the Parousia. This in turn explains, Munck argued, the intensity of Paul's vocational self-consciousness and of his missionary endeavour.[64]

But this position has been criticised on two grounds. On the one hand, it must be conceded, Paul did have a very high sense of his vocational significance. But it is equally true that Paul recognised the limitation and interdependency of his vocation. Thus, as we have already seen above, his mission characteristically functioned as a collaborative rather than an individual effort. In 1 Cor 3:4-9, Paul describes the efforts of others like Apollos as complementary under God. Indeed Paul's sensitivity to spheres of labour, and his annoyance at violation of such spheres, is

itself an acknowledgement of the limits of his own contribution in the spread of the good news, (2 Cor.10:12-16; Rom.15:18-21). Even when he was imprisoned, he accepted the provocative endeavours of his opponents, so long as the proclamation continued, (Phil.1:15-18). Paul understood his part in the eschatological mission to be consequential, but not uniquely decisive.[65]

Besides, while Munck assumes a consistently future orientation for the eschatological dimension of Paul's missionary understanding, clearly for Paul, the most decisive event of the End had already taken place in Jesus Christ, and the determinative experience for his own life and mission had been when this recognition had been forced upon him by a personal messianic encounter and commission. For him the End had already arrived, eschatological expectation had given way to eschatological experience, and the long-expected ingathering of the nations was now being fulfilled. He conceived of his Gentile mission as eschatological in nature principally not by virtue of some connection with a yet future event but by virtue of its evident connections with a past one. Therefore, Paul can describe his mission as a direct extension of the messianic mission that God had already initiated in Christ (2 Cor.5:19-20).

What has now already been made available at the end of time in the Messiah is to be made available by Paul himself in a geographically defined outreach to the nations, in fulfilment of the Old Testament eschatological promises, and it is to be realised in representative communities that demonstrate the life of the new age. By thus fulfilling the eschatological promise of blessing to the nations, Paul in his mission helps to complete that task that in the divine economy is to precede the final denouement.[66]

---

[63] *Ibid.*

[64] J. Munck, *Paul and the Salvation of Mankind,* Atlanta: John Knox, 1954, p. 41.

[65] W. P. Bowers, *Mission,* p. 616.

[66] *Ibid.*

The clearest sign of the End having already arrived was, for Paul, the presence of the Spirit in the lives of Christians and in the churches. The Spirit is the firstfruit, the down-payment, the *pledge of our inheritance toward redemption as God's people* (Eph.1:14). The Church, as the community of the Spirit, lives in the tension between the "already" and the "not yet". One of the passages in which Paul elaborates on what it means to live in this tension is 2 Cor.4:7-10. The late Bishop Leslie Newbigin called this "the classic definition of mission."[67] And Bosch says the passage "clearly characterises the Pauline mission as an eschatological event: only within the horizon of the expectation of the end can the tension between suffering and glory be sustained." [68]

The Pauline Mission and Israel

Although the church's mission to the Gentiles, spearheaded as it was by Paul, was extraordinarily successful, its mission to the Jews gradually petered out, and there is reason to believe that by the sixth decade of the first century, there were hardly any Jews becoming Christian disciples.

It is very clear that Paul was deeply distressed by this state of affairs. His outburst in Rom.9:1-3 is perhaps the clearest expression of his pain and agony at the thought of the adamant unbelief of the large majority of his people. And these words introduce a discussion on the implications of the gospel of salvation by grace through faith for the historic covenant promises made to the chosen people, the Jews (Rom.9-11).

In this discussion, Paul first relates the theme of God's sovereign choice (9:6-30) to the rejection of Jesus as Messiah by the majority of Israel on the one hand and to the Gentiles coming to faith on the other (9:31-11:10). Then in 11:11ff.

he describes the "mystery" of Israel's eventual salvation and how it will come about. Paul begins by explaining the resolute unbelief of the Jews as the result of divine hardening of Israel's heart. However, Paul sees a positive outcome: one, by Israel remaining unbelieving, the Gentiles have been given the chance to hear the good news and to respond to it in faith; and two, the faith of the Gentiles will move Israel to jealousy, and they in turn will come to faith. When the full number of Gentiles have come in, says Paul, all Israel will be saved. When Paul's statements, about Gentiles and Jews, are taken together, it seems probable that he is thinking in representative terms.[69]

There are some scholars who argue on the basis of this passage that the Church has no mission to the Jews, for God will directly accomplish the salvation of Israel. However, the analogy of the olive tree makes it quite clear that this is an incorrect understanding of what Paul is saying. Paul makes no distinction between Jews and Gentiles, for he holds that all become part of the eschatological people of God by faith in Jesus. This is confirmed by a further observation: the main thrust of what Paul has to say in Rom.11:11f. is to warn the Gentile believers against any triumphalistic and arrogant attitude. God is sovereign, and just as he broke off some branches and grafted in others, he could break off the grafted branches if their attitude so warranted. The one and only criterion is faith.

It is likely that the use of the term "mystery" in Rom.11:25 relates to the interrelation of God's dealings with Jews and with Gentiles. Paul has already made the point that by Israel rejecting the gospel, the Gentiles were given the chance to hear it. Further, on the basis of Scripture, Paul holds that their response in faith to the gospel will stir Israel to envy and eventually to their own salvation. So Paul sees his own mission to the

---

[67]Leslie Newbigin, *Mission in Christ's Way,* Geneva: World Council of Churches, 1987, p. 24.

[68] David J. Bosch, *Transforming Mission,* p. 145.

[69] So. C.K. Barrett, *The Epistle to the Romans,* London: A. & C. Black, 1971, p. 224.

Gentiles as ultimately benefiting Israel. "The more (he) makes of (his) Gentile mission the more jealous will the Jews become, and this will lead in the end to what (he) desires – their salvation" (Barrett 1971:215).

The discussion comes to a climax in Rom.11:25-27. In these verses Paul makes the following assertions: a) Israel has experienced a hardening while the Gentiles respond to the gospel; and b) when the *full number has come in*, then all Israel will be saved and the end will come.

Conclusion: An Assessment

Bosch[70] attempts to identify some specific weaknesses of the first Christians in the area of mission:

- There is good reason to believe that Jesus had no intention of founding a new religion. The Twelve were to be the vanguard of all Israel, and, beyond Israel, by implication, of the whole ecumene. But at a very early stage, Christians tended to be more aware of what distinguished them from others than of their calling and responsibility toward those others. And in course of time, the Jesus community simply became a new religion, Christianity.

- Related to this first failure, was a second: what began as a movement turned into an institution.

- The Church proved unable, in the long run, to make Jews feel at home. Beginning as a religious movement that worked exclusively among Jews, it changed, in the forties of the first century, to a movement for Jews and Gentiles alike, but wound up proclaiming its message to Gentiles only.

These points are open to debate. For example, it is a moot point whether the transformation from a movement to an institution was not inevitable.[71] And Bosch himself concedes that after 70 C.E. Pharisaic Judaism became too xenophobic to tolerate anything but a hard-line, exclusive Jewish approach. So the Jews may have contributed to the situation as much as the Church may have.

Be that as it may, there is no gainsaying the observation that the rapid spread of the Christian faith in the first century C.E. was nothing short of remarkable, and several scholars have attempted to uncover the factors that contributed to this phenomenon.

D.S.Lim[72] for example, makes the following observations:

1. The prime agents in evangelism were the ordinary believers, (Acts 8:4;11:19-21), called "informal missionaries". As they gossiped the gospel with conviction and enthusiasm, people were converted and added to the church and its evangelistic force.

2. It is significant that the early church kept their structures simple. To begin with, they had no buildings to maintain, for they met in homes and ministered from house to house, Acts 20:20. Their limited resources were used to support itinerant ministers and the poor among them. As households came to faith, their homes served as centres for prayer and worship, pastoral care and fellowship, hospitality, and especially evangelism.

3. Further, the early Christians were not dependent on a priestly class or a few

---

[70] David J. Bosch, *Transforming Mission*, p. 50f.

[71] D.J. Tidball, "Social Setting of Mission Churches" in *Dictionary of Paul and His Letters*, ed. By Gerald F. Hawthorne, Ralph P. Martin & Daniel G. Reid, IVP, Leicester [DPL], 1993, p. 886.

[72] D.S. Lim, "Evangelism in the Early Church," in *New Testament and Its Developments*, ed. By R. P. Martin and Peter H. Davids, Leicester: IVP [DLNT], 1997, p.394f.

professional religious leaders. Each house church was led by mature adults who, though new in the faith, were capable of taking charge of the prayers and study of the Word in weekly gatherings and in fellowship with neighbouring house churches.

4. The Christians lived transformed lives and exhibited a self-sacrificial love that transcended race, social class, and gender, as shown in their agape feasts. Their witness of courage, endurance, and even joy and serenity in the face of persecution made an impact on their contemporaries.

5. They contextualised their message. To the Jews, Jesus was presented as the Messiah in fulfilment of the high expectations in first century Judaism. Jesus was introduced as the second Moses, (Acts 3:22; 7:37), the eternal Son of David, (Acts 2:25-36), the Son of Man, (Acts 7:56), and the suffering servant, (Acts 3:18;8:34). But to the Gentiles, the evangelists drew on Greek literature and Stoic and Epicurean philosophies when needed, (Acts 17:27-28). When speaking to the religious, they used words like mystery, fullness and eternal life. God was the Creator and provider of all and not dependent on people's idolatrous offerings, (Acts 14:15-17). To others they offered God's forgiveness, (Acts 17:31; 24:25), and freedom from demons, magic, and Fate.

6. Above all, they prayed together, (Acts 4:24-31; 12:12). They recognised that their desire, strength and boldness to evangelise came from above. All important decisions were marked by prayer.

PART II

Theological Studies

The Future of Mission and Mission of the Future: Christian Hope and Christian Mission

PAUL JOSHUA BHAKIARAJ

The Future of Mission

Christian mission is not an end in itself. Judging from the effort devoted to damage limitation and reconstruction of society based on alarmist interpretations of the world it is understandable if one is perhaps not led to believe so. Judging from the frantic activity of some well-meaning leaders and mission executives to impress the importance and urgency of mission, it is understandable if one is perhaps not led to believe so. Judging from the fact that pragmatic, business-like and result-oriented strategies hog the attention of our mission studies curriculum it is understandable if one is perhaps not led to believe so. In practice it seems that many of us work on the assumption that Christian mission is indeed an end in itself.

In contrast, however, to this pervasive ground reality stands scriptural precept. The World Council of Churches (WCC) Document on Mission and Evangelisation rightly states, "the biblical promise of a new earth and a new heaven where love, peace and justice will prevail (Ps 85.7-13; Is 32.17-18, 65.17-25 and Rev 21.1-2) is the end which invites our actions as Christians in history."[1] This well received and widely commended statement underlines the point that, the end of Christian mission is bound up with God's final action not tied to man's finite activity. It suggests that Christian mission is directed towards the end that God will bring about as opposed to the fulfilling of our own temporal agendas, however pious and sacred we may assume them to be. The goal towards which Christian mission works, is not the establishment of a healthy and conducive society for all by a mere rearrangement of existing societal resources but, is the reality that our Sovereign God will usher in, by a decisive exertion of His power and authority, when He will conclusively establish His own radical reign over all of creation. All this suggests that the danger of relying on latent resources rather than the final act of transcendent providence, to shape glorious futures is always present.[2] Our directives could subtly usurp God' designs. Futurology, or our ability to conceive and engineer the future is not the dynamic that animates our mission effort rather it ought to be the grand eschatological hope we possess as disciples of Jesus Christ. The vision of His kingdom established and His name being worshiped unceasingly is the end to which the Church is to be yearning. That perfect *shalom*, which was the original intent of creation, in the end, is indeed the new beginning[3] that divine providence has designed. This *telos* is the future of mission.

---

[1] See "Ecumenical Affirmation: Mission and Evangelism, 1982" in J Scherer and S. Bevans eds. *New Directions in Mission and Evangelism*, Vol. I., New York: Orbis Books, 1992 pp 36-51

[2] See Richard Bauckham & Trevor Hart, "The Shape of Time" in David Fergusson & Marcel Sarot eds. *The Future as God's Gift: Explorations in Christian Eschatology*, Edinburgh: T&T Clark, 2000, pp 41-72.

That, present reality is not what is meant to be, appears as a widely recognised notion. 'What is,' many agree is not 'what ought to be'. Nonetheless, the scriptures reiterate that 'what will be,' by the decisive action of God, can serve as the blueprint for 'what ought to be' in the now. The huge gulf that exists between the two (i.e. 'what is' and 'what will be') represents [or ought to represent] an implicit Christian yearning, a restlessness for what can be. On every occasion we utter the prayer our Lord taught us, pleading for His kingdom to come, is this not the yearning we express? When Paul in Romans 8:22-23 talks about creation groaning in pain, is this not that hunger for deliverance he alludes to? When we cry *Maranatha* is this not the desire, the longing of our hearts?

This deep yearning within us, expressed in these and other ways is eloquently answered by Christian hope. Hope provides us with resources to address these profound desires and engage with those struggles. Hope longs for God's answer to fundamental questions we face and realities we experience. Having been kindled by the mission of Christ when He displayed his Lordship by His life, death and resurrection, it looks forward to the completion of that mission in the final consummation when God will completely vindicate Himself. By looking forward to God's sovereign plan, hope presents in sharp relief the unfortunate shape of the present and consequently demonstrates its potential under the providence of God. Isaiah' vision recorded in 2:4, inscribed on the curved wall of the United Nations building in New York alludes to the potential this vision has in shaping the present. For disciples of Christ hope provides meaning to that temporary dialectic between present and future. Hope opens us to the eschatological future of God and His creation. The shape of this future then acts as the ground for the possibilities of the present and thus represents its defining principle. Gabriel Fackre sums up this understanding succinctly:

> The confidence that the end will truly consummate the purposes of God, as anticipated by Exodus and Easter, energizes the believing community to set up signs on the way to the kingdom and city. Hope moblizes, while despair paralyses. The content of the End —glorified bodies, the "holy city with the radiance of some priceless jewel" (Rev. 21:11), crystal waters and flourishing forests – renders unacceptable emaciated bodies, cities of the homeless and hapless, poisonous rivers and decimated forests.
>
> Eschatology makes us pilgrims and strangers in the wilderness short of the New Creation and disturbers of the facile peace of the way the things are.[4]

Echoing a similar sentiment Oscar Culmann says that hope for God's decisive action in the eschaton "constitutes the keenest incentive to action."[5] With hope as one of life's coordinates, we can live in a present that is shaped by God's promised future and not be determined entirely by our past. That is to say Christian hope for God's final glorification represents the "future of mission" and simultaneously moulds and determines "mission of the future."

Christian Hope and Christian Mission: Prospects and Problems

Hope for a new heaven and a new earth, characterised by the uncontested rule of God is then one of the most potent elements in the

---

[3] Jurgen Moltmann, "Is the World Coming to an End or Has Its Future already Begun? Christian Eschatology. Modern Utopianism and Exterminism" in David Fergusson & Marcel Sarot eds. *The Future as God's Gift*, pp 129-138.

[4] Gabriel Fackre, "I Believe in the Resurrection of the Body," *Interpretation* 46, 1999, pp 42-52.

[5] Oscar Culmann. "Eschatology and Missions in the New Testament" in Gerald H. Anderson ed. *The Theology of Christian Mission*, New York: McGraw-Hill Book Co, 1961, p 44.

missionary enterprise of the Christian Church. We may even say that hope represents an integral constituent of the warrant and motivation for Christian Mission. It stands, not as a mere appendage to our mission theology, but serves as a primary point of reference. The rediscovery of hope as a central theme in theology promoted by Jurgen Moltmann has much to teach those of us involved in reflecting on the missionary task of the Church. As Moltmann points out, "from first to last, and not merely in the epilogue, Christianity is eschatology, is hope, forward looking and forward moving, and therefore also revolutionising and transforming the present...it is the glow that suffuses everything here in the dawn of an expected new day."[6] However, notwithstanding this significant role it plays for Christian faith scant attention is paid vis-à-vis missiology.[7] Whilst it may be true to say that, on the one hand, in contrast to nineteenth century liberal theology when the "eschatology office" was mostly closed, twentieth century theology has seen the 'eschatology office' working overtime,[8] but on the other hand, might it be legitimate to maintain that it has been doing so largely without the services of a missions desk? Whilst the reality of Christian hope is being recognised as central to our faith and life, mission and missiology has not yet caught up with that development. Perhaps, one reason for this malaise is the problem associated with extreme forms of eschatological speculation. The fascination for this sort of futurology is a fact we painfully experience even today, evidenced by the recent

tragic events in various parts of the world. This holds true even in Christian circles, where "eschatology seems to lend itself to becoming a playground for fanatical curiosity;" *The Late Great Planet Earth,* by Hal Lindsey and the recent crop of *'Left Behind'* books, movies and paraphernalia being just two cases in point. However titillating and exciting they may be, not to mention the megabucks that it rakes in for the business houses that promote them, these productions have caused confusion, redirected the focus away from the fundamentals which in turn has also led to an attitude of resignation and apathy.[9] Here apocalyptic speculation rather than a theological grounded eschatology animates Christian living. Futurology as opposed to Christian hope drives many of our churches.

It will be clear that we need to move beyond and reconfigure the poles in our mission theology. At the beginning of the third millennium we find ourselves at a most propitious time to undertake such an exercise. In various locales and settings the world over, discussions are turning to the subject of hope. Society is tired of bad news and is exhausted from riding on doom and gloom, as was done in yesteryears. This preoccupation will have to give way for a fresh approach to gospel proclamation. What can be 'good' about the 'good news,' if talk of punishment, death and escape eternal damnation hogs most of our discussion? The time is right to put the 'good' back into the gospel news. It is time to proclaim the 'good news of the kingdom of Jesus Christ.' This chapter is an initial attempt at such an exercise. Here we

---

[6] *Theology of Hope*, London: SCM Press, 1967, p 16.

[7] See Van Engen' comment in footnote 14, Charles Van Engen, "Faith, Love and Hope" in Engen, Gilliand and Pierson eds. *The Good News of the Kingdom: Mission Theology for the Third Millennium*, New York: Orbis Books, 1993, pp 253-63.

[8] David Bosch. *Transforming Mission: Paradigm Shifts in Theology of Mission*, New York: Orbis Books, 1991, pp 498-99.

[9] *Transforming Mission,* p 504

[10] See for example Bruce Chilton and J.I.H MacDonald. *Jesus and the Ethics of the Kingdom*, London: SPCK, 1987, p 3; G.R. Beasely-Murray. *Jesus and the Kingdom of God*, Grand Rapids: Eerdmans / Exeter; Paternoster Publishing, 1986, p x; and I.H. Marshall. *Jesus the Saviour: Studies in New Testament Theology*, London: SPCK, 1990, p 213.

will first seek to discuss and understand the significance of hope for Christian faith and mission. Secondly, we will discuss the structure a theology of hope assumed in select episodes of mission history. Finally, we will briefly enunciate the shape of mission that such a perspective promotes. This study is submitted it must be clarified, as an initial proposal for reflection and not an exhaustive reflection and directive for action.

Christian Hope and Christian Faith

That the overarching theme of Jesus' life and ministry was the kingdom of God is perhaps one of the very few subjects on which there seems to exist a consensus among practically all New Testament scholars.[10] Although the precise nature of the operation of this kingdom may be a matter of disagreement, most if not all agree that "kingdom" refers primarily to the sovereign activity of God as ruler or king.[11] Jesus, who ushered in this reign through his life and ministry, demonstrated that here was God, as foretold in the scriptures, decisively acting to bring down the rule of Satan and initiate a journey towards realising His uncontested reign. Through his life and ministry he was making clear that the arrival of this kingdom signalled God's unprecedented presence in, and action for the world. For his contemporaries demon possession meant that, Satan, who was exercising his power over the world, was still alive and active. The exorcisms that Jesus carried out were therefore meant to prove that God was asserting his authority over the realm of this world. If the very pillars on which Satan's rule rested were being torn down, this signalled, in no uncertain terms, that the reign of God in Christ has come in power and authority. Alongside this *'power encounter'* between God and Satan, it would do us well to recognise that this rule was also a *'personal encounter'* between

God and human society. The rule Jesus ushered in was characterised by a humble openness and generosity that extended across man-made boundaries. The compassionate manner in which he dealt with the sinners, the tax collectors and the social outcast indicated that, in this kingdom, it was not the privileged elite of society nor the prominent religious leaders who were foremost, but rather that it was the despised and rejected who received God's special attention. The unfettered interaction he had with women, Samaritans and even publicans asserted that He had burst open societal distinctions that slotted people into a rigid social hierarchy. Indeed, he demonstrated that this reign of God made it possible for the last to become first and the least to become the greatest.

The phenomenal impact that this radical life and message had during His own lifetime, and indeed throughout subsequent generations does not detract from the fact that this kingdom, Jesus announced, had a future dimension as well. Although Jesus heralded that the reign of God was present in His life and ministry, that present reign did not however exhaust that reality. The consummation of this kingdom He introduced was reserved for a later date, when He would establish Himself as sovereign Lord over all the earth. Paradoxically the kingdom of God was 'here' and at the same time was 'yet to come.' It was present as well as promised. As C. Burchard suggests the 'already' and the 'not yet' of God's reign in Jesus' ministry belongs to the essence of his person and consciousness and, should not be resolved by forcing into alien categories. Indeed it is precisely in this tension that Christian hope finds its dynamic.[12]

The climax of the life and ministry of Jesus in his bodily resurrection proved both the authenticity of his life and provided the assurance

---

[11] I.H. Marshall, *Jesus the Saviour*, p 214.
[12] Cited in Bosch, *Transforming Mission*, p.32.

for this promised 'not yet.' If through His resurrection Jesus defeated death itself then, His promise of life everlasting could be taken on face value. So, when the first Christians preached the resurrected Christ, they were not merely communicating facts of history, they were speaking of a present and clear reality, of life in the power of the Spirit of the resurrected Christ they experienced. The resurrection not only meant that God vindicated the life and ministry of Jesus, but also that this new life they now experienced was furnished with a new paradigm. The victory assured for the end time had already invaded the present. Ordering one's life on the assumption that Jesus was Lord therefore, did not merely entail a patient and passive expectation for this end time victory. It was rather the commencement of an eventful journey in active co-operation with the Spirit of this risen Christ, in realising His victorious kingdom even in the "here and now."[13] Indeed the giving of the Holy Spirit was the pledge of this promised future of Christ. The church was now an eschatological community that lived in that reality because of Jesus Christ and through the Holy Spirit. The future promised by Christ was here; eternal life was experienced in the now. The resurrection confirmed that the declaration 'Jesus is Lord' implied that all other powers, be it spiritual, political or economic were rendered powerless before this rule. Absolute power could not be ascribed to anyone apart from God the Father of Jesus. The kingdom that Jesus brought to bear was superior to other powers seen and unseen and hence demanded total allegiance. It meant therefore that this encounter that Jesus mounted with the powers was also a *prophetic* one. However, this claim was not plainly obvious for all to see. The very existence of injustice and

strife, oppression and hardship was a mitigating factor. Whilst Satan was thought to be a defeated foe, his apparent activity on the earth and in the lives of men and women suggested the contrary. This tension then of Christ's Lordship, affirmed by some but yet not acknowledged by all, provides the backdrop for this hope. Christians look back to the life and ministry of Jesus Christ in the first century as the primary foundation on which they believe that He is Lord. Equally important is the aspect of looking forward to the future when Christ will confirm this Lordship in establishing his sovereign and uncontested rule. The past and present are woven into a cord that establishes and sustains the belief in the Lordship of Christ. Based on the life and ministry of Jesus,

> Faith believes God to be true, hope awaits the time when this truth shall be manifested; faith believes that he is our Father, hope anticipates that He will ever show Himself to be a Father toward us; faith believes that eternal life has been given to us, hope anticipates that it will some time be revealed; faith is the foundation upon which hope rests, hope nourishes and sustains faith.[14]

Christian existence, we can therefore say, is set between faith in a fulfilled redemption and hope for an awaited consummation, faith in what has taken place and hope for what will take place as based on and assured by the history of God. Besides love, which constitutes its dynamic, Christian life, to put it differently, revolves around the bipolar axis of faith, in Christ as Lord and Saviour, and hope that one day He will conclusively demonstrate that for all to see. Faith that Christ was indeed ushering in the kingdom of God through his life and ministry and hope that this same Christ will one day consummate

---

[13] In addition to Moltmann, for whom the resurrection is key to understanding eschatology (particularly see *Theology of Hope* pp 139 – 229), for an illuminating discussion on the significance of the resurrection for the notion of the kingdom of God see J. Mudimann "The Resurrection of Jesus as the Coming of the kingdom- the Basis of Hope for the Transformation of the World" in R.S.Barbour ed. *The Kingdom of God and Human Society*, Edinburgh: T & T Clark, 1993, pp 208-223.

[14] J. Moltmann, *Theology of Hope*, p 20.

this rule in power and glory. Faith that in the very onset of the kingdom, God's uncontested rule was taking concrete shape while the rule of Satan was forced to its irreversible retreat and, hope that this reality would be conclusively established at the promised return of Jesus Christ. Faith and hope situate the Christian' belief and love animates it. That is why the Apostle Paul asserts that faith, hope and love alone will last (I Cor.13:13).

Christian Hope and Mission Theology

If Christian hope is a cardinal constituent of the Christian faith, a biblically faithful theology of Christian mission will likewise maintain a similar configuration. Christian hope will constitute both a motivating force as well as a defining principle. First, as its motivating force, Christian mission will not be content to derive its raison d'être simply by looking back into history where its warrant is said to be embedded nor work under the compulsion of impending doom a selective reading of this history promotes, but will be seen as the call to join in the unfolding of a glorious future which has already invaded the present through Jesus Christ. Sadly though, an entrenched view found within the Church is the "negative reason for evangelisation."[15] Here it is not God's offer of abundant life and future promise that motivates evangelism but rather negative compulsions of escape from hell and eternal punishment. A burning passion to rescue souls from eternal perdition that awaits them if they do not accept Christ as their Saviour is the motivating force for evangelism. The resulting sense of 'duty' to Christ commands reduces mission to the 'law' of the gospel. In contrast to this 'law' or 'duty' stands the 'joy' of mission, which is invariably interjected when hope is included into the equation. Hope releases joy that

liberates us from the 'burden of the law.' Christian hope enables us to transfer our gaze, which has far too long been fixed solely on the past, to the promise of the future made by Christ. Though undoubtedly we must look back to the history of *missio dei* in the world, this backward gaze does not exhaust our vision as we engage in reflection and practice. The potential of the future is as significant as the actuality of the past. Every knee bent at the foot of the Master and every tongue expressing his sovereign lordship is an inviting vision. The vision of lamb and lion lying down next to each other and swords being moulded into ploughshares is more profoundly a reality that graciously invites and inexorably draws us to actively participate in its realisation. If, as Paul Minear says, "the deepest cry which the Holy Spirit arouses in man is the yearning cry for heaven, for direct contact with God's throne, for the victory of God over His demonic enemies, for an invitation to the marriage feast of the Lamb,"[16] mission is the act of demonstrating and announcing that in Jesus Christ one is able to take part in that feast right in the here and now even as one awaits that reality to arrive in all its fullness. This fulfilling joy frees us to concentrate on what we have been saved for rather than focus solely on what we have been saved from. In place of the negative reason, Christian hope furnishes us with a 'positive reason' for evangelism.

Second, as its defining principle this promised future provides us with a reference point and thus ably addresses the contradiction of the present. The dissatisfaction with the present and its prospects is a cause for the deep angst that plagues our lives. Society that is caught between the promise of human achievement and the pathos of its depravity has apart from immanent resources little cause for hope. In such a situation Christian hope creates an

---

[15] Cf. Peter Beyerhaus, *God's Kingdom and the Utopian Error: Discerning the Biblical Kingdom of God from its Political Counterfeits*, Wheaton: Crossway Books, 1992 p.18.

[16] Quoted in Johannes Verkuyl, *Contemporary Missiology: An Introduction*, Grand Rapids: Eerdmans, 1978, p 203.

eschatological unrest, a yearning, for divine promise right within the present . Far from being satisfied with the status quo this unrest draws us toward God's agenda for the world. Moltmann clarifies succinctly:

> Faith wherever it develops into hope causes not rest but unrest, not patience but impatience. It does not calm the unquiet heart, but is itself this unquiet heart in man. Those who hope in Christ can no longer put up with this reality as it is, but begin to suffer under it, to contradict it. Peace with God means conflict with the world, for the goad of the promised future stabs inexorably into the flesh of every unfulfilled present.[17]

This forward-looking movement that hope draws us into launches us back into that very world as inhabitants and agents of that future. Christian hope draws us out and sends us into the world. In being sent into the world we realise our agenda is not set by the world rather it is set by the fact and promise of Jesus Christ. God's kingdom and not human authority nor aspiration will supply its orientation and directive. Its defining principle will issue from divine presence and promise rather than immanent potential or prospects. Mission then will represent a proactive movement of change in that eschatological direction as opposed to being reactionary protests against the present misdemeanours of society, horrors of the past or the doom of prospective futures. As Bauckham and Hart explain, "By enabling us to locate ourselves within a different teleology, and hence to configure the meaning of the present differently, this God empowers us to live history differently... This discovery sets us free even now to be active in pursuit of correspondence to our eschatological destiny..."[18] Here mission may be seen as an invitation to indwell the promises of God in Jesus Christ. Mission will be that creative and liberative process of indwelling and being indwelt by that reality that originates from God and finds in Him its consummation, the Kingdom of God. Moltmann' words are again relevant here:

Missions perform their service today only when they infect men with hope. This kindling of live hopes that are braced for action and prepared to suffer, hopes for the Kingdom of God that is coming to earth in order to transform it, is the purpose of mission. It is the task of the whole body of Christians, not merely the task of particular officials. The whole body of Christians is engaged in the apostolate of hope for the world and finds therein its essence – namely that which makes it the Church of God.[19]

When Christian hope is a cardinal constituent of our mission theology, the church or the 'apostolate of hope' will have in that very dynamic and reality, by which she is constituted, its warrant and design for mission in the world. Christian hope furnishes both a motivation and a defining principle for Christian mission. To be sure the above does not exhaust the elements of a mission theology that reckons with hope. For lack of time and space we will not be able to describe in detail such a theology, suffice here to introduce briefly the basic strands that comprise its fabric.

1.The Source, Content and Goal of Mission. Mission grows out of the biblically revealed plan of the Triune God (Gen 12; Is 49; Mt. 28:18-20; Mk 16:15; Lk.24:46-49; Jn.3:16; Eph 1:9-10 and I Tim 2:4-6; Rev.5:9-10; 6:9-10; 19:1-10). Through the work of Christ people are ushered into the kingdom and are prepared for its final coming (Mt.25:34; I Cor.15:24-28). The ultimate goal that "God may be all in all" (I Cor. 15:28) will be the reality that invites our efforts. Mission then will be preoccupied with the worship and

---

[17] J. Moltmann, *Theology of Hope*, p. 21. Also quoted in Richard Bauckham & Trevor Hart, "The Shape of Time", p 62.

[18] Richard Bauckham & Trevor Hart, "The Shape of Time," pp 70-71.

[19] J. Moltmann, *Theology of Hope*, p 328.

of giving glory to this holy Triune God its source, director and goal, both by present and potential disciples.

2.The Dynamic of Mission. Mission will be possible only through the personal presence of the Son of God (Mt.28:20) in the person of the Holy Spirit (Jn.16:8-11; Acts 1:8). Making real the person of Jesus Christ and making efficacious his reality in our lives here and now the Holy Spirit forms us as the bride of Christ. Practices that nurture this spiritual reality we inhabit by meditation on and studying the word, prayer and worship (Jn.6:53-58; 15:1-8; 1 Cor.11:26; Eph 6:18-20) and practices that allow this Spirit to indwell the disciple both individual and corporate will be seen as non-negotiable. The centrality of the Holy Spirit in empowering us to engage with society and its powers and in funding that unrest for God's future promise will be its dynamic.[20]

3.The Prospects of Mission. Although we may be blessed with positive results in the here and now, we are not assured of total success (Jn.15:16). In fact we are warned that persecution and rejection will be our lot (Mt. 10:16-25; Jn 15:18-21). A willingness and readiness for sacrifice and martyrdom is therefore to be encouraged. Although victory won on Golgotha (Rev. 12:11) is our launching pad, the present interim, when Satan's rule is not yet conclusively stamped out, will harbour hazardous situations.

4. The Church in Mission. The Church is a foretaste of that heavenly reality and its life in mission paves the way for God's sovereign rule, which he will set when he comes in glory (Mt. 24:31). This new humanity (Rom 5:14; 2 Cor 5:17; Eph 2: 14-16) through its activity of love (Rom 13:8-10; 2 Peter 1:7) and justice serves as a sign of that kingdom. As a sign she not only points to the kingdom but also serves as a catalyst for change in the direction of the kingdom (Mt. 13:33; 1 Peter 2:9). The kingdom of God then forms the mission paradigm that the church inhabits.

5. Our Confidence for Mission. Mission takes place in the joyful confidence that Jesus Christ, on the basis of the victory He has already won (Col.2:15; Heb 2:14-16) and His approaching final victory at the consummation (1 Cor 15:25; Rev 19) will guide the work of His commissioned messengers step by step toward the fulfilment that God has prepared (Phil 1:6). Despite mitigating circumstances that suggest otherwise, there is no adversary who can thwart that victory (Is. 46: 9ff; 55:8-13; 1Cor. 15: 57ff).[21]

Displaced Hopes in Mission History

In his treatise on Christian hope, Moltmann notes that two forms of sin against hope are: "presumption" and "despair." "Presumption is a premature, self willed anticipation of the fulfilment of what we hope for from God. Despair is the premature, arbitrary anticipation of the non-fulfilment of what we hope for from God."[22] The turn of 20th century provides the context for discussing the first.

The Presumption of Progress

"Progress...is not an accident, but a necessity... What we call evil and immorality must disappear. It is certain that man must become perfect."[23] With these words, Herbert Spencer

---

[20] This point needs to be stressed here for it underlines the present experience of God through the Holy Spirit in the life of the believer and the church, a point at which, if some critiques of Moltmann are right, his thought at this point is open to sharp criticism.

[21] Cf. Peter Beyerhaus, *God's Kingdom and the Utopian Error*. p. 68. I'm indebted to Peter Beyerhaus for the idea on which these points are based.

[22] J. Moltmann, *Theology of Hope*, p 23.

[23] Quoted by David Bebbington. *Patterns in History: A Christian Perspective on Historical Thought* Leicester: Apollos Press, 1990, p 85.

propounded in 1851, what had by then become the dominant philosophy of history. This philosophy, as David Bebbington points out, was founded on three assumptions. First, in accordance with the Christian view, history was thought to be a linear progression of events. Human history was the account of the advance of the human condition from a primitive age to the highly developed civilisation of the enlightenment era. Second, was its high expectation of the future. The flow of history narrated the definite development of human beings over the years and on that basis it was believed that the future offered a similar prospect of development and progress. Third, progress was assessed and evaluated by the extent to virtuous qualities had been developed within human beings. The final stage, it was said, would be characterised by the full realisation of these exemplary qualities.[24] This idea of progress forged its way to the core of then contemporary Christian world-view. First, it seemed that the development of the industrial age, with its resultant benefits, was seen to derive its impetus from a Christian world-view. A Christian understanding of nature and the world enabled scientists and others to study and discover the inner workings of the world and exploit that for human development. This correlation between Christianity and advanced Western civilisation therefore held much promise as an excellent tool for Christian apologetics. At the turn of the century, most Christians had every reason to be confident that not only would this Christianity induced progress continue in the West, but also through the efforts of missionary endeavour it would find new avenues in other parts of the world. It is not surprising then to hear Lord Balfour, addressing the 1910 World Missionary Conference at Edinburgh thus:

> By common consent there is just now a great opportunity. Nations in the East are awakening. They are looking for two things: they are looking for enlightenment and for liberty. Christianity alone of all religions meets these demands in the highest degree.[25]

Secondly, for a large section of the American missionary force the Calvinist influence taught them that before the return of Christ there were to be three stages. The period of the apostles when the gospel was offered to the world constituted the first. They believed the second to be a period of the anti-Christ when he held sway over the world, and finally there would a great expansion of the Church, during which the anti-Christ would be defeated.[26] It was believed that beginning around the time of the mid-nineteenth century, the third stage, characterised by a steady expansion of the Church around the globe as a preparation for the coming of Jesus, was in operation. The three million or so church members in the continents of Asia, Africa and Latin America were sufficient proof. This progressive realisation of the kingdom of God was as a result linked directly to the propagation of the gospel. In turn this enabled a phenomenal increase in missionary numbers, from 300 in 1815 to about 21,000 in 1910![27] The well-known watchword of the 1900 New York Missionary conference, and subsequently for the Student Volunteer Movement, "the evangelisation of the world in this generation," not only demonstrated this belief, but also crystallised it for generations to come. It is clear that the missionary project of

---

[24] D. Bebbington, *Patterns in History*, pp. 68-9.

[25] Quoted in Rodger Bassham, *Mission Theology: 1948 –1975 Years of Worldwide Creative Tension Ecumenical, Evangelical and Roman Catholic*, Pasadena: Wm. Carey Library, 1979, p 16.

[26] Timothy Yates, *Christian Mission in the Twentieth Century*, Cambridge: CUP, 1994, p 9; see also D. Bosch, *Transforming Mission*, p 313.

[27] R. Bassham, *Mission Theology*, p 16.

this period owed part of its framework to such a worldview. For a Judeo-Christian based western civilisation history was conceived of in linear terms and Christian mission from the West was an integral part of this unfolding of linear history. It was conceived as the victorious envoy of Christ and thus derived part of its warrant from that belief. Numerical expansion of the Church and the transmission of western values and technology vindicated this progress and hinted at the bright future it promised. This we submit smacks of 'presumption.' If presumption, as Moltmann says is the "premature, self-willed anticipation of the fulfilment of what we hope for from God," Christians at the turn of the century, seem to have been presumptuous of their "self-willed" activism to propel the missionary movement forward. They believed they could contribute to a progressive realisation of the kingdom of God. Unfortunately though this kingdom assumed the shape of the "kingdom of the Anglo-Saxon" which was in the business of bringing "light to the Gentiles by means of lamps manufactured in America."[28]

The Despair of Failure

Primarily as a reaction to the aggressive and often insensitive methods of mission employed, by many western missionaries, some African and Asian Christians called for a "moratorium on mission." Speaking at a Kuala Lumpur conference in 1971, the Philipino leader Emerito Nacpil boldly asserted, "the present structure of mission is dead, and the first thing that we ought to do is to eulogise it and then bury it." This strong reaction on his part was motivated as he said by the fact that mission was a "symbol of the universality of Western imperialism among the rising generations of the Third World." Mission, according to him, was in fact the greatest enemy

of the gospel, and the "most *missionary* service a missionary can do is to go home."[29] This call was echoed by the African leader John Gatu and the All African Council of Churches endorsed this view in their 1974 Lusaka Assembly, adding that "after a hundred years of missionary activity in Africa, the churches are still unable to stand on their own feet" and therefore "the call for a moratorium is a demand to transfer the massive expenditure ...in the churches in Africa to programme activities manned by African themselves."[30] Arguably it was a sense of despair, prevalent among many Asian and African Christians, at the visible failures of the modern missionary movement that gave rise to this call for a moratorium on mission. Hopes for a society that respected all its members and provided an opportunity for all to realise their full potential that lay shattered, issued in a sense of despair. Despair at the 'non-fulfilment' of what promised to be a genuine catalyst for the upliftment of millions had in fact turned into a 'benevolent monster.' Although not everyone shared in the optimistic western conception of the kingdom of God, they nevertheless held firmly to the belief that the gospel was able to bring about radical changes in individuals and societies; Christianity, as a departure from oppressive religious and other structures, was for many a ticket to a genuine humanisation. When this did not materialise, hope yielded to despair which in turn prompted calls for such actions as the 'moratorium on mission.'

Presumption of Progress Yet Again

A contemporary danger that we would do well to be mindful of is the grand and ambitious future that global capitalism seems to offer. Capitalism's triumphant onslaught appears to be taking the world into a new era of opportunity and freedom. Nations the world over, are

---

[28] H. Richard Niebuhr, quoted by T. Yates, *Christian Mission*, p 10.

[29] Emerito Nacpil, Quoted in D.Bosch. *Transforming Mission*, p 518.

[30] The Lusaka Report, 1974. Quoted in R. Bassham, *Mission Theology*, p 142.

embracing this reality for all the promise that it offers. The Church is not immune to these developments. Indeed it would be foolish not to acknowledge that Christian mission, has already shown itself susceptible to these pressures. Evidence is available that we seem to be putting a great deal of effort and monetary resources into grand programs, aided by facilities that this technological advance provides. For example, programs that plan to evangelise the world within certain timeframes are doing the rounds and 'marketing the church' is now the new mantra. Alarmingly presumption riding on the back of global capitalism is already seen to be at work.

Despair Yet Again

Moving to contemporary times, arguably, we find prevalent another form of despair. The ideology of religious pluralism is fast becoming popular, even gaining a degree of consensus. Religious plurality as an empirical fact is a reality that we cannot dispute, however religious pluralism as an ideology is a concept that is debated fiercely. The ideology of religious pluralism, simply put, states that Christianity which has for long conceived of itself as the 'only true religion,' has to give way to a belief that all religions are adequate and equally valid approaches to the one true reality. Proponents of this view have been influential in changing the course of Christian history such that traditional understanding of Christian mission of preaching the gospel and subsequently establishing Christian disciples (Mt 28:14) among all peoples has come to be radically questioned. Here mission is restricted to humanitarian acts in the fields of health, education. It is done not with the view to making disciples of Christ but, rather to enable the Buddhist to be a better Buddhist and the Hindu to be a better Hindu. It may be argued that this situation is not cause for despair but, calls for a fresh conception of mission, indeed a new

opportunity for mission. Whilst a call for a fresh conception of mission may not be totally inimical to our consideration nor the need for inter-religious dialogue and action, we nevertheless maintain that it does not have biblical warrant nor sufficient theological rationale, in terms of, to name at least one, a theology of hope. Here the integral link between "Christology" and "eschatology" is collapsed and in turn both poles of Christian theology are negated. If the basic foundation and primary standard of biblical eschatology is Jesus Christ' life, death and resurrection, then a theology of mission constructed with Christian hope as a central dimension will accord a centrality to this Jesus Christ. Eschatology finds its basis and source in the life and resurrection of Jesus Christ. Christology finds in eschatology its horizon and this supplies it with its universal implication.

> Christian eschatology speaks of Jesus Christ and *his* future. It recognises the reality of the raising of Jesus and proclaims the future of the risen Lord. Hence the question whether all statements about the future are grounded in the person and history of Jesus Christ provides it with the touchstone by which to distinguish the spirit of eschatology from that of utopia.[31]

In this postmodern quest for utopia many Christians are left with a sense of despair. A "despairing surrender of hope [that] wears the face of smiling resignation," a resignation that prides itself in realism and confines itself to maintaining the status quo. As Moltmann rightly clarifies despair does not need to take on a grave appearance. "It can be the mere tacit absence of meaning, prospects, future and purpose." Mission thus conceived is characterised by a hope that "does not find its way to the source of new, unknown possibilities" but satisfies itself with "trifling, ironical play with existing possibilities." This "un-adventurous play," we may predict

---

[31] J. Moltmann, *Theology of Hope*, p. 17.

along with Moltmann, "will end in boredom, or in outbreaks of absurdity."[32] When one looks around this absurdity appears to be alarmingly evident within the church. Immanent patterns of thought and experience are employed as pointers to, even determinants of, the possibilities of the future and this in turn fills the vacuum that the absence of genuine hope for God's future in Christ leaves.

Mission of the Future

By now it will be obvious that a mission theology in which Christian hope plays a significant role will occasion a radical rethink of our mission practice. The interpretative relationship between theology and practice will need to be worked to reap the gains that a fresh and faithful reading of the scriptures has brought to bear on our theological understanding. Christian hope that situates our faith and provides a significant coordinate for mission theology will as a result shape and determine our mission practice in no insignificant manner. To such a discussion let us turn.

Missio Dei

Perhaps the foremost element this eschatological perspective compels us to acknowledge in our practice is the notion of *Missio Dei*. We have noted that Christian hope is placed in God's action, *missio dei,* rather than human activity. In the beginning God created all that there is *ex nihilo*; in the cross and resurrection "new creation" is brought into being. The final consummation of *missio dei* will take place when he establishes His absolute rule over all. Clearly all three phases of this *missio dei* are based on His action, not on human activity. In its conception, execution and completion God is the source, the dynamic and the goal. One major impulse in the development of the concept of

missio dei originated from the Barthian influenced, German delegation to the 1938 International Missionary Council (IMC) meeting at Tambaram, South India. In contrast to various forms of triumphalism that were evident within the missionary movement they emphasised that "only through a creative act of God His Kingdom will be consummated in the final establishment of a New Heaven and a New Earth." They went on emphatically to assert: "only this eschatological attitude can prevent the Church from being secularised."[33] Coupled with other influences it initiated a radical rethink of the basis of mission. Subsequent conferences and deliberations established for us that it was not ecclesiology or soteriology that provided the context of mission but the doctrine of the Trinity. Mission is not primarily an activity of the church but an attribute of God.[34] The Church does not have a mission, it does not possess the salvation it seeks to share with the world. Rather mission is a privilege it enjoys by virtue of being formed by the mission of the Triune God. The gift of participating in that creative and liberative task is bequeathed to the church, the body of Christ. Disciples of Christ are now called to participate in the awesome act of pointing to and witnessing about this reality. To participate in mission is to indwell God's eternal love expressed to all people, indeed all of creation. It is to be a channel of that grace which she herself has received and now inhabits. It is a call to point to the hope that she lives in and with which she looks forward to the future.

From this concept of *Missio Dei* issue a number of directives for mission practice. Since Christian mission is not ours but the initiative of God it implies that we can claim no ownership of it. Though we may readily subscribe to this notion, it is surprising that often our actions speak

---

³² J. Moltmann, *Theology of Hope*, p. 24.

³³ Tambaram Series, Vol I: *The Authority of the Faith*, Quoted by D.Bosch, *Transforming Mission*, p. 390.

³⁴ D. Bosch, *Transforming Mission*, p. 390.

rather differently. We tend to assume the opposite is the case. Here mission is owned, governed and directed by desires and ambitions that are perhaps not as spiritual as the task deserves. They often become a false veneer for less noble desires. Allied to this, is also the tendency within some churches to venerate tradition over scriptural precept. Whilst tradition can be a potent resource for mission, in some cases however it takes captive the imagination and will of the church. The priority of mission yields to the compulsion of maintenance of tradition. Maintaining rituals rather than engaging in mission becomes the primary preoccupation. Hence the church is reduced to a voluntary club or a cultural artefact of a certain class or group with little or no concern for those outside.

The concept of *Missio Dei* offers a timely corrective. If Christian mission is God's mission, His agenda and not ours, temporal fortunes will constitute our permanent preoccupation. Mission will not serve to advance our personal or corporate misplaced ambitions but the kingdom of God. The reality of the kingdom of God, its values and ethos will form the parameters for our visions and efforts. Here neither Church nor mission can possess a life of its own for it source, dynamic and goal is derived from the sovereign God of heaven and earth, the coming king. Moltmann' words are apt:

> The risen Lord is always expected by the Church – the Lord, moreover, expected by the Church for the world and not merely for itself. Hence the Christian community does not live from itself and for itself, but from the sovereignty of Him who has conquered death and is bringing life, righteousness and the kingdom of God.[35]

Another form of negating the centrality of *missio dei* is the practice of equating one form of mission, even a successful form of mission as "the only" approach to mission. The propensity to subsume the whole missionary enterprise under a particular form of mission, like the postmodern idea of mission being "the effort to bring about the humanisation of peoples," perhaps falls prey to this temptation of assuming mission to be a human enterprise with little reference to God. A further point, which is associated to this, is the dichotomy that seems to exist between the concept of the "general mission of God" in creation and world history and the "particular mission of Jesus" in his life and ministry on this earth. The general mission of God, as is the case, can provide the warrant for "mission as humanisation of people." The particular mission of Jesus however, with its attendant "scandal of particularity," seems to fly in the face of this conception of mission and hence is sidelined. Conversely for many Christians, particularly those from the conservative constituency, mission is often seen in terms of stark contrasts. Those who have the light take the gospel to those heathen living in darkness; the "believers" go into the world to convert the "unbelievers." Little attention is paid to the fact that since mission is actually *Missio Dei,* God may perhaps already be at work in the lives of people where the missionary is seeking to go. *Missio Dei* provides a holistic perspective from which both the "general" and "particular" aspects of mission are held, not in competition but as complementary features of one whole. One cannot be understood without the other. The particular mission of Jesus specially His resurrection is where we find the interjection of hope into the human condition. It is from here that we can look back at creation and history where we find clues to the general mission of God. A resurrection Christology is a fundamental source and determinant for missiology and consequently eschatology that is born from that Christology funds and shapes missiology. As noted earlier they are mutually interpretative.

---

[35] J. Moltmann, *Theology of Hope, p.*325.

In the light of this therefore, humility is needed for we are eminently prone to usurp God's rightful place in our missionary task. Humility to concede that rather than the Kingdom of God, we often allow historical tradition or charismatic personalities to determine our priorities. Humility to acknowledge that God is always greater than our grand plans and strategies; and greater than our methodology, however effective they may be. Humility to also agree that until the future we hope for arrives, when God's final answer will be revealed, in our human frailty we may be providing imperfect answers. Furthermore we are required to display an attitude of humble respect, which will manifest an attentive ear and a loving heart, to the "other." Respect not only because he/she is a person made in the image of God but, also because that person is seen as the object and recipient of the love of God just as we see ourselves. We will allow for the fact that God has a relationship to this "other" prior to our encounter and seek to point to Him and according to His agenda.

Church and Mission

The second element we focus on is the relationship between Church and mission. The kingdom of God that was inaugurated by Jesus Christ found expression in the formation of the Church on the day of Pentecost. The Holy Spirit who indwelt the lives of the early Christians signalled that the beginning of the end had finally been initiated; the eschatological horizon had been firmly established pointing to the fact that God's kingdom was both 'here' and was 'to come.' In the interim the Church, through the power of the Holy Spirit, was to invite the world to participate in that "eschatological foretaste of the kingdom of God." This foretaste was not given in order that she would pride herself in being an exclusive community that dished out this experience as and when she so desired, but rather that she would act as a sign and instrument of that foretaste, that gospel. We are more trustees and stewards than beneficiaries.[36] Indeed mission itself was an "essential element in that eschatological divine plan of salvation."[37] The community that existed for the benefit of the outsider was to be a sign of God's design for His entire creation. Defining the Church as an "eschatological community" is done on the basis of the indwelling Holy Spirit and its missionary commission. Mission, which provides a primary focus for this eschatological orientation, will therefore necessarily be integral to its life. This recognition places on the whole Church, not an option to decide for or against mission, but rather to submit to its divine calling. Bishop Lesslie Newbigin expressed this succinctly, "the church is mission." It is illegitimate to talk about the one without, at the same time, talking about the other.[38] Mission is not an appendage to the other functions of the Church, an activity that can be pursued after establishing ecclesial structures and programmes. On the contrary mission is the heartbeat of God and hence the glorious privilege and awesome responsibility of the church.

If the church as a whole shares equally in the mandate to proclaim this vision of its coming king, certain sections of the Church are not to be understood, as was common in previous generations, as senders and others receivers. It is God, as the Johannine version of the great commission notes, that sent Jesus and it is Jesus who in turn sends, not just a select few but all His disciples, out into the world (John 20:21). The hegemony of the western missionary project,

---

[36] See Lesslie Newbigin, "The Kingdom of God and Our Hopes for the Future" in R.S. Barbour ed. *The Kingdom of God and Human Society*, pp 1-12.

[37] O. Culmann. "Missions in God's Eschatology" in N. E. Thomas ed. *Classic Texts in Mission and World Christianity*, London: SPCK, 1995, p 307.

[38] J.L.Newbigin. Quoted in D.Bosch, *Transforming Mission*. p 370.

in this understanding, finds no clear warrant and as a result stands inappropriate for the days ahead. In contrast to "territorial Christianity" we ought to affirm with Bishop Nazir Ali that mission is "from everywhere to everywhere."[39] Mission is from and to all six continents. By the same token, in contrast to much contemporary practice the mission effort of what has come to be called the Indian Instituted Churches will be seen in a more positive light. For long these groups have been called sects and have been thought of pejoratively. However, their phenomenal growth and advance has come to question the very signification of the term "mainline churches" to the older churches established churches. It is well recorded that Pentecostal and independent churches are the most vigorously growing sections of Christianity worldwide which may suggest that these new movements rather than older established churches seem to be the contemporary mainline.[40] The notion of partnership therefore will issue in a conceptual and practical rehabilitation of these independent groups by other churches. The church universal is the body of Christ, no one denomination or group of denominations can claim to be the real church. Hence a partnership, that will issue, not least in mutual respect and perhaps even integral collaboration in mission, is called for.

The Kingdom of God

This eschatological perspective interjects into our discussion the notion of *Kingdom of God*. We noted earlier that the concept of Christian hope was couched in the discourse about the kingdom of God. It is here that we are introduced to the character and shape of God's rule and its future that God has in store for all creation. The kingdom of God that was brought to bear in the life, person and teaching of Jesus was the framework that situated the faith and hope that Jesus' ministry nurtured in his followers. In our discussion about kingdom of God we noted the manner in which Jesus moulded it to represent it as a personal, a power and a prophetic encounter between God, the world and the evil one. This shape that Jesus imparted to the kingdom of God can serve as a model for our contemporary missionary engagement. The framework of the kingdom of God will then determine our mission.

The Bible teaches us that the kingdom of God ushered in by Jesus violated many of the social mores of 1st century middle-eastern society. Jesus' free and fair interaction and relationships with folk from all sections of society meant that in this kingdom people mattered more than religious and social convention. Here the publican and prostitute were valued just as the priest and Pharisee were thought to be important. The leper and lame stood on equal footing as the lord and lieutenant of the government. This approach to human relationships based on unconditional love, which stood in marked contrast to common practice of the day was revolutionary. It brought restoration to a Samaritan woman with questionable morals and to a blind beggar with sparse resources. The criteria for receiving this personal touch from Jesus do not lie in our religious or social status, our standing in society nor our personal abilities on the contrary it resides in our brokenness, our need for healing and our contrite heart. It is the sick that need a physician! It follows then the mission that adopts this paradigm will reinstate real people with real needs to the centre. Often programs and institutions take precedence over people, agendas for promulgating certain projects and practices that serve institutions, rather than the true welfare

---

[39] M. Nazir Ali, *From Everywhere to Everywhere*, London: Wm Collins & Sons, 1991. p.

[40] For a detailed discussion see Roger Hedlund ed. *Christianity is Indian: The Emergence of an Indigenous Community*, Delhi: MIIS/ISPCK, 2000; Roger Hedlund, *Quest for Identity: India's Churches of Indigenous Origin, the Little Tradition in Indian Christianity*, Delhi: MIIS/ISPCK, 2000, & O.L. Snaitang ed. *Churches of Indigenous Origin in North East India*, Delhi: MIIS/ISPCK, 2000.

of people, hog the priority. Mission becomes a program centred and institution fostering enterprise. Attention shifts from meeting personal and societal need to addressing institutional concerns. Elongation of institutional fortunes and program shelf-life attract more attention than people. Jesus' life and ministry is an example of this rebuttal of misplaced priorities. Social convention and institutions, even religious ones, were sidelined because they did not focus on people. For Jesus people were His priority. Should not this set of priorities also characterise our mission effort in the 21ˢᵗ century?

Another significant aspect of the Kingdom of God was its opposition to Satan's influence over creation. A power encounter with the spiritual forces that exercised malevolent influence was mounted. This was particularly evident in Jesus' interaction with sickness and demon possession. He was demonstrating that God was here to defeat Satan's rule and offer to creation His life in place of sin and death. Whereas sin and death was the legacy that Satan's rule bequeathed to creation, Jesus came to offer life abundant, life in all its fullness. For their part His followers adopted this self-same model (for e.g. Acts 4). The Holy Spirit now empowered His disciples to wage warfare against the evil one in a similar mode. Centuries later however, as a result of the Enlightenment and the philosophy that it advocated theologians came to dismiss all talk of spiritual realms as being mythical and possessing little if any relationship to contemporary reality. Rudolf Bultmann's effort to demytholigise scriptures was widely imbibed thus rendering this dimension of Christian mission as dated and inappropriate for modern society. In recent times however, signs of a recapitulation are evident. This is a welcome development and has to be encouraged but at the

same time caution has to be applied to avoid an unhealthy obsession with spiritual warfare, which is also perhaps evident in some sections of the church. Just as the Jesus' model suggests, a power encounter with evil forces at work today will be part of our strategy in Christian mission. For too long we have limited ourselves to a verbal proclamation of the gospel message, expecting people to 'believe' the message. The idea that all we need to seek for is intellectual assent to a set of propositions has stunted the gospel message and rendered it to an extent impotent. In the light of our understanding of the kingdom of God we would do well to recognise that the struggle we face is not merely against visible powers, social pressures and intellectual barriers to belief. More profoundly as the apostle Paul says in, Ephesians 6:12, it is against spiritual forces and evil powers. Christian mission that engages in spiritual warfare will take part in concentrated prayer, engage in a personal confrontation, and this does not have to take on dramatic overtones alone, it could just as well assume more quiet approaches, and also expend efforts to rehabilitate ones that were affected.[41] Healing that Jesus brings does impact many and as a result issues in restoration and wholeness to society broken with hurt and hopelessness.

The third dimension, we noted, about the kingdom of God was its prophetic encounter. In establishing His rule, Jesus was in effect nullifying the absolute sovereignty of other powers. Their hold on creation and society was now losing its grip, the kingdom of God demanded total allegiance. God and mammon could not dwell side by side; the latter has to give way for the former. However, this was not immediately apparent. Earthly rulers still governed and evil forces still had a palpable influence. The promise of God's design for the

---

[41] For a fuller discussion see http://www.gospelcom.net/ lcwe/dufe/index.html

Papers presented at the "Deliver Us From Evil" Consultation held under the auspices of Lausanne Committee for World Evangelisation.

final stage suggested that the establishment of uncontested rule was reserved for later. Whilst powers were displaced they were not destroyed; that was reserved for later. However, the fact that the kingdom of God ushered in by Jesus stood in direct opposition to all other powers that claimed ultimate authority meant the interim was when the Church was to serve as a sign a and instrument of that future; indeed to represent a foretaste of that reality. The kingdom of God negated a plurality of powers with equal standing. The Church was to be a prophetic voice in this interim, pointing to the ultimate reality of the total sovereignty of God.

Over the years some Christians have appreciated the imperative the kingdom of God issues in this regard. The prophetic stand they took claimed for the kingdom of God ultimate status and denied all other powers that exalted position. In seeking to live under that rule they subverted these other authorities and powers and their claim to ultimate authority. Christian mission that seeks to point to and work under that kingdom of God will necessarily take this prophetic role seriously. We need prophets who would raise their voice against injustice, oppression and depravation in areas as diverse as economic, political, social, psychological and environmental spheres of society. Prophets who would stake their life on the authority of the kingdom of God and serve as signs of that kingdom. For Christian mission under such a compulsion, a vision of divine promise can constitute a wholesome goal to work towards. For too long we have operated on the assumption that the gospel deals with privatised individuals and has nothing to say to societal structures and public systems. We have preached an individualistic gospel, which was neither biblical nor adequate to the problems of the world. It drove us into religious ghettos and promoted ascetic

mentalities. This myopic vision has robbed us of significant contributions Christian mission could have possibly made to society. One obvious by product of that myopic vision is the dichotomy that exists between evangelism and social concern. These two aspects of Christian witness have been set in opposition against each other and at times even seen as mutually exclusive. In contrast if the eschatological perspective of the kingdom of God, is brought to bear we find both in the Jesus model and the vision of the future redemption is an inclusive reality, one whose remit includes individuals and indeed all of creation, then perhaps we could move out of that dead end. The evangelism school, which insists on the priority of preaching the gospel and the conversion, must realise, as Newbigin has asserted:

> That the centre of attention in the Bible is not the destiny of the human soul considered as an atomic entity: it is the completion of God's whole purpose in a consummation which gathers up the story both of the human soul and the cosmos. [42]

To those who maintain the priority of social action, the pattern set by Jesus is a model. Preaching in his life was a necessary corollary to all healings and exorcisms. The works in and of themselves did not establish that it was the coming of the kingdom of God that has brought in this new reality. A call to repentance and discipleship, the precondition to being part of this kingdom of God, was not dispensed with in a desire to impact maximum numbers. The *personal, power* and the *prophetic* dimensions of the kingdom of God are to be held together in creative tension. The kingdom of God is a reality that stands against all powers that claim ultimate authority and allegiance. To enter into that is to stand against the world and its systems which enslave and degrade. Christian mission needs to

---

[42] J.L .Newbigin. "Christian Faith and World Religions" in G. Wainwright ed. *Keeping the Faith,* London: SPCK, 1989, p 333.

regain that prophetic edge which comes with acknowledging the true extent of the character of the kingdom of God.

Jesus Is Lord

Besides *Missio Dei* and the *Kingdom of God*, the third practice that the reality of Christian hope compels us to acknowledge is to declare that *Jesus is Lord*. In a sense this flows from the centrality of the kingdom of God but yet is distinct enough for separate mention. The declaration that Jesus is Lord finds in the resurrection its basis. As we noted above, the resurrection establishes that if Jesus has defeated death and its progenitor sin, He then stands as victorious over all forms of bondage that has taken humankind captive. No foe or enemy can thwart that kingdom now for He has proved it in the resurrection. This resurrection was indeed a revelation. The messiah in whom the disciples had put so much trust was dead. Their hopes were dashed and it seemed that they were made fools before the world. However, Easter revealed that this Jesus was no captive slave of death and Satan. He was in fact victor over these very powers. Death was now a temporary phase and resurrection was the portal into God's future promised to all disciples of Christ. The declaration *Jesus is Lord*, the constant cry of the early disciples, reassured them that despite mitigating factors such as the treacherous times of persecution they underwent, they were disciples of *Jesus the Lord*. This declaration that has come down to us over the ages, is as real as it was for the first disciples. In this declaration we affirm that no matter what contemporary circumstances may seem to indicate Jesus nevertheless remains Lord. Our faith in Jesus as Lord rests in the fact of the resurrection and our hope that one day He will be Lord over all confidently proceeds on that basis. Faith and hope revolve around the pole of the resurrection. It is here that faith finds its rationale and hope its dynamic.

Like the early disciples, we in south Asia live in treacherous times. All around us we find rival claimants to seats of absolute power. We find sin abounding, strife on the increase, oppression present in political structures just as is in social systems. Pain and heartache is common, genuine joy and peace rare. It is apparent that sin has held sway over much of life, as we know it. If anything it seems to increase as the days go by. Evidence such as this mitigates against the declaration that *Jesus is Lord*. Indeed when one looks around at the harm the church is placed under, it may be rather incredulous that this declaration is being made at all. The church has come under increased pressure to abdicate its self-understanding, retract its claims and revise its missionary calling. Violence and overt pressure has been applied in addition to subtle and more covert force to compel her to do so. Unfortunately even within the church at times sin has a power that is almost second to none. Some structures and systems within the church even add to the ever-widening grip of sin on our lives. Both from the outside and the inside it appears that the foundational structure of the church, its affirmation that *Jesus is Lord*, is being threatened and questioned perhaps like never before. In such a situation that Church will have to constantly call back to memory this declaration that *Jesus is Lord* and one day He will be Lord conclusively. She will need to repeat this in the face of ominous threats, not only for herself but also for the world at large. *Jesus is Lord* not of the church alone, not of our private spiritual experience alone but of the whole cosmos. Christian mission that takes place in such a milieu can take comfort that our Christian hope provides for us a language that can address this apparent paradox. Hope enables us to live in a tension of Christ's lordship established but yet to be fulfilled. When Christians are killed and jailed for their spiritual stance and activity Jesus remains Lord. When the people and structures of the Church are used for evil purposes even then

Jesus remains Lord. We know that He is Lord because He defeated death and rose from the grave. Death was a prelude to the resurrection; he could not experience resurrection unless he underwent death and rejection. The apparent victory of sin over Jesus and God's design for creation lasted but a few days. Just as for Jesus we must remember that Good Friday came before Easter and there was Holy Saturday in between. It is for no inconsequential reason that we call the day of Jesus' apparent defeat as 'Good Friday.' Indeed it was proved to be good in the light of Easter. The apparent victory of evil today, is simply that—apparent. Christian Hope looks forward to the second Easter when the true victor will establish His uncontested kingdom and rule over forever it in justice and peace. The first provides adequate foundations for our belief in the second. This eschatological future that we look forward to re-ignites our passion for and proclamation of the Lordship of Jesus Christ. It suffuses us with a dynamic that enables us stand even engage in mission, in the face of apparent defeat and hopelessness. Christian hope serves as the fuel propelling us forward to proclaim the Lordship of Jesus Christ. Living and acting with that hope then effectively subverts the power of lesser claimants to absolute power. It deconstructs the claims of these powers and renders their character impotent in the final analysis.

Conclusion

Rediscovering genuine Christian hope will occasion a radical revaluation of our mission theology and practice. We will affirm that God's mission, beginning from creation and moving up to its consummation in a "New Heaven and a New Earth," does not merely provide a comfortable assurance of "pie in the sky when we die." More profoundly it constitutes the horizon that provides our orientation, the assurance that enables our faith, the incentive that compels our action, and the goal to which all our efforts, indeed all of history, is directed. This recognition will enable us to decipher displaced hopes of previous efforts in mission and even alert us to similar dangers present in contemporary tendencies. It will also bring us back to living by the centrality of *Missio Dei* seen at work throughout history, the non-negotiable paradigm of the *Kingdom of God* expounded in the life and ministry of Jesus Christ and the foundational affirmation, that was so characteristic of the early disciples, *Jesus is Lord*. As a result impetus for mission will stem from the work of God progressing toward its grand finale, confidence in mission will arise not in successful methods or strategies but, in the history of God in as seen in the life of Jesus Christ made effective in the ministry of the Holy Spirit in the here and now, design for mission will be that vision of God's uncontested rule and, the object of mission will be to fulfil our calling as citizens of that kingdom. Mission, in this reckoning, will rightly begin with God, will be genuinely directed by him, and finally be brought to an end when He conclusively establishes Himself as Lord of all the universe.

CHAPTER 9

Theology of Mission in Historical Perspective: A Survey of Theological Trends as Traced in Major Conferences on Mission in the 20th Century in Relation to South Asia

ROGER E. HEDLUND

What is the theology of mission? Van Engen, who raises this question, says that theology of mission as a discipline began only in the 1960s.[1] Mission theology is missiological theologizing which "serves to question, clarify, integrate, and expand the presuppositions of the various cognate disciplines of missiology."[2] In this chapter we will survey a number of major 20th century conferences on mission to determine the theological trends that impinge on South Asia.

Beginnings

Missionary conferences were convened throughout the twentieth century beginning as early as 1900. Triumphalism was rampant at the turn of the century. At the Ecumenical Missionary Conference at New York, an optimistic portrayal of the progress of the missionary movement in India (and Further India) was presented.[3] Reports described the missionary impact on society. The demise of Hinduism was expected—a sentiment both uncharitable as well as poorly informed. A.T. Pierson, for example, published a series of books on the "miracles of missions" in which he celebrated the "transformation of Tinnevelly" but ignored the larger context in which mission takes place.[4]

In a similar hopeful vein, a Canadian National Missionary Conference in 1909 spoke of India's preparation for the Gospel. Reform movements were cited as evidence of the transformation of Hinduism. Methodist Bishop Thoborn was expectant of an ultimate Christian victory. Samuel Zwemer, however, noted the rise of a rampant new Hinduism as a rival missionary religion.[5]

Looking back, Zwemer rather than Thoborn was the more perceptive prognostician. Optimism gave way to realism following the Great War. No longer was Christian mission the immediate equation for creating God's Kingdom on earth. Nevertheless, despite a more sober tone, a positive note still is discerned at a National Missionary Congress in 1916 at Washington, D.C., which produced chapters on the Muslim World and on the Hindu World. The latter, by John P. Jones, reiterated great

---

[1] Charles Van Engen, *Mission on the Way: Issues in Mission Theology*, Grand Rapids, Baker Books, 1996, p.18.

[2] *Ibid.*, pp.22,23.

[3] *Ecumenical Missionary Conference, New York, 1900*. Report of the Ecumenical Conference on Foreign Missions, Held in Carnegie Hall and Neighbouring Churches, April 21 to May 1. Vol.I of 2 vols., New York: American Tract Society; London: Religious Tract Society; 1900. See chapter 21, "India and Further India," pp.502-524.

[4] Arthur T. Pierson, *The Miracles of Missions*, New York: Funk & Wagnalls Co., 1901.

[5] Canadian National Missionary Conference, *Canada's Missionary Congress*, Addresses Delivered at the Canadian National Missionary Congress, held in Toronto, March 31 to April 4, 1909, with Reports of Committees. Toronto: Canadian Council, Laymen's Missionary Movement

opportunities today in India and India's attraction to the Gospel.[6]

Edinburgh 1910

The culmination of the "Great Century" of Protestant missions (the 19th century) was the World Missionary Conference at Edinburgh in 1910. Edinburgh was an inclusive meeting. Questions of doctrine and polity were excluded, not as a compromise but as expedient. The emphasis was on consultation and cooperation. It was possible to work together despite differing views — a significant point for developments that were to follow in India during the twentieth century.

At Edinburgh participants accepted one another's confession of Christ. Yet Edinburgh was not entirely devoid of theology. A consensus was assumed on essentials, e.g. the world's need of Christ, God's offer of salvation, the missionary obligation.... The Conference did not require any elaborate justification for missions. "The evangelization of the world in this generation" was both the theme and the purpose of the World Missionary Conference. There was no debate about the meaning of mission. The aim and purpose of missionary activity was the evangelization of the peoples of earth.

Commission IV was devoted to the missionary message in relation to other religions. The Report on this Commission has been recognised as a masterpiece, among the most brilliant in the series, especially in its sympathetic treatment of Hinduism.[7] Missionaries are needed who will understand Hinduism and have the wisdom to appreciate its nobler qualities.

Diversity was recognized within Hinduism. The higher castes responded differently from the so-called lower castes. Edinburgh was committed to evangelization. Testimonials from converts were scrutinized. Factors bearing on conversion were noted: dissatisfaction with the old religion, uselessness of idol worship, the attractiveness of the new religion, a sense of sin, a new relationship to God as Saviour. Caste was noted as a significant barrier to conversion. "Edinburgh optimistically believed in the unanswerable appeal of the life of Christ to Hindus."[8]

The methodology of the Commission is particularly commendatory. The experiences of converts were sought as well as of missionaries and others in direct contact with Hindus. This gave the Conference a sense of ground reality. Hinduism's multiplicity was recognised, "not one religion but many," each requiring a different approach. "The popular religion of the village, ceremonial, and ritual Hinduism, the religion of the home, the social expression of religion, and a highly speculative and mystical religion—each demanded a different response from the Christian perspective."[9] In addition, it was noted, millions of Sudras and outcastes are not Hindus so much as animists.

Hinduism's spiritual view of life, in contrast to the materialism of the West, was seen as a positive point. The Hindu's quest for God, a desire for union with God, should be the basis for the encounter between Hinduism and the gospel. The *bhakti* tradition, the concept of *moksha* and the mystical dimension should be taken seriously.[10] The challenge of Hinduism was compared to that of the encounter with Hellenism

---

[6] *Men and World Service*, Addresses at the National Missionary Congress, Washington, D.C., April 26-30, 1916. New York: Laymen's Missionary Movement.

[7] See comments by Gairdner and others in Roger E. Hedlund, *Roots of the Great Debate in Mission: Mission in Historical and Theological Perspective*, Revised Edition, Bangalore, Theological Book Trust, 1993, pp.28-29.

[8] *Ibid.*, p.29.

[9] Wesley Ariarajah, *Hindus and Christians: A Century of Protestant Ecumenical Thought*, Amsterdam, Editions Rodopi, and Grand Rapids, Eerdmans, 1991, p.19.

[10] *Ibid.*, pp.26-29.

in the early Christian era. Edinburgh spoke of new possibilities driving Christians "to discover new dimensions that they had never seen before."[11]

Edinburgh was nevertheless highly optimistic, at some points influenced by the fulfillment theories of Farquhar and others. For the most part, the tremendous findings of Edinburgh remain a rich but forgotten treasure. Edinburgh, as Ariarajah states, "did not engage in apologetics," and did not unfairly judge the other faiths, but cultivated an attitude of listening and learning from them.[12] That stance has much to commend itself to us today.

Following the seminal World Missionary Conference at Edinburgh in 1910, a series of continuation conferences were held in Asia. In India such conferences took place at Madras, Bombay, Jubbulpore, Allahabad, Lahore and Calcutta. Reports were given on evangelization and related themes pertinent to engagement with Hinduism and Islam. The Bombay report mentions the needs of the outcaste masses. Jubbulpore called for special attention to the evangelization of one million Muslims in the region. Lahore noted the urgency of mass movements and the need for new types of literature for both Hindus and Muslims. The India National Conference also focused on the needs and opportunities of the mass movements.[13] It appears that the continuation conferences were primarily concerned about the outcastes (Dalits, "untouchables"), and secondarily for the Muslims, but gave little visible attention to major Vaishnavite, Saivite and diverse Hindu groups.

The World Missionary Conference at Edinburgh voted into existence a Continuation Committee which was to further the initiatives began at Edinburgh. A series of continuation conferences were conducted in India, Burma, Singapore, China, Korea, Japan and in other parts of the world. In 1912 the *International Review of Missions* began publication. The other most significant accomplishment was formation of the International Missionary Council (IMC)[14] which emerged in 1921. The IMC was an organ for cooperation between churches and mission societies of widely different traditions. The IMC did not try to resolve doctrinal differences. It followed the pattern set at Edinburgh and let the Churches themselves settle the doctrinal issues. However, Edinburgh's consuming passion for the evangelization of the world is not so evident in the IMC.

Jerusalem 1928

The next major world conference was called by the recently formed International Missionary Council and took place at Jerusalem in 1928. Gone was the earlier optimism, shattered by the Great War. The choice of Jerusalem for the first IMC conference might have been to compensate for Protestantism's perceived neglect of Islam.[15] Muslims, however, interpreted the event as a plot against Islam. "That Jerusalem was a closed meeting of the Council and allowed no visitors only heightened Moslem suspicions of its purpose."[16]

Jerusalem's central concern was with the *Christian* message. The conference declared, "Our message is Jesus Christ." Jerusalem

---

[11] *Ibid.*, p.23.

[12] *Ibid.*, p.29.

[13] *The Continuation Committee Conferences in Asia 1912-1913*, A Brief Account of the Conferences Together with Their Findings and Lists of Members, New York. Published by the Chairman of the Continuation Committee, 1913.

[14] The history of the IMC is written by William Richey Hogg, Ecumenical Foundations: A History of the International Missionary Council and its Nineteenth Century Background, New York, Harper, 1952.

[15] Roger E. Hedlund, *Roots of the Great Debate.*, p.62.

[16] William Richey Hogg, *Ecumenical Foundations*, p.251.

welcomed "every noble quality in non-Christian persons or systems" as rays of the light of Christ and proof that God is nowhere without witness even where He is unknown or rejected.[17] Secularism was identified as the common foe of all religions.[18] The religions were not the central focus. If anything, Jerusalem was uncertain about the religions. Along with respect, enrichment and appreciation, there was also the notion of fulfillment. Jerusalem's message, states Ariarajah, was a bundle of theological contradictions. "Edinburgh's penetrating insight portraying the encounter with other faiths as a challenge to the Christian faith itself was completely lost at Jerusalem."[19]

Jerusalem was more theological than Edinburgh, but was less interested in questions of evangelization. By focusing on Jesus Christ, Jerusalem endeavoured to appeal to everyone and hoped perhaps to reconcile opposing views.

At Jerusalem the so-called younger churches from Africa, Asia and Latin America were equal participants along with the sending churches of the West in planning for the Christian world mission.[20] The missionary was placed within the indigenous church, but mission became church centric.

Jerusalem's greatest contribution may have been in what transpired following the conference.

In India the Mass Movement Survey directed by J. Waskom Pickett[21] under the auspices of the National Christian Council of India and the oversight of Bishop V.S. Azariah,[22] and with the cooperation of the International Missionary Council, was a direct outcome of Jerusalem.[23] The purpose was to assemble and evaluate information regarding the mass movements so as to help leaders of the Church and missionary organizations to think through the issues and to shape policies and programmes accordingly.[24] The outcome was a vindication of the values of such movements together with identification of weaknesses and dangers and how to achieve larger possibilities.[25]

Madras 1938

The IMC conference on the World Mission of the Church at Tambaram, Madras, in 1938, corrected some of the deficiencies of the Jerusalem meeting. At Tambaram, Jerusalem's vagueness gave way to certainty. The non-Christian religions, largely overlooked at Jerusalem, were approached with respect and appreciation at Tambaram, but with a call for conversion.

If Jerusalem's major contribution was in what took place after the conference, at Madras it might be in what transpired in advance. Dissatisfied with Jerusalem's uncertainty, the IMC had

---

[17] "The Christian Message," The Statement Adopted by the International Missionary Council at Jerusalem, Easter 1928, Report of the Jerusalem Meeting, Vol. I, The Christian Life and Message in Relation to non-Christian Systems. See Roger E. Hedlund, *Roots of the Great Debate.*, p.77.

[18] William Richey Hogg, *Ecumenical Foundations*, pp.241,249.

[19] Ariarajah, *Hindus and Christians*, p.50.

[20] *Ibid.*, p.253.

[21] The story of Pickett's contribution is by Arthur Gene McPhee, "Pickett's Fire: The Life, Contribution, Thought, and Legacy of J. Waskom Pickett, Methodist Missionary to India," Ph.D. dissertation, Asbury Theological Seminary, 2001.

[22] For a study of Azariah's role, see Susan Billington Harper, *In the Shadow of the Mahatma: Bishop V.S. Azariah and the Travails of Christianity in British India*, Grand Rapids and Cambridge, Eerdmans, and Richmond, Surrey, Curzon Press, 2000.

[23] See John R. Mott's "Foreword" to *Christian Mass Movements in India* by J. Waskom Pickett, Lucknow: Lucknow Publishing House, 1969 reprint, pp. 5-8.

[24] J. Wesham Pickett, *Christian Mass Movements in India.*, p.12.

[25] *Ibid.*, pp.319-348

commissioned Hendrik Kraemer to prepare a clear statement on the Christian message and approach. *The Christian Message in a Non-Christian World* was a culmination of Kraemer's experience as a missionary in Indonesia and as a theologian. Kraemer's approach was to evaluate all religions in light of the revelation of Jesus Christ. The heart of the Christian message, said Kraemer, is the Word made flesh, the Incarnation is the decisive moment in world history. "The message of the Gospel is that God by His creative act of reconciliation and atonement in Jesus Christ, reconciling the world unto Himself, not imputing men's trespasses unto them, opened a way of reconciliation when there was no way."[26] Kraemer struggled with the theological problem of how God reveals Himself in the non-Christian religions if, in fact, He does so reveal Himself. In Kraemer we find a tension between the essential missionary attitude of respect and appreciation on the one hand and the essential Christ centric core on the other. "The argument of value does not coincide in any way whatever with that of truth."[27] Kraemer drew a line of radical discontinuity between the religions and the revelation of God in Christ. Religions have produced lofty ideals and great ethical systems, but also "the most abhorrent and degrading filth that perverted human imagination and lust can beget."[28]

Kraemer shows a deep understanding of Hinduism, its diversities and commonalities, philosophy and literature, sects and cults. Kraemer is impressed with the *bhakti* -theology of Ramanuja. The impressive similarity of *bhakti* -religion to Christianity is noted. Yet there is a radical difference: the absence of Jesus Christ and His new Kingdom. "Faith in the *bhakti* -religion and faith in the New Testament cannot be compared."[29] *Bhakti* -religion proclaims God as love and the possibility of receiving God's favour, but knows nothing of the biblical experience of salvation in which a holy God reconciles lost sinners to Himself.[30] At the popular level, superstitious practices and magic dominate the lives of millions; The Brahman has enormous authority, and the guru is god.[31]

India, however, was undergoing change. Indian nationalism was a growing factor during the era in which Kraemer wrote. Ambedkar's movement for social equality was essentially a cry for freedom which was deterred by Gandhi's misunderstanding of conversion and an almost universal acceptance of the doctrine of *karma*.[32] The Arya Samaj, Ramakrishna Mission, Hindu Mission and others were examples of a resurgence of Hinduism inspired by nationalism and the ideals of the Indian ethical and religious heritage. The slogan of the Hindu Mahasabha was "Hindustan for the Hindus."[33] Already religion was becoming politicised. The Hindu religious resurgence was essentially "a resurgence of religious nationalism."[34] Radhakrishnan, India's modern philosopher, endeavoured to combine the best from the ancient Hindu tradition with modern thinking, including elements borrowed from Christianity and Islam, "in a delusive synthesis" which symbolises "the chaotic and confused state of religious thinking and life in India" at that tumultuous moment in history.[35]

---

[26] Hendrik Kraemer, *The Christian Message in a Non-Christian World*, Grand Rapids, Kregel, 1961, p.76.

[27] *Ibid.,* p.106.

[28] *Ibid.,* p.113.

[29] *Ibid.,* pp.170-172.

[30] *Ibid.,* p.173.

[31] *Ibid.,* pp.234-235.

[32] *Ibid.,* pp.236-240.

[33] *Ibid.,* p.242.

[34] *Ibid.,* p.243.

[35] *Ibid.,* pp.244-245.

Regarding Islam, Kraemer noted that it had become a great syncretistic combination of theocratic legalism, mysticism and popular religion formulated as a modification of Christianity and Judaism. Islam presented a formidable challenge to Christian mission. Even the most nominal Muslim was ready to kill or die in defence of Islam.[36] However Kraemer also pointed out a major problem within Islam in the tension between the secularization of theocracy and the presence of mysticism in Islam.[37]

Kraemer was prominent at Tambaram and his thinking is said to have had a profound impact at this "most widely representative assembly of Christians ever gathered."[38] Not everyone agreed with Kraemer's position. Delegates from India were uneasy with Kraemer's radical discontinuity. The Madras "Rethinking Group" in particular challenged Kraemer's concept in the 1939 publication of *Rethinking Christianity in India*. Subsequently Indian Christian Theology has developed in a different direction. Vengal Chakkarai, for example, argued for *continuity*, rather than discontinuity. Comparisons between Hinduism and Christianity as rival faiths are futile. If Hinduism satisfies the spiritual needs of its followers, asks Chakkarai, why bring in Christianity at all? "The answer," he states, "is not that we want to bring the Hindu from one religion to another but that when God Himself calls people they obey."[39] The attraction is not to Christianity but to Christ. "Christ cannot oppose

Hinduism nor does He."[40] The "Rethinking Group" espoused a radical appreciation for the values in Hinduism.[41] P. Chenchiah, in particular, was anxious to retain his Indian-Hindu cultural heritage. For Chenchiah, direct experience of Christ rather than dogmas was the essential Christian core.[42]

Tambaram was able to identify values and glimpses of God's light in the non-Christian religions, but it failed to attain Edinburgh's previous level of comprehension of the formidable challenge of Hinduism to Christian faith.[43] It remained for persons like E. Stanley Jones to better articulate the Gospel of Jesus Christ in the Hindu context beyond the confines of the conference.[44]

Transition

The world mission conferences of the International Missionary Council continued at Whitby, Canada, in 1947, and at Willingen, Germany, in 1952. Both met in the wake of the Second World War. Neither one offered any special section devoted to the other religions. A final IMC meeting was held at Ghana in 1958 as a preparation for merger with the World Council of Churches (WCC).

The WCC is heir to the IMC, which during four decades had laid the ecumenical foundations.[45] The integration took place at the Third World Assembly of the WCC at New Delhi in 1961. Thereafter, a series of world conferences

---

[36] *Ibid.*, pp.215-219.

[37] *Ibid.*, pp.225-226.

[38] William Richey Hogg, *Ecumenical Founcations.*, pp.293,294.

[39] V.Chakkarai, "Christianity and Non-Christian Faiths," 1938, reprinted in *Asian Expressions of Christian Commitment* edited by T. Dayanandan Francis and Franklyn J. Balasundaram, Madras, CLS, 1992, p.114.

[40] *Ibid.*, p.118.

[41] See V.C. Rajasekaran, *Reflections on Indian Christian Theology*, Madras, CLS, 1993. Also P. Chenchiah, V. Chakkarai, and A.N. Sudarisanam, *Asramas Past and Present*, Madras: CLS, 1941,1996 reprint.

[42] Robin Boyd, *An Introduction to Indian Christian Theology*, Madras: CLS, 1975, 147.

[43] Wesley Ariarajah, *Hindus and Christians.*, p.88.

[44] Jones, who was present at Tambaram, apparently was not satisfied with the ecclesio-centrality of the Conference on the World Mission of the Church. See Wesley Ariarajah, *Hindus and Christians,* p.91ff.

[45] William Richey Hogg, *Ecumenical Foundations*, p.375.

were continued by the Commission and Division of World Mission and Evangelism of the WCC at Mexico City in 1963, Bangkok in 1972, Melbourne in 1980, San Antonio (Texas) in 1989, and Salvador (Brazil) in 1996. The conferences, programmes and documents which followed were not focused upon the religions so much as they were concerned about relationships between sending and receiving Churches. The weakness in the *missio dei* and "Missionary Structure of the Congregation" approaches which evolved during this era is that they fail to specify the work of God in the world, as Lalsangkima Pachuau points out.[46]

Gradually the WCC interest in mission *per se* appears to have diminished. Neither the Fourth Assembly of the WCC at Uppsala in 1968 nor the Salvation Today Conference of the CWME at Bangkok in 1972 evidenced interest in the communication of the Gospel among non-Christians but were concerned rather about questions of humanization.[47] Increasingly the emphasis has turned more toward inter-religious dialogue and related questions. For twenty years or more the WCC has sponsored Christian-Muslim conversations. The WCC Sub-Unit on Dialogue under the direction of Stanley Samartha from India and Wesley Ariarajah from Sri Lanka has given considerable attention to Hindu-Christian issues. Consultations on dialogue and related topics are an important source. Ecumenical engagement with Hinduism is seen in the assemblies and related conferences of the

WCC where one finds the imprint of D.T. Niles, P.D. Devanandan and M.M. Thomas.[48]

More than one stream emerged from Edinburgh.[49] A series of *evangelical* world conferences, beginning in the 1960s, with various sponsors, also continued the Edinburgh heritage.[50] These include conferences at Wheaton in 1966, Berlin in 1966, Lausanne in 1974, Pattaya in 1980, Edinburgh in 1980, Amsterdam in 1983 & 1986, Manila in 1989, Seoul in 1995, and South Africa in 1999. From this stream, three are of particular relevance: Lausanne, Pattaya and Manila.

Lausanne 1974

Lausanne 1974, the International Congress on World Evangelization (LCWE), has been called the most important evangelical gathering in the twentieth century.[51] The Congress was a pivotal event calling attention to the two billion unevangelized inhabitants of the globe. Lausanne contradicted the opinion that the geographical spread of Christianity had nullified the need for cross-cultural mission. The immensity of the task was demonstrated by the data compiled by careful research during several years prior to the Congress.

Underlying all was a theological foundation. Evangelical theologians from East and West, South and North presented studies on Scripture, hermeneutics, God, humanity, Christology, atonement, salvation, the Kingdom, the Church, evangelism, conversion, ethics, prayer,

---

[46] Lalsangkima Pachuau, "Missiology in a Pluralistic World: The Place of Mission Study in Theological Education," *International Review of Mission* LXXXIX, 355, October 2000, pp.539-555.

[47] Orlando Costas commented that virtually no one was satisfied with the outcome. See Orlando E. Costas, *The Church and Its Mission: A Shattering Critique from the Third World*, Wheaton, Tyndale, 1974.

[48] See Wesley Ariarajah's helpful discussion of these events and personalities as well as of pertinent conferences of the East Asia Christian Council (now Christian Council of Asia) in Wesley Ariarajah, *Hindus and Christians.*, pp.101-162.

[49] See Roger E. Hedlund, *Roots of the Great Debate.*, p.121.

[50] Normal E. Thomas, "World Mission Conferences: What Impact Do They Have?" *International Bulletin of Missionary Research*, October 1996, pp.146-154.

[51] Rodger C. Bassham, *Mission Theology: 1948-1975, Years of Worldwide Creative Tension Ecumenical, Evangelical, and Roman Catholic*, Pasadena, William Carey Library, 1979, p. 209.

apologetics, universalism, culture. The Theology of Evangelization Papers and Reports comprise one of the richest contributions of the Congress. The Lausanne Covenant reiterated the evangelistic mandate and acknowledged the urgency of evangelizing the neglected two-thirds of the human race yet to be evangelized. The Covenant emphasised the need to believe, obey, proclaim and "make disciples of every nation." Evangelism was seen as proclamation "with a view to persuading" and resulting in obedience to Christ, incorporation into the Church and responsible service in the world.

> Lausanne evoked expressions of opinion from the whole evangelical community as participants struggled with the issues of mission theology in the world today. The fruit of the discussions in the Lausanne Covenant show that evangelicals have developed a mature, positive, and well-rounded theology of mission. While continuing to stress the authority of the Bible and evangelism, the Covenant also focuses on Discipleship and church renewal as key elements in the total mission of the church. The strength of evangelical voices from Latin America, Africa, and Asia at Lausanne demonstrates that debate within the worldwide evangelical community will be diverse and varied, yet with all bound together in the task of involving 'the whole Church to take the whole Gospel to the whole world.'[52]

Lausanne stimulated a number of national and regional congresses and other consultations. These included the 1977 Pasadena Consultation on the Homogeneous Unit Principle, the 1978 Willowbank Consultation on the Gospel and Culture, the 1978 North American Conference on Muslim Evangelization, and the LCWE Consultation on World Evangelization (COWE) at Pattaya, Thailand, in 1980. The latter was primarily a strategy meeting consisting of 17 mini-consultations each of which produced a separate report. Pattaya was dominated by academicians rather than practitioners but nevertheless focused upon a world of unevangelized peoples beyond the social or spiritual outreach of any existing church.[53]

Other LCWE-related events include the International Consultation on Simple Life-Style at London in 1980, the Consultation on the Relationship between Evangelism and Social Responsibility at Grand Rapids in 1982, both co-sponsored by the World Evangelical Fellowship (WEF). The 1983 Wheaton Conference on the Nature and Mission of the Church was convened by the WEF but with LCWE as a co-sponsor. Each of these assemblies produced publications (including an *Unreached Peoples* annual series published by MARC-World Vision) which have allowed for a greater stimulation and dissemination of evangelical thinking on the varied dimensions of mission.

Manila 1989

The second LCWE International Congress on World Evangelization, Lausanne II, in Manila, in 1989, was a multi-variegated programme of celebration with more than 4,000 participants from nearly every political nation: a manifestation of the extension of the Kingdom of God and the impact of world evangelization. Notable features included emphasis on prayer, on suffering, on mission under repressive conditions, holistic evangelism, social concern as part of the evangelization process, ministry in a context of world poverty. Manila failed to focus adequately on the pluralistic religious context of Asia. Yet Asia is the birthplace of the major world religions and home for a majority of the world's unevangelized peoples! Nevertheless the Congress produced the Manila Manifesto that, as a companion to the Lausanne Covenant,

---

[52] *Ibid.*, p.295.
[53] Waldron Scott, "The Significance of Pattaya," *Missiology*, January 1981, pp.64,70.

contains some crucial theological content. The Manifesto is explicitly Christocentric, openly evangelical, consciously eschatological, intentionally holistic, decidedly ecclesiological, but weakly missiological.[54] Its missiological deficiency stems from its failure to fully realize the significance of the religious context of modern Asia.

Despite these weaknesses, the Manifesto and the Congress enunciated the mandate for evangelical social responsibility, provided meaningful exposure to a world of poverty and oppression, highlighted the call to mission under the most difficult circumstances including the witness of suffering and martyrdom, and asserted the indispensable role of the Holy Spirit in accomplishing the mission of Christ in the world.

Asian Conferences

Other more recent conferences in Asia and India also should be scrutinized. The Asia LCWE conducted a series of Asian Leadership Conferences on Evangelism (ALCOE). ALCOE-IV at Kuala Lumpur in 1996 expressed concern over the needs of Asia which has the world's largest populations and the largest blocks of major world religions including Buddhism, Hinduism and Islam. A major address was devoted to a Christian response to the resurgence of Asian religions and cultures.[55]

Indian Conferences

In India an All India Congress on Mission & Evangelisation was conducted by the Evangelical Fellowship of India (EFI) in 1977 at Devalali in Maharashtra. In his strategy paper on the Gospel and India's Religious Culture, Saphir Athyal addressed several issues including our attitude to other religions, questions of inter-religious dialogue, and implications of the Hindu concept of the essential unity of all religions.[56] In 1988 the EFI again convened an All India Congress on Mission & Evangelization, this time at Union Biblical Seminary (UBS), Pune. Again, in 1999, the All India Congress on the Church in Mission took place in New Delhi, sponsored by EFI. The Congress gave a general overview of 50 years of the Church in mission in India. It discussed some of the more urgent challenges and prospects for mission. Significant, was the initiating of networks to facilitate and encourage the work of mission. Prominent among them was the one on Women and the one on Holistic Mission. Efficacy of these efforts remains to be seen in the years to come.

WCC, CWME

Ecumenical initiatives also continued. At the 1975 Nairobi Fifth Assembly of the World Council of Churches on the theme "Jesus Christ Frees and Unites," speakers such as Moderator M.M. Thomas as well as Bishop Mortimer Arias acknowledged the impact of Lausanne 1974. Nairobi has been described as a swing back from the extremes of Upsala and Bangkok. "Few disputed that the world and its problems and possibilities must be the arena for mission. However, there was a renewed emphasis on evangelism, and the church as God's agent for mission."[57]

This focus continued at the Commission on World Mission and Evangelism (CWME)

---

[54] For amplification of these points see Roger E. Hedlund, *Roots of the Great Debate in Mission*, Bangalore, TBT, 1993, pp.415-416.

[55] Hwa Yung, "The Resurgence of Asian Religion and Cultures—A Christian Response" in *Taking the Whole Gospel to Asia Today, The Fourth Asian Leadership Conference on Evangelism, Kuala Lumpur, October 21-25, 1996*, New Delhi, Asia Lausanne Committee, 1997.

[56] Saphir P. Athyal, "The Gospel and India's Religious Culture," Strategy Paper 2, in *Go Forth and Tell: Christ Jesus, Saviour, Lord and King*, Report of the All India Congress on Mission and Evangelization, Devlali, January 12-19, 1977.

[57] Rodger C. Bassham, *Mission Theology 1948-1975.*, p.105.

conference at Melbourne in 1980 around the theme, "Your Kingdom Come." Melbourne has been described as Christological, methodological and ecclesiological but focusing on the evangelistic mission of the Church with a plea for the validity of specialized mission agencies as part of Church structure.[58] The documents indicated a dual commitment to evangelization and to the poor. Melbourne was concerned for world evangelization holistically defined, and will be remembered for its focus on the poor in relation to the Kingdom.

The Sixth Assembly of the WCC at Vancouver in 1983 gathered around a Christological theme, "Jesus Christ—the Light of the World." Prior to Vancouver the CWME had released a significant document, "Mission and Evangelism: An Ecumenical Affirmation," which was viewed by evangelicals as a new sign of hope for the Ecumenical Movement.[59] At the same time, however, the WCC appeared to advocate religious pluralism as the basis for dialogue,[60] which led some to conclude that frontier mission and evangelism were not WCC priorities.[61] Advocates of religious pluralism tend to assume "a nearly synonymous relationship between faith and culture."[62] Despite a close relationship between them, a distinction must be made.

The failure to differentiate between the gospel and human cultures has been one of the great weaknesses of modern Christian missions. Missionaries too often have equated the Good News with their own cultural background. This has led them to condemn most native customs and to impose their own customs on converts. Consequently, the gospel has been seen as foreign in general and Western in particular.[63]

In 1989, prior to the LCWE event at Manila, the CWME convened at San Antonio, Texas, in continuation of the Melbourne conference. The theme, "Your Will Be Done: Mission in Christ's Way," enunciated the Trinitarian nature of Christian mission and the centrality of Jesus Christ. Delegates were reminded "millions of our fellow men and women have not heard, even once in their lives, the Christian message."[64] Need for continued dialogue with evangelicals was pressed. Non-Western delegates at San Antonio urged a bold confession of Christ and, (in answer to the vague theocentrism of Hick, Knitter and Cantwell Smith), an explicit evangelism of people of all faiths.[65]

The Seventh Assembly of the WCC at Canberra in 1991 was devoted to a neumatological theme, "Come, Holy Spirit—Renew the Whole Creation." A renewed emphasis on the Holy Spirit in the WCC was most welcome. The Canberra theme, neglected by mainline Protestant traditions, is important in the Orthodox tradition as well as in the Pentecostal-Charismatic movement.[66] Study materials released in advance linked the Assembly theme to issues of justice, peace, liberation and renewal of the whole creation. A sensational plenary address and

---

[58] Jacques Matthey, "Melbourne: Mission in the Eighties," CWME, XI-XVII.

[59] Arthur F. Glasser, "Ecumenism: Signs of Hope?" *Theology News and Notes* March 1988, 15-17,27.

[60] Stanley Samartha, The Other Side of the River: Some Reflections on the Theme of the Vancouver Assembly, Madras, CLS, 1983, p.38.

[61] James A. Scherer, "The Mission Focus at the Vancouver Assembly of the WCC," *Missiology* October 1983, p.530.

[62] Van Engen, *Mission on the Way*, p.179.

[63] Paul G. Hiebert, *Anthropological Insights for Missionaries*, Grand Rapids, Baker, 1985, p.53.

[64] Address by the Conference Moderator, Anastasios of Androussa, Plenary Presentation in *The San Antonio Report, Your Will Be Done: Mission in Christ's Way* edited by Frederick R. Wilson, Geneva, WCC Publications, p.112.

[65] David J. Bosch, "Your Will Be Done? Critical Reflections on San Antonio," *Missionalia*, August 1989, p.135.

[66] T.K. Thomas, "The WCC Assembly Theme, Sub-Themes and Issues," *National Council of Churches Review* November 1990, pp. 604,605.

invocation by Professor Chung Hyun-Kyung of Korea confused the Holy Spirit with the spirits of earth, air and water and people killed by violence.[67] The WCC Canberra theme was a fitting sequel to the previous Melbourne conference on "Your Kingdom Come" and the San Antonio consultation on "Mission in Christ's Way."

Pentecostals

Not to be overlooked are the Pentecostals. The modern Pentecostal movement began as a missionary movement! Even before the formation of the first Pentecostal denomination, Pentecostal Christians were engaged in missionary sending.[68] Pentecostal fire, ignited at Azusa Street, Los Angeles, in the first decade of the twentieth century, spread rapidly to the ends of the earth! The Pentecostal Revival took seriously the command of Christ to evangelize the world.[69] Within 100 years the Pentecostal-Charismatic movement has grown to become the second largest body of Christians, larger than all other Protestants, exceeded only by the Roman Catholics. In India today the Pentecostals comprise the fastest growing section of the Church, and the Charismatic Movement has a growing impact in the Roman Catholic Church. The largest Protestant congregations in Bangalore, Chennai and Kolkata are Pentecostal. In Mumbai the New Life Fellowship is a rapidly multiplying urban house church phenomenon. These churches are actively engaged in various social programmes which benefit the poor and

marginalized. Pentecostal theology is essentially a theology of the Acts of the Apostles. The baptism, gifts, and fruit of the Holy Spirit are for Christian character building and are essential for the ministry of the Church and for carrying out mission. The indigenous church principles of Melvin Hodges facilitate lay initiative and leadership innovation. Pentecostal ecclesiology encourages the ministry and training of the laity. The Pentecostals provide a participation model for developing local leadership in the living situation.[70] The dominant theme of the Book of Acts is "the expansion of the church through missionary witness in the power of the Holy Spirit."[71] The Pentecostal approach takes seriously the problems of spirit possession and demonic manifestations. A missiology of power rather than mere argument and intellect is both revolutionary and relevant. Pentecostal missiology postulates a theology of the Kingdom. "The Kingdom in pneumatological terms has to do with the witness of the Church in the Spirit's power and the universalization of mission under His direction."[72] Pentecostals, the poor, and phenomenal church growth are linked together because of the disposition of the poor toward repentance and faith by which they enter the Kingdom.[73] The Holy Spirit as the Advocate of Jesus Christ is central in this redemptive activity. Pentecostal theology seems particularly suited to the task of penetrating the unevangelized blocks of the majority communities of South Asia. The witness of the laity, a willingness to live by faith, the disciplines of fasting and prayer, deliverance

---

[67] Chung Hyun-Kyung, "Come Holy Spirit, Renew the Whole Creation," *National Council of Churches Review*, June-July 1991, pp.1076-1087.

[68] Gary B. McGee, *This Gospel Shall Be Preached: A History and Theology of Assemblies of God Foreign Missions to 1959*, Springfield, Gospel Publishing House, 1986.

[69] See L. Grant McClung, ed. *Azusa Street and Beyond: Pentecostal Missions and Church Growth in the Twentieth Century*, New York, Bridge Publishing, 1986.

[70] Lesslie Newbigin, "Theological Education in a World Perspective" in *Missions and Theological Education in World Perspective*, edited by Harvie M. Conn and Samuel F. Rowen, Farmington, Michigan, Associates of Urbanus, 1984.

[71] Paul A. Pomerville, *The Third Force in Missions: A Pentecostal Contribution to Contemporary Mission Theology*, Peabody, Hendrickson Publishers, 1985, p.72.

[72] *Ibid.*, p.150.

ministries and miraculous healings all serve to authenticate the message of Christ.[74] Pentecostal theology is relevant in India.

Roman Catholics

Roman Catholic theology of mission historically centered in the Church as the ark of salvation. The Second Vatican Council of the 1960s brought indelible change into the Catholic Church. The new Catholicism manifested a new openness toward the Bible, toward Jesus Christ and Protestants. Inevitably this led also to questions about the religions. Two documents are specifically concerned about mission. *Ad Gentes*, the Decree on the Missionary Activity of the Church, highlighted the task of taking the gospel to the two billion human beings who had not yet heard the gospel message.[75] *Nostra Aetate*, the Declaration on the Relationship of the Church to Non-Christian Religions, affirmed the truth and values to be found in Hinduism, Buddhism, Islam and Judaism.[76]

Two trends followed Vatican II. Trend one reiterated the classic missionary activity of planting the Catholic Church among the nations. Trend two was toward inter-religious dialogue rather than conversion as the goal of mission. Catholic mission thinking in India has been deeply stirred by Karl Rahner's "implicit Christianity" proposition[77] and Raymond Panikkar's "cosmic Christ" postulate. According to Panikkar, "The good and *bonafide* Hindu is saved by Christ and not by Hinduism, but it is through the sacraments of Hinduism.... Hinduism has also a place in the universal saving providence of God."[78] Theologians in India built upon Panikkar, Rahner and aspects of Vatican II to foster a new indigenous theology. Ishanand Vempany projects all the world's religions as heirs of God's covenant with Adam, Noah and Abraham.[79] Catholic mission theology in India today generally follows the second trend, is dialogical and open toward the other religions. After Vatican II the Catholic Church began to accept a theology of religious pluralism and the work of the Holy Spirit "outside the visible boundaries of the Church."[80] Response to the spirituality of India means that the meaning of Jesus Christ must be translated into the living experience of Christians and the Christian community. Not arguments but a deep experience of Jesus will touch the soul of India.[81]

In India and Asia the Catholic Church has produced important writers on mission,[82] has convened significant conferences on mission,[83]

---

[73] *Ibid.*, pp.152-153.

[74] P.T. Abraham, "Indigenous Cross-Cultural Missions in India and Their Contribution to Church Growth: With Special Emphasis on Pentecostal-Charismatic Missions," Ph.D. dissertation, Fuller Theological Seminary, 1990.

[75] Walter M. Abbott (ed.) *The Documents of Vatican II*, London-Dublin, Geoffrey Chapman, p.597.

[76] *Ibid.*, pp.660-667.

[77] See Karl Rahner, "Salvation of the Non-Evangelized" in *Sacramentum Mundi, An Encyclopedia of Theology*, Vol.4, Bangalore, Theological Publications in India, 1975, p.80

[78] Raymond Panikkar, *The Unknown Christ of Hinduism*, London: Daron Longman and Todd, 1964, p.54.

[79] Ishanand Vempeny, *Inspiration in the Non-Biblical Scriptures*, Bangalore, Theological Publications in India, 1973, p.138.

[80] Thomas Mampra, "Mission in a Pluralistic Society," in *A Missiology for the Third Millennium*, edited by Thomas Aykara, Bangalore, Dharmaram Publications, 1997, p.80.

[81] *Ibid.*, p.81.

[82] Consider, for example, Swami Abhishiktananda, Michael Amaladoss, D.S. Amalorpavadass, Anato Karokaran, Sebastian Karotemprel, J. Mattam, Raymond Panikkar, M. Vellanikal, Ishanand Vempeny and others.

[83] For example, the 1971 Nagpur Theological Conference on Evangelization. See J. Pathrapankal, ed., *Service and Salvation*, Bangalore, Theological Publication in India, 1973.

and has seen the emergence of new mission journals[84] and institutes.

From outside of India, issues of social justice and need for structural changes in society were raised by Latin American theologians of liberation. Liberation theology found a resonance among Indian and Sri Lankan theologians, e.g. John Desrochers, Aloysius Pieris, Samuel Rayan, George Soares-Prabhu, Felix Wilfred, others. Dalit theology was to emerge as an Indian expression of Liberation theology among Protestants as well as Catholics Vatican II was revolutionary for theology of mission in India.

Issues Arising

Missiological theologizing moves in many directions. No uniform theology of mission can be derived from the mission conferences of the twentieth century. Nevertheless certain major theological themes can be discerned with their divergent trends.

God. Theological questions did not surface at Edinburgh. A degree of unanimity was assumed. That was no longer true at Jerusalem where considerable uncertainty was evident, consistent with the theological liberalism of the times. Jerusalem's divergent viewpoints found a Reaction at Tambaram in the radical discontinuity of Kraemer's Biblical realism that placed the revealed God of the Bible in a different category from the conceptions of God in the world religions. Indian theologians, from Tambaram onward, were more positive toward the religions, finding in them glimpses of truth as well as human searching for the Ineffable. From Jerusalem a transition is discerned from a Trinitarian and Christocentric theology of mission to an enlarged Theocentric approach leading to the ideology of Religious Pluralism which is prevalent today.[85] God then is the Mysterious Other believed by Christians to be revealed as Father, Son and Holy Spirit, known to Muslims as Allah, but perceived by Hindus as Brahman. Parallel responses in different cultural settings to the same Mystery, plural ways of salvation, each one valid for its adherents, according to Samartha.[86] It is difficult, however, to see how the pluralist paradigm can promote dialogue with non-theistic religions (Buddhism), with primal religions (tribal religions, Wicca) or the militantly monotheistic ones (Islam). Pluralists appear to have adopted the assumptions of *advaita Vedanta* as the basis for dialogue.[87] Over against the pluralist assumption, evangelical theology of mission was explicitly Christocentric and Trinitarian.

World. The arena of mission is the world. The century opened with a burst of enthusiasm. The world was in process of conversion. In a short time the Christian mission would bring the followers of all world religions and ideologies

---

[84] These include *Indian Missiological Review* more recently reincarnated as *Mission Today,* as well as *Third Millennium* and other popular and theological periodicals devoted to mission.

[85] See George David, "Unitive Pluralism and the Challenge of Mission to Hindus" in *Many Other Ways? Questions of Religious Pluralism* by IM. Bage, R. Hedlund, P.B. Thomas, Martin Alphonse and George David, Delhi: ISPCK, 1992, 59-68. Literature on religious pluralism is vast; e.g., S. Wesley Ariarajah, *The Bible and People of Other Faiths,* Maryknoll: Orbis, 1990; Gavin D'Costa (ed.), *Christian Uniqueness Reconsidered: The Myth of a Pluralistic Theology of Religions,* Maryknoll: Orbis, 1990; Jacques Dupuis, *Jesus Christ at the Encounter of World Religions,* Maryknoll: Orbis, 1991; John Hick, *A Christian Theology of Religions: The Rainbow of Faiths,* Louisville: Westminster John Knox Press, 1995; Paul F. Knitter, *No Other Name? A Critical Survey of Christian Attitudes toward the World Religions,* Maryknoll: Orbis, 1986; Lesslie Newbigin, *The Gospel in a Pluralist Society,* Geneva: WCC, 1989; Vinoth Ramachandra, *The Recovery of Mission,* Carlisle: Paternoster, 1996; S. J. Samartha, *One Christ—Many Religions: Toward a Revised Christology,* Bangalore: SATRI, 1992; S. Immanuel David (ed.) *Christianity and the Encounter with Other Religions: A Select Bibliography, Bangalore: UTC, 1988.*

[86] S. J. Samartha, *One Christ — Many Religions,* pp.95-96.

[87] Vinoth Ramachandra, *The Recovery of Mission,* p. 13.

into the fold of Christ and usher in the Kingdom of God on earth. Edinburgh exuded this postmillennialist optimism, which was shortly shattered by the First World War and the Russian Revolution. An optimistic estimate of the human condition continued, however, in proposals for inter-religious cooperation which surfaced at Jerusalem. The new Communist ideology proposed to bring the new socialist human without recourse to religion. Human society was viewed as redeemable without Divine intervention. To a large extent this remaining optimism was dispelled by the devastation of the Second World War. The outcome for Christian mission was a mantle of pessimistic gloom which became darker with the eviction of missionaries from China following the Communist revolution. The apparatus of mission was diverted into post-War rehabilitation and humanitarian aid and into building new structures for mission-church relationships. Simultaneously new initiatives in mission began, especially from North America, but increasingly from the younger churches of Africa and Asia.

Church. Edinburgh celebrated a century of missionary advance. The presence of significant leaders such as V.S. Azariah moved the Conference toward a greater awareness of the worldwide Church. Questions of faith and order issued in a follow-up stream leading eventually to the formation of the World Council of Churches. The ecumenical movement is rooted in Edinburgh. Meanwhile church leaders became prominent in the conferences of the International Missionary Council at Jerusalem and Tambaram. A gradual shift from the mission to the church takes place. Edinburgh was a gathering of missionaries and mission agencies. Jerusalem was not. Mission became church-centric. Gradually

the missions were excluded except as departments of churches. With increasing secularization in the West, however, eventually the church too was by-passed for a secular society in which the world set the agenda for the church. By the close of the century came a swing back to the centrality of the church as the base for mission in the world. This was discernable in conferences of the World Council of Churches following the 1974 Lausanne Conference of World Evangelization. The impact of Pentecostals and other evangelicals from around the world brought a greater awareness of the role of the church in mission.

Mission. Mission at the outset clearly meant the evangelization of the non-Christian world. From Jerusalem onward the definition was not clear. Mission became the doing of good deeds, building neighbourly goodwill, humanization efforts, programmes of social and political action, inter-religious dialogue and inter-church relationships. Stephen Neill's famous maxim arose out of this context of confusion: "If everything is mission, nothing is mission."[88] At Lausanne the evangelistic intentionality of the Christian witness was restored. Theology of mission at Lausanne centered in the Kingdom of God,[89] but focused on world evangelization.[90] Following Lausanne, mission became increasingly holistic. Evangelicals and ecumenicals arrived at a degree of consensus.[91] Social justice and evangelism were on the agendas of both. The participation of Pentecostals and other evangelicals along with the Orthodox in the WCC brought a more balanced understanding of mission within the world body. Dialogue is an aspect of mission but not its totality. Evangelization is a comprehensive span of activities centered in witness to Jesus Christ

---

[88] Stephen Neill, *Creative Tension*, London, Edinburgh House, 1959, p.81.
[89] Charles Van Engen, *Mission on the Way,* p.138.
[90] Gerald H. Anderson, "Christian Mission in A.D. 2000: A Glance Backward," *Missiology* XXVIII, July 2000, p.281.
[91] *Ibid.*.

as Saviour and Lord. Mission at the start of the third millennium once again is more clearly Christocentric.

Scripture. Authority for mission is derived from the Bible which also delineates salient aspects of missionary witness. The place of the Bible in mission is assumed. Evangelical conferences especially stress the place of the Bible as the foundation of Christian belief and practice. Recent biblical studies have brought a greater awareness of the Old and New Testament documents as the foundations of mission.[92] Not the use of the Bible as proof-texts, but the full sweep of the biblical revelation undergirds the Christian mission. A Christian theology of mission must be biblical as well as contextual. The Bible witnesses to Jesus Christ who is central in Christian mission. Bible translation has been a significant contribution of Christian mission from Ziegenbalg onward.

Conclusion

Mission conferences, it seems, are action oriented and less prone to theological reflection. This is not necessarily wrong. Mission itself means catering to human needs,[93] including the need for the proclamation of the gospel. The urgency of the human needs agenda, however, tends to crowd out theological cogitation on mission. The India Missions Association offers little or nothing of theological reflection on mission.

The development of new missiological initiatives helps to fill the void. These include mission studies in theological institutions in India as well as the formation of the ecumenical Fellowship of Indian Missiologists, efforts buttressed by large-scale missiological projects overseas along with the serious academic study of mission in renowned universities in the West.[94]

A further hopeful sign is the advent of Pentecostal scholars who participate in the theological debate. The shift from North to South and from West to East brings a fresh dimension. For too long theologizing was dominated by agendas set by a Western secularist and nominalist Christianity. New Christian movements are characterised by enthusiasm and missionary zeal. Increasingly, mission today is from Africa, Latin America and Asia to Europe and North America. One projection claims there are 1500 intentional missionaries (mostly from Africa) at work in Britain today.[95] Asian Christian missionaries today are found in Los Angeles and Chicago, Birmingham and London. Issues such as witchcraft, healing, dreams, possession, signs and wonders will be part of the new theological agenda—similar to the earliest Christianity of the New Testament and the post-apostolic age.[96]

Missiological theologizing in South Asia also will have to interact with critical issues of contextualization and indigeneity.[97] Neither can mission theology avoid the challenges of massive

---

[92] Donald Senior and Carroll Stuhlmueller, *The Biblical Foundations of Mission*, Maryknoll, Orbis, 1984; Andreas J. Köstenberger, "The Place of Mission in New Testament Theology," *Missiology* XXVII,3, July 1999, 347-362.

[93] G. Dyvasirvadam, "Mission in Transition: A Contextual Appraisal" in *Mission Paradigm in the New Millennium* edited by W.S. Milton Jeganathan, Department of Mission and Evangelism, Church of South India, Delhi, ISPCK, 2000, p.3.

[94] See Lalsangkima Pachuau, "The Study of Christian Mission in the Last 50 Years—Retrospect and Prospects" in *Mission Paradigm in the New Millennium*, edited by W.S. Milton Jeganathan, Department of Mission and Evangelism, Church of South India, Delhi, ISPCK, 2000, 112-120.

[95] Philip Thomas, "Missiology: Philip Jenkins and the Next Christendom," Family.missiology@family-bbs.net, November 2, 2002.

[96] *Ibid.*

[97] See Arthur Jeyakumar, "Lessons from the History of Protestant Christian Missions in India during the Twentieth Century" in *Mission Paradigm in the New Millennium* edited by W.S. Milton Jeganathan, Department of Mission and Evangelism, Church of South India, Delhi, ISPCK, 2000, 137-149.

poverty and exploitation. "The worsening situation of poverty in our land is so great that it demands a united and concerted effort of all of us together."[98] High on the agenda will also be reflection and action dealing with the struggles of India's "broken" people, the Dalits, for dignity and security.[99] Theological implications of masses of unevangelized populations must be considered. The priority of the Church's evangelistic mission today is threatened by the philosophy of Hindutva and the political power of the Sangh Parivar.[100] Academicians and missiological scholars are required who will articulate an appropriate response. They must do so reflecting the spirit of Christ with the church as a hermeneutical community. "For the church to be believable, it will need to be conscious of Christ's lordship in the midst of God's people and to conduct its mission as an expression of the fruit of the Spirit."[101]

Sources:

Aykara, Thomas (ed.) *A Missiology for Third Millennium*, Bangalore, Dharmaram Publications, 1997.

Bassham, Rodger C. *Mission Theology: 1948-1975 Years of Worldwide Creative Tension Ecumenical, Evangelical, and Roman Catholic*, Pasadena, William Carey Library, 1979.

Hedlund, Roger E. *Roots of the Great Debate in Mission: Mission in Historical and Theological Perspective*, Bangalore, Theological Book Trust, 1993.

Hedlund, Roger E. "Contours of Evangelism and Church Planting in Today's India," EFI All-India Congress on the Church in Mission, New Delhi, Hamdard University, 23-27 November, 1999.

Hedlund, Roger E. "Twentieth Century Mission Conferences: Models for Engagement with Hinduism and Islam," Consultation on the Indian Church in her context: The Emergence, Growth and Mission of the Church in a Pluralistic Context, Union Biblical Seminary, Pune, 14-16 February 2002.

Hogg, William Richey, *Ecumenical Foundations: A History of the International Missionary Council and its Nineteenth Century Background*, New York, Harper, 1952.

Jeganathan, W.S. Milton (ed.) *Mission Paradigm in the New Millennium*, Published for Department of Mission and Evangelism, Church of South India, Delhi, ISPCK, 2000.

Van Engen, Charles, *Mission on the Way: Issues in Mission Theology*, Grand Rapids, Baker Books, 1996.

---

[98] William Moses, "Mission in the Indian Context Today," in *Mission Paradigm in the New Millennium* edited by W.S. Milton Jeganathan, Department of Mission and Evangelism, Church of South India, Delhi, ISPCK, 2000, p.161.

[99] An entire issue of *Indian Missiological Review*, March 1995, was devoted to this issue. See also Santishree D.N.B. Pandit, "Dilemmas of Dual Identity of Dalit Christians in India," *Dharma Deepika* December 1997,39-48; A.M. Abraham Ayrookuzhiel, "Dalit Liberation—Some Reflections on their Ideological Predicament, *Religion and Society*, June 1988, 47-52; as well as books and publications by James Massey, John C.B. Webster, and others.

[100] P. Moses Manohar, "Political Challenges and Mission Perspectives" in *Mission Paradigm in the New Millennium* edited by W.S. Milton Jeganathan, Department of Mission and Evangelism, Church of South India, Delhi, ISPCK, 2000, p.307.

[101] Charles Van Engen, *Mission on the Way*, p.257.

CHAPTER 10

Toward a Normative Christology for Asia

JACOB PARAPALLAY

Introduction

The word of God is not bound (2Tim 2:9). This truth is confirmed by the infinite ways in which God's Word finds expression in the world. Above all, it is true in the unique expression of the Word in Jesus Christ. He transcended everything that bound him, even death. The early theologians of the Church interpreted Jesus Christ as the Messiah of Jewish expectations as well as the fulfilment of the hope cherished by the Gentiles of all times. Ignatius of Antioch (d. C.E. 110), for example, proclaimed Jesus Christ as the "ground for hoping that [all of humanity] may be converted and win their way to God." Further, he affirmed that Jesus was "our common name and common hope" (Ephesians: 10.1; 1.2).

The followers of Jesus Christ believe that he is indeed the common name and common hope meant for the whole of humanity. They encounter him as the Way, the Truth and the Life. They experience him as the beginning and the end of their lives, and therefore, the ultimate meaning of their lives. They confess him as the Lord of history and the universe, who lived and died at a particular time in history and yet is alive after his death, leading all to the fullness of life. He is the alpha and the omega, the beginning and the end. But something that is bound up with this transforming experience of Jesus Christ is that it must be shared, it must be proclaimed in a meaningful way that the same Jesus Christ can be encountered by the people of all cultures and languages. In the multi-religious society of the Roman Empire, the early Church found creative ways to theologise and proclaim the universal significance of Jesus Christ. When the Roman Empire accepted Jesus Christ as its Lord and Saviour, Christianity became a mono-religious culture without any challenge to its claims about Jesus Christ from outside. It had to face only the internal challenges with regard to the wrong interpretations of the person of Christ expressed through the heresies. The Christological heresies were the inadequate ways of interpreting the mystery of Christ proclaimed by the New Testament witnesses. But the dogmas formulated in the early councils responded to the challenges from within.

The strongest challenge to a mono-religious culture of Christianity came from Islam and later from the religions which the West encountered in the colonial era. The colonisers could not find Christ's presence in the religions of their colonial subjects as it would have probably hampered their claim to superiority, not only in military might, but also in religion and culture. With their absolute and exclusive claims about Christ and Christianity, they had reduced Christ to a tribal God and Christianity to a sect. If everything is Christified through creation and incarnation (Jn 1: 9, 14), to separate Christ through any exclusivism or to compare the incomparable with any one else would be an affront to the Christic experience of the believer. There are some Christians who still live in a utopia of a monoculture and eurocentrism scuttling the process of an effective and meaningful proclamation of Christ in multi-religious and multi-cultural societies of Asia. In the name of preserving orthodoxy some prevent the working of the Spirit to unfold the truth and the richness of the mystery of Christ in every age and every culture.

For those who are seriously committed to the proclamation of Jesus Christ that all people of Asia can encounter him as the ultimate meaning of their life, it is imperative that they proclaim him in a language meaningful to the people of various cultural, religious, socio-economic and political contexts of Asia. Therefore, the complex Asian context must be taken seriously for any meaningful Christological reflection in Asia. There need not be and cannot be one Christology for Asia. Though Jesus Christ is one, Christologies can be many depending on the contexts of Christic experience and Christological reflection. In fact, there are many Christologies in the New Testament itself.

What makes any Christology normative is that it is founded on the totality of New Testament witness about "who Jesus Christ is" and "what he has accomplished for humans through his life, death and resurrection," as well as on the content of the symbols of faith about him in the Christian Tradition. Such a normative Christology can become meaningful and relevant only when it takes into account the context of its articulation seriously. Therefore, a Christology that is authentically Christian and meaningful for the Asian context can emerge when those who found the ultimate meaning of their lives in Jesus Christ systematically reflect on: 1. the situation from which the people of Asia seek salvation or liberation; 2. how and why Jesus Christ is the Lord and Saviour who brings about true liberation from the situation of misery and un-freedom .

A Universal Quest and a Particular Answer

The quest for meaningfulness is another way of expressing the fundamental human desire for wholeness and harmony. There is an existential experience of dissatisfaction and consequent restlessness stemming from fears and anxieties about life and ultimate questions about life. Therefore, there is an undeniable quest for an integral wholeness or salvation which is not only otherworldly experience but also this-worldly, not only individualistic but also communitarian, not only oriented towards material welfare but also spiritually satisfying. The awareness that all is not right with the world and human society, the haunting thought of possible meaningless death and uncertain future beyond the grave heighten the quest for an integral wholeness, liberation or salvation. How one perceives the present situation of uncertainty and existential angst and the desire for wholeness or liberation are determined by one's religious, cultural, social and economic context.[1] It is an undeniable fact that the *Weltanschauung* of a particular people determines what they consider to be ultimately significant for their lives. This is evident in the way the people of different cultures and traditions experienced and articulated the significance of Jesus Christ for their lives

The decisive answer to the existential question raised by Jesus, "Who do you say that I am?"(Mt 16:15) is responded to in various ways by the apostolic community. It was a decisive answer because it gave a new meaning to their own lives and changed their understanding of God, human beings and the world. It was an existential answer because their understanding of the identity of the person of Jesus was intertwined with their self-understanding about themselves and the ultimate meaning of their lives. It was concerned about their existential search for salvation, wholeness and a practical orientation to their lives. For the believers, the question raised by Jesus of Nazareth was the most fundamental question a

---

[1] K.H. Ohlig, "What is Christology?" *Theology Digest,* 43:1, 1996, p.15.

human person can be confronted with. It is another way of articulating the same question human beings ask themselves concerning the meaning of their lives. The ultimate answer to the question, therefore, affects the totality of the person who encounters Jesus. Paul's Damascus, encounter is a typical case. Here the questioner was Paul and not Jesus. Whether in Caesaria Philippi or on the road to Damascus, it is not the question that is important but the answer. In both cases the answer is "from above". It is a gift. It is given to the individual person in a particular context even though the quest for meaningfulness is universal.

The seekers of all times and all cultures express in different ways the quest of humans for an ultimate answer to the mystery of life. The various world religions that emerged in Asia have something in common: they all admit that life in this world, in the final analysis, is not satisfactory; there is a longing for liberation and wholeness; and finally, there are different ways to attain liberation. Christianity, being one of the religions born in Asia, admits that God, the Ultimate Reality, has mysterious ways to lead humans to liberation even, those who deny the existence of any Ultimate Reality. But it also claims that the way of Jesus is not just another way to liberation but the Way. Unlike other great Teachers and Founders of Religions who showed the way to the attainment of liberation, he is *the Way,* he is the liberation as his name suggests (Jesus = *Yehoshua = God is saviour or God saves*). Hence, the Christians claim that Jesus Christ is the unique saviour or liberator. However, if Christianity is seen as a religion like any other religion and its founder like any other founder of a religion, the claims to superiority, exclusiveness and uniqueness, etc., become untenable. Jesus Christ is encountered by the disciples as the revelation of the Ultimate Reality, the beginning and end of everything that exists, the ultimate meaning of life and not the founder of a religion. Christianity, in its true sense, cannot be a religion but a community of transformed people who experience the ultimate meaning of their lives in the abiding presence of the one who is the Absolute yet became relative, trans-historical yet became historical, eternal yet became temporal, immortal yet became mortal. The mystery of this paradox surpasses all articulations and all comparisons. It is to be experienced and lived. Deep silence can be the loudest proclamation of this Christic mystery. An authentic Christology for Asia should not yield to the temptation of the western mind to analyse the mystery of Christ that surpasses all understanding, to define the indefinable and to make claims about having a clear and complete knowledge of the mystery as everything about it seems to be neatly categorised and formulated. An Asian Christology needs to be more symbolic and evocative than descriptive and dogmatic. It must lead to new inner visions and the ontological transformations of the persons than production of mere doctrines and speculations. The approaches of the New Testament writers and the early Churches to articulate their Christ-experience from their own particular contexts give an insight into the process of developing a normative Christology for Asia.

The Contextual Christologies in the New Testament

Confronted with the resurrection experience, the apostolic community struggled to express the content of their experience. In the light of the resurrection they began to understand Jesus in a new light. It was a difficult task. They had no terminology to express this mystery. At the same time they found themselves deeply involved in the mystery of the risen Jesus. He is the one with whom they had shared their life during his ministry. But he is also different. This difference made all the difference in their lives. They had no words to articulate it. So their understanding of the person of Jesus is expressed in some of the confessional formulas of the New Testament. The struggle of the apostolic community to proclaim him as Messiah or Christ immediately after the resurrection experience was that the political expectations related to the Messiah were not fulfilled in Jesus. He is the Messiah or Christ but not according to the expectations of the Jewish people. Though each of the evangelists, Paul and other authors of the New Testament have their own ways of communicating in a systematic way that Jesus is the fulfilment of their expectations, there is no real systematic reflection on the person of Jesus Christ. However, the catechetical need of the community and the challenges they had to face in proclaiming the reality of the risen Jesus determined the New Testament Christologies.

One of the initial attempts was to confess that Jesus was a prophet. We cannot take it for granted that it was so obvious that he was a prophet, mighty in word and in deed. He was killed as a criminal. For the Jews, he was accursed by God as he was hanged on a tree (Dt 21:22). But the resurrection experience was so compelling that from the initial confession as a prophet they began to proclaim him as the future Messiah or the Christ (Acts 3:20). They had to concede to the fact that the political expectations associated with the Messiah were not fulfilled in him. So only in future he would be Messiah. So it was a future Christology. But a further reflection on the experience of the resurrection confirmed that he is the expected one. So he must be confessed as the Christ. In order to make such a proclamation that he is the Christ, they needed to change, first of all, their mind-set about the Kingdom, which Christ would come to establish. They did change. The experience they had of the risen Jesus was so overwhelming that in its blinding light the shades of an illusory political kingdom they had expected gradually vanished. He became more important for them than their vision of the kingdom. So they proclaimed that he is the Messiah but his kingdom is not of this world. So in their proclamation they moved from

a future Christology to a present Christology. At resurrection Jesus is, indeed, Christ.

Was he Christ before resurrection? Their answer was in the affirmative. They were raising a question about the Christhood of the historical Jesus of Nazareth. In the beginning of this reflection they affirmed that at baptism by John He was Christ. The theophany at the baptism scene is an expression of this faith-affirmation (Mk 1:9ff; Mt 3:16-17). Was he Christ before baptism? The infancy narratives of Matthew and Luke, though couched in Middrashic language, affirmed that he was Christ from the moment of conception in his mother's womb. John would take this line of Christological reflection further when he proclaims that he is the Logos, who was with God from the beginning (Jn 1:1ff). Thus he will not only be the future Christ but He is also the present Christ of resurrection, the past Christ of baptism and of conception, and even pre-existent Christ. The New Testament reflections on the person of Jesus reached their climax in the Gospel according to John. All that we need to know about Jesus for our salvation seemed to have been communicated that we "may believe that Jesus is the Christ, the Son of God (Jn 20:31).

Normative Christologies in the Christ in Christian Tradition

The question "who is Jesus Christ?" was raised only in the context of his significance to his followers. The believers experienced him as the ultimate meaning of their lives. In him they experienced a complete transformation of their lives from alienation to communion, fragmentation to wholeness, meaninglessness to meaningfulness, death to life. "Only those who receive Jesus soteriologically can speak the confession that Jesus is the Christ."[2] Therefore, in the Christian Tradition, the identity of Jesus Christ was of utmost importance and normative Christologies developed due to the responses of

---

[2] *Ibid.*

particular peoples to their soteriological concerns. Before we discuss the possibility of a normative Christology for Asia, it is important to see the various normative Christologies of the Christian Tradition to understand the process of their development and to recognise the legitimate need to develop a normative Christology in the Asian context.

The Normative Christology of the Jewish Christianity

In the Jewish world-view the existential human situation had a beginning and would have an end. Whole life is historically oriented. Therefore, history is not only important but also the whole drama of Yahweh's intervention in the creation that takes place on the stage of history. Each human being has to play his or her role in history. Since history has a beginning from Yahweh, he also will bring about its eschatological fulfilment. In this linear understanding of history that moves towards its final fulfilment human beings realise that they have reversed the process of this movement of history by not playing their part according to God's plan, His law. The corruption of history was by the misuse of human freedom by taking the one way road to self-destruction and the destruction of others and the world. Thus, the history of suffering and guilt form the background of the Old Testament yearning for Yahweh's redemptive intervention in history. All Jewish expectations centred around the coming God's reign to set right the course of history which was ravaged by the evil powers, whether human or diabolic, causing dissatisfaction, restlessness, sickness and meaninglessness in life. God's reign brings about wholeness by "God's being with us" (Emmanuel) or by Yahweh's presence in history as the Saviour (Yehoshua or Jesus).

The Jewish Christians, with the background of the Jewish expectation for the definitive intervention of Yahweh in history, could clearly recognise the fulfilment of their expectations in the person and mission of Jesus. They identified him as the expected Messiah, the 'Son of Man' who would come at eschatological times as the Son of David to set history right by transforming it from a destructive history to salvation history. Jesus is enthroned as 'Son of God' for these transformative functions. Jesus' complete surrender to the Father by His obedience to Him, His fulfilling of the Father's will by His preaching and death on the cross were considered significant events that brought about salvation. So every kingdom-centred action of Jesus became salvific and therefore significant to the lives of those Jewish Christians who accepted Him as Lord and Saviour. In Jesus they encountered not only the ultimate meaning of history, but also the ultimate meaning of their own lives as they realised that they were participating in the fulfilment of history in its God-given pattern. Jesus was believed to be the alpha and omega of history, and therefore its centre and meaning. "God's lordship dawned in Jesus. Jesus was also designated 'son of God,' in the Jewish sense of kingly enthronement as 'son of God.' In His historical function Jesus appeared as 'son of God.'"[3] His historical life of obedience to His Father even to His death on the cross, His deeds of power over sickness, evil spirits and nature besides His power to forgive sins are the signs that a new course of history of God's reign has begun with Him. Thus He is absolutely significant in the experience and articulation of a Jewish-Christian as His personal saviour and the saviour of history.

The Normative Christology of the Hellenistic Christians

If the Jewish world-view had a historical orientation, the Hellenistic world-view had a Cosmo-centric orientation. What we call Hellenistic culture was a complex mixture of

---

[3] *Ibid.,* 16.

various cultural traditions of the Roman Empire, which had their unity in Greek thought and language. In the context of the Hellenistic culture the cause of the human experience of frustration and meaninglessness in life was interpreted differently and consequently the understanding of liberation from this situation was also different. What caused the misery of the human situation was not any criminal misuse of freedom and the consequent corruption of history, but the lack of right knowledge, the limitations of their beings as finite, as being mortal and the fact of being caught up in the evil matter. Each person as a microcosm suffered from the limitations of being that hindered his or her full integration into the macrocosm of which the human person was a part. Hence liberation consisted also in acquiring of true knowledge to extricate oneself from the imprisonment in matter and in securing immortality, thus becoming deified.

In this context of Hellenistic culture, Jesus Christ would be significant only if He could be the mediator of true liberation from the limitations of the human predicament, indeed, humanness itself. Therefore, the Hellenistic Christology developed as an answer to the Hellenistic soteriological concerns. In this Christology, Jesus Christ was seen as the mediator between the microcosm and macrocosm, matter and spirit, finite and infinite, relative and absolute. In the Greek philosophical tradition *Logos* had the function of mediation between those pairs of polarities. It was, therefore, easier for the Greek Fathers to show that Jesus Christ was the *Logos* that brings about this mediation.[4] Apologists like Justin, Theophilos of Antioch and Athenagoras could make use of the symbol, Logos, to interpret the meaning of Christ as logos incarnate.[5] Justin, for example, considered Logos as *logos spermatikos* (seeds of Logos) which united

---

[4] Influenced by the Platonic idea of world as the image of the perfect idea of the world, Philo considered that this perfect Image as the Logos and the biblical understanding that human beings are the image of God would then mean that they are the image of the image or Logos (eikon *eikonos*). So Philo could say, "the Image of God is the Logos through whom the whole universe was framed". The Logos has two dimensions, according to Philo. The Logos, as thought in God or as unuttered, pre-existent Word, the Logos *endeathetos,* and the which is uttered and through which the world comes into being, the Logos *prophorikos*. The synthesis of *logos, dabhar,* and also *Sophia* achieved by Philo provided the needed new meanings to the Christ-symbol in the new context of Hellenistic world. As there are similarities between Philonic Logos and Johannine Logos there are also differences. Johannine Logos which become flesh (Jn 1:4) is not only not an ideal and personified Logos that Philo's syncretism provided, but a real pre-existent and personal one. However, the Christ symbol would not have been interpreted by the Johannine community in terms of the Logos if this was not somehow present in the cultural context of the community, providing new meaning to their experience of Christ, the symbol of God.

The logos-Christology of the Prologue of John influenced the interpretation of the symbol Christ leading to orthodox doctrinal statements about the divinity of Christ, sometimes, even at the cost of orthopraxis. Since the symbol *is* and *is not* the reality, if we stop at the *is* dimension of the symbol and articulate dogmas and doctrines based on it eclipsing the *is not* dimension, the vision of the Reality becomes blurred and confused. Most of the christological controversies have their origin in the metaphysical understanding and elaboration of the *is* dimension of the symbol Christ. Faith seeking understanding often sought the help of metaphysics to explain the plausibility and intelligibility of the faith claims by 'locating them with in the interpretation of being itself'. Since metaphysics can deal only with the *is* dimension of the symbol, leaving the *is not* dimension, it gives the illusion that everything about the reality is expressed. Such an approach had dangerous consequences both in practical life as well as in the vision and encounter of reality. It leads to a maximalist's reading of the dogmas, arrogant exclusivism and stark absolutism. Dogmas stifle. Symbol liberates. The liberating capacity of the symbol emanates from its *is not* dimension. The Logos-symbol expresses the *is not* aspect of the reality of the symbol Christ. When logos-symbol was ontologized by Arius its symbolism was ravaged. The Church's reaction to Arian heresy as expressed in the Council of Nicea (C.E.325) using ontological categories like *ousia, homoousios* etc., was necessary to preserve the content of the apostolic faith but deprived the symbol of its power to evoke transforming vision and encounter.

[5] J.N.D. Kelly, *Early Christian Doctrines*, V Edition, London: A. & C. Black, 1989, pp. 95-101.

human beings to God, to explain who Christ was. For him, the same *logos* which was the source of relation between God and human beings and gave them the awareness of God, became incarnate.[6]

An incarnational Christology fitted well with the Hellenistic soteriological expectations of deification. Jesus Christ, being both divine and human, pre-existing as Logos (Jn 1.1ff, Phil 2.6ff), as the Lord, as the Son of God and as Son of Man of earthly existence, could fulfil the soteriological need because he is "Word became Flesh" (Jn 1:14). He is the enanthropesis of the divine Logos according to Origen. So the Chalcedon Council's (CE 451) Christological formula that Jesus Christ, One person in two natures "without confusion or change, without division or separation, perfect in humanity and perfect in divinity,"[7] could adequately express the significance of Jesus Christ in the Hellenistic Christianity's cultural context.

In the incarnational Christology the very incarnation itself was soteriological. Though the historical death and resurrection of Jesus was also considered redemptive, emphasis was on the fact of liberation brought about by incarnation. For example, Clement of Alexandria says, "the Word...became man so that you might learn from man how man may become God."[8] Christ bestows immortality as well as knowledge. Thus human beings are deified by incarnation. According to J.N.D. Kelly, "Clement's soteriology issues in a Christ-mysticism in which the Lord's passion and death have little or no redemptive part to play."[9] Athanasius affirmed that the Word became human that we might be made God.[10] Hellenistic Christology with its incarnational soteriology responded to the quest for significance experienced and articulated in

the Hellenistic cultural milieu. Though not divorced from the Jewish-Christian christological concerns Hellenistic Christology was conditioned by the Hellenistic world-view. In the Hellenistic context that was most meaningful Christology that brought thousands to encounter Jesus mission command of Jesus if she continues to proclaim Jesus and His message in a language alien to the peoples of these contexts.

Normative Christologies in Syrian Christian Tradition

The cultural contexts of both Western Syria and Eastern Syria determined the soteriological concerns as well as the Christologies of the Syrian Christian tradition. *The Christology of the West Syrian Christological Tradition:* Western Syria had a Semitic heart but a Hellenistic mind. Aramaic was the language of the ordinary people. The educated spoke Greek and articulated their thought in Hellenistic categories. With Antioch as its cultural centre, it developed a Christology different from that of East Syria because of its specific cultural context. Here, there was an organic synthesis of Hebrew and Greek world-views. The ontological categories of thought inherited from the Greeks were used to express historical concerns. The Jewish-Christian soteriology of historical fulfilment was indeed the liberation of the human nature from the predicament of finiteness and imperfections. Imperfections were believed to be caused by the misuse of human freedom leading to acts that are wicked and sinful. Therefore, liberation from the limitations of human nature involved liberation from the sinful state of human beings. Jesus Christ is significant in this context only if He is able to bring about an ontological transformation as well as moral regeneration of human beings. In fact,

---

[6] *Apologia* I,5,4; 8. *Apologia* II, 10,1; 13,4.

[7] J. Neuner and J. Dupuis, *The Christian Faith*, V. Edition, Bangalore:TPI, 1992, Nos 614,615.

[8] J.N.D. Kelly, *Early Christian Doctrines*, p. 184.

[9] *Ibid.*

[10] H. Bettenson, *The Early Christian Fathers*, London: Oxford University Press, 1956, p.384.

it was this belief that Jesus Christ was fulfilling this expectation of human beings for an integral liberation that triggered the Christological reflections of many Antiochene theologians like Diodore, Theodore of Mopsuestia, John of Antioch and other.

The Hellenistic idea of God's absolute transcendence and the monolithic monotheism of Judaism[11] probably influenced their initial reluctance to accept an incarnational Christology with its full implications. Instead of a *logos-sarx* Christology of the Alexandrians they preferred a *logos-anthropos* Christology which would safeguard the transcendence of the Logos and the autonomy of the human being. Who Jesus was and what He did were to be significant only if His life and death proved to be acceptable to God. Jesus' life of obedience to the Father even unto death proved His response to His vocation. His resurrection from the dead verified that God had approved and accepted His person and mission. Jesus became Son by His surrender to the Father or Sonship was conferred on Him by the Father. So in the beginning West Syrian Christology moved in the direction of adoptionism. For Paul of Samasota who championed the adoptionistic Christology, "Jesus Christ and the Word are other and other *(allos kai allos)....*The Word is... from above; Jesus Christ the man is from below."[12] God adopted human Jesus through Logos so that human beings could attain integral liberation by following Him.

Arius attempted an integration of Hellenistic incarnational Christology and Antiochene adoptionistic Christology. He was trained in Antiochene Theology but worked as a priest in Alexandria. He proposed a Christology which safeguarded the transcendence of the Absolute

of Hellenistic-Christianity and the strict monotheism of the Jewish-Christian tradition. At the same time he found a place for Jesus in the scheme of God's intervention in history for human liberation. Jesus was the embodiment of the created Logos and was given the honorific title Son of God. It was an ingenious idea. No wonder then, he could take along almost half the number of believers of his time to his side as they found this Christology very attractive.

Adoptionism and Arianism faced the question of the soteriological concerns of Antioch and Alexandria intelligently but heterodoxically. They suggested an artificial synthesis of traditions for their intellectual satisfaction without recognising the paradox of God's revelation in Jesus Christ, "a stumbling block to the Jews and folly to the Gentiles" (I Cor 1:23). They were not faithful to the Apostolic tradition. So the Council of Nicea (C.E.325) had to affirm that salvation in Jesus Christ is significant only if Jesus Christ was the pre-existent Logos, one in being with the Father *(homoousios),* begotten, not made. After the Council of Nicea, the Syrian theologians abandoned the adoptionistic Christology and began to expound the *Logos-anthropos* Christology differently. They were at variance in explaining the type of presence of Logos in Jesus, but were unanimous in affirming that He was fully human like any other human being with a rational soul. If not, He had no significance for humanity.

Theodore of Mopstuestia insisted that salvation consisted in the restoration of the authentic humanity which was the work of Christ, the man, in His life, death and resurrection because He had been "one of us, who came from out of our race" and our nature.[13] Both the Antiochene and the Alexandrian traditions were

---

[11] R.A. Kereszty, *Jesus Christ – Fundamentals of Christology,* ed by J.A. Maddux, New York: Alba House, 1995, p. 189.

[12] *Adversus Haereses,* IV:184-5; R.A. Kereszty, 1996, p.189.

[13] J. Pelikan, *The Christian Tradition – A History of the Development of Doctrine: I. The Emergence of Catholic Tradition (100 – 600),* Chicago: The University of Chicago Press, 1971, p. 235-236.

in agreement that the very purpose of incarnation was the salvation of humankind. For both of these traditions the validity of the Christological doctrine depended on its congruence with the salvific work of Jesus. It was common to their understanding that salvation was achieved when human beings could receive immortality and impassability. But in their Christological doctrine they differed.

Following the theological reflections of Theodore, Nestorius insisted that Logos indwelt the man, Jesus, as in the temple, interpreting John 2:9, where the man Jesus was referred to as the temple which could be destroyed but would be raised up. He supported his argument with Col 2:9, "In Him [the man who was assumed] the whole fullness of deity dwells bodily.[14]" For Nestorius, if Jesus was really human and indeed He was, there could only be an empirical union between Logos and the human Jesus and therefore divine predicates could not be attributed to the human Jesus. It was the opposite side of the Alexandrian view.

The *Logos-Sarx* Christology of Apollinarius (d. 390) insisted that Jesus had only one nature, the Logos, replacing the human soul and mind. According to him, "the divine energy fulfils the role of the animating spirit and of the human mind."[15] Cyril of Alexandria insisted on the one subject of incarnation, the Logos. Both divine and human predicates had the same subject. But in the Antiochene theological reflection, any unity that destroyed the distinction between human and divine would make salvation through Christ impossible. "As a complete human being, Jesus can be held up as a pattern for His followers."[16] Though the councils of Ephesus (CE 431) and Chalcedon (CE 451) condemned the extreme

Antiochene position, they had integrated some of its concerns into their doctrines.

West Syrian Christological tradition that opposed the Chalcedonian formula of "the hypostatic union of two natures in one person," moved in the direction of monophysitism. Eutyches (d.448), as its spokesman, seemed to have asserted that before the union the Lord was of two natures, but after the union He was of one nature (mono-physis). After the Council of Chalcedon, the Alexandrian ideas spread especially among the monks in Western Syria. The anti-Chalcedonian party installed Peter the Fuller, a Greek, as the Patriarch of Antioch in 470. He was driven out later but again assumed office till his death in 488. His successor, the Syrian Philoxenus, was the most virulent opponent of Chalcedon. In 512 another opponent of Chalcedon, the Greek monk Severus of Pisidia, became the patriarch of Antioch. He was considered to be the father of moderate monophysitism.[17] Fierce opposition to the Chalcedon Council and to Leo's Tome by successive Antiochene patriarchs considering them as godless, blasphemous and unorthodox as they spoke of two natures in Christ, led the West Syrian Church to settle down with monophysitism. This monophysitism in Christological thinking was expressed in its liturgical life.

The Christology of the East Syrian Christological Tradition

The original theological tradition of West Syria was inherited by the East Syrian tradition. East Syria had a unique Christian tradition "which retained relative autonomy in comparison with the Greek West and had virtually no contact at

---

[14] *Ibid.*, pp.252-253.

[15] J.N.D. Kelly, *Early Christian Doctrines*, p. 292.

[16] U. Linwood, *A Short History of Christian Thought*, New York: Oxford University Press, 1986, p. 82.

[17] W. de Vries, "The Reason for the Rejection of the Council of Chalcedon by the Oriental Churches," in P. Fries and T. Nesoyar, eds., *Christ in East and West*, Macon: Mercer University Press, 1987, p. 9.

all with the still more distant Latin West."[18] It had developed an "archaic" Christology in opposition to the Jewish charges that the Christians were worshipping an ordinary man as God. Aphrahat, the Persian sage (d.c.345), affirmed the Christian faith against Jewish opponents. For him, Jesus was God *(Alaha)* and Lord *(Marya)*. In his instructions he told his people, "But it is certain for us that Jesus, our Lord, is God *(Alaha)*, Son of God *(Bar Alaha)* and king, prince, light of light, creator (Bare)and counsellor and leader and redeemer and shepherd and gatherer and gate and pearl and lamp; and with many names is he named."[19] Aphrahat introduced the Syrian term *kyana* almost in the same sense of Greek *physis* to explain Christ's manner or condition of being as God and human, pre-existent, humiliated and finally exalted. In Him we can also find the presence of a spirit-Christology which is a decisive character of oriental Christology. Ephraem the Syrian (d.373) also used the term *kyana* in his hymns, sometimes meaning the unity of the person and at other times meaning two natures.[20] However, after Chalcedon, the East Syrian Church adopted the Nestorian Christological formulas at the Council of Seleukeia-Ctesiphon in C.E. 486. Though the founder of the East Syrian Christology, Babi the Great (d. 628)[21] praised Leo for eliminating the teachings of Dioscorus of Alexandria through the Council of Chalcedon. Katholikos Iso'yabb III rejected the Chalcedonian formula because it proclaimed the unity of the *hypostasis* in Christ. According to Elias of Nisibis (975-1049), the East Syrians in Persia rejected

the teachings of the heretic Cyril and the formula of Chalcedon forcibly effected by the emperor, as they found these teachings blasphemous.[22]

Christology was determined by the doctrine of Trinity. Those who opposed Chalcedon, whether the monophysites of West Syria or the Nestorians of East Syria, affirmed that the Chalcedonian formula did violence to the Trinitarian dogma by confessing two natures in Christ. According to them, "the doctrine of hypostatic union, even in the form adopted at Chalcedon, compromised the relation of the divine hypostases within the Trinity and threatened the impassability of Logos and therefore of the entire Godhead."[23]

It was the anthropological significance of Christ that was at stake in the fourth and fifth century debate about Christ. The question was about the origin and destiny of human beings, the two transcendent poles of human existence in history upon this earth.[24] Those who found in Jesus Christ their origin and destiny affirmed that He was God. Whatever, they thought, diluted the divinity was unacceptable to them, even the affirmations about His true humanity. Greek Christianity's reverence for tradition, the close link between "the faith believed in the divine liturgy, taught in theology and confessed in dogma" greatly influenced the life and thought of the Orient.[25]

Syrian Christian tradition both in its Monophsystic and Nestorian orientation continued to hold the significance of Christ for human salvation understood in terms of

---

[18] A. Grillmeier, *Christ in Christian Tradition*, Vol 1, 2nd Revised Edition, London, Oxford: Mowbrays, 1975, p. 214.

[19] *Demonstrationes* XVII,2; A. Grillmeier, *Christ in Christian Tradition*, p, 215.

[20] *Hymn.* 10,3; 11,9; A. Grillmeier, *Christ in Christian Tradition*, p. 335.

[21] G. Chediath, *The Christology of Mar Babai the Great*, Kottayam: Oriental Institute, 1982.

[22] A. Grillmeier, *Christ in Christian Tradition*, p. 12.

[23] J. Pelikan, *The Christian Tradition...*, p. 268.

[24] P.M. Gregorios, "The Relevance of Christology Today," in *Christ in East and West*, ed. By P. Fries and T. Nersoyan, Macon: Mercer University Press, 1987, p. 100.

[25] J. Pelikan, *The Christian Tradition..*, p. 341.

deification through configuration with Christ. Deification through mystical union with God was the main theme of the writings of Dionysius the Areopagite which influenced the Syrian tradition from the sixth century onwards. According to Dionysius, Eucharist was the main sacrament of deification. Eucharist itself was defined as "a participation in Jesus, the communion of the most divine Eucharist."[26] Such communion permitted one to share in "the most perfect form of deification" and "enabled him to ignore any but the most basic demands of the body and to grow, by means of this sublime deification, into a temple of the Holy Spirit."[27] Thus the Syrian tradition saw the significance of Jesus Christ as the mediator of this deification which was effected through the participation in the Eucharistic celebration.

Along with the influence of Cyril on the Christological thinking of West Syria, his Eucharistic theology also found wide acceptance. Salvation was mediated through the Eucharistic body of Christ. Cyril wrote that every week when they celebrated the Eucharist, Christ came among them both visibly and invisibly: invisibly as God, visibly as being again in body, allowing them to touch His holy flesh, in the *homologia kai anamnesis* of His death and resurrection.[28] Monophysite tradition received an intense religious fervour from such a dynamic faith of Cyril who affirmed that every Eucharist is a reincarnation of Logos whose flesh is given to the communicant. In fact, "the key to Cyril's christological interpretation of sacramental theology lay in His emphasis upon the life-giving power conveyed by the sacraments especially the Eucharist."[29]

In the Nestorian tradition of East Syria too, the Eucharist was of first importance. Before Nestorius, Theodore had already expounded a Eucharistic theology with the doctrine of real presence and sacramental transformation of bread and wine into the body and blood of Christ by the descent of the Holy Spirit who changes them into "the power of spiritual and immortal nourishment."[30] In the *Book of Heraclides,* Nestorius insists that "what we receive in the Eucharist is His body and blood which are of one substance with ours, so that thereby we made to share in His resurrection and immortality."[31] It is obvious that when a tradition sees the significance of Jesus Christ only in His mystical role for the individual believer's deification or immortality, Christ's significance in His prophetic role for the wholeness of the society and the world would be neglected. Eucharistic celebration, which provides the means for the transformation of human beings to make them worthy to participate in the impassable and incorruptible nature of God, would become the only and real concern of Christian existence.

The Normative Christology in the Latin Tradition

As Jewish, Hellenistic and Syrian Christian traditions had their culturally conditioned soteriological concerns, the Latins had their own. Hence their soteriological concerns determined their understanding of the significance of Christ. Though the Gospel was proclaimed in Rome in the first century itself, it did not develop its own theology.   was under the influence of Hellenism and Hellenistic theology. But in the second century with the resurgence of the Latin language

---

[26] *Ibid., p. 346.*

[27] *Ibid.*

[28] H. Chadwick *History and Thought of the Early Church,* London: Variorum Press, 1982, p. 155 [XVI].

[29] J. Pelikan, *The Christian Tradition,* p. 341.

[30] *Ibid.*

[31] H. Chadwick, *History and Thought of the Early Church,* p. 157 [XVI].

and thought in North Africa, the Latins began to develop their own theology. In their cultural tradition the humans and the world were under the divine law *(ius divinum)* which had established an order *(ordo)*. Through misbehaviour, sacrilege and rebellious actions the humans had destroyed this order.[32] Therefore, the existential situation of misery and meaninglessness was interpreted by the Latins as disorder caused by offences against the divine order. The divine legal power needed to be re-established to bring about order. In this cultural context, Jesus Christ could be significant only if He would mediate salvation by re-establishing the order in the name of God by His atoning death.

For Augustine (d.430), the most prominent representative of the Latin tradition, the original order was destroyed by the original sin of Adam. So human beings became "corrupt, vitiated, lost and dead" and they had no power to re-establish the order. Jesus Christ, being God and man could pay for human guilt and re-establish the order. In this new Christology the Hellenistic Christological categories like two natures were used, but for a different soteriological purpose. But the Hellenistic Christology's understanding of the ontological transformation of humans and the world by the fact of incarnation itself had no relevance for the Latin Christology. The soteriological concern of the Latins was juridical restitution, justification and redemption from guilt.[33] Jesus, the God-man, could pay for the human guilt as demanded by the just Judge, the righteous God. Pope Leo I expressed this Roman understanding in his Tome to *Flavius* that became a part of the Chalcedonian formula. He wrote,

> And, in order to pay the debt of our fallen state, the inviolable nature was united to one subject to suffering so that, as was fitting to heal our wounds, one and the same 'mediator between God and men, the man Christ Jesus' (1 Tim. 2.5) could die in one nature and not in the other. The true God, therefore, was born with the complete and perfect nature of a true man; He is complete in His nature and complete in ours...[34]

For Leo, the destroyed order could be restored only by the God-man who could conquer the devil, the author of sin and death. In fact, on the cross, according to Leo, the devil was tricked as the devil thought that he was victorious over this human being who died on the cross without realising that it was God-man who could not be subdued by sin and death. By his claim for the soul of Christ who was sinless, the devil forfeited his right over the souls of all sinners and thus they are saved from his domination.[35]

According to Gregory the Great (540-604), God deceived Satan by baiting the hook of Christ's Deity with the worm of His humanity.[36] The Roman concern for lawful rights and legal restitution in the understanding of soteriology reached its extreme when Gregory the Great declared that the devil must be given his due. What Paul wrote, "you are bought by a price" (I Cor 6:20) was understood as referring to a price paid to the devil who had legal rights over human beings who freely sold themselves to the devil. Gregory says, "God in His goodness would restore us again to freedom. There was a kind of necessity for Him not to proceed by way of force, but to accomplish our deliverance in a lawful way. It consists in this, that the owner is offered all that He asks as the redemption price of His property."[37]

---

[32] Ohlig, K-H, "What is Christology?" *Theology Digest,* pp-18-19.

[33] *Ibid.,* p. 19.

[34] J. Neuner, J. Dupuis, Ithe Christian Faith, pp. 164-165.

[35] U. Linwood, *A Short History of Christian Thought,* p. 110.

[36] *Ibid.,* p. 110; G. Aulen, *Christus Victor*, London: SPCK, 1945, pp.68-70.

[37] G. Aulen, *Christus Victor*, p. 65.

While Athanasius considered that the demons existed in the external world and needed to be defeated by the crucified Christ, Augustine explained the power of Satan both in the outside world and within human beings. Only Christ, both divine and human, could accomplish this task of legal battle, rescue human beings and establish the lost order. Thus the Latin Christology, according to K-H.Ohlig, used the categories like two natures, divine and human, for a soteriological schema quite different from logos-anthropos Christology and soteriology. The divine and the human natures were no longer soteriological terms but Roman legal titles, juridical conditions to make adequate payment or atonement for our guilt and effect the restoration of the order.[38]

With the Christianization of Europe, the Latin interpretation of soteriology was internalized and later it was spread through missionary enterprises in the colonial era. In the Middle Ages, Anselm of Canterbury (1033 - 1109) and Thomas Aquinas (1225 – 1274) gave new explanations of justification through satisfaction, but the basic Roman legal framework remained unaffected. Anselm rejected the idea of paying a price to the devil and proposed a positive way of atonement through the perfect sacrifice of Christ, in his classical book, *Why God Became Man*. In the context of the feudal society of his time, Anselm expounds his Christology based on the Latin justification Christology. According to Anselm, God's honour and the moral order of the universe had been degraded by human sins. God's mercy could forgive this but His justice would not allow this. Without proper satisfaction or the voluntary payment of debt, the original order cannot be restored. No human being could do proper satisfaction as all were born in sin. So Jesus Christ, the God-man, who was sinless and

immortal, freely offered himself as an oblation and satisfied God's justice so that God is love could flow and restore human beings and creation.

Peter Abelard (1079 - 1142) criticised the classical Latin theory of satisfaction as well as Anselm's theory of Christ's atoning sacrifice. For him we are transformed by the infinite love of God manifested through the incarnation of the Son. Only Luther (1483 - 1546), in his theory of atonement, integrated Abelard's view. However, Anselm's understanding of atonement continued to have its influence on the theological reflection of the succeeding centuries, with various modifications.

Thomas Aquinas modified Anselm's theology of satisfaction by expounding that God could have forgiven human beings without due satisfaction, but it was most fitting for Him to demand it.[39] According to Aquinas, more than the sinlessness of Christ, who had beatific vision from His mother' womb, the greatness of the love of Christ expressed in His passion and suffering was the direct principle satisfaction.[40] The later Western Christian tradition, whether Catholic or Protestant, followed without much changes the Leonian, Augustinian, Anselmistic and Thomistic theology of satisfaction or atonement which was culturally conditioned by the Roman system of juridical world-view. The Latin Christology with its predilection for understanding and explaining the significance of Christ in terms of legal categories like justification, satisfaction, or restitution for the offence against divine order influenced the whole Western theology until present times.

A Normative Christology in the Asian Context

Asia is the continent of many religions. All the religions in Asia admit that humans need

---

[38] K-H. Ohlig, "What is Christology?" *Theology Digest*, p.19.
[39] *Summa Theologiae*, III, Q I, 2a 2.
[40] *Ibid.,* III, Q 8, a3; Q 68, a 1.

liberation from the situation of misery and wretchedness. They offer philosophical or religious explanations for the situation of misery or misfortune and the way in which one can experience liberation from this situation. They concern themselves with the questions of the ultimate concerns of life and life-after. The basic concern of liberation from this world of misery overrides the interest in the transformation of this world. The prophetic dimension of the religions and their capacity to create a new world give way to an apocalyptic vision which lulls the spirit in the face of misery. The poor are fed on hopes for a better life hereafter. A normative Christology for Asia must, therefore, address not only the ultimate liberation but also a liberation from the socio-cultural, economic and political oppression and injustice. The rich and the powerful continue to maintain the structures and systems of domination bequeathed to them by colonisers and have become agents of neo-colonialism even at the cost of their own national interests. In most Asian countries a rich minority controls the means of production as well as political power, condemning the vast majority to abject poverty and exploitation. Most of the countries of Asia have become victims of international militarism and arms race at the cost of socio-economic development and friendly relationships with neighbouring countries.[41] The quest of the people is for an integral liberation. Perhaps, like the Syrian Christology which made a synthesis of the Hellenistic and Jewish-Christian soteriological concerns, a normative Asian Christology must synthesise the soteriological concerns of the Asian Religions and the quest for a historical liberation of the poor and the marginalized who form the majority of the people of Asia.

The fundamental question that the normative Christologies of the Jewish, Hellenistic, Syrian and Latin Christian traditions raised was about the role of Jesus Christ in liberating humans from the situation of misery and misfortune. They were clear about their situation of misery from which they needed liberation. In encountering Jesus Christ they experienced the liberation they were searching for. So they articulated their Christology, who the person of Jesus Christ is, from the perspective of their liberation experience. Similarly, the normative Christology in the Asian context emerges from the experience of liberation from the historical and cosmic bondage through Jesus Christ.

The sufferings that make human life miserable in this world are caused by ignorance *(avidya)* according to Hinduism, and by desire *(tanha or trshna)* according to Buddhism. There are complex religio-philosophical systems that analyse the various aspects of these root causes of misery and misfortune and propose ways and means to liberate oneself from this situation. Most such systems suggest that one can liberate oneself from the situation of suffering and reach the ultimate liberation. A few others may suggest that God's grace is needed for the ultimate liberation. Are humans themselves responsible for their own suffering and the sufferings of others or are they like puppets in the hands of a puppeteer who controls their destiny? The emphasis of these religions seems to be that the situation of suffering is given or destined by the Supreme reality or the whole structure of humans is such that they desire for what they are not and what they have not and end up in causing misery for themselves.

Does Jesus Christ offer anything new to the poor of Asia which the older religions of Asia cannot give? Is He just another apocalyptic visionary or a true prophetic missionary? Can Jesus address the quest for ultimate liberation and questions of poverty? The fundamental Christian *Kerygma* is that Jesus Christ is Lord and Saviour. But the question is how to proclaim this *kerygma*

---

[41] F.J. Balasundaram, *The Prophetic Voices of Asia, Part I*, Bangalore: A.T.C., 1993, pp.8-14.

meaningfully in the Asian context. A normative Christology of Asia needs to be the articulation of the Christic-experience of the people in a way that it proclaims Jesus whom the poor and the oppressed can encounter as their historical liberator and as the Christ, the Logos, whose presence is "known" or "unknown' in the religions of Asia. How does Jesus Christ as the self-emptying of God respond to the situation of suffering in the Asian context, whatever be the cause of suffering.

Is Jesus Christ just another God competing with a myriad of gods and goddesses of the Asian continent for supremacy? Can we discover what God has said about Jesus from the history of His people, from their struggles, from their hopes and frustrations? What God has said about His Son must be heard in unheard of ways and must be seen in hitherto unseen ways that we do not force God to reveal, through the familiar framework of our minds. It is simply letting God be God. The religion of His time could not recognise in Him the revelation of God because He had failed to fit into their understanding of God. So the Christology of the Asian context must reveal *the radical newness* of God's self-revelation in Jesus Christ as well as the voice of God breaking the silence from below, in the voice of the voiceless and the sigh of the oppressed.

The Christ of the Asian Reality

In the eighties, the Third World theologians evaluated the various Christological models of the Asian context and found them inadequate in responding to the plurality of religions and the pervasive poverty of Asia.[42] The "fulfilment theology" of the 1930's with its recognition of the Christ-of-the religions, was an initiative to counteract the "civilization theology" of the Western missionaries and colonizers. But it failed to recognise the Christ-of-the-poor. The ashramic Christ of the late 60's was a protest against the "development theology" of neo-colonialism. The ashramic movement, recognizing greed as the enemy within, embraced voluntary poverty and simplicity but refused to see the structural greed of systems and structures and failed to participate actively in the struggles of the poor for liberation. The "inculturation Christology" of the late 70's in opposition to "liberation Christology" failed to see that in Asia culture and religion are not monolithic and there is a link between religion and socio-cultural, economic and political liberation. Further, there are many cultures and classes in one religion itself and many religions in one culture. Therefore, a normative Christology for Asia must articulate the vision of Christ who is the Christ-of-the-religions-and-the-poor.

Aloysius Pieris has rightly pointed out that, "The religiousness – especially in Asia – is for a greater part Meta-theistic or, at least, non theistic if not, at times explicitly atheistic. The common thrust, however, is *soteriological,* the concern of most religions being *liberation (vimukti, moksha, nirvana)* rather than speculation about a hypothetical liberator."[43] Therefore, soteriology or the concern for liberation becomes the foundation of theology. In the common concern of all Asian religions and secular ideologies for liberation, what is the vision of Christ that promotes the cause of integral liberation. "Is he an oriental pantocrator? A western divine prophet? The private God of the Christians? The Universal Saviour? A Man for other?"[44] Answers to any of these questions positively or negatively would deform the figure of Christ. The mystery of Christ

---

[42] A. Pieris, "Non-Christian Religions and Cultures in Third World Theology – II, *Vidyajyoti* 46/5, 1982a, pp.166-170.

[43] A. Pieris, "Non-Christian Religions and Cultures in Third World Theology – II, *Vidyajoyti 46/5, 1982b, p.241.*1982b: 241.

[44] R. Panikkar, "Christophany for Our Times," *Theology Digest* 39/1, 1992, p.4.

cannot be limited to any titles or any particular function of Christ. However, the figure of Christ that is encountered, lived and interpreted in any cultural, religious, social, political and economic context makes Him the liberative force against all types of alienation. The liberative figure of Christ must energize the elements of integral liberation in all religious traditions of Asia, so that each religious tradition can contribute its unique share for the wholeness of all. Further, the Christ of the Asian reality must identify with the poor in their struggle against everything that alienates them from themselves, and against the systems and structures that prevent them from living a dignified and fuller human life.

Some Characteristics of a Normative Asian Christology

Taking into serious consideration the soteriological concerns of the Asian religions and the cry of the poor and the marginalized for historical liberation, a normative Christology of the Asian context must reveal the involvement of the God, in the history, culture , religion and socio-economic and political situation of the people, leading them to integral liberation. Such a God is revealed in Jesus Christ as the self-emptying, *kenotic* God. Some elements of this kenotic Christology can be spelt out:

1.In Jesus Christ the infinite became finite, the Absolute became relative, God became human, the Word became flesh (Jn 1:14). As He came not to be served but to serve (Mk 10:45) the self-emptying figure of Christ (Phil 2:6ff) is to be encountered as the servant and not the master of everything perfect, good, true, beautiful and authentically liberative in all religious traditions whether Great or Little, meta-cosmic or cosmic, unitive or messianic.[45] He is not only not against the liberative potential of Asian religious traditions, but has the power to actualise it in reality.

2. A kenotic Christ can reveal the power of the powerless, can identify with them and energize them to struggle for a fuller human life, at the same time liberate them from the forces of alienation within themselves as well as within the structures and systems which enslave them.

3. If Jesus Christ is truly God and truly human as the Council of Chalcedon confesses and proclaims, He cannot be but what He revealed himself to be in history, the servant of God, humanity and cosmos. In him is the self-disclosure of God that God is the servant of all and everything. This is the radical *kenosis*, the paradox of Christic revelation, a stumbling block to the Jews and folly to the Gentiles but, indeed, the power of God and wisdom of God (I Cor 1:25). Self-emptying is the essence of the Trinitarian Oneness. "There is no other name" that reveals the mystery of God as a kenotic God except the one who, being Lord become servent of His own creation. The newness, decisiveness, normativeness and the universal validity of Jesus Christ consists in His servanthood of everything that is authentically human, be it culture, religion, systems or structures. The self-emptying servanthood of God is expressed in the foot-washing of the disciples at the Last Supper (Jn 13: 3-15). This revelation subverts all human categories of discrimination: superiority and inferiority, higher class and lower class, high caste and low caste, pure and impure, patriarchalism and matriarchalism, male and female, Christian and Pagan, believers and non-believers, civilized and uncivilized, etc. It challenges the religious and secular structures that perpetuate the systems of discrimination and dehumanization and energizes the forces of liberation whether religious or secular.

4. The kenotic Christ can fulfill the longing of the Asian people for liberation from greed, acquisitiveness, egoism and the fragmentation of reality. He can reveal the value of an ethical

---

[45] M.M. Thomas, *Man and the Universe of Faiths,* Madras: CLS, 1975, p.33.

religiosity for integral liberation over cultic and gnostic religiosity. Jesus of Nazareth revealed a God who is anthropocentric and not self-centred, because He was by nature a self-emptying God. A kenotic Christ can perform His prophetic function in the Asian context by challenging all religions including Christianity to be authentically anthropocentric and discover the God of the humans in the cosmos and in human suffering.

5. The kenotic Christ can energise all those who encounter Him to promote everything authentically human and liberative in various religious traditions, cultures, and socio-political and economic systems with respect, love and a self-emptying attitude. Such an encounter with the kenotic Christ would empower them to identify themselves with those who are committed to fight against the forces of un-freedom and build a new society where the self-emptying of God is the source and model for communion and communities of justice, love, compassion, fellowship, peace, reconciliation and, indeed, wholeness and harmony.

Scripture reveals to us a kenotic God in Christ who came to serve. His service to the people of all religions is the newness of a radically different revelation of God who is to be acknowledged as the ultimate meaning of human life and the mediator and unifier of all that is authentic, good, true and beautiful in all religions and cultures. Thus, Jesus Christ can be recognised and proclaimed as the mediator and the unifier of all authentic religious traditions by His hidden presence in them and through the work of His Spirit in them. The revelation of the kenotic Christ without His historical incarnation can be manipulated by vested interests to support any systems of oppression and injustice whether religious, cultural, social, economic or political. The challenging *newness* of the revelation in Jesus Christ is that God seeks the integral liberation of human beings not from beyond the

cosmic and historical context, but from the centre of the cosmos and from the heart of human history. God suffers when humans suffer because in His radical kenoisis He shares everything that humans live and breathe except the alienation humans choose for themselves. This is the *paradox* of Divine Revelation in Christ that Paul speaks about in I Corinthians in 1:23, "a stumbling block to Jews and foolishness to Gentiles." Asia can only respond to a God who reveals himself from within its own context. Probably, the Christology of the kenotic Christ that God opted for and that all humans can respond to, if they make themselves free from the false values of their systems and structures. It overcomes the temptation of the Christians to present Jesus Christ in a triumphalistic way and as an alien God to the cultures and religions of Asia.

Conclusion

A normative Christology for any culture must be in continuity with the living Tradition of the Church expressed through the Scripture, traditions, worship, way of lived-faith, practice of charity, etc. The various Christologies in the New Testament show how difficult it was for the disciples to articulate their experience of the risen Lord. The Christologies of the Jewish, Greek, Syrian and Latin Christian traditions show the development of normative Christologies as the reflection of their Christic experience as the answer to the quest for liberation, understood from the context of their religio-cultural context. A normative Christology for Asia remains in continuity with these living traditions that form the totality of the Christian articulations about the mystery of God revealed in history.

The kenotic Christology, proposed in this chapter, takes into consideration the biblical revelation of God in history as a self-emptying God who shares everything that is cosmic and human. He is not an outsider to Asia but its heart and soul. He can be recognised in the quest of its cultures and religion for an integral liberation. He can be recognised in the struggles of the poor and the marginalized for a fuller and dignified human life.

The *newness* of the revelation in Jesus Christ is that He is God's self-communication in a way hitherto unknown to humans. He encounters humans as a self-emptying God, a paradox to human attempts to understand Him through philosophies and systems. His self-emptying is so radical that He can be recognised by His followers in the mystic and prophetic religions of Asia, in Buddha's silence and in the systems that deny His existence but are committed to human welfare. A kenotic Christology challenges all systems and structures both religious and secular that prevent humans from unfolding themselves and becoming authentic humans. It preserves, promotes and integrates everything that is true, beautiful and good in Asia's cultures and religions as they are the fruits of His Spirit active in them. He lets His disciples gather all the fragments, that nothing may be lost. Thus a normative Christology for Asia, like other Christologies of Christian Tradition, emerges from the Asian context and challenges the disciples to bear witness to their Christic experience by a life committed to the kenotic Christ and to suffer the consequences of that commitment that they may have life and have it in abundance.

CHAPTER 11

Emerging Catholic Missions and Missiologies in India

AUGUSTINE KANJAMALA, SVD

Introduction: The Context of India and the Issues

India is perhaps the most complex nation in the world because of its nearly unimaginable pluralism and contrasting, often conflicting, diversities at every level. Today's population of one billion originated from six distinct racial types and some degree of mixing, with the predominance of the Aryan race in the Indo-Gangetic plain in the North and the Dravidian race in the South. Eighteen official languages, including English, plus1652 dialects create a veritable tower of Babel. The geographical as well as linguistic isolation of innumerable communities in the early period, with hereditary occupations originally laid the foundation for the present day, nearly 4000 jatis and 500 tribal communities. Such a social situation was gradually reorganized and legitimized as *Varnashrama dharma* by priestly authors of the Hindu sacred Scriptures. Minority religious communities like Muslims, Christians, Sikhs, Biddhists, Jains, Jews, Parsis and Animists co-exist with the dominant Hindu community 60 percent, wrongly reported as 85 percent by Census Reports. With 40 percent illiteracy, half of the illiterate population of the world is found in this country. Yet, in contrast, it boasts of the third largest scientifically and technically qualified personnel among nations. India's rank is 134th out of 174 countries figuring in the Human Development Index (HDI) prepared by the United Nations Development Program (UNDP).

Such a mind-boggling complexity and diversity pose great challenges, to every one concerned, including Christian missionaries. Today's rapidly changing scenario provokes serious questions about mission. What is happening to proclamation of the Gospel of Jesus Christ in the Post Vatican Council II period? What do the missionaries in the field think about the relationship between proclamation and inter-religious dialogue; between proclamation and human liberation? What new methods of evangelization are initiated or emphasized by the missionaries because of new theological orientation and direction given by the Catholic Bishops Conference of India (CBCI) and national as well as regional mission institutes and their renewal programme? What are some of the contradictions and tensions between missionary vision on the one hand and praxis on the other? Which are the main theological /missiological trends that are being taught, circulated and published by Indian theologians? Is missionary work among non-Christians still relevant if salvation is possible in any religion?

Searching for answers the CBCI commission for Proclamation conducted a national survey during 1993-94 in 40 sample dioceses out of 130, in the 12 ecclesiastical regions of all the three individual / ritual churches. Our analysis below is based on the data collected from 1690 priests, 4127 sisters and 9050 lay people. The research sample is drawn from 10 percent of the priests, 5 percent of the sisters and nearly 0.1 percent of the lay people. Over 15,000 people actively participated in the massive survey by answering questionnaires, through personal interviews and group discussions.[1] The near consensus that emerged from 40 independent diocesan surveys, with minor local variations, confirms the validity of the methodology of the survey.

Trends in numerical growth and spatial distribution

The nature of Christian missionary activity and responses of the people were naturally influenced by various social factors, like ethnicity, caste, class, religion, and culture. The oldest Church, the Syrian Church on the Malabar coast, with its traditional claim to apostolic origin and upper caste background, constitutes nearly 69 percent of Kerala Catholics as well as one-fourth of India's Catholic population (nearly 15.6 million). 31 percent of the Kerala Catholics belong to the Latin Rite Church which originated in the sixteenth century. No wonder that nearly 50 percent of Indian priests and nearly 60 percent of Indian religious sisters originate from this southern corner of India,[2] though that is beginning to decline.

In the beginning of the 16th century, under the Padroado system, (*Jus Commissionis,* 1494) the Portuguese missionaries created new communities on the Western coast, beginning with Goa which became the center for further expansion to the rest of Asia. The latest data shows that over 1.3 million Catholics areas are mainly concentrated in Bombay, Goa, Mangalore and Poona. They constitute about 10 percent of the Catholics of India. Goa is also the home of large number of missionaries, but in recent years vocations are diminishing.

After observing the remarkable success of the Gossner Evangelical Lutheran missionaries

from Berlin, Belgian Jesuit missionaries penetrated into the deep jungles of Chotanagpur Plateau in 1885. Numbers were below one hundred then, but social involvement, particularly providing legal protection to the Adivasis and their land from exploitation and oppression of landlords and rajas, a mass conversion movement began under the leadership of Constans Lievens. Today there are nearly 1.1 million Catholics in Chotanagpur and neighboring regions. Nearly 75 percent of the Christians in the Hindi region are converts from the Adivasis of Chotanagpur and about 20 percent from the dalits. In U.P. the largest state with around 140 million population, including 16 percent Muslims, the 0.15 percent Christian presence is like a drop in the ocean. But Chotanagpur region is the new catchment area for increasing number of religious missionary vocations, balancing the decline elsewhere in India.

Today about 18. percent of the Indian Christian population is in the North East in contrast to 7 percent half a century ago. Around 75 percent of them belong to the Baptist and the Presbyterian Churches, which have had over 160 years of missionary service. One-fourth of the Christian population here is Catholic, thanks mainly to the missionary ventures of the Salesians of Don Bosco. During the post-independence era the Catholic population here multiplied over 17 times - from about 60,000 to 1.04 million, constituting around 7 percent of the Indian Catholic population. In three small states the Christians constitute the majority: Nagaland 87 percent, Mizoram 86 percent and Meghalaya 64 percent.[3] But in overall terms of the 31.5 million

---

[1] The author, in his capacity as the Secretary to the Catholic Bishops Conference of India (CBCI) Commission for Proclamation, conducted a national survey with the help and collaboration of a team each in 40 dioceses. Most of our data was collected during this research.

[2] O. Degrijse, *Going Forth. Missionary Consciousness In the Third World Catholic Church*, New York, 1984, pp. 44-46.

[3] I. Rajan, "Demographic Profile of Indian Christians: An Over View," in *Indian Missiological Review*, 1989, p. 127; Jayaseelan L., "Conflict Situation in Northeast India: the Church's Response," *Vidya Jyothi*, July 1999, p. 515.

population in the seven N.E. states, only 13.6 percent are Christian.

In the 17-18th century period, under the *Propaganda Fide*, (1622) great missionaries like Robert De Nobili, John De Britto and a few other pioneers directed their missionary experiments of adaptation and work among the upper castes of Madurai in Tamil Nadu. The new missionary method resulted in limited success, both in terms of number as well as inculturation. In contrast, the work of the missionaries in the 19th and 20th century among Dalits, sparked off a mass conversion movement to the Christian churches. One fifth of the Catholics of the country are in Tamil Nadu and majority of them come from the dalit background.[4]

Our study clearly shows an imbalance in the geographical spread of the Christian population as well as missionary personnel. For instance, in 1881 only 0.7 percent of the Indian population was Christian and probably 90 percent of them were found in South India; by 1971, after mass conversion movement of nearly 100 years, this figure suddenly increased to 2.7, out of these 60 percent are in South India, 8 percent in the North (Hindi Belt), 7.3 percent in the Western Zone, 5 percent in the East zone, 18 percent in the North-East region, and 3 percent in the extreme North.[5] Probably there will be little change in the structure of the Christian as well as Catholic population of the country in the near future, with the minor exception of North East India. According to the 1991 Census Report on Religion, the Christian population declined from 2.7 percent in 1971 to 2.32 percent in 1991. At the beginning of the year 2000 the Catholic population is estimated to be around 15.6 million, constituting 1.8% of the Christian population of India (about 25 million).

All over India the number of conversion was regularly increasing for over 100 years until 1971. They have been on the decline during the past 30 years. This phenomenon coincides with the liberal missiological spirit of Vatican II as well as systematic opposition by some state governments and Hindu fundamentalists.

Institutionalization, pastoral ministry and primary proclamation

Institutionalization is one of the major trends in the Catholic Church in post-Independence India. Some of the major indications[6] are: during the last 5 decades Catholic dioceses have grown from 56 in 1950 to 130 in 1996; dispensaries have increased to 10 fold (1469 in 1990); hospitals have also increased 10 fold to reach the mark of 593 (in 1990); growth rate of high schools is six fold (2,081 in 1990); colleges and institutions of higher learning have increased 8 fold (289 in 1990). The only exception to this trend of phenomenal growth of institutions is the field of primary and middle schools (about 25 percent growth).

A large number of priests and religious personnel are engaged in these institutions. Not only the old churches but also some of the new churches are very busy and burdened with administration and pastoral ministry. Consequently they have little time, even if they wish, for proclamation "Ad Gentes." The new mission territories are passing through the process of deepening the faith, from charisma to institutionalization, after the period of mass movement to the church. Institution building is required to render various services to the new Christian communities. *Mission Ad*

---

[4] A. Kanjamala,"Future of the Christian Mission in the Hindi Belt," *Verbum SVD*, Bonn-St. Augustin, 1993, No. 1, pp. 45ff.

[5] A. Kanjamala, "Trends in Numerical Conversions" in *Integral Mission Dynamics*, New Delhi, 1995, pp.610-616. All the statistical data in this book is tabulated by the author from different sources, mainly the *Catholic Directories of India*, regularly published by the CBCI.

[6] *Ibid.*, pp. 425ff.

Gentes therefore is not a priority as it was in the past.

Today about 20,000 Catholic priests, 80,000 nuns, 2000 brothers and a large number of catechists constitute an cadre of full time workers. 60 percent of the priests, 69 percent of sisters and 56 percent of brothers are concentrated in South India where 68 percent of India's Catholics and 25 percent of India's total population live. The rest of the mission areas suffer from shortage of personnel. During the last 20 years, because of the new missionary thrust in the South, there is a small shift in the distribution of missionary personnel. There is an overall 5 percent shift of missionary personnel, particularly from the Syro-Malabar Rite Church, in favour of other regions of India since 1980 when 65 percent of priests and 75 percent of sisters were working in the four Southern states.. The challenges to those who are responsible for planning and distribution of missionary personnel still continue.

Christian schools educate 10-12 percent of the students of this country, 15 percent of the sick people are being cared for by the Christian hospitals, particularly by religious sisters. Undoubtedly the influence of these institutions goes far beyond the minority character of Christianity. The institutional Church in India is as powerful as it is influential. The quality of life-style and witness and the spiritual influence of the men and women behind these institutions are more important than the institutions themselves. There is a danger that these institutions might become centres of conflict and rivalry for power, money, and prestige and of oppression if they are not permeated with the spirit of Jesus Christ.

Mission Ad Gentes – The Gentile Mission

The Vatican Council defined missions as follows:

> 'Missions' is the term usually given to those particular undertakings by which the heralds of the Gospel are sent out by the Church and go forth into whole world to carry out the task of preaching the Gospel and planting the Church among peoples or groups who do not yet believe in Christ. Their undertakings are brought to completion by missionary activity and are commonly exercised in certain territories recognized by the Holy See.
>
> The specific purpose of this missionary activity is evangelization and planting the Church among those people and groups where she has not yet taken root (A. G. 6).

During the past 150 years a good number of Hindus, Muslims, Parsis and others in general have shown appreciation for the teachings and the person of Jesus but only a few are interested in conversion to visible membership in the Church. Yet along with the missionaries and British administrators the Hindu reformers questioned many shocking social evils prevalent in the Hindu society, like child marriage, sati (widow burning), polygamy, prohibition of widow remarriage, temple prostitution, untouchability and so forth. Raja Ram Mohan Roy, K. N. Sen, M.C. Parekh, P.C. Muzoomdar, R. Tagore, Ranade, M. K. Gandhi and many others are daring examples. A purification process of Hinduism (Suddhi) stimulated by the challenges of missionaries and the Gospel of Jesus Christ still has relevance for today's India. The "Ethical Christology" (R.R.M. Roy), the "Oriental Christ" (P. C. Mazoomdar), the "Mystical and Ascetic Christ" (S. Radhakrishnan) and many other inspiring and appealing images of Jesus will have perennial attraction for every sincere seeker of God. Pope John Paul II said in Delhi on November 6, 1999, "No individual, no culture is impervious to the appeal of Jesus who speaks from the very heart of human condition" (EA.14). Since a majority of the followers of the great religions of India finds it difficult to accept Jesus as the only manifestation of God, and the only saviour, a pedagogy of gradual presentation of Jesus, as a prudent methodology of evangelization, is recommended by the Pope. (EA.20)

In recent times Hindu fundamentalism with its aggressive philosophy of Hindutva is on the rise. Arya Samaj, founded by Dayananda Sarasvati in the last century with the motto "Back to Vedas," Rashtriya Swayamsevak Sangh (R.S.S.) founded by K.B. Hegdewar, the Hindutva ideology of Veer Savarkar and similar movements were working to reorganize Hindus, to fight missionaries and reconvert Christians and Muslims to Hinduism. Hindu fundamentalism charges that Muslim and Christian colonizers together dominated or destroyed Hindu culture and religion for the past 1000 years. Hindutva aims to create the noble Hindu Rastra (Ramarajya) through its method: Hinduize all politics and militarize Hinduism. However the last election manifesto (1999) had to give up some of their aggressive traits to arrive at a consensus common agenda of National Democratic Alliance (N.D.A.) of 24 political parties.[7] The Sangh Parivar is expressing its displeasure with the liberals and many strains among the party members are surfacing.

There is also an alarming increase in incidents of persecution of missionaries. The burning to death of the Australian missionary G. Staines and his two children in January 1999; murder of Fr. Arul Doss in September 1999, both in Orissa; raping and attacks on Sisters in Jhabua district, M. P., murder of Sr. Rani Maria in M. P., attacks on Christians, burning of Bible and Churches, attack on Christian schools and other institutions, false accusations about conversions and other nefarious activities in Gujarat in December 1998-99, are widely reported.[8] It is not by accident that these atrocities are committed mostly in the cow belt. The protest meetings organized in the various parts of the parts of country by the Christians and their deputations to the government authorities had no significant impact. Christians in many areas are living in fear and panic. Under political pressure a few thousand Catholics reconverted to Hinduism particularly in the Hindi belt. However, it should not be overlooked that a majority of Hindus either appreciate or at least tolerate the Christian mission. It will be a gross error to paint all Hindus as fundamentalists and communalists.

Dalit conversions today seem to be on the decline, contrary to the false accusations of Hindu fanatics. A good number of Dalit Catholics have left the church or hide their identity for various reasons, including obtaining socio-economic benefits like job reservations and scholarships for education from the government. Some significant differences are noticed about the marginalization of the Dalit Christians and conflict between them and caste Christians, depending on the presence or absence of caste Christians who are unfortunately responsible for perpetuating caste culture in the Church.

Many problems in today's Church and mission go back to the oppressive caste culture and structure of Hinduism which permeates the Indian ethos. A minority community of Christians, in spite of their conversions, is powerless to fight the prevailing caste culture. The dominant castes are worried that the tribals and dalits, the traditional source of cheap labour, are escaping from their clutches because of education and other liberating services of Christian missionaries.

It is unfortunate that the issue of conversion is again being politicized by the Sangh Parivar. The missionaries are being accused of proselytisation, using unfair means such as fraud, force and allurement, particularly among the poor and uneducated. If such practices occur it must

---

[7] *India Today*, July 15, 1991, pp. 40ff.

[8] For a chronology of recent attacks on Christians, see, *Then They Came for Christians*, by Rajni Desai, Bombay, April 1999, pp. 95-98

be categorically denounced. At the same time the Church strongly believes in the freedom of the individuals and communities to choose their religion. If the Indian Constitution and government give the tribals, dalits and other backward communities the right to vote and choose their government, are not these people capable of choosing their religion? Article 25.1 of the Indian Constitutions states: "All persons are equally entitled to freedom of conscience and the right to freely to profess, practice and propagate religion." The Christian approach to proclamation to other religions is one of genuine respect: "respect for man in his quest for answers to the deepest questions of his life, and respect for the action of the Spirit in man" (EA. 20).

The Methods of Evangelization

According to diverse circumstances of time, place, challenges of people and creativity of the missionary, methods of evangelization keep on changing. Under the influence of the recent movement, "New Evangelization 2000" (Jesu Krist Jayanti 2000) and other revival factors, the proclamation of Jesus Christ and His Gospel has received certain fresh impetus. Mission in the specific sense is marked by three parameters: (a) territorial (over 60 percent of the world's population lives in Asia, of which only 2.5 percent are Christians); (b) worlds of new social phenomena: e.g., in urban areas new forms of culture, communication and life style are emerging; (c) cultural fields of communication with new culture and psychology (R. M. 37). "New" evangelization means new in vigour and new in forms and expressions.

Charismatic Retreat Movement

The charismatic retreat movement started on a large scale in Potta, Kerala, and continues to attract many. It is estimated that per year over 50,000 non-Christians come to Potta alone. The Potta team travels and preaches outside Kerala and even abroad. New centres are mushrooming

because it is a powerful form of witnessing, praying and healing. Many Hindus, Muslims and people of other religions actively participate in the retreat and give public witness to the favours and blessings received from Lord Jesus Christ. There are also other categories of charismatic retreat centers.

Why is the charismatic movement very popular? One probable answer is that the liberalism and rationalism of the post-Vatican II period and the emerging consumerist culture of the neo-rich have not satisfied the religious thirst of the masses. A sense of failure is noticed. People seem to be searching for religious experiences such as conversion to God, inner healing from certain compulsive bad habits, reconciliation and reunion among family members which are some of the main features of the charismatic gatherings and prayers.

Even if there is the possibility that the charismatic movement may be short lived, like many other past religious movements, a few lessons from the trend can be derived: 1) God experience and spirituality is the foundation of mission work. 2) Mission is a community experience and community building process. 3) The Word of God is central to proclamation. The Catholics must be grateful to the Protestant Churches for deepening this awareness.

Proclamation through mass media

UNDA / OCIC India has over 100 members. Out of these around 40 communication centres are working rather efficiently. Around 65 percent of the communication centres and their trained personnel are in South India. In the north where the need is more, only a few centres have been founded and are functioning well. The Gospel broadcasts over 'Radio Veritas' (Manila), in different Indian languages and over 'Radio Sri Lanka,' are well received by millions of listeners in India, including people of different religions.

Catholic Information/Enquiry Centres

There are around 40 Catholic information centres, half of which are in South India. Till 1985, on an average, 40-50 thousand inquiries were made to these centres per year. Well-prepared lessons and Christian literature are supplied to the enquirer. On an average around 30 adult baptisms per year are reported from these centers. In 1991 there were 43,432 inquiries out of which 61 percent were in South India and 20.6 percent were in the Hindi belt (North). For many educated non-Christians who are curious to know more about Jesus, postal correspondence is a peaceful method to deepen their knowledge and devotion to Christ and avoid possible reactions from their family members and friends.[9]

Humanization and Social Transformation

The Vatican Council and over a dozen recent social encyclical letters of Popes have legitimized the church's responsibility for all the spheres of human life: social, economic, cultural, religious and political. The traditional "other-worldly" concept of salvation is being replaced by an integral concept of salvation and liberation. Openness to problems of the world, appreciation of positive elements in world religions and cultures, respect for freedom of conscience and human dignity were the major contributions of the teachings of the second Vatican Council.

The post-Vatican liberation theology of Latin America gained a significant number of followers in the third world countries including India. As a result some missionaries have entered into radical social action for the transformation of unjust structures. But radical commitment to the poor and social justice has created a kind of polarization between the "salvation of souls missiology" and the "social mission" of the Church in some dioceses.

"People-centred" and "institution-centred" mission is another dichotomy accentuated by them. However with the decline of communism/socialism, there is a decline in the radical grass-root missionary approaches of the 1975-1990 period. The beginning of a return to institutionalized mission work is recently observed, for example, starting English medium schools even in rural areas at the insistence of the so called poor. With globalization of the economic policies of the country, the process will be accentuated since the importance of the English language is being appreciated even by some state governments.

Christian Ashrams

Being urged by numerous post-Vatican national as well as regional seminars and theological consultations on the Church in India and its mission today, the number of Christian/Catholic ashrams has increased to over 100. Ashrams are places of intensive spiritual life and search for God. Elements of traditional Christian monasticism and Hindu monasticism are incorporated into these new experiments. Inculturation of liturgy, spirituality, life-style, and dialogue with people of other faiths are among the major concerns of the ashramites.

The number of priests and religious personnel committed to full time ashram life is very small; yet the number of those who spend at least some time of their life in prayer and contemplation is on the increase. Large numbers of visitors from the West, particularly the youth is also seen. There are a few ecumenical ashrams, where membership is extended not only to Christians of different denominations but also to Hindus and other religious groups. At the same time it is observed that missionaries in general spend not much time for collective reflection on

---

[9] Nediyakalayil, V.,"Report on the Catholic Enquiry Centres," in *Paths of Mission in India Today*, edited by A. Kanjamala, Bombay, 1996, pp. 195ff.

mission theology, mission methods and life style. There seems to be a lot of action without adequate reflection and prayer.

The radically different contexts as well as the complexity of Indian Society, the varying needs of peoples, and cultural diversity demand as well as justify plurality of methods in the service of one mission of Jesus Christ. Proclamation of Christ, dialogue with religions, struggle for liberation of the poor, evangelization of cultures, concern and commitment to the integrity of creation are being recognized and approved as integral parts of the one and same mission.

Mission Theology

Mission theology is a believing and praying community's sincere and systematic articulation of the meaning and relevance of the Word of God in an ever-changing situation of peoples with their own different world-views and life views. The history of missions was a history of Christian encounters with diverse religions and cultures. A systematic study of the interactions between the Word of God and the servants of the Word of God and the recipients of the Word of God are constitutive elements of a dynamic, contextual and relevant missiology.

Contemporary mission theology particularly in the Third World is characterized by an inductive methodology, starting "from below" (influence of the Antiochean school of theology and the current challenges of social sciences) in contrast to the deductive methodology, starting "from above" (influence of the Alexandrian school of theology). Such a shift in paradigm naturally introduces certain definite challenges in the identity of Christian mission as well as methods of evangelization.

There are significant variations of views about the goals of missionary activity. While the vast majority of priests and sisters 84 percent are gradually moving away from the traditional ecclesio-centric approach to the mission, a very small minority seems to be closer to the traditional position. Such a difference is one of the sources of tensions and even serious conflicts. In a few dioceses the problem of conflicting perceptions is further exacerbated by the fact that there are significant regional differences in the perception of the source of salvation as well as the goals of mission.

The most powerful traditional motivation of mission- salvation of souls- is gravely weakened by the new theology which affirms that salvation is possible for the sincere followers of one's own religion (NA 1; AG 2; LG 16; GS 22; DP 29). "God wills the salvation of all" (Tim.2:4). Like St. Peter, the Church as well as missionaries is gradually realizing: "In truth I see that God shows no partiality. Rather, in every nation whoever fears him and acts uprightly is acceptable to him" (Acts 10:34-35).

Around 66 percent of priests and 74 percent of religious sisters maintain that all religions are means of salvation for their sincere followers. In contrast, a minority 16 percent of the priests and religious sisters continue to subscribe to the traditional view. The majority of the lay people 58 percent who have little opportunity for updating their catechism continue to uphold the traditional views on mission. *Extra Ecclesiam Nulla Salus* – "No salvation outside the Church" – was the traditional axiom taught by St. Cyprian in the 3rd century, reinforced by the theology of St. Augustine and strictly interpreted and adhered to by the Church until very recently. The council of Florence, 1438-1445 officially taught: "The Roman Catholic Church firmly believes, professes and teaches (sic) that outside the Church no one, neither pagan nor heretics, nor schismatic can attain eternal life, but will go to the everlasting fire which was prepared for the devil and his agents."[10] Unfortunately a few

---

[10] K. Rahner, J. Neuner, *Teaching of the Catholic Church*, Ranchi, 1969, p.212

Catholics as well as a few Protestants, and members of some sects still continue to hold onto this grim view. For them conversion of the pagans (an unfortunate term) and baptism into the Church is the top priority.

A quarter of a century ago, the Asian Bishops defined mission as triple dialogue: (a) dialogue with the great religious traditions of the people of Asia; (b) dialogue with the poor, the deprived and the oppressed; (c) dialogue with living traditions, the cultures and with the life realities of the people in whose midst we serve.[11] From the middle of the 20th century, under the influence of the comparative study of religions, dialogue with the world religions is understood as one of the methods of proclamation. The Vatican Council acknowledged that there exist "elements which are true and good" (O. T. 16), "elements of truth and grace" (A. G. 9), in other religions. Missionaries are thus exhorted, "to learn by sincere and patient dialogue what treasures a bountiful God has distributed among the nations of the earth" (A.G. 11). Therefore "any sense of mission not permeated by such a dialogical spirit would go against demands of true humanity and the teaching of the Gospel."[12]

The Synod of the Bishops in Rome affirmed: "action on behalf of justice and participation in the transformation of the world fully appears to us as a constitutive dimension of the preaching of the Gospel, that is, of the mission of the Church for the redemption of the human race and its liberation from every oppressive situation."[13] Missionary emphasis is gradually shifting towards witness, presence and service, particularly among the poor and oppressed. A shift from the past preoccupation with number and quantity to quality of Christian life and service is evident today. Working for liberation and humanization of the poor, marginalized and oppressed is becoming a major mission trend in a poor country like India.

Among the three major motivations for evangelization (Church-centred, Christ-centred, Kingdom of God centred), Christ-centred mission is the most powerful motive among Catholic missionaries. Around 70 percent of the missionaries on the all India level consider that making Christ known is their first priority.

The second priority of the missionaries is the promotion of the values of the Kingdom of God— 65 percent. The link between these two approaches is clear to most of the respondents. The Vatican Council's teaching that God's saving love extends to sincere followers of all religions has been accepted by most of our respondents— 66 percent of the clergy and 74 percent of religious sisters. Religious women, in responding to the questionnaire, in general expressed more liberal attitudes and opinions, probably due to lack of any systematic education in theology, unlike the clergy. Ultimately the vitality of the mission depends on the love that urges the missionary (2 Cor 5:14).

Church-centred mission gets only the third priority. Merely 16 percent of the missionaries, priests and sisters, consider this as most important. The main exception to this trend is the North East where church-centred mission gets a higher rating 36 percent because this is a responsive area in the traditional sense. Nearly two-thirds of the tribal population in the N. E. has embraced Christianity in this century. Decline in ecclesio-centrism, the main model in the pre-Vatican missiology, implies crucial changes in traditional ecclesiology and related attitudes to Church authorities, like bishops and priests. Naturally there are reactions to these new trends, particularly from the hierarchy.

---

[11] FABC, Taipei, 1974, No.9-24.

[12] Vatican Secretariat for dialogue, An Attitude of the Church Towards Followers of Other Religions, 1984, No.2

[13] "Justice in the World," 1971, No.6

Mission theology, being a human construct, in response to the "signs of the time" (G.S.4), cannot but be plural. It is important to keep in mind that the priorities listed above in no way intend to be exclusive: "Where God is accepted, when the gospel values are lived, where man is respected there is the Kingdom. It is far wider than Church's boundaries. The Church is an instrument for the realization of the Kingdom."[14] The Church is also the privileged place where the values of the Kingdom of God becomes more transparent and visible; a sacrament of the reign of God. Like Christ, the light of the world, the mission of the Church begins by becoming the light of the world. (L.G. 1; Is.42: 6; 49:6). Accordingly three inter-related models are distinguished:

(1) The mission of Jesus was predominantly Kingdom-centred. He spoke 116 times about the Kingdom of God, a metaphor of Messianic liberation that was familiar to the oppressed people of Israel (Mk 1:14; Mt 24:14). Jesus spoke about it in various parables (Mt 13:1-53). And St. Paul explains: "For the Kingdom of God is not a matter of food and drink, but of righteousness, peace and joy in the Holy Spirit" (Rom.14: 17).

(2) The apostolic mission was mainly Christ-centred, being overpowered by the resurrection experience of Jesus Christ (Acts 1:22; 4:12; 5:27-32 etc.). St. Paul spoke about Christ 379 times. His mission was highly Christo-centric.

(3) In the post-Constantine era Church became a central concern and ecclesio-centrism was the major model during the colonial mission.

The summary of Jesus' mission is the Good News (Mk. 1:14ff; Lk. 4:18) of the arrival of God's Kingdom (*Basileia*). The Kingdom is not a territory, nor is it an ideology. It means God's sovereign rule or reign to restore the whole creation and the whole of humanity to its original state as it was in the beginning of creation (Gen. 1-2). The expected human response to Jesus proclamation of the Kingdom is one of conversion (*metanoia*), primarily a change of heart, and not a change of religion, but a turning to God to accept his offer of love and entrust and submit our lives to God's will. Baptism is primarily a sign of inner conversion, a rite of admission into the new Spirit-filled community by the outpouring of the Holy Spirit at the time of the Pentecost. Baptism replaced the rite of circumcision as an external sign of admission into Judaism. Conversion and baptism means a participation in the death of Christ to sin as well as the old world (Rom. 6:3). The heart of the mission consists of Good News, Kingdom and Conversion. Two broad types of missiologies are operative in the contemporary Indian debate.

(1) The official teachings: mission documents of Vatican Council II (particularly L.G., A.G., N.A. and G.S.) the mission encyclical letters of Popes (particularly E.N., R.M.), Synods of the Bishops, and the collective teaching of the C.B.C.I. which claim to be biblical, apostolic and dogmatic in nature.

(2) In contrast to these, the grass root missionaries, struggling with the challenges of life situations, as discovered in the national survey, develop their own praxis and practical missiologies, shaped by daily experiences and reflections. How the tensions and conflicts between these two missiologies are resolved is usually left to each one. And the contemporary spirit of pluralism and individual freedom provide enough room for such solutions.

---

[14] Jacques Dupis,*Vidya Jyothi*, Vol. 56, p. 456.

Tensions, Conflicts and Crisis in the Indian Mission

Interest in the direct proclamation of Jesus and his Gospel seems to be on the decline in general (R.M.2). The findings of our survey in various dioceses support this view of Pope John Paul II. On the All India level only 33 percent of the missionaries are happy with the missionary atmosphere in their dioceses. However, a higher level of satisfaction was expressed in the Chotanagpur region (45 percent of the priests and 36 percent of the sisters) and in the North East (56 percent of the priests and 76 percent of the sisters). These areas are still quite responsive to missionary initiative.

The decline in the missionary spirit to some extent is due to various modern social and cultural factors. However, "The dampening of missionary zeal is due ultimately ... to the fact that the power of the Word is choked by the cares of the world and the delight in riches (Mt. 13:32) that is, by consumerism and the lure of power and money among those who should be servants of the Word," observes the final statement of the recent CBCI consultation on evangelization in Pune.[15] The renewal of the missionary spirit will depend on the renewed life of faith and love of Jesus Christ. "Missionary drive has always been a sign of vitality, just as it's lessening is a sign of crisis of faith" (R.M. 2).

The President of the Vatican Secretariat for Evangelization, in his address to the Cardinals in Rome on 4-5 April 1991, accused India of being the epicenter of new heresies. The emerging Indian mission theology of the Kingdom of God is also much suspected by some members of the hierarchy of India. "The Kingdom of God" - Chapter II of the recent mission encyclical, *Redemptoris Missio* by Pope John Paul II, was indirectly answering some of the missiological issues raised by theologians, including Indian theologians. The Pope draws attention to the tension that is observed between the proclamation of the Kingdom and proclamation of Christ. The Pope says (No.18):

> The preaching of the early Church was centred on the proclamation of Jesus Christ with whom the Kingdom is identified. There is a need to unite the proclamation of the Kingdom of God....and the proclamation of Christ-event (the Kerygma of the Apostles). The two proclamations are complementary (R.M. 16). But many who speak about the Kingdom are silent about Christ.

This cryptic silence and arbitrary detaching of the Kingdom of God from Jesus Christ, the sacrament of the Kingdom, is systematically challenged by the Pope.[16] The recent theology of the Kingdom of God is akin to the 19ᵗʰ century liberal Protestant missiology which accentuated the proclamation of the Kingdom of God without upholding the centrality of Jesus Christ.

According to the Vatican II theology of the local Church (L.G. 26) the bishop is the final authority, responsible for mission in his territory (A.G. 30). If he is not seriously interested, there is no organization in India with a common vision and coordinating authority to direct the work of proclamation. The traditional duty of *Propaganda Fide* to coordinate missionary activities in specific territories is abrogated by the new Cannon Law and traditional responsibility is not officially handed over to any corresponding body in India. We are in a state of disorganization. Since the CBCI Commission for Proclamation has no legal authority, who will coordinate the work of Proclamation at the all India level remains an unanswered question. Evangelization is perhaps the only task which can unite the whole church in India.

---

[15] A. Kanjamala, *Paths of Mission in India Today*, p.1996, 294.

[16] A. Kanjamala,"Redemptoris Missio and Mission in India," in *Redemption and Dialogue*, edited by W.R. Burrows, New York, 1993, pp. 198-199.

Serious conflicts between the pre-Vatican and Post Vatican II theologies of mission are observed in many dioceses. This is one of the major sources of personnel conflicts, for example, between Bishops and missionaries; between old priests and young priests; between priests and catechists (also laity); between Rome and the Indian Church. The conflict between traditionalists and modernists (liberals) seems to be on the increase in the context of growing scientific rationalism and individual freedom. While the missionaries, along with the official Church, recognize and uphold the centrality and uniqueness of Christ's redemptive acts on the one hand as well as the possibility of salvation outside the visible Church on the other hand, no clear answers to the question regarding the relation between these two views are provided. We are in the beginning of a transition from the past missiology of exclusivism (there is no salvation outside the Church) to the post-Vatican missiology of inclusivism (all those who are saved, even those members of other religions, are saved through the power and grace of Jesus Christ).

Because of the prolonged tensions and conflicts about 10 percent of the priests in a few dioceses resigned from their priesthood and religious life or migrated to other dioceses abroad. (Of course this might not have been the only reason). But it is a clear indication of the serious frustration not only of those who have left, but also of some of those who continue to work in these dioceses. Unfortunately, the spirit and morale of these dioceses are declining. The lay people are also getting confused and searching for clear and definitive answers. The sprouting of numerous small sects, both in the cities as well as in villages, seems to be an attempt to find alternative expressions of religious needs like certainty and anchor in the Word of God,

experiencing peace, joy and fellowship in small communities, in contrast to impersonal worship in large parishes.[17] The early Christian communities provide inspiring models as well as justifications for the promotion of Basic Christian Communities or Small Christian Communities. (Acts 2: 42-47; 4: 32-35).

A close affinity between the prevailing mission theologies and the responsive / non-responsive regions is observed, e.g., Church centered missionary approach gets low priority among the missionaries in the Hindi Belt and comparatively high priority in the North East. The missionaries also expressed a corresponding sense of satisfaction, dissatisfaction or frustration during my personal interviews with them.

India is a highly person-oriented society. Traditionally, personal contact between the missionaries and the people was an important method of evangelization. But these days contacts between missionaries and the people are on the decline. Institutionalization of missionary activities and modern travel and other conveniences partly explain the situation about which people are unhappy. Very few missionaries are ready to venture into frontier areas with poor amenities. The young missionaries of today manifest various characteristics of the emerging "soft culture" in contrast to the "tough culture" of earlier missionaries. The future of the mission will depend to a considerable degree on the committed laity who are in a better position to influence every sphere of society with the values of the Gospel (A.G. 2). In spite of the theology of "The People of God" (LG), the style of exercising authority, particularly in the old Churches, seems to be non-participatory. Often the quality of human relations does not inspire genuine confidence in the leadership nor is it favourable for building communities. In a male clergy dominated Church and mission, lay

---

[17] P. Parathazam, "The challenge Neo-Pentecostalism," *Vidya Jyoti*, March 1997, pp. 317-20.

people, particularly women, seem to be treated as second class missionaries. The rise of the laity in the western Church might be due to the recent fall in the number of clergy.

The most dangerous socio-political phenomenon in India today are: a) Communalism/fundamentalism; b) Increase in crime and violence, particularly against Scheduled Castes, Scheduled tribes and women; c) Rampant corruption in public life; d) Consumerism among the elite and neo-rich whose religious and ethical values are fast declining.[18] The deteriorating social environment is bound to influence the attitudes, values and behaviour of missionaries. In fact they require a deep-rooted spiritual resourcefulness in a rapidly secularizing society.

Regionalism/ethnocentrism in the Church and mission is on the increase. Dalit conflicts, tribal re-awakening, rite conflicts and tensions between the missionaries from the South and the indigenous people in the North are gradually increasing. The recent dalit liberation movement, headed by dalit Catholics as well as other leaders, has become a controversial issue. Its impact is slowly but surely spreading from Tamil Nadu to Pondicherry, Andhra Pradesh and other neighbouring states, challenging the marginalization and the oppression of the dalit Catholics by the upper caste Catholics who are in the minority.

A major breakthrough in the missionary activity of the Kerala Church after Vatican Council II is the missionary movement of the Oriental Churches to North India. Accusations against the southern domination in the north Indian mission are raised. Many missionaries hailing from the south and working in the north do not speak the local language and dialects of the people well. Often there is a lack of appreciation of the local culture. Social and cultural distance of the missionaries and the local people is easily noticed. Those who are working in the English medium schools are further alienated from the common people. Thinking and feeling with the local people and participating in their life style can help to reduce cultural conflicts. Instances of incongruity between the missiological vision of the official Church on the one hand and the actual practices of many missionaries on the other hand, became clearer through the survey and interviews. For instance, the goals and objectives of dialogue with people of other faiths: for some missionaries dialogue is only a means of proclamation; for others it is an end in itself.[19] In the perspectives of the Vatican authorities the 'Congregation for the Evangelization of the Peoples' is accorded higher status than the "Pontifical Council for Inter-Religious Dialogue."

The split between the Gospel and culture is one of the tragedies of our time (E.N.20). The real challenge for the missionaries is how to transform the secularization of the collective conscience of the people through the power and influence of the Gospel values, in other words, evangelization of the cultures.

Signs of Hope

Tensions, conflicts, confusion of vision, breakdown of values, or anomie in individuals as well as institutions are undoubtable indications of transition from the traditional system to a not yet clear and stable system. The crisis situation is also a time of new and creative opportunities. Our Christian hope should help us to rise above the pessimism which the contemporary missionary crisis tends to generate. It is not easy nor is it necessary to reconcile all the tensions, as long as these are reasonably contained. But

---

[18] R. Kottari, "From Religion to Religiosity," *Jeevadhara*, January, 1990, p. 115.

[19] A. Kanjamala, "Unity and Universality as a goal of Inter-religious Dialogue," *Mission and Dialogue*, edited by L.N. Mercardo, Manila, 1989, pp. 174 ff.

there can be no compromise on the centrality of the proclamation of the Kingdom of God and the proclamation of the person of Jesus Christ which are the two sides of the same reality. (D.P.63). Pope Paul VI wrote: "There is no true evangelization if the name, the teaching, the life, the promises, the Kingdom and the mystery of Jesus of Nazareth, the Son of God, are not proclaimed," EN. 22).

Granted that there are certain crises in the Indian mission, the post-Vatican era is also characterized by many signs of hope. For over two-thirds of the missionaries, the priority in mission is to make Jesus Christ known and to work for the realization of the values of the kingdom of God. Openness to other religions and cultures is on the increase and it reduces the social distance and conflicts between Christian missionaries and people of other religions. According to our sample, about 20 percent of the priests and sisters either organized or participated in inter-religious dialogue and prayer during the year of the survey. However, its practice is not very significant except for the dialogue meetings, mostly among the educated urban elite, on certain occasions like Gandhi Jayanthi, Divali, Christmas, Id, and other important religious festivals.

The radical commitment of some missionaries to the poor and the oppressed, moved by the spirit of compassion and service and without any ulterior motives of conversion, is another challenging trend. They "rejoice with those who rejoice, weep with those who weep" (Rom. 12:15). It is bound to weaken the false accusations from certain fundamentalist quarters about the hidden agenda of the missionaries. While there are a good number of Christian missionaries who are working in solidarity with the poor and the marginalized, the number of

Hindus committed to such situations and people is negligible.

The following are some of the major social trends in India which the Christian missionaries initiated a long time ago and are also now collaborating with: a) Dalit liberation movement b) Tribal liberation movement c) Women's liberation movement d) Protection of environment and ecology. The Spirit of life, freedom, justice, peace and righteousness can be discerned in the struggles of various people of good will. It must be kept in mind that every quest of the human spirit for truth and goodness and in the final analysis for God is inspired by the Holy Spirit. The Gospel of liberty is being preached to the poor and the marginalized (Lk. 4:18). The missionaries can be proud and happy that they have made significant contributions to restoring dignity to those who were suffering the pain and agony of dehumanization for centuries.[20] The people of the "little traditions" are given a new identity by becoming members of the universal church. Many tribal and dalit communities which were traditionally divided, even fighting against each other, are now being united under the umbrella of the Church. In such situations mission has undoubtedly worked as an agent as well as a sign of unity.

Further, the survey shows, in comparison with priests, the religious Sisters manifest more missionary involvement through their non-institutional forms of ministries and outreach programmes. Sisters in general are showing more interest in family visits. Their contact and involvement in non-institutional ministry is evaluated to be 3 to 4 times more than that of priests. A much higher percentage of sisters speak about the love of Christ to their students in schools, to the patients in hospitals and dispensaries as well as in informal settings. The

---

[20] A. Kanjamala,"Spirit of God in the Contemporary Social Movements," *Spirit of God and Mission Spirituality for the New Era* edited by P.A. Augustine, Indore, 1999.

mission of the future will not be as sacrament-oriented as in the past; for example, the number of baptisms, holy masses, confessions and other sacramental activities will be small. The future of the mission in India will be considerably shaped by the life, witness, commitment and work of religious Sisters who constitute about 80 percent of the full time workers in the Catholic mission fields.

The number of those who adopt new and creative forms of missionary methods is on the increase. Our study of 40 Catholic Inquiry Centres shows that 40-50 thousand adults of other religions are searching to deepen their knowledge of Jesus Christ through correspondence courses. Around 1,500 letters received annually from listeners of the Hindi programmes of "Radio Veritas," Manila, indicate that thousands of Indians of all religions are listening to the Gospel of Christ regularly. The charismatic retreat movement and their large regional and national conventions are occasions of proclamation and public witnessing. Large numbers of Christians as well as people of other faiths attend these. The lives of many people are remarkably transformed, as a consequence of their experience of personal conversion.

It is heartening to note that, following the directions of Vatican Council the number of those who study the Word of God and pray in families and Small Christian Communities (SCC) is on the increase. The publication of the Bible or a portion of it in all Indian languages and various dialects has considerably increased during the last quarter of the century.

Though Jesus was an Asian and the seed of Christianity was planted in the Indian soil nearly 2000 years ago, certain anti-missionary groups are trying to label Christianity (also Islam) as foreign. Granted that historical inaccuracies are part of their manipulative strategy, one cannot deny the fact that during the dynamic missionary era of the last 500 years, the Church / mission put on mainly foreign garbs with minor exceptions. The Catholic Church is making conscious and systematic efforts during recent decades to create an authentically Indian Church with an Indian style of thinking (theologizing), modes of liturgical worship, administration and life style. Though the Church is not tied down to any particular culture, the use of the local culture is obligatory on the part of the evangelizer as the best medium for communicating the Gospel as well as expressing appreciation for cultures (G.S. 53-60; E.N. 20). The recent efforts of inculturation seem to be, to some degree, fruitful in the young Churches of North India but it is being resisted in South India where the pressure of traditions, and unenlightened lay people cannot be easily ignored by the Church authorities.

The number of Indian missionaries going to foreign countries is on the increase. Accurate data about them is not yet available. Recruitment of indigenous vocations has turned India from being a mission receiving country to a mission sending one. Most of these missionaries are going to African and South American countries. European and North American Churches are asking for Indian missionaries, and the services of a few who are ministering there are quite appreciated. Of all the third-world Churches, the Indian Catholic Church and mission seems to be the most dynamic, with its emerging theological articulations, large number of dedicated missionary personnel and Indian contemplative spirituality, sustained by the rich and ancient religious and cultural atmosphere of India. The recent foundations of Mission Society of St. Thomas the Apostle (Palai Diocese), Heralds of Good News (Khammam Diocese) and a few other indigenous women missionary societies are expressions of renewal of the missionary spirit.

All these and many other developments uncovered by the national survey, but not reported here, are signs of hope. Undoubtedly, the Holy Spirit, the principal agent of mission (R.M. ch.3), is at work in every human heart (R.M. 28, 29). One of our missionary tasks will be the discernment and discovery of the life and love enhancing presence of the Spirit in the religions and cultures of the people even before the arrival of the missionary (A.G. 4), but obscured by the darkness of "the sin" of the world (Jn.1:29).

In a world tormented by so many problems and tempted to pessimism our message of Good News is, "God is love" (1 Jn.4:8) - Jesus Christ as the incarnation of God's love. Our mission is to make God's love visible and effective in every human condition and in every strata of society in whatever way we can. Our missionary goal is to create a "new heaven and a new earth" (Rev. 21:1-4) through the transformation of restless human hearts and unjust social structures (EN. 18). We dare to walk various paths of mission as made visible and possible through our Lord Jesus Christ. We are well aware that in the third millennium Christian mission to all the people of India, with a preferential love for the poor, will be a very demanding vocation.

Some Major Observations

The success or failure of the past missionary activities could be ascertained from two perspectives. First, the Christian Mission in the traditional and popular sense of preaching the Gospel of Jesus Christ to pagans, and their conversion and baptisms to the Church seems to be a failure to a considerable degree. Such a view, of course, springs from an organizational and numerical (quantitative) understanding of the Church's evangelizing mission. Two, on the other hand, if one understands success of mission in terms of change of hearts and minds and transformation of Indian social structures and acceptance of new values of life, then, every strata of Indian society was undoubtedly changed, in

different degrees of course, under the impact of Christian mission and British administration. This is a qualitative appreciation of the mission. Such an approach to the Christian mission in our country will be, probably the main trend in the future. Indian historian, K.M. Panikkar, in spite of his sharp criticism of the Christian mission, expresses his appreciation in the following words:

> The inheritance that India has stepped into is only partly Hindu and Indian...modern India does not live under the Laws of Manu. Its mental back ground and equipment, though largely influenced by persistence of Indian tradition have been modeled into their present shape over a hundred years of western education... Its social ideals are not what Hindu Society had for long cherished but those assimilated from the West... The religious beliefs of Hinduism have been transformed substantially during the course of the last hundred years. In fact it will be no exaggeration to say that the new Indian state represents traditions, ideals and principles which are the result of an effective, but imperfect synthesis between the East and West. The work of the missionaries among the aboriginal tribes may said to have created a tradition of social service which modern India has inherited. If the Indian constitution includes special provisions for the welfare of the tribal communities...much of the credit to such activities must be given to the missionary.[21]

It will not be an exaggeration to state that the Indian Constitution, modeled on many Western Constitutions, has incorporated the spirit and value systems of Christendom. The prolonged encounter between the Christians and Hindus contributed towards the rediscovery of the riches of ancient India and its crowning with secular values of liberal Christianity.

---

[21] Panikkar, K.M., *The Foundation of New India*, London, 1963, pp.15-16; 53; M.H. Srinivas discusses the impact of Christian mission on India in the context of the process called "Westernization," in *Social Change in Modern India*, Berkeley, 1973. See also, Jain, G., *The Hindu Phenomenon*, New Delhi, 1994.

One of the most radical missiological changes in the last 30 years has been the relegation of the Church-centred mission, from the first priority at the beginning of this century, to the third place at the end of the century. The views, attitudes and methods of the Indian missionaries today are closer to the position of Pope Paul VI in his apostolic exhortation, 'Evangelization in the Modern World' (EN 1975) than the stand taken by Pope John Paul II in *Redemptoris Missio* (1990).[22] The views and opinions elicited from over 15,000 respondents of the survey, further confirm this conclusion.

Until very recent times, mission theology, mission policies and missionary involvements came almost exclusively from Europe and America. The post-Vatican ethos has encouraged systematic theological reflections in response to Indian realities. "All India seminar on Church in India Today," Bangalore, (1969), "International Theological Seminar on Mission Theology and Dialogue," Nagpur, (1971), "All India Consultation on Evangelization," Patna, (1973), and "Paths of Mission in India Today," Pune, (1994), and many other national and regional deliberations are a few examples. Theological / missionary institutes, and theological publications from India have proliferated and are making their unique contributions towards the shaping of new mission theologies by responding creatively to the fast changing context and vibrant religious traditions, beliefs and practices of South Asia. The Indian theologians are sincerely trying to articulate a relevant missiology for the contemporary situation. As a result India is emerging as the most influential country in the Third World, with the largest number of missionaries as well as creative theologians, in spite of objections from certain ecclesiastical quarters.

For Christians, particularly for the missionaries, the greatest missionary revolution of this century is the discovery of other spiritual worlds, with their coherent meaning system. Recognition of these religions, with positive attitudes of openness and programmes of dialogue and partnership, in contrast to the closed and aggressive approach of the colonial mission, has laid the foundation for building a new civilization of Brotherhood and Sisterhood. We are all related to one another as members of one human family (NA. 1). We are entering the age of mutual mission.

More than 1300 years ago Brahmin missionaries and traders travelled and colonized South East Asia – Malay Peninsula, Cambodia, Sumatra, Java, Bali and Borneo. Buddhist missionaries were sent to China, East-Asian countries and Sri Lanka even before the arrival of Christian missionaries in the first century A.D. After the prolonged encounter with the Christian missionaries, Hinduism itself has again recently emerged as a missionary religion. Over a century ago Swami Vivekananda traveled to America, contrary to tradition, to preach and propagate Hinduism; and that historic event was gradually formed into a movement by thousands of Hindu missionaries and their converts in America, Europe and elsewhere. In our own time, Mahatma Gandhi and many other illustrious sons and daughters of Bharat, have happily assimilated what is best in Christianity while remaining strictly faithful to their religious tradition. The Catholic mission, after an unsuccessful attempt at adaptation and inculturation in the 17ᵗʰ century by Robert De Nobili, John De Britto and others, again is making notable endeavors to absorb "elements of goodness and truth which such religions possess by God's providence" (O.T. 16; A.G. 11) in a process named inculturation. These acts of challenge, purification, appreciation and symbiosis are some of the features of the age of mutual mission. "Since the responsibility for the future of humanity rests on all, we cooperate with

---

[22] A. Kanjamala,*"Redemptoris Missio and Mission in India,"* 1993.

those of other religions and convictions in facing contemporary problems."[23] The paradigm shift identified in this study is the beginning of a "Copernican revolution" in the Indian mission field.

Searching for an Alternative Model of Mission in India in the 21st Century

The main emphasis and characteristics of traditional mission are: (1) Proclaiming Jesus Christ, baptizing non-Christians to the Church for the salvation of souls; (2) planting the Church where it did not exist and ensuring its institutional strength; (3) interior transformation and new life in the Spirit through sacramental life and acts of charity.

In a rapidly changing and challenging context, India is searching for an alternative model of mission. By an alternative model, I mean a new model mission which is able:

● To interpret traditional mission theology with the help of Indian philosophical/ religious categories and cultural idioms, including the idioms of the tribal cultures.

● To find new ways of organizing as a Christian community and relating to people belonging to other faiths.

● To express new ways of feeling about mission, local peoples, and their cultures.

● To search for new priorities in the realization of the various constitutive elements of mission. This could provide an integrated as well as a new vision of the mission, which would also demand a new life style.

The alternative may be envisaged as a *qualitative* model of mission in contrast to the traditional *quantitative* models for measuring missionary success. It involves alterations as well as promoting new priorities. The future of the mission in India in all likelihood is not going to be marked by a great increase in quantitative results such as numbers of converts, but in quality. Numerical conversion and numerical strength, which was the top priority during the colonial mission, is not outright rejected here; but it might have only a limited relevance and scope in the future. How should we understand the emerging alternative model?

First, proclamation and working for the realization of the Kingdom of God are the highest priorities in evangelization. However, it does not follow that the Kingdom of God is detached from Jesus Christ. In the Risen Lord who proclaimed the Kingdom, we have the concrete initial unfolding and realization of the Kingdom in history. Ours is a country that loves and respects the person of Jesus and his message of love, compassion, forgiveness, and selfless sacrifice. In a person-oriented mission thus announcing Jesus and his gospel, whenever and wherever it is possible, should be understood as an integral part of the mission of the Church. The message of Jesus is universal; i.e., to be offered with love to all who are invited to respond freely.

Second, mission begins with the conversion of the heart and mind of the missionary according to the values taught by Jesus, particularly the Sermon on the Mount. In the past, mission emphasized the conversion of the object of the mission – non-Christian people. In the future, conversion must begin with the subject of the mission – missionaries. Missionaries who have not experienced God as unconditionally loving and forgiving (Lk. 15:11-32) and are therefore unable to communicate this experience of God are not credible. Rather they are suspected. In this regard, the last chapter of R.M., "Missionary Spirituality," is very important. "The missionary is a universal brother (sister)" (R.M. 89). The true missionary is a saint (90). The exhortation that "The missionary must be a contemplative in

---

[23] *SVD Constitutions*, Rome, 1983, No. 114.4.

action" (91) is very appropriate in the Indian religious ethos with a predilection for contemplation and mysticism. Mission begins with credible witnesses. "You shall be my witnesses…to the ends of the earth" (Acts 1:80).

Third, by providing the Gospel vision of life, the world, and society, the Christian mission should continue to challenge certain evils in Indian society as it did in the past. That is a prophetic role that many, perhaps because of their minority status, are afraid to exercise. By providing the model of action for the liberation of the Dalits, tribals, and other marginalized communities, however, the Christians contribute to creating a new social consciousness and social philosophy, one that reflects Kingdom values. Missionaries, particularly those who live and work in the midst of the people in non-institutional setups, play a significant role in this regard. The life, teaching, and example of Jesus – mirrored in the life of good religious people – can inspire and motivate others to collaborate with our noble services. If Saint Francis Xavier was the model for many Catholic missionaries in the past, Mother Theresa of Calcutta is one of the most loved and admired missionary ideals and models for the future.

Fourth, dialogue with people of different religious traditions and cultures should help to overcome the traditional Christian ethnocentrism – especially certain types of ecclesiocentrism. This will hopefully heal the wounds created by colonial arrogance and superiority and lead to mutual enrichment as different groups appreciate one another's spirituality and thus prepare the ground for universal brotherhood and sisterhood. Fullness of life, love, and light that Jesus promised will be gradually realized like the growth of a mustard seed or the yeast that leavens the dough (Lk. 13:18-21).

Conclusion

India is emerging as the most influential country in the third world, with its largest number of missionaries as well as creative theologians. All the above mentioned and many other developments uncovered by the national survey we conducted are signs of hope. We are also well aware that Christian mission to all the people of India, with a preferential love for the poor, in the third millennium will be a very demanding vocation. Facing these awesome opportunities and challenges in the 21ˢᵗ century we find inspiration and strength in the words of our Risen Lord, "I am with you always, until the end of the age" (Mt 28: 20).

CHAPTER 12

Contemporary Promises and Challenges in Global Christianity

TIMOTHY C. TENNENT

Introduction

The church which closed out the 20th century looks vastly different from what it did even 100 hundred years earlier. Indeed, as William Temple observed, the globalization of Christianity is "one of the great facts of our time." When William Carey, the father of the modern missionary movement, went to India at the turn of the 19th C. only one percent of the entire world's Protestants lived in all of Asia, Africa and Latin America *combined*! Today the majority of Christians live outside the Western world. In fact, 67 percent of Protestants today live in Asia, Africa and Latin America. The visible Church of Jesus Christ that has now entered the twenty-first century is a church that is predominantly non-white and non-European in its cultural, ethnic heritage.

The success of the 19th century missionary movement has stimulated many remarkable developments which if thrown out onto the table like snapshots might include such pictures as a thriving Latin American *Protestant* church sending out their own missionaries. Brazilians, for example, are now being sent out as missionaries to the Muslim world. Another snapshot would surely be of one of the thousands of house churches in China or even the current trend of a few public churches that have refused to register as TSPM churches. A third snapshot might be a picture of African bishops at the 1998 global Anglican conference in Lambeth rebuking

N. American Anglican bishops for their faithlessness to the gospel (At the 1978 Lambeth Conference there were 80 bishops from Africa, at the 1988 Lambeth there were 175; at the 1998 Lambeth there were over 300 African Bishops – the complexion of the global church is changing!).[1] We could put many such snapshots on the table for discussion. Some of these pictures are well known and quite visible such as the tens of thousands of Koreans at a prayer mountain. Other pictures are equally dramatic but quiet and almost beneath our radar such as the thousands of families from Kerala or Tamil Nadu in South India quietly moving toward North India to learn a new language and culture and plant a church. The pictures are dramatic. Some tell well-rehearsed stories; some are stories we are still trying to understand. But, make no mistake about it, the non-Western church is on the rise, and the people of God from the Southern continents are on the move. Indeed, these are all pictures well worth our celebration. I am sure that Lausanne 2004 which will meet in Thailand will be yet another picture of this great story called the church of Jesus Christ.

But the very globalization of Christianity has also given rise to new challenges and problems that heretofore we have not adequately discussed or, in some cases, not taken seriously enough. Our very language tells us that we are in a new era and we are grasping for an adequate vocabulary. Take, for example, the frequent use

---

[1] Africa, with 335 million Christians, is second only to Europe in the number of Christians on any continent. See D. Barrett, "Status of Global Mission, 2002" in *IBMR*, Vol. 26, No. 1, January 2002, pp. 22, 23.

of the words "former" and "post" in our discussions. We speak of the *former* Soviet-Union, the *former* Yugoslavia and so forth. Likewise, the word "post" says volumes about the "seam of history" (if I might borrow a phrase from Samuel Huntington[2]) upon which we stride. We now live in a *post*-Western, *post*-denominational, *post*-Christendom, *post*-colonial era in the missionary movement. New questions are being raised… new challenges are being posed… new leaders are now on the global stage. This has contributed substantially to the rise of missiology as a field in its own right rather than mission studies being merely tacked on in an ancillary way to an otherwise Western church history curriculum.

This chapter will seek to point out what I see as three exciting developments or promising elements in the new reality of the world Christian movement. Then, in the latter part of the chapter I will point out three potential pitfalls or challenges which the globalization of Christianity presents.

First, the Globalization of Christianity Testifies to the Translatability of the Gospel

Christianity is the only world religion whose primary source documents (NT) are in a language other than the language of the founder of the religion. In other words, the NT texts are not in Aramaic, but in Koine Greek. This is unheard of among world religions. Muhammad spoke Arabic and the Qur'ân is in Arabic; the Brahmin priests in India spoke Sanskrit and the Upanishads are in Sanskrit. Jesus spoke Aramaic and yet the primary documents that record Christ's teachings are not in Aramaic, but in Koine Greek. This makes a vitally important theological point about the translatability of the Christian gospel which so dramatically contrasts, for example, with the

Muslims who maintain the Qur'ân is untranslatable and the Word of Allah can only be conveyed in Arabic. At the very outset of the Christian message the linguistic translatability of the message is testified to and even enshrined in our primary documents. However, the translatability of the gospel is even more profound than the testimony of the English or Ibo or Hindi Bibles that are carried by believers around the world. We sometimes mistakenly assume that the translatability of the Christian message happens only on the linguistic level – as represented by, perhaps, the mission of the Wycliffe Bible Translators. However, the *kerygma* is not only *linguistically* translatable, it is also *culturally* translatable, i.e. to say the gospel is delivered not only in the 'enscripturated' text – but also in the proclamation and witness of a believing community – the members of which belong to a particular culture. As Andrew Walls has pointed out, the gospel is not just that God became a man, but that God "became a *particular* man."[3] He didn't just walk on the vague sands of time; he walked as a Jew on the real sands by the Sea of Galilee in the first century. He spoke a particular language and lived within all of the variegated nuances of a particular culture.

Indeed, the incarnation is the great testimony to translatability. The gospel is translated not only into a new language, but God also fully steps into the culture in Jesus Christ and in the lives and witness of new, believing communities around the world. One of our Gordon-Conwell graduates is a man named Stuart Foster. He is now in his eighteenth year working among the Lomwe people in Mozambique. He is completing the very first translation of the OT into the Lomwe language for the Lomwe believers. But let us not forget that not only is the text of the gospel being *read* by the Lomwe, but the gospel is also being

---

[2] See, Samuel P. Huntington, *The Clash of Civilizations and the Remaking of World Order*, New York: Simon and Schuster / Touchstone, 1997.

[3] Andrew Walls, "The Translation Principle in Christian History" in *The Missionary Movement in Christian History*, Maryknoll, New York: Orbis Press, 1996, p.27.

received and experienced by real Lomwe people – within a particular cultural context. They are coming to faith in Christ and becoming members of a heavenly kingdom and yet, at the same time, are still Lomwe. They see themselves, quite appropriately, as fully members of a Mozambique culture even while being fully Christian. Of course, the gospel continues to sit in judgement over the evils of the Lomwe culture just as it does over the evils of our culture, but, in the mystery of translatability, the gospel also takes root in a particular culture and becomes indigenized – the eternal gospel becomes clothed in yet another particular cultural expression moving us one more step toward the fulfillment of that great vision of John who saw in Rev. 5:9 "*men and women from every tribe, language, people and culture before the Lamb.*" Even in the presence of God in the apocalyptic Kingdom - even as the echoes of their common worship of Jesus Christ are still in the ears of the Apostle, they are still seen standing there in the particularity of the cultural context into which they were born.

For Deeper Missiological Reflection

Precisely because translatability is about much more than putting the Bible into vernacular languages it poses some very important questions about the language of Christian discourse in the many newly emerging centers of Christianity. This is particularly true in places like sub-Saharan Africa or in India where there are so many vernacular languages within rather close geographic parameters. Some have felt that using English (or in some cases French) as a language of discourse serves to unite the church and promote wider discussions than is possible in a more restricted – largely oral based vernacular language. This is a recapitulation of attitudes held in the past about Latin or Greek. Others argue that the vernacular is essential for any authentic indigenization of the church because the

vernacular language alone assures us that deep and meaningful theological dialogue can take place between the gospel and the culture. I sense this tension in a very particular way in my work in India. From the beginning of modern Protestant missions the missionaries in India were divided between the Orientalists (like William Carey) who gave their lives to promoting a vernacular discourse and the Anglicists (like Alexander Duff) who believed that English was the key to breaking the fetters of Hinduism (and Hindu linguistic paradigms) and promoting a genuine and widespread Christian discourse in India. In South India, English clearly dominates Christian discourse in terms of Christian publications and the medium of higher theological education. In North India, the Hindi language is a more powerful and unifying force and therefore we are seeking to promote Hindi medium education, offering a Serampore affiliated Hindi medium Bachelor's degree alongside our English medium program. We are working hard to not only translate key theological works into Hindi, but also to promote indigenous works written by North Indians for North Indians. We are also promoting what I call contextualized translations whereby we are receiving permission to translate some works into Hindi, but adapting them to the N. Indian context by using Indian allusions, Indian illustrations, Indian references to political and social realities and so forth. All of this, in my view, helps to reinforce the point that the Day of Pentecost was not just a *sociological* or *psychological* event so that men and women from around the world could hear the gospel in their own tongue. Pentecost is fundamentally a *theological* event that testifies that when God speaks to us, He speaks in the vernacular. "Divine communication is never in a sacred, esoteric, hermetic language; rather it is such that 'all of us hear...in our own languages...the wonders of God'."[4]

---

[4] Kwame Bediako, *Christianity in Africa: The Renewal of a Non-Western Religion*, Orbis Press: Maryknoll, New York: 1997, p.60. Also, quoting Acts 2:11.

Second, the globalization of Christianity testifies to the serial nature of Christian growth

Church history tells us that the story of Christian history is one of serial rather than progressive growth. That is to say, Christianity did not begin as a small band which has gradually expanded in an even kind of progression from a central core like a large stone which has been dropped in the middle of the lake and continues to move in an even progression outward from that original center. What we find, in fact, is that the church's history is the story of advance and recession. It is the story of stunning and unexpected advances in one corner and shocking decline and recession in another. Areas of previous weakness become areas of great strength and vice versa. This phenomena is, by the way, unique among major world religions like Islam and Hinduism which have an historical locus in a particular place and there is an historical consistent central core from which the religion emanates.[5] The advance and recession motif is so common that a few examples should suffice. The recession of the Church in the Middle East subsequent to the birth of Islam is the most obvious example. The birthplace of the Apostle Paul, the stomping grounds of the Pauline missionary journeys, the recipients of the seven letters to the seven churches in Revelation, the cities of the early ecumenical councils... all of these places are now predominately Muslim. Indeed, in the 9th century you would have forgiven an observer of the world scene had he told you that the globalization of Christianity was probably a lost cause. Even by the time of Martin Luther, there were more Muslims than Christians in the world, as a pre-Society of Jesus, pre-Padroado[6] world witnessed a Christianity essentially isolated in Western Europe. The long struggle of how Western Christianity re-asserted itself as a global faith is one of the great testimonies of the modern missionary movement (both Catholic via the Society of Jesus and Propaganda Fide and Protestant through the Mission Societies). Today, we are experiencing the explosive emergence of a vital African church. Likewise, Korea which until the modern era had no known Christians, is today the home of many of the largest churches in the world. Thus, the serial nature and changing locus of Christianity should be noted. The center of Christianity has shifted from Jerusalem to Antioch to Constantinople to Rome to West Europe, to North America and now to the non-western world.

This should not surprise us, but we should also note the profound theological and missiological implications of this observation. This means that those of us in the Western world have to adjust to the growing reality that we are no longer at the center of the world Christian movement. Even this realization must be, in part, a recognition that this is not an unfamiliar theme in church history. Indeed, the growth of the church frequently occurs at the margins or edges, not at the center of the church. It was not the church in Jerusalem that exploded in the first two centuries - it was the church in Antioch, the church on the frontier of the whole Jewish-Gentile exchange. It was in Antioch that the disciples were first called Christians and where the church grew from a single house church to over one quarter of a million believers by the end of the second century. Today even though the Western church continues to dominate theological education and global leadership, the growth of the church is in the non-Western world. Yet, the very growth of the church outside the West may be a catalyst for our own renewal as we become partners with our brothers and sisters

---

[5] For a more detailed analysis of this point see, Lamin Sanneh, *Translating the Message: The Missionary Impact on Culture*, Maryknoll, New York: Orbis Books, 1991.

[6] Luther was born in 1483. The Padroado was not established by Paul Alexander VI until 1493; The Jesuits were founded in 1534, but did not receive Papal approval from Pope Paul III until Sept. 27, 1540.

in the wider global church. In short, I believe that the growth of non-Western Christianity is surely a divinely appointed development which will finally break the global movement free from the chain of association which has led our Muslim and Hindu and Buddhist friends to accuse Christianity of being a western religion with a white face. That accusation is increasingly sounding strange with the rise and prominence of the non-Western church. As Kwame Bediako has keenly observed, the church today is growing and living out its witness in areas which are marked by three realities: "economic poverty, political powerlessness and religious pluralism,"[7] all areas not normally associated with Western Christianity.

For Deeper Missiological Reflection

The geographic shift of the center of Christianity to the Southern continents raises vital missiological questions about the nature of non-Western theologizing. The theological activity coming from the Southern churches can no longer be viewed as tangential to the main work of theology in the West. Nor can it be caricatured as merely expressions of a 'peoples theology' whether Liberation theology, Minjung theology or Dalit theology. Instead, we are experiencing what John Mbiti has called "new centres of Christian universality." We are seeing the emergence of many honest theological engagements and more profound reflections that are helping us all to understand the universal nature of theological reflection. I am particularly interested, for example, in the discussions going on between African theologians concerning Christology.[8] The African theologians have written extensively on the role of the ancestors in the development of an African Christology. Christ as the "supreme ancestor" is not a theme that is discussed in traditional Western theologies. The discussion about the relationship between a believer's 'natural' and 'spiritual' ancestors is quite illuminating. Once an African comes to Christ can (or should) the ancestral 'power-lines' be laid down differently? Can an African believer be connected to new, *spiritual* ancestors, that great cloud of witnesses who have gone before us, with Christ Jesus as the head, or is there an on-going connection with the 'living dead' in the African tradition since, even in Africa, God has not left himself without a witness (General Revelation), not to mention ancient African believers such as the Ethiopian Eunuch or Augustine (Special Revelation)? The range of African responses to this question form a spectrum of responses from Byang Kato[9] to Bolaji Idowu,[10] from John Mbiti[11] to John Pobee.[12] From these men we hear Christological formulations which, for the most part, strike our Western ears as quite odd: Christ as Chief,[13]

---

[7] Kwame Bediako, *Christianity in Africa: The Renewal of a Non-Western Religion*, Maryknoll, New York: Orbis Books, 1997.

[8] I am highlighting Christology, but there are many issues being wrestled with in African theology today. For an overview see, for example, *Issues in African Christian Theology* edited by Samuel Ngewa, Mark Shaw and Tite Tienou.

[9] Byang H. Kato, *Theological Pitfalls in Africa*, Kisumu, Kenya: Evangel Publishing House, 1975, and *Biblical Christianity in Africa*, African Christian Press, 1985.

[10] E. Bolaji Idowu, *Towards an Indigenous Church*, London: Oxford University Press, 1965.

[11] John Mbiti, *Bible and Theology in African Christianity*, Nairobi: Oxford University Press, 1986. See also "Some African Conceptions of Christology," in *Christ and the Younger Churches* edited by G. F. Vicedom, London: SPCK, 1972: pp.51-62.

[12] John S. Pobee, *Toward an African Theology*, Nashville, TN: Abingdon, 1979.

[13] See G. F. Vicedom, ed., *Christ and the Younger Churches*, London: SPCK, 1972, pp.51-62. See also, Francois Kabasele, "Christ as Chief" as found in *Faces of Jesus in Africa* edited by Robert J. Schreiter, Maryknoll, New York: Orbis Books, 1984, pp.103-115.

Christ as Master of Initiation,[14] Christ as the Great Ancestor.[15] These writers decisively demonstrate that Africa is producing a truly indigenous discourse with a range of views and perspectives which is necessary for a vibrant theological discourse.

Third, the globalization of Christianity reminds us of the truth in the well-known phrase, "it takes a whole world to understand a whole Christ."

The globalization of the Christian faith has brought many new Christians to the theological table and those who are eager readers of the Bible have helped us to hear the gospel afresh and learn to appreciate new insights from our brothers and sisters around the world. As the church of Jesus Christ emerges as a global reality, it is only right that they begin their own struggle to define and understand not only the perennial issues of the Christian faith, - questions like – the nature of faith, the mystery of the incarnation, the atonement, the life of the church, the role of the sacraments, etc... but they also begin to ask some new questions which have arisen out of the particularity of their own cultural context. Theology is, after all, the task of asking relevant questions of the text of Scripture and organizing the evidence of Scripture into a coherent response which, while addressing a particular question, is still true to the larger unchanging, supra-cultural core of the gospel message. This has always been one of the great challenges to Christianity... How do we preserve the sacred *kerygma* which from the very beginning was delivered into a particular cultural context and was revealed in a particular language – how do we preserve that universal proclamation/*kerygma* which is for all peoples and all tongues and all tribes and all nations when it moves out of its original language and cultural context into an entirely new linguistic and cultural context?

How the early church handled this is, of course, one of the great chapters in the life of the church. Indeed, one of the most important missiological events in the 1st century church was, of course, the transition of the Christian church from its predominately Jewish historical and cultural context to one which burst forth onto the new frontiers of the Gentile world, introducing new vocabulary, new questions, new cultural matrices, and new people-groups into the lifeblood of the church. The tension between the Jewish frontier and the new Gentile frontier was met at the famous Jerusalem Council. The successful decision of the Jerusalem Council in Acts 15 provided the launching pad which would lift Christianity out of a small corner of the Mediterranean world and thrust it, in due course, into every language, people and ethnic group in the world. That is the missiological enterprise. The decision of Acts 15 was difficult, it was risky, but it was also consonant with the Great Commission. If they had missed the missiological moment in Acts 15, Christianity would be known only as a small historical footnote in some dusty volume which would have described a group of 1st century Jews who were known as the Nazarene sect. But, instead, the early church chose to honor its Judaic roots and covenantal heritage, even while breaching its walls. It is now a matter of record that the early church, though fully rooted in the Jewish historical and cultural context, chose not to absolutize that culture or that heritage and they chose to not make it normative for all future believers. Their achievement was remarkable. What we are experiencing today is merely a reprise of an ancient theme in the church.

---

[14] See Kwame Bediako. "Jesus in African Culture: A Ghanian Perspective" *Emerging Voices in Global Christian Theology*, edited by as found in William A. Dryness, Grand Rapids: Zondervan, 1994, pp.91-121. See also Anselme T. Sanon, "Jesus, Master of Initiation," in *Faces of Jesus in Africa*, p.93.

[15] Charles Nyamiti, *Christ as Our Ancestor: Christology from an African Perspective*, Gweru: Mambo Press, 1984. See also Francois Kabasele, "Christ as Ancestor and Elder Brother," in *Faces of Jesus in Africa*, pp.119-124.

The unchanging *kerygma* encounters new languages and new cultures and emerges with new vitality as it proceeds to demonstrate its translatability to yet another generation.

Challenges that Face an Increasingly Globalized and Non-Western Church

We now turn to three potential pitfalls or at least special challenges that face an increasingly globalized and non-western church.

First, the Challenge of theological dis-coherence

Despite our celebration of the integrity of the national churches around the world and the emergence of new indigenous churches, none of these movements emerge out of a historic vacuum. Even the house churches in China and the rapidly growing AIC – African Independent Churches (African Indigenous / Initiated) have not emerged in a vacuum. Nevertheless, we are seeing today the emergence of churches that are historically - along with the rest of the globe - in the 21st century. It has, as a matter of the plain historical record, been over 2000 years since the birth of Christ – and the church today is a reflection of that shared history. However, we have churches that exist in a kind of first century context theologically and experientially even though they are living in the 21st century of Christianity as viewed through the widest lens. There are churches openly struggling with the relationship of the humanity to the deity of Christ or with the personality of the Holy Spirit or any number of issues which were debated in the great ecumenical councils of the church. These issues represent, for us, battles that have been fought and mostly won – but for many of the younger churches they are just engaging in their first theological skirmishes. Even in our own church history, the Western church is only now beginning to recognize and appreciate the Christology of the ancient, but non-Chalcedonian, Assyrian Church of the East.[16]

In what way can Chalcedon be re-visited or appropriately discovered and appropriated by these younger churches? They are living in a gulf of historical dis-coherence, i.e. they are living historically post-Chalcedon, but are pre-Chalcedonian in their own theological formulation. I suppose it is fair to say that many of these groups theologize along the margins of orthodoxy and, in some cases, are clearly heretical by any of the biblical, historical and creedal standards which we might use to measure historic orthodoxy. Of that we can perhaps all agree. We are not seeking to legitimize heresy. The challenge is in how do these churches emerge into the bright light of full-orbed orthodox faith? Do we give them a crash course in Chalcedon? Can the famous Latin formulations function with a kind of universal status for the larger cross-cultural context? Can we accept the reality of the rise of non-Chalcedonian churches who are hammering out an indigenous, *dynamic equivalent* of Chalcedon? Some mission scholars strongly advocate for a *laisse faire* approach. As long as the younger churches are eager readers of the Bible, they argue, then heresies will eventually work their way to the margins of the church's life and eventually orthodox faith will become normative. To circumvent their own theological development and discovery will only impede the long term goal of indigeneity. Other mission scholars, on the other hand, argue quite the reverse and insist that we are all recipients of prior struggles in the life of the church which emerged in a different cultural context and, quite frankly, a different language than our own. The

---

[16] See the joint declaration issued by Pope John Paul II and His Holiness Mar Dinkha IV, Patriarch of the Assyrian Church of the East where a common Christological declaration was signed on November 11, 1994. See *Information Service* N.88 (1995/I) 1-6. See also *Does Chalcedon Divide or Unite? Towards Convergence in Orthodox Christology* edited by Paulos Gregorios, William H. Lazareth and Nilos A. Nissiotis, Geneva: World Council of Churches, 1981.

proceedings of Chalcedon and the debates of Constantinople and Ephesus sometimes sound strange to our ears. But part of being a global Christian is to accept the historical line in which we all stand. The sooner these younger churches learn to appreciate and benefit from the voice of history, the sooner they will fully take their place on the stage as full members of the global Christian community which extends not just in space around the globe, but in time back to the first century.

For Deeper Missiological Reflection

My own doctoral research focused on the work of the 19th century Bengali theologian Brahmabandhav Upadhyay. He once wrote,

> We are of the opinion that attempts should be made to win over Hindu philosophy to the service of Christianity just as Greek philosophy was won over in the Middle Ages...The task is beset with many dangers. But we have a conviction and it is growing day by day, that the Catholic church will find it hard to conquer India unless she makes Hindu philosophy hew wood and draw water for her.[17]

The result was a thoroughgoing re-examination of orthodox Christian theology, but re-stated using the language and thought-forms of Vedantic philosophy, particularly advaitism of Śankara. I will mention two examples, both of which I have published in summary form in articles as well as a more extensive study in my book, *Building Christianity on Indian Foundations*.[18] The first is in the language used to describe the Trinity. There are four technical terms that are associated with the orthodox Trinitarian statement: person, substance, begotten and proceeding.[19] All of these terms are immensely difficult to translate into Indian languages with the necessary precision. The word 'person' for example is often translated as 'individual' which it cannot mean in the orthodox statement. The word 'begotten' will invariably utilize a word with sexual connotations. The word 'substance' is often translated as something solid and material which is not at all what was meant by the Greek word *'ousia'*.[20] The word 'proceeding' is invoked because of a long-standing theological and philosophical debate between the Eastern and Western branches of the Church. It is an important debate, but one in which the Indian church has not participated, so the terminology seems alien to them. In short, the orthodox formulations can be *translated* into Indian languages, but truly capturing the essence and heart of the formulation is exceedingly difficult.

Brahmabandhav Upadhyay looked for indigenous vocabulary within the Sanskritic tradition to express the orthodox view. He found this in the famous description of Brahman in the later Upanishads wherein Brahman is described as *sat* (being or reality), *cit* (intelligence or consciousness) and *ananda* (bliss).[21] Thus, *sat, cit* and *ananda*, often designated by the term *saccidananda*, is widely regarded as the most complete description of Brahman in all of Hindu

---

[17] *Sophia* Monthly 4, No. 7, July 1897, pp.8, 9.

[18] Timothy C. Tennent, *Building Christianity on Indian Foundations: The Legacy of Brahmabandhav Upadhyay*, Delhi: ISPCK, 2000.

[19] These terms are central to the Westminster Confession. See Westminster Confession II.3. For a full text of the Westminster Confession, see Robert L. Dabney, *The Westminster Confession and Creeds*, Dallas: Presbyterian Heritage Publication, 1983.

[20] For a full exposition of the problems of translating Latin doctrinal formulations into the Indian context see the excellent book by Robin Boyd, *India and the Latin Captivity of the Church*, Cambridge University Press, 1974.

[21] *Vajrasucika* Upanishad, 9. Radhakrishnan, ed., *The Principal Upanishads*, Delhi: Harper Collins, 1996, pp.937, 938.

sacred literature.[22] Time does not permit in this lecture to demonstrate how he used this vocabulary to express the orthodox doctrine, but it is widely believed to be one of the most remarkable expressions of indigenous theology ever to emerge out of India. While there are gaps in his theology, I remain convinced that Upadhyay comes close to achieving a "dynamic equivalent" of the traditional Trinitarian formula. Indeed, it is largely for his work regarding the Trinity that Upadhyay has been called the "father of Indian Christian theology".[23]

A second area where he devoted significant time is in the doctrine of creation. The doctrine of creation has always been a difficult area for Christians in the Indian context. The physical world is often characterized as being illusory as reflected in the Sanskrit word '*maya*', which is the most common word used to describe the physical world in the Hindu tradition. Upadhyay argues convincingly that the original usage of the word '*maya*' by Sankara was not illusory, but contingent. There is obviously a huge theological difference between the word as illusion and the world as contingent. It is upon this basis that Upadhyay goes on to identify Sankara's *maya* with 'contingent being' in Thomas Aquinas. The argumentation is complex and involves a fluency in both Indian and Western religious traditions, so it is not possible to explore this in a single paper. However, it is a testimony to genuine and vital indigenous theologizing. . Upadhyay's ingenious connecting of the well known *advaitic* distinction between *paramarthika* and *vyavaharika* with the Thomistic distinction between necessary existence and contingent existence is sufficient evidence alone to dispel the myth that non-Western theologizing is marked by "single issues" or is superficial.

This is the first challenge which the rapid globalization of Christianity brings to us. It may be summarized in a nutshell by asking the question, "How do the younger churches 'catch up' or benefit from the great theological stream which has preceded them?" How can the non-Western church best be given the theological space necessary for authentic theologizing? Isn't the full maturation of the "fourth self" – self-theologizing - long overdue?[24]

Second, the challenge of historical discoherence in our celebration of church history.

The rise and vitality of the non-Western church has occurred simultaneously with the decline of the church in the Western world. This is, as we recall, a testimony to the serial growth of the Christian movement and it, therefore, should not surprise us. Yet, the Western world has for centuries been the locus of theological discussion and still provides much of the leadership for the global church. Furthermore, without in any way taking away from the theological contributions of the Eastern and Uniate churches, the globalization of Christianity has been notably pursued by the Western church, whether it be the sacrifices of Jesuits or the modern Protestant missionary movement. Thus, the non-Western church owes its existence, in part, to the sacrifices and labors of the Western church. Western missionaries taught their converts about Western church history and about the Western church experience. In the process, Western church history has taken on a kind of universal status even on the mission field. I have

---

[22] *Saccidananda* is a religious formula similar to an *adesa*, i.e. a compact presentation of truth, often contained in a single word or phrase, which summarizes the essence of a teaching. The formula *saccidananda* does not appear in the earlier Upanishads, but it was used by later Vedantists to summarize the essence of Upanishadic teaching regarding the Absolute as *Sat, Cit, Ananda*.

[23] K. P. Aleaz, "The Theological Writings of Brahmabandhav Upadhyaya Re-Examined," *Indian Journal of Theology*, vol. 28, No.2, April-June, 1979, p.77.

[24] Paul G. Hiebert, *Anthropological Reflections on Missiological Issues*, Grand Rapids: Baker Books, 1994, p.46.

seen first hand dozens of young Christians around the world struggling to learn the nuances of Western church history who, at the same time, do not know much at all about their own church history or how their history fits into the larger picture of the Western church experience. I have the privilege of teaching not only at Gordon-Conwell, but also for the last fifteen years at a seminary in India. It is, therefore, with some irony that I (an outsider and Westerner) do a considerable amount of lecturing about Indian Christian theologians, because many Indians – even though their church history dates back to St. Thomas who came to the Malabar coast of S. W. India in 52 A.D., often do not know much else about their long history on the sub-continent. So, one can see that the first problem is intricately related to the second. The first problem is essentially a theological one, the second is an historical one –but they are two sides of the same coin. How can one develop theologically and own the faith unless your own church history can be celebrated? You see, the non-Western world Christian movement is not just younger churches which are only one or two generations old. The church in the East is older than much of the Western church and hundreds of years older than anything in N. America. Christianity came to India in 52 A.D. The church in India is almost as old as the gospel itself, but it is only since the 19ᵗʰ century that the Indian church has broken free from its captivity to Syriac liturgy and foreign cultural forms and truly become indigenized in Indian soil.[25] But there were many vital skirmishes in the Indian Church between the Eastern and Western church which are so important in the history of the Indian Church. However, what does the modern evangelical movement in India (which is often Pentecostal in its experience and Arminian in its theology) do with their long, largely Syriac, and liturgical

past? What do the new evangelicals in Russia do with the long history – religiously and culturally - with the Russian Orthodox church? After the iron curtain fell dozens of evangelical mission boards rushed into Russia like it was an untouched mission field with no Christian history, only to find the Russia Orthodox church there with a history longer than the history of the churches represented by these missionaries. What do the new house churches in China do when they reflect on the antiquity of the gospel in China brought by Nestorians who were themselves on the theological margins of the Western church and were missionaries to China, in part, because they were expelled because of their disputes with Western Christological orthodoxy? As the influence of the Western church declines, the study of non-Western church history will begin to take on new prominence and our own history will begin to be re-told from their perspective. Yet, this historical reassessment is vital if we are to wrestle with the theological dis-coherence mentioned earlier.

For Deeper Missiological Reflection.

One of the more important aspects of the historical context of the non-Western church (and increasingly the Western church as well) is the presence of non-Christian religions. Evangelical theologians in the West have not been sufficiently engaged in the whole field of inter-religious dialogue. Evangelicals need to discover that genuine dialogue can occur in a way which is faithful to historic Christianity while being willing to listen and genuinely respond to the honest objections of those who remain unconvinced. All too often dialogue is discouraged because non-Christian religions are dismissed out-of-hand as examples of human blindness and the fruit of unbelief. The result has been an avoidance of any serious dialogue lest

---

[25] Although understanding what "indigeneity" means in the Indian context is complex, as the Croonan cross incident in ancient Kerala testifies.

Christians unwittingly place the gospel on an equal footing with other religions. But, in the context of global religious pluralism this defensive posture is no longer tenable. Christianity is a faith for the world. It flourishes when challenged by unbelief, ridicule, and skepticism. Christianity can handle the tough questions. We can no longer afford the "luxury" of any kind of cultural, ideological or religious apartheid whereby we conveniently isolate ourselves from the beliefs and practices of the world we live in. We are called to bear witness to Christ in the Hindu world, the Islamic world, the secular world and so forth. Paul's spirited defence of the gospel on Mars Hill (Acts 17) and John's creative application of the *logos* to the incarnation (John 1) demonstrate how deeply the earliest Christians understood the context to which they were called to witness. To meet similar challenges in our own day, we need to humbly learn from our non-Western brothers and sisters how the gospel can be defended and creatively communicated in the midst of a wide range of cultural, philosophical and religious challenges.[26]

Third, what contributions may best be made by Western Christians to the world Christian movement?

This third major problem that we face is a more practical one and is essentially missiological in nature. What is the contribution of the Western world in the world Christian movement and the fulfillment of the Great Commission? The emerging vitality and growth of the church in the non-Western world and the emergence of the non-Western church as major players in missions, including their emergence as a sending movement has changed how we understand our own role in missions today. How do we best formulate missions strategy in light of the global situation we face? If Western Missionaries represent the

"sunrise" of the world Christian movement, what do we do now that we are seeing the bright noonday light of the non-Western church and the first shades of dusk settling over the Western church? We are used to doing the ministry and showing those on the field how we do it here. The West still provides a significant portion of the financial support for much of the missionary effort in the East, even that being advanced by the indigenous churches. Yet, simultaneous with the rise of missions giving in the West, we also have the decline of missionary personnel in the West and the rise of non-Western missionaries who, as indigenous agents, are prepared to bring the gospel to their own (or culturally near/related) people. The fact that we are seeing a rise in the overall global missionary force is a matter of great celebration. More people are crossing cultural boundaries with the Christian gospel today than in any other time in human history. However, some churches in the West think somehow our role has been reduced to funding, as if we can write a check and more or less "buy" our obedience to the Great Commission. However, this obscures three basic missiological facts which the N. American church needs to hear. First, there are thousands of unreached people groups who have no indigenous, viable church within their social, cultural and linguistic sphere. In short, despite all of the efforts of the 19th century missionary movement, one of the greatest needs in missions today is the need for cross cultural church planting. We continue to need personnel from East as well as West to rise to the challenge to give themselves fully to a cross-cultural, pioneer, church-planting ministry. Second, the N. American church needs to realize the growing missiological need in Western Europe where our own ethnically near brothers and sisters are calling for assistance in reaching a mushrooming new kind of post-Christian

---

[26] For more on this, see my recently published book, *Christianity at the Religious Roundtable,* Grand Rapids: Baker Books, 2002.

paganism. Today, despite the great Christian heritage in the Western European past, there are fewer evangelical Christians in Poland than in Nepal. There are fewer evangelical Christians in Spain than in Japan. Third, we can continue to play a vital role in the equipping and training of national leadership. We must not forget that the long term goal is viable churches among all the people groups in the world. Today the global *evangelistic* thrust is way ahead of the *church planting* thrust. There are thousands coming to Christ today and not being incorporated into a local church. There are millions watching the Jesus film, reading Christian literature, hearing Christian radio and responding to the gospel. The Western world has the resources, the experience and the personnel to step up to the plate and help in training and discipling a whole new generation of leaders around the world to pastor and disciple this growing evangelistic wave. Like the Macedonian man of long ago, the global church is calling us over to help and assist in producing growing, mature, viable churches. Let us rise and meet this great challenge.

Conclusion

This essay has sought to outline in rather broad terms some of the promises and challenges related to the globalization of Christianity and the rise of the non-Western church which are relevant for the missiological task. There are other areas not mentioned here which I also think deserve far more development. Nevertheless, these are some of the more pressing challenges we currently face in the early twenty-first century.

PART III

Historical Studies

CHAPTER 13

The History of Christianity in India: An Overview from a Protestant Perspective

DANIEL JEYARAJ

Christianity in India has a long and diverse legacy. From the beginning it is linked inseparably with the worldwide movements of Christianity and the socio-cultural history of India. This essay seeks to describe briefly the story of the Orthodox, Roman Catholic, Protestant and Pentecostal traditions in India.

Beginnings of the St. Thomas Traditions

The modern State of Kerala [earlier also known as Malankara or Malabar] was a meeting of different cultures. Jews were living there for a long time. There was a flourishing sea and land trade between Palestine and Kerala. It is believed strongly that Thomas, one of the twelve apostles of Jesus Christ, came to the place of Cranganore near Cochin in AD 52, played an important role in the conversion of a few inhabitants, founded seven churches (e.g., the Syrian churches at Cranganore, Nirnayam, and the like), ordained a few pastors and moved to the southeastern port city of Chennai. After a brief time of ministry he is said to have been martyred in AD 72. In the absence of concrete, contemporary, verifiable historical evidence, there have been different theories[1] to explain the mode of Thomas' travel, the place of his work, the nature of his ministry and the consequences of his work.[2] Memories of Thomas' ministry in India are found in the folksongs, legends and reports of Eastern Church representatives[3] and later by European travelers (e.g., the Franciscan Montecorvino in AD 1290s). It is evident that the St. Thomas Christians trace their origin to the very beginning of Christianity itself.[4]

When the Roman Emperor Constantine made Christianity a state religion in AD 313, he also showed kindness towards Christians living under the rule of Persian kings. Christians did however, experience troubles and persecutions. Several Christians immigrated to other parts of the world. It is possible, according to an account (AD 1721) by the Jacobite Mar Thoma IV that two groups

---

[1] For more information see A.M. Mundadan, *History of Christianity in India — From the Beginning up to the Middle of the Sixteenth century (up to 1542)*, Bangalore: Theological Publications in India; Published for Church History Association of India, 1984; Assisi Francis Thonippara, *Saint Thomas Christians of India—A period of Struggle for Unity and Self-rule (1775–1787)*, Bangalore: Pontificia Universitas Gregoriana, 1999.

[2] Muiyacami Teyvanayakam, *Christianity in Hinduism —A Conspiracy Exposed and a Confrontation*, Chennai: Dravidian Religion Trust, 1997.

[3] K.V. Koshy, *St. Thomas and the Syrian Churches of India*, Delhi: Indian Society for Promoting Christian Knowledge, 1999.

[4] Wilhelm Germann, *Die Kirche der Thomaschristen—Ein Beitrag zur geschichte der orientalischen Kirchen*, Gütersloh: Bertelsmann, 1877; Leslie Wilfried Brown, *The Indian Christians of St. Thomas—An Account of the Ancient Syrian Church of Malabar*, Cambridge: Cambridge University Press, 1956; revised edition: Cambridge: Cambridge University Press, 1982. Placid J. Podipara, *Die Thomas-Christen*, Würzburg: Augustinus Verlag, 1966; Edouard R. Hambye, *1900 Jahre Thomas-Christen in Indien*, Freiburg: Kanisius-Verlag, 1972.

of Christian settlers reached South India. In AD 345, Thomas of Cana (i.e., Knai Thomman), probably a wealthy merchant, led about 400 (Jewish) Christians of the Orthodox Church in Eastern Syria to the southern parts of Kodunganallur in Kerala. The followers of Thomas of Cana were and still are still known as *Knanaya* Christians. The second migration happened in AD 823 and was led by two Syrian bishops Mar Sapor and Mar Piruz. Both groups of settlers got land and other social privileges that helped them develop a distinct Christian community in South India. Their Syrian bishops were using East Syrian liturgy, but adapted themselves to the socio-cultural situation of India, including the institution of caste. The ritual celebration of *Qurbana* (i.e., Eucharist) was a central part of the liturgy.[5] While the bishops were non-Indians, other chief ecclesiastical executives (e.g., Archdeacons, priests, etc.) were Indians. Their ecclesiastical tie with the Edessean Church in Northern Arabia with its legendary book entitled *Acts of St. Thomas*,[6] the Chaldean Church in Iraq and the Persian Church in Iran, has an extremely complex history. Adherence to Syriac liturgy and worship hampered the growth of the Christian theology in India. The Orthodox traditions continued undisturbed until the arrival of the Portuguese in India.

Beginnings of the Roman Catholic Traditions

The fifteenth century marked several changes in India. Vasco da Gama (1469–1524), the Portuguese sailor who came to Calicut in Kerala twice, succeeded in signing a trade treaty with the local king Zamorin (May 1498 and February 1502).[7] In the meantime (AD 1500) eight European Franciscan monks reached Kerala and began to work among the St. Thomas Christians. They liked the idea of Portuguese *Padroado* (patronage) according to which the Portuguese government was to establish mission centers and churches, appoint clergy and support them in all possible ways. Vasco da Gama's followers were zealous colonizers. They captured important cities on the West Coast, establishing their political and religious headquarters in Goa. Slowly, they got the port cities of Mylapore and Nagapattanam and the like on the East Coast.[8] In the course of time, several Roman Catholic Orders (e.g., Dominicans, Carmelites, Augustinians, etc.) founded their institutions in several parts of India. Many of them worked mostly among the European traders and colonialists. However, with the arrival of the Jesuits (1542),[9] Roman Catholic Christianity began to spread not only along the West and East Coasts, but also into the heartland of India.

---

[5] Johannes Madey and Georg Vavanikunnel, *Qurbana oder Eurcharistiefeier der Thomaschristen Indiens*, Paderborn: Sandesanilayam, 1968; Johannes Maday and Georg Vavanikunnel, *Qurbana—Die göttliche Liturgie der Thomaschristen ostsyrischer Überlieferung (Syro-Malabarische Kirche)*, 2ⁿᵈ rev. ed., Paderborn, Ostkirchendienst, 1992.

[6] A.Frederik J. Klijn, *Edessa—Die Stadt des Apostels Thomas—Das älteste Christentum in Syrien*, Neukirchen-Vluyn: Neukrichener Verlag, 1965.

[7] Kingsley Garland Jayne, *Vasco da Gama and his Successors 1460–1580*, London: Methuen, 1910; Sanjay Subrahmanyam,Ed.: *Sinners and Saints—The successors of Vasco da Gama*, Delhi: Oxford University Press, 1998.

[8] Frederick Charles Danvers, *The Portuguese in India—Being a History of the Rise and Decline of·Their Eastern Empire*, London: W.H. Allen & Company, 1894, rpt. New Delhi: Asian Educational Services, 1988; A. Mathias Mundadan, *The arrival of the Portuguese in India and the Thomas Christians under Mar Jacob 1498–1552*, Bangalore: Dharmaram College, 1967; A. Mathias Pearson, *The Portuguese in India*, Cambridge: Cambridge University Press, 1994; Stephen, S. Jeyaseela: *Portuguese in the Tamil Coast — Historical Explorations in Commerce and Culture 1507–1749*, Pondicherry: Navajothi, 1998.

[9] Joseph Wicki, ed. *Documenta Indica*, Romae: Monumenta Historica Societatis Iesu, 1948–1988; Anand Amaladass, ed. *Jesuit presence in Indian History: Commemorative Volume on the Occasion of the 150ᵗʰ Anniversary of the New Madurai Mission 1838–1988*, Anand/Gujarath: Gujarat Sahitya Prakash, 1988; Charles J. Borges, *The Economics of the Goa Jesuits 1542–1759 — An Explanation of Their Rise and Fall*, New Delhi: Concept Publication, 1994.

At the request of the King of Portugal and as the Apostolic Nuncio (special emissary of the Pope), Francis Xavier, a Spanish nobleman and one of the founders of the Society of Jesus, reached Goa in 1542.[10] Xavier was not keen on encouraging Indian Christians to become ordained priests; but he had numerous catechists and helpers. Due to Xavier's charisma and the relentless work of his helpers, large numbers of *Parava*s (fisher-folk, pearl-fishers and seafarers) living along the West and East Coasts became Roman Catholics. Portuguese traders and soldiers helped the *Parava*s and kept them away from those who used to trouble them.

The Roman Catholic Church in India was growing. European Jesuit priests and Indian helpers trained at St. Paul's Seminary in Goa, were serving the Christians. The Jesuit missionary Henry Henriques (1520–1600) worked among the Roman Catholics in the port city of Tuticorin (i.e., *tûttukudi*, 1548–1600) and became a master of the spoken and written form of the Tamil language.[11] He is considered to be the father of modern Tamil prose as well.

In the meantime, Babur's grandson Akbar became a powerful Mughal Emperor. As he was consolidating his empire, he wanted to bring about the unity of the minds of his subjects who belonged to various political ideologies, as well as religious and cultural identities. In 1579, the Jesuit missionaries, Rudolfo Aquaviva, Antonio Monserrate and Francisco Henrique, brought European culture and paintings to Akbar's court. Akbar allowed them to build a chapel for their worship. When the third group of Jesuits went to the Mughal Court in 1595, Jerome Xavier (1549–1617), who was a nephew of Francis Xavier, became famous. He summarized the Roman Catholic teachings in Persian and used paintings to illustrate several episodes in the life of Jesus Christ. The Jesuit could not record conversion stories of Akbar or his ministers; however, Akbar permitted his subjects to become Christians.

Encounter between the St. Thomas Christians and the Roman Catholic Traditions in South India

While the successors of Akbar were busy maintaining, expanding and strengthening their vast empire in the northern parts of India, various events took place in the southern parts. After the battles at Talikotta in 1565, the Vijayanagar Empire lost its power and influence. The Sultans of Deccan played an important role in dismantling the power of the Vijayanagar Empire. The Mughal Emperors had appointed their deputies in major centers of politics and commerce. Royal Telugu Nayaks (territorial lords) were mostly vassals of the Mughal emperor and paid him annual tribute. These Nayaks ruled the famous South Indian cultural centers of Madurai and Tanjore and patronized either Shaivism or Vaishnavism.

In Kerala, St. Thomas Christians and Roman Catholics were getting to know each other in trade and in church life. Due to the increased interaction between the *Padroado* clergy and St. Thomas Christians, grave differences in ecclesiastical administration, questions about loyalty and identity, about the number of sacraments and the mode of administering the Lord's Supper became obvious. When the Portuguese *Padroado* clergy noticed that St. Thomas Christians would not easily give up their Syriac liturgy and accept their Latin forms of worship, they became aggressive. The Portuguese clergy and colonizers suspected

---

[10] Georg Schurhammer, *Francis Xavier—His life, His Times*, translated by Joseph Costelloe, Four Volumes, Rome: Jesuit Historical Institute, 1973–1982; Luis M. Bermejo, *Unto the Indies—Life of St. Francis Xavier*, Anand/Gujarath: Gujarat Sahitya Prakash, 2000.

[11] Henry Henriques, *Adiyâr varalâru* [Tamil: History of the Servants], ed. S. Rajamanickam, Tuticorin: Tamil Literature Society, 1967.

and systematically oppressed St. Thomas Christians.[12]

Aleixo de Menezes became the Prelate of the Sea of Goa (1595–1610). Fuelled by the Counter Reformation spirit of the Council of Trent (1545–1563) and euro-centric worldviews, he directed his *Padroado* zeal to violently subdue the identity of St. Thomas Christians, and to purge the perceived doctrinal and ecclesiastical impurities of the Syrian Church in Kerala. He gathered a Synod at Udayamperur, commonly known as the Synod of Diamper (June 1599),[13] and imposed his version of Roman Catholic (Latin) Christianity on St. Thomas Christians. The Syriac manuscripts and liturgies were burned. The Synod of Diamper and its consequences became a battleground for both friends and foes. Their dealings with the Syrian Christians led to further rivalry and divisions.

The chief division took place with the *Coonon Cross Oath* (Oath at the Hunchbacked Cross) on January 3, 1653, in Mattanchery.[14] The religious and cultural identity of St. Thomas Christians was increasingly threatened and they looked for an opportunity to revolt against the oppressive measures of the Jesuits. The majority of the discontented St. Thomas Christians gathered, under the leadership of their Archdeacon Thomas a Campo and twelve priests, at the Church of Our Lady of Life in Mattanchery, tied a rope to the cross, and made a solemn vow, never again to be under the power of Francis Garzia, the Roman Catholic bishop.[15] These priests ordained Thomas a Campo as their bishop. This was the major split. Those remaining in the Roman Catholic Church were known as the *Palayakuttukar* (people of the old group). The *Putukuttukar* (people of the new group) swore their loyalty to West Syrian [Jacobite] Orthodox Church, and formed the Syrian Orthodox Church in Kerala.[16] Many other splits were to follow.

The history of Christianity in South India, however, was not marked only by strife. Inland, especially in the Temple City of Madurai in the Tamil country, the Jesuit missionary Roberto de Nobili (1577–1656) laid an enduring foundation for establishing the Christian presence.[17] He arrived in Madurai in 1605/6. In order to impress upon the Brahmin elite that Christianity was not a religion of low people or of the European *Parangi*s (people given to wine, women and wealth) he changed his lifestyle. He learnt Telugu, the language of the Nayak ruler and merchants in Madurai; Tamil, the language of the common

---

[12] Teotonio R. De Souza, "The Indian Christians of St. Thomas and the Portuguese Padroado: Rape after a century-long dating (1498–1599)," *Christen und Geürze — Konfrontation und Interaktion kolonialer und indigener Christentumsvarianten*, ed. Klaus Koschorke, Göttingen: Vandenhoeck and Ruprecht, 1998, pp.31–42; Rowena Robinson, *Conversion, Continuity, and Change - Lived Christianity in Southern Goa*, Walnut Creek: Altamira, 1998.

[13] Michael Geddes, *The History of the Church of Malabar*, ed., London: Printed at the Prince's-Arms in St. Paul's Churchyard for S. Smith and B. Walford, 1694; Jonas Thaliath, *The Synod of Diamper*, Roma: Pont. Institutum Orientalium Studiorum, 1958, V.C. George, *The Church in India before and after the Synod of Diamper*, Alleppey: Prakasam Publications, 1977; Scaria Zachariah, ed., *The Acts and Decrees of the Synod of Diamper 1599*, n.p. [in Kerala]: Indian Institute of Christian Studies, 1994; George Nedungatt, ed., *The Synod of Diamper Revisited*, Rome, Pontif. Institute Orientale, 2001.

[14] Jacob Kollaparambil, *The St. Thomas Christians' Revolution in 1653*, Kottayam: Catholic Bishop's House, 1981.

[15] Karl Werth, *Das Schisma der Thomaschristen unter Erzbischof Franciscus Garzia—Dargestellt nach den Akten des Archivs der Sacra Congregatio de Propaganda Fide*, Limburg/Lahn: Pallotiner Verlag, 1937.

[16] David Daniel, *The Orthodox Church of India—History*, 2ⁿᵈ rpt., New Delhi: Rachel David, 1986.

[17] S. Rajamanickam, *The First Oriental Scholar [Roberto de Nobili]*, Tirunelveli: De Nobili Research Institute at St.Xavier's College, 1972; Thomas Anchukandam, *Roberto De Nobili's Responsio (1610)—A Vindication of Inculturation and Adaptation*, Bangalore: Kristu Jyoti Publications, 1996; Roberto De Nobili, *Preaching wisdom to the wise—Three treatises*, Saint Louis: Institute of Jesuit Sources, 2000.

people; Sanskrit, the language of Indian religions and liturgy. His greatest contribution was the creation of a Christian vocabulary in Sanskrit, Tamil and Telugu. He became a forerunner of inculturation. De Nobili's methods of accommodation were controversial. His superior, Bishop Francis Roz of Angamali-Canganore supported him in Madurai, and later in Goa and so he was able survive the vehement attacks against his methods. The troubles of the Jesuits with the St. Thomas Christians, however, did not affect De Nobili's function. While they were trying to 'latinize' the Syrian Christians, De Nobili concentrated his efforts on the people of non-Christian faiths.[18] De Nobili's Madurai Mission targeted the larger public and established strong Roman Catholic centers.[19]

In 1656, the Pope sent Carmelite missionaries from Rome to the Roman Catholics among the Syrian Christians. These missionaries who wanted to bring about reconciliation, had re-gained most of the dissenters by 1662. The same year, Pope Gregory XIV founded the *Propaganda Fide* (i.e., Sacred Congregation for the Propagation of the Faith) in Rome. It signalled the growing tension between the Pope and the Portuguese King over maintaining missions in the Eastern Hemisphere, and led to the rivalry between the Roman Catholic Orders, hindering their missionary work in South India. By the end of the seventeenth century, however, the Roman Catholic Church was firmly established in South India.

Beginning of the Protestant Traditions

Protestant churches were engaged in their own mission, i.e., maintaining and consolidating their territorial Christianity, and occasionally attempting to reach the Jews or Turks with the gospel of Jesus Christ. Their multiple conflicts — with Roman Catholic Counter Reformation on the one hand, and among themselves sapped their energy. Europe appeared to be Christian only on the surface; popular religiosity was mostly non-Christian. Only a few individuals thought about global Protestant missionary activity, for example, Ernst Justinian von Welz (1621–ca. 1668), an Austrian nobleman settled in the South Germany, who wrote about the importance of Protestant global mission.

Without Pietism there might not have been European cross-cultural mission activity in the eighteenth century. Pietism emphasized a personal heart religion that is based on sound intellectual study of the Bible. Pietists were willing to share their Christian faith and material resources with those who did not have them.

The context of eighteenth century India was complex.[20] The Mughal Emperor, Aurangazeb, died in 1707. His viceroys, especially, the Nizams of Hyderabad and the Nawabs of Arcot/Carnatic became powerful. The Nawabs of Arcot requested the soldiers of the English East India Company to help them collect revenues and suppress any revolt. The officials of the EIC, mostly colonizers, traders and (uneducated) soldiers, who came to India in order to become

---

[18] Until the suppression of the Jesuits in 1773, it accomplished more in a hostile environment than the Jesuit missionaries to the Mughul Court in their almost 200 year history. For further information see Payne, C.H. Translator: *Jahangir and the Jesuits*, London: George Routledge & Sons, 1930.

[19] For a "critical" study on De Nobili see Zupanov, Ines G: *Disputed Mission — Jesuit Experiments and Brahmanical Knowledge in Seventeenth-century India*, New Delhi: Oxford University Press, 1999.

[20] Joseph Thekkedath, *History of Christianity in India—From the Middle of the Sixteenth to the End of the Seventeenth century (1542–1700)*, Bangalore: Theological Publications in India, published for Church History Association of India, 1982; Hamby, Edouard Rene: *History of Christianity in India—Eighteenth Century*, Bangalore: Theological Publications in India, 1997.

rich and return to England with their riches as Nabobs, were greedy, and charged large sums of money for the service. When the Nawabs were unable to pay cash, they had to give lands, often, feudal kingdoms, to the East India Company (EIC). Ultimately it was the ordinary people who suffered greatly — at the hands of the cruel revenue officers of the Nawabs of Arcot, the EIC, the local princes and the feudal lords. The EIC in Madras and the French East India Company in Pondicherry were engaged in prolonged wars. Finally, the EIC won and established its power in South India. In the war-torn areas, however, bribery, corruption, nepotism and deliberate violence were not uncommon. In this situation, the Protestant church began to take its shape.

Bartholomaeus Ziegenbalg and Henry Plütschau reached Tranquebar (in Tamil: *Tarangkampadi*, "village on the sea shore"), a Danish colony (1619–1845), which covered the area of forty square kilometers in 1706.[21] When Ove Gedde, the Danish envoy met Ragunatha Nayak of Tanjore in 1619, they signed a trade treaty and agreed that the Danes in Tranquebar should have full freedom to practice their Lutheran belief. Their trade interest did not allow them to have missionaries in the colonies. However, the influence of P.J. Spener was felt in the Royal Court of Denmark, when Franz Julius Luetkens, a friend of Spener, became a court chaplain. He was instrumental in convincing King Frederick IV to send missionaries to Tranquebar. Luetkens wrote to his friends in Berlin to find appropriate missionary candidates. Ziegenbalg and Plütschau were identified and were persuaded to go to Copenhagen. After much difficulty, the Danish Bishop Bornemann ordained them as Danish missionaries who were

supposed to adhere to the Danish Church Order and the teachings enshrined in the Symbolic Books of the Lutherans. Regarding sending missionaries to Tranquebar, neither the Danish king nor the Danish clergy consulted the Board of Directors of the Danish East India Company in Copenhagen. They became enraged, and sent secret directives to Johann Sigismund Hassius (1704–1716), their chief executive in Tranquebar. In the name of neutrality and non-interference in the religious and social life of the inhabitants of Tranquebar, Governor Hassius was directed to suppress the work of the missionaries from the very beginning.[22]

Tranquebar was a plural society. In the colony, there were fifty-one temples, where Shaivites, Vaishnavites and devotees of the popular religions worshipped their deities. Moreover, there were two mosques. Roman Catholic (Indian) Christians and Protestant Europeans constituted a negligible minority. Ziegenbalg founded *Jerusalem*, the first Lutheran church that was meant for Indians in 1707. By 1718, *New Jerusalem* a second, more spacious church building was dedicated for Christian worship. Ziegenbalg and Plütschau enabled the believers by printing Christian literature – the Tamil New Testament and the theology of J.A. Freylinghausen. In 1716 they founded a seminary and Aaron, one of its students, was ordained in December 1733 as the first Protestant pastor.[23]

Soon, the Christians of the Tranquebar mission moved to different parts of India, and missionaries established other churches e.g. Fort St David at Cuddalore. The German missionary, Benjamin Schultze, became the founder of the Lutheran church in the city of Madras (1726). Rajanaikkan, a soldier in the service of the king

---

[21] Daniel Jeyaraj, *Inkulturation in Tranquebar—Der Beitrag der frühen dänisch-halleschen Mission zum Werden einer indisch-einheimischen Kirche (1706–1730)*, Erlangen: Verlag der Evangelisch-Lutherischen Mission, 1996.

[22] Anders Nørgaard, *Mission und Obrigkeit—Die Dänisch-hallesche Mission in Tranquebar 1706–1845*, Gütersloh, Gütersloher Verlagshaus Gerd Mohn, 1988.

[23] Daniel Jeyaraj, ed. *Ordination of the First Protestant Indian Pastor Aaron*, Chennai: Lutheran Heritage Archives, 1998.

of Tanjore, founded the first Lutheran church in Tanjore (1727/8). The Swede, John Zecharias Kiernander became the founder of the Lutheran Church in Calcutta. Missionary Christian Frederick Schwartz was instrumental in establishing Lutheran churches in Tiruchirapalli (1762). One of his women converts, Clarinda, founded a church in Palayamkottai (1785). Throughout the eighteenth century, fifty-four Tranquebar missionaries, about fourteen ordained Indian pastors, many Indian catechists and numerous women and men established the Protestant church in India in spite of the continuing anti-Christian sentiments.[24] The Word of God translated into Tamil was the major instrument in sustaining the mission of the churches that resulted from the Tranquebar Mission.[25]

Owing to the Danish wars with neighboring nations and the change of European worldviews, the Tranquebar Mission began to decline in South India. However, Calcutta with the British presence was showing new life and became an important city. At that time, one of Ziegenbalg's sons was the Director of the Danish East Indian Company at Frederick's Nagar ("City of Frederick," i.e., modern Serampore), not far away from Calcutta. He had been requesting for a pastor. The above-mentioned Kiernander, who knew Robert Clive as a clerk in Cuddalore, went to Calcutta in 1758. He built a church naming it *Beth Tephilla* (house of prayer), which is known today as *Lal Girija* (the Red Church) or the Old Mission Church in Calcutta.

By the end of the eighteenth century and at the beginning of the nineteenth century, the Rite Controversy had weakened the Roman Catholic Church. The Jesuits were suppressed (1773); there were no adequate replacements. Some Roman Catholics went to Protestant Churches both in North and South India. But the Roman Catholic missionary orders that were not linked to the EIC, were free to develop their educational, medical, and other philanthropic work and were active in the presidencies of Madras, Calcutta and Bombay.

This was the background in which the first Baptist missionary, William Carey, arrived in Calcutta (1793). The British in Calcutta, however, did not recognize Carey because he belonged to a dissenter group of Christians (Baptists) who criticized the Anglican Church in Great Britain. The Anglican leaders in Calcutta, Charles Grant, David Brown and others, looked instead for their own missionaries from the SPCK[26] and in 1797, William Tobias Ringeltaube (1770–1816), a Lutheran pastor from Halle (Saale) in Germany, was sent by the SPCK to Calcutta. However, his stay in Calcutta was short.[27]

---

[24] For more information on the Tranquebar Mission see J. Ferdinand Fenger, *History of the Tranquebar Mission — Worked out from the Original Papers — Published in Danish and translated into English from the German of Emil Francke — Compared with the Danish Original,* Tranquebar: Evangelical Lutheran Mission Press, 1863; 2nd ed., Madras, M.E. Press, 1906; Arno Lehmann, *It began at Tranquebar—The story of the Tranquebar Mission and the beginning of Protestant Christianity in India published to celebrate the 250th anniversary of the landing of the first Protestant missionaries at Tranquebar in 1706, translated by M.J. Lutz,* Madras: The Christian Literature Society, 1956.

[25] D. Dennis Hudson, *Protestant Origins in India—Tamil Evangelical Christians 1706–1835,* Grand Rapids: Eerdmans/ Curzon, 2000.

[26] Eyre Chatterton, *A History of the Church of England in India Since the Early Days of the East India Company with Thirteen Illustrations,* London: Society for Promoting Christian Knowledge, 1924; Mildred E.Gibbs, *The Anglican Church in India, 1600–1970,* Delhi: Indian Society for Promoting Christian Knowledge, 1972.

[27] Ringeltaube joined the London Missionary Society (founded in 1795), and came as their first missionary to South India. He reached Tranquebar in 1804 and asked the Tranquebar Missionaries for help and guidance. Johann Balthasar Kohlhoff advised him to look after the Lutherans in Tirunelveli (at that time belonging to SPCK). There he met Vedamanikam Maharasan (died 1827), the founder of the Protestant Church in Mylaladi (now mostly known as Marthandam, in Kanyakumari District of Tamil Nadu). Ringeltaube and Maharasan worked together. After 1816 Ringeltaube's whereabouts were not known.

Carey laid the foundation for a new model of missionary enterprise. Influenced by the diaries of David Brainard (1717–1747), the example of the Tranquebar missionaries and the zeal of the Moravians, Carey became a forerunner in establishing 'faith-missions.' In this sense, he became the father of the modern faith-missionary movements all over the world.[28]

As soon as Carey's New Testament in Bengali was printed in 1801, Lord Wellesly, the founder of the Fort William College in Calcutta, invited Carey to teach Bengali to English civil servants. There he came to know other learned Indians and sought their help for his Bible translation projects. With their help, the Serampore mission published, by 1834, six versions of the Bible and twenty-three versions of the New Testament, in Indian languages. Like the Tranquebar missionaries, Carey and his colleagues established schools for Indian children. Carey founded the first English newspaper *The Friend of India* (later known as *The Statesman*) and sought to educate the public mind. He joined Indian social reformers such as Raja Ram Mohan Roy in conspiring for the abolition of the burning of widows (i.e., *sati*). In 1805, Carey encouraged the Asiatic Society of Bengal to consider publishing an English translation of the Sanskrit epic Ramayana. His contribution to Bengali prose literature has been phenomenal. By reviving the language, he helped revive the mind of the Bengalis. Carey and his colleagues were great pioneers in several fields of knowledge,[29] and certainly was an important factor in the decision of the EIC in 1813 to allow British missionaries to come to India, and in 1833 to permit any Protestant missionary to any place in India. The eighteenth century became a century of great Protestant missionary activity in India.

Encounter between the Protestant and St. Thomas Traditions in South India

In the beginning of the nineteenth century, the political situation in Kerala changed. The EIC appointed their residents, Colonels Macauley and John Monroe, who asserted the political, military and economical power of the EIC in Kerala. At the request of Macauley, Monroe and Buchanan, the Church Missionary Society (CMS, founded in 1799 in London)[30] sent Anglican missionaries Thomas Norton and Benjamin Bailey (1816), Joseph Fenn (1818) and Henry Baker (1819), not to proselytize, but to help the Jacobite Christians. They taught in the seminary at Kottayam founded by Munroe (1813), established English medium schools,[31] translated the New Testament and the Book of Common Prayer into Malayalam, and had them printed in their own mission press. During their brief stay in England (1826–1833), CMS sent Joseph Peet and W. J Woodcock as missionaries. However, they were unsympathetic towards the Jacobite Christians and the rift between the two parties became permanent. Those who followed the Anglican ideals of the CMS missionaries and chose to give up their

---

[28] S. Pearce Carey, *William Carey — The Father of Modern Missions*, ed. Peter Masters, London: Wakeman Trust, 1993. His magnificent work entitled *An Enquiry into the Obligation of Christians to Use Means for the Conversion of the Heathens* (1792) inspired numerous missionaries. His dictum "Expect great things from God and attempt great things for God (based on Isaiah 54:2–3)."

[29] For an example see Sunil Kumar Chatterjee, *William Carey and Development of the Concept of Educational Museum in India — Religious pamphlets as source materials of church history*, Serampore: Carey Museum, Serampore College, 1982; Sunil Kumar Chatterjee, William Carey and Serampore, Calcutta: Ghosh Publishing Concern, 1984; Malay Dewanji, *William Carey and the Indian Renaissance*, Delhi: Published for William Carey Study and Research Centre & Christian Institute for the Study of Religion and Society by ISPCK, 1996; Ruth and Vishal Mangalwadi, *Carey, Christ and Cultural Transformation*, rev. ed., Carlisle: OM, 1997.

[30] Brian Stanley and Kevin Ward, *The Church Mission Society and World Christianity 1799–1999*, Grand Rapids: Eerdmans/Curzon, 2000.

[31] K.V. Eapen, *Church Missionary Society and Education in Kerala*, Kerala: Kollet, 1985.

orthodox identity formed an Anglican diocese in 1879.[32]

There was yet a larger group that wanted to follow the reformation ideas of the CMS missionaries, but also desired to keep their orthodox identity. Their leaders were Professor (Malpan) Palakunnutu Abraham (1796–1845),[33] who was teaching Syriac at the seminary in Kottayam, and Professor (Malpan) Kaithayil Geevarghese. Abraham Malpan revised the liturgy of the Eucharist and celebrated it in Malayalam in his native town. He was opposed (by Metropolitan Chepat Mar Dionysius), but he sent his nephew, Deacon Matthew who ordained him as the Metropolitan with the name Mathews Mar Athanasius. Once the successors of Matthew's Mar Anthanaisus established the annual Maramon Convention (ca. 1895/6), the reform churches began to grow and gave much importance to cross-cultural evangelism and mission. The Evangelistic Association (1889) was an important missionary organ of the reformed Christians who, in 1899, adopted the new name *Mar Thoma Church*.[34]

Growth of Protestant Traditions in the nineteenth century

The Industrial Revolution (1700–1900), the French Revolution (1770–1799) and the American Independence (1776), changed the outlook of Europeans. While on the one hand, people did not attach much importance to the established church traditions. On the other hand, cross-cultural Protestant missionary interest began to increase. It had some influence on the change in the policy of the EIC (in 1813 and 1833), which coincided to some extent with the Second Great Awakening in North America and was helpful to the history of Christianity in India. Pastors such as Charles Simeon of Cambridge had a positive influence on the minds of the public towards mission. The Clapham Sect in England played a decisive role in changing the policy of the EIC. They established the London Missionary Society (1795), the above-mentioned Church Missionary Society (1799) and the British and Foreign Bible Society (1804). The American Board of Commissioners for Foreign Mission (ABCFM, 1810) sent its first missionary Adoniram Judson to Calcutta in 1812. After 1833, the ABCFM missionaries came to Madurai, Vellore and Punjab. Christians in Germany, Switzerland, Denmark and Scotland were important in establishing the Basle Mission (1815) and the Evangelical Lutheran Mission in Dresden began to send their missionary representatives to India. Alexander Duff of the Church of Scotland reached Calcutta in 1830 and founded his famous college.[35] The Scottish mission established several institutions of higher learning (e.g., Wilson College in Bombay in 1832,[36] Madras Christian College in 1837, St.

---

[32] J.W. Gladstone, *Protestant Christianity and People's Movements in Kerala: A Study of Christian Mass Movements in Relation to neo-Hindu Socio-religious Movements in Kerala 1850–1936*, Trivandrum: India Seminary Publications, 1984.

[33] M.M.Thomas, *Towards an Evangelical Social Gospel—A New Look at the Reformation of Abraham Malpan*, Madras: Christian Literature Society, 1977.

[34] For information about churches in Kerala see Eugène Tisserant, *Eastern Christianity in India—A History of the Syro-Malabar Church from the Earliest Time to the Present Day—Authorized adaptation from the French by E. R. Hambye*, Bombay: Orient Longmans, 1957; V.C. George, *Christianity in India through the Ages*, Kuravilangad/Kottayam: Fr. Joseph Vadakkekara, 1972; Juhanon Mar Thoma, *Christianity in India and a Brief History of the Mar Thoma Syrian Church*, rev. ed., Madras: K. M. Cherian, 1968; Anthony Korah Thomas, *The Christians of Kerala—A Brief Profile of All Major Churches*, Kottayam: Thomas, 1993.

[35] A. A. Millar, *Alexander Duff of India*, Edinburgh: Canongate Press, 1992.

[36] Missionary John Wilson, the founder of this college, was also a social reformer; for further information see John Wilson, *History of the Suppression of Infanticide in Western India under the Government of Bombay: including notices of the provinces and tribes in which the practice has prevailed*, Bombay: 1855.

John's College in Agra, etc.).[37] Several other Protestant denominations (e.g. Presbyterians, Methodists, Congregationalists, Salvation Army and Friends) established their work in India during the nineteenth century as well. These missionaries did great work in increasing the number of Indian Christians and influencing Indian society, but their denominational identity was perpetuated over against Christian identity. Competition and duplication of work resulted in wastage of money and personnel. Instead of concentrating their work on people of non-Christian faith, they spent most of their efforts and resources on Christians only.

Several church and students movements in North America and Western Europe encouraged the Protestant missionary movement. For example, the Young Men's Christian Association (1844), the Evangelical Alliance (1846) and the Young Christian Women Association (1855)[38] were some of the important institutions that provided a large number of missionary personal. They concentrated their efforts on younger generations of people and helped them realize the human bond across national, political, cultural and ideological boundaries.

The second half of the nineteenth century was different in certain respects. In 1854, Sir Charles Wood introduced an educational dispatch[39] that promoted Western education and the education of women. Three years later, the University of Madras was established (1857) and the Indian board of the university recommended three missionaries, Hermann Gundert,[40] Peter Percival and J. Richard, as university professors.

After the First War of Indian Independence, during which in 1857 political power in India passed from the EIC to the British Crown, Empress Victoria declared that her government would not favor any person on the basis of his/her religious faith. Hence, all the religions were considered to be equal. This marked a change in the Christian and non-Christian relationship in India. The social and religious hierarchy of India's privileged —the Brahmins and a few of the higher castes got into the service of British India because they had access to education and religious scriptures. Christians had to look for other non-governmental ways of influencing Indian society.[41]

One of the ways of witnessing in a non-Christian, largely hostile environment was to seek co-operation among different missionary agencies to understand each other's distinctive doctrinal convictions and to look for opportunities for cooperation. The Madras Conference was important because it discussed the issues of the church in India and missionary cooperation in concrete terms. For example, missions chose specific geographical areas in

---

[37] *The Church of Scotland in Calcutta—Its history and work*, Calcutta: Thacker, Spink and Co., 1903; James McMichael Orr, *The Contribution of Scottish Missions to the Rise of Responsible Churches in India*, Edinburgh: The Author, 1967.

[38] Later, the Student Volunteer Movement for Foreign Missions (1888), the Student Christian Movement (1889), and World Student Christian Federation (1895) played an important ecumenical role.

[39] J.C. Ingleby, *Missionaries, Education and India—Issues in Protestant Missionary Education in the Long nineteenth century*, Delhi: Indian Society for Promoting Christian Knowledge, 2000.

[40] Albrecht Frenz, ed., *Hermann Gundert—Brücke zwischen Indien und Europa—Begleitbuch zur Hermann-Gundert-Ausstellung im GENO-Haus Stuttgart vom 19. April bis 11. Juni 1993 in Verbindung mit der Dr.-Hermann-Gundert-Konferenz Stuttgart 19. bis 23. Mai 1993*, Ulm: Süddeutscher Verlagsgesellschaft, 1993.

[41] For further information see Geoffrey A. Oddie, *Social protest in India British Protestant Missionaries and Social Reforms 1850–1900*, New Delhi: Manohar, 1979; Gerald Studdert-Kennedy, *British Christians, Indian Nationalists and the Raj*, Delhi: Oxford: Oxford University Press, 1991; Bernard Palmer, *Imperial Vineyard—The Anglican Church in India under the Raj from the Mutiny to Partition*, Lewes: Book Guild, 1999; Jeffrey Cox, *Imperial fault lines—Christianity and Colonial Power in India 1818–1940*, Stanford: Stanford University Press, 2002.

which to concentrate their work. Apart from the regional conferences, there were other decennial conferences in Allahabad (1872/73), Calcutta (1882/3), Bombay (1892/93) and Madras (1902). All these conferences helped the participants to realise that Christians in India constituted only a (negligible) minority and that denominational disputes and "sheep stealing," would only weaken their Christian witness.

In 1857, some prominent Nadar Christians of Tirunelveli protested against western influence over the Indian Christian church and founded the *Nattu Sabai* (new church) – an indigenous/ national assembly. They believed that their faith in Jesus Christ as Lord did not repudiate their association with their non-Christian cultural environment. Nilakantha Sastri Goreh (Christian name, Nehemia Goreh, 1825–1895) believed in the concept of *praeparatio evangelii*, i.e., God in his providence prepared Indians through their religious systems to accept Jesus Christ. God let the 'divine light' shine in the hearts of all Indians. They should not quench it, but get to know the True Light (i.e., Jesus Christ). Others such as Pandita Ramabai (1858–1922) became a Christian and founded the Mukti Mission (1888); she translated the Bible into Marathi, and created a spiritual movement among women and girls. In 1864, the American Episcopal Methodists ordained Indian Christians to be pastors of their churches. They gave these pastors ecclesiastical and administrative self-identity and self-determination. Bhavani Charan Banerji (Christian name, Brahmabandhab Upadhyaya, 1861–1907), a Hindu convert to Christianity understood the Trinity within Sanskrit categories of *Saccidananda*. These and other Christians spearheaded the inculturation of the Gospel of Jesus Christ in India. Thus, nineteenth century Christianity in India, was a minority religion, but full of life and reflection.

Churches in the twentieth century

At the beginning of the twentieth century, increased interdependent international commerce, transportation and communication helped the peoples of different continents come closer. The Anglo-American Conferences (in New York in 1854, Liverpool in 1860, London in 1878 and New York in 1900) underlined the importance of a world missionary conference. The first International Missionary Conference at Edinburgh in 1910 involved mostly representatives of global missionary agencies and a few non-Western delegates. The optimism of some western Christian leaders to change the destiny of humankind was evident, while Indian delegates such as V.S. Azariah (1874–1945)[42] voiced their critical views. In 1948, the World Council of Churches (WCC) was constituted in Amsterdam. Although the WCC does not have any legislative power, it is an assembly of Protestant churches that accepts and confesses Jesus Christ as God and Savior according the scriptures, and are willing to glorify together the Triune God. Such international events have influenced Christians in India too.

Indian Christians have had to respond to the challenges of their country in the twentieth century in the arena of many political changes. The Indian National Congress that was founded in 1885 became a dominant political party. The rising Indian nationalism made Indian Christian leaders think about their own mission agencies. In February 1903, Rev. Samuel Pakianathan of Tirunelveli became the first Indian missionary of the Indian Missionary Society, and went to the Dornakal area of the Telugu country. The Protestant Church in Tirunelveli was exposed to self-administration, self-support and self-propagation. Henry Venn, the secretary to the CMS in London, experimented, in Tirunelveli (1867), the process of transferring power to

---

[42] Susan Billington Harper, *In the Shadow of the Mahatma—Bishop V.S. Azariah and the Travails of Christianity in British India*, Grand Rapids: Eerdmans/Curzon, 2000.

Indians. There were many levels of circle councils (village, regional and district). Each council had missionary/clergy and lay representatives. Gradually, the existence of two distinct Anglican missions — the CMS and the Society for Propagating the Gospel (SPG) — was ended. Slowly, but steadily, Christians in Tirunelveli were forged with determination.

In 1905, V.S. Azariah and seventeen representatives from different churches in India met and constituted the National Missionary Society (NMS). Their declared purpose was to undertake interdenominational and cross-cultural missionary work in India and neighboring countries, create earnest missionary zeal for Christians, train them to give money for mission and related works. The ordination of Azariah as the first Anglican Indian bishop in 1912 was a great event for the history of Christianity in India.

The National Missionary Council came into being in Nagpur in 1914. It was to represent all Protestant missionary agencies in India. However, in 1923, the name was changed to National Christian Council of India, Burma, and Ceylon.[43] In the course of time, Burma and Sri Lanka formed their own national councils of churches. As a result, in 1979, the National Council of Churches in India (NCCI) was constituted. The NCCI represents all the non-Roman Catholic churches in India and is the forum for all ecumenical churches to speak their prophetic voices affirming their rights and responsibilities in secular and democratic India. At the same time, they may raise their voices against all forms of injustice, exploitation, dehumanization and ecological destruction. The NCCI speaks for religious freedom for all people, especially for minorities. Many other national Protestant organizations cater to the spiritual and social need of Indians (e.g., Evangelical Fellowship of India (EFI), the Union of Evangelical Students (UESI), the Christian Literature Society (CLS), the Evangelical Literary Society (ELS), and the like.

During the First World War the British treated the German missionaries as people of an enemy nation. As a result Lutheran churches came to be known as The Tamil Evangelical Lutheran Church in 1919.

The Third International Missionary Council met at Tambaram in 1938. There was an ongoing dialogue on the views of the Dutch Reformed missionary Henrik Kraemer (1888—1965) who emphasized the discontinuity of God's revelation in and through the faiths of non-Christian peoples. Biblical revelation was so unique and final, that it does not need any other substitute. Indian theological thinkers such as A.J. Appasamy, P. Chenchiah, and V. Chakkarai began to take the challenge of Kraemer seriously.[44] They took several Sanskrit religious categories to express the Christian message. The debate about the relationship of the Gospel of Jesus Christ to the faiths of non-Christian peoples continues, and will continue for a very long time.

By 1947, India had obtained its political independence from the British Crown. The partition of Pakistan in the same year was a painful experience during which Christians tried to reconcile warring parties, showed hospitality and voiced their concern for a reconciled society.

The Presbyterian, Anglican and Congregational Churches in South India constituted the Church of South India (CSI, September 27, 1947), which is considered to be the second greatest wonder after the Pentecost.[45]

---

[43] Kaj Baago, *A History of the National Christian Council of India 1914–1964*, Nagpur: National Christian Council, 1965.

[44] For further information see G.V. Job, and et al.: *Rethinking Christianity in India*, Madras: Sudarisanam, 1938.

[45] K.M. George, *Church of South India—Life in Union 1947–1997*, Delhi: Jointly published by Indian Society for Promoting Christian Knowledge and Christava Sahitya Samithi at Tiruvalla, 1999.

In September 1977, the CSI completed the thirty years period of experimentation. Now it is one organic church. Following the model of the CSI, the Church of North India (CNI) was constituted on November 29, 1970.[46] It included Presbyterians, Anglicans and Congregationalists of the London Missionary Society, and also the Baptist and Brethren Churches of North India, and the Methodist Churches of British and Australian conferences. Both the CSI and the CNI administer parishes, hospitals, and educational and vocational training institutions. Moreover, these churches relate to ecumenical institutions such as the Christian medical colleges at Vellore and Ludhiana, the United Theological College at Bangalore, and other institutions such as the Madras Christian College in Tambaram. They foster unity among Christians and show them effective ways of credible witness among the people of non-Christian faiths.

The Roman Catholic Church continued to expand in the twentieth century. In 1944, the Catholic Bishops' Conference of India (CBCI) was established in New Delhi to represent the Roman Catholic Church and its various missions, and to voice the solidarity of other churches and minorities. With the knowledge of the Pope, Roman Catholic delegates attended the third assembly of the WCC held in New Delhi in 1961, and witnessed the integration of the International Missionary Council with the WCC. The underlying message had a profound theological shift that emphasized the fact that the mission belongs to the church. Since Second Vatican Council (1962–1965), many conferences about evangelism, inter-religious dialogue and the like have been organized.[47] The Council permitted the Roman Catholic Churches in India to use local languages in liturgy, theology and all other works. Roman Catholic scholars joined the Protestant scholars in translating the Bible into many Indian languages. Moreover, Roman Catholic Christians have tried to relate the Biblical message to the Indian cultural and religious context.

The history of Christianity in the seven northeastern states of India (Assam,[48] Nagaland,[49] Meghalaya,[50] Mizoram,[51] Manipur, Tripura and Arunachal Pradesh) is a fascinating reality.[52] The inhabitants have their own distinct cultures that are saturated with primal religious views and practices. The Roman Catholics had their mission centers in this region for a long time.[53] By the middle of the nineteenth century, American Baptists and Welsh Presbyterians

---

[46] Dhirendra Kumar Sahu, *The Church of North India—A Historical and Systematic Theological Inquiry into an Ecumenical Ecclesiology*, Frankfurt am Main: Peter Lang, 1994.

[47] For example see Mariasusai Dhavamony, ed., *Evangelization, Dialogue and Development. Selected papers of the International Theological Conference, Nagpur (India), 1971*, Roma: Pontificia, Università Gregoriana, 1972.

[48] Mathew Muttumana, *Christianity in Assam and Interfaith Dialogue — A Study on the Modern Religious Movements in North East India*, Indore: Satprakashan Sanchar Kendra, 1984.

[49] Puthenpurakal, Joseph: *Baptist Missions in Nagaland — A Study in Historical and Ecumenical Perspective*, Calcutta: Firma KLM Private, 1984; Ramkhun Pamei, *The Zeliangrong Nagas — A Study of Tribal Christianity*, New Delhi: Uppal Publ. House, 1996.

[50] Sebastian Paredom, *Inculturation of the Church in Meghalaya, North East India*, Saltzburg: Universitaet-Dissertation, 1986.

[51] Gwen Rees Roberts, *Memories of Mizoram — Recollections and Reflections*, Cardiff: The Mission Board, Presbyterian Church of Wales, 2001.

[52] Frederick S. Downs, *History of Christianity in India—North East India in the nineteenth and twentieth centuries*, Bangalore: Theological Publications in India, published for Church History Association of India, 1992; F. S. Downs, edited by Milton S. Sangma, and R David, *Essays on Christianity in North-East India*, New Delhi: Indus Publishing House, 1994.

[53] For an example see David Syiemlieh, *A Brief History of the Catholic Church in Nagaland*, Shillong: Vendrame Institute Publications, 1990; Sebastian Karotemprel, Sebastian, ed., *The Catholic Church in Northeast India 1890–1990 —A Multidimensional Study*, Shillong: Vendrame Institute, 1993.

began working in Assam and Meghalaya. A large number of Assamese, Garos and Nagas embraced the Christian faith, and found a new identity. Before the beginning of the First World War there were many waves of revivals among the Khasis in Meghalaya, the Mizos in Mizoram, and the Ao Nagas in Nagaland. The churches were growing at a phenomenal rate. By the middle of the twentieth century, the Baptists[54] and Presbyterians had their own administrative and mission structures. Christians found their new identity to be edifying and community building.

Beginnings of Pentecostal Traditions

It is not yet firmly established as to when the Pentecostal traditions began to assert their presence in India.[55] Some scholars wish to see the connection with the supposed arrival of the Apostle Thomas in India in AD 52. Yet others like to record all the "Pentecostal-like" events in the history of Christianity in India (e.g., revivals through the contact of the St. Thomas Christians with the Roman Catholics, the Anglicans, the revival at Mukti Mission of Pandita Ramabai in 1905, etc.). Most of them agree that Pentecostalism is a twentieth century phenomenon. Among the several strands of Pentecostalism that came to India, two influences — American and Swedish— seem to be important.

The North American Pentecostal connection is very influential. Pentecostalism came to India through the followers of William Seymour (1870–1922) of the Azusa Street Mission in Los Angeles. Prominent among them was George Berg, who had the experience of Spirit baptism at the Azusa Street Mission in 1908. He went to Bangalore. His visit to Kottarakara in Kerala in 1909 marks the actual beginning of a Pentecostal movement in Kerala. Another North American missionary from the Azusa Street Mission was Robert F. Cook, who ministered in Bangalore and Kerala from 1913 onwards. Cook's association with the Assemblies of God was short-lived. The churches belonging to the Assemblies of God owe much to the tireless missionary work of Mary Weems Chapman, who came to Madras in 1914 and traveled to almost all the major Indian cities. She lived in Kerala (1921–1927) and trained several young Indian Pentecostal preachers (e.g., C. Mannasseh, P.V. John, etc.), who carried on her work successfully. Later, several overseas missionaries and Indian Pentecostal leaders took on the leadership and spread their movement far and wide.

The Swedish Pentecostal connection is also important. The visit of Karl Swan, the Swedish pastor-theologian, to Kerala in 1934, established a firm relationship. Two Pentecostal pastors from Kerala, K.C. Cherian and K.E. Abraham, went to Sweden (1936) and preached in numerous Pentecostal churches. K.E. Abraham founded the Indian Pentecostal Church of God. Like Swedish Pentecostal churches, the emerging Pentecostal churches have congregational polity.

Pentecostals uphold certain Indian ethos and morality (e.g., avoiding adultery, preserving gender segregation, ascetic lifestyle, etc.). The Pentecostal "brothers" and "sisters" have many things common with the religious orders of the Shaivites, Vaishnavites and of popular religions. Their guru-pastors are supposed to be holy. They are expected to have power to drive out evil spirits and cause revivals. Their theological training institutes (e.g., The Southern Asia Bible College in Bangalore) attach importance to mission. Pentecostal movements in North India implement

---

[54] Milton S. Sangma, *History of American Baptist Mission in North East India 1836–1950*, Two Volumes, Delhi: Mittal Publications, 1987 and 1992.

[55] For a comprehensive study on South Indian Pentecostalism see Michael Bergunder, *Die südindische Pfingstbewegung im 20. Jahrhundert—Eine historische und systematische Untersuchung*, Frankfurt am Main: Peter Lang, 1999.

not only evangelization, but also philanthrophy. Nowadays there are numerous Indian-initiated Pentecostal missions that are active among the Dalits and tribals.

Issues that Confront the Church in India

On January 26, 1950, India became a secular democracy. The constitution that guarantees basic rights for all people and religions has become a unifying factor that bonds people who speak at least 1652 languages and belong to about 3000 ethnic groups. Though only a minority of politically powerful people chose to promote religious traditionalism, nationalism, fundamentalism and communalism, the larger population must stand for the secular and democratic nature of India. Article 25 of the Indian Constitution enables all Indians — subject to public order, morality and health — to preach and practice their religion. There has been no unanimous agreement on the issues related to religious conversion. Indian civil courts have interpreted conversions in different ways.

The second half of the twentieth century, especially the last decade of the twentieth century, has witnessed more atrocities against Christians who constitute a minority, and who, according to available statistics, continue to decrease numerically (1971, 2.6 percent, but in 2001 only 2.3 percent). India's population has now crossed 1.2 billion (2003). Attacks on church properties, priests, nuns, pastors and overseas missionaries have been repeated. Those who indulge in such violence think that they are true patriots. They neglect the 2000-year history of Christianity in India, Christian contribution to nation building, education, medical and other humanitarian services. From 1967 onwards many so-called 'Freedom of Religion' bills have been introduced

for debate and implementation. The States of Madya Pradesh, Orissa and Arunachal Pradesh have had such a bill for about thirty years. After the demolition of the Babri Masjid on December 6, 1992, the relationship between those who call themselves 'Hindus' and the Muslims has deteriorated significantly. There were violent conflicts between the Muslims and the so-called 'Hindus' in Mumbai (former Bombay) in 1993. In 1996, the Bharatiya Janatha Party tried to introduce a freedom of religion bill in Maharashtra. The awful killings of numerous Muslims and the 'Hindus' in the State of Gujarat during February – April 2002, and the Muslim attack on the Swami Narayan Temple in September 2002, will remain scars in the memory of India for a long time. In October 2002, the government of Tamil Nadu successfully passed an anti-conversion bill that prohibits any religious conversion, especially of the already marginalized Dalits, tribals and women, using force or allurements. Most of these anti-conversion bills are unconstitutional because they deny Indians their right to think differently, and to live a dignified life.

Religious nationalism and fanatic fundamentalism that divide and polarize people have not spared the ethos of education, employment, law courts, and mass media. Other pressing issues that face India as a nation are over looked. In this context, the church in India is to realize its mission of peace, justice and reconciliation. The church has been and will be continuing its efforts — in collaboration with all people of goodwill — to redress social, cultural and economic evils not only for Christians, but also for all the people. Indian Christian leaders such as K.T. Paul, P.D. Devanandan,[56] M.M. Thomas,[57] Stanley

---

[56] Paul David Devanadan, *The Gospel and Renascent Hinduism*, London: Edinburgh House Press, 1959; *Preparation for Dialogue —A Collection of Essays on Hinduism and Christianity in New India*, edited by Nalini Devanandan and M.M. Thomas, Bangalore: The Christian Institute for the Study of Religion and Society, 1964.

[57] Madathilparampil M. Thomas, *The Acknowledged Christ of the Indian Renaissance*, London: S.C.M. Press, 1969; *My Ecumenical Journey 1947–1975*, Trivandrum: Ecumenical Publishing Centre, 1990.

Samartha[58] and many others have shown the various ways of Christian participation in socio-cultural activities and have motivated the global church to re-think their mission.

The theological seminaries in India[59] are beginning to understand the impact of issues related to theologies of the Dalits, tribals and women.[60] They need to train ministers who are willing to make a positive change in their parishes and neighborhood. Many church leaders are slaves of their own caste identity and they promote nepotism. Their activities do not promote the mission of the church nor does it seem to have a spiritual force that can transform people. Coordination, mutual responsibility and reciprocal accountability in sharing funds, personnel, knowledge and technical resources will help India greatly. The effects of globalization are real.

Theological training revolves around the missiological issues of understanding the biblical text in the light of its own cultural and historical background, of Christian history and theology, interpreting and communicating it clearly and authentically to hearers/receivers of a particular context. This holistic mission needs to be committed to the biblical authority and to emphasize salvation of the individuals and transformation of social structures.

The relationship between the Gospel and culture is another major issue. Christianity is not a colonial or western religion; it is an Asian faith. While Indian churches cannot deny their past, which coincided with colonial powers such as the Portuguese, we can create: theology, art, music and literature that help us see an Indian church. The distinctiveness of the cross of Jesus Christ, which judges, refines and reforms every culture, cannot be identified fully with any culture. The creative tension between the Gospel and culture is important. The examples set by Indian poets such as H.A. Krishna Pillai[61] and Narayana Vaman Tilak[62] should be continued with renewed determination.

The union conversation between the CSI and the Lutherans,[63] between the CSI, CNI and Mar Thoma Churches should be continued and encouraged. Other denominational unions (e.g., the Council of Baptist Churches in North East India, and the Pentecostal churches) should look for ways of united witness.

---

[58] Stanley J. Samartha, ed., *Living Faiths and Ultimate Goals—Salvation and World Religions*, New York: Orbis Books, 1974; "Between Two Cultures— Ecumenical Ministry" *in a Pluralisic World*, Geneva: WCC Publ., 1996.

[59] Siga Arles, *Theological Education for the Mission of the Church in India 1947–1987 — Theological education in relation to the identification of the task of mission and the development of ministries in India: 1947–1987 with special reference to the church of South India*, Frankfurt am Main: Peter Lang, 1991.

[60] John B. Webster, *A history of the Dalit Christians in India*, San Francisco: Mellen Research University Press, 1992; G. K. Ghosh, *Dalit Women*, New Delhi: A.P.H. Publishing Corporation, 1997.

[61] David Devadoss, *Life of Poet H.A. Krishna Pillai*, Madras: Madras Law Journal, 1946; Aiyadurai Jesudasen Appasamy, *Tamil Christian Poet: the life and writings of H. A. Krishna Pillai*, Published: London: United Society for Christian Literature/ Lutterworth Press, 1966.

[62] J.C. Winslow, *Narayan Vaman Tilak — The Christian poet of Maharashtra*, Calcutta: Association Press, 1923; H. L. Richard, *Christ Bhakti—Narayan Vaman Tilak and Christian Work Among Hindus*, Delhi: ISPCK, 1991; H.L. Richard, *Following Jesus in the Hindu context — The Intriguing Implications of N. V. Tilak's Life and Thought*, Pasadena: William Carey Library, 1998.

[63] *The Holy Spirit and the Life in Christ — Papers submitted to the joint theological commission of the church of South India and the Lutheran Churches, July 1953*, Madras: Christian Literature Society, 1953; *Unity in Faith and Life — The Joint Theological Commission of the Church of South India and the Federation of Evangelical Lutheran Churches in India — The meeting at Bangalore March 1954*, Madras: Christian Literature Society, 1955; J.R. Chandran, *The C.S.I. - Lutheran Theological Conversations 1948–1959 — A selection of the papers read together with the agreed statements and an introduction*, Madras: The Christian Literature Society, 1964.

There has been much scholarly reflection about radicalism, fundamentalism, inclusivism, exclusivism and Christ-centered syncretism. What is needed is not another theory, but credible role models of Christians who are ready to build bridges, and find opportunities for mutual learning and teaching.[64] As Christians participate in *missio Dei* (the mission of God), they are encouraged to be faithful and authentic witnesses of Jesus Christ. It is a life long event that requires following theological guidelines:

The *missio Dei* as the source; Jesus Christ who embodies fully God's intention in mission; the Holy Spirit who is the source of power; the church as God's instrument in mission; and human culture as the medium through which all communication of the gospel must be made.[65]

Thus, the legacy of the church in India will continue in the future, not only for its own sake, but also for the sake of the worldwide church.

---

[64] Miroslav Volf, "Be particular," *The Christian Century*, January 25, 2003, 33: "Religions are embraced and practiced in no other way except in their concreteness. To speak in a Christian voice is neither to give a variation on a theme common to all religions nor to make exclusively Christian claims in distinctions from all other religions. It is to give voice to the Christian faith in its concreteness, whether what is said overlaps with, differs from or contradicts what people speaking in a Jewish or Muslim voice is saying. Since truth matters, and since a false pluralism of approving pats on the back is cheap and short-lived, we will rejoice over overlaps and engage others over differences and incompatibilities, so as to both learn from and teach others."

[65] Wilbert R. Shenk, "Mission Strategies," *Toward the 21ˢᵗ Century in Christian Mission*, edited by James M. Philips and Robert T. Coote, Grand Rapids: Eerdmans, 2000, 218–234, quoted from p.230.

CHAPTER 14

Church-Mission Dynamics in Northeast India

LALSANGKIMA PACHUAU

The story of the churches in Northeast India is a complex account. The region is inhabited by diverse ethno-cultural groups, and varying ecclesiastical traditions have come into being. To comprehend the life and activities of the churches, one must have a sense of the rich ethnic background and manifold religious characters of the region. We will first look into the general background of the region and the people, and then account for the life and witness of the churches. Because our intention is to describe the missionary life of Christian churches in the region, we emphasize the contributions of the so-called 'native' or indigenous Christians. This is not in any way to discount the immensity of the western missionaries' contribution, but to recognize the role of the churches as they exist today. I will try to be as descriptive and objective as possible, saving the few observations I have for the concluding comments. Not in anyway to limit mission to proclamation and church planting, our attention will, however, be drawn mainly to these activities since they represent deliberate activities of witness to the Gospel across the religious and cultural boundaries in the region.

The Region and the People

Bordered in the north by Bhutan, Tibet and China, in the south and southwest by Bangladesh, in the east and southeast by Myanmar, the region we identify as Northeast India lies in the eastern corner of India. Linked to the rest of India by a small land-strip, there are seven states in the region, namely Assam, Arunachal Pradesh, Meghalaya, Manipur, Nagaland, Mizoram and Tripura. Often referred to as 'the seven sisters', some suggest that the eighth sister has been conceived with the recent birth of the state of Sikkim. Since the state of Sikkim, slightly removed territorially, is too recent an addition to the region, we will not consider it as part of the region.

Northeast India displays a distinctive "geo-ethnic character."[1] About three-quarters of the region is covered by hilly terrain and one quarter is made up of the four plains areas.[2] While the hill areas are the abode of the people so-called 'tribals', in the plains are sanskritized or hinduized non-tribals. The four plains are: the Brahmaputra valley and Barak (Surma) valley of Assam, the Tripura plains and the Manipur plateau. While the major part of Assam is composed of plains, large parts of Tripura and Manipur are hilly too. The population of the region is concentrated on the plains. According to the 1991 census, more than 71 percent of the region's population live in the plains of Assam, about 14.5 percent in Manipur and Tripura, and the remaining 14.5 percent in the hills of the remaining four states, namely, Arunachal

---

[1] Annanda C. Bhagabati, "Emergent Tribal Identity in North-East India," in *Tribal Developments in India: Problems and Prospects*, edited by B. Chaudhuri, Delhi: Inter-India Publications, 1982, p.218.

[2] N.K. Das, *Ethnic Identity, Ethnicity and Social Stratification in North-East India*, New Delhi: Inter-India Publications, 1989, p.28.

Pradesh, Meghalaya, Mizoram, and Nagaland.[3] Because the major proportion of population in these four hill-states is tribal, some anthropologists call them "tribal states."[4] The proportion of tribal population to the state population in these four states, according to the 1991 census report is 94.75 percent in Mizoram, 87.7 percent in Nagaland, 85.53 percent in Meghalaya, and 63.65 percent in Arunachal Pradesh.[5] If one compares these figures with the tribal population of 12.82 percent in Assam,[6] there appears to be a wide difference in tribal population. This, however, is not true since this 12.82 percent of Assam's tribal population represents roughly 35 percent of the tribal population of the region.

The distinction of the people into tribal and non-tribal is problematic when one looks at the racial composition of the population. The major portion of the indigenous people, both tribals and non tribals are of mongoloid racial stock. They are believed to have migrated from north and east of their present homeland. Indo-Aryan immigrants from the present day Bangladesh and other parts of India constituted the largest racial group. Other than these two, the Mon-Khmer group in the present day Meghalaya is the other

dominant race.[7] Linguistic composition of the region is extremely diverse. In the words of F. S. Downs, "No one even knows precisely how many languages are spoken."[8] Though a greater number of the people speak what Downs calls "Sanskrit-based languages (mainly Assamese and Bengali)," the numerous languages spoken by various groups of people are identified as belonging to the Sino-Tibetan group of languages.[9]

Religions of the People

The religious composition of the region also more or less follows the geo-ethnic character of the region. With the exception of Arunachal Pradesh, the vast majority of people identify with one of the 'six major religions of India': Hinduism, Islam, Christianity, Buddhism, Jainism, and Sikkhism. While almost all the tribal people in the so-called 'tribal states' of Mizoram, Meghalaya, and Nagaland are Christians, the number of Christians among the non-tribal people in the plains of Assam, Manipur and Tripura is relatively small and insignificant. In the case of Manipur where the region is more evenly divided into the plains region—inhabited mainly by non-tribals—and the hill region, inhabited by tribals,

---

[3] According to the Census of India 1991, the region's total population was 31,386,911. Assam has 22,294,562, Manipur and Tripura combined 4,571,541. See *Census of India 1991, Series-1 India, Paper 1 of 1991: Provisional Population Totals*, New Delhi: Amulya Ratna Nanda, Registrar General & Census Commissioner, India, 1991, p.3.

[4] K. S. Singh, "Tribal Perspectives," in *Continuity and Change in Tribal Society*, edited by Mrinal Miri, Shimla: Indian Institute of Advanced Study, 1993, p.6.

[5] *Census of India 1991, Series 1, Paper 1 of 1992, Vol. 1, Final Population Totals*, New Delhi: Amulya Ratna Nanda, Registrar General & Census Commissioner, Ministry of Home Affairs, India, 1992, pp.15-19. These numbers, however, do not agree with the information contained in the recently published book of the Anthropological Survey of India. According to the latter, tribal population in the four states are as follows: 93.55% in Mizoram, 83.99% in Nagaland, 80.58% in Meghalaya, and 69.82% in Arunachal Pradesh. See K. S. Singh, *The Scheduled Tribes, People of India*, National Series Volume III, Delhi, Bombay, Calcutta, Madras: Oxford University Press, 1994, p.3.

[6] See *Census of Indian 1991*, pp.15-19; *The Statistical Outline of India, 1994-1995*, edited by J. K. Mukhopadhyay, 21st ed., Bombay: Tata Services Limited, 1994, p.53.

[7] R. Gopalakrishnan, *The North-East India: Land, Economy and People*, New Delhi: Har-Anand Publications, 1991, pp.82-83.

[8] F. S. Downs, *History of Christianity in India, Vol. V, Part 5, North East India in the Nineteenth and Twentieth Centuries*, Bangalore: The Church History Association of India, 1992, p.1.

[9] D. Tyagi and M. Banerjee, "The North-East: Anthropological Perspectives," *Indian Association of Social Science Institute Quarterly* 12, 1994, p.44.

the Christian percentage is relatively high. The majority of the Christians in Manipur are tribals, and the figure of the tribal population matches the number of Christians. There are 632173 tribals (34.41 percent of the population), and the Christian population is 626669 (which is 34.11 percent of the population) in the 1991 census report. The following tabulated from the 1991 census report, 10 shows the religious composition of the seven states of Northeast India:

	Hindus	Muslims	Christians	Sikhs	Buddhists	Jains	Others
Arunachal Pradesh	37.04%	1.38%	10.29%	0.14%	12.88%	0.01%	36.22%
Assam	67.13%	28.43%	3.32%	0.07%	0.29%	0.09%	0.62%
Manipur	57.67%	7.27%	34.11%	0.07%	0.04%	0.07%	0.77%
Meghalaya	14.67%	3.46%	64.58%	0.15%	0.16%	0.02%	16.82%
Mizoram	5.05%	0.66%	85.73%	0.04%	7.83%	N	0.27%
Nagaland	10.12%	1.71%	87.47%	0.06%	0.05%	0.10%	0.48%
Tripura	86.50%	7.13%	1.68%	0.03%	4.65%	0.01%	N

Religious Composition of the Seven States of Northeast India

From the table, we can notice several things. With the exceptions of Arunachal Pradesh and Tripura, the tribal people are largely Christian and the non-tribals largely non-Christian. Among the hill states, Arunachal Pradesh and Meghalaya have a good number of 'other' religious persuasions. The report identifies these as indigenous religions, often referred to as 'animism', found mostly in the rural areas. Except in Arunachal Pradesh and Tripura where there is a good number of "indigenized" Hindus,[10] most Hindus and Muslims in the hill states are immigrants and government officials who settled in the region for official duties. In terms of religious composition, Arunachal Pradesh can be said to be the most mixed in the region. According to Chander Sheikhar Panchani, three religions are harmoniously co-existing in Arunachal Pradesh, these are Hinduism in the foothills, 'Animism' in the central stretch of the hills, and Buddhism in the higher Himalayan frontiers.[11] Amidst strong resistance, the Christian population in the state is fast growing too. The Christian percentage was 0.79 percent in 1971, 4.32 percent in 1981,[12] and by 1991, it had grown to 10.29 percent.

Christian Churches in Northeast India

The total Christian population of Northeast India, which is roughly 4.3 million, accounts for about 22.7 percent of Indian Christians.[13] With roughly 1.2 million, Meghalaya has the highest number of Christians followed by Nagaland with about one million. Among the seven states, Christians numbered the least in Tripura with about forty-seven thousand.

Although there were few visitations made by Roman Catholic missionaries in the past, it was the Protestant mission bodies which first made established mission works in the region in the mid-nineteenth century. Colonial administrators

---

[10] C. S. Panchani, *Arunachal Pradesh: Religion, Culture and Society*, Delhi: Konark Publishers Pvt. Ltd., 1989, p.200.

[11] *Ibid.*

[12] *Census of India 1981*, Series-1 India, Paper 3 of 1984, *Household Population by Religion of Head of Household*, New Delhi: V. S. Verma, Registrar General & Census Commissioner for India, 1984, pp.xiv-xv.

co-operated with mission works in a number of ways. At the initiative of David Scott, the first Commissioner of the East India Company in the region, Serampore Mission started mission stations in Guwahati (Assam) and in Cherrapunji of Meghalaya. Later, in the implementation of the comity arrangement, a concept by which one mission agency is responsible for one territory or one people, the colonial government also played an important role. Until recently, such a comity understanding prevailed among Protestants resulting in regionalizing of denominations. The three largest denominations are the Baptist Church, established by the American Baptist Mission, Roman Catholic Church, and the Presbyterian Church, founded by the Welsh Presbyterian (formerly Calvinistic Methodist) Church mission. The Baptists of American Baptist origin are now organized under the Council of Baptist Churches in Northeast India (CBCNEI), and the Presbyterians as the Presbyterian Church of India (PCI). According to F. S Downs, by 1990, 43 percent of the Christians in the region belong to CBCNEI, 26 percent to the Roman Catholic Church, and 23 percent to the Presbyterian Church of India.[14]

The Baptist Churches belonging to CBCNEI dominate the Christian population in the state of Nagaland, the Garo Hill district of Meghalaya, the larger part of Manipur hills, and a large number of pockets Christian communities in the Brahmaputra valley of Assam. Until the middle of the twentieth century, the Catholic presence was more or less confined to Assam and Meghalaya. Since then, the Catholic Church has been rapidly spreading in other parts of the region. The second largest Protestant denomination, namely the PCI, dominates the Khasi-Jaintia districts of Meghalaya, the relatively thick-populated northern Mizoram, and the Cachar district of Assam. Although lesser in numbers than the Baptists, Presbyterian churches are also well-established in the southern part of the Manipur hills. The British Baptist Missionary Society established the Baptist Church of Mizoram in southern Mizoram. Historically and denominationally related to the Mizoram Baptist Church are a few independent churches in the southern-most district of Mizoram.

It is of special interest that the evangelization of Tripura and Arunachal Pradesh were initiated and carried forth largely by Christians of Northeast India. In Tripura, the evangelization process begun by the Mizo Christian community was later joined and continued by the New Zealand Baptist Mission under the name Tripura Baptist Christian Union. In the Brahmaputra valley, other mission agencies of Baptist denominations, namely the Australian Baptist Mission and the Baptist General Conference of America, have also been working, and from them the North-Bank Baptist Association has come into being. Following their immigrant-members from southern Bihar (now Jharkhand), the Gossner Evangelical Lutheran Church and the Lutheran Santal Mission also established churches and were involved in evangelistic work among tea garden labourers in Assam. The Anglican presence in Northeast India is meager, indeed there was no significant mission effort by any of the Anglican mission agencies. With this bird's eye view of Christian presence in Northeast India as a background, we will briefly look into the history of evangelization of the region giving attention to the role of native Christians in the work of evangelization. This will be followed by a portrayal of the missionary endeavours of the churches in the region.

Evangelization of Northeast India: A Brief Historical Account

Until the independence of India, territorialization of mission agencies continued

---

[13] According to the 1991 Census report, there were 18,895,917 Christians in India of which 4,301.895 (or 22.77 percent) are in Northeast India. See *Census of India 1991, Series-1 India, Paper 1 of 1995, Religion*, pp.xii-xix.

under comity arrangement. The continuation of comity became impossible with the result that no one denomination now owns any particular territory. However, the heritage of comity is left in the region among the Protestants with most major denominations dominating the territories where their mission-forebears operated. As we deal with the historical account, it should be underlined that until the Independence of India, excepting the princely states of Manipur and Tripura, all parts of Northeast India belonged to the state of Assam. Nagaland became a state in 1963, followed by the implementation of the Re-organisation Act in the early 1970s by which the present states of Meghalaya, Mizoram and Arunachal Pradesh were sliced out of Assam. In dealing with these seven states, we will be using their present names since they were distinct districts anyway.

Assam:

At the invitation of David Scott, the Serampore Mission started rather small-scale mission works by opening a school in Guwahati in 1829. The school was soon closed in 1836 by which time another school had already been opened in Cherrapunji (Meghalaya). Following the amalgamation of Serampore Mission with the Baptist Missionary Society in 1837, the school was closed again, and the Cherrapunji mission was abandoned in 1837.[15] Around the same time in 1836, the American Baptist Mission appeared in upper Assam (northeastern part of Assam) with the intention to reach China. With the failure to move beyond the region, the missionaries of the American Baptist Mission gradually turned their

attention to some tribal groups in the border area of present day Nagaland and Arunachal Pradesh, and to the Assamese of upper Assam.[16] At the missionaries' request, the Mission Board also decided to adopt Assam as its field in 1841, abandoning the work among border tribals and in upper Assam.[17] Christian growth among the Assamese was slow and the missionaries were frustrated. The only sign of success in Assam was among the tribals. Since the second half of the nineteenth century, Christianity saw growth among the migrant tea garden labourers from Chhotanagpur district of Bihar, and among Kachari and Garos settling in Assam area.

Garo Hills (Meghalaya):

In 1847, Francis Jenkins, the successor of David Scott as the Commissioner of the region, opened a school in Goalpara near the Assam-Garo Hills border. A number of Garo boys were enrolled as students.[18] After they completed their studies, through the reading of a tract probably prepared by the Serampore Mission, which one of them found in a dustbin, and subsequent inquiry into Christianity, two of the Garo boys, Omed Watre Momin and Ramkhe Watre Momin converted to Christianity. They were baptized in 1863 at Guwahati. The two converts requested American Baptist missionary Miles Bronson to send a missionary, but no missionary was available. The two resigned their jobs, proceeded to Garo Hills, and began evangelistic work among their people amidst severe opposition. When Bronson finally visited them in April of 1867, he baptized 37 Garos, formed the first Garo Church and ordained Omed to be the minister of the

---

[14] Downs, *History of Christianity in India*, p.69, footnote no. 15.

[15] John Hughes Morris, *The History of the Welsh Calvinistic Methodists' Foreign Mission, to the End of the Year 1904*, Carnarvon: C. M. Book Room, 1910, pp.72-75; O. L. Snaitang, *Christianity and Social Change in Northeast India*, Shillong: Vendrame Institute, 1993, p.67.

[16] Milton S. Sangma, *History of American Baptist Mission in North-East India (1836-1950)*, Vol. 1, Delhi: Mittal Publications, 1987, p.30.

[17] *Ibid.*, p.45.

[18] *Ibid.*, p.188.

church.[19] In reporting his visit, Bronson exclaimed: "During my whole missionary life I have never seen anything so wonderful as the work now going on among the Garos. Those two Garo assistants Omed and Ramkhe, have worked quietly and faithfully on amid ridicule, reproach, and even threats of personal violence...."[20] The organisation of a Garo Baptist Church was followed by the adoption of the Garo hills as the mission field of the American Baptist Mission. In other words, the arrival of missionaries was preceded by evangelization by the "native evangelists" and the adoption of the area as a mission field by the establishment of a church. Garo Hills was one of the few areas in Northeast India where we find significant Christian presence in the nineteenth century.

Khasi and Jaintia Hills (Meghalaya):

The earliest Khasi converts were introduced to Christianity by Krishna Pal of the Serampore mission. They were from the foothills of Khasi land (now part of Bangladesh), and were baptised in 1813. After the abandonment of Serampore Mission's station in Cherrapunji, Khasi and Jaintia hills came to be adopted by the Welsh Missionary Society,[21] which sent its first missionary, Thomas Jones, in 1841. As in other places of Northeast India, reduction of the language to written form and formal education at the primary level became the preliminary and basic means of evangelization. The growth of Christianity was slow in the early years and oppositions were often violent.[22] There were only twenty Christians at the end of the first decade (1841-1851).[23] The standard of church membership was high, and the missionaries made no haste in baptizing new converts.[24] Whereas there were 1659 'Christians' in 1880, the 'communicants' were only 400.[25] Numerical growth began from the last two decade of the nineteenth century. In 1891, there were 6862 Christians of which 2147 were communicants. The number grew to 15678 Christians and 4945 communicants in 1901, and 17800 Christians and 6180 communicants in 1904.[26] Among the factors for the growth of Christianity among the Khasis, major progress made in the field of education,[27] the effect of the great earthquake of 1897 and the revival movements of 1905-07 and the 1950s are considered significant.[28]

The commitments of early Khasi converts are worth mentioning. There were women converts in the matrilineal system of the society who lost

---

[19] Krickwin C. Marak, "Christianity among the Garos: An Attempt to Re-read the Peoples' Movement from Missiological Perspective," in *Christianity in India: Search for Liberation and Identity*, edited by F. Hrangkhuma, Delhi: ISPCK, 1998, pp.161-166.

[20] "Report on Assam: Mission to Assamese," *Baptist Missionary Magazine* XLVII, No. XI, December 1868, pp.254-262, reproduced in *History of Christianity in Nagaland: A Source Material*, compiled by A. Bendangyangbang Ao, Mokokchung: Shalom Ministry, 1998, p.2.

[21] This was the original name given in 1840. The name was changed to Welsh Calvinistic Methodist's Foreign Missionary Society in 1843. See B. L. Nongbri, "Thomas Jones: A 'Scandal' to the Church – A 'Hero' to the People," Unpublished paper originally presented at a seminar in John Roberts Theological Seminary, 22 September, 1998, p.3. For convenience sake, we will use its popular name "Welsh Mission" henceforth.

[22] Downs, *History of Christianity in India*, pp.73-74.

[23] Joseph Puthenpurakal, "Christianity and Mass Movement among the Khasis: A Catholic Perspective," in *Christianity in India: Search for Liberation and Identity*, edited by F. Hrangkhuma, New Delhi: ISPCK, 1998, p.202.

[24] Morris, *The History of the Welsch...*, p.91.

[25] J. Fortis Jyrwa, *The Wondrous Works of God: A Study of the Growth and Development of Khasi-Jaintia Presbyterian Church in the 20th Century*, Shillong: Mrs. M. B. Jyrwa, 1980, p.29.

[26] Morris, *The History of the Welsch...*, p.197.

[27] Downs, *History of Christianity in India*, pp.74-75.

[28] O. L. Snaitang, "Christianity among the Khasis: A Protestant Perspective," in *Christianity in India* edited by F. Hrangkhuma, New Delhi: ISPCK, 1998, pp.240-246.

their rights of inheritance, and prospective chiefs such as U Borsing of Cherrapunji sacrificed their thrones because of their Christian identity.[29] The zeal to evangelize their own people began early, and soon developed into the creation of a 'Home Mission' at the end of the nineteenth century. To commemorate the new (twentieth) century, a 'Century Fund' was collected, amounting to more than Rs.10,000.00 in 1901 for Home Mission. By 1940, as many as 24 new churches were planted with more than 2500 new converts through the work of the Home Mission.[30] Since the 1920s, Khasi Churches have also made a significant contribution to the National Missionary Society of India.[31] Not only did the Khasi evangelists greatly contribute to the evangelization of the Khasi-Jaintia hills, but also in cross-cultural evangelism. In the history of Christianity in Mizoram, for instance, the Khasi contribution is noteworthy. Along with the first Welsh missionary, D. E. Jones, was a Khasi evangelist, Rai Bhajur, who sacrificed a high ranking government job and good salary to serve in Mizoram at a minimal income.[32] In addition to the work of a few Khasi missionaries, Khasi Christians who worked with the British government in Mizoram made significant contributions too. As a reputed church historian of Mizoram, Saiaithanga, said, "In the establishment of Mizo Church, the Khasis played significant role, we do not forget them."[33]

By the end of the nineteenth century, the only place where Christianity had made its presence significantly felt, was in the present day Meghalaya. Although a good number of Assamese had converted to Christianity, their number was insignificant in relation to the overall population. About 70 percent of Christians in the region at the beginning of the twentieth century were in Meghalaya.[34] Christian works made their headway in other parts of Northeast India only in the twentieth century.

Nagaland:

Various factors including a promise of 'harvest', conflict between some missionaries, and lack of response from the Assamese led to the drawing of attention to the Ao-Nagas of present day Nagaland.[35] The names of Edward Winter Clark and his wife Mary Mead Clark have been associated with the pioneering endeavour among the Ao-Nagas. However, the real pioneer who first landed among the Ao-Nagas with the Gospel was an Assamese convert who has been referred to as Clark's 'assistant.' His name was Godhula, who seemed to have been given an Anglicized 'Christian name,' Rufus Brown. In the fashion of traditional missionary hagiography, Godhula was only an 'assistant,' and Clark was the missionary and the real pioneer. One cannot discount the great contribution of the Clarks nor should one minimise Godhula's great pioneering work. After learning basic Ao language, Godhula proceeded to Ao-land without the permission of Clark in October of 1871. Suffering threats to his life as well as isolating 'imprisonment,' Godhula managed to get across his message of peace and love of the God whom he called 'the Bread of Love.'[36] After a few other trips, the first group of converts, nine in number, were brought to Clark and were baptized

---

[29] *Ibid.*, p.242; Downs, *History of Christianity in India*, p.73.

[30] Jyrwa, *The Wondrous Works*, p.38.

[31] *Ibid.*, 42.

[32] Snaitang, "Christianity among the Khasis," p.242.

[33] Saiaithanga, *Mizo Kohhran Chanchin*, third reprint, Aizawl: Mizo Theological Literature Committee, 1993, p.14.

[34] Downs, *History of Christianity in India*, p.80.

[35] Joseph Puthenpurakal, *Baptist Missions in Nagaland: A Study in Historical and Ecumenical Perspective*, Shillong: Vendrame Missiological Institute, 1984, pp.57-62.

[36] *Ibid.*, pp.63-69,213.

on the 10th or 11th of November 1872. "The immediate prospect of more baptisms," says Puthenpurakal, "induced Clark" to visit the Ao village where Godhula worked. And on December 22, 1872, 15 others were baptized.[37] Clark moved to Ao-land in 1876 and started evangelization work through preaching, schools, and literature work. He continued to utilize the "help" of Assamese and had 15 Assamese "assistants" or "helpers" starting with Godhula in the early evangelization work of the Ao-Nagas.[38] The early years did not see much conversion, and the succeeding missionaries in fact dismissed almost all the members of this early congregation to give way for a radical reformation of the church.

With Clark's motivation, other mission stations were opened among the Angamis, and for a brief period among the Lothas. Although C. D. King, the pioneer missionary among the Angami-Nagas who started his work from 1879, had the advantage of the British administration's protection and support, no visible fruit could be seen immediately due mainly to his inability to master the Angami language as well as the political instability in the region. For a brief period, i.e., from 1885 to 1887, missionaries were also posted in Wokha town among the Lothas. By the end of the nineteenth century, there were almost no Naga Christians outside the Ao tribe. After the drastic reformation in 1894, according to F. S Downs, there were only two Ao-Naga members in the church in 1895. A renewal movement again came about through the work of a young native convert by the name of Caleph. Along with his Assamese friend Biney, Caleph led evangelistic preaching tours, which greatly helped the growth of Ao communicant members. The number of Ao communicant church members grew to some 200 at the end of the nineteenth century.[39] The combination of preaching tours and education helped to revitalize and reform the Ao church. In the first half of the twentieth century, the earliest phenomenal growth among the Nagas came about among the Sema tribe. Through what Puthenpurakal calls "a chain of reaction," lay "native" evangelists carried the work of evangelization, leading to what he calls "a mass movement" among the Semas.[40]

While the growth of churches among the Aos was gradual and began from the first decade of the twentieth century, the growth among Semas and Lothas, dating from the 1930s, was impetuous and spontaneous. The hard resistance by Angamis also began to break down from the 1930s.[41] The major growth of Christianity among these tribes, as well as the initiation and growth among other Naga tribes, began after the Independence of India in 1947, and after the missionaries left Nagaland in the early 1950s. The contribution of Naga Christians in the evangelization of Nagaland is enormous. As early as 1898, the missionary report on Ao-Nagas said "all our churches are now self-supporting."[42] What may be called "mass evangelization" among the Semas was done mostly by the natives. By 1951, Christians in Nagaland numbered 98,068; in 1971 the figure rose to 3,44,798,[43] and to

---

[37] *Ibid.*, p.65.

[38] *Ibid.*, p.72.

[39] Downs, *History of Christianity in India*, pp.101-102.

[40] Puthenpurakal, *Baptist Missions in Nagaland*, p.104.

[41] Downs, *History of Christianity in India*, p.108.

[42] Quoted by Puthenpurakal, p.116. Puthenpurakal seems to have doubted this statement and added "We have to understand by this, that the local Christians contributed part of the salaries of the native evangelists, supplied bamboo or thatch or freely offered unskilled labour when a village chapel or a school had to be built." Perhaps, such an observation is made because Puthenpurakal, a non-native, does not understand the communitarian nature of tribals. In the light of our observation of the tribals' selfless commitment to their community, the statement should not be doubted.

[43] Downs, *History of Christianity in India*, p.108.

1,057,940 by 1991.[44] The Christian percentage of 87.47 in Nagaland is the highest in India. The fact that the major expansion of Christianity took place in the second half of the twentieth century when all foreign missionaries had left Nagaland is a living witness to the role of Naga Christians in the evangelization of Nagaland. P. T. Philip describes how Christian churches came into being among various Naga tribes leading to formation of new Baptist Associations saying it was the work of Nagas for Nagas. It was certainly through the works of Naga missionaries (or "evangelist" as they were called), mainly of the Ao tribe, that the Baptist Associations of Sangtam, Chang, Konyak, Phom, Yimchunger, and Kheamungan came into being.[45]

Mizoram:

The pioneer missionaries to Mizoram, J. Herbert Lorrain and F. W. Savidge, belonged to a private missionary agency called the Arthington Aborigines Mission, founded, funded, and directed by Robert Arthington, Jr.[46] The two reached Mizoram in January 1894 and worked for about three and a half years. Due to differences in mission goal with their sponsor Arthington, Lorrain and Savidge offered the area to the Welsh Mission which had earlier planned to adopt the district. The first Welsh missionary to Mizoram, David Evan Jones, along with a Khasi 'evangelist', U Rai Bhajur, came and replaced the Arthington missionaries in 1897. When the southern district of Mizoram was transferred to the Baptist Missionary Society, the two pioneer missionaries went back to Mizoram as the first two Baptist missionaries in 1903.

Missionaries of the two mission societies worked cooperatively in Mizoram creating an atmosphere where the people underwent similar spiritual and ecclesial experiences. The first baptised Christians received their baptisms in 1899.

As in other places of Northeast India, it was the first converts who made headway to evangelizing their people. One of the first two Mizo converts by the name of Khuma is said to have visited almost all the villages in Mizoram with a simple message of invitation to each individual he met and houses he visited, "Believe in Jesus Christ."[47] In a letter dated 17 November 1902, Jones wrote, "Today six young men went out two by two, to the North, to the West, and to the East to preach the Gospel throughout the land."[48] By 1903, the small congregation appointed four evangelists and supported them with a salary of Rupees three each. Starting in 1910, a group of Mizo evangelists employed by a certain Mr. Watkin Roberts were sent across the border to Manipur and Tripura, becoming cross-cultural evangelists. The contributions of this group will be dealt with while discussing mission work in Manipur and Tripura.

A series of revivals starting with the effect of the Welsh Revival of 1904 became most instrumental in converting the whole Mizo tribe to Christianity. The first revival in the series began in 1907, the second in 1913, the third began in 1919 lasting for about a decade, and more or less overlapped with the fourth which began in the early 1930s. The revivals helped to convert all the Mizos into Christianity, and also indigenized Christianity, bringing about a distinctly Mizo

---

[44] *Census of India 1991, Series-1 India, Paper 1 of 1995, Religion,* p.xvii.

[45] P. T. Philip, *The Growth of Baptist Churches in Nagaland,* Gauhati: Christian Literature Centre, 1976, pp.140-169.

[46] For a biography of Robert Arthington Jr. and a brief story of the Arthington Aborigines Mission, see Lalsangkima Pachuau, "Robert Arthington, Jr. and the Arthington Aborigines Mission," *Indian Church History Review* 28, No. 2, December, 1994, pp.105-125.

[47] Saiaithanga, *Mizo Kohhran Chanchin,* p.16.

[48] Quoted in J. M. Lloyd, *History of the Church in Mizoram (Harvest in the Hills),* Gospel Centenary Series No. 1, Aizawl: Synod Publication Board, 1991, p.57.

Christianity.[49] Teams of lay converts affected by revivals went about sharing their revival-experience with their fellow-tribe members spreading Christianity from village to village. In a matter of about sixty years, the whole of the Mizo tribe is considered to have become Christian.[50]

There are a few distinct tribes in the southernmost part of Mizoram among whom two mission agencies operated. While the Baptist Missionary Society undertook its work among the Lai people, a third mission society undertook its work among a distinct Lakher (also called Mara) tribe since 1907. This mission agency, named Lakher Pioneer Mission, was started by its pioneer missionary R. A. Lorrain, the brother of the Baptist pioneer missionary, J. H. Lorrain. The former began the society on the advice and support of the latter. R. A Lorrain and his wife started to work among the Lakher tribe from 1907, and the Church they established came to be called the 'Independent Church of Maraland'. Following a major split in the church, the larger group which has the majority members, came to be called the 'Evangelical Church of Maraland'. A large part of the Lai churches established by the Baptist missionaries has also withdrawn from the Mizoram Baptist Church, now organising themselves under the name Isua Krista Kohhran Lairam (IKKL).

Manipur

The two princely states of the region of Northeast India during the British Colonial rule, namely Tripura and Manipur, did not welcome missionaries. While missionaries managed to enter Manipur with great difficulty, Tripura remained close. William Pettigrew, the pioneer missionary in Manipur, was from the Arthington Aborigines Mission. He entered Manipur in February 1894 and started his work among the Meitei people (the non-tribal residents of the Manipur valley). Pettigrew changed his denominational affiliation from Anglican to Baptist before he entered Manipur. Due to impending opposition from the Meitei Hindus, the British Political Agent asked Pettigrew to move to the hills, and he worked among the Tangkhul Nagas from 1896. By this time, Pettigrew had joined the Baptists and the American Baptist Mission had adopted him as its missionary and Manipur as its field.[51] Slow and steady was the progress of mission among the Tangkhuls. The early converts, including some from the Kuki tribes, then took their new faith to their people. Because of his political and secular activities, such as helping in the census, and serving as a commissioned officer of the British army during the First World War,[52] Pettigrew was unable to do much mission work. Due to political restrictions, only a few other missionaries were permitted to enter Manipur, and the major evangelistic work was done by the natives. The first Kuki to become a Christian was Ngulhao who is reported to have caused the conversions of at least 334 persons. Similarly, it is also reported that it was the effort of the first Thadou Kuki convert, Nehseh, that the oldest church among the Thadou Kuki came into being.[53] The same was true with the Zeliengrong Nagas and

---

[49] For a detailed treatment of the revivals and their contribution to Mizo Christianity, see Lalsangkima Pachuau, *Ethnic Identity and Christianity: A Socio-Historical and Missiological Study of Christianity in Northeast India with Special Reference to Mizoram*, Frankfurt am Main: Peter Lang, 2002, pp.111-143.

[50] Saiaithanga, *Mizo Kohhran Chanchin*, p.21.

[51] Lal Dena, *Christian Missions and Colonialism: A Study of Missionary Movement in Northeast India with Particular Reference to Manipur and Lushai Hills 1894-1947*, Shillong: Vendrame Institute, 1988, pp.33-35.

[52] *Ibid.*, pp.37, 39.

[53] Th. Lamboi Vaiphei, *Advent of Christian Mission and Its Impact on the Hill-Tribes of Manipur*, n.p: The Author, 1997, pp.63-65.

Mao Nagas of the northern and northwestern part of Manipur.[54] Large-scale growth of Christianity among these tribes took place after the First World War.

As mentioned above, an independent missionary agency named Thadou-Kuki Pioneer Mission, founded by Watkin Roberts with the help of Mizo Christians, came to work in South Manipur. This new undenominational agency was "manned entirely by native workers" mainly sent from Mizoram, and established itself in the area.[55] At one time, it clashed with the American Baptist Mission, but when it became clear that the American Baptist Mission could not look after the area, the tension was resolved. When this new mission agency extended its work to the neighbouring states of Assam and Tripura, it changed its name to North-East India General Mission (NEIGM), in 1919.[56] However as conflict and dissension arose within the mission, and further clashes erupted with other Protestant missions due to the allegation of a breach of comity agreement, the NEIGM could not continue its work. In 1922, the mission was suspended from the comity of Protestant Foreign Missions in Bengal and Assam.[57]

Tripura and Arunachal Pradesh

The two states have a certain commonality and will be treated together. The two states have received the most missionary attention from other states of the region, in recent decades. Christians are small in number, there has been significant progress in church growth. These two states have

experienced vehement opposition to missionary activities at different points of time.

As said before, the state of Tripura has the least number of Christians in Northeast India mainly because the state did not permit missionaries until 1938.[58] The earliest Christian presence in the state, and subsequent mission work, began with Mizo immigrations to the northern border area of the state in the early part of the twentieth century. The first Mizo immigrants were non-Christians, and a team of Mizo evangelists frequented the village, resulting in a gradual conversion of the villagers. A good number of the second group of immigrants, including the Chief himself, were Christians. From this group of Mizo Christians emerged the pioneer missionaries to the other tribal groups of Tripura.[59] A missionary ('evangelist'), supported by the Mizo Christians, started evangelistic work among the Darlong tribe in 1917. The North-East India General Mission (NEIGM), whose early story we have narrated above, sent its missionary to work among the Mizo immigrants in 1918, and among the Darlong tribe in 1919. Other missionaries of NEIGM followed, and most of them became pastors and teachers.[60]

In the meantime the New Zealand Baptist Mission, which was working across the border in present day Bangladesh, succeeded in gaining permission to work in Tripura in 1938, and it immediately established a mission station near Agartala.[61] Gathering a small number of Christians, about one hundred in number, mainly

---

[54] *Ibid.*, pp.68-82.

[55] Lal Dena, *Christian Missions and Colonialism*, p.51.

[56] For a detailed treatment of the NEIGM, see Th. Lamboi Vaiphei, *Advent of Christian Mission*, p.51.

[57] Lal Dena, *Christian Mission and Colonialism*, p.53.

[58] M. J. Eade, "Golden Jubilee – Tripura Baptist Christian Union," *Tripura Baptist Christian Union: Golden Jubilee Souvenir, 1938-1988*, Agartala: Tripura Baptist Christian Union, 1988, pp.10-12.

[59] Z. Lianthanga, *Tripura a Kohhran lo din tanna leh Chanchintha a darh zel dan*, Vanghmun: Jampui-Sakhan Baptist Association, n.d. [1996], pp.4-6.

[60] *Ibid.*, pp.8-23.

[61] Eade, "Golden Jubilee," p.12.

Garos and Kukis residing in the state, the New Zealand Baptist Mission formed the Tripura Baptist Christian Union (TBCU) in December 1938.[62] Until the last missionary left Tripura in the early 1970s, TBCU was led by the New Zealand Baptist Mission. The Darlong Church joined TBCU in 1940,[63] and the Mizo Church, then called Jampui Presbytery, in 1944.[64]

The present Arunachal Pradesh, known in the past as North East Frontier Agency, has a long but insignificant interaction with Christian mission activities. Its remote location, ethno-linguistic diversity, and difficult accessibility for outsiders have prevented it from significant interaction with outsiders including Christian missions. The so-called 'Chinese aggression' of 1962 resulted in drawing the attention of the Indian government to the state leading to an unprecedented effort to develop the state economically. Beginning in the 1960s, but especially in the early 1970s, notable conversion to Christianity took place among the Adi and Nishi tribes. Christianity and the modernizing (or westernizing) tendency associated with it was considered by some, especially among the Adis, as a threat to their traditional identity. As a reaction to Christian conversion, the Adi Cultural and Literary Society came into being vowing to preserve, consolidate, and develop indigenous culture. This was followed by the formation of other similar organisations to protect indigenous culture and

promote tribal welfare.[65] The development contributed to Christian persecutions which intensified in the 1970s. Churches reported numerous kidnappings and torture of Christians, dispossessions of their belongings and burning of their houses.[66]

Elsewhere in India, two North Indian states, namely Orissa and Madhya Pradesh, enacted what may be called anti-conversion acts called Freedom of Religion Acts, and were involved in legal defence of the Acts in the Supreme Court.[67] The legal battle ended with the Supreme Court's judgement made in 1977. A year before this judgement, i.e., 1976, a state-level cultural conference was organised in Arunachal Pradesh by the Adi Cultural and Literary Society. The conference demanded Indigenous Faith Protection legislation, and the subsequent proposed bill was very similar to those in Orissa and Madhya Pradesh. Two years later, the Arunachal Pradesh State Assembly passed the 'Indigenous Faith Bill',[68] with a slight change in the concept of conversion. Conversion, according to this new Bill, includes a renouncing of indigenous faith and adopting another faith or religion. Among the various indigenous faiths listed, Buddhism and the Hindu (Vaishnava) sect are included.[69] The inclusions of such well-known non-indigenous faiths attest the religious motive behind the anti-Christian cultural revival movement. The *Rashtriya Svayamsevak Sangh* (RSS) and other Hindu fanatic groups are thought

---

[62] Hnehliana, "Tripura Baptist Christian Union," *Tripura Baptist Christian Union: Golden Jubilee Souvenir, 1938-1988*, Agartala: Tripura Baptist Christian Union, 1988, p.59.

[63] Lianthanga, *Tripura a Kohhran* , p.7.

[64] Eade, "Golden Jubilee," p. 2.

[65] Atul Chandra Talukdar, "Tribal Cultural Revival in Arunachal Pradesh," in *Impact of Christianity on North East India*, edited by J. Puthenpurakal, Shillong: Vendrame Institute Publications, 1996, pp.486-87.

[66] *Ibid.*, p.488.

[67] For a discussion on these legal conflicts and the subsequent outcome, see Lalsangkima Pachuau, "Ecumenical Church and Religious Conversion: A Historical-Theological Study with Special Reference to India," *Mission Studies* XVIII-1, No. 35, 2001, pp.190-92.

[68] Talukdar, "Tribal Cultural Revival," p.488.

[69] Solomon Doraisawmy, *Christianity in India: Unique and Universal*, Madras: The Christian Literature Society, 1986, p.104.

to be behind the anti-Christian movement and persecutions.[70]

Roman Catholic Church in Northeast India

Because the Roman Catholic Church in the Northeast has no particular region of operation, especially after Independence, a specific account of its work and expansion, albeit briefly, is considered imperative. The Catholic presence in the Northeast dated the earliest, but those were temporary in intention and nature. The first missionary society assigned specifically for the region was The Foreign Missionaries of Milan (PIME), and the missionaries of this society reached Guwahati in 1872, but due to a jurisdiction dispute, no tangible work was done. From 1889, mission work in the entire region of Northeast India was assigned to the German Society of Catholic Education, popularly known as Salvatorians.[71] It was the Salvatorians, in the words of F. S. downs, who began "Catholic missionary work proper."[72] During the First World War, the German Salvatorians were repatriated, and the work was entrusted temporarily to the Belgian Jesuits (1915-1922) until charge was handed over to the Salesians of Don Bosco, in 1922. The Salesian Brothers were joined by Salesian Sisters in 1923.[73]

While numerical growth of Christians was slow under the Salvatorians,[74] we began to see the pace of growth picking up with the Jesuits,[75] and a major growth from the first decade of the Salesians' work.[76] Until the Independence of India, Catholic mission work was confined almost exclusively to present day Assam (or Assam plains) and Meghalaya. Spectacular growth has been experienced by the Catholic Church in Northeast India after the Independence of India. Some new Orders joined the effort, strengthening the work together with diocesan clergy. In 1945 (after the Second World War, but before Independence), there were 70,194 Catholic Christians who increased to 713,837 in 1990.[77] From the Assam plains and Meghalaya, the Catholic Church soon moved out to Manipur and Nagaland, where it has been enjoying rapid growth.

Churches' Missionary Activities Today

In a popular Prayer Guidebook entitled *Operation World: The Day-by-Day Guide to Praying for the World*, the author, Patrick Johnstone commented enthusiastically on the Mizo people. He said, "No nation on earth has sent out a higher proportion of their people as missionaries. There may now be nearly 1,000 Mizo missionaries serving in other parts of India and beyond."[78] There may in fact be more than 1,000 missionaries sent out and supported by the Mizo Churches at present, although we do not exactly know if that number, out of a population

---

[70] *Ibid.*, p.104ff.

[71] George Kottupallil, "A Historical Survey of the Catholic Church in Northeast India from 1627 to 1969," in *The Catholic Church in Northeast India, 1890-1990*, Shillong: Vendrame Institute; Calcutta: Firms KLM Pvt. Ltd., 1993, pp.31-35. While Kottupallil calls the Salvatorians 'German Society of Catholic Education,' other writers including F. S Downs call it 'Society of the Divine Saviour'.

[72] Downs, *History of Christianity in India*, p.92.

[73] Kottupallil, "A Historical Survey of the Catholic Church," pp.36-53

[74] *Ibid.*, p.41.

[75] Downs, *History of Christianity in India*, p.105.

[76] There were 5488 Catholic Christians in 1922 when Salesians took over. The number increased to 24,459 in 1933. See Kottupallil, 50.

[77] Downs, *History of Christianity in India*, p.120.

[78] Patrick Johnstone, *Operation World: The Day-by-Day Guide to Praying for the World*, Grand Rapids, MI: Zondervan Publishing House, 1993, p.286.

of about 700,000 people,[79] represents the highest proportion in the world. Although our description will highlight that the Mizos' contribution is unique even among the churches in the region of Northeast India, churches in other states of the region have also been making significant contributions to the entire Christian missionary effort. As described before, in the history of the evangelization of the region, the indigenous people played an immeasurable role. Passion for mission is ingrained in the very lifeblood of the region's Christianity, and almost all denominations take the mission task seriously.

The history of Northeast India after the Independence of India has been plagued by various political insurrections.[80] With a variety of political, a number of so-called 'insurgent groups' have 'revolted' against the government of India. The insurgency and the counter-insurgency measures have brought immeasurable sufferings to the people. From state to state, foreign missionaries were expelled and banned as they were suspected to have played clandestine roles in these movements. From the early 1970s, no foreign missionaries were permitted in the region. This turn of events has challenged, and even compelled, the churches to continue and enhance indigenous missionary endeavours. It forced the churches to be self-supporting and self-governing and moved them to selfhood and self-propagation. The missionary zeal displayed from the beginning received new impetus as concerted missionary efforts among the churches came to be made after foreign missionaries left the region.

In Mizoram, all the four Protestant churches we have described above, namely the Mizoram Presbyterian Church (of the Presbyterian Church of India), the Baptist Church of Mizroam, Evangelical Church of Maraland, and the Isua Krista Kohhran Lairam, have been actively engaging in mission work. From the Presbyterian Church Synod, today there are 845 mission workers (375 so-called 'missionaries' and 470 'native workers' or 'evangelists') working in the various 'mission fields' and also in partnership with other churches or mission agencies. With those undergoing training, and those working in the mission office and training centres in Aizawl, the total number is 968.[81] This number does not include 182 missionaries under the Home Mission project working inside Mizoram among the non-Mizo people.[82] Thus, by the middle of the year 2002, the aggregate of those directly engaging in mission works from the Mizoram Presbyterian Church, is as many as 1027 persons.

According to the official church report of the Baptist Church of Mizoram in March 2002, there are 418 mission workers (187 'missionaries' and 231 'native workers' or 'evangelists'). Of these, 98 missionaries and 44 "native workers" are working inside Mizoram among non-Mizos, and four in the mission office.[83] The Evangelical Church of Maraland (ECM) in the southernmost part of Mizoram has about 62 mission workers

---

[79] The population of Mizoram in 1991 was 689,756. See *Census of India 1991, Series-1, India, Paper 1 of 1992, Vol. 1, Final Population Totals*, New Delhi: Census Commissioner, India, 1992, p.17.

[80] For further study on insurgency and Christianity in Northeast India, see Lalsangkima Pachuau, *Ethnic Identity and Christianit*, pp.29-58, 145-175.

[81] This was according to the report of the Synod Mission Board Coordinator at the 9th Missionary Retreat, May 22-26, 2002. Also see "Mizoram Synod," *Kristian Tlangau* 90, July 2002, pp.2-3. It indicates a slight increase from the grand total of 941 reported in the Synod meeting of December 2001. See "Synod Mission Board Report," *Mizoram Presbyterian Church Synod, Synod Khawmpui Vawi 77-na, 2001: Programmes & Agenda, Appendix & Reports*, Durtlang Kohhran Biak In, Nov. 29-Dec. 9, 2001, p. 72.

[82] "Home Mission Report," Mizoram Presbyterian Church, 2001, p.130.

[83] T. C. Laltlawmlova, "B.C.M. Mission and Evangelism Department Report, 2001-2002," *Baptist Church of Mizoram Assembly 106-na: Report[s]*, Rahsi Veng, Lunglei, March 6-10, 2002, p. 15. Also see the General Secretary's report: K. Thanzauva, "Baptist Church of Mizoram: Annual Report 2001-2002," especially p. 5.

(50 'missionaries' and 12 'native workers') of its own, besides a few others in partnership with the Indian Evangelical Mission. Furthermore, the Church has a vibrant counterpart church in the Myanmar side of the boundary, which has as many as 54 mission workers.[84] Like the ECM, the IKKL also gives its main attention to Myanmar where it works mainly among the Matu tribe. It has as many as 72 missionaries in Myanmar. It also works in the Bangladesh side of the Indian border, and is part of recent joint missionary work in China. In other parts of India, IKKL is working in Manipur in partnership with some native Baptist churches.[85] Beside these four mainline Protestant churches, there are other denominations such as the Salvation Army, the Pentecostals, Seventh-Day Adventist, and other indigenous denominations. Understandably in a lesser degree, most of these churches also engage in mission work. A number of independent non-denominational and inter-denominational mission agencies exist among Mizo Christians, which are also making significant contributions.

Not only do Mizo Churches have relatively more missionaries, their centralized system of church governance has made it easy to know the number of missionaries. Whereas local congregations have the tradition of working in close consonance with the central 'governing' office and abiding by the democratic governance at the centre, the case is different in churches among the Nagas, the Khasis, the Garos, the Kukis and others. Be it the Khasi Presbyterian or the Naga Baptist Church, each congregation is more or less independent, and in some cases the cooperating body functions only as a conciliar body. This has a bearing on the collection of information on their mission activities. At the Synod level of the Khasi Presbyterian Church, and at the Council level of the Baptists belonging to the CBCNEI, there are departments or divisions dealing with mission and evangelism, but the role such departments play is insignificant in comparison with the work done at the local or district level. Thus, we have no consolidated official reports or written documents to depend on, and we have to rely mainly on verbal interviews.

In the case of the Nagas, the Nagaland Baptist Church Council was formed in 1937[86] under which the Home Mission Board was created in 1960.[87] The Home Mission Board was transformed into the Nagaland Missionary Movement (NMM) in 1971[88] to become the representative missionary body of the NBCC. However, many missionaries are not affiliated to NMM, and most congregations engage themselves in mission work independently or as Association (of regional or ethnic churches). At present, the NMM leadership is working on coordinating various missionary activities of individual churches and Associations. In an interview conducted by this author,[89] the present Director of NMM, Hevukhu Achumi, stated that a survey is underway at present and the exact number of missionaries cannot be ascertained yet.

---

[84] These are calculated from the list of mission workers in different places, "Evangelical Church of Maraland: Mission Field Liata Hriatuhpa Zydua Moh List," circulated by the Church.

[85] H. Lalsangliana, "Mission Rawngbawlna Lam," in *Church Unification's Souvenir (IKK-LBK).*, edited by Th. Vanlalzauva et al, Lawngtlai: Isua Krista Kohhran Lairam, 2001, insert pages.

[86] Renthy Keitzer, *The Triumph of Faith in Nagaland*, An NBCC Jubilee Publication, Kohima: Nagaland Baptist Church Council, 1987, p.10.

[87] *Ibid.*, p.33.

[88] *Ibid.*, p.35. The life and works of the NMM from 1970 to the mid-1990s are briefly described in "The Formation of the Nagaland Baptist Council," in *From Darkness to Light* edited by Alongla P. Aier, n.p. Kohima: Nagaland Baptist Church Council, 1997), 117-128.

[89] A telephone-interview on June 29, 2002 around 9:00 A.M. in Bangalore.

Achumi estimated that "more than 300 missionaries and 500 to 600 evangelists [native workers]" are at work in the field, supported by Baptist Churches in Nagaland. Of the "more than 300 missionaries," 56 are missionaries of the NMM, and the rest are sent out and supported by local churches and Associations. A scheme to coordinate all the missionary activities of the churches has been worked out by the NMM,[90] and Achumi said that the organisation is presently working on its implementation. Though few in number, missionaries of the NMM are distributed in many parts of India and abroad. Outside of Nagaland, missionaries of the NMM are working in the states of Assam, Arunachal Pradesh, Sikkim, West Bengal, Orissa, Uttar Pradesh, Andaman and Nicobar Islands, and Andhra Pradesh. Outside India, missionaries are working in China, Nepal, Thailand, Cambodia, Bhutan (the Indo-Bhutan border area) and Hong Kong.[91]

In Manipur, churches under the former NEIGM and Manipur Baptist Convention (MBC) have been actively engaging in mission work, especially among the non-Christian Meiteis in the Imphal valley since the early 1960s. In 1980, the Manipur Baptist Convention appointed a full time "Evangelistic Secretary"[92] to coordinate the churches mission activities. Although MBC as a body has sent out only 15 mission workers, church conventions under MBC are making notable contributions. What one of its leaders reported in 1983 appeared to have bore fruit and

continues to do so. He said, "...the M.B.C. is now operating missionary activities in full swing on its frontiers.... The workers are faithfully sowing the seed of the living Gospel hoping for good germination in due course."[93] Responding to the inquiry of the present author, Paojangam Haokip, the Mission Secretary of the Kuki Baptist Convention, put together statistics of missionaries using the *Annual Report of Manipur Baptist Convention, 2000-2001*.[94] According to these statistics, there are as many as 576 mission workers employed by various churches. Of these, 234 belong to churches under the Manipur Baptist Convention (a member body of the CBCNEI). The remaining 342 belong to various independent churches some of which were the products of the former NEIGM, and the Presbyterian Church in Manipur. The Kuki Baptist Convention has the highest number with 97, followed by Evangelical Baptist Convention (an independent Baptist church not related to the Manipur Baptist Convention/CBCNEI) with 84 mission workers.

To account for the present mission engagement of the Khasi-Jaintia Presbyterian Church is extremely difficult. If one looks at the Synod's report, there is nothing noteworthy. The present enumeration is based purely on an interview[95] with David M. Syiem, Pastor of Khasi Congregations outside Meghalaya in Northeast India, who was assisted by Mr. Lyndan Syiem.[96] David Syiem is considered to be the most knowledgeable person regarding the mission

---

[90] "The Formation of the Nagaland Baptist Council," in *From Darkness to Light*, ed. Alongla P. Aier (n.p. [Kohima]: Nagaland Baptist Church Council, 1997, pp.125-126.

[91] The list, excepting Arunachal Pradesh, was provided by Achumi in the aforementioned interview. Neither Achumi nor the pamphlet issued on the occasion of "Mission Week," May 1-7, 2002 mention Arunachal Pradesh. But the "1997 Mission Field Overview" lists seven missionaries in Arunachal Pradesh. See "The Formation of the Nagaland Baptist Council," in *From Darkness to Light*, p.127.

[92] R. R. Lolly, *The Baptist Church in Manipur*, n.p.: Mrs. R. Khathingla Lolly, 1985, pp.99-103.

[93] *Ibid.*, p.103.

[94] The statistical report was conveyed to this author in the form of an e-letter dated August 16, 2002.

[95] Interview with David M. Syiem and Lyndan Syiem by the author on Sunday July 21, 2002 at the United Theological College, Bangalore, India.

[96] Mr. Lyndam Syiem, a faculty member of Thomas Jones School of Mission and Evangelism, was, at the time of the interview, working on his Master of Theology (Missiology) degree.

work of the Khasi churches. According to David Syiem, there are 40 cross-cultural missionaries sent out by the Synod and churches in the Synod. Nine of these are directly commissioned and supported by the Synod and the remaining 31 by local churches and districts. These missionaries are working in various parts of Assam, Uttar Pradesh, and Nepal. As we have indicated before, more than 30 percent of Meghalayans are non-Christians, and the churches are exerting significant efforts among these people. The two interviewees estimated that not less than 300 mission workers—mainly supported by Presbyteries—are working inside Meghalaya, most of whom are working in the district of Jaintia Hills and the southern region of the state (Bangladesh border area). The interviewees could also identify seven other missionaries working among non-Khasis. Thus, we can estimate that there are about 350 mission workers belonging to the Khasi-Jaintia Presbyterian Church.

There are a number of Protestant churches considered to be "indigenous"[97] in the Khasi-Jaintia area of Meghalaya, among which the Church of God and the Church of Jesus Christ have sent out notable numbers of missionaries. The two interviewees estimated that there are 15 to 20 cross-cultural missionaries and more than 50 workers in the Home Mission from these two churches. As we have said, the Protestant communities in the Garo Hills district of Meghalaya are dominated by the Garo Baptist Church (of the CBCNEI). Indeed, we have previously noted that the Garo Baptist Church has been a mission-minded church from its inception. Although the church leaders have been lamenting lack of continuing enthusiasm in evangelism, it has been making its contributions on a relatively smaller scale.

Concluding Observations

This review of Church-Mission dynamics in Northeast India calls forth a number of observations. First, one is struck by the localized character of mission activity. From the early history of Christianity in the region, as we have narrated above, witnessing the Gospel to neighbours has been strong. Depending on the strength of Christianity in each state, priority was always given first to what is commonly called 'Home Mission' (mission within one's state or territory). When one looks at the overall missionary programme, the main recipient-people of the missionaries' efforts are within the Northeast India region itself. Tripura and Arunachal Pradesh received the highest number, followed by Assam and Manipur. An interesting manner of mission work in the region is the multi-directional traffic of mission work. Although states like Manipur, Tripura, and Assam are the major recipients of missions, missionaries are also sent from these states. The geo-ethnic characters we have described before also play a role here. Missionary work is directed mainly from the Christian hill-tribal-areas to the non-Christian plains-areas. The main exception is the state of Arunachal Pradesh which is the only tribal state in the hills dominated by non-Christian religions.

A second area of interest is the role of Christianity in the 'modernization' or 'Westernization' of the tribal people. Colonial rule, Christianity and education are the main agents of change or modernization of the tribals. The three work in close proximity, and are often confused. While the purpose and functions of the three are definitely different, their impact on the societies and the manner by which they influence the social life of the people are hardly distinguishable. The missionaries' contribution in the field of education is significant. They were the ones who transformed most languages to written form, imparted basic civic sense and duty to the people, and introduced formal education,

---

[97] See O. L. Snaitang, ed., *Churches of Indigenous Origins in Northeast India*, Delhi: ISPCK, 2000.

thereby opening windows of knowledge to the tribal people which have enabled them to interact with the wider world. The missionaries were also given great opportunities. In places like Mizoram, for instance, the colonial government left the entire educational work in the hands of the missionaries. On their part, missionaries, however, gave utmost attention to evangelism, and education was meant mainly for *preparatio evangelica* (or preparation for evangelism). In most cases, Protestant missions gave almost exclusive attention to primary education, the main motive being to help the people read the Bible. While this was effective for evangelism, its inadequacy is felt even today in failing to bring wholistic social development. Mizoram has the second highest literacy rate in the country, but the state is also one of the least developed states economically.

The perceived foreign allegiance of Christians is another factor that should be considered. The national majority blamed Christianity and the colonial heritage for insurgency movements in the region. Many alleged Christian missions played clandestine roles in the secessionist movements in Northeast India. During the last five decades of insurgency in the region, no credible evidence to support such a belief has been produced. In this connection, it is important to recognize the role played by education. Education developed self-consciousness, brought a sense of selfhood and created a desire to progress. The identity consciousness of the culturally and racially distinct people became a major factor in the ethnopolitical movements in the region.

Finally, an observation on the understanding and practice of mission is in order. A cominant militaristic triumphalism permeates the sense of mission among the Christians of Northeast India, which results in a one-sided theory and practice of mission. The exclusivistic understanding of mission as evangelism, and evangelism narrowly-understood as consisting mainly of verbal proclamation, prevailed in the mission enterprise of Northeast Indian Christians. The arrogance of Christian triumphalism that colored a great part of the modern missionary movement of the nineteenth century persists among the mission-minded Christians. The militaristic language and concept dominate the understanding of mission which is viewed as a battle for Christ to conquer new lands as an extension of God's Kingdom. As a battle, mission must be successful, and successful at any price. The emotive conquest-spirit, which suits the mindset of the people who were traditionally warring people, also steers them to an imperialistic mode of mission practice. Thus, the missionary enterprise in Northeast India gives little or no attention to cultural awareness and sensitivity. Most mission literature, lyrics and preaching relate mission with salvation of the lost souls, and Christian mission, above all, is a battle to win the 'lost souls'. Conversion and church planting are dominant as goals of the mission enterprise, and all other activities are used to aid these chief ends of mission. Success of missions is measured according to the number of new baptisms and churches planted. No critical examination or theological reflections are allowed to interfere in the missionary enterprise. One is either engaged in the battle or outside the battle-field. A wide breach between critical theological thinking and mission practice exists, and theological education fails to make connection with the missionary endeavours.

CHAPTER 15

Mission as Transformation:
A Historic Model Among Subaltern and Dalit Communities

SAMUEL JAYAKUMAR

Introduction

This chapter deals with understanding and practice of Christian mission among Indian Dalit and subaltern communities. The purpose of this essay is to help us to increase our understanding of mission and improve our practice in the light of mission history. Firstly, we will consider the importance of the past for practicing Christian mission in the future. Secondly, we will examine transformation as a model for contemporary mission practice among the poor and marginalised.

Importance of the past in view of the future

What lessons do we learn from the Christian past for our understanding and practice of tomorrow's mission? The significance of the question lies in the fact that as always, even today the gospel of Christ has been proclaimed in a pluralistic context and very often in hostile environment. In India right now, a might reaction is building up against Christians. Communal incidents such as setting fire to churches, raping of Christian nuns and the killing of Christian priests and missionaries and converting churches into Hindu temples are Common.[1] According to Professor Robert Eric Frykenberg, nowhere today are threats to Christian survival more serious than in India.[2]

But it is not that persecution of Christians is altogether a new phenomenon. Christian evangelism always took place in the context of persecution and various other struggles.[3] Furthermore, always, the gospel of Christ has to be combating social injustice and oppressive cultures. However, now in this country the outcastes and the tribals no more have the freedom to critique and give up their own traditional oppressive culture.[4] Our struggle for social transformation is becoming much harder, more than ever before. These are some of the reasons why Christians should consider their history seriously in order to learn lessons for carrying out the future missionary responsibilities. According to Eric Sharpe, ever since Luke compiled his orderly account of the

---

[1] Philip Jenkins has rightly observed that? "Fears that Christians might take even deeper inroads among the poorest go far towards explaining the recurrent persecutions and mob violence directed against the churches across India, actions that often occur with the tacit acquiescence of local police and government. Matters have deteriorated sharply since 1997, when the Hindu nationalists enjoyed an electoral upsurge." See P. Jenkins, *The Next Christendom: The Coming of Global Christianity,* Oxford: Oxford University Press, 2002, p. 184.

[2] R. E. Frykenberg, "Christianity in South India Since 1500: Historical Studies of Transcultural Interactions Within Hindu-Muslim Environments," *Dharma Deepika,* Vo.3, No.7, December, 1997, p.3.

[3] Jesus said persecutions are expected while proclaiming the good news of salvation. Mathew 10:16-22; Mark 13:9-13; Luke 21:12-17.

[4] Cf.V.Mangalwadi in G.E.Veith, Jr, *Fascism: Modern and Post-Modern,* Mussoorie: Good Books, 2000, pp.23f. R. E. Hedlund, *India's Churches of Indigenous Origin: Quest for Identity,* Delhi: ISPCK. 2001, pp.92-93.

mission and the ministries of Jesus and his apostles, mission history has been an important discipline.[5]

Scholars and practitioners of mission continue to see the importance of history for articulating contextual theologies while they are aware that tradition and history cannot take the place of the Word of God. But Scripture has to be interpreted in the light of history. Historical experiences not only provide a basis for Christian faith and practice, but also a source for doing theology in context.

> The Christian tradition, embodied in the Scriptures and the history of their interpretation in different ages and places, expresses and carries forward —like the scientific tradition— certain ways of looking at things, certain models for interpreting experience. Unlike science it involves us in questions about the ultimate meaning and purpose of things and human life.[6]

Remembering, retrieving, actualizing and preserving the past is one of the crucial means by which Christian communities can empower themselves. R. E. Frykenberg has rightly pointed out this fact.

> What we call "forgetting", in a collective sense, happens when any community fails to transmit to posterity what its members understands about themselves and events in their past. "Remembering" by enhancing and preserving its own history, is one of the crucial means by which a community empowers itself.[7]

Unless we are aware of our origin (from where we have come) and destiny (to where we are going), we cannot meaningfully live in the present and plan for the future. Without history and traditions we not only lose our roots, but also the route.

On the other hand, there is a tendency to exaggerate the negative side of missionary history. Mission history has been considered as a negative backdrop rather than a positive example.[8] From the turn of twentieth century there has been a growing undue polarization over the meaning of Christian mission. Since the Edinburgh Missionary Conference, the traditional models of missions came under severe criticism, especially, through out the latter half of the century. However those models have to be very carefully studied in order to learn new lessons for the future missionary activities especially among the Two-Thirds world's poor. Often we have to look back and learn from the past history, particularly the interaction of Christian faith with other forces. As Soren Kierkegaard said, "life can only be understood backward but it must be lived forward". Learning from history, especially the history of evangelical involvement is critically important for the mission practitioners in Two-thirds world in the 21st century. According to Wolffe this is possible:

> The evangelical tradition has an objective historical coherence and vigor which means that it can be studied in a focused way without being 'ring-fenced' by tight conceptual separation from the remainder of Christianity. ... The reality is that evangelicalism both influenced and was influenced by the wider experience of professing Christianity, and no history can

---

[5] E. J. Sharpe, "Reflections on Missionary Historiography," *International Bulletin of Missionary Research*, Vol 13, No.2, (April, 1989), p.76. There is a diagnostic view of history for understanding the present problems of the subalterns. Accordingly, for the present maladies, the problem lies in the past. Then, the past becomes relevant for the present. Diagnostic view perceives history as a curative science for it provides solutions for the present crisis.

[6] V. Ramachandra, *Engaging Modernity*, Carlisle: Paternoster, 1996, p.150.

[7] R. E. Frykenberg, *Christianity in South India*, p.3.

[8] S. Jayakumar, *Dalit Consciousness and Christian Conversion: Historical Resources for a Contemporary Debate*, Delhi: ISPCK and Oxford: Regnum, 1999, pp.363ff. There are several reasons why such exaggeration should be avoided. See Kwame Bediako, *Jesus in African Culture*, Accra: Asempa, 1990, pp.5-7.

be properly rounded unless it begins by acknowledging this fact.[9]

Mark Noll's study of the *Nineteenth Century History of Evangelical Christianity from 1792 to 1910* that is from the publication of William Carey's *Enquiry into the Obligations of Christians to use means for the Conversion of the Heathens* to the convening of the World Missionary Conference is worth considering. Noll considers 19th century mission history as a decisive period nothing to equal, which had been seen in the history of the Christian faith. He contends that,

> In grand historical terms, the nineteenth century opened Western evangelicals and evangelical movements to the world. That opening broadened and refined what it meant to be an evangelical. It multiplied occasions for redeeming power and for obfuscating power. It transformed evangelical engagements with culture from a fairly a narrow range of interactions with Western European, British, and North American social and linguistic structures into a bewildering variety of associations with local societies on every continent in the world.[10]

Thus, modern mission history is significantly important, and in the following section we will draw some lessons from it.

Mission as Transformation

The term, development and progress are not suitable to describe the kind of change Christian mission has impacted in some of the societies. In some cultures the gospel of Christ addressed the basic social structures and relationships. *Transformation* is the concept that could cover the all round transformation the Christian mission was intended to bring about.

Transformation is a realistic mission model. It treats society as a real entity stained by personal and social sin. This avoids both the utopian vision of building God's kingdom with all its fullness on the earth and the pessimistic view that the world is un-redeemably evil that results in escapism and disengagement from society.[11] Mission as transformation challenges the evil structures of the world and aims to transform it by the power of the Gospel.

Evangelicals defined *transformation* as "the change from the condition of human existence contrary to God's purposes to one in which people are able to enjoy fullness of life in harmony with God." Its goal is the Biblical vision of the Kingdom of God.[12] For Vinay Samuel "transformation is to enable God's vision of society to be actualized in all relationships: social, economic and spiritual, so that God's will may be reflected in human society and his love be experienced by all communities, especially the poor." [13]

Victorian missionaries as pioneers of the Transformation *model*

The contention of the writer is that the Victorian Protestant Christian missionaries were the first to understand mission as *transformation*. While they had other understandings such as mission as *rescue, light* and *witness*, they were not unaware of a *transformation* model.

The nineteenth century missionaries were increasingly involved in educational activities along with evangelistic work especially among

---

[9]John Wolffe, "Historical Method and Christian Vision," M.Hutchinson and O.Kalu,ed., *A Global Faith: Essays on Evangelicalism and Globalization,* Sydney: Centre for the Study of Australian Christianity, 1998, p.103.

[10]Mark Noll, "Evangelical Identity Power, and Culture in the 'Great' Nineteenth Century," Unpublished Paper, *Oxford Consultation, Currents in World Christianity, July 14ᵗʰ - 17ᵗʰ, 1999,* pp.1, 28.

[11]"Not Development But Transformation," *Mustard Seed,* October, 1983.

[12]Vinay Samuel and Chris Sugden, ed., *The Church in Response to Human Need,* Oxford: Regnum, 1987, p.9.

[13] Vinay Samuel and Chris Sugden, ed., *Mission as Transformation,* pp 227-228.

the poor and oppressed communities. At the same time, in India, the British Raj was educating the Brahmins and upper-castes. While the missionaries concentrated on vernacular preaching, teaching and education, the Raj was concerned about English medium higher education. The aim of the Raj was different from the missionaries. The policy of the Raj was to civilize and educate the elite — to provide an input that would arrest the decline of the great Indian culture.[14] In other words, its intention was to *rescue* the culture from further decline and deterioration. Contrasted with this secular and political solution, the missionaries believed in a Christian answer. While the colonialists aimed at the reformation of society through knowledge, the missionaries desired the transformation of individuals, families and communities through conversion to Christ.

> The aim of Christian mission then is not to civilize aboriginals in the sense of imposing on them a Western way of life or any other way of life that is alien to them. It is rather to draw out the distinctive qualities within them and help these to grow and flower.[15]

Although the missionaries shared the indigenous and colonial view of Indian society as characterized by *kaliyugam*, a culture of despotism and decline, unlike the Raj they did not attempt to retain the so called *sanatan*, 'abiding', primordial civilization.[16] Instead they attempted to transform it into a visible *koinonia*, Christian communities. The first missionaries to South India were, for the most part, committed to their transformational approach because they had a reason for it:

> We may add, that so long as caste and the dispositions fostered by it remain in the native Christian Churches, the 'heathen' [non-Christians] can not but entertain degrading thoughts about Christianity: for they see that the 'rudiments of this world' - a sinful [evil] *Yugam* are retained, not withstanding our proclaiming Christianity to be the only and true way of wisdom. The 'heathen', when they look upon native Christian congregations, cannot say, as the 'heathen' [non-Christians] of old respecting the first Christians - 'see how they love each other!'[17]

The first generation Dalit Christians of South India confessed that, "Christianity has brought us fellowship and brotherhood. It has treated us with respect, and it has given us self-respect. It has never despised us because of our lowly origin, but on the contrary has held us as individuals who are valuable before God and man as any man of any origin."[18] Mission as transformation involved community building. "It is the total commitment to the social community, to build communities, to build and bring change."[19]

[14]T. A. Metcalf, *Ideologies of the Raj*, Cambridge: CUP, 1996, pp.1-27.

[15] MacNaughton, "Foreign Missions and their work among the Tribal People," in M. M. Thomas and W. Taylor,ed., *Tribal Awakening*, Bangalore: CISRS, 1965, p.172.

[16]P. van der Veer, "The Foreign Hand", in C .A. Breckenridge and P. van der Veer, ed., *Orientalism and Postcolonial Predicament*, Philadelphia: UPP, 1993, pp.23-44. T. M. Metcalf, *Ideologies of the Raj*, Cambridge: CUP, 1996, pp.1-27, 66ff.

[17]J. Rhenius, *Memoir of C. T. E. Rhenius* London: James Nisbet, 1841, p.211. Transformational mission was supported not by the British government, but by private Christians. The Missionary societies were happy that the government is not involved in this "holy task." They knew that, it is not the duty of the government to convert the people of India. They rejoiced that pure and impure motives, religious zeal and worldly ambition were not so mixed up. For them the duty of evangelizing India lies at the door of private Christians: the appeal is to private consciences, private effort, private zeal, and private example. Therefore the transformation is a mission carried about by the Church and the government. Eugene Stock, *History of the CMS*, Vol.II, London: CMS, 1899, p.210.

[18] V. S. Azariah, "Open Letter to Our Country Men...," Indian Witness, September 17, 1936, p.598.

[19] Vinay Samuel and Chris Sugden, *Mission as Transformation*, p.231.

The Victorian missionaries gave special attention to building up strong church communities in the mission field. As a result, during the nineteenth century in South India in the areas of missionary work, with the help of the local missionary each of the outcaste villages had its own corporate church life with independent activities: village schools, morning and evening prayer in each village, Bible study and classes for catechumens."[20] The village congregation was a kind of *koinonia*, fellowship of believers devoted to Scripture and worship. It was a community living based in Biblical principles of equality, liberty and fraternity for the all-round advancement of the poor believers.[21]

Mission as transformation involves translating the message into the language and culture of the people.

In some subaltern societies right from the outset, the evangelistic task depended upon preaching the Gospel in the language of the natives. Then, the missionaries had to promote vernacular literacy among them by establishing schools and translating and printing books, pamphlets and Bibles so that they could read them. So the European missionaries first introduced reading and writing among some of the marginalized communities because they did not know it at all.[22] In South India, the missionaries would seem to have preserved native culture by reviving the vernacular, Tamil language, which was at that time in decline.[23] As

Mark Noll contends, in a like manner in many societies the contribution of the missionaries to the vernacular stabilized shaky local cultures so that the natives could nurture and revitalize their cultural identities.[24] Lamin Sanneh concludes that missionaries revived the indigenous cultures of African communities by recovering their vernacular languages.[25] Mission as transformation was understood and practiced by the 19ᵗʰ century missionaries and native leaders. A recent historical study relating to South India makes it clear that, the 19ᵗʰ century missionary contribution to vernacular literacy, training of native leaders, education and health care brought a substantial transformation among the Dalits.[26]

Preaching, an agent of transformation

The missionaries served the people with the confidence that, "if they preach to them, Christ and Him only, in all His fullness of power and love, some measure of success will follow."[27] The result of preaching in the common language was that thousands of poor and oppressed who were ostracized as outcastes used the opportunity to listen to the Gospel, and not only become Christians but to become a people of a new society comprised of small Christian communities.[28]

Furthermore, preaching and the formation of Christian congregations among the Dalits contributed to the emergence of a new alternative Christian society – a kind of community between new Christians and the established power structure. In many ways it was a society counter

---

[20] A. F. R. Bird, "Telegu Mission," 1922-1923, *SPG-DL*, p.6.

[21] Stephen Neill, *Under Three Flags*, p.77.

[22] S.Rajamanickam, "Indian Church History – Problems and Historical methods," *ICHR*, Vol.VIII, No.1, July, 1980, pp.19-22.

[23] See S. Jayakumar, *Dalit Consciousness and Christian Conversion*, pp.159-164.

[24] Mark A. Noll, *The Scandal of the Evangelical Mind*, Michigan: W. B. Eerdmans, 1994, p.251.

[25] For a detailed discussion of this subject see Lamin Sannah, *Encountering the West*, London: Marshall and Pickering, 1993, chapters 2 and 3.

[26] S.Jayakumar, *Dalit Consciousness and Christian Conversion*, pp.151-221.

[27] Bishop Spencer, May 3, 1841, *C/IND*, Madras, Box 11.

[28] S.Jayakumar, *Dalit Consciousness and Christian Conversion*. p.173.

to the then existing violent Brahminical Hindu social order. The outcaste communities who were once considered by society as polluted and fit for nothing, made effective use of Biblical images such as 'New Creation' and 'Sons of God' given by the missionaries to increase their self-worth and dignity which had been denied to them for centuries.[29]

Some of the nineteenth century missionaries who worked in India among the poor and marginalized people did regard themselves as agents of a new creation or agents of social change; and changes were seen in the lives and situation of their converts.[30] For Forrester, the missionaries were 'political radicals' and 'social revolutionaries' who sought social and political revolution without being in the least mindful of the consequences.[31] In fact they were committed to social transformation of society through conversion of people to Christ. They worked with the hope that if persons accepted Christ, they would be better people and their society would progress. As Bishop Neill contended, the missionaries gave themselves to the preaching of the Gospel, in the confidence that 'the moral transformation wrought by the Gospel would in time solve economic and social problems.' [32]

The need then of Dalits was not a false hope or even a positive feeling, but faith and confidence in a tangible personal God, the Saviour who removes guilt, both real and false, such as *karma*. Proclamation of the Gospel provided the poor and the oppressed with a general confidence that life is meaningful and that it was possible to change one's quality of life by one's efforts. Bishop Picket came up with similar a conclusion after undertaking a through study of Dalit conversion movements:

The depressed classes in India are desperately poor. But their chief economic need is not financial; it is an antidote to the poisonous ideas that have made them incapable of struggling successfully with their environment. As severe as is the physical oppression to which they are continuously subjected, the depressed classes could not have been reduced by its operation alone to the low state in which they have lived for centuries. Much more devastating than physical oppression has been the psychological oppression inflicted by the Hindu doctrines of karma and rebirth, which have taught them that they are a degraded, worthless people suffering just retribution for sins committed in earlier lives. It is, then, a true instinct that makes the depressed classes respond more eagerly to the preaching of the Christian Gospel than to any direct ministry to their social and economic ills. The concepts that the Christian Gospel gives them of themselves and of God in relation to their sufferings and sins are worth incomparably more to them than any direct social or economic service the Church could offer.[33]

Christian education as a means of transformation

Education brought the intended inner transformation in the lives of the Dalits. For example, a girl who had been educated in a boarding school had a remarkable influence in her home village. Very often she was the only person in the place who could read, write and sew. She was able to perform many acts of kindness for her village people.[34] The missionaries themselves witnessed the transformation wrought by the schools. Margoschis noted that:

---

[29] S.Jayakumar, *Dalit Consciousness and Christian Conversion*, p.110, 217-218.

[30] G.A.Oddie, *Social Protest*, Delhi: Manohar, 1979, p.19.

[31] D.B.Forrester, *Caste and Christianity*, London: Curzon Press, 1980, pp.24-25.

[32] Stephen Neill, *Under Three Flags*, New York: Friendshp Press, 1954, p.52.

[33] J. W. Picket, *Christ's Way to India's Heart*, Lucknow: Lucknow Publishing Co., 1938, p.173.

[34] A. Margoschis, "A Concise Report of the Mission Districts," *SPG-R*, 1986, p.1-3.

On going to a strange village, not visited before, I have often been able to detect at once a girl who has been educated in the boarding school, for her manner, language, and general appearance is so utterly different to that of the other girls in the same village.[35]

Similarly, Indian leaders such as Bishop Azariah experienced the importance of Christian education for the transformation of Dalit communities. Azariah maintained that rural upliftment and the awakening of outcaste villagers were effected through Christian education. He wrote:

Through Christianity too illiteracy is being chased out of rural India. It was well known that the first thing done for a village which desires to join the Christian Church is to send a resident teacher there to instruct the village in the Christian Faith and open a school for their children. The teacher and his wife – if he has one – are truly the introducers of Light and Learning.[36]

The purpose of education among the outcaste Christians of Dornakal was to empower as well as enlighten the Dalit converts so that they might be restored to personal awareness. Moreover, he wanted the education given to them to prepare them for life, believing that thus trained, Christians would become centres of light wherever they were. Hence he maintained:

Any education given to such people must, we believe, include education to prepare them for life. Our aim then is to produce through this school a new generation of men – men who will not be ashamed of manual labour, men who will be willing to go back to the village with knowledge of some handicraft, and settle down there to earn an honest livelihood and to become centres of light, in their turn, creating a sturdy, self-respecting rural Christian manhood.[37]

Christian education greatly awakened the Dalits' consciousness of the injustice and deceit caused by the caste Hindus. Azariah's co-workers reported that the young adults who learnt to read and write, generally at night schools in due course began to question their Hindu masters about their 'debts' and became aware in many cases of how they had been deceived.[38] Azariah observed that Dalit Christians "on account of integrity, command higher field wages; that Christian labourers are in demand for transplantation and harvesting because they do not require close supervision."

For the most part missionary education gave the Dalits access to new knowledge and fresh information by providing a wider perspective to think beyond the boundaries of their caste and village loyalties, and to become ambitious and adventurous in their lives. Hence a large number of Dalits migrated to Ceylon, Malaysia and Burma to seek better fortunes. Thus mission education introduced the Dalits to a wider world — beyond the Brahmins. It gave them access to new information and power – especially in the areas of Western scientific knowledge that was becoming increasingly important. In the new order of western related knowledge, the missionaries were giving the Dalits an important advantage – at least positioning them alongside the Brahmins if not ahead of them. It opened up new boundaries, horizons and opportunities. Those who were educated by the missionaries became educators, Church workers, government clerks, businessmen and some even became policemen.[39] How otherwise else did people who were told they could only be sweepers get the motivation and notion that they could only be and do something different? The fact that they

---

[35] A. Margoschis, "Nazareth Report," *SPG-R*, (1878), p.345.

[36] V. S. Azariah, "Church in Rural India," *DDM*, Vol.5, No.10, October 1928, p.4.

[37] V. S. Azariah, *SPG-DL*, India 11, February 27, 1930, p.2.

[38] A. F. R. Bird, *Telugu Mission*, p.7.

[39] D. A. Christudhas, *Caldwell Athiyachar,* p.140

went in the new professions as a result is critically important.

Christian higher education prepared the nation for self-rule. As Kumaradhas has pointed out, in South India the education that the missionaries provided actually promoted the elements of political consciousness. At the turn of the century, the emancipated Dalit Nadars, in particular, along with the Christians of upper-caste background, provided leadership to the Christian community in general in the matter of the emerging national politics.[40]

Training the local leaders brings transformation in the larger society

The training and educating of native leaders enabled the outcaste Christian communities to manage their affairs on their own; first in the Church and later in the larger society. Communitarian and congregational life such as worship, prayer and learning together facilitated mutual pastoral care. Also, this enabled them to develop leadership qualities to manage their affairs independently.[41]

As Bishop Neill observed, it was impossible to overestimate the normal service rendered by the native workers and their wives. The husband and the wife together carried out an immense amount of work such as running the village school, conducting morning and evening services, women's fellowship, and Sunday school, apart from guiding and advising their flocks in their problems on regular basis.[42]

Health care illustrates that in general missionaries' practice of mission was wholistic in nature

To this day deaths result in some of the Dalit villages, especially in the rural India where there is no medical dispensary, as a result of inappropriate treatment by untrained native physicians. The absence of good medical care also created the serious problem that local physicians were frequently able to persuade the sick or their relatives to perform local traditional and religious ceremonies to effect cures, in the belief that sickness was caused by the influence of evil spirits.

The fear of ghosts permeated every aspect of the lives of the Dalits. For instance, if a person was sick, according to their custom, success in treating the disease depended upon the observance of the popular saying "|*Noykkum par, peykkum par*". In other words, the patient was not only to be treated for disease but for 'demon-possession.' Every native physician was also a priest who confronted the ghost while he treated the disease with his medicine and magic. This was a common challenge faced by the missionaries.[43]

Introduction of modern medicine and scientific understanding of pestilence and plague, removed the fear of demons among the Dalits, and also contributed positively to their all-round health and well-being.[44]

Conversion leads to social transformation

From what we have seem, the nineteenth century missionaries who worked among the various Dalit and subaltern communities believed in the direct relation between conversion to Christ, new identity and awareness, and social transformation.[45]

At the end of the nineteenth century the models mentioned above, namely, preaching,

---

[40] Y.V. Kumaradhas, "The Swadeshi Movement," *ICHR*, Vol.XXII, No.1, p.5.

[41] S. Jayakumar, *Dalit Consciousness and Christian Conversion*, p.218.

[42] Stephen Neill, *Under Three Flags*, p.107.

[43] A. Margoschis, *Tinnevelli Mission*, p.18.

[44] S .Jayakumar, *Dalit Consciousness and Christian Conversion*, p.218.

[45] *Ibid.*, p.218

education, training of native agents, and medical work, were identified by many missionary societies as the most fruitful ones for transforming the lives of the oppressed communities of South India. The missionaries continued with these methods and so enabled the poor and the oppressed to develop a new consciousness and identity which induced social transformation. This is true of various peoples of the Indian sub-continent.[46] For instance recently a majority of the Malto tribe's conversion to Christ enabled transformation and revitalization of their society.[47] They were converted to experience total transformation; to regain their lost freedom and equality; for deliverance from fear of spirits; desire for moral and dignified life; and desire to return to the higher form of their faith.[48]

Conclusion

Bishop V. S. Azariah reported from his missionary experience that the outcaste believers were a witness to the upper-caste non-Christians outside the church. He wrote that:

> ...the inner change, a change of heart in either the oppressor or the oppressed, could alone permanently change the vicious circle in which the rural life is moved. In some areas testimony has come ...that the non-Christian zamindar, landlords, became friends ... and Christians are treated with respect by caste people who once despised them and called them untouchables.[49]

Consequently at many occasions upper-caste people could witness to the new spiritual joy, hope and the character exhibited by the Dalit Christians. They could sense the change wrought by their conversion to Christ. Even the upper-castes wanted to experience the same change in their lives. Thus the Dalits commended the Gospel to their oppressors.

> They have seen what new spiritual joy and hope and what new strength of character Christianity has brought to their less fortunate neighbours, and they believe that they have found a way of deliverance for themselves from the ignorance and fears and superstitions that have kept them in chains so long.[50]

The above affirmation of the poor believers reveals the observable change ushered in by Christian mission among the people of both low and high caste background. The chief cause of this change in attitude by the high caste people was due to the impression made upon them by the remarkable change in the lives of their outcaste neighbours as a result of their conversion to Christ.

When the Dalit Christians began to live a dignified life the caste Hindus, as well as caste Christians began to change their opinions and attitudes towards the Dalits.[51] Thus a transformed life-style becomes a witness to others. This concurs with the Biblical principle of what is a witness. Peter commended his readers that, "Maintain good conduct among the Gentiles ... they may see your good deeds and glorify God in the day of visitation" (1 Peter 2:12). Commenting on this passage D. Senior and C. Stuhlmueller point out that, "Despite the threat posed by the majority culture, the Christians must be actively involved in society and offer it witness. The substance of this witness is the good deeds of the Christians and

---

[46] Frederick and Margaret Stock, *People Movements in the Punjab*, Bombay: GLS, 1979, p.25.

[47] At present there are about 40,000 Christians among the Malto tribe. For details see M.Raju, "Christianity and Social Transformation of the Maltos of Bihar, India." Unpublished M.A. thesis, All Nations Christian College, Open University, 1995.

[48] E. Sunder Raj, Quoted in *ibid*, p.100.

[49] V. S. Azariah, *Church in Rural India*, Dornakal: Diocesan Press, 1928, p.5.

[50] *Movements Among the Caste Villagers*, p.12.

[51] V. S. Azariah, "A Charge Delivered," 1923, pp.1-24.

their sense of hope."[52] This is the kind of testimony the poor and the oppressed bore to the upper-caste majority.

The twenty-first century ushers in new challenges for mission practitioners for ministry among the Dalits and subaltern communities. The proclamation of the gospel must continue unhindered combined with engaging in socio-economic and political liberation of the Dalits and subaltern communities.

---

[52] D. Senior and C. Stuhlmueller, *The Biblical Foundations for Mission*, p.300.

CHAPTER 16

Mission, Inter-Cultural Encounter and Change in Western India: A Case Study of Local in Relation To Global Church History

MOHAN D. DAVID

The new phenomenon of writing global church history has arisen because mission histories until recently had been written from the western or the metropolitan point of view. But now, since most churches (from about 1950), especially in Asia, are no more organically connected with the western church, it has become imperative to look at the history of Christianity of the nonwestern world and interpret it from the indigenous point of view. This way of writing church history emphasizes the study of the local, regional or national history in its multitude of relationships, and then relates these to the experiences in similar situations elsewhere. In this way it can arrive at generalizations which are able to understand the local from the general and the global perspective. What was so far considered periphery has now become the center. Global church history "will make a synthesis that brings the many local expressions of the church into global relationship."[1]

To say that more Christians live in the former unevangelized continents of Asia and Africa today than in the continents of Europe and American continents accounted for 93 percent of the world Christian's population and the continents of Asia and Africa accounted for 5.2 percent of the world christen population. Now the latter accounts for 29.2 percent, while Europe and the Americas still account for the majority – i.e. 67.2 percent of the world's Christian population.[2]

The mid-twentieth century marks the watershed of modern world history. For the West this meant the end of the political domination over the non-western world. For Asia and Africa this meant the beginning of a new life with the freedom to decide their own destiny. India, after becoming politically free in 1947, adopted a secular, democratic republican constitution and has been striving to build a prosperous society on the model of the West.

In the history of Christianity it has been the same. Up until 1950 the history of Christianity in India was essentially the history of the denominations of the western church, such as the history of the Methodist church in India, the history of the American Presbyterian church in India or the history of the Anglican church and the like. In other words Indian church history was the extension of western church history. But after 1950, with the withdrawal of the foreign missionaries, Indian church history has become indigenous church history. It is on account of this that the Church History Association of India planned to write the history of Christianity in five

---

[1] Wilbert Shenk, "Towards a Global Church History", *International Bulletin of Missionary Research*, 20. 2 April, 1996, p.50.

[2] David Barrett, *World Christian Encyclopedia*, Oxford: Oxford University Press, 1983, p.726.

volumes. Though the first two volumes and some sections of the fourth volume are published, the effort is beset with difficulties to evaluate since we are too near the time and the Indian church is still in the process of adjusting itself to its new responsibilities. In some respects the Indian church seems to be drifting for want of spiritual leaders and lack of vision. It is still groping in the dark because it has not succeeded in changing its inherited attitudes and inhibitions in order to be free to innovate and take a leap forward.

Christopher Columbus was unfortunate to die without enjoying the benefit of his momentous discovery. The American continent should have been rightfully named after him, but someone else was given the underserved honor. Sixty years later when Charles V was glorifying over his Spanish empire in the Americas, Francisco Lopez Gomara whispered in to the emperor's ear that outside of the divine creation of the universe and the coming of the Lord Jesus Christ into the world, the greatest event in human history was the discovery of the new continent by Columbus. That interpretation of the discovery made by Columbus triggered the imagination of the Spanish king and Columbus was at once raised to a high level of fame and glory, but it was too late; the great discoverer was already in the grave. But he was given recognition, even in its true creative perspective and this changed the entire understanding of the significance of what Columbus had done. A historian has to creatively interpret and connect the facts and put them in proper perspective so that the historical significance of an event receives its due recognition in the chain of events that have shaped the course of human history.

One of the serious handicaps of the historian's craft, unlike that of an economist or sociologist, is his dependence on the availability of sources. One can write a fairly authentic history of Christianity in India by sitting in London or in New York because most of the missionary archives are situated in these two countries. But for writing the history of Christianity in India of the past fifty years, I doubt whether the same thing can be said. In the Indian church we have yet to develop an understanding of the significance of maintaining church archives. When I was president of the Church History Association of India (CHAI), we made an effort to conscientize the church authorities regarding the need for the preservation of church records, but I do not think we succeeded.

Indian Church History in the Global Context

Writing the history of Christianity in India in the global context means to emphasize the need to write local, regional and national church history. In many parts of India scientific local or regional history has not been attempted. For example, so far there has been no comprehensive history of Christianity in Maharashtra; but there are some aspects in the history of Christianity in Maharashtra that have national and global significance.

Maharashtra provided to be the hardest ground in the whole of India for the gospel. The strongest and sustained opposition to Christianity came from Maharashtra, mostly from the Brahmin community. Maharashtra produced most of the outstanding Brahmin leaders of India, even more than Bengal.

Maharashtra was the only state in India that was ruled by the Brahmins for over a century before the British captured it in 1818. The Brahmins who had been the rulers, administrators and leaders of the society- both in the secular and religious spheres – greatly resented the fact that the British had usurped the political power from them. Poona Brahmins were the harshest critics and the worst opponents of British rule, and were treated with much contempt by the dominating Brahmins. Untouchability is the lowest depth to which the degradation of a human being can be carried. To be poor is bad but not so bad as to be untouchable. The poor can rise above their status. An untouchable cannot, said Dr. Ambedkar.[3] The two staunchest depressed class protestors against Brahmin dominated Hindu social system rise from Maharashtra.

The renaissance, reformation and enlightenment which Western Europe had gone through made Europe the harbinger of modernization. The industrial revolution and the new technology, together with the progressive ideas of nationalism and liberalism released by the French revolution had made Europe the leader of the new or the modern era. Colonialism helped Europe attain hegemony in the world. Western civilization built on the basis of the Greco – Roman and Judaeo – Christian civilization was recharged by the spirit of renaissance and reformation. It had totally modernized and transformed medieval Europe. The British rulers and the Christian missionaries brought this effervescent and dynamic civilization to India.

India never produced its own renaissance or reformation. Asia, says Sinai, "has never given birth to those political and social revolutions which have inaugurated a new epoch of civilization, which have changed the lives, the habits and values of whole peoples. Asian history is the history of being inert, being without sufficient resilience to defy destiny. It experienced no dramatic turning points in its history, no new social forces arose to alter the destinies and outlook of its peoples."[4]

India at the time of the advent of the British rule and the missionaries was still a medieval society with a feudal economy. Its society, untouched by the transforming effect of any revolution suddenly had this conclusive experience and was forced to begin the process of modernization. In India, this modernization revolution came like an avalanche on the Hindu social system and the Hindu society.

In history, time and space are of great significance. In India the ninteenth century was the time when the missionaries brought the gospel. While being the severest critics of the Hindu society, missionaries introduced western education which opened Indian minds to the spirit of renaissance and reformation and the ideas of the enlightenment. This was responsible for the change.

The coming of the British and the missionaries was considered providential by both. Missionaries felt that God had provided them the opportunity to Christianize the people of Asia and Africa. Initially the Indian response to the gospel was positive, and Alexander Duff was able to convert some upper castes and Brahmins in Calcutta. This initial response made many feel, including the British officials, that India would soon become Christian. It was also believed that if the Brahmins who occupied the top positions in the social hierarchy were converted, the rest of the Indian society would follow. But the greatest opposition came from the Brahmins and they turned away from Christianity. At the same time they were the first to benefit by the educational efforts of the missionaries.

Many Indian leaders, especially from Maharashtra, such as Ranade, Gokhale, and Chandavarkar considered the British rule as Godsent for the renewal and strengthening of Indian society. The role of the missionaries in the reawakening of Indian society was no less significant. M. N. Srinivas, a renowned sociologist, in his book *Social Change in Modern Indian* states that "Evangelical Christianity is regarded characteristically western, and it is indisputable that Christian missionaries played a crucial role in India's modernization".[5] The missionaries were quick to pounce on the evils of Hindu society and to denounce them in order

---

[3] B.R. Ambedkar, *Writings and Speeches* , Vol. V., Bombay: Unpublished writings, 1989, pp.411-412.

[4] I.R. Sinai, *The Challenge of Modernization*, New York, 1964, p.45

[5] M.N. Srinivas, *Social Change in Modern India*, Los Angeles, 1967, p.52

to prove the superiority of the gospel. The social evils included sati, child marriages, prohibition of widow marriage, the dowry system, and the seclusion of women, female infanticide and the caste system.

This was the first time that Hinduism faced such a blatant attack and found itself defenseless. The British government did not want to interfere with the socio-religious life of the people. Even the social legislation like the abolition of sati was introduced by the government under pressure from missionaries and leading Hindus like Ram Mohan Roy. It is this severe encounter between Hinduism and the gospel brought by the missionaries that was responsible for generating the forces of reform and modernization of the Indian society.

Nevertheless, the entire credit for ushering the process of modernization of the Hindu society cannot be attributed to the missionaries alone. Western education, which introduced the ideas of rationalism and liberalism, also played a significant role in the process of Indian modernization. It alone, however, could not have created this change, what forced Hindu society to rethink its socio-religious practices were the fear of the missionary and the superiority of Christian teachings. Ram Mohan Roy, who opposed conversion, was greatly enamored of the teachings of Christ. He believed that the teachings of Christ, if adopted by Indian society, would be the best for the progress of the Hindu society and advocated it in his book *Precepts of Jesus: A Guide to Peace and Happiness.*

How to Assess the Work of Christian Missions?

If one has to assess the success or failure of the Christian missions in India or in Maharashtra in terms of the number of converts to Christianity, the picture tends to be a rather pathetic one. After 150 years of missionary efforts in India, Christians constitute only 2.32 percent of the

population; in the whole of Asia Christians constitute 9 percent, while in Africa Christians constitute 48 percent, and Christianity continues to grow in Africa.[6] But if Christian missions are assessed in terms of a leavening effect, the result is mind-boggling. The magnitude of this success has not been adequately emphasized. Normally mission work has been evaluated in terms of the number of converts gained. The leavening work has been evaluated in terms of the number of converts gained. The leavening effect can be seen in the transformation of Indian society the Christian missionary work was able to bring about.

Three responses

The missionary criticism of Hindu society, together with the enlightenment spread by western education, produced three responses from Indian society. The first was progressive, the second was reactionary and the third manifested itself in the emergence of the movement for the emancipation of the low castes.

The leaders of the progressive movement took the missionary criticism of the Hindu society positively and tried to reform and purify the social system as they found. The missionaries rightly pinpointed the Hindu practices that were irrational, even inhuman, and not based on the Hindu scriptures. The first such reform movement in Mahrashtra was the Paramahansa Mandali, a secret society founded by the upper castes. It was a weak movement since the leaders did not have the courage to come out openly with their reformist ideas. When their names were published the members disbanded the society for fear of social ostracism. Prarthana Samaj was begun in Bombay in 1867 by the leading upper caste Hindu reformers led by Mahadev Govind Ranade, the greatest Indian leader between the time of Ram Mohan Roy and Mahatma Gandhi. No important event took place in Maharashtra without his

---

[6] *World Pulse*, Wheaton: World Pulse.33. 10. May 15, 1998, p.6

knowledge. The Sarvajanik sabha, founded in 1870 in Poona, and of which he became a guiding spirit, looked after the social, economic and political regeneration of the society in Maharashtra. Because of the success it achieved, A.O. Hume thought of organizing the first session of the Indian national congress at Poona, but it had to be shifted to Bombay at the last moment because of the outbreak of plague. Hume founded the national social conference in 1887 to discuss social reform questions, since the congress decided to discuss only political matters. Ranade believed that social progress would enable India to achieve its political goals.

Ranade was a religious man, and like Ram Mohan Roy wanted Hinduism to be reformed and freed from its corrupt practices. Ranade did not go to any mission school, but the deep influence of Christianity on his life and thinking was obvious. His object was to humanize, spiritualize and liberalize Hindu society. Though he did not acknowledge Christian influence openly, he had made a good personal study of the Bible and his devotional and personal life clearly indicated the deep influence of Christian teachings. His younger colleague Justice Chandavarkar mentions that he, Ranade and Telang read from the Bible every day and even preached from the verses in the New Testament at some of annual meetings of the Prarthana Samaj.[7] Justice Telang in a conversation with Justice Chandavarkar stated: "I remember the time when the older generation of our students read the Bible more carefully than is now the case. Take our friend Ranade, for instance. He has the Bible at his fingers' ends as it were".[8]

Justice Chandavarkar, President of the National Social conference, paying tribute to the missionary efforts for bringing change in the Indian society stated: "it is now the fashion in some quarters to cry down the missionary....if today there is an awakening among us on the subject of religion and society, that is a great deal due to the light brought by him....To the Christian missionary...is due to a great extent the credit of the religious and social awakening of which the school of hindoo Protestantism of the present day is the fruit".[9] This group of progressive leaders, who also included R.G. Bhandarkar, P.B.M. Malabari and G.K. Gokhale, believed that British rule was providential. Malabari, the champion of the Age of Consent bill, openly acknowledged his indebtness to Dr.John Wilson, the most outstanding missionary and orientalist ever to come to western India. Malabari wrote: "how much we owe to Christian missionaries! We are indebted to them for the first start in the race of intellectual emancipation. At a time when doubt and distrust are taking the place of reasoned enquiry among the younger generation of India, I feel bound to acknowledge the benefits I have derived from contact with the spirit of Christianity".[10]

The second response to the missionaries was reactionary and conservative. It was anti-Christian and anti-British. The leaders of this group gave first preference to political reforms and opposed the efforts of the progressive group. They included Vishnubua Brahmachari, Vishnushastri Chiplunkar, and B. G. Tilak. Chiploonkar was the bitterest critic of the missionaries and conversion. He ridiculed the missionaries in general, and John Wilson in particular in his book of essays called *Nibandhmala*. He and Tilak opposed the British and condemned conversion.

---

[7] N. G Chandravarkar,. *Speeches and Writings*, Bombay, 1911, p.331

[8] *Ibid.*

[9] *Ibid*, 43-45.

[10] *Dnyanodaya,* Ahmednagar: Dnyanodaya, 1920, p.34.

The third response was one from the depressed classes, or the low castes, who found for the first time some outside intervention favouring their liberation. The person who led the movement was Jotirao Phule, a product of the Scottish mission school in Poona. He modeled his work of running schools for the low castes and women on the kind of work the missionaries carried on in Poona and Ahmednagar. Phule did not favour conversion to Christianity. He was the first leader in India to be called a Mahatma (Great soul) and Gandhi was the second.

Change of Worldview of Christians and Hindus

The missionary visit to a village often was the most important event in the history of the village, exposing the villagers to a foreigner for the first time in centuries. The missionary work in Maharashtra was responsible for reorienting the worldview not only of the newly emerging indigenous Christian communities but also of the Hindu community; this was because the missionary worked both among the masses in the villages and among the elites in the cities. This is perhaps the most significant achievement of the inter-cultural encounter in 19th century Indian society.

The religious life of the indigenous Christians changed their mode of worship, their ethical and moral values, and their attitudes to others; indeed, their very purpose of life underwent a change which in turn changed their worldview. Christians living in even the remotest villages in India became a part of the world Christian community. Some Indian Christians were sent abroad. Their close contact with the missionaries further helped to globalize their outlook. It was to the missionaries that they looked for direction and financial assistance. This was more true in the case of those who worked in the missions or the mission institutions.

It was in the missionary educational institutions that the deepest and most successful inter-cultural encounters took place, encounters which changed the views and attitudes of all those who attended the missionary schools. It was in the missionary schools that the minds of the students were stimulated to think, and seeds of new ideas were sown by criticizing the inhuman and irrational social and religious practices in Indian society – even while the students studied secular subjects. Education became the most powerful instrument of changing the worldview of the Hindu community. To this may be added the writings and periodicals published by the missionaries. In fact, the pioneering contribution of missionaries to the growth of modern Indian language and to Indian journalism is widely acknowledged.

Mission histories tend to gloss over the very significant contributions made by the mission hospitals in changing the worldview of the Indian people. The mission hospitals were not only important centers of healing but also served as the places where the gospel was best preached in practise. One of the best examples of inter-cultural encounter that helped to change the worldview was the proclamation issued by the ruler of Kolhapur, removing the discrimination based on the caste. In this he was guided by his observation of the practices in the mission hospitals at Miraj where patients, irrespective of their caste and creed, were made to share rooms. A Brahmin and a low caste patient sleeping side by side was inconceivable, but it happened.

Attitudes towards Human Suffering

The missionary work in alleviating the sufferings of victims of famine, plague and other calamities and their attitude of compassion to all kinds of suffering changed the Hindu approach and attitude to suffering. In Hinduism, according to the law of Karma, it is necessary for a person to suffer in order to atone for the bad deeds of the past life and so to make one's soul free from Karma and to attain the final bliss. Even the sufferings of a low caste person were explained away in the same manner.

This entire concept and attitude of a Hindu to human suffering changed under the influence of the gospel. Hindu reform organizations took up plague and famine relief work, like the missionaries. They even took up educational and medical work on the model of the missionary institutions.

The most significant achievement of missionaries came in changing the Hindu attitude to the low castes. By befriending the low castes and by treating them as equal human beings and children of one God, the missionaries showed the way. It took time to change the Hindu view, but change certainly did take place. Most Hindu reformers spoke against caste discrimination but did not practice it. Gandhi was the greatest champion of the untouchables. But India had never experienced such silent social convulsion and revolution which the missionary was able to bring about in the society.

Hindu social reformers and leaders in modern Mahrashtra as well as other regions of India began to establish institutions on the model of mission institutions in order to steal the thunder from the mission work. Such institutions undertook to carry on the same kind of educational, medical, social upliftment and other welfare and humanitarian work which the missions had undertaken. The social reform organizations in Maharastra such as Prarthana Samaj, Satyashodhak Samaj, Deccan Education Society, Sarvajanaik Sabha and all-India Organizations like Brahmo Samaj, Arya Samaj and Ramakrishna Mission patterned their organization and work on the model of the Christian missionary institutions.

The Movement to Remove Untouchability

Let me illustrate the extent of the impact of inter-cultural encounter of Christianity with Hinduism in the mammoth movement for the removal of untouchability, a movement which to be one of the most significant achievements in the process of the modernization of the society.

Under the impact of the educational work of the missionaries in Maharashtra – even in the remotest villages – two major movements developed. One was the social reform movement started by the upper castes known as Prarthana Samaj which rejected Caste system, advocated inter-dining among caste groups, worship of one God, rejection of idol worship and education of women. It conducted its organization on the model of a missionary organization. At its meetings it conducted prayers, sang songs and even at times sermons were preached from the Bible. But when it came to practice the members failed as their family members rejected their objectives. This upper caste reform movement, though it fought against social evils, left a wide gap between what it preached and what it practised. Its success with regard to the removal of caste distinctions was minimal, while in other matters it was influential. It also attracted liberal intellectual leaders and reforms of Maharashtra.

A second movement which exclusively devoted itself to the upliftment of low castes was founded by Jotirao Phule, who himself came from the low caste. It needed a great deal of courage, vision and determination to launch a movement to defy, oppose and fight against the existing oppressive system. Phule could not have started his movement if the socio-political conditions had not changed under the influence of the British government and of the ideas of equality propagated by the missionaries.

Phule, while still a student at the Scottish mission school in Poona, learned his first lessons of he equality of all human beings as children of God and came to realize the injustice of the caste system. He was influenced by Thomas Paine's *The Rights of Man* as well. He made some good friends among the upper castes while in school. Phule was closely associated with the missionary institutions, first as a student and then as a teacher in mission schools. No doubt he gained his inspiration first by what the missionaries taught about the equality and dignity of all human beings. When he started his first girl's school he went to Ahmednaagar to see and study how the girl's school begun by the American Marathi mission was conducted.

The incident that triggered the spirit of the fighter in him took place when he had just finished schooling. He went to attend the marriage of a Brahmin friend, and while walking along with others in the marriage procession; the relatives of his friend spotted him and berated him, as a low caste, for joining. The young Jotirao was hurt deeply and couldn't bear the insult. He went home and related that incident to his father and wept bitterly, even though his father tried to console him.

Phule decided to fight against such an unjust caste system and its prejudices. Slavery in America was racial, but the caste system that dehumanized the low castes in India was religious, and had been developed by the Brahmins in the course of several centuries. He began to write extensively, giving a historical account of how corrupt and inhuman practices had been developed by the Brahmins for their own advantage. In his book *Gulamgiri* (slavery), published in 1873, he states: "Anyone who will consider well the whole history of the Brahmin domination in India, and the thralldom under which it has retained the people even unto the present day, will agree with us in thinking that no language could be too harsh by which to characterize the selfish heartlessness and the consummate cunning of the Brahmin tyranny by which India has been so far governed. How far the Brahmins have succeeded in their endeavors to enslave the minds of the Sudras and the Atisudras, those of them, who have come to know

well to their cost. For generations past they have borne these chins of slavery and bondage".[11] The main objective in writing the book, says Phule, was to make the shudras and atisudras understand how the Brahmins for centuries by their hegemony had subjected them to various kinds of sufferings, ignominies, pain and humiliation. Once they realized this, they would be able to work to make themselves free of this painful enforcement of slavery. Interestingly, he dedicated his book to the people of America as a tribute for abolishing slavery in 1865.

Thus began the silent but certain revolt against the caste system imposed by the Brahmins. The movement flowed in two streams. One was anti-Brahmin movement led by the Maratha leaders like Shahu Maharaj, the ruler of Kolhapur and Vithal Ramji Shide; the other was spearheaded by Jotirao Phule and his followers for the removal of untouchability. In order to carry on his fight in an organized manner he established the Satyashodhak Samaj (Truth Seeking Society) in 1873.

The Prarthana Samaj, a socio-religious movement of the upper castes, also advocated the abolition of unjust caste practices as one of its programs. Satyashobhak Samaj of the low castes aimed mainly at the abolition of caste abuses and improvement of the conditions of the low castes through education and better employment. Jotirao was not a member of the Prarthana Samaj, nor did the leaders of the Prarthana Samaj support Satyashodhak Samaj.

For Jotirao it became his life's mission to fight for the liberation of outcastes and women through education and removal of their disabilities. For exposing the craftiness of Brahmanism and their efforts to keep the outcastes oppressed, and for demanding the removal of abuses against them, he has been called the Martin Luther of India. No one

---

[11] Y. D Phadke,. *Mahatma Phule: Samagra Vangmaya*, Bombay, 1974, p.122

previously had dared to attack and expose the duplicity of Brahmanism as he did.

How does the missionary influence come in this? Phule's movement began to gather support from the Mahars and Mangs of Maharashtra mainly because of the vast efforts made by the Christian missionaries in rural Maharashtra to conscientize them through the missionary schools. These schools were mostly meant for the lower castes, though upper castes also took advantage of them. The missionaries were the first in the villages of Maharashtra to start schools and teach the low castes about their rights as human beings. Phule did not have the resources to work extensively in the villages like the missionaries. He had two schools in Poona which were later handed over to the government. So clearly, it was the missionaries who prepared the ground for the low caste movement in Maharashtra, a movement which came to be spearheaded by Jotirao in the 19ᵗʰ century.

The missionaries had already waged a struggle on behalf of the Mahar and Mang converts in rural Maharashtra, and fought in the courts to secure the basic rights of drawing water from the village water tanks or wells and the use of public places. The missionary efforts to secure the rights of the untouchable converts, and their success in this, served as the source of encouragement for the non-Christian untouchables to become conscious of their rights and to fight to secure them. Jotirao and his Satyashodhak Samaj thus became the champions of the cause already espoused by the missionaries.

Another leader who was influenced by the missionary effort and took up the cause of the untouchables was Shahu Maharaj, the ruler of the state of Kolhapur. He was greatly impressed by the educational and medical work of the American Presbyterian mission in his own state. He became a close friend of the medical missionaries of the Miraj hospital. He gave them land and other facilities for carrying on their work, and even entrusted the education of his children and those of the chiefs of his state to the missionaries, sending them to the mission school at Kolhapur. He was amazed by the work of Dr. Wanless of Miraj hospital, the man responsible for insisting that all patients irrespective of caste should share the same floor and even sleep in proximity to each other. Brahmins initially resisted, but soon fell in line. There was total castelessness in the hospital in a caste-ridden society. Under this inspiration Shahu Maharaj issued a proclamation in 1919 that in all public places in the state of Kolhapur there would be no discrimination on the basis of caste. For the purpose he gave the illustration of the mission hospital at Miraj.[12] He also established boarding schools for the education of the children of the low castes. The missionaries created an awareness among the low castes about their rights; Phule popularized the movement and gave the low castes an organization; Shahu Maharaj gave the movement a legal status.

Ambedkar and Safeguards for the Low Castes

One of the humiliating practices that hurt low castes children most even in government school, was to forbid them to sit in the classroom along with caste children – indeed, to make them to sit outside the class room or in a separate enclosure lest their touch pollute the high casters. This was a practice carried out in all non-missionary schools despite the government regulation against it. Dr. B.R. Ambedkar, the chairman of the drafting committee of the present Indian constitution, had suffered this ignomity as a child, and these bitter feelings remained till the end with this most brilliant Mahar of Maharashtra.

Ambedkar received the greatest shock of his life when he found that, despite the best education in econonmics and law from the USA and UK,

---

¹² *Kolhapur State Gazette*, Kolhapur: Kolhapur State Gazette, October, 1919, p. 169.

no one in Baroda was ready to give him a house because he was a Mahar. The ruler of Baroda who had supported his education offered him a job. But Ambedkar had to return to Bombay since he could find no place to stay in Baroda. So he decided to set up his legal practice in Bombay. As the champion of the untouchables he clashed with Gandhi. He began his crusade against untouchability in 1920s just at the time when Gandhi emerged as the new leader of the Congress Party and the country. 1920s was the time when mass conversion to Christianity was taking place among the low castes in India. Gandhi was a staunch Hindu and opposed conversion. To counteract the missionary effort to convert the low castes, he took up the cause of the untouchables, called them Harijan (God's people), and began to work for the removal of untouchability. He differed from Ambedkar on the question of securing separate political electrates for the untouchables in the elected bodies as a separate minority community like the Muslims and Sikhs. Gandhi wanted them to be treated as part of the Hindu community and not a separate community.

One of the main reasons that encouraged Gandhi and other leaders involved in the removal of untouchability was the living testimony of over five million Christian people in India who came from the untouchable section of society. Their level of education, success and progress made in various areas of life proved that they, as women and men of India, could be equal to any upper caste person when an opportunity was given.[13] Ambedkar was unhappy with Gandhi's efforts in this regard, and declared at Yeola in 1935 that though he was born a Hindu he would not like to die a Hindu. Ambedkar had great respect for Christianity, had made a good study of it and believed that the teachings of Jesus were superior to Hinduism. He had also appreciated how some members of his community who had become Christians had changed and benefited.[14] He even once toyed with the idea of becoming a Christian along with his people. Ultimately, in 1957 and a few weeks before his death, he became a Buddhist. Once he addressed a group of missionaries in Maharashtra and said:

> The Jews to whom Christ came were an oppressed people. My people are an oppressed group; therefore Jesus' advice to the multitudes who followed him becomes of vital interest to me. Jesus taught non-violence. To me that is the unique thing in His message. Look at Jesus not from the standpoint of theology but of society. If taken seriously, Jesus' unique message could not only save my people but it could build the kingdom of God on earth.[15]

Ambedkar further said that Jesus was the first to teach the gospel of non-violence and he is the first ever to advocate such a method to meet violence and oppression. "Gandhi is not the originator of non-violence, Jesus Christ is."[16]

It becomes more than clear from the above that the awareness created by the missionaries among the Mahars and Mangs in villages in Maharashtra sowed the seeds of the unrest that led to the launching of their liberation movement. Phule gave a shape to it, Shahu Maharaj encouraged it and Ambedkar inherited this great legacy and carried it to conclusion with the help of Gandhi and other liberal Indian leaders, in 1955 the practice of untouchability was made a criminal offense by an Act passed by the Parliament. No doubt, the liberalism and enlightenment of the members of the Constitution that proved for reservation policy in education

---

[13] R. M. Bennett, *The Church in India*, Toronto: 1954, p.21-22

[14] Ambedkar, *Writings and Speeches*. Vol. v., Bombay: unpublished writings,1989, p.420

[15] *Western India Notes*, xx., Kolhapur: January 1939, p.3.

[16] *Ibid.*

and employment opportunities for the low castes in order to help them to overcome the handicap they had suffered for centuries.

This inter-cultural history, one which illuminates the universal meaning of incarnating the life of God as revealed in Jesus Christ and which has transformed the life of the people in Mahrashtra and India, can be one way of presenting Global church history.

CHAPTER 17

Holy Spirit Led Mission in North India

JAMES MASSEY

In this story we are concerned with the Panjab of old, where once five rivers full of water flowed. But at the time of partition in 1947, when Panjab was divided politically into two Panjabs, its five rivers were also divided in two parts. Two-and-a-half-rivers are left with the Indian Panjab, and the rest have gone to Pakistan. But in spite of this division, the wheatlands on both sides still thrive and the overall progress in the cities and villages continues. On both sides, Panjabis are still Panjabis. Therefore our concern here for the old undivided Panjab is indeed justified.

A more appropriate name for the land of five rivers is 'Panjab' (not the generally anglicised usage – 'Punjab'), because it is a compound of two Persian words, *Panj* meaning 'five' and *ab* meaning 'water' or 'river'. Therefore the name Panjab can be rightly translated as 'the land of the five rivers'. The five rivers of Panjab are Jhelum, Chenab, Ravi, Beas and Sutluj. So this actually is the story of these five rivers.

The narration of this story is divided into the following three parts:

(I)   Historical Background

(II)   Spirit Movement

(III) The Future Missional Task

Historical Background

The Panjabi Christian community is among the younger Christian communities in India. It was the American Presbyterian Church (A.P. Mission), which sent the first missionary, John C. Lowrie, to Panjab. Lowrie arrived in Ludhiana on November 5, 1834 and established the first mission station in Panjab.

References have been made to Christianity in Panjab even before the advent of John C. Lowrie. The earliest reference is from a Panjabi source, which we find in the writings of the first Sikh theologian, Bhai Gurdas (A.D. 1546-1637), who said in one of his writings (*Var* or ballad 38:11):

Isai (Christian) *Musai* (Jews)
Haumaim (self-centered) *Hairane* (confused)

This reference to Christianity does give us a clue that there were Christians in and around Panjab during the 17th and 18th centuries, and it also reveals the kind of possible life these Christians were living. But we are not sure to which Christians Bhai Gurdas referred. Around that time there were some Jesuit priests living in the court of the Muslim Moghul Emperor Akbar (A.D. 1556-1605). Their relationship with the Muslim religious leaders was not cordial. For example, John Clark Archer in his book on the Sikhs, states that one Padri Rodolph challenged an *ulema* (Muslim Scholar) to prove which of the two revelations was true declaring that he would carry the Bible through the fire afterward if the *ulema* would carry the Koran in the same way, through the fire.[1]

---

[1] John Clark Archer, *The Sikhs in Relation to Hindus, Moselems, Christians and Ahnadiyya. (A Study in Comparative Religion),* Princeton, , 1941, p 165.

According to the Apocryphal 'Acts of Thomas', it is also said, the Apostle Thomas came to Panjab during the reign of King Gundaphorus, the last Parthian ruler, in the middle of the first century. It is true that the 'Acts of Thomas' as a document is apochryphal in nature, but it is also true that King Gundaphorus was a historical person because some coins from his time and a stone with an inscription of his name and the date A.D. 46 have been found, and are now in the Museum in Lahore, Pakistan. On the basis of King Gundaphorus' historicity, a strong view has been expressed by some historians like J.N. Farquhar, that St. Thomas possibly came to Panjab travelling by sea and also preached and converted some people. But later on, because of the invasion of the Kushans, he left Panjab via Socotra and went to Malabar in South India. It is also believed that converts or Christians of St. Thomas were wiped out by the Kushan invasion.[2]

But it is really difficult to prove the above story of St. Thomas and the Christians' presence in Panjab during the first century, because of the non-continuity of any Christian tradition from that time. We do not even have any proof which shows that the Roman Catholic priests, present in Akbar's court, were able to establish any church or Christian community. Therefore, the real story of Christianity in Panjab actually began with the arrival of John C. Lowrie. Almost all church historians have accepted this as a fact and therefore our concern here in this story is with Christianity in Panjab, from November 5, 1834 onwards to the present time.

Before we move on to discuss the main part of the 'Holy Spirit led Mission Story', it will be good to refer to an address given on October 29, 1834 by Dr. Elijah P.Swift, Secretary of the American Missionary Society to the first batch of missionaries that included the Rev. James Wilson, the Rev. John Newton and Miss Julia Davis. An extract from this address is quoted in *History of A.P. Missionaries in India* by John Newton (1886). This address helps us to know the political and geographical context of the 19ᵗʰ century, when in fact Christianity entered Panjab. We are reproducing this extract here:

> It is also gratifying to know that Northern India, and especially the Seik (Sikh) Nation, the field, and the people to which you repair, present encouragements of the most inviting character...The Seiks occupy a considerable part of the province of Lahore in the north-westerly part of Hindostan, a territory 320 miles in length and 220 in breadth; a part of Multan adjoining it on the south-west, and part of Delhi in the south-east...The country of the Siek nation, therefore, comprises the warm alluvial and fertile plains of the Punjab, and the high and salubrious elevations of the south base of the Himalayas, to which a mission intended for the Sieks might doubtless be removed if any important advantage were likely to grow out of such an arrangement.[3]

Newton himself gives the reason why they favoured Panjab as their mission field. He also refers to a long history, which serves as the background to the religious and social context of Panjab:

> After much consideration they chose the Punjab. No other section is so full of historic interests as this. It was from here that Hindooism spread over the whole Peninsula. It was here that the great battle was fought, which is described in the Mahabharat. It was through Punjab that every successful invasion of India has taken place, except the British. It was here that the tide of Alexander's victories terminated. But such

---

[2] Cyril Bruce Firth, *An Introduction to Indian Church History*, Madras, 1981, pp 1-17.

[3] John Newton, *Historical Sketches of the Indian Missions of the Presbyterian Church in the United States of America*, Allahabad, 1886, p. 4.

considerations had little influence on the first Missionaries in the selection of their field of labour... This seems to have been due mainly to the fact that this was the land of Sikhs — a people of fine physique, and unusually independent character; a people, moreover, who had already, in principle at least, discarded the old idolatry of Hindooism, and broken in some measure, the bonds of caste; and therefore might be considered to be in a favourable state to be influenced by the preaching of Christian Missionaries.[4]

After John C. Lowrie, the missionaries from other Christian traditions also came to Panjab. The Church Missionary Society of the Church of England started its work at Simla and Kotegarh in 1840 and Amritsar in 1850, the American United Presbyterians at Sialkot in 1855, the Scottish Presbyterians at Chamba in 1863, the New Zealand Presbyterians at Jagathri in 1911, English Baptists in 1891 (later on taken over by New Zealand Presbyterians in 1923), the Methodist Church in Southern Asia worked in Lahore in 1881 and other Christian traditions like the Salvation Army had their missions at Lahore and Dhariwal. The Roman Catholics worked in Lahore, Amritsar and Jullunder Cantonement. Thus by the end of the first quarter of the 20th century, Gospel work by different Christian missions began all over the Panjab.[5]

Spirit Movement

The basic task of Christian missionaries was (and, of the Christian Church, even today is) to proclaim the Gospel of Christ and to win human beings to faith and obedience in Him. This is exactly what Christian missionaries came to do in Panjab. But interestingly, things in Panjab did not turn out as expected. To begin with the missionaries were interested only in preaching the Christian Gospel to the upper caste people. A pioneer missionary of the United Presbyterian Church of U.S.A. admitted this truth after his first thirty years experience of missionary work, when he said:

> In concluding these remarks, about my own evangelistic work in the last decade. I may say briefly that I began with my eye upon the large towns and cities, but have been led from them to the country villages. I began with the educated classes and people of good social position, but ended among the poor and the lowly.[6]

The result of the above missionaries' approach was that from 1834 till 1885 —in 61 years, they had only 477 communicant members and many of these were not Panjabi Christians. Even the first person to be baptised in Ludhiana on April 30, 1837 was a Bengali upper caste Hindu. But then after 1885 we see a quick change in numbers which grew and grew. To understand this change is important because …in the beginning this not only troubled the missionaries; it was also a factor that almost shook the whole of Panjabi society. Through this we believe God's Spirit reveals its movement very clearly, and we see God's working and His option for the poor, lowly and downtrodden turning this whole affair into a movement of the Spirit. But in the beginning this 'Spirit Movement' (which church historians have labelled – 'Christian Mass Movement') was not a happy sign for Christian missionaries in Panjab because there were very few so-called upper castes who accepted the Gospel. The best example of the latter is the famous Sikh convert Sadhu Sundar Singh whom the well known missionary C.H. Loehlin has referred to as "The Panjabi Church's gift to world Christianity."[7]

---

[4] *Ibid.*

[5] C. H. Loehlin, "The History of Christianity in the Panjab," in *The Singh Sabha and Other Socio-religious Movements in the Panjab, 1850-1925,* edited by Gardha Singh, Patiala, 1984, pp 318-319.

[6] Andrew Gordon, *Our Indian Mission, 1855 – 1885,* Philadelphia, 1888, p 446.

[7] Loeklin, "The History of Christianity in the Punjab," p. 224.

In reality the Panjabi Christian community/Church comes from a Dalit background and it is because of the 'Spirit or Holy Spirit led Movement' among the Panjabi Dalits, in which an early Panjabi Dalit Christian, namely Ditt, played a major role. It is to him that J. Waskom Pickett referred when he observed that the real founder of the Church in Sialkot was "not Gordon, but Ditt."[8] Sialkot district was the first place where the United Presbyterian Church in the USA started their mission work.

The scope and length of this article will not allow us to go into the many details of the response or responses of Panjabis to the Gospel, instead, we will narrate two case histories here, to show how this call came, and who responded. These cases are of Ditt and Sadhu Sundar Singh respectively.

Ditt

After the A.P. Mission which began its work in Panjab on 5ᵗʰ November, 1834 through the first missionary John C. Lowrie in Ludhiana, the work of the United Presbyterian Church of America (U.P. Mission) began on August 8, 1855, with the arrival of its first missionary, Andrew Gordon, in Sialkot, Panjab. Interestingly, as a result of these missions' work beginning from 1834 till 1885 (as mentioned earlier), there were only 477 communicant members. But from 1885 onwards the number increased by thousands. The number of Christians belonging to all missions increased in the same way. In 1881 Christians in Panjab numbered 3796, in 1901 there were 37,980 and in 1921 this number went up to 375,031.[9] What was the reason behind this increasing number of Christians? The answer to this question lies in the story of Ditt. The source is the first missionary Andrew Gordon himself. Here only the main points of the story are given.[10]

The story of Ditt began when a Hindu of the *Jat* caste (a Panjabi upper caste) by name Nattu, was baptized on November 17, 1872 by the Rev. J.S. Barr. Nattu was not only from a high caste, he was also the son of a *Lambardar* (village head) and legal heir to his father's property and position. Missionaries were very happy, but later on they were unhappy, because Nattu forfeited his right to be his father's heir. For them he proved a failure, 'a weak brother'. But this was not true, because he became an instrument in bringing a person into the Christian fold, who later became one of the main leaders responsible for the present Church or Christians of Panjab. This man's name was Ditt.

Ditt was from a small village named Shahbdike, which was about two miles from a larger village named Mirali, and thirty miles from Sialkot, (now in Pakistan). Ditt was born around 1843. Gordon introduces him in these words: "...a man of the low and much despised *chura tribe*, by the name Ditt, a dark man, lame of one leg, quiet and modest in his manners, with sincerity and earnestness, well expressed in his face, and at that time about thirty years of age." By profession, Ditt was a dealer of hides. He came into contact with Nattu, who taught him about Jesus Christ, and in June 1873 Nattu took him to Sialkot for baptism.

The Rev. S. Martin was hestitant to accept Ditt for baptism. After all, his Christian teachings were based on the teachings of 'a weak brother Nattu'. But at the same time, Ditt's knowledge of Christianity was quite sound. He also appeared, to Martin, an honest person. Still he wanted to delay his baptism, for which Ditt was not willing. In the words of Gordon: "Mr. Martin finally decided to baptize Ditt not because he saw his way decidedly clear to do so, but rather because he could see no scriptural ground for refusing."

---

[8] J. Waskom Picket, *Christian Mass Movement in India,* New York, 1933, p 56.
[9] John C.B. Webster, *The Christian Community and Change in Nineteenth Century North India,* Delhi, 1976, p 47.
[10] Gordon, *Our Indian Mission,* pp 421-32.

Martin faced another problem when immediately after the baptism, Ditt asked permission to go back to his village instead of staying in a protected mission compound. This was a new thing for Martin. The practice was that a new convert stayed with the missionary for more instruction and protection. Martin's worry was how this poor illiterate man would deal with opposition. Anyhow, Ditt returned to his village and this action of his proved to be the starting point for a Christian movement among the *ex-churas* (Dalits) of Panjab.

On reaching home, Ditt did face bitter opposition from his own relatives. For example, one of his fellow villagers rebuked him by saying: "Oh Ho. You have become a *Sahib*" (gentleman). Others said: "You have become a '*be-I-man*'" (one without religion). His own sister-in-law said: "Alas, my brother, you have changed your religion without even asking our counsel; our relationship with you is over. Henceforth you shall neither eat, drink, nor in any way associate with us. One of your legs is broken already, so may it be with the other." But Ditt did not care about any opposition. Instead he witnessed his new faith in Christ openly and boldly, both to his family members and others. The result was amazing. Three months after his baptism in August 1873, he had to walk 30 miles for the sole purpose of introducing his family and friends to the missionaries. Martin examined them, and was fully satisfied and gave them baptism.

Ditt's work of buying hides from different places took him to many villages. Wherever he went on business, he preached about Christ also. By 1884, eleven years after his baptism, he brought into the Christian faith more than five hundred persons from his caste. By 1900 half the people of his community had accepted Christ, and by 1915 almost all the Dalits, known as *churas,* of Sialkot district had became Christians.[11]

The missionaries it seemed were not interested in the Dalits becoming Christians. Some were really troubled about it, and also about the way God's Spirit was working. This we see from a letter of J.C.R. Ewing, who writing to the Board of Foreign Missions on March 19, 1884, described this trend of poor, low castes becoming Christian as "raking in rubbish into the church."[12] Some other missionaries in their reports even hesitated to mention these converts' social background and they were shown as 'common villagers' or 'illiterate menials.'[13]

But the conversions continued and today in Panjab we have more than 3,00,000 Christians on the Indian side, of which 99 percent come from the Dalit background. The larger numbers of Panjabi Christians are in the Panjab on the Pakistan side, who also share the same background.

But the above attitude of the missionaries concerning the conversion of the Dalits had a twofold effect on Panjab Christianity. It left a negative cultural spot, which the Panjabi Christians even today would ignore, because they are afraid to talk about the past, which would reveal their low social background. When I say 'negative cultural spot', I mean that though the missionaries accepted the above trend as part of their mission work at a later stage, they were not fully convinced till the end. For the sake of a few from the so-called privileged castes, they were forced to maintain double standards in the church. The real problem occurred in the Holy Eucharist and Church services, which were, after all, the only occasions when the two groups of Christians

---

[11] Picket, *Christian Mass Movement,* pp 47-49.

[12] As quoted in Webster, *The* Christian Community and Change, p 60.

[13] Mark Juergensmeyer, *Religion as Social Vision, The Movement against Untouchability in the 20th Century, Panjab,* Berkeley, 1982, p 188.

could meet. According to Mark Juergensmeyer, the missionaries solved the problem in two ways:

> By establishing worship services for those who spoke English and those who spoke only Panjabi, which de facto eliminated the lower castes from English-speaking services; or failing this by ensuring that upper caste converts would sit at the front in the church so that they would use the communion implements first, before they become polluted by the Christians of lower castes.[14]

Besides the above administrative methods to deal with the problem, the missionaries used other methods also to solve the problem such as establishing 'mission compounds,' 'Christian colonies' and 'Christian villages' for the rural people. These can still be found today, for example, the village Santokh Majra established in 1870 near Karnal and a Mission compound in Jullunder.[15]

Establishing separate places for these Panjabi Christians helped to create a very distinctive Christian culture, which projected an image reflecting the 'Churas culture' which means the culture of the sweeper or lower class, although there were among them a few who had belonged to other castes.

Sadhu Sundar Singh

Sadhu Sundar Singh was a Christian convert from a Sikh background. '*Sadhu*' means 'holy' or 'Saint' or 'ascetic', and this title was used for a non-formal order of wandering holy men belonging to different religious faiths. Therefore as Sundar Singh, adopted this style of life after becoming a Christian. He was popularly known as 'Sadhu' by others. He was born on September 3, 1889 in a village named Rampur, which is about 15 kilometers from Ludhiana in Panjab. His father Sardar Sher Singh was a rich farmer.

His family practiced the Sikh religion. His life as a Christian began on September 3, 1903 (the day of his baptism) and he witnessed to his Christian faith rigorously till 18ᵗʰ April 1929, when he was last seen, before undertaking his missionary journey to Tibet. Sadhu Sundar Singh's conversion and life story is another example of the 'Spirit Movement.'

Sadhu Sundar Singh's mother was a very religious woman. It was she who influenced him the most and her influence continued to be with him throughout his life. She was very fond of him and was his guide for his religious life. She used to tell him that he should not be superficial and worldly like his brothers…but seek peace of the soul and love religion, and that one day he would become a holy Sadhu. These words of his mother always echoed deep down in his soul throughout his life.

Sundar Singh was fourteen years old when his mother died and then began the religious crisis in his young life. But after that, he started the study of various Sikh and Hindu scriptures with greater zeal. His Guru (religious teacher) told his father that his "son will either become a fool or a great man." He even learnt the practice of Yoga under the guidance of a Hindu *Sannyasi* (ascetic). All these hard efforts of Sundar Singh were in search of peace, which never came.

He was then sent to Ludhiana to study in a mission school. There he was given the New Testament as a text book, which he refused to study. He was warned by others not to study the Bible. He developed a complete hatred towards Christianity. He even burnt a portion of the Bible. When he saw missionaries coming to preach the Gospel, he used to abuse them. All these things he did even against the advice of his father. But his answer was: "The religion of the West is false; we must annihilate it."

---

[14] *Ibid.*

[15] Webster, *The Christian Community and Change*, pp.72-74.

But then came the day, a great day of decision, the 16th of December 1904; a day when Sundar Singh felt a great inner pain, a restlessness and unhappiness. Nothing could give him peace. He went to his father on the evening of 17th December and told him he had come to say good-bye, because by the morning of 18th December, he would die. He said that no religion or money or comfort was of any help in giving him peace. His intention was to commit suicide by putting himself on the railway lines in front of a train that used to pass by his village at five o'clock.

So on 18 December at three o'clock he rose and took a cold ceremonial bath according to the Hindu and Sikh customs. Then he prayed to God saying, "O God – if there be God, show me the right way and I will become a Sadhu, otherwise I will kill myself." He continued to pray for a long time and there came an answer to his prayer.

Suddenly at about 4:30 in the morning a great shining light appeared in his small room. At that moment he could not understand what this light was, so he continued to pray. But then he saw a figure of a human being in the shining light. At first he thought this human figure was Buddha or Krishna or some other divinity to whom he was praying. He was going to prostrate in front of that human figure, but then, to his amazement, he heard these words from the mouth of the human figure addressing him: "*Tu mujhe kyun satata hai? Dekh main ne tere liye apni jan salib par di*" ("why do you persecute me? I have given my life for you upon the cross.") At that moment, when he heard these divine words, Sundar Singh recognised Jesus who was looking at him with love and then the thought came to him: "Jesus Christ is not dead, He is alive, and this is He Himself;" and he fell at His feet and worshipped Him. In an instant Sundar Singh felt his whole being changed and he was filled with divine life, peace and joy in his inner soul. He rose from his feet but by that time Christ had disappeared.

This vision of Christ was the turning point of Sundar Singh's life. After this he dedicated his whole life to Christ and the work of preaching the Gospel. But he was sent away from his house. His family not only rejected him, they even tried to poison him, but God saved him. He was formally baptised on September 3, 1905 at Simla and after that, on the next day he left on his mission.[16]

There are many Indian scholars who have written wonderful books with originality of ideas regarding indigenous or contextual Christianity or how the Christian religion should be related to the Indian soil. But in the case of Sadhu Sunder Singh, he lived indigenous Christianity as its true follower. It was not a matter of intellectual exercise for him, it was in fact part of his real life. Some have even compared him with St. Paul and St. Augustine who were proud of their being Jewish and Roman respectively. The same is true about the Sadhu.

Why have Indians rejected the Christian faith? — Because it has no relation with the soil of our country in general. The Sadhuji said that Indians do need the Water of Life, but not in the European cup. About the practical steps of contextualization of Christianity, Sadhuji said that Christians should sit down on the floor in the Church. They should take off their shoes instead of their turbans. They should use Indian music and an informal address should take the place of sermons.

Sadhuji always wore a saffron robe and turban and even during travel to the West, he wore the same. Not only in his external appearance, but even the appearance of his total personality was such that it was said about him, that he looked "as if he had stepped straight out from the pages of the Bible."

Once in a Western country town, he visited a house; when he went and knocked at the door

---

[16] Friedrich Heiler, *The Gospel of Sadhu Sundar Singh,* Abridged Translation, reprint, Delhi, 1989, pp 41-44.

of that house, a maid servant came to open the door and after opening it, she immediately rushed inside, leaving the Sadhuji standing at the door and told her mistress (*malkin*): "There's someone, who wants to see you, Ma'am. I can't make anything of his name. But he looks as if he might be Jesus Christ."

A true *Chela* (disciple) of a true Guru (Teacher), he became the image of his Guru. How many disciples or followers can have such claims.[17]

The Future Missional Task

The Gospel continues to challenge the Panjabi Christians. The Panjabi Church/ Community is basically a Dalit Church/ Community, which historically comes from a background of the crushed and oppressed, by the caste system. It belongs to the so called *chura* community, considered to be not only the lowest part of Panjabi society, but also outside the pale of human society. Because according to the Indian caste system they are 'out-caste,' therefore considered untouchables and also historically regarded as 'non-human beings.' The following words of St. Paul addressed to the Christians of Corinth are in a sense applicable to the Panjabi Christians also:

> Consider your own call, brothers and sisters: not many of you were wise by human standards, not many were powerful, not many were of noble birth. But God chose what is foolish in the world to shame the wise; God chose what is weak in the world to shame the strong; God chose what is low and despised in the world, things that are, so that no one might boast in the presence of God. He is the source of your life in Christ

> Jesus, who became for us wisdom from God, and righteousness and sanctification and redemption. (*1 Corinthians 1:26-30 NRSV*).

These words of St. Paul are true in the case of Panjabi Christians, but as a community they still have to taste the fuller redemptive aspects of the Gospel. This is where they are faced with a major ongoing challenge. The future missional task of the Church has to be to bring complete salvation to these Christians, as a community, because even though most of the Christians are now third or fourth generation Christians, their overall life — religious, social, economic and political has not changed. This is basically because the whole Gospel, which can change one's whole life has not been preached to them. They have been fed on 'half salvation,' which could only show them the way to heaven (in other words) along with individual piety. This only provided a way of escape in their psychological self instead of bringing any real change in their life, spiritually, as well as temporally.

Also, the Church both in India as well as in Panjab has to work out a new mission strategy, based upon the newly discovered social and religious composition of the Indian people. Because, till now, various missionary movements and churches have based their mission programmes on a myth, that India has a majority of people (about 85 percent), who are Hindus and that too, that all of them are followers of the classical Brahmanical religious traditions. But the *Mandal Commission Report (page 61)* had made it clear that the truth is not as it looks. According to the Commission's findings, the percentage and the composition of the Indian population is as follows:

i)	Dalits and Tribal Communities	22.56 percent
ii)	Non-Hindu religious communities (Muslims, Christians and others)	16.16 percent
iii)	Forward and Upper Caste Hindus	17.58 percent
iv)	Hindu Other Backward Classes (OBC)	43.70 percent

---

[17] B.H. Streeter and A.J. Appasamy, *The Sadhu, A Study in Mysticism and Practical Religions*, reprint, Delhi, 1987, pp ix-xi.

Till now all our missions, as well as the theological task, have been focused upon 17.58 percent of the Indians (which include 5.52 percent Brahmins, who are the real followers of Classical Hinduism). Today we have to reverse, our base from this minority and turn our attention to the other 82.42 percent people of India, who include Dalits, Tribals, religious minorities and OBC in order to work out our Church programmes. This needs a bigger and bolder commitment to our missional task. This challenge becomes more pertinent for Panjabi Christians, because they share their culture and social roots with 82.42 percent of the people. This of course also imposes a challenge to be Global Christian Community: to change their view for their missional commitment in India as well as in the Panjab.

CHAPTER 18

Nationalism and Christianity: The London Mission Society and Conversion in 19th Century South Travancore

Y. VINCENT KUMARADOSS
ELIZABETH SUSAN ALEXANDER

Nationalism undeniably continues to be a powerful ideological force in today's world, especially in the post-colonial nations. However, a variety of trends within the pale of nationalism, specifically in the context of its interaction with ideological formations such as Christianity, remain unexplored. In fact, nationalism cannot merely be adjudged as having a monolithic, anti-colonial content and there can be "multiple histories of nationalism and colonialism" depending on specific contexts.[1] In nationalist historiography the notion of the 'nation' and 'nationalism' are invested with "an aura of utmost sacredness" endowing 'nationalism,' with a monolithic anti-colonial content. It is necessary, however, to recognize that neither the "domination exercised by the colonizers, nor the hegemony of the nationalist movement over the political life of the 'nation' was ever complete, and, that even under colonial conditions, relations of power were "multi-layered" and not merely 'mediated' by colonialism and nationalism.[2] The 'master narrative' of 'nation' and 'nationalism' can even be more a "fetter" than an "aid in understanding the past," being unable to "accommodate the multiple histories played out" in the complex shifting political life of a 'nation' under colonial conditions.[3]

The need for multiple histories of nationalism and colonialism is demonstrated in this paper by reflecting on certain events sparked off by the evangelizing efforts of the Protestant missionaries among the Shanars[4] of South Travancore during the 19th century, when this princely state was under the overlordship of the British. At one level the study shows that the relationship between different actors in the specific historical milieu in question, namely the Protestant Missionaries representing the London Missionary Society (LMS), the Shanar converts, the Princely state and the British Residency cannot be simplified or essentialised – for example, 'missions are the handmaid of imperialism,' the converts are anti-national and so on. In fact the relationships were shifting and changing into both conflict and cooperation, depending on specific historical contingencies. The second important point that emerges in the course of this narration is that it could be misleading to simplistically assume that 'nationalist' or colonialist concern underlay every

---

[1] M.S.S.Pandian, "Meanings of 'colonialism' and 'nationalism': An Essay on Vaikunda Swamy Cult," *Studies in History*, Vol.8, No.2, 1990, p-167. The present paper basically posits on this article.

[2] *Ibid.*

[3] *Ibid.*, p.185.

[4] The Shanars of South Travancore are known today as Nadars. During the 19th century, most of them, who were poor, were known as 'Shanars' and the rich among them held the title of 'Nadans' or landholders. With the Shanars accomplishing social and economic advances through the late 19th and early 20th centuries, they, as a caste group, adopted the name 'Nadars.'

political power struggle. In the actual terrain of politics encounters could be multilayered and cannot be merely explained in terms of nationalism.

Let us start with the Protestant missionary impact on the Shanars in South Travancore. Shanars being one of the lower castes in South Travancore, their social condition was extremely oppressive and degrading. Intervention by the missionaries was one of the major factors that gave them scope to defy the old order and contest caste- based practices such as denying them access to public places like roads, law courts and schools, preventing them from living in multi-storeyed houses, sanction against wearing an upper cloth to cover their upper torso, imposition of discriminative taxes and extraction of free labour *(ooliyum).*[5]

It was indeed true that when Ringeltaube, the first LMS missionary to Travancore commenced his mission, the British Residents such as Major MaCaulay and Col. Munro evinced great interest in the growth of Christianity and used their official position to help the London Missionary Society immensely with permission to erect churches and the gift of almost tax-free paddy lands. The British residents were also instrumental in ameliorating the social disabilities of the Shanar and other lower caste converts to Christianity. In 1812 Col. John Munroe issued a proclamation permitting the Shanar women who had converted to Christianity, to cover their breasts, a practice denied to them traditionally.[6] This was followed by a series of Government proclamations issued by the British Residents, exempting the Christians from paying the burdensome poll tax (1814), abolishing certain other discriminatory taxes imposed on the lower

castes and exempting them from *ooliyum* service.

It was however, not always true that the British officials collaborated as if in conspiratorial bond with the missionaries in furthering the spread of Christianity and indulging in conversion projects. There were British officials who did not tolerate the missionary presence and openly opposed the missionary efforts. In 1858-59, when the lower caste Shanars were resisting the combined onslaught of the petty state officials and armed gangs of upper caste Nairs, demanding the right for their women to use breast cloths, the British Resident Gen. Cullen, in keeping with his overall contempt for missionaries, refused to support the Shanars and the missionaries who stood with them in their struggle. In fact, the London Missionary Society characterized him as one who was more opposed to the missionary effort than the "bigoted Brahmins."[7] Also, it is not really true that the missionaries always looked for political patronage from the British officials. For instance, James Dawson, one of the LMS missionaries, refused to be the successor of Ringeltaube because he thought that Col. Munro exercised control over the mission and "wished the natives to be made Christians from political motives."[8]

The relationship between the London Missionary Society and the Travancore state was also one of shifts and changes. Velu Thampi, the Dewan of Travancore, refused to give permission to Ringeltaube to erect a church. He then launched a revolt against the British during the first decade of the nineteenth century. He proclaimed that the British, in order "to put up crosses and Christian flags in pagodas, compel inter- marriage with Brahmin women without reference to caste or creed, and practice all the

---

[5] Dick Kooiman, *Conversion and Social Equality in India: The London Mission Society in South Travancore in the Nineteenth Century,* New Delhi: Manohar, 1989.

[6] *Ibid.,* p-149.

[7] *Ibid.,* pp.146-147.

[8] *Ibid.,* p.56.

unjust and unlawful things which characterize Kaliyuga."[9] But subsequent Travancore rulers who were more under the British control than ever before, granted several concessions to missionaries and converts.

However, to the anti-British, 'nationalist' indigenous elite — upper caste Nairs supported by the Travancore state — it seemed that the Missions/Church and British political authority were overlapping. Even the civilising mission of the Church/ missionaries could not be supported as it threatened to subvert the pre-existing relations of power by winning the low caste converts freedom from the very degrading, dreaded and discriminative caste based practices that ensured the upper castes their traditionally privileged position. Their 'nationalism' became exclusive as the upper caste Nairs repeatedly targeted not only British political authority and the missions/Church that they saw as undifferentiated, but also the Shanar converts, the local adherents of the White Man's religion.

Dubbing the Shanar converts as 'anti-national' because they entered the Church giving up their indigenous faith in preference to an 'alien' religion which was also the religion of the British rulers, is not sustainable. Firstly, the Church cannot be merely reduced to a 'colonial' and 'anti-national' position. For example, the missionary reform and modernizing agenda aimed at propagating Protestant ethics and values such as equality, freedom, civic life etc, were not opposed to the nationalist ideals in any way. Secondly, the Shanar converts' allegiance to the Church/Mission was not complete. This was evident from the fact that in a number of cases a large number of Shanars rushed to the London Mission Society congregation, whenever

missionary efforts were perceived to be of help in shedding their caste based disadvantages. But, when they found these advantages to be petering off, they returned to their original faith.[10]

In 1814 when the poll tax on the low caste Christians was abolished, about one thousand families joined the Church, but when this advantage was subsequently extended to the Hindus also, only twenty of these families remained within the Church.[11] Similarly once the lower caste Christians were exempted from contributing free labour (*ooliyum*) for the preparations for Hindu festivals, there was a sudden rush of lower caste people to the LMS Church during those months when extraction of corvee for Hindu festivals would reach their peak, these converts leaving the congregation when the festival preparations got over. In 1818 when Rev. Mead was appointed as a civil judge in Nagercoil, about 3000 Shanars entered the Church expecting favours. Once the short-lived experiment of appointing missionaries as judges was abandoned and Mead relinquished his post, most of the new converts left the Church.[12] For the lower caste converts, the notion of 'national' and 'colonial' did not matter as they moved towards their new faith to gain temporal advantages and alter the existing situations of power in their own favour, which set them against the indigenous elite.

While the missionary efforts to ameliorate the disabilities of the Shanar converts had reached their climax in the nineteenth century in South Travancore, some Hindu Shanars took recourse to a heretical Hindu cult called the Muthukutty Swamy cult, which challenged the caste based inequities.[13] The founder, Vaikunda Swamy (1809-1851), claimed to be reborn as a son of Vishnu to salvage the Shanars from their

[9] C.M. Agur, *Church History of Travancore*, Madras: SPG Press, 1903, p.51.
[10] Dick Kooiman, *Conversion and Social Equality*, p.73-74
[11] *Ibid.*, p.73.
[12] *Ibid.*, p.74.
[13] M.S.S.Pandian, *Meanings of 'colonialism' and 'nationalism,'* pp.177-179.

oppression and degradation. In his preachings Vaikunda Swamy opposed the excessive taxes and *ooliyum* services imposed on the Shanars by the Travancore king. He unleashed virulent attacks on traditional Travancore society and the Travancore ruler, for which he was imprisoned for a while. He condemned several traditional practices such as idol worship, devil worship and animal sacrifice, betraying a close resemblance to the Christian belief and missionary preaching.

Within its territory the cult articulated the same aspirations as the Shanar Christians. Vaikunda Swamy vehemently opposed the denial of the right to Shanar women to wear the shoulder cloth. Inspired by the revolt of Shanar Christians and the Muthukutty Swamy cult, the Hindu Shanars joined the protest by wearing the upper cloth. Significantly, during the turbulent period of riots in the 1850's, which erupted on account of this protest, both the Hindu and Christian Shanars joined hands in fighting out the Nair opponents. Despite the united front and commonalities, only the Christian Shanars seemed to have provoked the wrath of the upper caste Hindus, while the adherents of the Vaikunda Swamy cult were left untouched. Not a single instance of any attack on the places of worship of this cult can be traced, while instances of attacks on Christians and churches proliferated. The cult was so popular that the London Mission Society reported in 1864:

> Some years ago a palmyrah climber named Muttukutti claimed to be an incarnation of Vishnu and deceived many people. His followers have erected pagodas in many places. As they regard Muttukutti as an incarnation of Vishnu, they affirm that the worship of Muttukutti is really a worship of the Supreme being.... This impostor is one of the chief obstacles to the spread of the Gospel in these parts.[14]

A large number of poor Shanars flocked towards this cult because the Church that gave them scope to question the caste-based disadvantages was ravaged by the upper caste Hindus. In order to safeguard themselves from the upper caste assaults, and subvert the hierarchisation of Hindus, the vulnerable Shanars found an alternative in the heretical Vaikunda Swamy cult and continued to protest against oppression. Though Vaikunda Swamy boldly accused the local rulers of being oppressors and the colonizers (British) of being 'white oppressors,' he never launched any systematic campaign against the latter.

It is significant to note that these were the modalities through which a section of the Shanars resolved the violent conflict with the traditional power holders of indigenous society as a result of the Protestant missionary activated aspirations. The London Missionary Society / Protestant Church articulated the interest of the subordinated classes, the Shanars. The LMS/ Church turned overtly political as an ally of the colonial power, the British and succeeded in securing some liberties for the Shanar Christians. But it was the 'nationalist' indigenous elite, led by Velu Thambi Nair (hailed as a 'nationalist' and anti-British) who suppressed them. The vision of freedom of the indigenous elite led by Velu Thambi Nair and others was different from the Shanars vision of liberation. While the former sought freedom from British colonial power, the Shanars sought freedom from the upper caste domination constituted by the indigenous elite. Indigenous elite nationalism was not only directed against the British colonial power but also against the Shanar Christians. For the upper castes colonialism meant an erosion of their pre-existing power; at the same time it meant a possibility of empowerment for Shanars. Thus there was no one history of colonialism and nationalism, but at

---

[14] As quoted in M.S.S.Pandian, *Meanings of 'colonialism' and 'nationalism'*.......... p-181

least one for the Shanars and another for the Nairs.

The above account establishes that it is misleading to simplify and essentialise the interactions between the different actors in this narration – namely the Church, colonialism and the indigenous society — into any strait-jacketed explanations. One cannot ignore the complexities of these multi-layered encounters which acquired different dimensions in different historical situations.The lines of demarcation within the 'national' and 'anti-national' paradigm blur as one traces the history of the Shanars who used their new faith to alter the existing situations of power in their own favour. The parameters of their politics were in fact removed from the concerns of nationalism and colonialism. The Church and the Vaikunda Swamy cult were both forms of protest employed by the subordinate Shanars of South Travancore. The most poor and vulnerable sought fulfillment of their aspirations in the popular Vaikunda Swamy cult that disapproved of both the local oppressor and white oppressor, while the Shanar Christians looked for a solution in the Church. While they did not completely adhere to the civilising mission of the Church, because they were unwilling to totally relinquish their cultural past, they did not view the Church as antithetical to the 'nation.' The Shanar Christians opposed the indigenous elite who opposed the colonizers, but they were not allies of the colonizers or 'anti-national.'

CHAPTER 19

History of Christian Mission in Sri Lanka

G.P.V. SOMARATNA

According to legend, the first Christian mission to Sri Lanka took place in the Apostolic period. St Thomas is believed to have been the first missionary to Sri Lanka. However, the preaching of the apostolic age would not have brought about lasting results. Missionary activity would have been confined to the very small Greek speaking trading community inhabiting the ports of the North Central coast of Sri Lanka.

Anuradhapura Christianity (4th to 7th centuries)

The second wave of missionary activity took place around the fifth century A.D. when the Persian Christian traders moved across the Indian Ocean during the period prior to the emergence of Islam in the seventh century. The Persians were Nestorians. Therefore their Christological beliefs differed from Orthodox Christianity. Their missionaries came from Persia. According to available sources, missionaries continuously served the Christian communities in Matottam, Vavuniya, Anuradhapura, and Sigiriya towns for more than two centuries. This Christian community ceased to exist some time after the fall of Persia to the Muslims in the seventh century.

Thereafter, till the arrival of the Roman Catholic missionaries, there was no tangible missionary presence in Sri Lanka except the visit of Friar Maringoli who was on his way back from China to Europe.

Portuguese Era (1505-1658)

The lasting presence of Christianity owes its origin to the Roman Catholic missionaries who arrived in the country in the sixteenth century. The first missionaries were the Franciscan friars who arrived in the island in 1543 at the invitation of the king of Kotte. The next were the Jesuits who began working in Mannar in the 1540s. The Jesuits were officially permitted by the Portuguese government in 1602 to work in other parts of the country. This was because the Portuguese government had the *dejure* authority to co-ordinate the missionary activities under the *padroado* privilege granted to the king of Portugal by the Pope. The Augustinians (1604) and the Dominicans (1606) also began missionary work in Sri Lanka. The island continued to receive missionaries from Portugal till the termination of Portuguese rule in 1658.

The Roman Catholic missionaries were able to make revolutionary advances in the spread of the Christian faith in the second half of the sixteenth and the first half of the seventeenth centuries. They had more than 120 resident priests at the time the missionaries were forced to leave the country. These missionaries were able to organize congregations and set up churches in all parts of the country which came under Portuguese rule.

The Roman Catholic mission was the first of the modern missions to Sri Lanka. Therefore, they did not face the prejudices and objections which the later generation of missionaries had to face. The external trappings of their religious practices were very close to Sinhala Buddhist and Tamil Hindu observances. Therefore, it was not difficult to transfer allegiance from one faith to the other. The majority of their converts came from the fishing community in Tamil and Sinhala areas. The Hindu laws of pollution pertaining to the caste system and the Five Buddhist precepts made them outcasts of the traditional society. But when the Portuguese left the country the people of the fishing community were able to enjoy the cultural privileges which were previously confined to the farmer caste.

The Roman Catholics were able to introduce Judaeo-Christian concepts, values, social habits and the biblical vocabulary to the Sinhala and Tamil languages. The next generation of missionaries was able to build upon the solid foundation laid by the Roman Catholic fathers during a period of over a century.[1]

Dutch Period (1642-1796)

The next stage of missionary activity began with the advent of Dutch Reformed Christianity to the island. The Dutch East India Company was able to capture the southern part of the island in 1642 from the Portuguese. The first ministers of the Dutch Reformed Church began working from that time. However, their activities really began with the total expulsion of the Portuguese from the island in 1658. The missionary activity depended on the goodwill of the Dutch East India Company which ruled the maritime provinces of the island. In fact, during this period political and economic motives overshadowed religious interests. The Dutch ministers were more interested in suppressing and reconverting Roman Catholics than in evangelism among the local population.

The Dutch, however, maintained the educational establishment set up by the Roman Catholics. They also translated the Scriptures into the vernacular languages and made them available to the people in printed form. Schoolmasters and Christian workers who were needed for work among the local people, were trained in the seminaries set up for the purpose.[2]

However, their work did not produce the desired results as the Dutch form of Christianity without external expressions of piety was not attractive to the people. Instead, the Roman Catholic Church, the practice of which was banned by the Dutch government, prospered clandestinely with the help of the Oratorian missionaries who arrived in Sri Lanka incognito. They were able to revive the Church and attract more believers to their congregations than the state supported Dutch Reformed Church. The Oratorians had an average of about 16 priests in the island whereas the number of ministers of the Dutch Reformed Church averaged around six. The loyalty of the Catholics and their steadfastness in the faith were a credit to the Oratorians who dedicated their time and energy to the welfare of the Catholics. Outstanding missionaries like Joseph Vaz, now the saint of Sri Lanka, and Jocome Gonsalvez, the literary genius in the vernaculars, provided inspiration for the later generations of Catholic priests. Venerable Joseph Vaz was instrumental in introducing a system of local leaders who would function in the absence of priests to care for the flock. Gonsalvez provided a large number of books and pamphlets in Sinhala and Tamil for the improvement of the quality of the faith of the Catholics.

During the Dutch period, another Protestant missionary organization had a promising start. The Moravians, who came to the island in 1740, began working in a suburb of Colombo and were able to attract a large number of people, including Dutch residents, to their meetings. The Dutch ministers who were alarmed by the loss of their members to the Moravian community, soon got

---

[1] V. Perniola, *The Catholic Church in Sri Lanka* , 12 volumes, Dehiwela: Tisara Publishers, Sri Lanka, 1983-2000
[2] Van Goor, *Jan Kompanie as Schoolmaster: Dutch Education in Ceylon 1690-1795*, Groningen: Wolters-Noordhoff, 1978

the government to expel them from the country, thereby terminating their work prematurely.

British Era (1796-1948)

When the Dutch rule came to an end in 1796, the government statistics indicated the conversion of the total population of the maritime provinces of the island to the Dutch Reformed faith. These numbers were misleading as people sought baptism in order to comply with government regulations which demanded registration in Church records to own and inherit property. These unrealistic high numbers shrank drastically as soon as the British allowed freedom of religious practice in their territory in 1806.

At the turn of the nineteenth century, the Catholics were the largest Christian community in the Island despite the oppressive policies of the Dutch government. The Dutch Reformed faith soon became confined to the Dutch descendants of the country. Nevertheless, the first generation of British authorities, who were guided by the statistics in the Dutch records, were alarmed by the lack of spiritual care for the large number of Protestants scattered throughout the country. Therefore, they made an attempt to encourage missionaries to come over to Sri Lanka from Europe, to care for them.

The first to arrive in the country were five missionaries from the London Missionary Society, in 1804. This society did not send any missionaries after this initial batch. The next mission was that of the Baptists (1812). The Wesleyan Methodist (1814), American Board of Foreign Missions (1816), Church Missionary Society (1818) and the Society for the Propagation of the Gospel (1848) were among the next set of Protestant missionaries. These missionaries were instrumental in setting up a branch of the Bible Society (1812), Religious Tract Society (1814), and Vernacular Education Society (1821) in order to facilitate their evangelical work. The other missionary societies which began work in the island during the British period were Salvation Army (1883) and the Assemblies of God (1924). All these missionary bodies continued to supply missionary personnel and material support throughout the British period and even after independence.

These missionaries learned Sinhala and Tamil, set up printing presses, opened schools and began preaching tours. They published Sinhala and Tamil grammars, dictionaries and school textbooks in order to enable the people to read and write in their own language. This was intended to be the base for introducing the scriptures to them. Bible translations were prepared, continuously revised, published and issued to the public at very low cost.

Education has been their chief activity almost from the outset, and it has made notable contributions to scholarship, discipline, social values and ethics of the people of the country. Their newspapers, books, journals and other publications together with the missionary educational set up, brought about revolutionary changes in the country. The newly literate middle class took over the administration from the traditional aristocracy. The village schools produced schoolmasters, clerks, and entrepreneurs. A large number of non-Christians sought the benefits of missionary education. The pioneering work done by the missionaries for the education of women brought enlightenment to the family. In fact, towards the end of the nineteenth century, every religion in Sri Lanka tried to imitate the methods and policies followed by Protestant missionaries in order to enhance the position of its faith. Non-Christians were attracted to the Victorian forms of ethics and social behavior which permeated Sri Lankan society through Christian missionary activities. Some non-Christians even sought solemnization of marriage according to Christian tradition. The history of Sri Lanka in the nineteenth century can easily be called the Christian century considering the predominance of Protestant Christian culture in almost all areas of society.[3]

The nineteenth century was a difficult period for the Roman Catholics. The Oratorian missionaries who functioned well in an underground Church environment found themselves to be misfits when the church was given freedom and forced to function in the open. They could not compete with the vigorous Protestant missionary organizations. Being Goans, they were familiar with the Portuguese language, but were unable to offer English education which the Catholics of the country demanded. By this time, the enthusiasm of the pioneer Oratorians was no longer present among the Catholic missionaries of Goan origin. Furthermore, the majority of them, by this time, were not proficient in Sinhala or Tamil. Therefore, the Congregation of the Propaganda of Faith in Rome took action to send missionaries from Europe to face the new challenge. The European missionaries had a difficult task at the beginning since they found it hard to secure the co-operation of the Oratorians. However, the termination of the Goan Oratorian order in 1834 by the Portuguese government did help to some extent. Among the European missionaries, Sylvestrine Benedictines (1838) and the Order of Mary Immaculate (1942) were the most prominent. Towards the end of the eighteenth century, the Jesuit order also began their work in the country. Women's orders like the Sisters of the Holy Family (1863) and the Good Shepherd Nuns (1867) concentrated on the education of girls. Sisters of St Peter, St Mary, St Mary Terese, St. Jane and St Agnes, also arrived in Sri Lanka in the 1880s to serve in the orphanages, leprosaria, hospitals and correctional institutions in addition to their involvement in education and parish work.[4] The beneficial impact of their activities was not confined to the Roman Catholic community.

Twentieth century

The only new Christian mission introduced in the first half of the twentieth century was the Assemblies of God (1925). It was a Pentecostal denomination which emphasized the spiritual gifts. Together with the Ceylon Pentecostal Mission, which was an indigenous body, they were active among the urban middle class and the poor in the estate sector of the hill country. However, they gained very few converts from outside the Christian community. The majority of their converts were from already established Christian denominations. The Ceylon Pentecostal Mission deserves special mention because they sent Sri Lankan missionaries to India, United Kingdom, United States, France and Malaya in a period when the missionary movement was dominated by the West.

In the first half of the twentieth century the traditional Christian missions, Protestant as well as Roman Catholics, devoted their attention to wholistic mission. In that venture, they gave less attention to evangelism and more attention to social enhancement programs. The educational establishment took a major portion of their time and energy. The Americans had an excellent medical mission in Jaffna.

By the time of independence in 1948, the Christians had a privileged position in the educational, professional, and entrepreneurial positions of the country. Nearly one and a half centuries of Protestant and Roman Catholic missionary work had brought about a society of Christians who had experienced 'redemption and lift'' which the other communities in the Island envied.[5]

---

[3] K.M. de Silva, (ed.) *University of Ceylon: History of Ceylon*, Vol. 3, Colombo : University Press, 1974, pp. 66-76.

[4] Bede Barcatta, *A History of the Southern Vicariate of Colombo: Sri Lanka*, Kandy: Monrefano, 1991.

[5] K.M. de Silva, *Sri Lanka: A Survey*, New Delhi: Oxford University Press, 1977.

Independence

Sri Lanka gained independence in 1948. Together with independence, parliamentary democracy was also introduced. Therefore, the majority were able to elect their own representatives to govern the country. The Buddhist nationalists had developed an anti-missionary attitude since the latter part of the nineteenth century. These negative attitudes re-emerged after independence. Their main aim was to terminate the philanthropic and educational establishments run by the Christian missions. Their agitation bore fruit in 1961 with the nationalization of Christian mission schools. A *coup dé tat* organized by some disgruntled Christian leaders of the Security Forces in 1962 made the government take serious restrictive measures as regards Christian missions, as baseless rumors connected the coup with the American CIA. Restrictions were imposed on the visas granted to foreign missionaries. The period of austerity which curtailed foreign travel and imports continued till 1977.

There was a trend away from evangelism in the 1960s as a result of nationalist opposition. Missionary movements, both Roman Catholic and Protestant, responded with service activities in the inner cities, refugee camps, settlements, health, welfare, vocational and recreational services. A lack of evangelism and the inclusive tendencies of missionary theology contributed to the reduction of the percentage of Christians in the population of the country in the 1960s and 1970s.

The charismatic movement, which began in Europe and America in the 1960s took nearly a decade to make its appearance in Sri Lanka. In the 1970s, the need for evangelism increased again as a result of the universalist attitude that dominated the mainline churches. The real impact began to be felt in the 1980s. The new evangelical missions emerged in all parts of the country. The estate sector, rural areas and the urban poor benefited from these new missions. Local leaders have led the missions in this era. The foreign element has been confined to leadership training, literature and financial support. The most outstanding support to the Christian mission in this era has come from America. Korea also has had a share in providing personnel, training and financial support. The traditional missionary countries like Britain, France and Holland have continued their historical connections, though on a low key.

The history of the Christian mission in Sri Lanka is long. It is a clear example of each generation finding its own purpose and living out its Christian faith. The foreign missionaries made a great impact in the initial stages of the Christian mission. Christians today owe a great debt of gratitude to the fathers who brought the faith to this land. They introduced a new life style to the people with ethics and values based on the Judeo-Christian tradition. The final result was 'redemption and lift' to the people in Sri Lanka.

PART IV

Religious Studies

Religious Pluralism & Contemporary Theological Issues that Impinge on Missiology for the 21st Century

IVAN M. SATYAVRATA and ABEY GEORGE

Introduction

The plurality of religions and cultures has been an integral feature of life within the human community since time immemorial. The Christian church has had to address this fact since its earliest inception. In recent years the issue has assumed growing importance in the contemporary world of theological reflection. In the South Asian context today the Christian response to the multi-cultural social reality has become an important and urgent concern.[1]

The Phenomenon of Religious Pluralism

Stanley Samartha is probably the best representative of a growing number of modern theologians who regard religious pluralism simply as "…part of the larger plurality of races, peoples and cultures, of social structures, economic systems and political patterns, of languages and symbols, all of which are a part of the total human heritage…the fact that different religions respond to the mystery of ultimate reality in different ways…"[2]

Ken Gnanakan, on the other hand, clearly distinguishes between the socio-cultural phenomenon of *plurality*, and various forms of *pluralism* as a theological posture which insists that we "…cast aside all the unique claims that we make about Christ and accept on equal terms similar claims of all other religions."[3]

The issue then is: what should be our attitude as Christians to the diverse faiths of our neighbours in the society in which we live? Is it right for Christians to continue to hold to the conviction that Jesus Christ is the *only* way to God — the *only* mediator between God and man in the present environment? There are also a vast number of related questions that arise in consequence, such as: Does confessing 'Jesus is Lord' mean that Krishna or Buddha or Allah is not? Does the fact that Christ is *my* Saviour imply that He is the *only* Saviour? If Christ is the only way to God, what about the millions of people who lived, for instance, in India in the years BC? If every religion claims to be the only true one

---

[1] Alan Race attributes this sudden surge in interest in the issue, to three major reasons. Firstly, the changing patterns of mobility have shattered older conceptions of the religious history of the world, which viewed the faiths as being largely confined to specific cultural and geographical boundaries. Secondly, at an academic level, there has been an accumulation of a wealth of knowledge concerning the beliefs and practices of non-Christian faiths. Finally, there seems to be a new missionary consciousness that a number of ancient faiths are manifesting throughout the world, Alan Race, *Christians and Religious Pluralism: Patterns in the Christian Theology of Religions*, London: SCM, 1983, p.viii.

[2] S.J. Samartha, *One Christ – Many Religions*, Bangalore: SATHRI, 1992, p. 4.

[3] Ken Ganakan, *The Pluralistic Predicament*, Bangalore: TBT, 1992, p.3. This distinction between the empirical reality of religious plurality and the philosophical/theological response to the social phenomenon, would seem to be an important one, although not followed too closely in this paper in keeping with the practice of most authors in this field. For further discussion on the 'kinds' of pluralism viz. empirical, cherished, and philosophical, see D. A. Carson, *The Gagging of God: Christianity confronts Pluralism*, Grand Rapids, MI: Zondervan, 1996.

and sees its mission as converting those of other faiths, will it not lead to further religious fanaticism and strong feelings of hostility in society?

While we cannot address all of the implications of an issue of such complexity in one monograph, this paper will attempt to identify and address the critical theological questions, especially as they relate to missiology for the twenty-first century.

Responses to Religious Pluralism

There is little debate today that Christianity was born into, and continues to exist in a religiously pluralistic world. In this pluralistic environment Christianity continued to hold on to the centrality of the original constituting fact of the Christian faith – the Christ-event – and claims concerning its decisiveness, which have given the Christian faith its intrinsic missionary nature.

Questions regarding the decisiveness and normativity of Christ thus have significant consequences for the Church's understanding of its mission. The historical particularity of Christianity received its first serious challenge during the Enlightenment. How could a loving God fail to offer salvation to all? In the early nineteenth century, Friedrich Schleiermacher sought to answer this question by correlating Christianity as the fulfillment of public truths.[4] God, he argued, is salvifically available in some degree in all religions, but the gospel of Jesus Christ is the fulfillment and highest manifestation of this universal religious awareness. By the late nineteenth century, however, historicism, with its heightened awareness of cultural and religious relativities, challenged the inclusivists' normative claim that Jesus Christ is the fulfillment of religion. It was argued that since we are at every moment purely historical creatures, religious claims can only be viewed as our culturally conditioned apprehension of the divine, allowing for a plurality of possible responses to the noumenal reality – different but all equally valid responses.

Religious claims have been consequently relegated to the 'private' sphere, so that today religious beliefs have become little more than a matter of personal taste.[5] During the past two decades a large number of theologians have "crossed the theological Rubicon"[6] – away from insistence on the superiority or 'decisiveness'[7] of Christ and Christianity toward a recognition of the independent validity of other ways. The implications of this shift are enormously significant. It is in this context that the church is required to forge an urgent response; to sketch to some degree of clarity a proper Christian response to the phenomenon of plurality and provide a clear theological basis for explaining the relationship between Christian faith and other religions.

During the early half of the twentieth century the discussion regarding the relation of the Christian faith and other religions was cast in terms of discontinuity (Hendrick Kraemer), fulfillment (John Farquhar), and mutual appreciation (William Hocking).[8] However, since

---

[4] Friedrich Schleiermacher, *Christian Faith*, Par. 7-9, as cited by Dennis L. Okholm and Timothy R. Phillips, eds, *Four Views on Salvation in a Pluralistic World*, Grand Rapids, MI: Zondervan, 1996, p. 8.

[5] Chris Wright, *What's So Unique About Jesus?* Eastbourne: MARC, 1990, pp. 9-11.

[6] Paul F. Knitter and John Hick, eds., *The Myth of Christian Uniqueness: Toward a Pluralistic Theology of Religions*, Maryknoll: Orbis Books, 1988, p. viii.

[7] The term "decisiveness" of Christ, rather than "uniqueness" or "finality," is preferred in this paper – as defended convincingly by O. V. Jathanna, *The Decisiveness of the Christ-event & the Universality of Christianity in a World of Religious Plurality*, Berne: Peter Lang, 1981, pp. 22-35.

[8] Hendrick Kraemer, *The Christian Message in a Non-Christian World*, New York: Harper & Brothers, 1938; John Nicol Farquhar, *The Crown of Hinduism*, London: Oxford, 1913; William Hocking, *Re-thinking Missions: A Layperson's Inquiry After 100 Years*, New York: Harper & Brothers, 1932.

the publication of the definitive work of Alan Race and Gavin D'Costa in the last quarter of the century, the threefold categorization of exclusivism, inclusivism, and pluralism have tended to provide the framework for the debate.[9]

Exclusivism

This view relates salvation and/or liberation exclusively to one particular tradition, so that it is an article of faith that salvation is restricted to this one particular "community", the rest of humankind being either left out of account or explicitly excluded from the sphere of salvation.[10] According to Alan Race, not even the most detached reader of the New Testament would fail to gain the impression that the overall picture of Christian faith that it presents is intended to be absolute or final, indicated both in general themes and by specific texts (Acts 4:12; John 14:6). It counts the revelation in Jesus Christ as the sole criterion by which all religions, including Christianity, can be understood and evaluated.[11]

The most emphatic and influential expression of such a view is seen perhaps in Cyprian's famous dictum *extra ecclesiam nulla salus*, and Karl Barth, the Swiss theologian, is often presented as the most important spokesperson of this "conservative" view, because at least in the early phase of his thinking (his later thoughts, it is held by many, betray an incipient inclusivist tendency), he drew a dividing line between the Christian faith and the others. He saw the gospel as coming vertically, from above, out of God's unapproachable transcendence, and therefore disclaimed all religions as autonomous attempts of natural, sinful man to realize his salvation through his self-chosen ways.[12]

Perhaps one of the most influential proponents of this view, particularly in our own context, is Lesslie Newbigin. He accepts the term 'exclusivism' to describe his thought, although he differs with other 'exclusivists' on topics such as the nature of Scripture, the presence of truth in the non-Christian religions, and the possibility of non-Christians being ultimately saved. For him, the decisiveness of Christ means that He is the unique and only Saviour.

The exclusivist theology of religion has come to represent the most clear cut of all theories in this field. It involves no complicated theory about the nature of religious experience; it appeals to what for many is a self-evident biblical witness; it gives a central function to the person of Christ; and the internal logic of its argument appears consistent and coherent; and, finally it is the position which corresponds most closely to what has generally been held to be orthodox Christianity for centuries.[13] Its most serious weakness appears to be its failure to take seriously the empirical data of other religions.

Inclusivism

This view is both an acceptance and a rejection of the other faiths. On the one hand it

---

[9] Alan Race, *Christians and Religious Pluralism*; Gavin D'Costa, *Theology and Religious Pluralism: The Challenge of Other Religions*, Oxford: Blackwell, 1986. Like all other categorizations, this classification too has a limited function, since the nomenclature often conceals normative truth claims of those who define the terms of classification. See Gavin D'Costa, "The Impossibility of a Pluralist view of Religions," *Religious Studies* Vol. 32, pp. 223-232. Both pluralism and inclusivism have been shown to be inadequate labels of the views they purport, yet used continually for want of better words, and exclusivism has often been associated with arrogance, intolerance, and dogmatism, See, Gerald H. Anderson and Thomas F. Strasky, eds, *Christ's Lordship and Religious Pluralism*, Maryknoll, N.Y.: Orbis, 1981, p. 148ff.

[10] Frank Whaling, ed. *The World's Religious Traditions: Current Perspectives in Religious Studies*, Edinburgh: T. & T. Clarke Ltd., 1984, p. 150.

[11] Alan Race, *Christians and Religious Pluralism*, p. 10.

[12] Karl Barth, *Church Dogmatics*, Vol. 1:2/17, as quoted by Peter Beyerhaus, "The Authority of the Gospel and Interreligious Dialogue," *Trinity Journal*, Vol. 17, No. 2, 1996.

accepts the spiritual power and depth manifest in them, so that they can rightly be considered as possessing elements of divine light and truth. On the other hand, it rejects them as not being sufficient for salvation apart from Christ, for Christ alone is Saviour. To be inclusive is to believe that all truth, Christian and non-Christian, belongs ultimately to Christ.[14]

One of the foremost proponents of this view is the leading Roman Catholic theologian, Karl Rahner, whose view became popularized by his concept of "lawful Religions" and "anonymous Christians" that emerged in the documents approved by the Second Vatican Council. According to this view, God has freely and finally communicated himself in his revelation in Christ.[15]

How is this possible? Rahner maintains that Jesus Christ is present in the non-Christian religions too:

> Such a presence of Jesus Christ throughout the whole of salvation and in relation to all people cannot be denied or overlooked by Christians if they believe in Jesus Christ as the salvation of all people, and do not think that the salvation of non-Christians is brought about by God and his mercy independently of Jesus Christ. This presupposes only that these non-Christians are of good will, even when this good will has absolutely nothing to do with Jesus Christ.[16]

The essence of this view is to be found in its two equally strong convictions: (i) the operation of the grace of God in all the religions of the world, towards salvation; (ii) the decisiveness of the manifestation of the grace of God in Christ, which makes universal claim as the final way of Salvation. A wide variety of forms of inclusivism may be distinguished, ranging from the more cautious views of Gavin D'Costa and Clark Pinnock to those of Raimundo Panikkar and J. A. T. Robinson, which reflect certain features of pluralism.[17]

Pluralism

Christianity in this theory represents only one cultured response to the divine initiative; it cannot claim a monopoly of religious truth.[18] This view is the belief that the world religions are true and equally effective in reaching liberation/freedom/ salvation. A verse from the *Bhagavad Gita* aptly summarizes this view: "Howsoever man may approach me, even so do I accept them; for, on all sides, whatever path they may choose is mine."[19] John Hick has been a provocative advocate of the pluralist perspective. According to this view any form of religion or quasi-religious world-view is granted equal status on the

---

[13] Alan Race, *Christians and Religious Pluralism*, p. 24. Quite convincingly argued in Adrian Hastings, "Pluralism: The Relationship of Theology to Religious Studies," in *Religious Pluralism and Unbelief*, London: Routledge, 1990, pp. 235-238.

[14] Alan Race, *Christians and Religious Pluralism*, p. 38. According to John Hick, inclusivism represents "the nearest approach to a consensus among Christian thinkers today." *The Metaphor of God Incarnate: Christology in a Pluralistic Age*, p. 88. Clark H. Pinnock suggests a number of positive features that have helped make it a success. See "An Inclusivist View" in *Four Views, edited by Okholm and Phillips*, p. 101f.

[15] He does not limit salvation to those who have responded to the revelation in Christ. What he fundamentally affirms is that salvation, wherever present, is always of Christ, for Christ alone is the Saviour.

[16] Karl Rahner, *Foundations of Christian Faith*, New York: The Crossroad Publishing Company, 1993, pp. 312f.

[17] Gavin D'Costa, *Theology and Religious Pluralism*; Clark H. Pinnock, *A Wideness in God's Mercy: The Finality of Jesus Christ in a World of Religions*, Grand Rapids: Zondervan, 1992; Raimundo Pannikkar, *The Unknown Christ of Hinduism*, London: Darton, Longman and Todd, 1964.

[18] Alan Race, *Christians and Religious Pluralism*, p. 76.

[19] *Bhagavad Gita*, 4.11, quoted in John Hick and Brian Hebblethwaite, eds. *Christianity and Other Religions: Selected Readings*, Philadelphia: Fortress Press, 1980, p. 190.

assumption that all of them strive for the salvation of the human race in its natural environment.[20]

Hick arrives at these conclusions on the basis of a twofold assumption. First, he recognizes the impossibility of ever reaching any measure of comprehensiveness even in theory, as long as the theology of religions is dedicated to a theo-centric basis. For not all religions have concepts of a supreme deity (cf. Buddhism's original atheism). Thus while replacing God with "Reality" – a more abstract term, agreeable to all, he moves to a soterio-centric model. Secondly, he changes the definition of salvation – transformation of humankind from self-centredness to Reality-centredness. "It can no longer be established simply by defining salvation as inclusion within the scope of the divine pardon bought by Christ's atoning death…this kind of arbitrary superiority-by-definition [is] no longer defensible."[21]

A pluralist would typically, then, attempt to negate Christocentric Christianity. The strategy, therefore, is to reduce Christ, and magnify God – in actuality 'the Real'. Thus, incarnation, for example, becomes a mere mythological event, though it does serve as a powerful metaphor of a divine *kenosis*, and of human openness and responsiveness to the will of God.[22]

The essence of a pluralistic view of religion is then, the belief that Christianity cannot be regarded as the only religion that provides salvation. Salvation/liberation is mediated distinctively and uniquely by various religious traditions.

Critical Issues In Religious Pluralism[23]

We will focus on four crucial issues:

The Question of Christ's Decisiveness

The question of Jesus – his particularity and universality – is undoubtedly the central issue in the debate on religious pluralism. Harvey Cox, in his book, *Many Mansions*, highlights the centrality of the issue as follows:

> For the vast majority of Christians, including those most energetically engaged in dialogue, Jesus is not merely a background figure. He is central to Christian faith. Not only do the Christian dialoguers recognize this, but so do their Muslim, Buddhist, Shinto, Hindu, and Jewish conversation partners. Wherever one starts…any honest dialogue between Christians and others will sooner or later – and in my experience it is usually sooner – have to deal with the figure of Jesus.[24]

The challenge of plurality has driven many theologians today to a renewed search for new, alternative Christologies that are not bound by the perceived limitations of the traditional understanding of the decisiveness and normativity of Jesus Christ.

Christianity has historically maintained that Jesus of Nazareth was not simply a great religious and moral teacher in first-century Palestine, but that, in an admittedly mysterious sense, he was the eternal creator God who became man – he was God incarnate. The influence of this view of Christ within the Christian community is clearly reflected in the great historic creeds and

---

[20] Peter Beyerhaus, "The Authority of the Gospel and Interreligious Dialogue," p. 138.

[21] John Hick, ed. *The Myth of God Incarnate*, London: SCM, 1977, p. 23. For a penetrating analysis of Hick's view, see Gavin D'Costa, *John Hick's Theology of Religions: A Critical Evaluation*, Lanhalm: University Press of America, 1987.

[22] John Hick, *The Metaphor of God Incarnate: Christology in a Pluralistic Age*, London: SCM, 1993, pp. 61-71.

[23] This section seeks merely to introduce the critical issues involved in the discussion. It does not purport to provide any conclusive solutions to all of the questions raised.

[24] Harvey Cox, *Many Mansions: A Christian's Encounter With Other Faiths*, Boston: Beacon Press, 1988, pp. 7-8.

confessions of the Christian faith.[25] The Westminster Confession of Faith (1646), for instance, affirms that Jesus "is very God and very man, yet one Christ, the only Mediator between God and man."[26] The Lausanne Covenant (1974), similarly, affirms that "Jesus Christ, being himself the only God-man, who gave himself as the only ransom for sinners, is the only mediator between God and man."[27]

Pluralists such as Hick and Knitter[28] would undermine such a Christology claiming that Jesus, while a great – perhaps even the greatest – religious leader, is ultimately in the same category as other great religious figures. Certainly God (or, the "Real", as Hick would prefer) was present and active in Jesus, but then, the same can also be said of Gautama Buddha, Muhammad, or Confucius.

The claim being made increasingly in such quarters is that Christians should no longer talk of God's work in the lives of neighbors of other faiths in purely negative terms. God's self-disclosure in the lives of neighbors of other faiths and in the secular struggles of human life should also be recognized as real and theologically significant. The problem then is to try and understand the particularity of God's revelation in Jesus Christ within the larger framework of God's universal love for all humankind.

One alternative, perhaps, would be to recognize God alone as Absolute and to consider all religions to be relative. This means that religious particularities are not denied, but the ambiguity of the historical phenomena of religions, is acknowledged. The relativization of religions would liberate their respective adherents from a self-imposed obligation to defend their particular community of faith over against others, in order to be free to point to the ultimacy of God who holds all things and all people in his embrace. In face of the sense of the paramount need for human unity, the claim of one group to have the truth, "that one religious tradition has the *only* answer"[29] not only seems preposterous, but is also seen as potentially disastrous.

In the context of the ever-increasing attack on what is commonly referred to as 'fundamentalism' (read 'exclusivism'), it would surely be 'safe' to politely accept all religions as being credible paths to God. "It is not through our *a priori* doctrinal formulations on God or Christ," writes Professor Christopher Duraisingh, "but rather through our collective human search for meaning and sacredness, that the 'universe

---

[25] Belief in historic Christology does not mean that every line of a creed is beyond criticism, or is inspired. The contexts in which the great historic creeds were formulated are in several respects significantly different from those of today. Thus, it cannot be expected that these creeds settle questions arising in the contemporary church. They are, however, essential for the Church's historical understanding of its faith and identity.

[26] Robert Shaw, *An Exposition of The Westminster Confession of Faith*, Scotland: Christian Focus Publications, 1992, p. 97.

[27] J. D. Douglas, ed. *Let the Earth Hear His Voice: International Congress on World Evangelization, Lausanne, Switzerland*, Minneapolis: World Wide Publications, 1975, pp. 3-4.

[28] John Hick contends that Jesus is not literally God incarnate but rather simply a human being who was open to the presence and reality of God to an unprecedented degree. See John Hick, "Jesus and the World Religions," in *The Myth of God Incarnate*, ed. John Hick; *An Interpretation of Religion*, New Haven: Yale University Press, 1989; John Hick, *God Has Many Names*, Philadelphia: Westminster, 1982. Paul Knitter views Jesus "not as exclusive or even as normative, but as *theocentric*, as a universally relevant manifestation (sacrament, incarnation) of divine revelation and salvation, Paul Knitter, *No Other Name? A Critical Survey of Christian Attitudes Toward the World Religions*, Maryknoll, N.Y.: Orbis, 1985. Also his "Toward a Liberation Theology of Religions," in *The Myth of Christian Uniqueness*, ed. Hick and Knitter, Maryknoll, N.Y.: Orbis, 1987, and "Theocentric Christology: Defended and Transcended," in *Journal of Ecumenical Studies* 24 ,Winter 1987, pp. 41-52.

[29] Stanley J. Samartha in *International Review of Mission*, July 1988, p. 315, quoted by Lesslie Newbigin, *The Gospel in a Pluralist Society*, Grand Rapids, MI: Eerdmans, 1990, p. 156.

of faiths' could be adequately understood."[30] It is precisely at this point that the need emerges to orient this search from a position of faith-commitment. A common search cannot surely mean a search that abandons any specific clue and simply agrees to search.[31] There is no "theological helicopter" that can help us to rise above all religions and to look down upon the terrain below in lofty condenscension.[32] All serious seeking involves dependence on some clue or truth-criterion. Christians for their part believe that the decisive clue, the true and living way, has been given in Jesus.

The most common reason for a lack of toleration of any exclusive claims in our present day world is the belief that a claim to absolute truth must be oppressive. The fact is quite to the contrary. The Christian claim is that in Jesus the absolute truth has been revealed amid the relativities of human cultures, and that the form which this truth took was not that of dominance and imperial power but that of one whose power was manifest in weakness and suffering. The Church therefore does not claim to *possess* absolute truth: it claims to know where to point for guidance in the common search for truth.[33]

Perhaps the most serious theological crisis facing the Church today is the need to articulate its understanding of the decisive significance of Christ in relation to the other great religions of the world. If an extreme form of exclusivism were the best response, then, as Lesslie Newbigin writes,

It would be not only permissible but obligatory to use any means available, all the modern techniques of brainwashing included, to rescue others from this apalling fate. If we hold this view, it is absolutely necessary to know who is saved and who is not, and we are then led into making the kind of judgments against which Scripture warns us.[34]

The church must thus find a way to affirm the unique truth of the decisiveness of Jesus Christ and at the same time temper its confident outright rejection of the possibility of truth and grace being mediated outside the church. The Christian tradition bears witness to a *particular* understanding of God as revealed in Christ, while allowing for the possibility of the knowledge of God or 'points of contact' in non-Christian religions. The decisiveness or finality of Christ, however, remains a core affirmation essential to the Christian self-understanding and theological identity.

The Question of Salvation

Of great importance in any discussion on salvation is the question of the meaning of the word itself. What does the term "salvation" mean? On the one hand, it is felt that the concept differs vastly from one religion to another.[35] On the other hand, it has been argued that there is a common core structure to all religions, which "are fundamentally alike in exhibiting a soteriological structure. That is to say, they are all concerned with salvation/liberation/ enlightenment/ fulfillment."[36]

---

[30] Stanley J. Samartha, *Ibid.*, p. 399.

[31] Lesslie Newbigin, *The Gospel in a Pluralist Society*, p. 158.

[32] Stanley J. Samartha, "The Lordship of Jesus Christ and Religious Pluralism" in *Christ's Lordship & Religious Pluralism* edited by Anderson and Stransky, p. 29.

[33] Lesslie Newbigin, *The Gospel in a Pluralist Society*, p. 163.

[34] *Ibid.*, p. 173.

[35] See Hans Kung, et al. *Christianity and World Religions: Paths of Dialogue with Islam, Hinduism, and Buddhism*, Maryknoll, N.Y.: Orbis Books, 1993.

[36] John Hick, *The Second Christianity*, London: SCM, 1983, p. 86.

The pluralistic theology of religions looks at the various religious traditions as representing many different paths leading to the same ultimate goal. It does not consider distinct ultimate ends as possible goals to which the different traditions would lead. The theocentric paradigm considers God (or, the Real) as constituting this common goal.[37]

Alister E. McGrath, however, claims that the different religions do not merely offer different ways of achieving and conceptualizing salvation; they offer *different salvations* altogether. Do Christianity and Satanism really have the same understanding of salvation? The Buddhist vision of *nirvana* and the Christian hope of resurrection to eternal life are obviously different.[38] Can all the routes to salvation be equally "valid" when the goals to be reached in such different ways are so obviously unrelated?[39]

Another major question would be as to whether salvation is possible outside Christianity? How does one perceive the often-quoted words of Cyprian of Carthage: *extra ecclesiam nulla salus*. Closely related is the question of the scope of salvation for those who have never heard the gospel. Again the opinions on this issue are diverse. If we define salvation in terms of forgiveness and acceptance by God because of Jesus' death on the cross, then it becomes a tautology that seems applicable only to Christianity. Conversely, if we define salvation as an actual human change, a gradual transformation from natural self-centeredness to a radically new orientation centered in God and manifested in the "fruit of the Spirit", then it may be that salvation is taking place within all of the world religions.[40] On this view, which is not based on theological theory but on the observable realities of human life, salvation is not a juridical transaction inscribed in heaven, nor is it a future hope beyond this life, but it is a spiritual, moral, and political change that can begin now.

Pluralism, thus, maintains that salvation in all religions is more or less alike. They are contexts within which men and women have been transformed, in varying degrees, from self-centeredness to Reality-centeredness. Their soteriological power can only be humanly judged by their human fruits; more or less equally within each of the great traditions.[41] Inclusivism believes that because God is present in the whole world, God's grace is also at work in some way among all people. It entertains the possibility that religion may play a role in the salvation of the human race, a role preparatory to the gospel of Christ, in whom alone fullness of salvation is found.

---

[37] See also Hick's work *The Rainbows of Faith*, London: SCM, 1995, pp. 17f.

[38] "A Particularist View: A Post-Enlightenment Approach" in *Four*, Okholm and Phillips, pp. 170f. While allowing for the possibility of some knowledge of God outside the Christian community, he insists that the notion of salvation varies considerably from one religion to another. In some religions, for instance, there is often no discernable transcendent element associated with their notions of salvation. Also, the English term *salvation* is often used to translate Sanskrit or Chinese terms with connotations and associations quite distinct from the Christian use of the term. These divergences are masked by the process of translation which often suggests a degree of convergence that does not exist. See, pp. 163-166.

[39] It would be a Herculean task to attempt a detailed discussion of such differences. Suffice it to note that all religions present themselves to their followers as paths of salvation/liberation. The two concepts are juxtaposed here, firstly, because the combined notion is easily applicable to diverse traditions, no matter how different their respective concepts; and secondly, the double concept has the advantage of combining such complementary aspects as: the spiritual and the temporal, the transcendent and the human, the personal and the social, the eschatological and the historical. Jacques Dupuis, *Toward a Christian Theology of Religious Pluralism*, Maryknoll, N.Y.: Orbis Books, 1997, p. 306.

[40] "A Pluralist View" in *Four Views on Salvation in a Pluralistic World*, edited by Dennis L. Okholm and Timothy R. Phillips, pp. 43.

[41] *Ibid.*, pp. 44f. A question that could be asked at this point is, of course, as to what criteria does one employ to indentify/define these "human fruits."

According to Ludwig Wittgenstein, the 'form of living' to which a word refers and within which it is used, is of decisive importance in establishing its meaning. The particularities of a way of life are of controlling importance to our understanding of concepts.[42] Salvation being the case in point, its use and associations within the Christian tradition especially in worship, point to a distinctive understanding of what the Christian faith is understood to confer on believers, its ultimate basis, and the manner in which this comes about.

Therefore, the distinctive character of each religion, and the concepts therein, must be affirmed.[43] Buddhism, for instance, offers one style of 'salvation', just as Christianity offers another. It is no criticism of Buddhism to suggest that it does not offer a specifically Christian salvation, just as it is not in the least imperialist to state that the Christian vision of salvation is not the same as the Buddhist. It is essential to respect and honor differences here and to resist the ever-present temptation to force them all into the same mould.[44]

The word *salvation*, as we have already seen, is meaningless unless its context is identified. It is, to use Wittgenstein's phrase, necessary to establish the 'form of living' that gives the word its distinctive meaning. Salvation in the Christian sense of the term is thus indeed possible for those outside the Christian community only in Christ

– the entire enterprise of evangelism being directed to the proclamation of this good news. How can the salvation in Christ be applied to those who have never heard the gospel of Christ? Several Indian Christian thinkers, and converts in particular seem to be convinced that this category of people would be judged on the basis of their response to the light which they possess apart from explicit knowledge of the Christ event.[45]

The Question of Revelation and Truth

In the present day religiously pluralistic world, a pervasive sense of skepticism about the possibility of the knowledge of truth is almost a tenet of faith. In this environment of uncertainty and relativity, the Christian claim of possession of the truth seems rude, at best, and derogatory, at worst. The pivotal point around which the whole debate revolves is the claim of Christ to be the Truth. A closer look, however, would reveal two equally pressing issues here. First is the question of Revelation itself. What constitutes revelation? Is there salvific value in it? Is there divine revelation in other religions? Closely tied with this issue is that of 'truth' itself. How do we, for instance, determine truth?

Looking first at the question of revelation, biblical scholars from the region need to revisit a number of well-known New Testament passages that point to a natural or general revelation among

---

[42] Refer, Ludwig Wittgenstein, *Remarks on Colour*, edited by G. E. M. Anscombe, trans. L. L. McAlister and M. Schuttle, Oxford: Blackwell, 1977, 3:302. See also for a detailed study on Wittgenstein's understanding of the close association of the *Lebensform* ("form of living") on the concepts and words used: Fergus Kerr, *Theology after Wittgenstein*, Oxford: Blackwell, 1988.

[43] If salvation is understood as "some benefit conferred upon or achieved by members of a community, whether individually or corporately," all religions offer "salvation." All religions – even quasi-religions – offer *something*. It is therefore important to note that it is improper to use the term *salvation* as if it were common to all religions. Salvation thus understood would be a particularity, not a universality.

[44] This is essentially Mark Heim's thesis in *Salvation: Truth & Difference in Religion*, Maryknoll, N.Y.: Orbis Books, 1997.

[45] See especially K. M. Banerjea's view in "The Relation Between Christianity & Hinduism, repr. in T. V. Phillip, *Krishna Mohan Banerjea: Christian Apologist*, Bangalore: CISRS, 1982, pp. 181-201; and, Sadhu Sundar Singh's view recorded by B. H. Streeter and A. J. Appasamy in *The Sadhu: A Study in Mysticism and Practical Religion*, repr./ed. Delhi: Mittal Publications, 1987, pp. 129-130, 232.

the Gentiles (Rom. 1:18ff., 2:12-16; Acts 14:15ff., 17:27ff.; John 1). According to Brunner, this original revelation – reflected in conscience, beauty and order of nature, relationships – is the originating and sustaining force behind all world religions.[46] Paul Tillich's case for a general revelation within all religions is widely known: "Religion is the state of being grasped [every human being capable of so doing] by an ultimate concern, a concern which qualifies all other concerns as preliminary and which itself contains the answer to the question of the meaning of life."[47]

One of the more influential proponents of general revelation is Wolfhart Pannenberg. His approach is different from the ones discussed thus far due to his emphasis on human experience as essentially historical. Elucidating his concept, Paul F. Knitter writes that, for Pannenberg, revelation is given in the process of *history*. It results from an interplay between, on the one hand, a person's natural "openness" and "quest for more" and, on the other, the concrete events of history. This interplay provides humanity with a revelation of the divine.[48]

Closely related to the question of universal revelation is that of the salvific value of Scriptures. Can theologians acknowledge the 'sacred scriptures' of other religions as the 'word of God'? and, if so, to what extent and in what way? To answer these questions Jacques Dupuis[49] appeals to the notion of progressive, differentiated revelation. Meanwhile, according to him, one must maintain that the religious experience of the sages and seers *(rishis)* of the nations is guided and directed by the Spirit. Their experience of God is an experience in God's Spirit. These scriptures represent the sacred legacy of a tradition-in-becoming, not without the intervention of divine providence. They contain words of God to human beings in the words of the rishis, inasmuch as they report secret words uttered by the Spirit in human hearts, but words destined by divine providence to lead other human beings to the experience of the same Spirit.[50] Consonant with this view are the findings of the Research Seminar on Non-Biblical Scriptures held in Bangalore:

> In the non-Christian communities of India Scriptures are considered as privileged and authoritative means of salvation. Through a living contact with these religions we are coming to realize in our Christian experience that the Holy Spirit is operative in them and that they are manifesting in diverse ways the one mystery of God...This working of the Spirit does not entail complete adequacy...yet this action of the Spirit brings to these scriptures an over-all religious authority for these communities as God-given means leading them to their ultimate destiny.[51]

---

[46] Emil Brunner, *Revelation and Reason*, London: SCM, 1947, pp. 117-119.

[47] Paul Tillich, *Systematic Theology*, Vol. I, pp. 153-155 as quoted by Knitter, *No Other Name?* p. 99.

[48] *Ibid.*, p. 99.

[49] Jacques Dupuis, *Toward a Christian Theology of Religious Pluralism*, pp. 244-253. In light of the view that God is *the Truth*, it must also follow, naturally, that the same God who spoke in history through his prophets, also spoke to seers in the secret of their hearts. All truth comes from *the Truth* and therefore must be honored. Revelation is thus progressive inasmuch as the history of revelation, in its various stages – cosmic, Israelite, Christian – bears the seal of the influence of the Holy Spirit.

[50] *Ibid.*, p. 247. He, however, maintains that what is suggested here is not tantamount to saying that the *whole* content of the sacred scriptures of other traditions is the word of God in the words of human beings. In the compilation of the sacred books of other traditions, many elements may have been introduced that represent only human words concerning God. Still less being suggested is that the words of God contained in the scriptures of other traditions represent God's decisive word to humankind.

[51] For details of the findings, see: D. S. Amalorpavadass, *Research Seminar on Non-biblical Scriptures*, Bangalore: NBCLC, 1975, p. 684.

Into this environment of 'scriptural pluralism', at worst, and 'scriptural inclusivism', at best, comes the biblical Christian claiming that only in Jesus Christ, and through him, does the fullness of revelation exist. The letter to the Hebrews states (Heb.1:1) the word uttered by God in Jesus Christ – in the Son – is God's decisive word to the world. And Vatican II comments that Jesus Christ "completes and perfects" revelation *(complendo perficit)*.

Thus, an open theology of revelation and sacred scriptures, in contrast to the exclusive 'biblio-christo-centric' view, will posit that while uttering His decisive word in Jesus Christ, and besides speaking through the prophets of the Old Testament, God has uttered preparatory words to human beings through the prophets of the nations – a word whose traces can be found in the sacred scriptures of the world's religious traditions. The sacred scriptures of the other religions, thus, would not have the official character that we ascribe to the Old Testament, and whether they can be called 'divine words', or sacred scriptures' from the theological point of view, remains a moot question.

The Question of Dialogue

Of profound importance again in the multireligious context that we live in, is the issue of inter-religious discourse and dialogue. Among those who have identified the concerns of comparative religion with the concerns of world peace, international harmony and universal brotherhood, an important name is that of Dr. Sarvapalli Radhakrishnan. According to him, any student of religion attempting to engage in dialogue with adherents of another faith system must "treat all religions in a spirit of absolute detachment and impartiality."[52] But his impartiality is not that of the phenomenologist, attempting to accept the believer's own faith-stance whatever that may be. It means, instead, to "surrender our exclusive claims" and to come to it with a 'clean (blank) mind', because comparative religion will teach us that religion is a universal phenomenon. It will further show us that behind all the expression of religion there is the "…same intention, same striving, the same faith."[53]

Others who fail to see any possibility of approaching the dialogue with a 'blank mind' refute Radhakrishnan's view. For them, it is a profound mistake, as in the words of Norman Anderson: "…to imagine, and still more to postulate, that those who want to participate in a fruitful dialogue must endeavour to come to it with blank minds, or to suppress their personal convictions or distinctive testimony.."[54]

Again, Visser't Hooft aptly put it thus:

Martin Buber, who has given us what is probably the most profound analysis of the nature of dialogue has made it very clear that the presupposition of genuine dialogue is not that the partners agree beforehand to relativise their own convictions, but that they accept each other as persons…As a Christian [therefore] I cannot do this without reporting to him what I have come to know about Jesus Christ.[55]

John Hick, however, stands diametrically opposed to the view mentioned above. According to him, "Christianity must move emphatically from the confessional to the 'truth-seeking' stance

---

[52] Sarvappalli Radhakrishnan, *East and West in Religion*, 1933, p. 16, as quoted by Eric J. Sharpe, *Comparative Religion: A History*, Gloucester Cresent, London: Gerald Duckworth and Company Ltd., 1986, p. 259.

[53] Eric J. Sharpe, *Comparative Religion: A History*, London: Gerald Duckworth and Co. Ltd., 1986, p. 259.

[54] Sir Norman Anderson, *Christianity and World Religions: The Challenge of Pluralism*, Leicester, EL: InterVarsity Press, 1984, p. 185.

[55] W. A. Visser't Hooft, *No Other Name: The Choice Between Syncretism and Christian Universalism*, Philadelphia: The Westminster Press, 1963, p. 86.

in dialogue."[56] Lesslie Newbigin immediately challenges such a view in his book *The Open Secret,*[57] in which he views the confessional and the truth-seeking stance as not necessarily incompatible in the search for the truth. An individual who adopts what Hick terms the 'confessional stance, starts out – as every thinking man must – from what knowledge he already has, from what his past experience has led him to accept, from what he has thought through for himself and has lived out in company with others. He is, however, now prepared to examine the basic validity and implications of these convictions in the light of the truth, seeking dialogue with others whose experiences, meditation and community life have led them to very different conclusions.[58]

It would, in fact, appear to be difficult, if not impossible, to approach a dialogue of any consequence with a completely open mind. It is quite human and natural to start from some 'frame of reference'. No intelligence, however critical or original, can operate outside such a fiduciary framework.[59]

Two major models of dialogue emerge: *Firstly,* that arising out of the necessity for adherents of various religions to interact with one another for the sake of political affiliations. Both in specific national and global contexts, adherents from a diverse spectrum of religions need to maintain close links in their move towards a political achievement. The dialogue that rises in such a situation is one that aims "to establish such socio-ethical principles which are endorsed by the moral teachings of the authorities of all major religions."[60] Such a dialogue may be compared,

to a certain extent, with Hans Kung's proposal of a 'global ethic'. The function of such an interaction, however, would be primarily to help usher in world peace and stability; and has therefore become an activity worth engaging in.

Secondly, the dialogue type that is an indispensable aspect of Christian mission to the people of other religions. The prime biblical example of such dialogue may be the Athenian discourse of Paul, both with the Jews, and Epicurean and Stoic philosophers. Such dialogue, however, must be differentiated from the evangelistic activity itself. At most, it may be seen as a prelude to evangelism, or better still, a stepping-stone. As stated in the historic Lausanne Covenant:

> Our Christian presence in the world is indispensable to evangelism, and so is that kind of dialogue whose purpose is to listen sensitively in order to understand. But evangelism itself is the proclamation of the historical, biblical Christ as Saviour and Lord, with a view to persuading people to come to him personally and to be reconciled to God.[61]

The functions of such a dialogue with which we are concerned are several: to establish contact with the non-Christian listener; to explore their traditional and present religious convictions to which we have to relate our message; to enable us to differentiate between genuine elements of divine truth, deriving from God's original revelation to mankind, on the one hand, and dangerous error, on the other; and, to enable an adequate and appropriate presentation of the gospel.

---

[56] Quoted in, Sir Norman Anderson, *Christianity and World Religions,* p. 185.

[57] *The Open Secret*, Grand Rapids, 1978, p. 186.

[58] Sir Norman Anderson, p. 186.

[59] Michael Polanyi, *Personal Knowledge,* London, 1958, p. 267.

[60] Peter Beyerhaus, "The Authority of the Gospel and Interreligious Dialogue", p. 143.

[61] Peter Beyerhaus, p. 143. Cf. Article 31 "Inter-religious Dialogue," Pope John Paul II, *Ecclesia In Asia: Post-Synodal Apostolic Exhortation*, November 1999.

Implications For Missiology

To begin with, the question of the universality or particularity of Christ presents us with perhaps the most crucial missiological implications. Is it theologically and morally possible (or even permissible) to hold that Jesus was indeed God incarnate, and that salvation is mediated exclusively through him? Must adherents of other religions too recognize him as their Lord? How then must Christians respond to competing claims of "lordship" and testimonies of grace received from other "saviours" by people of other faiths? These are questions that must trouble the minds of all thinking Christians. Bishop Stephen Neill sums up the matter well:

> Christianity maintains that in Jesus the one thing that needed to happen has happened in such a way that it need never happen again in the same way. The universe has been reconciled to its God. Through the perfect obedience of one man a new and permanent relationship has been established between God and the whole human race. The bridge has been built. There is room on it for all the needed traffic in both directions, from God to man and from man to God. Why look for any other?

Of related importance is the issue of whether God has revealed himself in non-Christian religions. General revelation, described in Romans 1 and Psalm 19, for instance, affirms that there exists *bona fid e* knowledge about God in the human heart. A study of most religions would show undoubtedly, evidence of genuine appropriation of truth. Now then, is there salvific value in the truth found in other religions? The answer to this question would, of course, involve not only the question of truth, but also how salvation is understood. If salvation/liberation in various religious reflects different forms of essentially the same, and this salvation is *in* Christ and *by* Christ, then the truth in the other religions must be regarded as insufficient for salvation.[62]

The question that logically follows is regarding the destiny of those outside of Christ. Two major implications are worth noting here. First, since only a small section of humanity will have the opportunity to embrace Christ consciously, only an even smaller number will actually do so. Secondly, is it appropriate to then claim that a vast majority of humankind is therefore automatically and eternally lost? Most Christians would hesitate to condemn those outside to eternal damnation, for two prime reasons: first, it involves judging a matter that must be left to God himself, and second, several passages in the scripture (e.g. Matt.25) warn that one should be careful about overly confident pronouncements on this matter.[63]

If, however, salvation is "possible" outside the explicit knowledge of Christ, how does that impact the motivation and purpose of Christian missions?[64] What is the responsibility of Christians towards people of other religions? Is mission to be limited solely to the humanization of society, the eradication of social ills, the provision of education, healing, and economic development? What basis then remains for evangelism, church growth, and urgency for the conversion of the greatest possible number of individuals and their incorporation into the Church?

---

[62] There are various questions that arise as a result: What, then, is the source and intent of this revelation? Of more practical consequence is the issue of the value of this revelation in communicating the truth of Christ in continuity with the pre-Christian aspirations of those who may be drawn to Christ.

[63] Millard J. Erickson, for instance, among several others, claims that scripture allows for a "theoretical possibility" of salvation apart from contact with God's special revelation in Jesus Christ. See Millard J. Erickson, *Christian Theology*, however, Vol. I, Grand Rapids, MI: Baker Book House, 1983, p. 172.

[64] It must be noted here that, historically, it was the conviction concerning the "lostness of man" – man apart from Christ automatically condemned to hell – which provided a strong incentive for Christian missions.

Another related issue is that of tolerance. Is there anything in the Christian particularist claim that requires intolerance towards others? Harold Netland[65] points out that there is no necessary connection between disagreeing with the beliefs of a particular group and the radical mistreatment of members of that group.

Conclusion

The issue of religious pluralism and its attendant implications will continue to be a matter of persistent debate for a long time to come. It may well be the central theological issue facing the Church if not globally, certainly for the Church in South Asia, on the threshold of the third millenium. The Church's success or failure in maintaining the theological dialectic between its distinctive Christian confession and its social and cultural acceptance in the religiously plural South Asian context is not merely an academic question, but one which directly impacts its future survival.

Religious Pluralism is here to stay, and a socio-political reality that the Church has to come to terms with as we enter the new millennium. On one hand, there is room for a warm openness towards our brothers and sisters of other faiths. Such welcome and openness would only be a reflection of the greatness of the grace of God as it has been shown to us in Jesus. It is important for each Christian to be eager to cooperate with people of all faiths in all endeavours that are in line with the Christian understanding of God's purpose in history. Moreover, it is this context of such shared commitment that is most conducive to Christian mission and meaningful dialogue.

On the other hand, faithfulness to the Christian tradition, experience, humanity, conscience and, most of all, to our Lord himself, requires that we uphold the normativity of God's decisive word and action in the historic Christ-event. The theological challenge is, perhaps, most aptly summed up by Jacques Dupuis as he quotes Edward Schillebeeckx:

> The unity, identity and uniqueness of Christianity over against [the] other religions...lies in the fact that Christianity is a religion which associates relationship to God with a historical and thus a very specific and therefore limited particularity: Jesus of Nazereth. This is the uniqueness and identity of Christianity, but at the same time its unavoidable historical limitation. [However]...the God of Jesus is a symbol of openness, not of closedness. Here Christianity has a positive relationship to other religions, but at thesame time its uniqueness is nevertheless maintained...[66]

---

[65]Harold Netland, *Dissonant Voices,*Grand Rapids, MI: Eerdmans, 1991, pp.308f.

[66] Edward Schillebeeckx, *Church: The Human Story of God*, London: SCM Press, 1990, p. 167, as quoted by Jacques Dupuis, p. 386f.

CHAPTER 21

A Christian Supplement to the Buddhist Search:
Ecclesiastes in the Light of the
Buddha's Four Noble Truths

M.S. VASANTHAKUMAR

Christian mission, however one defines it, needs contextualised messages.[1] Unless the mission considers its local context seriously and formulates its missiology accordingly, it will not be effective and relevant to the people to whom it hopes to bring the message of Jesus Christ. It has been often pointed out that in many countries Christianity is still an imported "potted plant" and not a "transplanted plant"[2] in the local soil. Since the traditional Christian theology[3] is typically western, it is irrelevant to the non-western countries to a great extent. Therefore various attempts have been made in recent decades to contextualise the Christian message and consequently several indigenous theologies emerged in the Third World. In such contextualised theologies, the context of the people is considered as the decisive factor in formulating theological and missiological concepts.[4] In fact, such contexualisations are extremely vital and valuable since our living contexts are different to that of the contexts of the Bible and traditional Christian theology. This essay is an attempt to contextualise the Christian message to the Buddhists, using the book of Ecclesiastes in the light of Buddha's Four Noble Truths.

As far as the Buddhists are concerned, the typical traditional Christian theology is irrelevant to their contexts and insensitive to their ethos. It does not make much sense to the Buddhist mind since the fundamental dogmas of both religions differ to a great extent. Traditional Christian theology depends on divine initiative in human salvation. God's self revelation to humanity and divine substitutionary activities in relation to people's redemption are stressed in Christianity. It also highlights the depravity of human nature to the extent that without divine aid people are unable to achieve salvation by their own efforts.

---

[1] Defending the contextualised messages does not mean that the central and essential aspects of the Christian gospel need changes. On the contrary, it is indigenising the gospel in terms of making it relevant to the context. In other words, it is taking the context of the listeners seriously and being sensitive to their ethos.

[2] This famous dictum of Daniel T. Niles is cited in Douglas J.Elwood, *Asian Christian Theology: Emerging Themes*, Philadelphia: Westminster, 1980, p. 27.

[3] Traditional Christian Theology, or Missiology and Traditional Christianity in this essay refer to the western theology we have received from the missionaries of the colonial period.

[4] Interpreting the biblical text in the light of the contemporary context does not mean that the original context of the text is ignored or forgotten. On the contrary, it is being faithful to the biblical text and becoming flexible to the contemporary context at the same time. As John Stott has admonished "we are called to the difficult and even painful task of double listening. That is, we are to listen carefully both to the ancient Word and to the modern world, in order to relate the one to the other with a combination of fidelity and sensitivity" (*The Contemporary Christian*, Leicester: Inter Varsity Press, 1992, p. 13).

But Buddhism, on the other hand, while rejecting the existence and activities of God, focuses on human beings and their ability to achieve redemption from the sufferings that are pertaining to the existence of living beings. According to Buddhism, people are inherently good and have the ability to achieve their salvation without any help from God, or any reference to God. Buddhism rejects the theistic position of Christianity and the constitutional nature of human beings as taught in the Bible.

Since traditional Christian theology begins with the subject of God, Buddhists find it difficult to comprehend its fundamental message, for the simple reason that their mind is not ready to accept the theistic notions of Christianity at once. Hence the starting point of Christian missiology in Buddhist contexts should be anthropology and not theology or the God-centred gospel message. As God had contextualised himself and become a man to reach human beings, Christian missiology must incarnate itself in Buddhist conceptual spheres in order to relate to them in a meaningful way. In this respect, the book of Ecclesiastes could become a bridge which could take the Christian message to the Buddhist mind in a meaningful way, for this Old Testament wisdom literature deals with a familiar subject to the Buddhists, even though it proposes a different solution to the human predicament.

The Methodology of Qohelet and the Buddha

Qohelet (author of the book of Ecclesiastes) and the Buddha had employed almost the same methodology to analyse human existence and propose solutions to its predicament. The Buddha explained the Four Noble Truths after his enlightenment in consequence to his intense meditation on human life which he had experienced, observed, and analysed. Likewise, Qohelet's depictions were based on his own personal experiences and observations. Hence both had discovered the same facts about human life, but analysed and proposed solutions differently according to their religious and cultural contexts. Since the Buddha had denied the existence of God and human soul, his teachings do not have any reference to these concepts. Qohelet, however, due to his Hebraic religious background, had made reference to these aspects. Nevertheless, the Buddhists could appreciate and comprehend Qohelet's writings, due to their familiarity with the similar analysis of the Buddha.

The Buddha had experienced and observed both the pleasurable as well as pathetic life of human beings. His early life was filled with extravagant luxury and extreme pleasure. He was protected from seeing pain and suffering, and prevented from contact with death and decay. Nevertheless, his satisfaction from the earthly pleasures enjoyed in his lovely palace decreased as time went by, and he began to search for a deeper meaning to his existence, instead of just being satisfied with enjoying the pleasures. When the Buddha was twenty-nine years of age, he went beyond the protecting walls of his palace and for the very first time saw real life in the form of four people – old, sick, dead, and an ascetic – which shocked him greatly. He was extremely sorrowful over what he saw. Hence, he renounced all the pleasures of the royal life, left his wife and son and travelled to various places studying under various Brahmanic sages. Yet his studies did not provide satisfactory answers to his quest concerning the meaning of life. Then he practiced the extreme forms of asceticism of the Jains. He went beyond all the ascetics in self mortification, but was unable to find answers to his spiritual quest. After six years of his wandering ascetic life, he went to Bodh Gaya and meditated under a Bo tree for seven weeks until he was enlightened.[5]

---

[5] Bhikkhu Bodhi, *The Buddha and His Dhamma*, Kandy: Buddhist Publication Society, 1999, pp. 3-8.

The initial discourse of the Buddha after his enlightenment, known as the Four Noble Truths, contains his discovery of the condition, cause and cure of universal suffering. In fact, the Buddha's meditations concerning the human life, were based on his observations and experiences of life. Even four weeks after his enlightenment, the Buddha meditated on the truths he had discovered. Hence the Buddha used his mind to a great extent to discover the facts of human existence based on his personal experiences and observations.

As the Buddha observed and contemplated human life, Qohelet too used his eyes and mind to analyse the human predicament. He too, like the Buddha, had discovered the realities of human life subjectively by experiencing them in his own personal life, and objectively, by observing and investigating the lives of other human beings. His analysis and depictions were the product of human research similar to that of the Buddha. In fact, "he does not appeal to revelation or any kind of special insight into God or the world."[6] On the contrary he constantly remarks, "I have seen" (Ecc. 1:14; 3:10; 5:13; 6:1; 7:15; 10:5, 7) or similar expressions such as "I saw" (Ecc. 2:13; 3:16, 22; 4:4, 15; 8:10, 17; 9:13) "I see" (Ecc. 2:24) "I looked and saw" (Ecc. 4:1) and "I realized" (Ecc. 5:18). Qohelet's expression, "I applied my mind" in 8:9 refers to using his mind to evaluate his observation. It "serves to introduce a reflection."[7] Qohelet uses this expression to "indicate his focused, deeply personal, disciplined pursuit of the object of his study."[8] Hence it could be similar to that of Buddha's meditation.

Regarding his method of discovering the state of human dilemma, Qohelet remarked, "I devoted myself to study and explore by wisdom all that is done under the heaven" (Ecc.1:13). The expression "by wisdom" indicates that Qohelet's discovery was "characterised and guided by wisdom."[9] The two words that he employs to describe his method of investigation point to "the exhaustiveness of his study."[10] These words i.e. study (*lidros*) and explore (*tur*) though "near synonymous,"[11] have slightly different meanings. The first term means, "to penetrate to the root of the matter"[12] or "search deeply into something."[13] The second word means "to search thoroughly over the wide spread"[14] or "to investigate it from all sides."[15] Hence the two verbs refer to the "deepness and wideness of the search."[16] Qohelet, like the Buddha, had used his mind and wisdom to investigate the human predicament thoroughly. The phrase "all the things that are done under the sun" (Ecc.1:13), indicates the comprehensiveness of Qohelet's observations and investigations.

The Discoveries of Qohelet and the Buddha

The Buddha had depicted his understanding of human life as *dukkha* in Pali language, and Qohelet had expressed the same thing in Hebrew as *hebel*. Both *dukkha* and *hebel* have a wide range of meanings but fundamentally agree in

---

[6] Tremper Longman III, *Ecclesiastes: The New International Commentary on the Old Testament*, Grand Rapids: Eerdmans Publishing Company, 1998, p. 81.

[7] Roland Murphy, *Ecclesiastes: Word Biblical Commentary*, Waco: Word Books, 1992, p. 11.

[8] T. Longman III, *Ecclesiastes*, p. 78.

[9] *Ibid*. 79.

[10] Michael A. Eaton, *Ecclesiastes: Tyndale OT Commentaries*, Leicester: IVP, 1983, p. 62.

[11] T. Longman III, *Ecclesiastes*, p. 79.

[12] Robert Gordis, *Koheleth – The man and His World*, New York: Schocken Books, 1968, p. 209.

[13] M. A. Eaton, *Ecclesiastes*, p. 62

[14] *Ibid*. p. 62.

[15] R. Gordis, *Koheleth*, p. 209.

[16] E. W. Hengstenberg, *A Commentary on Ecclesiastes*, Evansville: Sovereign Grace, 1960, pp. 61-63.

their basic connotations. Therefore, the Buddhists could comprehend what Qohelet is saying about human life.

The analysis of the Buddha concerning the human life is summed up in the concept of *dukkha*. In fact, "everything he had taught is related to *dukkha*. For him the entire teaching is just the understanding of *dukkha*... and the understanding of the way out of this unsatisfactoriness."[17] Thus his inaugural address after the enlightenment expresses this aspect of human life. In it, the Buddha depicts the human condition as:

> Birth is *dukkha*, ageing is *dukkha*, sickness is *dukkha*, death is *dukkha*; sorrow, lamentation, pain, grief and despair are *dukkha*; association with the unpleasant is *dukkha*, dissociation from the pleasant is *dukkha*, not to get what one wants is *dukkha*; in short, the five aggregates of attachment are *dukkha*.[18]

According to the Buddha "the world is established on *dukkha*, is founded on *dukkha*."[19] For him human existence is nothing else other than *dukkha*. In fact, life according to Buddhism is *dukkha*; it dominates all life, and it is the fundamental problem of life.

The Buddhist texts divide *dukkha* into three aspects. They are, ordinary suffering (*dukkha-dukkha*), sufferings caused by changes (*Viparinama-dukkha*) and suffering as conditioned states (*samkhara-dukkha*). Birth, old age, sickness, death, association with unpleasant persons and conditions, not getting what one desires, grief, lamentation, distress—all such forms of physical and mental suffering which are universally accepted as suffering or pain are included in *dukkha* as ordinary suffering.[20] Sufferings caused by changes are the vanishing pleasant feelings or impermanent condition of happiness. "A happy feeling, a happy condition in life, is not permanent, not everlasting. It changes sooner or later. When it changes, it produces pain, suffering, and unhappiness. This vicissitude is included in *dukkha* as suffering produced by change."[21] The third aspect is the most important philosophical definition of *dukkha*. A person or a being, according to Buddhism, is a composite of five *skandhas* (matter, sensations, perception, mental formation and consciousness) and according to the Buddha these five aggregates themselves are *dukkha*.[22] Therefore, "*dukkha* and the five aggregates are not two different things; the five aggregates themselves are *dukkha*."[23] Since the combination of these aggregates constitutes a being, *dukkha* is fundamental to all existence.

Though the first Noble Truth points out that *dukkha* is inherent in the very fabric of life, Buddhist scholars insist that Buddha's doctrine is not totally pessimistic and opposed to the joys of human life.[24] Yet, they admit that according to the Buddha happiness too is included in *dukkha*. Buddhism "does not deny the existence of

---

[17] Piyadassi Thera, *The Buddha's Ancient Path*, Kandy: Buddhist Publication Society, 1996, p. 38.

[18] The Buddha's first sermon, the *Dhamma-cakka-pavattana-sutta* (Discourse Setting in Motion the Wheel of Truth) is recorded in the *Samyutta-nikaya* LVI. This is believed to have consisted of a brief statement of the Middle Way, the Four Noble Truths, and the Eight-fold Path and was delivered to his first five disciples in the Deer Park near the ancient city of Benares.

[19] *Samyutta-Nikaya*, I

[20] Piyadassi, *The Buddha's Ancient Path*, p. 43. "It refers to the uninvited models of physical pain... It also accommodates the span of daily anxieties and apprehensions that are a permanent feature of life in a complicated and perturbed world" (Matthews, *Craving and Salvation*, p.7).

[21] W. Rahula, *What the Buddha Taught*, p.20.

[22] Piyadassi, *The Buddha's Ancient path*, p.44.

[23] W. Rahula, *What the Buddha Taught*, p. 20.

[24] Piyadassi, *Buddha's Ancient Path*, p. 42; W.Rahula, *What the Buddha Taught*, p. 17-18.

happiness in the world… but it does emphasise that all forms of happiness (bar that of *Nibbana*) do not last."[25] Hence, according to the Buddha, human life is totally characterised and conditioned by *dukkha*.

Life, according to Qohelet, is *hebel* which is the "central keyword in the book of Ecclesiastes"[26] and generally rendered in English as 'vanity'. The NIV translates it as 'meaningless'. It occurs thirty eight times in the book[27] slightly over half of the number of times it appears in the entire Bible.[28] Qohelet applies this term to a number of areas of human activities and shows that there is no meaning and value in them. Hence the book begins and ends with the declaration, "vanity of vanities, all is vanity" (Ecc. 1:2; 12:8). The word "all" in these verses literally means 'the whole'. Hence "all earthly experience, seen as a unit, is subject to vanity."[29] According to Qohelet, vanity characterises all human activity. Hence he says, "I have seen all the things that are done under the sun: all of them are meaningless, a chasing after the wind" (Ecc.1:14).

Qohelet leaves nothing out. He cannot find meaning in anybody or in anything. Hence he asks, "what does man gain from all his labour at which he toils under the sun?" (Ecc.1:3). Such a rhetorical question is a typical feature of this book. The question is repeated in 3:9 and 5:16. Variants of the phrase (containing the word 'profit' or *yitron*) are found in Ecclesiastes 2:11; 2:13 and 10:11. "It often tends… to suggest a negation: there is no profit from one's hard lot, the toil inherent in human existence."[30]

The term translated as 'gain' (*yitron*) is also a key word in the book of Ecclesiastes. It occurs nine times in this book and nowhere else in the Old Testament. (Ecc. 1:3; 2:11, 13; 3:9; 5:9, 16; 7:12; 10:10, 11). It derives from a verb (*ytr*) which means 'to be left over' or 'remain.'[31] It is a commercial term, signifying 'profit', that is, what is left over after expenses are met.[32] Accordingly, in this earthly life there is no profit left over from people's work. Since the earthly realm is subject to vanity, "there is no hope of finding ultimate gain or satisfaction from its resources."[33] "However much we acquire, in the end we are left with nothing at all."[34] Hence Qohelet concludes that work, with which human beings are occupied in this world, is meaningless and gives no satisfaction.

In 2:18-23, Qohelet states another reason for work being unable to satisfy human beings. People are not in a position to enjoy their earnings because death forces them to leave their wealth to others. Consequently all one's efforts and earnings may be wasted by others. Hence work did not bring real satisfaction to Qohelet.

Qohelet tried to find meaning and lasting satisfaction in pleasure and set out to test its possibilities. But he found nothing that could bring real enjoyment. Hence he says: "I thought

---

[25] P. Harvey, *An Introduction to Buddhism*, Cambridge: Cambridge University Press, 1992. p. 48.

[26] R. C.Van Leeuwen, "Vanity" in *The International Standard Bible Encyclopaedia Volume Four*, ed.G.W.Bromiley, Grand Rapids: Eerdmans Publishing Company, 1993, p. 966.

[27] *Cf.* 1:1, 14; 2:1, 11, 15, 17, 19, 21, 23, 26; 3:19; 4:4, 7, 8, 16; 5:7, 10; 6:2, 4, 11, 12; 7:6, 15; 8:10, 14; 9:9; 11:8, 10; 12:8.

[28] R. Murphy, *Ecclesiastes*, p. lviii.

[29] M. A. Eaton, *Ecclesiastes*, pp. 56-57.

[30] R. Murphy, *Ecclesiastes*, p. 7.

[31] T. Longman III, *Ecclesiastes*, p. 65.

[32] M. J. Dahood, "Canaanite-Phoenician Influence in Qoheleth" in *Biblica* Vol.33 (1952), p. 221.

[33] M. A. Eaton, *Ecclesiastes*, p. 57.

[34] Stuart Olyott, *A Life Worth Living and a Lord Worth Loving: Ecclesiastes & Song of Solomon*, Hertfordshire: Evangelical Press, 1986, p.18.

in my heart, come now, I will test you with pleasure to find out what is good? But that also proved to be meaningless" (Ecc.2:1). Qohelet sought to find joy in drink, music, and sex. He also used his wealth to build houses, gardens, and enjoy all luxurious comforts (Ecc.2:2-9). His wealth and all the pleasures that money could buy him did not bring lasting satisfaction. Hence he says:

> I denied myself nothing my eyes desired; I refused my heart no pleasure. My heart took delight in all my work, and this was the reward for all my labour. Yet when I surveyed all that my hands had done and what I had toiled to achieve, everything was meaningless, a chasing after the wind (Ecc.2:10-11).

Human endeavours, as well as pleasures and comforts did not bring real enjoyment or lasting satisfaction. Hence Qohelet sought to find meaning in wisdom. Yet, that too disappointed him (Ecc.2:12-17).

> He sees the relative value of wisdom in comparison to folly in much the same way that he admits the reward of material pleasure. Further thought, however, leads him to contemplate the benefits of wisdom in the light of his impending death. Death renders all things, including wisdom, meaningless.[35]

Since both wise and fool share the same fate, Qohelet regrets that he couldn't find meaning in wisdom (Ecc.2:15-17). According to Qohelet, the human existence itself is characterised by vanity. Hence he depicts life on this earth as "all the days of this meaningless life" (Ecc.9:9). In Qohelet's analysis of human life, death plays a major role.

According to him, the fact of death often reminds him of the meaninglessness of this life. In fact, Qohelet's "thinking was affected by his fear of death."[36] Since both wise and fool die, Qohelet concluded that pursuit of wisdom is meaningless (Ecc.2:12-17). Similarly, considering the death of human beings and animals, since both die, Qohelet asserted that human beings have no advantage over the animals. (Ecc.3:19-21). Hence Human life itself is *hebel* for Qohelet.

The Meaning of *dukkha* and *hebel*

Since Qohelet and the Buddha had depicted human life in their respective languages, it is necessary for us to know the exact meanings of the terms they had employed in order to comprehend their messages correctly. The Buddha's depiction of human life as *dukkha* is generally understood as life filled with suffering or pain. But *dukkha* is one of the Pali words that cannot be translated adequately into other languages. No single word in English covers the wide range of meanings of *dukkha*. The common rendering of it as suffering or pain, "is an inadequate description of Buddha's general outlook."[37] In fact, it is "highly unsatisfactory and misleading."[38] "The word *dukkha* is rendered variously as ill, suffering, pain and so on, which may be correct in certain contexts. But in other contexts... the term is used in wider senses."[39] *Dukkha* "represents the Buddha's view of life and the world, [and] has a deeper philosophical meaning and connotes enormously wider senses.[40]

From Buddha's description about happiness, we can comprehend an important aspect of *dukkha*. Since Buddha saw happiness as *dukkha*

---

[35] T. Longman, III, *Ecclesiastes*, p. 94.

[36] *Ibid.* p. 94

[37] Bruce Matthews, *Craving and Salvation: A Study in Buddhist Soteriology*, Canada: Wilfrid Laurier Press, 1983, p.6.

[38] W. Rahula, *What the Buddha Taught*, p.16.

[39] D. J. Kalupahana, *Buddhist Philosophy: A Historical Analysis*, p. 37.

[40] *Ibid.* p. 17.

because of its impermanent nature, it could be deduced that according to Buddha *dukkha* means impermanence. When Buddha said that human life is *dukkha*, he explicitly pointed out that the five aggregates that constitute a person are *dukkha* for the basic reason that they are constantly changing and not permanent. Since the aggregates themselves are *dukkha*, it is evident that *dukkha* means impermanence too, for the aggregates are not permanent in themselves.

The changing, unstable nature of life is such that people are led to experience dissatisfaction, loss, and disappointment or frustration. Thus another aspect or meaning of *dukkha,* according to the Buddha, is unsatisfactoriness. In fact Buddhist scholars refer to *dukkha* as unsatisfactoriness.[41] They point out that "where it is said that the five aggregates of grasping are *dukkha*, the term is used in the wider sense of unsatisfactory."[42] Referring to the Buddha's sermon on the first Noble Truth, they remark, "here the word *dukkha* refers to all those things which are unpleasant, imperfect, and which we would like to be otherwise. It is both suffering and the general unsatisfactoriness of life."[43] "It is admitted that the term *dukkha* in the first noble truth contains, quite obviously, the ordinary meaning of suffering, but in addition it also includes deeper ideas such as imperfection, impermanence, emptiness, and insubstantiality."[44] Thus in addition to suffering and pain, Buddha's understanding of *dukkha* includes impermanence, unsatisfactoriness, and insubstantiality. In fact, the Hebrew term employed by Qohelet to depict the human predicament has all these connotations.

The Hebrew term *hebel* is generally rendered in English as vanity. Like the Pali expression *dukkha*, there is not a single word in English that will capture the full meaning of this significant Hebrew term. Hence different words are suggested by biblical scholars such as 'useless'[45] 'emptiness'[46] 'meaningless'[47] 'absurd'[48] 'futility'[49] etc. The term 'vanity' goes back to the Authorised Version's equivalent of Latin *vanitas*, which connotes emptiness and futility.[50] It is important to note that the modern use of the word vanity in the sense of empty pride or conceit was not in the original term. The Hebrew term literally means 'breath' or 'vapour.'[51] Hence it could mean "without substance or reality."[52] "Always it points to something which is insubstantial or transitory or in some sense futile... It can refer to any activity which seems

---

[41] Piyadassi, *Buddha's Ancient Path*, p. 38.

[42] D .J. Kalupahana, *Buddhist Philosophy*, p. 37.

[43] P. Harvey, *An Introduction to Buddhism*, p. 48.

[44] W. Rahula, *What the Buddha Taught*, p. 17.

[45] This is the rendering of the Good News Bible.

[46] New English Bible uses this word.

[47] New International Version has this word.

[48] Michael V. Fox argues for this term "The Meaning of *hebel* for Qohelet" in *Journal of Biblical Literature*, 105 [1986], pp. 409-427. A.Camus insists that this is the exact equivalent of *hebel, Qohelet and His Contradictions*, Sheffield: Almond Press, 1989.

[49] Revised English Bible and New Jerusalem Bible employ this term.

[50] R. C. Van Leeuwen, "Vanity"p. 966. New Revised Standard Version and New American Bible prefer this term and scholars such as J.L.Crenshaw, *Ecclesiastes: Old testament Library*, Philadelphia: Westminster Press, 1987, R. Gordis, *Koheleth: The Man and His World: A Study of Ecclesiastes*, New York: Schocken Books, 1968, R.E.Murphy, *Ecclesiastes: Word Biblical Commentary Volume 23*, Waco: Word Books, 1992, and C. L. Seow, *Ecclesiastes: Anchor Bible Commentary*, Garden City: Doubleday & Co., 1997 also employ this traditional word.

[51] Hence R. B. Y. Scott uses this term in his commentary, *Proverbs and Ecclesiastes: Anchor Bible Commentary*, Garden City: Doubleday & Co., 1965.

[52] L.O. Richards, *Expository Dictionary of Bible Words*, Hants: Marshall Pickering, 1988, p. 608.

to be pointless."[53] Biblical commentators explain this term as "a wisp of vapour, a puff of wind, a mere breath – nothing you could get your hands on; the nearest thing to zero. That is the 'vanity' this book is about."[54] And "whatever is left after you break a soap bubble is vanity."[55] Hence whatever disappears quickly, leaves nothing behind and does not satisfy is *hebel*, vanity. In Ecclesiastes "it is used for things that do not last, cannot be grasped, or are not worthwhile."[56]

Generally the word *hebel* has metaphorical use for that which is evanescent and unstable, hence in this book 'meaningless' 'frustration' or 'futility'.[57] *Hebel* occurs approximately thirty two times outside the book of Ecclesiastes.[58] In thirteen passages it characterises idols,[59] hence these passages attribute "uselessness or meaninglessness to the idols."[60] In the remaining passages too[61] *hebel* means meaninglessness and in some instances it connotes 'temporary' or 'fleeting'.[62] In the book of Ecclesiastes these ideas, meaninglessness and transitoriness, are conveyed by the term *hebel*. "A comparison with its use elsewhere makes it clear that Qohelet knows and uses all its nuances."[63] The Septuagint consistently translates it by one Greek word, *mataiotes,* which means emptiness, futility,

purposelessness and transitoriness. "The verdict of vanity in the book of Ecclesiastes includes brevity, unsubstantiality, unreliability, frailty, futility and deceit.[64] Hence, according to Qohelet, all is untrustworthy, unsubstantial; no endeavour will in itself bring permanent satisfaction, the greatest joys are fleeting; everything is meaningless and impermanent. This clearly captures the meaning of the term *dukkha*, used by the Buddha to depict human existence.

Qohelet also uses the phrase "chasing after the wind" to describe the term *hebel* in some instances.[65] In the Old versions this phrase has been translated as 'vexation of spirit'[66] *ruah* in Hebrew could mean 'spirit' or 'wind'. Hence the meaning would be "frustration by the insoluble (vexing of spirit), or ambition for the unattainable (striving after wind)."[67] Yet the contexts of this phrase in the entire book favour the second meaning: "Since the wind, changeable and invisible, yields nothing, even were it to be caught."[68] Hence it describes the utter futility and foolishness of trying to find meaning and satisfaction in this life. For the Buddha and Qohelet human life is filled with frustration, suffering, unsatisfactoriness, impermanence and insubstantiality.

---

[53] Robert Davidson, *Ecclesiastes and Song of Solomon,* Edinburgh: Saint Andrew Press, 1986, p. 9.

[54] Derek Kidner, *The Message of Ecclesiastes*, Leicester: Inter Varsity Press, 1976, p. 22.

[55] Warren W. Wiersbe, *Be Satisfied*, Wheaton: Victor Books, 1990, p. 15.

[56] R. Murphy & E. Huwiler, *Proverbs, Ecclesiastes, Song of Songs: New International Biblical Commentary*, Peabody: Hendrickson Publishers, 1999, p. 181.

[57] J. Stafford Wright, *Ecclesiastes: The Expositor's Bible Commentary*, Grand Rapids: Zondervan Publishing House, 1991, p. 1152

[58] T. Longman III, *Ecclesiastes*, p. 63.

[59] Deut.32:21; 2kings 17:15; Ps.31:6; 57:13; Jer.2:5; 8:19; 10:8, 15; 14:22; 16:19; 51:18; Jon.2:8; Zech.10:2.

[60] T. Longman III, *Ecclesiastes*, p. 63.

[61] 2 Kings 17:15; Job 9:29; 21:34; 27:12; 35:16; Ps.31:7; 39:6; 62:9; 78:33; 94:11; Pro.13:11; Isa.30:7; Lam.4:17.

[62] Ps.39:4-5; 144:4; Job 7:16; Pro.31:30;

[63] Kiel K.Seybold, ""hebhel" in *Theological Dictionary of the Old Testament*, ed. G.J.Botterweck & H.Ringgren, Grand Rapids: Eerdmans Publishing Company, 1978, p. 318.

[64] M. A. Eaton, *Ecclesiastes*, p. 56.

[65] Ecc. 1:14, 17; 2:11, 17, 26; 4:4, 6, 16; 6:9.

[66] See Revised Standard Version and the Authorised Version.

[67] M. A. Eaton, *Ecclesiastes*, p. 63.

[68] R. Murphy, *Ecclesiastes*, p. 13.

The Cause for *dukkha* or *hebel*

Qohelet and the Buddha not only discovered the reality of human existence, they also sought the root cause or reason for the human predicament. According to the Buddha it is the human desires or cravings that bring *dukkha*. The second noble truth in Buddha's initial sermon states this as follows: "The noble truth of the origin of *dukkha* is this: It is this thirst (craving) which produces re-existence and re-becoming, bound up with passionate greed".[69]

The cause or the origin of *dukkha*, desires or cravings is described as *tanha* in the Pali texts, which literally means thirst and "clearly refers to demanding desires or drives which are ever on the lookout for gratification."[70] *Tanha* includes not only desire for, and attachment to, sense-pleasure, wealth and power, but also desire for and attachment to ideas, views, opinions, theories, conceptions and beliefs. According to the analysis of the Buddha, all the troubles and strife in the world, from little personal quarrels in families to great wars between nations and countries, arise out of this selfish thirst.

Like the Buddha, Qohelet also sees human desires as the root cause for the human predicament. Though he does not express it in such phraseology, his descriptions resemble the Buddha's explanation. According to Qohelet's Hebraic orientation, human cravings or desires are nothing else than human will or selfish motivations in opposition to the divine will. Instead of constantly seeking and living according to God's will as the Bible admonishes, people live the way they want, and bring sorrows and unsatisfactoriness into their lives. Such a kind of life could be described in the Buddhist way of thinking as life conditioned by cravings. It is a life conditioned and characterised by human desires only. Qohelet describes such a life as lived 'under the sun', a phrase that occurs nowhere in the Bible except in the book of Ecclesiastes.[71] Like the term *hebel,* this expression, which is used by Qohelet 29 times, also expresses an important concept in the book of Ecclesiastes.[72] Qohelet thus restricts his remarks to terrestrial human activity and work. Qohelet's "frequent use of the phrase 'under the sun' highlights the restricted scope of his inquiry. His worldview does not allow him to take a transcendent yet immanent God into consideration in his quest for meaning."[73] Hence Qohelet's approach and that of the Buddha were almost the same. Both tried to find meaning in human life without considering God's dealings in human affairs. For the Buddha, human desires bring sorrows and frustrations, and for Qohelet, human desires are godless self-oriented motivations.

Proposed solutions to *dukkha* or *hebel*

The fundamental difference between the Buddha's and Qohelet's thesis is their proposed solution to the problem of the human predicament. According to the Buddha, one has to eliminate the cause of *dukkha* by his/her own effort, in order to get rid of it. This is clearly stated in Buddha's third noble truth, which is the noble truth of cessation of *dukkha*. This is the ultimate goal of the Buddhists, known as *nibbana*. Hence

---

[69] This explanation is found in many other discourses recorded in the early Buddhist scriptures.

[70] P. Harvey, *An Introduction to Buddhism*, p. 53. While elucidating the nature of *tanha* the Buddha identifies three aspects of cravings. Thus in the *Mahavagga* of the *Vinaya* the Buddha has said: It is this *tanha* which produces re-existence and re-becoming, and which is bound up with passionate greed, and which finds fresh delight now here and now there, namely, thirst of sense-pleasure (*kama-tanha*) thirst for existence and becoming (*bava-tanha*) and thirst for non-existence (self-annihilation, *vibhava-tanha*

[71] It is, however, conceptually similar to the expressions "under heaven" (Ex.17:14; Deut.7:24; 9:14; Ecc.22:3; 3:1).

[72] Ecc. 1:3, 9; 2:11, 17, 18, 19, 20, 22; 3:16; 4:1, 3, 7, 15; 5:14, 19; 6:1, 12; 7:11; 8:9, 15, 17, 9:3, 6, 9, 11, 13; 10:5.

[73] T. Longman, *Ecclesiastes*, p. 66.

nibbana is known also as "extinction of *tanha*."[74] According to the Buddha, *nibbana* is the cessation or the extinction of craving.[75] Since *dukkha* originates from cravings, the extinction of cravings brings an end to *dukkha*. "With the giving up of craving one also gives up suffering and all that pertains to suffering. *Nibbana*, therefore, is explained as the extinction of suffering."[76]

According to the teachings of the Buddha, in order to extinguish the cravings and experience *nibbana* one has to follow the path Buddha had prescribed. It is generally known as the Middle Path[77] or the Noble Eight-fold Path that is composed of eight categories such as right understanding, right thought, right speech, right action, right livelihood, right effort, right mindfulness and right concentration. The Buddha's entire teachings deal in some way or other with this path. These eight categories of the path should be followed simultaneously and not one after the other. They are all linked together and each helps the cultivation of the other. The Eight-Fold Path aims at promoting and perfecting the three essentials of Buddhist training and discipline. They are ethical conduct (*sila*), mental discipline (*samadhi*) and wisdom (*panna*).[78]

> It is a way of life to be followed, practised and developed by each individual. It is self-

discipline in body, word and mind, self-development and self-purification... It is a path leading to the realisation of Ultimate Reality, to complete freedom and peace through moral, spiritual and intellectual perfection.[79]

According to the Buddha one has to follow the eight-fold path to be emancipated from *dukkha*. Qohelet on the other hand, admonishes people to bring God into their lives to end *hebel* and enjoy life. In fact, he has divided the human life into two spheres as realms of God and man. "God is in heaven, and you upon earth (Ecc.5:2) is an underlying assumption throughout the text."[80] Earthly life without reference to God is depicted in terms of "under the sun" in the book of Ecclesiastes. Hence according to Qohelet, "life will never be meaningful 'under the sun' until we make contact with the one who is above the sun."[81] Under the sun life is characterised by *hebel*. Therefore human beings gain nothing 'under the sun' (Ecc.1:3); the 'earth' which is dominated by futility 'goes on for ever' (Ecc.1:4); no new thing can take place 'under the sun' (Ecc. 1:9-11). Qohelet sought out what was done 'under the sun' (Ecc.1:13) and evaluated what resources could be found 'under the sun (Ecc.1:14). His quest for pleasure likewise found no hope of gain 'under the sun' (Ecc.2:11); what is done 'under the sun' was grievous to him (Ecc.2:17).

---

[74] W. Rahula, *What the Buddha Taught*, p. 35. Etymologically *nibbana* (*ni+vana*) means 'freedom from cravings,' a 'departure from craving,' or in Sanskrit *nirvana* (*nir+va*) means 'to cease blowing' or 'to be extinguished, Piyadassi, *The Buddha's ancient Path*, p. 67.

[75] *Majjhima-Nikaya* 28ᵗʰ *sutta*.

[76] Piyadassi, *The Buddha's Ancient Path*, p. 68.

[77] It is the middle path because it avoids two extremes: "one extreme being the search for happiness through the pleasures of the senses, which is 'low, common, unprofitable and the way of ordinary people;' the other being the search for happiness through self-mortification different forms of asceticism, which is 'painful, unworthy and unprofitable.' Having himself first tried these two extremes, and having found them to be useless, the Buddha discovered through personal experience the Middle Path 'which gives vision and knowledge, which leads to Calm, Insight, Enlightenment, Nirvana," W. Rahula, *What the Buddha Taught*, p. 45.

[78] Ethical conduct is built on the conception of universal love and compassion for all living beings, which includes right speech, right action and right livelihood. Right effort, right mindfulness and right concentration are included in the mental discipline. The remaining two factors, right thought and right understanding constitute wisdom.

[79] *Ibid*. p. 49-50.

[80] M. A. Eaton, *Ecclesiastes*, p. 44.

[81] Selwyn Hughes, *Ecclesiastes: The Search for Meaning*, Surrey: CWR, 1993, p. 5.

When Qohelet described life under the sun, which is *hebel*, God is out of his account. But when God was introduced everything changed. Instead of frustration and meaninglessness there is a joyful life for human beings from God. Hence 'the hand of God' (Ecc. 2:24), 'the joy of man' (Ecc. 2:25; 3:12; 5:18, 20; 9:7; 11:7-9) and 'the generosity of God' (Ecc. 2:26; 3:13; 5:19) are also the dominating themes in Qohelet's thesis. On seven occasions Qohelet has declared that human beings have a joyful 'portion' from God (Ecc. 2:10, 21; 3:22; 5:18, 19; 9:6, 9) and on twelve occasions God is depicted as a Giver of joyful life (Ecc.1:13; 2:26 3:10, 11; 5:18, 19; 6:2; 8:15, 9:9; 12:7, 11). Intermingled with its pessimism, Qohelet's thesis contains "invitations to a different outlook altogether, in which joy and purpose are found when God is seen to be 'there' and to be characterised supremely by generosity."[82] Hence Qohelet has described God as the Giver of good gifts (Ecc.2:26), sovereign over everything (Ecc.7:13-14), and the Creator to whom people owe everything (Ecc.12:1,7).

Qohelet's Conclusion and the Buddhists

Qohelet's conclusion may sound strange to the Buddhists for he has a two-fold theistic advice to offer. One is to fear God and the other is to follow God's commandments. He also mentions the judgement of God.

> Now all has been heard, here is the conclusion of the matter. Fear God and keep his commandments for this is the whole duty of man. For God will bring every deed into judgement, including every hidden thing whether it is good or evil (Ecc.12:13-14).

Buddhists and the Concept of God

"Buddhism has no God to whom it can refer as Creator, Lord, Saviour etc, who can be described as omniscient omnipotent etc."[83] Nevertheless, Sri Lankan Buddhism has absorbed almost all the deities of Hinduism.[84] Therefore, the contemporary Buddhist assertion of the non-theistic character of their religion is intended mainly to emphasise the unacceptability of Christian theism. The Buddhists in Sri Lanka worship not only the Buddha, but also other deities in their pantheon. They make offerings to the statues and pictures of the Buddha and other Hindu deities and recite Pali verses.

> Sinhalese Buddhists state that their religion was founded by the Buddha, who was a human being and is now dead. Cognitively this position is held by every Buddhists [sic] from the most learned monk to the most ignorant layman. Yet they usually behave as if the Buddha appears to them as a powerful and omnibenevolent god, a supreme being who is still in some way present and aware. For instance, if assailed by dangerous demons a pious Buddhist will recite the qualities of the Buddha and thus keep any malevolent forces at bay.... Moreover, Buddhists have dealings with the Buddha in which they behave as if he were at least numinously present; in particular, offerings are made before the statues.[85]

---

[82] M. A. Eaton, *Ecclesiastes*, p. 45.

[83] Chandima Wijebandara, *Early Buddhism: Its Religious and Intellectual Milieu*, Kelaniya: The Postgraduate Institute of Pali and Buddhist Studies, 1993, pp. 108-109.

[84] *Cf.* Gananath Obeyesekere, "The Buddhist Pantheon in Ceylon and Its Extensions" in *Anthropological Studies in Theravada Buddhism*. M.Nash, ed., New Haven: Yale University of Southeast Asia Studies, 1966, pp. 1-26; Richard Gombrich & Gananath Obeyesekere, *Buddhism Transformed: Religious Change in Sri Lanka*, Delhi: Motilal Banarsidass Publishers, 1990, pp. 65-199. For some specific examples of Hindu borrowings of contemporary Sri Lankan Buddhism see Richard Gombrich, *Theravada Buddhism: A Social History from Ancient Benares to Modern Colombo*, London: Routledge, 1996, p. 146.

[85] Richard Gombrich, "The Consecration of a Buddhist Image" p. 23.The usual offerings to a Buddha image, which may be made at any time, are flowers, lights and incense.

In Sri Lanka every Buddhist monastery[86] has a temple with at least one statue of the Buddha, and most lay people have in their houses a small shrine or at least a picture of the Buddha with a tiny altar before it. In front of these representations of the Buddha people conduct themselves as if in the presence of an important person or God. The Buddhists' explanation for such conduct is that of respect for the memory of Buddha. But "the demeanour of the average worshipper is reminiscent of theistic devotion rather than of philosophic contemplation."[87]

> At least one ceremony is so obviously motivated by fear that it cannot be rationalised in terms of respect and affection for the memory of an omnibenevolent Buddha, whether dead or alive. This is the ceremony of consecrating a statue. Only when a statue has been consecrated can it be an object of worship, and this fact is sufficient to show that a Buddha statue is more than a mere reminder of the Buddha.[88]

In fact the very act of consecration indicates that the statue of the Buddha is being brought to life. The ceremony consists of only a single performance of painting the eyes or carving the pupils. Once this ceremony is over, the statue is considered nothing else than divine. "Before the Eyes are made, it is not accounted a God, but a lump of ordinary Metal, and thrown about the shop with no more regard than anything else... The eyes being formed, it is thenceforward a God."[89]

The consecration ceremony of a statue of the Buddha and the subsequent veneration of it clearly indicate the fact that the Buddhists worship the statue contrary to their rational explanations. In the meantime they worship the gods of spirit religion and Hinduism contrary to the teachings of the Buddha. Hence when Anagarika Dharmapala began to reform Buddhism in the nineteenth century, his primary objective was "to separate canonical teachings from popular religious practices."[90] The Buddhists in Sri Lanka generally avoid asking for worldly blessings from Buddha. They go to the gods and other cultic rituals for such purposes. Dharmapala pointed out the inconsistency of Buddhist doctrines and such religious observations of the people. Hence it was his firm conviction that "no intelligent Buddhist ... would ever care to invoke a god who is only a step higher in the evolutionary scale of progress than man."[91] Many of the rituals, which did not have a direct scriptural rationale, were dismissed as "excrescences survivals of Hindu practices, which were antithetical, or at least irrelevant, to Buddhism."[92]

Despite the reforms of Dharmapala the Buddhists still have their gods and engage in ritualistic ceremonies. In fact contemporary Sri Lankan Buddhism is a "composite of canonical Buddhism, deity worship and magical animism... It is a blend of cultic and occultic practices within a derived concept from orthodox canonical Buddhism."[93] Astrology, occultism and worship

---

[86] A Monastery is not merely where monks live but the complex of buildings associated with such living quarters. This complex includes a temple containing Buddha images and other religious art.

[87] R. Gombrich, "The Consecration of a Buddhist Image" p. 23.

[88] *Ibid.* p. 24.

[89] Robert Knox, *An Historical Relation of Ceylon*, p. 130.

[90] Sarath Amunugama, "Anagarika Dharmapala (1864-1933) and the Transformation of Sinhala Buddhist Organisation in a Colonial setting" in *Social Science Information*, 24 (1985), No: 4, p. 720.

[91] Ananda Guruge, ed. Return to Righteousness: A Collection of Speeches, Essays and Letters of the Anagarika Dharmapala, Colombo: The Government Press, 1965, p. 638.

[92] S. Amunugama, "Anagarika Dharmapala", p. 720 .

[93] T. Weerasingha, *The Cross & the Bo Tree*, p. 45.

of territorial spirits and gods are common features of Sri Lankan Buddhism.[94] Prior to the arrival of Buddhism in the 3rd century BC,[95] the religious belief of Sri Lanka was basically animistic and people's religious convictions were conditioned by their fear of gods and demons.[96] Even though by the first century BC Buddhism had spread into every part of the country,[97] the earlier animistic religion "flourished side by side among the masses and has persisted down to modern times."[98] "Instead of the Sinhalese leaving animism and becoming Buddhists, they conveniently converted their gods to Buddhism."[99]

> Its early developments in Sri Lanka Buddhism absorbed various cults, rituals, and ceremonies that had been practised in the country... This popular aspect of Buddhism in Sri Lanka developed into a system capable of serving the varied religious needs of society.[100]

Since the gods are higher than human beings they are sought for various practical problems and needs. It is not an exaggeration or an error to say that Buddhists in Sri Lanka need gods for their day to day practical life. They cannot live with philosophical explanations alone. Hence they worship the gods while trying to obtain *nibbana* through Buddha's eight-fold path. But rituals and ceremonies are the predominant features of contemporary Sri Lankan Buddhism. This clearly indicates their need for god or a supernatural being who could help them in the numerous problems and difficulties that engulf their lives. It is at this point that Qohelet's admonition to fear God will make sense to the Buddhists.

Sri Lankan Buddhists can comprehend Qohelet's admonition to some extent, for fear is something very close to them. As Tissa Weerasingha has observed, fear is the 'major felt need' among Sri Lankan Buddhists. For he remarks, "the belief system, which attributes evil, sickness, failure in enterprise, calamity to malevolent spirits, is the crucial reason why fear is such a realistic force in peasant life."[101] He goes on to say that "fears of spirit attacks constantly plague the Buddhist mind and is the major felt need among them."[102] In the Buddhist mind sickness is primarily related to the spirits when western or herbal medicine is unable to bring cure.[103] In the puberty rite, the girl is guarded by a female relative for fear of being inflicted by evil spirits. All deities in the Sri Lankan Buddhist pantheon, malevolent and benevolent alike, can cause misfortunes, which may afflict an individual, a household, or even a whole village. The planetary deities that are associated with one's horoscope are able to cause bad periods. Therefore Weerasingha points out,

---

[94] This aspect of contemporary religious life in Sri Lanka is well documented in Richard Gombrich & Gananath Obeyesekere, *Buddhism Transformed: Religious Change in Sri-Lanka*, Princeton: Princeton University Press, 1988.

[95] Buddhism was brought to Sri Lanka by Mahinda, the son of an Indian Emperor Asoka.

[96] S. Paranavitana, "Pre-Buddhist Religious Beliefs in Ceylon" in *Journal of the Ceylon Branch of the Royal Asiatic Society*, Vol. XXXI (1929), pp. 302-327.

[97] G. C.Mendis, *The Early History of Ceylon*, Calcutta: YMCA, 1954, p. 10.

[98] S. Paranavitana, "Pre-Buddhist Religious Beliefs in Ceylon", p. 305.

[99] T. Weerasingha, *The Cross & the Bo Tree*, p. 54.

[100] H. B. M.Ilangasinha, *Buddhism in Medieval Sri Lanka*, Delhi: Sri Satguru Publications, 1992, p. 183.

[101] T. Weerasingha, *The cross & the Bo Tree*, p. 60.

[102] *Ibid.* p. 65.

[103] Nur Yalman also deals with this aspect of Sri Lankan Buddhism (*Cf.* "The Structure of Sinhalese Healing Rituals" in *Journal of Asian Studies*, 23 [1964], p. 118). N.Yalman further observes, that "the Sinhalese villages do not like being watched while eating... (for) there are hungry demons hovering around specially when the food is being prepared or consumed, and they must not be allowed to see it, otherwise one might get ill" ("On the Meaning of Good Offerings in Ceylon" in *Social Compass*, 2 [1973], p. 288).

"the belief system of the Buddhists needs to be dealt with together with a definite release from the bondage of fear, if there is to be any successful communication of the Gospel."[104] All fears should be chased away except the fear of God, which Qohelet sees as the basis for meaningful life.

Fearing God is not being afraid of Him. It is to "respect, honour, and worship the Lord."[105] Since according to Qohelet's background the fear of God is also the beginning of wisdom (Pr.1:7; 9:10),[106] the Buddhists could gain wisdom by fearing God instead of rejecting Him. Further, the fear of God "is the realisation of His unchanging power and justice (Ecc.3:14)... [which] delivers from wickedness and self-righteousness (Ecc.7:8) and leads to a hatred of sin (Ecc.5:6f.; 8:12f.)."[107] Hence it would enable the Buddhists to extinguish evil desires, for which they strive by their own efforts.

The necessity of God could be explained to the Buddhists in relation to their doctrine of *anatta*. Lynn de Silva has correctly pointed out how this doctrine could help the Buddhists to understand the necessity of God. It is his contention that Christianity "carries the doctrine of *anatta* to its logical conclusion."[108] Thus de Silva argues, "if *anatta* is real, God is necessary; it is in relation to the reality of God that the reality of *anatta* can be meaningful."[109] De Silva points out the awareness people have towards the Transcendent Reality[110] and remarks, "this transcendental quality is to be found in man's relationship to God."[111] To substantiate his thesis, de Silva highlights the apparent difficulties in the Buddhist concept of *anatta* and supplements it by his Christian understanding of it, and says, "the biblical understanding of ... *anatta* can enable us to understand what the term God means."[112] Thus de Silva brings God into the picture and expects the Buddhists to realise the need for God within the Buddhist philosophical system.

Buddhism, while denying the self (this is the crux of *anatta*), teaches that man must depend on himself for his own deliverance. For de Silva this is "one of the deepest dilemmas in Buddhism."[113] So he asks, "What is the self that denies the self and at the same time asserts that it alone can save the self?"[114] The ultimate goal to which Buddhist morality is directed is *nibbana* and it is achieved by self-effort. According to Buddhism people have the power to achieve this goal. Therefore de Silva says, "to deny the self and to affirm self-sufficiency is a contradiction."[115] According to him it is the Bible which takes the doctrine of *anatta* seriously and points out the inability of human beings to save themselves. Thus he remarks,

> In fact it can be shown that the Bible takes what is implied in the doctrine of *anatta* more seriously than Buddhism does, for the biblical teaching is that man is nothing by himself and can do nothing by himself about his salvation. The doctrine of *anatta*

---

[104] T. Weerasingha, *The Cross & the Bo Tree*, p. 60.

[105] T. Longman III, *Ecclesiastes*, p. 282.

[106] Psalms 110:10 also has the two aspects of Qohelet's conclusion

[107] M. A. Eaton, *Ecclesiastes*, p. 156.

[108] L.de Silva, "Good News of Salvation to the Buddhists", p. 450.

[109] L.de Silva "Emergent Theology in The Buddhist Context" p. 226.

[110] De Silva has dealt this in detail in his *Why Believe in God*, Colombo: Christian Study Centre, 1970.

[111] *Ibid*. p. 228.

[112] L.de Silva, "Emergent Theology in The Buddhist Context" (booklet), p. 58.

[113] L.de Silve, "Good News of Salvation to the Buddhists" p. 450.

[114] *Ibid*. p. 450.

[115] *Ibid*. p. 451.

therefore points to the truth that man cannot save himself by his own efforts and is in need of saving grace.[116]

De Silva positively affirms, "it is in relation to the unconditioned (God) that the full depth and significance of *anatta* can be understood."[117] That is to say, in view of *anatta*, God becomes indispensable. Thus by emphasising *anatta* Christians could make an attempt to convince the Buddhists of the necessity of divine help in attaining the ultimate goal in religious pursuit.[118] In fact, Qohelet's conclusion could be communicated to the Buddhists by explaining the full implications of the doctrine of *anata*.

In contemporary Sri Lanka the Buddhists' ultimate goal of *nibbana* is considered as a present living experience. According to them, "*nibbana* is a state to be attained here and now; in this very life and not a state to be attained only after death.[119] A person can attain *nibbana* "even while alive, by rooting out lust, hate and delusion."[120] Accordingly when a person totally eradicates lust, hate and delusion he is liberated from the shackles of *samsara*, from repeated existence.[121] Hence *nibbana* becomes a "living experience" and it is characterised by four special attributes: happiness, moral perfection, realisation, and freedom.[122] Likewise, life with God according to Qohelet has the same happiness, joy and freedom. Hence he concludes his thesis with the two-fold admonition of fearing God and following his commandments. Since the Buddhists in Sri Lanka appeal to the gods for a prosperous and peaceful life, Christians can introduce to them Jesus Christ who came to give humanity a meaningful life.

> Jesus Christ is the ultimate answer to Qohelet's conclusion of meaninglessness under the sun. Jesus emptied himself of his divine prerogatives to subject himself of the world "under the sun" in order to free us of the chaos to which God subjected the world after the fall into sin (Cf.Gal.3:3 and Rom.8:18-27).[123]

Buddhists and the Laws of God

Qohelet's second admonition, keeping God's commandments, is not difficult advice for the Buddhists, for they too have similar commandments in the Eight-Fold Path which the Buddha had enumerated in his Fourth Noble Truth. God's commandments in the Book of Ecclesiastes are not restricted to the Mosaic Law but refer to "all that is known to be God's Will."[124] God has revealed His will both in human conscience and in His word. Ecclesiastes 3:11 speaks about the divine work in human hearts. Romans 2:14-15 explicitly states that God has written his commandments in the hearts of people who do not have the Book of Law which was given to the Jews:

> Indeed, when gentiles, who do not have the law, do by nature things required by the law, they are a law for themselves, even though they do not have the law, since they show that the requirements of the law are written on their hearts, their conscience also bearing witnesses, and their thoughts are accusing, now even defending them.

---

[116] *Ibid.* p. 451.

[117] L.de Silva, "Emergent Theology in The Buddhist Context" (booklet), p. 58.

[118] De Silva has elaborated this concept in more detail in his *Why Can't I Save Myself – The Christian Answer in relation to Buddhist Thought*, Colombo: Christian study Centre, 1967.

[119] Lily de Silva, *Nibbana As Living Experience*, Kandy: Buddhist Publication Society, 1996, p. 2.

[120] Piyadassi, *The Buddha's Ancient Path*, p. 70.

[121] *Ibid.* p. 71.

[122] L. de Silva, *Nibbana as Living Experience*, p. 2.

[123] T. Longman III, *Ecclesiastes*, p. 284.

[124] M .A. Eaton, *Ecclesiastes*, p. 156.

Hence the non-Christians, "although they do not have the law in their hands, they do have its requirements in their hearts, because God has written them there."[125] The Bible clearly teaches that God has revealed himself to all human beings[126] which is theologically known as General Revelation.[127] Thus, God's existence and some of his attributes are known to all human beings, and "the basic requirements of the law are stamped on human hearts."[128] Therefore it could be concluded that the moral teachings of the Buddha were related to this phenomenal and mysterious work of God in human hearts despite his denial of God. Hence, by explaining the nature of the ethical teachings of the Buddha via general revelation, Christians could communicate the commandments of God to the Buddhists. It could be done by pointing out the similarities of the ethical teachings of the Buddha with those which are found in the Bible. In fact many have seen the similar teachings of both religions, but

wrongly concluded that this phenomenon was due to Buddhist influence on the biblical writings.[129] The similarities were not necessarily borrowings from one religion by another, they were mainly due to the general revelation of God.

In fact, according to the Bible all religions are nothing other than human responses to divine revelation even when they do not conform to the Judeao-Christian standards.[130] They are "a mixture of human response and divine revelation."[131] As the Bible declares, and human experience demonstrates, people are religious because of the intuitive awareness they have regarding the divine. This innate knowledge is due to the divine image within the constitution of human beings,[132] and the divine self-disclosure in human conscience.[133] Human religions do have diabolical and immoral aspects, but they are due to the sin, ignorance and fallibility that are inherent in human nature. Nevertheless, people with all their errors and evils seek God in response

---

[125] John R. W. Stott, *The Message of Romans*, Leicester: Inter Varsity Press, 1994, p. 84.

[126] Cf. Romans 1:19-20; Psalms 19:1-4; Acts 14:15-17; 17:22-31.

[127] General Revelation is defined as "God's communication of himself to all persons at all times and all places... It refers to God's self-manifestation through nature, history and the inner being of the human person," Millard J.Erickson, *Christian Theology*, Grand Rapids: Baker Book House, 1988, pp. 153-154.

[128] Everett F.Harrison, *Romans: The Expositor's Bible Commentary Volume 10*, Grand Rapids: Zondervan Publishing House, 1976, p. 31.

[129] For instance, Anagarika Dharmapala thought that Jesus' Sermon on the Mount was adopted from Buddhist sources. He remarked that the beatitudes harmonise with the Eight-fold Path (A.W.Guruge, ed., *Return to Righteousness: A Collection of Speeches, Essays and Letters of Anagarika Dharmapala*, Colombo: Ministry of Education & Cultural Affairs, 1965, p. 696). Likewise, Holger Kersten, whose writings are popular among the Sri Lankan Buddhists, insists that "the Buddhist thought is found in Jesus' teaching" (*Jesus Lived in India*, Dorset: Element Books, 1995, pp. 99-102). According to him "the Sermon on the Mount is a condensed version of Buddhism" (Kerston with E.R.Gruber, *The Original Jesus: The Buddhist Sources of Christianity*, Dorset: Element Books, 1995, p. viii). It is his contention that the Q source in the synoptic tradition as well as the Gospel of Thomas were the oldest material containing the original teachings of Jesus and that they are highly influenced by Buddhism (*Ibid.* pp. 111-112). Particularly, he asserts that Dhammapada and an extended collections of teachings based on Dhammapada is found in the Q source (*Ibid.* pp. 123).

[130] According to Romans chapter 1 idolatry and immorality are the natural consequences of the total or partial rejection of the divine revelation.

[131] C. Wright, *Thinking Clearly About the Uniqueness of Jesus*. Crowborough: Monarch Publications, 1997, p. 109.

[132] The Bible explicitly states that human beings are created in the image of God (Genesis 1:26-27). Though the Fall has affected the divine image to a considerable extent (Genesis 3), it is not totally destroyed by human sin but distorted because of it. Even after the Fall, human beings are depicted as possessors of the divine image (Genesis 9:6, James 3:9).

[133] According to Psalm 19:1, Romans 1:18-20 God has revealed himself both in creation and in human conscience. Paul says that the non-Jewish communities had divine laws inscribed in their hearts (Romans 2:14-15). The similarities between the ethical precepts of Moses and Hamurabi were also due to this phenomenon.

to divine revelation, and it is the responsibility of Christians to recognise this religious instinct without condemning it and attributing everything in other religions to Satan. In this respect, the greatest apostle of Christianity, Paul, set an excellent example in Athens. Although that city was full of idols, and idolatry was condemned by God, Paul, who was greatly distressed by the religious practices of the people (Acts.17:16), instead of condemning them, commended their religious observances (Acts.17:22). Paul was not endorsing or sanctioning idolatry, but neither was he approaching the non-Christians with a polemical mentality. In Paul's approach, "we have a respectful recognition of religious endeavours,"[134] for it was "a cultured compliment to the distinguished audience."[135] Such a positive attitude and broadmindedness are vital when encountering the people of other faiths.[136] With such an attitude the Christians can use the book of Ecclesiastes to help the Buddhists to find an answer to their spiritual Quest.

---

[134] W.J.Larkin, *Acts: The IVP New Testament Commentary.* Downers Grove: Inter Varsity Press, 1995, p. 255.

[135] J.D.G.Dunn, *The Acts of the Apostles: Epworth Commentaries.* Peterborough: Epworth Press, p. 234

[136] In Acts 17:22 the Greek word translated as 'religious' (*deisidaimonesterous*) could be used either in a good or bad sense. The KJV rendering 'Ye are too superstitious' implies criticism. Hence "it is an unlikely way to start an evangelistic speech" (A.Fernando, *Acts: The NIV Application Commentary*, Grand Rapids: Zondervan Publishing House, 1999, p. 475). F.F.Bruce, however, citing an ancient writer Lucian, says, it cannot be a complimentary expression, for "it was forbidden to use complimentary exordia in addressing the Areopagus court, with the hope of securing its goodwill" (F.F.Bruce, *The Books of Acts: The New International Commentary on the NT*, Grand Rapids: Eerdmans Publishing Company, p. 355). Nevertheless, we cannot be certain about how far Paul was abiding by this prohibition and the NIV rendering is more positive. Moreover, the Athenians' reputation for religious piety is well attested (W.J.Larkin, *Acts: The IVP New Testament Commentaries*, p. 255). Hence Paul was expressing commendation in his address, as K.Grayston has pointed out, "to provide a way into his address that would engage the attention of the audience" (Quoted in I.H.Marshall, *Acts: Tyndale New Testament Commentaries*, Grand Rapids: Eerdman Publishing Company, p. 285).

CHAPTER 22

Muslim-Christian Relations in the Context of Mawdudi's Islamism[1]

David Emmanuel Singh

The new ideas of secularism, democracy and nationalism in the subcontinent were facilitated by European colonisation. These ideas not only made space for the plurality of nations and laws, but also created space for religious visions. Many Muslim intellectuals considered plurality as a problem. Mawdudi (1903-1979)[2] for instance, responded to this perceived problem by formulating an integrative political ideology,[3] we might call 'Islamism'.[4]

The British had for some reason ignored the diversity of religious visions and clubbed various religious sub-groups together into neat categories called Hinduism, Islam, Christianity etc. Muslim elites largely ignored low caste converts when they were in power. But, when the British came to power they clubbed the Indian Muslim sub-groups with the Muslim elite.[5] The Muslim elite now out of political power, realising the importance of numbers in the increasingly democratic climate had to deal with plurality within Islam. They responded by attempting to educate the nominal Indian Muslims, a process of education called 'Islamization.'

In this paper I shall outline Mawdudi's integrative political theory. I shall also attempt to show how the strictly integrative ideology of Islamism and Islamization might have been compromised and that this compromise might not have been incidental. Perhaps at the centre of the whole matter is the principle "endogamous circles", which we might employ to explore the issue of Muslim-Christian relations.

Mawdudi's Political Theory

Mawdudi's political theory is based on three principles:

(i).   No person, class... entire population of the state...can lay claim to sovereignty. God alone is the real sovereign; all

---

[1] "Prefatory Reflections on Muslim-Christian Relations in the Context of Mawdudi's Islam" by David Emmanuel Singh was published in *Dharma Deepika*, Vol.1, No.1, 2000, and is used with permission.

[2] Mawdudi was founder and chief ideologue of the *Jamiat-i islami*, an organisation of the elite Muslims, which through its publication and propaganda still exercises immense influence over South Asia and beyond. Mawdudi is widely known as one of the great thinkers of the world of Islam in this century. [See W C Smith, *Islam in Modern History*, New York: The New American Library, 1957, p.236].

[3] For instance, Namik Kemal (d. 1888), Jamal al-Din al-Afgani (d. 1897), Muhammad Abduh (d. 1905), Rashid Rida (d. 1935), Muhammad Iqbal (d. 1938), the Egyptian Muslim Brotherhood founded in 1928 by Hasan al-Banna (d. 1949) and Jamaat-e-Islami founded by Mawlana Mawdudi (d. 1979).

[4] See in particular M. Hoebink, "Thinking about Renewal in Islam: Towards a History of Islamic Ideas on Modernisation and Secularisation" in *Arabica: Journal of Arabic and Islamic Studies*, tome XLVI, Fascicule I, January 1999, pp. 29-62. See also Scholars have used the term in this sense. Haldun Gülalp, *Political Islam in Turkey: The Rise and Fall of the Refah Party*, in The *Muslim World*, vol. LXXXIX, no. 1, January, 1999, pp. 22-41.

[5] See Henry Hughes Presler, *The Mid-India Practice of Toleration*, Delhi: ISPCK, 1996. [Henceforth cited as *The Mid-India Practice of Toleration*].

others are...subjects; God is...the lawgiver and the authority of absolute legislation vests in Him.

(ii). An Islamic State must, in all respects, be founded upon the law laid down by God through His prophet.

(iii) The government which runs such a state will be entitled to obedience in its capacity as the political agency set up to enforce the laws of God....[6]

Elsewhere Mawdudi presents these three principles as follows:[7]

1.   Unity (*tawhid)*

2.   Prophethood (*risala*)

3.   Vicegerency (*khilafa*)

The three principles mean that God alone has the right to command and forbid; people are under obligation to obey Him only.[8]

Mawdudi's theory stands as an antithesis to secular democracy which regards people as sovereign. Democracy demands among other things that the determination of right and wrong, consequent law making and its execution, lie in the hands of the people. This sort of popular sovereignty has no place in Mawdûdî's vision of Islamic polity.

The traditional belief that God intended man to be the *khalifa* (vicegerent) of God on earth is rooted in the Qur'anic and hadith account of Adam's creation.[9] Vicegerency involves a certain exercise of authority and rulership. Vicegerency to him is a "collective right of all those who accept and admit God's absolute sovereignty over themselves and adopt the divine code, conveyed through the prophet, as the law above all laws...."[10] Vicegerents are the totality of Muslim believers who submit to the One Sovereign and His laws received through the Prophet having repudiated all previous national, ethnic or cultural norms. Thus all believers possess the right to be vicegerents. Mawdûdî calls the resulting polity Islamic democracy.[11]

A realm where the three principles of *tawhid, risala* and *khilafa* exists as described above is the "Kingdom of God or theo-democracy."[12] This 'kingdom' is universal in scope because one God is sovereign over all.[13] It does not recognise geographical, linguistic or colour differences. Anyone who submits automatically joins the community of vicegerents that runs the Islamic State.[14] Since the scope for Islamic polity is universal, there is space for its expansion through the vicegerents. Thus Mawdudi says: "Administrators of the Islamic state must be those

---

[6] *Islamic Law,* p. 146.

[7] Mawdudi, *Human Rights in Islam*, Aligarh: Crescent Publishing, 1976. [Henceforth cited as *Human Rights]*, p. 7

[8] Mawdudi, *Islamic Law and Constitution*, trans. Khurshid Ahmad, Lahore: Islamic Publications, 1960, henceforth cited as *Islamic Law*, p. 145. The section on the political Theory of Islam in the book was an address delivered at Shah Chirag Mosque in Lahore, October 1939, i.e., before independence. It was printed as a tract titled *Political Theory of Islam*, Pathankot: Maktaba-e-Jama'at-e-Islami, nd. [Henceforth cited as *Political Theory]*; see p. 27. Mawdudi quotes the Qur'an to support his point- see *Islamic Law*, p. 145 and Surah 22:40 and Surah 3: 154

[9] Surah 2:30-35. References to Adam and angels are found in Surah 7:11. Satan refusing to prostrate (*sujûd*) to Adam in Surah 15:26-33. See also *The Translation of the Meaning of sahih al-bukhari* (Arabic-English), New Delhi: Kitab Bhavan, 1980. Henceforth cited as *sahih al-bukhari*, See vol. IV, LV- "The Prophets", Chapter 1, pp. 341-347,

[10] Mawdudi, *The First Principles of the Islamic State*, trans. Khurshid Ahmad, Lahore: Islamic Publications, 1978; [henceforth cited as *First Principles]*, p. 25.

[11] *Ibid.* p. 26.

[12] *Islamic Law*, p. 147.

[13] *Ibid.* p. 154.

[14] *Ibid.* p. 156

whose whole life is devoted to the observance and enforcement of this law...."[15] Although Mawdûdî takes pains to maintain that vicegerency refers to the 'whole community of believers,' this assertion is conceptual. The sovereign God is not personally involved in the execution and establishment of His law. There is therefore, a need for people to see that God is recognised and His laws, received through his prophet, are obeyed. The notion of vicegerency as applied to all the believers conceptually fills this gap: "Every believer of God is a Caliph...."[16]

It seems apparent that a state where the entire population is said to govern itself on the basis of the divine laws would be ungovernable. Mawdudi qualifies his notion of vicegerency. The product of this qualification ultimately turns out to be elitist.[17] He speaks of the appointment of an *amir* as the head of an Islamic State and the Islamic Consultative Assembly (*majlis al-shura*) chosen by the people.[18] To begin with, his list of qualifications for the rulers is discriminating. A person can be chosen as the vicegerent of vicegerents only if <u>he</u> is:

- Muslim
- Male
- A sane adult
- An obedient believing (Muslim) citizen of an Islamic State

Those who gain the confidence of the community of vicegerents undertake the role of the *amir* and the *shura*. In contrast to the 'popular sovereignty' in secular democracy, theo-democracy involves 'popular vicegerency.'[19] Salient features of Mawdudi's secular democracy in contrast to theo-democracy may be represented as follows:

Theo-Democracy	Secular Democracy
Sovereignty vested on one God	People are sovereign
All believers are vicegerents of God	- do -
All vicegerents obey the divine laws revealed **through the prophet**	People make their own law
The chosen fulfil the wishes of the sovereign God [acting on behalf of all]	Government fulfils the wishes of the people

---

[15] *Ibid.* p. 155.

[16] *Ibid.* p. 158

[17] Mawdudi's elitism can be said to be rooted in the Qur'an (Surah 2: 30; 7:129 and in particular 6:165). The more esoteric Islamic traditions however do not subscribe to Mawdudi's sort of elitism. Certain Sufi sources redefine the notion of vicegerency to avoid elitist interpretation. Cf. Yasien Mohamed, "Knowledge and Purification of the Soul: An Annotated Translation with Introduction of Isfahani's *Kitab al-dharia ila makaim al-sharia (58-76; 89-92)*" in *Journal of Islamic Studies*, 9 (1), 1998, 1-34. Here the vicegerency is connected to the idea of inner purification of souls (*taharat al-nafs*). Sufism in this sense was extremely democratising.

[18] *Human Rights*, p. 11

[19] *Human Rights*, p. 9

The Context for Mawdudi's Islamism and Islamization[20]

Freedom Struggle and Democratic Nationalism in the Subcontinent

Born in 1903 in Hyderabad, India, Mawdudi lived through the years of intense struggle for political freedom from the British. By the time Mawdudi began writing, nationalism was already beginning to establish itself and assume a near sacred character. Mawdudi's ideas communicated through his papers and speeches furnished a sharp ideological contrast.[21]

The fundamental critique of nationalism offered by Mawdudi was that people construct it. Such people ignore God and the revelatory laws of God:

> These principles have blighted the sacred ideals for which the messengers of God have endeavoured since the earliest of times. These Satanic principles have stood as formidable obstacles and powerful adversaries against the moral and spiritual teaching embodied in the heavenly books, and against the law of God.[22]

According to Mawdudi, if nationalism brings people together, it also divides them on the basis of their territorial claims. Laws of One God, in contrast, bring people of different language, ethnic, cultural and religious backgrounds closer together on the basis of their common relation to the Sovereign: "The law of God...has always aimed at bringing together mankind into one moral and spiritual frame-work and make them mutually assistant to one another on a universal scale."[23]

A predominant image of the product of nationalist ideology that Mawdudi had in his mind was that of Socialism and Nazism. Mawdûdî lived during a time when these were powerful ideologies. Nehru's nationalism was clearly designed after the Soviet Socialist model. Mawdudi found these repugnant and believed that these ideologies represented godless human attempts to usurp divine authority and law.[24] Nationalism as Mawdudi saw it, involved veneration of the states or fatherlands instead of one God, charismatic leaders took the place of prophets, who unlike the prophetic revelation brought plural and often conflicting versions of constitutions. Thus he felt there was a need for integrative Islamism.

Impermanence of the Nations: The Case of the Subcontinent

On the tenth of May 1947, a few months before Independence and the division of India and Pakistan, Mawdudi delivered a speech in East Punjab.[25] The audience consisted of Hindus, Muslims, Sikhs etc. The situation of Punjab was highly volatile. Hardly three months after this speech the birth of the two nations caused inexpressible sufferings to millions. In his speech, entitled "Nations rise and fall- why?"[26] Mawdudi outlined his theory giving reasons for the impermanence of nations. The tone of the speech was mild because he was addressing a mixed

---

[20] The term Islamization here refers to aggressive propagation of central ideas of Islamism, namely *tawhid, risala* and *khilafa* (including certain essential practices) among the Muslim masses.

[21] Mawdudi's began his writing first at the age of 17 when he became the editor of a daily paper *Taj* and little later *Al-jamiat*. At the age of 26 he published his first scholarly book, *Al-jihad fi-al-Islam*. He began his most influential monthly journal *tajuman al-Qur'an* in 1932.

[22] Mawdudi, *Nationalism and India*, Malihabad: Maktaba-e-Jama'at-e-Islami (Hind), 1948, p. 21.

[23] *Ibid.* p. 22

[24] *Ibid.* p. 25. Although Mawdudi is critical of Nazi and socialist ideologies, his political theory is also fundamentally ideological. This is so because his interpretation of Islam represented the elite Muslims (*ashrafs*) interests vis-à-vis the low caste Indians who converted to Islam (*ajlaf*).

[25] East Punjab was roughly the area that fell within India after independence.

[26] Mawdudi, *Nations Rise and Fall— Why?* Delhi: Markazi Maktaba Islami, 1978. [Henceforth cited as *Nations Rise*].

crowd. One can detect, however, his central critique- human desire to stake out sovereign territories, create laws and act independent of God. To Mawdudi, the rise of the nation states was a necessary evil. One Sovereign God however, remains ultimately in control of the nation above the claims of powerful individuals and groups who usurp God's role and submit to their own laws rather than God's. [27] Provisionally, till the establishment of the divine realm is realised fully, God evaluates the nations by using a simple yardstick: "Construction pleases God; destruction displeases Him." [28] God as the real Master of the universe supports every constructive effort of nations even when they do not recognise God and are led by people other than Muslims. But nations not ruled by God inevitably engage in destructive tendencies thus inviting God's judgement, leading to the nation's fall and establishment of Islamism.[29]

Mawdudi illustrates his theory of 'construction' and 'destruction' by giving his interpretation of causes of the rise and fall of nations. The theory seems rather simplistic because Mawdudi does not provide deeper bases for his theory of 'construction and destruction.'[30]

- The Aryans were God's instruments in increasing 'constructive' dimensions of greater India

- When their constructive energy was spent and they actually became instruments promoting 'destruction,' [for instance, the high castes ruling over of the low castes on

the basis of the laws of *Manu*] God sent Muslims to India.[31] But the Muslim rulers and the aristocrats succumbed to the same temptation as their predecessors and thereby increased the destructive tendencies. They were punished because they had a narrow vision. They were Muslims, but wereguilty of limiting their influence to politics and had no wide integrative vision.[32]

The British were permitted to assume power in India to undo the damage done by Muslim rulers. God expelled the British from India because they were found guilty of the same tendencies as their predecessors.

The 'freedom' of India from foreign rulers was, according to Mawdûdî, not final. It was for him one among many changes God was bringing about to cause reformation of human life and human movement towards recognising the ultimate divine Sovereignty-laws:

> This moment…is one of those turning points in history when the real sovereign of the earth brings the rule of one authority to an end and decides to transfer the administration of a country to a new authority… God did not…install these foreigners in power without a purpose, nor is he ousting them without reason. God did not dispossess the natives of their rule with out a cause, nor will he reinstate them in power without a design. The people of India stand as candidates for power today. The Hindus, the Muslims, the Sikhs- all demand power…. But this is not a permanent dispensation….[33]

---

[27] *Ibid.* p. 2.

[28] *Ibid.* p. 3

[29] The constructive tendency has to do with the effort of the vicegerents of God to establish, maintain, and develop virtues and prevent and eradicate evils 'abhorrent to God'. See *Human Rights*, p. 9

[30] *Nations Rise,* pp. 9-17.

[31] This point will be elaborated later in the paper.

[32] Mawdûdî's theory of fall and rise of states seems to apply to Muslim majority states like Turkey as well. See, Haldun Gülalp, *Political Islam in Turkey: The Rise and Fall of the Refah Party,* in The *Muslim World,* vol. LXXXIX, no. 1, January, 1999, pp. 22-41.

[33] *Nations rise.* pp. 16-17.

Islamic Revolution: The Final Dispensation

In his address to the students of Aligarh Muslim University (close to Delhi), Mawdudi identifies Islamism as the final dispensation through which God will establish his Kingdom.[34] The world, according to him, is soon going to witness the final burst of Islamic revolution. God will then establish good and constructive elements of life, the highest of which is in recognising that there is One God and that all human beings need to submit to His laws. Islam as the final revolution will not just be political and administrative like the Muslim rule in India that was replaced by the British; it will effect a total ideological transformation of the world. The model for this final success of the universal Islamic revolution comes from the early Islam of Arabia- from Muhammad's own time:

> It seems strange that, while during the space of thirteen years, only three hundred persons embraced Islam, in the latter ten years the whole country of Arabia adopted this religion wholesale.... The matter is quite plain. So long as life had not been actually planned and organised on the basis of this new ideology people could not understand what this novel type of leader wanted to do. ...Only men of...understanding...could believe in Muhammad...men whose realistic vision could see clearly that the salvation of mankind lay in this new creed. But when a complete system of life was built up on this ideology and people has [sic.] actual experience of it...it was then that they understood... [and] it became impossible to deny this open reality. Gentlemen! This is the method by which Islam seeks to bring about Islamic revolution.[35]

Interestingly, Aligarh University was a source and a centre for Muslim ideology that supported the Indian national Freedom movement. The Aligarh movement was parochial from Mawdûdî's integrative Islamist vision point of view. Mawdudi attempted to draw the attention of ideologues and students alike to his conviction that political 'freedom' was a mere phase in the experience of nations. Freedom of India and Pakistan was not to be the end of the divine vision envisaged by the Prophet. Islamic revolution was not just for political authority. Islamic political authority merely creates an environment for the establishment of the true understanding of Islam (submission to One God). Thus Islamism incorporated every aspect of human life on earth. Nothing was conceived outside its pale.

Mawdudi theorized that just as the establishment of Islam as a political entity in Madina ensured the phenomenal growth of Islam during Muhammad's own time, the establishment of Islamic political rule in a nation like Pakistan would enhance the effects of Islamic revolution. Mawdudi expected a change of heart among the ideologues and students of Aligarh University. Thus, in his final remarks he clearly placed before them his hope of Islamic revolution:

> I am...addressing the students of Aligarh and placing before them the plan of that movement for bringing about a social revolution of an Islamic nature. I have done my duty and communicated to you whatever I had in mind. The responsibility of changing our hearts does not lie on me.[36]

Just as the birth of Madina, the first Islamist city state, led to the expansion of Islam in Arabia during the prophet's own time, Mawdudi hoped Pakistan could well become the modern Madina. He understood the creation of a Muslim state [Pakistan] in terms of the nascent Muslim polity in Madina. The tiny community in Madina understood its role in terms of the entire universe

---

[34] Mawdudi, *Process of Islamic Revolution*, Pathankot: Maktaba-e-jamaat-e-Islami, 1947.

[35] *Ibid.* p. 54-55.

[36] *Ibid.* p. 57.

when the entire life of Madinese Muslims was infused by the new ideology. Creation of Pakistan provided a positive environment within which Islamism could take birth and expand.

Awareness of Plurality within Islam and the Role of the Elite in India

It was clear however, that 'Islamism' could not be applied to India immediately. Thus in India a different strategy had to be used.[37] The influx of democratic ideals had exposed intra-religious incompatibilities between the elite Muslims and the Indian converts to Islam organised in their respective sub-groups. Awareness of intra-religious plurality might have been one of the background impulses leading to the development of Mawdudi's political theory and its application on the masses of Indian Muslims who were seen as harbouring 'heterodoxy' and thus representing a challenge for the elite Muslims.

When applied to Islam in India, Presler's theory of 'disjunction' throws light on Mawdudi's Islamization of the Indian Muslims. H. Presler has written about two kinds of 'disjunction.'[38]

1. Disjunction between religions: Religious groups or endogamous circles [EC] do not associate with each other on account of ethnic, economical, social or theological disjunction.

2. Disjunction between sub-groups within a religion: Sub-groups within a particular religion remain distant from each other on account of ethnic, economical, social or theological disjunction.

Diagram I below, illustrates that when a religious community or EC adopts a dominant religion it brings with it its old social, economic, ethnic and theological baggage and assumes the role of a sub-group within the religion of their choice. Thus some of the old incompatibilities continue. Factors that keep people distant from each other (1) also keep co-religionists (2) distant from each other. But in the second case, the incompatibilities are tolerated or ritually justified, thereby creating a positive environment. Mutual crossing-over of individuals between sub-groups becomes possible without having to permanently break away from their respective groups.

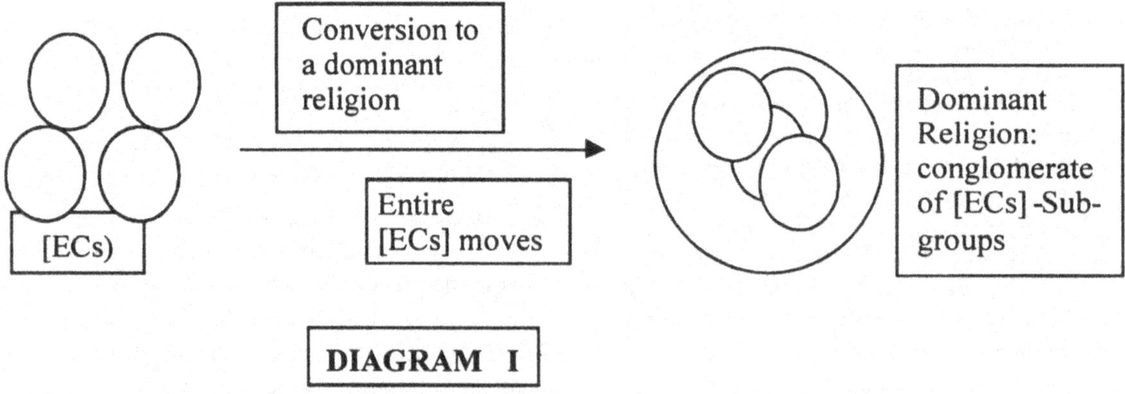

---

[37] See Mawdudi, *Let Us Be Muslims*, ed. Khurram Murad, Delhi: Markazi Maktaba Islami, 1987. This is a translation of Mawdudi's *khutbat*. It is a collection of ordinary details of what it means to be a Muslim for common Indian converts to Islam.

[38] *Practice of Toleration.*

The Diagram II below shows that pre-Islamic Arabs were divided into tribes and clans based on ancient kinship, traditions, rivalries, feuding and violence. These disjunctions were in theory disciplined by 'egalitarian Islam.'[39]

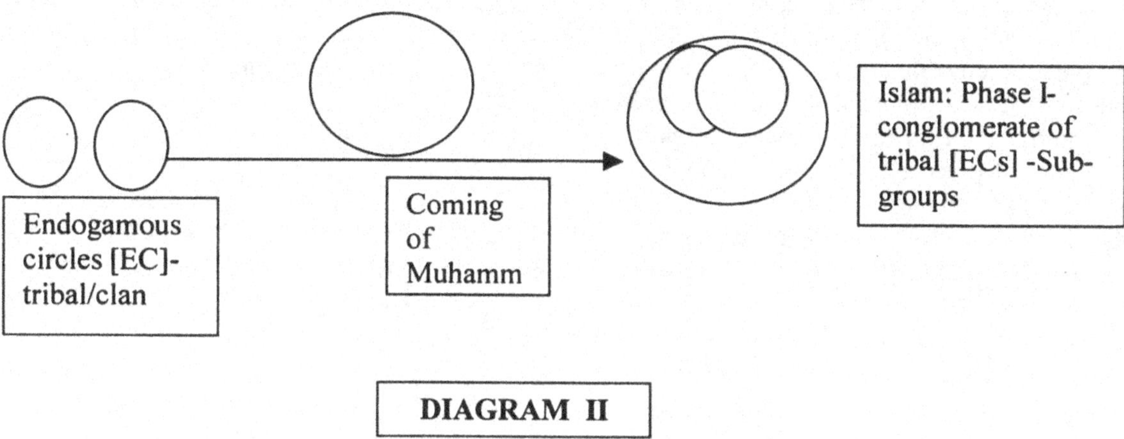

DIAGRAM II

Diagram III below shows that when 'ritually equal' Muslim Arabs conquered Aryan Persians in 640 CE, they encountered newer kinds of incompatibilities.[40] For instance, inequalities based on urban, economic, social, racial and theological differences and uniquely Aryan notion of *varnadharma*.[41] A fusion of two cultural groups took place and the Persian Aryan system was adopted in practice. The Persian serfs continued as a distinct subgroup within the system but the distinctions were tolerated.

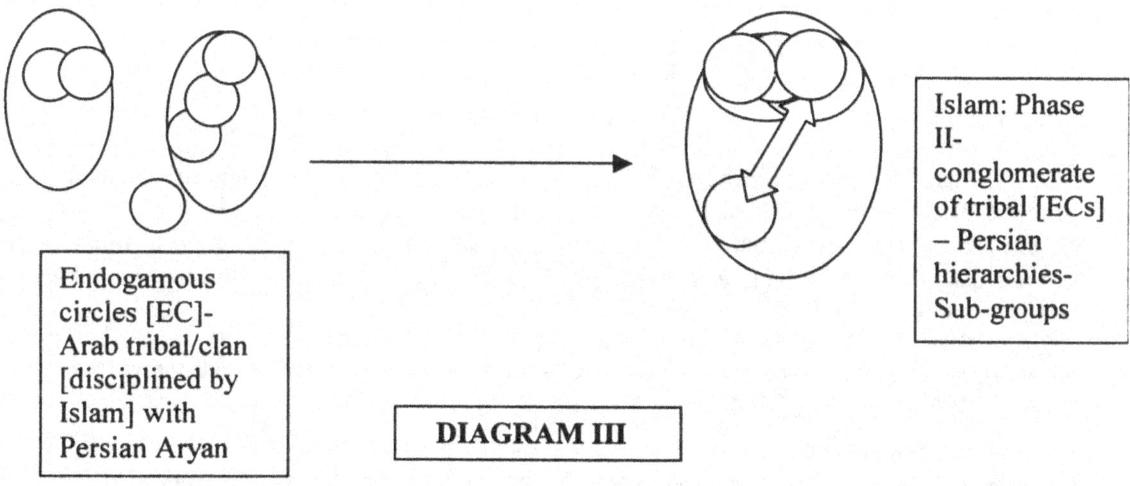

DIAGRAM III

---

[39] See Surah XLIX, p.13; IX, p.2.

[40] See *Practice of Toleration.*

[41] A way of life and subgroup incompatibilities based on colour in a particular religious system. For instance white denoting highest class, red denoting ruling elite, gold denoting business class and black or brown denoting out-castes-servants-slaves.

Consequently, beginning from the 12th century, Muslims conquerors of the Indian subcontinent were distinctly divided into- Religious doctors (*Ulama'* and Sufis), nobility (ruling class), merchants and serf sub-groups. A complex socio-political system harbouring sub-group disjunction was already within India when Muslims arrived because the Aryans had preceded Muslims into India. This system was based on colour and racial disjunctions and is also called 'Caste.'[42]

The Diagram IV below shows that a large number of Buddhists and the low-castes in the subcontinent converted to Islam. These converts were placed alongside the serfs in the social hierarchy that was already existent within Islam. Foreign Muslim rulers, though a minority in the subcontinent's Islam, naturally saw themselves as racially superior (*ashraf*)[43] to the great numbers of low-caste Muslims converts (*ajlaf*).[44] This system allowed the low-caste converts to continue their distinctive practices and also permitted crossings-over of the *ashrafs* to the 'heterodox' institutions of the *ajlafs*.[45]

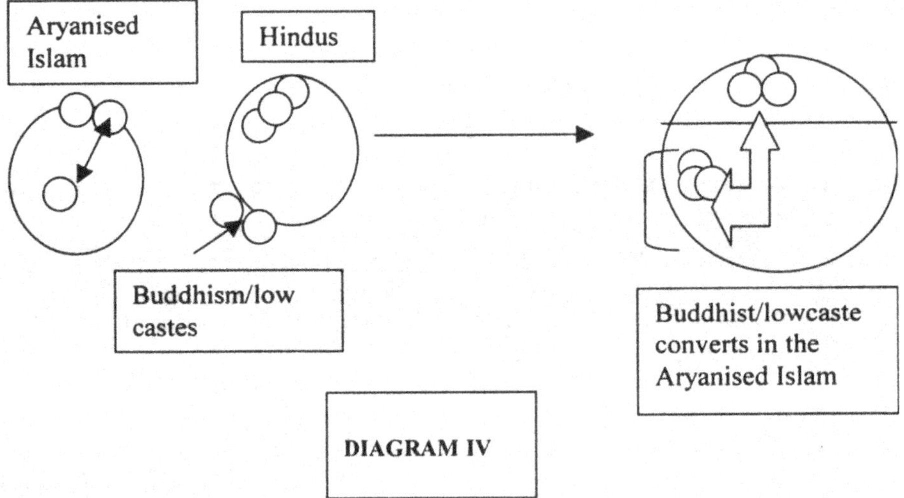

The shifting of the power balance from the *ashraf* to the British after the so-called 'Mutiny' in 1857 CE was a grave crisis for the *ashraf* ruling class. When *ashrafs* were ruling over a majority of non-Muslims and the kingdom was stable, the state sponsored a religious ideology, which was more universalistic.[46] But, when a minority of Muslim elite rulers were outnumbered by the

---

[42] Aryans used the term *dharma* [from *dhree-* meaning 'to hold' or 'that, which holds']. This system containing complex incompatibilities was called *varnadharma*. *Varnadharma* or caste in India contained within it four basic sub-groups corresponding to the Aryan Persian sub-groups-

Level I: *Brahmins, Khshatriyas, Vaishyas* [Minority/belonging to the original Aryan stock]

Level II: *Sudras*[Majority/original inhabitants who were conquered and integrated in the system]

[43] The foreigners were divided into class groups similar to the Indian caste. *Ashrafs* were one of several levels among them. For the sake of convenience I am using the term *ashraf* to refer to the entire group of Muslim foreigners.

[44] See Yoginder Sikand, "The Changing Nature of Religious Authority in Twentieth Century South Asian Islam" in *The Bulletin*, vol. 16, nos., 1 and 2, January-June 1997, pp. 5-22. Henceforth cited as "South Asian Islam".

[45] See appendix I: CASE I

[46] A. Kevin Reinhart in his *Before Revelation: The Boundaries of Muslim Moral Thought*, Albany: State University of New York Press, 1995.

Muslim converts from among the ruled states and the elite political power was becoming destabilised, the elite became more inward looking and their religious policy became more religiously militant and 'orthodox.' They began to see a disjunction between themselves and the *ajlafs*, which had been ignored in most cases. They felt that the *ajlafs* were weakening the elite Muslims' combined economic and ideological power in a context of the rising external political challenge. The *ajlafs'* ideological visions were considered heresies and they were blamed for having caused the wrath of God upon Islam on account of the un-Islamic practices that they had imported into Islam.

The *ashrafs* undertook a massive programme of Islamization in a bid to purge the *ajlafs* of 'un-Islamic' practices, thereby creating conditions for the return of Muslim political power. It was for this reason that Islamization was singularly led by the *ashrafs,* among whom Mawdûdî was one of the most important figures.[47] Islamization was a tool through which the *ashrafs* attempted to integrate the *ajlafs* within his vision of 'Islam.' Mawdûdî's 'democracy' was in this context an attempt to integrate vast numbers of Indian converts in concept, within his Islamic political ideology. In reality it was no different from the Pakistani elite who hungered for power. His was an ideologically 'Islamic' alternative to create a way in which the elite would continue to remain powerful politically.[48]

Two factors to do with the colonial administrators must be kept in focus in this background, because these aided the process of Islamization:

1. When the British established their paramountcy in the subcontinent:

   a. The British were a minority ruling over a majority made up of disparate religious traditions, ethnic, and language backgrounds. They subscribed to a political ideology which sought to create space for plurality.

   b. The British law supervened *shari 'ah* in principle

   c. The Muslim ruling classes were stripped of political power

   d. The British left them in charge of their religion and customs to regulate religious-personal- family matters.[49]

This arrangement was beneficial for both parties. It was an opportunity for the British to circumscribe the influence of *shari 'ah*, but for the Muslim elite it was an opportunity to extend their influence over the vast majority of Indian Muslim who were largely ignored. It was the only way that the elite could continue to wield influence over the masses.[50]

2. Loss of *ashraf* political power narrowed the actual gulf between the *ashrafs* and the *ajlafs*. The British aided this process by identifying subjects under religious categories such as Hindus, Sikhs, Christians and Muslims. Thus the *ashrafs* and the *ajlafs* were statistically clubbed together, just as the high and low caste Hindus were clubbed together. The statistical swelling of Muslim numbers achieved something significant. It caused a powerful movement called

---

[47] See Altaf Gauhar, "Mawlana Abul Ala Mawdudi- A Personal Account" in *Islamic Perspectives: Studies in Honour of ...Mawdudi,* eds. K Ahmad and Z. I. Ansari, Delhi: Markazi Maktaba Islami, 1987, pp.265-288

[48] *Ibid.*

[49] There is evidence for this process of mutual benefit from the British administration in Malaysia. See "South Asian Islam", pp.7-9 and 9-10.

[50] Evidence for this process in the British colonies like Malaysia is found in William Roff's work. See William R Roff, "Patterns of Islamization in Malaysia, 1890s-1990s: Exemplars, Institutions, and Vectors," in *Journal of Islamic Studies*, 9 (2), 1998, 21-228.

Shuddhi.[51] With the coming of the British secular democratic ideals first began to show signs of appearing. Appearance of democratic ideals convinced the elite among Hindus and Muslims that their numerical strength was an important criterion for political participation and power. The high caste Hindus saw Muslim numbers swelling as a result of the British census and interpreted this to mean that Muslims were increasing in power. They therefore launched the *Shuddhi* campaign. Significantly, the revivalist *Arya Samaj* (Fellowship of Aryans) led this movement. A Gujarati (West Indian) Brahmin, Swami Daynand Saraswati (1824-1883) was the founder of the *Samaj*. Swami Shradhananda, his disciple started the actual *Shuddhi* campaign in 1923. *Arya Samaj* and *Shuddhi* concentrated on the recovery of *aryadharma* (Aryan religion with its caste system), which meant re-conversion and reintegration of common Muslims back into the caste hierarchy so as to increase the high-caste political clout.

The *ashrafs* reacted to this. Their political rule was taken away from them and now their power base, which was centred on the great number of the Indian converts to Islam, was threatened by *shuddhi.*[52] Thus the Islamic political theory of Mawdudi, in its basic form represented the *ashrafs'* attempt to recreate conditions for strengthening the elite Muslim political base in places where they had ruled prior to the coming of the British.

What seems evident is that Mawdudi's 'political theory' was in part a vision of a small minority of elite Muslims who saw themselves as racially pure Arab-Aryans. Mawdûdî's notion of One sovereign God was part of the *ashraf* attempt to Islamize *ajlaf* and reform the plurality of religious visions within Islam of the subcontinent that had according to him, compromised on the uniting vision of Islam. The multiplicity of religious routes were perceived as sources of weakening of elite power and influence. This meant that the majority of Indian Muslims remained notionally linked to the elite or 'orthodox' institutions, but they preserved and frequented the 'heterodox' institutions where the *pirs* (dead saints) and *mujavirs* (mediums) exercised immense power over the masses. Assertion of the sovereignty of One God-one law crystallised in this context. The continuance of the heterodox institutions is evidence of the fact that Islamization never fully replaced the 'heterodox routes'. What it succeeded in achieving was to create a new sense of conceptual and uniform religious identity among the Indian Muslims. The Muslim masses after Islamization became aware of the essentials of Islamic beliefs and practices as defined by the elite. The essential content of such a reformation was the focus on one God-one law. The *ashrafs* however, allowed the 'heterodox' routes to exist within Islam in practice and often themselves crossed over to them in times of crisis.[53]

The two Foci of Mawdudi's Political Theory and the People of other Faiths

It has been noted above that Mawdudi's political theory had two foci: one for those states where Muslims were a majority and the other for those states where they were in a minority. India and Pakistan were his immediate test cases. In the former case Mawdûdî felt that the integrative

---

[51] A movement led by the high-caste Hindus who sought to reconvert the *ajlafs*.

[52] *Ibid.* pp. 10-11.

[53] On the political plane movement of sub-groups continue into larger and more dominant entities can also be demonstrated using examples from works done on North Africa, Middle East and Turkey. See, *Palestine Documents*, ed. Zafarul-Islam Khan, New Delhi: Pharos and Institute of Islamic and Arab Studies, 1998 and Yezid Sayigh, *Armed Struggle and the Search for State: The Palestinian National Movement, 1949-1993*, Washington, DC: Institute for Palestine Studies and Clarendon Press, 1997.

Islamist ideology had a favourable environment for its establishment.[54] It was from here that such an integrative vision was to grow beyond the state territories to realise the full universal potential of Islamism.[55]

In his vision of the universe there was ideologically no place for plurality of political and religious disjunction. In his Islamist vision for the majority Muslim states, Mawdudi had to grapple with the reality of plurality. Mawdudi limited the scope of the minority communities' freedom by allowing plurality to exist only at the levels of human rights and religious faiths. He made sure that no *plural political version* existed in an Islamic state because that would have been dangerous for the central elite concern for power.

As already stated, the establishment of British power led to the application of universalism, and acceptance of plurality and compromise. After the British left, the governments of nations where Islam was in a minority like India and Thailand, chose the pluralist model of governance. This was an encouraging development for the minorities because the stable government instituted positive policies for the minorities.[56] Like the British then, the Indian government might have seen this as a way to *circumscribe the influence of religious law to family-personal affairs*, but recognition of such plurality also led to freedom for the elite Muslims to assert their power over the Muslim masses. Islamization was the outcome of this process.[57]

The secular system of governance finds itself on a stable ground because of the radical separation of religion from the state. Secular states are open to allowing plurality within them, because their system ensures that freedom of religion is an essential right of the individuals and constitutionally this right is not likely to interfere with the political governance. It is perhaps for this reason that in the US and the UK it is possible for Muslims to build religious institutions, engage in active *tabligh* (propagation), hold religious demonstrations, find asylum and publish and distribute religious materials freely.[58] The same level of freedom and appreciation of plurality, or ability to deal with plurality as enshrined by the secular ideology might still be difficult in the majority Muslim states because traditionally, Muslims states *do not separate religious rights from political rights*.[59] It is difficult for many Muslim states to fully conceive the British strategy of granting freedom to minorities purely within religious sphere in order to safe-guard the political interests.

The so-called 'constitution of Mecca'[60] is known to have been relatively more tolerant of the minorities than *al-shurut al-'umariyya* (stipulations of Umar) or the charter of 'Umar.[61] The 'charter of Umar' has been known to

---

[54] Mawdudi, *Islami Qanun awr Pakistan mén us ke nifadh ki 'mali tadabir* trans *Islamic Law and its Introduction in Pakistan*, Lahore: 1948/1955. For details of his vision of non-Muslims in Islamic States see Mawdudi, i*slami hukumat men dhimmiyon ke huquq* trans. *Rights of Non-Muslims in an Islamic State*, Lahore: 1948/1961.

[55] See Mawdudi, *ittihad-i-'alam-i islamil* trans. *Unity of the Muslim World*, Lahore: n.d/1967.

[56]For instance recognition of the religious holidays and establishment of *sharia* courts to govern the religious and family affairs of Muslims.

[57] One can see this process in action in the context of Thailand. See R. Scupin, "Muslim Accommodation in Thai Society" in *Journal of Islamic Studies*, 9 (2), 1998, pp.229-258.

[58] See Sanjay Suri "Fanatical Zeal in English Climes" in *Outlook*, June 1999, p.22.

[59] *Cf.*, Ibrahim M. Abu-Rabi', "Christian-Muslim Relations in the Twenty-first Century: Lessons from Indonesia" in *Islamochristiana*, 24, 1998, pp.19-35.

[60] *"dhimma"* in *EL2* II, pp.227-231. See also Mawdudi, i*slami dastur ki bunyaden* Trans. *Fundamentals of the Islamic Constitution* ,Lahore: 1952/1952 and d*asturi sifarishat par tanqid: islami awr jamhuri nuqta-i nazar se*, A Critique of the Constitutional Proposal from the Islamic and Democratic Viewpoints, Karachi: n.d.

[61] See text of Umar's charter on *etudes arabes*, 1991, pp.80-81.

represent a hardening of Muslim policy towards minorities even though in most likelihood it was an apocryphal document.[62] It became, in time, the basic 'Islamic' reference for rulers seeking to relate to non-Muslims. This was the period in which Islam, was not fully established as a political force. The Abbasids however, consolidated the Muslim Empire. In the context of greater security and political stability under them the policy towards the minorities was more lenient. Medieval Islam saw a reversal of the trend under the Abbasids, when the 'charter of Umar' began to be considered an essential part of *shari 'ah*.[63]

Today, the Muslim countries feel drawn to this charter primarily because traditionally the charter has been thought to be an essential part of *shari 'ah*. The *shari 'ah* is the sacred law. It is considered far and away the better choice to obey *shari 'ah* than the secular charters. Thus for instance, the issue of plurality is a concern stemming from the notion of respect for variant opinions and choices of individuals and groups. But for a *shari 'ah* abiding Muslim, concern to establish knowledge and obedience of One God is a matter of obedience to the law of the Sovereign.[64]

The charter itself is very discriminating against the minorities and clearly it meant to address rulers' concern to determine the nature of relations with minorities, of which Christians were chief.

> They shall not build new churches or convents or cells or hermitages (for monks) in their towns and the countryside around.

> They shall not renew those (of these places) that fall in ruins. They shall not hinder (the use) of their churches to Muslims.... They shall not give shelter to spies... They shall not teach their children the Koran. They shall not show (the sign of) their associationism (*shirk*)...They shall...stand up from their seats whenever they (Muslims) want to sit. They shall not try to resemble Muslims in anything as regards clothes, hat...the way of combing.... They shall not ride on saddle neither shall they gird themselves with swords nor possess any kind of weapon.... They shall not show their crosses or their books.... They shall not bury their dead near those of Muslms. They shall not strike their bells (hard)...neither shall that raise their voices while reading in their churches... should they infringe anything of the stipulations (*shurut*)...they will have no right to protection....[65]

The text limits freedom of Christians *both on the political and religious fronts.*

Mawdudi, in contrast, follows the British and the Indian strategy of limiting minorities' freedom to certain essential human rites and religious affairs. Minorities were however, kept out of participation in the political and defence affairs of the state. In contexts where Muslims were a majority, like in India, Mawdudi adopted a different strategy. He concentrated on Islamization of the Indian Muslim with an eventual hope of establishing elite power and hence the integrative Islamist vision. The examination of the Islamization process has however, shown that despite Islamization, intra-religious sub-groups with in Islam were allowed

---

[62] See G. Scattolin, "Sufism and Law in Islam: A Text of Ibn 'Arabi...on Protected People (*ahl al-dhimma*)," in *Islamochristiana*, 24, 1998, pp.35 ff.

[63] *Ibid.* pp.48-49.

[64] Mawdudi, *Four Basic Qur'anic Terms*, Delhi: Markazi Maktaba Islami, 1995. See note 22 on p.100 for Mawdudi's opinion on *shari?a* vis-à-vis the notion of human rights. See also Mawdudi, *insan ke bunyadi huquq* (Fundamental rights of Man), Lahore, 1963.

[65] See the text of Umar quoted in G. Scattolin, "Sufism and Law in Islam: A Text of Ibn 'Arabi...on 'protected people *ahl al-dhimma*", in *Islamochristiana*, 24, 1998, p.45.

to continue with their pre-conversion disjunction. The Muslim elite had to make certain adjustments, for Islamization did not succeed in replacing the 'heterodox routes'. Certain amount of socialisation and compromise took place and in the end the elite made space for plurality within Indian Islam.

Mawdudi's vision for minorities was, atleast in the religious realm more flexible than the charter of Umar. His Islamization also did not push the integrative vision too far in order to establish a 'monistic' religious entity. One feels that if an Islamic state chose to adopt Mawdudi's version of Islamism, there would not seem any reason for the Christians minorities to feel threatened. This is as long as they remain aloof from politics and do not carry their freedom beyond the delimitation of their own religious institutions, personal and family matters.

The discussion above has also indicated that Mawdudi' attempted to Islamize the *ajlaf* in order to bring about the greatest possibility of similarity centring on the belief in one God and certain external practices. His Islamization was not pressed further than this. The Indian Muslims were allowed tacitly to maintain their heterodox institutions, beliefs and practices, even those institutions that were clearly Hinduistic and idolatrous- religious practices and beliefs, which qualified the *ajlaf* to be included in a separate category of 'religion'.

Conceptually, the *ashraf-ajlaf* relations and the story of the tolerance and compromise in practice may be taken as a model for the relations between Islam and Christianity. To illustrate, one can look at Mawdudi's comments on the Israelite captivity and release from Egypt. Basing his argument on the OT, Mawdudi conjectures that about one fifth of the Egyptians had come to accept the faith of Joseph (Abrahamic faith). The number of Israelites who left Egypt was estimated to have been about two million and the population of Egypt, Mawdudi believed was about 100 million. All of the two million however, could not have been Israelites, for the 12 sons of Jacob could not have increased to this number even in four centuries. Mawdûdî's inference has that the majority of the two million Israelites were converts to the faith of Joseph. In this note Mawdudi, was careful not to call this faith Judaisim. He was not bothered about the distinctive these people had. His concern was to show that the two million of those who left Egypt were Muslims. To him, the people of the faith of Joseph/ Abraham were, included in Islam as a sub-group. [66]

To Mawdudi, it was normative to assert that since there is one God, there cannot be more than two visions of *din* (religion). If there are variant *dins*, logically they are to be considered false. To him the most basic idea of the true *din* was to be found in all the true revealed scriptures. Like the Qur'an, all revealed scriptures therefore, have the same theme and therefore they were *in their essence* Muslim:

> Allah Almighty is the *rabb* (Lord) and *'ilah* (God); that there is no *'ilah* but He, nor is there any other *rabb*...He, and He alone should therefore be accepted as one's *'ilah* and *rabb*.... It also demand that we should give our *?ibadah* to Him...and make our *deen* exclusive for Him and reject all other *deens*.[67]

To Mawdûdî, most prophets were given limited national assignments, but Muhammad and Abraham were given a universal mission. [68] The scriptures Abraham and Muhammad received, according to Mawdûdî, had universal scope in that both concurred in their concern to guide

---

[66] *Ibid.* n.11, p.98.

[67] *Ibid.* p.5

[68] Mawdudi, *Nationalism and India*, Malihabad: Maktaba-e-Jama'at-e-Islami (Hind), 1948, 26ff.

humanity to belief in One God and His sovereignty-law. [69]

Many Christian theologians have recognised the importance of Abraham for dialogue among the three monotheistic religions. An appeal to Abraham by Christian theologians is driven by a variety of motives- evangelism, dialogue for evangelism or dialogue for eventual reconciliation between individuals whose respective faiths it is believed, go back to a common father- Abraham. Tarek Mitri, reflecting the WCC agenda, explores the Abrahamic theme for the purpose of creating conditions for dialogue leading to better relations, particularly in the context of the Middle East. He presented a paper on the theme of Abraham in the monotheistic religions- Judaism, Christianity and Islam at the Middle Eastern council of Churches sponsored colloquium in Beirut in 1998. [70] He asked questions like- how should one consider theAbrahamic heritage today; does not this common root lead to ambiguity and confusion; how does one avoid confusion without giving up the notion of Abrahamic heritage? He warns against the Orientalist attempt at describing Islam as 'Hagarian Ishmaelism' in the present context of the Palestinian-Jewish relations. [71] That is, one must refrain from interpreting Ishmael and Hagar segments in the Bible that support the idea: "to Isaac the land, to Ishmael the desert." In the context of the Palestinian struggle, it is not just the Arab Muslims, but also Arab Christians who would have to live in the deserts! [72]

In 1987, the Bible Society organised a dialogue of Muslim-Christian scholars in New Delhi. Kenneth Thomas from United Bible Societies gave the keynote address. He pointed out that Hebrew-Christian prejudice is obvious in the way Christians interpret Genesis 16:12 negatively: "He shall be a wild ass of a man, with his hand against everyone and everyone's hand against him. And he shall live at odds with his kin." Thomas shows that if viewed properly against the Ancient Near Eastern background and rules of idiom, Genesis 16:12 will not support the negative idea of Ishmael. For instance, "Wild ass" is an object of admiration and qualification. The phrase "his hand against..." signifies independence. Looking particularly at the phrase "And he shall live at odds with his kins," Thomas further attempts to show that the phrase "on the face of is translated normally as "at odds with..." He suggests that it is an idiom referring to the direction, East, that is the other side of Jordan, if viewed from Palestine. This therefore, describes the place where Ishmael's descendants, the Arabs wiil live. Though it may seem innocuous in the first blush, it has enormous political consequences against the Palestinian cause. Mitri, a Palestinian Christian, would naturally disagree with this interpretation. Taken outside the Palestinian context, Thomas' insights, however, may well prove useful in dissolving Christian prejudice against Muslims. It might enable individual Christians— the spiritual descendents of Isaac; and the majority of Muslims (non-Arabs), the spiritual descendants of Ishmael, to see each other in a more familial light.

Further, one might suggest that Christians-Muslims seem much closer in their agreement

---

[69] Mawdudi"s point about Abraham's universal role being similar to Muhammad may have been influenced by the Qur'anic view of Jews and Christians as 'people of the book'. It is possible that Mawdudi considered Jewish-Christian visions of God and His laws to be as universal as Islam.

[70] Tareq Mitri, *"an al-hiwar fi 'amar Ibrahim wa 'amrina ma 'ahu"* (Dialogue on the issue of our relationship with Abraham) in *Islamochristiana*, 24, 1998, Arabic pp.1-10.

[71] See for details David Emmanuel Singh, "Bases and Objectives of Christian-Muslim Relations: An Approach." Presented the conference on 'The Indian Churches in the Twentieth Century' organised by *Theological Book Trust*, Asia Theological Association, Bangalore, December 1998 [To be published by TBT, Bangalore].

[72] *Ibid.* p.3.

over Mawdûdî's notion of One sovereign God and the common Abrahamic heritage than *ashraf-ajlaf.*

The following model suggesting relations between Muslims-Christians is undoubtedly problematic. Not all Christians or Muslims will be happy with it and it might also seem very simplistic to scholars. But the model does show how some non-academic common individuals among the Christians and Muslims actually think of each other. The model originated from my reflection on Presler's principles applied to Mawdudi's Islamization and my relations with common Muslims in the complex of about 80 flats where I live (the majority being Muslim).

The *ajlaf* institutions like the *dargahs* (tombs of the saints) and shrines are known to meet the common peoples' needs.[73] It has been pointed out that there are also times when the *ashrafs* representing the 'orthodox' institutions, beliefs and practices cross over to the side of the *ajlaf* institutions, beliefs and practices, temporarily, in times of grave crises.[74] The movement of individuals between 'orthodox' and unorthodox' institutions occurs spontaneously and naturally because both institutions are tacitly considered to belong to the larger environs of Islam containing sub-group plurality.

Many Christians and some Christian organisations, like the Henry Martyn Institute,[75] see reconciliation between Muslims and Christians as part of the process leading to meeting of needs.[76] Those among the individual Muslims in my experience who consider Christianity as a family of faiths within Abrahamic spirituality, do not bother much about the official positions reiterated by the elite. They subscribe to their traditional institutions, beliefs and practices and are loyal to them in practice, but they see no problem in seeking help from their Christian friends, asking for prayer, listening to a reading from the Bible etc., because of their belief that Christians are their family members.

Many Muslims and Christians consider themselves as being part of the Abrahamic faith in the local dialogical contexts where they live and work as neighbours.[77] Just as in the case of the *ashraf-ajlaf* sub-groups, mutual disjunction between Muslims-Christians, historically known to be divisive are temporarily ignored especially during times of personal crises and need. This is perhaps not a model that might be officially adopted. It is a picture of reality as it exists in some parts of the subcontinent I come from. It can be diagrammatically represented as below:

---

[73] For details on rituals and popular piety of common Muslims in the subcontinent, I think one of the best research so far done is by my colleague Y. S. Sikand, "Ritual and Popular Piety at the '*urs* of a Qalandar *Dargah* in South India" Unpublished research, Henry Martyn Institute, Hyderabad, India.

[74] See appendix I

[75] The Henry Martyn Institute of Islamic Studies was founded in 1930 in the subcontinent to train missionaries to work among Muslims. Today it is involved in promoting peace, harmony, and reconciliation through research and publications, interfaith dialogue, mediation services in the context of conflict and violence.

[76] Diane D'Souza, "Evangelism, Dialogue, Reconciliation: The Transformative Journey of the Henry Martyn Institute," Hyderabad: HMI, 1998.

[77] Treating Islam as a sub-group is not a new idea. John of Damascene (ca. 675-749 or 750) a dogmatic theologian from Eastern orthodoxy referred to Islam as a heresy and not as an independent religion. See J. D. Sahas, *John of Damascus on Islam,* Leiden: E. J. Brill, 1972, p. 132 quoted by Olaf Schumann, "Between Orthodoxy and Orthopraxy: Theological Problems between Christians and Muslims" in Lutheran World Federation Studies *Christian-Muslim Dialogue: Theological and Practical Issues,* Geneva: LWF, 1998, pp. 103-116.

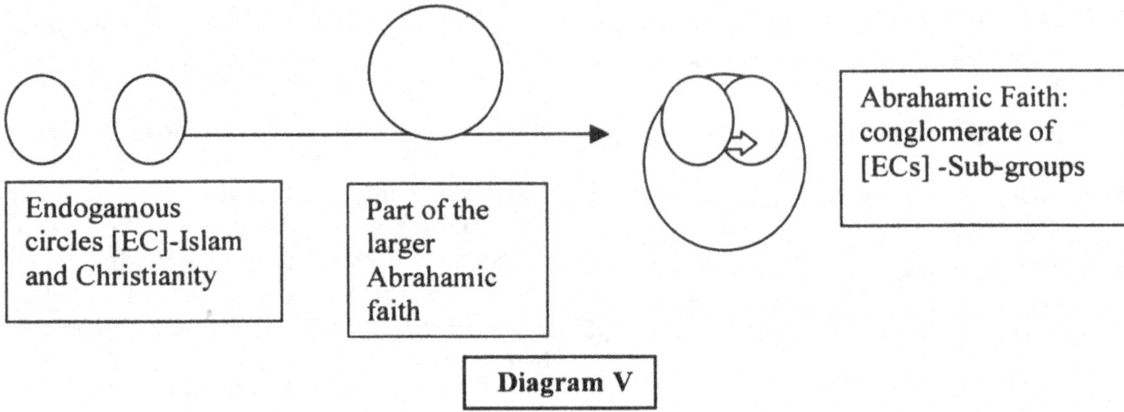

Conclusion

I began by observing that colonial rule facilitated the ideas of secularism, democracy and nationalism in the Muslim world. It was observed that Muslim intellectuals generally understood secularism, democracy and nationalism to involve ignorance about God, rule of the majority based on extra-revelatory sources and reification of national boundaries. While it seems true that secularism and democracy create space for plurality of laws and nations as also religious plurality. Muslim elite like Mawdudi treated plurality as a problem. In response to the perceived problem Mawdûdî, for instance, formulated an integrative ideology based on the idea of One sovereign God- one law.

The Muslim elite had largely ignored the Indian masses that converted to Islam during the various phases of their rule over the subcontinent. The Muslim elite became aware of the need for the Indian Muslim masses realising the importance of numbers in the increasingly democratic climate. But, the elite had to deal with the plurality that the converted Indian masses brought along with them into Islam.

In this context, I attempted to show that Mawdudi had a double objective. He sought to show that in places Muslims were a majority, Islamism could be applied in order to counter the effects of plurality bred by modern western secularism. His strategy for India however, was different. Using Presler's theory of disjunction I attempted to analyse Mawdudi's 'Islamization.' The analysis showed that Islamization did not succeed in removing 'pre-Islamic' disjunction from the Indian Muslim masses. The elite had to set aside their objective of removing plurality in the Indian Islam. Thus the 'heterodox institutions,' practices and beliefs continued among the converts. The compromise thus effected made it possible for some *ashrafs* to cross-over to the 'heterodox' institutions in times of crises.

Based on the above, Mawdudi's Islamism in its strict ideological garb is exclusive and does not allow plurality- political or religious. Mawdûdî, however, following the example of the British thought of granting limited freedom and protection to minorities in the realm of his Islamist state. He did so by circumscribing their freedom to the religious, personal and family front. Mawdudi's policy for minorities prevented them from participating in political and defence affairs of the state- that being an elite Muslims' preserve. Also in regions where Muslims are a minority, as in the case of India, Mawdudi's Islamization was not as strictly unitive as it sounds in theory. In the case of the *ajlafs*, a tacit compromise was made. The compromise was conducive to unofficial recognition of *ajlaf* with their plurality of beliefs and practices as a sub-group. The compromise also created conditions for *ashraf* individuals and families to cross over to the *ajlaf* institutions in times of need.

Mawdûdî's brand of Islamism was to be applied to a Muslim majority state, one can be sure that the minorities would be granted freedom in religious fields.

Taking Mawdudi's comments on Abraham, it is noted that in dealing with the Muslim-Christian relations, scholars normally take recourse to the idea of Abraham. Though the idea of Abraham needs to be used with some caution particularly in the context of the Palestinian cause, I said that it is universally recognised to be a useful point of contact.

In view of the analysis of *ashraf-ajlaf* relations and the failed Islamization of the *ajlaf,* there seems to be a similar possibility of using the idea of sub-groups involving Islam and Christianity within the larger Abrahamic spiritual heritage. The suggestion is that it is perhaps possible for Muslims and Christians to hold their historic mutual disjunction at abeyance in order to create conditions for *individuals* to engage in dialogue under more familial circumstance. Such a state of peace and trust where individual Christians or Muslims approach each other without any hidden agenda, as relatives, in reality, creates conditions for individuals to have their needs met in times of personal need or family crises, without having to convert.[78]

The model proposed above raises several issues and questions that may be further discussed. Some of them are noted below:

1. It has been pointed out to me that unlike Muslims in the Indian subcontinent, some Muslims in the Jewish-Muslim-Christian dialogue contexts resent Islam being seen as having common historical roots with the other two. While this idea may not be disturbing to the churches; it might disturb some Muslims. That is to say that some Muslims might not want to be included in the category of Abrahamic faiths.

2. The model might disturb churches if it were thought that Christianity and Islam are one faith with no distinctions, and therefore there was no need for proclamation and conversion.

3. The model might seem to some to have similarities to Marxist and revolutionary interpretations. If this model is promoted and used widely by churches it could be assumed to be in support of violent attempts to reshape Muslim communities.

   It might also be pointed out that in the Jewish-Christian interface, it might be assumed that Christians were usurping a covenant that was presented in the Torah as being Hebrew and by blood. The vast majorities of Christians and Muslims could claim neither.

4. There is a lot of discussion these days about contextualization and how new believers may be able to preserve their culture and past. The model might be useful in initiating a discussion on issues churches face in deciding what elements of the past practices and beliefs of believers could be allowed to continue. More importantly, the model might give churches a framework to understand why converts retain certain elements of their past faith and in a sense remain somewhat distinct from their co-religionists.

5. Some aspects of brahminical Hinduism or other religious traditions might seem highly monotheistic and closer to the Christian faith than popular Islam. What sort of covenant relationship could be designated for such

---

[78] See Appendix II

individuals so that churches do not leave the impression that all Muslims are on a higher ground in Christian eyes, than people of faiths other than Islam?

6. Would individual Christians like to use the model? If so how?

APPENDIX I

Case I

On campus C the graves are of two saints who were brothers. There is an unpaid *mujavir* whose brother acts as caretaker of the sacred site. Great numbers of illiterate people come from outside the campus on festival days (illiteracy rate of the city being 85 percent). The *mujavir* experiences ecstasy on celebration days. He divines sources and cures illnesses, promises remedies for personal difficulties, and gives flowers imbued with impersonal supernatural Powers. One festival evening, two Muslim strangers appeared among the crowds. Their clothing and bearing showed they were educated. They did not approach the graves nor consult the ecstatic, but stood apart. They covered their heads with handkerchiefs, recited the *fatiha*, and went away.[79]

Case II

Q: Are you escorting your respected wife to the shrine of Abdal-Qadiri-al-Jilani?

A: Yes. She is ill. Certain local Arab women oppose bringing her to a spirit medium at a saint's grave, in order to ask the spirit to intercede with God for her cure. They maintain that a careful reading of the Holy Qur'an will prove that spirit possession and mediums are not at all encouraged.

Q: But do not thousands of local Muslims come to this saint's grave for healing?

A: Yes, but the Arab women say that Indian Muslims have been living among Tribals and Hindus for centuries in this valley, and their practices have crept into local Islam. As Hindus ask their *pandas* (low caste priests) what is to be done for their sick, so do local Muslims ask the *mujvirs* to urge the saint to intercede with God.

Q: What do you reply to their objections?

A: It is puzzling. Maybe the Hindus borrowed our practice. I have thought so, since my pilgrimage to Mecca. On the ship were people of many nationalities, and after disembarking, I met even more. Most of those discussing this question with me said that Qadri (a religious order) shrines and *dargahs* (prayer shrines) are also found in their countries and are associated with mediums and healing.

Q: Would you permit me to put a question to your honourable wife?

A: [After looking at my white hair] Yes, ask her.

Q: Worthy sister! Did you decide to climb to the *dargah* on the top of this steep hill in spite of the objections of your Arab friends?

A: Sahib, what to do? I try not to counter their advice. But I am sick. Their views have not led me to health. If God is one, what is the harm in approaching Him through saints who might obtain divine favour for me? Besides, my husband urged me to approach this saint and I obey my husband.[80]

APPENDIX II

CASE: Muslims in the town of Y

Three months before I resigned as Secretary of the Bible Society of India-North West India Auxiliary from 1995-1998, a very dignified middle-aged man came to meet me. He knew my name and my interest in Islam. He told me he

---

[79] *The Mid India Practice of Toleration*, p. 16
[80] *Ibid.* p. 16-18

had come to meet me all the way from the town of Y. He said his name was Dr X and that he had come to share with me some stories that he thought would interest me. He said:

> I am a doctor and I live and work among a community that is very poor and cannot afford good medical treatment. My people live in the old Town of Y. Recently there was an outbreak of a serious disease in the locality. The poor families sought help from the local religious leader who told them the following story: 'Once there was a certain prince who announced his willingness to marry only such a girl who would not weep, even if her child died. By this requirement he hoped to find a wife who knew proper doctrine. As the news spread, the rank and file of women exclaimed! 'Where is such a mother who won't weep for her dead child?' Thus they showed their ignorance. At last a girl, well versed in our teachings, said, 'for what basic reason would one weep if one's baby dies? A child is a gift of God, Who may take back His gift; so why weep?' The prince married her. She gave birth to a son who died after two years. Neither the prince nor his wife wept.'
>
> He was telling them that God was all-powerful, and the best they could do was to submit to his will. Dissatisfied, they prayed to God earnestly to remove the disease and save them. Nothing happened. There was nothing I could do to save the people. I remembered Islam teaches that Jesus was one of the five Major Prophets of Islam [Adam, Abraham, Moses, Jesus, Muhammad]. Although Islam believes that Jesus was put on the cross and that he did not die, Christians say that Jesus died and was brought back to life. All we cared about was that Jesus was alive! We did not need to go to *dargahs* (tombs of dead saints) and unknown saints for healing. We believed that if Jesus were alive he would have heard our prayers from our homes and mosques! Scriptures tells us that Jesus alone had power to heal and raise the dead. Our religious leaders never teach this to us in *madaris* (religious schools) because they are fearful we would become Christians. I advised my people to pray to Jesus. We prayed at homes and in Mosques. Initially there was resistance, and then our leaders felt that as long as we prayed in our homes and mosques there was no threat to Islam. After all we prayed to Jesus, our own prophet. One by one people began to be healed till there was no trace of the disease. It is normal for us to pray to Jesus now. No one questions us. We believe Christians are our brothers. Our faith goes back to Abraham. But we are Muslim 'isawis (believers of Christ). We are not Christians because we are not baptised and we do not go to Church. Just as you say Jesus meets your needs, He meets our needs."

These cases raise a number of issues for those of us thinking about and practicing mission and inter-religious dialogue. I include some questions for reflection and discussion:

1. How does this story throw light on the theory of Ecs/ subgroups?

2. Does the story give any indication of whether Dr X had seen or read any Christian literature, scriptures and had discussed the issue with Christians?

3. Why do you think Muslims in Y decided to pray to Jesus?

4. Would pre-knowledge of Jesus be necessary in order for people to experience Jesus?

5. The story raises an important question: should Churches and para-church organisations seek baptised converts?

CHAPTER 23

The Christian Response to Hinduism

PAUL G. HIEBERT

Hindu holy men declared Sunday, December 6, 1992, auspicious, and more than 300,000 people gathered that day in Ayodhya, a pilgrim town north of Varanasi in North India.[1] Most wore the saffron color of Hindu nationalism. At midday, they broke down the police barricades around a mosque, which was reportedly built on the ruins of the temple that marks Rama's birthplace, and hammered it to the ground. The construction of a new Rama temple was to begin that evening. Violence triggered by the demolition killed 1,700 people across the subcontinent. Supporters justified the action as the liberation of Hindu sacred space to unify the nation. Critics decried it as communalism—the antagonistic mobilization of one religious community against another, and as an attack on Indian civil society. Later Hindu holy men began a *yatra*, a holy march, around North India which is to culminate in the construction of the temple, by force, if need be.

How are we to understand these events, and what implications do they have for the church in India and the world?

The Emergence of Neo-Hinduism

To understand recent events, we need first to define 'Hinduism'. S. Radhakrishnan wrote, "Hinduism is the way of life characteristic of an entire people, it is a culture more than a creed. It permeates every aspect of the individual's public and private life." As one author put it, "Hinduism has grown like some gigantic Banyan tree, with numerous spreading branches that put down their own roots, and yet remained, however tenuously, attached to the main trunk."[2]

Definitions of 'Hinduism'

The term 'Hindu' has been used in at least four ways.[3] The first definition was geographic—given to India by the invaders of India: the Turk, Persian and Arab Muslims, and the British rulers. 'Hindu' was the Persian word for 'Indian,' and was originally used of peoples living beyond the Indus River, not followers of a particular religion.[4] For the invaders from the West, Hindu meant 'Native to India.' Consequently, Muslims were divided into Arab Muslims (who could trace their descent from West Asia) and Hindu Muslims

---

[1] The roots of this was the Vishva Hindu Parishad (World Council of Hindus) which issued in April 1984 in Delhi a unanimous resolution for the "liberation" of three temple sites in north India, at Mathra, Varanasi and Ayodhya, because 1) these were historical sites in religious life [Ayodhya the birth place of Rama], 2) ancient Hindu temples stood there, and 3) Muslims under the Mugals destroyed the temples and built mosques on the foundations.

[2] Hugh Tinker, *The Banyan Tree: Overseas Emigrants from India, Pakistan and Bangladesh*, New York: Oxford University Press, 1977.

[3] For an excellent analysis of various definitions of 'Hinduism' see Robert Eric Frykenberg, "Constructions of Hinduism at the Nexus of History and Religion," *Journal of Interdisciplinary History*, 23:3, Winter, 1993, pp.523-550.

[4] David Ludden, ed., *Contesting the Nation: Religion, Community, and the Politics of Democracy in India*, Philadelphia: University of Pennsylvania Press, 1996, p.7.

(native converts). Similarly, the British referred to European and Hindu Christians. This practice of equating things 'Indian' with the term 'Hindu' has caused endless confusion.

The second definition is socio-religious. The most common description which Hindus give to their religion is *sanatana dharma*, 'eternal religion'. This refers to what is sometimes called Brahmanical Hinduism, a highly sophisticated worldview for categorizing all of life that emerged by the tenth century B.C. Robert Frykenberg notes:

> [Brahmanical Hinduism] lumped all mankind into a single category and then subdivided this category into a color-coded system of separate species and subspecies, genuses and subgenuses; and then ranked these hierarchically according to innate (biological, cultural, and ritual) capacities and qualities.[5]

Hinduism, here, is not a monolithic religion with formal doctrines and central institutions. Rather it is a worldview that incorporates different religious communities (*sampradayas*)—with their own gods, beliefs and practices—into a single hierarchical social system based on notions of purity and pollution associated with blood lines and caste.[6] Each Hindu's identity can be located ritually by religious duties appropriate for one's specific social status, ritual status, and age [one's *varnashramadharma*]. Religious practices revolve around many different deities [*devas*], sectarian traditions [*sampradayas*], and teachers [*gurus*] that form centers of caste and personal devotion. As David Ludden notes, "The ideas that define Hinduism as a religion, therefore, deeply discourage the formation of a collective Hindu religious identity among believers and practitioners. Hindu identity is multiple, by definition . . .."[7] This meaning of Hinduism is so pervasive and deeply entrenched that it remains the dominant force in rural Indian life today despite numerous attempts to destroy it.[8]

Many Indians have no place in this caste system. Tribals living in the mountains and forests, and untouchables in the villages are outside its pale. So, too, are Muslims, Christians, and Jews. Others, namely the once-born Sudras, are second class citizens in the community.

The third definition of Hinduism was a product of the West's encounter with the Indian civilization. European scholars translated the Vedas and defined Hinduism in terms of these ancient texts. They invented Hinduism as an exotic religious tradition that stood in contrast to the rational religions of the West.

The fourth definition refers to 'Neo-Hinduism', the religious movements which were born out of the encounter of Indian religious philosophy with western thought. It is this definition that will be used in this study.

Neo-Hinduism

The last decades of the nineteenth century and the beginning of the twentieth century marked the emergence of a new form of Hinduism as an Indian response to the confrontation of Christianity and the Enlightenment. To understand this rise of Neo-Hinduism it is helpful

---

[5] Frykenberg "Constructions of Hinduism," p.527.

[6] The Brahmanical (Sanskritic) name for this ranked ordering, *varnashramadharma*, was devised so long ago that its roots go back at least to the *Manu Smriti (Dharma Shastra)*, if not to the *Vedas* themselves. This worldview came to be regarded as virtually synonymous with *sanatana dharma* [Eternal Religion based on Cosmic Law] which has no founder, no universal doctrinal creed, and no particular institutional structure. Rather, it is a way of life and a highly developed religious worldview.

[7] Ludden *Contesting the Nation*, p.7.

[8] These movements include Buddhism led by Gautama Siddhartha, anti-Brahman Adi-Dravida (Tamilnadu), Adivasi ("Aboriginal People"), Islam, Sikhism, Christianity and Marxism.

to use A .F .C. Wallace's theory of revitalization [figure 1].[9] According to Wallace, revitalization movements arise when traditional worldviews are threatened by external forces. They are attempts to find meaning in life in the face of growing anomie.

Figure 1
Religious Revitalization Movements

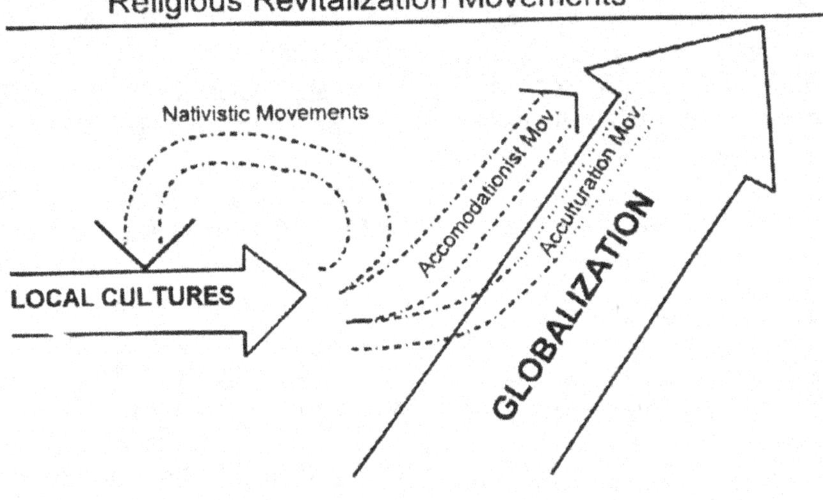

Wallace argues that when cultures and religions are overrun by more powerful ones, the people respond in several ways. The first response to massive outside cultural invasions is 'conversion movements' in which people change their allegiances to the new ideology. When the British conquered India and introduced the Enlightenment, some Indians adopted a modern secular scientific worldview. Most of these came from high Hindu castes. When missionaries brought the Gospel, others became Christians in Western based churches. Most of these were untouchables and tribals who had no status in the old Brahmanical order.

A second response is 'accommodation movements' in which people adopt many of the elements of the new religion or culture, but reinterpret these in terms of their old worldviews. In India this was seen in the rise of the Brahmo Samaj (Fellowship of Believers of the One True God)[10] and Prarthana Samaj (Fellowship of Prayer)—reform movements that emerged in the late nineteenth and early twentieth centuries.[11] These called for a radical transformation of Hinduism by submitting Hindu scriptures and teachings to the test of rationality. The result was a synthesis of Vedic idealism, Islamic monotheism and Christian ethics. These movements failed, however, to attract most orthodox Hindus.

A third response to 'cultural collision' is 'revitalization movements'. These look to the

---

[9] Anthony F. C. Wallace, "Revitalization Movements," *American Anthropologist*, 58,1956, pp.264-281.

[10] Founded by Ram Mohan Roy (1772-1833), sometimes called the Father of Modern India.

[11] For a discussion of India's quest for indigenous Christianity see Roger E. Hedlund, "India's Quest for Indigenous Christianity: Some Examples from the Recent Past," *Dharma Deepika*, January-June 2002, pp.19-29.

past, and seek to revive it through a new synthesis based on the old religion, but accommodating elements of the new. In India these are the movements that gave birth to Neo-Hinduism, such as the Arya Samaj and the Rama Krishna Mission.[12]

The Hindu revitalization movements were the result of India's encounter with the West. On the one hand, Neo-Hindu scholars were inspired by the recognition given to the Vedas and Upanishads by European scholars. They sought to create religious doctrines and institutions on the basis of the old texts, and organized Neo-Hinduism as a modern, formal 'high' religion. They rejected undesirable customs, such as idolatry and untouchable, as degenerate accretions to pure Vedic religion. They popularized their teaching by linking these to the great epics, the *Mahabharata* (with its *Bhagavad Gita*), and the *Ramayanam*, which are at the heart of popular Hinduism. On the other hand, these movements emerged out of the success of Christianity in winning untouchables. Hindu leaders became anxious about the landslide of the lower sections of Hindu society to Christianity, which, they said, weakened the solidarity of the society.

Neo-Hinduism and the Indian Nation State

Successful revitalization movements, in the long run, move in one of two directions. Some become increasingly religious in nature, detached from the socio-political arena in which they exist. Others become increasingly politicized as they seek to wrestle power from the dominant power around them. Both of these trends are evident in the Hindu revitalization movements.

Spiritualized Hinduism. One segment of Neo-Hinduism has become increasingly religious in nature, stressing the spiritual nature of Hinduism. This has its roots in the work of Dayananda (1824-1883), Ramakrishna (1836-1886), Vivekananda (1863-1902) and the Theosophists. Swami Dayananda Saraswati founded the Arya Samaj (1875) to defend and reform Hinduism. His watch-word was 'back to the Vedas', and his emphasis was 'India for Indians'. He wanted to remove Christianity and Islam from India, and make Hinduism the only religion there. K. David notes, he became "the spearhead of a dynamic type of Hinduism unifying all sections of Hindu society and attempting to bring to light the inherent vitality of Hinduism."[13] Vivekananda, a disciple of Ramakrishna, argued that Hinduism alone can claim to be the universal religion of the world because it is not built around the life of historical persons, but around eternal and universal principles. He instilled pride in Hindu culture and religion, and provided a stimulus for the national revival of Hinduism. Today Neo-Hinduism as a religious movement is centered around the Vishwa Hindu Parishad (VHP), the World Council of Hindus that coordinates the activities of Neo-Hindu movements and monitors orthodoxy.

One of the popular manifestations of Neo-Hinduism is the spread of 'guruism.' A great many charismatic Hindu gurus have major audiences in India, and have attracted Western followers. Among them are Ramana Maharishi (1870-1950), Swami Sivananda (founder of the Divine Life Society, died 1964) Ma Anandamayhi (considered by many to be a living deity), Satya Sai Baba, Rajaneesh and Bala Yogi.

A second expression of popular Neo-Hinduism is the move of religion from the home,

---

[12] India's Supreme Court has recognized Neo Hinduism as the legal representation of Hinduism. It gave an 'adequate and satisfactory definition' of Hinduism as: "Acceptance of the Vedas with reference; recognition of the fact that the means or ways to salvation are diverse; and the realization of the truth that the number of gods to be worshiped is large, that indeed is the distinguishing feature of the Hindu religion."

[13] K. David, "The Hindu View of Community: Classical and Modern," *Indian Journal of Theology*, 28,1979, p.178.

run by *purohits* who conduct family and caste rites, to temples, festivals, and religious fairs controlled by *pujaris*. Large temples have been revived and the celebration of nation wide Hindu festivals is increasing. Many now attract large numbers of pilgrims who take religious bus tours to visit famous shrines.[14] The most important actors in the temple movement are the priests and religious leaders of the VHP.

Politicized Hinduism. A second stream in Neo-Hinduism has become increasingly political in nature. In 1909 Pandit Malaviya founded the Hindu Mahasabha, which soon developed into a right-wing Hindu political party. In 1925, Keshav Baliram Hedgewar, a member of the Hindu Mahasabha, founded the Rastriya Swayamsevak Sangh (RSS), a Hindu religious movement which rejected cultural diversity and advocated the re-organization of the nation built on Hindu nationalism. In 1931 a young revolutionary in Maharasthtra, Vinayak Damodar Savarkar, was recruited for the RSS at Benaras Hindu University. He became its leader in 1940.

In his book, *Hindutva: Who is a Hindu?*, Savarkar popularized the concept of *Hindutva*, or Hindu nationalism. He argued that Aryans who came to the Indian sub-continent were a nation because they shared a geographical unity, racial features and a common culture.[15] He set out to create a Hindu national identity in which he hoped to make the RSS and Hindu society identical.[16] M. S. Golwalkar, a leader in the RSS, wrote:

> The ultimate vision of our work . . . is a perfectly organized state of society wherein each individual has been molded [sic] into a model of ideal Hindu manhood and made into a living limb of the corporate personality of society.[17]

The central vision of the RSS is a Hindu national state. Bhartiya Janwadi Aghadi writes:

> If there is one explosive idea that is setting the agenda for India today, it is *Hindutva*. . . . *Hindutva* has nothing to do with spirituality, but everything to do with political economy. . . . It has very little to do with Hinduism, but everything to do with an aggressive form of cultural nationalism . . . . It appears to be connected with India's past, but is actually an omen of the future . . . For some, *Hindutva* heralds the age of India's renaissance. For others, it reflects India's march towards fascism.[18]

If the RSS is the force behind 'Cultural Nationalism', the Bharatiya Janata Party (BJP), 'The Indian People's Party', is the political arm that is seeking to gain control of the nation and, through it, the people and cultures of India.[19] The

---

[14] Pilgrimage *or tirtha-yatra* is an ancient Indian tradition. Hsuan-tsang, who travelled in India between 629-645 A.D., Alberuni in his famous *Kitab-ul-Hind*, written about 1030 A.D. and Abul Fzl in *Ain-I-Akbari*, written in 1593 A.D., all conceded the importance of pilgrimage in Hindu tradition. The *Tirtha-Yatra* in the *Mahabharata* mentions 270 *tirthas*— sacred rivers, mountains, forests, and shrines where gods dwell, and where seekers go to be purified. The journies were long and arduous, requiring strength, stamina, and austerities of personal purification—fasting, sleeping on the floor, sexual abstinence, avoidance of the use of vehicles and walking barefoot.

[15] Savarkar based his vision of *Hindutva* on the Italian political theorist Giuseppe Mazzini (1807-1882), and Hitler's view that race is the most important ingredient of the nation.

[16] Vishal Mangalwadi, *India: The Grand Experiment*, Farnham, UK: Pippa Rann Books, 1997, p.289.

[17] M. S. Golwalkar, *We, or Our Nationhood Defined*, Nagpur: Bharat Prakashan, 1939, p. 88; quoted by Christopher Jaffrelot, *The Hindu Nationalist Movement in India*, New Delhi: Viking, 1996, p.59.

[18] B. J. Aghadi cited by Mangalwadi, *India*, 1993, p. 277.

[19] The BJP (formerly the Jana Sangh founded in 1951) and its allied Hindu organizations—the Vishva Hindu Parishad (VHP), Bajrang Dal (the VHP youth organization), Hindu Mahasabha, and Rashtriya Swayamsevak Sangh (RSS founded in 1925), together called the Sangh Parivar (brotherhood of interconnected Hindu nationalist groups affiliated with the RSS) —represent the effort by the Hindu nation to form a Hindu nation-state based on India's native culture. The Sangh

BJP's theory is that only *Hindutva* can keep the country together. The primary concern today is not so much BJP's present political clout, but the spread of its militant ideology among the intelligentsia, and its redefinition of the nature of the state. After Independence in 1947, India declared itself a secular civil state built on the western notion of a contract between the state and people as individuals. The BJP is now seeking to redefine the basis of the state in terms of communal entities. In other words, the government should have a contract with the different constituent communities, not with individuals. Mangalwadi writes, "In India . . . religion doesn't have much to do with Truth. Its purpose is to serve as social cement, to teach human beings how to live in a community by putting the community above individuals."[20]

The BJP argues that in the state, culturally diverse people cannot live together as equals. The idea that Islam and Christianity are foreign and alien is axiomatic among Hindu nationalists, who use this to justify the destruction of the Babri Masjid and burning of churches, and to argue Muslims and Christians are second-class citizens in India. In doing so they equate 'India' as an ancient civilization with 'India' as an independent national state. They favor a strong, centralized state based on cultural nationalism in which the safeguards of minority rights are eliminated, and the interests of the Hindu majority rule.

Since the BJP led coalition assumed power in 1997, there has a been a noticeable increase in violence against Christians. There has been a shift from a more or less peaceful co-existence of different religious and ethnic communities to a polity of hegemony and dominance, and from rational discourse to threats and violence.

Hindus of the Diaspora

Many Indians have moved outside the subcontinent. By the third century, Indians were trading with Ethiopia. In the eleventh century, the Cholas conquered the great Indonesian empire of Sri Vijaya, and established outposts of Hinduism in Bali and other parts of Indonesia. In the eighteenth century, Indian bakers and traders extended their activities to Burma, Malaya and Thailand, bringing their religion with them. Following the close of the slave trade, plantation owners and public works contractors found a new source of cheap labor in India. The result was Indian settlements around the world in which Hindu beliefs and practices were preserved. Indians also found new opportunities in Europe, North America and Australia. An estimated five to six million Indians now live outside India.

The Christian Church in India

The story of Christianity in India is a long and tangled one, extending from the time of Christ to the present. In this subcontinent Christianity has encountered great empires, sophisticated scholars, and some of the most profound philosophical systems on earth. Here Christianity has been forced to deal with religious pluralism that challenges its claim of the uniqueness of Christ, and with ethnic pluralism that challenges the unity of the church. In the encounter it has shaped and been shaped by India. In many ways India has been the testing ground for Christianity and the modern mission movement.

Protestant Missions and Churches

Protestant missions began in India in the early eighteenth century. They pursued two strategies: one to reach Hindus and the other to reach tribals.

---

promotes Hindu majoritarianism, cultural nationalism and national "unity in diversity" based on its own definitions of India's Hindu cultural heritage. It blames communalism on minority groups not willing to work under the rule of Hindu culture.

[20] Mangalwadi, *India*, p.44.

Mission to Hindus. Bartholomew Ziegenbalg and Heinrich Plutschau arrived in India in 1706 at Tranquebar, South East India. Their work was based on five principles: 1) education and church should go together, 2) the Scriptures and Christian literature should be translated and printed in local languages, 3) preaching should be based on a clear knowledge of the people's cultures, 4) definite personal conversions should be stressed, and 5) the establishment of churches with Indian ministers at an early date. The missionaries bought property, and built houses, schools and churches. They set up a printing press, and started philanthropic works. They trained and sent out native evangelists to the villages, and ordained their first Indian minister in 1733.

In 1793 William Carey, William Ward and Joshua Marshman established the Serampore Mission in North East India. They sought to spread the Gospel by every possible means, opening outstations and hiring Indian evangelists. They translated and printed the Bible, organized Baptist churches, studied the local culture, and trained indigenous leaders.

The development of truly indigenous churches was a priority from the beginning, but Protestant missions delayed the transfer of power to them, arguing that they were not ready for the responsibilities. The result was foreign control of mission churches, and increasing tensions between mission agencies and the churches. These were finally resolved when most mission agencies withdrew their control and personnel after Indian independence, and 'turned over' the work to Indian mission churches.

One consequence of this foreign control was that Christianity was shaped by western cultural practices and widely seen as a foreign religion associated with colonialism. Christian converts were often treated as aliens to their own land.

Mission to Tribals. The second Protestant mission strategy was to evangelize tribal societies found in the mountainous regions of North East India, and the hills of central India. British Welsh Presbyterians and American Baptists began evangelistic tours and establishing schools in the region, after 1836. The mission policy was to establish schools using the vernaculars to teach Christians how to read the Bible, and to train native evangelists and leaders for the rapidly growing churches. The government restricted where they could work under a 'discrete licensing policy', but as new areas were opened up by patrols, the missionaries extended their network of schools into the hills.Initially there was resistance to the gospel from tribal communities, but by the end of the century, Christianity was spreading rapidly among the tribes. The growth was based on an extensive educational system and a comprehensive indigenous church structure. Most of the Christian growth was the result of native evangelists and missionaries going to unreached villages and neighboring tribes, and occurred as group movements in which whole families and villages became Christian on the basis of corporate decisions.

During the twentieth century, Christianity continued to spread rapidly throughout the region. The methods most commonly used were to establish low level schools in which local leaders were trained, and itinerant evangelism by local evangelists. Relief and medical ministries were added, but there was concern lest people become 'rice Christians'. Christian revival movements (1906, 1913, 1919, 1929), often rooted in the singing of songs composed by the people, contributed much to the indigenization of Christianity in the region. By the twenty-first century, the majority of people in several North East Indian states considered themselves Christians.

Assessment. How can we assess the modern Protestant mission movement in India? There have been positive and negative outcomes. One contribution of Protestant missions has been the establishment of the Indian Church. Through the great sacrifices paid by those who went and those who supported the work, Christianity now plays an important role in Indian life, particularly in the South and North East. Christian missions have also built schools and hospitals throughout India to serve the general public.

A second outcome has been to bring Untouchables and tribals a sense of dignity and upward mobility. Today the children and grand-children of Untouchables are Christian doctors, lawyers, professors and government officials. Tribal communities have preserved their identities in the face of strong assimilative forces. Today, Christianity has become a vehicle for bringing together different tribes and castes in larger ecumenical structures such as the National Council of Churches, Evangelical Fellowship of India, the Church of South India, and the Church of North India.

Protestant Christian missions in India have also had serious weaknesses. One is their identification with western colonialism and civilization. No serious student of Christianity in India would argue that Christian missions and the Indian church did not benefit from the British Raj. While it may be technically correct, in terms of official policy, to say that the British were neutral in religious matters, there were many ways in which highly placed representatives of the British government assisted Christian missions, and the missionaries accepted that support gratefully. It is also clear that the missionaries did not consider themselves agents of the colonial power. Their primary purpose was the proclamation of the gospel. Frederick Downs writes, "The relationship between the missions and the government can best be described as cooperation in certain limited areas of mutual coincidence of interests. In other areas there was often conflict between the two."[21] What can be said is that Christian missions and the colonial government were there for their own purposes, and found each other useful.

'From the point of view of Indians, missionaries were often seen as agents of imperialism, and Indian Christians as traitors to their own cultures. Most national churches were under missionary control. Even the National Christian Council in India was governed by missionaries.

Another set of problems arose out of the principle of comity adopted by Protestant missions, by which they divided the land so as not to compete. One unintended consequence, however, was that tribes and castes often became identified with denominations. For example, in South India the Baptists became known as the church of the untouchable Madigas, and the Lutherans of the untouchable Malas. In Northeast India the Khasi and Mizo became Presbyterians, and the Nagas, Kuki and Garos became Baptists. Tribal and caste rivalries took the form of denominational rivalries.

A third set of problems arose out of the lack of adequately contextualizing the gospel and churches. Christianity came like a potted plant dependent on outside nurture and support. Many Indians saw it as a foreign religion, and as a religion of the Untouchables. The lack of contextualization meant that for many Christianity came to mean articulating the right beliefs and performing the right rites. The result was a lack of depth in discipleship, and little transformation of the Indian worldview in the light of the gospel.

Indian Initiated Churches and Missions

Hindu revitalization movements are trying to help Indians reaffirm their Indianness by identifying India with Hinduism. Protestant churches in India are also struggling with the

---

[21] Frederick S. Downs, *History of Christianity in India: North East India in the Nineteenth and Twentieth Centuries*, Vol.V, Part 5, Bangalore: Church History Association of India, 1992, 31.

tension of being Indian Christians, but also part of the global Church. Churches affiliated with western denominations are accused of being foreign and anti-Indian. In response, many churches in India are seeking to identify themselves with India. The result has been a rapid rise in Indian Initiated Churches.

Indian Initiated Churches

Many attempts have been made to form Indian-Christian churches affirming faith in Jesus Christ, but rejecting Western missionary control and retaining India culture and nationalism. Among the first were the Hindu Church of the Lord Jesus (1858), Yuomayam (1874), and Fellowship of the Followers of Jesus (1920). Recent movements include the Indian Pentecostal Church of God (1924), The Assemblies (Jehovah Shammah) started by Brother Bhakt Singh (1942), and the Nagaland Christian Revival Church. In recent years there has been an explosion of these Indian Initiated Churches which by the year 2000 had organized more than a hundred denominations.

Many of the Indian indigenous movements claim to be Christian, but some have sought to plant Hindu-Christian churches which worship Christ, but remain Hindu in identity. The largest of these was the Subba Rao movement begun in Andhra Pradesh.[22] Subba Rao conducted large healing ministries in the name of Jesus, but rejected baptism, and considered himself a Hindu.

Churchless Christians

In recent years, Herbert Hoefer, a Lutheran missionary in South India, studied the influence of Christianity outside the church. He writes:

> Our statistics have shown that there is a solid twenty-five percent of the Hindus and

Muslim population in Madras city which has integrated Jesus deeply into their spiritual life. Half of the population have attempted spiritual relationships with Jesus and had satisfying and learning experiences through it. Three-fourths speak very highly of Jesus and could easily relate to Him as their personal Lord if so motivated.[23]

Most of these silent followers of Christ are young, educated, poor people who have come in contact with dedicated Christians. The majority are women and high caste people. Many have experienced the confirmation of Jesus' place in their lives through physical healing, moral growth and a sense of forgiveness of sins. David Barrett and his associates estimate that there are more than four million 'radio believers', Hindus who take Bible correspondence courses and pray regularly to Jesus.[24]

Hoefer's findings have provoked a debate regarding the spiritual state of these 'churchless Christians'. Some questions are theological. Are these people indeed Christians? In Hinduism individuals are allowed to worship their own personal god (*ishta devata*), so a wife may believe in Jesus as her savior. But as a member of the family she must carry out the family duties of making evening offerings to the family and caste god (*jati* or *kula devata*). Second, should they be encouraged to be baptized when baptism means joining a church that itself is identified with *avarna* castes? Other questions relate to Christian ministry. How should the church minister to women in Hindu and Muslim homes who will be cast out or killed if they take a public stand for Christ? Should new homogeneous churches be planted for converts from different communities to win them, and make the unity of the church a

---

²² The present strength of the Subba Rao movement is not known.

²³ Herbert E. Hoefer, *Churchless Christianity*, Madras: Asian Program for Advancement of Training and Studies India, 1991, p.109.

²⁴ David Barrett, George Kurian and Todd Johnson (eds.), *World Christian Encyclopedia* 2ⁿᵈ edition, Vol. I, Oxford: Oxford University Press, 2001, p.361.

long term goal? These are not easy questions to answer.

Lessons from the Indian Church

What lessons can the global Church learn from the experiences of churches in India?

The Church as Local and as Global

The church in India, like the church in every country, is caught between the forces of being both global and local. The church must be native in every country, and yet remain part of one universal body. To the extent it is part of the world Christian community, it is seen as foreign by the local people. To the extent it identifies itself with the local community, it is distanced from the global community and is often distrusted as syncretistic.

The tension between local and global forces raises the question of the church's identity in the Indian context. The mission churches are tied to the global Church. The Thomas Church and Indian Initiated Churches represent movements to affirm the Indian identity of the church. The tension also raises the question of the Indian Christians' relationship to their national government. Should they affirm their Indian identity when that supports the establishment of a Hindu State, or should they support the secular state when that is seen by many as foreign?

Since World War II there has been a shift in relationship between Indian Mission Churches and parent mission agencies. Many of the churches still depend, to some extent, on outside funds, and enjoy participation in global activities. Indian nationalists argue that this proves the foreignness of Christianity in India. Indian Initiated Churches, on the other hand, are seen as more truly Indian, but they lack resources and global ties.

In recent years the two kinds of churches have moved towards the middle. After World War II most mission agencies turned ownership and control over to Indian leaders, who are now seeking to make their churches more Indian in character. The Indian Initiated Churches, on the other hand, have organized joint fellowships, and are setting up boards in the West to raise funds and to gain global visibility.

Not only must the church define itself in the Indian social context, it must define its message in the Indian cultural context without compromising the Gospel. Moreover it must communicate that Gospel in ways Indians understand as Good News. Most urban mission affiliated churches are copies of foreign churches. Indian Initiated Churches, on the other hand, are more Indian in their worship styles. Their theologies range widely from 'New Testament' churches to those in which Christ is the central god, but one among others.

The Challenge of Caste

Caste remains a central issue in the Indian churches. This is complicated by the fact that different castes and tribes are now often associated with different denominations to form ethnic-religious communities. Christianity has not brought an end to caste in the churches themselves.

Ethnic identities raise the question of evangelism and church unity. Following William Carey, Protestant churches required all converts to attend the same churches. In the 1960s Donald McGavran, a life-long missionary to India, began to advocate planting homogeneous churches aimed at reaching different caste groups. For the most part, the churches in India have publically rejected this strategy, but some have adopted this approach.

Divisions in the church based on ethnicity, class and gender are central issues in churches around the world. It is important that churches around the world examine their own responses to these powerful social forces, and decide how, theologically and socially, they must deal with the issues of the relationship between unity and diversity within the Church.

The Challenge of Religious Pluralism

Given the Hindu view that all religions lead to God, Indian theologians have sought for ways to understand and communicate the Christian claims of the uniqueness of Christ without being colonial and foreign. The issue of religious pluralism is now one of the greatest challenges to Christianity around the world. Indian theologians have also sought to do Indian theology within the context of global theology.

Persecution and Suffering

The current escalation of persecutions raises another critical set of questions for the Indian and the global church. How should Christians respond? If they turn to the secular government or foreign agencies for protection, they reinforce in the minds of many that they are a foreign presence in India. Many argue that the church should bear suffering without resorting to violence or help from the state. In so doing it can bear witness to love and forgiveness, a theme (*ahimsa*) deeply rooted in Indian culture. Others call for political responses.

The global Church must stand with Indian church leaders as they develop a Christian response to persecution. They point out that from a spiritual perspective, the decisive thing is not what happens to Christians, but how Christians respond to it. Persecution is an opportunity for the church to reflect on the implications of Jesus' teaching that we love our enemies. It is as a victim that Jesus prayed, "Father, forgive them, for they know not what they do." It is not easy for those of us living in comfort and security to say this, but we must learn from our persecuted brothers and sisters the theology of suffering and the cross. Hoefer writes, "Spiritual authenticity is the critical issue in the Indian mentality. It's the issue

that lies behind the guru-principle in Hinduism. It is also one of the dissatisfactions with the Western style of training and appointing spiritual leaders for a congregation."[25] In a land that highly values *ahimsa*, or nonviolence, the Christian response of love and compassion has been a powerful message to many observing the scene.

The global church must stand with Indian Christians in their persecution and suffering. It must minister to the traumatized victims of persecution, and recognize that they are the vanguard of Christian presence in India. It must also minister to the aggressor. Being a community committed to truth, it is incumbent for Christians to try to remove the prejudices and misconceptions that distort the attitudes others have towards them. There are times when protesting is necessary, but it must be spiritually based and redemptive in nature. The purpose is to confront the aggressor with the nature and implications of what he is doing and to open his eyes to what he is becoming, to bring him, hopefully, to repentance.

There is and will be continued persecution of the church in India. The critical question is how will the church and Christians respond. Will they seek to spare themselves from suffering, or stand as a witness to the gospel of love, forgiveness and reconciliation? Ironically, atrocities are a form of acclamation, an indirect authentication of the relevance and effectiveness of the Christian message.

Our Christian Mission in India

As Christians and churches in India and around the world, what is our mission in India? First, we must not forget that the task of evangelizing India is not complete. There are many who have not heard the Gospel, and many who have but who find it almost impossible to break out of the ideological grasp of Hinduism,

---

[25] Hoefer *Churchless Christianity*, p.36.

and the social webs of family and caste. The work is not finished, and the church in India cannot complete it alone. The good news is that the church in India is rapidly gaining a vision for missions. India, today, sends the second largest number of missionaries per country. Many of these go from the South and the North East to North and Central India. The global church must join with the church in India to proclaim the good news of salvation to every Indian. But outsiders must come as co-workers and partners in the Gospel.

In focusing on Hindus in India, we often lose sight of the millions of Hindus of the diaspora. They, too, need to hear the gospel, and they are often more open to receive it. For many of them Hinduism is more a cultural identity than a religious allegiance. Here a partnership between the Indian church and the global church can shape mission outreach that is seen as truly Indian.

Second, we must join the church in India as it develops a meaningful response to Hindutva. It is important that Indians see Christianity in India as truly Indian, not foreign. Indian Christians must model what it means to be good citizens who can contribute much to India by upholding healthy standards in public life, and by defending the marginal, weak and powerless.

Finally, we must recognize the impact of Hinduism on the rest of the world. Most church leaders are little aware of the challenges Hinduism poses in their communities.[26] Today the post-modern world, in its reaction to scientism and materialistic reductionism, is increasingly turning to Hindu beliefs and practices. In a pluralistic, relativistic world, the church must clearly bear witness to the uniqueness of Christ as the only way to salvation, but do so with humility and love.

The church is to live and to proclaim the gospel boldly until the end of this age. In each time and place, it must discern how best to communicate that good news, but the joy of participating in Christ's mission to the world remains its vision and hope.

---

[26] See "Everywhere a New Temple," *Hinduism Today*, December 1998.

CHAPTER 24

Inter-religious Dialogue

SEBASTIAN KAROTENPREL, SDB

Introduction

It is no exaggeration to say that human life and history constitute also the history of dialogue. Whatever is positive in human history is the product of dialogue in some form or another. Dialogue is at the heart of individual and societal development and fulfilment. All this is applicable to interreligious dialogue. This chapter will, therefore, examine the word, the concept, the theology, the practice, the ways and the limits of interreligious dialogue.[1]

The Word "Dialogue"

The word dialogue is derived from the Greek word *dialogos*, which means conversation between two persons. From its etymological meaning, the word dialogue has acquired ever-new connotations over the centuries. In fact, the incarnation is referred to as 'conversation' (*et in mundo conversatus est*).[2] It has acquired new epistemological, philosophical, anthropological, ontological and theological meanings. From the epistemological and philosophical angle,

---

[1] Bibliography on Interreligious Dialogue is very vast and hence we can indicate only a few titles here:

Johannes Augaard, *Witness and Dialogue in Ministry Perspective*, in *Ecumenica*. An annual Symposium of Ecumenical Research, Minneapolis, Augsburg Publishing House, 1969. William Burrows, ed., *Redemption and Dialogue. Reading Redemptoris Missio and Dialogue and Proclamation*, Maryknoll NY, Orbis, 1993. Congregation for the Doctrine of the Faith, *Dominus Jesus, on the Unicity and Salvific Universality of Jesus Christ and the Church*, Vatican City, Libreria Editrice Vaticana, 2000. Gavin D'Costa, *The Meeting of Religions and the Trinity*, Maryknoll, NY, Orbis, 2000. Mariasusai Dhavamony, *Interfaith Dialogue*, in *Studia Missionalia*, vol. 43, Pontificia Universita' Gregoriana, 1994. Jacques Dupuis, *Jesus Christ at the Encounter of Religions*, Maryknoll, NY, Orbis, 1991. FABC Documents, *For All Peoples of Asia*, ed. GB. Rosales and GG Arevalo, Quezon City/Maryknoll, NY, Claretian Publications/Orbis, 1992. Jose Kuttianimattathil, *Practice and Theology of Interreligious dialogue*, Bangalore, Kristu Jyoti Publications, Bangalore, 1995. Pontifical Council for Interreligious Dialogue, *Interreligious Dialogue. The Official Teaching of the Catholic Church (1963-1995)*, ed. Francesco Gioia, Boston, Pauline Books & Media, 1997. Pontificium Consilium Pro Dialogo Inter Religiones. *Pro Dialogo. Bulletin*, Vols, 27 (1974); 38 (1978); 43 (1980); 56 (1984); 77 (1991); 90 (1995). 92 (1996); 94 (1997), ss. *Religion and Society*, Vol. 12, 1995, *Interfaith Dialogue*, Bangalore, 1967.Vol.14, (967), *The Word of God and the Living Faiths of Men*, Bangalore, 1968. Vol.18 (1971), *Dialogue and Service in a Pluralistic Society*, Bangalore, 1972.

James Scherer and Stephen Bevans, ed., *New Directions in Mission and Evangelization, Vol. I, Basic Statements (1974-1991)*, Maryknoll, NY, Orbis, 1992. Leonard Swidler, ed., *Towards a Universal Theology of Religion*, Maryknoll, NY, Orbis, 1987. Norman Thomas, ed., *Classic Texts in Mission and World Christianity*, Maryknoll, NY, Orbis, 1995. Richard Wiles, *Christian Theology and Inter-religious Dialogue*, London, SCM Press, 1992. World Council of Churches, *Guidelines on Dialogue with People of Living Faiths and Ideologies*, London, SCM Press, 1979.

[2] See the Eucharistic Hymn composed by St. Thomas Aquinas,

Pange lingua. He speaks of the Word that became flesh and who dwelt among us as one who *conversed* with us: *Nobis datus, nobis natus, Ex intacta Virgine, Et in mundo conversatus est.* We must note, however, that the Latin word *conversatus* really means, *sojourned, lived, went about*, etc.

dialogue is seen as a method of arriving at truth by engaging in conversation with opposing positions or views. At the anthropological and ontological levels, truth is arrived at through a personal *I-Thou* dialogue.[3]

Theological Dialogue, Religious Dialogue, Interreligious Dialogue

We are here concerned with the religious and theological dimensions of dialogue. All human beings are in search of the ultimate truth and meaning in life. Such a search can be realized only in dialogue with one another. Christians who believe in a personal God hold that human beings are created with intelligence and freedom. The God of creation then enters into a constant saving dialogue with human beings endowed with intelligence and freedom in their search for truth and meaning in life. Human existence, we may say, is a constant search for the fullness of truth and meaning.

When God enters into human history in a recognisable and convincing manner, He reveals more specifically the truth about Himself and about human beings. Such revelation extends to their condition of brokenness, incompleteness, alienation, death and the fear of extinction on the one hand, and on the other, to the ultimate meaning of their existence and the means of achieving fullness of life and liberation.[4]

A Twofold Dialogue Between God and Humanity

Humanity has been in dialogue with its Creator who spoke to it in various ways, places, and times and through different persons.[5] God began a salvific dialogue in history with the people of Israel. But God who spoke in times past, Christians believe, has finally spoken through his Son, Jesus Christ. Thus He brought the saving dialogue with humanity to its fulfilment in His Son Jesus Christ. The Incarnation is the first step in God's new and existential dialogue with humanity in history, a unique, existential dialogue of life, by sharing in our very existence with all its enigmatic predicaments, its precariousness, vulnerability, anxiety, sin, suffering and death.

There has been, according to Christian faith, a concrete and historical (inter) divine-human dialogue between God and humanity through His Incarnate Son, which forms the new basis of interreligious dialogue. This new dialogue initiated through the Incarnation did not do away with the universal dialogue between God and humanity from its beginning. God has always been in search of humans and humans in search of God, and the mutual search and saving encounter continues to take place.

Towards a Definition of Inter-religious Dialogue

By interreligious dialogue we mean the dialogue that Christians enter into with the believers of other religions. It may be defined as a creative, transformative, purifying and mutually enriching encounter and exchange of each one's religious experience and its consequent spirituality, by the believers of different religions in a climate of mutual respect, trust, freedom, sincerity and love.[6] The goal of interreligious dialogue is authentic religiosity and thus the attainment of total liberation from evil in general and sin in particular, and the fullness of truth and life. Authentic religiosity has been called righteousness in the biblical sense of the word, peace or shalom, *dharma* (righteousness), *mukti* (liberation from *avidya* or the unreal), freedom from suffering and illusion of every kind, beatific

---

[3] *Cf.* Martin Buber, *I and Thou*, New York, Charles Scribner's Sons, 1958.

[4] *Cf.* Vatican Council II Pastoral Constitution on the Church in the Modern World *Gaudium et Spes*, nos. 4-18.

[5] *Cf.* Heb. 1: 1-3.

[6] *Cf.* R. L. Rowe, *The Miracle of Dialogue*, New York, Seabury Press, 1966, p. 105 ff.

possession of God or *moksha* in the fullness of life. Interreligious dialogue is meant to lead to the fullness of truth obscured by ignorance, prejudice, and passions. It leads to mutual enrichment by exposure to one another's religious values.

Interreligious Dialogue in a New Context

As Christianity spread into the Mediterranean world, then into the rest of Western Europe and Eastern Europe, and later gradually into the newly discovered continents of the Americas, it became the dominant religion of the West. In such a context of the dominance of Christianity as the major religion of the West, its relationship to other world religions was not fully appreciated. There arose a one-sided interpretation of Christianity as the exclusive means of salvation, and a generally negative interpretation of other religions. Christian theology of religions, generally speaking, appears mostly negative for over a thousand years, and more especially during the last five hundred years of Christian mission in its encounter with the great religions of the world and with the Traditional Religion(s).

Given such a negative theological climate, it is no wonder that interreligious dialogue was pushed to the periphery of theological reflection, and consequently did not sufficiently influence the Church's missionary approach and methods. But today, we have entered a new era in human history with radical philosophical, demographic, cultural and religious changes confronting us. It is in this changed context that interreligious dialogue has become a major theological and missionary concern. Dialogue has become a paradigm concept in Christian theology and acquired a new meaning, urgency and application in Christian mission.

The Emergence of the Theology and Praxis of Interreligious Dialogue

The word *interreligious dialogue* does not occur anywhere in the early documents of the Christian Churches till around 1965 or so. Thus for example it is not explicitly seen anywhere in the documents of the Second Vatican Council. But, the documents of Vatican II and the World Council of Churches have laid the theological foundations for interreligious dialogue.[7]

The Dogmatic Constitution on the Church, *Lumen Gentium*, says: "The Church is the light of all nations…the Church is a kind of sacrament or sign of intimate union with God, and of the unity of all mankind."[8] The Dogmatic Constitution on Divine Revelation *Dei Verbum*, 3 speaks of God who manifests Himself to all peoples and ceaselessly keeps the human race in His care.[9]

The Pastoral Constitution on the Church in the Modern World *Gaudium et Spes*, 3 says that the People of God is in solidarity with the entire human family in respect and love, by engaging with it in conversation about its various problems.[10] Again, it says that the Son of God in some fashion has united Himself with every human person and that the Holy Spirit is at work in the hearts of all peoples.[11]

Vatican Council II Decree on the Bishops' Pastoral Office in the Church *Christus Dominus*,

---

[7] For documents of the various Churches, cf. Conciliar Ecumenical Statements, Roman Catholic Statements, Eastern Orthodox and Oriental Church Statements, Evangelical Protestant Statements, in, James Scherer and, Stephen, Bevans, ed., *New Directions in Mission and Evangelization, Vol. I, Basic Statements, 1974-1991*, Maryknoll, NY, Orbis, 1992.

[8] Vatican Council II Dogmatic Constitution on the Church, *Lumen Gentium*, 1. Nos. 1-17 speak of the new dialogic attitude of the Catholic Church with all human beings.

[9] Vatican Council II Dogmatic Constitution on Divine Revelation *Dei Verbum*, 3.

[10] Vatican Council II Pastoral Constitution on the Church in the Modern world *Gaudium et Spes*, 3.

[11] *Ibidem*, no. 22

says that the bishops are called upon to approach all peoples, seek and promote dialogue with them. The mission of the Church is to *converse* with the human society. Bishops must carry on *conversations on salvation* with all peoples.[12] The Decree on the Church's Missionary Activity *Ad Gentes*, speaks of missionary activity as the discovery of the secret presence of God.[13] The Declaration on the Relationship of the Church to Non-Christian Religions *Nostra Aetate*, exhorts all the faithful to acknowledge and promote the spiritual good found among all believers through dialogue and collaboration.[14]

Gradually during the last 40 years or so, the concept of dialogue has entered into the theological language of the Churches in general. Structures for dialogue have been established in the major Churches and in the regional or continental assemblies of the various Churches.[15]

The World Council of Churches says that dialogue is a fundamental part of Christian service and not a secret weapon in the armoury of an aggressive Christian militancy. Rather it is a means of living our faith in the service of the community with one's neighbour.[16] Christians cannot but ask questions about the meaning of other religions and their salvific value: "What is the relation between the universal creative/ redemptive activity of God towards all humankind and the particular creative/redemptive activity of God in the history of Israel and in the person of Jesus Christ?"[17] Christians who are engaged in dialogue with other faiths must ask themselves penetrating questions about God's saving activity in the world and the role of other faiths in His general salvific plan for humanity.[18] Hence, dialogue is part of the mission of the Church.

The Orthodox Churches, in general, speak of dialogue with cultures rather than with religions. The Spirit of God is present among all peoples. All truth and goodness, no matter where they are found, come from the Holy Spirit. As St. Ambrose has said: "From the missiological perspective, the presence of the Spirit in creation makes the study of cultural, social and physical realties imperative."[19] Dialogue leads Christians to an attitude of appreciation of what is good in other cultures, without at the same time idealizing any particular culture:" Like St. Paul, when he proclaimed the gospel to the Athenians, we need not fear for our salvation when we enter into dialogue with people of other faiths and ideologies."[20]

The Evangelical Churches too speak of inter-faith dialogue as part of the evangelization work of the Church. Speaking of the uniqueness of Jesus Christ and witness to Him as the only Savior, the Manila Manifesto says: "We nevertheless are determined to bear a positive and uncompromising witness (I Tim. 2:5-7) to the uniqueness of our Lord, in His life, death and

---

[12] Vatican Council II Decree on the Bishops' Pastoral Office in the Church *Christus Dominus*, 13.

[13] Vatican Council II Decree on the Church's Missionary Activity *Ad Gentes*, 8-9.

[14] Vatican Council II Declaration on the Relationship of the Church to Non-Christian Religions *Nostra Aetate*, 2,

[15] For instance, The Pontifical Council for Interreligious Dialogue in Rome, The World Council of Churches' Office of Interreligious Dialogue, Asian Bishops' Conferences' (FABC) Office of Interreligious Affairs, Christian Council of Asia, etc.

[16] World Council of Churches, *Guidelines on Dialogue with People of Living Faiths and Ideologies*, Geneva, WCC 1979, 18.

[17] *Ibid*, 23.

[18] *Ibid*, 20.

[19] George Lemopoulos, ed., *The Holy Spirit and Mission*, Report of the CWME Orthodox Advisory Group, Geneva, WCC-CWME, 1990, n.7-10.

[20] *Ibid*, n. 12.

resurrection, in all aspects of our evangelistic work including inter-faith dialogue."[21]

The official pronouncements of the magisterium of the Roman Catholic Church and of the Pontifical Council for Interreligious Dialogue have been published into a very impressive volume.[22] The Federation of Asian Bishops' conferences (FABC) has dozens of *FABC Papers* containing the Statements of the FABC quinquennial Plenary Assemblies, and the statements of the FABC Office of Interreligious Dialogue. Similarly, The World Council of Churches, and the Evangelical churches have documents on interreligious dialogue.[23] To these we must add the immense amount of published literature on Interreligious dialogue.[24]

Structures of Interreligious Dialogue

Over the past forty years, numerous structures, centres and institutes for interreligious dialogue have been established or made available to all, Christians as well as people of other religions. We can mention here only the principal ones.

Several Ashrams or centres specifically meant for interreligious dialogue have been established recently, especially in India, Sri Lanka, Taiwan and Japan. They serve as centres for interreligious dialogue by sharing the scriptures of each religion. Competent persons in these centres hold special religious discourses and they offer opportunities for interreligious prayer meetings and lived experience of the spiritualities of the various religions.

At the level of Church, religious leaders and religious personnel, courses are offered in dialogue and religions so that today, there is a perceptible dialogue mentality within the Churches. Cultural centres in Korea, Japan, the Philippines, Malaysia, Indonesia, Thailand, India, Sri Lanka, etc., engage in dialogue at the level of culture, philosophy, fine arts, drama, song, painting, architecture, liturgical vestments, dancing, etc. They absorb many elements of indigenous, tribal, Hindu, Buddhist, Islamic, Jain, Sikh, Shintoist and Confucian cultures into liturgy, devotions, hymns, theology and sacred art.

Numerous theological journals, reviews, as well as research programmes, doctoral theses and publication centres all across Asia and elsewhere play a key role in promoting interreligious dialogue at all levels of the Church. The establishment of several theological faculties, especially in India and in the Philippines, facilitate research and publications on themes related to interreligious dialogue.[25]

National and continental theological associations, such as the Theological Commission of the FABC, Christian Council of Asia, EATWOT, Pontifical Institute for Arabic and Islamic Studies (PISAI), Departments of Christianity in secular universities, Henry Martin Institute of Islamic Studies, World Conference on Religion and Peace are important means of promoting interreligious dialogue.

A number of spirituality centres in Asia, Europe and America contributes to interreligious

---

[21] Lausanne Committee for World Evangelization, *The Manila Manifesto: An Elaboration of the Lausanne Covenant Fifteen Years Later*, Pasadena, LCWE, 1989, n. 3.

[22] Cf. Pontifical Council for Interreligious Dialogue, *Interreligious Dialogue. The Official Teaching of the Catholic Church (1965-1995)*, Boston, Pauline Books & Media, 1997; original Italian edition: *Il Dialogo Interreligioso*, Citta' del Vaticano, Libreria Editrice Vaticana, 1994.

[23] Some of these documents may be found in James Scherer- Stephen Bevans, eds. *New Directions in Mission and Evangelization, Basic Documents 1974-1991*, Maryknoll, NY, Orbis, 1992.

[24] For a very comprehensive treatment of Dialogue especially in India, cf. Jose Kuttianimattathil, *Practice and Theology of Interreligious dialogue*, Bangalore, Kristu Jyoti Publications, Bangalore, 1995.

[25] India alone has about 12 full-fledged theological faculties and publishes over 30 theological and missiological reviews.

dialogue. In such centres, Christians can have a lived experience of other spiritualities such as *Zen* meditation, *Yoga* practice, *Vipasana, Sadhana* Meditation, *Sufi* meditation of *fana and baqa.*

Interreligious dialogue is not limited only to theological, philosophical, and spiritual pursuits, but also to joint action for liberation and human promotion. Several groups are engaged in the promotion of human rights, the liberation of bonded and child labourers, the defence of legal and civil rights of indigenous/tribal peoples in several countries, and the protection of women against discrimination and economic exploitation. Other groups are involved in the struggle for economic and cultural equality by the Dalits from caste discrimination and exploitation. All such groups of persons committed to some form of liberation struggle continually enter into a new kind of dialogue, which is called dialogue of action. The dialogue of liberation and human promotion cuts across all religious affiliations and it is shaping a new kind of religious spirituality because it touches the core of all religions.[26] Swamy Agnivesh calls it a "spirituality of involvement," which is essential to all religions. As St. James has put it: "Religion that God our Father accepts as pure and faultless is this: to look after orphans and widows in their distress and to keep from being polluted by the world."[27] We may call it a "dialogue of engagement," as distinct from theological, cultural and spiritual dialogues, which are directly concerned with inner liberation.

Theology of Interreligious Dialogue

Since the establishment of the World Council of Churches in 1948 and the holding of the Second Vatican Council, the theology of interreligious dialogue has made immense progress and brought about profound changes in the Christian theology of religions and the Church's theology of mission and its methods. It is no exaggeration to say that the theology of interreligious dialogue is bringing about radical changes in our theological perceptions and the practice of mission at every level of the Church.

Early Stage

The decades immediately preceding the Vatican Council II may be considered as the first stage in the emergence of the theology of interreligious dialogue. During this period a number of theologians came to the conclusion that other religions are not altogether a mass of superstitions. Other religions have also rays of truth, elements of holiness, and grace.[28] They do have a role in the salvific plan of God for humanity in so far as they are a preparation for the Gospel. Religions of the world may be considered as a *preparatio evangelica.* Jesus Christ is the fulfiller of all human aspirations.[29] Hence Christianity is the crown and fulfilment of all the religions.

The Second Stage

With Vatican Council II, there has been a clear admission of the possibility of salvation for all.[30] All are given, in some mysterious way, the possibility of participating in the Paschal Mystery

---

[26] See the writings of Swami Agnivesh in India, of Aloysius Pieris in Sri Lanka on Asian Theology of Liberation, Minjung Theology in Korea.

[27] Jm. 1: 27.

[28] *Cf.* Jean Danielou, The *Lord of History: Reflections on the Inner meaning of History,* London, Longmans, Green and Co., 1958; The *Salvation of the Nations,* Notre Dame, University of Notre Dame Press, 1962.

[29] 29[23] Cf. J. N. Farquhar, The *Crown of Hinduism,* London, Oxford University Press, 1913; *A Primer of Hinduism,* Oxford, Oxford University Press, 1912. In *The Crown of Hinduism,* Farquhar argued that Hinduism finds its fulfilment in Christianity.

[30] *Cf.* Vatican Council II Dogmatic Constitution on the Church, *Lumen Gentium,* 16; Vatican Council II Pastoral Constitution on the Church in the Modern world *Gaudium et Spes,* 22.

of Jesus Christ and the Holy Spirit is at work in the hearts of all peoples, cultures and religions.[31]

The official admission of the possibility of salvation for all and the positive theology of other religions have laid the foundations for the present theology of interreligious dialogue. From this period onwards, interreligious dialogue is no more at the periphery of theological concerns and missionary methods. It begins to move to the centre of theological debate, and the search for new missionary methods. Dialogue calls for a new theological language and leads to a growing understanding of other religions and appreciation of their spiritualities.

The Third Stage

Broadly speaking, the third period in the development of the theology of interreligious dialogue covers the post-Vatican II years up to the present time. This period is marked by controversies about the new interpretations of Jesus Christ and their impact upon dialogue.

Dialogue according to Radical Religious Pluralism: Radical Religious Pluralism considers all religions as cultural expressions and variations of particular religious experiences. Human beings have an experience of and an insight into the Transcendent, the Real, the Mysterious, the Centre, the Sacred or the Ultimate. Such an experience finds varied cultural and historical expressions. Hence all religions are unique and equal. The "myth" religious experience is the new epistemological and hermeneutical tool and paradigm for unlocking and unravelling the problem of multiplicity of religious traditions.

According to Radical Religious Pluralism, since religions are philosophical and cultural expressions of the experience of the *Sacred*, all religions are equally valid and valuable. They are absolute norms for liberation and salvation for their followers. But one religion is not superior to another. All religions offer equally valid opportunities for religious experience, spiritualities and commitment to human promotion. Hence one religion cannot and should not have any claim to being superior or normative. Such claims have been the cause of religious wars, exploitation and marginalization of peoples. Dialogue, therefore, must be among equals.[32] Such are the conclusions arrived at by the advocates of Radical Religious Pluralism.

Dialogue of Mutual Fecundation: According to Raimundo Panikkar, Jesus Christ is the manifestation of the cosmotheandric reality. He is a perfect manifestation of the infinite *Brahman/ Logos*. But there are other manifestations of the same mystery of the Divine. Each manifestation is meant to lead human beings to the fullness of humanity, (*humanitas*), or *humanness*, which is also *christianness*. Hence Christ is one of the names of the multiple manifestations of the *Infinite* or the *Sacred*. Each is valid in so far as it leads to true humanness, according to Panikkar.

Dialogue is the way to discover this fundamental religious truth of the cosmotheandric mystery. Dialogue and not conquest or rivalry is the way to the recognition of the mystery of 'Christ'[33] hidden in all religions, including historical Christianity.[34]

---

[31] *Cf.* Vatican Council II Pastoral Constitution on the Church in the Modern World *Gaudium et Spes*, 22; John Paul II, Encyclical Letter on the Permanent Validity of the Church's Missionary Activity *Redemptoris Missio*, 28.

[32] *Cf.* John Hick, Paul Knitter, eds. *The Myth of Christian Uniqueness: Towards a Pluralistic Theology of Religions*, Maryknoll, NY, Orbis, 1987.

[33] It must be noted here that Panikkar uses the name "Christ" in a sense different from its traditional meaning.

[34] *Cf.* Raimundo Panikkar, The *Unknown Christ of Hinduism*, London, Darton, Longman and Todd, 1964; The *Unknown Christ of Hinduism: towards an Ecumenical Christophany, rev. ed.,* London, Darton, Longman and Todd, 1981: *The Trinity and the Religious Experience of Man*, Maryknoll, NY, Orbis, 1973; *The Intrareligious Dialogue*, New York, Paulist Press, 1978; The *Cosmotheandric Experience: Emerging Religious Consciousness*, Maryknoll, NY, Orbis, 1993.

The Mystery of God as Basis for Dialogue:The basis of dialogue, according to Bede Griffiths, is the mystery of the cosmic person, or the cosmic reality, known to Christians as the Holy Trinity. But the Hindus perceive the same reality as *sat-cit-ananda*. *Sat* is Truth (Reality), *cit* is Pure Consciousness and *ananda* is Bliss. The same ultimate Reality is perceived by Buddhists as *Trikaya* (literally three bodies or presences) or the doctrine of the eternal, indefinable, inaccessible Buddha (*Dharma-kaya*), the exalted, glorified Buddha (*Sambhoga-kaya*), and the illumined terrestrial Buddha (*Nirmana-kaya*), who remains on earth to teach disciples the way to the liberated state of nirvana.[35]

Here we have, Griffiths says, a dialogue of complementarity, namely, a dialogue that leads all to discover the complementary character of one and the same mystery of the Infinite, as expressed in different religions. But in the end, when we enter the mystery of God, all differences cease to exist.

The Eternal Logos and the Incarnate Logos: Some theologians seek another theological basis for interreligious dialogue, in the activity of the eternal *Logos* and the saving activity of the *Logos* Incarnate. *Logos* Incarnate is circumscribed by time and space and not available to those beyond the pale of the historical manifestation of the Incarnate *Logos*. The Incarnate *Logos* does not exhaust or terminate the saving activity of the eternal *Logos* who continues His saving work even after the Incarnation.

Such a Christological position, it is argued, would leave the ground open for dialogue with other religions. Thus the disturbing claim of uniqueness and universal applicability of Jesus Christ for all human salvation would be overcome. The language of uniqueness and universality is a language of faith and intelligible within a particular faith circle, but it need not be extended to include the believers of other religions in an ontological sense and in exclusive dogmatic formulations as in the past. Such exclusivism will only destroy any basis for interreligious dialogue.

The Spirit as Basis for Dialogue: Another effort to give a theological foundation for interreligious dialogue, appeals to a parallel saving activity by the Incarnate *Logos* and the Holy Spirit. The Incarnate *Logos* works out the salvation of Christians. But the Holy Spirit who was at work in the world, before the coming of the Incarnate *Logos*, does not suspend His saving activity with the coming of Jesus Christ. The Spirit continues His saving work even after His coming. Those who do not know Jesus Christ are illumined and led to salvation by the Spirit.

Such a theological position, it is argued by some, allows sufficient room for dialogue with the believers of other religions, without claiming any special privileges.

The Kingdom as Basis for Interreligious Dialogue: A theological basis for dialogue among religions is sought in the theological concept of the *Kingdom*. Advocates of this theological approach hold that the role of all religions is to usher in and serve the growth of the *Kingdom* of God, or the values that make up the *Kingdom* of God. These are: love, forgiveness, reconciliation, peace and mutual service. At the level of the *Kingdom* values, all human beings can be agreed. Hence, the protagonists of this approach hold that the Kingdom theology can serve as a common ground for dialogue with believers and even non believers.

The core of the preaching of Jesus Christ was the *Kingdom* of God. Jesus did not come to establish His own kingdom. It is argued hence

---

[35] *Cf.* S. G. F. Brandon, ed. *A Dictionary of Comparative Religions*, London, Weidenfeld & Nicholson, 1970, p. 156-7.

that the Church need not seek its own extension in an exclusive manner. Its mission today is to serve the Kingdom, be its witness, its servant and its manifestation. All those who are engaged in promoting the Kingdom of God can dialogue together and work together for peace.

Post-modern Culture as Basis for Dialogue: Western society is dominated today by what is known as Post-Modernism. It is not a philosophy, but a philosophical mentality and attitude to truth. It may be described:

> as a complex cluster concept that includes the following elements: an anti- (or post-) epistemological standpoint; anti-essentialism; anti-realism; anti-foundationalism; opposition to transcendental arguments and transcendental standpoints; rejection of the picture of knowledge as accurate representation; rejection of truth as correspondence to reality; rejection of the very idea of canonical descriptions; rejection of final vocabularies, i.e., rejection of principles, distinctions, and descriptions that are thought to be unconditionally binding for all times, persons, and places; and a suspicion of grand narratives, metanarratives of the sort perhaps best illustrated by dialectical materialism.[36]

Influenced by the post-modern mind-set, the Symbolic Christology of Roger Haight seeks to find a new basis for dialogue with Post-Modernity. He seeks to interpret Jesus Christ in terms and concepts that are intelligible to post-modern Christians and believers of other religions, mostly in the Western world. If Jesus is presented as the *symbol of God*, or the transcendent reality who or which may be interpreted by each one according to one's philosophical tendencies, then dialogue with post-modern society becomes possible. The

Christological formulations of the first centuries of Christianity can be, he insists, reinterpreted always keeping the "consistent intent of tradition in affirming that it was truly God who was at work in Jesus."[37]

Faith in Jesus Christ as a divine-human reality and in the Trinity is the result of the Christian experience of God and salvation: "Thus the affirmation of trinity is a function of the place of Jesus as the medium of Christian faith in God. Trinity is historically dependent upon christology. The doctrine is a product of historical development over centuries; that development is confusing, but it is no mystery; God is a mystery, doctrines are not."[38]

Haight hopes to bridge the gap between Christian faith and Post-Modernism with the concepts of symbolic theology and symbolic Christology. He says that the situation of religious pluralism is something positive, and not something to be overcome, because other religions are also mediations of God's salvation.[39]

Co-Relational Dialogue: The latest theological effort towards a genuine dialogue with religions is made by Jacques Dupuis. Dupuis' effort contains perhaps the most far-reaching possibilities for a genuine interreligious dialogue. The Christological groundwork for an eventual interreligious dialogue is based on what he calls a "Relational Christology," all saving grace is coming through Jesus Christ or at least it is *related* to Jesus Christ in the present economy of salvation. Such a relationship is constitutive of every saving grace from God for all peoples.

In the present dispensation of salvation, the saving grace for non-Christians is outside the Christian dispensation. Following E. Schillebeeckx, Dupuis argues that other religions

---

[36] Robert Audi, ed., *The Cambridge Dictionary of Philosophy*, Cambridge, Cambridge University Press, 1999, p. 725.

[37] Roger Haight, Jesus *Symbol of God*, Maryknoll, NY, Orbis, 1999, p. 479.

[38] *Ibid*, pp. 479-480

[39] *Ibid*, pp. 411-12.

are part of the universal salvific plan of God. Saving grace reaches other believers through these religions in the present dispensation. But eventually in the eschaton, it will merge into the Risen Christ: "an eschatological 'reheading' *anakephalaiosis* (Eph. 1:10) in Christ of all the religious traditions of the world will take place at the eschaton, and it will respect and preserve the irreducible character which God's self-manifestation through his Word and his Spirit has impressed upon each tradition."[40] Such a Christological position helps to overcome the unavoidable historical particularity of the unique saving revelation in Jesus Christ.

The event of Jesus Christ is constitutive of all salvation, especially his death-resurrection event that gives access to salvation for all humans. Hence, Dupuis holds that Jesus Christ remains God's universal sacrament of salvation. However, the uniqueness of Jesus Christ is not absolute but "constitutive" and "relational."[41] God's unique self-manifestation and offer of salvation in Jesus Christ are related to all other self-manifestations and offer of salvation.[42]

Thus Dupuis argues that relational Christology as explained above offers an adequate basis for dialogue with other religions without on the one hand reducing them to '*preparatio evangelica*' and on the other hand preserving the traditional faith of the Church on the uniqueness of Jesus Christ.

We have reviewed the most important theological efforts made during the recent decades to give a theological basis to the theology of interreligious dialogue. Whether they are adequate or not, and whether they are in accordance with the authentic traditions of the Churches is a different matter. We do not intend to give here a theological evaluation of each position. Their enumeration and brief description do not imply any approval nor is it conceded that they are of equal value.

Critical Observations on the Theologies of Interreligious Dialogue

Compatibility of Faith and Dialogue

As Christians we believe that the whole of the saving truth about God and human salvation has been revealed in Jesus Christ, especially in his death-resurrection and in the bestowal of the Holy Spirit. Hence it might appear that interreligious dialogue is *a priori* to be excluded as incompatible with Christian faith. But in reality, the definitive revelation in Jesus Christ calls for, and becomes the basis for dialogue with all peoples, religions and cultures, while retaining its uniqueness and universal application.

The offer of salvation is essentially dialogic. God's self-communication can take place only in the context of freedom. Given God's free offer of salvation to man, and man's freedom, even God does not impose His offer of salvation on human beings. It is offered in freedom and is to be accepted in freedom.

God's offer of salvation became concrete in Jesus Christ, especially in His death, resurrection and the bestowal of the Holy Spirit. Jesus fulfilled His mission of salvation in total freedom and respect towards His Father and all peoples. He came to show the way to a new righteousness, apart from the Mosaic religion, and apart from all that religions offer. The new righteousness consists in a new relationship between God and man, between man and man, in love, service and reconciliation. Its uniqueness, exclusiveness and universality do not make it any less a free offer, and hence any less dialogical. The proclamation and mediation of the salvation realized in Jesus

---

[40] Jacques Dupuis, *Towards a Christian Theology of Religious Pluralism*, Maryknoll, NY, Orbis, 1997, p.389.
[41] *Ibid*, pp.387-8
[42] *Ibid*, p. 388.

Christ, and its sacramental mediation, cannot but be dialogical.

It might appear that since we possess the saving truth and grace in Jesus Christ through faith and the sacraments, there is no need for dialogue with other religions and that there is nothing that Christians can learn from them. The possession of salvific revelation in Jesus Christ through faith does not imply that we grasp the whole mystery of Jesus Christ. Its verbalization in articles of faith and creeds, and its dogmatic formulations can never be fully adequate or perfect.

Besides, the mystery of God as revealed in Jesus Christ is present in other religions as part of the universal mystery of God and human salvation. It is through dialogue that we can have an insight into the whole mystery of Jesus Christ. The mystery of God, human salvation and the consequent spirituality traced out by the religions of the world, are not unrelated to God's self-revelation and self-communication in Jesus Christ. Hence our understanding and appreciation of them can only contribute to our knowledge and assimilation of the mystery of God and human salvation as revealed in Jesus Christ in the Christian tradition. That is what the Second Vatican Council has in mind when it says: "Men look to the various religions for answers to those profound mysteries of the human condition which, today even as in olden times, deeply stir the human heart ... What, finally, is that ultimate and unutterable mystery which engulfs our being, and whence we take our rise, and whither our journey leads us to?"[43]

Interreligious Dialogue and Christology

Every form of dialogue implies a particular theology and Christology. The recent theologies of interreligious dialogue are based on new Christologies that we have examined above very briefly. The Christian theology of dialogue implies a particular vision of God, a particular Christology and soteriology. It implies the mystery of God as Trinitarian and salvation in Jesus Christ. There is but one mystery of creation and redemption, which reconciles humanity with God in Jesus Christ, in his incarnation, death resurrection and the bestowal of the Holy Spirit.

A purely incarnational theology of the Logos uniting Himself to every human person is insufficient to support interreligious dialogue, as is assumed in some of the recent Christologies. It is from the fullness of the Logos that became flesh, lived among us, died for us, rose again for us and who sent the Holy Spirit to us, that we are saved. It is of the fullness of Jesus Christ, which includes His death and resurrection, that we are saved, that all people are saved. In other words, incarnational theology must be completed by soteriological Christology about the universal value of the reconciling death and resurrection of Jesus Christ for human salvation. Dialogue must be based on the whole Jesus Christ, the Logos who became flesh and died and rose for us. A universal theology of dialogue, which is based only on God or on the eternal Logos or on the Spirit at work in the world, is insufficient to support a comprehensive Christian theology of interreligious dialogue.[44]

The Teaching of the Churches on Dialogue

Within the Catholic tradition, the mainline Orthodox and the Protestant Churches there has been a constant growth in the theology of dialogue in recent years. Building upon the foundations of Vatican Council II, a number of official documents of the Catholic Magisterium

---

[43] Vatican Council II Declaration on the Relationship of the Church to Non-Christian Religions *Nostra Aetate,* 1.
[44] Cfr. Karotemprel, et al., *Cristologie e Missione Oggi,* Roma, Urbaniana University Press, 2001.
[45] Vatican Council II Declaration on the Relationship of the Church to Non-Christian Religions *Nostra Aetate,* 2.
[46] *Ibid,* 2.

deal with the theology of Dialogue. Interreligious dialogue is based on the firm conviction of the unity of origin, vocation and destiny of the human family.[45] All that is true in religions is also a reflection of "the Truth that enlightens all."[46]

In his Apostolic Exhortation *Evangelii Nuntiandi*, Pope Paul VI speaks of the positive function of the religions of the world as the living expressions of the soul of vast numbers of people, and their search for righteousness of heart. The religions of the world possess an impressive patrimony of deeply religious texts and a treasury of prayers.[47]

Other documents such as *Dialogue and Mission*,[48] *Dialogue and Proclamation*[49] and *Redemptoris Missio*[50] carry further the doctrine of interreligious dialogue. Interreligious dialogue is now considered to be an integral part of mission. They go further and say that dialogue is mission and mission is dialogical, even though dialogue does not exhaust the whole reality of mission. But dialogue, considered in itself, can be called mission since dialogue emphasizes the fundamental unity of God's plan of salvation for all. Inter religious dialogue calls all those engaged in dialogue to authentic religiosity. This is true evangelization because dialogue partners are transformed by Gospel values. Hence it may be called mission, in the broad sense of the word, even though no proclamation of Jesus Christ is involved in dialogue.

Thus *Redemptoris Missio* states that interreligious dialogue is part of the evangelizing mission of the Church. Dialogue and proclamation are two distinct expressions of evangelization, not to be confused, manipulated or regarded as identical, as though they are interchangeable.[51] They are intimately connected even though each retains its distinctiveness. "Dialogue is a path towards the *Kingdom* and will certainly bear fruit, even if the time and season are known only to the Father."[52]

Dominus Jesus in no uncertain terms affirms that the universal salvific will of the One and Triune God is offered and accomplished once for all in the mystery of the incarnation, death, and resurrection of Jesus Christ, the Son of God.[53] The statement of this central truth of Christian faith does not rule out dialogue: "Bearing in mind this article of faith, theology today, in its reflection on the existence of other religious experiences and on their meaning in God's salvific plan, is invited to explore if and in what way the historical figures and positive elements of these religions may fall within the divine plan of salvation."[54]

Dialogue will mark more and more the mission of the Church in the future especially in Asia where Christians live amidst followers of the great religions of the world. "In the climate of increased cultural and religious pluralism which is expected to mark the society of the new millennium, it is obvious that this dialogue will be especially important in establishing a sure

---

[47] Paul VI, Post-Synodal Apostolic Exhortation *Evangelii Nuntiandi*, n. 53.

[48] Secretariat for Non-Christians, *Dialogue and Mission: Attitudes of the Catholic Church Towards the Followers of Other Religions*, 1984.

[49] Congregation for the Evangelization of Peoples and the Pontifical Council for Interreligious Dialogue, *Dialogue and Proclamation*, 1991.

[50] John Paul II, Encyclical Letter on the Permanent Validity of the Church's Missionary Activity *Redemptoris Missio*.

[51] John Paul II, Encyclical Letter on the Permanent Validity of the Church's Missionary Activity *Redemptoris Missio*, n. 55.

[52] *Ibid*, n. 57.

[53] Congregation for the Doctrine of the Faith, *Dominus Jesus, on the Unicity and Salvific Universality of Jesus Christ and the Church*, Vatican City, Libreria Editrice Vaticana, 2000.

[54] *Ibid*, 14.

basis for peace and warding off the dread spectre of those wars of religion which have so often bloodied human history."[55] The Church in Asia is called upon to create suitable theological and practical models and methods of interreligious dialogue and mission in Asia. "It is therefore important for the Church in Asia to provide suitable models of interreligious dialogue - evangelization in dialogue and dialogue for evangelization - and suitable training for those involved."[56] Various elements of the Magisterium on interreligious dialogue and the theology of interreligious dialogue developed by theologians can help towards the formulation of such a theological basis and suitable methods of dialogue and proclamation.

A Theological Framework for Interreligious Dialogue

Trinitarian Basis for Dialogue

We may now sum up the theological basis for interreligious dialogue that we have been discussing. According to the Christian revelation the reality of God is Trinitarian. God is Father, Son and Holy Spirit. The whole creation and especially human beings are created in the image of God who is Trinitarian. Man is created in God's image and God calls us to share in his Trinitarian life. Salvation is ultimately God's self-communication. This self-communication has its source and pattern in God who is Triune. Christians believe that such self-communication is Trinitarian both in creation and salvation. Creation itself is an act of dialogue and salvation is the fulfilment of dialogue, namely, a shared divine life without end. Hence, creation,

redemption and eschatological salvation are dialogical events.

Christological basis of Dialogue

As Christians we believe that we are created in the image of the Son, who became incarnate. The Word was always present in the world. By His incarnation, the Son of God has in a mysterious manner united Himself with every human being.[57] All are, in a certain sense, intimately related to Jesus Christ. John Paul II in his first encyclical says: "Christ, the Redeemer of the world, is the one who penetrated in a unique unrepeatable way into the mystery of man and entered into his 'heart',"[58] Hence Christians must enter into dialogue with all peoples who are in some way already united to Jesus Christ.

Interreligious dialogue is, therefore, basically an intra-Christian dialogue. Those who are not baptized are not entirely strangers to Christians. They are already united to Jesus Christ. Hence dialogue with them is not a matter of choice, but of duty.

Pneumatological Basis for Dialogue

The Spirit of God is at work in all history, in every place and time. His presence and activity are universal, and he is not limited by the boundaries of the Church.[59] The Spirit of God scatters the seeds of truth and grace in the hearts of individuals, peoples, cultures and religions.[60] Hence interreligious dialogue is itself an activity inspired by the Spirit and an act of collaboration with the Holy Spirit.

Hence interreligious dialogue does not take place in a vacuum. The Christian who enters into

---

[55] John Paul II, Apostolic Letter at the Close of the Great Jubilee of the Year 2000, *Novo Millennio Ineunte*, 56.

[56] John Paul II, Post-Synodal Apostolic Exhortation *Ecclesia in Asia*, n.31

[57] *Cf.* Vatican Council II Pastoral Constitution on the Church in the Modern world *Gaudium et Spes*, 22.

[58] John Paul II, Encyclical *Redemptor Hominis*, n. 22.

[59] *Cf.* John Paul II, Encyclical Letter *Dominum et Vivificantem*, n. 53.

[60] *Cf.* John Paul II, Encyclical Letter on the Permanent Validity of the Church's Missionary Activity *Redemptoris Missio*, n.28.

dialogue is not initiating a new process of dialogue with other believers. It is the continuation of the dialogue that the Spirit of God has already begun in the hearts of all believers.

Kingdom of God as Basis for Interreligious Dialogue

God's mission to humanity, general and particular, has one single scope, namely, to usher in, nourish and bring to fulfilment the *Kingdom of God*. The ultimate purpose of the mission of Jesus is the fullness of the Kingdom, already realized in Him, but yet to be realized in history.[61]

All religions, in some way, seek to promote the *Kingdom* values of compassion, reconciliation, love, forgiveness, justice, respect and solidarity. The *Kingdom,* by its nature, tends towards communion among all peoples, with one another and with God. It is also the concern of all human beings, both individuals and communities and religious traditions. Working for the *Kingdom* means acknowledging and promoting what God Himself is doing in the world.[62] Dialogue with religions and collaboration with them is essential for the Church. The theology of *Kingdom* constitutes a very important basis for inter-religious dialogue. The *Kingdom* is the locus of interreligious dialogue.

Ecclesiological Basis for Interreligious Dialogue

The Church has been defined as a community of persons made one with the unity of the Father, the Son and the Holy Spirit.[63] It is also the sign and instrument of the same union with all peoples of the world. Her mission is fostering unity of all peoples, for all peoples constitute one single community with a single origin and goal. By her very nature the Church is called to dialogue with all peoples so that all may have the fullness of communion with the Father, the Son and the Holy Spirit.[64]

The Church is nothing but the community of those who have accepted the Kingdom of God in their lives. But the Church does not exhaust the Kingdom. The Kingdom extends to all places and communities of peoples who welcome its values. The Church is the visible locus and servant of the Kingdom wherever it exists. The Church constitutes the beginning of the Kingdom: "It is true that the Church is not an end in itself, since she is ordered towards the Kingdom of God of which she is the seed, sign and instrument."[65] The Church, therefore, essentially is related to and committed to dialogue with other religions, which are also partial expressions of the kingdom and its promoters.

Pilgrimage to the Eschatological Fullness as Basis for Dialogue

The Church is a pilgrim community; she is on an eschatological pilgrimage towards the fullness of salvific truth, goodness and harmony in the beatific vision and possession of God the Father, the Son and the Spirit. The Church is a pilgrim people.[66] Religions too consider themselves to be on a pilgrimage towards truth, goodness and fullness of bliss, *saccidananda*, and the fullness of life in some sense. All religions may be called *saccidananda* communities, namely, communities in search of the fullness of

---

[61] Cf. John Paul II, Encyclical Letter on the Permanent Validity of the Church's Missionary Activity *Redemptoris Missio*, n. 12 ff.

[62] *Ibid,* 16.

[63] *Cf.* Vatican Council II Dogmatic Constitution on the Church, *Lumen Gentium*, 4.

[64] Vatican Council II Declaration on the Relationship of the Church to Non-Christian Religions *Nostra Aetate*, 1.

[65] *Cf.* John Paul II, Encyclical Letter on the Permanent Validity of the Church's Missionary Activity *Redemptoris Missio*, n. 18.

[66] *Cf.* Vatican Council II Dogmatic Constitution on the Church, *Lumen Gentium*, 9-17, 48.

reality; truth as opposed to *avidya*, and bliss as freedom from all *dukha* or suffering and illusion. All religions are pilgrim communities moving towards the fullness of liberation, freedom from all illusions and from suffering.

If religions are perceived as pilgrim communities, it becomes evident that there is a common basis for dialogue between different pilgrim communities who are in search of the ultimate reality, truth and beatitude. Differences in philosophical perceptions, cultural expressions, linguistic formulations, symbols of worship and historical variations need not prevent a fruitful dialogue, while maintaining one's own faith conclusions and identity. The fact that the Church community is one that is gathered together by the Holy Spirit, gives it an identity of its own. But that does not prevent it from entering into dialogue with other faith communities in their pilgrimage towards the fullness of life in God.

Global Solidarity

In a world that is more and more interlinked and interdependent, multi ethnic, multi cultural and multi religious, dialogue is essential for co-existence, and for survival and progress. Negative exclusivism is a negation of the contemporary trends in the world and contrary to true religious values.

Hence Dialogue between religions, interdependence and collaboration are essential to world peace and prosperity of people. Thus *Ecclesia in Asia* rightly says: "Communion and dialogue are two essential aspects of the Church's mission, which have their infinitely transcendent exemplar in the mystery of the Trinity, from whom all mission comes and to whom it must be directed."[67]

Kinds of Dialogue

Interreligious dialogue takes place in different ways and at different levels. Each local Church must also develop a kind of interreligious dialogue according to the cultural, philosophical and religious contexts it lives in. But in general we may speak of some specific kinds of interreligious dialogue.

Dialogue of Life and Heart

Believers of different religions can live together in peace and harmony, respectful of one another's religious beliefs and practices. In so far as their religious expressions are good, they can also be appreciated and participated in. Dialogue of life and heart is spontaneous and arises out of a lived experience of pluralism of religions. Such dialogue of life and heart has always existed in the past among believers of all religions. While there have been all through history, expressions of religious fundamentalism, intolerance and persecution on the grounds of religious beliefs, it is also true that there have been many expressions of religious tolerance, dialogue, collaboration, mutual support and enrichment among the followers of various religions.

Dialogue of Religious Leaders

Meetings of religious leaders are another form of interreligious dialogue. Such meetings can be occasions of very fruitful interreligious dialogue and can also set an example to members of their religious communities to live in respect and amity. Recent times have witnessed several such meetings between the Roman Catholic, the Orthodox, the Protestant Church leaders and the religious leaders of Hindu, Buddhist, Islamic and other religious traditions. Meetings of religious leaders can promote mutual acquaintance, friendship, and appreciation of individuals and communities.

Dialogue between Religious Scholars, Theologians

Interreligious dialogue between scholars,

---

[67] John Paul II, Post-Synodal Apostolic Exhortation *Ecclesia in Asia*, n. 31.

theologians and experts representing different religious traditions is another expression of dialogue. Such dialogues help to clarify doctrinal and theological positions of each religion. There often exist serious misunderstandings of one another's theological position. These differences also shape one's negative attitudes towards other religions. Scholarly dialogues can dispel many prejudices; they can reveal fundamental, common religious denominators. They help to understand the theological language of each one and discover essential differences and at the same time, recognize underlying common theological grounds. Thus we come to realize that there is a common platform for dialogue, co-existence and collaboration in many areas of life.

Dialogue of Spiritualities

All great religions have fully developed spiritualities enriched by centuries of practice. Knowledge and personal experience of the spiritualities of one another can contribute immensely to mutual understanding, appreciation and enrichment. Thus, without compromising the essential identity of each religious tradition, Zen meditation, *Yoga* spiritual exercises, *Sufi* spirituality, Buddhist *Vipasana* etc., can be great sources of mutual dialogue and complementarity. In fact there is a growing use of them by believers of various religions.

Charismatic Meetings and Dialogue

In recent years, Charismatic prayers, retreats and scripture readings have brought Christians, Hindus and Muslims together especially in countries like India. The dialogue that takes place at such meetings have immense power to breakdown prejudices, appreciate the richness of other religious traditions and lead to inner healing, peace and harmony. At such meetings, popularly known as charismatic meetings, it would seem that the Holy Spirit takes over and leads people towards mutual respect and appreciation without the fear of being induced to abandon one's

religion and be converted to another. At the same time participants are enabled to benefit from healings of the spirit and body, illumination of the sacred scriptures, and most of all, spiritual fellowship.

Popular Religious Festivals

Popular religious festivals, pilgrimages and prayer meetings are also occasions and instruments for interreligious dialogue. Wherever and whenever these can be done without falling into religious syncretism, they can promote dialogue between believers. In today's world, there are many religious festivals, pilgrimages, and meetings, which bring believers of various religions, and even non-believers, together. They too serve as occasions of mutual understanding of other religions and their values. No doubt, there is the danger of syncretism in such participation. But we must recognize also the values and advantages of this form of dialogue. However, prudence and maturity are required in such a dialogue.

Dialogue through Spirituality of Involvement

There is a new kind of interreligious dialogue taking place among believers of all religions committed to human liberation, struggle for legal rights, human rights and human promotion. Religions not only define the human condition of evil and sin, but they propose also the means of liberation from all forms of evil, sin, ignorance and malice. To be involved in the struggle for human liberation is, therefore, to be deeply religious.

Persons involved in these activities are convinced that religion is essentially a spirituality of involvement to liberate people who are exploited, oppressed, marginalized and treated as second-class or 'classless' persons without rights. The struggle for human liberation forms part of the eschatological movement towards final human liberation. Such struggle is a form of spirituality and those involved in it share common bonds and goals. Hence dialogue among them is inevitable.

Dialogue through Asceticism

The recent call to joint fasting by Muslims, Christians and even non-believers on the last day of Ramadan has opened up a new kind and area of interreligious dialogue.[68] It offers to all an opportunity for a dialogue of Asceticism since all religions propose to their believers some form of asceticism such as fasting. Such a dialogue brings people to the heart of all religions, namely self-denial. Common ascetical practices lead people to inner purification and strength. Here again, participants share much common ground for mutual dialogue.

Dialogue through Sacred Scriptures

Many religions have a sacred book, which is believed to be divinely inspired in some way or another. The study and use of one another's sacred scripture brings about a better appreciation of the spiritual riches of other religions. Their study and use also reveal many basic similarities or even identities. All sacred scriptures, whether divinely inspired or not, are capable of inspiring all those who read and meditate on them. They are capable of purifying the lives of the believers. They are indeed an expression of man's search for God, truth and meaning in life. They also tell their faithful how God has been leading his people through all ages and places to the fullness of life. Dialogue through the sacred scriptures of the religions of the world holds promising results for the future of interreligious dialogue.

In conclusion we must say that there are many avenues and areas of interreligious dialogue open to the believers of all religions and to all people of good will. The enumeration of such areas of interreligious dialogue as given above is not intended to mean that there are no dangers involved in some forms of interreligious dialogue.

Requirements, Fruits and Limits of Interreligious Dialogue

Requirements for Genuine Dialogue

The documents of the World Council of Churches and those of the Catholic Church give detailed guidelines for interreligious dialogue. Thus the Kingston Statement sums up the guidelines for their member Churches:

It is Christian faith in the Triune God - Creator of all humankind, Redeemer in Jesus Christ, revealing and renewing Spirit - which calls us Christians to human relationship with our many neighbours. Such relationship includes dialogue: witnessing to our deepest convictions and listening to those of our neighbours. It is Christian faith, which sets us free to be open to the faiths of others, to risk, to trust, and to be vulnerable. In dialogue, conviction and openness are held in balance.[69] A very detailed set of guidelines is given by the Magisterium of the Catholic Church in several documents, especially in *Dialogue and Mission* and *Dialogue and Proclamation*.[70]

Self-identity of Faith: Dialogue partners must have a firm conviction of their own faith. If there is no such faith-identity, no dialogue is possible. Hence Christians believe that God has revealed Himself in Jesus Christ as the only source of salvation for all peoples. No doubt, others will have similar faith-conclusions. These must be respected.

---

[68] *Cf.* John Paul II, *Angelus Message*, on 18 November, 2001, *L'Osservatore Romano*, Call to fasting .

[69] World Council of Churches, *Guidelines on Dialogue with People of Living Faiths and Ideologies*, Geneva, WCC 1979.

[70] *Cf.* Pontifical Council for Interreligious Dialogue, *Interreligious Dialogue. The Official Teaching of the Catholic Church (1965-1995)*, Boston, Pauline Books & Media, 1997; original Italian edition: *Il Dialogo Interreligioso*, Citta' del Vaticano, Libreria Editrice Vaticana, 1994.

Attitude of Respect: All dialogue partners ought to bring to interreligious dialogue a genuine attitude of trust, respect and appreciation of the other as other. Respect for persons and their religious beliefs, whether they are authentic and well founded on reason or not, is essential for any fruitful dialogue.

Interreligious Dialogue and Mission: Dialogue and mission are intimately connected, but they preserve their specific distinctiveness. One does not negate the other. Dialogue is not to be instrumentalized for tactical or strategic reasons. Self-interest or a spirit of conquest and domination should not prompt it. When dialogue is prompted by the desire for truth, it will avoid all exaggerations.

Attitude of Openness and Conversion: Dialogue to be genuine, must be open to truth, and the whole salvific truth. Whatever is true and beautiful comes from God. The Spirit, we believe, has scattered His manifold gifts among all peoples. Hence great openness, humility and a spirit of conversion are required in every kind of dialogue. An attitude of openness to the whole truth is an essential requirement. Dialogue partners, as they make progress in dialogue, will realize that they have absorbed and assimilated into their lives only part of the saving truth and hence must be open to the whole truth.

One must also be true to oneself. There can be no glossing of irreconcilable differences, or false sense of irenism. Hence Dialogue calls for truthfulness and courage along with respect for others.

A Critical Spirit: Dialogue is not a path of roses. It calls for a respectful but critical spirit. While one is respectful towards the religious beliefs of the other, one must also be respectfully critical of what is not true, noble and good. The positive aspects of another religion should not make the dialogue partner blind to the shadowy or even dark areas of a concrete religion, whether in doctrine, in social justice or social customs that are contrary to human dignity. In a genuine dialogue, the same critical spirit must be used towards the practices and doctrinal positions of one's own religion. Thus Dialogue will lead to mutual purification of hearts.

Fruits of Dialogue

Dialogue has been called a path towards the *Kingdom of God*. The fruits of interreligious dialogue are many and they are already visible in breaking down barriers of prejudices, misunderstandings and removal of ill will. Dialogue can reap a harvest of genuine conversion.

Dialogue as a Corrective against Abuses: Religions tend to degenerate and become entangled in politics, power play, and self-seeking. Feudalism, caste-system, clericalism, despotism, nepotism and other personal and social evils have taken shelter under the name of religion in the past. Religions then become blind to political, economic, and social abuses and immune to pressures for reform and renewal. Genuine encounter and dialogue with other religions can reveal and heal the wounds of sin inflicted upon genuine religion and its practices.

A Comprehensive and Renewed Theology of Mission: Dialogue mentality has helped the Church to redefine Christian mission, its motivation, its scope and methods. There is today a greater and more comprehensive understanding of mission than in the past, thanks to the development of the theology of dialogue. In recent years, a more positive theology of religions compared to the negative theology of the religions in the past — and hence a more respectful approach towards them, has also emerged as a result of interreligious dialogue. The encounter and dialogue between religions have helped them to purify themselves from doctrinal aberrations, exaggerations and moral and social evils and lapses. Interreligious dialogue has helped them to become aware of exaggerated claims, compromises with the world, silence and connivance with grave evils of society.

Risks Involved in Dialogue

Dialogue and Mission: Interreligious dialogue brings with it some risks and dangers. It is good to be aware of them. One danger is the undervaluing of the need for mission. Mission is at times reduced to only dialogue. There was a time before the Second Vatican Council, when there was little official effort made towards dialogue with cultures and religions. Today there is a danger of having only dialogue without sufficient mission and proclamation *ad gentes*. There can be a tendency to glorify one's own culture and grant it priority over the demands of authentic religion. Culture, in so far as it is a human product, is also imperfect and subject to sinfulness and hence cannot be held superior to revelation.

Religious Indifferentism and Relativism: Dialogue, when not understood and not practised correctly, is in danger of falling into religious indifferentism and relativism in matters of faith. The document of the Catholic Church, *Dominus Jesus*[71] was intended to safeguard faith from degenerating into a theological opinion.

Syncretism: Christians must have the courage to enter into dialogue with the believers of other religions. While they seek to express and communicate the Christian message in dialogue and mission, by means of concepts, symbols, and images taken from indigenous cultures and intelligible to dialogue partners, there is always the danger of falling into syncretism.[72]

Dialogue and Faith Conclusions: Genuine Dialogue implies that each believer has absolutes in faith. All religions have their faith-conclusions, which have universal and normative application for others. Thus a Hindu believer may hold that his/her particular path of salvation has universal and normative value for believers of other religions. So long as this is done in charity, respect for others and general human solidarity, it does not hurt a Christian. Similarly, the Christian faith-conclusions and applications need not be offensive to any one, if held in charity, respect and mutual tolerance. It is the imposition of one's faith-conclusions that must be avoided.

Conclusion

God's salvific design for humanity is the foundation of all interreligious dialogue. Human existence is dialogical. If God enters into a dialogue of salvation with humanity, religions themselves cannot, therefore, be anything but dialogical. Despite the human search for truth and meaning in life, despite divine revelation at various times, places and to various persons in the religious history of the world and in Jesus Christ "in these last days", God and human salvation remain a mystery. The mystery of God and human salvation can only be approached in dialogue with God and with one another.

Truth, meaning and self-realization can be reached only in dialogue. Hence Christians have no other way to truth, meaning and salvation except the way of dialogue that God himself has established. It has always been so. But in our days it has become much more urgent and imperative, not to give up our religious certainties, but to relate them to other peoples' certainties and walk towards the fullness of God, which is our own fullness.

The urgency for Dialogue among believers of all religions has been dramatically illustrated by the Second Assisi Prayer Meeting by the

---

[71] *Cf.* Congregation for the Doctrine of the Faith, *Dominus Jesus, on the Unicity and Salvific Universality of Jesus Christ and the Church*, Vatican City, Libreria Editrice Vaticana, ns. 3-4.

[72] World Council of Churches, *Guidelines on Dialogue with People of Living Faiths and Ideologies*, Geneva, WCC 1979, 124-27.

leaders of all the Religions convoked by Pope John Paul II. Its concluding statement[73][74[59]] may be considered as a *magna carta* for interreligious dialogue:

1. We commit ourselves to proclaiming our firm conviction that violence and terrorism are incompatible with the authentic spirit of religion, and, as we condemn every recourse to violence and war in the name of God or religion, we commit ourselves to doing everything possible to eliminate the root causes of terrorism.

2. We commit ourselves to educating people to mutual respect and esteem, in order to help bring about a peaceful and fraternal coexistence between people of different ethnic groups, cultures and religions.

3. We commit ourselves to fostering the culture of dialogue, so that there will be an increase of understanding and mutual trust between individuals and among peoples, for these are the premise of authentic peace.

4. We commit ourselves to defending the right of everyone to live a decent life in accordance with their own cultural identity, and to form freely a family of their own.

5. We commit ourselves to frank and patient dialogue, refusing to consider our differences as an insurmountable barrier, but recognizing instead that to encounter the diversity of others can become an opportunity for greater reciprocal understanding.

6. We commit ourselves to forgiving one another for past and present errors and prejudices, and to supporting one another in a common effort both to overcome selfishness and arrogance, hatred and violence, and to learn from the past that peace without justice is no true peace.

7. We commit ourselves to taking the side of the poor and the helpless, to speaking out for those who have no voice and to working effectively to change these situations, out of conviction that no one can be happy alone.

8. We commit ourselves to taking up the cry of those who refuse to be resigned to violence and evil, and we desire to make every effort possible to offer the men and women of our time real hope for justice and peace.

9. We commit ourselves to encouraging all efforts to promote friendship between peoples, for we are convinced that, in the absence of solidarity and understanding between peoples, technological progress exposes the world to a growing risk of destruction and death.

10. We commit ourselves to urging the leaders of nations to make every effort to create and consolidate, on the national and international levels, a world of solidarity and peace based on justice.

---

[73] Concluding Statement of the Second Assisi Peace Meeting, held in Assisi on 24 January, 2002, cf. *L'Osservatore Romano*, 4-5, March, 2002, "*De Décalogue d'Assise pour la Paix*".

PART V

Contextual Studies

CHAPTER 25

Culture, Nation and Conversion Issues In Mission Today

S.M. MICHAEL SVD

Over the years the attacks on the Christian community in India are on the increase. A quick survey indicates that the trend of such attacks have increased since about March 1998. This coincides with the ascendancy of the Bhartiya Janata Party (BJP) at the Centre in Delhi. According to the United Christian Forum for Human Rights (UCFHR), the number of registered cases of communal violence against Christians in the 32 years between 1964 and 1996 was 38. This rose to 15 in 1997. In 1998, the number rose to 90. Nuns have been raped, priests executed, Bibles burnt, churches demolished, educational institutions destroyed and religious people harassed.

Who is behind this Violence?

Whether it be the hacking to death of Rani Maria in Indore, parading naked of Fr. Christudas in Dumka, attack on prayer halls, burning of Bibles in Gujarat, burning alive of Rev. Staines and his two minor sons in Keonjihar or hacking to death of Fr. Arul Doss, there is a pattern in the attacks against the Christian community in India. Several fact finding reports by Non-Governmental Organizations indicate that in all these cases, the chief instigators appeared to be from the bodies associated with the Hindu Right, namely, the Rashtriya Svayam Sevak Sangh (RSS), Vishwa Hindu Parishad (VHP), the irregular wing of the latter, the Bajrang Dal (BD), and the Hindu Jagran Manch (HJM). Together with the BJP these are often described as the Sangh Parivar.[1]

The fact is that the real cause of the communal riots is the rise of the Sangh Parivar (Hindu Nationalists Organizations). There was communal peace even in the early years after Partition. A Home Ministry review presented to the National Integration Council in 1968 noted: "From 1954 to 1960, there was a clear and consistent downward trend, 1960 being a remarkably good year with only 26 communal incidents in the whole country. This trend was sharply reversed in 1961." That was when riots erupted in Jabalpur – thanks to the Jan Sangh, the BJP's ancestor. Communal violence has not "looked back" since. According to Noorani, the attacks on Christians "mounted steeply after the Bharatiya Janata Party-led Government assumed office in March 1998."[2] The DGP (Director General of Police) of Gujarat, where the attacks on Christians were on a large scale, said: "the VHP and the Bajrang Dal were taking the law into their own hands."[3] This is also confirmed by the Archbishop of Delhi, Alan de Lastic, who said: "What I have noticed is that ever since this Government came to power at the Centre, the attacks on Christians and Christian missionaries

---

[1] See the following reports: "Then They Came for the Christians – A Report to the Nation" by AIFOFDR, 1999; Report of the United Christians' Forum for Human Rights (UCFHR) 1999; Violence in Gujarat – Hindu Jago Christi Bhago by Kamal Mitra for National Alliance of Women, 1999.

[2] A.G. Noorani, "RSS and Christians," *Frontline*, January 1, 1999, p.123.

[3] *The Hindustan Times*, August 6, 1998.

have increased."[4] The Director General of Police of Gujarat further confirms this. In an interview to Teesta Setalvad, co-editor of *Communalism Combat* on October 8, 1998, Gujarat's Director General of Police, C. P. Singh, said:

> One thing was clear in the pattern of incidents. It was the activists of the Vishwa Hindu Parishad and Bajrang Dal who were taking the law into their own hands, which posed a serious danger to peace in Gujarat. Many of the attacks on the minorities were after these organizations had whipped up local passions of conversions (by Christian missionaries) and allegedly forced inter – religious marriages — our investigations revealed that in most cases these were entirely baseless allegations.[5]

A member of the investigation team sent by the Minorities Commission revealed: "After initial reluctance, the officials named VHP and Bajrang Dal allegedly involved in the mob attacks on Christians and Muslims."[6]

Violence is an integral part of Hindutva ideology. According to one of the most prominent RSS ideologues, M.S. Golwalkar, violence "should be used as a surgeon's knife ... to cure the society." While the Sangh Parivar's animosity towards Muslims is well-known, its attitude towards Christians has taken many people by surprise. But, Vishwa Hindu Parishad (VHP) General Secretary Giriraj Kishore said in Chandigarh on November 25, 1998: "Today the Christians constitute a greater threat than the collective threat from separatist Muslim elements."

Why this violence against Christians?

When we scrutinize the pronouncements, news items and reports of the various Hindutva organizations on Christians for the last few years, we realize that the main issues raised by them against Christians are centred around three main areas, namely 'culture', 'nation' & 'conversion' in India. It is good to analyze these issues raised by Hindutva organizations and see how far they are valid in their accusations against Christians. This analysis may also shed some light on the real motive behind the violence on Christians.

(i) The Question of National Identity and Cultural Foundaton of Modern India

While the available anthropological knowledge on India reveals that India is a multi cultural, multi-racial, multi-lingual and multi-religious country, the Sangh Parivar questions this, and proclaims India to be a Hindu nation. Anybody who does not subscribe to this vision of the Sangh Parivar is considered an enemy of the nation.

This idea of a 'Hindu Rashtra', governed entirely by the principles of Hinduism, has been gaining more visibility in the last few years. The proposal put forward in the forty point 'Hindu agenda' during the Eighth Dharma Sansad of the Vishwa Hindu Parishad in February 1999 in Ahmedabad, included the demand to reinstate Bharat in its true *Sanatan* and righteous form. K.N. Govindacharya, the BJP and RSS ideologue declared that India is 'geo-culturally' a 'Hindu Rashtra.'[7] This idea of Hindutva implies that to be Indian is to be Hindu. To be an Indian, according to them, is defined by one's religion.

This is a very serious and grave error and an injustice to the citizens of India.[8] The inspiration behind the Hindutva ideology, 'to be Indian is to be Hindu', can be traced to Swami Dayananda Saraswathi (1824-1883), one of the first Hindu

---

[4] *Frontline*, 1999, p.123.

[5] *Communalism Combat*, Oct.8, 1998.

[6] *The Indian Express*, August 12, 1998.

[7] *Times of India*, January 30, 1999.

[8] Leela D'Souza, "The Debate on Conversions: Clarifying the Identity of India," *Third Millennium: Indian Journal of Evangelization* II,3, July-September 1999, pp.64-74.

revivalists of modern India. When several Indian elite raised the question of the cultural foundation for the modern India, some reformers were of the opinion that the re-creation of modern India should be on the basis of incorporating science and rationality into Indian culture. For example, Rammohan Roy (1772-1833) recognized some of the evil practices in Hindu society such as Sati, child-marriage and idol worship, and insisted on the need for reform in Hinduism and its society. He founded the Brahmo Samaj to restructure Hindu culture in terms of modernity. This challenged the presuppositions on which the orthodox Hindu system of conduct was based.

Opposing the modernist views, Dayananda Saraswathi urged a regeneration of Hindus through adherence to a purified 'Vedic faith'. The Vedic Aryans are described by Dayananda as a primordial and elect people to whom the Veda has been revealed by God and whose language – Sanskrit – is said to be the 'Mother of all languages'. They would have migrated in the beginning of the world from Tibet – the first land to emerge from the Oceans – towards Aryavarta. This territory, homeland of the Vedic civilization, covered the Punjab, Doab and Ganges basin. From this position, the Aryans would have dominated the whole world till the war of the Mahabharata, a watershed, opening a phase of decadence. The national renaissance implied precisely, for Dayananda, a coming back to the Vedic Golden Age.

The chief object of the Arya Samaj he founded in 1875 was to bring about social and religious revival through the renaissance of early Hindu doctrine, its favourite mottos being 'Back to the Vedas' and 'Aryavarta for the Aryans'.[9]

This view simply equated Indian culture with Hinduism and Hindu culture; all non-Hindu aspects were regarded as contaminating influences. The Arya Samaj is probably the first movement in India defining nationalism in terms of ethnicity.

These views of Dayananda Saraswati are the basis from which the later Hindu movements and organisations such as the Hindu Mahasaba, R.S.S., Shiva Sena, V.H.P., Bajrang Dal and BJP are formed.[10] The leaders of the Hindu nationalist movement based on a revival of Hindu culture openly acknowledged their identification of nationalism with Hinduism. Vivekananda, Aurobindo Ghose, Tilak, Savarkar, Hedgewar and Golwalkar are some of the prominent Hindu nationalists who identified India with 'Hindu'. For example, Golwalkar, one of the prominent ideologues of the RSS, made it crystal clear that India is a 'Hindu' nation. He suggested that Muslims and Christians be placed behind bars during the time of national crisis. His idea of the best solution to the minorities problem is contained in one word – assimilation. According to him they should be "wholly subordinated to the Hindu nation, claiming nothing, deserving no privileges, far less any preferential treatment – not even citizen's rights."[11]

In an interesting speech, a Hindu Mahasabha leader attempted to list the cultural changes which Indian Muslims would have to undergo in order to become acceptable nationals of the Indian (Hindu) state of the future. First, they would have to accept the *Ramayana* and *Mahabharata* as their epics and reject the Arabic and Persian classics. They would have to regard Ramachandra, Shivaji, and the Hindu gods Rama and Krishna as their heroes, and condemn various

---

[9] William Roy Smith, *Nationalism and Reform in India*, London: Yale University Press, 1938, p.57.

[10] S.M. Michael, "Culture, Religion and Politics in India: Rise of Hindu Cultural Nationalism," *Dharma Rajya* Vol.2, No.1, March 1998, pp.20-34,

[11] M.S. Goldwalkar, *We or Our Nationhood Defined*, 4th ed., Nagpur: Bharat Prakashan, 1947, pp.55-56.

[12] V.G. Deshpande, *Why Hindu Rashtra?* New Delhi: All India Mahasabha, 1949, p.10.

Muslim historical figures as foreign invaders or traitors.[12]

The present Sangh Parivar members express similar views about Christians in India. For example, the Bajrang Dal has threatened Christian-run educational institutions in Karnataka with dire consequences if they did not 'Hinduise' themselves by installing an image of Saraswati and beginning the day with Saraswati Vandana.[13] Rashtriya Swayamsevak Sangh leader Rajendra Singh declared at a RSS camp in Meerut on November 22, 1998, "Muslims and Christians will have to accept Hindu culture as their own if Hindus are to treat them as Indians."[14] Harsh Narain says: "Hindu culture alone deserves the credit of recognition as the national culture (*abhimanin*) of this country, as the culture owning and possessing this great nation, along with other Indian-born cultures like Buddhist and Jain cultures as its sub-cultures; Muslim and Christian cultures being in the nature of tenant-cultures. The distinction of master-parasitic culture has its own significance."[15] One can guess what he is hinting at.

The above position of the Sangh Parivar goes contrary to the historical facts. A simple scrutiny of Indian civilization will reveal that since the middle of the second millennium B.C. several streams of migrant groups and communities from different parts of the world migrated to the Indian sub-continent. The advent of the Aryans, the Tibeto-Burman speaking Mongoloid groups, the Kushans, the Sakas, the Greeks, the Huns, the Arabs, the Persians, the Turks and the Mongols at different points of time, testifies to the pervasiveness of the migration process during the successive periods of Indian civilization.[16] The

migrant groups and communities brought their respective traditions and behavior patterns from their native lands. In course of time they lost contact with their places of origin and underwent an extensive process of indigenization. The process of adaptation and interaction among the various groups brought about, on the one hand, India's characteristic diversity and, on the other, a composite cultural tradition. This fact is borne out by historical sources and contemporary surveys as well as research in folklore.

The Hindu nationalists want to deny the above fact for the simple reason that it goes against their interest of preserving the pre-eminent position which they are enjoying in the Hindu caste social order at the expense of tribals, dalits and other lower castes who are mainly Sudras. A quick look at the composition of Indian society will speak for itself. The Brahmins of India form only 6 per cent of Indian society, the other upper castes are 14 per cent. The Backward castes (Sudras) are 52 per cent; Dalits are 16 per cent and Tribals are 8 per cent of the Indian population.[17]

The subaltern groups mainly the backward castes, Dalits and tribals, view India completely differently from the Brahmins and other upper castes who dominate the Sangh Parivar. The leaders of the subaltern masses such as Jotiba Phule, Ramaswamy Naicker, Ambedkar and Swami Achchutanand incessantly and systematically exposed and condemned Brahminical Hinduism as a religion and culture of social slavery, and therefore an enemy of the people struggling to emerge as a modern nation.[18] The ideals and values and the customs and injunctions of Brahminical literature – the Vedas,

---

[13] P.R. Ram, *In the Name of Religion: Truth Behind Conversions and Acts of Violence*, Mumbai: EKTA, 1999, p.2.

[14] *The Asian Age*, November 23, 1998.

[15] A.G. Noorani, "RSS and Christians" p.127.

[16] Leela D'Souza, "The Debate on Conversions" pp.64-74.

[17] "The Revolution Against Caste," *Time*, April 13, 1992, p.11.

[18] S.M. Michael, *Dalits in Modern India: Vision and Values*, New Delhi: Vistaar Publications, 1999.

Upanishads, Ithihasas, Puranas and Dharma Shastras – as interpreted and upheld within the competetive politics of Hindu nationalists, appeared to these men as a pre-emptory call to reinforce and re-establish the Varna ideology of discrimination against the lower classes.

As a result of these conflicting visions of modern India, we observe today the emergence of two opposite socio-political and cultural forces in the Indian political arena. On the one hand, backward castes and classes are in search of a culture based on an egalitarian social and economic order with greater political participation; on the other hand, upper caste Hindus (Sangh Parivar) are equally strong in trying to retain control of their present position of privilege and dominance by reasserting ancient hierarchical Brahminic Hindu values. Thus, the contrasting interests of the upper and lower groups have polarized cultures in India, the former vigorously clinging to their traditional status, and the latter fighting for justice, equality and human dignity.

Now it may be easy to understand why Christian missionaries are attacked by the Hindu nationalist organizations such as RSS, VHP, Bajrang Dal, Shiva Sena, etc. The work of Christian missionaries among the downtrodden people of this country will go against the interests of the upper castes. That is why Pastor Rev. Graham Stewart Stains who was working among the lepers in a remote part of Orissa was burned to death, the nuns who are working in the remotest parts of India are raped; Christian educational and social institutions are ransacked and missionaries are humiliated.

(ii) The Issue of Conversion and Human Freedom

Another important issue on which Christians are targeted is conversion. Almost everyday there is one or the other news item in the Indian newspapers on the above subject. A number of

statements have been made by different Hindutva organizations. For example the eighth Dharma Sansad of the Vishwa Hindu Parishad (VHP) demands strict anti-conversion laws and a White Paper by the Central Government on the 'foreign conspiracy', behind conversions. The Prime Minister, Atal Behari Vajpayee, demanded a 'national debate on conversion' thereby implying that attacks on Christians are due to their conversion activities. Mr. Vajpayee said that if Christian missionaries continued with religious conversions, the government could not stop reconversions. VHP's Ashok Singhal argued that Professor Amartya Sen's Nobel Prize is a Christian conspiracy to open more missionary-run educational institutions to convert the poor. It was alleged that missionaries use force, fraud and allurements to convert people to Christianity. Funds obtained for welfare activities are used for conversion. All the same, conversion from Christianity to Hinduism is encouraged and supported by the Sangh Parivar as *Ghar wapasi* or homecoming.

The Pope's visit to India on 5 November 1999 was marked by the protest of the Hindutva organizations against forceful conversion by the Christian missionaries. Indian media was used in its fullness to create public opinion against Christians for their alleged forceful conversion activities. For example, M.V. Kamath, in his article, "Mission Impossible: Putting an End to Conversion Activity" published in the *Times of India* on 13 October 1999, justified the violence against Christian missionaries because they are engaged in conversion among the poor and the ignorant of India. He, not only demanded an apology by the Pope, but also a total stop and ban on Christian conversion activities.

Many of these pronouncements by various Hindutva oriented journalists, politicians and religious leaders completely ignore the inevitable socio-cultural dynamics and processes of human history and raise a lot of questions with regard to representation of facts, knowledge of Indian history and regard for human freedom.

We need to analyze the issue of conversion impartially. Human history points out that social change is an inevitable process. Inventions, discoveries, invasions, diffusions and assimilation are affecting the lives of people throughout the world. The process of conversions has to be seen in this broad context of social change. Usually, when conversion is discussed in India, it is done in the context of conversion to Islam and Christianity alone. In reality, however, conversion has been going on all through the history of India.[19] There have been cultural and religious encounters and interactions over the ages. India has been a sub-continent with a vast population of diverse levels of culture. The very cultural assimilation of influences emanating from the very ancient tribal populations of the vast Indian subcontinent and a succession of new arrivals – Aryans, Greeks, Scythians, Parthians, Shakas and Huns before the eighth century, as well as Arabs, Persians, Turks, Afghans and Mongols between the eighth and twelfth centuries – was a vital and dynamic process. Among the different migrants to India from ancient days, it was the Aryans who vigorously tried to establish a hierarchical order, *Varnashrama-dharma* as a universal social system in India.

What we today call and designate 'Hinduism' was not known till the medieval period. The term 'Hindu' was originally derived from the name Indus and was used successively by the Achaemenids, the Greeks and the Muslims to denote the population living beyond that river. Anthropological studies on India show that through a process of absorption, assimilation and conquest, a process of Sanskritization had been taking place in ancient India. Adivasis or Tribals and other indigenous people have been drawn into the orbit of a sanskritic world-view. Jayant Lele explains this process: "The Brahminic worldview had succeeded on several occasions in the past in capturing the diversity of cults, deities, sects and ideas (by making many compromises) under the rubric of *sanantana dharma.*"[20] Explaining this process of Brahminic incorporation, reinterpretation, appropriation and assimilation of tribal and other cultures, N.K. Bose says: "Once a tribe came under the influence of the Brahminical people and was converted into a caste enjoying monopoly in a particular occupation, a strong tendency was set up within it to remodel its culture more and more closely in conformity with Brahminical way of life."[21] Like the tribals who were assimilated into Hinduism, the non-Aryan i.e. the *Sudras* and *Ati-Sudras* were also assimilated and Sanskritized. The powerful upper-castes of a particular area exercised such an influence on the lower castes and outcastes that they also wanted to be integrated into the caste hierarchy by adopting the values and practices of the upper castes. This process is described as 'sanskritization' by the well known anthropologist M.N. Srinivas.[22] According to Romila Thapar, this "first step towards the crystallisation of what we today call Hinduism was born in the consciousness of being the amorphous, undefined, subordinate, other."

Even today this process of Hinduization of tribals is going on with full political support by the State and Central Governments.[23] The highest number of conversions was effected through the Hindu Census enumerators. The question in the

---

[19] S.M. Michael, *Anthropology of Conversion in India*, Mumbai: Institute of Indian Culture, 1998.

[20] Lele Jayant, *Hindutva: The Emergence of the Right*, Madras: Earthworm Books, 1995, p.xviii.

[21] Nirmal Kumar Bose, *Culture and Society in India*, Bombay: Asia Publishing House, 1967, p.214.

[22] M.N. Srinivas, *The Cohesive Role of Sanskritization and Other Essays*, New Delhi: Oxford University Press, 1989.

[23] Arjun Patel, "Hinduisation of Adivasis: A Case Study from South Gujarat" in *Dalits in Modern India: Vision and Values* edited by S.M. Michael, New Delhi: Vistaar Publications, 1999, pp.186-212.

census usually is: What is your dharma? Dharma is a word generally alien to tribals, particularly where formal education has not reached. Consequently, all *adivasis* (tribals), except those who are baptized into Christianity or Islam, are simply categorized as Hindu. Hence, from the above data, we can conclude that the biggest agent of conversion in Indian history has been the Brahminic Hindus.

When we turn to Christian conversion in India, we trace its presence from the first century. It is an ancient tradition that Saint Thomas, one of the twelve Apostles of Christ, came to India in AD 52 and established Christian communities in seven places. All the same the extensive diffusion of the message of Christ began only from 1498. The conversions that took place since then could be classified into four types, that is, of individuals, group movements, Christian Dalit conversion and Christian Tribal conversions. Most of the individual conversions are from Brahmin castes. The reasons for their conversion seem to be "the unsatisfactoriness of Hindu religion, though this may be reflection post-*eventum*."[24]

With regard to conversion movements to Christianity, several Hindu fundamentalists make the accusation that there were forceful conversions in the last 500 years. Studies of conversion movements indicate that this is a much more complicated problem. Firstly, we have to assess different historical periods and varied political regimes and the accounts are not the same for each. Further, the idea that missionaries came with the sword to convert, i.e. they always had the backing of the colonial state and the power to use military force to enforce conversions, is seriously challenged by the historical data. When we study the significant conversion movements in Indian Christian mission history, we understand the manifold factors which are operative in them. Conversion is never an isolated event.

While the Hindu fundamentalist organizations through their assimilation policy claim the tribals and dalits to be Hindus, the tribals and the dalits on the other hand reject this superimposed identity. The upper caste Hindus while trying to get the services of the dalits and tribals paid little attention to the alleviation of their deprived conditions. They are addressed as 'Backward Hindus'. Rejecting this identity, the tribals and dalits have found their own ways to move up in the social ladder of Indian society. The conversion movements among the Dalits and tribals have shown the potential of social change in religion.

The mass conversion of tribals to Christianity is related to the tremendous socio-economic and cultural changes brought about by westernization and modernization.[25] O.L. Snaitang, a Khasi, studying *Christianity and Social Change in North East India* finds that in a situation where radical changes were taking place, Christianity provided institutions, a new life style and ideology which protected the tribal society from the danger of detribalization and loss of identity.[26]

Some Hindu leaders are of the opinion that Christian conversions are only due to famines, poverty and starvation. But this is too simplistic and does not take cognizance of the complex phenomena of Christian conversions.

Sociologically, conversion is a process of change from one religion to another. It is something that is used by individuals to move forward in society, to free themselves from inherited shackles, to better themselves and their

---

[24] Andrew Wingate, *The Church and Conversion: A Study of Recent Conversions to and from Christianity in the Tamil Area of South India*, Delhi: ISPCK, 1977, p.13.

[25] Nali Natarajan, *Missionary Among the Khasis*, New Delhi: Sterling Publishers, 1977.

[26] O.L. Snaitang, *Christianity and Social Change in North East India*, Shillong: Vendrame Institute, 1993.

children. These shackles might be those of caste, of illiteracy, of economic slavery, of psychological apathy. But all these factors are always inter-linked and no one of them should be considered in isolation. The converts did not always perceive the spiritual and material components of conversion as separate things, but as a single phenomenon. It constituted no contradiction for them to use conversion as a leverage for upward social mobility.

Forceful conversion should be condemned. All the same, is it wrong if a group of people change their religion when they realize that their poverty and social degradation are due to the legitimized religious values and the structures of a given society? The prospect of radical change can only seem subversive to those who are committed to the status quo. It is understandable that the beneficiaries of the status quo resent radical changes. But to the oppressed and downtrodden, change is the lever of hope. At a time when the 'right to informed choice' is upheld even in routine matters, how can the right to freedom of choice be denied to millions in matters of ultimate significance?

Blaming the Church for accepting poor people into Christianity does not hold ground in the context of Indian democracy. Such sayings are an insult to the dignity of the poor. There is condescending paternalism in this idea that denies the poor the ability of making rational and intelligent decisions. Does our constitution discriminate against the poor in voting and choosing their representatives to parliament? Indian elections have proved the power and the wisdom of the poor and the ordinary. They have their own wisdom to choose and reject in spite of pressures and coercion. Hence, any underestimation of the capacity of the poor and the downtrodden by the upper caste Hindu fundamentalists is unwarranted.

Moreover, conversion movements are not only towards Christianity but also to other religions. Let us not forget the revolt of Dr. B.R. Ambedkar against Hinduism and his mass conversion to Buddhism in 1956. A deeper look into the history of India would reveal that Buddhism and Jainism were widespread in India, but today they are reduced to small minority religions because of the aggressive missionary activities of Brahminic Hinduism. The Arya Samaj and other Hindu organizations like the VHP promote conversion and reconversion (*Ghar Vapsi*) in their programs not only in India but in many parts of the world. There is so much misunderstanding, misinformation, rumors and political overtones with regard to Christian conversions. Hindu fundamentalists do not recognize the pluralistic nature of Indian society. Hence, they politicize even the very idea of conversion to Christianity. Behind this politicization there is a big agenda of Hinduization of India. This attitude is out of tune with the pluralistic tradition of India and contradicts the fundamental rights of the people of India.

Hence, the sweeping statements and accusations often made against Christians regarding conversion cannot be taken at face value. They must be subjected to rigorous questioning and analysis and once this is done we find that the issues are manifold and far more complex than what appears at the very first sight. We must not lose our objectivity in analysis and comprehension and must not allow truth and goodness to be saddled and dismissed or distorted by popular opinion or bias.

Conclusion

India is a sovereign nation. It has a written Constitution, the solemn pledges of our founding fathers; it is a document especially treasured for the broadness of its vision and the egalitarian values. This Constitution is drawn and promulgated in the context of the debate on the pluralistic nature of Indian society. The founding fathers of the Indian nation were well aware of the multi-cultural, multi-religious, multi-lingual and multi-ethnic nature of Indian society. Hence, it is very important to affirm the pluralistic nature of Indian society; and no religious group could claim India to be theirs.

Conversion has been taking place all through Indian history. Anthropological studies on India show that through a process of absorption and assimilation and conquest, tribals and other indigenous communities have been drawn into the orbit of Sanskritic Hinduism. Even today this process of Hinduization is going on with political support by the State and Central Governments. Moreover, conversion movements are not only towards Christianity but also to other religions. There is so much misinformation, rumors and political overtones with regard to Christian conversions. Hindu fundamentalists do not recognise the pluralistic nature of Indian society. Hence, they politicize even the very idea of conversion to Christianity. Hence, the sweeping statements and accusations often made against Christians on conversion require rigorous questioning and analysis.

Having said that, it is also very important to urge Christians to develop sensitivity on the issues of culture, nation and conversion in India. Christians in India should actively get involved in the political processes of the reconstruction of modern India as a strong and vibrant nation. The Church must collaborate with government agencies and other secular organizations to bring more life to the downtrodden people of India. In this context, the Christians in India can learn a lot from the pronouncements of the Holy Father during his 4-7 November 1999 visit to India.

Since the issue of religious conversions formed a core part of the controversy about the Papal visit, the Pope has done well to clarify the position of the Church on the issue. The Pope said freedom constituted the most noble prerogative of the human person and one of the principal demands of freedom was the free exercise of religion in society. "No state, no group has the right to control either directly or indirectly a person's religious convictions, nor can it justify [sic.] claim the right to impose or impede the public profession and practice of religion, or the respectful appeal of a particular religion to people's free conscience."[27]

Speaking about the relationship between the Church and cultures, the Holy Father points out that the Church has been imbibing positive elements of other religions apart from renewing cultures from within. "This engagement with cultures has always been a part of the Church's history. But it has a special urgency today in the multi-ethnic, multi-religious and multi-cultural situation of Asia where Christianity is still too often seen as foreign," the Pope said during the concluding session of the Asian Synod, an assembly of Asian bishops.

The Pope's call for dialogue is also very vital and relevant in the Indian context. This dialogue is to strive to discern whatever is good and holy in one another to promote peace and guarantee the world's future. The dialogue the Pope advocated was not intended to "attempt to impose our own views upon others, since such a dialogue would become a form of spiritual and cultural domination." However, this religious and spiritual interaction can be done without abandoning one's own convictions. "Holding firmly to what we believe, we listen respectfully to others, seeking to discern all that is good and holy, all that favours peace and cooperation."[28]

To conclude, we may say that the cultural context of evangelization in India is related to three main areas of Indian reality, i.e. culture, nation and conversion. These issues are highly

---

[27] As reported in the *Deccan Herald*, 8 November,1999: p.1.

[28] *Ibid.* pp.1,9.

politicized today. Christians need to be sensitive to these issues without compromising the vision of Jesus, engaging in dialogue, inculturating and discerning whatever is good and holy in other religions and cultures to promote peace and guarantee the world's future.

CHAPTER 26

Indigenous Christianity

ROGER E. HEDLUND

"Christianity has become a pluralist dispensation of enormous complexity, and religious statesmanship requires the flexible approach of translatability to foster this pluralism rather than opposing it as a threat." (Lamin Sanneh) [1]

The explosive growth of Independent Christianity in Asia, Latin America and Africa is highlighted in a recent publication.[2] Global Christianity today is centred in these three regions. This rapidly spreading Christianity is indigenous to Asia, Africa and Latin America. It is a vibrant faith, much of it Pentecostal or Charismatic, with considerable appeal to the poor and the marginalized.

In South Asia indigenous Christianity to a large extent—but not exclusively so—belongs to the so-called 'Little Tradition'[3] of religious studies. The 'Little Tradition' represents the practices and beliefs of Christian adherents which may be at variance with the dogmas and rituals of recognized 'Great Tradition' Christianity. Churches of the 'Little Tradition' may be looked upon as Christian expressions of popular folk religion, an equation which, however, can be questioned. The 'Little Tradition' consists of lesser-known churches and recent new movements of South Asian origin in contrast to the historic denominations and institutions constituting the 'Great Tradition'.

The history of Christianity generally is written from the standpoint of the 'Great Tradition'. Usually it is the story of Western Christianity, whereas the history of Christianity in the East is neglected and not well known.[4] Seldom is it written from the underside.[5] Yet the greatest growth of the Church today is taking place in the East and the South, in countries and peoples of Africa, Latin America and Asia, frequently among poor and disenfranchised,

---

[1] Lamin Sanneh, *Translating the Message: The Missionary Impact on Culture*, Maryknoll: Orbis, 1991, p.6.

[2] David B. Barrett and Todd M. Johnson, *World Christian Trends AD 30–AD 2200: Interpreting the annual Christian megacensus*, Pasadena, William Carey Library, 2001.

[3] 'Little Tradition' is a term coined by Robert Redfield and applied to India by Milton Singer and cultural anthropologists at the University of Chicago. See Robert Redfield, *Peasant Society and Culture*, Chicago, 1967, and Milton Singer, *When a Great Tradition Modernizes An Anthropological Approach to Indian Civilization*, New York, 1972. Redfield states, "In a civilization there is a great tradition of the reflective few, and there is a little tradition of the largely unreflective many." The two traditions intersect and are interdependent. One is the tradition of the philosopher, the other that of the little people. One is literary, the other oral. "Great and little tradition can be thought of as two currents of thought and action, distinguishable, yet ever flowing into and out of each other." (Redfield pp.41-43).

[4] Samuel Hugh Moffett, *A History of Christianity in Asia*, Vol.1: *Beginnings to 1500*, Second and Revised ed., Maryknoll: Orbis Books, 1998, p.xiii.

[5] See Roger E. Hedlund, "Christian History from the Under Side: Indian Instituted Churches & Indigenous Christianity," Keynote address, Conference on Subaltern Perspectives on Seminary Training, Centre for Dalit Solidarity, Dharmaram College, Bangalore, 23 October, 1998.

marginalized populations. "The emergence of independent churches around the world expressing indigenous forms of Christianity is undermining the equation of Christianity with Western culture."[6] India is one example.[7] Asian incarnations of the Gospel are embodied in various indigenous movements of the sub-continent.

India itself has seen numerous attempted incarnations of the Christian faith, some highly successful, others less so. Therefore the study of new religious movements of Christian origin is timely and promising. A majority of India's Christians are from the oppressed, the products of Tribal and Dalit conversion movements.[8] Conversion movements in India not infrequently have been movements of social protest, the response of Dalits and Tribals and the Poor to the call to a counter-culture, movements of affirmation in quest of dignity and equality. Numerous 'messianic' movements among tribal and other subaltern communities are examples of social protest movements which did not become explicitly Christian.[9] In India today, however, in North as well as South, a number of subaltern movements are taking place in which oppressed peoples are finding dignity in a new identity as disciples of Jesus Christ. For many, upward mobility resulted from conversion by which the downtrodden discovered new dignity and hope.[10] Not all conversions are among the oppressed, of course, nor are all the emerging churches of indigenous origins to be so classed, but nevertheless subaltern categories are prominent in the broad sweep of diversity among India's indigenous Christian movements.

Indigenous Christianity is a relatively new field for academic research in South Asia. A project highlighting the existence of numbers of 'Little Tradition' churches resulted in the publication of a series of books[11] as well as several articles in academic journals.[12] In India

---

[6] Paul G. Hiebert, "Missiological Education for a Global Era" in *Missiological Education for the 21st Century* edited by J. Dudley Woodberry, Charles Van Engen and Edgar J. Elliston, Maryknoll: Orbis Books, 1996, p.36.

[7] Roger E. Hedlund, "Indian Instituted Churches: Indigenous Christianity Indian Style," *Mission Studies* Vol.XVI-1,31, 1999:26-41.

[8] Estimates vary from perhaps 70 percent to as much as 80-90 percent.

[9] Stephen Fuchs, *Rebellious Prophets: A Study of Messianic Movements in Indian Religions*, Bombay: Asia Publishing House, 1965.

[10] Roger E. Hedlund, "Indian Christians of Indigenous Origins and Their Solidarity with Original Groups," *Journal of Dharma* Vol.XXIV,1 (1999):13-27.

[11] *Quest For Identity: India's Churches of Indigenous Origin, The "Little Tradition" in Indian Christianity* by Roger E. Hedlund, 2000; *Christianity Is Indian: The Emergence of an Indigenous Community* edited by Roger E. Hedlund, 2000; *Churches of Indigenous Origins in North East India* edited by O.L. Snaitang, 2000; *The New Wineskins: The Story of the Indigenous Missions in Coastal Andhra Pradesh, India* by P. Solomon Raj, 2003; all are published by ISPCK, Delhi.

[12] Journal articles include (1)"Subaltern Movements and Indian Churches of Indigenous Origins" *Journal of Dharma* XXII, I (1998):8-38; (2) "Indigenous Christian Movements in India" *Light of Life* May 1998, 51-57. (3) "Indian Christians of Indigenous Origins and Their Solidarity with Original Groups" *Journal of Dharma* XXIV,1 (1999) 13-27; (4) "Indian Instituted Churches: Indigenous Christianity, Indian-Style," *Mission Studies* XVI-1,31, 1999:26-42; (5) Chapter "The Search for Indigenous Church Models in India" in *Mission and Missions: Essays in Honour of I. Ben Wati* edited by J. Kanagaraj; Pune, Union Biblical Seminary, 1998; (6) Three Articles in the *New International Dictionary of Pentecostal/ Charismatic Movements* edited by Stanley M. Burgess, Zondervan, 2002; (7) An article in the *Dictionary of Asian Christianity* edited by Scott Sunquist, John Chew and Davi Wu, Eerdmans, 2001; (8) "Approaches to Indian Church History in Light of New Christian Movements," *Indian Church History Review* December 2000,153-170; (9) An entire issue of *Dharma Deepika* devoted to Indigenous Christianity, January-June 2002, viz. P.Daniel Jeyaraj, "Glimpses of Vedanayagam Sastriyar" 5-12; Grace Parimala Appasamy, "Christian Music of Tamil Nadu" 13-18; Roger E. Hedlund, "India's Quest for Indigenous Christianity" 19-29; Sudheer Merugumalla, "Christian Santhi Ashram" 31-

the 'Little Tradition' churches of indigenous origins (CIOs) are also designated as Indian instituted churches (IICs). In contrast to 'missionary' Christianity—i.e. 'Great Tradition' Churches and institutions that were the product of foreign missionary effort—indigenous Christianity has its own structures and cultural expressions which are frequently outside the orbit of the traditional Churches, hence overlooked by earlier studies which concentrated on Churches of the Great Tradition.[13] This phenomenon is more extensive and more influential than is generally realized.

Biblical and Theoretical Base

God identified with human culture in the Incarnation. The Christian gospel therefore affirms culture not in a unitary form confined to any one people or locality but as the totality of human social expressions. Christianity, from its inception, struggled with temptations of ethnocentrism and exclusive monoculturalism. The pivotal Jerusalem Council (Acts 15) established for all time the principle of full cultural diversity and validity. The Acts of the Apostles "is the story of the Christian movement as it began among the Jewish people and went on to become a faith for the whole world."[14] It did this not by imposing Jewish culture but by affirming the validity of non-Jewish cultures. Consequently biblical Christianity reserves no sacred space, neither Jerusalem nor Rome.

From its inception, Christianity translated itself out of its Aramaic, Hebrew and Judaic roots.[15] Translation has been the pattern ever since. "Missionary translation has characterized the spread of Christianity in both its Catholic and its Protestant forms."[16]

This was notably so in the case of William Carey, whose primary objective—and greatest achievement according to some—was the translation of the Bible into Bengali. The Bible was considered essential for creating an indigenous Church. Carey and the Serampore Mission laid the ground for the development of indigenous Christianity through their translations of the Bible into Bengali and scores of other South Asian languages, and the accompanying literary and publication activities which also were major contributing forces in a Bengali cultural awakening. Carey went beyond the elegant language of the educated elite to record the colloquial language of the masses which had its own diction and distinct style. "This work gave to spoken dialects in Bengali a status and a recognition such as was not given in the past."[17] Carey had a passion for developing the languages of India. He himself was involved in the translation of 29 Indian dialects, and additional translations were carried out by his associates. Serampore birthed a linguistic renaissance in India.[18] Through their multi-faceted activities, Carey and the Serampore mission contributed to

---

36; Solomon Raj, "Songs of the Pilgrim Churches" 37-42; Samanta Naik, "Churches of Indigenous Origins in Orissa" 43-46; Ravi Tiwari, "Christ-Bhakta Yesu Das" 47-60; Daniel Jeyaraj, "De Nobili Research Institute" 61-65; Jyothi Uday Kumar, "What Liberates a Woman? The Story of Pandita Ramabai" 66-70.

[13] See Roger E. Hedlund, "Approaches to Indian Church History in Light of New Christian Movements," *Indian Church History Review* December 2000,153-170.

[14] Introduction to the Acts of the Apostles in the *Good News Bible* , New York, American Bible Society, 1976, p.157.

[15] Sanneh, *Translating the Message,* p.1.

[16] *Ibid.,* p.3.

[17] N.R. Ray, "William Carey — A Linguist with a Difference" pp.153-156 in *Carey's Obligation and India's Renaissance* edited by J.T.K. Daniel and R.E. Hedlund, Serampore, 1993.

[18] S.K. Chatterjee, "Carey and the Linguistic Renaissance in India" pp.157-175 in *Carey's Obligation and India's Renaissance* edited by J.T.K. Daniel and R.E. Hedlund, Serampore, 1993.

a cultural renewal in Bengal which resulted in movements for social reform and political awakening throughout India. Carey's experiment at Serampore may be viewed as a progenitor of indigenous Christianity.

Indigenous Christianity is as old as Christianity itself. The earliest indigenous church was at Jerusalem.[19] As biblical scholar Lucian Legrand states, "The Christian faith was strictly indigenous only to Palestine!"[20]

The Jerusalem Church consisted of thousands of believing Jews gathered by the Twelve into a Messianic community.[21] Centered in the Temple and under the leadership of James, this initial 'Jerusalemite Judaeo-Christianity' community remained "solidly ensconced in Jerusalem."[22] Biblical scholars discern as well a 'Palestinian Judaeo-Christianity' under the direction of Peter, which was similar but less insular, venturing in witness beyond Jerusalem.

However it was 'Hellenistic Judaeo-Christianity' which most actively engaged in mission to the Diaspora. "This would be the Christianity of Philip and Stephen, Barnabas and Paul."[23] The Church at Antioch, where the community was given a distinct and separate identity as 'Christian', is the product of Hellenistic Judaeo-Christian mission.[24] The church at Antioch, quite different in character from Jerusalem, was a mixed community of Hellenized Jews and Greek Gentiles.[25]

But there were other churches equally indigenous to their context. The Book of Acts records the emergence of a church in Samaria through the ministry of Philip to a marginalized population.[26] We read of a church at Damascus, but know nothing of its origins.[27] Peter's Cornelius visitation resulted in an Italian Gentile household of faith.[28] Diversity of expression according to culture and circumstances is characteristic of the churches of the New Testament era. From Antioch the Christian mission "to the ends of the earth" commenced.

Jerusalem, however, questioned the resulting diversification with its apparent disregard for Jewish rites and tradition. Consequently a major international conference on mission was convened at Jerusalem to settle the issue.[29] Various options were considered. The decision to accept the Gentiles as equal members, without proselyte *cultural* conversion, validated the continuity of diverse human cultures and established a principle of multi-cultural liberty which would serve the formation of believing communities in any human society.

The Twelve chosen by Jesus are reminiscent of the twelve patriarchs and the twelve tribes, an obvious link with Old Testament Israel. Now, however, they are the prototypes of a new spiritual Israel in which not ethnicity but faith is the criterion for membership.[30]

---

[19] Acts 1:12-14.

[20] Quoted by J. Samuel Escobar, "A Missiological Approach to Latin American Protestantism," *International Review of Mission* LXXXVII, 345 (April) 1998:161-173, p.165.

[21] Lucien Legrand, *Unity and Plurality: Mission in the Bible*, Maryknoll: Orbis, 1990, p.100.

[22] *Ibid.*, pp. 94,95.

[23] *Ibid.*, p.94.

[24] Acts 11:19-26.

[25] *Jerome Biblical Commentary* Vol.II, p.190.

[26] Acts 8:5-25. In the eyes of Palestinian Jews of that time, the Samaritan were a despised "outcaste" community, and followers of a deviant cult.

[27] Acts 9:1.

[28] Acts 10:1-48.

[29] Acts 15:1-35.

[30] Legrand, *Unity and Plurality*, p.99.

Whatever their background, all believers were invested with royal and priestly dignity, "a chosen race, a royal priesthood, a holy nation, God's own people.... Once you were no people but now you are God's people."[31] Such, according to the New Testament, is the *ekklesia*, called from above by God, summoned from below into community.[32] According to Küng, the Old Testament people of God were legitimately succeeded by the new called-forth people of the Covenant assembled around Jesus Christ. The *ekklesia* is to be understood both as the whole New Covenant community and also as the local household community expressions of it.[33]

The New Testament Church exhibited a diversity of structures and worship patterns. There seems to have been considerable flexibility, for example, in offices and leadership functions. It is not surprising that throughout history the Church has known a variety of forms. What Küng relates concerning ecclesiastical offices[34] applies to the different cultural identities of the churches: they were truly *local*, i.e. indigenous, communities.

Cultural plurality is both acceptable and reasonable. A concern for unity is equally correct and compelling—a concern sometimes lacking among present-day Independent Churches. Multiple New Testament missions ought not to be misconstrued as irresponsible competition. Rather, here was an overflowing spiritual vitality "permeated by a basic concern for unity. This multiple mission was not content to express itself in anarchical abundance. The various tendencies sometimes collided in tumultuous confrontation, but the encounter was always accompanied by a quest for communion."[35] Underneath is an indelible unity, the bond of a common faith and purpose.

Contemporary indigenous Christian movements are legitimate heirs of this Biblical drive for unity in diversity. Nowhere has the contextual initiative been more evident than in Africa with its abundance of African Instituted Churches (AICs).

African Background

Indigenous Christianity thrives in Africa which has thousands of distinctly African denominations. The African phenomenon is well-documented in a number of university theses, books, and an ongoing spate of articles appearing in *Missionalia*,[36] published by the Southern African Missiological Society and the University of South Africa, as well as other periodicals.[37] Previously viewed as sub-Christian sects or cults, the African Instituted Churches today are understood as authentic Christian churches initiated by Africans and having African characteristics. "The African worldview does not permit the Western tendency to separate physical and spiritual, or personal and social."[38]

---

[31] I Peter 1:9-10.

[32] Hans Küng, *Structures of the Church*, New York: Thomas Nelson, 1964, p.12.

[33] *Ibid.,* p.11.

[34] *Ibid.,* p.207.

[35] Legrand, *Unity and Plurality*, p.94.

[36] Numerous articles have appeared. See, e.g., Obed Ndeya Kealotswe, "Corporate Personality in the African Independent Churches in Southern Africa, with special reference to the 'Head Mountain of God Apostolic Church' in Botswana," *Missionalia* 27,3, November 1999:299-312; Ulrich van der Heyden, "The Origins and Political-Religious Functions of an Independent Church, The Lutheran Ba-Pedi Church in the 19th Century," *Missionalia* 27,3, November 1999:377-389; Adrian Chatfield, "African Independency in the Caribbean, The Case of the Spiritual Baptists," *Missionalia* 26,1, April 1998:94-115.

[37] See studies by Allan H. Anderson and others at the University of Birmingham as well as other sources in the Appendix to this chapter.

[38] Allan Anderson, *Zion and Pentecost*, Pretoria, University of South Africa Press, 2000, p.29.

Aspects of an African worldview, ignored by Western theology, are taken seriously in the AIC's. Creed is less important than curing. Causation must be considered. The ancestors, spirits and divinities, dreams and visions, prophecy and divination are taken seriously. African healing traditions, an oral liturgy, music and dance, a narrative theology, and the inclusion of dreams and visions are elements also found in modern Pentecostalism.[39]

The African expression is significant in light of the world-wide emergence of Pentecostalism as the twenty-first century's dominant expression of Protestant Christianity. Hollenweger and Anderson have shown that modern Pentecostalism has roots in "the spirituality of nineteenth-century African American slave religion."[40] African Pentecostalism has its own distinctive character much more in common with the rest of the developing world than with the West, "predominantly a grassroots movement appealing especially to the disadvantaged and underprivileged."[41] Pentecostal spirituality has proven itself culturally adaptable and has incarnated itself into an African expression of Christianity.[42]

Pentecostalism is one type of indigenous Christianity. But not all indigenous Christian expressions are Pentecostal.

South Asian Heritage

At a very early time Christianity came to South Asia, where it adapted itself to the prevailing culture. The most notable example is the Thomas Christianity of South India. After carefully evaluating the sources and versions of the Thomas tradition, historian Mathias Mundadan concludes that the belief stands sufficiently validated that the Apostle Thomas preached, died and was buried in South India and that the community of Thomas Christians originated in the mission of St. Thomas in India.[43] Historically, indigenous Christianity has a 2000 year tradition in South Asia! Cult and culture combined to preserve a Christian community which is authentically Christian as well as thoroughly Indian.[44]

A second Indian tradition alleges an apostolate of St. Bartholomew possibly at Kalyan near present-day Mumbai. If so the history of the Bartholomew Christians presumably became intermingled with that of the Thomas Christians and later with the coming of the Portuguese merged with the Christians of Bombay.[45]

The other significant early South Asian Christian tradition is that of Pakistan which also claims a Thomas tradition. An early mission to the region is quite believable but not proven due to a poverty of primary sources.[46] A legend about

---

[39] Walter J. Hollenweger, "The Black Roots of Pentecostalism" in *Pentecostals after a Century* edited by Allan H. Anderson and Walter J. Hollenweger, Sheffield Academic Press, 1999.

[40] Allan H. Anderson and Walter J. Hollenweger (eds.) *Pentecostals after a Century: Global Perspectives on a Movement in Transition*, Sheffield Academic Press, 1999, p.23.

[41] Anderson, *Zion and Pentecost*, p.25.

[42] *Ibid.*, p.26.

[43] A.M. Mundadan, *From the Beginning up to the Middle of the Sixteenth Century*, History of Christianity in India Vol.1, Bangalore, Church History Association of India, 1989, p.64.

[44] Leslie Brown, *The Indian Christians of St. Thomas*, Madras, B.I. Publications, n.d., reprint of the Cambridge original, pp.3,5.

[45] Mundadan, *Ibid.*, p.66.

[46] John Rooney, *Shadows in the Dark:A History of Pakistan up to the 10th Century*, Pakistan Christian History Monograph No.1, Rawalpindi, Christian Study Centre, 1984.

Jesus in Kashmir is primarily the propaganda of Ahmadis or Qadianis, based on speculation regarding a supposed 'hidden life of Jesus' from age 12 to 29, and is not believable. As there are no reputable historical sources, it remains "a pure romantic fiction."[47] What is known is the existence of a token Christian presence in the region at the time of the Council of Nicea in the fourth century. There was also a missionary expansion of the Persian Church which penetrated at least as far as Afghanistan by the sixth century. Christian communities once existing in Baluchistan, Punjab and Sindh became isolated, declined, and died out by the eleventh century, probably absorbed by mass conversions to Islam. Were the Gypsies of Europe the last remnants of Christian refugees from Sindh and Punjab?[48] The question cannot be answered. What seems evident is that ancient Christianity once existed in the region prior to the advent of Islam.

Primitive Christian indigeneity is preserved in at least six South Indian Christian denominations that claim and accept the Thomas apostolic tradition as to the origins of Christianity in India. These include the Orthodox Syrian Church (in two sections), the Independent Syrian Church of Malabar (Kunnamkulam Diocese), the Mar Thoma Church, the Malankara (Syrian Rite) Catholic Church, the (Chaldean) Church of the East, the St. Thomas Evangelical Church (two factions), and a section (CMS) of the Church of South India as well as Indian Syrian Christians in Brethren, Independent and Pentecostal churches in India.[49]

As Felix Wilfred observes, the Thomas Christians are "of the soil" and as an integral part of the social and religious fabric of the region for nearly two thousand years have lived in harmony with the culture and traditions of their Hindu and Muslim neighbours.[50]

Indigeneity in Recent History

Ancient South Asian Christianity has experienced rebirth in countless reincarnations. A few examples may serve, notably from India, Sri Lanka and Nepal.

A broad diversity of indigenous Christianity is found in India, demonstrations of the ongoing translatability of the gospel. Attempts were made in Tamil Nadu, in Bengal and in Maharashtra to express historic Christianity through Indian cultural forms. At Madurai the brilliant Jesuit scholar, Robert de Nobili, completely Tamilized the gospel. Tamil Nadu had its own Vedanayagam Shastri and Krishna Pillai and others who enculturated the Protestant Christianity of the South. In Bengal the most radical attempts were the Christo-Samaj and the Church of the New Dispensation of Keshub Chunder Sen who, however, remained outside the Christian fold. In Maharashtra the Brahmin poet, Narayan Vaman Tillak, brought the richness of the Hindu *bhakti* tradition into the Church.

Others who in various ways appropriated the gospel in an Indian mode included Sadhu Sundar Singh, R.C. Das at Varanasi, Subba Rao in Andhra, Devadas of the Bible Mission at Guntur, Bro. Bakht Singh, and countless others. The story of Pandita Ramabai is one example.

In Maharashtra, Pandita Ramabai (1858-1922) was a social activist and radical advocate of women's rights and egalitarianism. A Marathi Chitpavan Brahmin convert to Christianity, her life has been a challenge to many. An articulate spokesperson on behalf of suppressed Hindu

---

[47] Rooney, *Shadows in the Dark*, p.67.

[48] *Ibid.*

[49] See Leslie Brown, *The Indian Christians of St.Thomas* and Other Studies of the St. Thomas Christians in India.

[50] Felix Wilfred, "Whose Nation? Whose History? in *The Struggle for the Past: Historiography Today* edited by Felix Wilfred and Jose D. Maliekal, Chennai, University of Madras, Department of Christian Studies, 2002, p.80.

women, her advocacy has earned her a place of honour in modern Indian history.[51] The distinctive contribution of Ramabai to indigenous Christianity in India is not so well known. The fascinating story of Ramabai has been told in several accounts and need not be repeated here.

In 1897 at Kedgaon, 35 miles beyond Pune, Ramabai launched a ministry for needy women and children. "Ramabai thus became the pioneer-founder of an indigenous national evangelistic mission in India — probably the first of its kind."[52] The Pandita Ramabai Mukti Mission continues to be active today meeting the needs of abused and abandoned women and children, a living institutional testimonial to the incarnational witness of Ramabai. A recent reconstructionist study identifies Ramabai as a prototype feminist who offered a devastating critique of Hindu patriarchy, "spokeswoman for the amelioration of women's status in Hindu society."[53] Ramabai is also important in the study of indigenous Christianity. Baptized in England, her understanding of Christianity was not confined to the Anglican Church. She was able to distinguish the Christian Faith from the Western traditions of the colonizers. In her conversion Ramabai neither rejected her own

cultural background nor identified with Western observances.[54] It is not surprising that the Mukti Church at Kedgaon emerges as an indigenous creation, distinct from "missionary" Christianity. Historically it is significant that here is an early expression of women's ministry and leadership.

In 1897 Ramabai invited Minnie Abrams, a Methodist "Holiness" missionary from America, to minister at Kedgaon.[55] In 1905 a spiritual revival at Mukti was to reverberate far beyond Kedgaon.[56] A first-hand account by Minnie Abrams describes the weeping and praying of the repentant Mukti girls as well as the dramatic manifestations which accompanied the new "baptism of the Holy Ghost and fire."[57] According to several authorities, Pentecostalism in India has its roots in Maharashtra at the Ramabai Mukti Mission, Kedgaon.[58] J. Edwin Orr documents the spread of the revival as the Mukti bands carried the message throughout the Maratha country. Characterised by emotional phenomena, the impact of the awakening was long-lasting in terms of conversions and changed lives.[59] Ramabai channeled the enthusiasm of the believing community into famine relief work as well as social rehabilitation.[60] In this way the spiritual

---

[51] S.M. Adhav, *Pandita Ramabai*, Madras, CLS, 1979, pp.238-241, provides a list of 114 books "about the life of Pandita Ramabai" which includes biographies as well as other compilations. See, e.g. Rajas Krishnarao Dongre and Josephine F. Patterson, *Pandita Ramabai, A Life of Faith and Prayer*, Madras, CLS, 1963; Nicol MacNicol, *Pandita Ramabai: A Builder of Modern India*, 1926.

[52] Adhav, *Pandita Ramabai*, p.18.

[53] Gauri Viswanathan, *Outside the Fold: Conversion, Modernity, and Belief*, Delhi, Oxford University Press, 1998, p.118.

[54] *Ibid.*, p.121.

[55] Basil Miller, *Pandita Ramabai, India's Christian Pilgrim*, Pasadena, World-Wide Missions, n.d., p.64.

[56] *Ibid.*, pp.86-87.

[57] Minnie F. Abrams, *The Baptism of the Holy Ghost & Fire*, Kedgaon, Pandita Ramabai Mukti Mission, second edition,1906, reprinted in 1999, pp.1-3.

[58] Ivan M. Saatyavrata, "Contextual Perspectives on Pentecostalism as a Global Culture: A South Asian View" in *The Globalization of Pentecostalism: A Religion Made to Travel*, edited by Murray W. Dempster, Byron D. Klaus, and Douglas Petersen. Carlisle, UK, Paternoster, Regnum Books, 1999, p.204. See also Gary B. McGee, *This Gospel Shall Be Preached: A History and Theology of Assemblies of God Foreign Missions to 1959*, Springfield, Gospel Publishing House, 1986, p.54.

[59] J.Edwin Orr, *Evangelical Awakenings in India*, New Delhi, Masihi Sahitya Sanstha, 1970, pp.111-114.

[60] Jessie H. Mair, *Bungalows in Heaven: The Story of Pandita Ramabai*, Kedgaon, Pandita Ramabai Mukti Mission, revised, 1993 reprint, p.79.

awakening had an enduring influence in Maharashtrian society.

Mukti Church continues today. The legacy of ministry to needy women and children continues. Training of members for ministry in the power of the Holy Spirit continues to be a distinctive emphasis. Mukti Church bears the Ramabai imprint of social vision combined with spiritual fervour. Mukti Church is a unique indigenous legacy of one of India's greatest women, Pandita Ramabai Saraswati, one of the makers of modern India.[61] India has many more examples.

Among the many Indian initiated Christian movements, the Indigenous Churches of India (the official name of the assemblies associated with Bro. Bakht Singh) must be mentioned, as well as numerous independent local assemblies and several break-away denominations in Andhra Pradesh. At Madras the Laymen's Evangelical Fellowship is an example of a significant holiness revival movement. Other similar new independent churches are found in many parts of India. The largest cluster consists of numerous indigenous Pentecostal fellowships, denominations and organizations. Some of these are off-shoots of the Indian Pentecostal Church of God (IPC) based in Kerala, others have emerged from the more exclusive Ceylon Pentecostal Mission (CPM). At Mumbai the charismatic New Life Fellowship is an indigenous house church movement that owns no property but has thousands of members functioning through cell churches throughout the city.

Questions have been raised concerning the authenticity of some new movements. Are the new "small church" movements fully Christian? Are they syncretic? Schismatic? Heretical? This bears investigation. Questioners tend to be judgmental, especially where new groups are perceived as "break-away" deviations from the mainstream. Biases aside, some evaluation in light of the norms of historical Christianity may prove helpful. To what extent are pre-Christian concepts and practices perpetuated among the new independent churches? Careful investigation also may alert indigenous leaders against non-indigenous heresies imported by popular preachers from the West.[62] Careful investigation may prove beneficial.

Sri Lankan Christian indigeneity has affinity to that of India as is illustrated by the history of Pentecostalism in Sri Lanka, in particular the origins of the Ceylon Pentecostal Mission.[63] According to historian Somaratna, the CPM began as a breakaway from the Assemblies of God led by Alwin R. de Alwis and Pastor Paul in 1923. The CPM espoused an ascetic approach to spirituality. Ministers were not to marry and they should wear white. They disdained the use of medicine and gave central importance to the doctrine of the second coming of Christ. Somaratna observes that testimonies of miraculous healing attracted Buddhists and Hindus, and the wearing of white was appropriate culturally in Sri Lanka where Buddhist devotees wore white to visit the temples. The CPM also instituted indigenous forms of worship.[64]

The CPM, despite its name, did not remain confined to Sri Lanka but spread to other countries including South India.[65] The CPM laid the foundation for other Pentecostal ministries

---

[61] So designated by Nicol MacNicol in his scholarly biography, *Pandita Ramabai*, Calcutta, 1926.

[62] See, for example, "Healing and Kenneth Hagin" by Keith Warrington, *Asian Journal of Pentecostal Studies* 3/1 (2000), 119-138.

[63] G.P.V. Somaratna, *Origins of the Pentecostal Mission in Sri Lanka*, Nugegoda, Margaya Fellowship, 1996.

[64] Somaratna, *Origins of the Pentecostal Mission*, pp.34-35, 40-41.

[65] Information provided by a stalwart member, Bro. Paul C. Martin, in a paper entitled "A Brief History of the Ceylon Pentecostal Mission" presented at the Hyderabad Conference on Indigenous Christian Movements in India, 27-31 October, 1998.

not only in Sri Lanka and India but beyond. Today, says Paul C. Martin, the CPM under various names, is one of the largest Pentecostal movements in the world with branches in several countries. While exact membership figures are not yet available, there are 848 branches worldwide (including 708 in India) and about 3,984 full-time ministers presided over by chief pastor C.K. Lazarus.[66] In addition there are numbers of independent assemblies and movements which have severed connections with the CPM. Some of these are prominent, such as the Apostolic Christian Assembly in Tamil Nadu, founded by Pastor G. Sundram, led today by Pastor Sam Sundaram, and many more.

Nepal is of particular note. Christianity in Nepal is in its first century! Prior to 1950 there were no Nepali Christians resident in Nepal. The story of the Church in Nepal is a record of efforts by Nepali Christians to reach their own people.[67] Nepal was closed to the outside, but Nepali people managed to seep out into India where a number of them were converted and became active evangelists. These Nepali Christians organized their own Gorkha Mission. Contacts developed along the border, and there were excursions into Nepal as well, but there was no place for Christians in Nepal.

Revolution in 1950 brought change and the first decade of the Church in Nepal. St. Xavier's School was started by the Catholics in 1951. Christian worship began in Kathmandu in 1953. Three Mar Thoma missionaries, trained in the Union Biblical Seminary at Yavatmal, India,

founded the Christa Shanti Sangh Ashram and took up residence in Kathmandu in 1953. Secret believers eventually were baptized. In 1953 the Nepal Evangelist Band received permission to open a hospital at Pokhara. In 1954 the United Mission to Nepal received permission to begin medical work. Other agencies followed, but primarily the story of the Church in Nepal is a record of Nepali Christians, many of them women, penetrating their country with the gospel.

The Nepali Church from its inception has been indigenous in character and outlook with emphasis on local leadership development. Discipleship schools and Bible schools were organized during the 1970s and 1980s. Kathmandu today has numerous small Bible training institutes, one or two seminaries, and at least one Christian university. The Association for Theological Education in Nepal serves to provide resources to meet the need of the growing Christian movement for training.

In 1991 there were more than 50,000 baptized believers in Nepal. The exact number of Christians is not known, but in 1996 it was estimated at about 200,000 Christians in Nepal, and more recently as many as 500,000 were reported, as well as response in the diaspora Nepali community in Northern India, Bhutan and other countries.[68] The witness of the gospel has advanced despite persecution, imprisonment and other hardships.[69]

The indigenous Christianity of Nepal has been described as Pentecostal or Charismatic in character from its very inception. Even before

---

[66] Martin, *op.cit.*, pp.5, 12.

[67] See Cindy Perry, *A Biographical History of the Church in Nepal*, Department of Intercultural Studies, Wheaton College, 1989.

[68] Cindy L. Perry, *Nepali Around the World: Emphasizing Nepali Christians of the Himalayas*, Kathmandu, Ekta Books, 1997.

[69] See Ramesh Khatry, "The Church in Nepal" in *Church in Asia Today* edited by Saphir Athyal, Singapore, ACWE, 1996; also Cindy Perry, "Nepal" in *A Dictionary of Asian Christianity* edited by Scott W. Sunquist, David Wu Chu Sing and John Chew Hiang Chea, Grand Rapids and Cambridge, Eerdmans, 2001; and Bal Krishna Sharma and Roger E. Hedlund, "Nepal" in *Evangelical Dictionary of World Missions* edited by A. Scott Moreau, Harold Netland and Charles Van Engen, Grand Rapids, Baker Books, and Paternoster, U.K., 2000.

Nepal opened its doors in 1951, Pentecostal missionaries in India were active on the Nepal border. Some of the converts were trained at the North India Bible Institute of the Assemblies of God at Hardoi. In Nepal converts were exposed to Pentecostal teaching. Besides the Assemblies of God, the Agape Fellowship and many independent churches are Pentecostal or Charismatic.[70]

Healing and exorcism are important dimensions of Christian witness in the animistic context of Tantric Hinduism and Tibetan Buddhism. It must be remembered that Christianity in Nepal is a first century Church.

Indigenous Christianity has proven adaptable and resilient. Christian witness is carried out through a variety of creative means. Investigation reveals empowerment activities among slum dwellers and street children, liberation of backward communities and tribals, encouragement of women's movements and Christ *Bhaktas*, use of indigenous communication media, employment of local proverbs and sayings, as well as the more traditional roles of community development, Bible translation, village schools, and church planting.

Churches of indigenous origins (CIOs) tend to be 'grass-roots' expressions of a popular Christianity of the 'Little Tradition'. Indigenous Christianity is an authentic signature of faith wherever the gospel has taken root. It was ever so from the beginning. "Once the church moved out from Jerusalem in the first century the gospel was almost never expressed except in translated form."[71] The phenomenon was true of what are now the established Christian traditions of America and Europe and is true as well of the emerging Christianity of Asia, Africa and the Pacific region.

Theological Implications

"Translation continues to be the primary means to discover the depth and extent of the gospel," states Mark Heim.[72] Translation, however, can be understood in different ways. One possibility is for the message to arrive as fixed and finished with little or no adjustment as it enters a new culture or language. Or there is the opposite possibility of a new 'alternative' gospel that is as adequate for the new context as the original gospel was for its situation. A third prospect is enrichment in which fresh insights and new aspects of the gospel emerge in each new cultural environment.[73]

This third expectation is what has actually happened in practice, even if denied in theory! As a sort of dialogue takes place between the gospel and culture, "historically it has been the diverse religious-cultural complexes Christianity has encountered that have been the primary context for theological development."[74]

An outstanding example was seen in the work of Brahmabandhav Upadhyay, already mentioned above, one of the greatest examples in Indian history of developing Christian theology by appropriating Hindu thought. In the opinion of the American scholar, Timothy Tennent, Brahmabandhav Upadhyay's "most important legacy is his attempt to enter into a positive dialogue with the *advaitic* philosophical

---

[70] Bal Krishna Sharma, "A History of the Pentecostal Movement in Nepal," *Asian Journal of Pentecostal Studies* 4,2, July 2001, pp.295-305.

[71] William A. Smalley, *Translation As Mission*, Macon, Georgia, Mercer University Press, 1991, p.154.

[72] S. Mark Heim, *The Depth of the Riches: A Trinitarian Theology of Religious Ends*, Grand Rapids & Cambridge, Eerdmans, 2001, p.137.

[73] *Ibid.*

[74] *Ibid.*

system."[75] It was Upadhyay's aim to utilize certain aspects of Vedic Theism as a platform to bring Hindus to the Christian (Catholic) faith.[76]

As Tennent states, "any imported theology ultimately proves insufficient since every culture asks the ultimate questions in its own way."[77] It follows that Christians in every culture have a right to do their own theologizing from within their own cultural setting. That in fact is what happened in the New Testament period as the gospel moved from Jerusalem into the larger Graeco-Roman world. That still continues to happen with every fresh incarnation of the Faith. "New concepts, new language, new categories and new metaphors are employed to articulate the Christian gospel."[78]

Upadhyay identified himself as a Hindu Christian: a Hindu by culture, a Christian by faith.[79] He was a 19th century theological pioneer. It is unfortunate that "the church of Upadhyay's day was unwilling to shed its foreign image and become rooted in Indian soil."[80] As a theologian, Upadhyay sought a synthesis of Vedic *advaita* with the theological system of Thomas Aquinas, two seemingly contradictory streams of thought.[81] "The result was a re-statement of the Christian faith using the language and thought forms of *advaitism*, while seeking to remain faithful to the teachings of Aquinas."[82] Upadhyay is an early example of indigenous theologizing, an essential requirement of an indigenous Church.

Mark Heim observes that a missionary's first task "is to become a converted member of the new culture, even of its religious heritage in so far as that is consistent with Christ."[83] That is one aspect. "The complementary side of the call for Christian mission is the search for the realization of the fullness of Christ. This view values the existence of Christian communities in varied cultures for the greater light that breaks forth on God's word and work from each new translation."[84]

In light of the present reality of the global presence of Christianity in its varied cultures, an exciting task awaits today to assimilate and unify "the fruit of these many transpositions of Christianity that exist within the Christian family."[85] The theological implications of indigenous Christianity are stupendous in their potential in the pluriform contexts of South Asia. "The fullness of Christ awaits unveiling," states theologian Mark Heim.[86] Our understanding of the incarnation remains incomplete until that takes place.

APPENDIX:

Bibliography of Select African sources

Tokunboh Adeyemo, "The African Church and Selfhood, " *Evangelical Review of Theology* 5,2, October 1981:212-223;

Allan Anderson, "Pentecostal Pneumatology and African Power Concepts: Continuity or

---

[75] Timothy C. Tennent, *Building Christianity on Indian Foundations: The Legacy of Brahmabandhav Upadhyay.* Delhi: ISPCK, 2000, p.367.

[76] Julius Lipner in his introduction to Upadhyay's life and thought in *The Writings of Brahmabandhab Upadhyay* Vol.I, edited by Julius Lipner and George Gispert-Sauch, Bangalore, United Theological College, 1991, p.xxxvii.

[77] Tennent, *Building Christianity on Indian Foundations*, p.2.

[78] *Ibid.*, p.3.

[79] *Ibid.*, p.10.

[80] *Ibid.*, p.13.

[81] *Ibid.*, p.146

[82] *Ibid.*, p.299.

[83] Heim, *The Depth of the Riches*, p.138.

[84] *Ibid.*

[85] *Ibid.*

[86] *Ibid.*, p.140.

Change?" *Missionalia* 19,1, April 1991:65-74;

Allan Anderson, "African Pentecostalism and the Ancestor Cult: Confrontation or Compromise?" *Missionalia* 21,1, April 1993:26-39;

Allan Anderson, "Challenges and Prospects for Research into AICs in Southern Africa," *Missionalia* 23,3, November 1995:283-294;

Allan Anderson, "The Hermeneutical Processes of Pentecostal-type African Initiated Churches in South Africa," *Missionalia* 24,2, August 1996:171-185;

Allan H. Anderson, "Frederick Modise and the International Pentecost Church: A Modern African Messianic Movement?" *Missionalia* 20,3, November 1992:186-200;

Allan Anderson, "The Mission Initiatives of African Pentecostals in Continental Perspective," *Missionalia* 28:2/3, August/November 2000:83-98;

Allan H. Anderson, "Types and Butterflies: African Initiated Churches and European Typologies," *International Bulletin of Missionary Research* 25, 3 (July 2001) 107-113;

Kwabena Asamoah-Gyadu,"'Fireballs in our Midst': West Africa's Burgeoning Charismatic Churches and the Pastoral Role of Women," *Mission Studies* 29,XV-1, 1998:15-31;

Daryl M.Balia, "Ethiopianism in South Africa: Roots of Black Theology," *Missionalia* 25,4, December 1997:585-597;

Hans-Jürgen Becken,"Beware of the Ancestor Cult! A Challenge to Missiological Research in South Africa," *Missionalia* 21,3, November 1993:333-339;

Hans-Jürgen Becken, "Sounds of the Double-Headed Drums," *Mission Studies* 24,XII-2, 1995:228-246;

Kwame Bediako, "The Roots of African Theology,"*International Bulletin of Missionary Research* 13,2, April 1989:58-65;

M.L.Daneel, "The Liberation of Creation: African Traditional Religious and Independent Church Perspectives." *Missionalia* 19,2, August 1991:99-121;

M.L. Daneel,"African Independent Churches Face the Challenge of Environmental Ethics," *Missionalia* 21,3, November 1993:311-332;

M.L.Daneel,"AIC Women as Bearers of the Gospel Good News," *Missionalia* 28:2/3, August/November 2000:312-327;

Lilian Dube-Chirairo, "Mission and Deliverance in the Zvikomborero Apostolic Faith Church," *Missionalia* 28:2/3, August/November 2000:294-311;

Stephen Hayes, "The African Independent Churches: Judgement through Terminology?" *Missionalia* 20,2, August 1992:139-146;

Ulrich van der Heyden,"The Origins and Political-Religious Functions of an Independent Church: The Lutheran Ba-Pedi Church in the 19th Century," *Missionalia* 27,3, November 1999:377-389;

Klaus Hock, "'Jesus Power — Super-Power!' On the Interface between Christian Fundamentalism and New Religious Movements in Africa," *Mission Studies* 23,XII-1, 1995:56-70; E.Ikenga-Metuh,"The Revival of African Christian Spirituality: The Experience of African Independent Churches," *Mission Studies* 14,Vii-2, 1990:151-171;

Jerisdan H. Jehu-Appiah, "The African Indigenous Churches and the Quest for an Appropriate Theology for the New Millennium," *International Review of Mission* LXXXIX, 354, July 2000:410-420;

Ogbu U.Kalu, "Estranged Bedfellows? The Demonisation of the Aladura in African Pentecostal Rhetoric," *Missionalia* 28:2/3, August/November 2000:121-142;

Byang H. Kato, "Christianity as an African Religion," *Evangelical Review of Theology* 4,1, April 1980:31-39;

Obed Ndeya Keolotswe,"Corporate Personality in the African Independent Churches in Southern Africa, with special reference to the 'Head Mountain of God Apostolic Church' in Botswana," *Missionarlia* 27,3, November 1999:299-312;

Dominique Kounkou,"A Missionary Challenge: African-Rite Christian Churches," *International Review of Mission* LXXXIX, 354, July 2000:459-466;

Robert Kipkemoi Lang'at, "The Doctrine of Holiness and Missions: A Pietistic Foundation of African Evangelical Christianity," *Evangelical Review of Theology* 25,4. October 2001:350-361;

Tobias Masuku, "African Initiated Churches: Christian Partners or Antagonists? Reflecting on the Unisa Dictionary Project with AICs," *Missionalia* 24,3, November 1996:441-455;

Tobias Masuku,"Listening to the Forgotten Voice: Some Views of African Independent Church Leaders on Theological Education," *Missionalia* 26,3, November 1998:392-411;

John Mbiti,"Dreams as a Point of Theological Dialogue Between Christianity and African Religion,"*Missionalia* 25,4, December 1997:511-522;

John S. Mbiti,"Christianity and African Culture." *Evangelical Review of Theology* 3,2, October 1979:183-197;

Joan Millard,"The New Jerusalem that was not Zion: Swedenborg and Africa," *Missionalia* 24,2, August 1996:225-232;

Matthews A. Ojo, "The Charismatic Movement in Nigeria Today." *International Bulletin of Missionary Research* 19,3, July 1995:114-118.

Matthews A. Ojo, "The Dynamics of Indigenous Charismatic Missionary Enterprises in West Africa." *Missionalia* 25,4, December 1997:537-561.

G.C. Oosthuizen, "Indigenous Christianity and the Future of the Church in South Africa." *International Bulletin of Missionary Research* 21,1, January 1997:8-12.

George C. Oosthuizen, "Southern African Independent Churches Respond to Demonic Powers." *Evangelical Review of Theology* 16,4, Octobert 1992:414-434.

C.O. Oshun, "Sprits and Healing in a Depressed Economy: The Case of Nigeria." *Mission Studies* 29,XV-1, 1998:32-52.

C.O. Oshun, "Healing Practices Among Aladura Pentecostals: An Intercultural Study." *Missionalia* 28:2/3, August/November 2000:242-252.

Christopher O. Oshun, "Joyfulness: A Feature of Worship Among African Independent Churches (AICs)." *Mission Studies* 18,IX-2, 1992:182-203.

Rufus Ositelu, "Missio Africana! The Role of an African Instituted Church in the Mission Debate." *International Review of Mission* LXXXIX , 354, July 2000:384-386.

Isabel Apawo Phiri, "African Women in Mission: Two Case Studies from Malawi." *Missionalia* 28:2/3, August/November 2000:267-293.

Gerald J. Pillay. "Pentecostalism within a South African Community: The Question of Social Change." *Mission Studies* 8,IV-2, 1987:39-51.

John S. Pobee, "Oral Theology and Christian Oral Tradition: Challenge to our Traditional Archival Concept." *Mission Studies* 11, VI-1, 1989:87-93.

Dr. Hennie Pretorius, "Zion: Profile and Self-Perception." *Missionalia* 28,2/3, August/November 2000:99-120.

Lamin Sanneh, "A Resurgent Church in a Troubled Continent: Review Essay of Bengt Sundkler's History of the Church in Africa." *International Bulletin of Missionary Research* 25,3, July 2001:113-118.

Ngoni Sengwe, "Identity Crisis in the African Church." *Evangelical Review of Theology* 7,2, October 1983:234-242.

David A. Shank, "The Legacy of William Wadé Harris." *International Bulletin of Missionary Research* 10,4, October 1986:170-176.

T. Jack. Thompson, "Xhosa Missionaries to Malawi: Black Europeans or African Christians?" *International_Bulletin of Missionary Research* 24,4, October 2000:168-170.

Tite Tienou, "Indigenous African Christian Theologies: The Uphill Road." *International Bulletin of Missionary Research* 14,2, April 1990:73-77.

Dawid Venter, "Globalisation and the Emergence of African Initiated Churches." *Missionalia* 26,3, November 1998:412-438.

Andrew F. Walls, "The Anabaptists of Africa? The Challenge of the African Independent Churches." *Occasional Bulletin of Missionary Research* 3,2, April 1979:48-51.

Andrew F. Walls, "The Challenge of African Independent Churches." *Evangelical Review of Theology* 4,2, October 1980:225-234.

G. Francois Wessels, "Charismatic Christian Congregations and Social Justice — A South African Perspective." *Missionalia* 25,3, November 1997:360-374.

CHAPTER 27

Christianity as Social Transformation in North East India

O.L. SNAITANG

Introduction

Tribal missiology is a study of changes in hill tribal societies; and about prospective areas of reflection for further research. The objective of this essay is to introduce the subject to those who would like to investigate more about the role of Christian missions and churches in social transformation among the people in a hill tribal region in the 19th and 20th centuries and some concerns for a viable tribal missiology.

Historical Background of the Hill People in the Pre-modern Era

Backwardness, neglect, isolation and alienation are different words but carry meanings in common. They all refer to the plight of India's Northeast.[1] Governments' continued apathetic attitudes to the region have in most instances become evident in underdevelopment, especially in transport and communication, science and technology, industry and closer contact with the rest of the country and the outside world alike. The apathy is also seen in areas of academic studies. Northeast India is still a less known subject not only in the larger academic educational curricula of the country but even in the context of theological studies.[2]

Northeast India is used here to mean the seven sister states of Assam, Nagaland, Manipur, Tripura, Meghalaya, Mizoram and Arunachal Pradesh. The region is bounded by China in the North, Myanmar in the east, part of Bangladesh in the south and West Bengal, Bangladesh and part of Bhutan in the west. Most of the people who inhabit the region are of Indo - mongoloid origins and had never been subjected to any outside political rule until the British conquest in the early part of the nineteenth century. Given the complexity of the traditions of the people in the region, this section is written on the assumption that traditional tribal culture was not a strong factor for people's unity.

The rooster shaped map of Northeast India gives an impression of a close knit geographical identity. The natural condition of the land however, does not foster a common identity among the people of the region. The unexplored

---

[1] For more information about the presence of Christianity in the region see C. Becker, *History of the Catholic Missions in North East India 1890-1915*, trans. and ed. by G. Standler and S. Karotemprel, 1923/1980; F. S. Downs, *Christianity in North East India : Historical Perspectives*, 1983;S. Karotemprel, *Albizuri Among the Lyngams: A Brief History of the Catholic Mission Among the Lyngams of North East India*, 1985; J. H. Morris, *The History of the Welsh Calvinistic Methodists Foreign Mission*, 1910; C. L. Hminga, *The Life and Witness of the Churches in Mizoram*, 1987; J. Meirion Lloyd, *History of the Church in Mizoram: Harvest in the Hills*, 1991; M. Muttumana, *Christianity in Assam and Inter-faith Dialogue*, 1984; M. M. Clark, *A Corner in India*, 1907; M. S. Sangma, *History of American Baptist Mission in North East India*, 1992; K. I. Aier, *The Growth of Baptist Churches in Meghalaya*, 1978; R. R. Lolly, *The Baptist Church in Manipur*, 1985; J. Puthenpurackal, *Baptist Missions in Nagaland*, 1984; R. Pamei, *The Zeliangrong Nagas: A Study of Tribal Christianity*, 1996; L. Jeyaseelan, *Impact of Missionary Movement in Manipur*,1996; O. L. Snaitang, *Christianity and Social Change in North East India*, 1993, and many others.

[2] See relevant articles in J. Puthenpurackal, *Impact of Christianity on North East India*, 1996.

virgin land was then covered with dense forests, vegetation, fruit trees and thick grass, making communication among people extremely difficult. The hilly terrain with rivers, rivulets and waterfalls in the hill areas and even in the plains, added beauty to the entire region, but had impeded contact and inter-action of people from different areas. Closer contact was further handicapped by the presence of ferocious animals like elephants, one horned rhinos, tigers, wild buffaloes, bears, snakes of various kinds, vultures and malaria infected mosquitoes. Besides that, the fear of demonic powers or evil spirits in the jungles, which was common among the tribes in the ancient past, did not facilitate the development of close and confident relationships while these factors have successfully prevented outside infiltration and interference in the internal affairs of the people, they have eventually contributed towards confining people to a single village or area within a limited geographical enclosure, thereby creating a self - contained identity in isolation.

A well structured political system - a system which might be compared to the present advanced parliamentary democracy, which functioned in traditional hill tribal societies, was also another significant factor which weakened the unity of the tribes, because it did not include the entire ethnic community but helped in perpetuating sub - ethnic separation. Its exclusiveness, independent character and at times imperialistic aggressiveness have unfortunately shut down any move for united action and partnership or for creating a spirit of togetherness.

The absence of any common intelligible language and a written culture among all the hill tribes had further intensified the people's cultural fragmentation. Many dialects were spoken in each tribe, some of which were not understandable in a community. This dimension reinforced tribal disunity and fostered innumerable sub - ethnic identities even among the same group of people. The self - enclosed dialectical situation was again aggravated by the subsequent disappearance of a written alphabet. In the ancient times, all good memories of the distant past, stories and songs, were simply passed on orally from one generation to another and in the process they had the effect of forming oral prose literature. However, most of the tribes could not recollect their poetic literature in full form except a repetitive humming of a two-line bhajan - like poems. In short, the hill people's life in the pre - Christian period was marked by the absence of a written alphabet, a written literature and a common intelligible spoken language.

What was true in the context of the traditional political structure, language or literature, was also true in the area of people's religious life and practices. That is, the traditional religious component could not bind the people together. God, in the primal faith, was not a God of the entire community. Some communities, like the Khasis of Meghalaya, claimed to have believed in the existence of one God. While there might have been some element of truth in their continued belief system, nevertheless, by the time the British Government and Christian Missions entered the areas in the first half of the nineteenth century, it was in many cases practically not a reality. A deity was usually identified with a particular clan or at the most, a single petty state. Each clan maintained its own secluded ground for keeping the cremated remains of deceased members. The family triadic gods - *U Thawlang* (a god from the side of the father), *Ka Iawbei* (a mother goddess) and *U Saidnia* (a maternal uncle god) were normally worshipped exclusively by members of a particular family and not by the whole community or by other members of the same clan, who somewhere in their history become dispersed and settled elsewhere in the region.

Superstitious belief in the existence of natural demons or spirits had enslaved the people and made them fearful, timid and insecure. It provided an occasion for the development of a wide range of rituals. Diseases like cholera, smallpox, malaria and other major ailments were mostly identified with a number of natural spirits and the causes for their rise attributed to human displeasure of the respective personified demons. The process of the healing technique was traditionally done therefore, through sacrifices, divination and other primal procedures. Unnatural death in any accident was viewed seriously as a deadly taboo. There was hardly any Good Samaritan spirit of service to those who were affected by unexpected injuries or death. In other words, tribal traditional religion did not sanction any inter-personal health care for the ill-fated victims but ensured ways for individuals to keep on the safe side.

Lack of proper hygiene in pre-modern society was also another significant feature which might be of some significance in the study of change in tribal traditional societies. Dwellings were constructed in a simple manner. They were small in size with neither partition of rooms nor construction of ventilation channels. In most cases, the surroundings did not have a proper drainage system. All sorts of domesticated animals could be found (in and) around the houses.

Another prominent feature of the pre-modern tribal history was the role of the barter economy. People used to exchange their goods or agricultural products in the markets to meet their simple needs. Human wants were very limited and the economic law of increasing utility appeared to have remained virtually outside their basic agenda because in the absence of any sophisticated life style in a community, people were generally endowed with a spirit of satisfaction.

Though the hill people had weak cultural milieu because of fragmentation in language, political organization or religion, nevertheless such development in their history is indicative of their long history of existence in the region. While there was no written record of how long they had been living in the region, the fact that they had been able to choose their own system of administration, mode of communication, religious beliefs and practices and had not scattered beyond their geographical boundary, were ample evidence of their long existence.

Another significant feature which gives pre-eminence to their strength is that cultural fragmentation is a sign of people's maturity in thinking, decision making, ruling and defending their own jurisdictional integrity and identity.

British Administration and Christian Missions

It was among these isolated tribes that western Christian Missions came for the purpose of evangelization. As we shall observe in the subsequent sections, their contribution in shaping the destiny of the hill people has been so significant. However, one may not fully understand the positive influence of Christianity unless a similar in-depth study is made of the cultural consequences following the imposition of the new administration in the early nineteenth century. Such argument is, however, by no means a suggestion that Christian Missions started their missionary work at the behest of the colonial powers, except the Serampore Baptist Mission that worked among the Khasis for a short period of time from 1813 to 1838.[3]

---

[3] Cf. F. S. Downs, The Mighty Works of God: A Brief History of the Council of Baptist Churches in North East India, 1971.

British Administration [4]

The impact of the British colonial presence among the hill people was remarkable. It shattered the age-old sub-ethnic cultural defenses and shook the deeply embedded primal self-contained identities. The British invaded the region and after subduing tribal chiefs, who had put up stiff resistance, annexed their territories, including the plains of Brahmaputra, Barak Valley and the plains areas of what is today, the Sylhet district of Bangladesh and placed them under a single administrative authority. Along with the administration came the army, engineers, clerks and a set of administrative establishments.

The introduction of a military power with guns, ammunitions and other military offensive equipment had far reaching effects on the tribes who depended on the use of bows, arrows and spears. The presence of the British military cantonment in the region was enough to shake the tribal world. For the first time in their history, these tribes were subjected to an alien administration. In the process, the British authority ushered in a new set up through the imposition of a written language, money economy, weights and measures, calendar year, food distribution system and a variety of food items, modern architectural buildings, clothing materials, dresses of various fashions, books and magazines, and a vast communication network. These new components had considerable impact on the primal people. Their main problem then was the adjustment to life under the British administration and of successfully functioning along with it. Once the traditional cultural components of the people with their territorial integrity and freedom were under siege the entire tribal milieu began to crumble.

Christian Missions

Christian missions entered the hill areas of the region at a time when the people were incapacitated culturally after the ushering in of the alien administration. The development did not take place in a planned manner. It was never conceived by any of the British officials, at least in the case of the Welsh Calvinistic Methodists Mission. While some writers like Nalini Natarajan would look at this phenomenon as a mere accident, others like J. H. Morris who conceived it theologically preferred to attribute it to divine providence.

The Serampore Baptist Mission was the first Protestant Mission which started missionary work among the Khasis in the year 1813 under Krishna Chandra Pal. But as a consequence of the demise of the last Serampore trio, Joshua Marshmann, in 1837, he could no longer provide continued supervision and the mission had to close down all its missionary activities in the region in the following year, despite its phenomenal progress.

Before the Serampore Baptist Mission withdrew its missionary operations, the American Baptist Mission had just begun its work in Upper Assam, in the year 1836. Its work soon spread to Nagaland, Manipur, Garo hills, Arunachal Pradesh and other parts of the region. The British Baptist Mission which began its work in Mizoram much later than the American Baptists, saw success in the southern region of Mizoram and expanded to the neighbouring tribes as well.

The Welsh Calvinistic Methodists Foreign Mission which was organised immediately after their withdrawal from the Congregational dominated London Missionary Society, started its independent missionary work among the Khasis in 1841 and helped fill up the gap left by

---

[4] See H. K. Barpujari, et.al., eds., *Political History of Assam* 1826 - 1919 Vol. I, 1977; S. Chaube, *Hill Politics in North - East India*, 1973; N. K. Barooah, *David Scott in North East India 1802 - 1831: A Study in British Paternalism*, 1970; R. M. Lahiri, *The Annexation of Assam 1824 – 1854*, 1975.

the Serampore Baptist Mission. Its mission work soon made significant impact in the Sylhet plain areas, northern Mizoram, hill areas of Manipur, Cachar hill tribes and other tribes of Assam. Its numerical growth and geographically wide spread have even necessitated a change in name from the previous 'Presbyterian Church in North East India' (PCNEI) to the 'Presbyterian Church in India' (PCI).

The Catholic Mission was another Christian Mission that contributed immensely to the people in this part of the country. Though its presence in the region was observed much earlier than the nineteenth century, nevertheless, its permanent missionary enterprise began only in the year 1890. Other Mission agencies (e.g. Anglican, the Salvation Army, the Seventh Day Adventists, the Pentecostal Mission and a number of indigenous Churches) that initiated work in the region have participated well in the ongoing process toward the development of a new tribal culture with a renewed universal outlook, exposure and creativity.

A Mission That is Integration [5]

As already indicated above, western missionaries have come to this region in response to their avowed commitment to the experienced divine commission and in the interest of their respective Mission bodies. With the exception of the Serampore Mission, other missions made an autonomous decision to enter the Northeast, and were self-supporting. There is no evidence of their being sponsored by the colonial powers.[6]

A passing introduction to the background of the Protestant Missions is not entirely out of place. These missions were direct products of the Pietist movement revivalism and evangelical awakening in Europe and in the United States of America. It was spiritual ideas that oozed out of these movements that had brought about drastic changes in the traditional static Christian outlook in the West for a world-wide spread of the faith. Closely related to the spiritual factor and influence, the social ideas and visions of the French Revolution and even of the Industrial Revolution also shaped most Protestant missionaries.[7] Their mission objective was clear, i.e., to preach the Good news of God's salvation to the heathens. As most of the missionaries were trained educationally, they had gone out for ministries overseas not with any confused visions but with a sound understanding of the mission strategies and the dynamism of implementation alike. That vision was well expressed in the starting of schools and colleges, the introduction of alphabets and production of books, medical services and other humanitarian works. All these activities were introduced with the objective of evangelising the tribes. New to the situation, the missionaries were not aware of the people's cultural incapacitation following the sudden onslaught at the hands of the mighty British power almost a generation earlier. However, the kind of means that they introduced in the process of evangelization had tremendous social consequences and contributed to national integration.

Language and the Creation of a Literate Society

Missionaries were pioneers in the introduction of a common language among most of the tribal groups in the region and in the development of modern literature in prose and poetry.

---

[5] For further detailed information, read F. S. Downs, *Christianity in North East India*; Nalini Natarajan, *The Missionary Among the Khasis*, 1977.

[6] Read F. S. Downs, History of Christianity in India: North East India in the Nineteenth and Twentieth Centuries Vol. V, Part 5, 1992, pp. 29ff.

[7] See J. P. Alter, "Liberty, Equality, Fraternity: Themes in Anglo - Saxon Protestant Missions in the Church in North India, 1800 - 1914 *Indian Church History Review*, VIII. I, June 1974, pp. 21ff.

Most Christian missionaries were experts in literature although they might not have had any idea about any of the oriental languages, like Sanskrit. Nevertheless, they were sure that preaching the Gospel to the natives would be futile and meaningless unless the people among whom they were working, knew something about the simple art of reading and writing. Much to their surprise, of course, hill tribes of the Northeast were without a common intelligible language or a written script. The story of having had a single spoken language and a written alphabet once upon a time, was already lost and what was left were mere nostalgic memories of the ancient past glory.

Now, the first thing that the missionaries did was to learn the dialect spoken by the people at the Mission station and adopt it as a common standard language for the entire community. The decision to universalise a particular dialect for the whole group was determined, not on the basis of its being superior or sweet sounding or the best, but because it was the only dialect which the missionaries could easily learn in order to communicate with the people at the station. In the context of a fragmented tribal society due to the large number of mutually unintelligible dialects, the process of universalising one dialect for the tribe led to tremendous social transformation and contributed to the development of a solidified community.

The universalisation of a dialect for the whole tribe went along simultaneously with the introduction of a written script in the Latin alphabet. Again, the decision to introduce the Latin letters instead of the Bangla alphabet which had earlier been adopted by the Serampore missionaries, had no connection with British colonial policy. As a matter of fact, British officers were strongly in favour of the imposition of the Bangla alphabet for the tribes.[8] However, the missionaries knew the Latin script better and did not know anything about the Bangla alphabet or any of the well known alphabets in India. Gradually, they carried out the production of books, booklets, hymn books, translation of the Scriptures and other publications in the respective languages of the hill tribes. These publications set a firm foundation for the creation of indigenous literature and at the same time, had the effect of bringing the people to a common sense of identity. As of today, the literary activities have grown widely and range from the production of various writings, journals, publication agencies, with the introduction of typewriting works, printing presses and the modern technological computer network as well to bookshops to distribute this literature. Literature has, therefore, solidified the once fragmented tribe.

Impact of Education

The role of educational institutions, viz. schools and colleges, in the social transformation of hill tribal societies, has been well acknowledged by people at various levels. Christian missionaries introduced school education realizing that unless the local people knew the basic art of reading and writing, the proclamation of the Gospel would not produce effective results. It was, hence, looked upon as one of the best means of evangelisation. A wide network of primary schools as initially started in many places in the hill region and some of the promising converts who completed the preliminary training were commissioned to work as resident primary teachers in different villages and as evangelists as well. The same school building was, in many cases, used for occasional evangelistic meetings, church services and for Sunday Schools. Christianity and education went side by side in the region and so many would tend accept both without any clear-cut distinction.

---

[8]Cf. *Proceedings of the Lieutenant Governor of Bengal, Education Department,* October 1863. Pro. No. 17 - 19.

Education has enabled the isolated hill people to know more about others and about themselves too. While the missionaries have given much importance to the study of the Holy Bible and Christian doctrines in school education, they have not ignored other academic subjects in the school curricula, like simple Arithmetic, English, History, and even some basic knowledge about elementary science. These attempts have been a blessing to the people, enabling them to go along with the new set up imposed from outside in addition to being instrumental for the creation of a literate community. All these subjects were no doubt important for the converts and members of the community at large, most of all, Arithmetic. It was imposed at a time when the tribal people were looking for some help and guidance in order to be able to function meaningfully in a changed environment.

The establishment of educational institutions and boarding houses also helped in filling up the gap left by the displacement of the traditional Morung institutions and other community-based group fellowships. They were also practical centres for inter-tribal relationships, contacts with other tribal groups and non-tribal communities as well. Missionaries took special interest in women's education and in the introduction of technical training schools for subsequent self-employment.

Impact of Medical Mission

Christian Missions were pioneers in providing medical services to the people. The medical mission first began in a humble way but in due course its was upgraded to the level of well established hospitals, and rendering services to people irrespective of class, caste and religious persuasions. The response to a venture of this kind of enterprise in the mission field has not been encouraging, at least in its initial stage, because of the people's firm belief in the role of evil spirits in the appearance of all sorts of human ailments and suffering. However, once they saw

that it was effective than their traditional healing techniques though sacrifices and herbal medicines, they began to go for the new healing methods. In this way, the medical mission had a significant influence upon the traditional worldview, and superstitions and added a new dimension to their rationality. It contributed to developing a changed attitude towards other human beings, even to those from the same ethnic group that would not have happened otherwise.

Cultural Consequences Following the Introduction of Faith and church Organisation

The traditional religious belief system was static and exclusive. Christian missionaries who expressed mild statements on most of the primal cultural elements were, however, not tolerant of the religious component. It was rejected outright. Rejecting the primal faith that did not foster tribal unity, Christian missions introduced an alternative (faith) that created a solidified society and an inclusive culture. The proclamation of the Biblical God ensured a fresh meaningful life and gave a new direction to a common goal.

The role played by the Word of God was also obvious. Its publication in the different tribal languages had been warmly received by the tribes as it unexpectedly replaced the chasm that had thus far been left unfilled and unfulfilled too. It transformed the people who were once plagued by a head cutting culture, intra-tribal feuds and, belief in the existence of evil spirits. It also brought renewal to the traditional people's life style and served as a guide book, a source material for divine knowledge, a treasury of hope and an authority on spiritual matters for the people.

The understanding of the church as a community of persons has transcended traditional clan - based institutions. Its catholicity is well expressed in its being inclusive of believers from all sub-ethnic or ethnic groups, men, women, children and people from all walks of life. Although the basic objective of developing a church was for religious services, yet the way in which it functioned in tribal societies was far beyond religious interests. The creation of a church went hand in hand with the imposition of church organisations. These new ecclesiastical structures were instrumental in breaking down primal institutional barriers and helped promote human fellowship. They were avenues in which members could come together for worship, discussion and participation in making resolutions in the interest of their respective Christian communities.

The salvific love of God that has saved people from tribal demons, has fostered human relationships and has also endowed people with a sense of mission, especially in areas in which Christianity is yet to get its foothold. It is this divine love which has transformed the ferocious tribes from head hunting to a new life of soul or heart hunting. As of today, Protestant Churches in Mizoram, Nagaland, Manipur and even Meghalaya, which are under the supervision of local leaders, are missionary minded not only among their own ethnic groups and in India, but also outside the country among different groups of people.

The Negative Impact of Christianity

However, there are other areas in which Christianity has not brought about healthy development. Most prominent has been the transplanting the western pattern of ecclesiastical differences. Before the end of the 19th century, Northeast India witnessed the intrusion of the Serampore Baptist, American Baptist and British Baptist traditions; the Welsh Calvinistic Methodists (later known as the Presbyterians), the Anglican tradition and the Catholic Mission. Whereas most of these missions worked among people in different areas, nevertheless the subsequent impact on the minds of the people

was so intense that it precipitated ecclesiastical animosity in due course.

While the development of Christian missions in most areas of the region produced a certain amount of mutual understanding, despite their differences, in Manipur there was unreconciled ecclesiastical conflict from the beginning of its operation.[9] Missions were subsequently productive in the fragmented tribal segment of the society. That is why indigenous churches in Manipur tended to be identified along with ethnic groups of people.[10] The church, therefore, has come to the region not in its fullness but in the form of denominations which gradually represent another form of tribalism.

The second major negative impact was the result of the missionary rejection of traditional religious component. Protestant Christian missions adopted a negative attitude towards the primal religion. The rejection was however, accompanied by the substitution of Christian elements, including the gift of the Holy Scriptures. Missionaries, in Nagaland, Manipur, Mizoram and Assam, have not totally set aside significant religious practices. The converts still retain and practice social dancing rituals in the Christian community; however the missionaries in Khasi Jaintia hills were so strict and rigid that they rejected completely even the socio-religious dances and sports. As a result, most Protestant Christians in Khasi-Jaintia hills no longer know how to perform them meaningfully.

Thirdly, the role of indigenous leadership has not been encouraging. In the first half of the twentieth century, Western Missions celebrated their centennial jubilees; missionaries, who had successfully prepared local leadership, had handed most administrative and pastoral responsibilities over to the native Christians — except in areas like the medical mission and

---

[9] Cf. Jeyaseelan, Impact of Missionary Movement, pp. 81-99.

[10] See a description on the rise of indigenous churches in Manipur in O. L. Snaitang, ed., *Churches of Indigenous Origins in Northeast India*, 2000, pp. 183-186.

theological education where local leaders were not readily available.

The new incumbents continued the activities in the areas which had already been set up by the missionaries and do not seem to have embarked on new projects. Although the post-missionary activity appears to have gained significant momentum, the basic misisonary thrust tended to gradually die down atleast among the major Protestant indigenized churches in Meghalaya. Instead, one witnessed their active involvement in fantastic open-air evangelistic meetings, crusades and healing services-activities which have already been introduced by churches of indigenous origins.

Another negative phenomenon in post-missionary Christianity was the resurgence of the tribal worldview in the context of the Christian community. The age-old tribal fragmented identities that had been smoothed over by the introduction of the new administration and Christianity began to resurface in the Christian church. Ecclesiastical structure had been one of the major solidifying means for the creation of a distinctive unified tribal identity. The splits in the post-missionary era were rather unfortunate and were an indication of subsequent breaking down in the community, for instance, the Bhois among the Khasis of Meghalaya, and the Lais in Mizoram, the Thadou Kukis among the Kukis of Manipur and many others.

Tribal Missiology in the Twenty First Century

Given the backdrop of the integrative role of Christianity among the isolated and culturally fragmented hill people and the myopic efforts of the post - missionary leadership, it is ironic to pass over the importance of social integrity in the study of a tribal missiology in the twenty-first century.

A renowned Greek philosopher, Socrates, once said "know thyself." Tribal missiology is a new subject. Its beginnings were in the life, struggles and history of the people. The movement grew out of the experience of the pain of being isolated, alienated and displaced, in the shadow of marginalisation, discrimination and ill-treatment, and also out of a struggle for a liberated life from various forms of vicious oppressive circles and a forward movement with hope and solidarity.

Northeast India's people should know themselves first. Most of us who have had a certain degree of knowledge tend to appreciate anything that comes from the West, think like the Europeans or Americans but act like those of the ancient past. Tribal missiology provides avenue for self - assessment of who the people were, for consciousness of where they have been, for a constructive awareness of why they are here today and where they should go from now!

Like the other marginalized peoples in mainline India, hill tribals share with them similar pains and sorrows for the fact that they have been left at a level of inhumanity for a long period of time and placed on the platform of under-development and continued backwardness. Western missionaries have helped a lot in liberating the people from the shackles of isolation and alienation, uplifting tribal social conditions and in developing a sense of unity in the community. But that is not the end of the movement. It is now the tribals who should understand themselves through an in-depth study, and dialogue, through well planned strategies and rational implementation. They should also see, understand and work from the perspective of unity.

Christianity in tribal areas, shaped by the missionaries, underscores not only social transformation but produces cultural synthesis as well. In this connection, knowing oneself is by no means an attempt at promoting communal rift in the solidified community or bolstering ecclesiastical administrative divisions on dialectical or linguistic patterns. The basic contents of the new faith have contributed to the process of building up the tribes to a common sense of ethnicity. In other words, the introduction of the redeeming and unifying love of God in Christ has transcended all petty claims of isolated identities in hill tribal societies and this faith offers a glimmer of hope in the fluid tribal scenario.

Missiology is a dynamic subject based on the model of Christ's principle of common life. Christ is for all people of the world. His concern is not exclusively for one group of people or clan but for the whole world. Therefore, Christianity which has been inclusive and excentric, should play a pivotal role in removing exclusivism, sectarianism, fanaticism and fundamentalism which have wreaked havoc in today's world and threatened to rip apart the basic tenets of the democratic-secular values of our country. Besides that, the basic theology of agape love which has the transformed tribal head-hunting life to soul redeeming mission is, in fact, an unexpected miracle. Christianity which has stamped out ill-feelings and communal enmity should have now served as a harbinger for conflict resolution, reconciliation, peace and for promoting communal harmony.

Keeping its broad-based outlook, tribal missiology espouses holistic ideas of mission. We have seen how Western missionaries have initiated not just prayer and singing but various means of shaping the destiny of the tribal people. Although their primary objective was for the evangelization of the tribes yet the impact that these activities had on the people were far beyond the religious objective. It touched upon every aspect of tribal culture and reinforced with dynamism cultural elements which enabled the people to function effectively in the changing modern set up.

In the Christian world the twentieth has been a century of ecumenism. Most Christian churches in India and elsewhere have begun to realize the importance of unity and have even joined together

to form one united church, like the Church of South India (1947), and the Church of North India (1970). But the development of this trend in Northeast India has been somewhat discouraging. Ecumenism in the region has become a model of missiological disunity because of a strong sense of denominational affiliation and tribalism. As we have indicated elsewhere, denominational Christianity was imposed by Western missionaries and had become ingrained in the thought patterns of the people. Even the broad-based ecumenical Christian Endeavour Union was introduced as a unit of a single denomination and continues to function so, even today. Denominationalism in ecumenical institutions is an indication of the ecumenical failure of tribal indigenized Christianity.

This dimension poses a serious challenge to churches in tribal areas and to missiological research, alike. The problem has been further compounded by lack of education, openness and interaction among leaders in different churches. One hardly witnessed the presence of a receptive spirit and equal respect in the process. A healthy ecumenical atmosphere may well be firmly established if the dominant churches and churches of little traditions are prepared to risk themselves for Christ's sake, to set aside all forms of denominational imperialism and ensure churches equal representation and involvement in all ecumenical institutions.

While the concern of tribal missiology for co-operative ecumenism is so intense and urgent, inter-religious dialogue requires similar, sufficient attention, as well. Northeast India is a home of almost all of the world's major religions. Multi-cultural communities are on the rise in major towns and cities.

Tribal missiological research should underscore the importance of dialogue with people of other faiths and looks at it with great seriousness. Any initiative of discussion, dialogue and research could well be a step forward for healthy development in inter-cultural relations, communal harmony and national integration.

Women enjoy a certain degree of liberty in the context of hill tribal societies. The matrilineal system of Meghalaya in particular ensured that women were privileged persons with respect to family lineage, inheritance of ancestral property, freedom of movement and occupation. However, the stigma of subordination and discrimination appears to have wreaked havoc in major decision making processes. Missionaries who have taken a pragmatic approach in their holistic mission among the hill people, have taken a special interest in the development of women through education and health care, but the predominantly patriarchal dominated church has still not shown positive preparation for promoting women leaders to the ordained ministry.

Time is now ripe for the removal of gender barriers in the church and society. Any imbalance in this aspect may well continue to endorse the shackles of the traditional system. However, given the presence of conflicting views against change in the society, it is highly important to make an in-depth study of this subject from a larger missiological perspective using the culturally integrative method. Any well established ancient tribal civilization requires proper shaping through education and exposure to the outside world so that any rapid change in the societal set up would come about proportionately with people's preparedness, thereby protecting them from the process of de-tribalisation.

Biodiversity should also be an inter-related subject of tribal missiology. Tribals are people of nature. Preservation, respect, and afforestation have characterized their relationship with nature. But the advent of modern agencies of change in the 19th and 20th centuries and the sudden rise of consumerism in the post-independence period have led to rampant destruction of the natural physical system and produced unhealthy development in the biodiversity order. Thus, this area of life which has so far not received serious attention, should stand equally uppermost in the tribal missiological agenda for the sustainability and very survival of humankind.

Conclusion

Tribal missiology is a complex and an inconclusive subject but it has been treated from a broad-based historical perspective seeing Christianity as social transformation in tribal societies. This chapter began with an objective examination of the pre-modern cultural setting of the people and assessed the changes brought about by British administration and Christianity. The introduction of various institutional means, like, novel features, alphabet, universalisation of one dialect for the entire ethnic group, literature, education and other means strengthened the once fragmented people with a common sense of unity. A study of tribal missiology should contribute further to that end and should by no means perpetuate tribal differences in the name of ecclesiastical administrative conveniences - a development which may rip the solidified community apart in the twenty-first century.

CHAPTER 28

Missiology for Twenty First Century Tribal India

NIRMAL MINZ

Tribal India has existed for thousand of years. The Aryan and Moghul colonials tried to ignore it. They rather looked down upon Tribal India and treated it as an unwanted region. The British colonial rulers treated Tribal India and its people as a special case needing a separate administrative treatment. The British government established the southwest frontier agency (SWFA) and northeast frontier agency (NEFA) as separate and special regions for the administrative of Tribal India.[1]

The nationalist leaders of free India took Tribal India quite seriously. While framing the Constitution of India, the constituent assembly provided a special section in the Constitution for the administration of Tribal India. The fifth schedule area under article 244 (1) and the sixth schedule areas of article 244 (2) have special provisions of administration different from the rest of the country. These schedule areas roughly cover the regions of Tribal India. This paper includes many more regions and areas besides the fifth and sixth schedule areas.[2]

Tribal India has undergone change due to constant contact with other peoples and cultures throughout history. A process of change has set in since the second half of the 19th and the whole of the 20th century in Tribal India. More radical changes are anticipated in its physical and socio-cultural life in the 21st century. Missiology for 21st century Tribal India will be discussed in this changing context.

Tribal India

For a better understanding of Tribal India and its problems and possibilities it is necessary to give a brief description of its geographical features and socio-cultural components.

Geographical Features of Tribal India

The backbone of Tribal India is made up of a wide strip of land from Bombay to Calcutta consisting of Vindyachal and Satpura and their ancilliary hills, mountains and river valleys; the Kaimur hills and valleys, extending to the Netarhat mountain ranges in Chotanagpur, and the Rajmahal hills in Santal Pragana. The famous Saranda jungle of Kolhan Singbhum in Jharkhand is found in this general region. Rivers like the Damodar and Barakar in the east, the Narmada and Tapti in the West, and the Mahanadi and Sone in the middle provide rich resources for waterpower generation. Forest resources – timber, leaves roots and fruits and plants with medicinal values are abundantly found in this region. Mineral resources – coal, iron, copper, gold, mica, manganese, boxite, uranium and others are abundantly found in this belt of Tribal India.

Moving towards the north from Bombay one finds the Arawali mountain range starting from

---

[1] British colonial government had a human consideraton in ruling India, particularly Tribal India. Therefore they isolated the tribals from the general rule of the country. But unfortunately they used the age-old exploiters as their agents in administering Tribal India, which had an adverse effect on the tribals.

[2] The schedule areas: 6th schedule area is in Assam, Meghalaya, Manipur, Mizoram and Tripura states within the Indian union. 5th schedule areas are found in the states of Andhra Pradesh, Bihar, Gujarat, Himachala Pradesh, Maharashtra, Orissa and Rajasthan. See Durgadas Basu, *Introduction to the Constitution of India*, New Delhi, 1999, pp. 279-281.

Gujarat extending up to Southern edge of Delhi. Beautiful sceneries with Mount Abu as the presiding peak in this region has provided the ancient homes of tribals in this region. Moving south one follows the western coast and on to Karnataka with Nilgiri mountain ranges and then on to both sides of the western Ghats in Tamil Nadu and Kerala. This region with luxurious vegetations has been the home of the tribals of south India. It has rich forest and water resources. The famous sandalwood forest of the Jawadi hills and the rich vegetations of Wynad district in Kerala are located in this region.

The Northeastern Tribal India is physically made up of the Garo, Khasi and Jaintiya hills of present Meghalaya, the hills and the valleys of Arunachal, Nagaland, Mizoram, Tripura, Manipur and part of Assam State. These mountain ranges are rich in mineral, forest and water resources.

And finally the hills and valleys of Himachal Pradesh and parts of the Jammu and eastern Kashmir valleys also are homes of tribal people. Tribals live in Lakshadweep and the Andaman and Nicobar Islands also.

Socio-cultural Components of Tribal India

Various authors show geographical distribution of tribal people.[3] The map attached herewith gives a fair idea of tribal population, but it cannot show the extent of tribal land. The distribution of tribal population is a background to discuss tribal movements.[4]

Tribal scholars and tribal organisations have identified seven major regions of concentration of tribal population in India.[5] These regions are as follows:[6]

- *North East Region:* The seven sisters, Assam, Arunachal, Nagaland, Meghalaya, Mizoram, Manipur and Tripura.

- *North:* Himachal Pradesh, Uttar Pradesh, Uttaranchal, North Bihar.

- *North Central Region:* This region is comprised of south Bihar, northern Orissa, eastern Orissa, Eastern Madhya Pradesh, and Western West Bengal.

- *Western Region:* This includes Maharashtra, Gujarat, western Madhya Pradesh and Rajasthan.

- *South Eastern Region:* southern Madhya Pradesh, Chatisgarh, eastern Maharasthra, northern Andhra Pradesh, and southern Orissa.

- South Region: *both sides of the western Ghats in Kerala and Tamilnadu, the Nilgiri area of Karnataka, and some parts of western Andhra Pradesh.*

- *Lakshadweep and the Andaman & Nicobar Islands.*

Tribals are the People among Peoples in India

Out of the total population of India the census record of 1981 mentions only 7.85 percent tribals in the country.[7] R.C. Verma lists seven major

---

[3] See R.C. Verma *Indian Tribes, Through the Ages*, New Delhi, Government of India, Director of Publication and Broadcasting, 1990, pp.13-18.

[4] K.S. Singh, ed. *Tribal Movements in India* Vol 1&2, inside cover page map, New Delhi, Manohar publications, 1982.

[5] N. Minz, R.D. Munda and other tribal scholars; Indian Confideration of Indigenous and Tribal People (ICITP) with its head quarter in New Delhi and their seven regional offices.

[6] Tribal communities mentioned in all seven regions of Tribal India are found in R.C. Verma, *Indian Tribes Through the Ages*, annexure II list of schedule tribes pp. 205-220. There are 476 tribal communities listed under the scheduled tribes list.

[7] *Ibid.*, p.13.

tribal communities in India with over 9 lakhs population.[8] (1) Bhils [52.32 lakhs], (2) Gonds [51.54 lakhs], (3) Santals [36.33], (4) Oraons [17.03 lakhs], (5) Minas [15.38], (6) Mundas [11.63 lakhs], and (7) Khonds [9.12 lakhs]. The census reports and records are not too reliable. The tribals claim that their population in India (Tribal India) will be not less than 9 to 10 Crores. The tribal communities in India belong to four language families. The Austric group Mundari family, the Dravidian family, Tibbato Burman (Monkhamer) family, and the Indo-Aryan family.

Basic Characteristics of Tribal Life

The kinship system is basic to tribal social organization. Marriage is endogamous to the Tribe and exogamous totem wise. Customary law is the principal governing rule of the tribe. Economically, most Tribals still practice hunting, gathering, fishing, jhum cultivation and small farming. Land and forest belong to God, and humans are stewards of nature, Earth is mother. Cultivation is carried on in cycles so that earth's fertility is preserved and rejuvenated.

The communitarian mode of Tribal life makes cooperation rather than competition essential for existence and survival. This comes out clearly in community ownership of land, cooperation in cultivation, and song and dance in the dancing ground.

Tribals practise primal religion. They worship and offer sacrifices to a supreme God, to minor spirits and the family deity. Evil spirits are pacified by offerings and sacrifices; favours are earned from good spirits. Ancestoral spirits form part of the corporate society of the tribal community. Each individual belongs to his or her ancestors and goes to join them after physical death. The ancestors are able to communicate with the living. Nature – humans – God/spirit are a continuum. They are separate yet belong together.

A Brief Historical Review of Tribal India

This review is not the history of Tribal India. It is to show how and to what extent Tribal India could withstand the onslaught of different political and cultural powers at different stages of history.

Early History: Tradition is the primary source of Tribal history. But this is not yet explored properly. Hindu religious literature is the second source, but this is too prejudiced to give a correct version of Tribal India. "In the great Sanskrit Epics of Valmiki and Vedvyasa the aborigines are denominated as monsters, monkeys and bears."[9] The Aryan invaders had no respect for Tribal India, though the latter had their own high civilization and culture. Mangobindo Banergee a historian of ancient India remarks, "the Rig Vedic people with pride of superior civilization have not a word of praise but have only hurdled various contemptuous expressions to denote the non-Aryan aborigines. They have ignored the contribution made by the primitive people to the stock of world culture."[10] Writing on the tribes of Chotanagpur the same author mentions, "The democratic aborigines the Mundas, the Oraons, the Hos, the Santals, the Bhumij have never known to recognize caste. Democracy is a marked feature of the pre-Aryan aboriginal Tribes and as such, caste hierarchy would presumably appear inconsistent with democracy."[11]

The Moghal Empire and Tribal India: The Moslem rulers were interested in wealth, pomp and glory in the plains of India. Tribal India

---

[8] *Ibid.*, p.19.

[9] S.C. Roy, *The Mundas and Their Country*, Ranchi, Catholic Press, reprint, 1995, pp.13-14.

[10] M. Banerjee, *An HistoricalOoutline of pre-British Chotanagpur (From earliest times to 1765)*, Ranchi Educational Publication, 1989, p.73.

[11] *Ibid*, p.80

seemed quite remote and inaccessible to them. "The slugged mountainous country of Chotanagpur had nothing to attract the Moslems, except beautiful natural scenery, until the land was known to contain diamonds."[12] This shows that Tribal India was not affected much even during the Moghul period of Indian history. It is only with the coming of the British Colonial Influence on Tribal India. The non-Tribal penetration of Tribal India began with the entry of petty kings. With these petty kings, small Zamindars, and courtiers entered Tribal India and began to grab land from Tribal families. Economic exploitation and social oppressions by non-Tribals had set in. Businessmen, money-lenders and various other groups also crept into Tribal India under the Aryan Kshatriya rulers. Agrarian problems had already begun and uneasiness was seen among tribals all over Tribal India.

In this socio-economic and political context in Tribal India, the British East India Company was given power to rule eastern India. "At this moment on the 12th August 1765, Shah Alam the Phantom emperor of Delhi, granted a 'Farman' conferring on the English East India Company the Dewani of Bengal, Bihar and Orissa which included Chotanagpur area".[13] With this Dewani the British trading company seized political power and ruled India for two hundred years.

The British government introduced roads and railways in the country. The railway line from Bombay to Calcutta went through the backbone of Tribal. Roads crisscrossed the country for administrative and military movement, and thus Tribal India was made accessible.[14]

Vernacular and English education was introduced throughout the country including Tribal India. The British system of education alienated the Tribals from the land and from their cultural ethos, as this education completely discarded the Tribal education system. The content of education was completely alien to Tribal India, but one had to go along with this system. In the meantime missionaries from America, England and Germany came to India and had begun their preaching, teaching and healing ministries in Tribal India.[15] The Government and Christian missions ran schools in Tribal India. Education made a big impact in tribal life; schools and boarding houses became the models for the upbringing of the children and youth. The youth dormitory and dancing ground [*Dhumkuria and Akhra*] were looked down upon as bad and outdated. This had its repercussions on the authority of the headman in the village, and thereby the village administration and social controls in Tribal India began to weaken. Socio-cultural values were affected. Trade, commerce and industries began to increase and expand in Tribal India. The first coal mine in tribal Bihar was started in 1885, and then an iron and steel industry was established in Jamshedpur by a Parsee, Jamshedjee Narawanji Tata, in Singhbhum District, in the heart of the central Tribal region. Coal mining and steel industries affected the tribals economically and socially. Tribal land was acquired with nominal compensation, and the people were displaced resulting in the socio-cultural disintegration of Tribal India. This was the beginning of major mining and mega iron and steel industries and power plants in Tribal India.

Labourers from Tribal India were recruited for the North Bengal and Assam tea gardens beginning from early 1920s. The railway reached Ranchi in 1907 and to Lohardaga in 1912. This

---

[12] *Ibid* p.201

[13] *An Historical Outline of pre-British Chotanagpur*, p. 248.

[14] S.C. Roy, *The Mundas and their Country*, Appendix IV, pp.liii,lvi.

[15] **Nirmal Minz**, *Rise up my people and claim the promise*, ISPCK, 1997, pp.16-24.

facilitated the resettlement of Tribal labourers from Chotanagpur, Orissa, and Chattisgarh to the tea gardens in Doors and Assam.[16]

The British colonial government was sympathetic to the tribal people in India. But they were rude in introducing their legal system in India. The introduction of individual ownership of land with a title, and law of inheritance, struck at the root of the Tribal land holding system and economic base. Introduction of a penal code and the judicial system shook the very foundation of tribal life in Tribal India. Land alienation began in a massive way. Forest laws took away the forest rights of the Tribal people in Tribal India. Worse, the anti-tribal people of the Aryan community were appointed as "grassroots" administrators in Tribal India. This led to tribal revolts against the local Aryan officials and the British government in general.[17]

The British colonial Government and the Christian missionaries joined hands in providing education, health and economic development programmes in Tribal India. Missionaries put tribal languages into written form, compiled grammars, and translated the Bible into Tribal languages. Education through the tribal mother tongue was carried on in the North Eastern tribal region. The German missionaries started the first printing press at Ranchi in Tribal India. The missionaries and the British Government tried to liberate the tribals of the central Tribal region by introducing land laws favourable to the Tribals and thus giving them self-confidence to fight against the injustices, exploitations and oppressions under which they had suffered for many centuries.[18]

Tribal India in Free India: India became independent on 15th of Aug.1947. Tribals had great hopes for a better future under free India. Reservations in admission for professional education, and in Government services and promotions, reserved constituencies for state Assembly and Lok Sabha seats, and special welfare measures and Development of Tribals are all enshrined, ensured, on principle.[19]But the policies and their implementations by the Government of India have hurt more than healed the age-old wounds inflicted upon the tribals.

Reorganizing states on linguistic lines took place in 1956 on the basis of Aryan and Dravidian languages. The tribal languages and cultural regions were not considered. Tribal India in this scheme was dissected into many pieces. The same tribe is divided between two, three or even four states. The Oraon tribe, for instance, was split between Bihar, Madhya Pradesh and Orissa. This is a great injustice. Consequently the freedom fighting of tribals within free India still continues till today.[20]

Education and Literacy: Education is a responsibility of the states. Except in the North East, education in the mother tongue is only in

---

[16] Sarkar, R.L., Christian Tea garden workers of tribal origin, ISPCK, Delhi, 1998, p.10.

[17] R.C.Verma, *Indian Tribes Through the Ages*, 1990. Tribal revolts/ annexure V, pp.225-28. & Singh, K.S., *Tribal Movements in India* Vol.2. Dr. Singh mentions altogether 25 Movements related to tribal in India.

[18] Roy, S.C., *The Munda's and their Country*, p.221

[19] R.C.Verma, *Indian Tribes Through the Ages*, 1990, p.125, constitutional safeguards: The protective provisions are contained in articles 15(4), 16(4), 19(5), 23, 29, 46, 164, 330, 334, 335,339(1), 371(A), (B), (C). Fifth schedule and sixth schedule articles 15(4), 16(4) and! 9(5) are exception to the fundamental rights of equality and freedom granted under part III of the constitution, provisions relating to developments of schedule tribes are contained mainly in article 275(1) first proviso and 339(2).

[20] K.S. Singh (ed), *Tribal Movements in India*, Vol. 1&2, Delhi, Manohar Publications, 1982.
See Vol.1. *Naga Movement*, p.39, *Mizo Political Movement*, p.129, *Khasi Solidarity Movement*, p.181, *The Bodo Movement*, p.253. Vol. 2. *Jharkhand Movement*, pp.1-86, *Gond Movement*, pp.161-186, *The Bhil Movement*, pp.263-272, *Tribal Autonomy Movement in Gujarat*, pp.243-260, *Tribal Mobilization and Political Awakening in Southern India*, pp.309-325.

lip service among the Tribal communities. North East India had been fortunate to have had foreign Christian missionaries who introduced education through the mother tongue in all the tribal languages in that region. There is no will to implement education through mother tongue in mainland Tribal India. The Bihar Government notified the introduction of primary education through tribal mother tongue in South Bihar in 1953, but it has never been implemented. Lack of primary education through the mother tongue among the Tribals of mainland India has handicapped them in making rapid progress in literacy and education in general.

Development: There is special constitutional provision for tribal development in India. Pandit Jawaharlal Nehru, the first Prime minister of free India, propounded the principle of *Panch Shila* for Tribal development in India.[21] But industries have been left out of the list. The Government of India has admitted the failure in implementing development programmes and schemes. To quote a Government report in this connection,

> In name of tribal developments we have spent a lot of money during the last several plans, but when accounting was made at the end of the last period of the safeguards to the tribals in the constitution, it was found that the actual benefits trickling down to the tribals have not been consistent with the promise we have made ....75% of the total benefits have not reached the tribals.... We cannot have development of this rate.[22]

Major Industrial Centers and Mega Power Projects: Major mining are found in Tribal India in Jharkand, Bihar and Madhya Pradesh. Major steel plants are located at the heart of Tribal India. National thermal power plants are found in the same region. Several river valley projects and dams to generate electricity and provide irrigation for the farmers are located in the mid-India Tribal belt.

India's Tribals favour economic development of the nation. These steel plants are the pride of our nation. But in establishing these plants, power stations and mega dams, Tribal India and tribal people were forgotten by the planners and implementing authorities in India. These mega steel plants and power stations have come up at the cost of the Tribals' land and socio-cultural life.

Massive tribal populations have been displaced by these mining and industrial projects of the nation. No proper compensation or rehabilitation were. Some have been disbanded and thrown into the streets as beggars. Former *maliks* (lords) of the land have been turned into unorganized labourers in brick kilns, agriculture workers, and construction coolies in North India. Development in the interest of the nation has been against the interests of the Tribal people. Government has acknowledged the adverse effects: "Again some of the big dam projects and hydel projects are not only affecting the forest ecology, the tribal population are not the beneficiaries of such development where the tribals live."[23] Urbanization is increasing in Tribal India very rapidly due to major mining operations and setting up of steel plants and power projects. The unprepared and uncared for tribals are becoming the backyard citizens in these centers of industries and commerce.

Assimilation Intentions of the Dominant Society: The written policy of the Government of India is to respect, promote and assist tribals in maintaining their languages and culture. But in practice an unofficial policy is working for the assimilation of tribals into the dominant caste society.

---

[21] S.S. Shasi, *Nehru and the Tribals*, New Delhi, Concept Publishing Company, 1990, p.18.

[22] *Ibid*. p.xxxiii (Introduction), quoted from Govt. Report – Approach to tribal Development in the sixth plan: A Preliminary perspective.

[23] *Ibid*. p.xxxii.

Hindutva and Religious Fundamentalism: Hindutva as an expressed ideology of the dominant society in India has endangered the very identity of Tribal India. Religious fundamentalism as perpetrated by the Vishwa Hindu Parishad, Bajrang Dal, and Rastriya Swayam Sevak organisations has adversely affected the tribal communities in India. Religious fanatics have been instigating traditional tribals to violence against their own people who are converts to Christianity.

Twenty First Century Tribal India

The editor of *Tribal Transformation in India* laments that policies of the Government and developmental programmes do not reach to the broad base of Tribal population who are the intended recipients.[24] Radical changes in Tribal life have not been all for the good or tribal society and culture. The onslaughts of modernity have vitiated age–old Tribal value systems. Haphazard development processes threaten their environment. The deepening crisis of identity has led to turmoil and unrest in the world of Tribal India.[25] Therefore the vision of 21st century Tribal India does not look so bright to a member of the Tribal community. The process of transformation is in fact a form of mutilation of tribal society. The assimilation policy wedded to urban–industrial development programmes will cause massive displacement leading to disintegration of tribal socio-cultural organizations and values.

Ashis Nandy, director of the Center for Development Studies, has observed that "one third of the country's 250 different tribes have been displaced. Some tribes are now entirely tribes of refugees and their deculturation and disintegration as communities are virtually complete."[26]

Tribal India in the Context of Globalization and Its Impact

Globalization is one major factor, which is going to make its impact in the world. India is already in the midst of economic liberalization and structural adjustments with world economic order. Amitabh Bachan, film star of the millennium has sensed the basic change of outlook in life at the turn of last century. He thinks that the evaluating principle of 21st century will be "material rather than ideal."[27]

Globalization is a world economic process. It will make a great impact on Tribal India. A major component of globalisation is the elimination of restrictions on the free movement across boarders of capital, goods, resources, technologies and services, but not of labour."[28] The multinational corporation, world banks, international monetary funds will be financing big industrial company and business houses in India. They have already begun to do so. The supreme ideology of the 21st century is going to be economics. "Whatever makes economic sense will be totally right; anything else will be totally unacceptable. In many ways this ideology already rules today. It is just that we are hesitant to openly recognize it."[29] In such a climate of thought and action, some reflective tribals are wondering about the future of tribal community.

---

[24] Budhadeb Chaudhury, ed, *Tribal Transformation in India*, Vol..I-V, New Delhi, Inter-India Publications, 1992, p.xii.

[25] *Ibid.* p. xiii.

[26] Ashis Nandy, "The Deracine," in Arthur C. Clarke, "Plus 2001 and Beyond," *The Telegraph Millenium Magazine*, January 2000, p.9.

[27] Amitabh Bachchan, "Idols of Decadence" in Arthur C.Clarke, "Plus 2001 and Beyond," *The Telegraph Millenium Magazine*, January 2000, pp.72-75.

[28] Helen Moussa and Patrick Talan, "Globalisation," *ECHOES, Justice, Peace and creation News*, Geneva, World Council of Churches, 12/1997, p.5.

[29] Imtiaz Ahmad, "Local colour," in Arthur C. Clarke, "Plus 2001 and Beyond," *The Telegraph Millenium Magazine*, January, 2000, p.19.

One concerned tribal asks, "what will be the condition of ancient traditions, social organizations and cultural heritage of tribals in Jharkhand region?"[30] The forest was the main economic resource of Tribal India for generations. But the nationalized forests of India are in the hand of multinational companies. World Bank forest projects will completely dislodge the age-old protectors of the forest – the Adivasis — from their right of possession of forest resources.[31] Globalization as a major economic process will massively move into Tribal India. Money not men, material and not human ideals, head but not heart are the new operative principles. Therefore, the very survival of Tribal people in the 21ˢᵗ century is in question. It is therefore necessary to stress the fact that the basic structure of the life and existence of all creation, and particularly of human society, is not by cutthroat competition but through cooperation among individuals, communities and nations. Tribal people have always lived by the principle of cooperation between man, nature and spirit. Such a vision of life helps to manage and reorganize life in a disintegrating situation.

Hindutva and Tribal India

The forces of Hindutva are very active in Tribal India, particularly in the central region from Gujarat to Bihar. "The proponents of Hindutva ideology argue that Adivasis originally belong to Hindu fold. Their conversion to Christianity is an irreparable damage to Hindu religion. Hence, it is morally correct to attack them, even physically, to stop this and to reconvert the Christian Adivasis back to Hinduism."[32] This is the second invasion of Aryans over Tribal people! A leading Indian sociologist clearly differentiates the "primal vision of the pre-Aryan people"—the Adivasis and Dalits— from Aryan and Dravidian Hinduism and all other religions.[33] We hold that Tribal people have had no religions affiliation with Hindus of any type. The Tribals have maintained their own religious faith, rituals and priests with worship in the home and occasional sacrifices in the sacred groves of the village. They have never built any temple and worshipped under the Brahmin priests in history. Therefore the claim of the proponents of Hindutva ideology is historically and theologically false.

Tribal India in the 21ˢᵗ century is going to face the subtle myth-making of Brahmanism to make the tribals believe that they are 'Kshatriyas and Hindus'.[34] "Old myths are being printed and propagated. Such as the vanaras of Ramayan the ancestor of the Mundas, and Hanuman's mother Anjani was born in the village Anjani in Lohardaga."[35] Such myth-making and revival of myths are being attached to the Adivasi history. Hanuman temples are also being built at almost each corner of the road in Jharkhand region, particularly in the vicinity of Government run Adivasi residential schools; all go to show the subtle inducement of tribal young students by the Hindus. Traditional tribals in Tribal India are at a kairos point in their history in many respects.

Revival and Resurgence of Traditional Tribal Religions

After one hundred and fifty years of contact with Christian missions, and in the turbulent

---

[30] Shishir Tudu, "Adivasi Identity and 21ˢᵗ century," *Prabhat Khabar,* 7 January 2000, p.6.

[31] Shunil, "Foreign Control Over for a New Move," *Prabhat Khabar,* Ranchi, 17ᵗʰ dec.1999, p.6.

[32] Sanjay Bosu Mullick, "Hinduism and the Mundas in Jharkhand (A response to the Hindutva conversion debate)." Seminar paper, New Delhi, Jawalhar Nehru University, 10ᵗʰ Oct.1999, Preface page one.

[33] T.K. Oommen, "Christians in the Indian Political Context," *People's Reporter*, Bangalore, Dec.16-31, 1999, p.8.

[34] Ajit K. Dandu, "Gahira(Jahila) Guru and His Sant Samaj Movement in Tribal Movements" in K.S. Singh, ed., *India* Vol.2, New Delhi, Manohar Publications, 1982, pp.197-207, specially pp.199 and 201.

[35] Bosu Mullick, "Hinduism and the Mundas in Jharkhand," p.12.

situation created by forces of Hindutva in Tribal regions of central India, there are signs of resurgence of traditional tribal religion. Tribal leaders have organized big public celebrations of Sarhul festival in Ranchi each year. They take out public processions through the main Road. The Saran Samitis are reclaiming the old burial grounds, sacred groves and trying to promote the public observances of seasonal festivals. This resurgent religious movement may pick up strength in future and this may present a challenge to missions in Tribal India.

Along with revival of tribal traditional religion, Hindutva is intensifying its anti-Christian activities primarily in Tribal India's central region – from Gujarat to Madhya Pradesh, Orissa and Bihar. Atrocities against Christians in this region are well documented by media (newspapers, radio and TV), and this trend seems to be intensifying.

Tribal self – Rule Laws: Tribals have had their own traditional village punch (gram sabha) in each village. The statuary punchayat Raj Act of 1973 has vitiated the very foundation of tribal community and identity resulting in confusion and disruption. However in 1996 an amendment of the Constitution (the Panchayat Extension Act No. 40 of 1996) provided that "Every Gram Sabha shall be competent to safeguard and preserve the traditions and customs, their culture identity, community resources, and customary mode of dispute resolution."[36] Along with this act of 1996, the constitutional provision for mother tongue primary education also must be taken seriously in 21st century. It will help promote literacy along with production of tribal literature in the mother tongue.

All tribal communities in Tribal India individually and corporately together must appropriate the Constitutional provisions in their favour and stand on them for a strong Tribal India in the 21st century.

Missiology for 21st Century Tribal India

Missiology for Tribal India will be discussed from three vantage points – first, foreign Christian missionary expansions; second, .Indian missionary undertakings in Tribal Indian; and finally missionary efforts from within Tribal India itself.

Roman Catholic missiologists have made a comprehensive study of the Catholic Church and her missionary obligations to the people of India with a specific section on the Tribals of India. They firmly hold, "missionary dynamics implies the sum total of the interactions between the missionaries and the people, relations between different Christian communities, and other people, the process of policy making and decision making, raising of funds and using them wisely, and a sense of oneness resulting from common experiences and shared culture."[37] Along with this comprehensive compilation of components, an evangelical Christian must also note the divine involvement in this dynamic process. In fact, without the triune God, Father, Son and Holy Spirit, involving Himself in mission undertakings, it cannot become a dynamic movement. In our understanding mission is *missio-dei*. The mission of God begins with His sending of Jesus Christ to this world to seek and save the lost. Jesus Christ, the crucified and risen Lord, sends His disciples, the believers in Him, and the community of faith to continue God's saving mission under the leading and guidance of the Holy Spirit.

Western Christian Mission in Tribal India (1840-1999)

Eastern Christianity came to India in the first century by the work of St. Thomas, the disciple

---

[36] B.D. Sharma, *Scheduled Areas, Self-Rule Laws Madhya Pradesh*, Sahyog Postal Cuter, New Delhi 1998, p.55.

[37] Augustine Kanjamala, ed., *Integral Mission Dynamics: An Interdisciplinary Study of the Catholic Church in India*, New Delhi, Intercultural Publications, 1995, Introduction, p.xxxii.

of our Lord.[38] Western Roman Catholic mission started in Goa. "It was with the arrival of the Portuguese in 1498 and the introduction of Padroado that the Latin Church in India was formally introduced and hierarchically established."[39] The Evangelical Protestant missionary movement in India started in 1706 at Tranquebar, Tamil Nadu by Lutheran Missionary Ziegenbalg from Germany in a Danish Colony. William Carey began his mission work under the Baptist Missionary Society from England at Serampore, West Bengal, in another Danish Colony from 1800. "The modern era of the missionary expansion of the Christian Church may conveniently be dated from 1792.... The publication of Carey's 'Enquiry into the Obligation of Christians to use means for the conversion of the heathen' may rightly be regarded as a landmark in Christian history".[40]

Western missionary work began in the Khasi hills in 1841 by the Welsh Presbyterian mission. The German mission started its work in Chotanagpur in 1845. The British Baptist Missionary Society, began its work in Mizoram in 1889, and the Welsh Presbyterian Mission in 1897. The American Baptist missionary work among the Nagas started in 1847. The Welsh Presbyterian Mission started its work among the Dheb tribes of Gujarat in 1841. The Free Church of Scotland began work in Nagpur among the Gonds and published a Gondi Grammar in 1866. The Moravian Brethren Mission worked in Kotgarh, Himachal Pradesh and other Centres.

The Basel Mission from Switzerland, the Church Missionary Society, and the American Reformed Presbyterian Church worked in the Nilgiri and Western Ghat hill ranges of Karnataka, Tamilnadu and Kerala from 1855. In the tribal regions of Orissa the British Baptist Missionary society began its work among the Konds from 1862.[41]

Western Christian Missionary: The First Friend of Tribals

Tribal communities in India had a bitter experience of contacts with other people in their history. The Aryans and the Semitic Moghuls came to exploit, oppress and suppress these simple honest tribals. Even the western traders and colonial government proved to be enemies who suppressed the tribals.

But the missionaries came with the Love of God in Jesus for all people including the tribals. Meeting the Christian missionaries in the middle of the 19th century, the tribals for the first time met a friend who came to care for their health, education and economic upliftment. Though the missionaries were ill-treated by the tribals, the former forgave the latter and continued serving them with love. And consequently some of the head-hunting tribes in North East India were won to Christ. The missionaries had to sacrifice their very life for the sake of Jesus Christ and to make Him known among the communities in Tribal India. The missionaries were the first people to recognize the worth of the tribal languages and took the initiative to give the Tribal languages a

---

[38] *Ibid* p.4.

[39] *Ibid* p.5.

[40] Ernest A. Payne, Introduction to the new 1961 facsimile edition of William Carey's *An Enquiry into the Obligation of Christians to use Means for the Conversion of the Heathens*, Leicester, 1792; Baptist Missionary Society Baptist House Oxfordshire, England, p.9.

[41] Nirmal Minz, *Rise Up My People and Claim the Promises— Advent of the Gospel among the Tribes of India*, ISPCK, Delhi, 1997, pp.17-25. This provides a summary of the beginnings of western Christian missions in Tribal India. One notes that the Roman Catholic Mission arrived in Tribal India after the Evangelical Protestant Missions pioneered. For instance the Belgian Jesuit Mission of the Roman Catholic Church was officially started in Chotanagpur in 1874. But the Roman Catholic way of massive educational, medical and socio-economic development work along with preaching the Gospel advanced more rapidly and drew many more members to the Catholic Church than the Protestant denominations, except in North East India.

written form with grammars and other books. This gave self-respect to the Tribal communities. Their languages were as good as any other language in India and in the world! Such recognition to tribal language encouraged and attracted the tribals to faith in Jesus Christ as their Saviour and Liberator from evil spirits, exploitative Zamindars, and other oppressors. A sense of belonging to the worldwide communion of believers provided them with a new identity and a sense of protection from the dehumanizing forces all around them. The tribals of Chotanagpur felt that God had heard their cry and had sent them a friend to stand by them and treat them with love and sympathy.

British Colonial Government was a Providential Arrangement for Western Christian Missions in Tribal India

The British government did not support the missions officially, yet individual officers had key roles in promoting and helping the missions to be established in some tribal regions. Local government officials welcomed and gave shelter to missionaries and assisted in many other ways in promoting mission concerns, particularly in education and health care services.[42] Missiologically, the precedence of the British Colonial Government in many parts of the world, including Tribal India, was God's own design for the propagation of the Gospel in those lands. In some particular cases, the British Government officially supported the programme of a mission society. Speaking of the SPCK and SPG in Assam, Bishop Talibuddin says, "The Society for the Propagation of Christian Knowledge (SPCK), the Society for the Propagation of the Gospel (SPG), had its official backing of the Church of England and was incorporated by the Royal Charter. Its main aim was to provide Anglican ministration to the British people abroad, and to evangelise the non-Christians."[43]

Prejudices of Western Missionaries Regarding Tribals

The missionaries were victims of the white man's feelings of superiority in the 19th and 20th century. Some missionaries and missiologists of that period looked down upon Tribal religion and culture. They thought that Tribal religion was the devil's workshop. They had negative attitudes to many tribal social and cultural customs. This is reflected in the missionary prohibition of traditional drums in Chotanagpur tribal churches. Derogatory terms (like "Kols" used by the Dikus) were used by German mission historians and missiologists.[44] Nevertheless the contribution of missionaries to language and literature in tribal languages is praiseworthy. The *Encyclopedea Mundarica* by Father Hoffmann of the Roman Catholic Mission, and Dr. Alfred Nottrott's translation of the Holy Bible in Mundari are monumental contributions to Mundari language and literature.

Preaching, Teaching, Healing and Development: Preaching, teaching and healing ministries along with socio-economic

---

[42] N. Minz, "Christianity among the Mundas, Oraons, and Kharias of Chotanagpur" in *Christianity in India*, edited by F. Hrangkhuma, Delhi, ISPCK, 1998, p.22. Mr. Hanington, the Deputy Commissioner at Ranchi Requested, Dr.Heberlin at Calcutta to send the German Missionaries to work among Adivasis in 1845. Also see Krickwin C. Marak, "Christianity among the Garos: An attempt to re-read peoples' movement from a missiological perspective," in *Christianity in India*, edited by F. Hrangkhuma, Delhi, ISPCK, 1998, p.156-157. David Scott, a British Government officer literally wanted to Christianize the Garos and run schools among them. He was quite instrumental in promoting mission work among the Garos.

[43] E.W. Talibuddin, "A missiological Reflection on the Anglican Church in North-East India from 1845-1970," *Indian Journal of Theology* Vol.40/ No.1&2, Serampore, 1998, p.90.

[44] L. Nottrott, *Die Gossner Sche Missions unter den Kolhs, 1845-1874*, Halle, Verlag Von Richard Mu"htmann, 1974. Also Johannes W. Holsten, "Die Kols Mission in Chotanagpur and Assam" in *Evangelista Gossner, Glaube and Gemeinde*, Gottingen, Bandenhocek & Ruprecht, 1949, p.226.

development of the Tribals were the basic methods in western missionary undertakings in the last century. The Evangelical Protestant missionaries were from a Pietistic background, yet the tribal socio-economic situation compelled them to attend to land issues and struggle against traditional local Zamindar's oppressive treatment of the tribals for many generations. Their sympathetic response to the tribal situation by the German missionaries and the Roman Catholic Jesuit Missionaries from Belgium attracted the tribals of Chotanagpur in large numbers. Missionary Constant Lievens is remembered with appreciation among all in Chotanagpur.[45]

Churches Established in Tribal India:

Churches and congregations in Tribal India are sustained by 150 years of missionary labor and a continuation of Christian ministry by tribal Christians in independent India. Tribal preacher-teachers, priests and pastors, sisters and brothers have made a notable contribution in spreading the Gospel among their own people. These preacher-teachers were the most effective carriers of the Gospel to their own relatives and friends, particularly at the early stage of missionary work in Tribal India.

Our non-Christian neighbours notice the transformation of tribal life. The inner change heart is reflected in the style of life and the healthy and clean practices adopted by the tribal Christians. Christianity was a timely intervention of God in Tribal India's history. Christianity has recreated their socio-cultural and religious history. A new beginning has been made in the social history of Tribal India. The Tribal Christian community is empowered and comparatively more able and equipped to adjust and live creatively in the modern world.[46]

Indian Missionaries to Tribal India

The western foreign missionary movements made a great impact on Tribal India. The establishment of denominational churches is a single factor to continue this impact in the future. With the independence of India the devolution of power from mission to church has taken place.[47]

Protestant churches in general are independent and claim to be rooted in the Indian soil. They keep fraternal relationships with the missions and churches abroad, and work in partnership with each other. The denominational Church bodies claim to be self-supporting, self-administrating and propagating the faith in the Indian context. The Second Vatican Council opened the way for the Roman Catholic Dioceses to live and serve as a local Church free from the bondage of the past. They have freedom to exercise all the powers of a local Church with full allegiance to the bishop of Rome, the Pope, as ultimate authority.

During the last fifty years in free India most of the denominational Church bodies kept busy maintaining properties and managing institutions. Attending to these tasks, mission and evangelism were not consciously taken as the primary task of the Church. This has slowed down the growth and expansion of the Church in India.

Indian Mission Societies and Indigenous Mission Work in Tribal India

The last quarter of 20ᵗʰ century Tribal India experienced a new upsurge of missionary work. A new trend also emerged in missiological thinking for mission to Tribal India. The contributions of the following scholars are important in this regard: S.A.B.Dilbar Hans, *Not Without Witness*, Madras, 1952; Fr. A. Van Exem,

---

[45] L. Tirkey, "Life and Work of Father Constant Lievens."

[46] Fidelis de Sa, *Crisis in Chotanagpur*, Bangalore, Redemptive Publications, 1975.

[47] T.V. Philip, *Protestant Christianity in India Since 1858*, pp.56-65.

Religious System of the Munda Tribe, Germany, 1982; C. Kerketta and R.Ced Kujur, *Durson Ke Liye Abhyajit*, Ranchi, 1994; Nirmal Minz, *Rise up my people and claim the Promises*, Delhi, 1997.

With the exception of Van Exem, all these writers are tribal Christians from Chotanagpur and Fr. Van Exem lived all his life and served among the Munda tribe. These authors have shown the basic values in tribal religion and put forth an appreciative attitude to tribal religion and cultural and social customs. Therefore these books are a transitional source to move from the Western ideology and theology of mission of the 19th and 20th century to a 21st century missiology for Tribal India.

Three Major Streams of Missions in India and from India to Tribal India Today

The first major stream consists of new denominational missions which are related to their respective Churches by reporting to its Bishop or President: the Nagaland Missionary Movement, the Zoram Evangelical Fellowship, the Presbyterian Synod of Mizoram, and some Pentecostal missions.

The second stream includes a number of Pentecostal-Charismatic mission agencies and their followers together with a large number of non-denominational or inter-denominational, indigenous, faith missions. Member of these organizations report directly to their leaders and supporting constituency. Well-known ones are the Friends Missionary Prayer Band (FMPB), Indian Evangelical Mission (IEM), the Gospel Echoing Mission Society (GEMS) and others.

Third are non-classical missions with roots in the west that continue in India. These include the Union of Evangelical students of India (UESI), Scripture Union, Global Outreach, Youth For Christ, Far East Broadcasting Association, Gospel Recording Association, Operation Mobilisation, India Every Home Crusade, Campus Crusade for Christ, Youth with a Mission, and Every Creature Crusade.

The western missionaries are coaches, teachers, colleagues and facilitators in the above missions.[48] The relevance of these missions is that the majority of Indian missionaries work among the tribals. Some people have criticized this because the Tribals make up only eight percent of the population of India. Emphasis on reaching the Tribals is not likely to change. "The goal of major missions like FMPB, IEM and others is tribal oriented."[49]

Some of the reasons given for the above situation in Indian missions are that missionaries are more equipped to reach the tribals. They get workers more easily from the Tribals communities themselves. These missionaries are concerned for the hopelessness, oppression and poverty of the Tribals and finally that the Tribals are easier to approach and more open to the gospel than most others. The above points have direct implications for mission for 21st century Tribal India.[50]

Indigenous Tribal Missionary Efforts in Tribal India

We have already noted that denominational Church bodies are established in Tribal India. There is no Tribal region without a

---

[48] K. Rajendran, *Which Way Forward Indian Mission? (A Critique of Twenty-Five Years 1972-1997)*, Bangalore, SAIACS Press, 1998, pp.56-57.

[49] *Ibid* p.72.

[50] S.D.Ponraj, *Tribal Challenges and the Church's Response*, Madhupur, Bihar, Mission Educational Books, 1996. Also see other books produced by the India Missions Association, the Church Growth Movement in India, and the Frontier Mission Centre.

denominational Christian community. The Indian missionary efforts of the last 25 years also have resulted in further founding of Pentecostal-Charismatic and Evangelical Christian communities in Tribal India.

Radio Ministry and Vishwavani Out reach Programmes: Radio ministry is effectively going on in all the major tribal languages of the Central, Western, and southeastern regions and in Northeast India. Radio programmers are heard in Sandal, Mandarin, Kudu, and the tribal languages of Gujarat and other states. This ministry by tribal missionaries themselves is effective. Many churches are planted and Christian communities formed in Tribal India through the radio ministry.

Faith and Prayer Healing in Jesus' Name: God's power in Jesus Christ is seen in Tribal churches. Simple lay believers pray in Jesus name, and the sick are healed. Through this ministry of churches in Sanna (Jashpur Dist), Udaipur, and Surguja district of Madhya Pradesh many congregations are newly established among the Kudux people.[51] The Potta Charismatic movement is active in this region to revive the congregations in established Roman Catholic parishes.

Jagat Jyoti led by Abraham Kandulna, a Zealous CNI layman, is working among the Mundas and Oraons and Sadams in this region. Jagat Jyoti has a support base and paid evangelists with two cadres: first, at the grassroot village level, missionaries work in the field; second, area coordinators look after a number of evangelists and assist them by their counselling and guidance. Mr. Abraham Kandulna is the director of Jagat Jyoti with its head office at Kathartoli, Ranchi.[52] Thousands of new converts are baptized and handed over to the nearest mainline denomination in the area as fruit of the labour by Jagat Jyoti.

The Evangelistic Campaign by A.G. Church with the Support of Pentecostal and Other Smaller Groups: The evangelistic campaigns of the Assemblies of God combine preaching the word of God with prayer for healing. People gather in thousands, and many of the sick who believe in Jesus' healing power get healed. This campaign is conducted in rural as well as urban areas. The A.G. Church is gathering a good harvest for Christ from Tribals and non-tribals in the Chotanagpur region. It has an urban base and rural outreach programmes. The A.G. Church is led and guided by Tribal missionary pastors with burning zeal for the Gospel.[53]

Mainline Churches and Mission Concerns: The main denominational churches are still dependent upon foreign assistance for mission and evangelism. The old foreign models of preaching teaching and healing ministries are continued even in Tribal India. Only the independent churches/missions are struggling to reach the unreached. The contribution of FMPB in mission to Tribals is very encouraging. They have continued their mission and evangelism

---

[51] Faith and Prayer healing ministry in our region started with an illiterate lady in Sanna. She had the Vision of Jesus and was commanded to pray for the sick. She began it and sick began to be healed. Group of faithful simple lay Christians gathered around her and have been going from village to village, organize prayer-healing ministry with spiritual songs and bhajans. Pastor and evangelist in this area joined and continue spreading the Gospel and establishing congregation. No outside preacher or inspiration had any influence in this movement. Roman Catholic, Lutheran and others join in this ministry of the Gospel Voluntarily. And the movement is going on. Potta Chrisma among Roman Catholic Congregations also works in this area.

[52] Mr. Abraham Kandulna was working with Vishwa Vani, Radio ministry. After sometime be felt the need of founding 'Jagat Jyoti' mission society of the tribal church to work among the tribals, financially supported by tribal Christians with prayer, and contribution regularly.

[53] Pastor Shanti Prakas Kachhap and Pastor John Toppo are the leading missionary pastors of the A.G. church in Ranchi. It is a mission with rapid growth with new congregations in and around, Ranchi.

among the Maltos of Raj Mahal in Santal Parganas, Bihar. They have reaped a good harvest there and a living Church has been established among these tribal communities.

A Reflection on Missiology for 21ˢᵗ Century Tribal India

Missiology for Tribal India must be discussed in the context of missiology in the modern world and modern India. The foreign missions have receded into the background, and indigenous Indian missions have presented themselves as a dynamic movement of the Spirit during the last 25 years in India. And the majority of Indian missionaries have gone into Tribal India. The variables of a Tribal missiology are discussed below. But before launching on this task we must reaffirm the biblical basis of the mission mandate in the present Indian and Tribal context.

Reaffirmation of Biblical Basis of Mission Mandate

The biblical basis of mission for all centuries is the *missio dei* (God's mission). The God of the Bible has revealed Himself to every generation of people. "In the past God has revealed Himself through Prophets, at many times in various ways, but in this last days, he has spoken to us by his Son, who appointed him heir of all things, a and through whom He made the Universe" (Heb 1:1-2). This speaking God is a sending God also. He sent finally, His own son Jesus Christ to this world and thus has intervened in the affairs of men in this world. The basic mission of sending Jesus Christ to this inhabited world is expressed as follows. "For God so loved the World that, He sent His only Son, that who ever believes in Him shall not perish but have eternal life"(John 3:16). The explicit purpose of coming of Jesus to this world is further expressed in the following passage, "for even the son of Man did not come to be served, but to serve and to give His life as a ransomed for many" (Mark 10:45). This vision of mission is to be implemented according to

Nazareth Manifesto spelled out by Jesus Himself. "The spirit of the Lord is on Me, because He has anointed Me to preach the Good news to the poor. He has sent Me to proclaim freedom for the prisoners, and recovery of sight for the blind, to release the oppressed and to proclaim the year of the Lord's favor" (Luke 4:18,19). Jesus fulfilled this mission by His word and deed, and finally sacrificed His life on the cross as a ransom for many in this world.

During His active ministry Jesus gathered his followers as disciples and sent them to fulfill the same mission giving them power and authority with programmes. "When Jesus had called the twelve disciples, He gave them power and authority to drive out all demons, and He sent them out to preach the kingdom of God and to heal the sick"(Luke 9:1,2). Spiritual power and authority both to preach and to heal the sick in the name of Jesus accompany this sending.

Then again Jesus sent his disciples, after the manner the Father sent him. Jesus said, "Peace be with you. As the father has sent Me, so do I send you" (John 20:21). The disciples and the believing community are sent into this world, into India, and into Tribal India, to fulfill the mission God. And finally Jesus commissioned His disciples and through them the community of believers in the following words, "Then Jesus came to them and said, all authority in heaven and on earth has been given to me. Therefore, go and make disciples of all nations, baptizing them in the name of the Father, and of the Son and of the Holy Spirit, Teaching them to obey everything I have commanded you. And surely I am with you to the very end of the age" (Matthew 28:18-20). The above is a comprehensive basis of mission to this world and therefore to Tribal India in the 21ˢᵗ century also. God's mission is still relevant, as He desires that all people, including the tribals of Tribal India, be saved. The scripture again points out, "This is right and acceptable in the sight of God our saviour, who desires every one to be saved and to come to the knowledge of the Truth. For there is one God, there is also one mediator between God and mankind, Christ Jesus, Himself human who gave Himself a ransom for all" (I Timothy 2:3-4).

This mission of God contains the message that is wholisitc in nature. Salvation in Jesus Christ is a wholistic (physical, mental and spiritual) health for a person, his family, his society and the whole environment in which he lives. Such a Gospel is urgently needed for people in Tribal India today in this third millennium. The believing communities in India and Tribal India must witness to Jesus Christ and serve people in His name. The small believing groups India are as weak as the early Christians community in Christian history. But Jesus provides a new strength for the church to continue the mission of God. He said, "But you will receive power when the Holy Spirit comes on you, and you will be My witnesses in Jerusalem, in all Judea, and Samaria, and to the ends of the earth" (Acts 1:8).

Time and again the Holy Spirit has moved Christians to be a witnessing and serving community among all people in this world. The nature of the Christian community is rooted in the very nature of God. Sending God, sending Jesus prompts Christians through the working of the Holy Spirit to send missionaries to un-reached peoples and groups.

Salvation is for the Individual and the Community as a Whole

The health of a person is linked with the health of the family, and in turn its welfare is dependent upon the physical, mental and spiritual health of a society, including its natural environment. Tribal people have an organismic understanding of life. Tribal India has a communitarian basis of human society. An individual person's socio-spiritual life will be much richer and better in a community which is regenerated in its inner life to face sin and evil and overcome it. The "mass movement" concept is out-dated now. It is known as a "people movement" to Christ under the direct inspiration of the Holy Spirit after hearing the word of God. Salvation of the village/ entire community is basic to mission to Tribal India. Therefore, evangelism and social action, witness and service are integral to the wholistic mission of God in Jesus Christ. Equal emphasis is required to transform the entire community along with the individual in our mission to Tribal India. The 21ˢᵗ century needs discipline of people groups in order that individuals will have a better possibility of Christian nurture to develop a Christ-like character and life-style.

Changed Situation in Tribal India

Because of the fact that all major tribal communities have come in contact with the message of the Gospel and that the denominational churches are established for about 150 years, there is a basic source for mission work in Tribal India. Tribal Christians form about 24.5 percent of the total Christian population of India. So even numerically there is a substantial Christian community in Tribal India. In the mainland, the strength of tribal Christians is much less than in North East India. Chotanagpur tribal Christians make up 10 percent of the total Christian population in India. The awareness to join in the common task of mission and evangelism in Tribal India has to be built up among tribal Christians. It is their primary responsibility to preach the Gospel as an obligation to their own kith and kin. Closer cooperation and partnership is urgently required between the denominational church bodies work as well as mission societies engaged in mission work among the tribals in the new millennium. Closer unity of all Christians is essential to the survival and progress of the mission of God in tribal.

Missionaries and mission societies from India are welcome to Tribal India. Many mission societies have found the Tribals to be open to the

Gospel. It is necessary to strike the iron when it is hot. Christians in Tribal India need igniting with zeal for the Gospel. The present situation of mission and evangelism in Tribal India demands more zealous missionaries from other parts of India.

The experience of foreign missionaries in the past and Indian missionaries to Tribal India is similar. It is the Tribal converts who have been effective witnesses to their relatives and friends in their own tribe. But programme of social action and wholistic service to the community requires outside help, both with personnel and finance. Therefore, collaboration and cooperation between Tribal Christians, missionaries from India and the outside world are urgently required in this millennium.

Mission is Divine Intervention and not a Colonial Expansion of the West in Disguise

Tribal India has become the target of the RSS, VHP and Sangh Pariwar. Objection to tribals becoming Christians is gathering momentum. When Prime Minister Atal Bihari Vajpayee had proposed a debate on 'conversion' in parliament, Mr.K.K.Chandi, a Gandhian Christian, responded with an article, "Is religious conversion violence, and does it breed violence among the non-violent?"[54] It is clearly shown in this article that discussion on conversion had taken place in 1935, and in the Constituent Assembly of India, and that the Constitution of India has insured the basic rights for individuals and minorities to profess and propagate their faith.

Missions and missionaries are accused of being the agents of expansion of western colonial powers in India. This accusation is coming from the fundamentalist forces of Hindutva, the dominant society in India. This force has always suppressed, oppressed and exploited the tribals in India. Now they are trying to make tribals Hindus, although historically and culturally tribals are different people with distinct religion of their own. Their religion is called "primal Religion" without any statues as the objects of their worship. The objections to conversion of tribals to Christianity is politically motivated and therefore must be taken with a grain of salt.

Christian mission is Divine Intervention in the life of a people and in a country. God has intervened in life of tribal communities in Tribal India. This intervention has done two major things to the tribals. First, their life is being transformed individually and group. One of the signs of this transformation is that their languages have been given equal status to any language in the world including English and Sanskrit. This provides them with a self-respect, which cannot be achieved in any other way. Second, the tribal people are incorporated into a world brotherhood of Christians of all nations and people. Such a status is again a transforming effect in the life of tribal people. They are made aware of their right and duties as respectable citizens in India. This divine intervention has a process of conversion of an individual and the whole community with a new and fresh understanding of life itself. "Conversion should be understood not as a demand for a change of religion but as a challenge to all turn to God from idolatry."[55] Mission as divine intervention places such challenges before the individuals and communities. And there are people who accept this challenge and get converted to God from idols. The same author discusses conversion on the basis of his field studies in Gujarat. On the basis of this study Mattan puts forward a renewed understanding of "baptism as a call not to a separate culture, but to a counter-culture with the goal of a fuller humanity."[56]

---

[54] K.K.Chandi, "Is religious conversion violence, and does it breed violence among the non-violent?" *People's Reporter,* Vol.12, No.22, Nov.16-30, 1999, p.1.

[55] J. Mattam, S. Kim., eds., *Mission and Conversion A Reappraisal,* Bandra, Mumbai, St. Pauls, 1999, p.9.

[56] *Ibid* p.12

Resurgence of Tribal Religion and Missionary Obligation

Tribal India is going through a religious crisis. On the one hand, a Hinduisation process is influencing it. On the other hand, a modern development and globalisation process is disturbing its old traditions and customs. When big dams, industrial complexes, mining operations and urbanization are encroaching upon the physical places of worship and ritual practices, educated tribals are waking up to save and preserve them through demonstrations and objections to the encroaching agencies. Many tribal festivals are taken into the streets in order to demonstrate their continuing relevance by a show of strength in public processions. Some tribals are reinterpreting traditional beliefs and practices for modern society.

This process of reflection on traditional beliefs and customs opens up a channel for communication between the traditionalists and the Christian missionaries in Tribal India. Missionaries should appreciate this resurgence and try to understand it form a divine perspective. Any resurgence will have new interpretations and understandings of the primal vision of life. The Gospel of Jesus Christ can come into this crisis situation with new hope for the future in the mind and heart of the Tribals. Apparent resistance to the Gospel will be an opportunity in God's design for the power of the Gospel to influence the leading members of the tribal communities in Tribal India.

Church and the Bible in Tribal India

So far denominational church bodies have been established in Tribal India. The Bible has been used by evangelical and Roman Catholic missionaries without being conscious of the historical and cultural gap between the tribals from the biblical world. Modern man has gone far away from the Biblical world and its images and symbols. But tribal man and his world are very close to the Biblical world. There is a smaller gap between them. Therefore, tribals can pick-up and make sense of the biblical images and symbols quite easily. In this regard, the Bible and its world of symbols and images provide a hope for the survival of the tribal people in the face of the devastatingly destructive forces of modern development. Therefore, the Bible should be translated and used in all the major tribal languages in India. The Biblical message gives hope for survival in the face of displacement, disintegration and destruction. And the church as the Body of Christ presents a new possibility with which to face the modern world. Tribal Christians can survive anywhere in India, even beyond the boundaries of Tribal India, in the fellowship of believers. "Christian world mission refers to the redemptive activities of the Church within the societies where the Church is found."[57]

Through the establishment of churches in Tribal India, the redemptive activity of the Church will continue no matter what comes. "The living God with whom we have to do is not the God of the philosophers but the God of Abraham, of Isaac, and of Jacob, the God who still addresses us when we read the Bible as believers in company with the whole Church, in missionary dialogue with the cultures of mankind and in reliance on the work of the spirit who takes the things of Christ and shows them to us."[58]

Conclusion

The home base of mission to Tribal India is the Church and congregations already found there. It is these Churches who have to bear the burden of mission among the tribals of Tribal India.

---

[57] Ralph Winter, "The Meaning of Mission," *Mission Frontier* Vol.2, India, Oct-Dec.,1998, p.11.

[58] Leslie Newbigin, "The Bible in the Church" in *Gospel in the World*, compiled by D.J. Ambalavanar, Madras, CLS, 1985, p.13.

The history of the Church teaches clearly and conclusively that the missionary epochs have been the times when the home church has been the most powerfully stimulated.... has not the time come for the church to give herself with greater earnestness than ever to the stupendous task of making Christ known and obeyed in all the world?....where ever you find a pastor with overflowing missionary zeal and knowledge, you will find an earnest missionary Church.[59]

Though the author John R. Mott wrote these statements in a completely different context, his words are true and relevant for the churches in India and those of Tribal India for the future of mission in 21st century Tribal India. As Ralph Winter remarks, "the most obvious surge toward an evangelism in the world today will come if Christian believers in every part of the world are moved to reach outside their churches and win their cultural near neighbours to Christ. They are better able to do that than any foreign missionary."[60] This emphasis and focus on the church and its nearest cultural neighbour is key to the future of mission and evangelism in Tribal India in the 3rd millennium.

Mission work in Tribal India is mainly dependent on God's instrument, the missionary in 21st century Tribal India. If the missionary is conscious of the immediate ministry of the Holy Spirit and has a commitment to the spiritual dimension in his/her church growth activities and programmes,[61] one may be assured of his/her work bearing fruit in Tribal India. "The time seems to be ripe for the churches in India and churches among the Tribes of India to consider a new paradigm on mission, with the millennium shift in India. The new paradigm must address itself to the unjust social, economic and religious structures in Indian society. It should wrestle with the evils of caste and tribalism in church and Society. The new paradigm must aim at the creation of a new human society in India with justice, peace and integrity."[62]

---

[59] John R. Mott, "The Pastor and the Modern Missions," *Mission Frontiers,* India, Vol.2, Oct-Dec.1998, p.31.

[60] Ralph Winter, "Cross–cultural Evangelism: The Biblical Mandate," *Mission Forntiers*, India, Vol.2, Oct.-Dec.1998, p.36.

[61] C. Peter Wagner, "My Pilgrimage in Mission," *International Bulletin of Missionary Research*, Vol.23, No.4, Oct.1999, pp.164-167.

[62] Nirmal Minz, *Rise up My People and Claim, The Promise, The Gospel Among the Tribes of India*, ISPCK, Delhi, 1997, p.123.

CHAPTER 29

Religious Freedom in Nepal Then and Now

RAMESH KHATRY

"Religion, after all, is the serious business of the human race,"[1] said the famous historian, Toynbee. From the beginning of creation, man has felt the need to worship a Being greater than himself. In times of crisis, man found solace in trusting God. Religion also provided man an ethical standard. Most religions prohibit murder, rape, theft, adultery, robbery, bribery, and other actions we call sins. People may debate and change their minds on what today counts as sin, but the fact remains that religion guides ethics. This world would degenerate into a jungle-community should all the religions cease to exist.

The advent of Karl Marx brought a change in the attitude of people towards religion. "Religion is the opium of the people."[2] This dictum by Marx is the cornerstone of the whole Marxist outlook on religion. Marx was responding to the nominal Christianity of the religious leaders during his time. They excelled in exploiting the simple people of Germany. Children worked eighteen hours a day on meager wages in factories that had 'Christian' owners. Rich Christian landowners exacted heavy penalties from people gathering wood to make a livelihood. Karl Marx developed communism because the Christians behaved no better. According to a Communist dictionary, religion is, "a specific form of social consciousness whose characteristic feature is a fantastic reflection in people's minds of external forces dominating over them, a reflection in which earthly forces assume unearthly forms."[3]

Marxism looks down on religion, making it a product of inherent weakness in man. "The appearance of religion in primitive society was conditioned by man's impotence in face of nature because of this low level of productive forces."[4] However, where true religion existed, people benefited.

One of the personal rights is the right to religion. Personal rights exist because God has given them. God willed that man should live as a free being. This means others should not hinder his freedom. Most states recognize God-given rights. They do not create them. They may write them into their constitutions so that people hindered in these rights may seek legal redress. Article 14 of the 1960 constitution of Nepal said, "Every person may profess his own religion as handed down from ancient times and may practice it having regard to the traditions. Provided that no person shall be entitled to convert another person from one religion to another."[5]

---

[1] Toynbee, "Civilization on Trial V" in *The Great Treasury of Western Thought*, ed. by MJ Adler and C. van Doren, New York: RR Bowker Co., 1977, p.1279.

[2] "The Attitude of the Workers' Party to Religion" in Marx, Engels, *Marxism*, Moscow: Progress Publishers, 1979, p.230.

[3] I. Frolov, ed., *Dictionary of Philosophy*, Moscow: Progress Publishers, 1984, p.357.

[4] *Ibid.*

[5] "The Constitution of Nepal," Kathmandu: HMG Press, 1981, p.8.

Marxists would have said that Nepal did not need the above article in its constitution. As Nepal progresses, gets stronger, it would drop off the scaffoldings of religion. However, adherents of religions in Nepal, other than Hinduism or Buddhism, would say otherwise. They considered the Article 14 of the 1960 Nepalese Constitution favourable to the Hindus or the Buddhists but discriminatory against themselves.

The Scope of This Paper

The thesis of this paper is that by prohibiting change, Article 14 of the 1960 Constitution mutilated the very definition of freedom, and did not in reality grant the genuine right of religion to the Nepalese Christian population. We shall deal with this article first.

Then we shall study the article relating to the Freedom of Religion in 1990 Constitution. This will enable us to evaluate how Nepali Christians fare in the present day.

The Historical Background

One of the characteristics of Hinduism has been its pride in toleration. The leaders of the faith boasted of it.[6] However, how these leaders practised toleration is another thing. Gandhi himself goes on to say in the next line, "Only Christianity was at the time an exception. I developed a sort of dislike for it."

While we applaud the frankness of Gandhi, we cannot help but think that this remark betrays his lack of toleration. To be fair we must admit Gandhi did not encourage persecution of Christians or of any other religious adherents. C F Andrews and Stanley Jones, both western missionaries, developed close friendship with him.

Can we regard the Hindus as truly tolerant in India when they are at loggerheads with devotees of every other religion? The Hindu-Sikh riots in Punjab, the Hindu-Muslim rows in Gujarat, the Hindu-Christian debates when the Pope visited India in January 1986 and November 1999 all point to the same fact. The Hindus' vessel of toleration does not hold much water!

History reveals that the Nepalese governments did not always treat Christians or Muslims badly. History gives ample proof that at one time the harassment of Christians did not exist.

The first Christian missionaries ever to come to Nepal were the Roman Catholic Fathers of the Capuchin Order. When they came, the present Kathmandu valley still had three kingdoms: Kathmandu, Bhatgaon, and Patan, The Capuchin Fathers had developed friendship with the three kings.

> "On certain occasions they reprimanded kings, nobles and common people for their unjust deeds, cruelty, and sin, while exhorting them to repent, seek God's forgiveness, and live a righteous life. They helped to negotiate peace between warring Kathmandu and Bhatgaon. Some of the Fathers, who had picked up some medical knowledge, brought medicines with them and gave free treatment to all who sought it. They treated royalty and commoner alike."[7]

The Malla kings favoured the Capuchin Fathers. Besides rent-free houses, the Fathers received gifts and protection. In 1737 the King of Bhatgaon gave them a decree of liberty of conscience:

> We, Jaya Ranjita Malla, King of Bhatgaon, in virtue of the document, grant to all European Fathers leave to preach, teach and

---

[6] Gandhi, M. K., *An Autobiography*, Ahmedabad: Navajivan Publishing House, 1959, p.24. M K Gandhi said the same, while relating the influence of his father on his life, "He had, besides, Musalman and Parsi friends, who would talk to him about their own faiths, and he would listen to them always with respect, and often with interest. Being his nurse, I often had a chance to be present at these talks. These many things combined to inculcate in me a toleration for all faiths..

[7] *Ibid.*

draw to their religion the people to us subject, and we likewise allow our subjects to embrace the Law of the European Fathers, without fear or molestation either from us or from those who rule in our kingdom. Nor shall the Fathers receive from us any annoyance or be obstructed in their ministry. All this however, must be done without violence and of one's own free will. Krishna Simha Pradhan, Prime minister, is the witness to the document, and Sri Kasi Nath is the scribe. Given on the 11th day of the month Mangasira, in year 861 of the Nepalese era; may the day be auspicious.[8]

The king of Kathmandu showed similar gestures:

> The King of Kathmandu likewise received the Fathers with friendly conversations [1737 A.D.] and in his eagerness to have them in Kathmandu gave them a house for residence [a permanent gift], transit facilities through his kingdom, and a written Decree of Liberty of Conscience. In this Decree His Majesty declares himself free of any malicious accusations given to the Fathers in the past [when they were expelled earlier], to have examined their religious books and declared them to be good. Then he states that no one shall harass or harm those who, of their own free will, embrace the way of life professed by the Priests.[9]

Though these documents were written roughly 260 years ago we see in them a modern outlook. Both the Malla kings recognised in the liberty of conscience the freedom to preach and practise one's religion. Also they recognised in their subjects the capacity to make their own choice as adults.

Were these governments more advanced than the panchayat government of 1960-1990 in granting total religious liberty? We believe they were. The decrees they presented to the Capuchin Fathers are surprisingly close to the United Nations Declaration of Human Right Article 18 we quoted earlier. The Right to Religion, if genuine, must include the option to preach and practise, and to accept or reject. In this the Malla kings have been examples to us.

From what we know, the Capuchin Fathers led ordinary Christian lives, doing the duties of priests. During roughly 55 years of stay in the three towns of the Kathmandu valley, they instructed and then baptised the adults who believed and requested it. Thousands of children with severe illnesses were also baptised when they were at the point of death. The Priests led these Christians in worship, in the use of the sacraments; shepherded them in life's way; and performed nine Christian marriages. The Fathers interceded to the king on their behalf when they were ostracised and helped them to get leased land to work."[10]

The advent of Prithivinarayan Shah brought a total change in the policies towards the Capuchin Fathers. We have to take into account the fact that the British were expanding their empire during this period. The Malla kings asked the British to help them to counter-attack the Gorkhalis, led by the Shah. The Gorkhalis defeated the British at the forts of Sindhuli and Hariharpur. "This British interference caused the Gorkhalis strongly to suspect the Capuchin Fathers of complicity in trying to get the British help...the suspicion of foreigners hardened more and more in these war years and developed into a policy, in King Prithivinarayan's time, of firm exclusion of Europeans and even Indians from the new, young Gorkha Kingdom...For a while King Prithivinarayan held the Fathers as hostages against a further possible attack by the British. The grants, decrees, and facilities which the

---

[8] J. Lindell., *Nepal and Gospel of God*, Delhi, Masihi Sahitya Sanstha, 1979, p. 24.
[9] *Ibid.*, p. 25
[10] *Ibid.*, p. 24

Mission experienced under the Malla kings were now no longer valid."[11]

Whether the Capuchin Fathers had any effective contact with the British or not still remains a mystery. The Capuchins were Italians; the imperialists, British. However, this did not make any difference. Both were foreigners alike, and that proved enough. The Capuchin Fathers asked for permission to leave the country and this was granted.

In February 1768 about 60 Christians with one Father crossed the boarder and settled near the town of Bettiah. The remaining Fathers held as hostages were released and allowed to leave. The clear intention of the Christians was again to return to their native land as soon as settled conditions of the new regime would allow. But such a return never happened.[12]

This incident set a new precedent — that of suspicion of adherents of other religions. This has continued to the present day.

The first two constitutions of Nepal have been more liberal than that drafted in 1960 A.D. The government of Nepal Act 2004 (1947 A.D.) does not talk much about religion, but it has no prohibitive clauses restricting the rights of the citizen:

> Subject to the principles of public order and morality this constitution guarantees to the citizens of Nepal freedom of person, freedom of speech, liberty of press, freedom of assembly and discussion, FREEDOM OF WORSHIP, complete equality in the eye of the law...[13] (Capitals mine)

What this constitution does not say is just as important. The adherence to the religions of the forefathers is not mentioned, neither the fact that a person cannot convert to the religion of his choosing. Maharaja Padma Shumshere Jung Bahadur Rana, the author and the grantor of the 1947 constitution said in the inaugural address, "With regard to Fundamental rights, we have tried to make provision for them in a manner similar to that which obtains in the advanced countries of the world. Our laws and regulations being incomplete in this regard, we have tried to make them approximate to those of India and other advanced countries."[14]

Judging by the contents, we can easily say, with religion in mind, that this was the most liberal constitution the people of Nepal had ever had. Padma Shumshere must be considered years ahead of any other Nepali constitution-framer.

The Interim Government of Nepal Act 2007 (1950) has striking similarities to the Government of Nepal Act 2004. Article 15[1] has, "His Majesty's Government shall not discriminate against any citizen on grounds of religion, race, caste, sex, place of birth or any of them."[15] Article 16[3] further declares, "Nothing in this section shall affect the operation of any law which provides that the incumbent of an office in connection with the affairs of any religious or denominational institution or any member of the governing body thereof shall be a person professing a particular religion or belonging to a particular denomination."[16]

These facts prove that discrimination on religious grounds did not exist as a government policy either in the Malla period or in the latter Rana period or during the reign of King Tribhuvan (the present king's grandfather). It is

---

[11] *Ibid.*, p. 35 - 36

[12] *Ibid.*, p. 36 - 37

[13] Neupane, P., *The Constitution and the Constitutions of Nepal.* Kathmandu: Ratna Pustak Bhandar, 1969, pp. 172 -173

[14] *Ibid.*, p. 201

[15] *Ibid.*, p. 147

[16] *Ibid.*

a sad commentary on the progress of the country that as the years went by it became more repressive in granting the true freedom of religion.

It is interesting to see how our neighbour India dealt with the issue. Perhaps there we shall find valuable lessons for us as well.

Lessons from India

Whatever happens in India cannot but affect Nepal. Nepal and India have an open border. Citizens of both countries may freely travel back and forth.

Although the majority in India belongs to Hinduism, the framers of the constitution purposely made India a secular state. What does 'secular' mean? Commenting on it Jawaharlal Nehru said, "The word...does not obviously mean a state where religion as such is discouraged. It means freedom of religion and conscience including freedom for those who may have no religion. It means free play for all religions..." [17] The word "secular" however, conveys much more to me...It conveys the idea of social and political equality.

Elaborating on articles 25-28 of the Indian Constitution, Nagendra Singh, a noted author on Indian law says, "This group of articles guarantees freedom of conscience and the right freely to profess, practise, and propagate religion, and to establish and maintain religious and charitable institutions. The State is not allowed to impose any taxes for promotion of particular or religious institutions… It guarantees freedom of conscience and religion; and to run one's own educational and religious institutions without interference from the State." [18]

This spirit present in the Indian Constitution was lacking in its counterpart in Nepal. At least

in two decisions the Supreme Court gives us a guideline. In His Majesty's Government [HMG] vs. Ramrati Kaharni [2023-2024BS] the court ruled that eloping with a Muslim man in India did not equal religious conversion. [19] In other words, Ramrati did not become a Muslim. And she was acquitted. This verdict gives another reason why Part 4, Chapter 19, No.1 of the *Muluki Ain* (Civil Law) should have been abolished and Article 14 of the 1960 Constitution amended.

Also, this woman who had lived with her Muslim husband for 16 to 18 years is declared a Hindu by the court. She has attended the mosque, listened to the sermons of the Mullahs for all those years, but she had not taken part in the Muslim rite which declared her a Muslim. Which comes first — mental conversion or the external rite? Since the law is vague on that, it is best abolished.

In HMG vs. Dalmaya Rai [2038 BS] some of the accused have become Christians in Malaya or Hong Kong while serving as mercenaries in the British Army. [20] However, their wives had become Christians while still in Nepal. The Supreme Court acquitted all the 18 involved on the basis that the accused practised Christianity at home without disturbing others.

This judgment is right. Firstly, it tallies with the internationally known standards of religious freedom. Secondly, the majority of religious people practise their religions first at home. If someone asks about their religion, they would naturally explain. The Christians in the above case seem to have done the same.

Nepalese Christians under the 1960 Constitution

What do the authorities say regarding "freedom," "liberty," "right," and "change"? "Freedom" is the "power of acting, in the

---

[17] Dash, S C, *The Constitution of India,* A Comparative Study, Allahabad: Chaitanya Publishing House, 1968, p.493.

[18] N. Singh, *Human Rights and the Future of Mankind,* Delhi: Vanity Books, 1979, p.75.

[19] HMG vs, Ramrati Kaharni [2023 -2024], a copy issued by the Supreme Court Kathmandu

[20] *Falgun,* Issue 11, pp. 747 -750

character of a moral personality, according to the dictates of the will, without other checks, hindrances, or prohibitions than such as may be imposed by just and necessary laws and duties of social life."[21]

The emphasis here is that there should be no obstruction other than necessary for public good. The definition presumes that a man has a moral personality. He has the faculty to choose and face the consequences. Failure to consider man as a moral personality means we regard him as a babe, unable to make a proper decision. Closely related to the concept of freedom is that of liberty.

Liberty is the "the power of the will to follow the dictates of its unrestricted choice, and to direct the external acts of the individual without restraint, coercion, or control from other persons.... The word "liberty" includes and comprehends all personal rights and their enjoyment...It embraces freedom from duress; freedom from governmental interference in exercise of intellect, in formation of opinions, in the expression of them, and in action or inaction dictated by judgment."[22] The fact that strikes the eye in this definition is that a government should not interfere and there is the option to self-expression.

The meaning of a "right" follows the same train of thought. "As a noun and taken in a person concrete sense, a power, a privilege, faculty, or demand inherent in one person and incident upon another. Rights are defined generally as powers of free action. And the primal rights pertaining to men are enjoyed by human beings purely as such, being grounded in personality and existing antecedently to their recognition by positive laws."[23]

Winston Churchill on being accused of not following his election pledges remarked, "Only a fool never changes his mind!" What does "change" mean? "An alteration, modification or addition, substitution of one for another,"[24] describes one dictionary. "Alteration... variety,"[25] states another.

Article 14 of the 1960 Nepalese Constitution prohibited the basic ingredient for freedom-change. It granted freedom for Nepalese to remain in the religion as handed down from ancient times. Applying that logic to any other field would prove disastrous.

Should the farmer not use any modern implements of agriculture because his ancestors used only the plough and the oxen? Should a lad born in the tailor family do nothing more than sew clothes all his life? Is not change necessary for progress? Would I relish my freedom at a dinner table if my host asked me to eat as much as I wanted, but only from the "dhal" dish? In practical terms, Article 14 of the 1960 Constitution did the same.

An educated modern mind might not relish Hinduism at all, but he had no choice but to remain a Hindu. Another might not like the behaviour and the examples of the Buddhist "lamas," but under the 1960 Nepalese Constitution he had to continue as a Buddhist.

Another faulty assumption in Article 14 was that "old is always gold." The Nepalese tradition of respecting the elders and ancient things has a lot to say in its favour. Not all that is ancient is necessarily bad, but not all is good either. The modern mind is creative as well as critical. It may choose and reject. It may delete and modify.

---

[21] H.C. Black, *Black's Law Dictionary*, St. Paul: West Publishing Co., 1979, p. 597

[22] *Ibid.*, p. 827

[23] *Ibid.*, p. 1189

[24] *Ibid.*, p. 210

[25] H. W. Fowler and F. G. Howler., *The Concise Oxford Dictionary of Current English*, Oxford: Clarendon Press, 1964, p. 198

It is no secret that Hinduism itself has undergone a lot of revision throughout its history. Perhaps the best way to study this is through the lives of two reformers of Hinduism.

First we shall look at the pioneer of Hindu reformation — Ram Mohan Roy. "... Roy was the first Hindu to break through the barrier between the East and the modern West. He advocated that India adopt European intellectual achievements in order to further its own development. His numerous activities had but one objective, to arouse India's spirit and to free it from the deadening stupor of medievalism."[26]

Here was a Hindu who realised the need for change. He took a drastic step — he adopted Western ideas. What was the result? "He was active in social reform and was instrumental in the abolition of 'suttee'..."[27]

Another Hindu reformer to win worldwide acclaim was Vivekananda. He noted that social work did not fit with the *maya* doctrine of Hinduism. So the Hindu logic of his day reasoned — if the world is an illusion why bother about it? The doctrine of *karma* helped in this negative attitude. If a man lies dying on the street, he is suffering for evil deeds committed in the previous life. So he deserves to lie there!

Vivekananda did not bother about social service till he went to Europe. The three years in the West changed him significantly. "The effect of his Western experience upon Vivekananda's thought became obvious after his triumphant return to India. Even before his departure he had begun to feel that the chief task of his order must be the regeneration of the Indian masses rather than personal meditation. Now he definitely stressed the prime necessity of social and educational work. For this purpose he founded the Ramakrishna Mission...The mission became an important philanthropic organization."[28]

Ram Mohan Roy, Vivekananda, and Radhakrishnan advocated cautious change in Hinduism to counter the effects of Christian social service. The man, who even though a Hindu, made social service the tenet of his life was Mahatma Gandhi. The doctrines of *karma* or *maya* did not prevent him from being deeply involved with the poor, the sick, and the outcasts. Gandhi incorporated many Christian ideals into his philosophy and life. "The Sermon on the Mount" taught by Jesus Christ was one of his favourite passages from the Bible. In all these cases, changed Hindus brought about lasting social reforms in their societies. Change is needed for progress.

The prohibition of change of religion ran counter to the United Nations' concept of freedom. "The ability or capacity to act without undue hindrance or restraint"[29] is presumed in the Universal Declaration of Human Rights, Article 18.

"Everyone has the right to freedom of thought, conscience, and religion. This right includes the freedom to change his religion or belief, and freedom either alone or in community with others and in public or in private, to manifest his religion or belief in teaching, practice, worship, and observance."[30]

Nepal is a party to the United Nations. Article 14 in the 1960 Nepalese Constitution stood in contradiction to the UN ideal by prohibiting religious change. Freedom does not exist if there is no option for change.

---

[26] H. Kohn, "Roy, Ram Mohan," *Encyclopaedia of Social Sciences*, Vol. 13, 1963, p. 447

[27] *Ibid.*

[28] F. Nishnun, "Vivekananda, Swami", *Encyclopaedia of Social Sciences*, Vol. 15, 1963, p. 270

[29] N. Webster, *Webster's Third New International Dictionary*, Massachusetts, Merriam- Webster Inc. Publishers, p. 906

[30] *Treaties and Alliances of the World*, New York: Charles Scribner's Son, 1974, n.a., p. 16

A famous Nepali author of law, Mr T B Singh, commenting on Article 14, rightly says, "Each should have the right to accept the religion of his choice."[31] However, Singh has lost his courage on the next page. "The restrictive clause of Article 14 has prohibited anyone from converting someone else. Together with this, no one, even by his own will, can change his religion."[32]

The confusion that rages in Mr. Singh's thinking should surprise none. He juggles words to prove the reality of Nepalese freedom of religion when it does not exist. How much simpler would it be just to admit so, instead of this attempt to hoodwink the readers?

The next paragraph in Singh's book offers the same recipe. He asserts, "According to Article 14 one can preach his own religion without disturbing other religions."[33] However, he goes on to the prohibition of conversion on the threat of punishment.

This brings us to what the Nepalese Civil Law [*Muluki Ain*] itself had to say. "No person shall propagate Christianity, Islam or any other faith so as to disrupt the traditional religion of the Hindu community in Nepal, or to convert any adherent of the Hindu religion to these faiths. In case an attempt is made to do so, a sentence of imprisonment for three years shall be awarded. In case conversion has already taken place, the sentence will be for six years. A foreign citizen, in addition, shall be expelled from the country. If any Hindu converts himself into any of the above-mentioned religions, he shall be imprisoned for a maximum period of one year. Where only an attempt has been made to convert, a fine of Rs.100 shall be imposed. Where conversion has already taken place, it shall be invalidated, and such a person shall remain in his Hindu religion."[34]

The *Muluki Ain* thus clearly enunciated the real situation of the freedom of religion (or lack of it) in the country. The pseudo-liberty the constitution granted had a commentary in the *Muluki Ain*. It does not bother a Hindu or a Buddhist. The latter is considered a blood brother of the former. However, Muslims and Christians have had a difficult time.

When does propagation turn into proselytism? If a Hindu walks into a church or a mosque and hears the exposition of the Scriptures; will that qualify as proselytism? If such a Hindu decides on his own to become a Muslim or a Christian, who should receive the blame? Is an exposition of the Bible in a room an attempt at conversion? These questions may sound foolish, but they don't to those who have been imprisoned or punished by this clause in the *Muluki Ain*.

The modernity that has come to Nepal has brought its woes as well. Mr Rewatiraman Khanal is realistic about modernity and the problems that it brings to the only Hindu kingdom in the world. "In this case, it is necessary to think about the problems of the present Nepalese society. Nepal has diplomatic ties with many countries in the world. Many Nepalese go to other countries to study, work, or trade. Therefore, we cannot rule out the influence of the customs and rules of the other countries on the Nepalese society. Although the majority of the Nepalese are Hindus, there are many adherents of other religion too."[35]

Mr Khanal had thought of these problems in the context of mixed marriages between the

---

[31]T. B. Singh, *The Constitution of Nepal and the Constitutional Law*, [Nepali], Kathmandu: Law Books Publishing Committee, 1983, p. 158

[32] *Ibid.*, p. 159

[33] *Ibid.*

[34] *The Muluki Ain*, [Nepali], Kathmandu: Law and Justice Ministry, 1983, p.241

[35] R. Khanal, *Muluki Ain*, Kehi Vivechana, Kathmandu: Sajha Prakashan, 1978, p. 366

followers of different faiths. However, although the government had made laws regarding the religion of children out of mixed marriages, it had failed to consider the adults who may change their religions due to the foreign influence. This lop-sided emphasis has caused untold misery to religious converts and leaders of Christianity and Islam. There is no doubt that in the name of religious toleration and freedom, active persecution of Muslims and Christians, more of the latter, continued in the country from 1960, if not earlier.

The Years of No Return: 1985-1986

On April 17, 1986, the *Rising Nepal* had this to say, "Morang district court has sentenced three foreigners each to three years' imprisonment on the charge of preaching Christianity. Likewise, the district court has sentenced four Nepalese each to one year's imprisonment on the same charge..."[36]

The mentioned Roman Catholic Christians were celebrating the renowned festival of Easter. Their function was interpreted as proselytism. Their arrest must have embarrassed the government, which had earlier begun a relationship with the Vatican. "Archbishop Agostino Cacciavillan has been appointed the Apostolic Pro-Nuncio of the Holy-See to the Kingdom of Nepal..."[37] heralded the same newspaper about one year prior to the incident.

How could the government, which established a relationship with the Vatican, continue to arrest Christians for whom the Holy Father took responsibility? Here again, the duplicity in the policy for religious freedom stood out crystal clear.

The Gorkhapatra, being in the vernacular, had been more free in printing the harassment of Christians. "Lalitpur district court sentenced Sahadev Mahat [Farping], and Gyan Bahadur KC known as Abraham [Kupondole] to three months imprisonment each for converting to Christianity. The court further said that they should give up Christianity and return to Hinduism..."[38]

Can a court force a person to re-convert to Hinduism? Does the court have the right to play God by asking the accused to forsake a religion he holds dear? Does the legislature or the constitution have the authority to act, as the Creator, by dictating which religion a person must adhere to? Do not such actions go against the very definition of freedom that the state claims to protect? The police and the government officers had put their feet in the mouth in their zeal to punish Christians.

The Gorkhapatra reported another similar incident, this time involving foreigners, "The Dhading district court cleared seven Nepalese and four foreign citizens and sentenced eight Nepalese for one year and five foreign citizens for three years. They were among the twenty-four accused of preaching Christianity in Kutal of Ree village panchayat..."[39].

Since the concerned this time were foreigners too, the matter became International news overnight. This damaged the reputation of Nepal as a tolerant Hindu state. If foreigners brought up as Christians, could not practise their faith, how could the government really claim that it granted religious liberty?

Pastor Nicanor Tamang must have received the most serious punishment ever for doing his duty as a Christian leader. A pastor serves the Christian congregation that attends his church. He does this by preaching from the Bible on the weekly day of worship, visiting the sick, organising relief for the poor, and conducting

---

[36] *The Rising Nepal,* April 17, 1986
[37] *Ibid.,* May 1,1985
[38] *The Gorkhapatra,* April 30, 1985
[39] *Ibid.,* Nov.22, 1985

religious functions like weddings and funerals. He also baptises people who confess Jesus as Lord and Saviour and those who want to become Christians. What did the *Rising Nepal* say about Pastor Nicanor? "Lalitpur district court has sentenced Nicanor Tamang, an Indian national from Sikkim currently dwelling at Jhamsikhel, Lalitpur, to six years' imprisonment on the charge of preaching Christianity."[40]

Someone familiar with Christianity cannot but laugh at the humour in the quoted sentence. What does a Brahmin pundit do but expound the Hindu Scriptures? What does a Christian pastor do but preach from the Bible? It is his duty to preach. The congregation pays the pastor a salary for his service. Should the Brahmin priest be imprisoned because he preached to the people gathered to hear him? Why should a Christian pastor get a six-year sentence for doing his duty? It was no excuse to say that the *Muluki Ain* prohibited preaching by a Muslim or a Christian. If the government claimed total religious liberty according to the United Nations charter, those offending laws should have been changed long ago.

Enough was enough for the Nepali Christians. The year 1985 gave them an opportunity to draw attention to their plight. The ex-president of the United States, Jimmy Carter, was coming to Nepal in October. An expatriate missionary couple arranged a meeting of key Nepali Christians, with the president in Soaltee Hotel. He was to have dinner with the king that very evening.

The next day, the Nepali press did its best to twist what the president had remarked regarding the Christians in the country. The Indian newspapers were impartial. *The Statesman,* had this remark from Jimmy Carter's press conference in Kathmandu, "On his human rights platform, he said he was concerned that members of minority communities in Nepal, like Christians, do not have full rights to worship as they please. He is opposed to the ban on voluntary acceptance of any religion which is in force in Nepal..."[41]

---

[40] *The Rising Nepal,* May 14,1985

[41] *The Statesman.,* Nov. 1, 1985. The letter delivered to President Jimmy Carter by Nepali Christians on October 29, 1985, was drafted by the author. It ran as follows:

'Dear Mr President:

The Bible verse that comes to us as we address you is - "... and who knows whether you have come to the kingdom for such a time as this" (Esther 4:14).'

'During your presidency you gave priority to human rights. The Christians in Nepal remember that more than even the Camp David Accord. Based on Christian principles, the United States successfully advocated freedom from British rule for India and freedom of religion for Japan. The persecuted Christian minority of Nepal humbly requests your kind mediation at this crucial period.

'Though a member of the UNO and a beneficiary of US aid, Nepal has consistently violated Article 18 of the Universal Declaration of Human Rights. The enclosed materials indicate that neither the Constitution of Nepal nor the civil law grants freedom of religious choice. "Every person may profess his own religion as handed down from ancient times and may practise it having regard to the traditions, provided that no person shall be entitled to convert another person from one religion to another," (Constitution, Part 3, Fundamental Rights and Duties, Art. 14). The Civil Law, not available in English, Part 4, chapter 19, On Conversion, Art.1 prescribes one year prison sentence for freely converting oneself to another religion, three years for an attempt to convert someone, six years for successfully converting others, and a return to Hinduism after punishment. Impetuous murderers and pastors get the same prison sentence of six years. Included is a partial report of harassment, torture, or imprisonment of Christians. Roughly 40 Christians, out on bail, await trial in various courts of Nepal.

'Neither have the Christian organizations, not recognized at best, escaped government censure. The Nepal Bible Institute building lies vacant since its closure in January 1983. Classes meet elsewhere in secret. Two churches continue services in spite of a ban. Christian gatherings have broken up after police intervention. Several appeals to His Majesty the King have fallen on deaf ears.

The audience Jimmy Carter granted to Nepali Christians was a great tonic to the church in Nepal. However, other American individuals too were advocating the rights of the church in Nepal.

The US State Department Country Reports on Human Rights Practices observed, "During 1984, some 40 Nepali Christians were arrested, mostly in western Nepal, for conversion and/or proselytization. They are currently free on bail awaiting trial and reportedly have the assistance of counsel. Numerous Christian voluntary organisations operate educational, medical, and social service facilities in Nepal, most of which are officially sanctioned by the government. In addition, foreign clergy are permitted to live and work in Nepal to serve the expatriate community. However, the government has made clear that open proselytizing by foreigners would result in their expulsion from the country."[42]

Amnesty International did not know the harassment of Nepali Christians till 1983. Since then, it kept up with the issue. "Amnesty International also received reports that Christians in some parts of Nepal had been arrested, accused either of proselytizing or of having changed religion, both of which may be deemed offences under Nepal's Constitution. Some of these detainees were reportedly released on bail, while others were freed without formal charges being brought. The local authorities appeared to exercise considerable latitude in determining the arrests and prosecution.

Amnesty International wrote to the government on 12 October 1983, making reference to internationally-established standards pertaining to religious freedom, and urging it to ensure that citizens of religious beliefs other than Hinduism had their rights peacefully to practise and teach their faith protected."[43]

The request of the Amnesty International came to the point. Nepal's religious laws did not conform to the "internationally-established standards pertaining to religious freedom." Compared to what other secular, democratic countries have, the religious right in Nepal is almost a skeleton. More flesh must go on it for the citizens to enjoy full religious liberty. Parts of the flesh are "their rights peacefully to practise and teach their faith."

Amnesty International's request suggests that people other than Hindus have a difficult time. Why should only the Hindus have the right to practise and teach their faith to others?

Nepal had declared itself as the zone of peace in 1986. That really had no meaning for the harassed Nepali Christians. However, 1986 became the year that instilled hope in the heart of the church in Nepal. No longer could persecution of Christians in Nepal remain a local incident.

'Sir, I am sure our King will respect your mediation on behalf of The Nepalese Christians. We rest confident that as the servant of our Lord Jesus and as the champion of justice and human rights, you will do what you can to help your brothers and sisters in Nepal. We shall pray for you as you seek his guidance.'

[42] "The US State Department Country Reports on Human Right Practices," Washington, 1985, p. 1347

[43] "Amnesty International Report," London: The Times, Sep 1984, p. 245.

25, 1985 had this to say about Amnesty's mediation for Nepali Christians, '...according to Amnesty International's information, Nepalese Christians have been arrested solely for participating in religious activities and peacefully professing their religious beliefs. For example, in mid-May, 1984, 12 persons attending a bible school in Pokhara, Dadeldhura district were arrested by local police authorities. Released on bail, eight of them were convicted by the

Dadeldhura District Court in March 1985, to six months' imprisonment. They are currently on bail awaiting appeal to a higher court.

'Arrests in similar circumstances have continued during 1985. Between January and May at least 22 Nepalese Christians were reported as having been arrested in different parts of the country.

'Amnesty International has expressed its concern on these matters to the Government of Nepal on several occasions, but has received no response.'

Accepting the invitation of Nepali Christian leaders, Christian Solidarity International brought in a delegation that consisted of David Atkinson, David Alton (Members of the British Parliament), two American congressional staff, two lawyers, three staff members, a pastor, and a businessman who financed their travel. In the process of meeting persecuted Nepali Christians, the group travelled over one thousand miles across Nepal and interviewed thirty-six Nepali devotees of Jesus. Somehow, Nepali Christians even five days walk away from the nearest bus station got news of their arrival. Christians in East Nepal travelled to Dharan to meet the delegation. One pastor showed the baton the police broke over his back while torturing him. Others displayed the scars on their bodies.

Although the delegation met many persecuted and tortured Christians, its attempt to meet the king and the royal Hindu high priest failed. They got as far as the foreign minister who admitted that he knew of persecution, but not to the extent discovered by the delegation.

The delegation's visit encouraged Nepali Christians immensely. Other Christians in the world had not forgotten them. Now they knew tangibly that others cared and prayed for them. Christians in Muslim and Communists countries too suffered as they did. Persecution had united them as never before and given them one voice. Neither was the Nepali press silent.

> According to...the press conference held at Soaltee Hotel, suppression and torture of Nepali Christians should stop, Christians should have the freedom to read and keep Bibles, Nepali Christians should have legal security, and Nepali laws should conform to the declaration of the United Nations Organisation...
>
> David Atkinson said...."Once we return to England, we will request the foreign minister to take this matter to the government. The foreign minister has plans to accompany Queen Elizabeth during her visit to Nepal...
>
> Nepali observers have taken these statements very seriously. Nepal is a Hindu nation. Even though Nepali law prohibits conversion, such cases do appear time to time. However, this is the first time that a delegation has come from foreign countries because 'Nepali Christians have been suppressed' and given straight directives as to what laws Nepal should make regarding their religion...Focusing on Nepal's diplomatic relations with the chief pilgrimage of Christians, the Vatican City, which has supported Nepal becoming a zone of peace, observers believe that nothing should disturb the traditionally religious tolerance of the country.[44]

Another newspaper thundered, "Since all religions are great and conversion merits legal punishment, Nepali Christians who have been converting illegally have been jailed. Hiding this fact, England's House of Commons member is surprisingly not ashamed to claim that these are in prisons for just 'becoming Christians'. The Central Census Department states that above 3900 Christians live in Nepal. Claiming this to be a lie, David (Atkinson) ridiculously asserts that they number twenty-five to thirty-five thousand. Saying that the present plight of Nepali Christians cannot remain a private or internal problem, the delegation has forewarned us about its intention to pressurise and interfere in this totally internal matter of Nepal...Not even one percent of what David says is true. No advocate of any religion has gone to jail just because of his faith, without doing wrong. However, those converting illegally, committing crimes, stealing idols and dealing in drugs have gone to prisons...and majority of Christians have suffered for such crimes...We do not understand why His Majesty's Government gave this delegation permission for this baseless

---

[44] *The Saptahik Bimarsha*, Jan 10, 1986.

'study'. Himself a Christian, Foreign Minister Subha has assured the delegation that he will look into this matter. This has greatly delighted the delegation, and revealed the mystery a bit further. Observers say that those believing in 'Bible first and guns later' should not receive such privilege in future."[45]

The World Hindu Council, which the queen of Nepal chaired, put out a statement, "Nepal is a free, sovereign nation. Its Constitution declares it a Hindu state, but all have the freedom to observe their own religion. In this holy land where there never has occurred a religious dispute, an attempt to provoke controversies of this nature is really sad. In the Kingdom of Nepal, no one has suffered discrimination because of his religion. The liberality of Hinduism can not even imagine such discrimination."[46] "Some Christian Nepali citizens have come to us and said that what the foreign delegation uttered is not true. Together with advocates of other religions, we have lived in harmony till now. It is not right that foreigners should come here and spread confusion."[47]

If Jimmy Carter's visit was a tonic to the Nepali Christians, the visit of the Christian Solidarity International's delegation scared the Nepal government to its backbone. In its frantic response, the Nepali press was admitting that the Christian church in Nepal is a force to reckon with. The Nepali church had begun to tread the path to greater freedom and liberty. It had progressed so much that going back became more arduous than continuing forward.

Christians Too — Become Nepali Citizens: 1987-1990

Known cases of persecution of Nepali Christians, following 1987 are numerous. Cited below are examples that were the most prominent and those that created a stir Internationally.

In early 1988, four Christians of Ratomate denied their faith in Jesus, five others remained loyal even through their knees bled from the beating, The police authorities had received orders from "above," meaning the palace, to deal severely with drug dealers, sellers of girls (to brothels in India), and Christians.

That same year, another incident drew international attention to the plight of Christians in Nepal. On October 27, 1988, two expatriate missionaries, a Canadian and an American, were trekking in east Nepal. They reported to a police checkpoint at Phidim as the Nepali trekking laws required. As if to earn medals for their work, the police made a thorough search of their belongings, and naturally found Christian literature and Bibles. The police drew up an accusation sheet, and locked the two expatriates and their porters in a cell ten feet square. Their first appearance before the judge took place so quickly that they could not even get lawyers to represent them and get their release through bail. Friends of these prisoners sent letters worldwide to publicize the case. They asked sympathizers all over the world to pray for these prisoners, another thirty Nepali believers in jails, and about two hundred out on bail; to write letters of protest to the Nepali ambassador in London, and to send lines of encouragement to the prisoners themselves. For the first time, other Nepali Christians in jails all over the country got letters from their brothers and sisters throughout the world.

The final hearing for the American and Canadian Christians took place on February 28, 1989. Their account of the trial read like a description of a Festival:

> Though we were put on trial for preaching Christianity, the trial became a forum for the Gospel...Our lawyer invited the curious local

---

[45] *The Matribhumi,* Jan 14, 1986.

[46] *The Gorkhapatra,* Feb 15, 1986.

[47] *The Saptahik Bimarsha,* Jan 17, 1986.

residents into the room to witness the proceedings. The small room was soon packed to the maximum. The witnesses all heard the Gospel message when the lawyer read from a Nepali text book on religions in Nepal. The subject he read? It was about Jesus, his birth, life, death, and resurrection. The onlookers listened carefully and nodded agreement as the lawyer read these truths concerning Jesus. 'If...(they) are to be sentenced because of the contents of the books they sold,' he argued, 'then all the teachers in Nepal should also be imprisoned for teaching from the text book.' How could the Judge disagree? Phidim and the Judge got zapped with the Gospel in that court room...'[48]

As if God were judging the autocrats of Nepal, politically the government started confronting problems never faced before. The transit and trade treaty between Nepal and India ran out on March 23, 1989. The government "in New Delhi brought trade between the two countries to a halt. Furthermore, the Indian government did everything in its power to make the transit through India of goods to Nepal from third countries difficult. In just a few weeks traffic dropped by half in Kathmandu because of the fuel shortage and endless queues of Nepalis sprang all over the capital waiting patiently for the weekly ration of kerosene."[49]

In addition to trouble with India, Nepal's reputation in the international arena started getting worse. *Asia Watch*, a unit of the Washington-based non-official *Human Rights Watch*, condemned Nepal in a hundred and four-page report. *Asia Watch* criticised some laws that the government of Nepal had recently passed: Public Security Act, Destructive Crimes Act, and the Treason Act.[50] For publishing this report of *Asia Watch*, the Nepalese government confiscated that particular issue of the *Times of India.*

In October 1989, the supreme court in Kathmandu sentenced three leaders each to six years in jail "on charges of propagating Christianity in ways injurious to Hindu religion" and two Christians to one year in prison for converting to Christianity.[51] The first three were reportedly "offering various allurements," the favourite charge applicable to any pastor or preacher. Even "peace through forgiveness of sins through the sacrifice of Jesus" qualified as allurement.

The climax in 1989 for the Christian community was yet to come. "On 12th November a shocking event took place in Bhaktapur, the neighbouring city in Kathmandu valley. One of the oldest Nepali churches was raided by two vans full of policeman and the whole congregation (of thirty-nine people) was arrested. They were then taken to the police station where the believers were forced to recant their faith and were made to bow down to an idol as the sign of public renunciation. Those who refused to comply were held under police custody. There were eight people — seven women and the pastor who refused. The pastor, who is seventy-six years old, stood up boldly, for which he was badly beaten. The seven women were released on bail after eleven days in custody, but the old man was not allowed to come out on bail."[52]

Beating the seventy-six year old pastor drew more condemnation than the beleaguered Nepal

---

[48] *Ibid.*

[49] William Raeper and Martin Hoftun, Spring Awakening, Viking Penguin, New Delhi, 1992, pp.20-21.

[50] *The Times of India*, Sept 7, 1989. 'Asia Watch recognises the right of all nations to take measures to protect national security in a state of emergency. But in Nepal, these laws are in force permanently in circumstances that do not involve a publicly declared national emergency that threatens the life of the nation.'

[51] The *Rising Nepal*, Oct 20, 1989.

[52] *Jubilee Campaign's* releases, dated Nov 21, 1989.

government would have liked. In addition to political warfare with India, the government was trying to fight the religious front too. In December, the BBC sent a television crew to meet and film the pastor's condition.

The political revolution was snow balling at an incredible pace. The country would become a democracy again after thirty years of royal dictatorship, but only after more human sacrifice. God had designated April 6, 1990, as such a day, when unsung martyrs would die in order that their countrymen and women may live. A great crowd was approaching the palace. Shree Nath and Gorakh Bahadur battalions dwelled in the palace compound to guard the king. In addition, the government had ordered paratroopers, some of who were taking aim from tree-tops unto the crowd below. All of a sudden, the soldiers started firing.

Perhaps, no one will know how many really died on that day. The BBC put the figure at fifty. However, others put it much higher. "Witnesses... say that they saw three army trucks loaded with bodies leave Kathmandu after Friday's protest.[53] For the first time, Nepalese had to endure a twenty-four hour curfew, violators of which met immediate deaths.[54]

That very night brought good news. "Shortly before midnight on 8 April, Nepal TV announced that the King had lifted the ban on the political parties. This was a sudden turn-around..."[55] Previously, plainclothes policemen infiltrated church services, beat Christians and put them to jails. However, that Saturday all hoped for genuine religious freedom, and a government committed to human rights. Many had prayed for such a day.[56]

If April 8, 1990, were the Black Friday to families of martyrs, the Easter Sunday coming two weeks later would be unique. Christians all over Nepal, the only Hindu kingdom in the world, would take part in the first Easter rally ever. They would march with placards and banners extolling Jesus. For the first time, police would treat Christians in procession as Nepali citizens, protecting instead of arresting them.

The State of Freedom of Religion Now: 1990 Following

The new Nepali Constitution would be drafted only by October of 1990. Interesting events happened before its release. Buddhists refused to consider themselves 'Hindus.' This meant that the percentage of the population of Hindus came down from over 90 to about 60. The Buddhists, Christians, and the Communists wanted a secular constitution. The Palace and the Nepali Congress were in favour of declaring Nepal a Hindu state. The latter won.

The new constitution was disappointing to Christians. Part 3, Article 19:1 gives freedom for each citizen to practise the religion of one's forefathers. Conversion from one religion to the other is prohibited. However, 19:2 states, "Each religious body can maintain its free identity under law, run and protect its own religious place and trust."[57]

This gives the right to Nepali churches and Christian organisations to register with the government. However, that has not been easy.

The Association for Biblical Education in Nepal got its registration only after three years of running from one office to another. Then, the authorities wanted the word "Biblical" deleted.

---

[53] *The Arizona Republic*, April 8, 1990.

[54] *Ibid*.

[55] Raeper and Hoftun, p. 68.

[56] Based on a newsletter by Mike Francis.

[57] The Constitution of the Kingdom of Nepal, 2047, (in Nepali) Law and Justice Ministry, 2053; 1996 A.D., pp. 13-14

When the registration finally took place in December 1998, the organisation I work in became the Association for Theological Education in Nepal (ATEN). Even then ATEN has not had the courage to get the land and building transferred to its name. The government-approved constitution of ATEN says that it can be shut down should it "cease to function." Closure depends on the character and mood of the Chief District Officer concerned!

There were about sixty Christians in jail even after Nepal became democratic in April, 1990. A British member of the parliament, David Atkinson, came in person to request their release during that summer. Since then, Christians have been locked up for a few days, mostly due to ignorance of the local officials, who did not yet know what rights the new constitution gave.

Sadly, the Civil Law has not changed. Chapter 19:1 still prohibits preaching to convert. It still prescribes three years in jail for the attempt, six years after success in conversion, and expulsion for foreigners after they serve their sentences. Another clause, 19:1a, is an addition to the old Civil Law. It awards three years in prison or three thousand rupees fine or both for disturbing a religious place or activity.[58]

So, both the 1990 Constitution and the new civil law give the government and the society ammunition to be used against Nepali Christians. The Nepali press usually has one anti-Christian article per week. Events in India, the murder of Graham Staines and his two sons, the return of the BJP government in majority, always have ripples in Nepal. The counterpart of Shiv Sena of India has become the Pashupati Sena in Nepal. The recent call by the Pope for more evangelisation of India inspired articles against him in Nepal. The present Prime Minister, Krishna Prasad Bhatterai, declared himself to be a staunch anti-Christian.[59] His predecessor, Sher Bahadur Deuba, did not claim so publicly, but was known for his anti-Christian stance. During the year, 1999, two Nepali churches were burnt down.

On the positive side, Prime Ministers Girijha Prasad Koirala and Manmohan Adhikari greeted Christians during Christmas. The evangelist Luis Pulau preached in an open-air meeting in Kathmandu. Christians air special radio programmes and hold celebrations in the City Hall during Christmas. The Easter rally continues.

The greatest threat to Nepali Christians now may not be hostile Hindus or governments. The easy flow of foreign money into the country after 1990 has weakened and splintered churches. Denominations, unheard of in the 1970's, have multiplied. Nominal Christians are on the rise. Though no Nepali Christian would like to return to the pre-1990 days of persecution, he/she has to agree that the democratic revolution has brought mixed blessings.

---

[58] *The Civil Law* (in Nepali), Law and Justice Ministry, 2054 (1997 A.D.), p. 226.
[59] Kanchan, April 1999, p. 1,4.

CHAPTER 30

Modern People Movements: A Jharkhand Case Study

R. GEORGE EDWARD

Introduction

When missionaries presented the Gospel of the Lord Jesus Christ to the animist Maltos, they saw them (as people) in their totality. They communicated the Gospel in such a way that it brought transformation to them in their every activity. They had to concentrate on their spiritual and social transformation. The chief numerical growth of the Church has been by a people movement through group conversion. It is a lay and liberation movement. The Gospel had an easy entrance and interpretation in Malto thought forms that led to wholesome conversions of the people into the new faith in Christ.

There are many analogies or bridges from within the Malto traditional religion, which can be used to explain the Christian Gospel to the Maltos. The goodness of the Lord Jesus Christ can effectively be communicated through the traditional religious framework of the Maltos. It is necessary, for effective communication, to explore some bridges from the basic assumptions that they hold. In the course of this exploration missionaries saw that there were some surprising parallels between Malto traditional religious practices and some practices discussed in the Bible. The missionary had to build from what was known in the Malto traditional religious practices to communicate what was unknown to the people, for communication commences where the people are, and not with a negation of their beliefs. David Burnett affirms this universal fact, "God starts where the people are in their own historical, cultural and personal context, in order to reveal himself to them in a way that is particularly comprehensible and meaningful."[1]

To a Malto man or woman religion means living aware of, encountering, and acknowledging the active reality of the spirits by their regular rituals and customs. Their religious beliefs are changing in response to internal social pressures and environmental changes, yet traditional beliefs and practices, handed down orally, still carry weight.

I write as a Christian missionary who has been working among the Malto people for about 19 years. My colleagues and I are encouraged by the Malto response to the Gospel. I want this study to lower barriers to meaningful communication of the Gospel, and help Gospel workers, whether newcomers or Malto, to communicate more effectively. The Church must present the Gospel in language and symbols that the people understand. This should transform the life of the Malto believers from within, making the Gospel part and parcel of their world-view, value systems and actions.

Maltos of Jharkhand

The Maltos[2] live on the Rajmahal hill tracts of the northeastern part of Jharkhand. Although

---

[1] David Burnett, *Unearthly Powers: A Christian Perspective on Primal and Folk Religion*, Eastbourne: MARC, 1988, p.22.

[2] Malto means 'of people'

they are also known as *Pahariyas*[3] and as *Maler*,[4] they increasingly call themselves, and want others to call them, by their more respected recent name, 'Maltos.' While Santals reside nearby in the valleys, Malto villages are scattered all over the Rajmahal hills, which are elevated from 500 feet to 1200 feet. Their population is about 1,10,000, with 95 percent in India and the other 5 percent in Bangladesh in the Chittagong Hill Tracts.[5] Their main four Indian districts are Sahibganj, Pakur, Godda and Dumka.

Maltos have three sub-groups, the Mal Pahariyas, Kumarbhag Pahariyas and Sawriya Pahariyas, each a distinct endogamous and linguistic group. The major distinction is over beef. **Kumarbhag Pahariya,** who do not eat beef, speak the Kumarbagh dialect of Malto, intermarry with Mal Pahariyas, but have no social dealing with Sawriya Pahariyas whom they look down on as unclean and unworthy to mix with. They are mainly in the south of Pakur district, in Godda and Dumka districts. **Mal Pahariyas,** speaking Mal Pahariya, and living mainly in the narrow strip from Litipara in Pakur district to Chandana in Godda District, have all kinds of social relationships with the Sawriya Pahariyas. They too do not eat beef. **Sawriya Pahariyas,** who do eat beef, are the largest community of Maltos with a population of about 86,799.[6] They live in the hill parts of Godda, Sahibganj, and Pakur districts, and retain more habits of their ancestors than the other two. Proud of their unbounded liberty in the matter of food, they call themselves the ***asal pahariyas,***[7] because they have not restricted themselves in what they may eat.

About 97 percent of Maltos are illiterate and few villages have electricity. An average village is 6 kilometres from the main road and public transport in the area is minimal. The people suffer from malaria, *kala-azar*, tuberculosis, and other mostly water-borne diseases. Infant mortality is high at approximately 250/1000. Poverty, powerlessness and exploitation by non-tribal people mark Malto lives. Their population is declining,[8] though not nearing extinction.

Though the Maltos live among the Austro-Asiatic Santals and the Indo-Aryans, their language is Dravidian, distinct from and not understood by either the plains people or the neighbouring Santals. Maltos can speak Santali, but Santals do not speak Malto. The name of the language of the majority of the people is '***mal saba.***' The word 'Malto' now implies not only the tribal identity, but also has positive connotations connected with literature, Christianity and improved living conditions, symbolic of their newly found dignity.

The language, unwritten till 1982, has been reduced to writing using Devanagri script and a number of literacy primers, storybooks, and songbooks have been introduced in the language. Now people learn to read and write in their own heart language as well as Hindi. Sawriya and Kumar Bagh people understand each other well, and church planting and Bible translation are going on in both dialects.

Bridges to the Maltos: Redemptive Analogies

Analogies with Malto traditional religion could explain the goodness of the Lord Jesus Christ. Communicating the Gospel message has

---

[3] Mountain people

[4] People

[5] George and Premila Edward, "Malto Narrative Discourse" in Robert Longacre, ed., *Textlinguistics*, Dallas: SIL Publications, 1988, p. 149.

[6] Peter Premraj, "Bihar Background" in S. Vasantharaj Albert, ed., *Bihar: Church and People Groups*, Madras: Church Growth Association of India, 1992, p. 21.

[7] Original Inhabitants

[8] Newman Bill, Alice and Edward, Survey on *Mal Pahariya Dialect*, Nashik: IICCC, 1995, p. 5.

taken into account the ways Maltos think and how they formulate their traditional ideas. And since communication commences where the people are, working from the known to the unknown rather than negating their beliefs, missionaries have begun to build from some surprising parallels with Bible practices.

God calls us to use what we find already in the people. As Eugene A. Nida points out, "The introductory use of points of contact is essential and valuable, as Paul found it meaningful to refer to 'the unknown god' of the Athenians, Acts 17:23."[9] Missionaries and local evangelists have built an intellectual bridge over which Christian understanding could migrate into the Malto world. They began to seek to modify the existing beliefs through the bridges they found which pointed the way to feeling and understanding biblical revelation. They have also realized the significance of establishing cultural substitutes, and have contextualised and made them part of the life of the people.

Unearthly Powers and Christianity

A tree or a stone or a river or a hill is not merely an inanimate object for a Malto person, but may possess unseen power. This power must be recognized, and patterns followed to avoid any harm, and in order to cope with the everyday activities of life. Malto awareness of unearthly powers may remain for centuries and rigidly held taboos may in time become superstitions or merely quaint customs, but the task is to show the Gospel not merely as intellectual truths, but to show Jesus Christ as the Lord of power. Their customary acceptance of spiritual powers can lead them to accept the spirituality of the God of Christianity.

The beliefs of the Malto society are codified orally and these codified beliefs make up the doctrine of the unearthly powers. In seeking to

understand the thinking of the animistic Malto, Christian workers interacted afresh with the Word of God to determine how to make the most-powerful Jesus Christ relevant within the Malto experience. People would see the difference between their unearthly powers and the power of the risen Christ. The Lausanne Committee for World Evangelization dwells briefly on this point:

> We wish to affirm, therefore, against the mechanistic myth on which the typical Western worldview rests, the reality of demonic intelligences, which are concerned by all means, overt and covert, to discredit Jesus Christ and keep people from coming to Him.[10]

It is worthwhile to note that the worldview of the Indian missionary is often not different from that of the Western. When such a missionary accepts the reality of the unearthly powers, he or she finds the first bridge to bring animistic Maltos to Christ. The dynamism and callousness of the unearthly powers always strike the mind of the people as their benevolence and they seek to establish fruitful relations with them. In this context of spiritual warfare, the Gospel message brings the people to the right knowledge about God and consequently right relationship with their Creator. People turn their attention and allegiance to the truth that sets them free from the clutch of the unearthly powers.

God

However, a major obstacle confronting missionaries in communicating the Gospel of Jesus Christ is that the Maltos already have their own cosmology and a range of gods, goddesses, deities and spirits. However, the notion of God held by the Maltos has provided one of the vital keys to an understanding of their deepist feelings and a take-off point for communication of the Gospel. William Reyburn points out,

---

[9] Eugene A. Nida, *Customs and Cultures,* California: William Carey Library, 1954, p. 261.

[10] The Willowbank Report, Wheaton: Lausanne Committee for World Evangelization, 1978, p. 21.

In fact, the missionary who will know his people will have to first know their God. How a people symbolise the supernatural, and the way they think and feel toward their God or gods is not only a clue to the stuff of which the society is made, but also an indication of what in Christianity will be immediately relevant.[11]

Gosanyi, 'god', is unique and cannot be seen or understood through carved images. God is Spirit. Christianity shares the Malto belief in the existence of God. The Malto concept of *gosanyi* is a '*being*' that is omnipotent, omnipresent and omniscient. This God is different from nature, is eternal and free from all limitations. This is the God of gods, faithful in his promises, providing security, delighting in those who do good things and offer regular and sincere sacrifices. Before him all are equal. Sometimes he punishes those who do wrong. Those who fear and obey this God can enjoy his presence and activities. He often visits those who look for him, and sometimes shows himself and his plans through dreams, calamities, accidents and sickness. The Malto concept of God corresponds to their perception of life. People are accountable to God for whatever they think or do, so they need to lead obedient lives.

The concept of *gosanyi* made a powerful bridge to make known the truth about God, when Christian missionaries explained that God is the living, eternal Being in whose presence all creatures live and move and have their being '(Acts 17:28). Maltos would recognise that *gosanyi* is this God. The Supreme Being, *gosanyi*, whom the Maltos had previously thought was distant and unknown, is now near through the Lord Jesus Christ. Because they fear the unearthly powers and want to be free, they are ready to hear about the loving and faithful Creator God who is not distant but always active in the world.

Maltos already see God as distinct from human creation, but their animism has no clear concept of the relation between the creature and the creator, which can be learnt from creation. "God created people in His own image, in the image of God, male and female, He created them" is a powerful bridge to help Maltos know of Christ and Truth. This is Clarke's point:

> Very prominent in the Christian doctrine is the statement that God created man in his own likeness. This conception is not peculiar to the doctrine of the Bible, for in any case where an intelligent creator is supposed to exist, it is necessarily implied that man, who is intelligent, bears resemblance to him. Even the myth of the savages affirms this.[12]

Christianity confirms Malto belief in the creation of the universe by *gosanyi* the 'Supreme Being.' Maltos already have, in their belief in the divine origin of the universe, a bridge to bring them to Christ. We can make clear that our Creator God is alive, still creating and providing, and indeed is the same One as the Heavenly Father, who is concerned for their needs.

Since Maltos already have a creator God, *gosanyi*, we may inject into this idea further biblical concepts. For example, in translating the Bible into Malto '*gosanyi*' is used for God.

In addition, the Malto's belief in spirit possession lays a foundation for the concept of the indwelling presence of the Holy Spirit who, however, cleanses and empowers people for daily living. In Malto thinking a spiritual being intrudes into a human body. The Gospel appeals with the news that Christ can live in a heart, but not in an overpowering coercive way. Rheenen observes that in Christianity:

> Creator God is never understood as possessing human beings. God is above such manipulative acts. He desires the allegiance

---

[11] William D. Reyburn, "The Transformation of God and the Conversion of Man", in W.A. Smalley, ed. *Readings in Missionary Anthropology*, Pasadena: William Carey Library, 1974, p. 26.

[12] William Newton Clarke, *The Christian Doctrine of God*, New York: Charles Scribner' sons, 1914, p. 137.

of those who are in charge of their own mental and physical faculties. God, as pictured in the Scriptures, indwells rather than possesses.[13]

The Christian message would help them understand that spirit possession is the ultimate grip of satanic forces on the human soul. The Maltos came to appreciate the character of God as revealed in the Bible through teaching. A clear distinction has been made between any association of the God revealed in the Bible with that of the spirits the Maltos worshipped. Missionaries and local evangelists insisted that the God of the Bible is always alive and active in the world, still creating and providing, and taking care of His people.

Sacrifice

Maltos know about sacrifice, a ritual to present an object to a spirit or deity or ancestor. Protection and provisions are the major concerns behind special celebrations held once or twice a year where libations are poured out at specific sports in the homes and the fields. The New Testament reveals that even a near-perfect sacrifice is never totally satisfactory. The necessary perfect and complete sacrifice was Jesus Christ, sacrificed once on the cross to take away the sins of many people (Hebrews 9:28). After this sacrifice, no more are needed. This truth has made a powerful bridge in communication of the Gospel message to the Maltos.

Every year Maltos sacrifice a buffalo, which they consider the greatest sacrifice to please *gosanyi* and to seek blessings and protection from the spirits. This sacrifice shares some similarities with the Christian concept of Christ's sacrifice on the cross, though the Christian God no longer expects animal sacrifice. Maltos also offer sacrifices to propitiate harmful spirits. Similarly Christ's death propitiated God and so reconciles humans with God. The idea of sacrifice has helped the animist Maltos to understand the meaning of reconciliation with God. As Burnett correctly points out; believers in Christ are not required to offer animal sacrifices, rather spiritual sacrifices acceptable to God through Jesus Christ, though they are anointed to priesthood in the world.[14]

Malto sacrifices were to ward off sickness, sufferings, and afflictions. When the Gospel is presented as powerful enough to meet all physical and spiritual needs, Maltos respond positively. Despite the fact that Christians do get sick sometimes, Christ's sacrifice guarantees that no ultimate harm comes to a Christian believer. Often Maltos are disappointed to find no benefit from their sacrifice, but they have no alternative belief. For Christians the benefits of Christ's sacrifice are guaranteed.

Maltos were frustrated and disappointed by the failure of their sacrifices. They could not get what they wanted to achieve or accomplish through their sacrifices to the spirits. Jacob Loewen remarks, "... because religion is so thoroughly integrated into the total fabric of life, there will be motivation for change only when a system frustrates an individual or a whole society at some rather crucial point."[15] When some frustrations and disappointments arose, Maltos were not only willing to counter change, they were actually looking for relief. This area of frustration for the Malto society became an open door for the Gospel.

Priest

A priest is an important religious official in Malto society. He discharges his priestly functions

---

[13] Gailyn Van Rheenen, *Communicating Christ in Animistic Contexts*, Michigan: Baker Book House, 1991, p. 241.

[14] Burnett, *Unearthly Powers*, p. 131.

[15] Jacob A. Loewen, *Culture and Human Values: Christian Intervention in Anthropological Perspective*, Pasadena: William Carey Library, 1975, p.7.

in connection with community rituals and ceremonies. Everybody respects him, since priesthood is determined by age, experience, freedom from serious deformity and good conduct. Public opinion is always sought to dictate who among the people are fitted to be priests. This reminds us of the principles for the Old Testament Levitical priesthood. People can go and tell the priest their problems, and he in turn will approach the spirits through prayer and sacrifice.

The priest takes the initiative for cursing the angry spirits who often inflict diseases on the village. He also holds a key position at festivals. Usually he is a person who knows about the spirits and has mastery over the rites and rituals with which he propitiates the spirits residing in the hills and forests of the local area. Besides pleading to the *gosanyi*, to bless the people, he also invokes the ancestral spirits to win their favour in all ceremonies, rituals, and religious undertakings.

The role of the priest as a ritual functionary to the Malto aids their perception of Jesus Christ as the High Priest to plead on their behalf. The author of the letter to the Hebrews persistently presents Jesus Christ as a priest who offers a perfect sacrifice, not on earth, but in the very presence of God the Father (Hebrews 8:1-7).

Rheenen points out that the animist priest holds special powers because of his relationship with the spirit world. Christians cannot use this practitioner because his power is not of God.[16] Maltos coming to Christ gain access to God and could introduce others to this privilege, but only Christ atones or propitiates or reconciles. They enter by virtue of His sacrificial work.

The Church in its role as the body of Christ is anointed for priesthood to the world, giving universal access to God. So when Maltos come to Christ, they no longer need the traditional priests, for they may all bring what Christ asks, the offering of praise. The Maltos understand the imagery of the priest well and it provides a meaningful bridge in the presentation of the Gospel to them.

Fear

Fear is a major fact of life in Malto society. Maltos fear spirits, and fear makes them superstitious in all aspects of life. The spirits of the deceased ancestors of other tribes are feared very much. But Christ liberates people from superstition. This is a powerful bridge to draw Maltos to Christ and encourages them into new hope and freedom. The phrase **'don't fear'** appears in the Bible about 366 times. Our Lord's promise to be with believers till the end of the world (Matthew 28:20), is a good example. Maltos longing to live undisturbed by malevolent powers now find safety in Jesus Christ. They understand that the Lord Jesus Christ is able to overcome the spirits, which dominate their very life, and release people from their bondage and fear. As a consequence, they voluntarily accept the lordship of Jesus Christ in large numbers.

Rheenen observes that animistic peoples live with an all-pervasive fear of ancestors, spirits, magic and witchcraft. However, for the Christian, 'perfect love drives out fear', 1 Jn. 4:18.[17] He points out that while animists fear disharmony, which tears society apart, the Christian message shows how people can truly live with both God and humans. In this harmony humans need not manipulate the divine, for the Christian learns to place his or her life dependently in the hands of the sovereign God.[18] Maltos love this. Personally trusting God is different from the Malto idea of sacrifice, for Christian sacrifices express thanks,

---

[16] Rheenen, *Communicating Christ,* p. 157.
[17] *Ibid.* p. 30.
[18] *Ibid.*

dependence and trust come what may. In Christ, fearful Maltos have the protection of a loving almighty God.

Some observers point out that tribal animists are shocked when bulldozers and tractors destroy sacred trees and push aside rocks while constructing a new road or dam. Christianity, however, presents God as the Creator of all things, who has put human beings in charge of His creation, as stated in Genesis 1:26.[19] Maltos find harmony when they are faithful to God, not when they fear created things. They realized the Christian God must be more powerful than the familiar spirits such as *Kanya Gosanyi, Kondo gosanyi, sinybatte gonsayi, rakse gosnayi, sittar gosanyi, mariya gosanyi, jarqe gosanyi, dasmi gosanyi, jitya gosanyi, kuri gosanyi, sitaam gosanyi, sagari kathu gosanyi,* and so village after village turned to the new faith.

Christ's assurance to His followers that He sets them free from the anxieties and fears that surround their lives appears powerfully to the Maltos. The Maltos are taught what to fear and how to respond appropriately as they are empowered to freedom from their fears. Maltos responded to the claims of Christ in groups when they saw that His power is much more superior to the spirits who always caused them fear. The Gospel assures them that there are no forces in the universe, natural or supernatural, real or imagined, which can endanger them. People are led to a trusting relationship with Jesus Christ and they enjoy and experience this assurance.

The Gospel message has become an important powerful force in the continuous restructuring of the Malto cultural environment and their worldview. As they grow in their faith in Christ, they discover new spiritual ways of managing their fear complex. This new style of life attracts others too to come to Christ in large numbers.

Concept of Sin

A major feature of Christian thinking, lacking in the Malto religion, is the concept of sin. Maltos regard nothing as specifically sin. They see theft and adultery as evil acts against the well being of an individual or the community, but they also have a god from whom they seek protection before they go out to steal. The concept of sin and its punishment both in this world and in the next world introduced by the Gospel proclamation draws the attention of the people.

Yet Maltos do have a concept of right and wrong, and a sense of estrangement from the Supreme Being. They do regard certain acts as offences. When they accept the idea that sin is not only an act that harms someone, but also shows how humans rebel against God, Maltos see themselves as sinners who need a saviour. Sin does not harm God but offends Him and earns His just anger. At this point they can see the meaning of the bridge message that Jesus Christ saves from sin. Rheenen rightly remarks on this:

> As an animist internalises the Christian message, his perceptions of sin and salvation change into different ways. First, his definition of sin and salvation are expanded and reformulated. He no longer defines sin only in terms of the social structure. Second, the animist's source of salvation changes. He no longer relies on other personal spiritual beings or impersonal forces for his salvation.[20]

Many of the older Maltos believe that the lack of social harmony in many areas has resulted from the younger people abandoning their traditional way of life and following the life-style of the non-tribal people of the *bazaar*. They believe that observing the traditional way of life is the natural order of things. They perceive the results of various types of behaviour and actions as both understandable and inevitable. Maltos view sin

---

[19] *Ibid.*
[20] *Ibid.* p. 275.

as the result of disturbing the balanced nature. In this context, the Gospel message that teaches a real and vital experience of living with God seems to be relevant to meet their needs in their own culture. Burnett's words are applicable to the ministry among the Maltos as he says, "The universal awareness of sin in primal societies, if understood within the context of their own culture, can provide a bridge for the presentation of the gospel."[21]

Blood

Most of the Malto people have a belief in the power of blood when it is poured out after sacrifices, but they all do not know exactly how this power can be known or realized. Here lies an important bridge for the presentation of the Gospel of Christ. This provides a redemptive analogy for the presentation of the Gospel to the people.

Blood is vital to life. In sacrifice, the Maltos believe shedding blood brings peace from *gosanyi*. This has been an excellent point of contact not only for Gospel preaching but also for theological discussions. When Maltos offer blood sacrifices to appease spirits, deities and ancestors, blood represents the solemn presentation of life to God. Sacrifices become effective by virtue of the death of the animal or fowl. Similarly the writer of the book of Hebrews emphasises that without shedding blood, sin cannot be forgiven (Hebrews 9:22). And furthermore Old Testament animal sacrifices became efficacious because of Christ's sacrifice. Maltos also believe that blood is a way to commune with gods and spirits. When they presented the Gospel missionaries and local evangelists used this, emphasising that Maltos could commune with God because of what the blood of Jesus achieved.

The sacrificial motif occurs in Christian Communion when Christians remember the blood of the covenant, which is poured out for many to forgive sins (Mt. 26:28). By the shedding of Jesus' blood on the cross, all the unearthly powers are defeated for any Malto who believes in Him. Maltos would certainly understand how the blood of Christ could atone for sin.

When confronted by the new message of the Gospel, change in their faith began. At this crisis point, the reaction to the Gospel message took the form of a violent but voluntary movement to Christ.

Rituals

Rituals are very important in Malto traditional religion. Maltos participate in them with zeal and devotion as rituals bring colour into their life. As Burnett says, "They are visible demonstrations of the religious beliefs of a people. They enact a drama of these beliefs and aspirations, and in so doing influence powers to achieve the desired ends."[22]

The ritual of marriage and burial rites are very important. Marriage involves the creation of new social networks and it creates potential problems in Malto society. Maltos have a number of rituals to solemnize their marriages but do not have any to solve their marital disputes. Their marriage rites do not emphasize the continuous ties of marriage. Their burial rites involve certain rituals of sacrifices to speed the dead on their way to the land of ghosts, and to control them until they arrive.

Everything that puts life, health or happiness in jeopardy has been transformed by the power of the Gospel the Maltos heard. It is remarkable to see that those customs which are culturally expedient, are adopted and certain cultural beliefs are cleansed to fit into Christian principles. For

---

[21] Burnett, *Unearthly Powers*, p. 87.
[22] *Ibid.* p. 93.

example, bathing before coming to worship, appearing in neat and clean clothes at religious gatherings, and offering unblemished goods and gifts to God. These customs provide a kind of continuity with their own tribal culture and are used to explain the Gospel to non-Christians each time the custom is observed. This is highlighted by Ganga Malto who says, "Now we stopped the unhygienic and superstitious treatment of wounds by applying cow-dung. We pray to God for healing and at times we visit hospital for treatment."[23]

Some of the rituals, which are neither unchristian nor culturally destructive, are retained with some modifications. The customary rule of disposing of a dead body in burial, postures of standing or kneeling, raising hands, closing eyes, observance of total silence in prayer and worship are some of the Malto customs that continue to be followed. Many customs and ceremonies connected with birth, puberty, marriage and death have been changed to thanksgiving prayer meetings in the churches or at their homes.[24] The Maltos have learned to bury their dead with a Christian service of prayer and thanksgiving meeting and with the hope of resurrection in the future. For the individual these customs serve to affirm his or her own cultural identity and heritage. All rituals and festivals may lay the foundation for the concept of reconciliation between God and the Maltos, which has been effected by Christ as our Mediator. Community rituals express their corporate identity as the group God is reconciling.

Some Christian rituals like communion services, harvest festivals, Bible verse competitions, festivals of the Holy Spirit, fasting prayer, all night prayer, Church dedications, house dedications, child dedications, memorial services, and thanksgiving services are excellent bridges to make known Christ to the Maltos. Another common ritual that touches the very means of livelihood of the people is the agricultural harvest festival during which thanksgiving offerings are made at in their gatherings for worship. Such bridges contribute to meeting their need for ritual. The missionaries have arranged parallel rituals as bridges to coincide with the traditional Malto festivals. This is one way of meeting the cultural void which the new convert may otherwise feel. Establishing Christian substitutes for Malto culture helps the people to grow in Christ, if these suit the context and become part of the life of the young Church. On seeing the new believers who give thanks to God for His gracious provision of a new harvest of maize, non-believers are attracted to the Gospel and later with along with their whole family or village, accept Christ.

Conducting a *dharma mela*[25] once a year is another good bridge to teach about God. A celebration would attract the people as they used to gather for their annual buffalo sacrifice festival. A dharma *mela* could include Gospel preaching, screening the 'Jesus' film, singing, dancing and fellowship meals.

There is always anxiety in the ritual of the animist Maltos, along with emotion and excitement. They greatly appreciate the emotion of the Christian life and the excitement of being a Christian without the anxiety.

David Burnett suggests three factors in developing rituals as bridges. They must illustrate Christian truth through symbols relevant both to the culture of the people and to the Scriptures. Although the coming of Christianity will challenge many social issues, changes should strengthen family and social relations as far as possible. And rituals should allow people to participate in Christian worship in ways which

---

[23] Ganga Malto, Chamarpahar, Interview, 25 December, 1995.

[24] R George Edward, *No Longer Forgotten*, Unpublished Material, Chennai, p. 16.

[25] Religious festival

are meaningful to them.[26] These factors have been considered before presenting the Gospel to the Maltos.

James chapter five contains an excellent example of a ritual that can enable Maltos to refrain from the strong pressure to revert. Sickness is a big issue. Instead of going to the shaman, missionaries have taught them to ask the church leader to pray for recovery and apply oil on the body, a well-known practice in both Christian and Malto custom. Both baptism and dedication are now considered as indications of the social acceptance of the children.

The Existence of Evil

Maltos believe evil spirits constantly disturb peaceful life, diverting people from contacting *gosanyi*, but Christ protects people from the attacks of the evil spirits. The Bible clearly speaks to the hearts of the animist Maltos, proclaiming Christ as Victor over the evil spirits and deities. Christ is more powerful than the forces of evil. No Malto wants to face evil. When the spirits and deities they used to worship fail to save them from evil, the good and righteous God who is totally against evil, helps them to challenge all sorts of evil in their life. When missionaries presented the good news of Christ as Victor over and Saviour from evil, they used it a good bridge to the Maltos.

The Gospel of Christ brought the Maltos the good news, that their guilt could be forgiven by God and people and that peace and forgiveness of sin could be established. It also provided the context in which they could get together for meaningful fellowship to establish greater group belonging. The existence of evil cannot harm them any more because of their belief in the most powerful God.

When the Maltos come to know that the God to whom they can commit their life has all the resources to overcome the powers of the evil, they turn to Him in large numbers.

Power Encounter

Animist Maltos may be convinced intellectually that Christ is the Lord of creation, but may remain uncertain whether He can or will be all-powerful in their daily lives. Miracles and healings in Jesus' name are a wonderful bridge to make Christ known as the Almighty Lord and they do draw Maltos to Christ. The movement to Christ has emphasized on power encounter and its related subjects such as spirit possession, casting out spirits, attacks of spirits and sorcery. Seekers and believers were taught to put their total trust in the Lord Jesus Christ. As Ponraj points out: "Faith on the Lord Jesus Christ and truth of the Bible was emphasized, since real spiritual power comes from one's understanding of the truth of the Bible and his or her faith in God who is the source of such power."[27]

In the village of Kasari a precious silver jewel was stolen from the house of the village headman. Having searched unsuccessfully everywhere in his house, he was very upset and called the missionaries who prayed with him. When he returned from the market the next day, he found a small package packed in a kerchief under his bed. He opened it and found his precious, missing jewel. Convinced that God had answered the prayer, he thanked the Lord Jesus, and began his Christian life.[28] Power encounters have played an important part in the spread of Christianity among the Maltos.

Missionaries showed that God's power is greater than that of the sorcerers. This power encounter communicated very effectively.

---

[26] Burnett, Unearthly *Powers*, p. 105.

[27] S.D.Ponraj, *Tribal Challenge*, Madhpur: Mission Educatonal Books, 1996, p. 22.

[28] R. George Edward, Personal Diary, October 1984.

Swamidoss remarks, "Power encounter is the encounter of God with men in supernatural ways where things happen superseding the laws of nature."[29] The power of God overcomes the powers of evil, and we must proclaim this and never let the Gospel appear impotent. Christ heals, delivers from the unearthly powers, and protects from all the invisible powers of spirits. The Lausanne Committee for World Evangelization confirms this method:

> People give allegiance to Christ, when they see that his power is superior to magic and voodoo, the curses and blessings of witch doctors, and the malevolence of evil spirits, and that his salvation is a real liberation from the power of evil and death[30]

Missionaries and local evangelists have witnessed an amazing response to the Gospel by the Maltos. Power encounter wonderfully showed the compassion of God. Barnabas' testimony is an example:

> When I was sitting at the outskirts of my village Pantheni one day, crying over my leprosy, my distant relative Gabriel Malto who had just become a Christian passed through our village. He saw me weeping, came and asked, "Why are you so sad? Just believe in the Lord Jesus Christ who can heal you from this dreadful disease. He is the most mighty Healer." I just put my trust in Him and prayed to Him, "O Lord, please heal me. I am not at all loved in the village. Nobody is giving me food." Within a month I was completely healed. My fingers and toes which, suffered from leprosy, became all right. Now this Premila sister teaches me to read and write. I learn with these healed fingers. Praise the Lord.[31]

Though this Barnabas died later of tuberculosis he was an active local evangelist, loved and respected in every village for his wonderful testimony. He had given a piece of land for a church building and another on which an English medium school for Malto children now runs.

In September 1984 a barren woman, Mesi of Kasari village, suffered badly from evil spirits. Neighbours brought her to an outreach meeting where missionaries prayed to God to deliver her. She began to recovery immediately and the evil spirits shouted, "All of us five spirits are driven out from this woman," and left her. This exhibition of God's power over evil spirits brought the whole of Kasari village to Christ, and as Mesi believed in Christ her whole life changed. Now she has two children and the whole village worships Jesus.[32] Miracles were the means by which a great spiritual victory was won in many villages.

In some villages seeing the Divine power stopped people opposing preachers. In Amdanta village, when people understood the power of God in healing a young man from *Kala-azaar*, they stopped opposing the telling of the Gospel in their village.[33]Power encounters help Maltos to understand that Jesus came to destroy the power of the evil spirits and to free humans from their stranglehold. They reveal to Maltos that Jesus Christ is the God of unequalled power, so that they may turn to Him. Magicians, witch doctors and shamans become powerless before the power of Christ. The Maltos are convinced intellectually that Christ is the Lord of creation and is able and willing to be all-powerful in their daily lives. As a result, they accept the Lord Jesus Christ *en masse*.

---

[29] Andrew W. Swamidoss, 'Power Encounter - Bible Perspective" in Jayapaul David, ed., *Planters* Vol. 2, No. 3, Oct. - Dec. 1996. p. 10.

[30] Willowbank Report, p. 525.

[31] Barnabas Malto, Pantheni , Interview, 25 February 1993.

[32] Edward, Personal Diary, June 1984.

[33] Premila Edward, Personal Diary, December 1986.

Land

Ideally a Malto family owns land to gain a living. Land, passes from father to son, or at least stays within the family. Maltos feel a close link with land and forest. They view the land as a gift from *gosanyi* for which they are collectively responsible, and then work on everybody's land in turn. Nobody can possess more land than they really need, since the poor receive generously from those who have more. This is the Bible message also (Leviticus 25).

God's resources belong to all, not to any individual. Fellowship is another feature here. They enjoy togetherness, also biblical. They set high value on land as permanent shelter. When Jesus offers an eternal dwelling with Him in God's presence (John 14:2-3), this attracts animist Maltos greatly, so this has become yet another strong bridge to reach them.

A Strong Sense of Community Life

Often animistic societies turn as communities to Christ, and the Gospel, interwoven with all of life, enables people to abandon spirit worship, witchcraft, sorcery and fear. Maltos emphasise unity and sharing. No individual is neglected. This sense of oneness may contribute towards unity in Christ, since co-operation is vital and normal for them. Traditional solidarity lay in collective sacrifices, drinking, singing, feasting, labour in fields, and house building. It is natural for Maltos to turn to Christ as whole communities. They understand God is reconciling the group, not merely the individual.

Ploughing, fishing, hunting and recreation activities are always done in a group. This has enhanced a strong sense of community life in Malto society. It has been a form of voluntary association and of collective or communal involvement, which result in a type of mutual partnership. It boosts their economic possibilities and reduces the monotony and tedium of their daily routine work.[34]

Collective communal endeavour has been a hallmark of the Malto economic system, and it has developed features of communal economies. In communal inheritance of property, the whole village is replenished through the collective share of land. This not only emphasises collective ownership of land but labour as well.[35] This valuable quality of inner interdependence is utilised to spread the Gospel. The role of an incentive is fulfilled by a sense of mutual obligation, sharing, and solidarity. Every individual is sensitive to the collective responsibility, which is always uniform.

The village headman is head of the social structure. If he turns to Christ, the whole community comes to Christ. This is one of the wisest bridges to reach the Maltos with the Gospel of Christ, for then the Gospel may grow unhindered. When missionaries and local evangelists took the Gospel message to the headmen, they decreased opposition, and increased the number of people the Gospel could reach.

Malto society ensures that individual members in a village do perform most of their social functions towards each other. This is the basis on which the wider network of social relationships is dependent for its success. This paves the way for a change in their overall development.

Foremost missiologist Donald McGavran observes that a change of religion involves a community change. Only as its members move together does change become healthy and constructive.[36] He adds that people become

---

[34] Edward, *No Longer*, p. 12.

[35] *Ibid.*

[36] Donald McGavran, "The Bridges of God" in Ralph D Winter, et al., eds., *Perspectives on the World Christian Movement*, Pasadena: William Carey Library, 1981, p. 275.

Christians as this group-mind is brought into a life-giving relationship to Jesus as Lord.[37] A change of religion has indeed strengthened the Malto social ties with their community. The Maltos accept Christ along with their families and their kinship groups.

Personal identity

Missionaries have identified with the people and in affirming Maltos identity they have built another bridge. Malto identity is a crucial issue now. People need religious and cultural awareness to maintain their tribal identity. Christian faith and values could help them to reshape their lives with new meaning and identity as 'Maltos in Christ.' Contemporary missions need strategies and principles that integrate tribal customs and Christian faith in a way that produces proved-Christians and not detribalized-Christians as alleged by others.

The initial movement towards Christianity sprang from the quest for a new identity. The rejection of the spirits gave a boost to the self-image of the converts. They have learnt to think of themselves as the children of God and to see their human dignity in a new light. Exem was of the opinion that this conversion was one of the major steps towards integrated renewal and progress and that people would try to live up to their newly acquired dignity and to qualify themselves better to tackle their problems.[38]

A Sense of Reconciliation in the Community

For Maltos, reconciliation means the well being of the community. It is a triangle of good relationship of the self with others and with **gosanyi,** sometimes achieved at great cost, yet worth pursuing. Sometimes they offer sacrifices or provide community meals to restore harmony. Living in reconciliation is also part of the Christian doctrine to which Maltos could readily relate.

The premium on reconciliation in the Malto community has ushered the people to acceptance of the Gospel message of Jesus Christ who has claimed to be the Prince of Peace. Both Christians and non-Christians live together harmoniously in many villages, enjoying intimate kinship, as differences between individuals, and differences of power and prestige seldom upset the Malto society. This does not mean that there are no personality clashes or domestic conflicts in any village. The prevalent sense of reconciliation provides a meaningful analogy with the concept of reconciliation with God through the Lord Jesus Christ.

Missionaries derive their structures for communicating the Gospel of the Lord Jesus Christ to the Maltos, from the Malto cultural roots. They attempt to resolve most situations of conflict with the culturally specific formula of reconciliation. This Malto socio-cultural trait has been a blessing to bring the people to Christ in large numbers.

Mother Tongue Communication

Malto language is the principal medium for all relationships, work, customary, and religious activities. When missionaries communicate in Malto, people are stimulated to listen enthusiastically and attentively. Presenting the Gospel in their own mother tongue has created a bond uniting the communicator with the people. This too has been a rewarding key to the life and thought of the Maltos, since whatever they hear in their "heart-language," they listen to. Using the mother tongue is also biblical (Acts 21:40, 22:2). George Cowan asserts that "use of the vernacular speeds up identification with and acceptance by the people."[39] It is true with the Maltos as well.

---

[37] *Ibid.*

[38] Exem, "*The Evangelization,*" p. 57.

[39] George M. Cowan, *The Word That Kindles*, New York: Christian Herald Books, 1979, p. 62.

Missionaries have recognized the legitimate role of the mother tongue in communication and the dignity of the Malto language that the people protected. Donald McGavaran rightly observes, "... proclaiming the gospel in the heart language of any group of people is certainly the first step in evangelization."[40] Maltos prefer to hear the Gospel preached in Malto rather than in Hindi or Santali.

Some Maltos know other languages, but the missionary who presents the Gospel in Malto has more influence and functions as a bridge builder. Accepting the language indicates acceptance of the people of that language, and consequently hastens the people's acceptance of the speaker. This aids rapport, and encompasses dignity and worth. One of the ever-present barriers to communicating the Gospel to the Maltos is cultural difference. This is reduced when speakers use the language that is integral to their personality and sense of personhood, closer to their life, and easier for them to understand. Communicating in Malto is certainly a most powerful force.

Washing the Feet

The Malto custom of washing feet is another important point of theological significance, a good bridge to point to Christ. In intimate relationships of greater love and respect, the host will anoint the guest's feet with mustard oil and wipe them with a towel,[41] just as Jesus did for his disciples at the Last Supper (John 13).[42] In both Malto and biblical culture it marks love, service and respect in welcoming guests. Maltos lead in this biblical action shared by few other cultures.

As the growing number of Malto Christians read the Scripture in their own mother tongue now, they will continue to reassess their own customs and beliefs as a people who remain part of their own culture, and yet are totally Christian. Their worship, ritual and practice express their life and feelings in ways which are meaningful and relevant to them.

Hope

In traditional Malto religion, sacrifices and rituals seek earthly happiness, successes and prosperity, and the people have no concept of life after death. It is non-existent and hence not a matter of concern. The Maltos do not feel certain of meeting loved ones again, after death. When the gospel is presented to the Maltos, they come to know that the new faith is able to meet their deepest spiritual needs and they share this view with their family members and friends.

The Christian God not only cares for people's present well being, but also for the future. The Christian view of the future can awaken in Maltos a welcome hope for the after-life, a marvellous point of contact. Eternal life by Christ's victory over death is an important theological lesson missionaries and local evangelists could present as a reward of obedience to the 'message.' Living free from revenge by the spirits has been attractive and markedly different from the traditional Malto burial without hope. The Gospel message has brought peace instead of fear, trust instead of dread, confidence instead of apprehension. Out of it comes a new life of fullness and hope, a new spiritual life for the Malto community as a whole and for every Malto individual.

Songs

Maltos love singing and songs are to them a rich endowment. They also love singing Gospel songs, which have happily formed yet another

---

[40] Donald McGavaran, "Discipling Without Dismantling the Tribe, Tongue and People" in M. Ezra Sargunam, ed., *Mission Mandate*, Madras: Mission India 2000, 1992, p. 165.

[41] Premila Edward, Personal Diary, February 1992.

[42] cf. Lk. 7:37-47.

wonderful bridge to Christianity. With simple music, a harmonium and some native musical instruments, the Gospel message readily appeals. But this still needs care. Songs with a Gospel message are carefully selected or composed in local tunes to complement the biblical truth. Music is at the heart of evangelism among the Maltos. It also, in an important way, affirms the 'Maltoness' of Malto Christians.

Malto believers are attached to their own traditional music, and have a hymnal with Gospel themes set to their own cultural tunes. So there is complete acceptance of their own musical heritage.[43] The recognition of native music as a legitimate activity of the Maltos has proved of immense social and survival value. Maltos have various native musical instruments like drums and flutes Men have a keen interest in playing on flutes, which are made of narrow bamboo tubes.

Songs were the bridge that softened the villagers of Chappande, Basco and Santola, who were earlier unresponsive to the Christian message. When they hear songs in their mother tongue, they feel refreshed after their day's labour in the forest or field. Songs attract people to gather, sing, and to listen to the Christian message the songs carry. Many non-Christian Maltos have purchased the Malto Christian songbook and sung along enthusiastically, later interested to know more about Christ.

Summary

Undoubtedly many of the homogenous people groups who were found to be responsive at a given point in Church history have similar historical, sociological, and cultural factors that have prepared them to be a responsive people like the Maltos. Mass conversion to Christianity did not take the believers out of their place but rather sent them back into it, the same people in the same place, and yet a new people with new convictions and new standards of life.

In the present situation of the proclamation of the Gospel to the animists, there are initially, two groups: the non-animist believer who shares the message with the animists and the animists who receive the message. Subsequently, the believing animist community who has an animist heritage emerges on the scene. Now it is the role and responsibility of the animist believer to communicate the Gospel of the Lord Jesus Christ meaningfully to the non-believers of his/her own community or to the other tribal people groups. This is the advantage of the holistic approach in communication of the Gospel to the animists.

It is a learnt experience that we must know and like the Malto person and culture if we wish to communicate the Gospel well and build a growing Church. Sensitively using Malto ideas and practices has built helpful bridges for Christianity making sense of the Gospel to Malto hearers and making it more emotionally convincing. Scornfully rejecting traditional religion as superstition or contrary to biblical practices is counter-productive and arrogant. The cultural bridges have become dynamic positives, meeting the deepest individual spiritual needs.

However, long-held animistic beliefs do not disappear overnight. Missionaries and Malto Christians need to be clear about which beliefs and customs stand under the judgement of Christ and which may be transformed or transfigured by the light of Christ. Rheenen states,

> The persistence and revival of animistic beliefs in the twentieth century demonstrate the need for qualified missionaries who understand the logic of animistic worldviews and who are prepared to powerfully proclaim God's victory over all the powers and forces as demonstrated by the life, resurrection and exaltation of Jesus Christ.[44]

---

[43] Edward, *No Longer*, p. 31.
[44] Rheenen, *Animistic Contexts*, p. 26.

The terrible intertribal genocide or massacres in 1996 in Rwanda and Burundi whose inhabitants were animist converts to Christianity in the East African revival in the 1930s, testify to the grave importance of a deep conversion of the whole culture. Superficial changes in belief may in the end lead to wholesale reversion and tragedy.

Missionaries and local evangelists allowed and guided the Maltos to develop customs and rituals that are consistent with both the Malto native culture and the teachings of the Bible. The combination of the factors of a responsive people group, the value of the Gospel to the context of the people, and the methods employed to reach the Maltos with the Gospel, led to the spread of Christianity on a large scale.

PART VI

Strategic Studies

CHAPTER 31

Apologetics in a Hindu Context

M. SUDHAKAR

I believe that the topic we are considering in this chapter[1] has great value and significance, because it is in the context of 'missions' that we are looking at apologetics and the role it plays in reaching out to our friends in the Hindu context where God has placed us as His witnesses. I think it is a part of God's sovereign plan that He has made some of us Indians and placed us among Hindu friends and has put some of us in close contact with Hindu friends in different parts of the world. It is in the Hindu context where God has placed us that we are expected to live as worshipping and witnessing individuals and communities. I Peter 2:9-10 talks about this 'double identity' of the Church and I believe that as individual Christians also we should be not only worshipping people but we should also be witnessing people. We (not just the Christians in India, but the worldwide Church of the Lord Jesus Christ) should be especially concerned about the Hindu friends because globally speaking, Hindus are the third largest religious group next only to Christians and Muslims and from the Indian perspective they are the largest religious group (about 82 percent of over one billion people). Not only this, there are Hindus in significant numbers in different parts of the world and Hindu gurus have tremendous influence on people all over the world. The following are some of the gurus who enjoyed and continue to enjoy great success in the west: J. Krishnamurthi, Chinmayananda,

Maharishi Mahesh Yogi (TM), Satya Sai Baba, Bhaktivedanta Swami Prabhupada (Krishna Consciousness), Balayogeshvar (Divine Light Mission), Bhagavan Rajaneesh, Pundit Ravi Shankar (Art of Living), Deepak Chopra, et al. It is in this context of having a special burden to reach out to the Hindu friends with the gospel (which is the power of God unto salvation) as the ambassadors and witnesses of the Lord Jesus Christ that we are focusing our attention on this particular topic.

In this chapter we will focus on the two broad subjects of apologetics and the Hindu context. I will try to answer different questions related to apologetics and then I will discuss the unique features of the Hindu context and will discuss just two specific apologetic issues that we need to deal with in the Hindu context. I will conclude with some suggestions for effective witnessing and evangelization in this context.

Apologetics

For many years now, I have been involved in the ministry of training Christians, especially professionals who are in secular settings, in the subject of apologetics and also the ministry of evangelism undergirded by apologetics and a lot of pre-evangelistic ministry. There have been many occasions when I had to answer a lot of questions that Christians have raised about apologetics. Quite often I had to explain what

---

[1] I wish to thank Dr. Roger Hedlund for choosing the topic for this chapter and for inviting me to write it. I have great appreciation for those who recognize that it is of critical importance for the Church to reach the Hindu friends in India and all over the world.

apologetics is all about and then I had to answer different questions like, does the Bible teach anything about apologetics? Can we win people through the application of apologetic principles in our evangelism? Are we not substituting for the work of the Holy Spirit when we try to convince people? and so on. So I thought we should address some of these important questions here, before we can look at Christian apologetics in a Hindu context.

What is apologetics?

Apologetics is a branch of Christian thought that deals with the conflicting worldviews with which Christianity interacts. The English word *apologetics* is derived from the Greek word *apologia*. This word might sound like the common word *apology* which means, as we all know, to say you are sorry. But the meaning of the word *apologia* (noun) is very different. It literally means 'a defense or an answer' or 'reason for doing or believing something'. This word is used with this meaning in 1 Peter 3:15, where Christians are commanded to "be prepared to give an answer (*apologia*) to every one who asks them to give the reason (*logos*) for the hope that lies within them." The word *apologia* is translated as 'answer' (NIV) and 'defense' (NASB, NKJV and NRSV). The verb form of this word, *apologeomai* means "to defend, to make reply, to give an answer, to make legal defense of oneself."[2] In the New Testament times, an *apologia* was a formal courtroom defense of something (2 Timothy 4:16). But in 1 Peter 3:15, Peter seems to be talking about giving an answer in the informal situations, and we see many examples of this in the New Testament. In the New Testament the Greek word occurs eight times as

a noun and ten times as a verb. This should help us to understand that we are not building a case for Christian apologetics from just one or two verses in the Bible and that it was very much taught and practised by the apostles. In fact, this truth will become obvious to anyone who takes time to study the use of this word in each of these eighteen places and to study Church History. The Church Fathers of the second and third centuries like Justin Martyr (100-165 AD), Clement of Alexandria (155-215 AD), Tertullian (160-225 AD), Origen (185-254 AD), et al are called 'apologists,' because they defended Christianity against all kinds of attacks by writing books that were called 'apologies'.[3] Throughout the history of the Church we can see God raising up people who dedicated their God-given intellectual abilities to the cause of defending Christianity and communicating God's truth clearly and convincingly.[4] This means that, following the example of these men of God, within the context of our interaction with others whose belief systems (worldviews) contradict Christian faith, when people ask us questions about our faith and raise objections against it, we have to give them reasons for our faith or make a rational defense of Christian faith and communicate the gospel convincingly. Let me summarize this discussion by quoting J. P. Moreland who says:

> The word *apologia* means "to defend something," for example, offering positive arguments for and responding to negative arguments against your position in a courtroom.... this is exactly how the apostle Paul did evangelism (Acts 14: 15-17; 17:2, 4, 17-31; 18:4; 19:8). He persuaded people to become Christians by offering rational arguments on behalf of the truth of the

---

[2] See A. J. Hoover, "Apologetics" in *Evangelical Dictionary of Theology*, edited by Walter A. Elwell, Grand Rapids: Baker Books, 1984, pp.68-69. Also refer to Peter C. Moore, *Disarming the Secular Gods*, Downers Grove: InterVarsity Press, 1989, p.13.

[3] See Earle E. Cairns, *Christianity through the Centuries*, Grand Rapids: Zondervan Publishing House, 1996, pp.103-111. Here you will find brief descriptions of the writings of the apologists.

[4] Refer to Lit-Sen Chang, *What is Apologetics*, San Gabriel: China Horizon, 1999, pp.23-46.

gospel. He even cited approvingly two pagan philosophers, Epimenides and Aratus (Acts 17:28), as part of his case for the gospel. In 1 Peter 3:15, the apostle does not suggest that we be prepared to do this, but *commands* it.[5]

If this is what apologetics is, then how does it help us in our evangelism or mission work?

What is the Role of Apologetics in Evangelism?

We are now focusing our discussion on the role of apologetics in evangelism, because I believe that evangelism is the heart of missions. The Christian missionary concern is the concern for the worldwide proclamation of the Gospel of Jesus Christ, so that people from every tongue and tribe might come to know Christ and follow Him as disciples. J. P. Moreland says, "For those of us who seek to be followers of Jesus Christ, the central demand of the New Testament should dominate our lives – the worldwide proclamation of the gospel."[6] It should be this evangelistic motivation that should drive us to the study and use of apologetics in our interactions with our friends of other faiths. In this context I would like to discuss a few ways in which apologetics helps us in our evangelism and thus in our missionary work.

Broadly speaking, apologetics has two main aspects to it: on the one hand, it concerns the countering of objections to the Christian faith; and on the other, it concerns setting out the attractiveness of the gospel. Thus apologetics has both a negative and a positive aspect to it and we should put both to effective use in our evangelistic discussions or encounters. In the context of giving a defense of his ministry to the Corinthians Paul says, "The weapons we fight with are not the weapons of the world. On the contrary, they have

divine power to demolish strongholds. We demolish arguments and every pretension that sets itself up against the knowledge of God, and we take captive every thought to make it obedient to Christ."[7] I think here Paul is talking about the negative and the positive aspects of the ministry of preaching the gospel and bringing people to Christ. Let me sum up this discussion about the two aspects of apologetics by quoting the Christian philosopher Stephen Evans who, after defining apologetics as the rational defense of Christian faith, says, "Some distinguish positive apologetics, which attempts to argue for the truth of Christianity, from negative apologetics, which merely attempts to remove barriers to faith by responding to critical attacks."[8]

So, negatively apologetics helps us to encounter and respond to the objections to Christianity that we come across in the market place of ideas – be it in the media or in the common place where we rub shoulders with our friends, colleagues, and neighbors. In other words, apologetics helps us to effectively respond to the hard questions people ask and thus to remove barriers to faith in Jesus Christ. When we give reasoned or thoughtful and convincing and yet gentle and respectful (1 Peter 3:16) answers to our friends, the intellectual blocks would be removed and they will come to a place where they can meaningfully consider the gospel and appreciate fully the attraction, coherence, and uniqueness of the Christian faith. This is very important, because people are deceived by the Devil to believe in all kinds of false ideas and worldviews and they cannot see the truth of the gospel because of the blindness that the evil one has caused (2 Cor. 4:4). The demolition of the intellectual strongholds and arguments is of

---

[5] J. P. Moreland, *Love Your God With All Your Mind*, Colorado Springs: Navpress, 1997, p.51.

[6] J. P. Moreland, *Scaling the Secular City: A Defense of Christianity*, Grand Rapids: Baker Book House, 1988, p.249.

[7] 2 Corinthians 10: 4-5 (NIV).

[8] C. Stephen Evans, *Pocket Dictionary of Apologetics & Philosophy of Religion*, Downers Grove: InterVarsity Press, 2002, p.12.

critical importance (2 Cor. 10:4-5), because the objections people raise and the questions they put forth stand between those people and a living faith in their true God and Saviour.

Unless we remove the intellectual obstacles, people will not come to the knowledge of the truth that we present to them. Gresham Machen said:

> False ideas are the greatest obstacles to the gospel. We may preach with all the fervor of a reformer and yet succeed only in winning a straggler here and there, if we permit the whole collective thought of the nation or of the world to be controlled by ideas which, by the resistless force of logic, prevent Christianity from being regarded as anything more than a harmless delusion.[9]

In our context, the collective thought of the nation or of the vast majority of Hindu people is controlled by the false idea that 'all religions are just different ways to reach the same God' or that 'all religions are equally true', and the implication is that there is nothing unique about Christ and Christianity. We are constantly challenged by the false ideas of relativism, syncretism and pluralism and we need to be equipped to clear these blocks and to go on to present the message of the uniqueness of Christ as the only mediator between God and man (1 Tim. 2: 1-6), as the Lord of all (Acts 10: 36), as the way and the truth and the life and as the only way to heaven (John 14: 6). We will deal with some of these ideas later on in this chapter. But here we are just arguing that there is a great need for us (Christians) to learn how to demolish the intellectual strong holds that are there in the minds of people, especially our Hindu friends, of course with gentleness and respect as the apostle Peter instructs.

This is exactly what the great apologists of our times, Norman Geisler and Ron Brooks, say. They argue that sometimes evangelism should follow pre-evangelism and that this involves answering questions and removing obstacles. They say:

> Before we can share the Gospel, we some times have to smooth the road, remove the obstacles, and answer the questions that are keeping that person from accepting the Lord. ... The objections that unbelievers raise are usually not trivial. They often cut deep into the heart of the Christian faith and challenge its very foundations. If miracles are not possible, then why should we believe Christ was God? If God can't control evil, is He really worthy of worship? Face it: if these objections can't be answered, then we may as well believe in fairy tales. These are reasonable questions which deserve reasonable answers.[10]

The questions mentioned by Geisler and Brooks may be different from the questions our Hindu friends ask us. But we have to accept the argument that sometimes we have to help people by answering questions and removing mental blocks before they can come to a place where they can consider the gospel seriously and respond to it. Now let us consider the positive aspect of apologetics.

Positively, apologetics is about setting forth the full wonder of the Christian gospel of redemption or salvation in a winsome manner. This means that we should take trouble to explain the central ideas or themes of the Christian gospel in a language that our friends can understand. In other words, we should make an intelligent, clear and convincing presentation of the gospel by bringing in the elements of reasoning and proving and thus make it relevant to our friends in the Hindu context. I believe that in all our interactions with other people, we should remember the fact that they are made in the image of God, and one of the implications of this is that they are intelligent. When we try to present the gospel we

---

[9] Quoted by J. P. Moreland, *Christianity and the Nature of Science*, Grand Rapids: Baker Book House, 1989, p.11.
[10] Norman L. Geisler and Ronald M. Brooks, *When Skeptics Ask*, Wheaton: Victor Books, 1990, pp.10-11.

should present it as truth first and then apply it to their needs and dilemmas. Moreland says that the gospel message should be presented to people primarily because it is true and not because it works, though the practical benefits of knowing Christ are certainly important. He thinks that "if we follow the New Testament example, we are to present the gospel as a rational message to be believed and we are to defend it against objections."[11]

The Apostle Paul presented the gospel in this fashion, and I call his approach 'the REPP approach'. It is an approach of Reasoning, Explaining, Proving and Proclaiming (Acts 17:1-4) so that people might be persuaded to accept the gospel truth and receive Christ. We should not miss out the fact that this was how Paul presented the gospel generally in his ministry. Commenting on Paul's evangelistic ministry in Corinth, John Stott says that he both taught and convinced people of the truth and that Paul himself summarized his preaching there in terms of 'trying to persuade people' (Acts 18 and 2 Cor. 5:11). Stott says that we have no liberty to invite people to come to Christ by closing, stifling or suspending their minds and that since God has made them rational beings, He expects them to use their minds. Stott concludes his analysis by saying:

> So then, the gospel is truth from God, which has been committed to our trust. Our responsibility is to present it as clearly, coherently and cogently as we can, and like the apostles to argue it as persuasively as we can. And all the time, as we do this, we will be trusting the Holy Spirit of truth to dispel people's ignorance, overcome their prejudices and convince them about Christ.[12]

We should never think that when we do apologetics and build a logical case for Christ we are substituting for or neglecting the work of God the Holy Spirit. We should do our part and expect God to do His part (1 Peter 3:15-16; 2 Tim. 2:24-26), because evangelism is a joint venture business where both humans and God are involved. I can say this confidently because the Bible makes it clear that generally humans are God's method, and He has entrusted the responsibility of proclaiming the gospel to humans. If this is not the case, Paul would not have spoken daily for two years in the lecture hall of Tyrannus (Acts 19: 9). This kind of an endeavour requires the full range of intellectual equipment. Neither Paul nor anyone else in the early Christian mission thought that argument alone could bring anyone into the kingdom of God. But they knew that argument could break down barriers which obstruct men's vision of the moral and existential choice that faced them, of whether to respond to Christ or not.[13] J. W. Montgomery says that a clearly reasoned presentation of the Gospel "is important – not as rational substitute for faith, but as a *ground* for faith; not as a replacement for the Spirit's working but as a means by which the objective truth of God's Word can be made clear so that men will heed it as the vehicle of the Spirit, who convicts the world through its message."[14] Commenting on this Paul Little says, "Apart from the work of the Holy Spirit, no man will believe. But one of the instruments the Holy Spirit uses to bring enlightenment is a reasonable explanation of the gospel and of God's dealings with men."[15]

This understanding of the positive aspect of apologetics should help us to recognize two things: first, that apologetics has a very important

---

[11] J. P. Moreland, *Scaling the Secular City*, Grand Rapids: Baker Book House, 1987, p.249.

[12] John Stott, *The Contemporary Christian*, Leicester: Inter-Varsity Press, 1992, p.59.

[13] Michael Green, *Evangelism in the Early Church*, Grand Rapids: Eerdmans, 1970, p.206.

[14] J. W. Montgomery, "The Place of Reason," in *HIS*, March 19966, p.16.

[15] Paul E. Little, *Know Why You Believe*, Downers Grove: InterVarsity Press, 1968, p.3.

role to play in our evangelism, which involves the effective and faithful proclamation of the Christian gospel and inviting people to respond; and second, that we need to learn about the worldviews that control the beliefs (religious ones in particular) and religious practices of the people, so that we can connect with them. We will discuss this further later on in this chapter. But here we just want to emphasize the point that if we follow the example of Paul and integrate apologetics into our evangelism (both one to one and one to many methods), we can see people being persuaded to accept the truth of the gospel and to receive the Lord. This is what we see in Paul's ministry. He argued persuasively in his gospel presentations (Acts 19: 8) and people were persuaded (Acts 17: 4). As I have already pointed out, Paul himself summarized his preaching in Corinth in terms of 'trying to persuade people' (Acts 18 and 2 Cor. 5:11). The verb 'to persuade' is the translation of the Greek verb *peitho* and it is used seven times in the book of Acts to describe Paul's evangelism (17: 4; 18: 4; 19: 8; 19:26; 26: 28; 28: 23, 24).[16] The meaning of this word is, "to convince someone to believe something and to act on the basis of what is recommended."[17] May this power of persuasion be present in our gospel proclamation as it was there in Paul's proclamation. So far we have considered a few questions related to apologetics. But now, in the remaining space of this chapter, we will focus our attention on the Hindu context and the apologetic issues that we need to address in such a context.

The Hindu Context

I have been a Christian for over 27 years and all these years I have been interacting with Hindu friends, and I have had the privilege of presenting the gospel both in one to one and one to many contexts and of seeing people from Hindu backgrounds coming to know Christ. I have used apologetics extensively and I have taught Christians (in the RZIM seminars on Apologetics) how to use apologetics in their evangelistic discussions with the Hindu friends. So, what I am going to say in the following paragraphs and pages is backed up by personal experience. I will also try to bring in what I have read that has a bearing on what I am going to say.

To begin with, let me say, on the basis of my own experience, that the Hindu context is a very complex context and that the questions you get from a Hindu (in the context of religious discussion in general and evangelistic conversations in particular) depend on the kind of Hindu she or he is. It may not be an exaggeration to say that you can have as many forms of Hinduism as there are Hindus. Maybe there is some exaggeration in my statement, but there is a lot of truth also in it. I have started my analysis of the Hindu context with this important point, because I want the readers to understand that we should not put people in boxes, and that we should not think that we can answer any Hindu, just because we have been able to answer some in the past.

Contrasting Hinduism with Islam and Christianity, Heinrich von Stietencron says, "With Hinduism, I am afraid, things get more complex and involved. Not only does it have no church, but it also lacks any universally binding doctrines. It offers instead many possible varieties of religious thought, belief, and action; and as we will see, it largely defies our concept of religion."[18] Keith Yandell, in the *Cambridge Dictionary of Philosophy*, defines Hinduism as

---

[16] See Ajith Fernando, *Relating to People of Other Faiths*, Mumbai: GLS Publishing, p.41.

[17] Johannes P. Louw and Eugene A. Nida, editors, *Greek-English Lexicon of the New Testament: Based on Semantic Domains*, vol. 1, New York: United Bible Societies, 1989, p.423.

[18] Heinrich von Stietencron, "What Is Hinduism? On the History of a Religious Tradition" in *Christianity and the World Religions*, edited by Hans Kung, New York: Doubleday & Company, 1986, p.137.

"the group of religious and philosophical traditions of India that accept the doctrinal authority of the Vedas and Upanishads, comprising the schools of Mimamsa, Sankya-Yoga, Nya-Vaishesika, and Vedanta (six in number, with the connection within pairs of schools, indicated by hyphenation, based on historical and conceptual linkages)."[19] In the same article Yandell says:

> ...the closest Indian term to 'philosophy' is *darsana* (seeing); the goal of philosophy is typically taken to be not simply understanding, but enlightenment (*moksha*), which involves escape from the reincarnation cycle and from karma. All the orthodox schools formally accept the doctrines that the individual *Atman* beginninglessly transmigrates from body to body unless it attains enlightenment and that in each lifetime the *Atman* acts and hence accumulates consequences of its actions that will accrue to it in future lifetimes (karma).... The classical Hindu philosopher typically in effect accepts some such proposition as the following: The Hindu scriptures contain the truth about the nature of what is ultimately real, about the nature of the human self, and about how to obtain the highest good.[20]

You can tell that there can be a plurality of religious beliefs and philosophical traditions within Hinduism and that there might be some common beliefs among all of them. Reflecting a similar understanding Dayanand Bharati says this: "Already we have enough religions here in India, more than any other country in the world; even just in Hinduism alone which is rightly called a parliament of religions."[21] Another Indian author, Manasseh, says that Hinduism, unlike other religions, is neither institutionalized, nor creed based, nor based on any single book and yet it survived mainly because of caste-bonds and rituals. May Indians prefer to call it *dharma* (a way of life).[22] We can say that Hinduism has got its own unique features among the world religions. For example, there is no single person or figure in Hinduism who is considered to be the founder or authority figure, unlike other religions like Christianity, Islam, Buddhism, Jainism and so on. There is no single book that all Hindus follow, and there is no single set of doctrines that all Hindus subscribe to, unlike the people of other religions like Judaism, Christianity, Islam, etc. Hinduism is not an organized religion, unlike other religions like Christianity, Islam, Judaism, and Sikhism. The reason we find Hinduism to be unique in so many ways is that it is not one religion, but a collection of religions or at least religious perspectives. Commenting on the diversity of religious views within Hinduism, Stietencron says this:

> Even within Hinduism, one person's sacred scripture is by no means necessarily someone else's. This individual may assign a minor role to a god whom another individual worships with deep devotion as the supreme divinity and Lord of the world. One man teaches that living creatures should never be harmed, while another man's altar drips with the blood of sacrificed goats and buffalos. One believer's Tantric practices are an abomination to others.[23]

Quoting another source, Manasseh says, "As Dr. S. Radhakrishnan puts it, 'The Hindu tradition by its very breadth seems to be capable of accommodating varied religious conceptions'."[24]

---

[19] Keith E. Yandell, "Hinduism" in *The Cambridge Dictionary of Philosophy* edited by Robert Audi, Cambridge: Cambridge University Press, 1999, p.383.

[20] Ibid., pp.383-384.

[21] Dayanand Bharati, *Living Water and Indian Bowl*, Delhi: ISPCK, 2001, p.3.

[22] P. Manasseh, *A Historical Overview of the Indian Religions*, Secunderabad: Hyderabad Academy of Biblical Studies & Research, 2001, p.5.

[23] Stietencron, "What is Hinduism?" pp.138-139.

[24] The source he quoted is D. S. Sharma, *Hinduism Through the Ages*, Bombay: Bharatiya Vidya Bhavan, 1973, P.236.

Stietencron suggests that we should understand Hinduism not as a religion, but as a collection of religions. He further says, "Though actually different, they are nonetheless bound together by geography and history, as well as by the socioeconomic conditions and cultural frames of reference that developed in their common space. These are religions containing elements of shared traditions, and religions that have continually influenced each other down through the ages . . ."[25] I think we should accept the thesis that Hinduism is not a religion but a collection of religions, because within Hinduism there are different conceptions or ideas of God like monotheism, polytheism, pantheism, and henotheism. Stephen Evans says, "Hinduism is more a group of religious traditions than a single religious faith, since within Hinduism one can find both theistic and monistic views of God . . ."[26]

Even the terms 'Hindu' and 'Hinduism' are not Indian terms and no Indian religion ever called itself 'Hinduism.' The meanings of these words have changed over a long period of time. It all goes back to the name of the great Indus River. Its old Sanskrit name was *Sindhu* and the Greek name was *Indos* and we owe our words 'India' and 'Indians' to this Greek name. The Persians in their language called the same river 'Hindu' and this word, as in Sanskrit, indicated the land through which the river flows. The plural of this geographical name stood for the people who lived there, the 'Hindus', the 'people of the Indus' or the people of 'India', the Indians. So, originally the word 'Hindu' appeared as a geographical term and once the Persian king Darius I extended his empire to the banks of the Indus, Hindus, the inhabitants of the land of the Indus (the Indians) were incorporated into the multination Persian state. From that time the Persians and other Persian-speaking people lumped all Indians together as 'Hindus.' Later on the Arabs also called India 'Al Hind.'

The shift in the meaning of this word began much later, took place very gradually, and was finally completed by the Europeans. When Persian speaking Muslims from Afghanistan and Central Asia invaded India, first around 1000 AD and then after 1200 AD, they subjugated large parts of India, but they could convert only a fraction of the people to Islam. Then the Muslims used the term 'Hindu' to characterize the Indians who would not convert to Islam and who were not Buddhists. Thus, in the Islamic context, the word 'Hindu' contained a distinct religious element. Finally, in the sixteenth century, the merchants and Christian missionaries who came from Europe got to know this expression for the majority of non-Muslims in India and for the first time they separated the terms 'Indian' and 'Hindu,' applying the former to the secular sphere and the latter to religion and then they derived the word 'Hinduism' from it.[27]

The forgone discussion, I hope, would help us to understand why there is so much difficulty in understanding what Hinduism is and why there are so many forms of Hinduism. I hope we can now understand why Basham says that although Hindus are one of the largest and one of the most important religious groups of the world, their faith is indefinable in a few words.[28] The fact that there are diverse religious views or perspectives within Hinduism might cause the reader to wonder if there are any common beliefs that all Hindus or at least a vast majority of them subscribe to and if there are any common apologetic issues, which

---

[25] Stietencron, "What Is Hinduism?" p.143.

[26] C. Stephen Evans, *Pocket Dictionary*, p.54.

[27] See Manasseh, *A Historical Overview*, p.5, and Stietencron, "What Is Hinduism?" pp.138-141.

[28] A. L. Basham, "Hinduism" in *The Concise Encyclopedia of Living Faiths*, edited by R. C. Zaehner, Boston: Beacon Press, 1959, p.225.

if we learn to deal with, would be generally helpful in our efforts to reach out to people in the Hindu context. I would say that there are a few strands of belief that are held in some form or another by a vast majority, if not all Hindus. I have seen that issues like reincarnation or transmigration of the soul, the corollary of reincarnation and the related issues of karma, moksha, avatars or manifestations of God, and the ultimate unity of all religions come up frequently in our interactions with our Hindu friends. There are some scholars who recognize this fact in their writings. For example, Stephen Evans says, "Generally, Hinduism is characterized by an acceptance of the doctrine of reincarnation, or transmigration of the soul, and the goal of the religious devotee is seen as the deliverance of the soul from the cycle of reincarnation."[29] Basham also recognizes some of these common threads of belief among Hindus.[30] Stietencron too admits that the Hindu people do not feel thrust into a brief and passing life and that the possibility of rebirth gives them a wider horizon to life and a different sense of time.[31] Now that we have looked at some common beliefs and issues that we encounter in a Hindu context, I would like for us to take a closer look at just two out of the many common apologetic issues that we need to learn to address.

The Common Apologetic Issues we need to learn to Address

Here I will explain the apologetic issues and show how we can address them one by one. I will try to be precise. But I hope that the students and general readers who read this chapter will try and get hold of some of the sources that are cited and study further to equip themselves and to help others.

Are not all Religions one or at least teach the same things?

This is one of the most common objections that people raise when we try to present the gospel in the Hindu context. For many Hindus 'all religions are one', to quote the words that Ramakrishna Paramahamsa (1834-1886) used and popularized. Commenting on Paramahamsa's understanding, Basham says, "The result of his experiments may be summed up in the slogan: 'All religions are one'." According to Paramahamsa, Hinduism, Christianity, Islam, Zoroastrianism, all repeat the same message, all led back to the same truth that was perceived by the mystic – the oneness of all religions in the Universal Spirit.[32] Elsewhere, in the same essay, Basham says that it is possible within a single all-embracing system, for many apparently opposed beliefs to exist side-by-side, and indeed even to be held by the same individual, and that synthesis is a part of the Indian genius.[33] Philosophically speaking, this thinking reflects elements of relativism, syncretism, and pluralism that deny any uniqueness to any religion and this is a big challenge that we have been facing and we continue to face in the Hindu context. This tendency is not new in India. Traditionally the slogan, 'any way will lead you to the destiny', has been applied to the different ways to God that are available for the Hindus to choose from. You can attain moksha or liberation through the *gnana marga* (the path of knowledge), or *karma marga* (the path of works), or *bhakti marga* (the path of devotion). In fact, *yoga* is also one of the ways to attain union with the Ultimate and it is technically called *ashtanga yoga*, because it is an eight-step process and the goal is union with the Ultimate or Brahman. But for some time now, this slogan is applied to different religions, which

---

[29] C. Stephen Evans, *Pocket Dictionary*, p.54.
[30] A. L. Basham, "Hinduism" p.225.
[31] Stietencron, "What is Hinduism?" p.246.
[32] Basham, "Hinduism" p.257.
[33] *Ibid.*, 230.

are considered to be like different routes to the same destiny (for example, you can reach the top of a mountain from any direction) or like different rivers that ultimately merge with the same ocean.

In this context it is very common to find people who would ask, "What is so unique about Christ or Christianity?" or "Why are you so narrow-minded and intolerant?" and so on. People make tolerance and pluralism great virtues. Stietencron says, "Nowadays many educated Hindus carry their individual tolerance still further by dropping any insistence that their religion is superior to the others. 'This is the right way for me', they will say; 'yours is the right one for you. We shall meet at the goal, in final salvation'." [34] He goes on to say that a characteristic feature of the great Hindu religions is that they never start out by assuming an irreconcilable opposition between two postulated truths and that any claim to absoluteness is alien to them. When they see unavoidable contradictions, they view them as lodged within the framework of complementary oppositions, and they try to integrate them into some comprehensive connections. He further observes that this attitude had led Hindus to develop an unusual capacity to assimilate foreign influences and other religions, while maintaining their own.[35]

I hope the readers can now understand or at least understand better why our Hindu friends often try to draw similarities or parallels between their belief system and the Christian faith. If Christianity is one among the religions and Christ is one of the ways, then there is no problem. But the moment we say that Christianity is the truth and Christ is the only way, then we are in for trouble. They will either say that we are narrow minded and intolerant, or they will try to show similarities to conclude that ultimately all religions are teaching the same things. For example, they will say, "You have 'trinity' and we have 'trimurtis' and you have 'incarnation' and we have 'avatars' and if you take time to look at these concepts carefully you will realize that there is no difference." If you are in the habit of talking to Hindu friends to present the gospel truth, I am sure you would have found yourself in a situation where you were bombarded with some of the above-mentioned questions and arguments, and you would have wondered how you could respond. How can we respond to this one basic objection that comes in different forms? In the next few paragraphs I will try to show how we can respond to this objection, remove the obstacles, and go on to present the gospel to our Hindu friends.

How do we respond to this objection?

One basic thing we have to learn more and more is the art of listening to our friends carefully and understanding what they are saying. Once we understand what the issue is we can address it effectively. Our Lord Jesus is a good example for us to follow in this regard. Jesus was a good listener and He posed questions in His interaction with people. In Luke 2: 46-47 we read about what Jesus did when He was in the midst of the doctors of the law in the Jerusalem temple. Luke says that Jesus was listening to them and asking them questions and that He gave answers (this means that He gave people opportunity to ask Him questions as well). In response to some of the questions our friends ask we need not always give lengthy answers. Sometimes we should ask them good questions that will force them to think through their beliefs and assumptions and to see where they are making mistakes in their thinking. If you study Matt. 21: 23-32 carefully you will understand what I am talking about. Let me give you some examples that will illustrate this point.

Once I struck a conversation with a fellow passenger in the train. He was a Hindu

---

[34] Stietencron, "What is Hinduism?" p.145.
[35] *Ibid.*, p.146

businessman and within a couple of minutes into the religious conversation we were having he said, "I believe all religions ultimately teach us the same things and there is no fundamental difference between religions."

I said, "Would you please tell me what you mean by that."

He said, "You see Mr. Sudhakar all religions teach us that God exists, that we should not harm others, that there is hell and there is heaven, that we should do good and go to heaven or be liberated."

Are there similarities between religions? I think that the answer is both 'yes' and 'no.' Let me explain what I mean. What I mean is that there are superficial similarities and if we go a little deeper, we will see that there are fundamental differences between religions. I helped my Hindu friend to recognize this by asking some more questions of clarification.

I said, "Sir, you mentioned a number of things, but what do you think is the most important topic in any religious discussion?"

He said, "I think it is God."

Then I said, "I agree with you. But would you please tell me what you mean by the word 'God' from your perspective!"

What he said in response was very interesting and I did not find a statement like that in any book that I read on Hinduism.

He said, "God is everything and nothing."

How does that sound? I was able to see a serious problem in this definition of God. There is an internal contradiction in it. But I did not say that to him. I tried to help him to see it himself. So I continued to question him, of course without being arrogant and in a non-threatening manner.

I said, "Sir can anything be what it is and what it is not?" To help him to understand what my question was, I pulled out a pen from my pocket and said, "Can this be a pen and not a pen at the same time?"

He thought for a while and then said, "Mr. Sudhakar, you are using too much of human logic in our discussion about God."

Once again I could see a contradiction in what he said, like in what he said about God. So, I asked him another question to make the contradiction clear to him. I said, "Sir, if you do not mind, I would like to ask you just another question." He responded positively, and I said, "Sir, is your statement, the statement that you have just made, a logical statement or an illogical statement?"

He thought for a longer time this time and seemed to have understood that even to say that we should not use logic we should use logic, because other wise what we say would be illogical or nonsensical. He finally said, "I think we should use logic in our discussion about God."

We had a little further discussion on the laws of logic or the principles of right thinking in our search for truth. We agreed that the use of logic in any meaningful conversation is inescapable. Now that we agreed on the basic principles of right thinking, I said that two contradictory statements about God (for that matter about anything else) cannot be true at the same time and showed to him how God cannot be Infinite-Impersonal and Infinite-Personal at the same time. In other words, I said that if God is an infinite person (as Christianity and other theistic religions teach), then God cannot be an infinite impersonal entity (as pantheistic Hinduism – Sankara's *Advaitha Vedanta* teaches). The discussion went on and I could point out to him many more contradictory beliefs. For example, in polytheistic Hinduism there are many finite personal gods, whereas in theistic religions like Judaism, Christianity and Islam, there is only one infinite personal God. Man is essentially divine according to pantheism where as according to Christianity man is not divine but a creature that has become sinful. I also pointed out to him that not all religions have a belief in God. For example, Buddhism does not talk about God and Jainism has no concept of a creator God, these are agnostic and atheistic religions respectively. Finally my Hindu friend agreed that all religions are not the same and that they are all not teaching the same things and he asked me if I could recommend any book that he could read on this subject. I told him about Mortimer Adler's book[36] and offered to send it to him by VPP (Value Payable Parcel). He thanked me for the good discussion we had, and the conversation ended on a very positive note. He gave me his personal phone number and said, "Please call me whenever you come to Bangalore." [I entrusted him to God (because very soon after this I went out of the country and got busy) and sent him the book and he received it.]

If you have followed the above summary of the dialogue carefully you would have noticed that the discussion was carefully controlled and guided towards truth and truth principles. This is what we need to learn to do. We should help people to recognize that truth cannot be different for different people or that truth does not change from place to place or person to person or country to country or culture to culture. In other words, truth is transcultural and universal. For example, two plus two equals four and only four, and it is the same for all people. If Gandhiji was born on the 2ⁿᵈ of October, that is the truth for all people everywhere. So also if the atom is divisible, it is divisible for all. It cannot be both divisible and indivisible. Truth is objective and hence does not depend on our personal and private opinions or feelings, but on the reality out there. Truth is the characteristic of propositions or statements where what is stated by a statement corresponds to the reality. If the statement does not correspond to

the reality, then the statement is false. This is the logic of truth[37] and this is the same for all the people either in the east or in the west. So, when it comes to truth claims you cannot be broad-minded, because truth itself is narrow and it excludes falsehood.

In fact, if all the religions were ultimately teaching the same things, then the talk about religious tolerance would be completely out of place. Why? Because, if all religions are ultimately the same, then who should tolerate whom and for what reason? Tolerance becomes relevant only where there are differences. There are not just differences, but fundamental differences between religions as has been discussed already, and when we deal with contradictory beliefs we have to be clear that two contradictory and opposite beliefs cannot be true at the same time. From the Christian perspective, we are not only to tolerate the people who hold different beliefs, but we have to respect them, because they are created in the image of God as free individuals. But to respect a person does not mean that we accept the false beliefs she or he holds and say that he or she is right. It rather means that we will be gentle and respectful while trying to show to them the internal contradictions that relativism and pluralism[38] suffer from and to guide them to the truth. This is vital in the present situation because globally also most of the people think that there is no absolute (unchanging) truth and that truth is a matter of perspective and hence truth is relative. The pressure to compromise is so intense that there are many so called Christian scholars who are suggesting that we should not insist that truth is exclusive and that Jesus is the only way for all people. For example, Stanley Samartha says this:

---

[36] Mortimer J. Adler, *Truth in Religion: The Plurality of Religions and the Unity of Truth,* New York: Collier Books, Macmillan Publishing Company, 1990.

[37] See Mortimer J. Adler, *Truth in Religion,* pp.10-39,69-92.

[38] See Paul Copan, *True For You, But Not For Me,* Minneapolis: Bethany House Publishers, 1998. In this book Copan deals with a lot of issues related to truth in a very concise and clear fashion.

Truth is no more defined in terms of exclusion. A religion that defines itself to be true by excluding others is outmoded. . . . Therefore the apprehension of Truth at a given point in history cannot claim exclusive validity. It can indeed, be valid, but not exclusive. No particular response to or formulation of Truth can claim to be unique, final or absolute. . . . To Christians this Truth is decisively manifested in Jesus Christ. No one asks them to dilute or betray this faith. But the function of Christology in a pluralist world is not to claim 'uniqueness' for Christ by proving that others are wrong or false, but to confess, explain, and help Christians to live in obedience to the Truth manifested to them in Jesus Christ.[39]

Samartha goes on to argue for a revised Christology in his book, and he is just one of the many who are trying to persuade Christians not to make any exclusive claims.

I think what Paul Little said many years ago is very relevant in the present context. He said:

We live in an age in which tolerance is a key word. Tolerance, however, must be clearly understood. (Truth, by its very nature, is intolerant of error.) If two plus two is four, the total cannot at the same time be 23. But one is not regarded as intolerant because he disagrees with *this* answer and maintains that the only correct answer is *four*. The same principle applies in religious matters. One must be tolerant of other points of view and respect their right to be held and heard. He cannot, however, be forced in the name of tolerance to agree that all points of view, including those that are mutually contradictory, are equally valid. Such a position is nonsense.[40]

This should help anybody to understand that Christ's claim that he is the way and the truth and the life (John 14:6) is a reasonable truth claim and that the Christian truth claims are reasonable as well. When it comes to responding to truth claims, we should understand that the only thing we can do with them is to either accept or reject on the basis of evidence. So we should help our friends to face the truth claims for what they are and to examine them closely, rather than saying that Christians are narrow minded. But we need to remember that our aim in doing apologetics is not to argue to win the argument but to win people over to Christ and we need not apologize for wanting to win others over to Christ. Right from the beginning, the Christian movement has been unashamedly committed to mission – that is, to the spread of the gospel and the winning of individuals to faith. Without this vision the fledgling Church would not have spread beyond the walls of Jerusalem. In accomplishing this mission apologetics plays a crucial role because it clears the ground, answers questions, builds bridges and enables the gospel invitation to be offered to people at the level of both heart and mind.[41] With this truth in our minds let us look at another example that will show how we can respond to the objections people raise and go on to present the gospel to them in a gentle and yet clear manner. This example will also show how we need to help one another as Christians in terms of equipping for effective witnessing.Once a Hindu lady became a Christian. Her community excommunicated her and the few who were on talking terms always tried to persuade her to return to Hinduism. She came in contact with a Christian who was teaching Chemistry in a college (he attended the RZIM seminar on Apologetics), and this man told her that she could share with him and his family whatever problems she was facing so that they could help her. A little

---

[39] S. J. Samartha, *One Christ – Many Religions: Towards a Revised Christology,* Bangalore: The South Asia Theological Research Institute (SATHRI), 2000, pp.119-120.

[40] Paul E. Little, p. 97.

[41] Peter C. Moore, *Disarming the Secular Gods,* Downers Grove: InterVarsity Press, 1989, p.20.

while after this, this lady went to another lady in the neighborhood who was a vegetable vendor. The vegetable vendor lady looked at the Christian lady strangely and started talking sarcastically. She said, "Oh! I came to know that you found a new God and left all our gods. I pity you. Your religious life must be very boring. You have to worship the same god all the time. But we in Hinduism have a rich variety. We can worship different gods and goddesses for different purposes at different times. For you it must be like eating the same vegetable every day." The Christian lady was dumbfounded. She did not know how to respond, and she quickly bought the vegetables she wanted and left, feeling frustrated. Later that evening she remembered the encounter she had with the Christian lecturer, and she went to his house and shared her experience with his family. They encouraged her in different ways, and the man told her how she could respond to the Hindu lady. He said, "When you go to the vegetable vendor lady the next time, say something like this: The last time we met, you compared God to vegetables. But is God like vegetables? Allow her to think for a little while and then say that God is more like a father than vegetables. Whether you like it or not, you can have only one father. You cannot have one father today and another father tomorrow. In the same way, there is only One Heavenly Father to all of us mankind and He is the Creator God. We all have to worship this true God. We cannot have different gods, and that is why I have committed myself to this one true God." This lady understood the point, and when she went to buy vegetables a few days later she followed the instructions and talked to the vegetable vendor lady. This time the vegetable vendor lady became dumbfounded. But the Christian lady was gracious and gentle and she guided the discussion carefully without hurting the other person, and finally shared her testimony of how she came to know God personally and became a Christian. This shows how even the uneducated folks in

India become philosophical in religious discussions and how with a little bit of critical thinking we can understand the mistakes people make in their thinking and help them to move in the direction of truth. Let us consider just another example.

Once I struck up a conversation with a fellow passenger in a train. He was a Hindu. Within a few minutes into the discussion, he said, "Sir, there is no difference between Christianity and Hinduism. You believe in 'trinity' and we believe in 'trimurtis' and you have 'incarnation' and we have 'avatars'. If you take time to look at these concepts carefully you will realize that there is no difference."

I said, "Sir, would you please explain what you mean by 'trimurtis'."

He said, "Sir, it is simple. We believe that Brahma creates, Shiva destroys, and Vishnu preserves."

Then I said, "Sir, is it one God in three persons, or is it three different Gods?"

He thought for a while and said, "I think it is three Gods."

Then I pointed out to him that there is a fundamental difference between Christianity and Hinduism because 'trinity' is the idea of One God existing in three Persons, and there is no conflict among the three persons of the Godhead. I explained to him how the three members of the triune Godhead are involved together in creation, revelation and redemption. I went on to ask him another question. I said, "Do you worship the 'trimurtis' equally?"

He thought for a while and said, "No."

Then, with his permission, I asked him another question. I said, "Would you please explain why you do not worship Brahma, Vishnu, and Shiva equally?"

He gave me the following explanation on the basis of some *purana*. He said, "Once there was a 'rishi' who performed 'thapasya' and gained powers over nature. He went to the world of Brahma. But Brahma was busy in his own affairs and did not care for the rishi. So the rishi got angry and cursed Brahma and said that no one on earth would worship him. Then the rishi went to the world of Shiva. Shiva received the rishi, but after a long time of waiting. So the rishi said to Shiva that he would be worshipped only by a few people on earth and that too in the form of a 'linga'. Finally the rishi went to the world of Vishnu. Vishnu recognized the presence of the rishi immediately and received him and entertained him. So the rishi was pleased with Vishnu and said that he would be the most popular god on earth."

I followed this explanation very carefully and said to him, "If you do not mind, I would like to ask you just another question." He responded positively and I asked, "Sir, please tell me whether it is the rishi that deserves worship or the trimurtis?" "Who is greater?" I asked.

He thought for a long time and kept quiet. Then I put my arm on his shoulder and told him that my intention in asking the question was not to silence him and that I was trying to get to the truth together with him. He was willing to talk to me further and I explained things clearly and showed him that there is nothing in common between the concept of 'trimurtis' and the concept of 'trinity' except for the fact that both the words start with the same letter. He agreed with me on this and I went on to discuss with him the fundamental differences between the Christian concept of 'incarnation' and the Hindu concept of 'avatars'. For example, incarnation is real, historical, permanent and a once for all time act of God, whereas avatars are multiple, not historical, and not permanent. Also, God taking humanity upon Himself makes sense, because God created Man in His image and likeness, whereas some of the avatars are in sub-human forms and one of them is half-human and half-animal. Moreover, can't God who is almighty and all knowing deal with the human problem of sin in one visit to the earth? Let me mention just one other fundamental difference. Avatars are for the purpose of punishing the wicked and saving the righteous (*Dusta sikshana, Sista rakshna*), whereas the incarnation is for the purpose of making the sacrifice or atonement once and for all for the sins of all mankind, because all have sinned and have fallen short of the glory of God. When I explained these things, this Hindu friend understood and agreed with me, and I could go on to present the gospel of God's grace revealed in Christ to this friend. Let us now focus on just another common apologetic issue (reincarnation) before concluding this chapter.

What about Reincarnation?

Reincarnation has been a widely accepted doctrine among Hindus and Buddhists and it was held by many Greek philosophers, who termed it *metempsychosis* – literally, 'change of souls'. According to Hinduism, all life is essentially one and the plant, animal, and human life are so interrelated that souls are capable of 'transmigrating' from one form of life to another. A person could have been an animal, plant, or mineral in some previous existence. One of the corollaries that go with reincarnation is the belief in *karma*. The idea is that there is some force in the universe that causes every human on earth to build credits or debits through his or her behavior. A person shapes the quality of life in the next incarnation through his or her actions in this incarnation. If one commits evil in this life, then retribution may be expected in the next; whereas performing good in this life will assure a better life in the next incarnation or *moksha* (liberation from *karma samsara*, the cycle of births and deaths and union with the Ultimate). Also from one life to another, the karmic debt gets accumulated. The soul can progress spiritually upward into another human body, or downward into animal, plant, or mineral bodies, depending upon its *karma*. Another corollary of reincarnation is the belief in the immortality of the soul. The soul is believed to have eternal properties of its own and so the potential for eternal life resides in the soul, which will inevitably live on with or without the body.[42] *Advaitha Vedanta* is the mother of reincarnation and according to it, ultimately, there is only one reality – the Brahman and there can be no fundamental distinctions between human beings, animals, earth, or God. According to this philosophy there is not even the 'I' 'Thou' distinction, because all reality is one. The Mahabharata supports this doctrine.

There are a number of problems with this doctrine. For example, there is no satisfactory explanation in Hindu thought as to when or how the first *karma* came into existence and automated the terrifying cycle of births and deaths (*karma-samsara*).[43] There is no means of knowing as to why one may be suffering any particular rebirth and how much karmic debt one has accumulated. So there does not seem to be any opportunity for us to correct past deeds or mistakes in the future and there is no positive hope for a better future or ultimate salvation. There is a very serious problem that *Advaitha Vedanta* faces. If all reality is ultimately one and there is no 'I' – 'Thou' distinction, then whose *karma* determines 'my' status in the next life and am I a real person? And who would merge or unite with whom? Leaving these problems aside we should see if there is any evidence that is offered in support of reincarnation.

As far as the evidence is concerned, the most popular literature on reincarnation is not very impressive. Some cases of retrocognition (knowledge of the past) are presented. But it is generally assumed that cognition implies presence. It is assumed that if some one has unexplained, detailed knowledge of persons, places, or things in the past, it must follow that he or she was actually there in some form. In other words, if I remember a past life, then it has to be my life that I remember.

But why should this be so? The theory of reincarnation stands or falls on the way in which cases of retrocognition are manipulated into 'proof' for the reality of past lives. If it could be shown beyond doubt that some of the best examples of retrocognition are cases where reincarnation is impossible, then it would not be necessary to look to reincarnation for an explanation. The case of Peter Hurkos is an example of retrocognition that actually excludes the possibility of reincarnation. Hurkos exhibited cognition that is similar to what is often cited as evidence by reincarnationists. But the knowledge he possessed was usually about people, places, and things that existed after his birth. Even more telling is the fact that he was capable of 'remembering' intimate details of the lives of two or more persons who lived simultaneously, and no one could possibly argue that he obtained his information during a previous life. Psychic research provides us with a great number of similarly documented cases, where people have experienced cognition of events and people in the distant past, the recent past, the present, and the future. In these instances reincarnation is the least plausible explanation and other explanations are more plausible.[44] There are a number of other reasons why reincarnation cannot be accepted and let me mention just one more. If reincarnation is true, then the experience of retrocognition should be typical (all of us should remember the

---

[42] See John Snyder, *Reincarnation Vs. Resurrection*, Chicago: Moody Press, 1984, pp.19-25.

[43] Acharya Daya Prakash Titus, *Fulfilment of the Vedic Quest in the Lord Jesus Christ*, Bhovali, U.P: Sat Tal Ashram, 1982, pp.19-21.

[44] See John Snyder, *Reincarnation vs. Resurrection*, pp.27-41. Also refer to Paul Copan, "*That's Just Your Interpretation*", Grand Rapids: Baker Books, 2001, pp.60-68.

past) and not atypical. But why is it that the experience of retrocognition is atypical (only a few people experience it)? I am afraid there is no answer to this question. We should use this knowledge in trying to help our Hindu friends who believe in reincarnation and become victims of all the ill effects this belief produces. The following three are the effects the belief in reincarnation has produced in people: 1) Relinquishing to the unseen fate, 2) Indifference towards and the attending lack of motivation for social concern and action, and 3) Putting off any serious attempt for liberation. Lokamanya Bala Gangadar Tilak suggested that *karma* and the desire for liberation from it are two contradictory things, because a man who is under the spell of karmic *avidya* or *maya* (ignorance or illusion) is hardly free to entertain any sincere desire for salvation.[45] We have to deal with our Hindu friends very compassionately and gently when we try to point out the problems with the doctrine of reincarnation. Let me now conclude with a few suggestions for effective witnessing among Hindu friends.

Suggestions for Effective Witnessing in the Hindu Context

There are a number of ways in which we can be effective in our mission of reaching the Hindu friends. Or there are a number of things we can do to be effective in reaching our Hindu friends. But I will mention only some that I think are the most important ones.

First, we must develop meaningful relationships with them.

We should have such good friendship with them that we can talk to them freely about anything and we can engage them in a sustained dialogue. This means that we should visit them

and they should be invited to our homes so that they can see the power of the gospel at work in our lives. Unless they see the difference the gospel has made in our lives they might not be able to see the truth of the gospel. George David says that we need to be friendly with the people of other faiths. He goes on to say:

> The tendency today is to prefer to communicate with people from a long distance. . . . the primary medium for the communication of the gospel is friendly, personal relationships with those we seek to communicate. The failure to enter into face to face, personal friendly relationships with Hindus is one of the major reasons why the church has failed to communicate with them. [46]

What I am saying is that we must identify with the people that we are trying to reach. This is what our Lord did and He said to His disciples that He was sending them into the world just as the Father sent Him (John 17:18; 20:21). Christ is the best example that we can follow. John Stott says that the incarnation of Christ is the model for mission. After talking about the way He identified with people, he says that Christ could not have become more one with us than He did and that it was the total identification of love. He goes on to say, " . . . our mission is to be modeled on His. Indeed, all authentic mission is incarnational mission. It demands identification without loss of identity. It means entering other people's worlds, as he entered ours, though without compromising our Christian convictions, values or standards."[47] Johns Stott talks about the need for entering into other people's thought world and says that we ought to be

> ... praying and working hard for a whole new generation of Christians thinkers and apologists who will dedicate their God-given

---

[45] See Acharya Daya Prakash Titus, *Fulfillment of the Vedic Quest*, pp.21-22.

[46] George David, *Communicating Christ among Hindus Peoples*, Chennai: CBMTM Publications, 1998, pp.7-8.

[47] John Stott, *The Contemporary Christian*, pp.357-358.

minds to Christ, enter sympathetically into their contemporaries' dilemmas, unmask false ideologies, and present the gospel of Christ in such a way that he is seen to offer what other religious systems cannot, because He and He alone can fulfil our deepest human aspirations.[48]

I think John Stott's emphasis here is on identifying ourselves with the people we are trying to reach, and this is not different from developing meaningful relationships with non-Christians. This cannot be overemphasized. But let me conclude this part by saying that according to Ray Bakke of the International Urban Associates, 90percent of the people who come to know Jesus do so through personal relationship and not through programmes.[49]

Second, we must not adopt the negative approach.

This negative approach is all about Christians trying to attack the whole of the belief system of the other person (especially the weaknesses or errors), giving the impression that the whole of his system (be it Hinduism or Islam or whatever) is false, evil and bad. We should understand that all the false systems are only counterfeits of the original (Christian theism or incarnational theism) and therefore they have at least some similarities to the original. And we should look out for the similarities or the truths that are common to them and us on which we can agree with them, and use these as bridges in our evangelistic dialogues or conversations with them. This way we won't 'cut their noses before offering them the rose to smell'. This does not mean that we compromise on truth issues. But this does mean that we should study the belief systems of the friends of other faiths so that we can learn about what they believe, where their systems have gone wrong and the truth they have within their system. Paul's

ministry is very helpful in our efforts to learn how to relate to and reach out to the friends of other faiths. His ministry in Athens (Acts 17:16-34) is particularly instructive because it is a description of his ministry to people from a completely different religious background. Paul was not afraid to clash with or challenge the thinking of his audience. Paul believed that unless he demolished those beliefs that cannot coexist with the gospel, he could not bring the Athenians to accept the good news of the gospel (2 Cor. 10:5). But it is important for us to notice that he begins on a very positive note. Ajith Fernando says:

> Paul had earlier found points of contact with the Athenians. He did so later too. He was not afraid to agree with his audience when he could, for his sharing of the gospel was not a competitive argument he was having with them. His aim was to direct his audience to accept the truth. He affirmed whatever glimmerings of truth they already had. But he knew that when he presented truth, he also had to show that the things that clash with the truth were untrue.[50]

To bring the critical and the constructive together in his evangelistic strategy Paul must have known both what he believed and what his audience believed. In his speech to the Athenians he quoted a non-Christian author or authors (Acts 17:28) approvingly. This speech also shows that he had a good understanding of the religion of the Athenians. So we must conclude that Paul studied and learned about the religions of the people to whom he preached the gospel. I think we must follow the example of Paul and many others in the history of the Church. Ajith Fernando says that in our efforts to get to know other religions reading the books written by the adherents of those religions themselves is the thing to do. He says that we must also read the books written by Christians. But he goes on to say:

---

[48] *Ibid,* pp.359 to 360

[49] Source of this information is the *MARC Newsletter,* August 2001.

[50] Ajith Fernando, *Relating to People of Other Faiths,* Mumbai: GLS Publishing, p.43.

But reading is not the only way to learn. Talking and being friends with people of other faiths is a good way to go beyond what the books say about these religions and to get a 'feel', a 'sense' of the way adherents of these religions think and act. Even more helpful is trying to share the gospel with them. We do not need to wait until we know these religions well to share the gospel. . . . we can learn a lot while witnessing to them. Listening forms an important ingredient of witness. As we listen to them share their convictions and also listen to their objections to what we say, we will begin to learn a lot about their beliefs.[51]

I think that in our efforts to become conversant with other faiths, we should combine both reading books and listening to our friends while trying to present the gospel to them.

Third, we should make sure that Christian 'presence' is established to make the Christian 'proclamation' effective.

Although Christianity has been in India for more than 20 centuries, Christians are still only about 3 percent and not all of them are Christians according to the biblical understanding. What are the reasons? The reasons are many, but the most important ones are the two I have mentioned in this section and the two that I will discuss now. The third reason is that the Christian 'proclamation' has not been backed up well enough by the establishment of the Christian 'presence'. What Paul says in Titus 2:9 when applied to our own contexts means that we should make the gospel more attractive by living distinctively Christian lives. This is how I think we should establish Christian presence as individual Christians. As a community also we should establish Christian presence by the way we relate to one another as God's people. Jesus says that if we love one another as He loved us the world will know that we are His disciples (John 13:34-35). What I am trying to say is that the lives we live (as individuals and as communities of God's people) should show to the world that the gospel we are preaching has transformed us. In the words of John Stott it means that the good news of Jesus Christ must be set forth both visually and verbally. Commenting on 1 John 4:12 Stott says, "The invisible God, who once made Himself visible in Christ, now makes Himself visible in Christians, *if we love one another. . ..* It is through the quality of our loving that God makes Himself visible today."[52] When love governs our relationships within the body of Christ, unity will also be a mark of the Church and this also helps the world to recognize that Christ is sent by the Father (John 17:20-23). This whole point can be summarized by saying that the gospel we preach becomes more attractive and acceptable to others if we practice it ourselves. In other words, integrity in our lives gives us personal authenticity and this makes our evangelistic efforts more effective. Conversely, if our lives contradict the message we preach, our evangelism will lack all credibility and it would be less effective.[53]

Fourth, our efforts to reach our Hindu friends must be based on strategic planning.

What I mean is simply that we should not focus all our efforts only on those who are easily reachable, but we should also have some definite plans to reach those who are more influential in the society and are hard to reach. In India most of our evangelistic and mission efforts are focused on the tribals and the downtrodden people. J. N. Manokaran observes that there is a tendency to "win the winnable" and increase the numbers.[54] I think he is right. We have neglected

---

[51] *Ibid.,* pp.90-91.

[52] John Stott, *The Contemporary Christian*, Leicester: Inver-Varsity Press, 1992, pp.255-256.

[53] *Ibid.,* p.254.

[54] J. N. Manokaran in "Urban Challenge—Reaching the Cities" published by the India Missions Association, p.12.

the intelligentsia and the professionals. I think there is a general misconception in India that Christianity is for the lower castes and the simple folks, because the missions and probably the Church have bypassed the thinking-educated segment of the Indian population. Manokaran observes that there are 300 million urban educated-class people in the country who can also be classified as middle and upper class people, who have the intelligence and the economic power to make decisions, to influence the government and its policies. These are the real influencers and they can change the course of Indian history. But they have not been targeted at all by the missions and the Churches, and the impression given is that Christianity is only for non-thinkers, tribals, for low-caste people and the marginal communities of the country who have no influence in the society to be effective agents of change.[55] I think it is time for us to think strategically like the apostle Paul did and to come up with some viable strategies to win the powerful and influential groups of people like politicians, journalists, businessmen, professionals etc. I think our Lord is not only interested in the tribals (seven to ten percent of the population) who live out there in the jungles, but He is also interested in the 'tribals' who live in the concrete jungles of our cities (20-25 percent). So we must make special efforts to reach them with the gospel so that our county might be influenced by the gospel.

We should also develop a strategy where we will have a lot of pre-evangelistic programs like talks, seminars, open forums, and lectures in secular settings where false ideas that have captured the minds of people can be addressed and a theistic framework can be established. This strategy helps us to remove the mental blocks from the minds of our friends of other faiths so that they might be better prepared to receive the gospel or at least consider it more seriously and openly. Moreland thinks that unless a person considers the possibility that a belief might be true, he or she can never take that belief seriously. He says:

> If a culture reaches the point where Christian claims are not even part of its plausibility structure, fewer and fewer people will be able to entertain the possibility that they might be true. . . . This is why apologetics is so crucial to evangelism. It seeks to create a plausibility structure in a person's mind, 'favourable conditions' as Machen put it, so the gospel can be entertained by a person.[56]

Lastly but most importantly, we should pray

We should pray for the strongholds of the evil one to be pulled down so that people might escape from the trap of the Devil who has taken them captive to do his will. The battle for the minds and lives of people is not a purely intellectual battle. It is a deeply spiritual one. We are actually trying to release people from the clutches of the evil one (2 Tim.2: 24-26), and we need the power that comes from God when we pray. I think, to take seriously the Great Commission to 'make disciples of all nations' (Matt. 28: 18-20), is to commit ourselves to all that we humanly can to ensure the gospel is preached in all its fullness and glory. May I encourage you to commit yourself to all that you can do.

---

[55] *Ibid.*

[56] J.P.Moreland, *Love Your God With All Your Mind*, Colorado Springs: Navpress, 1997, pp.75-76.

CHAPTER 32

Spiritual Warfare and Worldview[1]

Paul G. Hiebert

In recent years, there has been a renewed interest in the Gospel as power in the lives of people, and in spiritual warfare between God and Satan.[2] This comes as an important corrective to the earlier emphasis in many western churches on the Gospel as merely truth, and on evil as primarily human weakness. Both truth and power are central themes in the Gospel and should be in the lives of God's people. But much literature on spiritual warfare has been written by missionaries who are forced to question their Western denial of this-worldly spirit realities through encounters with witchcraft, spiritism, and demon possession, and who base their studies in experience, and look for biblical texts to justify their views. These studies generally lack solid, comprehensive theological reflection on the subject. The second is by biblical scholars who seek to formulate a theological framework for understanding spiritual warfare, but who lack a deep understanding of bewildering array of beliefs in spirit realities found in religions around the world. Consequently, it is hard to apply what their findings in the specific contexts in which ministry occurs. We need a way to build bridges between the biblical teaching and the particularity of different cultures.

Worldviews

Stories of battles between good and evil, and of power encounters between good gods and evil demons are found in most religions. In Hinduism, Rama battles Ravana, in Buddhism Buddha fights Mara, and in Islam Allah wars against Shaitan. As we read these stories, however, we sense that these myths differ greatly from the spiritual warfare referred to in Scripture. To understand these differences, we need to understand the worldviews in which they are embedded. Moreover, in reading Scripture, we need to examine our own worldview as it relates to the reality and nature of spiritual warfare lest we read into it our own understandings of war and warfare, and so distort its message.

Beneath the behavior and beliefs of human cultures are fundamental assumptions human communities make about the nature of reality—their worldviews. These help them make sense out of their experiences, give them a feeling of being at home, and reassures them that what they see is the way things really are. Worldviews shape how people see the world around them. They are largely implicit. They are what people look with, not what people look at.

---

[1] "Spiritual Warfare and Worldviews" by Paul G. Hiebert was published in *Direction Journal* Fall 2000, Vol.29 No.2, pp.114-24.

[2] See Neil Anderson, *Victory over the Darkness: Realizing the Power of Your Identity in Christ*, Ventura, CA: Regal, 1991; Arnold Clinton, *Three Crucial Questions about Spiritual Warfare*, Grand Rapids, MI:Baker, 1997; Charles Kraft, *Defeating Dark Angels: Breaking Demonic Oppression in the Believer's Life*, Ann Arbor, MI:Vine, 1992; A. Scott Moreau, *Essentials of Spiritual Warfare:Equipped to Win the Battle*, Wheaton, IL: Harold Shaw, 1997; David Powilson, *Power Encounters: Reclaiming Spiritual Warfare*, Grand Rapids:MI, 1995 and C.Peter Wagner,*Engaging the Enemy: How to Fight and Defeat Territorial Spirits*, Ventura, CA:Regal, 1991, to name a few.

People in different cultures have different worldviews. They do not all live in the same world with different words for the same things. They live in different conceptual worlds that see reality in radically different ways at the most fundamental levels.

It is important for us to understand the different worldviews that underlie current writings on warfare, and, in particular, the worldview we bring with us when we read Scripture. Our worldview determines whether such things as spirits or ancestors really exist on earth, and whether magic and witchcraft can actually make bad things to happen to us. We too often assume that our worldviews are biblical, when, in fact, they are largely shaped by the culture around us. We need to study Scripture to understand the biblical worldview that lies behind the descriptions of spiritual warfare found in it.

Worldviews of Spiritual Warfare

We will examine three current views of spiritual warfare found around the world that have distorted our understanding of spiritual warfare as it is found in Scripture. It is not possible here to examine the specific worldviews of spiritual warfare found in the cultures around the world. That is the task of each missionary as he/she ministers in specific human contexts. Our task, rather, is to examine the worldviews underlying the current debate on spiritual warfare, including our own, and to test them against biblical teachings on the subject. If we do not examine our own worldviews, we are in danger of reading our cultural understandings of war and warfare into Scripture and of distorting its message. We will briefly examine three worldviews underlying the current debate in the West regarding the nature of spiritual warfare to see how they have shaped the current debate regarding spiritual warfare.[3]

Modern Supernatural/Natural Dualism

The worldview of the West has been shaped since the sixteenth century by the Cartesian dualism that divides the cosmos into two realities—the supernatural world of God, angels and demons, and the natural material world of humans, animals, plants and matter. This has led to two views of spiritual warfare. First, as secularism spread, the reality of the supernatural world was denied. In this materialist worldview the only reality is the natural world which can best be studied by science. For modern secular people, there is no spiritual warfare because there are no gods, angels or demons. There is only war in nature between humans, communities and nations. Some Christians accept this denial of spiritual realities, and demythologize the Scriptures to make it fit modern secular scientific beliefs. Angels, demons, miracles and other supernatural realities are explained away in scientific terms. The battle, they claim, is between good and evil in human social systems. The church is called to fight against poverty, injustice, oppression, and other evils which are due to oppressive, exploitative human systems of government, business and religion.

The second view of spiritual warfare emerging out of this dualism is that God, angels and demons are involved in a cosmic battle in the heavens, but the everyday events on earth are best explained and controlled by science and technology (figure 1).

People pray to God for their salvation, but turn to modern medicine for healing and psychology for deliverance from so called demon possession, because demons, if they exist, exist in the heavens, not on earth. They are not a part of everyday life. Western missionaries influenced by this dualism denied the realities of witchcraft,

---

[3] For good reviews of current issues and literature see Robert Priest, *Missiology and the Social Science*, Edward Rommen and Gary Corwin, eds.. Pasadena, CA: William Carey Library,1996, and A. Scott Moreau, *Essentials of Spiritual Warfare: Equipped to Win the Battle*, Wheaton, IL: Harold Shaw, 1997.

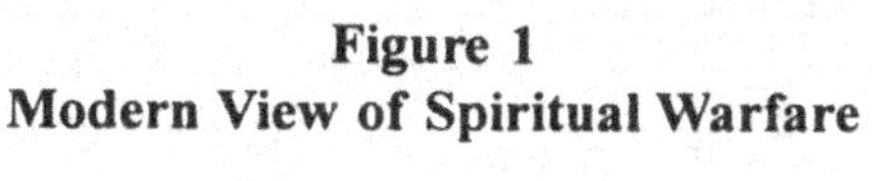

Figure 1
Modern View of Spiritual Warfare

Supernatural

Battle in the heavens between God, Angels, Satan and demons.

Natural

Battle on earth Between Church and World

spirit possession, evil eye and magic in the cultures where they served. Consequently they failed to provide biblical answers to the people's fears of earthly spirits and powers, and to deal with the reality of Satan's work on earth.

Tribal Religions

For most tribal peoples, ancestors, earthly spirits, witchcraft and magic are very real. The people see the earth and sky as full of beings (gods, earthly divinities, ancestors, ghosts, evil shades, humans, animals and nature spirits) that relate, deceive, bully and battle one another for power and personal gain. These beings are neither totally good nor totally evil. They help those who serve or placate them. They harm those who oppose their wishes or who neglect them or refuse to honor them. Humans must placate them to avoid terrible disasters. Spiritual warfare in animistic societies is seen as an ongoing battle between different alliances of beings (figure 2).

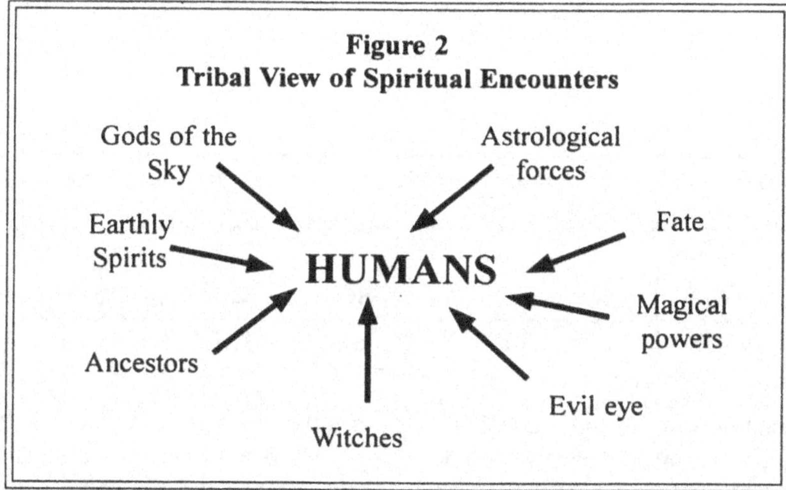

Figure 2
Tribal View of Spiritual Encounters

For the most part these alliances are based on ethnicity and territory. The battle is not primarily between "good" and "evil," but between "us" and "them." The gods, spirits, ancestors and people of one village or tribe are in constant battle with those of surrounding villages and tribes. When the men of one group defeat those of another, they attribute their success to the power of their gods and spirits. When they are defeated, they blame this on the weakness of their gods and spirits. We see this in the Old Testament in way the Arameans viewed their battles with the Israelites (I Kings 20:23,-30).

Land plays an important role in tribal views of spiritual warfare. Gods, spirits and ancestors reside in specific territories or objects, and protect their people who reside on their lands. Their powers do not extend to other lands. When people go on distant trips, they are no longer under the protection of their gods. When a community is defeated, the people are expected to change their allegiance to the stronger God and serve him. Conversions to new gods often follow dramatic "power encounters."

Some Christians interpret the biblical data on spiritual warfare using the traditional tribal themes of territory and power encounter. Satan is viewed as having authority over the earth, an authority he exercises through delegation to his demonic hierarchy. But, as Chuck Lowe points out,[4] this view of territorial spirits has little biblical justification. Belief in spirits who rule

territories and control people implies that these people are hapless victims of the cosmic battles of the gods, and that once they are delivered they will be ready to convert to Christ in mass. This sells human sinfulness short. Even if demons are driven out, humans call them back and renew their individual and corporate rebellion against God.

Belief in evil spirits now ruling geographic territories also denies the work of the Cross. Whatever delegated authority Satan had at the time of creation was taken away after the resurrection when Christ declared, "And now all authority has been given unto me (Matt. 28:16)." Satan now has no authority over the earth, only the authority given him by his demonic and human followers.

Cosmic Dualism

A third worldview of spiritual warfare is based on a cosmic dualism (figure 3).

<table>
<tr><td colspan="4">Figure 3
The Myth of Cosmic Dualism</td></tr>
<tr><td></td><td></td><td>GOOD</td><td>EVIL</td></tr>
<tr><td>Heavens</td><td colspan="3">Good People ← battle of power ← Central Evil gods
(fall out)</td></tr>
<tr><td colspan="4" align="center">↓</td></tr>
<tr><td>Humans</td><td colspan="3">Good People ← battle of Evil ← people power</td></tr>
<tr><td>Nature</td><td colspan="3">Good nature ← battle of ← Evil nature power</td></tr>
</table>

This is found in Zoroastrianism, Manicheism and Hinduism, and in cultures shaped by the Indo-European worldview, including those in the West. In it mighty gods battle for control of the universe: one seeking to establish a kingdom of righteousness and order, and the other an evil empire. The outcome is uncertain for both sides

are equally strong, and the battle is unending for when good or evil are defeated they rises to fight again. All reality is divided into two camps: good gods and bad ones, good nations and evil ones. Ultimately the division is not between cosmic good and evil—good gods and nations often do evil in order to win the battle, and evil gods and

---

[4] Chuck Lowe, *Territorial Spirits and World Evangelisation?* Borough Green, Kent, GB: Mentor/OMF, 1998.

nations do good. The real division is between 'our side' and 'the enemy.' If we win, we can establish the kingdom, and by definition it will be good. If the others win, they will establish what we see as an evil empire.

Central to this worldview is the myth of redemptive violence. Order can be established only when one side defeats the other in spiritual warfare. In other words, violence is necessary to bring about a better society—war is necessary to establish.[5] To win, therefore, is everything. The focus, therefore, is on the battle. The myths tell of the battles between the gods and spirits, and the effect of these battles on humans. Conflicts and competition are intrinsic to the world, and lead to evolution (biology), progress (civilization), development (economic), and prowess (sports).

Morality in the Indo-European battle is based on notions of "fairness" and "equal opportunity," not on some moral absolutes. To be fair, the conflict must be between those thought to be more or less equal in might. The outcome must be uncertain. It is "unfair" to pit a strong football team against a team of amateurs. Equal opportunity means that both sides must be able to use the same means to gain victory. If the evil side uses illegal and wicked means, the good side is justified in using them. In movies, the policeman man cannot shoot first. When the criminal draws his gun, however, the policeman can shoot him without a trial. In the end, both the good and the bad sides use violence, deceit, and intimidation to win the battle. In this worldview, chaos is the greatest evil, and violence can be used to restore order.

Indo-European religious beliefs have largely died in the West, but as Walter Wink points out, the Indo-European worldview continues to dominate modern western thought. It is the basis for the theories of evolution and capitalism, and is the dominant theme in western entertainment and sports. People pay to see sports games, and go home at the end claiming victory or making excuses for the loss. The story ends when the policeman unmasks the villain, and the cowboys defeat the Indians. Victory in the Indo-European myth is never final, however, nor is evil fully defeated. Evil always rises again to challenge the good, so good must constantly be on guard against future attacks.

Many current Christian interpretations of spiritual warfare are based on an Indo-European worldview which sees it as a cosmic battle between God and his angels, and Satan and his demons for the control of people and lands. The battle is fought in the heavens, but it ranges over sky and earth. The central question is one of power—can God defeat Satan? Because the outcome is in doubt, intense prayer is necessary to enable God and his angels to gain victory over the demonic powers. Humans are victims of this struggle. Even those who turn to Christ are subject to bodily attacks by Satan.

Biblical Views of Spiritual Warfare

Warfare is an important metaphor in Scripture and we must take it seriously. Eugene Peterson writes,[6]

> There is a spiritual war in progress, an all-out moral battle. There is evil and cruelty, unhappiness and illness. There is superstition and ignorance, brutality and pain. God is in

---

[5] See Gerald J. Lardson, ed. *Myth in Indo-European Antiquity.* Berkeley: University of California Press, 1974; Bruce Lincoln, *Myth, Cosmos, and Society: Indo-European Themes of Creation and Destruction.* Cambridge, MA: Harvard University Press, 1986.

Walter Wink *Engaging the Powers: Discernment and Resistance in a World of Domination,* Minneapolis, MN:Fortres, 1992.

[6] Eugene Peterson *Leap Over a Wall: Earthy Spirituality for Everyday Christians.* San Francisco, CA: Harper San Francisco, 1997, pp.122-123.

continuous and energetic battle against all of it. God is for life and against death. God is for love and against hate. God is for hope and against despair. God is for heaven and against hell. There is no neutral ground in the universe. Every square foot of space is contested.

The question is, what is the nature of this battle in biblical terms? One thing is clear, the biblical images of spiritual warfare are radically different from those in the materialistic, dualistic, animistic and Indo-European myths (figure 4). For example, in the Old Testament the surrounding nations saw Israel's defeats as evidence that their gods were more powerful, but the Old Testament writers are clear—Israel's defeats are not at the hand of pagan gods, but the judgment of Yahweh for their sins (Judg. 4:1-2; 6:1; 10:7; 1 Sam. 28:17-19; 1 Kings 16:2-3; 2 Kings 17:7-23). Similarly, the battle between God and Satan is not one of power (Job 1:1-12, Jud. 9:23-24). The whole world belongs to God. The gods of the pagans are, in fact, no gods. They are merely human-made images fashioned from wood and stone (Is. 44:46). Satan is a fallen angel created by God.

In the New Testament the focus shifts to a more spiritual view of battle. The Gospels clearly demonstrate the existence of demons, or unclean spirits, who oppress people. The exorcists of Jesus' day used techniques such as shoving a smelly root up the possessed person's nose to drive the spirit away, or by invoking a higher spirit through magical incantations (Keener 1993). Jesus, in contrast, simply drove the demons out on the basis of His own authority (Mk. 1:21-27; 9:14-32). He was not simply some mighty sorcerer who learned to manipulate the spirits through more powerful magic. He is the sovereign God of the universe exerting His will and authority over Satan and His helpers.

The Nature of the Battle

The Bible is clear: there is a cosmic battle between God and Satan (Eph. 6:12). There is, however, no doubt about its outcome. The dualism of God and Satan, good and evil, is not eternal and coexistent. In the beginning was God, eternal, righteous, loving and good. Satan, sin and sinners appear in creation. Moreover, God's creation is an ongoing process. The very existence of Satan and sinners, and the power they use in their rebellion is given them by God, and is a testimony to His mercy and love. Finally, whatever the battle, it was won at Calvary.

If the cosmic struggle between God and Satan is not one of power, what is it about? It is the establishment of God's reign on earth as it is in heaven. It is for human hearts and godly societies. God in His mercy is inviting sinners to repent and turn to Him.

The parable of the wayward son helps us understand the nature of the warfare we face (Bailey 1998). The father lavishes his love on his son, but the son rebels and turns against his father. The father is not interested in punishing his son, but in winning him back, so the father reaches out in unconditional love. The son wants to provoke the father into hating him, and thereby to justify his rebellion, but the father takes all the evil his son heaps on him and continues to love. When the son repents, he is restored back fully into the family (Luke 15:21-24). Similarly, God loves His rebellious creations, and longs to save them, not punish them. If He were to do less, He would be less than perfect love. In this battle for human allegiances, humans are not passive victims. They are active co-conspirators with Satan and his host in rebellion against God, and God urges them to turn to Him for salvation.

The Weapons of Warfare

Scripture makes it clear that the weapons of spiritual warfare are different for God and for Satan. Satan blinds the minds of humans to the truth through lies and deception. He tempts them with the pleasures of sin by appealing to their old nature. He intimidates them with fear by sending misfortunes. He accuses them of their sins. Above all, he invites them to worship themselves as gods (Gen. 3:1-7, 2 Tim. 3:2). God uses the weapons of truth to enlighten the mind, righteousness to combat sin, and peace and shalom to counter temptation. Above all, He invites all into the Kingdom of God in which Christ reigns in perfect love and justice. Satan and his followers [demonic and human] devise cultures and societies of rebellion that blind human minds. They seek to control those who turn themselves over to the rebellion, to keep sinners from converting, and to cause the saved to fall. Human rebellion is both individual and corporate. God and his followers [angelic and human] create the church as a counter-cultural community where Christ is recognized and worshiped as Lord, and where truth, love and righteousness reign. In the battle, God, His angles and His saints minister to protect and guide His people (2 Ki 6:17, Gen 24:7; 31:11-12; Dan 8:15-16, 9:20-23; Matt 1:20).

Power Encounters

At the heart of much of the current debate regarding spiritual warfare is the concept of 'power encounter.' Often this is seen in Indo-European terms (figure 5).

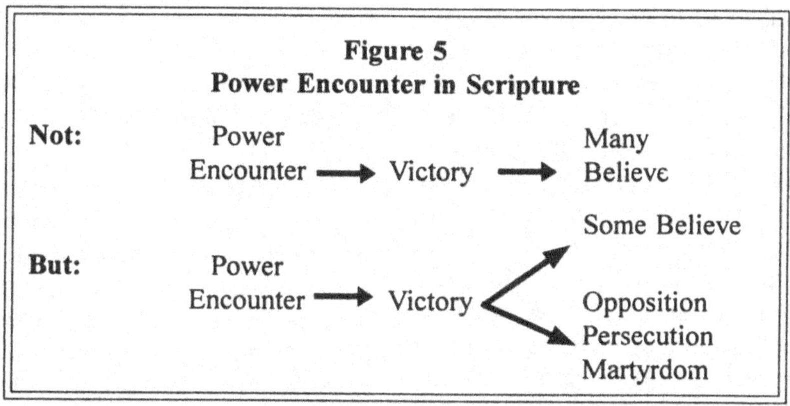

Proponents see such encounters as opportunities to demonstrate the might of God through dramatic healings, casting out of demons and divine protection, and assume that when people see God's miraculous interventions, they will believe. Scripture and church history show that demonstrations of God's power often lead some to believe, but they also excite the enemy to greater opposition leading to persecution and death. We see this in the book of Acts where victories are followed by persecution, imprisonment and death (appendix 1). Above all we see it in John where Jesus confronts the religious and political establishments and is crucified (appendix 2). In biblical spiritual warfare, the Cross is the ultimate and final victory (1 Cor. 1:18-25). If our understanding of spiritual warfare cannot explain this, we need to reexamine it. On the Cross Satan used his full might to destroy Christ, or to provoke him to use his divinity wrongly. Either would have meant defeat for Christ—the first because Satan would have overcome Him and the second because it would have destroyed God's plan of salvation through the use of unrighteous means.

The Cross as victory makes no sense in the Indo-European or tribal worldviews. In the Indo-European worldview (figure 6),

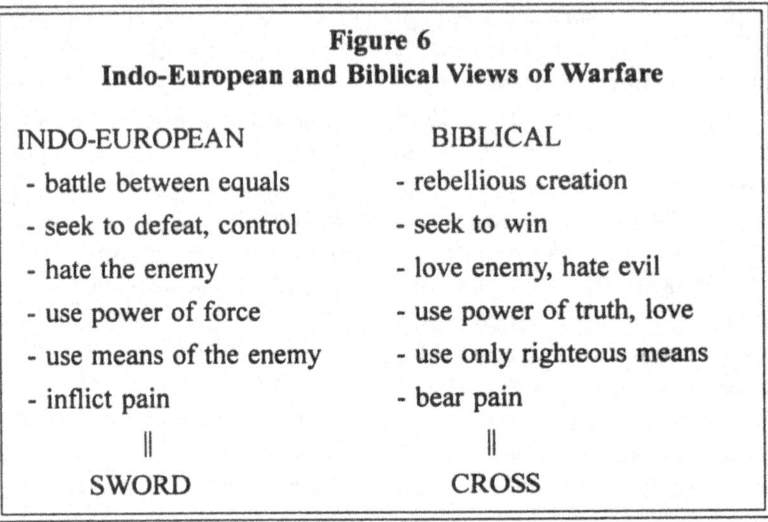

Christ should have taken up the challenge of His tormentors, called down His angelic hosts waiting ready in heaven, and come down from the Cross in triumph to establish His kingdom. In Scriptures the Cross is the demonstration of victory through weakness. At the Cross Satan stands judged because he put Christ, God incarnate as perfect man, to death. On the Cross Jesus bore the sins of the world and triumphed over all the powers of evil. His obedience unto death "rendered powerless him who had the power of death that is the devil" (Heb. 2:14). The Cross was Satan's undoing (Col. 2:15), but Satan's defeat was not an end in itself. Rather it removes the obstacles to God's purpose of creating people fit for His Kingdom (Gen. 12:1; Ex 19:3ff; I Peter 2:9). The Cross is the victory of righteousness over evil, of love over hate, of God's way over Satan's way. If our understanding of spiritual warfare does not see the Cross as the final triumph, it is wrong.

The biblical heroes in spiritual warfare are given in the hall of fame in Hebrews. Some overthrew kingdoms, escaped death by the sword, put whole armies to flight and received their loved ones back from death (Heb. 11:33-35). Even greater are the victors who were tortured, mocked, whipped, chained, oppressed, mistreated and martyred (Heb. 11:36-38). They were "too good for this world." In all these cases, victory lies not in defeating the enemy, but in standing firm in faith and bearing witness to Christ, no matter the outcome.

Christians and churches are in desperate need of showing God's power in transformed lives and in a Christlike confrontation of evil wherever they find it, whether demonic, systemic or personal. Here we face two dangers. On the one hand, we may avoid bold demonstrations of power for fear these may become magic. The church then is poor in the manifestations of God's might. On the other hand, in our zeal to demonstrate God's power we can run after the sensational and be tempted to use power for our own glory. Neither miracles nor the Cross can be taken out of the gospel without distorting it.

The Coming Kingdom

Finally, a biblical view of spiritual warfare points to the final establishment of the Kingdom of God throughout the whole universe. When we focus too much on the current battle, we lose sight of the cosmic picture in which the real story is not the battle, but the eternal reign of Christ. That vision transformed the early church, and it should be our focus in ministry today.

Appendix 1

Power Encounters in the Acts of the Apostles

Chapter

2:       Pentecost: power of the Holy Spirit —> ridicule, some believe

3:       Peter heals a crippled man —> put in jail, some believe

5:       Ananias and Sapphira die from God's judgment —>great fear in the church
[God judges evil in believers and the church as well as evil of Satan]

5:       The apostles heal many —> they are put in prison

6:       Stephen performs signs and wonders —> he is killed, and persecution spreads

11:      Growth of the church —> persecution, death of James

13:      Paul confronts Elymas —> proconsul believes

14:      Paul and Barnabas do signs and wonders —> some believe, Paul stoned

16:      Paul and Silas cast out a demon —> they are beaten and put in jail

17:      Paul preaches the Gospel —>some scoff, others believe

21:      Paul preaches and defends himself —> he is jailed and sent to Rome

Appendix 2

Jesus Confronts the Powers of Jerusalem and Rome
[Power Encounters in the Gospel According to John]

Chapter

1.   Birth: His birth as a king challenges Herod and earthly kingdoms.

2.   Overturns the tables; challenges the corrupt religious order which turned the court of evangelism into a market place

3.   Nicodemus: challenges the ignorance of a leader of the religious establishment.

4.   Samaritan woman: violates Jewish religious exclusivism.

5.   Heals on the Sabbath: confronts the legalism of the establishment.

6.   Feeds the five thousand: shows up the failure of establishment to care for the people.

7.   Feast of Booths: confronts the religious leaders and their unbelief.

8.   Preaches: challenges the merciless interpretation of the law.

9.   Heals. shows the powerlessness of the religious establishment.

10.   Confronts the Pharisees: challenges their teachings.

11.   Raises the dead: shows the powerlessness of the religious leaders.

12.   Triumphal Entry: challenges the leaders' understanding of God Kingdom.

13-19.   Jewish and Roman Leaders Conspire and kill Jesus.

20-21.   Jesus rises from the dead. defeats Satan and the political/religious establishments, establishes his kingdom.

                    Missiology for the 21ˢᵗ Century: South Asian Perspectives

Appendix 3

A Comparison of Evangelical Systematic, Biblical and Missiological Theologies

	Systematic theology	Biblical Theology	Missiological Theologies
SOURCE	The Bible is divine revelation	The Bible is divine revelation	The Bible is divine revelation
KEY QUESTION	What is the cosmic story?	What does Scripture say to these cosmic realities?	particular human situation?
METHOD	Abstract analogical logic	Historiography	Precedent teachings and cases
RESULTS	Helps develop the synchronic and understandings of a biblical worldview	Helps develop the diachronic understandings of a biblical world view	Helps develop missional vision motivation based on a biblical worldview
LIMITATIONS	Difficulty in bridging from: -structure to story, - universal to particular- explanation to mystery	Difficulty in bridging from: - story to structure- universal to particular Not missiological in nature	Difficulty in bridging from: - today to cosmic structure- now to cosmic time and story Not missiological in nature

CHAPTER 33

The Church's Role in Nation Building

C.V. MATTHEW

I

'Christian mission is a conspiracy against the nation of India; Christianity is an alien faith and its growth will necessarily result in the destruction of this ancient nation called India; Church in India is a threat to our national integrity and as a denationalizing entity it is inimical to the very existence of the nation.' Such allegations are put forward with more force and more frequently these days and it seems that more and more people are inclined to believe so.

The thesis of this paper is exactly the opposite—in the making of this nation called India it is the Christian faith and the Christians that contributed most positively and significantly.[1] Impartial political and social scientists and thinkers hold the view that India as a nation is only still in the making[2] and the idea of India as an 'ancient nation' is a pure myth, however pleasing it may sound. In this ongoing process of making or building this nation the Christian faith and Christians contributed immensely, notwithstanding the fact that they could have done far better. History bears witness to the fact that it is colonialism that brought about, as never before, greater political and territorial unity, cohesiveness and integrity in the subcontinent that finally paved way for the emergence of the modern sovereign republic of India. Colonialists brought about a larger 'British India' for commercial and administrative purposes and were not propelled by any altruistic motives. Therefore the Christian Church shall not claim any significant credit in this respect.[3] However, in several other areas of this nation making process the church has played a decisive and an enviable role. My intention here is to present a bird's eye-view of the contributions made by the Christian faith and its followers especially in the realm of ideas and values. The foundational materials used in building a nation are not bricks and mortars, i.e. not a strong treasury, nor a strong army nor an inexhaustible and formidable arsenal, though they may seem

---

[1] The scope of this paper is not to give a detailed, specific and exhaustive description of the various contributions (with the help of statistics and other means) the church and the Missions made to the nation of India. The concern here is to paint the larger and more general picture, showing the areas of accomplishments and deficiencies that may help us to be more contributive in the process of nation-building.

[2] In his brilliant article entitled "India Invented: Ostrich Approaches To National Unity," Arvind N. Das gives us a summary of the perceptive approach that both Pandit Nehru and Dr. Babasaheb Ambedkar had towards the 'Indian Nation', "Both Nehru and, much more clearly B.R. Ambedkar realised that India did not exist as a nation. What they were promoting was a vision of a nation-in-the-making, a new formation shaped by republican ideals and cast in the mould of a modernistic Constitution. Ambedkar was explicit on this issue. In believing that we are a nation, we are chasing a great delusion. We can only attempt to become a nation-in-the-making, he wrote on the eve of drafting the Constitution" (*The Times of India*. Bombay, Sept. 17, 1991).

[3] It must be noted that the church has played and does continue to play a significant role in controlling and neutralizing the political turmoil in North East India caused by cultural and civilizational differences and antipathies. Contrary to the communally prejudiced view prevalent in certain circles, the church in fact plays the role of a reconciler and integrator in North East India.

important. To be a nation, any community or society may require political unity or territorial integrity, one executive, one constitution, a common law, a means of viable transportation and easy communication. The Christian Church that is involved in building a nation has to be deeply concerned about these constituents, but more so about the most foundational aspects which are values and ideas. A nation is primarily built on principles, that is, on a worldview.

II

For precision and clarity in understanding I would like to state what I mean by the key words in the title.

'Church' refers to the entire ecclesiastical body of the Christian community in India; it is the Church in the Indian soil that is referred to. Wherever *'Church'* with capital *'C'* is used it stands for the total collection of all the Christian communities, bodies, institutions and associations; *'church'* with small *'c'* stands for the ecclesiastical bodies such as various denominations, local churches and nondenominational independent churches. No distinction is made between denominational traditions such as Roman Catholic or Orthodox or Protestant nor any distinction made on the basis of theological persuasions such as evangelical or liberal. *Indian Church* stands for the entire Christian mass of population in this subcontinent of India and its activities and the *Indian church* signifies the totality of the ecclesiastical or denominational entities.

A *'nation'* "is a body of people occupying a given area whose common interests are strong enough to make possible the maintenance of a single sovereign civil authority, i.e. a state which may and often does predate the nation as a historical reality."[4] *'Nation'* therefore in our present study refers to our country 'India' and her people—the sovereign republic of India.

'Nation-building' is defined as "the process of reinforcing the common bonds among the people of a nation state to the end that there may be general stability and prosperity so that the nation may participate usefully in the community of nations."[5] Nation building is an ongoing task of developing a nation in relation to its own people and also in relation to other nations in the world. In the words of Valerian Cardinal Gracias:

> National development does not consist merely in economic progress but means increasing possibility for *all* of living a fully human life on the physical (material), cultural, spiritual levels. It also implies the growing ability of a nation as whole to take its rightful place in the international field, economically, politically, culturally, i.e., to function with a proper degree of autonomy and prestige.[6] (The Role of Christian Colleges in Indian National Development. 1967. p.32).

Christian participation in the life of the society and therefore in the building of the nation "is a moral duty, a national obligation and the demand of enlightened self-interest," said P. D. Devanandan who relentlessly reminded the Church that she may discharge her responsibility to the nation.[7]

III

Having seen the general parameters of our understanding of Church and nation building, I consider it important to delineate a Christian or Biblical view of a developed nation. When the Church is involved in building a nation it must

[4] Bela Harmati, *The Role of the Church in Nation Building*, Report of an International Consultation held at the Njube Youth Center, Bulawayo, Zimbabwe, September 2-7, 1982, Geneva: LWF, 1983, p.8.

[5] *Ibid.*

[6] Valerian Cardinal Gracias, "The Role of Christian Colleges in Indian National Development," 1967, p.32.

[7] P.D. Devanandan and M.M. Thomas, *Christian Participation in Nation Building*, Bangalore: NCCI, 1960, p.49.

be on the foundations of and in concurrence with the Biblical values and principles. An exhaustive treatment of the subject here is beyond the scope of this paper and therefore I will only highlight the key principles involved in building a nation.

The foundation of God's throne, the Bible says, is righteousness and justice (Ps. 89:14) and a kingdom ('nation') is built on righteousness or destroyed by its absence (Pro. 11:11). It is law and justice that keep a nation steady and strong (Pro. 29:4). A nation is a good and equitable state when it is built on the principles of honesty, morality, justice and fairness (Pro. 29:12, 14; 31:2-5). Righteousness, morality, justice etc provide the foundation for a just and abounding nation. Its pillars are principles of human dignity and freedom, truth and knowledge, personal responsibility and stewardship, and the rule of law.

The Christian vision and commitment must be the building up of a "just, participatory and sustainable" nation.[8] The report of the Lutheran World Federation's consultation on the role of the church in nation building states that a nation is built, besides other factors, by common civil values, common symbols, common sense of progress, common participation in decisions, equality before the law, mutual respect for others and tolerance, and a feeling of freedom.[9] The Report goes on to say that fostering of moral and ethical values such as rectitude, honesty, love, tolerance, joy, reconciliation, forgiveness, righteousness and self-criticism will go a long way in building a just and progressing nation.[10]

These foundational biblical principles of righteousness and justice points to a particular worldview which implies the following in building up a strong and just nation.

The Principle of Individual Human Worth and Freedom. There must be an atmosphere of freedom for individual members to develop themselves as individual persons using all their talents and gifts and the resources available. Ultimacy or primacy cannot be given to any social order or set up to make individuals serve the system. If that happens then the individuals are enslaved to an oppressive system in operation. A nation has to recognize and ensure an individual's unique value and right to live by his or her conscience. Vishal Mangalwadi underscores this truth:

> Liberty is an indivisible whole. It begins with the mind—the freedom to think your own thoughts even if you disagree with society. It grows into a freedom to express your beliefs and thoughts, including the freedom of the press, in order to bring positive change to society. It continues into economic freedom, wherein you may apply your thoughts to harness natural resources for everyone's good.
>
> Finally, liberty bespeaks political freedom— the right of the individual to be protected from the oppressive power of the state, and the right to help shape policies and programs.[11]

The Programme of Dissemination of Knowledge and Educating the Citizens. The development of a nation is intrinsically related to the intellectual development of its members. Knowledge and intellectual development cannot be monopolized by a few and the rest denied its privileges. Pertaining to the utmost significance of education for *all* in a nation or community, H.G. Wells speaks thus:

> The modern citizen...must be informed first and then consulted. Before he can vote he

---

[8] B. Harmati, *The Role of the Church*, p.8.

[9] *Ibid.*, p.9.

[10] *Ibid.*

[11] Vishal Mangalwadi, *India: The Grand Experiment*, Surrey: Pippa Rann Books, 1997, p.142.

must hear the evidence, before he can decide he must know. It is not by setting up polling-booths, but by setting up schools and making literature and knowledge and news universally accessible, that the way is opened from servitude and confusion to that willingly co-operative state which is the modern ideal…Until a man has education, a vote is a useless and a dangerous thing for him to possess. The ideal community towards which we move is not a **community of will** simply; it is a **community of knowledge and will**….[12]

The Role of a Free Press. A free press is another dimension of this endeavor to disseminate the truth. Truth reforms, regenerates and liberates. Truth must be sought after, sifted, understood, disseminated and defended. A free press is absolutely indispensable for a just and democratic state. A tool for reformation, a voice of the voiceless, a defender of the truth, a check on the abuse of power by the powerful—these and many other causes are served by a free press, and the role of such a press in building a just and egalitarian nation can never be overemphasized.

The Principle and Practice of Stewardship. The resources available in any community—material, mineral and personnel—have to be harnessed and put to maximum use with efficiency should that community progress on the economic front. A positive approach to the world and life in it and a personal and responsible sense of stewardship of the resources available are inevitable for generating wealth and for providing enough for a welfare life. Nature and its resources cannot either be deified and held in awe and adoration on the one hand or defied and held in contempt and derision on the other. They must be taken as a trust given by the Creator God to individuals and to the community for better treatment—preservation, proliferation, promotion and righteous use.

The Principle of the Rule of Law. Cultural fascism or cultural nationalism, and despotism or dictatorship rest on the will and power of mortals, who always are a minority but a serious threat to the majority—the rest of the community or nation. It is the rule of law rather than the law of the ruler that ensures a just nation.

IV

Let me give a very brief sketch of the condition that prevailed in the subcontinent prior to and during the colonial period.

Politically there was no unity. Hundreds of kingdoms existed side by side with no sense of unity or any serious sense of interdependence. These were ruled by the royal caste under the guidance of the priestly caste while the common people had no say whatsoever in administrative matters. A fragmented, splintered, competitive and fighting political scenario prevailed with no sense of commitment to the 'state' (*desh bhakti*); loyalty was to the kings (*raj bhakti*). Any idea of a devotion to the land in general ('pan India' nationalism) was obviously absent.

At the **social level** the caste order was in complete command of the situation.[13] Being a discriminatory system, there was no equality of humans. The caste community was supreme; individuals existed for society and not the other way round. Many—the untouchables—did not have the rights and privileges that the livestock enjoyed. The low status and illiteracy of women wasted half of the total human resources.[14] Spirituality and education were the monopoly of

---

[12] H.G. Wells, *The Outline of History*, New York: Garden City Books, 1961, pp.587-588.

[13] For a succinct survey of the social disabilities the 'untouchables' suffered see, J.W. Pickett. *Christian Mass Movements in India*. Lucknow: 1933. Also consult *Dr. Babasaheb Ambedkar. Writings and Speeches Vol 5.* [*Untouchables or the Children of India's Ghetto and Other Essays on Untouchables and Untouchability. Social-Political-Religious*] Bombay: Govt. of Maharashtra, 1989.

[14] For details see Engelbert Zeitler *et.al*, eds., *Women in India and in the Church*, Pune: Ishvani Kendra, 1978.

the privileged few; and they were all male in gender. Some enjoyed almost divine status while the majority were demonized and kept away. Female infanticide was widely common. Child marriage, enforced widowhood etc were the order of the day. Medical care and public health programmes were not available to the majority. Infant mortality rate was high, resulting in creating a multitude of young widows. High birth rate was the only answer to the high infant mortality rate and the curse of short life span. Another heavy pressure upon the women! Status quo, in favor of the privileged, was maintained and the religious ideology of *Karma* and *Samsara* sacralized this stagnation while shutting out any scope for innovation and creativity. Mass illiteracy, poverty, backwardness, degeneration and dehumanization were the order of the day. P. D. Devanandan's societal diagnosis and prescription in post-independent times should surely help us to imagine how much worse the situation was a hundred or two hundred years before: Having observed that India's traditional societal structure was composed of three institutions viz., joint family, caste system and the village community he says, "In their rigid traditional forms, they militate against the new urges of individual freedom, material advance and social equality and should be replaced, by viable alternatives more adequate to the present needs."[15]

Philosophically, truth is unknowable and amoral, so held the highest philosophical tradition. This position stifled any urge for pursuing knowledge and morality. Rational enquiry and intellectual encounter with truth and application of this truth in daily personal and societal life were not concerns that merited attention of even the 'educated.' Freedom of individual conscience and free and open dissemination of knowledge were neither entertained nor encouraged. The Ultimate Reality is Silence and Unknowable and Indescribable, and therefore it did not inspire any attempt to articulate the truth in human languages; consequently none of the 'secular' or 'profane' languages (all languages other than Sanskrit) received any attention or patronage or development. Matter is evil and the farther a person was from the material world, the better he was in his spirituality. There was no sense in looking after the body with care because it in fact was looked down upon as a cage or prison house, hampering the release and salvation of the soul.

V

Into this setting, the Christian missionaries, following the footsteps of their Master who "went about doing good," arrived with a high sense of divine mission to do good to the people and to the community in the subcontinent. They had a different worldview, a worldview rooted in and emerging from the Gospel. The Church in pre-independent India laboured for a philosophical, moral and cultural regeneration of the worldview prevalent in the subcontinent and it is this commitment on the part of the Christians and their missions that helped the building up of the modern nation of India constitutionally committed to the principles of secularism, individual freedom of conscience, equality of all humans and genders, and constitutional parliamentary democracy.

The Christian contribution to the nation-building of India in terms of education has been widely acknowledged and appreciated. Education was an integral part of the missionary commitment, and church life and ministry. Churches and schools existed side by side; evangelism and education went hand in hand. In the length and breadth of this country Christians took the initiative and founded schools and other

---

[15] P.D. Devanandan, *Christian Participation in Nation Building*, p.139.

educational institutions and through the newly educated generations brought about radical changes in the value system and worldviews. Vishal Mangalwadi observes:

> ... it is important to understand that under early missionary statesmen, education was not a *strategy* in the sense of a *bribe* or *bait* for evangelization of India. It was an integral part of their theology, of what it means to serve God, love our neighbors and establish human culture...on the earth. Education was not brought to India to seduce Indians into the Church. It traveled naturally with the Gospel, because to preach the Gospel meant to teach all of God's truth, to reform the human mind and character.[16]

The open educational system in English medium, introduced and promoted by the missionaries, to quote D. S. Sarma the veteran Hindu scholar:

> ... broke the intellectual isolation of the Indian mind and brought it into contact with Western science, literature and history. The result of this was a great mental expansion similar to that which the European nations experienced at the time of the Revival of Classical Learning in the fifteenth and sixteenth centuries. A new world of ideas revealed itself to the wondering gaze of our young students in schools and colleges. In place of extravagant mythical geography, legendary history and pseudo-science with which they had been acquainted came sober and correct ideas about the configuration of the earth, the rise and fall of nations and the unalterable laws of Nature. In the light of this new knowledge many an evil custom in Hindu society, hitherto regarded as a decree of God, appeared in its true colours as the folly of man. Sati, infanticide, enforced widowhood, child marriages, untouchability, purdah, *devadasi*, the caste system and prohibition of foreign travel began to lose their tyrannical hold on the mind of the Hindus. And reformers arose who were

determined to purge the society of these evils.[17] (1973, p.61).

Take for instance, the education of women. What far-reaching and thoroughgoing effects it had! It assured the worth of women and their dignity. They received a new sense of equality. The potential in them became available for building the family and the nation and their active participation in public affairs resulted in an enhanced quality of life. Education of women resulted in better family ethos and lifestyle, and it has also helped arresting uncontrolled population growth. This naturally helped the economic aspect of life as well.

The Christian worldview acknowledges and appreciates the worth and beauty of the material world, human body, and life. The example of the Lord Jesus Christ going around *preaching*, *teaching* and *healing* motivated the Church to take all these three ministries seriously. The very preaching of the Gospel—that God loves everyone and has offered abundant life freely available for all—was revolutionary in this land of inhuman discrimination and untouchability. The healing ministry of the Church stood unparalleled and unrivalled.

The Christian contribution to the nation building of India is best appreciated when we note that it is with the Christian missions in India that the institution of press and journalism began in this country. "It was at the Serampore Mission in 1818 that we see the beginning of the modern Indian press, with the launching of *Friend of India* in English, *Sumachar Darpan* in Bengali, and the short-lived *Dig Darshan* in Hindi. The three periodicals, under the general editorship of Joshua Marshman, a colleague of William Carey, were inspired exclusively by a Christian presupposition that liberating power comes not from the barrel of a gun but from the Truth. The birth of the free press, thus, was a non-official

---

¹⁶ Mangalwadi, *India*, p.147.

¹⁷ D.S. Sarma, *Hinduism Through the Ages*, Bombay: Bharatiya Vidya Bhavan, 1973, p.61.

and non-commercial initiative."[18] The Gospel provides a worldview that generates and legitimizes such a vital institution as free press. In the development and promotion of native languages and dialects, whether in the North or in the South, whether in the plains or in the tribal belt, the Christian missionaries did yeoman services and caused the revival of literature.

In converting the subcontinent into a modernized economy and in instilling a formidable sense of personal responsibility and duty in looking after and multiplying material resources, the Christian faith has made indelible and conspicuous contributions. It is the Christian faith that declared a war against institutionalized and sacralized poverty in India. Caste system, mass illiteracy and low status and oppression of women had made India a land of, what Dr. Sam Higginbottom, the founder of the Allahabad Agricultural Institute and the author of *The Gospel and the Plough* refers to as, " appalling loss of human life, and stupendous economic waste."[19] The Gospel and the Christian understanding of spirituality that instills a high sense of stewardship and economic responsibility inspired the economic emancipation of poverty-stricken India.

In a splintered and warring subcontinent like India it is the Gospel and Christian statesmen who introduced and pushed the idea and practice of the rule of law—justice and not power as the ultimate principle of governance. Power is to serve the governed and not to lord it over and hurt them, teaches the Bible. The ruler is not absolute, for God alone is absolute and perfectly moral. Therefore even the ruler has to come under the authority of the law, the rule of the law. These and similar principles enshrined in our constitution are directly drawn from the Biblical

worldview and the significance of this contribution can hardly be exaggerated.

The God of the Bible and the Gospel proved efficient and vibrant agents of transformation that ensures the growth and vitality of this nation in the making. Sunder Raj gives a micro case:

> In South Tamilnadu, when the Chanar (sic.) caste of toddy tappers came to the Christian faith, the rampant drunkenness was not only wiped out but the whole caste's progression entirely changed to business, education and most leading careers of the day. This happened within a period of two generations. Penance, repentance, reconciliation with God and man forming the dominant part of the Christian worship and dogmas, have produced, however limitedly though, social and moral consciousness to the effect, that by all documented evidences Christians are relatively law-abiding, tax paying citizens.[20] (1985. p.20).

Turning to the major failures of the Church during this period, the most talked about issue is the general absence or lack of interest among the Christians in getting involved in the political affairs of the subcontinent, particularly in the independence struggle. This criticism is largely sustainable in most parts of India except in the case of the Syrian Christian community in the erstwhile princely state of Travancore. Perhaps the Christians elsewhere might have had their reasonable compulsions for staying away from active political participation considering the realities of the background that they came from and the subsequent fears that they might have entertained.

Another area where the church failed to a substantial degree, is in creating an egalitarian community within the church. Probably the church found it too heavy and difficult to resist

---

[18] *Ibid.,* p.180.

[19] Sam Higginbottom, *The Gospel and the Plough,* New York: Board for Foreign Missions of the Presbyterian Church in the United States, 1938, p.145.

[20] Sunder Raj, *The Confusion Called Conversion,* New Delhi: TRACI, 1986, p.20.

the caste dynamic infiltrating and affecting the very ethos and life of the church. Or the church might have been keen on numerical growth. Whatever might be the sociological excuses we may suggest, the church has to own up the moral responsibility for failing in this area and not being able to provide an egalitarian community of their own.

VI

In the post independent era, Christians continued the good works of the past and kept serving the society in building a healthy, educated and prosperous nation. In the medical, educational and social rehabilitation fields Christian contributions continue to shine. In caring for the widows, the aged, the destitute, the orphans, the lepers, the blind, the handicapped and retarded ones, and such despised, avoided and marginalized people the Church continues to serve in the old tradition of commitment and devotion. A new thrust witnessed during this period is the importance given to developmental projects. Besides the traditional programmes of rendering services to the needy and neglected, Christians in independent India turned their concerted attention to socio-economic development. Christian agencies like the World Vision of India and EFICOR illustrate the point. Several research institutes and action groups have been founded to do serious research works in the socio-economic field in order to promote well planned and relevant social services and developmental growth. Centre for Social Action (Bangalore), the Indian Social Institute (New Delhi), the Institute for Development Education (Madras), the Christian Institute for the Study of Religion and Society (Bangalore/Delhi), the Madras Institute of development Studies (Madras), the National Council for Applied Economic Research (New Delhi) and the like are some such institutes. We also see during this time special attention being given to developmental projects in rural and slum areas. In his survey of the development of Christian social thought in India Godwin Shiri acknowledges:

> There was an eagerness on the part of the Christian leadership of the churches to prove that Christian participation and the Christian community could contribute in building the nation. The churches all began to venture into new areas of social activities, including developmental projects. All these brought good 'credit' to Indian Christian community. Quite often Indian political leaders credited the churches for their educational and humanitarian activities.[21]

However, we must note that there are some serious omissions, deficiencies or misplaced priorities in our approach and activities. Let me mention just a few of them.

Christian educational institutions are mostly English medium institutions; in this area we are doing a commendable job but what we missed is a serious omission. Christian educational programmes are identified with English education which in certain circles is viewed as a vestige of colonialism and a 'foreign strategy' designed to hamper and destroy the growth of Indian languages and her culture. This fear and allegation may be unfounded; nevertheless the fact remains that our contribution to education through the medium of local languages of our country is very insignificant. We have, it seems, lost sight of the vision that the early missionaries had in opening and running schools in local languages. Unless the languages of India are developed, and thus the growth of the national culture fostered, the building of a healthy and self-confident nation will remain a mirage.

Another drawback is the fact that the majority of our educational institutions cater to the needs of the elite upper classes and castes in our cities and towns, and in the process the vast majority

---

[21] Godwin Shiri, *Christian Social Thought in India: 1962-1977*, Madras: CLS, 1982, p.8.

of our people in the villages and those who are poor are kept outside the gates of the centres of learning run by Christians.[22] This is a major failure on the part of the Church in our involvement in building this nation of one billion people of whom the majority is still in villages and slums. There is a need to fill our villages and slums with elementary schools and vocational training centres. When these millions are sidelined and avoided there is no serious 'nation-building' taking place here. If we do not take the place that belongs to us through our commitment to the Biblical worldview, the vacuum will be filled by some others!

The same charge may be leveled against our medical services. Who do we serve today? Having visited a number of leading Christian 'Mission' Hospitals in Kerala, the former director of the Christian Medical College and Hospital, Ludhiana, Dr. K.N. Nambudripad, lamented that these have become "five star hotels for the new rich and the middle and upper classes." This criticism is not untrue when we survey the emphasis of our medical ministries today. Instead of reaching every village and hamlet with community primary health centres for the care of the poor we are busy building up ultra super specialty hospitals to cater to the rich. In many places these have become commercial centres and not service points.[23] It is not these '5-Star Hospitals' that will bring development[24] to our nation, but unsung institutions like Christian Fellowship Hospital at Oddanchatram, near Palani in rural Tamil Nadu. B.H. Jackayya, in a report on the role of the Indian Church in nation building, makes the following sharp criticism, "Despite the fact that our church serves through institutions such as colleges, medical hospitals etc., these are no longer playing a vital role in nation building. Rather they have become

---

[22] "The Church should re-examine the policies of those of her educational institutions that cater more to the economic and social elite of the country. Her educational research and training programmes must pioneer new structures and non-formal methods to bring the benefit of literacy and learning to lower economic strata and to the rural areas so to be true to her evangelical missions through justice and development." (Christopher Duraisingh quotes Felix Wilfred's report on a workshop on 'Educational Institutions for Restructuring a Just Society' in his "Images of the Church in India: Assessment and Perspectives" in Ram Singh (ed.), *Christian Perspectives on Contemporary Indian Issues*, Madras: Institute for Development Education, 1983. p.158).

In his brilliant and penetrating address to the principals of Christian colleges (at a consultation held at Madras Christian College in 1967) Valerian Cardinal Gracias, Archbishop of Bombay had this penetrating admonition, "...we might ask ourselves if our institutions, not only in their ideals but in actual functioning, have been adequately Christian. There is always the temptation to forget one's roots—e.g. Christian institutions which began as orphanages, today appear as high class boarding schools, so restrictive and selective in admissions that there is no place for the poor in the inn. Consciously or unconsciously, under external pressures, it may very well be that the original image of our institutions, if not completely defaced, has been greatly disfigured" ("The Role of Christian Colleges in Indian National Development," 1967, p.21).

Vishal Mangalwadi does not mince words in his evaluation of many of our English medium schools: "English has become a vested interest. It is no longer a reforming force. Many (though by no means all) of the convents of Jesus and Mary, Peter and Paul are serving Mammon, not God. They love the honour which the upper castes Hindus give to them. Thus, in as much as they keep dividing India in two classes, and they keep enabling the upper castes to retain their grip on the levers of power, these institutions have become St. (*sic*) Lucifer's Convents." (*Missionary Conspiracy: Letters to a Postmodern Hindu*, Mussoorie: Good Books, 1996, pp. 300-01). For a detailed evaluation of the Christian sponsored English medium education and the question of the development of national languages, see Ibid., pp. 283-322.

[23] All of us know that it is the Christians who largely still go to the villages with medical mission. But the burden here is not to take comfort in that, but to highlight the point that a radical shift in our emphasis has taken place in the last few decades. Our priority does not seem to be any longer the health and wellbeing of the poor and the less privileged.

[24] The Montreux Consultation in 1970 defined development as a triad consisting of social justice, self-reliance, and economic growth. For a discussion see, Kurien, 1981. p.11-29. For a treatment on Church and Development consult the entire book.

prestigious institutions for the high and rich and a source of discord, disintegration, disunity; thereby they defeat the church's mission and ministry."[25] We have lost our constructive bias towards rural India. Nobel Laureate Prof. Amartya Sen categorically observed that until three traditional curses of our national life *viz.*, mass illiteracy, lack of primary health care and disappointingly limited and pathetic infrastructure are squarely dealt with the nation will not march towards progress and wellbeing. Endowed with the life-affirming Biblical worldview and with the missionary devotion and commitment, we are best equipped to challenge these roadblocks, I believe. The enslaved illiterates of our villages can be helped by effectively using means like *panchayati raj* so that a participatory developed nation may emerge. Social and developmental agencies, denominational churches and local churches—all should work together, complementing each other. Projects to help people to provide for themselves safe drinking water, primary health care and hygiene, primary education, housing and good access facilities can be adopted and executed not only by social agencies, but primarily so by churches. Indian churches need to take initiative in this area.

Our widely perceived reluctance to join hands with others and work towards the all round development of the nation is a major criticism that we must, with humility, accept. As a closed community[26] we seem to be very happy in our ghettos and spending ourselves in *our own* projects. We *run* our projects and do not want others to *interfere* in what we do! Of course, we do not *disturb* others in what they do! Either it is our 'holier-than-thou' attitude and the resultant spiritual arrogance or it is our 'minority complex'

and the subsequent sense of insecurity that prevents us from working together with others to maximize development and growth.

Yet another sector that the Christian community largely ignored and has not ventured into is the political life of the nation—parliamentary democratic political system, the legal and judiciary arena, and the civil administrative system. Clear vision, ability to think, discuss, debate and articulate convincingly and persuasively, right decision-making process, the power to execute them—these the political process provides. When Christians stay away from this crucial area of life, besides betraying our lack of wholesome commitment to the totality of life, we deny ourselves the privilege to decisively participate in the mission of nation-building. This is willful abdication, of responsibility, and that is criminal. Here too, the vacuum our absence creates will be filled by others—many a time by the ones we criticize and condemn, the all too familiar corrupt elements of our society. Corruption that eats away the vitals of our nation and our people cannot be fought by remote control; it calls for conviction, courage and humility to challenge and fight this demon head-on. In a parliamentary democratic system like ours the decision-making process is so vital that it demands our concerted involvement. "Politically literate Christians" are crucial for nation-building.[27]

Industry and commerce is another area that the Christian community has largely ignored. How can a strong nation be built without generating sufficient resources and spending and investing them wisely? Christian disinterest in this field is unjustifiable and inimical. The same may be said about the lack of contributions from Christians in the area of scientific researches and

---

[25] Jackayya, *The Role of the Church in Nation Building*, p.92.

[26] Christopher Duraisingh, in this context, refers to "Christians as a community alienated from the cultural and national ethos." See "Images of the Church in India," p.138.

[27] P.D. Devanandan, *Christian Participation in Nation Building*, p.49.

discoveries. We seem to be happy and settled with white-collar jobs that guarantee financial stability with which we create our security. We do not dare to venture into the unknown, labour hard and discover and generate new things and new resources. Nearly forty years ago we were encouraged, "If we can release ourselves to new fields like co-operatives, technical education, and developed forms of service to agriculture and small-scale industries in fruitful ways, and show that the spirit of Christian dedication and the framework of Christian fellowship can enhance their value for society and nation, we shall release healthy influences."[28]

In the process of building a free and just nation we have gone through times of great peril and darkness. There were times when human rights were abrogated and fundamental rights violated. These were serious threats to the just and free nation we wanted to build. At many such time the Christian community and the church-at-large failed to play her crucial prophetic role standing in the great tradition of the prophets of old, but preferred to remain silent;[29] 'our guilty silence' indeed.

Let me mention just one more area where the Christian community failed to penetrate and effectively contribute to the development of this nation. It is the field of art, architecture, literature, media and journalism[30]—media that can be effectively and powerfully used to fight corruption and create a viable and healthy worldview. It appears as though in this too, we have left others to do what they think might be profitable to them.[31] Though the Christians constitute one of the most literate communities in the nation, our creative involvement in these fields is pathetically negligible and insignificant.

The greatest challenge we face in the mission of nation-building today is essentially a triad: communalism, corruption and cultural fascism.[32] These forces are formidable and they will demolish and destroy our nation if not challenged and nullified. They can be countered, not by going nuclear, but by going moral and spiritual. The learned Cardinal said it long ago: "But the greatest need of modern India today, and a *sine qua non* of national development, is leadership given by men (used in the generic sense) of complete *moral integrity* and great moral courage."[33] This is the call and challenge before the Christian community in India as never before in seeking the welfare and good of our nation. Cardinal Gracias continues to remind us,

> We have only to ponder deeply on the Christian values enshrined in the Indian

---

[28] *Ibid.*, p.126.

[29] Duraisingh, "Images of the Church in India," quotes Fred Karat's observation about church's silence during the dark period of Emergency, " 'The Church and Christians seem to have been moved not by any considerations of right and wrong, of truth and falsehood, of human values, of the development of the poor, etc., but exclusively by considerations of their own security and that of the community's interests in the face of oppressive forces which seemed invincible,' " p.158.

[30] P.D. Devanandan's soft criticism runs thus, "The Indian Christian is criticised for taking little interest in, and for having made little contribution to literature and fine arts. This is in the main true. Yet we are thankful for Christian pioneers in literature, music, painting, and architecture who have made noteworthy contributions. The poems of N.V.Tilak, Vedanayaga Sastriar, Krishna Pillai, Gurnam Joshua, Kahanji Madhavji Ratnagrahi, the art of A.D. Thomas, Masoji and Wesley and others have made the Christian community conscious of what can be achieved," p.281.

[31] No wonder, every villain or drunkard in many Indian films, as though a general rule, is a guy with cross around his neck—a 'Christian!'

[32] Nearly thirty years ago Valerian Cardinal Gracias, "The Role of Christian Colleges in Indian National Development," listed two: "The greatest enemies to national development at present are two which are closely connected: Communalism in all its forms; and Corruption," p.32.

[33] *Ibid.*

Constitution with its recognition of the inviolability of each human person as the foundation of society, its defence of the rights of minorities and especially of freedom of conscience and freedom of religious belief and practice. Those values are not the logical outcome of Hinduism for all its religious tolerance: in the traditional thought of India, the individual has no intrinsic value of his own. It is the Christian doctrine of the immediate creation of each human soul and its unique 'embodiment' together with its redemption by Christ through union with the Paschal mystery of His death, resurrection and return to God, His Father and ours, that is the foundation of the modern democratic concept of man and society in India as elsewhere, however unconscious the modern democrats themselves may be of the fact.[34]

VII

As we stand at the very end of the second millennium and the threshold of the third, we have many things to **thank the Lord** for—the privilege and blessing of having a secular democratic republic as our nation and the privilege of contributing much to her blessings and development. At the same time, there is a crying need on our part to **acknowledge our failures**—both the sins of omission and commission—**and repent** for the same. If we repent and turn to the Lord He will heal the land and bless it, and empower us to serve our nation with commitment and devotion. We need a fresh **vision** for our **nation** in the 21ˢᵗ century—a **nation** that is made of *individuals, families, communities* and a mosaic of races, language groups, religious traditions and cultures; a **vision** born out of the Biblical worldview, a vision that honors Jesus Christ the Lord of the nations and history, a vision that seeks the wellbeing of our fellow citizens in a healthy environment and the

fulfillment of our national aspirations in healthy fellowship with one another (i.e. communal harmony); a vision that promotes a genuinely national consciousness, and social and national integration. It must be a vision that realizes truth, righteousness, justice, freedom, equality, mercy and love. *Shalom* for this country and for her people, everyone of them. The key is and shall always be the *right theology.*

> *"The people whose gods are inferior to mortal sovereigns can never aspire high. To the last, they are of the earth, earthy. As long as they cling to the earth, however high they may lift their head for a time in the struggle for life or space, they cannot win the higher spiritual race, which, after all, decides the fate of the nation."*[35] **Inazo Nitobe** [former Japanese ambassador to the League of Nations]

> "Then our sons in their youth
> will be like well-nurtured plants,
> and our daughters will be like pillars
> carved to adorn a palace.
> Our barns will be filled
> with every kind of provision.
> Our sheep will increase by thousands,
> by tens of thousands in our fields;
> our oxen will draw heavy loads.
> There will be no breaching of walls,
> no going into captivity,
> no cry of distress in our streets.
> Blessed are the people of whom this is true
> **Blessed are the people whose God is
> the LORD.**"
> (Psalm 144:12-15)

References and Bibliography

Ambedkar, Babsaheb (1989) Writings and Speeches. Vol. 5. Untouchables or the Children of India's Ghetto and Other Essays on Untouchables and Untouchability. Social-Political-Religious. Bombay: Govt. of Maharahstra.

---

[34] *Ibid.,* p.43.
[35] Inazo Nitobe, *The Japanese,* 1912, p.136.

Arles, Siga (1991) *Theological Education for the Mission of the Church in India:1947-1987.* Frankfurt: Peter Lang.

Chandran, J.R. (1991) *The Church in Mission.* Madras: CLS.

............................, *The Christian College and National Development.* (1967) Consultation of Principals of Christian Colleges. Madras: CLS.

............................, The Christian Mind Series (1994 November onwards) New Delhi: TRACI.

Das, Arvind N. "India Invented: Ostrich Approaches To National Unity" in *The Times of India.* Bombay, Sept. 17, 1991.

Desrochers, John (1994, 1995) *The India We Want to Build.* Vols.3. Bangalore: Centre for Social Action.

Desrochers, John & George Joseph (1988) *India Today.* Bnagalore: Centre for Social Action.

Devanandan, P. D. & M. M. Thomas, (1960) *Christian Participation in Nation Building.* Bangalore: NCCI.

Gnanadason, Aruna (ed.) (1990) *Ecumenism: Hope in Action.* Nagpur: NCCI.

Harmati, Bela (1983) *The Role of the Church in Nation Building. Report of an International Consultation held at the Njube Youth Center, Bulawayo, Zimbabwe, September 2-7, 1982.* Geneva: LWF.

Higginbottom, Sam (1938) *The Gospel and the Plough.* New York: The Board for Foreign Missions of the Presbyterian Church in the United States.

Hrangkhuma, F & Seabatian C.H. Kim (eds.) (1996) *The Church in India: Its Mission Tomorrow.* Delhi: CMS/ISPCK.

Jackayya, B.H. (1983) *The Role of the Church in Nation Building. Report of an International Consultation held at the Njube Youth Center, Bulawayo, Zimbabwe, September 2-7, 1982.* Geneva: LWF.

Kurien, C.T. (1981) *Mission and Proclamation.* Madras: CLS.

Kurien, C.T. (1974) *Poverty and Development.* Madras: CLS.

Mangalwadi, Vishal (1986) *Truth and Social Reform.* Mussoorie: Good Books.

Mangalwadi, Vishal (1996) *Missionary Conspiracy. Letters to a Postmodern Hindu.* Mussoorie: Good Books.

Mangalwadi, Vishal (1997) *India: The Grand Experiment.* Surrey: Pippa Rann Books.

Mangalwadi, Ruth & Vishal (1993) *Willaim Carey: A Tribute by an Indian Woman.* Mussoorie: Good Books.

Massey, James (ed.) (1994) *Indigenous People: Dalits.* Delhi:ISPCK.

Nehring, Andreas (ed.) (1994) *Fundamentalism and Secularism. The Indian Predicament.* Madras: Gurukul Summer Institute.

Nehru, Jawaharlal (1960) *The Discovery of India.* London: Meridian Books.

Nitobe, Inazo (1912) *The Japanese*

Raj, Sunder (1986) *The Confusion Called Conversion.* New Delhi: TRACI.

Sarma, D.S. (1973) *Hinduism through the Ages.* Bombay: Bharatiya Vidya Bhavan.

Schaeffer, Francis A. & Vishal Mangalwadi (1998) *Corruption Vs True Spirituality.* Mussoorie: Good Books.

Shiri, Godwin (1982) *Christian Social Thought in India: 1962-1977.* Madras: CLS.

Shourie, Arun (1994) *Missionaries in India: Continuities, Changes, Dilemmas.* New Delhi: ASA.

Singh, Ram (ed) (1983) *Christian Perspectives on Contemporary Indian Issues.* Madras:The Institute for Development Education.

Sumithra, Sunand (ed.)(1992) *Doing Contextual Theology.* Bangalore:TBT.

Thomas, M. M. (1978) *Revolution in India and Christian Humanism.* New Delhi: Forum for Christian Concern for People's Struggle.

Thomas, M.M. (1983) *The Ideological Quest Within My Christian Commitment:1939-1954.* Madras: CLS.

Varma, Pavan K(1998) *The Great Indian Middle Class*. New Delhi: Viking.

Villa-Vicencio, Charles (1992) *A Theology of Reconstruction. Nation-building and Human Rights*. Cambridge: University Press.

Wells, H.G. (1961) *The Outline of History*. New York: Garden City Books.

Zachariah, Mathai (ed.) (1971) *The Indian Church. Identity and Fulfilment*. Madras: CLS.

Zeitler, Engelbert *et.al* (eds.) (1978) *Women in India and in the Church*. Pune: Ishvani Kendra.

CHAPTER 34

Toward a Theology of Urban Mission in India

ATUL Y. AGHAMKAR

Introduction

At the beginning of the twentieth century little over ten per cent of the world's population lived in cities, but this scene changed drastically towards the end of the century. "Today we are on the threshold of living in a world that for the first time will be numerically more urban than rural."[1] This growth is primarily taking place in the non-Western countries. This rapid growth of urbanization will affect the non-Western world significantly since much of the Western Hemisphere is already urban. Hence the implications of urbanization for the non-western world are quite consequential. Although urbanization is not new, the degree and the speed with which the non-western countries are turning urban is new.

India, being part of Asia, is experiencing a tremendous urban growth. "In terms of absolute number of urban settlements and size of the urban population, India is possibly the largest urbanized nation in the world today."[2] This presents a tremendous challenge to the church in India — challenge that the church has been slow to respond, even though the implications of rapid urbanization are tremendous for the church and her future mission. Since urbanization is perceived to be an irreversible trend, it is imperative for the church in India to be informed, and properly equipped to respond to the challenge of urbanization. While doing that, it is equally important to enable the church to take theological reflections on the city seriously.

The Neglect of Urban Theology

Urban theology is comparatively a new field and not much has been produced in this area. Furthermore, what is available today is primarily written from the North American and European perspectives. Hence their applicability to the Indian context is limited. The urban context in North America is primarily an industrial, secular and post-modern; the issues raised by the American urban theologians are different from those that are faced in India.

Theological reflection on cities is not an easy task. Even though much contextual theology has been produced in India, rarely is this done keeping the urban context in mind. Indian theologians very seldom address urban issues and concerns causing the urban mission to suffer. What H.C. Koetsier said about Europe a decade ago applies precisely to the Indian context:

> There has been little theological analysis and reflection on what is happening in cities. It seems as if theology has lost interest in the world of the modern city. Only recently have a few theologians left their ivory towers of theological erudition to conform the turmoil of inner city life. Hence, churches have not been able to cope with the situation in the cities. They have withdrawn from the cities sociologically by migration and theologically

---

[1] John Palen, *The Urban World*, New York: McGraw-Hill, 1987, p.9.
[2] R. Ramchandran, *Urbanization and Urban Systems in India*, Delhi: Oxford University Press, p.1.

by a similar abandonment. Churches simply have not been willing to reflect critically and creatively on the challenges posed by them in the cities.[3]

The problem of urban theology in the Indian context is that her systems are so complex that one wonders where to start and upon what issues to focus. There are macro and micro issues, socio-political issues, religious issues of pluralism and discrimination and caste related issues. And of course the issues of poverty and affluence are very evident in the city. Added to these complexities is a church that is weak and divided.

The Neglect of Urban Missiology

Although cities have been in existence from ancient times, India has been considered to be a rural country, until recently. The major focus of Christian missions has been rural and tribal oriented and missionary societies have continued to focus on them. This has led to the unforgivable neglect of the city and consequently to the theological sidetracking of the city.

Most Indian theological reflection either neglects missiology, or undermines its importance. While the urban population of India is increasing at a staggering rate, the urban theological and missiological reflections have not yet picked up their pace making India one of the largest and yet most neglected mission fields today.

Cities acting as magnets, have attracted millions of people into their fold. People of different language, ethnic and religious groups, the poor and marginalized, as well as the rich affluent are found in our cities. As if the ends of the earth have come to the city, the most un-reached people groups are found within our city walls.

To make any substantial impact on our cities, we need to reflect on them both theologically and missiologically. What Ray Bakke said in this context is important: "The kind of mission work that pleases God and can expect his blessing is done carefully, on sound Biblical foundations. Developing a theology of the city is one of the ways to survive in urban ministry."[4] This is sadly missing in the Indian context.

The pace of urbanization in India is so rapid there is a danger that the urgency of doing urban ministry may cause Christian workers to neglect the Biblical and theological foundations. The needs and the demands of the city are so pressing that Christians are often tempted to move into the various cities for ministry without pausing to take theological and missiological bearings seriously.

This paper therefore attempts to examine the modern development of urbanization in India and provides a framework for Biblical, theological and missiological reflections on the city.

Urban Scenario in India

There was a time when most of the world's class cities were found only in Europe and North America. The process of urbanization took more than a century in Europe and North America, but in Asia, it is taking only decades. It is estimated that in the first decade of the twenty-first century, Asia will have more city dwellers than any other continent of the world.

Traditionally India was perceived to be a predominantly rural yet archaeological excavation shows that India had a well-developed Sindhu civilization with cities like Mohanjo Daro and Harappa. A number of ancient cities (e.g. Benaras, Ranchi and Madurai) have survived till today.

---

[3] H. C. Koetsier, "The Church Situation in European Cities," *Urban Mission*, 3.3. January 1986, p.5.

[4] Ray Bakke, *The Urban Christian*, Downers Grove, Illinois: Inter Most un-reached people groups are found in these cities, InterVarsity Press, 1987, p.62.

With the advent of the British, the pattern and the process of urbanization took a unique turn in India. The British grafted onto the indigenous cities their developed military and administrative centers. John H. Brush's scrutiny reveals a clear distinction between indigenously developed cities and cities that were developed by the British.[5] Among many contributions that the British made to the Indian urban scene were the modifications of the urban landscape of the existing cities with the introduction of the Civil Lines and the Cantonments.[6] Initially, the concentration of the British activities was primarily confined to the port cities like Bombay, Calcutta and Madras, but gradually, as the British established themselves firmly, they developed district headquarters 'cities' throughout India. This initiated a gradual process of urbanization in India.

Starting with the post Independence era, the modern phase of urbanization in India can be traced back to the Nehruvian policy of industrialization. In its first five-year plan, against the wishes of M. K. Gandhi, the then Prime Minister Jawaharlal Nehru, encouraged industrialization in India. With the emergence of industries in certain regions of India, urbanization spread rapidly. Consequently, the most industrialized regions became the most urbanized regions.[7] This explains why the leading industrial States (Maharashtra, Gujarat and Tamilnadu) have a very high urban population percentage.

In the early seventies rapid urbanization began to grip India. Millions of rural people migrated to Indian industrial cities. What Bogue and Zachariah said in this regard is true: "A discussion of urbanization in India fundamentally is a discussion of net rural-to-urban migration."[8] Today, India claims to have more than one third of her population living in the cities. "In terms of the absolute number of urban settlements and size of the urban population, India is possibly the largest urbanized nation in the world today."[9] These urban people by and large, are very open to change. Not only do the most urban people come under the influence of the modern ideologies of secularism, modernity and rationalism, these ideologies also directly or indirectly influence their attitude and behavior. This is an important point to note since this paves the way for better presentation of the gospel to urban dwellers.

Urban Christian Scenario in India

The epicenter of Christianity in India is gradually moving city-ward as we have already seen. As a result a number of Indian cities have developed a strong Christian presence. A government study[10] indicates that the Christian presence in is as follows: Kochi 36.25 per cent, Madras 10.0 per cent, Bombay 7.0 per cent and Bangalore 6.71 per cent. Apart from these major urban centers, the Christian population is also found in other cities. For example the estimated Christian population of Maharashtra in 1991 was 8,85,000 (Eight Lakh and eighty five thousand). Out of this about half of the Christians are found in Bombay alone. If the Christian population of Thane and Pune districts were added to Bombay,

---

[5] John H. Brush, "Morphology of Indian Cities" in *India's Urban Future*, edited by Roy Turner, Berkeley: University of California Press, 1962, p.59.

[6] R. Ramachandran, *Urbanization and Urban Systems in India*, Delhi: Oxford University Press, 1991, p.62.

[7] Prakas V. L. S. Rao, *Urbanization in India: Spatial Dimension*, New Delhi: Concept Publishing Company, 1983, p.53.

[8] Donald J. Bogue and K. C. Zachariah, "Urbanization and Migration in India," in *India's Urban Future* edited by Roy Turner, Berkeley: University of California Press, 1962, p.27.

[9] R. Ramachandran, *Urbanization*, p.1.

[10] *Census of India*, Series-1, Paper 4 of 1984: Household Population by Religion of Head of Household (Up to District, U.A. & City Level), 1981, p.83.

then over two thirds of the Christians of Maharashtra would be found in these three urban districts.[11] Obviously, there are sufficient indications that this trend will continue even in the coming decades.

The number of major Christian institutions: theological colleges, seminaries, missionary societies and Christian developmental organizations mean that significant Christian resources and personnel are available. But sadly, very little is being done from the missiological perspective. It is imperative then that the urban Christian constituency of India be informed and equipped to effectively minister to the urban populations. But before we get involved in city ministry, we must get our biblical and theological bearings in order.

Biblical Perspectives of Urban Mission

The Traditional Christian attitude towards the city has not been very positive. In the words of Harvie Conn, the "Anti-urban negativism" among Christian theologians,[12] not only weakened true biblical understanding of the city, but also contributed towards neglecting the city. Jaques Ellul's *The Meaning of the City*[13] is perhaps a classic example of such negativism. He perceived the city as nothing but a citadel of sin. Such negativism has crippled the balanced and positive reflection on the city from the Biblical perspective. Therefore we need to take time to understand the biblical approaches to the city and reflect on them theologically.

The City in the Bible

The Biblical account of the city is not uniform or systematic, but without understanding its urban focus, we cannot understand its message completely. Right after the story of the Creation and the Fall, the Bible mentions the first city that was ever built by man (Gen. 4:17). Then onward we cannot but see the importance the Bible gives to the urban places, urban contexts, and urban people. If we look at through the urban glasses, we will notice that from the book of Genesis to the book of Revelation, the Bible, apparently, is pro-urban. Understanding this urban emphasis of the Bible is crucial for developing a theology for the city.

According to Ray Bakke[14] the Bible includes over 1,200 references to cities, whereas Greenway[15] counted 1,400 references. Bakke further reports that at least 119 cities were recorded by name in the Bible. Prominent Biblical characters are seen as urban dwellers, urban ministers and urban planners. Hence the ultimate imagery of the Bible is strongly urban.[16]

The most frequently occurring term for "city" in the Old Testament is '*ir*' and is found some 1,090 times.[17] Interpreting the meaning of the word 'city' etymologically, one may come across several meanings. Kaiser suggests that "From the Cannanite cognate language Ugaritic comes the suggestion that the root represents an earlier laryngeal and '*g*' and hence the root *gyr*, meaning, 'to protect.'"[18] This appears to be in line with the purpose of the building of early Biblical cities.

---

[11] Paul Gupta and Tony Hilton, *The Unfinished Task in Maharashtra*, Madras: Council on National Service, n.d., p.95.

[12] Harvie Conn, "Genesis as Urban Prologue" in *Discipling the City: A Comprehensive Approach to Urban Mission* edited by Roger Greenway, Grand Rapids: Baker, 1992, p.13.

[13] Jaques Ellus, *The Meaning of the City*, Grand Rapids, Eerdmans, 1970.

[14] Raymond Bakke, *The Thailand Report on Large Cities*, Wheaton, Laussane Committee for World Evangelization, p.4.

[15] Roger Greenway, *Apostles to the City: Biblical Strategies for Urban Missions*, Grand Rapids, Baker, 1978, p.11.

[16] Frank Allen, "Toward a Biblical Urban Mission," *Urban Mission*, January 1986, p.8.

[17] Frank Frick, *The City in Ancient Israel*, Missoula, Montana: Deolars Press, 1977, p.25.

[18] Kaiser 1989, p.7.

Cain, the wanderer, built the first city in which to settle down and protect himself and his family members. Thus, etymologically it suggests that the city was a place of protection. Taking this thought further, Kaiser elaborates, saying: "Perhaps more to the point is the fact that the word 'city' in Hebrew is frequently modified by the adjective *mibsar,* meaning 'fortified' or 'that which cuts off abruptly.'"[19] Thus in this usage the city was a place where people would go for protection and safety.

Early City Builders in the Bible

Cain is considered to be the first builder of a city (Gen. 4: 17). The biblical account gives a background of this action. Cain kills his brother Abel and brings upon himself God's curse "You shall be a fugitive and a wanderer on the earth" (4:14). Ellul gives a vivid description of the context in which Cain built the city. Ellul contends that Cain built the first city "to satisfy his desire for security by creating a place belonging to him, a city."[20] In this way he wanted to settle down and protect himself. Ellul concludes saying, "The city is the direct consequence of Cain's murderous act and of his refusal to accept God's protection."[21] This building of a city is seen as a rebellion against God and His authority. Cain felt that the city might give him a sense of safety and protection. Through building this city, he tried to substitute his own security against the security God wanted to provide. "The city begins as a refuge from the insecurity of an open and hostile world."[22] The very act of building a city by Cain is often interpreted as an open rebellion against God.

The building of the first city by Cain is considered to be the beginning of the civilization and culture. Leupold is of the view that the beginning of civilization did make far greater strides among those alienated from God than among those who were devoted to Him.[23] So the city may have marked the beginning of civilization, but it also marks one more step further from God— a step toward self-reliance and self-confidence. Although some contend that the creativity with which Cain built the city can also be interpreted as part of the blessings God had given to his creation, in reality we see rebellion against God and his creation.

Nimrod is considered the second builder of the cities in the Bible. Though not much is recorded about him, we find from Genesis chapter ten that he was the first tyrant upon earth and was a great hunter. The meaning of his name itself throws some light on his character. "For the meaning of the vermiform *nimrodh,* without a doubt, is 'let us revolt.'"[24] To his name several cities are credited (Gen. 10:10-11). He did not build some of these cities; rather he captured and ruled them. Significant among them is Babel, or Babylon, and Nineveh. Interestingly, both of these cities reflect the arrogant and bloody characteristics of their founder, Nimrod. The biblical account depicts these cities as centers of concentrated sin and rebellion against God.

Goldingay argues that Genesis 4: 17-24 is an important passage because, "It tells us that the development of the city is the context in which families grow (e.g.Enoch, Irad, Mehujael, Methushael, Lamech)...."[25] Interestingly, we note

---

[19] *Ibid.*

[20] Ellul, *The Meaning of the City*, p.5.

[21] *Ibid.*

[22] John Goldingay, "The Bible in the City," *Theology*, January 1989, p.5.

[23] H.C. Leupold, *Exposition of Genesis*, Columbus, Ohio: Wartburg Press, 1942, p.214.

[24] *Ibid.*, p.366.

[25] Goldingay, "The Bible in the City" p.6.

that it was Cain and his descendants who began living in the city and that is where they raised their families. The city was the context in which early humanity developed its family, technology, art and culture. Early accounts in Genesis throw light on such urban development in which pre-patriarchal families evolved.

Tension Between Good and Evil in the City

Cities in the Bible demonstrate amazing contrasts and dichotomies. On the one hand, they are portrayed as the symbols of human arrogance, pride and self-sufficiency. Cities are understood as a mark of man's success and advance against God.[26] The building of cities is looked upon as a deliberate attempt to become independent of God and his authority. But on the other hand, they are the symbols of the blessings God had given to humanity to multiply and dominate the earth.

The tension between good and evil in cities is quite evident and runs throughout the Bible. Robert Linthicum puts it well when he says: "The essential Old Testament assumption about the city is that it is the battleground between Yahweh and Bale. The essential New Testament assumption is that the city struggles between God and Satan."[27] However, most cities mentioned in the Bible are not depicted as totally evil. Even in a city like Sodom, we see Lot and his family as the representatives of the good and the godly. Jerusalem is a good example of a city that demonstrates a vital tension between good and evil.

Jerusalem was considered to be the city of God, par excellence, but it was a city with a very bloody and evil background. And God allowed the city to be His dwelling place. As long as the city remained faithful and obedient to God, submitting humbly to His commands, and serving Him alone, it received blessings and became a channel of blessings to others. But when the urban dwellers of Jerusalem began oppressing one another, rebelling against God's commandments, cheating the fatherless and the orphans, God did not spare her from punishment and destruction (Jer.7: 3-7; 9:11).

There are two extreme views of cities — the negative and the positive. The view that is needed is one that will take into consideration both sides and yet strike a balance between the two. If we take the view that cities are the result of human rebellion against God and His authority, then we will agree with Jaques Ellul's interpretation that cities are nothing but citadels of sin and evil. But if we take the view that cities are the result of God's common grace as advocated by Greenway and others, then we will develop a sympathetic understanding toward the city. Harvie Conn further elaborates on this when he said that the cultural mandate given to Adam and Eve in the garden, to fill, rule and subdue the earth (Gen 1:28), was nothing more than a mandate to build the city.[28] Although we may not completely agree with Conn's interpretation, we cannot fail to see his positive approach to the city.

Gods dealing with the City People

In dealing with the city people, God demonstrates his concern for justice and righteousness. While loving them, He demonstrates His overall love for His creation. He desires that no one should perish (John 3:16). He demonstrates a clear concern for the poor and the oppressed. We see Him standing against those urban oppressors and condemning them because they oppress the poor and the widows (Prov. 28: 5, Isa. 1:17, Jer. 22:16, Mic. 6: 8, Luke 14: 12-14). He cautions those who do not show justice to the poor (Ex. 22:21-24) and warns those who indulge in corruption (Isa. 1:21-23, 10:1-3). He

---

[26] Ellul, *The Meaning of the City*, p.16.

[27] Robert Linthicum, *City of God, City of Satan*, Grand Rapids: Zondervan, 1991, p.27.

[28] Conn, "Genesis as Urban Prologue" p.15.

expects justice and fair treatment from the people and challenges them to change their hearts and ways (Jer 7:5-6).

Mercy is another characteristic of God that is demonstrated in dealing with the urban people. We see his mercy towards His own people of Israel even after they rebelled against his commands by running after the gods of other nations. God did not spare them for their sin of idolatry. However, having punished them, He opens His arms to accept them and show His mercy. He showed mercy to the people of Babel, and rather than punishing them for their rebellion and arrogance, He disperses them. We see God's mercy amidst judgment shown to the evildoers among the Ninevites, whereas we see Him judging and destroying the Sodomites, for their sinfulness and unrepentant hearts. So we see a logical connection between people's behaviors and God's response to them.

While condemning the evil systems and structures, God also cares and uses the systems of the cities. Jerusalem can be cited as a good example. He chose the city for His earthly dwelling place. He used her as His witness among the nations. But He rebuked the evil structures and systems that opposed Him and His purposes. Babylon can be seen as another striking example. Even though Babylon is described as the representative city of humankind—rebellious, greedy, violent, and idolatrous, we see God using it to punish the Israelites. He used Nebukhadnezzer, the king of Babylon as His instrument. Cyrus, the Persian king is another example of how God used this urban King for accomplishing His purpose. Coming to the New Testament era, we clearly see how God allowed Paul to use the provincial cities, their influence and networks for the spread of the Gospel.

The New Testament and City People

In the New Testament, we find the word 'polis' occurring about 160 times, most commonly in the gospel of Luke and the Acts of the Apostles. It is also found about 16 times in Matthew and 27 times in Revelation.[29] In the New Testament the city is closely associated with dense inhabitation of people enclosed by walls. The cities of the New Testament are much more diverse in character. The influence of Greek philosophy and civilization, as well as the Roman military dominance along with religious diversities were explicitly present in the New Testament cities.

The New Testament era is almost an urban era, particularly when it comes to the life and ministry of the apostle Paul. Roman and Greeks continued to exert their influences primarily through their cities. Trade routes connected major cities, and thus fast communication between the cities became an easy matter. Cities like Rome, Athens, Damascus and Jerusalem became the prominent centers of the world. The New Testament marvelously demonstrated the use of cities for the penetration of the Gospel. A few very prominent cities come to our attention when we begin to deal with New Testament Christianity. We will restrict our studies to two New Testament cities, i.e. Jerusalem and Antioch. Jerusalem, as we have seen, was the key and crucial center for Christianity during and after the time of Jesus. Antioch became the first Hellenistic city to have received the honor of being a prominent non-Jewish Christian center that remained influential and became a model for the missionary church.

The City of Jerusalem

The name Jerusalem occurs 139 times in the New Testament. It continued to be a center of

---

[29] Hermann Strathmann, "Polis" in *Theological Dictionary of the New Testament* Vol.VI, Grand Rapids: Eerdmans, 1968, p.259.

socio-politics as well as a religious centre for the Jews and remained a focal point of everything the Jews were and did. It is often seen as a battleground for both God and Satan.

Jerusalem during Jesus' Time

Jerusalem played a very important role in the life and ministry of Jesus and throws a significant amount of light on Jesus' attitude toward the city. "From Mark to John, Jerusalem occupies a growing place in the gospels. But it is in Luke that its role is more heavily underlined, as the hinge between the gospel and the Acts."[30] Jews in New Testament times attached a theocratic importance to Jerusalem. They considered Jerusalem as the center of the world for the purpose of God's redemption. During Jesus' time it had become a hub of Jewish religious and political activities, partly because in Jerusalem the highest seats of political and religious authorities were established.

When Jesus came to Jerusalem, "There He confronted the two theocratic institutions: the priests as functionaries of the cult (cf. Lk. 19:45 ff.), and the scribes as keepers of the Mosaic tradition (Matt 23)."[31] However, most significantly in Jerusalem was the temple, the presence of God on earth that brought a great influx of Jewish visitors to Jerusalem.

Beginning with Matthew's account, where we find Jesus being led by Satan into the temple in Jerusalem (Matt. 4: 5). Ellul has a point when he says that it is the Devil who takes Jesus into the city. He implies that Satan uses the holy city as a lure, a temptation for Jesus. Satan not only acts in the city but also in all holy places.[32]

However, we read in Matthew 16:21, that Jesus intentionally began moving toward Jerusalem. He did this deliberately, and volunteered to face the city. But the most significant words Jesus uttered in connection with Jerusalem are found in Matthew 24:37-39. Its parallel is also found in Luke 19: 41-44, which clearly depicts His intentions for the salvation of the city. His attempt to bring her under His wings is significant. He wants Jerusalem to be His, but on the contrary, we note that the city has rebelled and detached herself from Jesus. This broke His heart for He knew that by refusing to come to God, the city was opting for its own destruction and desolation. "The one-thousand-year history of Jerusalem from David to Herod could best be depicted as a continuing and lengthy rejection of any new way God might be at work in the midst of His people."[33] Thus a stubborn and arrogant attitude led Jerusalem to its own destruction. The history of Jerusalem is a great witness to the cycle of destruction and restoration.

In Mark's Gospel we find Jesus turning towards Jerusalem only after meeting with the disbelief of the Galilean towns (Mark 6: 1-6, 8: 11 ff.), and He announces that He will go to Jerusalem to suffer and be rejected by the elders and the priests. And yet He consciously goes there to complete the task that has been entrusted to Him—to offer His sacrifice (10:32). In the context of His death, He declares the punishment of the city and the abomination in the temple (13: 13-20). "Jerusalem here is the place of the great denial."[34] Interestingly we note that Jesus rarely made Jerusalem His 'home.' He frequently visited the city, ministered in the city and yet never

---

[30] Michael Join-Lambert and Pierre Grelot, "Jerusalem" in *Dictionary of Biblical Theology* edited by Xavier Leon-Dufour, London: Geoffrey Chapman, 1967, p.232.

[31] H. Schultz, "Jerusalem" in *New International Dictionary of New Testament Theology* Vol.2 edited by Collin Brown, Grand Rapids: Zondervan, 1979, p.329.

[32] Ellul, *The Meaning of the City*, p.114.

[33] Linthicum, *City of God, City of Man*, p.116.

[34] Join-Lambert and Grelot, "Jerusalem" p.132.

resided there. Even when at the time of His death, He had to leave the city and die outside of the city.

Jerusalem is important for Luke. It dominates the beginning and the end of the Gospel. The temple of God, which forms a central part of the ministry and deeds of Jesus, is referred to frequently in Luke. It is in Jerusalem that many of the great deeds and events took place. "In fact, if the story of Jesus is completed at Jerusalem with His sacrifice, apparitions and ascension (Lk 24: 36-53, Acts 1:4-13), it is from there that the story of apostolic testimony begins."[35]

Luke significantly portrays the importance of Jerusalem in the formation and spread of the early church. He shows that it was at the city of Jerusalem the apostles receive the Holy Sprit (Ac. 2) and thus they receive a sense of clear mission and began carrying the gospel from Jerusalem to Judea and to Samaria and the ends of the earth. It is in Jerusalem, Luke mentions that the first Christian church was established.

Jerusalem During Paul's Time

Jerusalem played quite a crucial role in Paul's life and letters. Paul recognized Jerusalem as the center of Christendom and got the permission from the priests to persecute the Christians. Jerusalem became the starting point for the missionary expansion during Paul's time. Commenting on the significance of Jerusalem, Charles H. Talbert points out that: "(a) It is from Jerusalem the universal preaching of the gospel is to begin (Luke 24:47; Acts 1:8). (b) Every new expansion of the church in apostolic times had to receive the approval of Jerusalem (e.g. Acts 8:12, 14-15; 11:1-2, 18, 19-21, 22; 15:2, 12ff.).

(c) Paul's entire ministry is given a Jerusalem frame of reference (9:27ff); his work at Antioch is undertaken at Barnabas' initiative (11:25 ff); his missionary commission is given by a church which Jerusalem approved (13:1-3); each of his missionary journeys ends at Jerusalem (15:2 18:22; 21:17); he recognizes the validity and appeals of the witness of the twelve (13:31); he refers difficult questions of Jerusalem (15:2), accepts Jerusalem decisions (21:23-26), and appeals to Jerusalem authority (16:5). In sum, Jerusalem controls the mission enterprise in Acts."[36]

Soon after his conversion, we see Paul becoming part of the community of believers, and being sent out by the church in Jerusalem to Antioch as their missionary. The idea of a New Jerusalem, the heavenly Jerusalem, is also introduced by Paul, especially in Hebrews 12:22. "Paul assumes in Galatians 4 the reality of a city which is God's city, for which the earthly city Jerusalem had been simply an advance metaphor. It corresponds closely with his statement that 'our citizenship is in heaven'" (Phil 3:20).[37] Paul, while being connected with the earthly Jerusalem, set his hopes for the heavenly Jerusalem. "In Jewish apocalyptic tradition heavenly Jerusalem was the pre-existent place where God's glory was always present. For Paul it was also the place of freedom from the law."[38] The book of Revelation gives a formal shape to the idea of New Jerusalem. In Rev. 3: 12 and 21:2 we read about the New Jerusalem as a heavenly city descending from heaven as the bride of the exalted Christ, and receiving as its citizens all those who have been marked as conquerors.

---

[35] *Ibid.,* p.233.

[36] Charles H. Talbert, *Reading Luke: A Literary and Theological Commentary on the Third Gospel,* New York, Crossroads Publications, 1982, p.100.

[37] Tom Wright, "Jerusalem in the New Testament" in *Jerusalem Past Present in the Purposes of God* edited by P.W. Walker, Cambridge, Tyndale House, 1993, p.69.

[38] Shultz, "Jerusalem" p.329.

The City of Antioch

Antioch in Syria was one of the most influential cities during Paul's time. It was one of the three greatest cities of the Greco-Roman world, and an early center of Christian expansion. It attained political importance and a high degree of commercial prosperity, which made it a wealthy and sophisticated metropolis in which Greek civilization flourished and came into close contact with both oriental culture and religious ideas.[39] Being cosmopolitan in nature, the city attracted people of different faiths and provinces. The city had a typical blend of different religious and philosophical groups.

Antioch had its own uniqueness and sinfulness too. The city was a typical Roman city, with a strong influence of Greek culture and religion. Green says, "It is almost a microcosm of Roman antiquity in the first century, a city which encompassed most of the advantages, the problems, and the human interests, with which new faith would have to grapple."[40]

Greenway and Monsoma point out that "Understanding Antioch is crucial for a biblical perception of urban mission, because patterns were established there that set the course of mission history and changed the religious map of the world."[41] It is a significant city, for it gives clues as to how the Gospel spread from the Jews to the Gentiles. Acts 11:19 says when persecution broke out as a result of the execution of Stephen, many Christian Jews fled to Antioch. As they settled in Antioch, they could not but share the gospel with their fellow-Jews in Antioch.

However, the most interesting phenomenon in the history of early Christianity took place at Antioch. Gospel was shared with the non-Jews in Antioch for the first time. This was not done with planning and deliberate intentions; rather it was a spontaneous movement arising from those simple Christians, who could not keep quiet about their faith in Jesus Christ. Not only was it at Antioch that the Gentiles heard the gospel for the first time, it was also the Antiochan church, not the Jerusalem church, that sent out the first missionaries. This makes Antioch a significant urban center from the Christian point of view. As in every city of the time, the infiltration of numerous religious and philosophical cults was very much evident at Antioch. As pointed out:

> There were cults of Zeus and Apollo and the rest of the Greek pantheon. There was also the Syrian worship of Baal and the Mother Goddess, and the mystery religions with their teachings on death and resurrection, initiation, and salvation. Occultism was common along with magic, witchcraft and astrology.[42]

The spirit of intellectualism, of mysticism and the reality of pluralism were characteristics of Antioch. Added to these was the inevitable practice of idol worship. Numerous gods and goddesses were worshipped in the city. Naturally, this led to immoral practices and corruption in Antioch. The city had a significant Jewish population. Thus the Antiochans were exposed early to Judaism and eventually to Christianity. McRay believes that there must have been about 22,000 to 65,000 Jewish people living in Antioch, where barriers of religion, race and nationality were easily crossed and where toleration may have been a matter of civic pride - it was a perfect base of operation for Christianity.[43]

It was perhaps Nicholus, who had been a proselyte to Judaism and one of the early converts

---

[39] Downey 1962, p.145.

[40] Michael Green, *Evangelism in the Early Church*, Grand Rapids, Eerdmans, 1970, p.114.

[41] Greenway and Monsma, *Cities: Mission's New Frontier*, p.31.

[42] *Ibid.*, p.32.

[43] J. McRay, "Antioch on the Orontes" in *The Dictionary of Paul and His Letters* edited by Gerlad Hawthorne and Ralph P. Martin, Downers Grove: InterVarsity Press, 1992, p.23.

to Christianity who was instrumental in bringing the gospel to the Antiochans (Acts 6:5). The Jews in Antioch were an influential community, attracting many Greeks and Hellenists to their faith. Thus we have a number of 'God-fearers' who may have been already receptive, and thus when the Gospel was brought to them, it made its inroads among this receptive segment of the city. "Some of the Greeks to whom the Word was preached were doubtless Gentiles who had attended the synagogues and were familiar with the background of the new teachings" (cf. Acts 17:4).[44] Whoever was responsible for bringing the gospel to Antioch, God chose Hellenistic Christians to move out of Jerusalem and to begin to make a significant influence for the Gospel.

The Antiochan church not only shows us how the Gospel reached them but how it spread from there to the 'uttermost parts of the world.' This brought a number of Jewish leaders to Antioch who witnessed the growth of the Antiochan Christians (Acts 11:22-24). Paul and Barnabas became actively involved in the life and ministry of the church and made Antioch, the center of their missionary activities among the Gentiles (Acts 13:3, 15:22-36; 18:22-23).[45]

It was from Antioch that the first missionary vision and action emerged. Paul and Barnabas were set aside as the first missionaries who went out, through the church in Antioch, as missionaries to the urban world of the first century. Greenway makes an interesting point in this context: "From Jerusalem witnesses were forcibly scattered abroad (Act 11:19), but at Antioch apostles were set apart, commissioned, and sent forth to the work (Act 13:2-3).[46] God used the Gentile church, Gentile soil and Gentile resources for the expansion of His kingdom.

Perhaps because of Paul's urban ministry exposure and experience at Antioch, he deliberately became an urban missionary, focusing on the cities of his time. It was Antioch that provided him with a model of what the church should be and in Antioch that Paul learned what it meant to bring the Gentiles to a saving faith in Jesus Christ. His Antioch experience was a molding experience for Paul. This made a lasting impression on the early church and became an instructive model for mission in the early church. Again what Greenway says is crucial: "At Antioch was demonstrated what God's grace can do in a highly urban and pagan environment, and through this gateway the gospel went forth to other cities, where the struggle and victory of Antioch were repeated over and over again."[47]

Jesus' Approach to the City People

"The mission movement of the New Testament was primarily an urban movement."[48] Overwhelming references in the New Testament to the cities point to the fact that God takes the cities seriously. In fact, we get the impression that God apparently has a soft corner for the city and its people. Often we stress the urban approach of Paul in the New Testament, but rarely do we consider Jesus' approach to urban people. Even casual readings of the Gospel show how frequently Jesus visited, ministered and preached and taught people in the cities.

The very fact that Jesus was born in the city of David (Lk 2:4 and 11) and went around preaching in all the cities and towns (Lk 8:1), and that a great multitude of people came to listen to Him from every city (Lk 8: 4), indicates the importance God attributed to the city. He appointed and sent His disciples into every city

---

[44] Downey 1962, p.147.

[45] McRay, "Antioch" p.24.

[46] Greenway, *Apostles*, p.41.

[47] *Ibid.*, p.42.

[48] Greenway and Monsoma, *Cities: Mission's New Frontier*, p.13.

(Lk 10: 1). He deliberately set His face towards Jerusalem. Frequent references to the urban places and urban people indicate Jesus' concern and love for the city people. Conn observes:

> Jesus raises the widow's only son from the dead in the city of Nain (Luke 7:11-17). A prostitute 'from the city' (Luke 7:37) receives His forgiveness of sins. To the cities He sends His disciples, empowered to heal the sick and announce the approach of the kingdom in the approach of Jesus (Luke 10:1,9,17). And at Calvary, 'outside the gate' of the city, He suffers 'to make the people holy through His own blood' (Heb. 13: 12).[49]

Jesus was also aware that not all those cities, and the people living in those cities would accept Him and be saved. Rather we come across a resistant crowd of urban people. We read in Matthew 8:34, that having performed a miracle in Gadarenes, the whole city responded by pleading with Him to leave the region. When it comes to preaching the good news of the gospel to the city people, Jesus warns His disciples of those urban people who will not receive them and their good news. (Luke10:13-16). He foretells that the cities of Chorazin, Bethsaida, and Capernaum will fare worse judgment than Sodom and Gomorrah (Math 10:15-; 11:24).

Often, urban theologians tend to focus on Jesus' concern and emphasis on the poor and the destitute. To a certain extent they are right, and we need to continue to give that emphasis while working in the city. He sent His disciples to the cities of Galilee (Matt 10:11); He himself taught and preached in the cities (Matt.11:1). He took time for the elite likes Nicodemus and discusses issues that pertain to the higher understandings (John 3:1-21). He intentionally stooped under the tree and asked an urban rich elite man Zacchaeus to take Him to his house (Lk.19:1-10). He frequently mingled with the Pharisees and had intellectual discussions and debates with them (Matt. 9:9-17). He healed a nobleman's son in the city of Cana (Jn. 4:46-54). Some of His best and closest friends whom He loved were from the city and were not necessarily poor (Jn.11:3). Often we come across urban women ministering to Him (Lk.8:3), and Him taking time to teach them (Lk.10:39).

Even though He focused primarily on the Jewish people in His earthly ministry, He never rejected the non-Jewish people. We read about Him healing the ruler's daughter (Mat 9: 18-25). We see Him healing a centurion's servant (Lk.7:1-9). As a matter of fact, He healed them, and often used them as examples to teach the Jewish people (Lk.7:9). Strikingly, we see Him talking with an urban Samaritan woman from the city of Sychar (Jn 4:1-43), discussing with the deeper truths about God.

Paul's Approach to the City People

If Christianity enjoyed its greatest success in the cities of the Roman Empire, it was Paul and his urban strategy, which were crucial in the process. The world, in which the apostle Paul ministered or opted to minister, was an urban world. Paul was an urban person, and partially depended on the city for his livelihood. Certainly there were villages and rural areas during that time, but the place and function of the urban centers were so significant that Paul wanted to make use of this urban network for the effective communication of the Gospel. He chose, and primarily ministered to, the urban dwellers of his time. "All the cities, or towns, in which he planted churches were centers of Roman administration, of Greek civilization, of Jewish influence, or of some commercial importance."[50] Expanding further, Allen notes Paul's intentional effort in bypassing some of the minor towns and villages and focusing on the provincially important cities.

---

[49] Harvie Conn, "Genesis as Urban Prologue" p.30.

[50] Roland Allen, *Missionary Methods: St.Paul's or Ours?* Grand Rapids: Eerdmans, 1962, p.13.

The centers he selected for establishing his churches were all centers of high influence. And finally, these were also the centers of the world's commerce in which a significant percentage of the Jewish community was involved.[51]

Secondly, we notice that Paul's strategy was to focus on certain groups of people. They were not necessarily ethnic groups but a certain receptive strata of the society. Granted that Paul's initial target group was the Jewish people in Diaspora, centered on the synagogue, we find that he did not receive an enthusiastic welcome from the Jews. However, he initially made contacts with some God-fearing Gentiles in the context of the synagogues. These contacts must have been very useful to him in developing further family-household contacts. Perhaps realizing that there was a segment of responsive Hellenistic, Greek speaking, Gentile people who were open and receptive to the Gospel, Paul focused on them. These people apparently were from the middle or lower classes of society.

Paul also targeted an influential segment of Roman society. While the appeal of the Gospel to the marginalized and poor was greater, the gospel seemed to have found its way among the elite and the rich also. Many of these men and women were influential in the contemporary society. Although I Corinthians 1:26 is often taken as a typical description of the kind of people in the early church, many other New Testament passages reveal that "The early Church contained not only 'unlearned and ignorant men' but many of the rich priesthood."[52] We note that some of these prominent men of the urban world made a significant impact for Christ and exerted their influence on society. Green further notes that the intellectuals also made their way slowly into the

Christian movement.[53] Although intellectuals and philosophers were not the primary targets of Paul's strategy, we definitely find them in the early church.

Thirdly, we must not lose Paul's focus on the family. Paul used one of the most effective methods of his time— the household evangelism. Again and again we come across examples of those families that were led to Christ through the ministry of Paul and other Christian workers. Perhaps the Acts of the Apostles best demonstrates Paul's focus on the family. We note the conversion of the households of Cornelius (Acts 10: 2-24), Lydia (Acts 16:12-15) the Philippian jailer, (Acts 16: 25-34) and Crispus (Acts 18:8). Paul's strategy clearly shows that he not only accepted the existing social systems but also used it effectively for the spread of the gospel. Paul not only targeted the urban families, but having reached them, he established churches, where he continued to equip and train family members for effective ministry. When these families were united and formed into churches, they began to exert a tremendous influence on relatives and friends. These households became centers of Christian faith and evangelism. Hedlund is right when he observed that, "The house church phenomenon of the New Testament (Rm. 16: 5-15; Col. 4:15; Phil 2) was an accompaniment of the family evangelism pattern."[54] (Hedlund 1985: 227). Paul approached urban people of his time, not necessarily as individuals but as family units. Perhaps he saw the salvation of the city in and through families and thus he put a tremendous emphasis on the family.

Conclusion

Reflecting theologically on the city is a crucial task. To reflect on the city, one has to

---

[51] *Ibid.*, pp.13-16.

[52] Green, *Evangelism in the Early Church*, p.119.

[53] *Ibid.*, p.120.

[54] Roger E. Hedlund, *The Mission of the Church in the World*, Grand Rapids, Baker, 1991, p.207.

understand the city both from biblical and contextual points of view. To understand the biblical approaches to city people, it is imperative that we see God's concern, love and compassion for them. The God of the Bible is a just and merciful God. While God is loving and merciful, He is also upright and just. In His dealing with arrogant, disobedient and corrupt people, who tend to continue in their sinful ways His punishment is evident.

God's perspective of the city includes His plan of salvation. The people of God in the city play significant roles in this plan. God wants His people to be witnesses in the city and to be instruments of change and vitality. If we want to make an impact on the city, we have to learn to look at the city from God's perspective.

While reflecting on the biblical approaches to the city, one has to take time to understand the contemporary urban context of India. The constant city-ward migration of people is presenting a tremendous challenge. Yet this can be perceived as an enormous opportunity for the mission of the church. As the church in India continues to get involved in the urban ministry, she must take her biblical and theological bearings seriously.

CHAPTER 35

Toward a Missionary Engagement with Science and Technology

VINOTH RAMACHANDRA

How will our children and grandchildren remember the last century? Will they remember it for two world wars, the Holocaust and numerous other acts of genocide? As the century which saw the rise and fall of communism, or the emancipation of women and the resurgence of ethnic minorities in many parts of the world? Will they look back upon it as the age of decolonization and the shift of the centre of gravity of Christianity to the Third World? As the age of non-governmental voluntary organizations?

The twentieth century will undoubtedly be remembered for all these things. But a good case can be made for saying that what has most distinguished it from earlier epochs has been the spectacular growth of organized science and the unprecedented speed of technological change. There are said to be more scientists alive today than there were in all the past put together. Similarly the difference in scale between the technological resources available in 1900 and those available today is staggering. The changes of the century in travel, communications, medicine, pharmaceuticals, weaponry, robotics, information processing, and genetic engineering, to take only a few obvious examples, reveal a social revolution which is proceeding unabated.

How are these changes to be explained? There is no single theory to explain technological growth. But most of the explanations advanced by historians invoke the complex interactions between economic needs and political interests on the one hand, and individual curiosity and ingenuity on the other. Since the early decades of the twentieth century a dramatic change has occurred *vis-á-vis* technological innovation. Until then scientific and technological breakthroughs were treated mainly as a matter of luck. But since then a significant part of the labour force in affluent nations has been directed at searching for new ways to produce goods and at new goods to produce.

The desire to cut costs and maximize profits leads business corporations to spend huge sums on research and development, while the urge to secure national prestige encourages governments to do the same. The universities generate an ever-increasing supply of professional scientists and engineers who are trained to value research and innovation and who advance their careers by securing grants from governments, private corporations and industrial foundations. Foundations team up with universities to free doctors from earning their living by treating patients, so that they can think of new ways to treat future patients. International rivalry, corporate profit, and personal ambition thus combine to produce a culture of ever-accelerating technological innovation.

Technological Optimism

There is a long line of technological *optimists* in the Western intellectual tradition, men who hailed technological change as progress not only in craft skills but in human flourishing. The ninth-century philosopher John Scotus Erigena believed that the mechanical arts could help fallen man to recover some of the original dominion over the earth which God had given Adam, and thereby recover for mankind its original image-likeness to God. In the thirteenth century the Franciscan scholar Roger Bacon linked this idea to the millenarian expectations which had been aroused by the abbot Joachim of Fiore: the development of the mechanical arts would both restore the image of God in man and also enable him to withstand the arrival of the Antichrist. In the nineteenth century, August Comte the founder of positivist sociology, announced that science would bring about humankind's ultimate regeneration.

It is interesting how often religious imagery and language is invoked in extolling the wonders of technology. In the veneration of technology, whatever form it may take, Christian eschatology is transformed into an expectation of redemption through technology. Oswald Spengler, known for his fascist writings in the years between the two world wars, declared that "Technology is eternal and unchangeable like God the Father, it saves humanity like God the Son, it illuminates us like the Holy Ghost."[1]

More recently, "People see the Net as a new metaphor for God," says Sherry Tuckle, a professor of the sociology of science at the Massachusetts Institute of Technology. The Internet, she says, exists as a world of its own, distinct from earthly reality, crafted by humans but now growing out of human control. "Like it or not, the Internet is one of the most dramatic examples of something that is self-organized. That's the point. God *is* the distributed, decentralized system."[2]

An article about the Internet in *Time* magazine put it like this: "For many, signing on the Internet is a transformative act. In their eyes the Web is more than just a global tapestry of personal computers and fibre-optic cable. It is a vast cathedral of the mind, a place where ideas about God and religion can resonate, where faith can be shaped and defined by a collective spirit. Such a faith relies not on great external forces to change the world, but on what ordinary people, working as one, can create on this World Wide Web that binds all of us, Christian and Jew, Muslim and Buddhist, together, interconnected, we may begin to find God in places we never imagined."[3]

Molecular biology has taken over from nuclear physics as the media's new "glamour science", and thousands of biotechnology firms have mushroomed almost overnight. It is widely believed that the Henry Fords and Bill Gates's of the twenty-first century will emerge form the biotech industry. The techniques for implanting modified or completely artificial genes into mammalian cells are advancing in laboratories all over the world. Genetically modified animals are being produced in large numbers every day. In a book significantly entitled *Remaking Eden* Lee Silver, an American molecular biologist, anticipates what the combination of genetic and reproductive technology will lead to over the next fifty years. If we are prepared to produce genetically engineered plants and animals, to enhance some valued property in them, why not extend the techniques to enhance the capabilities of human beings?

Initially, argues Silver, genetic engineering will be ethically acceptable only to treat those childhood diseases such as sickle-cell anaemia or cystic fibrosis that have a severe impact on the quality of life. However as the technology develops and peoples' fears subside, so "[the

---

[1] Quoted in E. Schuurman, *Technology and the Future*, Toronto: Wedge Publishing, 1980, p.359.

[2] Quoted in "Finding God on the Web", *TIME Magazine*, 16 December 1996, p.53

[3] *Ibid.*

range of genetic manipulation] will extend to the addition of new genes that serve as genetic inoculations against various infectious agents, including the HIV virus...The final frontier will be the mind and the senses. Alcohol addition will be eliminated, along with tendencies towards mental disease and antisocial behaviour like extreme aggression. Visual and auditory vacuity will be enhanced in some to improve artistic potential. And when our understanding of the genetic input into brain development has advanced, reprogeneticists will provide parents with the option of enhancing various cognitive attributes as well."[4]

Now this is typical technological "hype", often appearing in popular books written by scientists and the new breed of "futurologists". Observe how these comments transmit two dominant assumptions that have come to characterize a globalizing modernity. The first is the notion of the *technological fix*. All social and environmental problems can be fixed by technological innovation, including the problems created by technology. This is a view purveyed by many scientists and technologists and widely believed by the lay public. The more problems technology spawns, the more technology needed to solve them. In recent years this has been linked, in the field of popular medical journalism, to a naive *genetic determinism*: you are what your genes dictate. So, not only all diseases (like cancers), but all social problems from crime to racism can be eradicated at one stroke by developing gene-therapy drugs. The pharmaceutical companies obviously love it, and so does the political establishment; for it obviates the need to look at environmental and lifestyle factors behind the spread of cancers and to make costly policy decisions about changing unjust economic and social structures. This is bad

science, but the "technological fix" is very attractive to people who have no patience with human complexity.

For instance, when the first mapping of the human genome was announced by scientists in June 2000, an editorial writer for *The Times* of London, under the headline "Secrets of Creation", concluded with hundreds of other journalists that "this is a breathtaking moment for genetic science, for human health, even for philosophy... The greatest scientific journey of this century starts here, with this directory; as its alphabet is decoded, the prediction, treatment and understanding of disease should be revolutionised... It could, in particular, revolutionise the treatment of cancer, which is caused by malfunctioning genes."[5]

Genetic fatalism about disease is a myth that needs to be exposed. It is very unlikely that a simple and direct causal link between genes and most common diseases will ever be found. This message is not one that many scientist working in the field want the public to hear, since continued political support for funding genetic research depends on persistent public credulity.

The fact is that progress in exploiting the genome will be slow. Its importance lies not in the existence of a working draft of the genome-by itself, this tells us very little-but rather in its opening up the possibility for sequencing multiple copies of the human genome to discover variations among individuals in health and in disease. Even knowing this variation- a precondition for practical application- is of limited value, since the chief task of research must now be to study how variations in gene sequences interact with different environmental exposures, and gradations of each exposure, so as to alter the conditions of risk.

---

[4] L. Silver, *Remaking Eden*, New York: Avon Books, 1997, p.237.
[5] *The Times*, London, June 23 2000

For a more sober assessment of the possibilities of gene therapy, we turn to Sir David Weatherall who leads the Institute of Molecular Medicine at the University of Oxford: "The remarkable complexity of the genotype-phenotype relationship has undoubtedly been underestimated during the early period of the revolution in the biomedical sciences that followed the DNA era. It has led to many statements being made about the imminence of accurate predictive genetics that are simply not true... It is far from certain that we will ever reach a stage in which we can accurately predict the occurrence of some of the common disorders of Western society at any particular stage in an individual's life."[6]

Technological Fatalism

The second naive assumption propagated by technological optimists is a certain *technological fatalism*. This is curiously paradoxical; for on the one hand we are told that technology frees human beings, but on the other we are told that we cannot -and must not- resist the march of technology. Technological development, it is asserted, carries its own autonomy. The only value it recognizes is efficiency: does it work? If we *can* do something, technically speaking, then we *should* do it. But even if we choose not to, the inexorable march of technology, which is identified with the growth of knowledge, will eventually ensure that it is done. The technological "fix" and the technological "imperative" go hand-in-hand.

Therefore, it is not surprising that others have resolved the paradox by asserting that human beings are *not* free in a technology-dominated society. Many historians and philosophers of technology have, since the 1960s, drawn attention to the new enslavements of modern technology.

Science and technology have encouraged us to exaggerate the importance of a certain kind of technical-rational knowing and making; to substitute quantitative calculation for qualitative judgement; to replace truly human ends with impersonal technical means; to cleanse the world of religious meaning; it is destructive of nature, of traditional human cultures, and indeed of living human beings.

Thus, Mahatma Gandhi's indictment of Western technology (a criticism which can justifiably be charged with some hypocrisy, as Gandhi and his followers made considerable use of the railways and other modes of modern communications) resonates with many in the non-Western world: "It is not the British people who are ruling India, but it is modern civilization, through its railways, telegraphs, telephones, and almost every invention which has been claimed to be a triumph of civilization... Bombay, Calcutta, and other chief cities of India are the real plague spots... There was true wisdom in the sages of old having so regulated society as to limit the material condition of the people...Therein lies salvation."[7]

The American social commentator Neil Postman argues that contemporary fascination with modern technology has led us to the point of evacuating our world of all but technical meanings. The problem is not simply that we have surrendered certain sectors of social life to the logic of technology, but that increasingly everything that passes for culture in our wealthier societies is determined solely by technical logic. Postman calls this condition *Technopoly*: "Technopoly is a state of culture. It is also a state of mind. It consists in the deification of technology, which means that the culture seeks

---

[6] David Weatherall, "From Genotype to Phenotype: Genetics and Medical Practice in the New Millennium," *Philosophical Transactions of the Royal Society of London*, vol. 354, B, 1999, p.2008.

[7] Quoted in Stephen Hay, "Jaina Goals and Disciplines in Gandhi's Pursuit of Swaraj", Ch.5 of *Rule, Protest and Identity*, edited by Robb and Taylor, London: Curzon Press, 1978.

its authorization in technology, finds its satisfaction in technology, and takes its orders from technology. This requires the development of a new kind of social order, and of necessity leads to the rapid dissolution of much that is associated with traditional beliefs."[8]

Postman's critique builds on the work of one of the most profound critics of technology, the French sociologist Jacques Ellul. The latter was also a lay-theologian whose worldview was strongly shaped by Karl Bath and the European dialectical theology of the inter-war years. He felt that the principal tragedy of the modern world lay in the fact that our obsession with technology has completely eclipsed our ability to reflect about *what* we are doing with technology and *why*. We have become so fascinated by our technical capabilities, argued Ellul, that we have allowed ourselves to be absorbed into the technological apparatus. Technology for Ellul is more than tools, machines and gadgets. It is a closed, inter-locking system within which we have become trapped.

Central to this system is the dominance of *technique*. "Technique is the totality of methods rationally arrived at and having absolute efficiency (for a given stage of development) in every field of human activity."[9] Ellul vigorously rejects the idea that technology is only about using the most efficient means to achieve goals that we have agreed upon beforehand as a society. Rather, in a culture bewitched by technology the means become everything. Instead of the ends determining the means, the means determine the ends. "Technical civilization means that our civilization is constructed *by* technique, *for* technique, and is exclusively technique."[10]

Technology is defined by the "complete separation of the goal from the mechanism, the limitation of the problem to the means, and the refusal to interfere in any way with efficiency..."[11] A principal characteristic of technique is its refusal to submit to moral *judgements*. Technique never observes the distinction between moral and immoral use. It tends, on the contrary, to set up a completely independent technical morality. "Technique advocates the entire remaking of life and its framework because they have been badly made."[12]

Modern technology is not simply an extension of human tool-making but is a new account of what it is to know and to make. What has changed, compared to traditional tool-making cultures, is a uniquely manipulative relation to the world and an autonomous anthropocentric human self-understanding. In the modern technological environment we seem to have lost the possibility of encountering something outside of ourselves which might discipline, and thus give order to, our human making and willing. Technology has become self-legitimating, self-justifying. The closed system is self-promoting and self-propagating.

Ellul's vision of technology was almost wholly fatalistic. He saw no hope for human deliverance from this system short of direct divine intervention to bring history to its eschatological consummation. In a book he wrote not long before his death, he asked: "Is this a closed situation? Is there no way out? Is collective spiritual and material suicide the only result...? If we have any chance of emerging from this ideologico-material vice, of finding an exit from this terrible swamp that is ours, above all things

---

[8] N. Postman, *Technopoly: The Surrender of Culture to Technology*, New York: Vintage, 1993, p.71.
[9] J. Ellul, *The Technological Society*, trans. John Wilkinson, New York: Random House, 1964, p.2.
[10] *Ibid.*, p.128.
[11] *Ibid.*, p.133.
[12] *Ibid.*, pp.142-3.

we must avoid the mistake of thinking that we are free."[13]

So, paradoxically, both optimists and pessimists have contributed (by alternative routes) to the nurturing of a passive attitude among large sections of the public towards scientific research and technological innovation.

Research and Responsibility

The scientist, unlike most other professionals, is a producer of knowledge; and, so, he carries a greater moral responsibility than other professionals. Since he is the creator of awesome potentialities (for good or for evil), he cannot wait till those potentialities are actualized before he begins to explore their implications. For instance, a lawyer might have chosen to defend Hitler because of his belief that all human beings have a right to due legal process; or a doctor might have chosen to treat Hitler, even to save his life, because she has sworn the Hippocratic oath to treat all people alike irrespective of their moral character. But a scientist who has been devising, say, more efficient gas chambers or more advanced missile systems for the Nazis cannot, at the end of the day, disclaim responsibility for what Hitler did with those devices. The scientist shares in the responsibility for evil.

As self-centred human beings, it is easier to delight in the technical aspects of our craft than to face up to tough, challenging issues which may call for a spiritual maturity which as scientists we may lack. Looking back on the heady days of the Manhattan Project (the secret US project during the latter part of world war II to develop an atomic bomb), Robert Oppenheimer, its director, remarked a decade later: "When you see something that is technically sweet, you go ahead and do it and you argue about what to do about it only after you have had your technical success. That is the way it was with the atomic bomb."[14] Similarly, another physicist, Freeman Dyson comments: "Nuclear explosives have a glitter more seductive than gold to those who play with them. To command nature to release in a pint pot the energy that fuels the stars, to lift by pure thought a million tons of rock into the sky, these are exercises of the human will that produce an illusion of illimitable power."[15]

This combination of profound creativity with moral naïveté, intellectual passion with personal or national ambition, has made science an instrument of great violence today. Ironically, side by side with its massive benefits, in the name of science more suffering has been inflicted on human beings and other living creatures in the last century than in the entire history of humanity. Science is less and less a quest for understanding, a humble delight in the creation of God. It is tied to military power and huge commercial interests. The distortions of human sin are reflected in the misplaced priorities of scientific research. As Richard Bube, formerly of Stanford University, has written: "Much of scientific research today is motivated by one of two simple questions: (1) does the research promise financial profit in the near future (the industrialization of science)or (2) does it promise contributions to the military program (the militarization of science)?... This means that the choice of research topics and the directions of research efforts tends to be more or less directly influenced by military needs in a proportion out of balance with overall human needs."[16]

This is true also in poor countries such as India, China and Pakistan. It is estimated that

---

[13] J. Ellul, *The Technological Bluff*, Eng.trans. Grand Rapids: Eerdmans, 1990, p.128.

[14] Quoted in F. Dyson, *Disturbing the Universe*, Pan, 1979, p.78.

[15] *Ibid.* p.91.

[16] R. Bube, "Crises of Conscience for Christians in Science" in *Journal of the American Scientific Affiliation*, March 1989.

almost half of all scientists and engineers in the world today are involved in research connected to military interests. This represents a terrible waste of human talent, let alone of the earth's natural resources. We now possess the satellite technology to survey every square metre of our planet, but we are still unable to provide the cities of the world with safe and reliable electric power or a pollution-free public transport system.

The practice of science has to be weighed in the context of today's global realties. The world is becoming increasingly unequal. Less than twenty five per cent of the world's population consumes over eighty five per cent of its resources. Today, taking into account loans, outright aid, and repayments of interests, the poor countries send about $30 billion a year to the affluent countries in excess of what they receive from the latter. If the falling prices of the agricultural commodities of poor nations are brought into the calculation, the net South-to-North flow of capital would be around $60 billion a year. But to obtain a more accurate figure, one should also include the fortunes of Third World politicians and businessmen that are "exported" to banks in Europe and America, and the profits of multinational corporations which are sent back to their parent base in the North. How many people in the affluent nations realize that their extravagant living standards are being maintained largely by income from the poorest nations of the world?

Moreover, we need to add to this list the cost to the poor of the export to rich nations of engineers, scientists, architects, doctors and accountants, most of whom have been trained in state institutions at local taxpayers' expense. The poor nations produce not only raw materials for the affluent world, but also professional skills. Forty per cent of the scientists and engineers working at NASA are from the Indian subcontinent. One-third of all doctors in the US similarly come from that part of the world.

The unequal distribution of global wealth also determines the nature of goods that are manufactured. A large proportion of the affluent nations' GNP is devoted to consumer goods and the production of technologies to make these consumer goods. Since there are also gross inequalities within poorer nations, the same high-tech consumer products (motorcars, computers, camcorders, mobile phones, etc) are enjoyed by elites in countries where the basic needs of nutrition, sanitation and shelter for the great majority of its citizens have still to be met. Thus only a small portion of the world's resources flow towards the processing of basic goods required by half the world's people (and especially the world's children) for their survival.

According to the UN Human Development Report 2001 ("Making New Technologies Work for Human Development"), "Public research, still the main source of innovation for much of what could be called poor peoples' technology, is shrinking relative to private research. Gaining access to key patented inputs-often owned by private firms and universities in industrial countries- has become an obstacle to innovation, sometimes with prohibitive costs."[17]

One global industry that continues to make huge profits even in times of economic recession is the pharmaceutical industry. World sales of the larger pharmaceutical companies exceeds the GNP of many Third World nations. It is an unusual, if not unique, industry in that it requires someone outside it to promote its manufactures: neither "market forces" nor "consumer sovereignty" operate, because it is the medical doctor who decides which drug the consumer should buy. So, the medical profession has

---

[17] United Nations Development Program, *Human Development Report 2001*, Oxford and New York: Oxford University Press, 2001, p.98.

become the major target of the sales-promotion drives of these companies. Medical research, professorial chairs, seminars and symposia are often sponsored by pharmaceutical companies. Although over twenty per cent of its total sales derive from the Third World, less that one per cent of its total research and development expenditure is orientated towards Third World health priorities.

Countries in which clinical trials are now conducted are often too poor to pay for the medicines that are successfully tested and patented. And the people recruited for those trials very seldom get the kind of medical care that the participants in trials in prosperous countries can expect. The major international codes on human experimentation, including the principles proclaimed at Nuremberg in 1947 and the World Medical Association's Declaration of Helsinki in 1964, all say that the well-being of the subject should take precedence always over the needs of science or the interests of society, and that doctors must obtain "the subject's freely informed consent." But whether these codes covering the treatment of people who are the subjects of research can and should be applied in Africa and Asia has become a bitterly debated question.[18] As compensation to their subjects for enrolling in the research, should investigators be required to leave their subjects medically better off? Should the latter receive the benefits of treatment now, not in some distant future when pharmaceutical companies may, or may not, reduce the price of their drugs or vaccines so that citizens in poor countries can afford them?

We have noted that with recombinant DNA technology it is now possible to manipulate the genetic blue-print of living organisms to suit our own cultural, political and economic aspirations. Pharmaceutical and agri-business companies are staking out exclusive rights to patent genetic material taken from the Third World's forests. They are heavily lobbying governments to allow the patenting of all human, animal and plant tissue. This raises profound ethical questions which reach beyond the scientific community.

The use of this technology in human reproduction and genetic screening opens up the prospects of discrimination against those we consider "unimportant", even "useless", according to our warped scale of values (this is the real aspect of "playing God" in genetic engineering) and the exploitation of women in a commercial eugenics. The synthesis of new viruses and bacteria for use in biological warfare could lead to a genetic arms race every bit as horrific as the nuclear arms race. Cross-species genetic transfers go far beyond traditional breeding of animal and plant species, reducing genetically engineered animals to the status of manufactured products. Are human body parts and even a major portion of the human genome soon to become the patented property of a private company? That would indeed be the culmination of the consumer society, human inheritance itself turned into a saleable commodity.

Some Myths about Science

(A) *Science as self-legitimating*. There is something deeply ironic about the widespread belief that the practice of modern science is a threat not only to human dignity and significance, but to the entire Christian worldview which has, historically, under-girded that conviction of human significance. For the practice of science is primarily an act of faith. To embark on scientific work requires a basic assumption: namely, that there is a real world outside our minds and it is structured in an orderly and intelligible way. Moreover, this created order is contingent, not necessary. In other words, the universe does not

---

[18] See David J. Rothman, "The Shame of Medical Research" in *The New York Review of Books*, November 30, 2000, pp.60-4.

have to be the way it actually is. The rational structure of the universe needs to be *discovered*. It cannot be deduced in advance by logical reasoning. This calls for a basic posture of humility before the world whose rationality we seek to articulate through our theories and experiments.

Moreover, to embark on a career of scientific research one has to assume that the human mind is capable of unlocking the secrets of the universe. The very success of science has hidden from view the radical nature of this primary assumption. Physically speaking, humans are microscopic specks of dust on a very ordinary planet revolving around an average-sized star in a remote corner of a galaxy which comprises a hundred billion stars and which itself is only one among a similar number of galaxies. And, if the geological and neo-Darwinist theories concerning the formation of the earth and the emergence of life on earth are a reliable picture of what has happened on our planet, then human life is very recent on a universal time-scale.

Some astronomers and biologists proclaim that these discoveries have "put man in his place" and they pour scorn on the biblical emphasis on a human being's intrinsic value and dignity. For example, the astrophysicist Chandra Wickramasinghe, in an attempt to show that modern cosmology is a vindication of Buddhist philosophy, writes: "The sobering lesson of astronomy, a lesson that still continues to unfold, is that our planet and humans upon it are truly insignificant on a cosmic scale. Our egocentric, ethnocentric and anthropocentric interests must surely pale into total insignificance in a cosmic context."[19]

However, those who seem to delight in belittling human significance are not only committing the childish error of confusing size and age with value or importance; but they also fail to see that astronomy and evolutionary theory themselves are products of that same insignificant human mind! To use human theories to attack human significance is to destroy the very foundation of those theories. Darwin himself confessed to "the horrid doubt...whether the convictions of man's mind, which has been developed from the mind of the lower animals, are of any value at all are trustworthy. Would anyone trust in the convictions of a monkey's mind, if there are any convictions in such a mind?"[20] Surely the very success of science itself bears eloquent testimony to the significance of human thought. As the mathematician Blaise Pascal put it in the 17th century: "Through space the universe grasps me and swallows me up like a speck. But through thought I grasp it."[21]

Listen, too, to the philosopher-theologian Thomas Torrance: "Behind and permeating all our scientific activity, whether in critical analysis or in discovery, there is an elementary and overwhelming faith in the possibility of grasping the real world with our concepts, and, above all, faith in the truth over which we have no control but in the service of which our rationality stands or falls. Faith and intrinsic rationality are interlocked with one another."[22] Another scientist who has spoken eloquently on the faith of the scientist and the awe and sense of wonder that science invokes is the greatest physicist of the last century, Albert Einstein: "Without the belief that it is possible to grasp reality with our theoretical constructions, without the belief in the

---

[19] C. Wickramasinghe, "An Astronomer's View of the Universe and Buddhist Thought", *Ceylon Daily News*, May 15 1992.

[20] Francis Darwin, ed., *The Life and Letters of Charles Darwin*, London: Murray, 1887, 1:316, quoted in Philip J. Sampson, *Six Modern Myths About Christianity and Western Civilization*, Downers Grove, Ill: InterVarsity Press, 2000, p.21.

[21] B. Pascal, *Pensees*, trans.A .J. Krailsheimer, London: Penguin, 1966, No.113.

[22] T.F. Torrance, *Christian Theology of Scientific Culture*, New York: Oxford University Press, 1981, p.63.

inner harmony of the world, there can be no science. This belief has and always will be the fundamental motive for all scientific creation."[23]

The fact that science is possible is itself a fact that points us beyond science. Even when we use mathematics to unlock the secrets of the physical universe, something very strange is happening. For these mathematical patterns are abstract human creations, conjured up by human thought. Time and time again the breakthroughs in fundamental science have occurred because someone has chosen to trust a theory simply because of its elegance and simplicity from a mathematical point of view, and then discovered that it does indeed generate empirically successful results in the physical world around us. This "unreasonable effectiveness of mathematics" (a famous phrase of the Nobel laureate Eugene Wigner) is a source of wonder to many philosophically-inclined mathematicians and physicists.

The science journalist Timothy Ferris poses the question, "Why then does science work? The answer is that nobody knows. It is a complete mystery- perhaps *the* complete mystery- why the human mind should be able to understand anything at all about the wider universe... Perhaps it is because our brains evolved through the working of natural law that they somehow resonate with natural law... But the mystery, really, is not that we are at one with the universe, but that we are so to some degree at odds with it, different from it, and yet can understand something about it. Why is this so?"[24]

As Ferris observes, evolutionary psychology will not help. It may well be true that if there was no congruence between the workings of our minds and the way things really are we would have perished long ago in the evolutionary struggle. But what counts for adaptive cognitive strategies of survival relate to the world of our everyday experience (that is, the world of gravity and pain, rocks and trees). Euclidean geometry, arithmetic and simple mechanics can help in coping with that world. But we are not talking at this mundane level. We are dealing here with counter-intuitive theories about the behaviour of the subatomic world and of vast galaxies at distances we cannot even imagine, with strange entities such as "black holes", "gluons" and "quarks" all predicted by abstract and sophisticated mathematical ideas. How can gauge field theories or string theories be spin-offs from the evolutionary struggle for survival? Even the dream of men like Stephen Hawking to have a mathematical "theory of everything" simply begs the question. A theory of everything, if it is to be truly a theory of *everything*, must include within it the most intriguing question of all: from where does the desire of Hawking-like creatures, accidentally thrown up like flotsam in an obscure part of the universe, for an explanation of "everything"- and their confidence of success-originate?

Now, if we are creatures made in the image of the Creator God, and called by God to responsible stewardship, it is not presumptuous of men and women to seek to understand their creator's world. We would naturally expect some sort of a correspondence between the human mind and the physical universe which that mind explores. Both the rationality of the universe and the rationality of the explorer are grounded in the ultimate rationality and faithfulness of the Creator.

Therefore, given other grounds for faith in a God who is the Creator of the world, and whose character and relationship with humankind is disclosed in the biblical revelation, the entire scientific enterprise becomes perfectly

---

[23] A. Einstein, *The Evolution of Physics*, New York: Simon & Shuster, 1938, p.313.

[24] T. Ferris, *Coming of Age in the Milky Way*, New York: William Morrow & Co, 1988, p.385.

reasonable. It also accounts for the historical observation that modern science originated- and was nurtured- in a cultural environment deeply influenced by these biblical convictions. Outside of those convictions, the success of science itself cries out for explanation.

(B) *Science as total knowledge*. We have seen, therefore, people don't acquire knowledge for the first time when they start to study science. There is a whole background of knowledge, implicitly accepted, which undergirds their study. Many of the presuppositions of physical science- including the reality of the external world and of other minds, the value of intellectual enquiry, the trustworthiness of their memories and the reports of other colleagues both past and present, and much else besides- all count as knowledge, and it is only by treating this as knowledge that it becomes possible to do any science at all.

The scientific community is also undergirded by shared moral values: for example, truth-telling (in work and reporting of results), right of free expression and access to information, team-work, patience, honest debate and mutual criticism, and so on. Whenever these values have been flouted (and they have, as anyone familiar with the history of science knows) the scientific world is deeply shocked. So, the pretended "value-neutrality" of science is a dangerous myth.

Similarly, the success of scientific accounts of human origins and human behaviour cannot, logically speaking, be used to discount philosophical or theological discussions on what constitutes humanness. The physical scientist's *methodological* reductionism is a valid, useful and often necessary approach. It is normally how a scientist works. Each aspect of a complex phenomenon is analysed separately. But if she were to go on to claim that the adequacy of her story at its own physical level requires the theologian to deny the validity of his account of human beings, that would be a false move. For that would be to fall into the trap of *metaphysical*

reductionism: namely, the failure to perceive the hierarchical character of reality which requires description and understanding at several levels of meaning. Even within science, while it may be valid to reduce a complex whole to its component parts in order to discover underlying causal mechanisms, it is usually the case that the whole is much more than the sum of its parts. As we move to higher levels of complexity, new properties emerge which require new explanatory concepts and theories which cannot be reduced to lower-level accounts. Thus human sociology cannot be reduced to psychology, or psychology to biology, or biology to quantum physics.

Let us take some simple illustrations to show the logical absurdity involved in this move. A physicist may legitimately describe a Beethoven symphony as "longitudinal patterns of molecular vibrations in the air", but this is of no interest to any non-physicist and especially to a musician or musicologist. Indeed the latter will remind the physicist that she has quite simply missed the point of the work *as a whole*. This is not, however, a fault of the physicist, for the appreciation of music is outside the scope of physics. The concept of a symphony is not found in any physics textbook. But, granted that the physics-level description is true, there is a higher-level description which requires *new* concepts to do justice to all that is happening in the room. If, however, the physicist were to deny the musicologist's account simply on the grounds that musical concepts cannot be expressed in terms of physics, she would be committing the reductionist fallacy.

Similarly, an electrical engineer may explain the behaviour of a computer in terms of integrated-circuits and other components of its "hardware". The mathematician may say that the computer is behaving in a certain way because it is being controlled by a program ("software") which, let us assume, is working out the income tax returns of a company's employees. The income tax laws which determine the output of the computer cannot be reduced to the laws of electro-magnetism which determine the computer's circuitry. The two descriptions *complement* rather than contradict one another. Both are required, but for different purposes.

The theological concept of *creation* is a higher-order explanation of reality than the cosmological and evolutionary explanations of the natural scientist. The reason we say it is a "higher-order" account is simply because, even as the musicologist's analysis of music assumes that the physics-level analysis is true (there would be no music if there were no molecular vibrations in the air), so to say that we are persons created in the image of God assumes that the biological-level description is valid. Our personhood is *embodied* in physical and biological structures, just as Beethoven's symphony is embodied in the complex patterns of sound waves in the air or a mathematician's computer program is embodied in the integrated circuitry of the machine. What would happen if the computer were wrecked or the air sucked out of the room? The software could still be run on another computer and the symphony played in another place. Likewise, even when our bodies are destroyed in death, our Creator can re-embody our personhood in new structures of His choosing. That is His freedom, and it is the basis of our Christian hope.

Engaging with Technology

How do we witness to the rule of Jesus Christ over the technological world? To dethrone technology is not to shun it or to disparage its intellectual fascination or its power to set men and women free from drudgery and want, but rather, to reject its pseudo-autonomy and to seek to re-locate it within a wider perspective of a gospel-shaped wisdom.

Here are three basic affirmations we need to make about technology: (1) Technology is a

human activity. It is not an inexorable force that comes to us from outside of our collective life. And, like all human activity, it is not "value-neutral". It comes to us already value-loaded. Every piece of technology is the product of a human choice: to develop *this* technology rather than *that*. The choice reflects the values, interests and perceived needs of the society that gave it birth. Whenever we import a specific technology we are also importing a set of specific cultural values with it. But, since technology is a result of human choices, we can also make choices as to whether we should resist it, embrace it or adapt it to *our* social needs and interests.

Consider the mobile phone, ubiquitous symbol of the new global economy. As a (typical) press release from one mobile manufacturer describes it, "It's perfectly suited to talking to people, to receiving short messages, screening short movie clips, holding video conferences on the move, receiving headlines...eventually you will *simply say what you want whenever you want it and wherever you want it.*"[25]

Observe how this embodies an ideal of individual freedom and control which characterises modern Western societies. To say whatever we want, whenever and wherever we want it, is to be totally in control. With "texting" and the Internet now incorporated into our mobile phones, we can now become self-enclosed, self-sufficient, controlling centres. There are even news-gathering services on the Internet offering to download only news that is tailor-made to our individual interests and needs. Moreover, for all the advertising hype about mobile phones "bringing the world together", we have all endured the experience of a stranger in a crowded train or restaurant uttering sheer banalities (or even obscenities) at the top of his voice into his mobile phone, blissfully insensitive to the feelings of those around him. The mobile phone transmits

---

[25] Orange Press Release, 13 July 2000 *(my emphasis)*.

and reinforces the solitariness and individualism of the cultures that gave it birth.

The more complex the artefact, the more diverse are the human motivations it embodies. Behind every successful technology lies a network of social interests and interactions that developed along the way. To build complex strategic and tactical missiles in India, for instance, scientists had to recruit an array of social and technical allies: the political elites, the military establishment, engineering firms, commercial subcontractors and so on. These various social groups did not unilaterally decide to construct a missile program. But the presence of an external scapegoat (whether Pakistan or China) for the nation's internal woes generated momentum and served to legitimate the program in the eyes of the general public.

(2) Technology alters our perceptions of ourselves, of others and of the world. There is a dialectical relationship between the tools we use, our conception of the world and our self-consciousness. "To the man with the hammer, everything is a nail."[26] The widespread use of technology in the wealthier parts of the world has blurred the distinction between the natural (that which is given to human beings) and the artificial (those things made by human craft). As Oliver O'Donovan points out: " When every activity is understood as making, then every situation is seen as raw material, waiting to have something made out of it."[27]

Technological change is thus *ecological* change. It changes the culture, altering the structure of our interests, the character of our symbols, and the things we think about and think with. It fosters certain habits of mind (particularly a cognitive style that is highly pragmatic and sceptical) and discourages others. "Computers don't just do things for us", observes Sherry Tuckle of M.I.T, "they do things to us, including to our ways of thinking about ourselves and other people... Computer screens are the new locations for our fantasies, both erotic and intellectual."[28]

Consequently, it is not surprising that those who worship technology eventually develop machine-like personalities: emotionally under-developed, shallow in their relationships, driven by a desire to control and quantify every human situation, unable to appreciate beauty and value in anything outside the artificial. Technology can rapidly deliver vast amounts of material, but thoughtful assimilation takes time and effort. Pondering a subject, writes the sociologist Orrin E.Klapp, is "inherently slow, as suggested by synonyms like brooding, contemplating, meditating, deliberating, mulling things over". We end up with "a growing mountain of information about which people do not know what to think".[29]

Let us return to the mobile-phone concept of "communication". This has pushed aside the old-fashioned idea of "conversation" which was slow, messy and sometimes painful. The new communication is identified with "exchanging information", and this exchange is crisp, clear and instant. You say as little as possible to make sure you get what you want as fast as you can. To be "in 24-hour communication" has come to mean sending and receiving a tidal wave of "messages" every day. And, in the new language of the mobile world, it is the device, not the human user, that does the "communicating" via global networks. Learning is also being redefined as "information gathering". To learn now means to have the right information pushed at you as efficiently as possible, and the mobile utopian

---

[26] Postman, *Technopoly*, p.14.

[27] O. O'Donovan, *Begotten or Made?* Oxford: Oxford University Press, 1984, p.3.

[28] S. Tuckle, *Life on the Screen: Identity in the Age of the Internet*, London: Weidenfeld and Nicolson, 1996, p.30.

[29] Quoted in R. Jacoby, *The End of Utopia: Politics and Culture in an Age of Apathy*, New York: Basic Books, 1999, p. 165.

vision is about instant access to exactly the right information to suit your immediate needs.

The usefulness of the mobile phone is not in question. It is extremely valuable in some circumstances. But as more and more consumers adopt this technology uncritically, it is inevitably going to diffuse the associated ideas, images and ways of thinking. When the mobile phone becomes our primary mode of human communication, or "texting" becomes the epitome of good communication, then more important dimensions of human communication wither. It would be difficult, for instance, to sustain genuine dialogue between persons of widely divergent beliefs, because such dialogue involves argument and the hard intellectual effort to understand opinions different to ours. Moreover, as the American lawyer Stephen Carter warns, "It is easy to be rude online precisely because the people with whom we argue are faceless, somehow no more real than the machine that transmits their words to our screens. And so, safe behind our anonymity and taking advantage of theirs, we say things that we would not dream of uttering face to face."[30] These tendencies have profound implications for the future of democracy.

Similarly, the use of medical techniques of *in vitro* fertilization, gamete transfer and antenatal fetal screening subtly alter the nature of parenthood. And when we change the nature of parenthood, imperceptibly our attitude to our children changes. When a child is made through the process of embryo donation and *in vitro* fertilization, the child may be seen no longer as a mysterious and wonderful gift, but as the product of meticulous human planning. It is a product not of our *being* but of our *will*, an artefact, perhaps even a commodity at our disposal. And, like all commodities, it must be subject to a process of "quality control". If technology provides the knowledge that the fetus is abnormal, there is considerable pressure on the parents to see that that fetus is removed from the production line.

The very existence of fetal screening and the availability of abortion until even late in pregnancy tend to imply that the commitment of a mother to child is tentative or conditional. "Technology, then, has had the effect of encouraging a mother to distance herself from the child she carries. Instead of pregnancy being an inseparable attachment, which starts early on and grows throughout nine months, antenatal screening means that the relationship of the mother and child now begins with separation and distancing and moves only later to attachment, around the time of birth."[31]

(3) Technology must be subject to moral criteria. "Nihilism" designates the denial of any objective moral order or any truth beyond the sheer assertion of human willing in the midst of the ceaseless human struggle for survival. It is up to us to supply our own meanings and values. The only purposes in the world are of human making. Those who operate under the assumption that all human problems can be converted into technical problems amenable to technical solutions are also inclined to accept the nihilistic proposition that reality itself is a kind of human artefact, and that there is no truth or order in the world save that which we have managed to construct for ourselves.

As Christians we need to publicly challenge this view. In the Gospel we have an alternative understanding of reality. This should shape our ethical outlook. Just as there is a physical order to the universe that is independent of cultural perception, and whose intelligibility we articulate when we do science, so there is a moral order

---

[30] Stephen L. Carter, *Civility: Manners, Morals, and the Etiquette of Democracy,* New York: Basic Books, 1998, p.199.

[31] J. Wyatt, *Matters of Life and Death,* Leicester, UK: Inter-Varsity Press, 1998, p.98.

that not only transcends the human will but that actually makes sense of our willing, creativity and passion.

The neonatologist and medical ethicist John Wyatt has proposed an "ethics of art restoration" to counter the "Lego-kit" view of humanity prevalent in modern medical technology.[32] There is no intrinsic or "natural" order to a Lego kit. There is no right or wrong way of putting the pieces together. There is no masterplan built into it by the designers. It is delightfully value-free. The only two questions you may ask of any particular construction are: (a) can it be done? and (b) is it safe? Many medical researchers take for granted the Lego-kit view of the human body.

In Christian perspective, however, human beings are flawed artistic masterpieces. A masterpiece may get defaced, damaged or decayed with age; the frame may be riddled with woodworm and the varnish cracked and peeling. Professional art restorers, those skilled in restoring defaced masterpieces, work according to clear guidelines. What is normative here is the *intention of the original artist*. The restorer is obliged to use all the information and techniques at his disposal- X-ray analysis, historical records, chemical tests and so on- to determine the object's "original constitution", to assess what information the object itself embodies regarding the creator's intention. Only when the original artist's intention is discerned that the art restorer can decide what form of intervention is appropriate. Unethical restoration is the use of techniques and materials to alter or enhance the appearance of the work of art. Art restorers are not at liberty to improve the painting or sculpture they are working with, by adding an extra bit here or there. Operating within these constraints, they are free to use sophisticated and invasive technology. It may be necessary to replace an area of canvas with a new synthetic substitute modelled to resemble the original material. It may be necessary to remove the decaying, original varnish and to replace it with a polyurethane covering. What is paramount however is the aim to be faithful to the artist's original intention, to protect and maintain the true nature of the object.

This is an useful analogy of the role of the physician or surgeon. Wyatt writes: "The task of health professionals is to protect and restore the masterpieces entrusted to our care... we must use technology in a way which is appropriate to preserve the original design, the creation order which is embodied in the structure of the human body. However tempting it may be, however spectacular the consequences which might result, we are not at liberty to improve upon the fundamental design. With each new advance in medical technology we must ask the basic question: 'Does the use of this technology allow the artist's intention to be fulfilled, or does it change the design at a fundamental level?'"[33]

When applied to reproductive technology, Wyatt concludes that where surrogate parents and gamete (embryo or sperm donation) is used "the unique biological link between parent and child" is broken, as is the link between "baby making and love making" that is God's intention for us. Our desire to know, to probe the secrets of our human bodies and to combat disease are expressions of God-given freedom.[34] Yet sometimes we must be prepared to say "no" to some of the possibilities of human freedom. In O'Donovan's poignant words, sometimes God calls us "to accept exclusion from the created good as the necessary price of a true and unqualified witness to it."[35] By refraining from the use of reproductive technology, a childless

---

[32] *Ibid.* pp.31,87.

[33] *Ibid.* p.88

[34] *Ibid.* p.93

[35] O. O'Donovan, *Resurrection and Moral Order*, Leicester, UK: Apollos, 2nd edition, 1994, p.96.

couple may bear witness to God's creation order while having to pay the price of exclusion from some of the blessings of that order. The Church should recognize and honour the painful sacrifice that such couples make.

Another important criterion in technology evaluation must be the question of justice. Who controls the technology? Who has access to it? The main creators and controllers of technology have increasingly become large multinational corporations with more global reach than responsibility. Far from producing a solution to the gap between the world's "haves" and "have-nots", recent developments in robotics or agricultural technology may actually widen the gap.

The fault lies not with the technologies *per se*, but rather with the human context (economic, political, ideological) in which they are developed. Scientific and technological research *by themselves* do not lead to the enrichment of human life. It all depends on who has *control* over the fruits of research. Research and development that takes place within a grossly unequal economic order and/or a repressive political order will only tend to exacerbate those inequities and/or repression. The powerful consolidate their power, usually at the expense of the weak.

As an example of this tendency, consider the famous Green Revolution of the 1960s. Certain high-yielding "miracle seeds" were developed by agrarian research institutes in Mexico and the Philippines and introduced to other agricultural societies. Here was a technology designed to increase local food production and so alleviate malnutrition and rural poverty. However, these seeds, being artificially nurtured, required high doses of pesticides for protection against pathogens; they also needed good irrigation and high inputs of fertilizer. Most agricultural countries are economically poor and have to import fertilizers and pesticides. They also had to rely on foreign experts for advice and on seed banks owned by multinational institutes. So the import bills increased more rapidly than did agricultural exports. Moreover, the vast majority of subsistence farmers could not afford fertilizers and pesticides, nor did they have adequate irrigation facilities for their small-holdings; so they sold their land to the wealthier farmers. This resulted in more landlessness and worsening rural poverty.

To whom did the Green Revolution bring a lucrative harvest? The Indian writer Claude Alvares is blunt in his answer: "To those who designed the project, including American private foundations like Ford and Rockefeller; multinational corporations, who manufactured the seeds, equipment and nutrients; the banks who provided the credit and certain categories of very large farmers."[36] It is with hindsight that we realise that the alleviation of famine and rural poverty has much more to do with land reform, co-operative ownership of technology and the purchasing power of the poor than with the raising of national food productivity.

Concern for social justice includes not only issues of access, but also the way the costs and benefits of a given technology are distributed. It is the poor who live by the roadside who bear the costs of the motor-car (noise, pollution, the destruction of trees) without receiving any of its benefits. Nuclear power stations are sited in relatively remote areas and bring electricity to distant urban dwellers; but, in the event of radioactive leakage or a major explosion, it is the poor who live in the vicinity of the reactor (and do not benefit from its electricity) who will bear the overwhelming cost. (Moreover, an accident in a South Indian power station, on a day with a fairly stiff breeze, will also spell disaster for millions in Sri Lanka). These (and other)

---

[36] Claude Alvarez, *Science, Development and Violence*, Delhi: Oxford University Press, 1994, p.43.

examples raise moral and political issues that town-planners, engineers and policy-makers need to address with imagination, empathy and courage.

The introduction of new technologies in societies with grave disparities of income -and backed up by aggressive modern marketing techniques- only serves to generate envy, frustration and social violence. They become, unwittingly, instruments of human exploitation rather than of human participation and stewardship. This is why, contrary to the beliefs of many managers and technocrats around the world, technology can never be a substitute for imaginative and courageous political leadership. It is only when science and technology are seen as *servants* of a higher human vision that they can become truly liberating instruments.

Conclusion

Theologically understood human beings and the universe belong together. They form what we mean by *world* in its relation to God. And God has made the universe to express itself, to bring forth its own order in ever richer forms, and in that way to find its fulfilment as the creation of God. This is what takes place through us human beings, for we are "that unique element in the creation through which the universe knows itself and unfolds its inner rationality."[37] Moreover, astonishing as it may sound, the *telos* of the non-human creation depends upon human agency as it is directed by the Spirit of God (Rom.8:19). The created order will share in the fulness of the divine life as it is freely drawn into our reverent obedience to the creator.

Thus, for the Christian engaged in scientific and engineering research, there is a powerful sense of ultimate accountability in all that she does: accountability to the God of truth, justice and compassion who will call us to answer for what we have done with his creation. The scientific enterprise must be ruled by love: love of God and of neighbour. Where love is absent, science becomes demonic. It enslaves rather than liberates. Love of God includes respect for truth. It leads to integrity in work, so that fame, reputation and wealth (whether personal or national) are not the motivators in research. Love of neighbour means that global human need and respect for the integrity of creation takes priority over personal "self-fulfilment". It also means that sometimes the demands of justice will override human curiosity. Thus, certain areas of investigation have to carry legal restrictions because they can easily be abused or directly threaten human personhood: for example, non-therapeutic research on embryos, the elderly or the handicapped. The benefits that accrue through this kind of research need to be sought by other means which do not violate human dignity.

Historically, the scientific enterprise itself emerges from the world-view of biblical theism as a natural expression of obedience to God; and, it is seriously doubtful if that enterprise can have any coherence outside of such a theistic worldview. In biblical terms, the idolatry of science and technology as an end in itself and the shrugging off of moral accountability for one's work are a denial of stewardship. Technology, like every other human activity, participates both in the grandeur of human creativity and in the alienation that rebellion against the creator brings in its wake. It is not an autonomous discipline conducted in a vacuum. Young people entering the fields of science and engineering must be aware of the social, political, cultural and economic contexts of those fields.

The missiological challenge is not to renounce human creativity nor forego technological making; rather it is to insist that this creative activity be nourished by the love of God, the love of neighbour, and by the love of the world for the sake of God and neighbour.

---

[37] T.F. Torrance, *Reality and Scientific Theology*, Edinburgh: Scottish Academic Press, 1982, p.68.

CHAPTER 36

Bible Translation as Communication

CHRISTEENA ALAICHAMY

Introduction

Mission is about making God known to people who do not know Him as the true God, their creator. Mission is proclamation of God's Word to people of all nations, all tribes, people of all languages. The Bible is God's Word. Through His Word God has revealed Himself and His salvation by Jesus Christ His son. Therefore unless God's Word is communicated to people of all languages and cultures they cannot know God, believe in Him, receive forgiveness for their sins and become God's children.

Mission is about bringing people back to the God who has created them. God created man and woman, loved them and gave them everything they needed. He walked with them and talked with them. But this loving relationship was broken when Adam and Eve chose to disobey God's command and joined the rebellion begun by God's enemy, Satan. They became slaves to sin and to Satan. To come back to a life of freedom, life abundant with love, joy and peace, people need to know the Way back to God so they can be reconciled with Him. They are shown the Way in God's Word. Thus, God's Word is central to Mission. Our mission cannot be accomplished without God's Word in people's languages.

God chose to reveal Himself and His provision of salvation to all the people of His creation through the chosen people of Israel. He called Abraham and his descendants in order that they might know Him and then make Him known to people of all nations. He revealed Himself to them through His commands and dealings with them. This revelation of God constitutes the Old Testament of the Bible. To reveal Himself fully to humankind, to present a model of a life lived according to God's expectation and to give His life as a ransom to redeem humanity from slavery to sin and Satan, God sent His Son, Jesus Christ. Jesus' life and ministry, His choosing, training and sending his disciples to proclaim the Good News of Salvation to all, make up the New Testament of the Bible. Mission is proclamation of Jesus Christ as the only Way for people to be saved and teaching them to follow all that Jesus taught. Thus Mission revolves around the Bible, the Word of God.

The Bible was originally written in Hebrew and Greek. It needs to be translated into the languages of all the people groups of the world, in order for them to understand the Word of God and know God through it. Bible translation ministry, so important and integral for Mission, needs to be understood well and done effectively. As this is a vast subject, I limit my discussion to the following three topics:

1. God's work in history to give His Word to all people.

2. Translation as Communication.

3. Communicative translation of God's Word and its role in Mission.

God's Word for All People

God in His Mission uses His people to make His Word available and understandable to all. When we look at the history of the Church and of Mission we can see that God accomplishes His plan stage by stage, making His Word available and understandable to more and more people at each stage.

Availability

In the history of Bible translation at least six stages can be identified. In the first stage the Hebrew Old Testament was translated into the Greek language to make God's Word understandable to the Jews who no longer spoke Hebrew. In the second stage, the whole Bible was translated into the major ancient languages like Syriac, Coptic and Latin. In the third stage, the Bible was translated into the major European languages. In the fourth stage, it was made available in the major developed languages of the Americas, Asia and Africa, following the modern missionary movement. In the fifth stage, the Bible began to be translated into previously unwritten languages spoken by minority people groups. This was initiated by Wycliffe Bible Translators (WBT), an American organization doing Bible translation in Bible-less groups all over the world. Now, in the sixth stage, Bible translation, in the unwritten languages of minority people groups is being carried out by nationals in their own countries. This has become necessary as expatriate missionaries are often denied entry into many countries due to political and various other reasons. Thus translation of the Bible continues and will continue as an integral part of Christian Mission until God's Word becomes available for all people groups.

Understandability

People come to know God when they understand God's Word. Availability of the Bible in mother tongues of more people has made it possible for more people to understand the Word of God and know Him. When Bible translation went hand in hand with the mission movement the Churches were established, and stood firm, and as missionaries came up from new churches the mission movement continued. When the Bible was not translated the churches did not survive. Even in places where there were thousands of believers, the numbers went down and churches died , and people turned back to their old faith as they did not have the Word of God to grow in the Christian faith.

Giving God's word in people's own languages alone does not make it fully understandable. It can be made more or less understandable depending on how it is translated. In the history of the Bible translation movement, there has always been opposition to making the Bible more understandable. In the 4th century A.D. when Jerome made a new translation that was more understandable than other Latin Bibles, he was met with criticism and opposition. Not being literal was the criticism against him. Jerome was "in favor of a free translation style as opposed to one of slavish literalism."[1] His Latin translation, the Vulgate, was opposed not only by Augustine but also by the people. When one bishop used Jerome's translation of the book of Jonah, he was almost deposed because his congregation reacted against the modern translation.[2]

Jerome's Vulgate, though opposed at first, became in time the official Bible of the church. When Church and State merged in Rome during the time of Constantine, Latin, the language of the administration became the language of the church as well.

In the 14th century, John Wycliffe realized the need for people to understand God's word. In his time the Bible was only available in Latin and so only the clergy had access to it. The church and the traditions had the highest authority in the

---

[1] H. Roland, Worth, *Bible Translations: A History through Source Documents*, Jefferson, NC: McFarland and Company, 1992, p.29.

[2] *Ibid.*, p.35.

lives and beliefs of the people. The common people knew only what the clergy said to be right or wrong.

Wycliffe's efforts to make God's Word accessible and understandable to all horrified the clerics. One cleric wrote:

> This Master John Wycliffe translated from Latin into English... the Scriptures which Christ gave to the clergy and the doctors of the church that they might sweetly minister to the laity... Thence by his means it is become vulgar and more open to laymen and women who can read... Thus the pearl of the Gospel is scattered abroad and trodden underfoot by swine, the jewel of clerics is turned to the sport of the laity.[3]

Wycliffe was charged as a heretic and his translation, as the "crowning act of wickedness." He was also described as "doing the work of Antichrist by the expedient of a new translation of Scriptures into the mother tongue."[4] Though Wycliffe was not burned to death, his opponents did dig up his bones, burn them and cast the ashes into the current of the River Swift.

Phillips, who starts his book *Translators and Translations* with the account of the burning of Wycliffe's bones, powerfully brings out the two important facts regarding translators and translations. He says,

> The bone ash borne on the bosom of the *River Swift* on that day in 1428 could symbolize at least two important facts in relationship to translators and translations. The first of these is that Bible translation work has been accompanied by much misunderstanding. It has always been a labor of sacrifice and love... The bone ash swept along in the swirling waters of the *River Swift...* symbolizes the second fact that it is a process which never ends.[5]

In the second half of the 15th century the Reformation gave rise to a new awakening to make God's word accessible and understandable to all believers. Again a new translation was needed to be done for people to understand God's word. Tyndale's deep conviction that it would be impossible to establish the lay people in any truth unless the Scriptures were plainly laid before their eyes in their mother tongue, made him risk his life in the venture of translating the Bible afresh in English.[6] Tyndale's passion for making God's Word available and understandable to all can be seen by his powerful words to one of the learned theologians of his day. During an argument, Tyndale exploded, "If God spare me life, ere many years, I will cause the boy that driveth the plough, to know more of the Scriptures than you do."[7]

Tyndale had to go into voluntary exile, as his translation project was not welcomed in his own country by the official church leaders. He went to Germany, translated the Bible and sent the copies to England. By God's providence, Germany turned out to be just the right place for Tyndale to go. Martin Luther had also been translating and had printed the New Testament in German in 1522; Tyndale left in 1524 for Germany. Martin Luther did his translation in order to make common people understand God's Word. He did most of his translation in a secret and secluded place because of opposition from his opponents.

Though Tyndale's translation was opposed in the beginning, it was later included as the major part of the King James Version and this was

---

[3] J.B. Phillips, "Translator's Foreword" in *The New Testament in Modern English*, London: Geoffrey Bles, 1958, p.14.
[4] *Ibid.*
[5] *Ibid.*, pp.10-12.
[6] *Ibid.*, p.22.
[7] Eugene H. Glassman, *The Translation Debate: What Makes a Bible Translation Good?* Downers Grove: InterVarsity Press, 1981, p.14.

approved and used. Now, when the King James Version has become somewhat obsolete, God has raised people to produce new translations. Again they are not welcomed by all. Nida and Bratcher's *Good News Bible* which made the Bible more understandable in common, day to day language, was opposed for its deviation from the old translation. (There is an interesting anecdote of the members of a particular denomination who became indignant about the substitution in the *Good News Bible*, of the word 'blood' with 'death' (of Jesus). They literally buried the *Good News Bible* in a coffin and placed a sign, saying, "Here lies the *Good News Bible*, which died for lack of blood!") When Kenneth Taylor translated the *Living Bible* for more understandability than the *Good News Bible*, it was rejected by many. The reason for such rejection and tension between those who want to preserve the original and those who want to communicate it to the receptors, is different understandings of the translation process.

As every language keeps changing in course of time and as new knowledge regarding Biblical cultures and manuscripts are acquired, new translations are needed to make God's Word more understandable than before. Understanding the process of human communication and the process of translation will help to produce translations that will communicate effectively.

Translation as Communication

Making God's Word available in one's own mother tongue is not enough in itself. It should be understood by people in order for them to know God and follow Him. So it is imperative that the Bible be translated in such a way that it communicates God's intended message to the receptor in an understandable manner.

The Meaning in Translation

Communication concerns meaning. Meaning is communicated in translation. Therefore it is important to know exactly *what* meaning is to be communicated in translation. There are two types of meaning: the 'linguistic' meaning and the 'interpretive', or 'intended' meaning. Linguistics as a discipline concerns the word meaning, or the linguistic meaning. Dictionaries are compilations of word meanings. Semantics, a sub-discipline of linguistics, is all about this linguistic meaning. Grammar is about the way in which words combine to make more meanings. Words are assigned their meanings by consensus in the community. People of the same community communicate with each other because of the common meanings they have for words.

But in real life communication, words and sentences communicate much more than their conventional meanings. In human communication people interpret and understand what is intended and expressed by the communicator. What is interpreted by the receptor is the interpretive or communicative meaning. Because of the traditional understanding of "meaning" as being simply the word meaning, Dan Sperber and Dierdre Wilson refer to the meaning communicated as the "communicative intent."[8] They do not use the term *meaning* at all.

The Process of Human Communication

In human communication meaning is not transferred from one end to the other end, as in telecommunication. Instead, meaning is inferred or created in the mind of the receptor. David Berlo was the first to speak of human communication as a process of meaning creation. According to Berlo, "*Communication does not consist of the transmission of meaning*. Meanings are not

---

[8] Dan Sperber and Dierdre Wilson, *Relevance: Communication and Cognition*, Cambrdige, MA: Harvard University Press, 1986.

transmittable, and meanings are not in the messages, they are in the message user."[9] Colin Cherry was the first to refer to human communication as an inferential process.[10] Sperber and Wilson explain communication in inferential model as opposed to code model (telecommunication model). They conceive of human communication as ostensive and inferential. Meaning is not just encoded into the words to be decoded by the receptor as perceived in the code model. In human communication, according to Sperber and Wilson, the intended meaning, or the communicative intent, is inferred by the receptor by means of the cognitive environment from the ostensive evidence produced by the communicator on the basis of relevance. The cognitive environment of an individual is "a set of assumptions available to him" to process the communicator's intention.[11] These assumptions are known as World View assumptions by anthropologists.

As the basic assumptions or concepts in the mind of the receptor play a vital role in the cognitive process of communication, understanding the world view of the receptor is very important for effective communication. The inference is made by means of this previous understanding on the basis of contextual relevance. Human communication works this way in the primary communication situation where both the communicants share the same world view assumptions and the situational context gives the clue for the inference of the intended meaning. Cognitive environment interacts with the message, creating meaning in the mind. This connection or coupling is a significant factor for communication to take place.

In translation, which is secondary communication, on the other hand, there is a big communication gap between the original communicators and the present receptor due to cultural, temporal and linguistic differences. The translator needs to bridge this gap in his or her translation, so that the present receptors can understand the originally intended meaning in terms of their cognitive environment.

Translation Theories

Translation has been defined traditionally as decoding meaning from one language and encoding it into another language. I refer to these theories as linguistically oriented Bible translation theories. As more studies have been done in human communication, other translation theories have been developed that are communication oriented, to ensure effective communication through translations. I refer to these theories as communication oriented Bible translation theories.

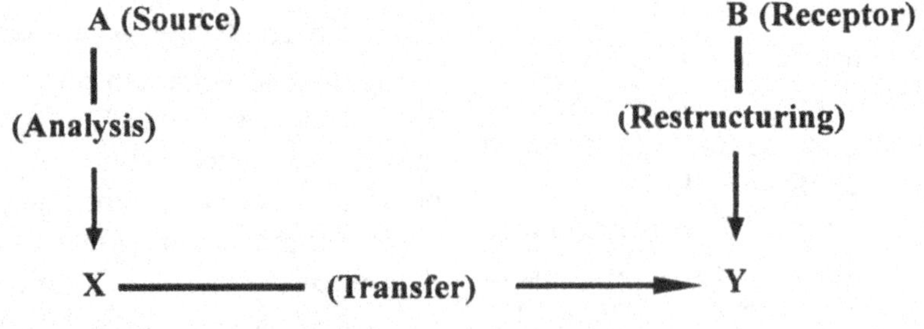

NIDA'S TRANSLATION MODEL (Nida and Taber 1974:33)

---

9 David Berlo, *The Process of Communication*, New York: Holt, Rinehart and Winston, 1960, p.175, (emphasis his).
10 Colin Cherry, *On Human Communication*, 2ⁿᵈ Edition, Cambridge, MA: The M.I.T. Press.
11 Sperber and Wilson, *Relevance: Communication and Cognition*, p.46.

Linguistically Oriented Bible Translation Theories: According to these theories translation is defined as a linguistic process of transferring meaning from one language to another language. In this approach, faithfulness in Bible translation is equated with communicating the word meaning, or linguistic meaning. Eugene Nida (1964, 1974, 1981, 1986), William A. Smalley (1991), John Beekman and John Callow (1974, 1981), Katharine Barnwell (1986), Mildred Larson (1984) and E. A. Gutt (1991) are the contributors to linguistically oriented Bible translation theory. 'Meaning' for them is the 'linguistic meaning' and they equate it with 'intended meaning'.

Gutt: E.A. Gutt[12] (1991) insists that translation is strictly a linguistic process. According to Gutt, to be faithful to the Word of God the translators should just reproduce the source text in the receptor language. He considers explication of implicatures inappropriate as he thinks that it will distort the original communicative intention.

Nida with Taber, Reyburn and de Waard: Eugene A. Nida and Charles R.Taber explain three stages of the translation process as follows:

(1) Analysis, in which the surface structure (i.e. the message given in language A) is analyzed in terms of (a) the grammatical relationships and (b) the meanings of the words and combination of words,

(2) transfer, in which the analyzed material is transferred in the mind of the translator from language A to language B, and

(3) restructuring, in which the transferred material is restructured in order to make the messages fully acceptable in the receptor languages.[13]

In their model Nida and Taber perceive translation as the transfer of linguistic meaning from language A to language B. The translator does not have to think about the communication gap between the original communicator and the present day receptor, and he or she is not required to do any addition or alteration to bridge that gap. Faithfulness for them is the reproduction of the linguistic meaning in the natural language of the receptors.

In fact, in spite of all his rich insights and understanding about various cultures of the world, Nida strongly opposes any bridging of the communication gap in translation. Nida and William D. Reyburn[14] reject the validity of any type of adaptations and restructuring in the text. Jane de Waard and Nida even recommend preserving some of the obscurity "to do justice to primarily religious languages":

> To do justice to primary religious languages, one must preserve in translating something of the transcendent quality of the forms. It would be wrong to eliminate all of the 'sublime obscurity' and rewrite primary religious language in the style of a text book on theology. Overzealous attempts to explain everything in the Scriptures may actually rob the primary religious language of the creative power to effect commitment and reorient human lives.[15]

According to Nida, the goal of the translator is to produce 'dynamic equivalence translation'. Nida defines 'dynamic equivalence translation' as "the closest natural equivalent to the source language message,"[16] and Nida expects this

---

[12] E.A. Gutt, *Translation and Relevance*, Oxford: Basil Blackwell, 1991.

[13] Eugene A. Nida and Charles R. Taber, *Theory and Practice of Translation*, 2nd Edition, Leiden, Netherlands: E.J. Brill, p.33.

[14] Eugene A. Nida and William D. Reyburn, *Meaning Across Cultures*, Maryknoll, NY: Orbis Books, 1981.

[15] Jane de Waard and Eugene A. Nida, *From One Language to Another: Functional Equivalence Translation*, Nashville, TN: Thomas Nelson, 1986, pp.22,23.

[16] Eugene A. Nida, *Toward a Science of Translating*, Leiden, Netherlands: E.J. Brill, 1964, p.66.

translation to produce an equivalent response among the receptors. Nida's contribution to translation theory is commendable in terms of using the natural equivalent forms of the receptor language, focussing on 'meaning' rather than form. As a linguist he has developed the translation theory in terms of finding the right words, grammatical forms and idioms of the receptor language to express the meaning of the text in the original language. Without the closest natural equivalent forms, translation cannot be done. Though the linguistic meaning may be equivalent to the communicative meaning most of the times, this is not always true.

Beekman and Callow: Beekman and Callow's 'idiomatic translation' also focuses on using the idiomatic natural expressions of the receptor language in translation, like Nida's 'closest natural equivalent translation'.[17] Their Semantic Structure Analysis (SSA) to understand the intended meaning of the Biblical text does not go beyond the linguistic meaning.[18]

Smalley: *William Smalley distinguishes three kinds of meaning as:*

... ideational (meaning as information), interpersonal or interactional (meaning as relationship between the people involved in the communication, the kind of communication they are involved in, the feelings and attitude they display) and textual (meaning as the way in which the communication is structured, the meaning which lies in the form itself).[19] (1991 : 124-125).

Smalley insists that "all three kinds of meaning are to be found both in the source text and in any translations."[20] He also rightly points out that Nida's dynamic equivalence translation has focussed mainly on ideational meaning. Ideational and textual meanings go to form the linguistic meaning. By the inclusion of the interactional meaning, Smalley extends the domain of translation theory to communication. However, he rejects the consideration of the cultural aspects of the communication context like the world view of the receptors that forms the major part of their cognitive environment. Thus his translation theory is still limited in terms of effective communication.

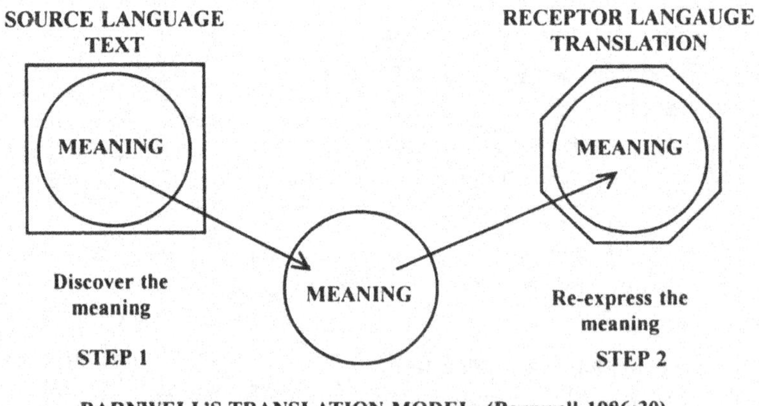

BARNWELL'S TRANSLATION MODEL (Barnwell 1986:30)

---

[17] John Beekman and John Callow, *Translating the Word of God*, Grand Rapids: Zondervan Publishing, 1974.

[18] John Beekman and John Callow, *Semantic Structure of Written Communication*, Dallas, TX: Summer Institute of Linguistics, 1981.

[19] William A. Smalley, *Translation as Mission: Bible Translation in the Modern Missionary Movement*, Macon, GA: Mercer University Press, 1991, pp.124-125.

[20] *Ibid.*, p.125.

Barnwell: Barnwell describes the translation process as involving two primary steps: Step 1: Study the source text and discover the word and grammatical patterns of the source language.

Step 2: Re-express that meaning using different word and grammatical patterns. The meaning should be expressed in a way that is clear and natural in the receptor language.[21]

These two steps imply that translation is primarily a linguistic process and the meaning in translation is confined to the linguistic meaning. However Barnwell also states very clearly that communication through translation involves the communication of what is stated explicitly in the text as well as what remains there implicit, unsaid because the author assumes that his or her audience already knows it. But she recommends such bridging of the communication gap only for societies among whom there are no churches and the literacy rate is very low. She says, "In an area where there has been no previous Christian contact, and where there are very few people who can read... the translator may decide to make more implicit information explicit in the text of the translation itself."[22] For the groups where there are churches and the literacy rate is high, she recommends that the bridging may be done by supplementary means such as glossary and illustrations, not in the text itself.[23]

Larson. Larson, although defining translation as a linguistic process without incorporating the communication factors, still acknowledges the need for bridging the cultural gap between the original and to-day's communication situation. She insists that the bridging should be done in the text itself. She is right in saying that "one of the challenges facing a translator is knowing when to supply the information which is implicit in the text."[24]

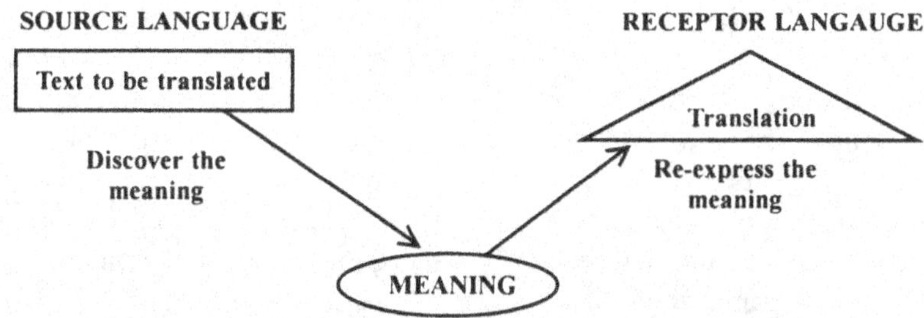

LARSON'S MODEL OF TRANSLATION MODEL (Larson 1984:4)

Thus from Gutt to Larson we see a shift from rejection to slow increase in communication focus. These are the main Bible translation theorists who influence the translation practice of the Bible Societies and Wycliffe Bible Translators. The following figure puts them in a continuum in terms of communication focus. Their lack of incorporation of communication factors in their definition and model of translation significantly affects their translation practice.

---

[21] Katharine Barnwell, *Bible Translation: An Introductory Course in Translation Principles*, 3rd Edition, Dallas, TX: Summer Institute of Linguistics, 1986, p.30.

[22] *Ibid.*, p.89.

[23] *Ibid.*

[24] Mildred Larson, *Meaning Based Translation: A Guide to Cross Language Equivalence*, New York: University Press of America, 1984, p.42.

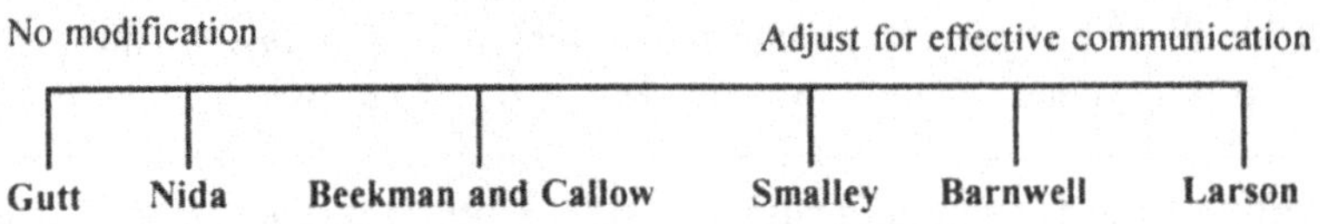

**THE CONTINUUM OF COMMUNICATION FOCUS IN
TERMS OF TEXTUAL MODIFICATION**

Communication Oriented Translation Theories. There are more Communication oriented translation theorists in the secular world than in the Christian World. In this approach, translation is cross-cultural communication. Unlike the linguistically oriented translation theorists, they are concerned not with preservation and reproduction of the original text, but with the recreation of that text for the receptors to understand the author's intended meaning. The importance of the interaction between the world view assumptions in the receptors' mind, and the communicated message, to create the meaning intended by the communicator in the receptors' mind, is taken seriously by the communication oriented translation theorists.

The significance of commonality for effective communication is readily taken into consideration in this approach. The lack of commonality increasing the communication gap between people of different cultures and necessitating bridging the gap in the translation, is acknowledged in this approach. So bridging the communication gap, leading to the recreation of the text whenever it is necessary, is recommended by these theorists.

Effective communication is crucial for international, socio-political and economic purposes. So the secular translation theorists are keen to incorporate communication factors in their theories. As translation is not mere transfer of linguistic meaning the translator's role is crucial in this approach. This has great implication for the practice of Bible translation. Holz-Mantaari's translator is an expert, and translation, the work of a team of experts. So she highly recommends that translators should be well trained and equipped for their job.[25] Hawson and Martin's translator is the cultural operator who mediates between the source and the receptor cultures.[26]

More than the secular translation theorists, the Bible translation theorists need to be concerned about incorporating communication factors in translation theory, so that the theory will guide the training and practice to produce communicative translations. We see that kind of communicative focus and incorporation of communicative factors in the translation theories of Daniel Shaw, Louis J. Luzbetak, Charles Kraft and Christeena Alaichamy.

Kraft. Following Berlo, Kraft considers meaning as not being contained in the words but rather created in people's minds. According to Kraft "Meaning is the structuring of information in the minds of persons."[27] "But words, like all information-bearing vehicles within cultures, derive their meanings from their interaction with the contexts in which they participate."[28]

---

[25] Justa Holz-Mantaari, *Translatorisches Handeln: Theories und Methods*, Helsinki: Suomalainen Tiedekatemia, 1984, p.366.

[26] Lance Hewson and Jacky Martin, *Redefining Translation: The Variational Approach*, London: Routlege, 1991.

[27] Charles H. Kraft, *Christianity in Culture: A Study in Dynamic Biblial Theologizing in Cross-Cultural Perspective*, Maryknoll, NY: Orbis Books, 1979, p.135, emphasis his.

[28] *Ibid.*, p.137.

Though Kraft describes the process of translation within Nida's theoretical framework, Kraft's dynamic equivalence goes beyond Nida's in its communicative focus. He insists that the task of the translator is the same as that of any other communicator.

> The task of the Bible translator is the same in essence as that of (1) God when he seeks to communicate in languages across the cultural-supracultural barrier, (2) any witness (such as the authors of scriptures, a missionary, or a "personal worker") who seeks to communicate the message of God to any person or group who stands on the other side of a cultural and/or psychological barrier, or (3) any preacher who seeks correctly and helpfully to interpret and apply the message to the lives of his hearers. All, if they are to communicate effectively, must be hearer oriented, presenting their (i.e. God's) message according to the basic principle of communication science ....[29]

KRAFT'S MODEL OF DYNAMIC EQUIVALENCE TRANSLATION
(Kraft 1979:275)

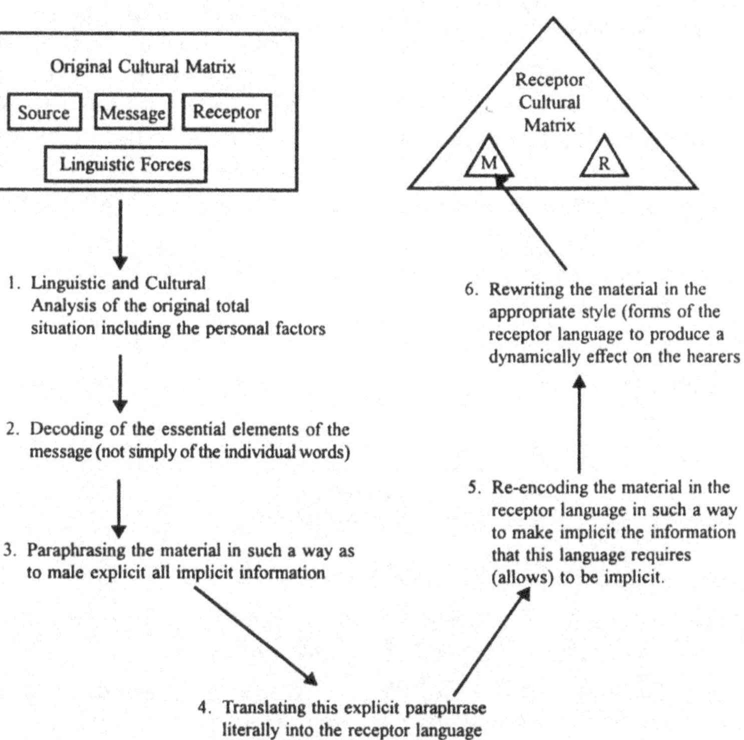

Kraft also has incorporated the bridging factor in his model of translation. He does not reject any needed modification in the text to make it convey the message across the communication gap. The adjustments he suggests are not limited to only linguistic differences or the figurative uses but also to cultural differences. Kraft strongly emphasizes,

> Whatever of paraphrase must (because of the requirements of the target language and culture) be included in the translation to make it equivalently intelligible and

---

[29] *Ibid.*, p.264.

impactful is legitimately to be called "translation". It should not be dismissed as "mere paraphrases" (in a negative sense) or (as in KJV) italicized as if it were optional matter inserted at the whim of the translator.[30]

Paraphrase is something said in a different way. So all translations are paraphrases of the original Bible in Hebrew and Greek. There are many who hold on to the King James Version as the perfect translation of the original. They reject the *Good News Bible* because it has made changes for more understandability. But Nida, the co-translator of the *Good News Bible,* rejects the *Living Bible* as a paraphrase, as it has additions and explication of implicatures for the sake of bridging the communication gap. Kraft, in fact, encourages Living Bible type translations. Kraft rightly says, "the translation that requires the hearer/reader to fill the necessary additional

understanding or to depend on experts for true meaning is inadequate."[31]

Shaw. Shaw calls the meaning to be translated, 'the source meaning', the meaning intended by the source, which includes the cultural meaning along with the linguistic meaning.[32] He says that the task of the translator is "to produce translations that meaningfully communicate the intent of the source."[33] Shaw states clearly how commonality ensures communication and the lack of it makes it less effective:

> ... in most aspects of life, where common knowledge is assumed, effective communication is an expected result. Where this common shared experience is lost in a cross-cultural interaction, communication is much less effective ... This matter of cultural diversity is of central importance if the scriptures are to be understood.[34]

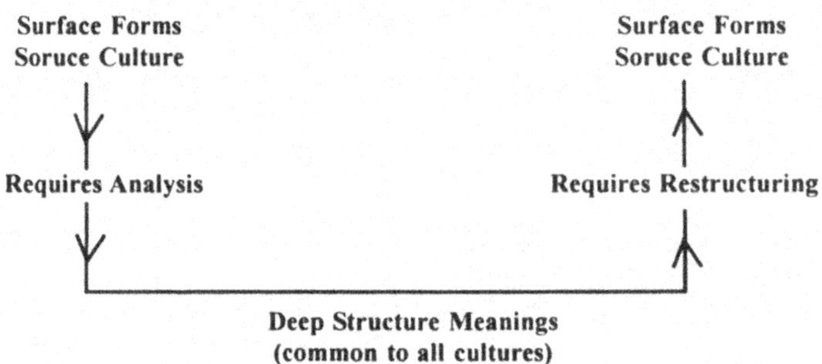

SHAW'S TRANSLATION MODEL (Shaw 1988:194)

This factor highlights the need for the translators to go deeper into the source culture as well as the receptor culture in order to successfully accomplish this task of mediation. Both Kraft and Shaw emphasize that Jesus' incarnational model is to be followed by the translators to enter the receptor culture, in order to bridge the cultural

gap in their translation, for successful communication.

Shaw emphasizes the need for making implied information explicit in the text. He points out that the criterion for making the implied information explicit in the text, is always understanding of the receptors. He says, "material

---

[30] *Ibid.,* p.272, emphasis his.

[31] *Ibid.,* p.269.

[32] R. Daniel Shaw, *Transcrulturation: The Cultural Factor in Communication and Other Communication Tasks,* Pasadena, CA: William Carey Library, 1988, p.193.

[33] *Ibid.,* p.29.

[34] *Ibid.,* pp.30-31.

is necessary to the extent that it provides understanding of what the source assumed."[35]

Luzbetak. Luzbetak declares that "good translations are always highly contextual translations."[36] Luzbetak insists that the translation should be made, focussing on the present day context. According to him, the original writers wrote their messages with specific "cognitive, emotive and motivational goals" to an audience of "specific social and cultural identities." "This culturally conditioned non-linguistic meaning, being first filtered through the cultural filtering of the translator's mind, must be expressed in terms of the culture of the society into whose languages the translation is being made."[37]

In order to produce such a contextual translation, Luzbetak insists that the translators need to "be sensitized" to the cultures involved in the translation context. Thus Luzbetak brings out the significance of going deeper into the source and receptor cultures to understand the meaning communicated by the source text and to recreate that meaning in the receptors, through the translated text. He also points out the translators' need to be aware of their own cultural frameworks in order to avoid the distortion which their own cultural background could cause in the process of communication. Kraft, Shaw and Luzbetak thus bring out the significance of understanding the source culture and the receptor culture along with becoming aware of the translator's own culture, in order to make the translation communicative for the receptor.

Alaichamy. In the model I have developed, Bible translation is described as tridimensional communication, not just cross-cultural communication.[38] Bible translation as communication involves spiritual, relational and technical (or professional) dimensions.

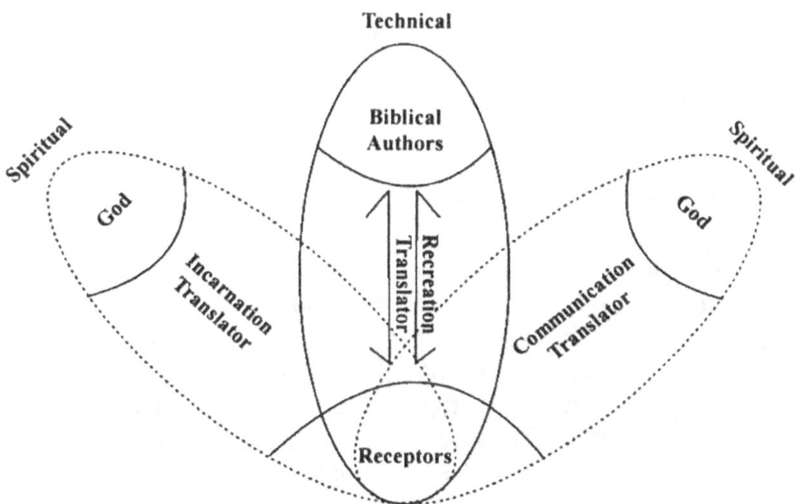

BIBLE TRANSLATION AS TRIDIMENSIONAL COMMUNICATION
Alaichamy (1996:111)

---

[35] *Ibid.*, p.211.

[36] Louis J. Luzbetak, "Contextual Translation: The Role of Cultural Anthropology" in *Bible Translation and the Spread of the Church* edited by Philip C. Stine, New York: E.J. Brill, p.109.

[37] *Ibid.*

[38] Christeena Alaichamy, "Communicative Translation: Theory and Principles for Application to Cross Cultural Translation in India," Ph.D. Dissertation, Pasadena, CA: Fuller Theological Seminary, 1997.

In the spiritual dimension, the Bible translator, as God's messenger to the people of the receptor culture, bridges the communication gap between God and the receptor culture people. In the relational dimension, the Bible translator, as an effective interpersonal communicator, relates with the people and understands their culture and world view. In the technical dimension, the Bible translator bridges the communication gap between the original Biblical authors and present day receptors by recreating the text in order to create the authors' intended meaning in the receptors' mind. Thus in all three dimensions the translator needs to be an effective communicator. Effective communication by Bible translation depends upon how effective the translator is as a communicator in all three dimensions.

The spiritual dimension presents Bible translation not just as a linguistic task done by linguists, but as missionary work done in obedience to God's command to communicate. In the spiritual dimension the translator is connected to God as well as to people in order to be His messenger to the people. The translator listens to God, depends upon Him, and receives the strength and wisdom to be His messenger. Following Jesus' model the translator lives with the people to reveal God to them. This living with the people is also essential for understanding the people's culture and world view. The insights for this dimension come from the Word of God and Cultural Anthropology. To be effective in this dimension the translator needs to follow the principles of living following Jesus's incarnational model.[39]

In the relational dimension the translator relates with the people. In this dimension, intercultural communication takes place, face to face. The translator needs to communicate successfully with the receptor culture people in order to learn all about their culture and world view. This dimension brings into focus the translator's spiritual, cultural and communicational sensitivity as the essentials for the success of his or her communication task. The spiritual dimension gives the inspiration, courage and strength for the translator to meet the challenges of this dimension. The insights for this dimension come from the Word of God and communicology (communication theories). To be effective communicators, the translators need to follow the principles of relating and the interpersonal and intercultural principles.[40]

The technical dimension is the one that translation theories are concerned with. This is the production part of Bible translation. This dimension presents Bible translation as cross cultural communication. The translator is the mediator or bridge between the original authors and the present receptor to close the communication gap that exists between them due to lack of commonality. On the source side, the translator crosses the gap to understand the author's intended meaning. On the receptor side, the translator crosses the gap and enter into the receptor's framework in order to be able to recreate the text in such a way that it will enable the coupling or interaction to take place in the receptor's mind. The coupling or interaction between the receptor's cognitive environment and the message in the text, creates the meaning that is intended by the original author, in the receptor's mind.

To understand the communicative intent, it is essential to understand not only the syntactic and semantic (linguistic) meaning, but also the pragmatic (cultural and communicative contextual) meaning. Sometimes understanding

---

[39] *Ibid.*, pp.120-129.
[40] Alaichamy, "Communicative Translation", pp.130-139.

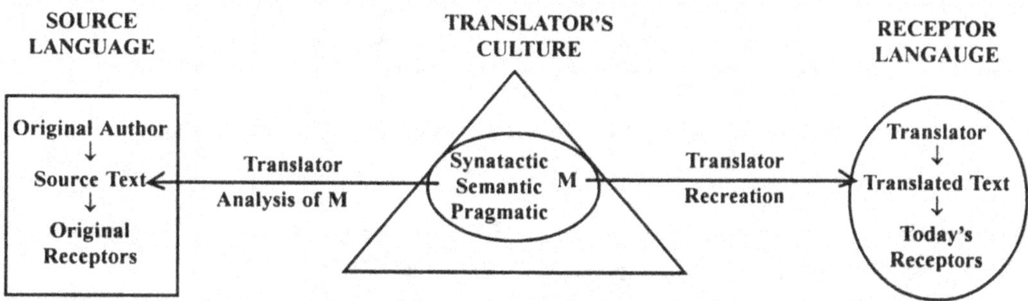

THE TRANSLATOR'S TASK IN THE TECHNICAL DIMENSION
Alaichamy (1997:142)

of the cultural background itself helps to understand the pragmatic meaning, and other times understanding of the whole communication situation is necessary to understand the pragmatic meaning.

Luke 7:36-50 and Mathew 22:1-14 can illustrate this point. In Luke 7:36-50 there is the description of a woman washing Jesus' feet with tears, wiping them with her hair, pouring expensive perfume over them and kissing them. Unless one understands the cultural context where the honored guest is expected to be welcomed by the host following cultural rules of hospitality, one cannot understand here the deep love and penitence the woman shows and the way in which Jesus contrasts her actions of love with the Pharisees' disregard for Him. But in Mathew 22:1-14, Jesus' words, "let the children first be fed, for it is not right to take the children's bread and throw it to the dogs," cannot be understood correctly just by understanding the cultural context. If one understands the cultural context one can know that by 'dogs' Jesus refers to the gentiles, but still one cannot understand Jesus' communicative intent. When one looks at the whole communicative context, it is clear that Jesus was saying that He was not only for the Jews, but also for the Gentiles.[41]

The translation principles for communicative translation include both the principles related to linguistic patterns as well as the principles of recreation. The translation principles related to linguistic patterns are dealt with elaborately by Nida (1964), Nida and Taber (1974), Beekman and Callow (1974 and 1981), Barnwell (1986) and Larson (1984).[42] Understanding the linguistic meaning is the first step and then this is used along with other cultural and contextual factors to understand the communicator's communicative intent. In the same way the communicative intent is communicated through the recreation of the text using the linguistic patterns of the receptor language. Therefore the principles of re-creation I have developed are in addition to the translation principles developed by others.[43] Thus the Bible translation theory has been extended by the inclusion of cultural, communicative and spiritual factors to make Bible translation communicate. Following is the continuum of communication focus of Bible translation theorists.

---

[41] For fuller discussion see Alaichamy, "Communicative Translation," pp.145-149.

[42] Nida, *Toward a Science of Translating*; Nida and Taber, *Theory and Practice of Translation*; Beekman and Callow, *Translating the Word of God* and *Semantic Structure of Written Communication*, Dallas, TX: Summer Institute of Linguistics, 1981; Barnwell, *Bible Translation*; and Larson *Meaning Based Translation*.

[43] Alaichamy, "Communicative Translation," pp.143-160.

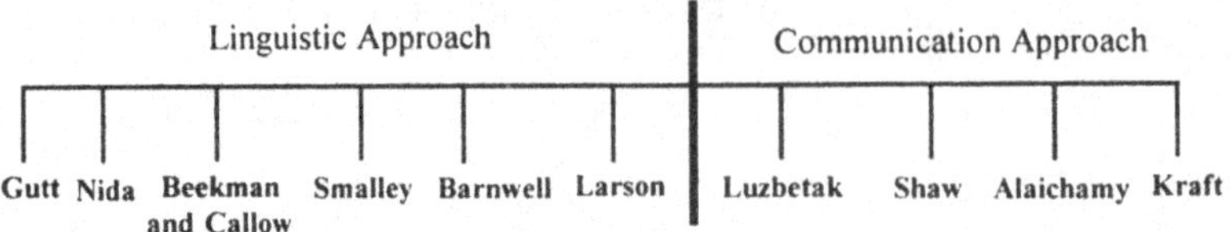

The Continuum of Communicative focus

I have placed Kraft in the extreme right as he goes to the extreme of approving even Clarence Jordan's cotton patch version as legitimate translation. Jordan has changed the whole primary communication to to-day's receptor culture. He has changed the names of Biblical characters and places to American names and places in America. It is not right to change the original communication like this. Rather the translation should bridge the communication gap to help the receptors to understand the original communication.

3. The Role of Communicative Translation in Mission

God's Word made understandable to people plays a vital role in all three stages of Mission, namely, Proclamation, Transformation and Continuation. The goals of mission are to proclaim the Word of God, transform individuals' lives and societies, and continuation of the mission by the church. These goals are achieved when contextualization takes place in all three stages. In contextualization, the Word of God gets connected to the context. In the proclamation stage the Word of God should be connected to the cognitive context, the existing concepts in peoples' minds. In the transformation stage the Word of God needs to be connected to all the areas of people's lives. This can be possible only if the Word of God is understood in its depth. Understanding is essential for obedience leading to action. Listening to God results in obeying. Mission continues when people listen and obey God. When they obey God and get involved in mission, they connect the Word of God to the lives of people around them.

3.1. Communicative Translation in Proclamation

In order for the Good News to be understood and for people to respond to it, it should be proclaimed in an understandable way. To proclaim the Gospel in an understandable way, the Word of God containing the Good News should be translated in such a way that the receptors easily understand the intended meaning.

When John Wycliffe translated the Bible into English and made it understandable, his disciples, called the 'lollards', went everywhere in England and preached it. When Wycliffe Bible translators went to the minority language groups, those local people who worked with them were the first ones to become Christians, because they understood God's Word.

When Bible translation went hand in hand with missionary work people understood the Gospel preached to them and responded in great numbers. In Mizoram, the response to the Gospel proclaimed was almost 100 percent because the missionaries translated the Word of God into Mizo as soon as they started their mission among them. In Billy Graham's evangelistic crusades the *Living Bible* was given to those who made commitment as new believers can understand it easily.

The Tamil Bible was the first one to be translated in the whole of Asia, by Zieganbalg in 1706. It underwent many revisions until 1948. Now it's language is outdated like the King James Version. Therefore, when Tamil Christians want to proclaim the Gospel to non-Christians, they have to consciously translate the Biblical concepts into today's Tamil language and the cognitive context of Tamil culture. In order for

Tamil non-Christians to understand the proclaimed message, it needs to be contextualized. The message should be formed in such a way that it will be connected to the cognitive context, their world view assumptions, so that the intended meaning will be created in their minds. The translation of key terms like 'God', 'sin', and 'being born again' should be related to the basic assumptions which are in their mind in order to help them understand what is being proclaimed. As the present Bible is not communicative in terms of the Tamil language and culture, it is very difficult to use the Word of God straight for proclamation. This may be one of the reasons for the lack of evangelism of their non-Christian neighbors by Tamil churches. Though we are in great need of another translation, the Christian community strongly opposes any attempt to produce new translations, because they do not understand that translation is communication and that communicative translation in turn will enhance communication of the Gospel.

3.2 Communicative Translation in Transformation

The first stage of Mission is accomplished when the Word of God is connected to the cognitive content of the receptors, resulting in their understanding of the message. This is contextualization in the proclamation stage. Contextualization should continue, leading to perfection or building up of the church in faith. The Word of God needs to be connected to all the areas of people's lives, their beliefs and practices. Paul Hiebert[44] defines this process of evaluation of old beliefs and practices in the light of the Word of God for the transformation of individual lives and societies, as 'critical contextualization'. The goal of translation is to help people apply God's Word to their lives, to change individuals' lives and societies.

In the communicative approach to translation, the cross-cultural translators are the messengers of God, and they live out God's Word among the receptors. They live in constant touch with God and connect people with God. Often the translation assistants with whom the translators relate closely are the first to come to know God and later become strong Christian leaders.

The translators, as effective interpersonal and intercultural communicators, build a trusting relationship with the receptors. With training in cultural anthropology and knowledge about culture change they can understand the receptor culture well and assist the new Christians in the process of critical contextualization. Critical contextualization is the responsibility of the insiders. However, as the translators will have gained the respect and trust of the insiders, they can be of great help to the local Christians in evaluating their culture in the light of God's Word.

The translation of the Bible done with the communication focus can itself communicate effectively to the people of the receptor culture. By using communicative translation of the Bible, the local evangelists and pastors can preach and teach effectively as they themselves can understand the message clearly. Once, in the early days of our translation ministry, we were teaching the local Christians using the Kukna scripture passages we had translated at that time. A local evangelist expressed his joy, saying, "I get deeper understanding of God's Word when you teach from the translation in my own language rather than from Gujarati. I am waiting to have the entire Bible in my language to gain still deeper understanding of God's Word."[45]

---

[44] Paul Hiebert, *Anthropological Reflections on Missiological Issues*, Grand Rapids, MI: Baker Books, 1994.

[45] See Paul Alaichamy, "Intermediate Language Translation Aids: An Experiment in the Indian Context," Ph.D. dissertation, Fuller Theological Seminary, 1997.

Unless this transformation phase of mission is achieved, syncretism and nominalism will be the result. In Nagaland, the Bible has been translated into many Naga languages, but it is said that these translations are not easily understandable and so are not used well by the Christians. Could this be one of the reasons for the increasing nominalism that threatens the Naga Church today?

3.3. *Communicative Translation for Continuation of Mission*

Lamin Sanneh testifies that the vernacular Bibles in African languages initiated and enhanced the indigenous missionary movement and that the Good News in Africa has been spread mainly by the local Christians and evangelists because they have a Bible that they can understand.[46] Churches become missionary churches when people understand the Word of God. In the late 12th Century, a rich merchant in Lyons, France, by the name of Peter Waldo, started a transformation movement when he got the Bible translated. He sold all his property, gave to the poor and started preaching the Gospel which he understood. Many listened and followed him, and they also preached the Gospel everywhere.[47]

In the later part of the 19th century the Santhali church in Bihar thrived on the Word of God when it was translated into Santhali by the pioneering Scandinavian missionaries. Today there are many churches and even graduate level theological training available in Santhali medium. On the other hand, even though the churches among the Bhil tribe of Central India, and the Kukna and Vasava tribes of Western India had thousands of believers in the early part of the 20th century, they later lost their vitality and were in danger of near extinction. Could the reason for this condition be attributed to the lack of the Bible in their mother tongues? Praise God, today active Bible translation ministry is being carried out among all these groups by Indian Christians.

Conclusion

Bible translation makes God's Word available and understandable to people of all cultures, so that they may know God. Therefore, Bible translation should be an integral part of mission. One Western mission agency has been working in one of the Northern Indian states for about a century. Recently a historian from the West came to write the history of this mission. He asked the missionary who has spent five decades of her life in that area, "Why has the Bible not yet been translated into the mother tongue of the people?" The missionary, although she had poured out all of her life for the people, felt sad that she had not even learned the language of the people. She and other missionaries had always carried out the missionary work in the major trade language of the region. Later, when a national Bible translation organization sent their translator to start translation work in the local language of that area, the missionary was overjoyed, saying that the mission would now be complete with the translation of the Word of God in the people's language.

---

[46] Lamin Sanneh, *Translating the Message: The Missionary Impact on Culture*, Maryknoll, NY: Orbis Books, 1989.

[47] Worth, *Bible Translations*, pp.49,50.

PART VII

Contemporary Issues

Understanding Religious Conversion: A Study of Theological, Anthropological and Psychological Perspectives[1]

SEBASTIAN C.H. KIM

Understanding religious conversion is important since it relates to the nature, function and meaning of religion in human life.[2] To understand conversion is not an easy task, since it involves not only the practical religious life of human beings, but also theological, psychological and socio-cultural dimensions.[3] Therefore any study of conversion needs to consider what these disciplines have to say. In this study, we shall examine the nature of conversion from three different perspectives: theological, socio-cultural, and psychological, respectively. Each will be considered according to the criteria of that particular academic discipline. Within these perspectives, different schools of thought will be discussed, these will be summarized at the end of each section, and, when appropriate, the study will show how the schools interact with one another. The purpose of this study is not to bring about a comprehensive, single definition of conversion, but rather to identify different definitions of conversion and bring them into interaction in order to understand conversion from different perspectives.

Theological Perspectives

Theological perspectives represent the debate within the church using the church's own disciplines.

a) *Representative view of Theologians: Conversion as theological reality, which induces a radical change of understanding of God, self and neighbours*

Historically, it could be said that the understanding of conversion changed in three stages: first - from the fourth century onwards - it was vocation, especially to the monastic life; secondly, transfer of allegiance from one religion to the other; and third, in the Pietist Movement it meant change of the moral and spiritual condition of self.[4] The Medieval RC theological understanding of conversion was shaped by Augustine who was "the first Christian theologian to take Paul's teaching on justification by faith seriously."[5] In reaction to Pelagius, Augustine formulated the doctrines of original sin and predestination which necessitated a radical conversion experience that only God could bring

---

[1] For the discussion on conversion in India, see author's recent book, *In Search of Identity: Debates on Religious Conversion in India*, New Delhi & Oxford: OUP, 2003.

[2] Eugene V. Gallagher, *Expectation and Experience: Explaining Religious Conversion*, Atlanta: Scholars Press, 1990, p.148.

[3] Lewis R. Rambo, *Understanding Religious Conversion*, New Haven: Yale University Press, 1993, 7; Gallagher, *Expectation and Experience*, p.131.

[4] J.G. Davies, *Dialogue with the World*, London: SCM, 1967, 50.

about. Martin Luther, while reacting to the church's abuse of power, was much influenced by Augustine's interpretation of Paul and maintained the otherworldly and individualistic understanding of conversion. Because the believer was now understood to have a direct relationship with God, independent of the church, "a personal and subjective experience of a new birth by the Holy Spirit" came to be expected.[6] John Calvin described conversion as a "transformation not only in external works, but in the soul itself, which is able only after it has put off its old habits to bring forth fruit conformable to its renovation."[7] The Pietism and Holiness movements stressed personal decision and there was a shift from "emphasis on God's sovereignty to God's grace."[8]

Karl Barth regarded conversion as "awakening" from the "sleep of death" which only is possible through the "power of the mystery and miracle of God."[9] It is the activity of God through His saving grace, a "movement" in which the individual participates rather than responds. Our role is to participate and let be in the presence of God. For Barth conversion signified a decisive change; conversion is not "improvement but alteration," it is something "new."[10] It is an axis where the two-way "movement" - "God is for

him, and he for God" - operates in reality.[11] The relationship is not only to God but also to fellowmen. In the process of conversion, human beings "cross the threshold of our private existence and move out into the open."[12] Therefore in Barth's view, conversion is a life-long process rather than an event. In *The Cost of Discipleship*, Dietrich Bonhoeffer portrayed discipleship in terms of a God-wrought "single-minded obedience" to God's call whatever the cost.[13] Though he does not use the word "conversion" it is clear that a life-changing event is envisaged: "When Christ calls a man, He bids Him come and die."[14] Bonhoeffer's context meant that his call to conversion was addressed first and foremost to "Christians" themselves. Bonhoeffer emphasized the ethical content of conversion. Christians are called to reject the cheap grace of religion and to live out their "secular calling" in a serving Christian community,[15] a "church for others,"[16] "to remain in the world in order to engage in frontal assault on it."[17] Bonhoeffer's legacy was taken up later by others and used to justify a secular Christianity in which conversion was "to the world."

Paul Tillich rejected orthodoxy and sought instead to rethink the "eternal truth" of Christianity for the contemporary situation. In the third part of his *Systematic Theology*,[18] he sees

---

[5] David J. Bosch, *Transforming Mission: Paradigm Shifts in Theology of Mission*, Maryknoll, NY: Orbis, 1991, pp.215-6.

[6] *Ibid.*, pp.241-2.

[7] John Calvin, *Institutes of the Christian Religion* Vol 1, trans. Henry Beveridge, London: James Clarke & Co., 1957, p.513.

[8] Bosch, *Transforming Mission*, pp.252-3, 278.

[9] Barth, *Church Dogmatics, Vol. IV/2*, p.555.

[10] *Ibid.*, p.560.

[11] *Ibid.*, p.561.

[12] *Ibid.*, pp.565-566.

[13] Dietrich Bonhoeffer, *The Cost of Discipleship*, trans. R.H. Fuller, 2nd ed, rev & unabrgd, New York: The Macmillan Company, 1959, pp.69-83.

[14] *Ibid.*, p.79.

[15] *Ibid.*, pp 228-244.

[16] Bonhoeffer, *Letters and Papers from Prison*, trans. R.H. Fuller, enlgd. ed., London: SCM Press, 1971, p.382f.

[17] Bonhoeffer, *The Cost of Discipleship*, p.238.

[18] Paul Tillich, *Systematic Theology*, Vol. III, Chicago: The University of Chicago Press, 1963.

conversion as becoming part of the "Spiritual Community,"[19] the community of Spiritual personalities, or those who manifest "Spiritual Presence"[20] and move toward the divine "ground of being" which is being "determined by" and "united in God" by faith and love.[21] He argues that two notions are brought together in the word conversion: first, in the Old Testament, in the realm of the socio-political, the turning away from injustice, inhumanity and idols to justice, humanity and to God; and in the New Testament, the turning from the temporal and oneself to the eternal and to God.[22] Karl Rahner argues that conversion is a "fundamental decision" with regard to God and a basic choice to "commit the whole life to God" but at the same time, since it is not possible to analyse it fully, it cannot be fixed at a definite moment in life.[23] He argues that wherever a person denies himself and loves his neighbour, wherever one renounces the idols of fear and hunger for life, the Kingdom of God is present. Conversion may therefore be unreflecting, implicit and "anonymous." Christ may not even be known, though "attained in his "Spirit".[24] Conversion is experienced "as a gift of God's grace" and at the same time as "a radical fundamental decision." Rahner emphasizes the ethical dimension of conversion and believes it

is gradual. Even a sudden conversion may be the result of a long-term process.[25]

Bernard Lonergan argues that conversion is central to theological method because it is "basic to Christian living," therefore "an objectification of conversion provides theology with its foundation."[26] He sees conversion as "resultant change of course and direction" and "existential, intensely personal, utterly intimate" but it is not "so private as to be solitary."[27] He points out that conversion is total; it "affects all of a man's conscious and intentional operations."[28] He divides conversion into three parts: first, *intellectual conversion* which implies the truth attained by cognitional self-transcendence; second, *moral conversion* which "changes the criterion of one's decisions and choices from satisfactions to values," third, *religious conversion* which is "being grasped by ultimate concerns," an "other-worldly falling in love" as well as "total and permanent self-surrender without conditions, qualifications, reservations."[29] Hans Küng believes that, in view of the kingdom of God - "the ultimate and definitive reality" - "a fundamental transformation" is expected.[30] This is "no more and no less than a fundamental, total orientation

---

[19] *Ibid.,*, p.217.

[20] *Ibid.,* pp. 107-110. Tillich uses prefers the term "Spiritual Presence" to "Spirit of God" since the Spirit of God is not a separated being, p107.

[21] *Ibid.,*, p 217.

[22] *Ibid.,* p.219.

[23] Karl Rahner, "Conversion" in Karl Rahner (ed.), *Encyclopedia of Theology: A Concise Sacramentum Mundi,* London: Burns & Oates, 1975, 291.

[24] *Ibid.,* p.292.

[25] *Ibid.,* p.294.

[26] Bernard Lonergan, *Method in Theology,* New York: Herder and Herder, 1972, p.130. See also "Theology in Its New Context" in Walter Conn (ed.), *Conversion: Perspectives on Personal and Sociological Transformation,* New York: Alba House, 1978, p.14. Lonergan points out that in any religion "it follows that reflection on conversion can supply theology with its foundation and, indeed, with a foundation that is concrete, dynamic, personal, communal, and historical," p14.

[27] *Ibid.,* p.130.

[28] *Ibid.,* p. 131.

[29] *Ibid.,* p. 240.

[30] Hans Kung, *On Being a Christian,* trans. Edward Quinn, London: Collins, 1977, pp.248-9.

of man's life toward God: an undivided heart..."[31] In order to emphasize this he prefers the word "conversion" to "repentance"[32] since conversion is not to be confused with "doing penance" or with a religious experience. "It is a decisive change of will, an awareness changed from the roots upwards, a new basic attitude, a different scale of values." It does not require confession but *faith*.[33] "Jesus' call to conversion is a call to *joy*" not a new list of duties, it is "a true liberation" of submission to God's will, which is "man's well-being."[34] Conversion is thus becoming truly human.

The eschatological theology of Jurgen Moltmann set down in *Theology of Hope*[35] does not include conversion as a theological category. But *The Spirit of Life*[36] includes a chapter on "The Rebirth to Life" which prefers "rebirth" to "conversion"[37] and equates it with new creation.[38] Rebirth due to the operation of the Spirit is described christologically as justification.[39] But to look at it purely christologically is to neglect the experience of the Spirit.[40] He seeks to rectify this omission, describing the experience of the Spirit as an ongoing one characterized by joy and peace, including peace with creation.[41] In his definition of the Spirit as the life-giver, Moltmann opens the way for the application of this rebirth to all people "who truly affirm and love life."[42] Moltmann argues for a rediscovery in Western theology of the immanence of the Creator in the creation and the cosmic orientation of the church. Thus he also infers the church's involvement in the struggle of creation for rebirth from ecological crisis.[43]

The emergence of Latin American Liberation Theology has led to a further reinterpretation of conversion. In his classic *A Theology of Liberation*, Gustavo Gutierrez calls for a "conversion to the neighbour, to social justice, to history" which is implied in our conversion to the Lord.[44] "Conversion means a radical transformation of ourselves; it means thinking, feeling, and living for Christ - present in exploited and alienated persons. To be converted is to commit oneself to the process of the liberation of the poor and oppressed... generously, but also with an analysis of the situation and a strategy of action." "Conversion is a permanent process" the fruitfulness of which "depends on our openness..."[45] Gutierrez points out that "our conversion process is affected by the socio-economic, political, cultural, and human environment in which it occurs." Authentic conversion demands a change in these structures,

---

[31] *Ibid.*, p.249.

[32] *Ibid.*, p.250.

[33] *Ibid., p.250.*

[34] *Ibid.*, p.251.

[35] Jurgen Moltmann, *Theology of Hope: On the Ground and the Implications of a Christian Eschatology*, trans. James W. Leitch, London: SCM Press, 1967.

[36] Jurgen Moltmann, *Spirit of Life: A Universal Affirmation*, trans. Margaret Kohl, London: SCM Press, 1992.

[37] *Ibid.*, p. 150.

[38] *Ibid.*, 147.

[39] *Ibid.*, 152f.

[40] *Ibid.*, 150-2.

[41] *Ibid.*,pp.153-5.

[42] *Ibid.*, p.xii.

[43] "The Scope of Renewal in the Spirit" in Emilio Castro (comp.), *The Wind of God's Spirit: Reflections on the Canberra Theme*, Geneva: WCC, 1990, pp.31-39.

[44] Gustavo Gutierrez, *A Theology of Liberation: History, Politics and Salvation*, London: SCM, 1973, p.118.

[45] *Ibid.*, p.118.

a break from our social class to "profound solidarity with those who suffer."[46] Conversion is thus not brought about by a "withdrawn or pious attitude" or "through purely interior and spiritual attitudes" but - in common with Bonhoeffer - by "thinking, feeling, living as Christ" for others.[47] Gutierrez thus affirms orthopraxis in reaction to orthodoxy, social action in place of piety and religion.

We can say that, in spite of differences, there are some common features in these views. *First*, conversion is a fundamental decision of one self whether it is initiated by God or within us. It is not an unconscious process which occurs beyond our intellect or reason. Although the spiritual process of regeneration and forgiving may take place beyond our understanding of empirical realm, the person acknowledges and realizes it. *Second*, the nature of conversion involves radical change of one's understanding of God, oneself and neighbours, whether these are simultaneous or not. In other words, through conversion one finds discontinuity of oneself from the past being, and a transformation takes place. It is a turning and changing of direction, which produces fruit of his new nature and new concept of self and identity in God. *Third*, conversion is an on-going movement or process rather than an once-for-all event. Although conversion can be seen as a decisive moment, it is understood as an event within the wider process of the work of God in human life, and these two are not separable. *Fourth*, conversion is a theological reality not only a phenomenological experience therefore it

may not be identified with personal feelings and emotions or sociological context alone. Rather it has to do with moral, intellectual and religious realization and awakening of self and direction. It is the divine act of God to bring humans into communion with him.

b) Ecumenical reinterpretations of conversion: Conversion as collective and ethical action, a simultaneous turning to God and to the world

The great missionary conference of Edinburgh 1910 took conversion as a central theme. The report of Commission IV, "The Missionary Message in Relation to Non-Christian Religions" was concerned primarily with the conversion of non-Christians to the Christian faith and included testimonies of some of these converts.[48] The central figure of the Conference, John Mott, in his closing address, had no hesitation in calling the delegates to "conquest" and "the expansion of Christianity."[49] But by the Tambaram-Madras conference of the International Missionary Council in 1938 such an approach was questioned. The report of the Layman's Foreign Mission Inquiry[50] led by W.E. Hocking and the book *Rethinking Missions*[51] he edited, were the subject of debate at Tambaram. Hocking not only shifted the ground away from individual conversion toward social involvement but also allowed for a christology that viewed Jesus as "the supreme religious teacher and exemplar of a life lived in union with God, whose example provides support for those who 'subsequently desire to carry out the same venture.'"[52] Such a christology was clearly at

---

[46] *Ibid.*, p.118

[47] *Ibid.*, p.118

[48] *The Missionary Message in Relation to Non-Christian Religions*. Report of Commission IV of the World Missionary Conference, Vol. 4, Edinburgh: Oliphant, Anderson & Ferrier for the WMC, 1910.

[49] "Closing Address" in *The History and Records of the World Missionary Conference*, Vol. 9, Edinburgh: Oliphant, Anderson & Ferrier for the WMC, 1910, pp.347-351.

[50] The Report was published in several volumes in New York and London by Harper & Brothers, 1933.

[51] W.E. Hocking, *Rethinking Missions: A Laymen's Inquiry After One Hundred Years*, New York: Harper & Brothers, 1933.

[52] Timothy Yates, *Christian Mission in the Twentieth Century*, Cambridge: Cambridge University Press, 1994, p.91.

odds with the Neo-orthodox approach of Hendrik Kraemer the author of *The Christian Message in a Non-Christian World*.[53] He condemned "the widely prevalent aversion to evangelization, to proselytism, to conversion, and the recommendation of 'sharing religious experience' or of social service as the only valid missionary methods," asserting that "the apostolic theocentric apprehension is the only valid Christian apprehension [therefore] the Christian Church has not only the right but also the duty to take conversion and evangelization as prime necessities for mankind."

The notion of conversion as a change of religion was to come under increasing challenge in the ecumenical movement in the years after World War II. The first challenge arose out of the realization of the complicity of the Christian church in the horrors of Nazi Germany. Secondly, the withdrawal of Britain and other European nations from the empire led to a less assertive tone and less certainty that Christian faith was best for everyone. It also meant that making converts became a politically sensitive issue and many countries became closed to such missionary effort. This challenge was further fuelled by entry of Eastern Orthodox churches into WCC from 1961. They had an aversion to proselytism borne of bitter experience of other Christian traditions seeking to convert their adherents.[54]

In response to the first challenge, the need for the conversion of the church, as underlined by Bonhoeffer became pre-eminent. At first the christo-centric theology of Barth seemed the only way to maintain a basis for conversion: the call was to Christ not to the church, the mission was God's, not the church's.[55] In 1952 the International Missionary Council defined mission as "witness," which understood as "proclamation, fellowship and service..."[56] "Service later became the dominant theme, especially under the influence of J.C. Hoekendijk.[57] The emphasis was on the responsibility of the convert not the privileges.[58] Interest in the fruit of mission in terms of measurable results gave way to preoccupation with the method and the attitude of the missionary, characterized by "presence and dialogue".[59] The goal of dialogue is emphatically not conversion but understanding and enriching one another.[60] In response to the second challenge, effort was made to reinterpret the meaning of conversion and to distinguish it from proselytism.[61] Emilio Castro made conversion a major theme of *The Ecumenical Review* and *The*

---

[53] Hendrik Kraemer, *The Christian Message in a Non-Christian World*, London: Edinburgh House Press, 1938.

[54] See the article by Petros Vassiliadis, "Mission and Proselytism: An Orthodox Understanding" in *International Review of Mission*, LXXXV/337, April 1996, where he strongly criticises the proselytising activities of Protestant groups. And also see *Common Witness: A Study Document of the Joint Working Group of the RCC and the WCC*, CWME Series No. 1, Geneva: WCC, 1980.

[55] *The Missionary Obligation of the Church*. Principle Statements and Findings of the International Missionary Council, Willingen, 1952, London: Edinburgh House Press, 1952, p.2.

[56] Bosch, *Transforming Mission*, p.511f.

[57] Hoekendijk pushed the concept of *missio Dei* to the point where mission became almost entirely secular, a process detailed by Bosch in *Transforming Mission*, 391f and Yates in *Christian Mission...*, p.196f.

[58] David Bosch summarises the new approach: "Conversion is... not the joining of a community in order to procure 'eternal salvation'... A Christian is not simply somebody who stands a better chance of being "saved," but a person who accepts the responsibility to serve God in this life..." *Transforming Mission*, p.488.

[59] Yates, *Christian Mission...* pp.133-162.

[60] Stanley J. Samartha, *Courage for Dialogue: Ecumenical Issues in Inter-Religious Relationships*, Geneva: WCC, 1981, pp.29-34.

[61] cf. Ans van der Bent, "The Concept of Conversion in the Ecumenical Movement: A Historical and Documentary Survey" in *The Ecumenical Review*, 44/4, Oct. 1992. Bent is concerned about the "unconverted elements" of our life and churches, and that the church re-examine the theological and psychological dimensions of conversion.

International Review of Mission.[62] He rejected any idea of the primacy of personal conversion over social responsibility, as it is a call for "the total community to change their way and comply with God's will," Castro thus brought conversion and social change together.[63] He pointed that conversion is not an improvement but a transformation which calls for the obedience in faith in Christ, and conversion is always relational therefore it is "incorporation into the saving and liberating mission of God in the world."[64] His concern was both ecumenical and social as he sees conversion as relational and dynamic rather than religious and static. Conversion for him was a change of attitude toward God and neighbour.

Philip Potter's argument, "Being turned to God is also being turned to one's fellow humans. Conversion entails the service of people," relates conversion to justice and peace, becoming "the new covenant people, a sign of the presence of the kingdom and a witness to the final promise of history."[65] Hyung-Kyu Park, with his strong *Minjung* theology background, persuasively comments that conversion is to dwell with the people around. Therefore conversion is "pilgrimage to liberation with Jesus and with the poor" to a community where justice and peace prevails and whence spiritual and other-worldliness of conversion is irrelevant to our context of injustice.[66] Jose Miguez Bonino sees conversion as discipleship. Through conversion God is incorporated into and participates in human beings which results in "the creation of a new creature."[67] He believes that conversion can take place through a communal praxis of the believers.[68] The common strand in all these approaches is that conversion a discipleship of personal commitment to acting according to divine ethics to bring about justice and peace in this world. Conversion is irrelevant if there is no discipleship for others since this is the heart of the reason for God's calling. Mary Motte sees conversion as "relocation, moving into another's space, and seeing life and all reality from that position" therefore "a way of living that opens to relocation and continuing change as one moves along the journey of life... the welcome of the other..."[69] There are suggestions of a further widening of the concept of conversion as "conversion to others and experience of the God of others."[70]

The important document "Mission and Evangelism: An Ecumenical Affirmation"[71] includes several paragraphs summarizing the ecumenical consensus on conversion. The proclamation of the Gospel includes "the announcement of a personal encounter... with the living Christ, receiving his forgiveness and making a personal acceptance of the call to discipleship and a life of service." But it

---

[62] Castro contributed an article on conversion the *ER* in 1967; devoted a whole issue to the subject as the editor of *IRM* in 1983; and in 1992 wrote a report on conversion in the *ER* as General Secretary of the CWME.

[63] *International Review of Mission*, LXXI/284, 1983, p.309. See also Emilio Castro, "Conversion and Social Transformation" in John C. Bennett, ed., *Christian Social Ethics in a Changing World: An Ecumenical Theological Inquiry*, London: SCM, 1966.

[64] "Report of the General Secretary: A Call to Conversion," *The Ecumenical Review*, 44/4, Oct., 1992, p.503.

[65] Philip Potter, "Turning to Freedom and Fullness" in *International Review of Mission*, LXXI/284, 1983, p.313.

[66] Hyung-Kyu Park, "Conversion as a Pilgrimage to Liberation" in *International Review of Mission*, LXXI/284, 1983, p.384.

[67] Jose Miguez Bonino, "Conversion, New Creature and Commitment" in *International Review of Mission*, LXXI/284, 1983, p.331.

[68] Bonino, "Conversion..." p.332.

[69] Mary Motte, "Conversion: A Missiological Perspective," *The Ecumenical Review*, 44/4, Oct. 1992, pp.453-454.

[70] Maria Clara Lucchetti Bingemer, "Preface - Third World Theologies: Conversion to Others" in K.C. Abraham,ed., *Third World Theologies: Commonalities & Divergence*, New York: Orbis, 1990, xiii.

[71] *International Review of Mission*, LXXI/284, Oct. 1982.

recognizes that many have very limited possibilities for personal decision-making (para.10). The statement stresses that though conversion may take on varied forms depending on the situation, it "happens in the midst of our historical reality and incorporates the totality of our life" and therefore always involves responsibility to one's neighbour (para.11). Conversion is a conscious decision that is endorsed by the Holy Spirit who brings about new birth. "Conversion [is] a dynamic and ongoing process" involving a new relationship with God and a new fellowship as well as a turning away from old securities. The change of life style is not only individual but also collective on the part of nations changing "from war to peace, from injustice to justice, from racism to solidarity, from hate to love..." (para.12). Lamenting the fact that "the life. of churches as well as... individual Christians" is a major obstacle to confessing Jesus Christ by non-Christians, the document declares that "the call to conversion should begin with those who do the calling" (para.13). The section concludes by stressing the benefits of conversion in this life in terms of giving meaning, endurance and assurance that death has no final power (para.13).

The ecumenical understanding of conversion could be summarized thus: *First*, the focus of Christian conversion should be on the kingdom of God rather than the church as an institution. *Second*, conversion is a two-way simultaneous action of turning to God and at the same time to the world, not one after the other. *Third*, the collective and ethical dimensions of conversion rather take precedence over the personal and spiritual ones. *Fourth*, the emphasis is on the conversion of Christians rather than conversion for non-Christians. *Fifth*, "peace" (between the religious communities) and "justice" in this world are important in understanding conversion. *Sixth*, transfer from one religious community to the other is an irrelevant issue since conversion is ethical rather than religious. *Seventh*, conversion has a positive aspect of turning to (God and neighbour) rather than a negative aspect of turning away (from sin).

c) *Evangelical responses to ecumenical discussion: Conversion as a transcendental reality that changes the whole of human life, intimately related to spiritual salvation*

Evangelism in the sense of calling individuals to respond to the gospel has always been close to the heart of the evangelical movement, so they had a strong interest in the traditional meaning of "conversion." Consequently they have not readily accepted ecumenical attempts to reinterpret the term or to avoid it altogether. This was first clearly articulated from North America at "The Congress on the Church's World Wide Mission" convened at Wheaton, Illinois in April 1966.[72] "The Wheaton Declaration" included a section on "Mission - and Proselytism." Equating proselytism with making converts, the Congress noted that the word was being used by "some religious groups and nationalistic forces," "in reaction to the dynamic witness of evangelicals." While repudiating "forced conversions" and use of "unethical means" to achieve conversion, it declared that "all followers of Christ must disciple their fellowmen" and "When we seek the conversion of unregenerate men, even though they may be attached to some church or other religion, we are fulfilling our biblical mandate."[73] It is clearly stated in the Declaration that those who are not converted are destined to go to hell: "We believe that if men are not born again they will be subject to eternal separation from a righteous,

---

[72] Harold Lindsell, ed., *The Church's Worldwide Mission*. Proceedings of the Congress on the Church's Worldwide Mission at Wheaton College, 1966, Waco, Texas: Word Books, 1966.

[73] *Ibid.*, p.225f.

holy God."[74] It opposes the "universalism" of the ecumenical movement.[75]

Anticipating a preoccupation with social issues at the forthcoming WCC Assembly at Uppsala, 1968, rather than a concern for "that great number of men, at least two billion, who have either never heard of Jesus Christ or have no real chance to believe in Him as Lord and Saviour," Donald McGavran published an article in which he charged that the WCC would "betray" the unevangelized.[76] He posed a "central question" to agents of mission: "How many of the lost are we bringing back to the fold? How obedient are we to our Lord's command to disciple the nations? How faithful are we to the mission of God, the mission to which our Lord gave His life."[77] McGavran believed that the drive to call for conversion had all but evaporated from the ecumenical movement. For many Evangelicals he was justified by subsequent events at Uppsala that, while incorporating some of the critique, consistently played down "world evangelization" in favour of "humanization". Disillusioned with the WCC, Evangelicals - led by Billy Graham and John Stott - convened probably the most representative evangelical gathering ever at Lausanne in Switzerland in 1974.[78] But nevertheless the carefully drafted Lausanne Covenant[79] reaffirmed in several places the need for mission to call for conversion:

To proclaim Jesus as 'the Saviour of the world' is not to affirm that all religions offer salvation in Christ. Rather it is to proclaim God's love for a world of sinners and to invite all men to respond to Him as Saviour and Lord in the wholehearted personal commitment of repentance and faith. (para. 3)

Evangelism... is the proclamation of the historical biblical Christ as Saviour and Lord, with a view to persuading people to come to Him personally and so be reconciled to God... to deny themselves, take up their cross, and identify themselves with His new community". (para. 4)

The goal [of world evangelization] should be... that every person should have the opportunity to hear, understand, and receive the good news.... the result will be the rise of churches deeply rooted in Christ and closely related to their culture. (paras. 9 & 10)

John Stott, architect of the Lausanne Covenant, explains the problems of conversion in mission,[80] stresses the importance of conversion as participating "in Christ" to receive the reconciliation which God offers in Christ. He uses the word "conversion" to imply the human response that involves repentance and faith, a conscious act and process rather than event. But this is always in relation to "regeneration" which is what God does in the

---

[74] *Ibid.*, p. 221f.

[75] *Ibid.*, p. 223f

[76] Donald McGavran, "Will Uppsala Betray the Two Billion?" in Donald McGavran , (ed.), *The Eye of the Storm: The Great Debate in Mission*, Waco, Texas: Word Books, 1972, pp.233-241. First published in *Church Growth Bulletin*, Special Uppsala Issue, May 1968.

[77] McGavran, "Will Uppsala Betray...," p.238.

[78] Lausanne was remarkable not only for its statement of evangelical solidarity - The Lausanne Covenant - but even more so for the extent to which it listened to ecumenical criticism and to Christian leaders from the Third World.

[79] J.D. Douglas, ed., *Let the Earth Hear His Voice*. International Congress on World Evangelization, Lausanne, 1974, Minneapolis: World Wide Publications, 1975.

[80] John Stott, *Christian Mission in the Modern World*, Downers Grove: Inter-Varsity Press, 1975, pp.109-110. The problems mentioned are: social snobbery over "evangelical enthusiasm," the association with proselytism, and the rise of syncretism and universalism.

process.[81] He rejects the idea of conversion as a psychological experience since God is part of this regeneration process. He also argues for the importance of community in conversion, but this is not purely a human community because it has a divine element. Conversion is thus both "turning away from the world" and at the same time "turning toward the world".[82]

Lesslie Newbigin, although very much part of the ecumenical movement, takes a stance on conversion which is closer to the evangelicals because he emphasizes the transcendent, divine dimension, conversion as a turning to God. He sees a certain naivety in modern society's rejection of any form of absolute truth and encourages "confidence in the Gospel" in the context of religiously pluralist society.[83] He points out that "all understanding of reality involves a commitment, a venture of faith," in this sense conversion is "radical".[84] In common with the ecumenical emphasis, he stresses that conversion is not merely "inward" but happening "always in the context of concrete decisions at the given historical moment."[85] It means, "being turned round in order to recognize and participate in the dawning reality of God's reign."[86] For Newbigin, conversion is simultaneously an "inward" and "outward" process, "a total change of direction" affecting "all areas of life." He rejects two stages of conversion, first religious and second ethical.[87] For him conversion is "primarily and essentially a personal event"[88] but it must involve joining the Christian community. He believes that conversion has a strong sense of "discontinuity" with the past.[89] It is a commitment to Christ and to follow him "with all who are so committed."[90] Conversion implies a decisive moment *and* a belonging. Newbigin understands that conversion is both personal and communal, both religious and ethical: these are not and should not be separated.

Applying cultural anthropology to conversion has been a major concern for recent missiologists, particularly among North American evangelical scholars. Donald McGavran developed his use of anthropology and statistics in the study of conversion in the light of his experience of mass conversions in India in the 1930s. Advocating the importance of cultural considerations in Christian mission, he promoted the "homogeneous unit principle." This points out that "men like to become Christians without crossing racial, linguistic, or class barriers."[91] He sees conversions as people movements which "result from the joint decision of a number of individuals ... all from the same people, which

---

[81] Stott, *Christian Mission...*, pp.109-116; see also Millard J. Erickson, *Christian Theology*, unabridged, one vol. ed., Grand Rapids: Baker Book House, 1983, 933-942. Erickson sees conversion as a combination of repentance and faith (e.g. Mark 1:15) and for him, repentance is not indispensable, it is a prerequisite for salvation. Faith is twofold: "giving credence to affirmations and trusting in God". And also see Donald G. Bloesch, in his article "Conversion" in Walter A. Elwell, ed., *Evangelical Dictionary of Theology*, Grand Rapids: Baker Book House, 1984, pp.272-273 Bloesch argues that conversion is a "sign" not a "condition" for our justification and it is both an event and a process, both personal and social, and only through God's intervention is it possible for us to be converted.

[82] Stott, *Christian Mission...*, p.121.

[83] Lesslie Newbigin, *The Gospel in a Pluralist Society*, London: SPCK, 1989, p.244.

[84] *Ibid.*, p.148.

[85] *Ibid.*, p. 93f.

[86] *Ibid.*,, p.96.

[87] Lesslie Newbigin, *The Open Secret: An Introduction to the Theology of Mission*, Grand Rapids: William B. Eerdmans, 1995, p.135.

[88] *Ibid.*, p.139.

[89] Newbigin, *The Finality of Christ*, pp. 89-90.

[90] Newbigin, *Open Secret*, p.140.

[91] Donald McGavran, *Understanding Church Growth*, Grand Rapids: William B. Eerdmans, 1970, p.198.

enables them to become Christians without social dislocation, ...and form Christian churches made up exclusively of members of that people."[92] He also argues that resistance from other religions to Christianity is not theological but socio-cultural, and "if social resistance can be overcome, the Gospel can be heard."[93] Therefore conversion, for him, is a series of multi-individual, mutually interdependent events. McGavran's interpretation of conversion as a people movement was welcomed and accepted by many contemporary missionaries but also caused controversy.[94] It is important to note that McGavran affirms the diversity of Christianity expressed according to the cultural patterns of people group, thus conversion pattern should be different from one group to another. Taking McGavran's view further, Charles Kraft, in his book *Christianity in Culture*, deals with conversion and sees that "the real issues are not theological but cultural."[95] He points out, first of all, that there is evidence that "no single set of specific forms" were imposed in the Bible account.[96] He sees conversion as "conscious allegiance to God," "a dynamic interaction between God and human beings," and the process of "maturation".[97] He also stresses that

conversion should take place "in community" and "in keeping with the culture." According to his theory of "dynamic equivalence," conversion must take different forms in different cultures if its meaning is to be preserved.[98] Kraft explores the possibility of breaking the barrier of the "form" of conversion that was established by Western Christianity in a particular cultural setting, and therefore cannot and should not be applied in any other cultural context.

However, Paul Hiebert, with much experience of missionary work in South India, sharply disagrees with Kraft on the issue of forms and meanings in Christian communication, saying that forms are often so integrated with meanings that it is difficult to separate them from one another. For Hiebert it is not sufficient to change the "form of conversion," its meaning also must be redefined in the encounter with another culture. Hiebert then tries to relate conversion and culture by introducing a "bounded set" and "fuzzy set" theory.[99] He sees that Western culture is dominated by the idea of the bounded set in which everything is in a clearly defined set pattern.[100] He advocates the "centered set" as the most appropriate to conversion. This has to do with relationship with the centre (Christ), "things

---

[92] McGavran, *Understanding Church Growth*, p.297. He quotes Latourette who points out the problem of nineteenth century Protestant individualism and says, "more and more we must dream in terms of winning groups, not merely individuals..."

[93] *Ibid.*, p.299.

[94] See Rene Padilla, *Mission Between the Times*, Grand Rapids: William B. Eerdmans, 1985, pp.142-169; David Bosch, "Church Growth Missiology", *Missionalia* 1, April 1988, 13-24; Lesslie Newbigin, *The Open Secret: An Introduction to the Theology of Mission*, Grand Rapids: William B. Eerdmans, 1995, pp.121-159; Peter Cotterell, *Mission and Meaninglessness: The Good News in a World of Suffering and Disorder*, London: SPCK, 1990, pp.152-169.

[95] Charles Kraft, *Christianity in Culture: A Study in Dynamic Biblical Theologizing in Cross-Cultural Perspective*, Maryknoll, NY: Orbis, 1979, p.329.

[96] *Ibid.*, pp. 124-8.

[97] *Ibid.*, pp. 334-8.

[98] *Ibid.*, pp. 344.

[99] Paul Hiebert, *Anthropological Reflections on Missiological Issues*, Grand Rapids: Baker Books, 1994, pp.107-136. Although the term "fuzzy" sets was introduced by Lofti Asker Zadeh in his article "Fuzzy Sets," *Information and Control* 8, 1965, pp.338-353, Hiebert developed the idea further in his anthropological explanation of culture and conversion. A fuzzy set has no sharp boundaries. Instead there are degrees of inclusion, categories flow into one another pp.111, 118.

[100] *Ibid.*, p.113.

related to the center belong to the set, and those not related to the center do not."[101] He sees that relationship to the centre is the key issue in conversion and believes that, according to the direction, he can draw a boundary. He concludes that "...conversion often looks more like a process than a point, and the church more like a fuzzy body made up of people with different degrees of commitment to Christ."[102] Hiebert makes a significant contribution to the study of conversion by pointing out that relationship to Christ is the vital issue, and not the socio-cultural and religious boundaries that define a person's conversion. In other words, a person's direction "toward" and relationship "with" Christ is the key concept not whether a person is in a particular religious boundary either because s/he was born there or because s/he moved into that boundary.

More recently, evangelicals have given great attention to questions of culture and history in conversion. Andrew Walls sees conversion as "translation" which means "application of new material and standards to a system of thought and conduct already in place and functioning".[103] This is not substitution, but transformation. Conversion is an incarnation, an "opening up of the functioning system of personality, intellect, emotions, relationship to the new meaning, to the expression of Christ"[104] and it is a continuous "turning" to God. On the issue of culture and identity in conversion, he sees the importance of belonging[105] in understanding conversion in the light of cultural diversity. Referring to Kwame

Bediako's work,[106] Walls also points out that Christianity needs to convert to the past, that is the culture and history of the converts needs to be integrated into their Christian faith.[107]

Evangelicals retain a strong conversion theology; they have reinterpreted conversion in several ways. *First*, the understanding has moved away from the early evangelical notion of a "radical change of one's past through a decisive experience of conversion" to more a more integrated understanding. Conversion is not a once-for-all decision but a continual "repenting" and "believing". In evangelical understanding, "change of heart", "change of religion" and "change of action" are all-important dimensions of conversion, but they tend to make "change of heart" primary, understanding that this will bring about the other changes. *Second*, there is great concern to be sensitive to "culture" as a factor in conversion. Conversion as traditionally understood and practised was a product of Western Christianity and cannot be applied unchanged to a different culture. Western patterns of conversion are now regarded by many as inappropriate. Instead there is a re-evaluation of the form of conversion in order to find a suitable model which functions in another culture to bring about a change of heart, orientation toward Christ and a personal relationship with Him. *Third*, there is an emphasis on the importance of the community in conversion. Evangelicals increasingly recognise that conversion in non-Western cultures is not merely an individual

---

[101] *Ibid.*, p.123.

[102] *Ibid.*, p.134.

[103] Andrew F. Walls, *The Missionary Movement in Christian History: Studies in the Transmission of Faith*, Edinburgh: T & T Clark, 1996, p.28. Also published in Philip C. Stine (ed.), *Bible Translation and the Spread of the Church*, Leiden: E.J. Brill, 1990, pp.24-39. See also Lamin Sanneh, *Translating the Message: The Missionary Impact on Culture*. Maryknoll: Orbis, 1989.

[104] Walls, *The Missionary Movement...*, p.28.

[105] Walls points out that most of non-Western culture has a notion of sense of identity driven from the community which can be describe as "I belong, therefore I exist". Walls, *The Missionary Movement...*, p.45.

[106] Kwame Bediako, *Theology and Identity: The Impact of Culture upon Christian Thought in the Second Century and in Modern Africa*, Regnum Studies in Mission, Oxford: Regnum Books, 1992.

[107] Walls, *The Missionary Movement...*, p.52f.

decision or a personal matter but very much to do with society. Conversion of whole communities may be more desirable than extraction of converts from their society. The church is not necessarily a religious institution or an alternative society but a community of believers in Christ. Therefore evangelicals are struggling to find ways to bring about a Christian community without disturbing cultural integrity or social peace, and while preserving the identity of the people group.

Although evangelicals focus on cultural aspects of conversion and convincingly argue for the need of re-defining conversion according to the cultural context, the question of "change of religion" remains. This is a particularly pertinent question in India today. Consider a Hindu born into the religious culture of Hinduism: for him, religion is part and parcel of culture. Can s/he stay in the Hindu community and be a believer in Christ? Does a Hindu need to be a Christian in order to be saved? What do we mean by Christian - is it not also a cultural as well as religious term? Is it possible to insist on "change of religion" without disconnecting him/her from Hindu society? Can the Christian community transcend other communities without being imperialistic? As Ray Anderson says, "[Evangelical] theologians have yet to restate the case for conversion to Christ in compelling and convincing terms."[108] The question of conversion thus continues to be a pressing one for evangelicals.

Socio-anthropological Perspectives

Sociologists and anthropologists have paid considerable attention to the study of conversion in recent years and have broadened its understanding.[109] One cannot understand any religious phenomenon without considering its social and anthropological environment, and conversion is no exception. In this section we shall consider debates that have taken place in the field of socio-anthropology.

Conversion as a means to re-conceptualizing group members' social identity, and a multi-individual and mutually interdependent decision that gives a group of people a new identity

Max Weber[110] was one of the first to see religion as a social phenomenon and therefore open it to sociological investigation. Weber does not use conversion as a category but he does see a religious community as arising out of "routinization" of a prophetic movement, which is "a process whereby either the prophet himself or his disciples secure the permanence of his preaching and the congregation's distribution of grace."[111] As the congregation develops after the prophet is gone, the need to maintain and enlarge the community leads to a threefold development by the priests: closing the canon in order to protect themselves from other intellectual doctrines; setting dogmas, particularly of soteriology, so that their community is unique and superior; and making it difficult for the congregation to transfer to another congregation by emphasizing the importance of membership.[112] For Weber, conversion needs to be understood in the light of the socio-political needs of religious leaders who want to keep and expand their congregation. He further argues that only Christianity developed a "comprehensive, binding and systematically rationalized dogmatics of a theoretical type

---

[108] Ray S. Anderson, "Evangelical Theology" in David F. Ford (ed.) *The Modern Theologians: An Introduction to Christian Theology in the Twentieth Century*, 2nd ed., Oxford: Blackwell Publishers, 1997, p.495.

[109] cf. Lewis R. Rambo, "Current Research on Religious Conversion" in *Religious Studies Review* 8, 1982, pp.146-159.

[110] Max Weber, *The Sociology of Religion*, trans. Ephraim Fischoff , Boston: Beacon Press, 1956, pp.60-74.

[111] *Ibid.*, p. 60.

[112] *Ibid.*, pp.69-71.

concerning cosmological matters, the soteriological *mythos* (Christology), and priestly authority (the sacraments)" because of the strength of priestly organization and its considerable political autonomy.[113]

In his detailed examination Robert Hefner[114] discusses some weakness in Weber's approach due to the underestimation of the complexity of "traditional religion" and the potential locality of "world religion." On the issue of prophets, Hefner rejects the idea that the prophetic role is unique to world religions since the prophets come from their own context and also prophetic revelation is not confined to world religions. He also argues that rationalization of the world religions need not necessarily provide the rationality of individual followers of the world religion. On the contrary, the traditional religion often meets people's deepest needs and desires. He sees world religions as the "longest lasting of civilization's primary institutions"[115] which have been remarkable self-sustaining systems drawing people from traditional religions. He argues that conversion is "not a deeply systematic reorganization of personal meanings but an adjustment in self-identification through the at least nominal acceptance of religious actions or beliefs deemed more fitting, useful, or true." It is "acceptance of a new locus of self-definition" and a "reference point for one's identity".[116] He further argues that conversion is not related to "ultimate conditions of existence", but to "commitment to a new kind of moral authority and a new or re-conceptualized social identity."[117] Moreover, religious conversion "always involves such authoritative acceptance of as yet unknown or unknowable truth."[118] He then agrees that the transcendental aspect of world religions is significant but only because it is linked to successful institutions, the combination of doctrine and social-organization is what distinguishes them from other religions.[119] For him the "problem of dignity and self-identification in a pluralized and politically imbalanced world lies at the heart of many conversion histories."[120] He then argues, "in such a context a religion that promises a new measure of dignity and access to the values and rewards of the larger society may find a ready following among peoples previously committed to local ways."[121] He sees that world religions survived by conversion - "defining the boundaries and membership of religious community; establishing the relationship of religion to political power; and controlling belief among a laity ignorant of or uninterested in official doctrine."[122] However, Hefner's understanding of conversion mainly deals with how and why local religions and beliefs merged into Christianity. It therefore cannot explain why there are conversions between the followers of one world religion to another, and why Christians "convert" to pagan activities or new religious movements.

---

[113] *Ibid.*, p.73.

[114] Robert Hefner, "Introduction: World Building and the Rationality of Conversion" in Robert W. Hefner (ed.), *Conversion to Christanity: Historical and Anthropological Perspectives on a Great Transformation*, Berkeley: University of California Press, 1993, pp.7-14.

[115] *Ibid.*, p.3.

[116] *Ibid.*, p.17.

[117] *Ibid.*, p.17.

[118] *Ibid.*, p.18.

[119] *Ibid.*, pp. 19-20.

[120] *Ibid.*, p.25.

[121] *Ibid.*, p. 27.

[122] *Ibid.*, p. 31.

Robin Horton[123] derived his controversial theory of conversion from examining "breakaway" African churches in Nigeria. He pointed out the weak analysis of Weber and others' arguments that "pre-Christian gods make little reference to regularity or predictability" and their tendency to equate a "multiplicity of gods with incoherence, and a single god with coherence."[124] In this theory, he divides African cosmology into two: the side that relates to the microcosm of the local community and its environment and the side which relates to the world as a whole, the macrocosm. In the first we find the lesser spirits and in the second the supreme being.[125] The relative importance of these two cosmologies in an individual depends on the extent of interaction of that person with the wider community. Horton goes on to show that deepening encounter with the macrocosm will lead to development of the macrocosmic side of the traditional cosmology. In specific terms he concludes, "acceptance of Islam and Christianity [in Africa] is due as much to development of the traditional cosmology in response to other features of the modern situation as it is to the activities of the missionaries."[126] And further, world religions are accepted only "where they happen to coincide with the response of the traditional cosmology to other, non-missionary, factors of the modern situation."[127] Therefore Islam and Christianity are merely "catalysts — i.e. stimulators and accelerators of changes which were 'in the air' anyway" - and not necessarily the end product.[128] So for Horton, people accept world religions not because of the attraction of the philosophy or ideology behind them. Rather, they serve the function of facilitating a necessary transition from a largely microcosmic worldview to the macrocosmology of modernity.

Eugene Gallagher[129] believes that Horton is right in looking at conversion in the light of cultural history. He believes Horton "blends an appreciation of the active self, with its search to make sense of change in terms of traditional views of the world, with a recognition of the powerful influence of long-term cultural and social trends."[130] In doing so, Horton provides an explanation of conversion not only based on psychology or sociology but also on cultural history, and "Horton offers an example of the integration of personal experience, individual deliberation, social context and historical development into a coherent explanation."[131] However, Humphrey Fisher[132] has questioned Horton's findings, by examining the phenomenon of Muslim conversion in Africa. He argues that Horton "over-estimated the survival... of original African elements of religion; ... [and] under-estimated the willingness and ability of Africans to make even rigorous Islam and Christianity their own."[133] He believes that Christianity and Islam

---

[123] Robin Horton, "African Conversion," *Africa*, XLI/2, April 1971, pp.85-108. See also his articles - "On the Rationality of Conversion: Part I," *Africa* 45/3, 1975, pp.219-235; "On the Rationality of Conversion: Part II," *Africa* 45/4, 1975, 373-399.

[124] *Ibid.*, p.98.

[125] *Ibid.*, p.101.

[126] *Ibid.*, p.103.

[127] *Ibid.*, p.104.

[128] *Ibid.*, p.104. See also his article "On Rationality of Conversion: Part I" in *Africa*, 45/3, 1975, 219-235, where he elaborates his argument further.

[129] Eugene Gallagher, *Expectation and Experience: Explaining Religious Conversion*, Atlanta: Scholars Press, 1990.

[130] *Ibid.*, p.104.

[131] *Ibid.*, p.106.

[132] Humphrey Fisher, "Conversion Reconsidered: Some Historical Aspects of Religious Conversion in Black Africa", *Africa*, XLIII/1 (Jan. 1973), pp.27-40.

[133] *Ibid.*, p.27.

played a much more active role in changing people's world-view. It was not that, in the process of moving into the "macrocosm," Islam played the role of catalyst by way of conversion. Rather it was through conversion that Africans began to move into the "macrocosm." He further argues that the tropical African attitude to Islam was not the conversion but rather adhesion. Although Islam in Africa did not demand radical change of Africans, nevertheless in the long run though Islam Africans were significantly changed in their cultural patterns.[134] He rejects the conclusions of an anthropo-social approach to conversion by adding a religious and historical dimension to conversion.[135]

It should be noted that, Jean and John Comaroff[136] have questioned the Weberian use of conversion as an analytic category of sociology. They argue that modern Protestant conversion is "an ideologically saturated" European construct used by the missionaries to interpret the results of their activity.[137] Citing Horton's work, they ask how well the term conversion grasps "the highly variable, usually gradual, often implicit, and demonstrably 'syncretic' manner in which the social identities, cultural styles, and ritual practices of African peoples were transformed by the evangelical encounter."[138] Africans, they suggest, were not constrained by the Western cultural assumptions undergirding the concept of conversion such as "that adherence to one religion excluded involvement in all others" - hence the need for

a civilising mission as well to inculcate such values. They conclude that since "the significance of conversion to Africans themselves cannot be assumed to conform to European preconceptions." Its usefulness in interpreting African experience is seriously undermined.[139] However, by interpreting conversion in relation to ideological problems, they neglect to appreciate people who experienced conversion as they made a conscious, intellectual and deliberate decision. The Comaroffs see conversion as if it is an ideological framework imposed upon Africans who had no choice but to accept it without their own reflection and evaluation. Certainly culture and logic are different from one society to another, but one can analyse this with certain tools since human societies have much more continuity and unity as well as interaction with one another than the Comaroffs seem to suggest.

In summary of these arguments it may be said: *First*, conversion in religious organizations has to do with extending or keeping its congregation. As Christianity became a world religion, there was a need to set a clear boundary by closing the canon, setting dogmas, and defining the privileges of membership or judgements for losing membership. Conversion was used to enforce the social structure of Christianity. *Second*, conversion is the reconceptualizing of a person's social identity as one enters into a society. Christianity has provided a distinctive transcendental doctrine as well as

---

[134] *Ibid.*, pp.33-4.

[135] See also Carol V. McKinney, "Conversion to Christianity: A Bajju Case Study" in *Missiology*, XXII/2, April 1994, pp.148-149 where she uses theories of Horton and Fisher but without giving her critique on them. Also Robert Hefner in his *Conversion to Christianity* sees the Horton-Fisher debate as a struggle between "intellectualist voluntarism and structural determinism" p.23. He criticises Horton's view of conversion as neglecting political and structural influences (from the western, and better organized social stucture) on conversion.

[136] Jean and John Comaroff, *Of Revelation and Revolution: Christianity, Colonialism, and Consciousness in South Africa*, Vol. 1, Chicago & London: University of Chicago Press, 1991.

[137] *Ibid.*, pp.249, 251.

[138] *Ibid.*, pp.249f.

[139] *Ibid.*, pp.250f.

social organization. Therefore people in search of self-dignity and identity joined it. In this process conversion has been a vital part of the Christian life, as a new member needs assurance. *Third*, there have been discussions on whether people themselves are the subject of conversion or whether they are just participating in a conversion movement as a passive object. And whether Christianity plays a vital role in conversion or if it simply serves the role of catalyst for historical and social change. *Fourth*, for some sociologists, conversion is not relevant at all since it is peculiar to Christianity (and Islam), which have been created to meet the need of a particular context of history, and thus it does not fit into the world view of most non-western cultures and religions.

Psychological Perspectives

The psychological study of religion has paid much attention to conversion because it is an "observable and behavioural phenomenon."[140] The focus has been largely "internal emotional dynamics, behaviour, self-identity, and impact of interpersonal and intellectual influences on the individual."[141] There have been many studies done on religious conversion[142] but here we shall limit ourselves to psychological perspectives on Christian conversion; namely psychology of religion and socio-culturally integrated psychology.

a) Perspectives from psychology of religion: Conversion as a subconscious process to meet a personal psychological crisis and an expression of a person's attempt to find an inner contentment while facing the wider complexities of life

Edwin Starbuck, in his book, *The Psychology of Religion,*[143] focused entirely on the empirical study of the conversion experience of Christians. He believed that "the psychology of religion sees in the scattered facts of religious experience an evidence that spiritual forces are at work." He believed that examining these facts objectively and in detail would enhance religion.[144] He assumed "religion is a real fact of human experience, and develops according to law."[145] On the basis of this conviction, Starbuck carried out extensive research on various aspects of Christian conversion experience.[146] He found that conversion is a distinctively adolescent phenomenon because of psychological and some physiological factors. He believed conversion occurred when a young person became aware of the wider world and had a sudden increment in ability to reason, and also when a person experienced a physiological transformation such as puberty.[147] Therefore he saw conversion as "primarily unselfing" and "the first birth of the individual into his own little world" as he becomes a conscious being. It is a "period of self-consciousness," moving "from a limited world of existence to a larger world of being", and the "surrender of personal will to be guided by the larger force".[148] For Starbuck, conversion is motivated by the "forces in human life and its surroundings which tend to break the unity and harmony of consciousness; and its unity once

---

[140] Wayne E. Oates, "Conversion: Sacred and Secular" in Walter E. Conn, *Conversion: Perspectives on Personal and Social Transformation*, New York: Alba House, 1978, p.149.

[141] Lewis R. Rambo, *Understanding Religious Conversion*, New Haven: Yale University Press, 1993, p.10.

[142] See Larry D. Shinn, "Who Gets to Define Religion? - The Conversion/Brainwashing Controversy," *Religious Studies Review*, 19/3, July 1993, pp.196-198.

[143] Edwin Starbuck, *The Psychology of Religion*, New York: The Walter Scott Publishing, 1914.

[144] *Ibid.,* p.6.

[145] *Ibid.,* p.16.

[146] *Ibid.,* pp.21-27. Starbuck analysed questionnaires of more than 2000 people from different backgrounds.

[147] *Ibid.,* pp.29-48.

[148] *Ibid.,* p.146.

destroyed, the contrast between what is, and what might be, gives birth to ideals and sets two selves in sharp opposition to each other." This then will lead a person to struggle and desire an alternative answer.[149] Although there was some weakness in his methodology and interpretation, this was one of the earliest scientific attempts to discover the psychological aspects of conversion which had till then been confined to the area of religious and theological studies. His study opened the possibility of looking at the phenomenon of conversion as part of personal psychological trends of maturity.

William James, who also made a significant contribution to the study of the psychology of conversion at the turn of the century,[150] endorsed the works of Starbuck,[151] and used his theories as a starting point for his own argument. He saw that individual experiences are first hand information and therefore have prime importance in the study of the subject. He sees the importance of self-surrender in conversion[152] and this occurs not only in a "conscious process of thought and will" but also in "subconscious incubation and maturing of motives deposited by the experiences of life."[153] In this manner, conversion is seen by theologians as due to "direct supernatural operations of Deity," but by psychologists as due

to the "subconscious" which does not transcend the individual's personality.[154] He also believed that the whole phenomenon of regeneration is a natural process, more or less "divine in its fruits".[155] Therefore he rejected the idea of sudden conversion as divine interaction and the idea that it is not in degree but in kind.[156] He saw it not as the presence of a divine miracle but as a psychological one.[157] In his opinion there were two ways to get rid of undesirable affections: either "an opposite affection should over-poweringly break over us" or "we give-up".[158] In this process complete division is established - between old and new life. And in this understanding of the human being as composed of "divided-soul," conversion is experiencing a "state of assurance" characterized by "a passion of willingness, of acquiescence, of admiration," a "sense of perceiving truths," and an "objective change".[159] For James, conversion is a subconscious psychological experience where a person, giving up him/herself, acquires a sense of satisfaction, and in turn, this experience is interpreted by others as a divine activity.

Robert Thouless[160] sees that psychological studies on conversion have been influenced by Freud's system of psycho-analysis.[161] He points out that although Starbuck's study has

---

[149] *Ibid.*, p.155.

[150] William James, *The Varieties of Religious Experience*, Cambridge, Mass.: Harvard University Press, 1985, which is a collection of papers delivered at Edinburgh University in 1901 and 1902.

[151] James wrote the preface for Starbuck's book in 1899.

[152] *Ibid.*, p. 173.

[153] *Ibid.*, p. 188.

[154] *Ibid.*, p. 174.

[155] *Ibid.*, p. 188.

[156] cf. James, *The Varieties of Religious Experience*, p. 187.

[157] "Sudden conversion is connected with the possession of an active subliminal self". James, *The Varieties of Religious Experience*, p. 195.

[158] *Ibid.*, p. 174.

[159] James, *The Varieties of Religious Experience*, pp.201-202.

[160] Robert H. Thouless, "The Psychology of Conversion" in Walter E. Conn, *Conversion: Perspectives on Personal and Social Transformation*, New York: Alba House, 1978, pp.137-147.

[161] Thouless, "The Psychology of Conversion", p.139. Thouless explains that he "considers that there is an active process of repression by which that which is painful or incompatible with the purposes of the main stream of consciousness is banished into a region called the unconscious from which it may influence behavior or the conscious process of thought but cannot be voluntarily made a part of the conscious stream of thought."

considerable weakness,[162] it nevertheless raised the important question of the psychological reasons for adolescent conversion. From this, in line with James, he points out that the core factor for such conversion is the "system of conflicts which result from the emergence into consciousness of the impulses connected with the sex instinct" and even, he suggests, "psychic change at adolescence which has been given a religious coloring."[163] However, he goes on to say that, while adolescent conversion is largely to do with change from a non-religious to a religious attitude, there is another dimension of "mystical conversion" which is to do with change "from a merely conventional acceptance of the socially approved pattern of religious life to an attitude in which the religious motive becomes dominant and in which religious belief and behaviour become more personal and even possibly idiosyncratic."[164] For him, mystical conversion has more religious elements than that of the adolescent one as well as a more positive attitude of searching for new concepts and meaning, but both of them are the result of an unsatisfactory condition of the psychological dimension of personal life which drives a person to act.

Led by James, the school of psychology of religion has focused on several points: *First*, conversion is primarily a psychological experience, a subconscious process which leads towards a unification of the divided self. *Second*, conversion is conditioned, more by psychological, biological and physiological aspects of human life, rather than outside information the person acquires through ideological, intellectual or religious dimensions. *Third*, conversion occurs in line with a person's psychological changes which are also influenced by his/her process of growing up. As a person moves from his/her small world of self to the appreciation of the wider world, the person experiences psychological stress and struggle. Conversion is the expression of a person's attempt toward an inner settlement as he/she encounters the complexity of life. *Fourth*, religion plays the role of catalyst, channelling the person's psychological struggle and desire through a rationalized ideal. In conversion, the process is psychological but it is interpreted as religious.

b) Psychology with socio-cultural perspectives: Conversion as both a personal and communal experience and conditioned by both subconscious dimension of human self and conscious dimension of an act of human will

Recently, psychologists have been challenged to include socio-cultural perspectives in their analysis of the human mind. Such psychologists insist that the approach of James and others is limited in their analysis of conversion because modern social science has uncovered the pertinent influence of the socio-cultural environment on a person's conversion. They try to bridge the psychological and the socio-cultural to formulate an integrated understanding of conversion.

Wayne Oates[165] identifies Starbuck's theory of conversion as "rapidation of growth".[166] He finds this unsatisfactory because he believes Starbuck over-identified conversion with a certain age group. He argues that other studies show that the age of crisis varies according to the kind of crisis and the person's context and some even suggest that the intensity of crisis in adulthood is

---

[162] Such as in his gathering of data from converts which lacked of systematic questionnaire methods; the biased approach of investigators who had a set, patterned idea of conversion; and use of a rather biased sample.

[163] Thouless, "The Psychology of Conversion," p.142.

[164] *Ibid.*, pp.144-145.

[165] Wayne Oates, "Conversion: Sacred and Secular" in Walter E. Conn, *Conversion*, pp.149-168.

[166] *Ibid.*, p.150.

even greater than in adolescence.[167] Also he points out that, contrary to Starbuck's assumption that conversion always lead into maturity, in many cases converts show immature behaviour because of "irrationality and intensity of beliefs".[168] In response to James's understanding of conversion as "unification of a divided soul," he sees "dissociated personality," in which one experiences dilemma within self, as an appropriate understanding for the study of conversion. There are the dilemmas of loyalty, authority and conflict over freedom and restriction.[169] These may not be subconscious, one may realize this dilemma consciously, and this calls for a "responsible decision" which is "integral to thoroughgoing conversion." This should be based on "specific relationship, of the self-as-a-whole to itself, to others, to institutions, and to God."[170] Wayne Proudfoot, also responding to James' theory,[171] sees that emotion consists of both psychological and cognitive components and points out that "assessments and interpretations are formative rather than consequent."[172] In other words, experience does not happen by itself, rather it must have been informed to the person before the conversion experience. He further suggests, "the explanatory scheme is firmly in place prior to the experience."[173] By analysing the testimony of a convert used by James, and the narrative of the Book of Acts 2:12-13, he concludes that in both

cases "the arousal was interpreted in religious terms and attributed to divine activity" and that attribution produced "conviction and behavioral consequences".[174] For Proudfoot, belief is prior to the psychological experience in the conversion process and religion plays an active and decisive role in conversion.

Meanwhile, Eugene Gallagher[175] states that James' theory is misleading because it "cuts off those individual lives from their participation in society and history," and moreover, "feelings, acts, and experiences prior to the moment of religious conversion exert a powerful influence on how that experience is understood, described, and explained."[176] Therefore for Gallagher, the prior circumstances are vital in understanding the particular experience of conversion. And he further points out that James' theory is deficient in considering the active participation of converts themselves in their process of conversion.[177] Paul Johnson,[178] on the other hand, sees that "crisis" is the key to understanding conversion. It is the "self-consciousness" which affects a person who desires to search for self-realization and yet faces "competing demands of a complicated world and the clashing desire of a complex inner life that give him no rest."[179]. And in this process of crisis, "a person feels that he is confronting Thou, while his fate hangs in the balance.... In such eruptive and decisive experiences the person may have a religions conversion to change the whole course

---

[167] *Ibid.*, p.154.

[168] *Ibid.*, p. 155.

[169] *Ibid.*, pp.156-8.

[170] *Ibid.*, p.158.

[171] Wayne Proudfoot, *Religious Experience*, Berkeley: University of California Press, 1985.

[172] *Ibid.*, p.102.

[173] *Ibid.*, p.104.

[174] *Ibid.*, p.105.

[175] Eugene V. Gallagher, *Expectation and Experience: Explaining Religious Conversion*, Atlanta: Scholars Press, 1990.

[176] *Ibid.*, , p.36.

[177] *Ibid.*, p.37.

[178] Paul E. Johnson, "Conversion" in Conn, *Conversion*, pp.169-178.

[179] *Ibid.*, p.170.

of his life."[180] He further claims, "no person is self-sufficient" and he must "depend upon resources beyond his own," therefore the "very existence of man from moment to moment is a crisis."[181] He defines conversion as "the outcome of a crisis.... unless a person is aware of conflict serious enough to defeat him, and unless he is concerned ultimately enough to put his life in the balance, he is not ready for conversion."[182] He sees conversion as a conscious approach to the fulfilment of self-awareness which one cannot reach because of one's own limitations.

Lewis Rambo, in his recent study[183] tries to reach an integrated understanding of conversion in interaction with different disciplines, especially psychology and sociology. In his search for a definition of conversion he states that it is "one of humanity's ways of approaching its self-conscious predicament, of solving or resolving the mystery of human origins, meaning, and destiny."[184] For him the central meaning of conversion is "change" and it offers a hope to people who are searching for "new life, new love, new beginnings". In conversion these take place in "a dynamic force field of people, events, ideologies, institutions, expectations, and orientations."[185] He concludes that conversion is "a complex process that transpires over time, shaped by the expectations of those who are advocating a certain type of conversion and the experience of the person who experiences the process."[186] He sees that there is "a constant dialectic between human experience and the person's environment."[187] Rambo's work demonstrates the complexity of the study of conversion because of its multiple understandings from many different disciplines and from different contexts.

From the perspective of an integrated psychology of conversion, some findings are: *First*, in the study of conversion, psychological approaches are not enough to deal with all dimensions of conversion experience. Conversion is primarily a personal and psychological experience but it also has communal and socio-cultural aspects that are vital to understanding the experience. *Second*, conversion is not only conditioned, by the subconscious dimension of human self, but also by the conscious dimension of an act of human will. It is not just determined by biological and physiological conditions of individuals but it is, by and large, governed by a responsible decision of a person who is well aware of his act and its consequences. *Third*, the experience comes as one already known rather than one rationalized or interpreted after the experience. In most cases, expectations of religious experiences lead into that particular experience, and therefore the realm of the subconscious is not a vacuum but must have been filled with information received already.

Summary and Conclusion

In our study we have examined three perspectives. From the theological perspective, *theologians* argue that conversion is a fundamental, conscious decision that brings a person into a radical change of understanding of God, self and neighbours. Conversion is first and foremost a theological reality. *Ecumenical discussions* have brought new perspectives on

---

[180] *Ibid.,* p.174.

[181] *Ibid.,* p.177.

[182] *Ibid.,* p176.

[183] Lewis R. Rambo, *Understanding Religious Conversion*, New Haven: Yale University Press, 1993.

[184] *Ibid.,* p.2.

[185] *Ibid.,* p.5.

[186] *Ibid.,* p.170.

[187] *Ibid.,* p.171.

conversion, particularly a focus on the kingdom of God rather than the church which highlights the ethical nature of conversion. Conversion is turning to both God and neighbour and is applicable to Christians as well as non-Christians. It is a positive "turning to" rather than a negative "turning from." The *evangelical response* has focused on the decisive nature of conversion as primarily a spiritual turning from the old life to the new life in Christ. Conversion is intimately related to eternal salvation in which God is active by his grace. And, for evangelicals, it is a transcendental reality that changes the whole human life.

From socio-anthropological perspectives, we have found that in *social history*, Christianity drew people into its community at first by adhesion and then by conversion, which meant abandoning the past. Over church history, conversion has been understood as the entrance to the social bounds of the church rather than merely a personal decision to accept Christ; therefore conversion is seen as the outcome of the social development of Christianity in competition with other political and social entities. *Sociologists and anthropologists* argue that conversion has been a means to keep and extend the congregation and hence reinforce the social structure of Christianity. Conversion is also a means to reconceptualizing the members' social identity and self-dignity. And there have been debates over the role of local people, social change and Christianity in conversion movements. Sociologists tend to treat social change as the dominant factor. Conversion is a multi-individual and mutually interdependent decision that gives a group of people a new cultural identity. By giving conscious allegiance to Christ, through a change of direction and relationships in conversion process, a person's world-view and value system are transformed.

Within the discipline of psychology, scholars in the *psychology of religion* argue that conversion is a subconscious process to meet a personal psychological crisis. Therefore it is conditioned by psychological, biological and physiological changes in the individual. Conversion is also an expression of a person's attempt to find an inner contentment while facing the wider complexity of life. And in this inner process, Christianity plays the role of catalyst and interpreter of the event. By contrast, those who want to integrate *psychology with socio-cultural perspectives* argue that conversion is not only a subconsious experience but is also the conscious act of person who is already informed about the consequences of his/her decision.

It could be said that there is no single and comprehensive definition of the nature of conversion but instead there are diverse understandings according to different disciplines of thought. Lewis Rambo represents this fact when he concludes:

Conversion is paradoxical. It is elusive. It is inclusive. It destroys and it saves. Conversion is sudden and it is gradual. It is created totally by the action of God, and it is created totally by the action of humans. Conversion is personal and communal, private and public. It is both passive and active. It is a retreat from the world. It is a resolution of conflict and an empowerment to go into the world and to confront, if not create, conflict. Conversion is an event and a process. It is an ending and a beginning. It is final and open-ended. Conversion leaves us devastated - and transformed.[188]

Complex and multi-faceted conversion may be but all those concerned with its study agree that, whatever it means and whatever the context, the understanding of conversion is vital to perceiving the mystery of human transformation and its consequences.

---

[188] Rambo, *Understanding Religious Conversion*, p.176.

CHAPTER 38

Human Rights and Religious Freedom in South Asia Today

JEANETTE PINTO

All human beings are born free and equal in dignity and rights. Human rights and fundamental freedoms are the birthright of all human beings; their protection and promotion is the first responsibility of governments. Human rights are not against anyone but for everyone. Governments must take steps to place human rights at the top of the international and national agendas. The declaration of human rights is a magisterial document approved in 1948 by over 50 United Nations members.

The preamble of the Declaration of human rights approved by the General Assembly of the United Nations in Paris on 10 December 1948, recognizes the inherent dignity as well as the equal and inalienable rights of all members of the human family as the foundation of freedom, justice and peace in the world. Article 18 states that everyone has the right to freedom of thought, conscience and Religion. This right includes freedom to change one's religion or belief and freedom to manifest one's religion or belief in teaching, practice, worship and observance. A careful observation indicates that the Declaration calls attention to two preoccupations of contemporary man: "a sense of the dignity of the human Person" and the need for "constitutional limits ....to the powers of the Government.[1]

Freedom is life. It is like water and air for the human being. It is impossible to live fully without it. Freedom dose not differentiate - it is not linked to colour, religion, political principle or social standards. The denial of human rights

and freedoms takes different forms. Groups defending human rights all over the world are required to spare no efforts in the struggle for human rights.

The pages of History are blotched with the blood of man who has been cruelly treated by one of his own kind. Strangely man is man's first enemy, and the deprivation of any freedom makes him a victim for the other. In matters of religion, not only have there been discussions debates and duels, but there have been wars fought. The Crusades are a historical fact.

This essay is an attempt to examine how human rights are the fundamental freedoms necessary for the full realization of all people. Everyone is entitled to them without any distinction of any kind. Christianity has contributed towards the concept and growth of human rights and this is discussed with special reference to the freedom of Religion. The area of study is India, a subcontinent in South Asia, which has a large mixed population with varied minority groups. It also focuses on the challenges before the church and the Indian Christian community.

The Freedom of Religion

The Indian constitution provides for the religious liberty of both the individual and associations of individuals united by common beliefs, practices and discipline. The basic guarantee of this right is found in Article 25 (1) and is not confined only to citizens but extends

---

[1] H.M. Seervai, *Constitutional Law of India*, Bombay, 1968, p. 476.

to "all persons" including aliens. Religious denominations as well as individuals have certain important rights; Collective freedom of religion is spelled out in Article 26. Then article 15 (1) of the Indian Constitution provides: "the state shall not discriminate against any citizen on grounds only of religion, race, caste, sex, place of birth or any of them".[2] Ensuing out of these provisions emerge a number of non-discrimination principles. Any clause that needs clarification would be referred to the Supreme Court, which will study the clause and declare it unconstitutional.

Freedom is a 'possession.' When a freedom is conferred, an absolute license is not given to do what one pleases irrespective of any other consideration. The Constitution guarantees an ordered freedom which if not exercised properly makes it punishable by law. Deliberate insult to the religious beliefs of any group of citizens would disrupt public order. Religion is pervasive and most often more influential than any other factor in social life. Freedom and tolerance in religious life would make difficult the growth of racial or religious chauvinism. In the field of religion, respect for the religious beliefs of each other alone would foster the democracy of religion.

The propagation of Religion

The Indian Constitution guarantees to all persons not only the freedom of conscience but the right to profess, practice and propagate religion.[3] However attitudes are different and there are several objections, especially to conversion. Firstly, much has been written, that conversions have tended to disrupt the established patterns of family caste, and village social life.[4] Secondly, Gandhi wrote, "In Hindu households the advent of a missionary has meant the disruption of the family.... change of dress, manners, language, food and drink."[5] This tended to make the Christian convert become denationalized and westerninsed - it meant they also gave up their national culture. Yet other criticism of conversions, are that they are motivated by political considerations as also that they are promoted by unethical or questionable methods. "Conversion and service go ill together,"[6] was a common expression of Gandhiji.

The *Niyogi Committee* report (1956) that dealt with missionary in India, stirred up a hornet's nest in Church circles due to the negative view it took of the subject.[7] Similarly a proposed but never enacted O.P. Tyagi Bill, as well as anti-conversion bills passed by the legislatures of Arunachal Pradesh, Orissa and Madhya Pradesh, raised the hackles of the Indian Christian community as they were seen to run counter to the freedom of religion guaranteed under the Indian Constitution. Oddly enough, these bills were termed "Freedom of Religion" bills, ostensibly at protecting all religions, but in reality intended to curb conversions to Christianity.

Om Prakash Tyagi introduced the "Freedom of Religion Bill" on 22nd December 1978. The Bill sought to prohibit "conversion from one religion to another by the use of force or inducement or by fraudulent means."[8] This proposal backed by the RSS was intended to offer tribals the 'protection of the state', against the missionaries.[9] There was strong agitation by

---

[2] *Ibid.* p. 482.

[3] D.E. Smith, *India as a Secular State*, Bombay, 1963, p. 163.

[4] See C. Rajagopalachari, ed., *Letter to Dr.Blaise Levai, Revolutions in Missions*, Vellore, 1957, pp.5-6.

[5] *Harijan*, 11 May 1935; Also see "Christian Missions: Their Place in India," Ahmedabad, 1941.

[6] *Harijan*, 25 May 1935; *Young India*, 19 January 1928, p.125.

[7] Lionel Fernandes, "Challenges Before the Indian Christian Community," unpublished paper presented...

[8] For complete text of the bill see *Orgainser*, 15 April 1979, pp.1-15.

[9] *Times of India*, 29 May 1979.

Christians and the Minorities Commission[10] and so the Janatha Party was forced to drop the bill. In the Union Territory of Arunachal Pradesh, the government had allowed a vote without the plans being submitted for administrative organization. The Tyagi bill was strongly criticized in the Lok Sabha.

The sore point with the Church authorities was that State agencies were being empowered to judge the merits of a sovereign personal decision in matters spiritual, while the onus of proof that the decision to convert was a free one, without inducement or fraud, was placed on both the converted and the converter. It was as though every conversion involved potentially guilty parties who had somehow to prove their innocence if they were to escape punishment. This was not acceptable under a liberal democratic Constitution.

Concept of a Secular State

The term 'Secular State' is used to describe the relationship which ought to exist between the state and religion. The secular state is a state that guarantees individual and corporate freedom of religion and so really it is the interrelation of the religion, the individual and the state.[11] It may help to visualize a triangle in which religion and the state form the base angels and the individual is at the apex.

There is no state religion in India. Religion is a matter of faith, but not necessarily theistic. Religious freedom goes hand in hand with religious tolerance. Secularism in the Indian constitution does not pose a threat to the propagation of religion. Our secularism is not intended to elevate our way of life into a kind of national religion, but assures one of the freedoms one enjoys in this sphere.

Is India a Secular State? Indeed a completely secular state doesn't exist. Despite various problems and issues India is secular in as much as it is a democracy. The ideal is embodied in the Constitution; it is being implemented in a substantial measure. There are problems, some inherited, some created, but there is a struggle to overcome them.

The secular state is in origin, a western and not an Asian concept, although certain elements of the secular state have a long tradition in Asia.[12] The word "SECULAR" however was introduced in the Indian Constitution on January 3, 1977, viz the 42nd Constitution Amendment Act, 1976, to make India a 'sovereign, socialist, secular democratic republic'. Although the word secularism was introduced late in the Constitution, India has been a secular state from the very beginning. Jawaharlal Nehru was the Architect of Indian secularism.[13] Articles 15, 16, 25, 26, 27, 28, 30 all revolved around the Freedom of Religion.

A South Asian Perspective

Asia is the "earth's largest continent and ...home to nearly two-thirds of the world's population". It is heir "to ancient cultures, religions and traditions," and a "cradle of the World's major religions".[14] The 20th century has brought about changes in the physiognomy of the continent, viz urbanization, mass emigration, tourism etc. resulting in greater poverty and exploitation of people.

In the past few years the world has witnessed considerable changes. The South Asian Region

---

[10] The minorities Commission had been established by the government in January 1978 for the regulation of religious and linguistic minority affairs.

[11] D. E. Smith, *India as a Secular State*, Bombay, 1963. p 4

[12] *Ibid.* p.22.

[13] N.S. Gehlot, ed. *Politics of Communalism and Secularism*, New Delhi, 1993, p.157.

[14] "Ecclesia in Asia," *The Examiner*, Vol.150 Number 46, Mumbai, p.4.

is characterized by extraordinary geographical, political and socio-economic diversity. Massive economic and demographic pressures compound the problems of maintaining political stability and institution building.

The region of South Asia accounts for a mere two percent of the global income but needs to support 22 percent of the global population.[15] It is a well known fact that diversity and complexity are its chief characteristics. In addition to this region's humanity of tribal groups, minorities and disadvantaged social groups have little hope for a better future, as they become victims for violators of rights.

India is a subcontinent, the largest of South Asian countries. Hinduism, Islam and Christianity are the chief religions of this region. The twin focus of this study is:

- To examine whether the people of India enjoy their fundamental human right to freedom of religion.

- If they do, to examine how much of the freedom they enjoy, or if they do not, to analyse the forces leading to the loss of this freedom.

A general review indicates that at the cost of progress, development and growth the fundamental freedoms and the birthrights of innocent, ignorant people have been ignored and trampled upon. Human rights become a major problem in South Asia once the western agenda is accepted. There is no doubt that western values have made inroads into Hindu society over the years. As Andre Beteille observed about caste: 'How does one account for the continued existence of asocial arrangement which everyone is eager to attack and no one is prepared to defend?.[16]

Minorities in India

The popular adage of Indian nationalism has been 'Unity in diversity; the composite Indian culture had defied the definition of the Indian nation. The question that looms large is whether India is a nation or not? India with its different languages, castes, creeds, religions, dress, beliefs climatic factors etc is really one entity a plurality of units, some more, some less. The less form a *minority*.

Minorities are essentially a phenomenon of democracy. Democracy implies the recognition of right of individuals and groups formed in different ways. In India one may ask "who are the minorities? They are religious political and social; thus Musalmans (Religious); Depressed classes (social); Liberals (Political); Princes (Social); Brahmans (Social); Non Brahmans (Social); Lingayats (social) Christians – Protestants and Catholics (Religious); Jains (Social?); Zamindars (Political?);… who are the majority in this medley?" M.K. Gandhi continues … "My list is not exhaustive. It is illustrative. It can be increased Ad Libitum."[17]

The word "minority" has an arithmetical connotation – a minority is a smaller part of a whole, and may be characterized by one or more traits or features. In every country there are unlimited numbers of minorities possessing both a numerical importance and certain characteristics or features.[18] The expression "prevention of discrimination" is qualified by the words "on grounds of race, sex, language or religion", but no such limitation is placed on the protection of minorities.

---

[15] Richard Reoch, ed., *Human Rights, The New Consensus*, London, 1994. p 139.

[16] Andre Beteille, "The Reproduction of Inequality: Occupation, Caste and family", *Contributions to Indian Sociology*, Vol.25, No.1, 1991, p.23.

[17] M. K. Gandhi, *Harijan*, 21 October 1939, p.312ff.

[18] Haksar, Urmila, *Minority Protection and International Bill of Human Rights*, Bombay 1974, p.26.

Protection of minorities is the protection of non-dominant groups, which while wishing in general for equality of treatment with the majority, desire a measure of different treatment in order to preserve basic characteristics which distinguish them from the majority of the population. The characteristics meriting such protection are race, religion and language. "To qualify for protection a majority must owe undivided allegiance to the government of the state in which it lives. Its members must be nationals of that state. If the minority wishes for assimilation and is debarred the question is one of discrimination and should be treated as such."[19]

Minorities of all types must be protected so that their members can exercise fully and equally the rights to which they are entitled like all other human beings. They must have the right to develop their own culture, speak their own language practice their own religion and participate on a basis of equality in the larger society in which they live. Minorities should get adequate representation so that possible biases in the system get neutralized and the minorities feel reassured. It is imperative that a quota of 25 percent is fixed for minorities in all wings of law enforcement machinery till a balance is restored.[20] Most important is that minorities must enjoy a sense of belonging.

Having thus far looked at the provisions for freedom of religion, what a secular state means, and about the minority in India, the thrust of the study will now be directed towards the Christians as a minority in the pluralistic society of India. The Christian faith is essentially built on fundamental openness to the Transcendent.[21] Often Christians and Hindus meet in a spirit of friendly, sincere and respectful dialogue, but more recently one cannot understand the phenomena of why Christians have become a target for attack. Is there some hidden agenda that has led to the debate on conversions? Why are the onslaughts on democratic and human rights in our country, India, growing daily? These and related issues will hereby be discussed.

Christians as a minority in Pluralistic India:

Let us examine the population table of the Census of India 1991.[22]

Table 1

INDIA: RELIGIOUS COMPOSITION OF POPULATION BY STATES AND UNION TERRITORIES, 1991

India/State/ union Territory	Hindus	Muslims	Christians	Sikhs	Others
INDIA	81.56	12.58	2.32	1.94	1.60
Andhra Pradesh	98.14	68.91	1.83	0.03	0.09
Arunachala Pradesh	37.04	1.38	10.29	0.14	15.15
Assam	67.13	28.43	3.32	0.07	1.05
Bihar	82.42	14.81	0.98	0.09	1.70
Delhi	83.67	9.44	0.88	4.84	1.17
Goa	64.68	5.25	29.86	0.09	27.29
Gujarat	89.48	8.73	0.44	0.08	1.27

---

[19] See document: *Commission on Human Rights*, pp 13-14.

[20] Khaid Ansari, "Rights vs Riots", *Times of India*, 13 November '99, Mumbai, p.10.

[21]"Christians and Hindus: Pilgrims in Dialogue for the Good of All," *The Examiner,* Vol.150 Number 45 Mumbai. p.5

[22] A report to the nation entitled, *Then They Came for the Christians*, All India Federation of Organisation for Democratic Rights (AIFOFDR) Mumbai, April 1999. Table 1. p.100.

India/State/ union Territory	Hindus	Muslims	Christians	Sikhs	Others
Haryana	89.21	4.64	0.10	5.81	0.24
Himachal Pradesh	95.90	1.72	0.09	1.01	1.28
Jammu& Kashmir	34.18	62.58	0.13	2.17	0.94
Karnataka	85.45	11.64	1.91	0.02	0.98
Kerala	57.28	23.33	19.32	0.01	0.06
Madhya Pradesh	92.82	4.96	0.65	0.24	1.35
Maharashtra	81.12	9.67	1.12	0.21	7.88
Manipur	57.67	7.27	34.11	0.07	0.88
Megalaya	14.67	3.46	64.58	0.15	17.14
Mizoram	5.05	0.66	85.73	0.04	8.52
Nagaland	10.12	1.71	87.47	0.06	0.64
Orissa	94.67	1.83	2.10	0.05	1.35
Punjab	34.46	1.18	1.11	62.95	0.30
Rajasthan	89.08	8.01	0.11	1.48	1.32
Sikkim	68.37	0.95	3.30	0.09	27.29
Tamil Nadu	88.67	5.47	5.69	0.01	0.16
Tripura	68.50	7.13	1.68	0.03	4.66
Uttar Pradesh	81.74	17,33	0.14	0.48	0.31
West Bengal	74.72	23.61	0.56	0.08	1.03
Andaman & Nicobar Islands	67.53	7.61	23.95	0.18	0.43
Chandigarh	75.84	2.72	0.78	20.29	0.37
Dadra & Nagar Haveli	95.48	2.41	1.51	0.01	0.59
Daman & Diu	87.76	8.91	2.86	0.10	0.37
Lakshadweep	4.52	94.31	1.16	N	0.01
Pondicherry	86.1	6.54	7.23	N	0.07

The Christians are just 2.32 percent, the second largest of the minority groups. Of the 32 states and Union territories only Mizoram and Nagaland have a Christian population of 85.73 and 87.47 percent respectively. Meghalaya has 64.58, Manipur 34.11 and Goa 29.86 percent respectively. The rest of the areas have a negligible number and some have a miniscule percentage. If numbers are a matter of threat to the minority, the Christians seem so ridiculously outnumbered next to the Hindus who number 81.56 percent. What kind of threat can the 'Lilliputian' be to 'Gulliver'?

A study of Table 2 [23] shows the changes in religious compositions of population in India between 1951-91.

Over a period of five decades the trend indicates a decrease in the Christian population – the drop being from 2.35 in 1951, to 2.32 in 1991. There is a decrease in numbers however small, and it does not support the so-called 'hue and cry of numbers of conversions' to justify why the numbers should have increased considerably.

A close look at the figures of the percentage of Christians in various states[24] again indicates the trend of a regular decrease. A special case in reference may be made of Goa where in 1961 after its independence from the Portuguese the Christian population was 30.07 percent. Recently during the Pope's visit to India there was much hype about the Hindu government wanting the Pope to apologize for Portuguese proselytization

---

[23] *Ibid.* p.101 (Table 2)
[24] *Ibid.* p.101 (Table 3)

in the 15th and 16th centuries. What is interesting is that the Christian population of Goa in the first place was much less than 50 percent of the majority.

Table 2

INDIA: CHANGES IN RELIGIOUS COMPOSITION OF POPULATION. 1951-91

Religious Community	Percentage of Total Population in					Trend
	1951	1961	1971	1981	1991	
Hindus	84.98	83.51	82.72	82.28	81.56	Regular decrease
Muslims	9.91	10.70	11.21	11.76	12.58	Regular decrease
Christians	2.35	2.44	2.60	2.44	2.32	Decrease
Sikhs	1.74	1.79	1.89	1.92	1.94	Regular decrease
Buddhists	0.05	0.73	0.70	0.70	0.77	Increase
Jains	0.45	0.46	0.47	0.47	0.40	Decrease

[Source: census of India, 1991: India: Religion, Paper 1 of 1995, xiv-xxiii and Census of India, 1971: India: Religion Paper 2 of 1972, 2-5 and Annexure, and Victor Petrov: India, Spotlight on Population, 1985.]

Table 3 indicates that over a period of 50 years there has been a regular decrease in Goa's Christian population and in 1991 it stood at 29.86.

Table 3

PERCENTAGE OF CHRISTIANS IN VARIOUS STATES, 1961-1991

Religious Community	Percentage of the Christians in				Trend
	1961	1971	1981	1991	
Andhra Pradesh	3.97	4.19	2.68	1.83	Decrease
Goa	38.07	3.97	31.35	29.86	Regular decrease
Kerala	21.22	21.05	20.56	19.32	Regular decrease
Manipur	19.49	26.03	29.68	34.11	Regular increase
Meghalaya	35.21	46.98	52.62	64.58	Regular increase
Mizoram	86.64	86.09	83.81	85.73	Decrease
Nagaland	52.98	66.76	80.21	87.47	Regular decrease

[Source: Census of India, 1991: India: Religion, Paper 1 of 1995, xiv-xxiii and Census of India, 1971: India: Religion Paper 2 of 1972, 2-5 and Annexure]

Very clearly the demographic profile of the Christian population in India shows a decline in numbers as a percentage of the total population. While the percentage of Christians is growing in certain states (north-east), it is declining in other states. (A.P., Goa, Kerala). The changes in demographic profile have little to do with mass conversion, and more to do with fertility rates among different communities. Economic status and education have also in a way contributed to people having smaller families.

While Christians constitute a majority of the population in three states *viz.* Mizoram, Meghalaya and Nagaland, these states constitute only 0.45 percent of India's total population. The Christian population in these three states constitutes only 14.71 percent of India's total Christian population. One cannot therefore understand the hysteria of the RSS over the supposed 'growth' in numbers of the Christian population. If numbers are not the threat then it is difficult to understand the reason for the attack on Christians.

Missionary Expansion in India and Hindu sentiment:

The Renaissance, Reformation and Enlightenment which Western Europe had gone through made it the harbinger of modernization. Also progressive ideas of nationalism and liberalization expressed in the French Revolution made Europe the leader of the New or Modern era. The British rulers and the Christian missionaries brought this effervescent and dynamic civilization and spirit to India. The time perhaps was not ripe for India and her people. Its society, untouched by the transforming effect of any revolution suddenly had this conclusive experience and was forced to begin the process of modernization. "It came like an avalanche on Hindu social system and the Hindu society" writes David.[25] Also according to Srinivas, "Evangelical Christianity is regarded characteristically western and it is indisputable that Christian missionaries played a crucial role in India's modernization."[26]

In the process the missionaries were quick to point out and denounce the evils of Hindu society to prove the superiority of the Gospel. The social evils of Sati, Child Marriage, Dowry system, Prohibition of widow remarriage, Female infanticide, etc. were all blots on Indian society. The blackest blot was the caste system. It was

the first time that Hinduism faced a blatant frontal criticism of their systems, and that too from foreigners. It may have come as an affront to the leading Hindus who found themselves defenseless in the face of truth. The missionary criticism of the Hindu society together with enlightenment and western education which was the forte of the Europeans Christians perhaps gave the Hindus a feeling of inferiority. Added to this it is possible the Hindus also harbored feelings of anger and resentment, which has now caused them to resort to targeting and attacking the Christians.

Human history has shown that social change is an inevitable process. The missionary with his love of God and man brought certain emancipation to the human heart. Dr. John Wilson an oriental missionary himself acknowledged, "The benefits derived from contact with the spirit of Christianity".[27] In this regard then, the fact that Christianity had a liberating effect and an attraction for the depressed classes or the low castes in India to liberate them from their despicable conditions.

The most significant achievement of the missionaries was in changing the higher caste Hindu attitudes towards the low castes. They befriended the low castes and treated them as equal human beings and as children of one God. The Hindu reformer spoke against the caste system but did not practise it. Indeed according to David, "India had never experienced such silent, social convulsions and revolution which the missionary was able to bring about."[28]

The caste system was a religious form of slavery, it dehumanized the low castes in India. Selfish, heartless Brahmins evolved it over several centuries for their own advantage. They

---

[25]"Evaluating Missions: Cross cultural Encounter and social Change in Western India," *India Church History Review*, Vol. XXIII, No.1, Bangalore, 99, p. 7

[26] M.N.Srinivas, *Social Change in Modern India*, Los Angeles, 1964, p. 45.

[27] Wilson John, *Dnyanodaya*, Ahmednagar, 1920, p.34.

[28] "Evaluating Missions: Cross Cultural…" *ICHR.* p.11.

also managed to enslave the minds of the Sudras and Untouchables. Christian missionaries preached to them of the love and compassion of Jesus. They worked tirelessly to liberate them from the sufferings, ignominies, pain and humiliation they suffered. They championed the cause of the untouchables and raised the dignity of this unfortunate human being known by different names all over the country.

Tribal response to Christianity and the Hindu reaction

Tribals in India as elsewhere are not a homogeneous group. The 'tribe' infact is not even defined properly. In India they are an administrative category. The British, until March 31, 1937, categorized them as 'backward classes'. It was under the Government of India Act, 1935, that they were first scheduled as tribes, a practice that was retained in independent India. This population is spread from east to west, from the Patkoi to the Aravalli range. The scheduled tribes constitute eight percent of the Indian population.[29]

The mass conversion of tribals to Christianity is related to socio-economic and cultural changes. Christianity provided institutions with a new life-style and ideology that protected tribal society. A freedom, long desired for, was now enjoyed. This would not have been looked upon with favour by the upper Hindu crust – perhaps they preferred "the shackles of caste, of illiteracy, of economic slavery and of psychological apathy"[30] to be part of their life. The upper classes lost their hold over 'labour' and 'muscle power', which they needed in order to lead comfortable easy lives.

Thus they found cause to blame the church for accepting poor people into Christianity, for raising their economic status, for teaching them to be self-reliant and for empowering them in various ways.

Dalit Struggle

One third of the total population of India, or over 300 million, are Dalits.[31] They are the invisible people kept as underdogs by the caste system for several millennia. It needs to be pointed out, however, that the Dalit struggle in the last few decades has been viewed with care and concern and Indian Christian theology is directed towards their struggle.

The Dalits see themselves as non-entities, non-persons and non-people in this country. They are discriminated against, "socially, religiously, politically, economically and above all ideologically[32] Bala Sundaram has rightly quoted Bishop M Azariah [33] that "the stigma they suffer is called wounded psyche". This psychic wound has been inflicted on the Dalits by people with vested interests, and by power-wielders. The reality is that the Dalits see themselves as exploited people, a defeated, dispossessed and deprived people who live in segregation. Today they are emerging from the culture of silence and they are becoming visible all over the country.

Dalits and Religion

The Dalits worshipped their ancestors and female deities. Historically the Aryans subjugated the Dalits for exploiting their labour. Over a period of time they became the outcastes and dregs of society suffering indignities, insults and inhuman treatment. They were soon denied worshipping-rights and access to temples. *Karma samsara*, the exploitative doctrine, determined their status. This meant no freedom for the Dalits,

---

[29] S. K. Chube, "The Scheduled Tribes and Christianity in India, *Economic and Political Weekly*, Vol. XXXIV No. 9, 27 February 1999.

[30] S.M. Michael SVD, "In the Interests of Freedom," *The Examiner*, Vol., 150, Number 44, Mumbai, p.13.

[31] F. J. Balasundaram, "Dalit struggle and its implications for theological education," *ICHR*, Vol XXXI, No. 2, p.117

[32] *Ibid.* p. 123.

[33] "*Towards a Dalit Theology,*" p. 228.

and it necessitated conversion to a religion other than Hinduism. This is why the Dalits embraced Christianity. Having converted to Christianity, they value their right to freedom of religion. Untouchability and long years of subordination have aroused Dalit consciousness, their journey being from 'rejection to resurrection'.[34]

The crucial challenge facing the Dalits today is that they are not a homogenous group. They are scattered all over the country and face linguistic, religious and cultural barriers. They are scattered in all religions - in Islam, Sikhism, Christianity, Buddhism and some even within the fold of Hinduism. They have now also become followers of the Varna ideology within their present groups of affiliation: Malas and Madigas of Andra Pradesh; Mahars and Mongs in Maharastra; Pulayas in the south; - each one claiming superiority over the other, forgetting that they were all once victims of the same ideology that they themselves now perpetuate.

Secularism vs Communalism

In a multi religious society like India, the concept of secularism has always been the most pressing need of our time. The menace of communalism has assumed many forms to identify itself with problems of caste, community, culture and language and this gave rise to numerous problems related to ethnic groups like the Bodos, Nepalese, Jarkhands, Gorkhas and so on.[35] Communalism in the Indian context has proved to be both ritualistic and institutionalized. It has also become politicized.

Today, 'Communalism' is seen as the opposite of 'Secularism.' Communalism involves the use of religion for the secular purpose of political order. The constitutional framework of the secular state in India has three basic components: freedom of religion, citizenship and separation of state and religion. Political parties have blatantly distorted and misused these basic components of the constitution. They probably have a hidden agenda in supporting Communalism, and therefore they aggressively attack the Christians.

Attacks on Christian communities and their institutions in Gujarat and some states of India have become a major concern for the secular polity of India. The attacks on Christians in Gujarat especially have targeted the tribals who were either ignored or taken for granted until now, but who have embraced Christianity, challenging the oppressive Hindu caste system. The communal attacks are the response of the business class to this challenge from the downtrodden.[36]

Hindutva as a challenge to Secular India

It is a known fact that four-fifths of all Indians are Hindus, and the Bharatiya Janatha Party (BJP) espouses Hindu nationalism. It seeks to restore Hindu pride and glory after eight centuries of Muslim conquest and 200 years of British colonial rule. This perhaps has made the party communal, xenophobic and abrasive. Other political parties desire the country to be multilingual, multi-religious and multi-ethnic. But the BJP wants 'one nation, one people and one culture.'[37] It says this composite culture, 'Hindutva', is supposed to encompass all religions, regions and languages in India. The BJP's methods of pervasion seem brutal, sometimes fomenting riots in which thousands have been killed.[38] The Bharatiya Janata Party is attempting to attract Muslims to its fold trying

---

[34] *Ibid.* p. 128.

[35] N.S. Gehlot, ed., *Politics of Communalism and Secularism*, New Delhi, 1993. p. vii.

[36] "India's New Government" *The Economist,* Vol 347, Number 8062,.

[37] "Who's Afraid of the BJ?" *The Economist*, p. 32.

[38] *Ibid.* p.32

several means, however, since the thrust of this study is focused on the Christians, the other minority groups will not be touched upon here.

Any social anthropologist or even an average discerning person knows that Muslims, Christians, Sikhs and Buddhists are not homogenous, in fact sectarian, linguistic and cultural differences prevail affecting their attitudes. The minority communities are often stereotyped as "fanatical" and "fundamentalist" and the acts of a few individuals are portrayed as that of the entire community.[39] For example recently there were many attacks on Christians by the Sangh parivar alleging that they were indulging in forcible conversions – the Christians have been stereotyped and described as being 'conversion – enthusiasts'. Every religious community has liberal, secular, fanatical and fundamentalist elements. Yet when it comes to the minorities, the entire community is held responsible for the acts of a few fanatical lunatics – the voice of the liberal and secular Muslims, Christians or Sikhs is not heard.[40]

The Church As An Agent of Change

There is little doubt that the Church in India has had an impact on society. The Roman Catholics, the Syrian or St. Thomas Christians and the Protestant Churches all had, through their missionaries, evangelized and converted a number of the local natives to Christianity. The Church also adopted a policy of outreach through the triad that included preaching, teaching and healing. In addition the missionaries followed the principles of 'Liberation theology' to free people from the various bonds and shackles they were tied down to in society. The Church, while it cherishes democracy and religious liberty, resists capitalism saying it is individualistic, materialistic and anarchic, and that it also fosters inequality.[41]

Christian Missiology: past and present encounters and responses

The missionaries, in their endeavour to spread Christianity, criticized Hinduism, especially the dehumanizing social and religious practices. They persuaded the Hindus to see the virtues of love, respect, equality and compassion for all in the tenets of Christianity. It was indirectly coaxing the Hindu to give up his religion and take to Christianity. Christian missionaries however failed in their efforts to win over the upper classes to Christianity, but it had the greatest appeal to the untouchable.

It is interesting to note how Christian missiology progressed in most parts of the world. The first stage was exploration, when the missionaries learnt the language, were sometimes misunderstood, persecuted, and even killed. The second stage was when they began to build Churches – a witness to Christ. In the third stage one sees a community of adherents formed. We see the Church emerging strong in the fourth stage. Schools and seminaries prepare leaders and the Word (Gospel) spreads.[42] Christian missionary work became closely linked to educational work, bringing about a cultural transformation of society. There was economic upliftment and empowerment of the weaker sections of society. Gradually the Indian Christian community emerged – no doubt heterogeneous but surprisingly those who became Christians were from almost every religious group, sect and tribe in India.[43]

---

[39] Asghar Ali Engineer, "The Media and the Minorities" *The Hindu*, 13 July 1999.

[40] *Ibid.* p.32.

[41] Banerjee, Brojendra Nath, "Economic Policy Reforms" *Religion and Society,* Bangalore, 1993, p.1.

[42] K. Farias, "The Christian Impact in South Konkan," *Church History Association of India*, (CHAI), Mumbai, 1999, p.284.

[43] A Report to the nation entitled, "*Then They Came for the Christians,*" All India Federation of Organisation for Democratic Rights (AIFOFDR) Mumbai April 1999. p. 93.

One cannot really evaluate mission work merely in terms of numbers of converts gained. The impact or effect of the Christian missions can be seen in the transformation of Indian society. The social hierarchy indicated that low castes were the dregs of society. Said Dr. Ambedkar, "untouchability is the lowest depth to which the degradation of a human being can be carried. To be poor is bad but not so bad as to be an untouchable. The poor can rise above his status. An untouchable cannot empower".[44] Seeing the untouchables and the downtrodden communities empowered was gradually becoming a threat to the upper classes. The missionaries and the Church now began to be perceived as enemies of the upper castes and hence anger has been directed towards them.

There has been a wave of carefully planned attacks on Christians across the country. There have been regular news items of attacks on Christians – heinous crimes or rape, burning of churches and Bibles, desecration of crosses, killing and destruction of property of the tribals etc. over the past year. The leaders of the Bhartiya Janata Party (BJP) and other Sangh Parivar affiliates have systematically whipped up hatred towards India's small Christian community, and have spread a number of blatant falsehoods to induce irrational panic and intolerance among the dominant Hindu community.[45] There is constant propaganda to point to the Christians as foreign agents and anti-national people. Most, or all of these attacks on Christians are by the Sangh Parivar leaders. Surely this indicates a state of insecurity that these leaders suffer from. Summarily it may be assumed that for helping to change the face of society, for uplifting the

economically weak, and for being an agent of change, the Indian Church has become a victim of the 'power hungry'.

In the 20ᵗʰ century peculiar problems have risen for the Churches and the missions in India. The proselytizing activities of the missionaries are viewed with distinct disfavour. Humanitarian work is welcome but conversion is considered obnoxious.[46] Price, who, in the 1920s, made an interesting study of how non-Christians reacted to Christianity in 'Oriental' lands, accordingly drew up these conclusions. He recorded that, "initially there are impulsive reactions, followed by indifference. Then there is resistance or passive opposition. Later one sees connivance or tacit co-operation and finally there is a readiness to join the new group."[47]

Christian Mission and transformation of the nation

Freedom of religion is not an absolute freedom. It is subject to the regulatory power of the state. For example, in the name of religion no act can be done against any public order, morality and health of the public, nor may religious freedom be used to practice economic exploitation.[48] To propagate one's religion is a fundamental right.

The mind of the Catholic Church is revealed in the Vatican Council document: 'Declaration of Religious Freedom' adopted in December 1965. The second article of this document makes important points. Every man has the right to religious freedom because he is a human person. No one is to be forced in any way contrary to his own beliefs. The foundation of these rights is the dignity of the human person.[49]

---

[44] B.R Ambedkar, *Writing and Speeches*, Vol. V, Bombay 1985, pp 411-412.

[45] A Report to the nation entitled, *"Then They Came for the Christians,"* All India Federation of Organisation for Democratic Rights (AIFOFDR) Mumbai April 1999. p. 89.

[46] P. Thomas, *Christian and Christianity in India and Pakistan*, London, 1954, p.243.

[47] Maurice T. Price, *Christian Missions and Oriental Civilizations*, Shanghai, 19245, pp.2-3.

[48] *"Commission for Evangelisation, Christianity in India: Its True Face,"* Catholic Bishops Conference of India (CBCI) Thanjhavur, 1981, p.59.

[49] *Ibid*, p. 63.

The Christians have failed to touch the heart of India. It was a non-Christian, a Hindu, who emerged as a leader for the nation. When a missionary asked Gandhi "What definite work would you suggest that a missionary should do for and among the masses?" His prompt reply was "The spinning wheel".[50] Strange but true, salvation began in a workshop in Nazareth; perhaps if we want India is to be converted it needs to tread the same path.

Gandhi made a distinction between making money and earning money. When given, money can harm, when earned by honest labour it helps increase self respect and develops character. What the starving millions of India need is not alms but honest work and living wages.

As a Christian community we need to reflect on whether we are, in truth, reflecting 'Life' as Jesus commanded. Gandhiji said to a Christian missionary:

> "Let your life speak to us even as the rose needs no speech but simply spreads its perfume. Even the blind who do not see the rose perceive its fragrance. That is the secret of the Gospel of the rose. But the Gospel that Jesus preached is more subtle and fragrant than the Gospel of the rose".[51]

Challenges in the area of human rights

There are a number of challenges facing the human rights community at the end of the second millennium. Firstly it may seem fair to categorize the human rights world as currently "caught between the rock of political intervention and the wide open sea of humanitarianism".[52] Secondly there seems to be an overt interest of financial institutions *viz* the World Bank in the role of human rights reporting. Thirdly, 'peace' is a major concern and so Non Government Organizations (NGOs) are working with the United Nations for the protection of human rights.

Mission of the Church Today

Religious freedom goes hand in hand with religious tolerance, and this tolerance requires patience to suffer even irreverent propaganda against one's own faith by the followers of other faiths. The process of dialogue, reflection, debate and negotiation could help resolve differences resulting in understanding, goodwill and respect for others. After all it is up to us to build a better tomorrow for our children by creating a better and safer world today. The Church also bears this responsibility.

The questions with which I began this paper are not merely academic debates they are now being enacted on the national stage. Yes, we are not by nature a secular people – religion plays too large a part in our daily lives for that – "but Indian secularism should mean letting every religion flourish, rather than privileging one above the rest..."[53]

India stands at the intersection of the most significant questions facing the world at the end of the twentieth century. If democracy leads to inefficient political infighting should it be sacrificed in the interest of economic well-being? Does religious fundamentalism help to assert a country's identity in the face of Western hegemony? Is there a case for pluralism and diversity amid cultural and religious traditions? Answers to such questions will determine what kind of a world the next century will bring.

The church needs to take a hard look at discrimination within its own fold against women generally. Church organization is a classic example of institutionalized and theologically

---

[50] Fr. Philip OCD, *Christianity in Free India*, Salem, 1947, p.25.

[51] *Ibid* ,p.24

[52] Richard Reoch,, ed., *Human Rights, The New Consensus*, London, 1994. p. 69.

[53] Shasi Tharoor, *India from Midnight to the Millenium*, New Delhi, 1997, p.361.

rationalized patriarchy. Women have held high offices in civil and professional life. They have proved themselves equal to their male counterparts. The church should consider their rights within reasonable limits according to Christ's teachings. It should also examine the subtle discrimination that prevails against Christians of tribal origin.

In a survey of the political culture of the Roman Catholic Christian Community of Mumbai,[54] it was observed that while political awareness was of a high order in the community, political involvement tended to be on the low side. Allegiance, egalitarianism and a sense of political efficacy were on a high side whereas appreciation of politicians and political parties was low. The church should train and motivate leadership in the community.

Biblical Basis for mission today

The Declaration of Religious Freedom, *'Dignitatis Humanae,'* December 7, 1965 indicates that the Church must concede to others the liberty of action, thought, speech and writing that it demands for itself.[55] This is one guideline for the Christians to follow. In addition to this let us not forget the directions given to the followers of Christ in the Holy Bible-The Great commission. "All authority has been given to me" says Jesus, and He urges his followers to "go and make disciples of all nations". He assures us of his presence "to the very end of the age."[56]

St. Paul in his message to the Ephesians tells us that our commitment as Christians is to build the body of Christ — 'Unity in the Body of Christ'. He urges that "every effort be made to keep the unity of the spirit through the bond of peace: there is one body and one spirit. He continues to remind us that there is "one Lord, one faith, one baptism; one God and Father of all who is over all and through all in all."[57]

When in prison St. Paul had one precious commodity, 'time', to think and reflect. Paul's letters from the prison have deep insights. He adopted a positive approach and showed Christian maturity. He urged that Christians live as "Children of Light" and attain to the "whole measure of the fullness of Christ"...[58] "then we will no longer be infants, tossed back and forth by the waves, and blown here and there by every wind of teaching and by the cunning and craftiness of men in their deceitful scheming."[59] He viewed Christian life as a kind of warfare and wanted his readers to prepare for combat with a dangerous opponent. He proposed "love and truth" to be the Christian's weapons. He listed the "sword of the Spirit" as an offensive weapon, all the rest were used for defence. He compared himself to "an ambassador in chains" and urged Christians to be fearless and make known the mystery of the Gospel.[60] This perhaps is the best fulcrum on which should revolve missiology for the 21ˢᵗ century.

---

[54] Unpublished Ph.D. Thesis, "Survey: Roman Catholic Christian community of Mumbai," Department of Politics and Public Administration, Pune University, 1981.

[55] *The Examiner*, Vol. 150, Number 44, Mumbai, p. 9.

[56] *Bible*, Matthew 28; 16-20.

[57] *Bible*, Paul to the Ephesians 4;1-6.

[58] *Ibid.*, 4:13.

[59] *Ibid* 4:14

[60] *Ibid* 6:19-20.

CHAPTER 39

Let There Be Life: Theological Foundations for the Care and Keeping of Creation[1]

PRAVEEN [SUNIL] KAPUR

Almost three millennia ago the prophet Isaiah said, "the earth mourns and withers, the earth lies polluted under its inhabitants, for they have transgressed the law ... The earth is utterly broken, the earth is rent as under, the earth is violently shaken" (Isaiah 24:4–5, 19). In chapter twelve, Jeremiah also speaks of the withering and mourning land having become desolate because of the destructiveness and wickedness of humans.

The world at large has come to realize the danger that it faces from the gruesome monster that is eating it up at an escalating rate. The need to know about this danger is not purely for the head, but more so for the heart of humanity. For even having the knowledge, many continue to be carefree. "Despoiling the earth is blasphemy, and not just an error of judgment, a mistake; it's sin against God as well as man."[2] We ought to confess our unbelief and ungratefulness towards God, because we have not cared for the rest of creation as we are called to do. The consequences are clear: the death of nature means the death of humanity itself.

The world is forever falling into the temptation of trying to turn "stones into bread." The task of Christianity is not, however, to produce new social conditions. New conditions do not produce a new person; new persons produce new conditions. The foundation for our environmental concern must be Jesus Christ and Him alone. It is upon this ground that we must build, and not on good works, or humanism, or science. For Jesus triumphed where the first man, Adam, failed. Adam had everything in his environment conducive to victory. Jesus had everything in the howling wilderness against Him. Yet, after forty days without food He triumphed over Satan.

The church at present seems to be impotent before the ecological crisis, for we are mistakenly using the wisdom of the world. The weapons of our warfare ought to be spiritual rather than carnal. Using the world's weapons, the church does not stand a chance. But using God's weapons (Eph. 6:14–17), the world will become weak. These are not the days for the church to turn inward, curl up in a corner, and passively await the end. The world has yet to see what the Spirit can do.

In getting a right perspective, Christians should not be among the destroyers of nature; rather we should treat creation with overwhelming respect and reverence. Nature should not be regarded as nothing more than a warehouse supplying the raw material for the transformation of society and history. Our interest in ecology must not be related only to survival. Our faith must inherently and necessarily be open

---

[1] The Title by "Let there be Life" was published originally in the *Evangelical Review of Theology* (*ERT*) 17:2, April 1993, pp.168-175 and is used with permission.

[2] John Stott, *Involvement: Being a Responsible Christian In a Non-Christian Society*, New Jersey: Fleming H. Revell Co., 1985, p.160.

to nature, as it was created for God's pleasure, praise, and glory.

The simplest and the oldest way in which God is manifest is through and in the Earth itself. God still speaks to us through earth and sea, birds of the air, creatures upon the Earth, if we can but quiet ourselves to listen and ponder, carefully and prayerfully, to the created order. Nature does not open up to us if we always come to it with our knives. "Man is the only being who can interpret creation. He is, so to speak, the language of nature. Nature speaks but silently. Man puts into words these silent utterances of nature"[3] (Ps. 19:13–14).

But all this language can be misinterpreted. As a devout man of God, Sadhu Sunder Singh talked in his writings as if God were speaking to him saying, "In the book of nature, of which I also am the author, I freely manifest myself, but for the reading of this book also spiritual insight is needed, that men may find Me; otherwise there is a danger lest instead of finding Me they go astray."[4] 'The happiness we derive from creation has its limits. God alone can completely meet the needs of the human hearts and satisfy them in perfection."[5] It is then folly to worship living things, like trees (Rom. 1:21–25, Jer 2:20)."To read other books you master painfully the language in which these books are written, but this is not so with the Book of Nature. It is written in a language which is simple and intelligible to all. Live with Christ and the Book of Nature will be clear to you."[6]

The Christian mystic seeks to find God meditating on the great wonders of God's creation, knowing that there must be a Creator, and that creation and Creator are not one and the same. God works in creation in a hidden way—

even more wonderfully within a converted soul. The Good News is all about the abundant life. Where then does this abundant life begin? Is it not here on Earth? Can we really experience this abundant life without nature, given our destructive attitude toward it?

Although the word "nature"—as we use it—appears nowhere in the Bible, to those who are open and receptive Scripture is full of references to it. Revelation comes from seeing how life works. To those who have eyes to see, the Bible says, "The heavens declare the glory of God, the skies proclaim the work of His hands" (Psa 19:1). The things made by God reveal God's nature and God's power: "Since what may be known about God is plain to them, because God has made it plain to them. For since the creation of the world God's invisible qualities — God's eternal power and divine nature — have been clearly seen, being understood from what has been made, so that men are without excuse" (Rom 1; 19–20).

All nature glorifies God, except for two of God's creations: the fallen angels who have no chance of redemption, and human beings who yet have a way to come back to God through Jesus Christ. One can learn from nature that has not sinned against its Creator and glorifies God in its beauty and honor! "On all the works He has inscribed his glory," says Calvin.

Nature glorifies God because of its immense variety. The numberless species visible and invisible in the world are a reflection of the infinite being of God, revealing God's numberless attributes. "The death of these creatures, great and small will leave a void in God's creation and in the imagination of men for generations to come."[7]

---

[3] Sadhu Sundar Singh, *Reality and Religion,* Madras: C.L.S., 1974, pp.22-23.
[4] Sadhu Sundar Singh, *At the Master's Feet,* Madras: C.L.S., 1983, p.11.
[5] Sundar, *Reality,* p.1.
[6] B.H. Streeter and A. J. Appasawmy, *The Sadhu ,* London: Macmillan, 1921, p.193.
[7] Francis A. Schaeffer, *Pollution and Death of Man,* Wheaton: Tyndale House Pub., 1970, p.21.

Without nature as interpreter of God's Word, it is difficult to understand God's mind. In Job 12:7–9, the animals are said to instruct us, as elsewhere they are said to minister to Jesus in the wilderness. Is there any reason not to take care of our interpreters, instructors, and ministers?

The whole of creation joins in the praise of God — the sun, moon, sea, land, fire, snow, human beings, and all creatures. Creation is our praise partner. All created things were given to humans to glorify God, and not to abuse, exploit, or destroy.

God is not left without witnesses. The beauty of nature testifies to God's glory. Our consciences attest to the living God, just as nature affirms the presence of God. "The heavens proclaim His righteousness, and all the people see His glory" (Psa 96:6). How clearly David often expressed the Lord of Glory in nature in the Psalms (Psa 29:39).

While both nature and our inner selves witness to God the Creator, we cannot remain silent while there is a destruction of the living witness of God in nature. With the death of nature, our fellow silent witness to the existence of God will disappear. Why do we not seem to care sufficiently to stop this annihilation of nature?

Do we prefer to reduce the Gospel to cold calculation, or to a series of prescriptions, or of laws and theories? Or can we tell a poetic story through nature that is close to the heart of humanity, that relates the Lord of Creation to human beings, that brings a fuller relationship and meaning rather than any analytical description would have done? It is much easier to create interpersonal bonds. Yet, not being able to relate to nature, we know even less the art of relating and communicating to the "crown of creation," human beings. As we tend to move away from nature, we become more and more impersonal and less and less communicative. The further away we have gone from the Garden of Eden, the harder it has become for us to relate to God, other humans, and nature. We can go back into the Garden only by repenting and accepting the death and resurrection of Jesus Christ, so as to be able to walk with God again "in the cool of the day" (Gen 3:8).

Much biblical wisdom comes from examples of nature manifesting order in human life. This kind of wisdom steers us rather than taking on the task of mastering our lives. It is rooted in experience and is practical, particular, and open. It observes orderliness, but does not seek to impose order. We must train ourselves to listen to be able to see the order in nature established by God.

One of the wisest men ever to live was Solomon. The fourth chapter of I Kings describes Solomon's wisdom. It is not Solomon's ability to render justice—not even his ability to rule effectively — that is highlighted in the summary of his wisdom. Rather, it is his encyclopedic knowledge of the environment. This is all the more striking when one contrasts the book of Proverbs. There the focus is on human life and experience.

Creation brings about relationship; God's plan for this world is relationship. In looking at the biblical view of the connection between humanity and nature, we notice that humanity and land animals were created on the same day (Gen. 1), out of the same dust or ground (Gen. 2:7–19), both having God's breath (Spirit) breathed into them (Gen. 2:7, Ps. 104:29–30, Job 34:14–15). Both have rationality and feeling (Gen. 3:1–5, Num. 22:28–30, Job 39:16–18); both have an awareness of God, though with animals it might bear different responsibilities and is less clouded with sin. In the end, both share the fate of death. In fact Ecclesiastes 3:19 claims "man has no advantage over the animal."

Human distinctiveness is by no means easy to define. It is clear that the world was not created only for human benefit (Job 39, Psalms 49). The kindness to animals required in Deuteronomy 25:4 and Proverbs 12:10 has no ethical base if animals exist only for human use.

Satan's purpose in all environmental problems is to destroy as many people as possible. Satan has always been a destroyer and a murderer. Millions are dying, faster than we can reach them with the message of the merciful Lord Jesus. A total disregard for the ecological balance hinders their chance to experience salvation and grace here on Earth. Still, the need to save the environment for God's glory is urgent. In our burden for those who do not know God, our involvement is not merely in saving forests; it is a commitment for the survival of humankind. Life in all forms is precious. Let us nourish it, and not be disillusioned by Satan into aiding his evil strategy. The Bible tells that the wrath of God will come upon the destroyers of the Earth and they will be destroyed (Rev 11:18b). Let there be life!

God's purpose in creation is love. God's very being is love. It is experienced in the inner relations of the Trinity and expresses itself in the bliss of love by bringing into existence the entire universe. But sin has distorted creation.

The fall disturbed humanity's harmonious relationship with nature. Now it appears as hostile, introducing elements of struggle and violence in our relationship with nature (Gen 3:15, 17–19; 9:2). Because we misuse nature, nature suffers and groans with pain, awaiting our full redemption as its own liberation from the burden of our sin. The Earth and it's creatures come to stand in an ambiguous relationship to humanity, being sustained by God, independent of human effort, but nonetheless suffering as a result of human disobedience to the Creator.

Of all the creatures on Earth, man is the most destructive and the root of the ecological crisis is human economic greed. In Numbers 35:33,

God clearly gives a command to us: "do not pollute the land where you are," yet today this is exactly what we do. Sin — our rebellious nature and rejection of God—has been the cause of the curse upon our land. In some ways, humanity has become an enemy of creation (Gen 9:2). Before sin entered, people lived in harmony with nature; today fear and terror supplant the previous harmony between persons and animals. If we continue to defile our land with sin, the land itself will vomit us out (Lev 18:25–30). On the other hand, blessings flow if we are faithful towards God. Morality, response to God, and the fertility of the Earth are all interrelated. If we obey God, the fruitfulness of the Earth will be a natural consequence. When we refrain from sinning against God, God blesses the land.

Our work is to preserve the blessing by being holy. The Bible tells us "the land must not be sold permanently, because the land is mine and you are but aliens and my tenants" (Lev 25:23). If we do not obey God, as Master and King, God has every right to throw us out of the land (Deuteronomy 11:13–17), just as Adam and Eve were thrown out.

God never misses the fall of a sparrow. The fact that God has not destroyed us for what we have done to creation should be assurance of God's love and highlights the need for us to respond willingly to it. In the judgment upon humanity, a reversal in the creation order is said to take place. The first to go will be humans, then animals, then the birds of the air and, finally, the fish of the sea. In the end, redemption for persons and a right relationship with nature comes only through God's son, which, in turn, ought to stop further misuse of knowledge and destruction of life. As Richard Bauckham says, "salvation is simply the completion of creation."[8]

The biblical record includes the hope that the present Earth and heaven will pass away, and

---

[8] Richard Bauckham, "First Steps to a Theology of Nature," *The Evangelical Quarterly* 58, July 1986, p.67.

the Lord will create new ones. This will be a better creation, populated with redeemed people. God is planning an immeasurably better thing than we can imagine. To those who love and obey God, God will say, "well done, good and faithful servant! You have been faithful in a few things. I will put you in charge of many things. Come and share your master's happiness" (Mathew 25:14–30). We must turn to God the Creator for a right relationship with nature, including other creatures: "A righteous man cares for the needs of God's animals" (Proverbs 12:10).

This Earth may be destroyed, but woe to us if we become the agents of destruction. Knowing that each one of us is ultimately going to die does not mean that we should not be taken care of, or that we should not care for ourselves. Even should the Earth one day come to an end, does nature also not have the right to be cared for and to live? Let there be life!

"The earth is the Lord's, and all it contains, the world and those who dwell in it," says the psalmist (Psa. 24:1). "Worthy art Thou, our Lord and our God, to receive glory and honor and power; for Thou didst create all things, and because of Thee will they exist, and were they created" (Rev. 4:11). All things were created for God's glory, says Isaiah 43:7. "The Lord has made every thing for its own purpose," says Proverbs 16:4. In contemplating nature, we see the meaning of coordination in this world and its manifold spaces. Everything is well arranged ecologically and has a purpose.

Psalm 104 provides commentary on the accounts of creation by portraying the importance of rocks and trees, birds and animals, for their own sake. Creation does not exist merely for the sake of human beings. Everything has a meaning, bringing glory to the Creator. There are animals, rocks, mountains, and stars that live without reference to humanity. There is life, because the life-giver has imbued everything with life. Without God, nothing can exist. God continues

to create and sustain everything that exists for God, by God, and human beings are only the vice-regents. Creation has its own independent value. For this reason, 'dominion' must never be confused with exploitation.

Jesus frequently referred to the natural world and environment, and there is much we can learn from His ministry. He made much use of the environment conveying the Gospel of the kingdom of God, and even nature obeyed Him. Not only did Jesus identify himself as a shepherd who laid down His life for His sheep, but Christ is also identified as the Lamb, one of the most gentle, the most harmless of all animals, who will wipe away every tear from our eyes.

The promise of God never again to destroy the life that God has created "as long as the earth remains," means that the creation receives from the Creator the promise of preservation. This is a promise of providential care. "Everything that exists in heaven or earth shall find its perfection and fulfillment in Christ" (Eph. 1:10 Phillips).

The death of creation is not normal, but do not weep. The Lamb has conquered. All of creation awaits transformation through the life of Christ. The church that is now Christ's body on Earth is the sign of that transformation already taking root in this world. In this upside-down world, the ethics of Jesus can turn things right side-up, or at least, save them from further destruction. To this end, we must develop a specifically bibical environmental ethic.

Some might ask, should we just preach the Gospel and not care, practically, for nature? Is it wrong to stress matters of conservation or environment? For nominal Christians, the weakness lies in the fact that having known the Creator, they have not loved the creation. Yet, God's handmade things are loved and preferred even more when one has an intimate relationship with the One who came and suffered here on Earth. God's covenant is with all creation as illustrated at the time of Noah. In Genesis 9:8–

17 we read that God says, "I now establish my covenant with you and with your descendants after you and with every living creature that was with you." Further, in verse 13, God promises, "I have set my rainbow in the clouds and it will be the sign of the covenant between me and the earth." It is absolutely false for a Christian to have a platonic view of nature. What God has made must not be despised by human beings.

Today's Christians have to seek for new ideas, ask new kinds of questions, and look at the unchanging Gospel in terms of their own culture. They must unfold new dimensions in relation to global ethical problems. In fact, for the Christian, the beauty of God is better understood in the light of many diverse cultures. Out of this might come a new spirituality that would illuminate the spiritual dimension of the world order. This could lead to the development of a planetary awareness, and work towards the redistribution of the Earth's wealth. This spirituality will see redemption not as the lifting of humanity out of nature, but as redeeming nature with and through human beings.

The work of the church is now to "Wake up! Strengthen what remains and is about to die" (Rev. 3:2). As other religions and national organizations maintain a concern for nature, how much more ought we to be concerned who are the sons and daughters of its Creator and who know that we will be accountable for dealing with God's creation.

The Old Testament prophets have shown that the Lord would reign through the anointed one as the Prince of Peace (Isa. 9:6–7). The zeal of the Lord will bring peace, not only to humanity, but to nature as well. "The wolf shall dwell with the lamb and the leopard shall lie down with the kid and the calf and the lion, the yearling together, and a little child shall lead them ... for the earth shall be full of the knowledge of God as the waters cover the sea" (Isa 11:6, 10). So the prophet's vision here is the harmony between humanity and the rest of creation, not of enmity, or of creation forced cruelly into providing a human task. The relationship will be restored. This vision does not speak of creation being destroyed. All are good; the cobra, the viper or the lion will not be able to harm each other. All these things will be united to the One who was to be a substitution for the curse of God to human beings, and the Earth as well, Jesus Christ of Nazareth who redeems the world.

Now therefore the church is called to participate actively with God, through Jesus Christ, in a great cosmic mission for a New Creation. From this time forth, Christians must read their Bibles for a fresh insight into the message of God's love for the entire cosmos in the light of our contemporary predicament.

CHAPTER 40

Women and Gender Issues in Christian Missions in India

SAMUEL THAMBUSAMY AND BEULAH HERBERT

Women and Christian Missions in India[1]

The origins of Christianity in India can be traced to the first few centuries A.D. with possible apostolic roots. In the subsequent centuries, the Roman Catholic missionaries and Protestant missionaries established mission stations and furthered the gospel. During the Worldwide Missionary movement in the late 18th and 19th centuries, Christian Missions revived their vigor and evoked tremendous response. The mission enterprise reached out to different geographical areas with varied approaches, but the focus on women and the work for women originated only in the second half of the 19th century. Until that time very "little had been done or could be done."[2] However, between 1821 and 1880, several societies[3] began operations for reaching girls and women in India. The growth of Missions and their labor for women is significant against the background not only of the oppressive social evils that existed at that time, but also in view of the prevalent societal apathy towards emancipation of women.

Women in Christian Missions

The beginnings: The missionary efforts to educate girls began with small initiatives by the wives of missionaries around 1813. This low-profile missionary endeavor of the missionary wives "extended to all womanhood wherever possible."[4] This is the first known work directly done for women and these efforts of wives of missionaries were momentous in the emancipation of women in India.

The Zenana Mission: In 19th century India, in noble and high caste families, men outside the family were not allowed to visit women in their quarters (*Zenana*).[5] In 1854, the policy of sending women to teach girls in the *Zenana* of Hindu families was adopted. The *Zenana* work was started in Calcutta and Mrs. Mullens and Miss. Toogood were prominent among the women involved in the work. The *Zenana* work comprised entirely of women who evangelized

---

[1] The history part was researched and written by Samuel Thambusamy.

[2] C.B. Firth, *Introduction to Indian Church History*, Madras: CLS, 1998, p.191. Even the little efforts taken by missionaries to educate girls and women were not popular and successful. These efforts did not find social approval and so failed to create a lasting impact. Ziegenbalg, the Lutheran missionary at Tranquebar pioneered a girl's school as early as 1707. His colleague Schultze taught girls at Madras in 1732. Mrs. Marshman (1818) at Serampore and Mrs. Wilson at Bombay initiated a few schools for girls. But these schools faced great difficulties. The students were mostly from the lower castes and even had to be paid for.

[3] Society for Promoting Female Education (1834), Indian Female Normal School and Instruction Society (1852), L.M.S. Ladies' Committee for Missions in India and China (1875), Ladies Society for Female Education, Free Church of Scotland (1837), Women's Union Missionary Society (1861), Baptist Female Missionary Society (1870), Church of England *Zenana* Missionary Society (1880).

[4] Hugald Grafe, *History of Christianity in India: Tamilnadu in the Nineteenth and the Twentieth Century* Vol. IV, Part II, CIIAI: Bangalore, 1990, p.205.

[5] Every large house of the noble and high caste families in India had a part apportioned to females where no male ever entered. The women lived in these quarters and not even the father entered these apartments.

and gave spiritual instruction to Indian women in their own *Zenanas*. The successful approach of *Zenana* Schools was soon employed in other towns as well and rapidly became an accepted method of reaching Indian women.

Initially, the missionary wives led the *Zenana* visitations. Soon, the growth of the *Zenana* visitations and, more importantly, their success, led to single women missionaries being sent to India in increasing numbers specifically for women's work. The Church of England *Zenana* Missionary Society (1880) and the *Zenana* Bible and Medical Mission[6] (1881) were founded. The two Societies divided the field between them with the *Zenana* Missionary Society working in the Punjab, Sind, the Central Provinces, Bengal, the Madras Presidency and South India and the other, in the Ganges valley. These two women's societies cooperated and collaborated with other Protestant societies in India and carried on the work among women. *Zenana* teaching was started in Tamilnadu by Indian Christian women (mostly pastors' wives) like Mrs. T.W. Sattianadhan and Mrs. Bauboo. The *Zenana* Missionary society soon took over the entire work among women in the Church Missionary Society church in Tirunelveli district of Tamilnadu.

The *Zenana* Missions in the homes effectively reached girls and women who would have otherwise not had an opportunity to listen to the Christian message in public at all.[7]

The Bible Women: The system of Bible women (ministry of female catechists) existed in Tranquebar. Miss C.C.Giberne, the first unmarried lady missionary in Tamilnadu, revived the system later in Tirunelveli district in 1844. The Roman Catholics also had two Indian women orders, namely, the Sisters of our Lady of Seven Sorrows and the Congregation of St. Anne

(*Annammals*) similar to the Protestant "Bible women." The sisters were trained to go to the surrounding villages for teaching women and children and for medical care. The Orders, in popular conceptions, were considered as a counterpart of the Protestant "bible women" and were called "Baptist widows."

Education

Besides the *Zenana* missionaries, many other women missionaries came to India. Miss. M.A..Cooke was the first woman missionary to come to India through the British and Foreign School Society as early as 1821. She began organizing schools for girls in Calcutta and very soon, many schools came into existence. Many other women missionaries carried the work of educating women. Notable among them is Isabella Thoburn (1840–1901), the first woman missionary of the Methodist Women's Foreign Missionary Society, who arrived in India in 1870. She devoted herself to the education of women and founded a school for girls in Lucknow. This school later became the first Christian College for women. She was the pioneer of higher education for women. Miss.C.C.Giberine taught at the teachers' training school at Kadachapuram, in Tirunelveli district of Tamilnadu. Indian women were trained and sent to teach in "day schools' in several places. These women served as missionaries in places where there were no churches.

Medical Missions

Clara Swain, another missionary from the Women's Foreign Missionary Society was the first woman medical missionary and began her work at Bareilly in 1870. She pioneered the medical care of Indian women by women. Sara Seward sent by the American Presbyterian

---

[6] The *Zenana* Bible and Medical Mission later became the Bible and Medical Missionary Fellowship and were taken over by male leadership. This is the present-day "Interserve," which still has a lot of women missionaries.

[7] The *Zenana* work had its own limitations especially when a lady opted for baptism against the wishes of her family. The 'secret Christian ladies' of Sivakasi are examples in this regard.

Mission and many others followed her. Efforts were also taken to train Indian women in medicine and medical care. Dr. Edith Brown and Miss Greenfield founded a School of Medicine in Ludhiana in 1894. Dr. Ida S. Scudder founded the medical centre for medical training of women at Vellore, which later became the Christian Medical College in 1945. This prestigious institution is the biggest single Christian medical enterprise in Asia to this day.

The Dohnavur Fellowship

Amy Carmichael (1867–1951) another *Zenana* missionary, was burdened for girls who were devoted to the gods and were used as temple prostitutes. From 1900, despite the risk involved she personally involved herself in the rescue of hundreds of such girls from the clutches of the *devadasi* system, as also abandoned children and boy temple prostitutes. As her work steadily grew the *Dohnavur* Fellowship of Women started in 1920. The Fellowship became the nucleus of the various activities of social upliftment of women in and around that area.

Outstanding Indian Women In Missions

There are several women who contributed to the life of the Church and its mission. Outstanding among them are Pandita Ramabai, Alice Sarabji Pennell, Ellen Lakshmi Goreh and others. We will briefly look at some of them.

Pandita Ramabai (1858 – 1922)

Ramabai was a Maratha Brahmin. Her parents, forced into a pilgrim life, wandered through the various sacred places and earned a living by reciting the *Puranas*. Hence, Ramabai learnt the Puranas and became well versed in the recitation of the *Puranas* and earned the title *Pandita*. She lost her parents and widowed early,

she returned to Poona. Ramabai had nurtured a desire to improve the condition of women, from her childhood, and she began advocating social reforms, especially the rehabilitation of widows through her associations with the *Prarthana Samaj*. She went to England for further training where she came under the influence of Christianity through the Sisters of St. Mary, and was baptized in 1883. She then went to America and through her well wishers started the Ramabai Association. She returned to India to continue her work among women with the support of the Association. She started Sarada Sadan, a home and a school for widows in Bombay that was later shifted to Poona in 1890. When the famine (1896) left hundreds of girls helpless, she developed a settlement at Mukti largely for girls. The Mukti Mission "has been instrumental in saving hundreds of women, girls and child widows from a fate worse than death."[8] Pandita Ramabai had contributed a lot to the emancipation of women and there was an impressive change in the position of women during her life.

Chandra Lela (1825 – 1907)

Chandra Lela was widowed at the early age of nine. Although she belonged to an orthodox Brahmin family, she was disillusioned with idol worship and turned away from it. When she encountered Christian Missionaries she received the gospel and became a missionary. She began to preach the gospel and drew large crowds.[9] She is said to have led more than a hundred thousand people to Christ.[10]

Women and Indigenous Missions

Apart from the pastors' wives and Bible women, in the latter part of the 20th century, in the 50's, women were recruited in their own right by some organisations like Scripture Union,

---

[8] John Caldwell Thiessen, *A Survey of World Mission*, Chicago: Moody Press, 1961, p.44.

[9] It was the novelty of hearing a woman speak in public that drew large crowds. John Caldwell Thiessen, *A Survey of World Mission*, Chicago: Moody Press, 1961, p.45.

[10] *Ibid.*, p.45

Union of Evangelical Students of India, Campus Crusade for Christ, Youth for Christ, Operation Mobilisation, Child Evangelism Fellowship, and India Every Home Crusade. However, it was only in the early 70's that the Indian Indigenous Cross Cultural Missions started recruiting single women in their own right in evangelism and Church planting in the context of cross cultural missions. At present we have a host of women contributing to missions through various avenues in the Church, para Church organisations and Cross Cultural Missions. For one, Dr. Mrs. Iris Paul of the Reaching Hand Society, Malkangiri, Orissa is a notable example.

Christian women have contributed a lot to the Christian Mission enterprise in India The emancipation brought about by Christian missionaries helped women to serve in hospitals as doctors and nurses and in schools as teachers and to participate in Mission. The contribution of women to the life of the Church and Missions cannot be overlooked or neglected. Firth writes:

> The service of women workers, missionaries, teachers, doctors, nurses, bible women and of the women's organisations in the churches has been one of the most effective agencies both in building up the Church's life and in bearing its witness to the non-Christian society by which it is surrounded.[11]

Contribution of Christian Mission to the Empowerment of Women

A striking feature of the Christian Mission enterprise is its impact on the condition of women in Indian society. Christian missionaries contributed a lot to the emancipation of women, primarily through education. They also pioneered medical care for women and played an important role in the liberation of women from socially approved and religiously sanctioned oppressive systems.

Education of women

Christian missions initiated the empowerment of Indian women through their educational endeavors. The missionaries educated women at a time when education was considered unnecessary for women. Some remarked, "Dear me they will teach the cows next" and "you might as well teach monkeys as women."[12] It took a long while to break through such concrete prejudices of the patriarchal Indian society against female education. It was particularly through the effort of the wives of missionaries and later other women like Isabella Thoburn (from 1870) who devoted themselves to educate women, that this was made possible. The education of women brought about a radical change in society.

Liberation

Widow Rehabilitation. The ignominy of widowhood in Indian society led to untold miseries of its widows. Often these widows were young because of the prevalent societal practice of child marriage. The Roman Catholic Church made the care of widows its special concern. It gave the lead in practising widow remarriage as early as 1843.[13] Such a breakthrough along with other factors contributed to the Widow Re-marriage Act (1856). The Order *Annammals* was exclusively for widows. Similarly, the Protestant Missionary C.C.Giberne employed widows and elderly women as teachers at the training school at Tirunelveli. The missionaries also contributed to the formulation of "the Age of Consent Bill

---

[11] C.B.Firth, *Introduction to Indian Church History*, p.195.

[12] Quoted by Arthur Jeyakumar in "Christianity among the Nadars," F. Hrangkhuma, ed., *Christianity in India*, Delhi: ISPCK, 1998, p.134.

[13] The wedding took place secretly in Trichirapalli. There was an uproar after the news about the wedding broke out. The subsequent discussions convinced those who opposed widow remarriage. In the next 20 years about 100 more marriages of widows took place.

(1891) and the Christian Marriage Restriction Act (1929)" which fixed the minimum age to consummate marriage. These bills raised the status of women.

Abolition of Sati. Christian missionaries vehemently protested against *satisahagamana* - the burning alive of a Hindu widow on the funeral pyre of her husband. William Carey opposed this horrific social evil from the day he became aware of the practice. He reported cases as they happened and built public opinion against it. The protests soon gained momentum abroad and in India as many others like Raja Ram Mohan Roy joined the struggle. Finally, in 1829, Lord William Bentick issued an order prohibiting *Sati*. Carey, being the official government translator immediately translated the order for the fear that a delay on his part could lead to the death of precious lives of women. Thus the practice of *Sati* was banned.

Dignity and self-worth. Caste rules in South Kerala and South Tamil Nadu imposed restrictions on the mode of dress. *Chanar* or *Nadar* women were allowed to wear just a coarse piece of cloth known as ' *mundu*' extending from the waist to the knee leaving the breasts bare. The women were required to uncover their bosom in the presence of upper caste men. Such a practice was humiliating and not honorable for the women. The missionaries encouraged the women to cover the upper part of their body by wearing blouses. They even trained the girls in the boarding schools to make and use a kind of loose blouse known as "fringe *ravikai*" with short sleeves, which was tied in front with a string. These blouses were sold to women at the cost of the material and given free to the poor. Besides,

the missionaries made many representations and petitions to the government to grant women this freedom and gave much publicity for this in England. Through the relentless missionary effort, the *Nadar* women were invested with dignity and self-worth. This in turn led to a movement for social upliftment among the entire *Nadar* community.

Similarly, Christian missions also liberated hundreds of girls under the clutches of the *devadasi* system. The work of Amy Carmichael is highly commendable. Amy Carmichael's care for the dancing girls contributed to the abolition of the *devadasi* system in Kanyakumari district (1930) and in the whole of Tamilnadu (1947).

Christian missionaries had a far reaching influence on Indian society. Non-Christians who were influenced by Christian Missionaries initiated many of the social reform movements that sprung up outside the Church. Firth rightly concludes:

Today girls education has become a rule rather than an exception, women graduates are plentiful and women are nowadays playing an increasing part in public life. It would be absurd to claim that this is entirely due to the example and the work of Christian Missions; but we may justly claim that Christians have been in the forefront of the movement for the emancipation of women.[14]

Women in Missions since 1947 [15]

Critical review of women in Missions since 1947:

Women have been part of Missions contributing significantly. However, Mission

---

[14] C.B. Firth, *Introduction to Indian Church History*, p194.

[15] This section has been taken from the track paper presented by Beulah Herbert for the Women in Church and Society track in the All India Conference On Church In Mission, New Delhi, 23 - 27 Nov. 1999. Several persons had gathered the material for the track paper that was in three parts. The part on Women In Society was contributed to by Augusta Paul, the section on Women in Missions by Ellen Alexander and the one on Women in Church by Leela Manasseh. The entire paper was put together and edited by Beulah Herbert. Mrs. Ellen Alexander contributed this section taken from the track paper.

agencies are run by and large by men. Apart from the early indigenous missions such as the Indian Missionary Society and the National Missionary Society founded by the late Bishop V.S. Azariah of Dornakal in the second decade of this century and the mission departments and boards of several denominations, there has been a proliferation of Indian indigenous missions in the South after the '50's. Till the early seventies the cross cultural mission agencies had no place for a single woman missionary in her own right. But now almost every mission agency in any part of the country recruits and employs single women missionaries. These women have been doing a great deal of work especially in linguistics and Bible translation and evangelising women and children. Most of the para-Church organisations that are not specifically categorised as cross cultural missions are also recruiting and employing women workers.

Interserve, formerly known as *Zenana Medical Mission* started as a women's missionary organization, but has been taken over by men. While Interserve has some women in leadership and in principle has no problem with female leadership, it does not have many women at the top.

The Union of Evangelical Students of India has had women but did not allow them to teach doctrine in mixed camps. But over the years change is taking place in its strong male leadership. It has women executive secretaries and presently allows women to teach doctrines. There is still a long way to go.

The number of women faculty and students in theological institutions is far less than the number of men. Marriage is pointed out as one reason. However, for several years some Institutions had women faculty teaching Christian Education and English. In many major theological colleges both the husband and the wife could not be on the faculty.

In many Mission organisations in which couples are recruited the woman does not have an identity of her own but is seen as a "staff wife"; not an equal but a second fiddle.

The emphasis of the role of women in Missions has been to be a support to the calling of the *man*; her place is in the home bringing up children and offering hospitality and if and when time permits she is asked to do other things. It is recognised that domestic responsibilities whether for the husband or the wife are important. However, the domestic role of the women has been emphasized to the negligence of the husband's responsibility in the domestic sphere and the negligence of training, capability and the needs of the wife.

Hurdles, needs and trends.

The role of women in missions thus far is a matter of praise to God since several women have been built and nurtured even though women have not been in leadership positions.

Some theological institutions and Mission Agencies, which like to have women in leadership, have a problem in finding women to take up leadership. In some others the women are ready but the hierarchy is not. The reasons can be:

- Years of biased teaching
- On marriage the woman follows her husband and takes on his calling
- Lack of acceptance of single women
- Culture
- Lack of opportunities for training and development to equip women to take leadership.

Many Institutions have made discriminations in the use of the library, kind of jobs, requirements of travelling work, the demand that the women leave the organisation when they get married and so on. Some of these issues are quite real and practical. However, these hurdles need to be crossed over by finding practical and realistic solutions and not by discriminatory trend setting.

When a woman gets married within the circle of missions irrespective of her training, calling and gifts she is expected to abandon all of it and fall in line with her husband's mission. This does not happen with Christians in the secular work force. While many women who are pastors wives and wives of workers in several para-Church organisations are given the freedom to take up secular work or in few cases be involved in different kind of Christian work, several cross cultural agencies curtail this freedom. It is recognised that in a cross cultural mission situation there is a great need for both the husband and wife to be involved in the work of the same agency. However, there are situations where there is the calling and the feasibility of the wife and the husband being involved in the work of different agencies, mission or secular. These situations should be recognised and the wife given the freedom to follow God's call for her.

The role of women in the corporate world has changed. The Church which should have given the world a biblical agenda, has unfortunately left us to follow the world. The world sees women as good managers, especially of people, because of their ability to be in touch with their feelings, relational abilities and their ability to make decisions.

Women in India can be classified into three types:

- *The contemporary woman* who is there, side by side with men, able to do everything as well as men.

- *The confused woman* not in a derogatory sense, but a woman still searching, seeking and sending out feelers for her identity and what she can and should do. She is inhibited by years of teaching and expectations from her society and culture, but wants to break out.

- *The complacent woman* is content in her own way and "could-not-care-less" about her role or status willing to go along.

Our mission organisations perhaps fall into the second group. Most of the missions do not have a clear and specific planned strategy for women. The role of women in ministry has been a neglected theme in missions according to a leading missiologist.[16] Two Indian missiologists write that it is pure excuse to say our culture does not accept women as leaders because our Indian culture has already accepted women as Prime Minister and cabinet minister and there are many women gurus in Hinduism.[17] However, most of the women are recognising their abilities and needs. There is a great need for their abilities to be recognised and needs to be met. This has to be addressed. Before our behaviour and attitudes change our thinking has to change, *the thinking that men can do better than women*. It is this thinking that prevents men and women from giving women opportunities for training and to use that training.

Challenges and Opportunities.

- Changes are taking place in Missions giving women opportunities to serve moving out of the kitchen into the classroom, boardroom and the field.

- Men and women in Society, in the Church and in Missions do not have to get into competition with one another or see others as a threat.

---

[16] Roger Hedlund, "Introduction" in Sam Lazarus,ed., *Proclaiming Christ,* p. xi quoted in Rajendran.K., *Which Way Forward: A Critique of 25 years 1972-1997*, Bangalore: SAIACS Press, 1998, p. 184.

[17] Jacob Kavunkal and F. Hrangkhuma, *Bible in Mission in India Today*, Bombay: St.Paul's Press, 1993, p.283 quoted in K. Rajendran, p. 184.

· The Gospel is about freedom and about giving and receiving. We need to give this freedom and space to one another to be the persons God wants us to be and do what God wants each one of us to do.

· We are called to be trendsetters. The Church turned the world ' upside down' or should we say the "right side up"? We need to set biblical trends, find new paths and give the world a map to follow.

· The New Millennium must be a year of Jubilee in which fathers set their daughters free, husbands set their wives free, sons set their mothers free not just in words of mere "tokenism", but in day to day living, practicality and reality.

Theology of Gender[18]

This section would consider the different aspects of Gender issues and Missions. There are various issues involved. They are —

· A consideration of a theology of gender

· A consideration of theology from a gender perspective

· A consideration of the gender perspective of the Communicator's culture

· A consideration of the gender perspective of the Receptor Culture

· And gender issues of practical nature to be dealt with in the receptor culture.

The theology of gender issues will be dealt with next to the theology from a gender perspective.

Theology from a Gender Perspective

There is a body of Christian doctrine handed down to us, through the centuries, which has largely been articulated by men. The various topics of Christian doctrine like God, Trinity, Christ, Sin, Salvation, Church and Ministry, and Ethics have not been considered from a gender perspective. In recent times, Feminist theologians, both men and women, have articulated these doctrines from a gender perspective. Such articulations have risen from a deep recognition of such a lapse. We shall briefly discuss these doctrines from a gender perspective. This paper will just deal with the doctrines from a gender perspective and not deal with a comprehensive survey of the whole of the Christian doctrine.

Doctrine of God. The primary questions that emerge out of the doctrine of God from a gender perspective are: Does God have gender and sexuality? Or does God transcend gender and sexuality? The biblical witness does not show anywhere that God is 'gendered'. It depicts God as one who transcends both gender and sexuality.[19] God being a Spirit does not have a biological nature of which sexuality is only an aspect. God also transcends the entire created order and so transcends gender and sexuality, which are parts of the created order.[20]

However, there have been attempts to depict God as in some way related to some aspects of sexuality. This view holds that sexuality is a part of the spiritual nature and hence deeper than the biological reproductive sexual nature. Such attempts have not been helpful in giving an adequate expression to the biblical revelation of God as a transcendent One, especially in the multi-religious South Asian context. The concept and origin of gods and goddesses depicted with maleness and femaleness[21] already exists in

---

[18] This part of the article has been contributed by Beulah Herbert, taperecorded by her, transcribed by Sam Thambusamy and edited by Beulah Herbert

[19] Aida Spencer, et.al., *Goddess Revival,* Grand Rapids: Baker Books, 1995, pp. 48-51. *Cf.* Miroslav Volf, *Exclusion and Embrace*, Nashville: Abingdon, 1996, pp.170–71, 173.

[20] Miroslav Volf , *Exclusion and Embrace*, Abingdon: Nashville, 1996, pp.170–71, 173.

[21] Chung, Hyun Kyung, *Struggle to be Son Again: Introducing Asian Women's theology*, New York: Orbis Books,1990, pp.48f citing Padma Gallop.

religions such as Hinduism and other Popular and Primal religions. Hence, an effort to depict God with some aspects of maleness and/or femaleness makes the theological task of explaining the uniqueness of a transcendent God extremely difficult. Moreover, this could possibly lead to a misinterpretation and misrepresentation. It was precisely for this reason that the Old Testament clearly affirmed the transcendence of God. The unequivocal affirmation of the transcendence of God is primarily to safeguard any misunderstanding of God in the midst of the prevalent Cannanite fertility cults and the other religions of the Ancient Near Eastern world.[22] Therefore, an attempt to affix gender and sexuality to God is not contributive to the understanding of God as the transcendent One.

The same can be said for the use of masculine and feminine terms, and other imageries to speak of God. To speak of God either in male and female imageries or in strict masculine and feminine terms[23] could only be done at the risk of compromising the transcendence of God. The categorization of humanity into masculine and feminine nodes springs from a Freudian psychoanalytic notion[24] rather than the Bible. The Bible does use imageries and metaphors to speak of God. For example, God has been depicted as a fatherly or motherly one or a compassionate, concerned and gracious one or midwife[25] etc.; but these imageries or metaphors in no way attribute any gender or sexuality to God.

In general, the teaching of the Bible is that God transcends gender and sexuality and any attempt to accede gender and sexuality to God and attribute maleness and femaleness to God runs contrary to the biblical witness.

Doctrine of Trinity. The three persons of the Holy Trinity have been depicted in various other ways.[26] Some Feminist theologians have reacted against the use of male terms in the conception of God as a Triune God - God the Father, God the Son and God the Holy Spirit. While some have used alternative terms like "Creator - Redeemer - Sustainer- Sanctifier- Friend" [27] for the three persons of the Trinity, others conceive the Trinity as one "Holy family".[28] The Holy Spirit is depicted as a female principle or person within the Godhead[29] and the Trinity is conceived as a "Holy family" - Father, mother and child.

However, the conception of God as the "Father - Son – Spirit" in no way attributes gender and sexuality to God. The "Father – Son" within the Trinity is in no way a biological relationship but rather represents the 'fatherly' relationship of "God - the Father", primarily to Jesus Christ.[30] God extends such a "fatherly" relationship to every believer who comes to God through Jesus. The alternative terms also do not bring such "relationality" when used for God. We have already seen that the biblical witness affirms that God, being a Spirit, transcends gender and sexuality. Therefore the Holy family depiction, that of "Father – Mother – Child" does not

---

[22] Aida Spencer et.al., *Goddess Revival,* pp. 85-92.

[23] Phyllis Trible, *God and the Rhetoric of Sexuality*, Philadelphia: Fortress Press, 1978.

[24] Miroslav Volf, ' Gender Identity' in *Exclusion and Embrace*, chp 4, Grand Rapids: Baker Books, 1995, pp.169-190.

[25] Aida Spencer, et.al., *The Goddess Revival,* pp.110 –113.

[26] Daphne, Hamson, *Theology and Feminism,* Oxford, Basil Blackwell,1 990, pp.71-72.

[27] Daphne, Hamson, *Theology and Feminism,* pp.92-96.

[28] Elizabeth Vendel - Molmann & Jurgen Moltmann, *Humanity in God,* New York:Pilgrim Press, 1983, p.101.

[29] Elizabeth A., Johnson, "The maleness of Christ" in Anne Carr and Elisabeth Fiorenza, eds, *The Special Nature of Women*, London: SCM Press, 1991, p.113.

[30] A. Lewis, *Motherhood of God, A report by a study group appointed by woman's guild and the panel on doctrine on the invitation of the general assembly of the Church of Scotland,* Edinburgh: St. Andrew Press, 1984, pp.17-18.

harmonize well with the biblical witness. Further, the use of the feminine noun '*sophia*' to point to "wisdom" and *logos*, a masculine term used to refer to the second person of the Trinity do not point to a female principle and are not to be taken to mean a female person or principle within the Godhead.

Christology. Some feminists have reacted to the maleness of Jesus Christ. While some have completely rejected a male Saviour for women, others like Rose Mary Ruether[31] have raised the question: Can a male Saviour save women? Others have recognized that Jesus had to be a male since Jesus had to be a human within a particular socio-cultural and historical context. Because God transcends sexuality and gender, there is no problem for God Incarnate to relate to men and women, the sexuality of Jesus of Nazareth being no barrier. Even a casual study of the actions and attitudes of Jesus within the framework of a male human person detailed in the Bible suggests that He cut across the division between men and women. Jesus related to women just as he related to men without any problem of inhibition and discrimination. So, Jesus Christ saves in and through transcending the human maleness of Jesus.[32] He is the saviour of women since both men and women relate alike to the same God.[33]

The doctrine of Sin and Salvation. Sin in Christian theology is understood as "rebellion", "disobedience" and even interpreted as "pride". This has led to reactions from the feminists, particularly to the notion of Sin as "pride". They maintain that it is meaningless to talk of "pride" to women who are abused, oppressed and subordinated. They opine that in the Feminist point of view, 'Sin' is not one of "pride" but rather to be understood as "not being assertive", "unwillingness to take responsibility", "allowing others to dominate and treat them as mindless children and slaves."[34]

Although the meaning of "Sin" may be different in accordance with the context, we cannot move away in essence from the biblical portrayal of Sin. The Bible portrays "Sin" as "arrogance", "over reaching" and "disobedience." Women, although oppressed, suppressed and abused, do have a fallen sinful nature of pride and disobedience in whichever particular form their sinfulness is expressed. In the missiological contexts "Sin" needs to be carefully interpreted and applied differently, keeping in mind the men and women we encounter within the specific socio-cultural contexts.

Salvation. Likewise Salvation is seen or argued by feminist theologians to be different. Salvation primarily means "deliverance" or "re-uniting with God". This may, in different contexts, acquire different interpretations and be applied appropriately. A feminist viewpoint need not be different and discontinuous from what has been interpreted through the centuries by male theologians. A feminist view may be continuous with the biblical interpretation of sin and salvation.

It is also argued that the concept of "sacrifice" is meaningless to oppressed women who have always been used to sacrificing themselves for the sake of others.[35] Although such sacrifices call for our due sympathies, we need

---

[31] Rosemary Ruether, "Can a male saviour save women" in *Sexism and God Talk: Towards a Feminist Theology*, Boston: Beacon Press, 1983 pp.116-134.

[32] *Ibid.* pp.137-138.

[33] Aida Spencer, *The Goddess Revival*, 1995. Compare Daphne Hamson's view that men and women are not alike *Theology and Feminism*, p. 132.

[34] Daphne Hamson, *Theology and Feminism*, p.121-131, 145.

[35] Elizabeth Wendel - Moltmann & Jurgen Moltmann, *Humanity in God*, pp.119-121.

to recognize that many women may sacrifice themselves without a heartfelt commitment to Jesus Christ. The sacrifice of Jesus Christ is rooted in God and springs from a deep love, commitment to God and not necessarily denial of self. The same may not be the case with every woman who sacrifices herself. It may be simply a "self abnegation" which once again is rooted in the self. Though their "sacrifice" is not to be belittled, questioned or denied, sacrifice and not self-abnegation is to be upheld. We need to see whether such women sacrifice themselves for the sake of others having committed themselves to God and whether it is an outcome of their situation of oppression and domination.

The doctrine of Ecclesia or Community. The Bible speaks of community for it is central to the people of God, their life and relationship with God. While some radical feminists envisage women's communities and churches, the Bible does not speak of separate *ecclesia* each separate for women and for men, but rather a community of women and men.[36] God created humanity as male and female. The community envisioned by God is also of men and women[37] - not men apart from women and vice versa. The radical feminists' claim of women's communities negates the true community[38] - one that consists of men and women. The true community is reconciled and made one, and is inclusive of both men and women, young and old and all other segments of society torn apart. The wholesome community displays mutual love, respect and trust. Women and men live and work together in harmony without enmity and competition. The community lives together and affirms true community extending reconciliation, healing and unity. The doctrine of community from a gender perspective should uphold a community, tearing down whatever keeps women and men apart.

Doctrine of Ministry. The concept of Ministry from a gender perspective should deal with the involvement of women in Mission and their participation in decision making both within the Church and outside the Church and in cross cultural missions as well. As this point is to be elaborated elsewhere, in this section on gender issues and the doctrine of ministry, it is not dealt with elaborately. Suffice it to say that women ought to be given equal opportunities with no segregation or restrictions laid upon their ministry and participation. In the ministry of the Church "giftedness" and "call" need to be affirmed, encouraged and promoted. Women should be given equal opportunity to involve and participate equally along with men in cross cultural missions and evangelism.

Christian Ethics. The missiological implications in the area of ethics relate to overcoming discrimination and working for gender equity which is truly to be seen in every aspect of ethics. Gender issues in themselves are an issue of ethics. In each receptor culture or community the particular issue of ethics may be different. Despite this, equal partnership of women without any gender discrimination has to be advanced within the particularity of the socio-cultural context of Mission. The particular concerns of Ethics from a gender perspective are of Gender Justice, Gender Equity and working towards a community of mutuality and equality.

Gender Perspective of the Communicator's Culture and Receptor Culture

Another key aspect of the gender issue which is pertinent to the missiological context is that of

---

[36] All the three works of Letty Russell. *Future of Partnership*, Basil Blackwell: Oxford, 1979; *Growth in Partnership*, Oxford: Basil Blackwell, 1981; *Becoming Human*, Oxford: Basil Blackwell, 1982.

[37] Letty Russell, *Growth in Partnership*, pp.66,70-71.Elizabeth Wendel-Moltmann & Jurgen Moltmann, *Humanity in God*, p.88, 95-106.

[38] For example the separatist movement of Mary Daly.

the culture of the gospel communicator. The gospel communicator would have resolved certain gender issues and this baggage should not be carried to the receptor culture or community. The dominant issue in the context of the gospel communicator need not necessarily be the same in the receptor culture. Issues dominant in the receptor culture need to be identified and dealt with accordingly. In the Indian culture women would not boldly talk to men let alone a stranger. However, in cross cultural mission encounters women are required to talk boldly to men. Women need to come out of their cultural mould and thinking and readily adapt themselves to the challenges of the missiological situation. For example the earlier white missionaries who came to India did not have the practice of covering their heads in their normal everyday life. But, upon their arrival, because of the demands of the Missiological context, they went about covering their heads like other Indian women. The missionaries covered their heads to identify with the Indian women. Secondly, they accepted the feature of the Indian culture wherein respectable women covered their heads. The missionaries did not want to be seen as questionable characters. Gender issues arising out of the existing social limitations and restrictions in the receptor culture or community are to be thought through. If they do not conflict with the basic gospel message these could be welcomed and accepted. The principle that governs is to see that the gospel is not discredited and does not become a stumbling block.

Although we need to be careful, we need to be conscious of the fact that the gospel does critique the oppressive elements of every culture and transforms them. The missionaries carried on a relentless struggle against certain socially accepted and religiously sanctioned practices in Indian society which were especially oppressive towards women. For example, the *Chanar* or *Nadar* women were required to uncover their bosom in the presence of upper caste men. The missionaries saw it as a humiliating practice and not honorable for the women. The case was fought by Amy Carmichael at the Palayamkotai Court and the rights were won for the *Nadar* women.[39] The missionaries also trained women to make and use a blouse. Similarly, other oppressive elements like child marriage, oppressive widowhood, *Sati* and the *Devadasi* system that existed in 19th century Indian society, were transformed by the power of the gospel.

There could be several practices in the receptor culture which deny rights to women and hinder an unfolding of a harmonious community. Every practice within a culture that does not truly reflect the biblical pattern of gender equality needs to be challenged and changed. The renewed community envisioned is to be one in which men and women live harmoniously with equality, love and partnership based on mutual trust and respect. Such a transformation of the receptor culture or community is to be worked out by constantly weighing each gender issue against the biblical injunctions.

Missiological Implications of Gender Issues

The questions that are foremost are: who is the woman in the receptor culture? and who is the woman in the communicator's culture? To begin with, it is important that the concept of woman – as one created in God's image equal to man, and also given the responsibility to take care of the created order – has to be worked out in the gospel communicator's culture, in the mission life of the communicator and in the receptor culture. It is not simply a woman having been created in the image of God but a woman (just as the man) having been created equally in God's image and having been made into a community, a

---

[39] The circular order of the Government of Travancore in May 1814 allowed a concession for the Nadar female converts to Christianity to wear *Kuppayam* (Jacket) .

community of mutuality and equal partnership. This needs to be worked out. The identity, the role and the relationship of women have to be spelt out in these cultures and in a situation of mutual equality according to the biblical norms of equality, mutuality and interdependence.

One major aspect of missiological concern is the gender issue. There is an urgent need for a theology of gender. Such a theology[40] should attempt to delineate the identity and the role of women and describe the relationship of women with men.

Identity and role of women. The identity of women is derived from the creation narratives found in Gen. 1, 2

- Women have been created in the image of God just as men have been created in the image of God.

- The sexual difference between men and women is only the second step since it relates to their biological reproductive nature. The "multiplying" that is spoken of follows the creation of humanity in the image of God as male and female.

- Both men and women carry the same social mandate for "dominion", "authority" and "rulership" (read better as stewardship).

- The creation of woman after the man as narrated in the second chapter of Genesis does not imply inferiority. Likewise the creation of the woman from the rib of the man is indicative of a "side-by side relationship" – shoulder to shoulder – in equal and mutual partnership. The exclamation of the man – "bone of my bone and flesh of my flesh" underlines the relationship between them and points

to the fundamental unity between men and women.

- According to the creation narrative in Gen. 2, woman has been created as a "helper". This in no way is used in the sense of a servant or a person of secondary role or status but rather used in the sense of a strong support.

- The naming of the woman does not symbolize any "domination" or "acquiring power" over the woman but rather it suggests the identification of her as a woman.

- In the last few verses of Gen 2 we read of the marriage relationship. The *'becoming one flesh'* is not merely physical aspect, but in every aspect of life. This oneness can be built only upon equality, mutuality and interdependence within that relationship. This oneness is not to be understood as an amalgamation or fusing of the two to the extent of annihilation of each but as a peculiar oneness of heart and soul and mind and life. The personal distinctiveness of each is maintained but also interdependence is upheld within such a relationality.

The Fall. Such a harmonious created order was disrupted during the Fall. The Fall described in Gen. 3 does not indicate any gender difference. The man and the woman are equally accountable and responsible for their disobedience and the decree of God after the Fall is not a cursing judgement, but a spelling out of the consequence of disobedience and Sin. The Fall has disrupted the harmonious relationship of both the man and the woman with God and with each other. As an outcome of the Fall the new sinful situation presents the domination of women by men and

---

[40] An egalitarian perspective is explicated by a number of persons such as Bilezikian, Mary Evans, Mary Hayter, Joy Fleming Elasky, Rebecca Merrill Groothuis, Aida Spencer, Miroslav Volf, Mary Stewart VanLeeuwen, Gretchen Gaebelein Hull.

manouvering, manipulation, domination and possession of men by women. This disrupted relationship is redeemed and reversed by Jesus Christ.

Jesus. The life of Jesus shows how God treats men and women as equal partners and how He gives equal opportunities to know, follow and love God. Jesus' attitude and actions invest women with status as truly belonging to the Kingdom of God as equal partners with men.

The New Testament. The New Testament Church valued the participation of women in accordance to the spiritual gifts apportioned to them by God through the Spirit. Opportunities for ministry were given according to their "call" and "giftedness". There are certain passages that seemingly restrict women from total participation in the life of the community. For example, I Cor.11; I Cor.14, and I Tim.2 need to be carefully interpreted in the specificity of the socio-cultural background of the Corinthian and the Ephesian churches. The question is whether these restrictions are "eternal principles" (for all men- at all times- in all places) or whether these restrictions are given to women in a particular situation in a particular context of society and Mission. Paul does not seem to restrict women to a subordinate role at all times. The Apostle had called women 'co-workers' and recognized them as his colleagues in ministry elsewhere in the New Testament. The basic principle is to be derived from Gal 2:28 which underlines that there is no discrimination between the two genders. Walls of separation and every other barrier that separates are broken down and both women and men are reconciled within the redeemed Community. Paul neither contradicts himself nor his master in upholding gender equality and gender justice.

Conclusion

The Christian mission enterprise reached out to women in India. Its focus and labor for women is significant against the background of both the oppressive social evils and societal apathy towards emancipation of women. Christian missionaries contributed a lot to the emancipation of women, primarily through Education. They pioneered medical care for women and played an important role in the liberation of women from socially approved and religiously sanctioned oppressive systems. Ever since, several Indian women have made enormous contributions to the life of the Church and its Mission. The role of women in missions thus far is a matter of praise to God. However, although women have been built and nurtured, women have not been incorporated in the leadership of administrative and decision-making structures. The Church should give the world a biblical agenda and help the world find new paths and a map to follow. There is an urgent need for a theology of gender. Such a theology attempts to delineate the identity and the role of women and describe the relationship of women with men. In the ministry of the Church 'giftedness' and 'call' need to be affirmed, encouraged and promoted. Women ought to be given equal opportunities with no segregation or restriction laid upon their ministry and participation. To facilitate this, it is important that the concept of woman - as one created equally as a man in God's image, and also given the responsibility to take care of the created order - has to be worked out. This working out has to take place in the gospel communicator's culture, in the mission life of the communicator and in the receptor culture. It is not enough to simply claim that a woman has been created in the image of God. It is important to go further and affirm that a woman is also created equally in God's image just as the man, and that women and men have been made to form a community, a community of mutuality, equal partnership, independence and interdependence put in practice. It is also equally important to spell out the identity, the role and the relationship of women according to the biblical norms of equality, mutuality and interdependence.

CHAPTER 41

An Alternate Reading of Poverty[1]

JAYAKUMAR CHRISTIAN

Before we take a fresh look at models of transformational initiatives among the poor, it is important for us to examine our understanding of poverty. Our understanding of the poor and their relationships must shape our models of transformation. How do we understand the people we seek to serve—the poor? What is the context of our transformational initiatives?

Poverty continues to defy simplistic descriptions, definitions and easy solutions. It continues to raise very uncomfortable questions for our continued reflection and response.

Essentially, poverty is about relationships. It is a flesh-and-blood experience of a people within their day-to-day relationships. Within these relationships, the poor experience deprivation, powerlessness, physical isolation, economic poverty and all other characteristics of poverty. This chapter seeks to examine the many dimensions of this relationship. It focuses on the nature and causes of chronic intergenerational poverty. The author hopes that this alternative reading of poverty will provide some defining parameters for constructing the next-generation paradigm of transformation.

Poverty – Captivity within the God Complexes of the Powerful

Any serious student of poverty is immediately confronted with the fact that all is not well with relationships in poverty situations. Even the "perfect social harmony" of the powerful is not without its cracks and flaws. For poverty is about a powerful minority, "less numerous, [which] perform[s] all political functions, monopolize[s] power and enjoy[s] the advantages that power brings" (Curtis 1981, 332). These powerful seek to play god in the lives of the poor, reinforcing each other to form a "god complex." To play god in the lives of the vulnerable is essentially an expression of the inherent ability of humans to be evil.

The Nature of God Complexes

Let me explain the term *god complex*. In poverty situations, the term refers to those who:

- seek to absolutize themselves.

- base their power on what Max Weber calls the "eternal yesterday" (Curtis 1981, 427) to influence the "eternal tomorrows" of the poor.

- seek to influence areas of the life of the poor that are beyond their particular scope of influence (Wrong 1979, 250). Among commercial sex workers, for example, the landlord may go beyond the moneylender role to act as the "protector" of the girls in the community, shielding them from the local police and the political powers. The commercial sex workers, however, have to buy this "protection." The landlord is going beyond his specific scope of influence.

---

[1] "An Alternate Reading of Poverty" by Jayakumar Christian was published originally in the book, *Working with the Poor*, edited by Bryant L. Myers, published by World Vision, 1999, and is used with permission.

- within poverty situations claim immutability. They operate under the assumption that they will never experience "power deflation,"[2] and their power can never be challenged.

- work in conjunction with others to keep the poor powerless, making it a "complex." It is the interplay of several power holders that keeps the poor powerless.

This tendency to absolutize power, influence eternal tomorrows, overflow scope-specific influence, claim immutability and fear power deflation are traits that are normally attributed to gods. In poverty situations the powerful seek to play the role of god in the lives of the poor.

Walter Wink's description of the "domination system" in his book *Unmasking the Powers* parallels the description of the god complexes in poverty relationships (Wink 1992).[3] Wink describes the "domination system" as a system that:

• demands that the world value power as an end in itself;

• requires society to become more like itself;

• acquires a sense of independence "beyond human control";

• assumes an identity of its own; and

• wounds the soul of its subjects (Wink 1992, 54, 40, 41, 41, 101).

These god complexes hold the poor captive. They feel threatened with any transformational initiative that undermines their foundations. They operate through people, systems and structures (Liddle 1992, 795). Religious systems, mass media, law, government policies and people in powerful positions all serve to reinforce the god complexes that keep the poor poor.

God complexes also have an ideological center, an inner reality that governs and holds together the structures, systems and people. This inner reality provides the logic for the structures and systems, and offers interpretations on ultimate values for life, events and processes. For example, the media, apart from marketing products passionately, also aggressively promote a particular interpretation of life's ultimate values. Since these ideological centers deal with ultimate values, I refer to them as "inner spiritualities" or "spiritual interiorities." Structures and systems are inextricably rooted in these spiritual interiorities. They form the "spirituality" of the various economic, social, political, bureaucratic and religious structures and systems. Therefore, apart from structure, systems and people, there is the "interiority of earthly institutions or structures or systems" (Wink 1992, 77). These inner spiritualities provide that underlying "spiritual dimension in the victimization of the poor and the power accruing activity of the systems" (Linthicum 1991, 19).

So god complexes are clusters of power (social, economic, bureaucratic, political and religious) within the domain of poverty relationships that absolutize themselves to keep the poor powerless. These god complexes hold the poor captive.

---

[2] "Power deflation," according to Anthony Giddens, is the "spiraling diminution of 'confidence' in the agencies of power so that those subordinate to them come increasingly to question their position" (see Cassell 1993, 223).

[3] Wink's primary thesis in *Engaging the Powers* is that we need to avoid the "cosmic personifications that disguise the power arrangement of the state [and the] . . . mystification of actual power relations that provided divine legitimacy for oppressive earthly institutions" (1992, 25). However, I do not see the need to depersonal- ize cosmic forces or principalities and powers to understand the relationship between cosmic forces and structures and systems. Wink's description of the domination system appears to be about the power of structures rather than the cosmic powers in structures. I will deal with the role of personal principalities and powers in poverty situations later in this chapter.

Redefining Who Rules

If poverty is about the god complexes of the non-poor and related structures, systems, people and spiritual interiorities, then our transformational initiatives must seek to reverse these god complexes. Transformation is about challenging the god complexes that cause the human spirit to bow down to any other than its Creator. This challenge must involve encounters with persons, structures, systems and spiritual interiorities that perpetuate the god complexes. Transformation is more than a bundle of successful "sustainable" programs—it is an encounter of conflicting spiritualities.

If transformational initiatives must challenge god complexes within poverty situations, then establishing the kingdom of God must be a valid alternative. God's kingdom does not co-exist with other kingdoms and god complexes. The kingdom of God is that radical alternative to oppressive god complexes. Proclaiming the absolute nature of the King of the kingdom of God in the face of these god complexes is the most radical of all options. The kingdom of God challenges all other initiatives that seek to absolutize themselves in the lives of the poor. If we are to challenge the god complexes, then the kingdom of God is not peripheral to our models of transformation —it is the core.

Establishing God's rule will also involve an encounter at the spirituality level and will challenge our flawed understanding of power. It is important to communicate the kingdom's understanding that all power belongs to God (Ps. 62).

This understanding of poverty and consequent model of transformational response to the poor makes our involvement more than simple development work. It is a prophetic ministry of a dependent community—challenging the god complexes.

Some questions for our consideration

- Do our transformational initiatives consistently express the reign of God among us?
- Are we enabling communities to discover and live under the reign of God?
- Are we seeking to reverse the god complexes that keep the poor poor?
- Do we tend to become a god complex ourselves over the poor?
- ·Do our development teams believe and express a redefined understanding of power—power as defined by the Word?
- Do we train our teams to understand and analyze the structure, systems, people, values and spiritual interiorities that characterize a god complex?
- Do our definitions of sustainability and empowerment include equipping the poor to deal with structure, systems, people, values and spiritual interiorities?

Poverty – The Result of Broken Relationships

Another important mark of poverty situations is broken relationships. The poor are excluded from the mainstream of society, and their sense of community is marred.

Exclusion from the Mainstream

First, let us examine the exclusion of the poor from the mainstream of society. It is a "systematic process of disempowerment" (Friedmann 1992, 30), excluding the poor from the economic, political, social, bureaucratic and religious mainstream of society. It is also a selective process.

This exclusion of the poor is rooted in the world's rejection of the wisdom of the poor as not worthy of any attention. As Len Doyal and Ian Gough rightly point out, the voice of the poor is regarded as "damaged goods" by the powerful—blemished either by ignorance or self-interest, consequently giving way to abuses of power (1991, 11).

The poor also exclude themselves by not participating in social and political processes. The poor do not speak up; they may even decline to sit down with the powerful. Weak, powerless and isolated, they are often reluctant to push themselves forward (Chambers 1988, 18).

Society uses different social systems to exclude the poor. The legal system is probably the most commonly used tool in this process. The "legality" of economic systems excludes the poor. Legality becomes a privilege available only to those with political and economic power; those excluded— the poor—have no alternative but illegality (Llosa 1989, xii).

Apart from legal systems, the education system is also designed to ensure inter-generational exclusion of the poor from the mainstream. Poor children are excluded from this system, thus creating the future poor. Arguing that curriculum development is always both political and pedagogical, Paulo Freire concludes: "It is the very structures of society that create a serious set of barriers and difficulties, some in solidarity with others, that result in enormous obstacles for the children of subordinate classes to come to school (Freire 1993, 30).

Fragmentation of Community

Apart from excluding the poor from the mainstream, the sense of community among the poor is always under attack. For the poor, being a community is an integral part of who they are— their basic unit and their survival mechanism. The powerful always threaten the sense of community in poverty situations.

Power threatens community; it is divisive. When power encounters poverty, the community base is eroded. As Sik Hung Ng points out, power breeds conflict. Humans oppose humans in the struggle to attain, share or influence power. "Power is, therefore, divisive and leads to antagonism and conflict" (Ng 1980, 85).

The poor's response to exploitative expressions of power also results in the disintegration of the community. They either "exit," or express "loyalty" or "voice" their response (Chambers 1983, 142, 143). Each of these fragments the community further.

The very nature of power, the role of the elite and the response of the poor all contribute toward eroding the community base.

Redefining Community

If poverty is about broken relationships— exclusion from society's mainstream and the fragmentation of community—then our transformational initiatives must result in rebuilding community. We must move beyond community organizing to something more radical and fundamental.

The Christian faith offers the most radical of responses to these situations, namely, the formation of covenantal communities. The covenantal community that the Christian faith offers is a community of unequals with trust, celebration and redemption as its chief characteristics. I suggest that creating covenant communities (patterned after Yahweh's covenant with Creation) must be an integral part of our response, both among the poor and between the poor and the non-poor.

Jesus rebuilt community by challenging the very lines that divided people. He further made those lines a religious issue about which God was deeply concerned. While issue-based community organization techniques exploit numbers and mobilize people around issues, covenantal communities deal with issues without reducing the poor to mere numbers. Personhood is valued; diversity is celebrated and not exploited. Rebuilding relationships demands investing in relationships. A key question for us, therefore, is this: Have our models of transformation enabled us to invest in relationships and build covenantal communities that do not gloss over issues but instead create celebrating communities?

Some questions for our consideration

- Do our teams express a true sense of community—a covenantal community?

- Do we have a way of being a reconciled team ourselves?

- Do we have a way of healing each other so we can become agents of healing rather than multiplying hurt?

- Do our definitions of and strategies for sustainability, empowerment and community organization include building covenantal communities - communities among the poor as well as between the poor and the non-poor?

- Do we facilitate "win-win" relationships within poverty situations?

- Do our offices and centers become places for healing broken relationships?

Poverty – The Result of Hopelessness and Distorted History

It is impossible to understand inter-generational poverty without raising the question of time. Deep-seated hopelessness in poverty situations demands our attention. Unfortunately, hope and hopelessness are often thought of as belonging to the realm of the future. Human experience, however, suggests that hope and hopelessness are more than a state of mind or a thing of the future. Hope and hopelessness shape the powerlessness of the marginalized today.

Hopelessness is Today's Experience

First, hopelessness prevents meaningful action today. It results in disinterested action, lack of desire for change and low aspirations. This cycle of hopelessness and lack of interest in changing the present pushes the marginalized into extreme powerlessness. Hopelessness is more than a future thing; it shapes the present and perpetuates powerlessness.

Second, powerlessness is vicious. Powerlessness destroys hope today. Powerlessness and hopelessness reinforce each other to hold the poor in permanent captivity within a vicious cycle of deprivation. Further, the powerful do everything to crush any glimmer of hope among the poor, since hope among the poor is a threat to the powerful. Hopelessness causes powerlessness, and powerlessness destroys hope. This vicious circle of hopelessness and powerlessness among the poor destroys the very energy needed to live.

Hopelessness is a Product of History

Hopelessness is rooted in the history of a people. The future is shaped in a laboratory called history. History is an important dimension for understanding poverty and hopelessness in poverty situations. The relationship between history and poverty is not a new arena in poverty studies.[4] There are several ways in which different forces within a people's history have an impact on their present. I focus here intentionally on *interpreted-remembered* and *shared* aspects of history at the *micro-level* that shape poverty relationships.[5]

---

[4] Marxists, the dependency school and liberation theologians have contributed much to understanding the role of the historical processes in causing poverty.

[5] First, in poverty studies the focus must be both on macro- as well as microrealities. However, in the past the focus has been very much on the macro-level historical process, with very little attention given to micro-level historical process. In this chapter I have kept my focus on: (a) the micro-level, thus keeping the focus at the grassroots level, (b) the interpretations of history rather than the objective aspects of history. At the micro-level the focus is not on history as foolproof objective evidence but on particular interpretations of history. Therefore, this study understands history as *interpreted* and looks at its impact on the present and the future, (c) the *remembered* aspects of history that are crucial. The remembered aspects of interpreted history shape the day-to-day lives of the poor. This history is stored in the community's "memory", and (d) history in the form available as community property. History is a *community process*. The community shares this remembered history.

History is distorted in many ways. Let me highlight a few ways in which history is distorted as it relates to the powerlessness of the poor.

First, the *substance* of remembered and interpreted history tends to marginalize the poor, the girl child and women. The powerful not only exercise power but also set the agenda and rules for the exercise of power within poverty relationships. Marvin Olsen in *Power in Modern Societies* (Olsen and Marger 1993) calls this form of power that sets the agenda and rules "meta power." Meta power is the ability to "shape the aggregate action and interaction possibilities of those involved in the situation" (ibid.36). The powerful shape the rules for relationships and define the wants of the poor. They ascribe meaning to life situations, which then shape poverty relationships.

Second, the *process* of history-making also becomes a source of powerlessness. While it is true all humans are free to make history, in reality some humans are much freer than others to do so. In the bargain, those who "do not make history . . . tend increasingly to become the utensils of historymakers as well as mere objects of history" (Wright 1993). In this major venture of the powerful to write and rewrite history, the powerless become mere objects. Therefore, the history-making process itself is a source of powerlessness for the poor.

Third, the *opportunity* to read reality is also curtailed by the powerful. Paulo Freire defined literacy as the "reading of the world," and concluded that much of the education system does not enable the poor to read their own world (Freire 1993). The poor read the world through the lens that the powerful have lent them. In his famous conscientization strategy for liberation from oppression, Freire advocates that "each man [must] win back his right to *say his own word, to name the world*" (Freire 1990, 13). Years of intergenerational poverty seriously cramp the ability of the poor to even name their reality. It is a distorted reading of reality and history - a reading from the perspective of the powerful.

Finally, the socioeconomic *cost* of these distortions of history is very high for the poor. When the poor become mere tools in the hands of history-makers, the rest of their life also gets defined by the "station" assigned to them in the histories written by the powerful. Even rules for life situations and relationships are molded by history.

Redefining History

For a community characterized by hopelessness and shaped by distorted histories, the kingdom of God provides a liberating alternative. As followers of the Lord Jesus Christ we can reread distorted history with God as the point of reference. This becomes an alternative perspective to reading the history provided by the powerful. It is an alternative to a world that constantly tells the poor that even God has forsaken their communities and families.

This rereading of history must affirm that God is active and interested in the history of the poor. This rereading of history must also recognize that history is not the savior; salvation comes from the Lord of history. Rereading history is more than rewriting it from the poor's perspective. Neither the victor nor the vanquished is the valid starting point for the rereading project. History written from the perspective of the powerless will only mean reversing the format, not transforming history. The challenge is to read history while affirming that God is active in the histories of people.

Rereading history while affirming God's action in history opens up the possibility for the powerless to imagine the future anew. It affirms that the future need no longer be a mere extension of distorted versions of history. The new future need not be out of bounds to the poor. The marginalized, who have constantly been denied this history-making role and have become tools in the hands of the world's history-makers, now have a new opportunity to imagine a future characterized by hope.

Imagining a new future is a ministry of "prophetic imagination." This prophetic imagination must precede any concrete response (Brueggemann 1978, 45). It is a response that "is empowering the poor in a manner which encourages and enables them to take the *long view*, to enhance and not degrade resources" (Chambers 1991, 5, emphasis added). Only then can the poor dream of a new future.

In this task of imagining a new future, the prophet of God provides leadership. It is the vocation of the prophet to keep alive the ministry of imagination and hope and to provide a liberating alternative to what has been for generations thought of as the only thinkable reading of history and reality, that of the powerful (Brueggemann 1978, 45).

Some questions for our consideration

- Do we consciously enable the poor to see God in their history, even as we facilitate the use of our analytical tools (participatory learning and action, dream mapping and so on)?

- Do we consciously challenge the world's message/disinformation that God is not involved in the histories of the poor?

- Do our teams function in a way that affirms what God has done and is doing among our colleagues?

- Do our definitions and strategies for sustainability and empowerment include equipping the poor to reread their history and reality so they can imagine a new future?

- Do our transformational initiatives minister hope in the midst of despair?

- Do our teams initiate hope-based action?

Poverty – Result of Marred Identity of the Poor

Poverty is about personhood and identity. By marring identity the powerful seek to inflict permanent damage to the poor. Let us examine a few ways by which the poor's identity is manipulated and marred.

The Process of Marring

First, flawed social norms and a people's worldview are used to mar the identity of the poor. In the Indian context, the caste system is the mould used for shaping social norms. In various cultures, religion and traditions have served as major tools to reinforce these norms. For example, a community's caste traditions, accompanied by fear of shame, perpetuate intergenerational temple prostitution in parts of India.[6] When traditions, fear of shame and marred identity combine, powerlessness is the product. The powerless have no option but to submit.

Second, years of marginalization mar the identity of the poor. The fact that girls are born with a distinct social disadvantage leaves a negative imprint on their minds. This is more than stunting of their aspirations and awareness. It also affects the poor's ability to reflect critically and analyze their situation. Years of exploitation have reduced the marginalized to dull, submissive living objects. Their perpetual exploitation freezes their minds. Consequently, self-image and identity are shaped by the hurt and pain that the poor carry in their minds. Dullness of the mind

---

[6] Journalist Saritha Rai, narrating the story of a community of prostitutes in the Kolar area (Karnataka, India), points out that the *jathi sampradaya* (the caste tradition) has been used to maintain the institution of prostitution in this village for generations. Caste traditions require that poor families dedicate at least one girl to the trade of prostitution. Fear and shame accompany these traditions. Consequently, traditions and the fear of shame have for generations shaped the identity of this community (see Saritha Rai, "Turning a New Leaf: A Village Steeped in Prostitution Finds a New Life," *India Today* 17, no. 6 [1992], 10).

along with hurt and pain serve to perpetuate powerlessness among the poor.

Third, the powerful intentionally reduce the poor to mere objects.

> In their unrestrained eagerness to possess, the oppressors develop the conviction that it is possible for them to transform everything into objects of their purchasing power; . . . for the oppressors, what is worthwhile is to have more—always more—even at the cost of the oppressed having less or having nothing. For them, *to be is to have* and to be the class of the "haves" (Freire 1990, 44).

The poor become less than human in the process, their identity defined by the mere object status assigned to them (Freire 1990, 20, 55).

Fourth, marring the poor's identity is a prelude to further exploitation. It seems natural that any exploitation and oppression must deal with the question of the identity of the oppressed. Once the oppressor ascribes a "low identity" to the poor, then all consequent acts become "legitimate" behavior. For example, the girl child becomes "unwanted" before she is exploited by the oppressor. The wives of the landless become "property" before the landlord abuses them sexually. The landless become debtors before they are abused and humiliated by the moneylender.

To summarize, powerlessness is a product of the poor's marred identity. Through oppressive social norms, stunting of the mind, retarding reflective ability and reducing the poor to mere objects, society mars the identity of the poor.

Redefining Identity

Transformational initiatives must address issues of identity; they should facilitate clarifying the identity of the poor. Our point of reference for this process of identity clarification is the knowledge that all are made in the image of God.

Further, this image is a gift from God; the image of God is not earned. Quality standards such as empowerment and sustainability need redefinition as well, if they are to deal with the issue of marred identity.

Some questions for our consideration

- Do we relate with the poor in a way that consistently and consciously affirms that the poor are made in the image of God?

- Do we affirm or mar the identity of our staff or members of our team? Do we equip our staff to rightly divide the Word, teach from the Word, and link the Word to the context?

- Do our definitions and strategies for sustainability and empowerment include clarifying the identity of the poor?

- Do our transformational initiatives challenge the lie that the world promotes, namely, that the poor are not made in the image of God?

Poverty – The Result of Inadequacies in a People's Worldview

Poverty is a much broader concept than sociopolitics and economics. A survey of various development theories suggests that the roots of poverty can be traced to a people's worldview. This is not a simple ethnocentric statement; it is an acknowledgment that a people's worldview is a powerful tool for perpetuating chronic poverty. Development ethicists[7] and community psychologists are calling development practitioners to consider seriously worldview-related issues (Rappaport 1987, 139–42).

Worldview is a practical tool within the culture of a people (Kearney 1984, 66). Worldview serves as a framework to explain, evaluate, validate, prioritize commitments,

---

[7] Dennis Goulet suggests that these moral options ought to be exercised around three vital issues. They are the criteria of the good life, the basis for just relations in society and the principles for adopting a proper stance toward the forces of nature including technology (Goulet 1989, 45).

interpret, integrate and adapt to various realities and pressures of life (Kraft 1989, 183).

Let me illustrate the role of worldview in perpetuating poverty by examining one theme in popular Hinduism. (I use Hinduism only as a case in point for this analysis. All cultures have their elements of fallenness).

Karma (willed activity, reaping the result of one's past deeds) is probably the most frequently studied of all beliefs of the Hindu poor. The Upanishads[8] summarize well the underlying philosophical basis of karma:

> By the holy deeds, he becomes holy; by sinful ones, sinful. It is for this reason that they say that a person consists merely of desires *(kama)*; as his desire is, so his will *(kratuh)*; as his will is, so his deed (karma); as his deed is, so his evolution (quotation from Upanishads iv, 4,2, in Prabhu 1940, 20).

The karma of a person affects the person's physical existence now—size, shape, color, appearance and so on. Karma also affects the "social position, including the class or caste into which we are born. It even affects whether we are born as humans or as some lower or higher form of life" (Reichenbach 1990, 51). "Karma is not a mechanical principle but a spiritual necessity. It is the embodiment of the mind and will of God. God is its supervisor. . . .Justice is an attribute of God (Radhakrishnan 1927, 53).

The belief in the migration of the soul (*samsara*) further intensifies the negative effects of the karma theory. Average Hindus dread future births and deaths since they reckon that the soul has to go through several million births and deaths with no necessary assurance of progress (Appasamy 1942, 115–20).

Karma and Poverty

In poverty situations worldview assumptions based on karma hold several negative implications for the poor. Karma theory interprets the "person- group" aspect of society in terms of the results of past karma. Karma classifies society into two categories—those whose karma is good and others, like the poor, whose karma is bad. Among the non-poor this karmabased understanding of person-group enables them to believe that the poor are paying for their bad deeds of the past, that poverty is the result of the bad karma of the poor. The non-poor believe their wealth, irrespective of how it is acquired, is the fruit of their good karma.

Therefore, in a community where karma is a defining worldview, poverty becomes a natural consequence. Such cause-effect relationships can be traced in all poverty situations. Poverty is a worldview issue.

Redefining Worldviews

Poverty challenges cannot be adequately responded to if we do not confront the worldview inadequacies of the people involved. A worldview-level understanding of the causes of poverty demands going beyond the traditional "being culturally sensitive" stance. We need tools to analyze worldview-level inadequacies, both among the poor and the non-poor. Transformational initiatives must intentionally pursue worldview-level encounters.

---

[8] According to the studies of Bruce R. Reichenbach, the theory of karma is embedded in five basic presuppositions:

   a. All actions for which we can be held morally accountable and which are done out of a desire for their fruits have [negative] consequences.

   b. Moral actions, as actions, have consequences according to the character of the actions performed: right actions have good consequences, wrong actions have bad consequences.

   c. Some consequences are manifested immediately or in this life, some in the next life and some remotely.

   d. The effects of a karmic action can be accumulated.

   e. Human persons are reborn into the world (Reichenbach 1990, 13–23).

This critique of worldview-level inadequacies almost immediately calls for a reference point that can guide the critique and serve as the alternate point of view. For followers of Jesus Christ, this must necessarily be the Word of God. We must become the hermeneutical community who will study the Word of God in context, who will provide leadership in this process of confronting poverty at the worldview level.

Some questions for our consideration

- Do we equip our staff teams and the communities with which we work to analyze the worldview of the poor and the non-poor in poverty situations?

- Do our baselines include gathering and analyzing data related to the community's worldview?

- Do we know how to analyze our own worldview themes and challenge inadequacies on the basis of the Word?

- Do our sustainability and empowerment definitions and strategies include challenging sensitively the meaning ascribed by the community to various aspects of reality that perpetuate poverty?

- Do our programs affirm those aspects of culture and worldview that do not perpetuate poverty, but instead affirm values that are consistent for creating a world that does not tolerate poverty?

- Do we develop and use various means within programs to address worldview inadequacies?

- Do we consciously develop the skill of the staff teams rightly to divide the Word and allow the Word to critique the community's worldviews, as well as our own?

Poverty – The Result of Exploitation by Principalities and Powers

Any effort to understand the meaning of poverty must grapple with yet another dimension of reality, namely, the role of principalities and powers in poverty situations.

Mission anthropologist Paul Hiebert's analysis of the different perceptions of reality and the "excluded middle" triggered several reevaluations of traditional perceptions of the causes of poverty. According to Hiebert, the influence of Enlightenment thinking, dualism and a mechanistic perception of reality influenced mission thinking. Consequently, the dualistic view of reality excluded important dimensions of reality, including the middle tier. Hiebert describes this middle level as including beings [which] are forces that cannot be directly perceived but thought to exist on this earth. These include spirits, ghosts, ancestors, demons, and earthly gods and goddesses who live in trees, rivers, hills and villages. These live not in some other world or time, but are inhabitants with humans and animals of this world and time. . . . This level also includes supernatural forces such as manna, planetary influences, evil eyes and the powers of magic, sorcery and witchcraft (1982, 41).

Most Christian missions are built on a fragmented and dualistic perception of reality. On the other hand, for the Hindu poor, all of life is directly or indirectly related to the work of spiritual power: sickness, a failed business and social ostracism can all be explained in terms of spiritual power working against the poor. Demons, shamans, witch doctors and gods mediate this spiritual power.

Poverty is not only rooted in the fall of humans but is also a result of the present working of the Evil One. Missiologists and grassroots practitioners affirm that "behind all poverty is the devil . . . [and] the ultimate cause of poverty is the devil himself" (Duncan 1990, 9). Therefore, authentic and sustainable involvement among the poor will involve confrontation with the powers of the Evil One. "The Son of God was revealed for this purpose, to destroy the works of the devil" (1 John 3:8).

Through the years there have been several debates on the identity of the cosmic powers.[9] A common view is that God created the powers, and they were meant to serve God's purposes. However, after the Fall the powers were set against God's purposes and were particularly directed against God's creation. "Now they are 'behaving' as though they were the ultimate ground of being" (Mouw 1976, 89). The powers seek to absolutize themselves. They are enemies of Christ (Ps. 110:1, Eph. 6:11–12, 16; 2:2; 4:27; Arnold 1989, 56). References to the powers also indicate that there is a plurality of powers (Mouw 1976, 86). The powers belong to the kingdom of Satan (Kraft 1992, 19) and wield control over people. I have opted to understand principalities and powers as personal beings (Arnold 1992, 77) and forces (Arnold 1988, 44–51) that have a dominating influence on persons, social organizations and groups (Kraft 1992, 19), and structures.

Poverty, Principalities and Powers

There are several ways in which the Devil and his forces influence persons. Let me confine myself to the role of the principalities and powers in poverty situations.

First, the powers reinforce various deceptions that have roots in a people's belief system. They blind the mind (2 Cor. 4:4). The poor are made to believe that their *varna* (each of the four original castes of Hindu society) and their duty (*sav-dharma*) define their identity. The Devil and his forces are great deceivers (2 Tim. 2:26; Gal. 4:3; Eph. 2:12). They keep the poor enslaved, captive and under deception about their role in society, their place in the hierarchy of *varnas* and their place in God's presence (Arnold 1992, 93). The deception these powers perpetuate to keep the poor powerless is well illustrated by the experiences of poor communities. Through these deceptions the prince of the power of the air (Eph. 2:2) seeks to keep the poor powerless. Often these

---

[9] Heinrich Schlier develops the thesis that the "air" in Ephesians 2:2 is the principal medium by which the powers exercise their control on the affairs of humans (Schlier 1961, 12). H. Berkhof proposed that these powers are structures of earthly existence, and Paul's emphasis is not so much on the personal-spiritual aspects of nature as on the role of the powers in conditioning earthly life (Berkhof 1962, 18). Oscar Cullmann (in *Christ and Time*) proposed that the powers were both human authorities and angelic powers (Arnold 1989, 44). Wesley Carr in a recent work claims that the powers should not be understand as referring to any evil or demonic force but as pure angelic beings who surround the throne of God (Carr 1981). John Howard Yoder focuses his attention on the "revolutionary subordination" of the church to the "powers." Referring to the identity of the "powers," Yoder points out that they are fallen. However, "the Powers [are] not simply something limitlessly evil. The Powers, despite their fallenness, continue to exercise an ordering function" (Yoder 1972, 143–44). Richard J. Mouw suggests that Paul depersonalizes the power while he identifies these powers as the forces that "'stand behind' and 'influence' the political life [and] . . . other areas of human social life" (Mouw 1976, 87). Clinton E. Arnold, in his survey of the concept of power in Ephesians, concludes that Paul does not "demythologize the 'powers' and make them equivalent to the abstract notions of 'flesh' and 'sin' or see them as some kind of spiritual 'atmosphere.' The flesh and the devil (with his power) work in confluence leading humanity into disobedience from God" (Arnold 1989, 69). Finally, Walter Wink's three-part work suggests that spiritual powers are not some separate heavenly or ethereal entity but the "inner aspect of material or tangible manifestations of power" (Wink 1984, 104). Wink identifies such an understanding about powers as a mark of an integral worldview based on the views of Carl Jung and others. They are "withinness or interiority in all things, . . . [the] inner spiritual reality [that is] inextricably related to an outer concentration or physical manifestation" (Wink 1992, 5). Wink suggests that there are three types of manifestations of powers. They are the outer personal possession, collective possession and the inner personal demonic (Wink 1986, 43). For Walter Wink, powers are that spiritual interiority of the domination system, which shapes the day-to-day life of all humans.

deceptions lead people away from God. As Heinrich Schlier suggests, it is the nature of these powers to "present and interpret everything in the universe which they dominate in their own light and in their own way" (Schlier 1961, 32).

Second, the principalities and powers attack the body through disease (Matt. 9:32, 33; Luke 13:16; 2 Cor. 12:7). This is probably why churches that minister to the health and physical well-being of their members attract the poor. The poor and the non-poor alike are vulnerable to exploitation by the principalities and powers in this area. For the poor, however, sickness has greater socioeconomic costs. It pushes them to the edge of survival. It creates dependence on moneylenders, high debts, absence from work and other negative economic implications. They become dependent on village priests and witchcraft, which in turn drain the poor financially.

Third, the role of the powers in influencing people through compulsive dependence on certain habits is also well known. The cost of maintaining compulsive behaviors is high and erodes the poor's financial base. The poor do not have the same options that the non-poor have. These habits and destructive options spell vulnerability and powerlessness for the poor, who already grapple with economic crises, and result in perpetual socioeconomic captivity of households (Schlier 1961, 33).

Fourth, the Devil attacks relationships that were meant to serve as positive agents in shaping identities. He sows seeds of enmity between people and keeps the poor, who are already on the fringe of society, divided. While not blaming the Devil for all the disunity in the community, it is necessary to recognize that unity and brotherhood are not the Devil's cup of tea. Marred relationships are a mark of abiding in death (1 John 3:14), while unity and brotherhood are a sign of life.

Fifth, the Devil also exploits curses that people cast on each other. "A curse is the invocation of the power of Satan or of God to affect negatively the person or thing at which the curse is directed" (Kraft 1992, 75). Very often, the effects of curses on the poor have serious socioeconomic costs (e.g., the Bhils in western India define themselves as "cursed people"— cursed by God before Creation).

Sixth, cosmic principalities and powers seek to control the will of the poor. "The ultimate aim of the enemy is not simply to control people's minds but to get at their wills" (Kraft 1990, 272). By capturing a person's will, the Devil seeks to influence choices in life. Within popular Hinduism karma, *samsara* (the cyclical understanding of time and events) and other such beliefs aid the Devil. Consequently, hopelessness and powerlessness set in.

Seventh, the Devil and his forces seek to cripple the identities (Kraft 1992, 82) of persons involved in poverty relationships. The principalities and powers deceive the poor into believing they are not made in the image of God. This lie is easier to sell when the poor believe God has forsaken them. The poor "feel nonexistent, valueless, humiliated [and believe that they] . . . are stupid, ignorant people who know nothing . . . like oxen who know nothing" (Wink 1992, 101). In this context powerlessness is an issue of identity and reinforced by cosmic powers (Wink 1992, 103). Often, the Devil feeds on the "spiritual garbage" (Kraft 1990, 276) in the person and the community, abusing marred identities, hurt from broken relationships and the pain of captivity to a harsh religious belief system. The principalities and powers play a crucial role in intensifying the powerlessness imposed by society on the poor, reinforcing oppression and carrying it to its logical end of marring the poor's will and identity.

Apart from influencing persons involved in poverty relationships, the principalities and powers also affect the context within which these relationships take place. The term *context* here refers to structures and systems, which are very much a part of any poverty situation. There has been much debate on the role of the powers in relation to the structures and systems.[10]

There are four aspects to the role of principalities and powers vis-à-vis structures that I would like to consider here. The powers:

1. influence structures and systems through people. They manipulate a culture's social, political, economic, religious and even artistic subsystems by acting through individuals (Wagner and Pennoyer 1990, 256).

2. shape the interiority of structures and systems. This interiority is not a reference to the powers, as Wink suggests, but the powers influence these interiorities. The powers ensure that relative powers always seek to absolutize themselves (become god complexes), socio-economically and politically exclude the poor, cause the community to become noncommunity, mar the identity of the poor and so on.

3. exploit belief systems and worldviews, and manipulate the context of poverty relationships (1 Cor. 8:4, 5; 10:19–20; Arnold 1992, 94). However, the powers also exploit any form of idolatry, irrespective of which religious system nurtures it.

4. have access to poor families through symbols and articles of significance. The powers empower various symbols and forms within religious systems. These symbols and forms are not as neutral as they appear.

Redefining the Role of the Principalities and Powers

The role of principalities and powers in poverty situations demands that we recognize that transformation is essentially a battle—a battle against principalities and powers. Transformational initiatives must then be an effort to unmask the principalities and powers. We need to confront the Devil and his forces in the context of poverty relationships.

We must pray for our staff members as they confront the Devil. Prayer and fasting must become essential tools for transformational initiatives. The gifts of the Spirit should be used within the context of confronting poverty. The whole armor of God must become the dress code for all those who seek to confront the principalities and powers.

Christian involvement among the poor cannot ignore this aspect of poverty situations. If

---

[10] Recent interpretations suggest the powers work through economic and political structures, as well as influence social patterns, cultural norms and group habits. "These structures of existence are then viewed as the objects of our spiritual struggle and may be regarded as demonic" (Arnold 1992, 167). On the other hand, there are others who have held the view that powers must only be dealt with in the context of setting individual souls free from the grip of darkness (see survey, McAlpine 1991, 55). C. Peter Wagner points out that the devil and his forces influence nations and keep the minds of the unreached blind. Wagner argues, based on his reflections on passages like Daniel 10:10–21, that the "territorial spirits and their dominance of geographical areas are taken for granted as the history of Israel unfolds". (Wagner and Pennmoyer 1990, 79). However, Walter Wink, as mentioned earlier, is of the opinion that the powers are the inner spirituality that inhabits structures and systems. He suggests that unless we depersonalize the cosmic powers, it will be difficult to justify any involvement in setting right the inadequacies in structures and systems (Wink 1992). Clinton E. Arnold, commenting on the influence of the powers over nations and territories, suggests that the powers influence structures and systems by influencing people (Arnold 1992, 202). Thus the influence of the powers "extends to human institutions and organizations, the social and political order" (Arnold 1992, 81). There is much ambiguity about the role of the powers in relation to structures and systems. Richard Mouw points out that this ambiguity is not due to defects in current theological understanding, but due to "the perils inherent in attempts to duplicate Paul's exact views, given his lack of systematic presentation on the subject" (1976, 88). Since the focus of this paper is on the role of the personal principalities and powers, I would like to consider their role as such without reducing them to structures of existence or interiorities. These personal cosmic powers do influence structures.

poverty is the result of the exploitative role of the cosmic powers, there is no way we can be involved in poverty situations without the anointing of the Holy Spirit. We must live in daily obedience to the Holy Spirit. There is a need to be "spiritual" at the core of our response.

Some questions for our consideration

- Do we recognize that our transformational initiatives are a battle with the principalities and powers and that these same initiatives require unmasking the principalities and powers?

- Do we "use" prayer and fasting as tools for social action, going beyond personal spiritual disciplines?

- Do we help our staff recognize and use the gifts of the Spirit as valid development skills?

- Do we require staff members to wear the whole armor of God as their uniform?. Do we provide prayer cover for front-line staff in the battle? Do we recognize at leadership includes providing prayer cover for staff members and their families?

- Do our definitions and strategies of sustainability and empowerment include communicating the message to the powers that Jesus is Lord?

Poverty – Captivity of the Poor in a Web of Lies

Throughout the analysis of poverty relationships in this chapter the common theme has been the underlying death and distortion of truth and the perpetuation of lies. Lies are the thread that links the perpetuation of god complexes, the distortion of history, the marring of identity, the fragmentation of relationships, the role of the principalities and powers and the inadequacies in worldview themes. Flawed assumptions and interpretations (lack of truth) that are rooted in religious systems, the worldview of a people and the work of the principalities and powers sustain oppressive relationships.

A helpful image to represent the captivity of the poor in a world of flawed assumptions and interpretations is the idea of a web. In the context of poverty relationships, this web is essentially a web of lies—that social status is divinely sanctioned, that poverty cannot be changed, for example. Both the poor and the non-poor believe these lies and thus ensure perpetuation of the powerlessness of the poor.

Various worldview themes reviewed in this chapter and the principalities and powers that reinforce these themes form the web of lies.[11] It is a web of lies within which the poor are held captive. It is a web of lies that is more than a cognitive level deception. It is a web that affects the lives, attitudes and relationships of the poor. The structures, systems, people, and principalities and powers involved in poverty relationships nurture this web, which is rooted in the worldview of a people. It is seen as an expression of God's justice and believed to be a spiritual necessity. It affirms the status quo.

Redefining Truth

If poverty is the captivity of the poor in a web of lies, then the most appropriate response of the church will involve proclaiming the truth. Transformational initiatives must proclaim truth in public places. They must proclaim the truth about the identity of the poor—that they are made

---

[11] I use the term *lie* to qualify particular assumptions within the worldview of persons within poverty relationships. My understanding of poverty situations, in the light of scriptural affirmations about humans being made in the image of God and other such foundational truths, suggests that the term *lie* aptly describes the contrary assumptions that create and sustain poverty and powerlessness. However, there is need for further comparative inquiry between biblical affirmations and worldview assumptions within poverty relationships.

in the image of God. Transformation must go beyond the transfer of power to the very redefinition of power. Our work must show that we recognize that we are in the business of communicating truth to the cosmic powers (Eph. 3:8– 10). We are involved in the task of proclaiming the Truth that sets us free. This ministry of proclaiming truth within poverty situations is the task of a prophetic community. Transformation must seek to establish truth and righteousness in poverty situations.

Some questions for our consideration

- Do we recognize that we are called to be a prophetic community, to proclaim the truth?

- Do our definitions and strategies include reordering the relationship between truth and power, establishing truth in public life and proclaiming Truth as the basis of all relationships?

- Do we proclaim truth within poverty relationships?

- Do we live and express truth within ourselves? Do we have the strength to challenge the lies that exist in our midst?

What have we learned about Poverty?

This chapter suggests that we need to understand poverty holistically before we seek to develop a holistic response to the poor. It suggests broadening the scope of our inquiry into poverty to include examining:

- the captivity of the poor in the god complexes of the non-poor, structures, systems and the cosmic powers;

- the impact of broken relationships (exclusion from the mainstream and the fragmentation of community base);

- the role of hope or hopelessness, as well as distorted interpretations of history;

- the impact of the marred identity of the poor;

- the relationship between poverty and inadequacies in the worldviews of the poor and the non-poor;

- the role of principalities and powers;

- the captivity of the poor in a web of lies.

This chapter also suggests that this perspective about the causes of poverty demands a response that is radically different from our traditional transformational development programs and initiatives. I have suggested that we must reexamine our definitions and strategies for transformational initiatives, empowerment, sustainability and other parameters for our involvement.

Transformational development: Our definitions of transformational development must include initiatives that express the reign of God, create covenantal communities, follow a God who is active and Lord over history in imagining a new future, restore the image of God in the poor, encounter worldview inadequacies, are involved in a spiritual battle with the cosmic powers through the enabling power of the Holy Spirit, and, finally, proclaim the Truth that liberates.

Measurements of sustainability: These measurements must include the impact on structures, systems and people, as well as spiritual interiorities that characterize god complexes, relationships in the community, the role of the poor in society, the identity of the poor, perception among the poor and the non-poor about the histories of the poor, inadequate aspects in worldviews, the role of the principalities and powers, and the role of truth in public life.

Empowerment: The various aspects of poverty examined here also call for a fresh look at our definitions of and strategies for empowerment. Our empowerment strategies must include redefining the very nature of power itself. It is important to examine issue-based community organizational strategies that tend to demonize the powerful and build sacred images around the causes of the powerless. We need to work toward building covenantal communities with both the poor and the non-poor, communities that celebrate diversity without glossing over issues of oppression and exploitation. Empowerment should include challenging the lines that divide the poor, and the poor from the non-poor. Further, empowerment also means equipping the poor to challenge all tendencies to absolutize powers, to exclude the poor from society's mainstream and to divide communities. The poor must be empowered to reread history, affirming God's action in the history of the poor. Empowerment must include equipping the poor to critique their worldview and challenge the principalities and powers and all forces that perpetuate lies in public places.

Three Key Implications for An Overall Approach to Poverty

In closing, let me place before you three key implications of this analysis of poverty relationships for an overall approach to poverty.

Our Response to the Poor must Address the Whole Context of Poverty

We must recognize that poverty is about relationships, and goes beyond mere statistics. My analysis suggests there are several key players and factors in any poverty situation. The god complexes need to be addressed, broken relationships need to healed, forces that mar the identity of the poor must be challenged, the lines that divide must be actively ignored, covenantal communities with poor and non-poor must be formed, the cosmic powers need to be unmasked and truth must shape and inform public life. If we are to address poverty adequately, transformation must have an impact on the context of poverty as well. Transformation cannot be merely an event or a series of disconnected events; transformation must address the whole. Transformation has to affect every person involved in any given situation.

Therefore, our focus should be more than just transformation—it should be on initiating *ripples of transformation*—a series of well planned transformations that influence the whole context of poverty, the poor and the nonpoor, the structures, systems, people, cosmic powers and spiritual interiorities. Further, if our focus is on ripples of transformation, then our work among the poor is about *movements, not just projects*.

It is time for the Christian response to the poor to mature into initiating movements rather than being content with successful projects. We need to pursue ripples of transformation instead of being content with sporadic transformational events. The challenge is to create a world that does not tolerate poverty—not just transform the poor.

Poverty Demands a Response that is Essentially Spiritual at Its Core

Another theme emerging from this inquiry into poverty is the fact that there are fundamental spiritual issues underlying poverty relationships. The god complexes are molded by spiritual interiorities. Broken relationships and marred identities are essentially a challenge to God's intention for creation. Worldviews, and especially a worldview's religious roots, make our encounter with poverty an encounter not just at the worldview level but an encounter of religious persuasions. Poverty is about truth, and transformation an encounter of truths. Finally, poverty demands an encounter with the principalities and powers.

Therefore, I suggest that poverty by its very nature demands a spiritual response. We need to respond at a level that goes deeper than our traditional level of engagement. We need to expand our scope from addressing dignity issues to clarifying the very identity of the poor. Our community organization has to go beyond mobilizing the poor to creating covenantal communities that are patterned after Yahweh's covenant with His people. We need to move from flesh and blood strategies to including "communicating the mysteries" to the powers in heavenly places. Transformation also includes worldview level engagement with the proclamation of truth.

In many ways this model of transformation demands an engagement or encounter at the level of spiritualities. Transformation is about calling attention to defining the nature of the spiritual—a spirituality that shapes and molds all of life (attitudes, relationships, worldview and behavior). We cannot be agents of transformation without a fundamental undergirding at the spiritual level. There can be no sustainability and empowerment without addressing the spiritual. This is just more than evangelism plus social action.

It is an analysis of poverty that recognizes the all-pervading nature of spiritualities and a model of transformation that is essentially spiritual in nature.

Transformation must include Transforming the Agents of Transformation

This issue is closely related to the theme of spirituality. The emerging model of transformation is not only spiritual, but also demands an investment of the person. For example, rebuilding relationships and forming covenantal communities demands investing in relationships. A key question, therefore, is, Have our models of transformation enabled us to invest in relationships? If we will have to challenge a flawed understanding of power then we need to demonstrate what the new understanding is. If we are to clarify identities we need to affirm the image of God in ourselves, as well as in our colleagues. If transformation is about truth then we need to live truth; we should not gloss over lies as the "usual organizational politics."

Years of work among the poor have taught us that limiting our investment among the poor to just money makes the poor beggars, and limiting our investment to programs makes the poor glorified beggars (beneficiaries), but if we believe transformation is about transforming lives then we must intentionally invest our lives. Only life can reproduce life.

If transformation is about investing lives then we must pay attention to the quality of our lives. We must graduate to becoming communities where celebration, diversity and accountability are important hallmarks. If we are called to proclaim truth we must recognize we are fulfilling the prophetic function; we need to become a prophetic community that knows the discipline of standing in "the counsel of the Lord" before rushing to help people. If our transformation is about challenging principalities and powers, then we must be equipped with the whole armor of God, the gifts of the Spirit and prayer and fasting as tools for social action.

If our transformational initiatives must have the mark of integrity, then the agents of transformation must continuously be transformed themselves. We are involved among the poor and the oppressed as obedient followers of the Lord Jesus Christ. Transformation is about obedience and discipleship. Let transformation begin with us.

References and Recommended Readings

Appasamy, A. J. 1942. *The Gospel and India's Heritage*. New York: Macmillan.

Arnold, Clinton E. 1989. *Ephesians—Power and Magic: The Concept of Power in Ephesians in the Light of Its Historical Setting*. Grand Rapids, Mich.: Baker House.

————. 1992. *Powers of Darkness: Principalities and Powers in Paul's Letters*. Downers Grove, Ill.: Inter Varsity Press.

Berkhof, H. 1962. *Christ and the Powers*. Scottdale, Pa.: Herald Press.

Brueggemann, Walter. 1978. *The Prophetic Imagination*. Philadelphia: Fortress Press.

Carr, Wesley. 1981. *Angels and Principalities: The Background, Meaning and Development of the Pauline Phrase hai archai kai hai exousiai* SNTSMS 42: Cambridge University Press.

Cassell, Philip. 1993. *The Giddens.* Stanford, Calif.: Stanford University Press.

Chambers, Robert. 1983. *Rural Development: Putting the Last First.* Essex, UK: Longman Scientific and Technical.

————. 1988. *Poverty in India: Concepts, Research and Reality.* Sussex, UK: Institute of Development Studies.

————. 1991. "In Search of Professionalism, Bureaucracy and Sustainable Livelihoods for the 21st Century." *IDS Bulletin* 22, no. 4: 5–11.

Christian, Jayakumar. 1994. "Powerlessness of the Poor: Toward an Alternative Kingdom of God Based Paradigm for Response." Pasadena, Calif.: Fuller Theological Seminary.

Cullmann, Oscar. 1964. *Christ and Time.* Philadelphia: Westminster Press.

Curtis, Michael, ed. 1981. *The Great Political Theories.* Vol. 2. New York: Avon Books.

Doyal, Len, and Ian Gough. 1991. *Theory of Human Need.* New York: The Guilford Press.

Duncan, Michael. 1990. *A Journey in Development: The Bridge Series.* Melbourne, Australia: World Vision.

Friedmann, John. 1992. *Empowerment: The Politics of Alternative Development.* Cambridge, Mass.: Blackwell.

Freire, Paulo. 1990. *Pedagogy of the Oppressed.* New York: Continuum.

————. 1993. *Pedagogy of the City.* New York: Continuum.

Goulet, Dennis. 1989. *The Uncertain Promise: Value Conflicts in Technology Transfer.* New York: New Horizons Press.

Hiebert, Paul. 1982. "The Flaw of the Excluded Middle," *Missiology* 10, no. 1.

Kearney, Michael. 1984. *Worldview.* Novato, Calif.: Chandler and Sharp.

Kraft, Charles H. 1989. *Christianity with Power: Your Worldview and Your Experience of the Supernatural.* Ann Arbor, Mich.: Servant Publications.

————. 1990. "Response to 'In Dark Dungeons of Collective Captivity' by Pennoyer." In Wagner and Pennoyer, *Wrestling with Dark Angels.*

————. 1992. *Defeating the Dark Angels: Breaking Demonic Oppression in the Believer's Life.* Ann Arbor, Mich.: Servant Publications.

Kuppuswamy, B. 1992. *Social Change in India.* 4th edition. Delhi: Konark Publishers.

Liddle, R. William. 1992. "The Politics of Development Policy." *World Development* 20, no. 6.

Linthicum, Robert C. 1991. *Empowering the Poor: Community Organizing Among the City's "Rag, Tag and Bobtail."* Monrovia, Calif.: MARC.

Llosa, Mario Vargas. 1989. "Foreword." In *The Other Path: The Invisible Revolution in the Third World,* edited by Hernando De Soto. New York: Harper & Row.

McAlpine, Thomas H. 1991. *Facing the Powers: What Are the Options?* Monrovia, Calif.: MARC.

Mahadevan, T.M.P. 1956. *Outlines of Hinduism.* Bombay: Chetna.

Mills, C. Wright. 1993. "The Structure of Power in American Society." In *Power in Modern Societies,* edited by Marvin E. Olsen and Martin N. Marger. Boulder, Colo.: Westview Press.

Mouw, Richard J. 1976. *Politics and the Biblical Drama.* Grand Rapids, Mich.: Wm. B. Eerdmans.

Mills, Wright C. 1959. *The Power Elite.* New York: Oxford University Press.

Myers, Bryant. 1991. "The Excluded Middle," *MARC Newsletter* 91, no. 2: 3.

Newbigin, Lesslie. 1966. *Honest Religion for Secular Man*. Philadelphia: Westminster Press.

Ng, Sik Hung. 1980. *The Social Psychology of Power*. London: Academic Press.

Olsen, Marvin E., and Martin N. Marger. 1990. "In Dark Dungeons of Collective Captivity." In *Wrestling with Dark Angels: Toward a Deeper Understanding of the Supernatural Forces in Spiritual Warfare,* edited by C. Peter Wagner and F. Douglas Pennoyer. Ventura, Calif.: Regal Books.

Olsen, Marvin E., and Martin N. Marger, eds. 1993. *Power in Modern Societies*. Boulder, Colo.: Westview Press.

Prabhu, Pandharinath. 1940. *Hindu Social Organization: A Study in Socio-Psychological and Ideological Foundations*. Bombay, India: Popular Prakashan.

Radhakrishnan, Sarvapalli. 1927. *The Hindu View of Life*. Bombay, India: Blackie & Sons Publishers.

Rao, Nagaraja P. 1983. "Hinduism and the Common Man." In *The Gospel Among Our Hindu Neighbours,* edited by Vinay Samuel and Chris Sugden. Bangalore, India: Asian Trading Corporation.

Rappaport, Julian. 1987. "Terms of Empowerment/Exemplars of Prevention: Toward a Theory for Community Psychology." *American Journal of Community Psychology* 15, no. 2:121–48.

Reichenbach, Bruce R. 1990. *The Law of Karma: A Philosophical Study*. Honolulu: University of Hawaii Press.

Schlier, Heinrich. 1961. *Principalities and Powers in the New Testament*. London: Nelson.

Wagner, C. Peter, and F. Douglas Pennoyer, eds. 1990. *Wrestling with Dark Angels: Toward a Deeper Understanding of the Supernatural Forces in Spiritual Warfare*, Ventura, Calif.: Regal Books.

Wink, Walter. 1984. *Naming the Powers: The Language of Power in the New Testament*. Philadelphia.: Fortress Press.

———. 1986. *Unmasking the Powers: The Invisible Forces that Determine Human Existence*. Philadelphia: Fortress Press.

———. 1992. *Engaging the Powers: Discernment and Resistance in a World of Domination*. Philadelphia: Fortress Press.

Wrong, Dennis H. 1979. *Power: Its Forms, Bases and Uses*. New York: Harper & Row.

Yoder, John Howard. 1972. *The Politics of Jesus*. Grand Rapids, Mich.: Wm. B. Eerdmans.

CHAPTER 42

Religious Nationalism in South Asia

T. K. OOMMEN

I

Broadly speaking South Asia may be identified as the region of "Indian civilization" presently divided into eight states. The insider-outsider polarization in South Asian polities is primarily discerned in terms of religion and language or a combination of the two. Of the two, religious identity is more pertinent for a discussion on religious nationalism and hence I shall focus principally on it. The linguistic identity will be referred to only when it exists in conjunction with religious identity. The population of the South Asian states is drawn from different religions although all the states have one dominant religion, as is evident from table 1.

Table 1:
POPULATION (PERCENTAGE) OF SOUTH ASIA BY RELIGION
(MID- 1980)[A]

S.No.	Country	Hindu	Muslim	Buddhist	Christian	Others
1.	India N=694,309,000	78.8	11.6	0.8	3.9[B]	4.9[c]
2.	Bangladesh N=84,803,000	12.7	85.9	0.6	0.5	0.3
3.	Pakistan N=82,952,000	1.3	96.8	0.0	1.8	0.1
4.	Burma N=35,195,00	0.9	3.6	87.2	5.6	2.7
5.	SriLanka N=15,465,000	16.0	7.2	66.9	8.3	1.6
6.	Nepal N=14,232,000	89.6	3.0	6.1	0.0	1.3
7.	Bhutan N=1,327,000	24.6	5.0	69.6	0.1	0.7

The South Asian countries listed in the table may be divided into three categories based on their dominant religious collectivities: Hindu (India and Nepal), Muslim (Pakistan and Bangladesh), and Buddhist (Bhutan, Burma, and Sri Lanka). British India was divided into the states of India and Pakistan in 1947 after prolonged and bloody inter-religious conflicts between Hindus and Muslims. While Pakistan gave formal legitimacy to Islam as the state religion, the Indian state opted for secularism, which meant according equal respect to all religions and/or the state keeping equal distance from all religions. However, religion as the sole determinant of state formation could not be sustained for long even in the case of Pakistan. Thus in 1972, after 25 years of its emergence, Pakistan was split into two, this time based on geography and language, although both the new states, Pakistan and Bangladesh, are populated predominantly by Muslims.

As the basis of state formation changed form religion to language, the problem of non-Bengali Muslims (usually referred to as Bihari Muslims whose mother tongue is one of the dialects of Hindi) remains unresolved to this day. Curiously however, even the aspirations of Bengali Hindus and Chakma[1] Buddhists could not be fully accommodated in Bangladesh. That is, the state of Bangladesh, having temporarily rejected religion as the basis of 'national' identity in favour of linguistic identity to wrest freedom from the co-religionists of Pakistan, had to reclaim its religious identity to gain authenticity as a "nation".[2]

In Pakistan the saliency of the religious factor took a more virulent form.[3] Not only were the aspirations of religious minorities, such as Hindus and Christians, not fully accommodated, but even Muslim protestant sects such as the Ahmedias[4] were labelled heretics and apostates and declared non-Muslims. The case of Muslim refugee migrants from India to Pakistan, usually referred to as Mohajirs, is equally problematic, in that they are treated as outsiders and their nativity claims within the territory under the jurisdiction of the state of Pakistan is contested. Thus, both in Bangladesh and in Pakistan the rupture between insiders and outsiders based on religion is clear and vivid.

The case of Sri Lanka illustrates even more acutely the rupture between insiders and outsiders in South Asia. While the original inhabitants[5] of the island state have been marginalized and reduced to a microscopic minority, all the contending groups—Sinhala Buddhists, Tamil Hindus, and Tamil Muslims—are migrants from India. This common 'regional' background does not however in any way dilute the religio-linguistic identity conflicts. The current turmoil in Sri Lanka is geared not simply to reinforcing these identities within the framework of the polity. At least a section of the Tamil Hindus are aspiring for and demanding a sovereign state. Even if they succeed in achieving their objective in a distant future the problem of religio-linguistic identity cannot be solved as there will be Tamil Hindus in the Sinhala Buddhist areas and vice versa. To

---

[1] Although the population of all tribes in Bangladesh is distributed into more than one religion, the Chakmas and the Marwas are predominatly Buddhists inhabiting the Chttagon Hill Tracts bordering India and Bangladesh, see H. Hussain, "Problem of National Integration in Bangladesh", in S.K. Chakravarty and V. Rarain , eds., *Bangladesh: History and Culture*, New Delhi: South Asian Publishers,1986, pp. 196-211; U. Padnias, *Ethnicity and Nation-Building in South Asia*, New Delhi: Sage Publications, 1989.

[2] See Chakravorty and Narain, *Bangladesh: History and Culture*, 1986.

[A] Compiled from the data provided by David B. Barrett, ed., *World Christian Encyclopedia*, OUP, Nairobi, 1982, pp.165, 179, 202, 370, 507, 635.

[B] The percentage of Christians is inflated as it includes "Crypto-Christians" (affiliated to the Church but unknown as such publicly to the state or society). For example, in India, Crypto-Christians are estimated to represent 1.1 per cent of the total population, with the percentage of those professing Christianity at 2.8, which approximates the official count. In India Crypto-Christians and animists are usually counted as Hindus.

[c] Of this nearly 2 per cent are Sikhs.

[3] See A. M. Weiss, *Islamic Reassertion in Pakistan* State, New York: Sycracuse University Press, 1986.

[4] Ahmedias do not accept the Islamic belief that Mohammed is the last prophet and uphold that Gulam Ahmed who lived just a century ago was a prophet. According to unofficial estimates, the Ahmedias constitute around three per cent of the population of Pakistan and are largely drawn from the Sunnis, the Muslim sect that accounts for about 80 per cent of Pakistan's population

[5] The veddas, the original inhabitants of Sri Lanka, totaled 3,971 in 1907 but shrunk to mere 800 by the mid 1960s

complicate matters, both Christians and Muslims are dispersed throughout the territory of Sri Lanka, and the former are drawn from both Sinhalese and Tamils.[6]

The case of India is admittedly more complex, not only because of her stupendous size but also because of her staggering cultural diversity. Although 83 per cent of Indians are Hindus, the Muslim population is nearly 12 per cent, India being the second largest Muslim country in the world. Christians constitute less than three per cent of the total population but they count over twenty-five million. The followers of Sikhism, the youngest of the religions of Indian origin, who assert their religious identity with vehemence, number about fifteen million. Several migrant religions have made India their home. In fact, 80 per cent of the world's Zoroastrians live in India. Indian religious diversity makes it extremely difficult to insist that Hinduism is the sole native religion of India. However, Hindu nationalists view those who profess other religions as outsiders.[7]

The situation in regard to the three remaining South Asian states, Bhutan, Burma, and Nepal, is somewhat less complicated although all of them are multi-religious as is evident form table 1. For one thing, inter-religious conflicts have been less virulent in these states in the past and an ethos of harmonious relationship between religious groups still persists. For another, their linguistic diversity is limited in comparison to other South Asian states.

The general point that emerges from the foregoing description is that state formation in post-colonial South Asia is based on religion. Even in those cases where it is not explicit, religion has great potency in molding the societal ethos. The fact that religious identity is often bolstered by linguistic identity invariably reinforces the insider-outsider wedge, as is evident form the following points.

First, the tendency to identify specific languages exclusively with particular religions is common. For example, Sanskrit is identified with Aryan Hinduism, Tamil with Dravidian Hinduism, Urdu with north Indian Islam, Pali with Sinhala Buddhism, Punjabi (written in Gurumukhi) with Sikhism. The coupling of religion with language led to the crystallization of a series of complex and competing identities.

Second, the above often leads to particular religio-linguistic groups staking their claim on a specific territory as their exclusive homeland, often ignoring the equally legitimate claims of other groups. Such are the claims of Sikhs in Punjab and Muslims in the Kashmir Valley (India), Tamil Hindus in Jaffna (Sri Lanka), Sindhi Muslims in Sind (Pakistan), Chakma Buddhists in the Chittagong Hill Tracts (Bangladesh). These claims are invariably defined as anti-national and perceived as threats to the 'nation', that is the state. Admittedly, state policy towards these religio-linguistic collectivities would be coercive, even downright oppressive. Understandably, such a state policy would draw its legitimacy from the majority of the population belonging to the dominant religious collectivity.

Third, for South Asian states the cut-off points of history vary, notwithstanding their common civilizational history, depending upon which religious collectivity constitutes their dominant population. Pursuantly, "national" reconstruction is neither a New Beginning nor a New Revolution but the re-conquest or the

---

⁶ See S.J. Tambiah, *Sri Lanka: Ethnic Fratricide and the Dismantling of Democracy*, New Delhi: Oxford University Press, 1986.

⁷ See T. K. Oommen, *State and Society in India: Studies in Nation-Building*, New Delhi: Sage Publications, 1990:(a) pp. 43-66.

rediscovery of an appropriate past depending upon who constitutes the national mainstream. Thus, if for India and Nepal the re-conquest dates back to the era of Aryan Hindu advent some five thousand years ago, to Sri Lanka, Burma, and Bhutan the nodal points of history vary depending upon the time at which Buddhism (or its dominant form) became the 'national' religion.[8] For Pakistan and Bangladesh, the cut-off point of history is more recent, the medieval period, when Muslim rule was firmly established in the Indian subcontinent. The differing layers of history invoked by the different states for national reconstruction influence their policies towards religious collectivities. These policies in turn legitimize the cognition about insiders and outsiders, that is, the brand of religious nationalism they pursue.

I have noted above that the seven South Asian countries are populated by people drawn mainly from three religions. One cannot however find any pattern based on religious composition and the nature of state policies. This contradicts the familiar stereotype that some religions (e.g. Hinduism) are catholic and tolerant and some others (e.g. Islam) are fundamentalist and rigid.

Pakistan and Bangladesh are the two Muslim majority states of the region that are relevant to our discussion. Pakistan is an Islamic state, in that it is a state with Islamic laws but not a theocratic state, because the ordained priests *ulema* are not given the responsibility for running the state although their opinion is often sought in the formulation, interpretation, and application of state laws. The state in Pakistan is, however, expected to enable the Muslims to order their lives 'in accord with the teachings and requirements of Islam as set out in Holy Quran and Sunnah...'[9] The objective of the state in Pakistan is clearly laid down in her constitutions.

The first constitution of Pakistan promulgated in 1956 explicitly referred to it as an Islamic Republic. Although this reference was omitted from the constitution of 1962, after eleven years the 1973 constitution declared Islam as the state religion and prescribed that, (a) the president and prime minister ought to be Muslims, and (b) that all laws should be brought in conformity with the values of Islam. In fact in 1981 President Zia ul-Haq stated that the purpose of the state of Pakistan is to promote the ideology of Islam.[10] Subsequent governments of Pakistan have reiterated this position and reinforced this orientation.

The state of Pakistan emerged in 1947 with the explicit intention of protecting the interests of Muslims. Therefore, it should surprise none that its Islamic orientation persists. In contrast, Bangladesh emerged to safeguard the interests of a linguistic category, the Bengalis. Given this thrust, adequate assurance was given in the constitution to safeguard the interest of the Hindu and Christian Bengalis too. Indeed, the constitution that Bangladesh adopted in 1972, soon after its emergence as an independent state, describes it as a secular and socialist state. From 1975 onwards however the military regime of Bangladesh took definite steps towards

---

[8] If for Sri Lanka this nodal point is around the third century BC (see W.Rahula,"Buddhism as State Religion'in W. Rahula, *History of Buddhism as State Religionl, Colombo: M.D. Gunasena and Co*, 1956, pp, 62-77, for Bhutan it is AD seventh century (see B. J. Hasrat, *History of Bhutan*, Education Department, Government of Bhutan, Timpu, 1980. pp. 34-45, and for Burma it is AD eleventh century when Thervada Buddhism firmly entrenched itself there. See D. E. Smith, *India as a Secular State*, Bombay: Oxford University Press, 1965, pp. 3-11.

[9] The Pakistan constitution was rewritten several times. For an account of this, see M.D. Ahmed, "Conflicting Definitions of Islamic State in Pakistan," in W.P. Zingal (ed.) *Pakistan in its Fourth Decade*, Hamburg: Des Deutschem Orient Institutes, 1983, pp.127-46; R. Raja, "The Continuous Process of Re-writing the Constitution" in W. P. Zinglaed,1983, pp.1-15.

[10] See L. Wolf-Philips,"Constitutional Legitimacy in Pakistan" in W.P. Zingal, ed., 1983, pp. 16-63.

Islamization.[11] This trend culminated in May 1988 when a bill was passed declaring Islam as the state religion of Bangladesh. Thus the eroded saliency of religion in the context of the conflict between the two wings of Pakistan was gradually recovered by the new state of Bangladesh. The point to be noted is that although Bangladesh started as a secular state, right from the outset the Islamic ethos prevailed and was eventually institutionalized.

The constitutions of both Pakistan and Bangladesh guarantee to every citizen the right to profess, practice, and propagate his religion. In Bangladesh however religious minorities voice complaints of discrimination by the state. The situation in Pakistan is more problematic, in that not only do non-Muslim religious minorities complain about discrimination based on religion, but revolts against Muslim sects themselves are not unknown.[12] Thus there is a wide gulf between constitutional guarantees and social praxis and social praxis is determined by the compulsions of statecraft that cannot ignore the pressures exerted by the dominant religious collectivity.

The three Buddhist majority states of South Asia too vary in regard to the official status accorded to religion. Thus though Buddhism is the official religion of Bhutan right from the outset, its official status has been shifting in Burma. In 1948 although several legislations supporting Buddhism were introduced in Burma only in 1961 was it declared the state religion. However, in 1962 this recognition was withdrawn and the principle of equal respect for all religions was adopted as the state policy. However,

Buddhism was declared a state religion subsequently. If the official status of Buddhism in Burma has fluctuated, in post-colonial Sri Lanka it has been more or less stable in that no explicit official recognition was given to Buddhism.[13] However, the predominant tendency is to identify Sinhala Buddhism as the "national" religion. As one commentator puts it, Buddhism is for "all practical purposes the official religion"[14] of Sri Lanka. The general point is that although Buddhism occupies the dominant place in all the three states it has differing official status in each. However, state policy facilitates the process of dominance by the majority religious collectivity irrespective of the nature of their polity: monarchy (Bhutan), military dictatorship (Burma), and democracy (Sri Lanka).

The two Hindu majority South Asian states too vary enormously when it comes to according official status to religion. Nepal is a monarchical Hindu state in which the monarch must be an adherent of Aryan culture and Hindu religion. In contrast, India has no state religion and equal respect to all religions is a constant refrain in the constitution. It is clear that South Asian states, with the exception of India, have either explicitly adopted a state religion or have accorded pride of place to the religion of the majority/dominant religious collectivity. Does this Indian exceptionalism make any difference in actual practice?

II

Today's India is a result of division of territory of the subcontinent to create a religion-based

---

¹¹ For a discussion of the shift from the 'secular' to the Islamic thrust fo the state in Bangladesh, see M. Talukdar , "Bangladesh Politics: Secular and Islamic Trends," in S. K. Chakravorty and V. Narain, eds, 1986, pp. 47-73. and K. M. Mohsin, 1986, pp. 28-41.

¹² In 1953, Pakistan Punjab witnessed widespread anti-Ahmediya riots. For an account of these, see *Report of the Court of Equity (Munior Commission) constituted under the Punjab Act 11 of 1954 to Enquire into the Punjab Disturbance of 1965: 3-11,* Supdt. of Government Printing, Punjab, 1954.

¹³ This is a recent development in that from third century BC to AD nineteenth century only a Buddhist had the legitimate right to be the king of Sri Lanka. See Rahula, 1956, pp. 62-77.

¹⁴ G Obeyesekere, "Religious Symbolism and Political Change in Ceylon," *Modern Ceylon Studies,*1970, p.62.

polity, namely Pakistan as noted earlier. The 'communal riots' that followed uprooted around fifteen million people, perhaps the largest displacement of people in human history. Between 1946 and 1951, six million Muslims left Indian territory for Pakistan and nine million Hindus and Sikhs came to India from Pakistan, Pakistan eventually becoming an Islamic state. Given this background, it goes to the credit of emerging free India that no constitutional recognition was accorded to Hinduism, the religion of its overwhelming majority. And yet, religious nationalism is alive and kicking in India. Three religious collectivities in India claim that they are nations.

Hindu[15] identity is neither entirely new nor completely old; it is a conjoint product of both contemporary construction and the givens of the past. The cultural symbols and the values that embody them have a recognizable trajectory, some of which are newly constructed to cope with the challenge posed by the Semitic religions. On the other hand, some of these values and symbols are revivals of old ones. It is this past- present linkage that imparts to the new identity its vibrancy and vitality, on the one hand, and its ambiguity and ambivalence, on the other. This is evident from the differing boundary demarcations of Hinduism, which fall on a continuum. That is, there are a series of Hindu identities and not just one ideal type. Let me list the three most prominent ones.

First, according to some Hindu nationalists, Hindus are simply the original and obvious inhabitants of Hindustan, that is, India. "Hindu society living in this country since time immemorial is the national ... society here.... The same Hindu people have built the life values, ideals and culture of this country and, therefore, their nationhood is self-evident."[16] Further, "[w]e, Hindus, have been in undisputed and undisturbed possession of this land for over eight or even ten thousand years before the land was invaded by any foreign race."[17] Viewed thus, Hindus are simply a people who occupy their homeland and share a lifestyle. This all-embracing definition does not have religious content, Hindus being a people of a designated land, as the Germans or the Greeks are.

Second, Hindus are all those who pursue religions of Indian origin, including the primal vision. Thus Savarkar contends: "Hinduism must necessarily mean the religion or the religions that are peculiar or native to this land .... [1]t should be applied to all the religious beliefs that the different comminutes of the Hindu people hold."[18] In this conceptualization, the inextricable linkage between the community of faith and the country of residence is taken to be the essence of the Hindu nation. But such a proposition would be rejected by the "non-Hindu" religions of Indian origin and some have openly challenged it (e.g., Sikhs); hence the following clarification:

> Sikhs are Hindus in the sense of our definition of Hindutva and not in any religious sense whatever. Religiously they are Sikhs as Jains are Jains, Lingayats are Lingayats, Vaishnavas are Vaishnavas; but all of us racially and nationally and culturally are a polity and a people.... We are Sikhs and Hindus and Bhatratiyas (Indians). We are all three put together and none exclusively.[19]

Clearly this studied ambivalence and cultivated ambiguity is a political project designed to avoid

---

[15] Notwithstanding the well-known fact that the terms Hindus and Hinduism are appellations invented by conquering or colonizing outsiders to refer to the inhabitants of the then India, today these are terms that connote a particular religious collectivity and corpus of belief system and ritual practices specific to them.

[16] D. R. Goyal, *Rastriya Swayam Sewak Sangh*, Delhi: Radhakrishna, 1979, p.40.

[17] M. S. Golwalkar, *We or Our Nationhood Defined, Bharat Prakashan, Nagpur,* 1939, p.49.

[18] V. D. Savarkar, *Hindutva*, New Delhi: Bharat Sahitya Sadan, 1949, pp.104-5.

[19] *Ibid.*, p125.

possible wedges and potential conflicts between religions of Indian origin. Be that as it may, this definition of Hindu is both inclusive (all those who profess religions of Indian origin) and exclusive (all those who profess religions of "alien" origin).

The third conceptualization of Hindu is more restrictive and substantially exclusivist. It includes (a) only twice-born Brahmins, Kshatriyas and Vaishyas or, at best, also ritually-clean Shudras, (b) of Aryabhumi, that is, North India. It excludes the Panchamas (those of the fifth order) that is, the ex-untouchables currently counting a hundred and forty million[20]; the Adivasis (the original inhabitants), presently accounting for seventy five million[21]; and Dravidian Hindus of South India, numbering around two hundred and fifty million.[22] This conceptualization questions the internality of a substantial proportion of "Hindus"; they are rendered "outsiders".[23] Clearly, such a definition of Hindu falls short of the requirements of a political project; it divides the Hindus of India into different "nations."

To avoid the extreme exclusivist orientation of this conceptualization, neo-Hindu reformers have attempted to accommodate non-Hindus through Shuddhi (ritual purification). But the innovation is applicable only to (a) ritually unclean untouchables; (b) the tribal communities, that is, Vanvasis (forest dwellers) who claim primal vision as their religion; and (c) those who have been converted into "alien" religions. For the Dravidian clean caste Hindus, Shuddhi is irrelevant. Thus once again one encounters the ambiguity of boundary and ambivalence of attitude in defining Hindu and Hinduism. The caste and linguistic factors invoked in defining Hinduism erode the saliency of religion.

Hindu is thus defined at least in three different ways invoking different variables: territory, religion, and caste or language. All of them pose problems in defining Hindu as a nation or nationality, and I shall list them presently. But what is common to all the three conceptualizations is that they deny equality to one or another segment of the population.

It is true that 83 percent of the Indian population is classified as Hindu in the census.[24] To begin, it may be noted that the claim that India is the Hindu homeland was made with reference to undivided India in which the proportion of Hindus was much less than that in divided India. On the other hand, undivided India had the largest Muslim congregation in the world. Even after partition, India remains the second largest Muslim country in the world. Similarly, 80 percent of the world's Zoroastrians live in India. Hindu nationalists counter this point by suggesting that these people are outsiders which raises the

---

[20] According to the Hindu doctrine of creation, Brahmins emerged from the mouth of the creator, Kshatriyas from the hands, Vaishyas from the thighs, and Shudras from the feet. This chaturvarna (four colour) scheme does not even account for the untouchables, belonging to the fifth varna.

[21] The four-hundred or so tribal communities of India claim that they are the original inhabitants (Adivasis) of the land. This claim is not accepted by Hindu nationalists, who insist that Aryan Hindus were the original settlers, and consequently, label the tribal communities as forest-dwellers (Vanvasis).

[22] Population of India speaks languages belonging to four families: Indo-Aryan (73 percent), Dravidian (25 percent), Austro-Asiatic (1.5 percent), and Tibeto-Chinese (0.5 percent). Dravidian languages are spoken mainly in the four South Indian states: Kerala (Malayalam), Karnataka (Kannada), Tamil Nadu (Tamil), and Andhra Pradesh (Telugu). The Dravidian movement, which opposed Aryan domination, considers Dravidian Hinduism distinct from Aryan Hinduism.

[23]T. K. Oommen, *State and Society in India, 1990a*, pp.43-66.

[24] This figure is problematic because the Indian census automatically counts all those who do not belong to one of the world religions as Hindu. In the British Indian census there was a religious category variously designated as "animist", "tribal", "primitive", etc., which counted two to three percent of the population, which was about twenty-five million people in those days. This category is absorbed under the rubric of Hinduism from the 1951 census onward.

question as to the time span required for the nativization of a people in a country.

The Zoroastrians have been in India since the eighth century. The Muslims came to the Kerala coast as early as the seventh century. The Syrian Christians of Kerala claim to be converts since 52 A.D. At any rate, an overwhelming majority of Muslims and Christians are converts from Scheduled Castes and Scheduled Tribes, the original inhabitants of India. Therefore, if one takes the criterion of nativity seriously, a majority of the Muslims and Christians have a better claim to be Indian nationals because the Aryan Hindus, who claim to be the original inhabitants, came to India only some 3,500 years ago.

The attitude of Hindu nationalists varies enormously in regard to the different religious categories, viewed in terms of their sources of presence and modes of incorporation. All religions of Indian origin are considered as Hinduism according to one of the conceptualizations as noted above. However, this expansionist orientation in defining Hindus is resented by some, the most obvious case being that of the Sikhs in independent India, as they too claim to be a nation based on the criterion of religion. The Hindu-Sikh conflict, then, is to be viewed as the competing claims of two religious nationalisms. Be that as it may, the Sikh accusation that Hindu nationalists are antidemocratic is equally applicable to Sikh nationalists, as both tend to be hegemonic.

Generally speaking, Hindu nationalists have an attitude of indifference and even tolerance toward the 'migrant' religions — Jews, Zoroastrians and Bahai's — not simply because their numbers are very small and hence they do not pose any threat, but also because they have

not claimed any part of the Indian territory as their homeland and have not indulged in proselytization.[25] However, the Hindu nationalists have had an uneasy relation and a hostile attitude toward Christians and Muslims, although it has varied in intensity. The negative attitude toward Indian Christians during the colonial period was part of the hostility toward British rulers, as both were co-religionists and hence an instant object of suspicion. The persisting hostility toward Christians after the exit of the British can be traced to the continuing missionary activity, often geared to proselytization. This hostility is moderated by two factors. First, Indian Christians never defined themselves as a nationality and second, have not demanded any special benefits from the state on the basis of religion. (However, Christian converts from the Scheduled Castes and their spokespersons do demand such benefits now, as conversion has not improved their material conditions).

The Hindu nationalists' attitude to the Muslims is very negative for several reasons. First, they number over a hundred million and constitute perhaps the single most important vote bank against Hindu nationalism. Second, the presence of two Muslim majority states— Pakistan and Bangladesh— as immediate neighbours makes the relationship between the Hindu majority and the Muslim minority uneasy, ambivalent, and even tricky. Third, Hindu nationalists hold the Muslims responsible for the vivisection of India, the sacred and ancient land of the Hindus. Fourth, Indian Muslims have not entirely given up the claim to nationality even after partition, although they are territorially dispersed. The effort to consolidate Muslims as a nationality is pursued by projecting (although

---

[25] It may, however, be noted that the Bahai's did pursue the project of proselytization in the 1960s in the region of Malwa in central India. Consequently, their number increased from a small figure in the 1950s to 400,000. See W. Garlington,"The Bahai faith in Malwa" in G.A. Oddie, ed., *Religion in South Asia*, Delhi: Manohar Publishers, 1977, pp. 101-18. But due to the hue and cry which followed, the Bahai's abandoned the proselytization project in India.

wrongly) Urdu as the exclusive language of Muslims. Finally, the claim by a section of Kashmiri Muslims that Kashmir is their exclusive homeland, the secessionist movement in Kashmir believed to be abetted and sustained by Pakistan, the special privilege conceded to Kashmir under article 370 of the Indian constitution, have all soured the relationship between Hindu nationalists and Muslim nationalists.

The Hindu nationalist hostility to other religions is thus not simply based on their "alien" origin but anchored as well to the proclivity they unfold in claiming that they too are nations. Thus interreligious hostility in independent India is most pronounced between Hindus, on the one hand, and Sikhs and Muslims, on the other, both of who define themselves as nations or nationalities. It is important to recall here that Sikhism is the youngest religion of Indic origin, further, the definition of Hinduism by the Indian Constitution, the Hindu Code Bill, and Hindu nationalists includes Sikhism along with Jainism and Buddhism.

Hinduism, although not proselytizing, is migratory. At least twenty million Hindus live outside the Indian subcontinent, the traditional sacred land of Hinduism. In some of the countries (e.g., Fiji, Surinam, Mauritius) they constitute majorities. Would it be correct to say that those Hindus who have settled outside the Indian subcontinent cease to be Hindus because they do not live in their ancestral homeland? The absurdity of the question is patent, but it emanates from the assumptions made by Hindu nationalists. At any rate, where does one put agnostics, rationalists and secularists in the scheme of Hindu Rashtra or, for that matter, in any nation constructed on the basis of religion? Finally, the Hindu nationalist claim implies the annexation of Nepal, the Hindu majority neighbor, as a part of consolidating the Hindu nation!

It is also not true that only Islam and Christianity have colonized new territories and in that process either annihilated or marginalized native populations. The dominant religions of Sri Lanka are Buddhism and Hinduism (both of Indian origin), and the original inhabitants of the country, the Veddas, constitute just one percent of Sri Lankan population today. In the process of Aryanizing India, the native population was stigmatized. Buddhism has been vigorously proselytizing, and Hinduism acutely assimilative. Therefore, religion-territory conterminality is not axiomatic even in the case of religions of Indian origin. The Hindus belong to a multiplicity of speech communities; that is, there are several Hindu nations. To grapple with this problem, Hindu nationalists project Sanskrit as the common ancient language of all Hindus and Hindi written in Devnagri script as the national language of India. But they encounter several difficulties and severe resistance in this context.

The fallacious claim about religion-territory conterminality is also implied in the claims advanced by Muslims and Sikhs that they are nations. As hinted above, the alien migrant element in the Muslim population of South Asia is negligible, and the overwhelming majority of Muslims are converts from local castes and tribes. Therefore, the claims of Muslims that particular areas of the Indian subcontinent are their homeland is legitimate and authentic because they have a moral claim on these territories, although not as Muslims. If the Muslims were not natives and mere migrants eager to return to their homeland (as the Jews did in the wake of the Zionist movement), they would not have succeeded in staking their claim. But there are several difficulties in advancing the claim that Muslims *qua* Muslims constitute a nation.

First, none of the areas claimed by the Muslims as their homeland (as in the case of other religious groups) was populated exclusively by them even after substantial transfer of Hindu and Sikh populations from these areas. Therefore, the claim that these areas were or are Muslim homelands is not tenable— not because Islam is an "alien" religion, but because nativity and nationhood cannot be defined in terms of religious faiths and affiliations. The so-called Muslim homeland is as much the homeland of non-Muslims of that region.

Second, even if a section of the Muslims are migrants to India, to the extent that (a) the migration occurred several centuries ago and since (b) they identify with the territory presently inhabited by them as their homeland, the claim ought to be accepted as legitimate. Because there are several alien elements among Hindus— Kashmiri Pandits, Maghi Brahmins, and Rajputs to mention but a few – whose nativity is not questioned by Hindu nationalists, this is no concession to the alien elements in the Muslim population.

Third, Pakistan, which emerged in 1947, although populated predominantly by Muslims, could not be sustained as one 'nation' for long because of the absence of geographical contiguity and linguistic uniformity. In fact, Islam became an irrelevant variable in maintaining the unity of Muslim Pakistan, leading to its split mainly based on territory and language.

Fourth, the Hindi-speaking Muslims, popularly referred to as Bihari Muslims, instantly became alien elements in Bangladesh, the state of the Bengali-speaking Muslims. Even the Hindi/ Urdu speaking Muslims who migrated to Pakistan from India are not accepted as natives and remain Mohajirins, the stigmatized outsiders. Thus Muslim nationalists deny nativity even to co-religionists who are migrants from outside. This clearly points to the unsustainability of religious nationalism.

Fifth, the predominantly Muslim but multilingual Pakistan continues to have serious tensions and conflicts among its different linguistic groups — Punjabis, Sindhis, Baluchis, and so on — that is, the nations that constitute the state of Pakistan. Each of these collectivities defines its respective linguistic region as its homeland. Thus it is clear that homeland can be anchored only to speech communities and not to faith communities.

Once India was partitioned, no territory within could be claimed as a Muslim homeland, save the Kashmir valley. However, this claim is ambivalent for two reasons. First, Kashmir itself is partitioned and apportioned between India and Pakistan for geopolitical reasons. Second, there are others in Kashmir (e.g., Kashmiri Pandits) who stake their claim with equal intensity and authenticity that Kashmir is their homeland too. In such a situation the only route available to those who falsely claim that the Kashmir valley is an exclusive Muslim homeland is to intimidate, terrorize, and flush out those who make counterclaims. In the exodus of Kashmiri Pandits from Kashmir what one witnesses is the inevitable consequence of the perverse notion that there exists conterminality between territory and religion, that is, territorialization of religion. Admittedly, territorialization of religion leads to ethnification of minority or weak nations.

After partition, the Muslims of India did not have a decisive majority in any part of India except in the Kashmir valley and the Laccadives and Minicoy Islands. But Muslims constituted about 12 percent of India's population, amounting to around seventy million people in the 1950s. That is, while their absolute number was substantial, they were thinly dispersed all over the country. This situation was susceptible to their getting assimilated within the linguistic regions (nations) they inhabit. This necessitated the invention and maintenance of new symbols to preserve their socioreligious identity. Urdu, written in Persian Arabic script, is the most important symbol the Muslims invoke to highlight their cultural specificity and nationality within India. But the project remains ineffective in investing nationhood on Muslims on an all-India basis because not only that the principle of geographical contiguity is imperiled but also the majority of Indian Muslims are *not* Urdu speakers.

The Sikh claim to nationhood, too, assumes religion-territory conterminality, but the Punjab claimed to be the Sikh homeland, was a Muslim-majority province before India's partition, with 51 percent Muslims in 1921. By 1961, although the Muslim population was reduced to a mere two percent in the Indian Punjab (both because of the re-allocation of territory and migration), the Sikhs constituted only 33 percent, and the Hindus were still in majority with 64 percent. As religion was not accepted as the basis of constituting politico-administrative units in independent India, the only hope was to carve out a Sikh majority province by invoking language as the criterion. The Sikh leadership therefore staked their claim for a separate province based on Punjabi language. A separate Punjabi-speaking state was formed in 1966 in which the Sikhs constituted only a thin majority of 53 percent. Thus, in spite of two successive partitions, the Punjab still cannot be viewed as the exclusive homeland of Sikhs; they do not constitute a decisive demographic majority, and the remaining 47 percent of non-Sikh population, too, considers Punjab as its homeland. But, a fatal error by Punjabi Hindus in disclaiming their real mother tongue — namely, Punjabi — and on falsely insisting that Hindi is their mother tongue provided a thin veneer of legitimacy to the crystallization of the idea that the Punjab is the Sikh homeland.[26] There is another reason why the Sikh claims to the Punjab, as their homeland is untenable. Although 78 percent of the Sikhs of India live in Punjab, the remaining 22 percent are dispersed all over India. This demographic dispersal of Sikhs may be traced to two factors. First, in the wake of partition a substantial proportion of the Sikhs who migrated to India settled outside the Punjab. Second, the Sikhs are an enterprising migratory community in search of economic opportunities. The logical corollary of insisting that Punjab is the exclusive homeland of the Sikhs is to render instantly the Sikhs outside Punjab and the non-Sikhs inside Punjab aliens, outsiders, and refugees.

The point is claims to nationhood by a people are based on their moral claim on a specific territory as their homeland. Such a claim cannot be sustained by a religious collectivity because of the disjuncture between religion and territory. Pursuantly, the claim to nationhood by Hindus, Muslims and Sikhs based on the assumption and argument that the whole of India or specific parts of India constitute their exclusive homeland is untenable.

III

Once the untenable assumption that religious collectivity is a nation is accepted, an appropriate strategy, namely, communalization of politics, has to be invoked. Communalism has a positive as well as a negative referent. In South Asia, communalism is invariably viewed as a negative force as it is juxtaposed against nationalism; it may be defined as the tendency on the part of a religious collectivity to claim that it is a political community.[27]

It is necessary and useful to distinguish between at least three different variants of communalism as a political force as they fall into a hierarchy of threat to the state.[28] First, a religious community defines itself as an autonomous political community, that is, an entity entitled to have its own sovereign state. This implies secession from the multi- religious polity to which it is currently attached and hence may be

---

[26]See B.R.Nayyar, *Minority Politics in the Punjab*, Princeston: Princeston University Press, 1966.

[27] L. Dumont, *Religion, Politics and History in India*, The Hague: Mouton and Co, 1970.

[28] T. K. Oommen 1990a, *State and Society in India*, pp.112-23.

designated as *secessionist* communalism. The Muslim demand for Pakistan and the Sikh demand for Khalistan are examples of this variety of communalism.

The second variant of communalism is the proclivity on the part of the religious collectivity to define itself as a nation, that is, as a cultural entity with a territorial base. This is often articulated in the argument that in order to maintain its cultural specificity the nation should have a separate politico-administrative arrangement, which could be a district or a province within the federal polity.[29] The demand for a separate Punjabi Suba, although couched in linguistic terms, was essentially a demand for a separate Sikh province within India. To the extent that the demand is geared to preserve the cultural specificity of a religious collectivity and a separate province is viewed as a tool to achieve that end, this type of communalism may be designated as *separatist* communalism.

The third variant is the demand by a religious collectivity to be recognized as a specific entity suffering from material deprivations, the eradication of which could be met through measures such as political representation, employment quotas, distribution of land, industrial licenses, and so on. In this context, mobilization of the religious collectivity is attempted as an interest group geared to the welfare of its members. Therefore, this variety of communalism may be labelled *welfarist* communalism.

I am persuaded to distinguish between these three types of communalisms because their implications vary vastly for the state, the nation, and the religious community. The three types of communalism can be organized on a continuum of hierarchy of threat to the state, and consequently state responses differ radically in each case.[30] Generally speaking, the state would oppose tooth and nail secessionist communalism and would spare no effort to liquidate the movement. This can be easily discerned in the response of the Indian State and Hindu nationalists to secessionist movements in the Punjab and in Kashmir. The opposition to separatist communalism is less virulent. If the mobilization by the concerned religious community is massive and visible and if the countermobilization by the opposing community is weak, the state in all probability would concede the demand. The formation of the Punjabi Suba exemplifies this pattern of response. Finally, governments of multireligious democratic societies are compelled to allow religious collectivities to function as interest groups and to concede the demands they make. This response pattern is called for either because the demands made are perceived as legitimate or because the political clout of the community as a vote bank is substantial. The state response to the demands made by religious minorities in the context of the policy of protective discrimination (e.g., bringing the neo-Buddhists under the purview of the reservation policy), providing the requisite recognition to languages claimed by religious minorities as a part of their cultural heritage (e.g., the recognition given to Urdu), or "protecting" the minorities from "intimidations" of the state legal system (non-implementation of a uniform civil-code) are examples of the Indian state recognizing religious collectivities as "legitimate" interest groups.

---

[29] Thus Kushwant Singh writes: "The only chance of survival of the Sikhs as a separate community is to create a state in which they from a compact group, where the teaching of *Gurumukhi* and Sikh religion is compulsory where there is an atmosphere of respect for the traditions of their *Khalsa* forefathers" in *History of Sikhs:* Vol.2, Princeton, Princeton University Press, 1966, p.305. Here state does not refer to sovereign state but only provincial state.

[30] T.K.Oommen, *Protest and Change: Studies in Social Movements*, New Delhi: Sage Publications, 1990b, pp.183-209.

Of the three communalisms listed above two imply religion-territory association. Thus, secessionist communalism is geared to the establishment of an exclusive state for the religious collectivity, which implies its legal claim over its presumed homeland. In the case of separatist communalism, the claim over the homeland by the religious collectivity is essentially moral in that the "nation" is to function within the territorial boundaries of the multinational state of which it is a part. However, a religious community operates merely as an interest group when it recognizes the impossibility of carving out a separate state or nation for itself because it cannot stake and sustain any legal or moral claim on a contiguous territory. Generally speaking the interest group orientation and demographic dispersal of a religious group within the territory controlled by the state coincide.

The point to be noted is that the nature and content of communalism is inextricably bound up with the religious collectivity's territorial base and spread, which in turn has profound implications for the polity. If secessionist communalism invariably invites state repression, welfarist communalism usually augments democratic culture. Separatist communalism may graduate into secessionist or may be scaled down into welfarist depending upon the manner in which the demands are framed and articulated, and on the state response to them. That is, the nature of the state— democratic or authoritarian— and the style of framing and pursuing the demands by the mobilized collectivities will critically mould the process.

The claim to nationhood or nationality by a religious collectivity willy-nilly implies that the process of evolving and imposing a common life-style on a culture on an Independent India has been articulated in different contexts and forms. I shall pursue the present discussion with special reference to Hindus and Sikhs, and this for two reasons. First, the claim to nationhood by these religious collectivities has not yet been realized, unlike the case of the Muslims in the Indian subcontinent. Second, the Hindus and Sikhs were, and to a certain extent even today are sharing a common life-style; yet every effort is made to overemphasize their specificities, while ignoring the commonalities.

The Hindu advocacy of homogenization has been articulated in different ways. If in the 1960s and the 1970s the preferred phrase was "Indianization," now it is "Hindutva." Hindu nationalists insist that the advocacy is disassociated from and devoid of any narrow religious context and content but refers to a life-style common to the people of India as a whole; hence, a Hindu is one who follows this life-style.

If life-style includes matters of dress, food, worship styles, art forms, marriage and family patterns, there is very little common even to the Hindus of different regional-linguistic areas, not to speak of the different religious communities of India. This, however, is not to deny that there exists a civilizational unity encompassing, the multiplicity of the collectivities inhabiting India, but this envelops the people of South Asia as a whole and is not confined to the geographical area under Indian state. Perhaps an example will lend clarity to the point I am making. Brahmins constitute the only pan-Indian Varna (Caste), and even they differ vastly in, say, food habits. Thus if the majority of Brahmins traditionally were vegetarians, the Bengali Brahmin was a fish-eater and the Kashmiri Pandit a meat-eater. That is, vegetarianism is not common to all Hindus, not even to Brahmins. But beef is a taboo for believing Hindus, and they do not consume it. (The fact that beef was not a taboo in ancient India and it constituted a part of the regular diet is not relevant here.)

Against this background it is important to recall that there have been several mobilizations against cow slaughter in 'secular' independent

shall list only three of them here.[32] First, to homogenize invariably means to establish the hegemony of the dominant collectivity, with the attendant annihilation of the weak and minority collectivities or at best their assimilation into an artificially contrived cultural mainstream, leading to the eclipse of their identity. Second, most state-societies, as they are constituted, draw their population from diverse sources. Therefore, assimilation and annihilation endanger the principle of diversity and block the task of developing pluralism and democracy. Third, contemporary societies are constantly exposed to alien influences and hence characterized by frayed edges and loose textures. The ongoing process of globalization is bound to intensify this trend. In such a situation the only viable option is to celebrate diversity, foster pluralism, nurture inter-group equality, and reinforce democratic trends.

It is fairly clear by now that cultural relativism is a necessary corollary of homogenization; 'relativization' is the tendency to rehabilitate tradition in its totality in terms of original vision and purity. It often provides justification to all kinds of inhuman and disparaging practices:[33] be it, *sati* (the practice of the Hindu wife committing suicide by jumping into the funeral pyre of her husband), untouchability, maintenance of particular diets, dress patterns, and so on, all of which are justified in the name of religion. Thus, cultural relativism in the context of religion has two dimensions. First, it advocates values and practices that are patently inhuman and irrational in the contemporary context. Second, it insists on practices that are incongruous and anomalous in modern society, which practices are justified by invoking religious texts formulated and injunctions adumbrated in an entirely different

context. This is often referred to as religious 'fundamentalism', which may be defined as the tendency to adhere to the text ignoring the context. The Hindu conservative elements often justify and legitimize practices such as sati and untouchability in the name of tradition and values of pristine Hinduism. The Sikh adherence to the keeping of the five *Ks— Kesh* (unshorn hair and beard), *Kanga* (comb), *Kachh* (knee-length pair of breeches), *Karah* (steel bracelet), and *Kirpan* (sword)—also smacks of cultural relativism. Admittedly, relativism fosters conformity and advocates anachronistic life-styles.

The ideology of homogenization, then, is not only geared to the standardization of values, norms and practices, but it also implies (a) the revival of obsolescent traditional values, norms and practices that are not relevant to the present, and (b) the imposition of those values on others, both 'deviant' co-religionists and religious minorities. This is so because the reference point of homogenization advocated by religious nationalists invariably relates to the original vision and practices of their founding fathers, ignoring the context of the latter's advocacy. That is, religious nationalisms carry with them the inevitable tendency of revivalism. Further, religious nationalists endeavor to create a societal ethos buttressed by the values of the dominant religion within the polity. Neither Hindu nor Sikh nationalism is an exception to this inherent tendency; therefore neither is likely to survive in a modernizing world, nor are other religious nationalisms.

IV

The gist of my argument is that religious nationalism as a project is bound to fail because its domain assumptions— namely, that there is conterminality between religion and territory and

---

[32] T. K. Oommen, "Reconciling Pluralism and Equality," *International Review of Sociology* (1),New Series, 1992, p.154.

[33] See R. Redfield, *The Primitive World and its Transformation*, Ithaca: Cornell University Press, 1957.

that a religious collectivity is a political community— are wrong and empirically unsustainable. The process of cultural homogenization is a prerequisite to encapsulate and contain all the religious groups within the ken of religious nationalism. This in practice means imposing the life-style of the majority over the minority religious groups. Further, given the fact that the frame of reference of religious nationalisms is invariably anchored to what is believed to be the original vision of the founding fathers, it necessarily prompts relativism, that is, reviving and preserving the traditional beliefs and rituals even as they are embedded in unjust and inhuman values. Admittedly, religious nationalism carries with it the seeds of religious fundamentalism. For these reasons religious nationalism is not sustainable in a world in which democracy has emerged as a universally accepted and acclaimed value.

CHAPTER 43

Conclusion:
Recasting Mission & Missiology,
Elements of an Agenda for the Asian Church in the 21st Century

ROGER E HEDLUND and PAUL JOSHUA BHAKIARAJ

Previous chapters in this book have engaged with a wide variety of pertinent biblical, theological, historical, religious, contextual and strategic issues that impinge on mission and missiology in this 21st century. This constructive and critical discussion will doubtless, as it is meant to, serve as a valuable resource for the church as she comes to increasingly recognise the reality of the times she lives in, the resources she possesses and the challenge that she faces. To conclude this discussion on *Missiology for the 21st Century* this chapter seeks to draw together the foregoing and in so doing offer the Asian Church some proposals as we move further ahead into that century. Here we seek to reflect particularly on some resources, contexts and perspectives for the Asian Church. To summarise the basic intent of this combined effort and to proffer a possible way forward, the first section will focus on some resources of the church, the second will concentrate on the context she finds herself in and finally in the third a proposal will be made suggesting fresh perspectives be adopted as we move further into the 21st century.

The 21st Century Church

As early as 1978 extant signs suggested to some perceptive scholars that, *The Coming of the Third Church* [1] was imminent. Among them was Swiss Catholic missionary to Africa, Walbert Buhlmann, who pointed out then that, analogous to a Copernican shift that took place during the early years of the 1st century, when the Hebraic-Jewish base of the Church gave way to a Greco-Roman base, and again later around 11th-12th century when that Mediterranean base gave way to a European one, a third shift was underway. This shift, he predicted, would replace the Church "European-American base with one from the majority world of Africa, Latin America and Asia. This "epoch-making"[2] shift initiated by these "surprise packets"[3] of world Christianity would usher in this third church that will be characterised by its young, dynamic but poor people.[4]

Now whether or not Buhlmann was considered a prophet is not clear, one thing is certain though, the observation made over two and a half decades ago has proved to be, in truth, "prophetic." In the time that has lapsed since he wrote that book, a shift of the centre of gravity of the world Church from the west to the two-thirds world, as predicted, has taken place. Christianity is now predominantly a southern religion, a religion of the poor. Echoing Buhlmann' thesis, scholars such as Andrew Walls, Lamin Sanneh, Dana Robert and others have also

---

[1] Walbert Buhlmann, *The Coming of the Third Church*, New York: Orbis Books, 1978
[2] *Ibid.* p. ix
[3] *Ibid.* p. 4
[4] *Ibid.* pp. 22-23

been pointing out this seemingly obvious, but ignored, fact.[5] In their acclaimed *Encyclopaedia*, David Barrett et al also provide extensive statistics to corroborate the fact of this new reality.[6] Writing recently, historian Philip Jenkins rightly observes: "The era of Western Christianity has passed within our lifetimes, and the day of Southern Christianity is dawning. The fact of change is undeniable: it has happened and will continue to happen."[7]

Whilst Africa and Latin America may stand at the forefront of this movement in numerical strength, the Asian Church has also been at the centre of this shift. This geographic and demographic ecclesiastical reversal embraces the Asian region, with its complex religious, ethnic, cultural, socio-economic diversity. From tribal groups to urban populations, from adherents of other religions to adherents of none, there appears to be a steady growth in the number of Asian followers of Christ. Whilst one may not be entirely sure whether Barrett's estimates, which suggest that in India alone there are 62 million Christians, about six percent of the total population, can be taken at face value, the Indian Church has nevertheless seen significant growth. Conversion movements are not historical artefacts of years gone by alone, they continue even today. Perhaps the same can be said of other countries in the region. Nepali Christianity is said to have seen a 16 percent growth over the last year, Chinese Christianity has witnessed a growth

of about seven percent and the list could go on.[8] Compared to the so-called Christian west where a rapid decline of Christianity is painfully evident, Asia represents a region of remarkable church growth. Just as regular reports highlight rapid expansion of African churches, so also it is not uncommon to hear, for example, of the development of mega churches in places like Chennai, Manila, Seoul and Singapore. Christianity in Asia stands with her sister churches in Africa and Latin America to stake its claim to be a centre of global Christianity.

That this is the new reality of the 21ˢᵗ century church is due in large part to the contribution of the Asian Christians themselves. In this challenging context of religious, ethnic, cultural, socio-economic diversity Christian mission is carried out by a vast number of Asian Christians. Contrary to those who think that mission is not native to the Churches of Asia, it can be demonstrated that mission is integral to the Asian Churches. Ken Miyamoto suggests that because they were "receivers" rather than "senders," most Asian churches failed to develop a clear understanding of mission and social thought.[9] However, that may be a rather myopic observation. Mission has been understood severally among Asian churches and India maybe a typical case in point. Historically the Orthodox Church has comprehended mission in terms of the life and witness of its members.[10] The Church

---

[5] Andrew Walls, *The Missionary Movement in Christian History: Studies in the Transmission of Faith*, New York: Orbis Books, 1996; Lamin Sanneh, *Encountering the West: Christianity & the Global Cultural Process: The African Dimension*, New York: Orbis Books, 1993; Dana Robert, "Shifting Southward: Global Christianity Since 194," *International Bulletin of Missionary Research* 24; April 2000, pp. 50 –58.

[6] David Barrett, George T. Kurian and Todd M. Johnson, *World Christian Encyclopedia*, 2ⁿᵈ edition, New York: OUP, 2001.

[7] Philip Jenkins, *The Next Christendom: The Coming of Global Christianity*, New York: OUP, 2002. pg. 3

[8] See Patrick Johnstone, *Operation World*, Carlisle: Paternoster Press, 2001.

[9] Ken Christoph Miyamoto, "This-Worldly Holiness and the Missio Dei Concept in Asian Ecumenical Thinking" in *Ecumenical Missiology: Contemporary Trends, Issues & Themes*, ed. by Lalsangkima Pachuau, Bangalore: United Theological College, 2002, p.99.

[10] Metropolitan Geevarghese Mar Osthathios, "Contribution of the Orthodox Church to World Mission" in *Blossoms from the East:Contribution of the Indian Church to World Mission* FOIM VI, ed. by Joseph Mattam and Krickwin C. Marak, Mumbai: St. Pauls, 1999, p.158.

in worship is a light in the world; according to the Orthodox perspective, "liturgy is mission." Reiterating that notion, the president of the Mission Board of the Orthodox Malankara Church in India speaks of a potential evangelistic thrust in India and throughout the world in the new Millennium.[11] The Mar Thoma Syrian Evangelistic Association, organized in 1888 by the Mar Thoma Church, continues its missionary engagement with society employing varied methods of holistic mission. Formation of the Indian Missionary Society (IMS) and the National Missionary Society (NMS), movements that are still active even today, during the first decade of the twentieth century, were indigenous expressions of their commitment to mission by Indian Protestant Christians. Likewise launching of agencies such as the Indian Evangelical Mission (IEM) and Friends Missionary Prayer Band (FMPB), a few decades later, are significant efforts of a next generation of Indian Christians. The India Missions Association (IMA) an umbrella body of such agencies, had about 150 affiliated mission organisations in 2002 and by February 2003 this increased to 182.[12] This figure does not include the number of unaffiliated agencies throughout the region. In all these cases, mission efforts adopt a variety of approaches, but incarnational identification with the poor and helpless, solidarity with the disenfranchised, empowerment of the oppressed, serving the needy, and communicating the Christian message to all seems to be characteristic of each one. Christian mission in all its kaleidoscopic variety

is alive and well in the Asian continent.

Increasingly, another striking aspect of the Church at the dawn of the 21st century is that burgeoning Pentecostal-Charismatic congregations largely fuel its growth. Pentecostalism during the twentieth century has emerged from the status of a marginalised movement to become a major tradition of Christianity. With 193 million members in 1990, the Pentecostals were the largest Protestant group of churches in the world.[13] In addition to these denominational Pentecostals if one includes mainline Charismatic Protestants and Catholics, the total is more than 372 million, which is 21.4 percent of the world's Christians.[14] A decade ago, out of an estimated 4 million full-time Christian workers, 1.1 million were Pentecostal-Charismatics. "Fully one fourth of all full-time Christian workers in the world are from the Pentecostal-charismatic persuasion."[15] David Barrett has shown us that at the start of the 21st century Pentecostals and Charismatics constitute the second largest body of Christians in the world, exceeded only by the Roman Catholics in size.[16] This "Pentecostalisation" of the church is no less true in Asia as it is in Latin America and Africa.

In the conclusion of his 1997 revision of his study of the Pentecostal-Charismatic Movements, Vinson Synan states that "Christian affairs of the twenty-first century may be largely in the hands of surging Pentecostal churches in the Third World and a Roman Catholicism inspired

---

[11] Geevarghese Mar Osthathios, "Orthodox Perspectives on Mission and Evangelism" in *The Community We Seek: Perspectives on Mission*, ed. by Jesudas M. Athyal, Tiruvalla: Christava Sahitya Samithi, 2003, p.119.

[12] K. Rajendran, "Preparing the Future Church/Mission Leadership and its Impact upon India." Paper presented at the CMS Consultation on Issues in Mission Leadership, Union Biblical Seminary, Pune, 9-11 January 2003, p.2.

[13] Vinson Synan, *The Spirit Said Grow: The Incredible Pentecostal-Charismatic Factor in the Global Expansion of Christianity*, Monrovia: MARC, 1992, p.1.

[14] *Ibid.*, pp.10-11.

[15] *Ibid.*, p.13.

[16] David B. Barrett & Todd M. Johnson, *World Christian Trends AD 30-AD 2200: Interpreting the Annual Christian Megacensus*, Pasadena: William Carey Library, 2001.

and revivified by the charismatic renewal."[17] Another authority on Pentecostalism Allan Anderson emphatically asserts: "Pentecostalism is *not* a predominantly western movement, but both fundamentally and dominantly a *Third World* phenomenon."[18] It comes as no surprise then that this southern Christianity is predominantly a church of the poor and powerless. The poor are the ones, who more often than not, seek out and subscribe to the Pentecostal experience and message, for in it they find resources to address the angst that characterises their life. Pentecostalism offers to them a wherewithal that enables them to cope and engage with the harsh realities of life. The healing that is available through faith in Christ, a camaraderie that is offered through community and dignity derived from direct access to divinity coalesce to furnish a coping mechanism that is eminently attractive to those whom society tends to neglect. Employing their respective academic specialisations, the American theologian Richard Shaull and Brazilian sociologist Waldo Cesar have ably demonstrated how this has come about in Latin America. For his part Cesar describes the condition of the poor and disenfranchised in Latin America, elucidating how Pentecostalism provides meaning and liberation in their everyday lives. Shaull complements that with his theological exposition of Pentecostalism' reshaping of beliefs and practices in the service of the poor and goes on to also discuss how the experience promoted by Pentecostals provides the basis for transformation.[19]

Transformation also occurs on the cultural front, for this southern Pentecostalism is stamped by a diversity of localized cultural expressions. In the hands of the Pentecostals the gospel finds in local cultural idioms vehicles for expression and modes of existence that renders it relevant within the diversity of world cultures. Christianity, which has long been thought of as synonymous with western society, is now being adopted as an indigenous response to the human spiritual quest. Since these new Christian movements are often of the Little Tradition initiated by local initiatives, spontaneous and rooted in the cultures and spirituality of the people, they are accepted and adopted as having a home grown logic and indigenous integrity. This fresh construal provides Christianity a credibility that appeals to sections of society that were once outside the pale of Christian influence. The gospel is now freed to incarnate itself into a variety of cultures and worldviews. The Pentecostal stress on pneumatology, suggests Anderson, nurtures this freedom to "incarnate the gospel anew into the diverse cultures: to believe in the power of the Holy Spirit is to believe that God can and wants to speak to peoples today through cultural mediations other than those of Western Christianity. Being Pentecostal would mean to affirm such spiritual freedom." [20]

Freedom and liberation that issues from southern Pentecostalism combine to form a force that is proving to be attractive as it is fulfilling. If all this promise is to be harnessed further, the 21ˢᵗ century Church is set to move into exciting

---

[17] Vinson Synan, *The Holiness-Pentecostal Tradition: Charismatic Movements in the Twentieth Century*, Grand Rapids/Cambridge: Eerdmans, 1997, p.298.

[18] Allan Anderson, *The Gospel and Culture In Pentecostal Mission in the Third World*. Paper presented at the 9ᵗʰ Conference of the European Pentecostal Charismatic Research Association, Missions Academy, University of Hamburg, Germany, July 1999. [Emphasis in the original].

[19] Richard Shaull and Waldo Cesar, *Pentecostalism and the Future of the Christian Churches:Promises, Limitations, Challenges,* Grand Rapids: Eerdmans, 2000.

[20] Allan Anderson, *The Pentecostal Gospel and Third World Cultures*. Paper read at the Annual Meeting of the Society for Pentecostal Studies, Springfield, Missouri, 16 March 1999.

and adventurous times, developing into a potent movement that could alter the shape of the world to come. The Church in the region, indeed the world Church has in Asian Christianity a valuable *resource* as she moves further into the 21st century.

The 21st Century World

The future of the world is no longer what it used to be! Rapid change has altered not just the way we live in the world but also the manner in which we envision the future of that world. As leading sociologist Antony Giddens has rightly noted, "we live in a world of transformations."[21] Predicting the future is then an onerous task that is to be attempted with great caution. However, if we intend to recommend certain *perspectives* for Christian mission in the 21st century, an analysis of the *context* will doubtless aid in our effort. That is not to say that a study of realities around us alone enables us to discern the way forward. While context analysis may assist in gospel proclamation it does not determine that vocation. The good news of the kingdom Jesus Christ preached and exemplified in and through his life remains ever true. Its vitality and efficacy does not wane with the winds of change that passing time brings. However, by the same token whilst we assert the truth of the unchanging gospel we simultaneously affirm the need for a contextualising of that gospel. Contextualisation will not be possible if that context is not taken seriously and understood for all it represents. Understanding the context will be then an important exercise that occupies our attention. This is what we turn to now. The broad contours offered here are neither exhaustive in its breadth nor comprehensive in its depth. Our remit here will be only to highlight some of the most significant global issues that will invariably shape

the future. It is true that local situations may present additional demands that attract our attention and exact particulars may vary from place to place, but as we increasingly come to terms with the reality of the "global village" we inhabit, we will realise that these global issues will in some shape or form influence our lives. Transcending national, cultural and economic boundaries, they will inform and determine the nature of the world we inhabit. Indeed that is why they are *global* issues.[22] Short of burying our heads in the sand, it appears that we can do little to escape its influence.

Globalisation

It does not take a seasoned commentator to recognise that globalisation is a reality that has most decidedly made its presence felt. The term "globalisation" means different things to different people. For some it refers to the global spread of modern technology and ease of communication that has prompted. Others use it as a term to denote global cultural interaction of societies. Still others treat it as the historical development of capitalism by which rich nations exploit poorer ones in myriad ways. For all the ambiguity of the term, two facts are certain. First globalisation has brought the world community together like never before. Today the term "global village" is not merely a cliché but present reality. Second, it is primarily economic factors that seem to have facilitated this connectedness. Much like the *Pax Romana* that existed during the 1st century and the *Pax Britannica* during the 19th century that indelibly shaped and seemingly held the world together, the 21st century world appears to be increasingly cemented by a *Pax Economica*. Potent forces of the market economy, which is now hailed as the meta-answer for the world, appear to bring and hold together nations in a

---

[21] Anthony Giddens, *Runaway World: The Reith Lectures*, 1999. http://news.bbc.co.uk/hi/english/static/events/reith_99/week1/week1.htm The lectures were subsequently published as Anthony Giddens, *Runaway World: How Globalisation is Reshaping our Lives*, London: Profile Books, 2002.

[22] See the discussion in John Seitz, *Global Issues: An Introduction*, Oxford: Blackwell, 2001.

unified framework that allows each one to compete, at least theoretically, on level footing. Hitherto political, economic and ethnic boundaries seemed more rather than less impervious to external influence and control. Today however, we find that they present no serious obstacle to the growth of capitalist market economy. Whereas socialism raised walls between nations, capitalism appears to bring them down. Though it is true that globalisation also has political, cultural and technological dimensions, and as Giddens says, "is a complex set of processes,"[23] the economic seems to predominate and drive it forward. Economics is the engine of globalisation. Giddens himself admits: "Economic influences are certainly among the driving forces, especially the global financial system." [24]

To be sure, globalisation has issued in tremendous opportunity for many. The success in the world market of Indian companies, like Infosys and Wipro Technologies, and the many Chinese corporations manufacturing goods as diverse as toys and electronics, are some of its spoil. Likewise scores of nations have found it to provide the ticket to prosperity and success. Asia has harnessed some of those benefits for itself. Indeed Asia has been touted as a region of the future, the area that holds much economic promise, even economic threat to some western nations. The roar of the "Asian Tigers" of international business is growing louder. Simultaneously however, "globalisation... isn't developing in an even-handed way, and is by no

means wholly benign in its consequences."[25] For all its reputation as a harbinger of good news for many, globalisation has occasioned much oppression and hardship for many more. The rich march ahead to greater economic prosperity and power whilst the majority poor find themselves being sucked further into a spiral of acute powerlessness and poverty. Giddens rightly notes that globalisation "creates a world of winners and losers, a few on the fast track to prosperity, the majority condemned to a life of misery and despair."[26] A telling example is the banana trade, which is said to be "symbolic of the wide injustices in international trade today."[27] In this multi billion dollar industry 90 percent of the income remains in the west, 34 percent goes to the distributor and retailer, profit margins for the multinational corporations are pegged at 17 percent, while the actual producers of the fruit earn a meagre five percent even though they bear all the risk involved.[28] Workers in Ecuador, one of the largest producers of the fruit for export, earn just 1$ a day and some independent farmers get less while Chiquita, Dole and Del Monte the three giant fruit companies enjoy profits from two thirds of the world exports.[29] It is not only large multinationals that promote injustice such as this but local entrepreneurs are often as guilty. Unscrupulous businesses in our own nations exploit vulnerable and desperate children and women for super-fat profits. The carpet industry, which thrives on the export market that globalisation has made possible, for example, has one of the worst track records in exploitation of

---

[23] *Ibid.*

[24] *Ibid.* For a brief exposition of the economic basis of Globalisation, also see Peter Heslam Globalisation: Unravelling the New Capitalism, Cambridge: Grove Books, 2002. For a perceptive and telling indictment on the linkage between globalisation and poverty see Vandana Shiva, *'Poverty & Globalisation' Reith Lecture for 2000* http://news.bbc.co.uk/hi/english/static/events/reith_2000/lecture5.stm

[25] *Ibid.*

[26] *Ibid.*

[27] See http://www.bananalink.org.uk/trade/btrade.htm

[28] See http://www.newint.org/issue317/facts.htm

[29] *Ibid.*

children. Infamous manufacturing bases in India, Pakistan and Nepal are notorious for the deplorable conditions children as young as eight work in. Long hours, inhuman conditions, enforced labour and outrageous wages are only some of the hardships that young ones endure.[30]

There can be no doubt that, "globalisation is not incidental to our lives today…it is the way we now live."[31] Consequently, globalisation and the attendant change it issues to political life, sociological processes, economic activity and religious devotion will be one of the primary forces that determine the shape of the world.

Conflict

We have already highlighted poverty and injustice as being attendant features of globalisation. Add to that combination, violent conflict and we have a lethal cocktail that is destructive as it is real. Indeed, recent world events have already demonstrated that violent conflict is indeed a clear and present danger not some distant prophecy of doom and gloom merchants. The post 9/11 world is teeming with tensions of one sort or another. Regional tensions also add to that tinderbox. Violence perpetrated by Hindu right wing groups in India, Islamic extremists in Indonesia and ethnic rivalry among Christians in Africa appears not to have abated, but finds yet more reason to rear its ugly head terrorising people and communities and at times even holding nations to ransom. For all the progress we have achieved in technology and medicine we are unable to cure the growth of an unhealthy "tribalism" within our societies. Major wars afoot in the world are symptoms that this tribalism animates whole communities and promotes conflict, often of the violent sort. In their challenging book, *Jihad vs. McWorld: How*

Globalism & Tribalism Are Reshaping the World, Benjamin R. Barber and Andrea Schulz[32] have argued that in the globalised world two forces of 'race' and 'soul' vie for supremacy. The first scenario that:

> …holds out the grim prospect of a re-tribalization of large swaths of humankind by war and bloodshed: a threatened balkanization of nation-states in which culture is pitted against culture, people against people, tribe against tribe, a Jihad in the name of a hundred narrowly conceived faiths against every kind of interdependence, every kind of artificial social cooperation and mutuality: against technology, against pop culture, and against integrated markets; against modernity itself as well as the future in which modernity issues.

is pitted against the second, characterised by:

> …on rushing economic, technological, and ecological forces that demand integration and uniformity and that mesmerize peoples everywhere with fast music, fast computers, and fast food—MTV, Macintosh, and McDonald's—pressing nations into one homogenous global theme park, one McWorld tied together by communications, information, entertainment, and commerce.[33]

Though their thesis smacks of a reductionistic or simplistic interpretation of the state of play, Barber and Schulz nonetheless have put their finger on what could well become the diabolical duo of the 21st century. Jihad, or whatever it is called in other parts of the world, ostensibly provides a mechanism that responds to the onslaught of McWorld' global homogenising mission. These forces, that seem to be both tearing the world apart while paradoxically also bringing it together, play into each other' court. "Jihad not only revolts against but abets McWorld, while

---

[30] See http://www.unicef.org/sowc97/report/shapes.htm

[31] opt. cit.

[32] New York: Balantine Books, 1996

[33] *Ibid.*, p..4

McWorld not only imperils but re-creates and reinforces Jihad."[34] As a result, the world has been "squeezed between these opposing forces" and "has been sent spinning out of control."[35] As noted, we will recognise that this tribalism is not targeted against McWorld in west alone, it has also found violent expression in Asia as well. The Christian community in India and Pakistan for example has been at the receiving end of this tribalist violence. If Barber and Schulz are right these wars will continue to animate much of global interaction and will increasingly demand our attention. Add to all this, the crusading spirit of modern American politics and one feels that we are on a fast track to total destruction. As much as we would desire to avoid and see the end of conflict, extant signs demand we recognise violent conflict as a primary force that will profoundly shape and determine the world we live in.

Population Growth & Urbanization

A third global issue of the 21ˢᵗ century world is rapid increase in population and an accompanying urbanization, particularly in the majority world. At the turn of the 20th century world population was pegged at 1.6 billion, while at the end of that century it was 6.1 billion. It is said that this number could rise to more than 9 billion in the next 50 years. In 1800, the vast majority of the world's population, approximately 86 percent, resided in Asia and Europe, with 65 percent in Asia alone. By 1900, Europe's share rose to 25 percent, due to the increase that the Industrial Revolution encouraged. At the same time some growth was also seen in the American continent. World population growth accelerated after World War II, when the population of the majority world began to increase dramatically. A

billion people were added between 1960 and 1975 and another billion were added between 1975 and 1987. One will notice that each additional billion was achieved in shorter periods of time. The 2000 growth rate of 1.4 percent, when applied to the world's 6.1 billion population, will yield an increase of about 85 million people annually. This large and increasing population will ensure that growth will remain high for several decades to come.

Between 2000 and 2030, it is said that nearly 100 percent of this annual growth will occur in the majority world. Rates of 1.9 percent and higher, mean that populations will double in about 36 years. While Asia's share of world population may continue to remain around 55 percent in the next century, Europe's share that has declined sharply could drop even more during the 21st century. Africa and Latin America each would gain part of Europe's portion and by 2100, with Africa capturing the greatest share of that.[36]

Findings of the Population Division of the UN's Department of Economic and Social Affairs suggest that, "virtually all the population growth expected at the world level during the next 30 years will be concentrated in urban areas. Also, for the first time in the world's history, the number of urban dwellers will equal the number of rural dwellers in 2007."[37] Urbanization is set to radically transform the landscape of the world. In 1950, 30 percent of the population lived in urban areas, by 2000 that increased to 47 percent. It is estimated that by 2030 that proportion will reach 60 percent. The world's urban population, which was estimated at 2.9 billion in the year 2000 is expected to reach 5 billion by 2030. When compared to increase in population estimated, it implies that urban areas will absorb almost all

---

[34] *Ibid.* p.5.

[35] *Ibid.*

[36] Details provided here are adapted from information found at: http://www.prb.org/Content/NavigationMenu/PRB/Educators/Human_Population/Population_Growth/Population_Growth.htm

[37] See http://www.un.org/esa/population/publications/wup2001/WUP2001-pressrelease.pdf

this population increase. In 2000 about 75 percent of the population of northern countries lived in urban areas. That is set to increase to 84 percent by 2030.

With population growth taking a negative turn in these northern nations, it means this dramatic urbanization will take place in the majority world. Urban population here is expected to increase by 2.0 billion persons, almost as much as the increase in world population, which is estimated at 2.2 billion. Urban growth rate here reached 3 percent per year in period between 1995 and 2000, compared to 0.5 percent in northern nations. In the future growth rate will continue to accelerate averaging 2.4 percent per year during 2000-2030, while growth rate in rural areas will reach only 0.2 percent. The proportion of urban dwellers, which was estimated at 40 percent in 2000, will increase to 56 percent by 2030. With 37 percent of their respective populations living in urban areas in 2000, Africa and Asia are considerably less urbanized and, consequently, are expected to see rapid rates of urbanization during the period 2000-2030. It is expected that by 2030, 53 percent and 54 percent, respectively, of their population will live in urban areas. With 26.5 million inhabitants, Tokyo is the most populous city in the world, followed by São Paulo (18.3), Mexico City (18.3), New York (16.8) and Mumbai (16.5). By 2015, Tokyo will remain the largest city with 27.2 million inhabitants, followed by Dhaka, Mumbai, São Paulo, Delhi and Mexico City, all of which are expected to have more than 20 million inhabitants.[38] It is instructive to note that four of the six largest cities will be found in Asia and three in South Asia, with India being home to two!

It must be understood that this urbanization does not merely imply a change in geographical location alone. 'Push' and 'pull' factors, the lack of resources in rural areas and conversely the availability of jobs and amenities in urban settings that facilitates this change, occasions a profound transformation. From psychological to political, economic to environmental, urbanization issues in a complex transformation of consciousness, life style and outlook that is perhaps yet to be comprehensively understood by scholars. One thing is certain though, urbanization will be a primary factor that determines the character and structure of the world in the days to come.

Ecology

The 6.1 billion or so people together with all other life forms on the planet today are dependent on the world's ecosystems. Air, water, food, minerals, energy and animal life are some of the resources on which we survive. However steady growth of the global population, inappropriate use of land and excessive water and energy consumption have led to air pollution, water shortage, climate change, global warming and destruction of the ozone layer.

Time and space do not allow us to go on discussing issues related to energy, bio diversity, agriculture, bio-technology and other major ecological concerns. However, one common thread that seems to run through these various issues we have noted is that destruction of these precious eco systems seems to be almost concomitant to our contemporary life styles and world affairs. Development that has been advocated and pursued seems to result in an insensitive destruction of the environment. Apparent progress is purchased at a huge cost. Though it may have taken time, this fact has been recognised for what it represents. In 1992 one major advance made by the third UN environmental conference held in Rio de Janeiro,

---

[38] These details have been adapted from information found at: http://www.un.org/esa/population/publications/wup2001/WUP2001-pressrelease.pdf

also known as the Earth Summit, was the adoption of the concept, "sustainable development." Sustainable development means "development that meets the need of the present without compromising the ability of future generations to meet their own needs."[39] It recognises the need for a judicious approach to development that takes into consideration the needs both of the now and the future, of present and future generations. Having made that laudable beginning, it will take conscious and concerted determination by each community in every nation to turn around global ecological destruction we have unleashed on nature. This is one major global issue that will attract attention in the days to come.

Health & Biotechnology

Since it was announced about 25 years ago at the WHO and UNICEF sponsored "International Conference on Primary Health Care" in Alma-Ata, in the former USSR, "*Health for all*" has indeed become an achievable target rather than a distant dream. Over that period, considerable strides have been taken in advancing the prospects of global health. Some countries have reduced their child mortality by half, reduced child malnutrition by one-third, and raised school enrolment by one-fourth. Life expectancy worldwide has leaped from 48 years in 1955 to an average of 66 years. Whereas in 1974, only 5 percent of children in southern nations were immunized against polio, tetanus, measles, whooping cough, diphtheria and tuberculosis, by 1995 worldwide immunization rates increased to 80 percent, and in some southern nations increased to anywhere between 30-70 percent. There has been a 99.8 percent decline in reported polio cases worldwide and it remains endemic only in about ten countries.[40]

Although much progress has been achieved many are the grave challenges that lie ahead. More than a billion people continue in extreme poverty with women and children being the worst affected. It is said that one-third of all children suffer from hunger and malnutrition which in turn severely inhibits their ability to survive childhood let alone realize their full potential as adults. The malevolent sceptre of HIV/Aids that hangs over many nations is perhaps one of the greatest human disasters. There are 42 million people living with HIV/AIDS worldwide. 38.6 million of these are adults, 19.2 million are women and 3.2 million are children under the age of 15. Five million new infections with HIV occurred in 2002 of which 4.2 million were adults and 2 million of them were women. A total of 3.1 million people died of HIV/AIDS related causes in 2002. Sub-Saharan Africa has the highest number of HIV positive individuals (29.4 million people living with HIV/AIDS) followed by South and South-East Asia (6 million). In North America there are 980,000 people living with HIV/AIDS, 570,000 in Western Europe and 1.2 million in Eastern Europe and Central Asia. The number of HIV positive individuals in Australia and New Zealand has remained constant since 2001 (15,000 people). In Latin America and the Caribbean the figure is 1.5 million and 440,000 respectively. East Asia and the Pacific have 1.2 million people living with HIV/AIDS. North Africa and the Middle East have 550,000 people living with HIV/AIDS.[41]

One may recognise that the majority world carry just under 90 percent of the global burden, yet these countries receive only 10 percent of the worldwide health resources to combat the epidemic. As in many other areas biotechnology has made significant advances. Antiretroviral treatment is available for those suffering from

---

[39] See http://www.un.org/esa/sustdev/documents/agenda21/english/agenda21chapter1.htm and following chapters.

[40] See http://www.unfoundation.org/programs/child_health/challenges.htm

[41] See http://www.who.int/hiv/en/

HIV/AIDS. However as a WHO report points out, "the failure to deliver antiretroviral (ARV) treatment for AIDS to the millions of people who need it is a global health emergency. We have the medicines to treat people for a dollar a day or less but these medicines are not getting to the people who need them." The report also clarifies that, "some six million people in developing countries have HIV infections that require antiretroviral treatment. But fewer than 300,000 are being treated. In sub-Saharan Africa, where most of the people in need of treatment live, only 50,000 people are receiving it."[42] Unprecedented advance in medical technology is to be lauded, but often this knowledge remains within the reach of the wealthy nations. Giant corporations fiercely guard these assets and further perpetuate gross inequality as a result. To counter that the Doha Declaration of the WTO provided the mechanism for weaker economies to manufacture a wide range of drugs to safe guard public health. Antagonism it has raised however proves that corporate interests were threatened by these measures and obstacles are being placed in the implementation of those agreements. One notable exception has been the historic Human Genome Project. An international undertaking started in 1991, the Human Genome Project aims to map all human genes and identify the 3 billion DNA pairs of these mapped genes. The potential for an economic bonanza was clear right from the start, but wisdom prevailed and commercialisation of the data was not attempted. However, this is but one exception. The recently concluded WTO meeting at Cancun, Mexico the one held previously at Seattle in 1999 and further the lawsuit some American pharmaceutical giants lodged against the South African government is sufficient evidence that the big business of biotechnology will remain a potent force in the world community.

Aligned to this are the many ethical dilemmas that biotechnological advance has raised. We have increasingly come to understand how such advances present us with complex moral situations for which we seem to be least prepared. For example genetic engineering not only poses complex challenges to traditional worldviews but also impacts social and psychological frameworks, not to mention the risk that it presents to human and animal life and the natural environment. With advances being made at such a rapid pace, the 21st century certainly promises to be an era of characterised by massive change and an accompanying rise in ethical dilemmas.

Religions

In many popular studies of the future a striking omission is the role world religions will play in society. For example in *Preparing for the 21st Century*, Paul Kennedy lists population explosion and shifting demographic patterns; the communications revolution and the rise of the multinational corporation; world agriculture and the burgeoning field of biotechnology; robotics, automation and the changing face of industry; the growing threats to the natural world and the danger posed by global warming; and the decline of the nation-state as being the global issues of the future.[43] Though he does mention it, religion figures neither as a major resource nor as a global issue. Contrary to his predictions, history has demonstrated that world religions continue to exert a potent influence on society including social, economic and political life. The future seems unlikely to alter this fact.

Earlier when we discussed conflict as a global issue, we noted that religion would be a vital part of that equation. It would not only fuel conflict but also be transformed by it. We do not need to elaborate on that here. In much the same way it appears that, since religion is central to

---

[42] See http://www.who.int/mediacentre/releases/2003/pr67/en/

[43] New York: Random House, 1993.

defining of norms, values and meaning and in providing ethical resources for individual and corporate life, it will necessarily play a significant role in society' response to global issues. Take for example the debate on population control. Among the 18,000 delegates who attended the United Nations sponsored Conference on Population and Development held in Cairo in September 1994 two vocal groups, the Catholic Church and a few Islamic nations (some nations like Saudi Arabia, Lebanon, Iraq and Sudan did not attend), were instrumental in shaping the declaration in keeping with their own ideologies. The Vatican forced a debate on abortion supported in part by the Muslims, who admitted though that abortion could be allowed in some circumstances. The Vatican worked to prohibit abortion being advocated as a form of birth control. For their part some Islamic nations worked against a draft, which they saw as belittling Islamic family conventions. Phrases, which might have suggested permission for homosexuality or promiscuity, were removed and finally they were able to introduce a clause in the final document, stating that it should be consistent with "full respect for the various religious and ethical values and cultural backgrounds" of the signatory countries.[44]

Or consider the religious basis for the environmental crisis facing the world. As far back as 1967 Lynn White was one of the first to indict Christian theology for its complicity in the exploitation of nature. In the essay *The Historical Roots of our Ecological Crisis*,[45] White explained how attitudes developed during the Middle Ages in the Latin West led to the rise of science and technology which in turn resulted in the threat to human existence and ecological balance. A contrast was made between the many ancient religions in which the world is filled with gods and spiritual powers. Gods control the fertility of the land and hence if you want a good crop, you solicit the cooperation of these divine beings. However, for theological views current then nature became neutral, emptied of spirits and of spiritual significance. It became an object to be exploited for man's benefit. White's thesis is that the Bible displaced the spirits from trees, fields, mountains, and streams, leaving humanity as the only place where spirit resides. Consequently Christianity in its western form became the most anthropocentric religion the world has ever seen. Combined with cultural inclinations in northern Europe it encouraged the 'dominion' of nature, the results of which we live with today.

Although Oxford theologian Alister McGrath has ably critiqued this thesis asserting that it is enlightenment rationality rather than Christian theology which is the culpable agent,[46] it must be mentioned that White went on to suggest however, that religion was both the root and the remedy of the present crisis. For all the ecological damage unleashed, Christianity also provided an alternative view exemplified in St. Francis' view of the interdependence of created beings where flowers, birds, and nature all have a part to play in the praise of God. Rather than follow the former, this latter model, he suggested, would be most appropriate for the future.

In addition to this instrumental role that religion plays, its essential role in society is also of great import. Though the propriety, perhaps even legitimacy, of religious life may be questioned by groups of atheists, religion has played a profoundly significant role in the lives of the vast majority of the world' populace.

---

[44] See http://www.iisd.ca/linkages/Cairo/program/p00000.html

[45] *Science*, Vol.155; pgs.1203-1207, March 10, 1967. Also see Lynn White, "The Historical Roots of our Ecological Crisis" [with discussion of St. Francis; reprint, 1967] in *Ecology and Religion in History*, New York: Harper & Row, 1974.

[46] *The Reenchantment of Nature: The Denial of Religion and the Ecological Crisis*, New York: Doubleday, 2002.

Religion is a foundational resource of the world community. It secures for life in general a transcendental orientation providing meaning and significance, furnishes a moral outlook that translates into ethical imperatives for the well-being of the world. These resources whatever shape or form they possess serve as fundamental co-ordinates for human society and as a result for the world at large. To be sure religion will have to engage with the changing world and will have to address issues that were perhaps hitherto considered outside its pale, nevertheless its value, as an immense resource and fundamental feature of the world community cannot be neglected nor sidelined. In the 21st century world religions will come to play a profoundly significant role and foolish we would be to ignore its potential.

There is no doubt that the matrix comprised of these global issues will most certainly determine the nature and shape of life in the 21st century. If each issue on its own is complex and has far reaching consequences for human society and the natural world the effect of all of them put together will confound us all the more. We do not have to stress that this multifaceted and exacting context defies simple and neat characterisation. Consequently glib and superficial answers will not do. Attending to the global issues of the 21st century in all its complexity will require a colossal effort from all sections of society. What exactly will transpire in this century is not clear, but one thing is: the future promises to be both exciting as well as challenging. It is in this challenging *context* that we are called to participate in mission.

Recasting Mission & Missiology

If, as was suggested, Asia is the continent in which a great deal of the expansion of the Church will occur and also the arena where global issues will increasingly become a pressing concern it behoves us to be cognizant of this '*double imperative*' we face. That the Asian church is multiplying is to be celebrated. The selfless toil of those behind this development is to be lauded and their example emulated. Furthermore, celebration ought to provide additional motivation for continued rededicated service. However, celebration would be incomplete if critical scrutiny of the inner dynamics of this development is not attempted. Research and analysis will not only lay bare these dynamics but also serve as a tool for instruction both within the continent and around the globe. Celebrating God's providence locally can enhance appreciation, stimulate reflection and promote emulation globally. Contextual demands that make this imperative doubly significant require an adequate response. Piecemeal and reactionary answers will serve only to either alienate us or hasten our descent. Since these demands will stretch the Church in more ways than one, all her resources will have to be summoned to mount that response. A response that will have to possess a theological depth as it is comprehensive in interdisciplinary breadth. Ironically just when she is experiencing phenomenal growth the Asian church seems to be faced with perhaps the most serious challenge she will ever face. On the wings of the 21st century come opportunity and threat, promise and peril. The potential for lasting impact is therefore immense. Building on her rich and eventful heritage the Asian church is strategically poised to instigate an unprecedented transformation of the continent and the world.[47] Andrew Walls' comment is as relevant in Asia as it is for Africa:

> What happens within the African [and Asian] churches in the next generation will determine the whole shape of church history

---

[47] It is instructive to note that two leaders; Lesslie Newbigin and Paul Heibert who have made a significant impact on western theology and missiology, have done so after extensive experience in Asia, which shaped them profoundly. They stand as models for us Asian missionary-scholars.

for centuries to come; what sort of theology is most characteristic of the Christianity of the twenty-first century may well depend on what has happened in the minds of African [and Asian] Christians in the interim.[48]

Echoing a similar sentiment Walbert Buhlmann observes:

> ...now the third millennium will evidently stand under the leadership the Third Church, the Southern Church. I am convinced that the most important drives and inspirations for the whole church in the future will come from the Third Church.[49]

If Asian Christianity is presented with so paradigmatic a role, her response will be of no small consequence. The need to recognise the gravity of the situation cannot be overemphasised. As Walls' and Buhlmann's comments imply, her response to this "double imperative" will not only determine her life and presence in the region but also shape the nature and character of worldwide Christianity as well. Hanging in the balance here is no less than the world Church' prospects, not simply the fortunes of one regional expression of that body. The question is: how is she going to formulate her response? Old answers may not suffice for today we are faced with new questions and greater responsibilities. Old strategies may not be appropriate for today we are faced with new situations and greater opportunities. Neither will mere rearrangement of structures and resources suffice. If many inherited systems and resources are not entirely appropriate for the challenges ahead, mission and missiology will require a major overhaul. Whilst theological continuity, going back to the Christ himself, is to be cherished and maintained a radical discontinuity with questionable theology and methodology will be necessary. Mission and missiology will have to creatively engage with and construct a fresh approach to both the vitality of the Asian church and the profound challenge of the 21ˢᵗ century. In short, what is required is a *recasting of mission and missiology.*

Accordingly in this final section of our discussion we table a proposal for the Asian church as she faces such a momentous responsibility. This proposal is not so much a set of concrete steps, a 'how to' list that promises instant success and progress. To be sure there are many of that around; suffice to say that promoting pre-packaged strategies hatched in incubators in western nations for global consumption is a mockery of mission, it smacks of capitulation to McWorld rather then humble submission to the Gospel. On the contrary, what is recommended here is a set of three suggestions that would offer the urgent need of recasting mission and missiology suggestive *perspectives*. These suggestions attend not so much to actual strategy, though that may be implicated in these suggestions, but perhaps more to the attitudinal stance we need to adopt, not so much to the mechanics of execution but more to the dynamics of position as we seek to engage in mission and missiology in the 21ˢᵗ century.

Expand our Missiological Horizon:

To critically and creatively engage in mission and missiology in this 21ˢᵗ century the first suggestion we make is to "expand our missiological horizons." Horizons that guided our mission effort in the past have served us well. Part of the success that we have come to recognise here is due, at least in part, to such resources. That is, however, not to say it did not lead to questionable developments. D.T. Niles' parable of the gospel as seed is suggestive here. Niles

---

[48] Andrew Walls, "Towards an Understanding of Africa's Place in Christian History" in John. S. Pobee, ed., *Religion in a Pluralistic Society*, Leiden; Brill, 1976, pp. 180-189. Chapter 5, "Africa in Christian History: Retrospect and Prospect" in his *The Cross-Cultural Process in Christian History*, New York: Orbis, 2002, also deals with that same theme.

[49] *The Coming of the Third Church*, p. 6.

spoke of the gospel as a seed you sow. If the gospel was sown in the Middle East you have as a result Middle Eastern Christianity; if sown in Europe you have European Christianity. The problem was, when some missionaries came to Asia they brought their own flowerpots and not the seed. As a result you had European flowerpots planted all over Asia. Horizons for the seed of the gospel were determined in Europe and America and foisted on us. They were forged in response to issues that were alien to our contexts and irrelevant to our concerns. The agenda thus set for us did not always gel with our own experience nor provided adequate answers to our own questions. This in turn occasioned a grave disservice to the cause of the gospel.

Take, for example, the commercialisation of the gospel, symbolised by the commodification of heaven. Adopting this strategy, evangelists offer the prospect of heaven against the threat of hell, as the bonanza available for those who make 'a decision for Christ'. To simplify the mechanics of one's journey there a few spiritual laws are thrown in detailing the steps to achieve that heaven. Salvation offered by Christ is broken down to simple propositions and packaged together to aid in its favourable reception, and thus you have an eminently marketable product. Concerns for the favourable reception of this message blind one's eyes to concerns of theological veracity. Form overrides substance. It is plain to see how in this instance the gospel is watered down to a four-step plan of self-actualisation and salvation provided by Christ is reduced to "pie in the sky when we die." In analysing the history of this commercialisation of religion, Laurence Moore identifies its roots in the development of market economy in America. "The forces," he observes, "that drew everything in American society into the web of monetary exchange inevitably changed some aspects of religion"... religion was itself taking

on aspects of a commodity." Far from being an insignificant or inconsequential development, Moore found this process to be a rather pervasive shaping of religion. "Religions' systematic and expansive complicity," he concludes, "in mechanisms of market exchange is surely the most important aspect of the particular kind of secularisation that has characterised the nineteenth and twentieth centuries."[50] It is clear that this insidious commercialisation is not only a travesty of the gospel but offers little by way of spiritual sustenance and fulfilment. Asian preference to focus on the mystical and a quest for spiritual depth have in this shallow gospel little interest.

If that was one extreme example of acquiescence to one culture, at the other end we find a similar development except this time Christianity falls prey to an Asian cultural bondage. In their effort to rid themselves of unhealthy associations with western Christianity some Asian Christians adopted an uncritical attitude to their own culture and background. Forms of Christianity thus developed were so immersed in Asian cultures that it was hard to differentiate the gospel from other worldviews of the region. In working against one disfiguration they unwittingly created another. The caricature they drew of others turned out to be a mirror reflecting their own image. An example of this is found in the *Nattar Sabai* begun by Arumainayagam Sattampillai in 1857 at Nazareth in South India. It is alleged that in reaction to disciplinary action, taken against a catechist by an SPG missionary, Sattampillai led a break away movement to establish his own church. Here an amalgamation of Hindu and Jewish practices was adopted to express a unique belief that represented, perhaps more than anything else, an attempt by some leaders of a particular caste to gain ascendancy in their social status. Sattampillai mixed Hindu and Christian creation beliefs to

---

[50] *Selling God: American Religion in the Marketplace of Culture*, New York: OUP, 1994, p. 91

establish for the Nadars divine status and thus clinch the moral and spiritual high ground that he assumed they lost with the arrival of western missionaries. Arguably it was caste pride and social ambition that motivated Sattampillai to employ Christian and Hindu resources to "establish the claims of the community to higher status through mythological reconstruction of a kingly past."[51]

In these cases we find the gospel subsumed under cultural compulsions. Horizons are determined by extrinsic cultural impulses rather than internal theological rationale. They suggest that the attempt at recasting mission and missiology will, in the expansion of horizons, find a potent stimulant. It may seem odd that the term 'expand' rather than 'narrow' is employed, for focussing on the gospel may appear, to some, to necessitate a restriction and curtailment of vision. On the contrary, we submit that, when culture is allowed to determine horizons a restriction of the gospel and, not as may be claimed, an expansion is the result. In contrast to a narrow "cultural Christianity" we would argue for the expansion of our horizons as founded on and motivated by the gospel of Christ. If, as we believe, the gospel of Christ is God's answer for fallen creation we will agree that the cultural captivity of the gospel, whether western or eastern, has indeed narrowed its horizons. The placing of cultural demands on the gospel, whilst may have appeared successful in the short term by way of apparently enhancing its appeal, has in the long term indeed hedged the gospel into manmade confines. In focusing on the gospel therefore, an expansion of horizons is not only urged but also nourished. Since the gospel is God's "yes" to His world, its comprehensive character and spiritual depth is ensured. Divine source rather than its contextual association is the guarantee and assurance of its meaning and relevance.

An expansion of horizons in the first instance would necessitate we *rediscover the gospel*. Our comprehension of the gospel is limited to the extent we seek within culture the primary framework to understand the world and respond to it. To the extent we focus instead on the gospel as the reality that provides our orientation and dynamic we will be able to cogently address, engage and even judge the world and its systems. We will do well to understand that our remit is not so much to evaluate the gospel on cultural norms but more to allow the gospel to enliven even transform culture based on its own internal criterion. This liberating gospel of Jesus Christ is to be rediscovered as the measure of our life and message. Internal dynamics of the gospel, not external compulsions of context are its plumb line. Mission thus promoted will be founded and determined by gospel centric precepts rather than culturally motivated preference. In this insistence we will unearth resources not only to counter aberrations of the gospel we have promoted in the past but also engage in integral mission in the future. For too long we have been trafficking a substandard gospel. Under the influence of various impulses we have been taken captive by an anthropocentric preoccupation. Humankind rather than God was the centre of that universe. The gospel was forced to serve our purposes rather than fulfil the desire of its author. Man became the measure of all things and his fulfilment and actualisation gained pre-eminence. Rediscovering the gospel and its attendant expansion of our horizons will enable us to encounter God afresh. Rediscovery of that answer, the divine 'yes' will transform our narrow individualistic obsessions to an expansive theocentric passion. This gospel we will discover speaks to us as individuals, speaks to society at large and indeed even addresses eminently the global issues we noted. Reliance on the gospel

---

[51] M. Thomas Thangaraj, "The History and Teachings of the Hindu Christian Community Commonly Called Nattu Sabai in Tirunelveli" in *Indian Church History Review*, June 1971, pp. 43- 68.

to meet the challenges of the 21st century will not leave us stranded on the highway to despair and doom. On the contrary we will find here resources more than adequate for the complex and immense task that faces us. A rediscovery of the gospel will lead to enhanced worship and witness, which in turn will have far reaching impact.

Rediscovery of the gospel in turn necessitates a *submission to the gospel*. To encounter the gospel afresh in all its vitality and yet fail to submit to it would not only be unfortunate but also leave the exercise only half done. Not to mention the responsibility Luke 12:48, "to whom much is given much will be required," entails. Submission to the gospel plays then a role of equal importance. A rediscovered gospel will call for radical change to our theology and methodology of mission; submission to that gospel will ensure that this change is carried through. Rediscovery would show up the need for some unpopular and hard decisions and actions, submission would provide the resolve to follow that through. Many of us often find it easier to follow conventional wisdom because it happens to be safe and is accepted by the majority. This, as we are only too well aware, is done sometimes at the cost of our allegiance to the gospel, perhaps unwittingly but sometimes even knowingly. Submission to the gospel is not then a passive acceptance of received tradition but an active and critical engagement with the gospel, tradition and context. Submission is a creative and constructive process by which we allow the gospel to inhabit and inspire our primary affections, our mental faculty and our praxis. To facilitate that we would need to adopt a *hermeneutic of submission*. Submission to the gospel then is elevated to a foundational tenet that is to be adopted. It becomes a primary determinant of the life of discipleship not just an occasional pious platitude we rehearse. In contrast to a *hermeneutic of subjection* to foreign

agendas we had to endure in the past and at times even to this day, and in contrast to a *hermeneutic of suspicion* of hidden agendas we pursued as we came to recognise various forms of subjection, for the 21st century we recommend a *hermeneutic of submission* to gospel agenda. The hermeneutic proposed here will entail not just a faithful reading of the gospel but also put in place a commitment to follow through with its exacting imperatives. This hermeneutic of submission, will not have to labour its own trajectory right from scratch. To be sure it would recognise God's providential leading in the past through all agents and celebrate that but at the same time seek to not only name but also negate any capitulation to alternate agendas. A hermeneutic of submission will facilitate the move from a preoccupation with reactive criticism to proactive construction of authentic contextual identity founded on the gospel. A hermeneutic of submission will facilitate one to critically engage with the past, confidentially grapple with the present and boldly move ahead into the future. It will be characterised by, what the late South African missiologist David Bosch called, a "bold humility." Based on gospel foundations and animated by a gospel dynamic it will facilitate the creation of fresh, relevant and broad horizons.

Employ a Missiological Imagination:

When we begin our effort at recasting mission and missiology it may come to our notice that many of the resources we possess lack an imagination fit neither for contemporary times nor for the reality of the gospel. The straightjacket of convention, and worse convention imposed from outside, grants little freedom to employ a missiological imagination. We find our imagination stunted even disabled by structures we have inherited. Ever since Emperor Constantine won the battle of Milvian Bridge in AD 312 and the subsequent favour he bequeathed to the church, large sections of the church have been co-opted into an establishment mode.

Church and State were closely knit together; its ethos was one of power and superiority over against society. The church was an institution enjoying special royal sanction and its personnel elite purveyors of privilege and power. This entrenched view was furthered when Christianity expanded to the far corners of the world courtesy of colonialism. By virtue of its correlation with the political conquest of western powers Christianity was inextricably tied with the foreign ruler, the religion of the man or woman on the throne. Efforts to disseminate the gospel assumed this state as providential and comfortably sailed on that tide. To be sure there were exceptions to the rule. Ancient traditions of St. Thomas churches or pioneers like William Carey often reaped the ire of governments and society by standing outside its pale, but unfortunately we in Asia have inherited what has come to be called the "Christendom model"[52] of church and mission. Though many notable contemporary exceptions, particularly among the little tradition or churches of indigenous origin exist, more than just vestiges of that model remain even today. In more recent times, although political realities may have changed, we are increasingly coming to realise that our alliance with western economic power seems to offer an eminent substitute in this changed scenario. Like in times past when we relied on the cultural and political advantage of alliance with the ruler, we now assume that alliance with the economic powerhouse of the west is the answer. The Christendom model of mission appears to have gained in global capitalism a ready ally that will facilitate and fund its dominance. Western political power is substituted by western economic power, which in this global village takes on the role of an omnipotent hero, the harbinger of salvation.

It is striking to note that in just a couple of centuries after Jesus' ignominious death on a cross we find Christianity sporting a visage so dissimilar, even opposed to its humble origins. Small and often poor communities that spread rapidly throughout the Mediterranean bringing the gospel to bear on their life and society ushered in a revolution of grace and peace. These communities had neither imperial privilege nor vast financial resources. For the most part they were a despised minority meeting secretly in catacombs and private homes. They were often accused of being cannibals and/or sexual pleasure seeking perverts, even accused of being behind Rome' destruction by fire. Their leaders were often thrown in prison for disturbing the peace and instigating riots. Yet despite this acute disadvantage and severe stigma the early church was able to fulfil its missionary calling. This "Apostolic Community model" of mission from below was instrumental in changing the face of the then known world. Soon however, it was lost to the seemingly more powerful top-down methodology of Christendom. Unfortunately even today we find this true in the church. Illusions of grandeur promoted perhaps not so much by political power but by economic potential and communication technologies are sweeping our churches. We have not succeeded in loosing the "God-complex" of Christendom that situates our arrogance and pretence that we not only possess the privilege but also the right to run rough shod over others in society. This has debilitating effects on our missiological imagination. In contrast we submit that, an "apostolic community model" of mission, described in the New Testament writings and followed on into the early church, will not only reinstate the ethos of the gospel, where the weakness of the cross is its power, but will also facilitate a revitalisation of our missiological imagination as well. For the 21ˢᵗ century what we need is a paradigm shift from the 'Christendom model' to an "apostolic community

---

[52] For a fuller discussion on a Christendom model of mission see David Bosch, *Transforming Mission: Paradigm Shifts in the Theology of Mission*, New York: Orbis Books, 1991, pp.274 ff

model" of mission. Here small and despised Christian communities empowered by the Spirit will be able to give out of their position of poverty and disadvantage. Minority status will not be a hindrance; indeed it will be its leverage for mission. Brokenness and vulnerability will be its platform; grace and peace will be its message. Here we will rely neither on the political power of the establishment nor on the purchasing power of our economic status. Our devotion to Christ and Spirit-endowed dynamic alone will fund our existence and evangelism. As in the early church this disadvantaged status will provide fertile ground for the growth of a creative and liberative missiological imagination; an imagination that will be founded and funded by a cross-shaped discipleship; an imagination that will doubtless nurture new possibilities and fresh discoveries faithful to the gospel and meaningful to the times. Just as the early church was able to impact society despite their almost insignificant societal status we in Asia in the 21st century will from our position of insignificance and poverty impact our nations and indeed the world. The lack of power and resources will not hinder but rather empower our missiological imagination to create new vistas for service. If that is to happen we will first need to *adopt a new model*, the apostolic community model we find in the scriptures and in the early church.

The second responsibility that such an engaged missiological imagination sets before us is the need to *create a new language*. By virtue of its links with political and military power of Christendom, in Christian mission we have become accustomed to the use of strong militaristic and war related language. We spoke from our positions of power and privilege as we waged war on non-believers. Derogatory of the other, this language set the tone for much of our mission effort. Some wise and perceptive leaders have recommended we desist from such a practice.[53] Though we fully agree with that statement, what we are suggesting here is not confined to such a practice alone. Our recommendation goes further and perhaps more precisely touches the heart of the issue of imagination. As various studies have demonstrated language is as much a determinant of reality as it is a tool to describe that reality. Language creates worlds as much as it describes them. In creating worlds it also situates identity and fosters culture. Language prescribes as much as it describes. It is a most basic and fundamental dimension of our world, our reality just as much as it is a fundamental determinant of our world, our reality. Consequently our use of language in Christian mission plays no small part in determining its nature and shape and also the goal we strive for. If a fresh model is to be adopted this new language we create will assume an integral role in its formation and structure. It will not only describe that new model, that new reality but also prescribe what shape it ought to take. Furthermore, for the 21st century that lies ahead no less than a new language will be necessary to attend to its imposing demands; a new language not only to describe that world but also to open it up for a missiological engagement. This new language will have to create a world that brings the gospel to bear on our society with creative imagination. A new language that would not only portray the compulsions and motivations of sinful human systems but also inject a dynamic to address even counter those systems and point society towards the integral gospel of Jesus Christ. A new language that not only exegetes the gospel but also the context of the world and in turn facilitates the critical and constructive engagement between the two. Lamin Sanneh has eloquently demonstrated how the translation of the Bible into the vernacular has occasioned a

---

[53] A "National Consultation on Mission Language and Biblical Metaphors" convened by The Evangelical Fellowship of India in Bangalore, October 4 -7 2000, issued a declaration that was later published in their *AIM Magazine*, December 2000.

revitalisation of indigenous cultures and traditions.[54] Before that transpired however, he amplifies, the problem of employing concepts and terms mined from indigenous quarries, was to be faced. In accepting and employing the vernacular, for the translators, it meant in essence creating a new language. Besides divesting one language of its apparent privilege of being a conduit of divine revelation and endowing another with that right, it also meant constructing a fresh vocabulary, a vocabulary that at once described and prescribed the mode of Christian faith; a vocabulary that drew the various societies into a fuller appreciation for its own worth and potential. This new language, he goes on to assert, not only affirmed the value of the vernacular but also unleashed a potent revitalisation of local cultures. A new language grew a new people.

A fecund imagination this new language points to, will find in the scriptures its training ground. If, as we asserted, the gospel of Jesus Christ is the basis for life and witness, education of our imagination can find no better school than the scriptures. It is here that spiritual frameworks and interpretative resources are to be found and nurtured. It is here that this new language finds it source and substance. The effort at cultivating our imagination will find here in the story of God's dealing with His children the necessary stimuli and orientation. In that sense then this new language will, in essence, be an old language, a language Jesus Christ conversed in. It will be a language that finds in His person and life its basic script. But, since we have allowed historical processes and societal compulsions to obliterate much of its razor edge sharpness, originality and relevance we will have to create that language afresh. Akin to rediscovering the gospel, suggested earlier, this will require the marshalling of all our resources. In returning back to that

source our imagination will need to be exercised so as to begin that act of language creation. The process does not promise to be simple nor clear-cut, but one thing is certain, creating a new language will require the employ of a missiological imagination and in so doing Christian mission can be assured of making significant strides in the days ahead.

Engender a Missiological Vocation:

When the Swiss theologian Emil Burnner said: "The church exists by mission as a fire exists by burning," he was indeed pointing to a theological truism. The existence of the church in the world is bound inextricably with mission. The delegates of the International Missions Council who met at Willingen, Germany, as far back as 1952, also rightly asserted: "there is no participation in Christ without participation in His mission to the world. That by which the Church receives its existence is that by which it is also given its world mission."[55] Mission is constitutive of the church's definition, for not only is she founded by mission, but also lives by mission.[56] This implies then that a fundamental determinant of the church will be its missionary engagement with the world. A going out of herself for the sake of others will be the stamp characterising her shape. After centuries of almost total neglect of the missiological vocation, significant strides were taken, by those who initiated and worked the modern missionary movement. They succeeded in reforming the notion of the church in keeping with biblical precept. Mission was back on the agenda. For the most part however, even here the assumption that mission was one of the many responsibilities granted to the church was prevalent. Mission was done in the mission field out there among the heathen. This "them" and "us" attitude as a result perpetuated the notion

---

[54] *Translating the Message: The Missionary Impact on Culture*, New York: Orbis Books, 1989.

[55] International Missionary Council, *The Missionary Obligation of the Church*, London: Edinburgh House, 1952, p.3.

[56] For a classic study on this issue see, Johannes Blauw, *The Missionary Nature of the Church: A Survey of the Biblical Theology of Mission, Foundations of the Christian Mission*, London: Lutterworth Press, 1962.

that mission was a special grace endowed to an elite few rather than the gift lavished on all of Christ's followers; it was undertaken by those who received a "special call" for missionary service and absolved the rest from participating in it. Paralleling the so called "clergy" and "laity" divide evident in many sections of the church is the "missionary" and "non-missionary" divide that continues to plague us. In stressing the need here to engender a missiological vocation, we are in effect highlighting the imperative to return to a biblical understanding of mission. This is not the time to rehearse a theology of missiological vocation, suffice to highlight that in the calling of Abraham lies the foundations for a framework to understand the Church's missiological vocation. One will notice that the reason behind Abraham's, and consequently his descendants, calling, as found in Genesis 12, was for the welfare of the nations. Abraham and Israel were chosen for a cause, to be a blessing to the nations. Old testament scholar Chris Wright cogently explains:

> The affirmation is that Yahweh, the God who had chosen Israel, was also the Creator, Owner and Lord of the whole world (Deut. 10:14f), and that Yahweh had chosen Israel in relation to his purpose for the world, not just for Israel. The election of Israel was not tantamount to a rejection of the nations, but explicitly for their ultimate benefit. Thus, rather than asking if Israel itself 'had a mission', in the sense of being 'sent' anywhere, we need to see the missional nature of Israel's *existence* in relation to the mission of God in the world. Israel's mission was to *be* something, not to *go* somewhere.[57]

By virtue of following on in that lineage of God's chosen people and constituted as the body of Christ, the Church's missional vocation then is (or ought to be) a fundamental strand in our ecclesiology, whatever precise shape that may take. As in the early church we will need to recover that fundamental posture of mission as central and not peripheral to our character; the Church does not have a mission, it is a missionary agent.

One imperative that presents itself is the need therefore to *release all God's people* for mission. If we dwell on the model, as exemplified in the biblical narrative we find that the nomenclature itself, of the "apostolic community" model, is rather suggestive. "Apostle" means "one who is sent;" coupled with the term "community" we then have a "community sent by God" to partner with Him in His mission. Just as Abraham and Israel was chosen for a cause, so also the Church is called with a purpose, the purpose of blessing the nations. This body of Christ is then a sign and an instrument of that blessing.[58] As a sign she celebrates that blessing bequeathed to her and models her life on that dynamic of the gift of grace. As an instrument she channels that blessing, that gift of grace to the world through her life and witness. Just as this gift of being part of that body is not the preserve of a certain elite group but is freely given to all, so also this gift of sharing the blessing is for all and not reserved for a special few alone. Just as each member of the body of Christ enjoys a similar status before God, so also each member enjoys the privilege of being a partner with that triune God in blessing the world. The priesthood of all believers is a doctrine that attests to this very truth. It seeks to do away with a hierarchical conception of the church where the priest represents the people to God and God to the people. It establishes that the whole body of Christ stands on an equal footing both in matters of our standing before God and our calling in the world. All God's

---

57 See http://www.martynmission.cam.ac.uk/COldTest.htm

58 Here I employ terminology used by Bishop Lesslie Newbigin, though I limit myself, for reasons of time and space, in fleshing out those concepts. See *A Word in Season: Perspectives on Christian World Mission,* Grand Rapids: Eerdmans, 1994, p. 33.

people are priests and prophets. This is, however, not to say that all Christians are required to become "cross-cultural missionaries," moving to a new geographical location to engage in evangelism. To be sure there is much value in that calling and that is not being denounced here. On the contrary, this idea of conceiving all God's children as missionaries has not so much to do with one's location but one's vocation. As Christians who are the body of Christ, whatever career we may follow, whatever socio-economic or ethno-cultural background we may possess and whichever geographical location we choose to live in we are blessed with a missional vocation. As Abraham was called to be a blessing even as he was a wealthy businessman, so are we called to bless the world with the gospel even as we pursue our respective careers in the world. When Bishop Lesslie Newbigin spoke of the "congregation as the hermeneutic of the gospel"[59] in effect he underlined the necessity of conceiving mission as the work of all God's people. For Newbigin, it was not the professional priest or missionary that is responsible for sharing the gospel alone, it is the congregation that shoulders the task of living out the gospel. The gift of the gospel that has touched and transformed members of the congregation is to be shared to the world by that very congregation, which believes it. Those who look at the congregation in its internal and external life should find here a cogent exposition of that gospel and through that come to understand and indwell its reality. As the congregation disperses into the world they will be empowered to live and share that gospel in their respective realms of work and influence. In those realms they will embody the gospel and thus participate in God's mission to the world. As much as their leaders they will also have a role to play in the task of the congregation. In such a scheme leaders will be necessary, but their role, as Newbigin asserts, will be to "lead the

congregation as a whole in a mission to the community as a whole, to claim its whole public life, as well as the lives of all its people, for God's rule."[60]

The second imperative that this stress on missiological vocation leads us to is the need to *construct new structures* for mission. Partly because we have tended to work on the assumption that mission is the special calling on certain people alone and carried on "out there" in the so called "mission field" by those who leave their home to live and serve as missionaries there, the structures we presently have understandably perpetuate that very system. To be sure these structures have contributed significantly to God's cause and there is no reason why their existence is to be questioned per se. However, if all God's people are to be released for the calling that the gospel places on them, these structures we note do not necessarily offer a way forward. In Acts 6 and 15, for example, we see how, like us today the apostles, faced with either initiating change or the disruption of mission and ministry, under the guidance of the Holy Spirit, created new structures to facilitate the advance of the gospel. Concerned that they would be forced into a "neglect of ministry" (Acts 6:2), the apostles constructed structures that would not hinder but enhance their missional calling. The freedom to construct these new structures was based on the priority of the gospel over inherited systems and structures. The advance of the gospel and not ecclesiastical tradition was foremost in their mind. This provided them the freedom to venture into uncharted waters and launch new initiatives. In a similar vein mission history tells us how some pioneers went about setting fresh structures in place to further the cause of the gospel. Sometimes this attracted the ire of many within ecclesiastical hierarchy and no small consequence was the result. But under the guidance of the Holy Spirit these stalwarts

---

[59] See Ch.18 in *The Gospel in a Pluralist Society*, London: SPCK, 1989
[60] *Ibid.* p.238

promoted an advance of the gospel through those very structures.

Simultaneously however, we would do well to understand that new structures are not to be constructed just for the sake of novelty and independence. Proliferation of Christian organisations betrays an unhealthy move, in some circles, to see in these new organisations the key to independence and freedom. The lack of trust and genuine partnership leads to rivalry and suspicion, which in turn breed questionable practices. In contrast we need to understand that structures, as these biblical and historical examples demonstrate, are to serve and facilitate the advance of the gospel rather than hinder and obstruct it. Mission structures are to enable Christ' followers to live more faithfully in this 21st century world and not serve to either debilitate the spread of the gospel because of a dearth of suitable mechanisms or distort it through the creation and manipulation of questionable mechanisms. Structures are to be seen as integral to faithful gospel proclamation rather than of mere instrumental value. The utilitarian approach to mission structures does more damage than good to the cause of the gospel. A deeper understanding of the role and use of structures is needed for the very constitution of our structures, not only tell a story but also impact the ethos of the work and people within them. To use sociological language, mission structures are both "determinants" and "variables" of Christian mission. It behoves us therefore to pay sustained attention to the motives, nature and use of structures in Christian mission. Astute biblical and theological reflection is required when new structures are to be founded and old ones altered. The construction of new structures is to be undertaken with utmost prayer and care.

The Promise of Mission and Missiology in the 21st Century

At the beginning of the 21st century we stand at a crucial moment. Old paradigms are being questioned and fresh ones are being actively sought. In many ways we may be living through a truly "watershed moment" and no less than a recasting of mission and missiology will suffice. We have discussed some elements of an agenda for that future, after noting the nature of some resources we possess and the shape of the context we inhabit. Our discussion has highlighted the fact that recasting mission and missiology will be no simple exercise, it will stretch us in more ways than one and will require the marshalling of all our faculties both individual and corporate. We will need to draw from the wells of our resources to address that world we inhabit. For all the uncertainty that we are faced with, one thing is sure: the future promises to be interesting as it promises to be challenging.

When, at the end of His personal earthly mission, Jesus invited His disciples to join Him in mission by sending them into the world, the affirmation He pronounced was intended to provide assurance and cultivate confidence among that motley crew. He declared: "All authority in heaven and on earth has been given to me," and then went on to assure them with these words: "And surely I am with you always, to the very end of the age" (Matthew 28: 18 & 20). If we have any confidence in our missionary engagement in this new century it's founded on this very pledge. It is the presence and power of Christ that is our assurance and confidence. Along with the gift of mission comes divine empowerment. It would be unfortunate and rather foolhardy if we rely on our own resources, depend on our own ability to understand the context or trust in our perspectives alone. More dependable, incisive and perceptive than our human faculty is divine promise. We have been called, constituted and commissioned by that promise and it will be our privilege and joy to rely and depend on that promise as we engage in mission and missiology in the 21st century.

SELECT BIBLIOGRAPHY

Books & Reference Works

Abraham, K.C., ed., *Third World Theologies: Commonalities and Divergences*. Paper and Reflections from the Second General Assembly of the Ecumenical Association of Third World Theologians, December, 1986, Oaxtepec, Mexico. Maryknoll: Orbis, 1990.

Amaladoss, M, T.K. John and G. Gispert-Sauch, eds., *Theologizing in India*. Selection of Papers presented at the Seminar held in Poona on October 26-30, 1978. Bangalore: Theological Publication in India, 1981.

Amalorpavadass, D.S., *Theology of Evangelisation in the Indisan Context*. Bangalore: National Biblical Catechetical and Liturgical Centre, 1973.

Amalorpavadass, D.S., *Evangelisation of the Modern World (Synod of Bishops, Rome, 1974)*. Bangalore: National Biblical Catechetical and Liturgical Centre, 1975.

Amalorpavadass, D.S., *Gospel and Culture: Evangelization, Inculturation and "Hinduisation"*. Bangalore: National Biblical Catechetical and Liturgical Centre, 1978.

Anderson, Gerald H., ed., *The Theology of the Christian Mission*. Nashville: Abingdon, 1961,

Anderson, Gerald H. and Thomas F. Stransky, eds., *Mission Trends No.1: Crucial Issues in Mission Today*. New York: Paulist Press, Grand Rapids: Eerdmans, 1974.

Ariarajah, S. Wesley, *Hindus and Christians: A Century of Protestant Ecumenical Thought*. Amsterdam: Editions Rodopi, Grand Rapids: Eerdmans, 1991.

Athyal, Abraham P. and Dorothy Yoder Nyce, eds., *Mission Today: Challenges and Concerns*. Chennai: Gurukul, 1998.

Athyal, Jesudas M., ed., *Mission Today: Subaltern Perspectives*. Mission Evangelism Studies, Vol. II. Thiruvalla: Christava Sahitya Samithi, 2001.

Aulén, Gustaf, *Christus Victor: An Historical Study of the Three Main Types of the Idea of Atonement*. New York: Macmillan, 1977.

Baago, Kaj, *Pioneers of Indigenous Christianity*. Bangalore: Christian Institute for the Study of Religion and Society, 1969.

Barrett, David B. and Todd M. Johnson, *World Christian Trends .AD 30-AD 2200: Interpreting the Annual Christian Mega-Census*. Pasadena: William Carey Library, 2001.

Barrett, David B., George T. Kurian and Todd M. Johnson, eds., *World Christian Encyclopedia—A Comparative Survey of Churches and Relgions in the Modern World: Vol.I, The World by Countries, Religionists, Churches, Ministries, Vol.II, The World by Segments, Religions, Peoples, Languages, Cities, Topics*. Oxford: Oxford University Press, 2001.

Bassham, Rodger C., *Mission Theology: 1948-1975, Years of Worldwide Creative Tension Ecumenical, Evangelical, and Roman Catholic*. Pasadena: William Carey Library, 1979.

Bosch, David J., *Transforming Mission: Paradigm Shifts in Theology of Mission*. Maryknoll: Orbis, 1992.

Bürkle, Horst and Wofgang M.W. Roth, eds., *Indian Voices in Today's Theological Debate*. Lucknow: Lucknow Publishing House, 1972.

Burrows, William R., ed., *Redemption and Dialogue: Reading* Redemptoris Missio *and* Proclamation. Maryknoll: Orbis, 1993.

Castro, Emilio, *Sent Free: Mission and Unity in the Perspective of the Kingdom*. Madras: CLS, 1988.

Christian, Jayakumar, *God of the Empty-Handed: Poverty, Power and the Kingdom of God*. Monrovia: MARC World Vision, 1999.

Clarke, Andrew D. and Bruce W. Winter, eds., *One God, One Lord in a World of Religious Pluralism*. Cambridge: Tyndale House, 1991.

Conn, Harvie M and S.F. Rowen, eds., *Missions and Theological Education in World Perspective*. Farmington: Associates of Urbanus, 1984.

Coward, Harold, ed., *Hindu-Christian Dialogue: Perspectives and Encounters*. Maryknoll: Orbis, 1990.

Daneel, Inus, Charles Van Engen and Hendrik Vroom, eds., *Fullness of Life for All: Challenges for Mission in Early 21st Century*. Amsterdam: Rodopi, 2003.

D'Costa, Gavin, ed., *Christian Uniqueness Reconsidered: The Myth of a Pluralistic Theology of Religions*. Maryknoll: Orbis, 1990.

Dempster, Murray W., Byron D. Klaus and Douglas Petersen, eds., *Called and Empowered: Global Mission in Pentecostal Perspective*. Peabody: Hendrickson, 1991.

Dempster, Murray W., Byron D. Klaus and Douglas Petersen, eds., *The Globalization of Pentecostalism: A Religion Made to Travel*. Oxford: Regnum, 1999.

Douglas, J.D., ed., *Let the Earth Hear His Voice: International Congress on World Evangelization Lausanne, Switzerland*. Official Reference Volume: Papers and Responses. Minneapolis: World Wide Publications, 1975.

Downs, Frederick S., *History of Christianity in India Vol. V, Part 5: North East India in the Nineteenth and Twentieth Centuries*. Bangalore: Church History Association of India, 1992.

Dupuis, Jacques, *Who Do You Say I Am? Introduction to Christology*. Maryknoll: Orbis, 1994.

England, John C., Jose Kuttianimattathil, John M. Prior, Lily A. Quintos, David Suh Kwang-sun, and Janice Wickeri, eds., *Asian Christian Theologies: A Research Guide to Authors, Movements, Sources. Volume 1: Asia Region 7th-20th centuries; South Asia; Austral Asia*. Maryknoll: Orbis, Delhi: ISPCK, Quezon City: Claretian, 2002.

Fernandez, Francis and Jose Varickasseril, *Mission: A Service of Love, Essays in Honour of Goerge Kottuppallil, S.D.B.* Shillong: Vendrame Institute Publications, 1998.

Frykenberg, Robert Eric, ed., *Christians and Missionaries in India: Cross-Cultural Communication since 1500*. Grand Rapids & Cambridge: Eerdmans, 2003.

Fuchs, Stephen, *Anthropology for the Missions.* Allahabad: St. Paul Publications, 1979.

Grafe, Hugald, *History of Christianity in India Vol. IV, Part 2: Tamilnadu in the Nineteenth and Twentieth Centuries*. Bangalore: Church History Association of India, 1990.

Guder, Darrell L., *Be My Witnesses: The Church's Mission, Message, and Messengers*. Grand Rapids: Eerdmans, 1985.

Hambye, E.R., *History of Christianity in India Vol. III: Eighteenth Century*. Bangalore: Church History Association of India, 1997.

Hedlund, Roger E., *Quest for Identity: India's Churches of Indigenous Origin, The 'Little Tradition' in Indian Christianity*. Delhi: ISPCK, 2000.

Hedlund, Roger E., ed., *God and the Nations: A Biblical Theology of Mission in the Asian Context*. Delhi: ISPCK, Revised 2003.

Hedlund, Roger E., *Roots of the Great Debate in Mission: Mission in Historical and Theological Perspective*. Revised and Enlarged, Third Edition. Bangalore: Theological Book Trust, 1997.

Heim, S. Mark, *The Depth of the Riches: A Trinitarian Theology of Religious Ends*. Grand Rapids and Cambridge: Eerdmans, 2001.

Hiebert, Paul G., *Anthropological Reflections on Missiological Issues*. Grand Rapids: Baker, 1994.

Hiebert, Paul G., R. Daniel Shaw and Tite Tiénou, *Understanding Folk Religion: A Christian Response to Popular Beliefs and Practices*. Grand Rapids: Baker, 1999.

Hogg, William Richey, *Ecumenical Foundations: A History of the International Missionary Council and its Nineteenth-Century Background*. New York: Harper & Brothers, 1952.

Hollenweger, Walter J., *Pentecostalism: Origins and Developments Worldwide*. Peabody: Hendrickson, 1997.

Hrangkhuma, F., ed., *Christianity In India: Search for Liberation and Identity*. Delhi: ISPCK, 1998.

Jeganathan, W.S. Milton, ed., *Mission Paradigm in the New Millennium*. Department of Mission and Evangelism of Church of South India. Delhi: ISPCK, 2000.

Jongeneel, Jan A.B., *Philosophy, Science, and Theology of Mission in the 19th and 20th Centuries, A Missiological Encyclopedia Part I: The Philosophy and Science of Mission*. Frankfurt: Peter Lang, 1995.

Jongeneel, Jan A.B., *Philosophy, Science, and Theology of Mission in the 19th and 20th Centuries, A Missiological Encyclopedia Part II: Missionary Theology*. Frankfurt: Peter Lang, 1997.

Kanagaraj, Jey J., ed., *Mission & Missions: Essays in Honour of I. Ben Wati*. Pune: Union Biblical Seminary, 1998.

Kanjamala, Augustine, ed., *Paths of Mission in India Today*. Mumbai: St. Pauls, 1996.

Kanjamala, Augustine, ed., *Integral Mission Dynamics: An Interdisciplinary Study of the Catholic Church in India*. New Delhi: Inercultural Publications, 1995.

Karotemprel, Sebastian, ed., *Following Christ in Mission: A Foundational Course in Missiology*. Bombay: Pauline Publications, 1995.

Kavunkal, Jacob, *To Gather Them Into One: Evangelization in India Today, A Process of Building Community*. Indore: Satprakashan Sanchar Kendra, 1985.

Kavunkal, Jacob and F. Hrangkhuma, eds., *Bible and Mission in India Today*. FOIM Series I. Bombay: St. Pauls, 1993.

Kavunkal, Jacob and F. Hrangkhuma, eds., *Christ and Cultures*. FOIM Series I. Bombay: St. Pauls, 1994.

Kraft, Charles H., *Christianity in Culture: A Study in Dynamic Biblical Theologizing in Cross-Cultural Perspective*. Maryknoll: Orbis, 1979.

Küng, Hans, Josef van Ess, Heinrich von Stietencron and Heinz Bechert, *Christianity and World Religions: Paths to Dialogue*. Maryknoll: Orbis, 1993.

Larkin, William J. Jr. and Joel F. Williams, eds., *Mission in the New Testament: An Evangelical Approach*. Maryknoll: Orbis, 1998.

Legrand, Lucien, *Unity and Plurality: Mission in the Bible*. Maryknoll: Orbis, 1990.

Luzbetak, Louis J., *The Church and Cultures: An Applied Anthropology for the Religious Worker*. Techny: Divine Word Publications, 1970.

Malipurathu, Thomas and L. Stanislaus, eds., *The Church in Mission: Universal Mandate and Local Concerns*. Anand: Gujarat Sahitya Prakash, 2002.

Marak, Krickwin C. & Plamathdathil S. Jacob, eds., *Conversion in a Pluralistic Context: Perspectives and Perceptions*. Delhi: ISPCK, 2000.

Martinson, Paul Varo, ed., *Mission at the Dawn of the 21st Century: A Vision for the Church*. Minneapolis: Kirk House, 1999.

Mathew, C.V., *The Saffron Mission: A Historical Analysis of Modern Hindu Missionary Ideologies and Practices*. Delhi: ISPCK, 1999.

Mathur, Hari Mohan, *Anthropology and Development in Traditional Societies*. New Delhi: Vikas, 1995.

Mattam, Joseph and Sebastian Kim, eds., *Dimensions of Mission in India*. FOIM III. Bombay: St. Pauls, 1995.

Mattam, Joseph and Sebastian Kim, eds., *Mission and Conversion: A Reappraisal*. FOIM IV. Mumbai: St. Pauls, 1996.

Mattam, Joseph and Sebastian Kim, eds., *Mission Trends Today: Historical and Theological Perspectives*. FOIM V. Mumbai: St. Pauls, 1997.

Mattam, Joseph and Krickwin C. Marak, eds., *Blossoms from the East: Contribution of the Indian Church to World Mission*. FOIM Series VI. Mumbai: St. Pauls, 1998.

Mattam, Joseph and Krickwin C. Marak, eds., *Missiological Approaches in India: Retrospect and Prospect*. FOIM Series VII. Mumbai: St. Pauls, 1999.

Michael, S.M., *Culture and Urbanization*. New Delhi: Inter-India Publications, 1988.

Moreau, A.Scott, Tokunboh Adeyemo, David G. Burnett, Bryant L. Myers and Hwa Yung, eds., *Deliver Us from Evil: An Uneasy Frontier in Christian Mission*. Monrovia: MARC World Vision, 2002.

Mundadan, A.M., *History of Christianity in India Vol.I: From the Beginning up to the Middle of the Sixteenth Century*. Bangalore: Church History Association of India, 1989.

Myers, Bryant L., *Walking with the Poor: Principles and Practices of Transformational Development*. Maryknoll: Orbis, 1999.

Myers, Bryant L., ed., *Working with the Poor: New Insights and Learnings from Development Practitioners*. Monrovia: World Vision and LCWE, 1999.

Neely, Alan, *Christian Mission: A Case Study Approach*. Maryknoll: Orbis, 1995.

Neill, Stephen, *A History of Christian Missions*. The Pelican History of the Church, Vol.6. Middlesex: Penguin Books, 1964.

Neuner, J. and J. Dupuis, eds., *The Christian Faith in the Doctrinal Documents of the Catholic Church*. Bangalore: Theological Publications in India, 1976.

Newbigin, Lesslie, *The Gospel in a Pluralist Society*. Geneva: WCC Publications, Grand Rapids: Eerdmans, 1989.

Nida, Eugene A., *Customs and Cultures: Anthropology for Christian Missions*. Pasadena: William Carey Library, 1979.

Pachuau, Lalsangkima, ed., *Ecumenical Missiology: Contemporary Trends, Issues and Themes*. Bangalore: United Theological College, 2002.

Panikkar, Raymond, *The Unknown Christ of Hinduism*. London: Darton, Longman & Todd, 1968.

Panikkar, R., *Myth, Faith and Hermeneutics: Cross-Cultural Studies*. Bangalore: Asian Trading Corporation, 1983.

Pathrapankal, J., ed., *Service and Salvation: Nagpur Theological Conference on Evangelization*. Bangalore: Theological Publications in India, 1973.

Perniola, V., *The Catholic Church in Sri Lanka*. Original Documents Translated into English. *The Portuguese Period* Vol.1, 1505-1565; Vol.2, 1566-1619; Vol.3, 1620-1658;. *The Dutch Period* Vol.1, 1658-1711; Vol.2, 1712-1746; Vo.3, 1747-1795; *The British Period* Vol.1, 1795-1844; Vol.2, 1845-1849; Vol.2, 1850-1855. Dehiwala, Sri Lanka: Tisara Prakasakayo. 1989-1995.

Perry, Cindy L. *Nepali Around the World: Emphasizing Nepali Christians of the Himalayas*. Kathmandu: Ekta Books. 1997.

Peskett, Howard and Vinoth Ramachandra, *The Message of Mission: The Glory of Christ in All Time and Space*. Downers Grove: InterVarsity Press. Delhi: ISPCK. Chennai: MIIS. 2003.

Phillips, James M. and Robert T. Coote, eds., *Toward the 21st Century in Christian Mission: Essays in Honor of Gerald H. Anderson*. Grand Rapids: Eerdmans, 1993.

Pittman, Don A., Ruben L. F. Habito, and Terry C. Muck, eds., *Ministry and Theology in Global Perspective: Contemporary Challenges for the Church*. Grand Rapids & Cambridge: Eerdmans, 1996.

Pomerville, Paul A., *The Third Force in Missions*. Peabody: Hendrickson, 1985.

Puthenpurakal, J. *Mission in the Documents of the Catholic Church*. Shillong: Vendrame Institute Publications, 1997.

Ramachandra, Vinoth, *The Recovery of Mission: Beyond the Pluralist Paradigm*. Carlisle, UK: Paternoster, 1996.

Sanneh, Lamin, *Translating the Message: The Missionary Impact on Culture*. Maryknoll: Orbis, 1991.

Schreiter, Robert J., *Constructing Local Theologies*. Maryknoll: Orbis, 1985.

Senior, Donald and Carroll Stuhlmueller, *The Biblical Foundations for Mission*. Maryknoll: Orbis, 1984.

Shaull, Richard and Waldo Cesar, *Pentecostalism and the Future of the Christian Churches: Promises, Limitations, Challenges*. Grand Rapids and Cambridge: Eerdmans, 2000.

Shenk, Calvin E., *Who Do You Say That I Am? Christians Encounter Other Religions*. Scottdale: Herald Press, 1997.

Shenk, Wilbert R., *Changing Frontiers of Mission*. Maryknoll: Orbis, 1999.

Somaratna, GPV, *The Events of Christian History in Sri Lanka*. Nugegoda, Sri Lanka: Margaya Fellowship. 1998.

Spencer, Aída Besançon and William David Spencer, eds., *The Global God: Multicultural Evangelical Views of God*. Grand Rapids: Baker, 1998.

Stott, John, ed., *Making Christ Known: Historic Mission Documents from the Lausanne Movement 1974-1989*. Carlisle: Paternoster, 1996.

Stott, John and Robert T. Coote, eds., *Gospel and Culture*. Papers of a LCWE Consultation on Gospel and Culture. Pasadena: William Carey Library, 1979.

Sugden, Chris, *Seeking the Asian Face of Jesus: The Practice and Theology of Christian Social Witness in Indonesia and India 1974-1996*. Oxford: Regnum, 1997.

Sugirtharajah, R.S., ed., *Asian Faces of Jesus*. Maryknoll: Orbis, 1995.

Tennent, Timothy C. *Building Christianity on Indian Foundations: The Legacy of Brahmabandhav Upadhyay*. Delhi: ISPCK, 2000.

Thekkedath, Joseph, *History of Christianity in India Vol.II: From the Middle of the Sixteenth Century to the End of the Seventeenth Century*. Bangalore: Church History Association of India, 1988.

Thomas, M.M., *The Acknowledged Christ of the Indian Renaissance*. London: SCM, 1969.

Thomas, Norman E., ed., *Classic Texts in Mission and World Christianity*. Maryknoll: Orbis, 1995.

Thampu, Valson, *Rediscovering Mission: Towards A Non-western Missiological Paradigm*. New Delhi: TRACE, 1995.

Tippet, Alan, *Introduction to Missiology*. Pasadena: William Carey Library, 1987.

Trompf, G.W., ed., *The Gospel Is Not Western: Black Theologies from the Southwest Pacific*. Maryknoll: Orbis, 1987.

Van Engen, Charles, *Mission on the Way: Issues in Mission Theology*. Grand Rapids: Baker, 1996.

Van Engen, Charles, Dean S. Gilliland and Paul Pierson, eds., *The Good News of the Kingdom: Mission Theology for the Third Millennium*. Maryknoll: Orbis, 1993.

Van Engen, Charles and Jude Tiersma, eds., *God So Loves the City: Seeking a Theology for Urban Mission*. Monrovia: MARC World Vision, 1994.

Van Engen, Charles, Nancy Thomas and Robert Gallagher, eds., *Footprints of God: A*

Narrative Theology of Mission. Monrovia: MARC World Vision, 1999.

Van Rheenen, Gailyn, *Communicating Christ in Animistic Contexts*. Grand Rapids: Baker, 1991.

Verkuyl, J., *Contemporary Missiology: An Introduction*. Grand Rapids: Eerdmans, 1978.

Verstraelen, F.J., A. Camps, L.A. Hoedemaker and M.R. Spindler, eds., *Missiology, An Ecumenical Introduction: Texts and Contexts of Global Christianity*. Grand Rapids: Eerdmans, 1995.

Walls, Andrew F., *The Missionary Movement in Christian History: Studies in the Transmission of Faith*. Maryknoll: Orbis, 1996.

Wilfred, Felix, *Beyond Settled Foundation: The Journey of Indian Theology*. University of Madras: Department of Christian Studies, 1993.

Wilfred, Felix, *Asian Dreams and Christian Hope: At the Dawn of the Millennium*. Delhi: ISPCK, 2000.

Wilfred, Felix and Jose D. Maliekal, eds., *The Struggle for the Past: Historiography Today*. University of Madras: Department of Christian Studies, 2002.

Yates, Timothy, *Christian Mission in the Twentieth Century*. Cambridge: Cambridge University Press, 1996.

Periodicals of South Asian Interest

- *al-Mushir* (Christian Study Centre, Rawalpindi, Pakistan, from 1967?)

- *Annual Bibliography of Christianity in India* (Heras Institute, St. Xavier's College, Bombay, 1981-1989)

- *Bangalore Theological Forum* (United Theological College, Bangalore, India, from 1968)

- *Bibliographia Missionaria* (Pontifical Missionary Library, Urban University, Vatican City, from 1936)

- *Dharma Deepika* (Deepika Educational Trust, Chennai, India, from 1995)

- *Dialogue* (Ecumenical Institute for Study and Dialogue, Colombo, Sri Lanka, from 1974)

- *Ecumenical Review, The* (World Council of Churches, Geneva, Switzerland, from 1948)

- *Evangelical Review of Theology* (Theological Commission, World Evangelical Alliance, India, now UK, from 1976)

- *Exchange: Bulletin of Third World Christian Literature and Ecumenical Research* (Missiology Department, Inter-University Institute, Leiden, The Netherlands, from 1972)

- *Indian Church History Review* (Church History Association of India, Bangalore, India, from 1967)

- *Inian Journal of Theology* (Theology Department, Serampore College, India, from 1958

- *Indian Missiological Review* (Sacred Heart Theological College, Shillong, India, 1979-1998)

- *International Bulletin of Missionary Research* (Overseas Ministries Study Center, New Haven, USA, from 1976)

- *International Review of Mission/s* (Commission on World Mission and Evangelism, World Council of Churches, Geneva, Switzerland, from 1912)

- *Ishvani Documentation and Mission Digest* (Ishvani Kendra, Pune, India, from 1982)

- *Jeevadhara* (Kerala, India, from 1971)

- *Jnanadeepa: Pune Journal of Religious Studies* (Jnana Deepa Vidyapeeth, Pontifical Institute of Philosophy and Religion, Pune, India, from 1998).

- *Journal of Asian Mission* (Asia Graduate School of Theology, Quezon City, Philippines, from 1999)

- *Journal of Dharma* (Dharmaram College, Bangalore, India, since 1975)

- *Journal of the Henry Martyn Institute* (Henry Martyn Institute, Hyderabad, India, from 1981)
- *Logos* (Sri Lanka, from 1979)
- *Missiology, An International Review* (American Society of Missiology, USA, from 1972)
- *Missionalia* (South African Missiological Society, University of South Africa, from 1973)
- *Missio Nordica: Bibliography of Nordic Mission Literature* (Nordic Institute for Missionary and Ecumenical Research, Uppsala, Sweden, from 1989?)
- *Mission Studies* (International Association for Mission Studies, Frederiksberg, Denmark, from 1984)
- *Mission Today* (Sacred Heart Theological College, Shillong, from 1999)
- *Religion and Society* (Christian Institute for the Study of Religion and Society, Bangalore, India, from 1953)
- *South Indian Folklorist* (Folklore Resources and Research Centre, Palaymkottai, India, from 1997)
- *Studia Missionaria* (Pontifical Urban University, Rome, Italy, from 1952)
- *Third Millennium* (Bishop's House, Rajkot, Gujarat, India, from 1998)
- *Vidyajyoti Journal of Theological Reflection* (Vidyajyoti Institute, Delhi, India, from 1975)
- *Voices from the Third World* (Sri Lanka, from 1977)

INDEX